FREDERICK FORSYTH
THE FOUR NOVELS

BY FREDERICK FORSYTH

The Biafra Story 1969
The Day of the Jackal 1971
The Odessa File 1972
The Dogs of War 1974
The Shepherd 1975
The Devil's Alternative 1979

FREDERICK FORSYTH
THE FOUR NOVELS

The Day of the Jackal
The Odessa File
The Dogs of War
The Devil's Alternative

Complete and unabridged

Hutchinson
London Melbourne Sydney Auckland Johannesburg

Hutchinson & Co. (Publishers) Ltd

An imprint of the Hutchinson Publishing Group

17-21 Conway Street, London W1P 6JD

Hutchinson Group (Australia) Pty Ltd
30-32 Cremorne Street, Richmond South, Victoria 3121
PO Box 151, Broadway, New South Wales 2007

Hutchinson Group (NZ) Ltd
32-34 View Road, PO Box 40-086, Glenfield, Auckland 10

Hutchinson Group (SA) Pty Ltd
PO Box 337, Bergvlei 2012, South Africa

The Day of the Jackal
First published 1971
© Frederick Forsyth 1971

The Odessa File
First published 1972
© Danesbrook Productions Ltd 1972

The Dogs of War
First published 1974
© Danesbrook Productions Ltd 1974

The Devil's Alternative
First published 1979
© Ahiara International Corporation SA 1979

This edition first published 1982
Author's introduction to this edition © Frederick Forsyth 1978, 1982

Typeset by Book Economy Services
Burgess Hill, Sussex.

Printed in Great Britain by The Anchor Press Ltd
and bound by Wm Brendon & Son Ltd,
both of Tiptree, Essex.

British Library Cataloguing in Publication Data
   Forsyth, Frederick
      The four novels of Frederick Forsyth.
      I. Title
      823'.914[F]   PR6056.0699
ISBN 0 09 145720 3

Contents

Author's Introduction

My first novel, *The Day of the Jackal*, must remain, I believe, one of the most accidental novels ever written. For this reason its almost immediate and continuing success is all the more bewildering – to me if to no one else.

Most authors of whom I have read or heard interviews appear to have consciously dedicated themselves to a career as a professional writer. Most seem to have a sort of compulsion, a dedication, a commitment; many disclose that only through writing can they achieve any sort of fulfilment and that if kept for long away from their writing, they pine.

My own case is completely and mysteriously the opposite. I decided, in January 1970 with little hope of any success, to try my hand at a single, one-off novel, for no better motive than that I happened to be broke and without many prospects after twelve years in journalism. I dashed off *The Day of the Jackal* in thirty-five days, virtually without notes, relying on my memory and keeping the plot in my head. That, so far as I was concerned, was that. If it failed, so what. If it succeeded in making a few pounds, so much the better. The compulsion to write another one was a minus quantity.

That it was published at all was due in major part to the astuteness of Mr Harold Harris of Hutchinson, for after four rejections I had decided by September of 1970 that at Christmas I would put the manuscript in a drawer and return to full-time journalism. It was a witness of his further acumen that having read it, he suggested that I sign on with him for another two novels. I did, and having signed felt obliged to fulfil the contract. Without that signature I would probably have rejoiced in the success and the royalties of *Jackal*, pocketed the latter and moved on to something else. Because of that contract, *The Odessa File* and *The Dogs of War* came to be written.

By the summer of 1973 I had written three novels within forty months, and was extremely tired. With my contract honoured, I decided to call it a day, at least as far as novel-writing was concerned. In any case, I was getting married and leaving the country for a long rest in the sun of Spain.

Over the next four years I pottered about, modernizing an old Irish manor house, starting a family and writing only five film treatments and a short story. It was in 1977 that I began more and more to toy with an idea in my head about the influence on world events of wheat, energy and terrorism. By the spring of 1978 I had a story in my head, but was still undecided whether or not to write it in novel form. It was my wife who settled the question. While aware that in my writing periods I become grievously uncompanionable, she was also of the view that when I have a story trying to get out, I am even worse. So in April 1978 I started the series of journeys and secret meetings that were necessary to garner the factual research I needed. By mid October I was ready, and on the 28th sat down to write, finishing on the 12th December. From a phrase that had come to my attention during the researches, I called it *The Devil's Alternative*.

This fourth book was something of a departure, for I felt it necessary to set the action in the near future instead of the recent past. That inevitably meant hazarding a few predictions. Surprisingly, some of them have come true since the time of writing, and others appear to be not too far off. The fall of the Shah of Iran, the arrival of Britain's first woman premier, the successive Soviet wheat crop failures, the US embargo of grain shipments to Russia, the Kremlin's conquest of Afghanistan, the increasing Russian crackdown on Jews, dissidents and non-Russian nationalists, the steady splintering of the façade of the Soviet empire – all these are presaged in the fourth of these novels and are perhaps more pertinent to our age.

Over eleven years have passed since I sat down to tap out *Jackal* on a borrowed table; yet I still cannot muster a shred of that compulsive urge to write, that committed dedication to place words on paper which, I am sure, marks the true professional novelist or writer. So though I would like to count myself as a professional (once) in the matter of flying aeroplanes and as a reporter, as a novelist I seem destined to remain a quite damnably lucky amateur. For this reason alone, and there are others, the continuing success of my novels surprises me even while I have to take note of the fact of it.

I'm delighted for all that to see the four now appearing between the same covers, and wish that anyone dipping into them for the first or even second time will find some entertainment between their pages.

January 1981

THE DAY
OF THE JACKAL

To my Mother and Father

Contents

PART ONE
Anatomy of a plot

1

It is cold at six-forty in the morning of a March day in Paris, and seems even colder when a man is about to be executed by firing squad. At that hour of March 11th, 1963, in the main courtyard of the Fort d'Ivry, a French Air Force colonel stood before a stake driven into the chilly gravel as his hands were bound behind the post, and stared with slowly diminishing disbelief at the squad of soldiers facing him twenty metres away.

A foot scuffed the grit, a tiny release from tension, as the blindfold was wrapped around the eyes of Lieutenant-Colonel Jean-Marie Bastien-Thiry, blotting out the light for the last time. The mumbling of the priest was a helpless counterpoint to the crackling of twenty rifle bolts as the soldiers charged and cocked their carbines.

Beyond the walls a Berliet truck blared for a passage as some smaller vehicle crossed its path towards the centre of the city; the sound died away, masking the 'Take your aim' order from the officer in charge of the squad. The crash of rifle fire, when it came, caused no ripple on the surface of the waking city, other than to send a flutter of pigeons skywards for a few moments. The single 'whack' seconds later of the *coup-de-grâce* was lost in the rising din of traffic from beyond the walls.

The death of the officer, leader of a gang of Secret Army Organisation killers who had sought to shoot the President of France, was to have been an end – an end to further attempts on the President's life. By a quirk of fate it marked a beginning, and to explain why it must first be necessary to explain why a riddled body came to hang from its ropes in the courtyard of the military prison outside Paris on that March morning. . . .

The sun had dropped at last behind the palace wall and long shadows rippled across the courtyard bringing a welcome relief. Even at seven in the evening of the hottest day of the year the temperature was still 23 degrees Centigrade. Across the sweltering city the Parisians piled querulous wives and yelling children into cars and trains to leave for the weekend in the country. It was August 22nd, 1962, the day a few men waiting beyond the city boundaries had decided that the President, General Charles de Gaulle, should die.

While the city's population prepared to flee the heat for the relative cool of the rivers and beaches the Cabinet meeting behind the ornate façade of the Elysée Palace continued. Across the tan gravel of the front courtyard, now cooling in welcome shadow, sixteen black Citroën DS saloons were drawn up nose to tail, forming a circle round three-quarters of the area.

The drivers, lurking in the deepest shade close to the west wall where the shadows had arrived first, exchanged the inconsequential banter of those who spend most of their working days waiting on their masters' whims.

There was more desultory grumbling at the unusual length of the Cabinet's deliberations until a moment before 7.30 a chained and bemedalled usher appeared behind the plate-glass doors at the top of the six steps of the palace and gestured towards the guards. Among the drivers half-smoked Gauloises were dropped and ground into the gravel. The security men and guards stiffened in their boxes beside the front gate and the massive iron grilles were swung open.

The chauffeurs were at the wheels of their limousines when the first group of Ministers appeared behind the plate glass. The usher opened the doors and the members of the Cabinet straggled down the steps exchanging a few last-minute pleasantries for a restful weekend. In order of precedence the saloons eased up to the base of the steps, the usher opened the rear door with a bow, the Ministers climbed into their respective cars and were driven away past the salutes of the Garde Républicaine and out into the Faubourg St Honoré.

Within ten minutes they were gone. Two long black DS 19 Citroëns remained in the yard, and each slowly cruised to the base of the steps. The first, flying the pennant of the President of the French Republic, was driven by Francis Marroux, a police driver from the training and headquarters camp of the Gendarmerie Nationale at Satory. His silent temperament had kept him apart from the joking of the ministerial drivers in the courtyard; his ice-cold nerves and ability to drive fast and safely kept him De Gaulle's personal driver. Apart from Marroux the car was empty. Behind it the second DS 19 was also driven by a gendarme from Satory.

At 7.45 another group appeared behind the glass doors and again the men on the gravel stiffened to attention. Dressed in his habitual double-breasted charcoal-grey suit and dark tie Charles de Gaulle appeared behind the glass. With old-world courtesy he ushered Madame Yvonne de Gaulle first through the doors, then took her arm to guide her down the steps to the waiting Citroën. They parted at the car, and the President's wife climbed into the rear seat of the front vehicle on the left-hand side. The General got in beside her from the right.

Their son-in-law, Colonel Alain de Boissieu, then Chief of Staff of the armoured and cavalry units of the French Army, checked that both rear doors were safely shut, then took his place in the front beside Marroux.

In the second car two others from the group of functionaries who had accompanied the presidential couple down the steps took their seats. Henri d'Jouder, the hulking bodyguard of the day, a Kabyle from Algeria, took the front seat beside the driver, eased the heavy revolver under his left armpit, and slumped back. From then on his eyes would flicker incessantly, not over the car in front, but over the pavements and street corners as they flashed past. After a last word to one of the duty security men to be left behind, the second man got into the back alone. He was Commissaire Jean Ducret, chief of the Presidential Security Corps.

From beside the west wall two white-helmeted motards gunned their engines into life and rode slowly out of the shadows towards the gate. Before the entrance they stopped ten feet apart and glanced back. Marroux pulled the first Citroën away from the steps, swung towards the gate and drew up behind the motor-cycle outriders. The second car followed. It was 7.50 p.m.

Again the iron grille swung open and the small cortège swept past the ramrod guards into the Faubourg St Honoré. Arriving at the end of the Faubourg St Honoré the convoy swept into the Avenue de Marigny. From under the chestnut trees a young man in a white crash helmet astride a scooter watched the cortège pass, then slid away from the kerb and followed. Traffic was normal for an August weekend and no advance warning of the President's departure had been given. Only the whine of the motor-cycle sirens told traffic cops on duty of the approach of the convoy, and they had to wave and whistle frantically to get the traffic stopped in time.

The convoy picked up speed in the tree-darkened avenue and erupted into the sunlit Place Clemenceau, heading straight across towards the Pont Alexandre III. Riding in the slipstream of the official cars the scooterist had little difficulty in following. After the bridge Marroux followed the motor-cyclists into the Avenue General Gallieni and thence into the broad Boulevard des Invalides. The scooterist at this point had his answer. At the junction of the Boulevard des Invalides and the Rue de Varennes he eased back the screaming throttle and swerved towards a corner café. Inside, taking a small metal token from his pocket, he strode to the back of the café where the telephone was situated and placed a local call.

Lieutenant-Colonel Jean-Marie Bastien-Thiry waited in a café in the suburb of Meudon. He was thirty-five, married with three children and he worked in the Air Ministry. Behind the conventional façade of his professional and family life he nurtured a deep bitterness towards Charles de Gaulle, who, he believed, had betrayed France and the men who in 1958 had called him back to power, by yielding Algeria to the Algerian nationalists.

He had lost nothing through the loss of Algeria, and it was not personal consideration that motivated him. In his own eyes he was a patriot, a man convinced that he would be serving his beloved country by slaying the man he thought had betrayed her. Many thousands shared his views at that time, but few in comparison were fanatical members of the Secret

Army Organisation which had sworn to kill De Gaulle and bring down his government. Bastien-Thiry was such a man.

He was sipping a beer when the call came through. The barman passed him the phone, then went to adjust the television set at the other end of the bar. Bastien-Thiry listened for a few seconds, muttered 'Very good, thank you' into the mouthpiece and set it down. His beer was already paid for. He strolled out of the bar on to the pavement, took a rolled newspaper from under his arm, and carefully unfolded it twice.

Across the street a young woman let drop the lace curtain of her first-floor flat, and turned to the twelve men who lounged about the room. She said, 'It's route number two.' The five youngsters, amateurs at the business of killing, stopped twisting their hands and jumped up.

The other seven were older and less nervous. Senior among them in the assassination attempt and second-in-command to Bastien-Thiry was Lieutenant Alain Bougrenet de la Tocnaye, an extreme right-winger from a family of landed gentry. He was thirty-five, married with two children.

The most dangerous man in the room was Georges Watin, aged thirty-nine, a bulky-shouldered, square-jowled OAS fanatic, originally an agricultural engineer from Algeria, who in two years had emerged again as one of the OAS's most dangerous trigger-men. From an old leg-wound he was known as the Limp.

When the girl announced the news the twelve men trooped downstairs via the back of the building to a side street where six vehicles, all stolen or hired, had been parked. The time was 7.55.

Bastien-Thiry had personally spent days preparing the site of the assassination, measuring angles of fire, speed and distance of the moving vehicles, and the degree of firepower necessary to stop them. The place he had chosen was a long straight road called the Avenue de la Libération, leading up to the main cross-roads of Petit-Clamart. The plan was for the first group containing the marksmen with their rifles to open fire on the President's car some two hundred yards before the cross-roads. They would shelter behind an Estafette van parked by the roadside, beginning their fire at a very shallow angle to the oncoming vehicles to give the marksmen the minimum of lay-off.

By Bastien-Thiry's calculations a hundred and fifty bullets should pass through the leading car by the time it came abreast of the van. With the presidential car brought to a stop, the second OAS group would sweep out of a side road to blast the security police vehicle at close range. Both groups would spend a few seconds finishing off the presidential party, then sprint for the three getaway vehicles in another side street.

Bastien-Thiry himself, the thirteenth of the party, would be the lookout man. By 8.05 the groups were in position. A hundred yards on the Paris side of the ambush Bastien-Thiry stood idly by a bus-stop with his newspaper. Waving the newspaper would give the signal to Serge Bernier, leader of the first commando, who would be standing by the Estafette. He would pass the order to the gunmen spreadeagled in the grass at his feet. Bougrenet de la Tocnaye would drive the car to intercept the security police, with Watin the Limp beside him clutching a submachine gun.

As the safety catches flicked off beside the road at Petit-Clamart, General de Gaulle's convoy cleared the heavier traffic of central Paris and reached the more open avenues of the suburbs. Here the speed increased to nearly sixty miles per hour.

As the road opened out, Francis Marroux flicked a glance at his watch, sensed the testy impatience of the old General behind him and pushed the speed up even higher. The two motor-cycle outriders dropped back to take up station at the rear of the convoy. De Gaulle never liked such ostentation sitting out in front and dispensed with them whenever he could. In this manner the convoy entered the Avenue de la Division Leclerc at Petit-Clamart. It was 8.17 p.m.

A mile up the road Bastien-Thiry was experiencing the effects of his big mistake. He would not learn of it until told by the police as he sat months later in Death Row. Investigating the timetable of his assassination he had consulted a calendar to discover that dusk fell on August 22nd at 8.35, seemingly plenty late enough even if De Gaulle was late on his usual schedule, as indeed he was. But the calendar the Air Force colonel had consulted related to 1961. On August 22nd, 1962, dusk fell at 8.10. Those twenty-five minutes were to change the history of France. At 8.18 Bastien-Thiry discerned the convoy hurtling down the Avenue de la Libération towards him at seventy miles per hour. Frantically he waved his newspaper.

Across the road and a hundred yards down, Bernier peered angrily through the gloom at the dim figure by the bus-stop. 'Has the Colonel waved his paper yet?' he asked of no one in particular. The words were hardly out of his mouth when he saw the shark nose of the President's car flash past the bus-stop and into vision. 'Fire!' he screamed to the men at his feet. They opened up as the convoy came abreast of them, firing with a ninety-degree lay-off at a moving target passing them at seventy miles per hour.

That the car took twelve bullets at all was a tribute to the killers' marksmanship. Most of those hit the Citroën from behind. Two tyres shredded under the fire, and although they were self-sealing tubes the sudden loss of pressure caused the speeding car to lurch and go into a front-wheel skid. That was when Francis Marroux saved De Gaulle's life.

While the ace marksman, ex-legionnaire Varga cut up the tyres, the remainder emptied their magazines at the disappearing rear window. Several slugs passed through the bodywork and one shattered the rear window, passing within a few inches of the presidential nose. In the front seat Colonel de Boissieu turned and roared 'Get down' at his parents-in-law. Madame de Gaulle lowered her head towards her husband's lap. The General gave vent to a frosty 'What, again?' and turned to look out of the back window.

Marroux held the shuddering steering wheel and gently turned into the skid, easing down the accelerator as he did so. After a momentary loss of power the Citroën surged forward again towards the intersection with the Avenue du Bois, the side road where the second commando of OAS men waited. Behind Marroux the security car clung to his tail, untouched by any bullets at all.

For Bougrenet de la Tocnaye, waiting with engine running in the Avenue du Bois, the speed of the approaching cars gave him a clear choice: to intercept and commit suicide as the hurtling metal cut him to pieces or let the clutch in a half-second too late. He chose the latter. As he swung his car out of the side road and into line with the presidential convoy, it was not De Gaulle's car he came alongside, but that of the marksman bodyguard d'Jouder and Commissaire Ducret.

Leaning from the right-hand side window, outside the car from the waist up, Watin emptied his submachine gun at the back of the DS in front, in which he could see De Gaulle's haughty profile through the smashed glass.

'Why don't those idiots fire back?' De Gaulle asked plaintively. D'Jouder was trying to get a shot at the OAS killers across ten feet of air between the two cars, but the police driver blocked his view. Ducret shouted to the driver to stick with the President, and a second later the OAS were left behind. The two motor-cycle outriders, one having nearly been unseated by de la Tocnaye's sudden rush out of the side road, recovered and closed up. The whole convoy swept into the roundabout and road junction, crossed it, and continued towards Villacoublay.

At the ambush site the OAS men had no time for recriminations. These were to come later. Leaving the three cars used in the operation they leapt aboard the getaway vehicles and disappeared into the descending gloom.

From his car-borne transmitter Commissaire Ducret called Villa-coublay and told them briefly what had happened. When the convoy arrived ten minutes later General de Gaulle insisted on driving straight to the apron where the helicopter was waiting. As the car stopped, a surge of officers and officials surrounded it, pulling open the doors to assist a shaken Madame de Gaulle to her feet. From the other side the General emerged from the debris and shook glass splinters from his lapel. Ignoring the panicky solicitations from the surrounding officers, he walked round the car to take his wife's arm.

'Come, my dear, we are going home,' he told her, and finally gave the Air Force staff his verdict on the OAS. 'They can't shoot straight.' With that he guided his wife into the helicopter and took his seat beside her. He was joined by d'Jouder and they took off for a weekend in the country.

On the tarmac Francis Marroux sat ashen-faced behind the wheel still. Both tyres along the right-hand side of the car had finally given out and the DS was riding on its rims. Ducret muttered a quiet word of congratulation to him, then went on with the business of clearing up.

While journalists the world over speculated on the assassination attempt and for lack of anything better filled their columns with personal conjectures, the French police, headed by the Sûreté Nationale and backed up by the Secret Service and the Gendarmerie, launched the biggest police operation in French history. Soon it was to become the biggest manhunt the country had yet known, only later to be surpassed by the manhunt for another assassin whose story remains unknown but who is still listed in the files by his code-name, the Jackal.

They got their first break on September 3rd and as is so often the case with police work it was a routine check that brought results. Outside the town of Valence, south of Lyons on the main road from Paris to Marseilles, a police road-block stopped a private car containing four men. They had stopped hundreds that day to examine identity papers, but in this case one of the men in the car had no papers on him. He claimed he had lost them. He and the other three were taken to Valence for routine questioning.

At Valence it was established that the other three in the car had nothing to do with the fourth, apart from having offered him a lift. They were released. The fourth man's fingerprints were taken and sent to Paris, just to see if he was who he said he was. The answer came back twelve hours later: the fingerprints were those of a twenty-two-year-old deserter from the Foreign Legion, who faced charges under military law. But the name he had given was quite accurate – Pierre-Denis Magade.

Magade was taken to the headquarters of the Service Régional of the Police Judiciaire at Lyons. While waiting in an anteroom for interrogation, one of the police guarding him playfully asked, 'Well, what about Petit-Clamart?'

Magade shrugged helplessly. 'All right,' he answered, 'what do you want to know?'

As stunned police officers listened to him and stenographers' pens scratched across one notebook after another, Magade 'sang' for eight hours. By the end he had named every one of the participants of Petit-Clamart, and nine others who had played smaller roles in the plotting stages or in procuring the equipment. Twenty-two in all. The hunt was on, and this time the police knew who they were looking for.

In the end only one escaped, and has never been caught to this day. Georges Watin got away and is presumed to be living in Spain along with most of the other OAS chiefs among the civilian settlers of Algeria.

The interrogation and preparation of the charges against Bastien-Thiry, Bougrenet de la Tocnaye and the other leaders of the plot were finished by December and the group went on trial in January 1963.

While the trial was on the OAS gathered its strength for another all-out attack on the Gaullist Government and the French Secret Services fought back tooth and claw. Under the pleasant norms of Parisian life, beneath the veneer of culture and civilisation, one of the bitterest and most sadistic underground wars of modern history was fought out.

The French Secret Service is called the Service de Documentation Extérieure et de Contre-Espionage, known for short as SDECE. Its duties are both those of espionage outside France and counter-espionage within, though each service may overlap the other's territory on occasion. Service One is pure intelligence, subdivided into bureaux known by the initial R for Renseignement (Information). These subdivisions are R.1 Intelligence Analysis; R.2 Eastern Europe; R.3 Western Europe; R.4 Africa; R.5 Middle East; R.6 Far East; R.7 America/Western Hemisphere. Service Two is concerned with counter-espionage. Three and Four comprise the Communist Section in one office, Six is Finance and Seven Administration.

Service Five has a one-word title – Action. This office was the core of the anti-OAS war. From the headquarters in a complex of nondescript buildings off the Boulevard Mortier close to the Porte des Lilas, a dingy suburb of north-east Paris, the hundred toughs of the Action Service went out to war. These men, mainly Corsicans, were the nearest thing real life ever got to the fictional 'tough guy'. They were trained to a peak of physical fitness, then taken to Satory Camp where a special section shut off from the rest taught them everything known about destruction. They became experts in fighting with small arms, unarmed combat, karate and judo. They underwent courses in radio communication, demolition and sabotage, interrogation with and without the use of torture, kidnapping, arson and assassination.

Some spoke only French, others were fluent in several languages and at home in any capital in the world. They had the authority to kill in the course of duty and often used it.

As the activities of the OAS became more violent and brutal, the Director of the SDECE, General Eugène Guibaud, finally took the muzzle off these men and let them loose on the OAS. Some of them enlisted in the OAS and infiltrated into its highest councils. From here they were content to provide information on which others could act, and many OAS emissaries on missions into France or other areas where they were vulnerable to the police were picked up on information provided by Action Service men inside the terrorist organisation. On other occasions wanted men could not be inveigled into France and were ruthlessly killed outside the country. Many relatives of OAS men who simply disappeared believed ever after that the men had been liquidated by the Action Service.

Not that the OAS needed lessons in violence. They hated the Action Service men, known as the Barbouzes or Bearded Ones because of their undercover role, more than any policeman. In the last days of the struggle for power between the OAS and the Gaullist authorities inside Algiers the OAS captured seven barbouzes alive. The bodies were later found hanging from balconies and lamp-posts minus ears and noses. In this manner the undercover war went on, and the complete story of who died under torture at whose hands in which cellar will never be told.

The remainder of the barbouzes stayed outside the OAS at the beck and call of the SDECE. Some of them had been professional thugs from the underworld before being enlisted, kept up their old contacts, and on more than one occasion enlisted the aid of their former underworld friends to do a particularly dirty job for the Government. It was these activities that gave rise to talk in France of a 'parallel' (unofficial) police, supposedly at the orders of one of President de Gaulle's right-hand men, M. Jacques Foccart. In truth no 'parallel' police existed; the activities attributed to them were carried out by the Action Service strong-arms or temporarily enlisted gang bosses from the 'milieu'.

Corsicans, who dominated both the Paris and Marseilles underworld and the Action Service, know a thing or two about vendettas, and after the slaying of the seven barbouzes of Mission C in Algiers a vendetta was declared against the OAS. In the same manner as the Corsican under-world helped the Allies during the landings in the South of France in 1944 (for their own ends; they later cornered most of the vice trade along the Côte d'Azur as a reward) so in the early sixties the Corsicans fought for France again in a vendetta with the OAS. Many of the OAS men who were pieds-noirs (Algerian-born Frenchmen) had the same characteristics as the Corsicans, and at times the war was almost fratricidal.

As the trial of Bastien-Thiry and his fellows wore on, the OAS cam-paign also got under way. Its guiding light, the behind-the-scenes instigator of the Petit-Clamart plot, was Colonel Antoine Argoud. A pro-duct of one of France's top universities, the Ecole Polytechnique, Argoud had a good brain and a dynamic energy. As a lieutenant under De Gaulle in the Free French he had fought for the liberation of France from the Nazis. Later he commanded a regiment of cavalry in Algiers. A short, wiry man, he was a brilliant but ruthless soldier, and he had become by 1962 operations chief for the OAS in exile.

Experienced in psychological warfare, he understood that the fight against Gaullist France had to be conducted on all levels, by terror, dip-lomacy and public relations. As part of the campaign he arranged for the head of the National Resistance Council, the political wing of the OAS, former French Foreign Minister Georges Bidault, to give a series of inter-views to newspapers and television across Western Europe to explain the OAS's opposition to General de Gaulle in 'respectable' terms.

Argoud was now putting to use the high intelligence that had once made him the youngest colonel in the French Army and now made him the most dangerous man in the OAS. He set up for Bidault a chain of interviews with major networks and newspaper correspondents, during which the old politician was able to put a sober cloak over the less palatable activities of the OAS thugs.

The success of Bidault's Argoud-inspired propaganda operation alarmed the French Government as much as the terror tactics and the wave of plastic bombs exploding in cinemas and cafés all over France. Then on February 14th another plot to assassinate General de Gaulle was uncovered. The following day he was due to give a lecture at the Ecole Militaire on the Champ de Mars. The plot was that on entering the hall he was to be shot in the back by an assassin perched among the eaves of the adjacent block.

Those who later faced trial for the plot were Jean Bichon, a captain of artillery named Robert Poinard, and an English-language teacher at the Military Academy, Madame Paule Rousselet de Liffiac. The trigger-man was to have been Georges Watin, but once again the Limp got away. A rifle with sniper-scope was found at Poinard's flat and the three were arrested. It was stated at their later trial that, seeking a way to spirit Watin and his gun into the Academy, they had consulted Warrant Officer Marius Tho, who had gone straight to the police. General de Gaulle duly attended the military ceremony at the appointed time on the 15th, but made the concession of arriving in an armour-plated car, to his great distaste.

As a plot it was amateurish beyond belief, but it annoyed De Gaulle. Summoning Interior Minister Frey the next day he hammered the table and told the Minister responsible for national security, 'This assassination business has gone far enough.'

It was decided to make an example of some of the top OAS conspirators to deter the others. Frey had no doubts about the outcome of the Bastien-Thiry trial still going on in the Supreme Military Court, for Bastien-Thiry was at pains to explain from the dock why he thought Charles de Gaulle should die. But something more in the way of a deterrent was needed.

On February 22nd a copy of a memorandum which the director of Service Two of SDECE (counter-espionage/internal security) had sent to the Interior Minister landed on the desk of the head of the Action Service. Here is an extract:

'We have succeeded in obtaining the whereabouts of one of the main ringleaders of the subversive movement, namely ex-Colonel of the French Army, Antoine Argoud. He has fled to Germany and intends, according to information from our Intelligence Service there, to remain for several days....

'This being so it should be possible to get at Argoud and perhaps seize him. As the request made by our official counter-espionage service to the competent German security organisations has been refused, and these organisations now expect our agents to be on the heels of Argoud and other OAS leaders, the operation must, in so far as it is directed against the person of Argoud, be carried out with maximum speed and discretion.'

The job was handed over to the Action Service.

In the mid-afternoon of February 25th Argoud arrived back in Munich from Rome where he had been meeting other OAS leaders. Instead of going straight to Unertlstrasse he took a taxi to the Eden-Wolff Hotel where he had booked a room, apparently for a meeting. He never attended it. In the hall he was accosted by two men who spoke to him in faultless German. He presumed they were German police and reached into his breast pocket for his passport.

He felt both arms grabbed in a vice-like grip, his feet left the ground and he was whisked outside to a waiting laundry van. He lashed out and was answered with a torrent of French oaths. A horny hand chopped across his nose, another slammed him in the stomach, a finger felt for the nerve spot below the ear and he went out like a light.

Twenty-four hours later a telephone rang in the Brigade Criminelle of the Police Judiciaire at 36 Quai des Orfèvres in Paris. A hoarse voice told the desk sergeant who answered that he was speaking for the OAS, and that Antoine Argoud, 'nicely tied up', was in a van parked behind the CID building. A few minutes later the door of the van was jerked open and Argoud stumbled out into a circle of dumbfounded police officers.

His eyes, bandaged for twenty-four hours, would not focus. He had to be helped to stand. His face was covered with dried blood from a nose-bleed, and his mouth ached from the gag which the police pulled out of it. When someone asked him, 'Are you Colonel Antoine Argoud?' he mumbled 'Yes'. Somehow the Action Service had spirited him across the frontier during the previous night, and the anonymous phone call to the police about the parcel waiting for them in their own parking lot was just their private sense of humour at work. He was not released until June 1968.

But one thing the Action Service men had not counted on; in removing Argoud, despite the enormous demoralisation this caused in the OAS, they had paved the way for his shadowy deputy, the little-known but equally astute Lieutenant-Colonel Marc Rodin, to assume command of operations aimed at assassinating De Gaulle. In many ways it was a bad bargain.

On March 4th the Supreme Military Court delivered its verdict on Jean-Marie Bastien-Thiry. He and two others were sentenced to death, as were a further three still at large including Watin the Limp. On March 8th General de Gaulle listened for three hours in silence to appeals for clemency by the lawyers of the condemned men. He commuted two of the death sentences to life imprisonment, but Bastien-Thiry's condemnation stood.

That night his lawyer told the Air Force colonel of the decision.

'It is fixed for the 11th,' he told his client, and when the latter continued to smile disbelievingly, blurted out, 'You are going to be shot.'

Bastien-Thiry kept smiling and shook his head.

'You don't understand,' he told the lawyer, 'no squad of Frenchmen will raise their rifles against me.'

He was wrong. The execution was reported on the 8 a.m. news of Radio Europe Number One in French. It was heard in most parts of Western Europe by those who cared to tune in. In a small hotel room in Austria the broadcast was to set off a train of thoughts and actions that brought General de Gaulle nearer to death than at any time in his career. The room was that of Colonel Marc Rodin, new operations chief of the OAS.

2

Marc Rodin flicked off the switch of his transistor radio and rose from the table, leaving the breakfast tray almost untouched. He walked over to the window, lit another in the endless chain of cigarettes and gazed out at the snow-encrusted landscape which the late arriving spring had not yet started to dismantle.

'Bastards.' He murmured the word quietly and with great venom, following up with another *sotto voce* string of nouns and epithets that expressed his feeling towards the French President, his Government and the Action Service.

Rodin was unlike his predecessor in almost every way. Tall and spare, with a cadaverous face hollowed by the hatred within, he usually masked his emotions with an un-Latin frigidity. For him there had been no Ecole Polytechnique to open doors to promotion. The son of a cobbler, he had escaped to England by fishing boat in the halcyon days of his late teens when the Germans overran France, and had enlisted as a private soldier under the banner of the Cross of Lorraine.

Promotion through sergeant to warrant officer had come the hard way, in bloody battles across the face of North Africa under Koenig and later through the hedgerows of Normandy with Leclerc. A field commission during the fight for Paris had got him the officer's chevrons his education and breeding could never have obtained, and in post-war France the choice had been between reverting to civilian life or staying in the Army.

But revert to what? He had no trade but that of cobbler which his father had taught him, and he found the working class of his native country dominated by Communists, who had also taken over the Resistance and the Free French of the Interior. So he stayed in the Army, later to experience the bitterness of an officer from the ranks who saw a new young generation of educated boys graduating from the officer schools, earning in theoretical lessons carried out in classrooms the same chevrons he had sweated blood for. As he watched them pass him in rank and privilege the bitterness started to set in.

There was only one thing left to do, and that was join one of the colonial regiments, the tough crack soldiers who did the fighting while the conscript army paraded round drill squares. He managed a transfer to the colonial paratroops.

Within a year he had been a company commander in Indo-China, living among other men who spoke and thought as he did. For a young man from a cobbler's bench, promotion could still be obtained through combat, and more combat. By the end of the Indo-China campaign he was a major and after an unhappy and frustrating year in France he was sent to Algeria.

The French withdrawal from Indo-China and the year he spent in France had turned his latent bitterness into a consuming loathing of politicians and Communists, whom he regarded as one and the same thing. Not until France was ruled by a soldier could she ever be weaned away from the grip of the traitors and lickspittles who permeated her public life. Only in the Army were both breeds extinct.

Like most combat officers who had seen their men die and occasionally buried the hideously mutilated bodies of those unlucky enough to be taken alive, Rodin worshipped soldiers as the true salt of the earth, the men who sacrificed themselves in blood so that the bourgeoisie could live at home in comfort. To learn from the civilians of his native land after eight years of combat in the forests of Indo-China that most of them cared not a fig for the soldiery, to read the denunciations of the military by the left-wing intellectuals for mere trifles like the torturing of prisoners to obtain vital information, had set off inside Marc Rodin a reaction which, combined with the native bitterness stemming from his own lack of opportunity, had turned into zealotry.

He remained convinced that given enough backing by the civil authorities on the spot and the Government and people back home, the Army could have beaten the Viet-Minh. The cession of Indo-China had been a massive betrayal of the thousands of fine young men who had died there – seemingly for nothing. For Rodin there would be, could be, no more betrayals. Algeria would prove it. He left the shore of Marseilles in the spring of 1956 as near a happy man as he would ever be, convinced that the distant hills of Algeria would see the consummation of what he regarded as his life's work, the apotheosis of the French Army in the eyes of the world.

Within two years of bitter and ferocious fighting little happened to shake his convictions. True, the rebels were not as easy to put down as he had thought at first. However many fellagha he and his men shot, however many villages were razed to the ground, however many FLN terrorists died under torture, the rebellion spread until it enveloped the land and consumed the cities.

What was needed, of course, was more help from the Métropole. Here at least there could be no question of a war in a far-flung corner of the Empire. Algeria was France, a part of France, inhabited by three million Frenchmen. One would fight for Algeria as for Normandy, Brittany or the Alpes Maritimes. When he got his lieutenant-colonelcy Marc Rodin moved out of the bled and into the cities, first Bone then Constantine.

In the bled he had been fighting the soldiers of the ALN, irregular soldiers but still fighting men. His hatred of them was nothing to what consumed him as he entered the sneaking, vicious war of the cities, a war fought with plastic bombs planted by cleaners in French-patronised cafés, supermarkets and play-parks. The measures he took to cleanse Constantine of the filth who planted these bombs among French civilians earned him in the Casbah the title of Butcher.

All that was lacking for the final obliteration of the FLN and its army, the ALN, was more help from Paris. Like most fanatics Rodin could blind himself to facts with sheer belief. The escalating costs of the war, the tottering economy of France under the burden of a war becoming increasingly unwinnable, the demoralisation of the conscripts, were a bagatelle.

In June 1958 General de Gaulle returned to power as Prime Minister of France. Efficiently disposing of the corrupt and tottering Fourth Republic, he founded the Fifth. When he spoke the words whose utterance in the mouths of the generals had brought him back to the Matignon and then in January 1959 to the Elysée, 'Algérie Française', Rodin went to his room and cried. When De Gaulle visited Algeria his presence was for Rodin like that of Zeus coming down from Olympus. The new policy, he was sure, was on the way. The Communists would be swept from their offices, Jean-Paul Sartre must surely be shot for treason, the trade unions would be brought into submission and the final wholehearted backing of France for her kith and kin in Algeria and for her Army protecting the frontiers of French civilisation would be forthcoming.

Rodin was as sure of this as the rising sun in the East. When De Gaulle started his measures to restore France his own way, Rodin thought there must be some mistake. One had to give the old man time. When the first rumours of preliminary talks with Ben Bella and the FLN filtered through Rodin could not believe it. Although he sympathised with the revolt of the settlers led by Big Jo Ortiz in 1960, he still felt the lack of progress in smashing the fellagha once and for all was simply a tactical move by De Gaulle. Le Vieux, he felt sure, must know what he was doing. Had he not said it, the golden words Algérie Française?

When the proof came finally and beyond any doubt that Charles de Gaulle's concept of a resuscitated France did not include a French Algeria, Rodin's world disintegrated like a china vase hit by a train. Of faith and hope, belief and confidence, there was nothing left. Just hate. Hate for the system, for the politicians, for the intellectuals, for the Algerians, for the trade unions, for the journalists, for the foreigners; but most of all hate for That Man. Apart from a few wet-eared ninnies who refused to come, Rodin led his entire battalion into the military putsch of April 1961.

It failed. In one simple, depressingly clever move De Gaulle foiled the putsch before it could get off the ground. None of the officers had taken more than a passing notice when thousands of simple transistor radios were issued to the troops in the weeks before the final announcement that talks were being started with the FLN. The radios were regarded as a harmless comfort for the troops, and many officers and senior NCOs approved the idea. The pop music that came over the air from France was a pleasant distraction for the boys from the heat, the flies, the boredom.

The voice of De Gaulle was not so harmless. When the loyalty of the Army was finally put to the test tens of thousands of conscripts spread out in barracks across Algeria turned on their radios for the news. After the news they heard the same voice that Rodin himself had listened to in June 1940. Almost the same message. 'You are faced with a choice of loyalties. I am France, the instrument of her destiny. Follow me. Obey me.'

Some battalion commanders woke up with only a handful of officers and most of their sergeants left.

The mutiny was broken like the illusions – by radio. Rodin had been luckier than some. One hundred and twenty of his officers, NCOs and rankers remained with him. This was because he commanded a unit with a higher proportion of old sweats from Indo-China and the Algerian bled than most. Together with the other putschistes they formed the Secret Army Organisation, pledged to overthrow the Judas of the Elysée Palace.

Between the triumphant FLN and the loyal Army of France there was little left but time for an orgy of destruction. In the last seven weeks, as the French settlers sold their life's work for a song and fled the war-torn coast, the Secret Army exacted one last hideous revenge on what they had to leave behind. When it was over there remained only exile for the leaders whose names were known to the Gaullist authorities.

Rodin became deputy to Argoud as operations chief of the OAS in exile in the winter of 1961. Argoud's was the flair, the talent, the inspiration behind the offensive the OAS launched on Metropolitan France from then on; Rodin's was the organisation, the cunning, the shrewd commonsense. Had he merely been a tough fanatic he would have been dangerous but not exceptional. There were many others of that calibre toting guns for the OAS in the early sixties. But he was more. The old cobbler had sired a boy with a good thinking brain, never developed by formal education of army service. Rodin had developed it on his own, in his own way.

When faced with his own concept of France and the honour of the Army Rodin was as bigoted as the rest, but when faced with a purely practical problem he could bring to bear a pragmatic and logical concentration that was more effective than all the volatile enthusiasm and senseless violence in the world.

This was what he brought on the morning of March 11th to the problem of killing Charles de Gaulle. He was not fool enough to think the job would be easy; on the contrary, the failures of Petit-Clamart and the Ecole Militaire would make it much harder. Killers alone were not hard to find; the problem was to find a man or a plan that had one single factor built in that would be sufficiently unusual to penetrate the wall of security now built up in concentric rings round the person of the President.

Methodically he listed in his mind the problems. For two hours, chain-smoking before the window until the room became cloudy with a blue haze, he set them up, then devised a plan to demolish or circumvent them. Each plan seemed feasible under most of the critical examination to which he submitted it; each then disintegrated under the final test. Out of this train of thought one problem emerged as virtually insurmountable – the question of security.

Things had changed since Petit-Clamart. The penetration of the Action Service into the ranks and cadres of the OAS had increased to an alarming degree. The recent abduction of his own superior Argoud indicated the lengths to which the Action Service was prepared to go to get at and interrogate the leaders of the OAS. Even a blazing row with the German Government was not avoided.

With Argoud already fourteen days under interrogation the whole OAS leadership had had to go on the run. Bidault suddenly lost his taste for publicity and self-exposure; others of the CNR had fled panicking to Spain, America, Belgium. There had been a rush for false papers, tickets to far places.

Watching this, the lower ranks had suffered a staggering setback to morale. Men inside France previously prepared to help, to shelter wanted men, to carry packages of arms, to pass messages, even to provide information were hanging up the phone with a muttered excuse.

Following the failure of Petit-Clamart and the interrogation of the prisoners three whole *réseaux* inside France had had to be closed down. With inside information the French police had raided house after house, uncovered cache after cache of weapons and stores; two other plots to kill De Gaulle had been swamped with police as the conspirators sat down to their second meeting.

While the CNR made speeches in committee and burbled about the restoration of democracy in France, Rodin grimly faced the facts of life as exposed in the bulging briefcase by his bed. Short of funds, losing national and international support, membership and credibility, the OAS was crumbling before the onslaught of the French Secret Services and police.

The execution of Bastien-Thiry could only worsen morale. To find men prepared to help at this stage would be hard indeed; those prepared to do the job had their faces engraved on to the memory of every cop in France and several million citizens beside. Any new plan set up at this stage which involved a lot of planning and co-ordination of many groups would be 'blown' before the assassin could get within a hundred miles of De Gaulle.

Arriving at the end of his own argument, Rodin muttered, 'A man who is not known....' He ran through the list of men whom he knew would not flinch from assassinating a president. Every one had a file thick as the Bible in French police HQ. Why else would he, Marc Rodin, be hiding in a hotel in an obscure Austrian mountain village?

The answer came to him just before noon. He dismissed it for a while, but was drawn back to it with insistent curiosity. If such a man could be found . . . if only such a man exists. Slowly, laboriously, he built another plan around such a man, then subjected it to all the obstacles and objections. The plan passed them all, even the question of security.

Just before the lunch-hour struck, Marc Rodin shrugged into his great-coat and went downstairs. At the front door he caught the first blast of the wind along the icy street. It made him flinch, but cleared the dull headache caused by the cigarettes in the overheated bedroom. Turning left he crunched towards the post office in the Adlerstrasse and sent a series of brief telegrams, informing his colleagues scattered under aliases across southern Germany, Austria, Italy and Spain that he would not be available for a few weeks as he was going on a mission.

It occurred to him as he trudged back to the humble rooming house that some might think he too was chickening out, disappearing from the threat of kidnap or assassination by the Action Service. He shrugged to himself. Let them think what they wished, the time for lengthy explanations was over.

He lunched off the boarding house Stammkarte, the meal of the day being Eisbein and noodles. Although years in the jungle and the wilderness of Algeria had left him little taste for good food, he had difficulty cramming it down. By mid-afternoon he was gone, bags packed, bill paid, departed on a lonely mission to find a man, or more precisely a type of man, whom he did not know existed.

As he boarded his train a Comet 4B of BOAC drifted down the flight path towards Runway Zero-Four at London Airport. It was inbound from Beirut. Among the passengers as they filed through the arrivals lounge was a tall, blond Englishman. His face was healthily tanned by the Middle East sun. He felt relaxed and fit after two months enjoying the undeniable pleasures of the Lebanon and the, for him, even greater pleasure of supervising the transfer of a handsome sum of money from a bank in Beirut to another in Switzerland.

Far behind him on the sandy soil of Egypt, long since buried by the baffled and furious Egyptian police, each with a neat bullet hole through the spine, were the bodies of two German missile engineers. Their departure from life had set back the development of Nasser's Al Zafira rocket by several years and a Zionist millionaire in New York felt his money had been well spent. After passing easily through Customs the Englishman took a hire car to his flat in Mayfair.

It was ninety days before Rodin's search was over and what he had to show for it was three slim dossiers, each encased in a manila file which he kept with him permanently in his briefcase. It was in the middle of June that he arrived back in Austria and checked into a small boarding house, the Pension Kleist in the Brucknerallee in Vienna.

From the city's main post office he sent off two crisp telegrams, one to Bolzano in northern Italy, the other to Rome. Each summoned his two principal lieutenants to an urgent meeting in his room in Vienna. Within twenty-four hours the men had arrived. René Montclair came by hired car from Bolzano, André Casson flew in from Rome. Each travelled under false name and papers, for both in Italy and Austria, the resident officers of the SDECE had both men top-listed on their files and by this time were spending a lot of money buying agents and informers at border checkpoints and airports.

André Casson was the first to arrive at the Pension Kleist, seven minutes before the appointed time of eleven o'clock. He ordered his taxi to drop him at the corner of the Brucknerallee and spent several minutes adjusting his tie in the reflection of a florist's window before walking quickly into the hotel foyer. Rodin had as usual registered under a false name, one of twenty known only to his immediate colleagues. Each of the two he had summoned had received a cable the previous day signed by the name of Schulz, Rodin's code-name for that particular twenty-day period.

'Herr Schulz, bitte?' Casson enquired of the young man at the reception desk. The clerk consulted his registration book.

'Room sixty-four. Are you expected, sir?'

'Yes, indeed,' replied Casson and headed straight up the stairs. He turned the landing to the first floor and walked along the passage looking for room 64. He found it halfway along on the right. As he raised his hand to knock it was gripped from behind. He turned and stared up into a heavy blue-jowled face. The eyes beneath a thick single band of black hair that passed for eyebrows gazed down at him without curiosity. The man had fallen in behind him as he passed an alcove twelve feet back and despite the thinness of the cord carpet Casson had not heard a sound.

'Vous désirez?' said the giant as if he could not have cared less. But the grip on Casson's right wrist did not slacken.

For a moment Casson's stomach turned over as he imagined the speedy removal of Argoud from the Eden-Wolff Hotel four months earlier. Then he recognised the man behind him as a Polish Foreign Legionnaire from Rodin's former company in Indo-China and Vietnam. He recalled that Rodin occasionally used Viktor Kowalski for special assignments.

'I have an appointment with Colonel Rodin, Viktor,' he replied softly. Kowalski's brows knotted even closer together at the mention of his own and his master's name. 'I am André Casson,' he added. Kowalski seemed unimpressed. Reaching round Casson he rapped with his left hand on the door of room 64.

A voice from the inside replied, 'Oui.'

Kowalski approached his mouth to the wooden panel of the door.

'There's a visitor here,' he growled, and the door opened a fraction. Rodin gazed out, then swung the door wide.

'My dear André. So sorry about this.' He nodded to Kowalski. 'All right, Corporal, I am expecting this man.'

Casson found his right wrist freed at last, and stepped into the bedroom. Rodin had another word with Kowalski on the threshold, then closed the door again. The Pole went back to stand in the shadows of the alcove.

Rodin shook hands and led Casson over to the two armchairs in front of the gas fire. Although it was mid-June, the weather outside was a fine chill drizzle and both men were used to the warmer sun of North Africa. The gas fire was full on. Casson stripped off his raincoat and settled before the fire.

'You don't usually take precautions like this, Marc,' he observed.

'It's not so much for me,' replied Rodin. 'If anything should happen I can take care of myself. But I might need a few minutes to get rid of the papers.' He gestured to the writing desk by the window where a thick manila folder lay beside his briefcase. 'That's really why I brought Viktor. Whatever happened he would give me sixty seconds to destroy the papers.'

'They must be important.'

'Maybe, maybe.' There was nevertheless a note of satisfaction in Rodin's voice. 'But we'll wait for René. I told him to come at 11.15 so the two of you would not arrive within a few seconds of each other and upset Viktor. He gets nervous when there is too much company around whom he does not know.'

Rodin permitted himself one of his rare smiles at the thought of what would ensue if Viktor became nervous with the heavy Colt under his left armpit. There was a knock at the door. Rodin crossed the room and put his mouth to the wood. 'Oui?'

This time it was René Montclair's voice, nervous and strained.

'Marc, for the love of God . . .'

Rodin swung open the door. Montclair stood there dwarfed by the giant Pole behind him. Viktor's left arm encircled him, pinning both the accountant's arms to his side.

'Ça va, Viktor,' murmured Rodin to the bodyguard, and Montclair was released. He entered the room thankfully and made a moue at Casson who was grinning from the chair by the fire. Again the door closed, and Rodin made his excuses to Montclair.

Montclair came forward and the two shook hands. He had taken off his overcoat to reveal a rumpled dark-grey suit of poor cut which he wore badly. Like most ex-Army men accustomed to a uniform he and Rodin had never worn suits well.

As host Rodin saw the other two seated, in the bedroom's two easy chairs. He kept for himself the upright chair behind the plain table that served him for a desk. From the bedside cabinet he took a bottle of French brandy and held it up enquiringly. Both his guests nodded. Rodin poured a generous measure into each of three glasses and handed two to Montclair and Casson. They drank first, the two travellers letting the hot liquor get to work on the chill inside them.

René Montclair, leaning back against the bedhead, was short and stocky, like Rodin a career officer from the Army. But unlike Rodin he had not had a combat command. Most of his life he had been in the admin-istrative branches, and for the previous ten years in the pay-accounts branch of the Foreign Legion. By the spring of 1963 he was treasurer of the OAS.

André Casson was the only civilian. Small and precise, he dressed still like the bank manager he had been in Algeria. He was the co-ordinator of the OAS-CNR underground in Metropolitan France.

Both men were, like Rodin, hardliners even among the OAS, albeit for different reasons. Montclair had had a son, a nineteen-year-old boy who had been doing his National Service in Algeria three years previously while his father was running the pay-accounts department of the Foreign Legion base outside Marseilles. Major Montclair never saw the body of his son, it had been buried in the bled by the Legion patrol who took the village where the young private had been held a prison by the guerrillas. But he heard the details of what had been done to the young man afterwards. Nothing remains secret for long in the Legion. People talk.

André Casson was more involved. Born in Algeria, his entire life had been wrapped up in his work, his flat and his family. The bank for which he worked had its headquarters in Paris, so even with the fall of Algeria he would not have been out of work. But when the settlers rose in revolt in 1960 he had been with them, one of the leaders in his native Constantine. Even after that he had kept his job, but realised as account after account closed and the business men sold out to move back to France that the heyday of French presence in Algeria was over. Shortly after the Army mutiny, incensed by the new Gaullist policy and the misery of the small-time farmers and traders of the region, fleeing ruined to a country many of them had hardly seen across the water, he had helped an OAS unit to rob his own bank of thirty million old francs. His complicity had been noticed and reported by a junior cashier, and his career with the bank was over. He sent his wife and two children to live with his in-laws at Perpignan, and joined the OAS. His value to them was his personal knowledge of several thousand OAS sympathisers now living inside France.

Marc Rodin took his seat behind his desk and surveyed the other two. They gazed back with curiosity but no questions.

Carefully and methodically Rodin began his briefing, concentrating on the growing list of failures and defeats the OAS had sustained at the hands of the French Secret Services over the past few months. His guests stared gloomily into their glasses.

'We simply must face facts. In the past four months we have taken three severe blows. The frustration of the Ecole Militaire attempt to free France of the Dictator is merely the latest in a long list of such attempts which have failed even to get off the ground. The only two in which our men have even got within spitting distance of him have been fouled up by elementary mistakes in planning or execution. I don't need to go into the details, you know them all as well as I do.

'The kidnapping of Antoine Argoud has robbed us of one of our most astute leaders, and despite his loyalty to the cause there can be no doubt that with modern methods of interrogation, probably including drugs, used on him, the whole organisation stands in jeopardy from the security standpoint. Antoine knew everything there was to know, and now we have to start again almost from scratch. That's why we are sitting here in an obscure hotel rather than in our headquarters in Munich.

'But even starting from scratch would not be so bad if it were a year ago. Then we could call on thousands of volunteers full of enthusiasm and patriotism. Now that is not so easy. The murder of Jean-Marie Bastien-Thiry will not help matters. I do not blame our sympathisers too much. We promised them results and have given them none. They have a right to expect results, not words.'

'All right, all right. What are you getting at?' said Montclair. Both listeners knew Rodin was right. Montclair realised better than any that the funds gained in robbing banks across Algeria were expended on the costs of running the organisation, and that the donations from right wing industrialists were beginning to dry up. More recently his approaches had been met with ill-concealed disdain. Casson knew his lines of communications with the underground in France were becoming more tenuous by the week, his safe-houses were being raided and since the capture of Argoud many had withdrawn their support. The execution of Bastien-Thiry could only accelerate this process. The résumé given by Rodin was the truth, but no more pleasant to hear for all that.

Rodin continued as though there had been no interruption.

'We have now reached a position where the prime aim of our cause to liberate France, the disposal of Grand Zohra, without which all further plans must inevitably abort, has become virtually impossible by the traditional means. I hesitate, gentlemen, to commit more patriotic young men to plans which stand little chance of remaining unrevealed to the French Gestapo for more than a few days. In short, there are too many squealers, too many backsliders, too many recusants.

'Taking advantage of this, the Secret Police have now so completely infiltrated the movement that the deliberations of even our highest councils are being leaked to them. They seem to know, within days of the decision being taken, what we intend, what are our plans, and who are our personnel. It is undeniably unpleasant to have to face this situation, but I am convinced that if we do not face it we shall continue to live in a fool's paradise.

'In my estimation there is only one method remaining to accomplish our first objective, the killing of Zohra, in a manner that will by-pass the whole network of spies and agents, leave the Secret Police stripped of its advantages and face them with a situation of which they are not only unaware but which they could hardly frustrate even if they knew about it.'

Montclair and Casson looked up quickly. There was dead silence in the bedroom, broken only by the occasional clatter of rain against the window-pane.

'If we accept that my appreciation of the situation is, unfortunately, accurate,' continued Rodin, 'then we must also accept that all of those we now know as being both prepared and capable of doing the job of eliminating Grand Zohra are equally known to the Secret Police. None of them can move inside France as other than a hunted animal, pursued not only by the conventional police forces but betrayed from behind by the barbouzes and the stool-pigeons. I believe, gentlemen, that the only alternative left to us is to engage the services of an outsider.'

Montclair and Casson gazed at him first in amazement, then dawning comprehension.

'What kind of outsider?' asked Casson at length.

'It would be necessary for this man, whoever he is, to be a foreigner,' said Rodin. 'He would not be a member of the OAS or the CNR. He would not be known to any policeman in France, nor would he exist on any file. The weakness of all dictatorships is that they are vast bureaucracies. What is not on the file does not exist. The assassin would be an unknown and therefore non-existent quantity. He would travel under a foreign passport, do the job, and disappear back to his own country while the people of France rose to sweep away the remnants of De Gaulle's treasonable rabble. For the man to get out would not be vastly important, since we would in any case liberate him after taking power. The important thing is that he be able to get in, unspotted and unsuspected. That is something which at the moment not one of us can do.'

Both his listeners were silent, gazing each into his private thoughts as Rodin's plan took shape in their minds also.

Montclair let out a low whistle.

'A professional assassin, a mercenary.'

'Precisely,' replied Rodin. 'It would be quite unreasonable to suppose that an outsider is going to do such a job for the love of us, or for patriotism, or for the hell of it. In order to get the level of skill and of nerve necessary for this kind of operation, we must engage a true professional. And such a man would only work for money, a lot of money,' he added, glancing quickly at Montclair.

'But how do we know we can find such a man?' asked Casson.

Rodin held up his hand.

'First things first, gentlemen. Evidently there is a mass of detail to be worked out. What I wish to know first of all is if you agree in principle to the idea.'

Montclair and Casson looked at each other. Both turned to Rodin and nodded slowly.

'*Bien.*' Rodin leaned back as far as the upright chair would allow him. 'That then is the first point disposed of – agreement in principle. The second concerns security and is fundamental to the whole idea. In my view there are increasingly few who can be regarded as absolutely beyond suspicion as the possible source of a leak of information. That is not to say I regard any of our colleagues either in the OAS or the CNR as traitors to the cause, not as such. But it is an old axiom that the more people know a secret, the less sure that secret becomes. The whole essence of this idea is absolute secrecy. Consequently the fewer who are aware of it the better.

'Even within the OAS there are infiltrators who have achieved responsible positions and who yet report our plans to the Secret Police. These men's time will come one day, but for the moment they are dangerous. Among the politicians of the CNR there are those either too squeamish or too gutless to realise the full extent of the project they are supposed to have become committed to. I would not wish to put the life of any man in danger by gratuitously and unnecessarily informing such men of his existence.

'I have summoned you, René and you, André, here because I am utterly convinced of your loyalty to the cause and your ability to retain a secret. Moreover for the plan I have in mind the active co-operation of you, René, as treasurer and paymaster is necessary to meet the hire that any professional assassin will undoubtedly demand. Your co-operation, André, will be necessary to assure such a man of the assistance inside France of a small handful of men loyal beyond doubt in case he should have to call on them.

'But I see no reason why details of the idea should go further than we three. I am therefore proposing to you that we form a committee of ourselves to take the entire responsibility for this idea, its planning, execution and subsidisation.'

There was another silence. At length Montclair said, 'You mean we cut out the entire Council of the OAS, the whole of the CNR? They won't like that.'

'Firstly, they won't know about it,' replied Rodin calmly. 'If we were to put the idea to them all, it would require a plenary meeting. This alone would attract attention and the barbouzes would be active to find out what the plenary meeting was called for. There may even be a leak on one of the two councils. If we visited each member in turn it would take weeks even to get preliminary approval in principle. Then they would all want to know the details as each planning stage was reached and passed. You know what these bloody politicians and committee men are like. They want to know everything just for the sake of knowing it. They do nothing but each one can put the whole operation in jeopardy with a word spoken in drunkenness or carelessness.

'Secondly, if the agreement of the entire council of the OAS and the CNR could be obtained to the idea, we would be no further forward, and nearly thirty people would know about it. If, on the other hand we go ahead, take the responsibility and it fails, we shall be no further back than we are now. There will be recriminations no doubt, but nothing more. If the plan succeeds we shall be in power and no one will start arguing at that time. The exact means of achieving the destruction of the dictator will have become an academic point. In brief then, do you two agree to join me as sole planners, organisers and operators of the idea I have expounded to you?'

Again Montclair and Casson looked at each other, turned to Rodin and nodded. It was the first time they had met with him since the snatching of Argoud three months earlier. When Argoud had taken the chair Rodin had kept quietly in the background. Now he had emerged as a leader in his own right. The chief of the underground and the purse were impressed.

Rodin looked at them both, exhaled slowly and smiled.

'Good,' he said, 'now let us get down to details. The idea of using a professional mercenary assassin first occurred to me on the day I heard over the radio that poor Bastien-Thiry had been murdered. Since that time I have been searching for the man we want. Obviously such men are hard to find; they do not advertise themselves. I have been searching since the middle of March, and the outcome can be summed up in these.'

He held up the three manila folders that had been lying on his desk. Montclair and Casson exchanged glances again, eyebrows raised, and remained silent. Rodin resumed.

'I think it would be best if you studied the dossiers, then we can discuss our first choice. Personally, I have listed all three in terms of preference in case the first-listed either cannot or will not take the job. There is only one copy of each dossier, so you will have to exchange them.'

He reached into the manila folder and took out three slimmer files. He handed one to Montclair and one to Casson. The third he kept in his own hand, but did not bother to read it. He knew the contents of all three files intimately.

There was little enough to read. Rodin's reference to a 'brief' dossier was depressingly accurate. Casson finished his file first, looked up at Rodin and grimaced.

'That's all?'

'Such men do not make details about themselves easily available,' replied Rodin. 'Try this one.' He handed down to Casson the file he held in his hand.

A few moments later Montclair also finished and passed his file back to Rodin, who gave him the dossier Casson had just finished. Both men were again lost in reading. This time it was Montclair who finished first. He looked up at Rodin and shrugged.

'Well ... not much to go on, but surely we have fifty men like that. Gunslingers are two a penny....'

He was interrupted by Casson.

'Wait a minute, wait till you see this one.' He flicked over the last page and ran his eye down the three remaining paragraphs. When he had finished he closed the file and looked up at Rodin. The OAS chief gave away nothing of his own preferences. He took the file Casson had finished and passed it to Montclair. To Casson he passed the third of the folders. Both men finished their reading together four minutes later.

Rodin collected the folders and replaced them on the writing desk. He took the straight-backed chair, reversed it, and drew it towards the fire, sitting astride it with arms on the back. From this perch he surveyed the other two.

'Well, I told you it was a small market. There may be more men about who do this kind of work, but without access to the files of a good Secret Service, they are damnably hard to find. And probably the best ones aren't even on any files at all. You've seen all three. For the moment let us refer to them as the German, the South African and the Englishman. André?'

Casson shrugged. 'For me there is no debate. On his record, if it is true, the Englishman is out ahead by a mile.'

'René?'

'I agree. The German is a bit old for this kind of thing now. Apart from a few jobs done for the surviving Nazis against the Israeli agents who pursue them, he doesn't seem to have done much in the political field. Besides, his motivations against Jews are probably personal, therefore not completely professional. The South African may be all right chopping up nigger politicians like Lumumba, but that's a far cry from putting a bullet through the President of France. Besides, the Englishman speaks fluent French.'

Rodin nodded slowly. 'I didn't think there would be much doubt. Even before I had finished compiling those dossiers, the choice seemed to stand out a mile.'

'Are you sure about this Anglo-Saxon?' Casson asked. 'Has he really done those jobs?'

'I was surprised myself,' said Rodin. 'So I spent extra time on this one. As regards absolute proof, there is none. If there were it would be a bad sign. It would mean he would be listed everywhere as an undesirable immigrant. As it is, there is nothing against him but rumour. Formally, his sheet is white as snow. Even if the British have him listed, they can put no more than a question mark against him. That does not merit filing him with Interpol. The chances that the British would tip off the SDECE about such a man, even if a formal enquiry were made, are slim. You know how they hate each other. They even kept silent about Georges Bidault being in London last January. No, for this kind of job the Englishman has all the advantages but one. . . .'

'What's that?' asked Montclair quickly.

'Simple. He will not be cheap. A man like him can ask a lot of money. How are the finances, René?'

Montclair shrugged. 'Not too good. Expenditure has gone down a bit. Since the Argoud affair all the heroes of the CNR have gone to ground in cheap hotels. They seem to have lost their taste for the five-star palaces and the television interviews. On the other hand income is down to a trickle. As you said there must be some action or we shall be finished for lack of funds. One cannot run this kind of thing on love and kisses.'

Rodin nodded grimly. 'I thought so. We have to raise some money from somewhere. On the other hand there would be no point getting into that kind of action until we know how much we shall need. . . .'

'Which presumes,' cut in Casson smoothly, 'that the next step is to contact the Englishman and ask him if he will do the job and for how much.'

'Yes, well, are we all agreed on that?' Rodin glanced at both men in turn. Both nodded. Rodin glanced at his watch. 'It is now just after one o'clock. I have an agent in London whom I must telephone now and ask him to contact this man to ask him to come. If he is prepared to fly to Vienna tonight on the evening plane, we could meet him here after dinner. Either way, we will know when my agent phones back. I have taken the liberty of booking you both into adjoining rooms down the corridor. I think it would be safer to be together protected by Viktor than separated but without defences. Just in case, you understand.'

'You were pretty certain, weren't you?' asked Casson, piqued at being predicted in this manner.

Rodin shrugged. 'It has been a long process getting this information. The less time wasted from now on the better. If we are going to go ahead, let us now move fast.'

He rose and the other two got up with him. Rodin called Viktor and told him to go down to the hall to collect the keys for rooms 65 and 66, and to bring them back up. While waiting he told Montclair and Casson, 'I have to telephone from the main post office. I shall take Viktor with me. While I am gone would you both stay together in one room with the door locked. My signal will be three knocks, a pause, then two more.'

The sign was the familiar three-plus-two that made up the rhythm of the words 'Algérie Française' that Paris motorists had hooted on their car horns in previous years to express their disapproval of Gaullist policy.

'By the way,' continued Rodin, 'do either of you have a gun?'

Both men shook their heads. Rodin went to the escritoire and took out a chunky MAB 9 mm that he kept for his private use. He checked the magazine, snapped it back, and charged the breech. He held it out towards Montclair. 'You know this flingot?'

Montclair nodded. 'Well enough,' he said, and took it.

Viktor returned and escorted the pair of them to Montclair's room. When he returned Rodin was buttoning his overcoat.

'Come, Corporal, we have work to do.'

The BEA Vanguard from London to Vienna that evening glided into Schwechat Airport as the dusk deepened into night. Near the tail of the plane the blond Englishman lay back in his seat near the window and gazed out at the lead-in lights as they flashed past the sinking aircraft. It always gave him a feeling of pleasure to see them coming closer and closer until it appeared certain the plane must touch down in the grass of the undershoot area. At the last minute the dimly lit blur of grass, the numbered panels by the verge-side and the lights themselves vanished to be replaced by black-slicked concrete and wheels touched down at last. The precision of the business of landing appealed to him. He liked precision.

By his side the young Frenchman from the French Tourist Office in Piccadilly glanced at him nervously. Since the telephone call during the lunch-hour he had been in a state of nerves. Nearly a year ago on leave in Paris he had offered to put himself at the disposal of the OAS but since then had been told simply to stay at his desk in London. A letter or telephone call, addressed to him in his rightful name, but beginning 'Dear Pierre . . .' should be obeyed immediately and precisely. Since then, nothing, until today June 15th.

The operator had told him there was a person-to-person call for him from Vienna, and had then added 'En Autriche' to distinguish it from the town of the same name in France. Wonderingly he had taken the call, to hear a voice call him 'my dear Pierre'. It had taken him several seconds to remember his own code-name.

Pleading a bout of migraine after his lunch-hour, he had gone to the flat off South Audley Street and given the message to the Englishman who answered the door. The latter had evinced no surprise that he should be asked to fly to Vienna in three hours. He had quietly packed an overnight case and the pair of them had taken a taxi to Heathrow Airport. The Englishman had calmly produced a roll of notes, enough to buy two return tickets for cash after the Frenchman had admitted he had not thought of paying cash and had only brought his passport and a chequebook.

Since then they had hardly exchanged a word. The Englishman had not asked where they were going in Vienna, nor whom they were to meet, nor why, which was just as well because the Frenchman did not know. His instructions had merely been to telephone back from London Airport and confirm his arrival on the BEA flight, at which he was told to report to General Information on arrival at Schwechat. All of which made him nervous, and the controlled calm of the Englishman beside him, far from helping, made things worse.

At the Information desk in the main hall he gave his name to the pretty Austrian girl, who searched in a rack of pigeon-holes behind her, then passed him a small buff message form. It said simply: 'Ring 61.44.03, ask for Schulz.' He turned and headed towards the bank of public phones along the back of the main hall. The Englishman tapped him on the shoulder and pointed at the booth marked *Wechsel*.

'You'll need some coins,' he said in fluent French. 'Not even the Austrians are that generous.'

The Frenchman blushed and strode towards the money-change counter, while the Englishman sat himself comfortably in the corner of one of the upholstered settees against the wall and lit another king-size English filter. In a minute his guide was back with several Austrian banknotes and a handful of coins. The Frenchman went to the telephones, found an empty booth and dialled. At the other end Herr Schulz gave him clipped and precise instructions. It took only a few seconds, then the phone went dead.

The young Frenchman came back to the settee and the blond looked up at him.

'On y va?' he asked.

'On y va.' As he turned to leave, the Frenchman screwed up the message form with the telephone number and dropped it on the floor. The Englishman picked it up, opened it out and held it to the flame of his lighter. It blazed for an instant and disappeared in black crumbs beneath the elegant suède boot. They walked in silence out of the building and hailed a taxi.

The centre of the city was ablaze with lights and choked with cars so it was not until forty minutes later that the taxi arrived at the Pension Kleist.

'This is where we part. I was told to bring you here, but to take the taxi somewhere else. You are to go straight up to room 64. You are expected.'

The Englishman nodded and got out of the car. The driver turned enquiringly to the Frenchman. 'Drive on,' he said, and the taxi disappeared down the street. The Englishman glanced up at the old Gothic writing of the street name-plate, then the square Roman capitals above the door of the Pension Kleist. Finally he threw away his cigarette half smoked, and entered.

The clerk on duty had his back turned but the door creaked. Without giving any sign of approaching the desk the Englishman walked towards the stairs. The clerk was about to ask what he wanted, when the visitor glanced in his direction, nodded casually as to any other menial, and said firmly 'Guten Abend.'

'Guten Abend, mein Herr,' replied the clerk automatically and by the time he had finished the blond man was gone, taking the stairs two at a time without seeming to hurry. At the top he paused and glanced down the only corridor available. At the far end was room 68. He counted back down the corridor to what must be 64, although the figures were out of sight.

Between himself and the door of 64 was twenty feet of corridor, the walls being studded on the right by two other doors before 64, and on the left a small alcove partially curtained with red velours hanging from a cheap brass rod.

He studied the alcove carefully. From beneath the curtain, which cleared the floor by four inches, the toe of a single black shoe emerged slightly. He turned and walked back to the foyer. This time the clerk was ready. At least he managed to get his mouth open.

'Pass me room 64, please,' said the Englishman. The clerk looked him in the face for a second, then obeyed. After a few seconds he turned back from the small switchboard, picked up the desk phone and passed it over.

'If that gorilla is not out of the alcove in fifteen seconds I am going back home,' said the blond man, and put the phone down. Then he walked back up the stairs.

At the top he watched the door of 64 open and Colonel Rodin appeared. He stared down the corridor for a moment at the Englishman, then called softly, 'Viktor.' From the alcove the giant Pole emerged and stood looking from one to the other. Rodin said, 'It's all right. He is expected.' Kowalski glowered. The Englishman started to walk.

Rodin ushered him inside the bedroom. It had been arranged like an office for a recruiting board. The escritoire served for the chairman's desk and was littered with papers. Behind it was the single upright chair in the room. But two other uprights brought in from adjacent rooms flanked the central chair, and these were occupied by Montclair and Casson, who eyed the visitor curiously. There was no chair in front of the desk. The Englishman cast an eye around, selected one of the two easy chairs and spun it round to face the desk. By the time Rodin had given fresh instructions to Viktor and closed the door, the Englishman was comfortably seated and staring back at Casson and Montclair. Rodin took his seat behind the desk.

For a few seconds he stared at the man from London. What he saw did not displease him, and he was an expert in men. The visitor stood about six feet tall, apparently in his early thirties, and with a lean, athletic build. He looked fit, the face was sun-tanned with regular but not remarkable features, and the hands lay quietly along the arms of the chair. To Rodin's eye he looked like a man who retained control of himself. But the eyes bothered Rodin. He had seen the soft moist eyes of weaklings, the dull shuttered eyes of psychopaths and the watchful eyes of soldiers. The eyes of the Englishman were open and stared back with frank candour. Except for the irises, which were of flecked grey so that they seemed smoky like the hoar mist on a winter's morning. It took Rodin a few seconds to realise that they had no expression at all. Whatever thoughts did go on behind the smoke-screen, nothing came through, and Rodin felt a worm of unease. Like all men created by systems and procedures, he did not like the unpredictable and therefore the uncontrollable.

'We know who you are,' he began abruptly. 'I had better introduce myself. I am Colonel Marc Rodin. . . .'

'I know,' said the Englishman, 'you are chief of operations of the OAS. You are Major René Montclair, treasurer, and you are Monsieur André Casson, head of the underground in the Métropole.' He stared at each of the men in turn as he spoke, and reached for a cigarette.

'You seem to know a lot already,' interjected Casson as the three watched the visitor light up. The Englishman leaned back and blew out the first stream of smoke.

'Gentlemen, let us be frank. I know what you are and you know what I am. We both have unusual occupations. You are hunted while I am free to move where I will without surveillance. I operate for money, you for idealism. But when it comes to practical details we are all professionals at our jobs. Therefore we do not need to fence. You have been making enquiries about me. It is impossible to make such enquiries without the news of them soon getting back to the man being asked about. Naturally I wished to know who was so interested in me. It could have been someone seeking revenge, or wishing to employ me. It was important to me to know. As soon as I discovered the identity of the organisation interested in me, two days among the French newspaper files in the British Museum were enough to tell me about you and your organisation. So the visit of your little errand boy this afternoon was hardly a surprise. *Bon.* I know who you are, and whom you represent. What I would like to know is what you want.'

There was silence for several minutes. Casson and Montclair glanced for guidance at Rodin. The paratroop colonel and the assassin stared at each other. Rodin knew enough about violent men to understand the man facing him was what he wanted. From then on Montclair and Casson were part of the furniture.

'Since you have read the files available, I will not bore you with the motivations behind our organisation, which you have accurately termed as idealism. We believe France is now ruled by a dictator who has polluted our country and prostituted its honour. We believe his regime can only fall and France be restored to Frenchmen if he first dies. Out of six attempts by our supporters to eliminate him, three were exposed in the early planning stages, one was betrayed the day before the attempt, and two took place but misfired.

'We are considering, but only at this stage considering, engaging the services of a professional to do the job. However, we do not wish to waste our money. The first thing we would like to know is if it is possible.'

Rodin had played his cards shrewdly. The last sentence, to which he already knew the answer, brought a flicker of expression to the grey eyes.

'There is no man in the world who is proof against an assassin's bullet,' said the Englishman. 'De Gaulle's exposure rate is very high. Of course it's possible to kill him. The point is that the chances of escape would not be too high. A fanatic prepared to die himself in the attempt is always the most certain method of eliminating a dictator who exposes himself to the public. I notice,' he added with a touch of malice, 'that despite your idealism you have not yet been able to produce such a man. Both Pont-de-Seine and Petit-Clamart failed because no one was prepared to risk his own life to make absolutely certain.'

'There are patriotic Frenchmen prepared even now . . .' began Casson hotly, but Rodin silenced him with a gesture. The Englishman did not even glance at him.

'And as regards a professional?' prompted Rodin.

'A professional does not act out of fervour, and is therefore more calm and less likely to make elementary errors. Not being idealistic he is not likely to have second thoughts at the last minute about who else might get hurt in the explosion, or whatever method, and being a professional he has calculated the risks to the last contingency. So his chances of success on schedule are surer than anyone else, but he will not even enter into operation until he has devised a plan that will enable him not only to complete the mission, but to escape unharmed.'

'Do you estimate that such a plan could be worked out to permit a professional to kill Grand Zohra and escape?'

The Englishman smoked quietly for a few minutes and stared out of the window. 'In principle, yes,' he replied at length. 'In principle it is always possible with enough time and planning. But in this case it would be extremely difficult. More so than with most other targets.'

'Why more than others?' asked Montclair.

'Because De Gaulle is forewarned – not about the specific attempt, but about the general intention. All big men have bodyguards and security men, but over a period of years without any serious attempt on the life of the big man, the checks become formal, the routines mechanical and the degree of watchfulness is lowered. The single bullet that finishes the target is wholly unexpected and therefore provokes panic. Under cover of this the assassin escapes. In this case there will be no lowering of the level of watchfulness, no mechanical routines, and if the bullet were to get to the target, there would be many who would not panic but would go for the assassin. It could be done, but it would be one of the hardest jobs in the world at this moment. You see, gentlemen, not only have your own efforts failed, but they have queered the pitch for everyone else.'

'In the event that we decide to employ a professional assassin to do this job . . .' began Rodin.

'You have to employ a professional,' cut in the Englishman quietly.

'And why, pray? There are many men still who would be prepared to do the job out of purely patriotic motives.'

'Yes, there is still Watin and Curutchet,' replied the blond. 'And doubtless there are more Degueldres and Bastien-Thirys around somewhere. But you three men did not call me here for a chat in general terms about the theory of political assassination, nor because you have a sudden shortage of trigger-fingers. You called me here because you have belatedly come to the conclusion that your organisation is so infiltrated by the French Secret Service agents that little you decide remains secret for long, and also because the face of every one of you is imprinted on the memory of every cop in France. Therefore you need an outsider. And you are right. If the job is to be done an outsider has to do it. The only questions that remain are who, and for how much. Now, gentlemen, I think you have had long enough to examine the merchandise, don't you?'

Rodin looked sideways at Montclair and raised an eyebrow. Montclair nodded. Casson followed suit. The Englishman gazed out of the window without a shred of interest.

'Will you assassinate De Gaulle?' asked Rodin at last. The voice was quiet but the question filled the room. The Englishman's glance came back to him and the eyes were blank again.

'Yes, but it will cost a lot of money.'

'How much?' asked Montclair.

'You must understand this is a once-in-a-lifetime job. The man who does it will never work again. The chances of remaining not only uncaught but undiscovered are very small. One must make enough for this one job both to be able to live well for the rest of one's days and to acquire protection against the revenge of the Gaullists. . . .'

'When we have France,' said Casson, 'there will be no shortage. . . .'

'Cash,' said the Englishman. 'Half in advance and half on completion.'

'How much?' asked Rodin.

'Half a million.'

Rodin glanced at Montclair, who grimaced. 'That's a lot of money, half a million new francs. . . .'

'Dollars,' said the Englishman.

'Half a million dollars?' shouted Montclair, rising from his seat. 'You are crazy?'

'No,' said the Englishman calmly, 'but I am the best, and therefore the most expensive.'

'We could certainly get cheaper estimates,' sneered Casson.

'Yes,' said the blond without emotion, 'you could get men cheaper, and you would find they took your fifty per cent deposit and vanished, or made excuses later as to why it could not be done. When you employ the best you pay. Half a million dollars is the price. Considering you expect to get France itself, you esteem your country very cheap.'

Rodin, who had remained quiet through this exchange, took the point.

'*Touché*. The point is, monsieur, we do not have half a million dollars cash.'

'I am aware of that,' replied the Englishman. 'If you want the job done you will have to make that sum from somewhere. I do not need the job, you understand. After my last assignment I have enough to live well for some years. But the idea of having enough to retire is appealing. Therefore I am prepared to take some exceptionally high risks for that prize. Your friends here want a prize even greater – France herself. Yet the idea of risks appals them. I am sorry. If you cannot acquire the sum involved, then you must go back to arranging your own plots and seeing them destroyed by the authorities one by one.'

He half-rose from his chair, stubbing out his cigarette in the process. Rodin rose with him.

'Be seated, monsieur. We shall get the money.' They both sat down.

'Good,' said the Englishman, 'but there are also conditions.'

'Yes?'

'The reason you need an outsider in the first place is because of constant security leaks to the French authorities. How many people in your organisation know of this idea of hiring any outsider at all, let alone me?'

'Just the three of us in this room. I worked out the idea the day after Bastien-Thiry was executed. Since then I have undertaken all the enquiries personally. There is no one else in the know.'

'Then it must remain that way,' said the Englishman. 'All records of all meetings, files and dossiers must be destroyed. There must be nothing available outside your three heads. In view of what happened in February to Argoud I shall feel myself free to call off if any of you three are captured. Therefore you should remain somewhere safe and under heavy guard until the job is done. Agreed?'

'*D'accord*. What else?'

'The planning will be mine, as with the operation. I shall divulge the details to no one, not even to you. In short, I shall disappear. You will hear nothing from me again. You have my telephone number in London and my address, but I shall be leaving both as soon as I am ready to move.

'In any event you will only contact me at that place in an emergency. For the rest there will be no contact at all. I shall leave you the name of my bank in Switzerland. When they tell me the first two hundred and fifty thousand dollars has been deposited, or when I am fully ready, whichever is the later, I shall move. I will not be hurried beyond my own judgement, nor will I be subject to interference. Agreed?'

'*D'accord*. But our undercover men in France are in a position to offer you considerable assistance in the way of information. Some of them are highly placed.'

The Englishman considered this for a moment. 'All right, when you are ready send me by mail a single telephone number, preferably in Paris so that I can ring that number direct from anywhere in France. I will not give anyone my own whereabouts, but simply ring that number for latest information about the security situation surrounding the President. But the man on the end of that telephone should not know what I am doing in France. Simply tell him that I am on a mission for you and need his assistance. The less he knows the better. Let him be simply a clearing house for information. Even his sources should be confined uniquely to those in a position to give valuable inside information, not rubbish that I can read in the newspaper. Agreed?'

'Very well. You wish to operate entirely alone, without friends or refuge. Be it on your own head. How about false papers? We have two excellent forgers at our disposal.'

'I will acquire my own, thank you.'

Casson broke in. 'I have a complete organisation inside France similar to the Resistance during the German occupation. I can put this entire structure at your disposal for assistance purposes.'

'No thank you. I prefer to bank on my own complete anonymity. It is the best weapon I have.'

'But supposing something should go wrong, you might have to go on the run. . . .'

'Nothing will go wrong, unless it comes from your side. I will operate without contacting or being known to your organisation, M. Casson, for exactly the same reason I am here in the first place; because the organisation is crawling with agents and stool-pigeons.'

Casson looked fit to explode. Montclair stared glumly at the window trying to envisage raising half a million dollars in a hurry. Rodin stared thoughtfully back at the Englishman across the table.

'Calm, André. Monsieur wishes to work alone. So be it. That is his way. We do not pay half a million dollars for a man who needs the same amount of molly-coddling our own shooters need.'

'What I would like to know,' muttered Montclair, 'is how we can raise so much money so quickly.'

'Use your organisation to rob a few banks,' suggested the Englishman lightly.

'In any case, that is our problem,' said Rodin. 'Before our visitor returns to London, are there any further points?'

'What is to prevent you from taking the first quarter of a million and disappearing?' asked Casson.

'I told you, messieurs, I wanted to retire. I do not wish to have half an army of ex-paras gunning for me. I would have to spend more protecting myself than the money I had made. It would soon be gone.'

'And what,' persisted Casson, 'is to prevent us waiting until the job is done and then refusing to pay you the balance of the half-million?'

'The same reason,' replied the Englishman smoothly. 'In that event I should go to work on my own account. And the target would be you three gentlemen. However, I don't think that will occur, do you?'

Rodin interrupted. 'Well, if that is all, I don't think we need detain our guest any longer. Oh . . . there is one last point. Your name. If you wish to remain anonymous you should have a code-name. Do you have any ideas?'

The Englishman thought for a moment. 'Since we have been speaking of hunting, what about the Jackal? Will that do?'

Rodin nodded. 'Yes, that will do fine. In fact I think I like it.'

He escorted the Englishman to the door and opened it. Viktor left his alcove and approached. For the first time Rodin smiled and held out his hand to the assassin. 'We will be in touch in the agreed manner as soon as we can. In the meantime could you begin planning in general terms so as not to waste too much time? Good. Then *bonsoir*, Mr Jackal.'

The Pole watched the visitor depart as quietly as he had come. The Englishman spent the night at the airport hotel and caught the first plane back to London in the morning.

Inside the Pension Kleist Rodin faced a barrage of belated queries and complaints from Casson and Montclair, who had both been shaken by the three hours between nine and midnight.

'Half a million dollars,' Montclair kept repeating. 'How on earth do we raise half a million dollars?'

'We may have to take up the Jackal's suggestion and rob a few banks,' answered Rodin.

'I don't like that man,' said Casson. 'He works alone, without allies. Such men are dangerous. One cannot control them.'

Rodin closed the discussion. 'Look, you two, we devised a plan, we agreed on a proposal, and we sought a man prepared to kill and capable of killing the President of France for money. I know a bit about men like that. If anyone can do it, he can. Now we have made our play. Let us get on with our side and let him get on with his.'

3

During the second half of June and the whole of July in 1963 France was rocked by an outbreak of violent crime against banks, jewellers' shops and post offices that was unprecedented at the time and has never been repeated since. The details of this crime wave are now a matter of record.

From one end of the country to the other banks were held up with pistols, sawn-off shotguns and submachine guns on an almost daily basis. Smash and grab raids at jewellers' shops became so common throughout that period that local police forces had hardly finished taking depositions from the shaking and often bleeding jewellers and their assistants than they were called away to another similar case within their own manor.

Two bank clerks were shot in different towns as they tried to resist the robbers, and before the end of July the crisis had grown so big that the men of the Corps Républicain de Sécurité, the anti-riot squads known to every Frenchman simply as the CRS, were called in and for the first time armed with submachine guns. It became habitual for those entering a bank to have to pass one or two of the blue-uniformed CRS guards in the foyer, each toting a loaded submachine carbine.

In response to pressure from the bankers and jewellers, who complained bitterly to the Government about this crime wave, police checks on banks at night were increased in frequency, but to no avail, since the robbers were not professional cracksmen able to open a bank vault skilfully during the hours of darkness, but simply thugs in masks, armed and ready to shoot if provoked in the slightest way.

The danger hours were in daylight, when any bank or jeweller's shop throughout the country could be surprised in the middle of business by the appearance of two or three armed and masked men, and the peremptory cry 'Haut les mains'.

Three robbers were wounded towards the end of July in different hold-ups, and taken prisoner. Each turned out to be either a petty crook known to be using the existence of the OAS as an excuse for general anarchy, or deserters from one of the former colonial regiments who soon admitted they were OAS men. But despite the most diligent interrogations at police headquarters, none of the three could be persuaded to say why this rash of robberies had suddenly struck the country, other than that they had been contacted by their 'patron' (gang boss) and given a target in the form of a bank or jeweller's shop. Eventually the police came to believe that the prisoners did not know what the purpose of the robberies was; they had each been promised a cut of the total, and being small fry had done what they were told.

It did not take the French authorities long to realise the OAS was behind the outbreak, nor that for some reason the OAS needed money in a hurry. But it was not until the first fortnight of August, and then in a quite different manner, that the authorities discovered why.

Within the last two weeks of June, however, the wave of crime against banks and other places where money and gems may be quickly and unceremoniously acquired had become sufficiently serious to be handed over to Commissaire Maurice Bouvier, the much-revered chief of the Brigade Criminelle of the Police Judiciaire. In his surprisingly small work-strewn office at the headquarters of the PJ at 36 Quai des Orfèvres, along the banks of the Seine, a chart was prepared showing the cash or, in the case of jewellery, approximate re-sale value of the stolen money and gems. By the latter half of July the total was well over two million new francs, or four hundred thousand dollars. Even with a reasonable sum deducted for the expenses of mounting the various robberies, and more for paying the hoodlums and deserters who carried them out that, still left, in the Commissaire's estimation, a sizable sum of money that could not be accounted for.

In the last week of June a report landed on the desk of General Guibaud, the head of the SDECE, from the chief of his permanent office in Rome. It was to the effect that the three top men of the OAS, Marc Rodin, René Montclair and André Casson, had taken up residence together on the top floor of a hotel just off the Via Condotti. The report added that despite the obvious cost of residing in a hotel in such an exclusive quarter, the three had taken the entire top floor for themselves, and the floor below for their bodyguards. They were being guarded night and day by no less than eight extremely tough ex-members of the Foreign Legion, and were not venturing out at all. At first it was thought they had met for a conference, but as the days passed SDECE came to the view that they were simply taking exceptionally heavy precautions to ensure that they were not the victims of another kidnapping as had been inflicted on Antoine Argoud. General Guibaud permitted himself a grim smile at the sight of the top men of the terrorist organisation themselves now cowering in a hotel in Rome, and filed the report in a routine manner. Despite the bitter row still festering on between the French Foreign Ministry at the Quai d'Orsay and the German Foreign Ministry in Bonn over the infringement of German territorial integrity at the Eden-Wolff Hotel the previous February, Guibaud had every reason to be pleased with his Action Service men who had carried out the coup. The sight of the OAS chiefs running scared was reward enough in itself. The General smothered a small shadow of misgiving as he surveyed the file of Marc Rodin and nevertheless asked himself why a man like Rodin should scare that easily. As a man with considerable experience of his own job, and an awareness of the realities of politics and diplomacy, he knew he would be most unlikely ever to obtain permission to organise another snatch-job. It was only much later that the real significance of the precautions the three OAS men were taking for their own safety became clear to him.

In London the Jackal spent the last fortnight of June and the first two weeks of July in carefully controlled and planned activity. From the day of his return he set himself among other things to acquire and read almost every word written about or by Charles de Gaulle. By the simple expedient of going to the local lending library and looking up the entry for the French President in the *Encyclopaedia Britannica*, he found at the end of the entry a comprehensive list of reference books about his subject.

After that he wrote off to various well-known bookshops, using a false name and a forwarding address in Praed Street, Paddington, and acquired the necessary reference books by post. These he scoured until the small hours each morning in his flat, building up in his mind a most detailed picture of the incumbent of the Elysée Palace from his boyhood until the time of reading. Much of the information he gleaned was of no practical use, but here and there a quirk or character trait would emerge that he noted in a small exercise book. Most instructive concerning the character of the French President was the volume of the General's memoirs, *The Edge of the Sword* (Le Fil de l'Epée) in which Charles de Gaulle was at his most illuminating about his own personal attitude to life, his country and his destiny as he saw it.

The Jackal was neither a slow nor stupid man. He read voraciously and planned meticulously, and possessed the faculty to store in his mind an enormous amount of factual information on the offchance that he might later have a use for it.

But although his reading of the works of Charles de Gaulle, and the books about him by the men who knew him best, provided a full picture of a proud and disdainful President of France, it still did not solve the main question that had been baffling him since he accepted in Rodin's bedroom in Vienna on June 15th the assignment to go through with the assassination. By the end of the first week in July he had still not worked out the answer to this question – when, where and how should the 'hit' take place? As a last resort he went down to the reading room of the British Museum and, after signing his application for permission to research with his habitual false name, started to work his way through the back copies of France's leading daily newspaper *Le Figaro*.

Just when the answer came to him is not exactly known, but it is fair to presume it was within three days from July 7th. Within those three days, starting with the germ of an idea triggered by a columnist writing in 1962, cross-checking back through the files covering every year of De Gaulle's presidency since 1945, the assassin managed to answer his own question. He decided within that time precisely on what day, come illness or bad weather, totally regardless of any considerations of personal danger, Charles de Gaulle would stand up publicly and show himself. From that point on, the Jackal's preparations moved out of the research stage and into that of practical planning.

It took long hours of thought, lying on his back in his flat staring up at the cream-painted ceiling and chain-smoking his habitual king-size filter cigarettes, before the last detail had clicked into place.

At least a dozen ideas were considered and rejected before he finally hit on the plan he decided to adopt, the 'how' that had to be added to the 'when' and 'where' that he had already decided.

The Jackal was perfectly aware that in 1963 General de Gaulle was not only the President of France; he was also the most closely and skilfully guarded figure in the Western world. To assassinate him, as was later proved, was considerably more difficult than to kill President John F. Kennedy of the United States. Although the English killer did not know it, French security experts who had through American courtesy been given an opportunity to study the precautions taken to guard the life of President Kennedy had returned somewhat disdainful of those precautions as exercised by the American Secret Service. The French experts' rejection of the American methods was later justified when in November 1963 John Kennedy was killed in Dallas by a half-crazed and security-slack amateur while Charles de Gaulle lived on, to retire in peace and eventually to die in his own home.

What the Jackal did know was that the security men he was up against were at least among the best in the world, that the whole security apparatus around De Gaulle was in a stage of permanent forewarning of the likelihood of some attempt being made on their charge's life, and that the organisation for which he worked was riddled with security leaks. On the credit side he could reasonably bank on his own anonymity, and on the choleric refusal of his victim to co-operate with his own security forces. On the chosen day, the pride, the stubbornness and the absolute contempt for personal danger of the French President would force him to come out into the open for a few seconds no matter what the risks involved.

The SAS airliner from Kastrup, Copenhagen, made one last swing into line in front of the terminal building at London, trundled forward a few feet and halted. The engines whined on for a few seconds, then they also died away. Within a few minutes the steps were wheeled up and the passengers started to file out and down, nodding a last goodbye to the smiling stewardess at the top. On the observation terrace the blond man slipped his dark glasses upwards on to his forehead and applied his eyes to a pair of binoculars. The file of passengers coming down the steps was the sixth that morning to be subjected to this kind of scrutiny, but as the terrace was crowded in the warm sunshine with people waiting for arriving passengers and trying to spot them as soon as they emerged from their aircraft, the watcher's behaviour aroused no interest.

As the eighth passenger emerged into the light and straightened up, the man on the terrace tensed slightly and followed the new arrival down the steps. The passenger from Denmark was a priest or pastor, in a clerical grey suit with a dog collar. He appeared to be in his late forties from the iron-grey hair cut at medium length that was brushed back from the forehead, but the face was more youthful. He was a tall man with wide shoulders and he looked physically fit. He had approximately the same build as the man who watched him from the terrace above.

As the passengers filed into the arrivals lounge for passport and Customs clearance, the Jackal dropped the binoculars into the leather briefcase by his side, closed it and walked quietly back through the glass doors and down into the main hall. Fifteen minutes later the Danish pastor emerged from the Customs hall holding a grip and a suitcase. There appeared to be nobody to meet him, and his first call was made to the Barclays Bank counter to change money.

From what he told the Danish police when they interrogated him six weeks later he did not notice the blond young Englishman standing beside him at the counter apparently waiting his turn in the queue but quietly examining the features of the Dane from behind dark glasses. At least he had no memory of such a man.

But when he came out of the main hall to board the BEA coach to the Cromwell Road terminal the Englishman was a few paces behind him holding his briefcase, and they must have travelled into London on the same coach.

At the terminal the Dane had to wait a few minutes while his suitcase was unloaded from the luggage trailer behind the coach, then wend his way past the checking-in counters to the exit sign marked with an arrow and the international word 'Taxis'. While he did so the Jackal strode round the back of the coach and across the floor of the coach-park to where he had left his car in the staff car-park. He hefted the briefcase into the passenger seat of the open sports model, climbed in and started up, bringing the car to a halt close to the left-hand wall of the terminal from where he could glance to the right down the long line of waiting taxis under the pillared arcade. The Dane climbed into the third taxi, which cruised off into the Cromwell Road, heading towards Knightsbridge. The sports car followed.

The taxi dropped the oblivious priest at a small but comfortable hotel in Half Moon Street, while the sports car shot past the entrance and within a few minutes had found a spare parking meter on the far side of Curzon Street. The Jackal locked the briefcase in the boot, bought a midday edition of the *Evening Standard* at the newsagent's in Shepherd Market, and was back in the foyer of the hotel within five minutes. He had to wait another twenty-five before the Dane came downstairs and handed back his room key to the receptionist. After she hung it up, the key swayed for a few seconds from the hook, and the man in one of the foyer armchairs apparently waiting for a friend, who lowered his newspaper as the Dane passed into the restaurant, noted that the number of the key was 47. A few minutes later as the receptionist bobbed back into the rear office to check a theatre booking for one of the guests the man in the dark glasses slipped quietly and unnoticed up the stairs.

A two-inch-wide strip of flexible mica was not enough to open the door of room 47 which was rather stiff, but the mica strip stiffened by a whippy little artist's palette knife did the trick and the spring lock slipped back with a click. As he had only gone downstairs for lunch the pastor had left his passport on the bedside table. The Jackal was back in the corridor within thirty seconds, leaving the folder of traveller's cheques untouched in the hope that without any evidence of a theft the authorities would try to persuade the Dane that he had simply lost his passport somewhere else. And so it proved. Long before the Dane had finished his coffee the Englishman had departed unseen, and it was not until much later in the afternoon, after a thorough and mystified search of his room, that the pastor mentioned the disappearance of his passport to the manager. The manager also searched the room, and after pointing out that everything else, including the wallet of traveller's cheques, was intact, brought all his advocacy to bear to persuade his bewildered guest that there was no need to bring the police to his hotel since he had evidently lost his passport somewhere in transit. The Dane, being a kindly man and not too sure of his ground in a foreign country, agreed despite himself that this was what must have happened. So he reported the loss to the Danish Consulate-General the next day, was issued with travel documents with which to return to Copenhagen at the end of his fortnight's stay in London, and thought no more about it. The clerk at the Consulate-General who issued the travel documents filed the loss of a passport in the name of Pastor Per Jensen of Sankt Kjeldskirke in Copenhagen, and thought no more about it either. The date was July 14th.

Two days later a similar loss was experienced by an American student from Syracuse, New York State. He had arrived at the Oceanic Building of London Airport from New York and he produced his passport in order to change the first of his traveller's cheques at the American Express counter. After changing the cheque he placed the money in an inside pocket of his jacket, and the passport inside a zipped pouch which he stuffed back into a small leather hand-grip. A few minutes later, trying to attract the attention of a porter, he put the grip down for a moment and three seconds later it was gone. At first he remonstrated with the porter, who led him to the Pan American enquiries desk, who directed him to the attention of the nearest terminal security police officer. The latter took him to an office where he explained his dilemma.

After a search had ruled out the possibility that the grip might have been taken by someone else accidentally in mistake for their own, a report was filed listing the matter as a deliberate theft.

Apologies were made and regrets were expressed to the tall and ath-

letic young American about the activities of pickpockets and bag-snat-
chers in public places and he was told of the many precautions the
airport authorities took to try to curb their thefts from incoming foreigners. He had the grace to admit that a friend of his was once robbed in a
similar manner on Grand Central Station, New York.

The report was eventually circulated in a routine manner to all the
divisons of the London Metropolitan Police, together with a description
of the missing grip, its contents and the papers and passport in the pouch.
This was duly filed, but as weeks passed and no trace was found of either
the grip or its contents no more was thought of the incident.

Meanwhile Marty Schulberg went to his consulate in Grosvenor
Square, reported the theft of his passport and was issued with travel
documents enabling him to fly back to the United States after his
month's vacation touring the highlands of Scotland with his exchange-
student girl-friend. At the consulate the loss was registered, reported to
State Department in Washington and duly forgotten by both establishments.

It will never be known just how many incoming passengers at London
Airport's two overseas arrivals passenger buildings were scanned through
binoculars from the observation terraces as they emerged from their aircraft and headed down the steps. Despite the difference in their ages, the
two who lost their passports had some things in common. Both were
around six feet tall, had broad shoulders and slim figures, blue eyes and a
fairly close facial resemblance to the unobtrusive Englishman who had
followed and robbed them. Otherwise, Pastor Jensen was aged forty-eight
with grey hair and gold-rimmed glasses for reading; Marty Schulberg was
twenty-five, with chestnut-brown hair and heavy-rimmed executive
glasses which he wore all the time.

These were the faces the Jackal studied at length on the writing bureau
in his flat off South Audley Street. It took him one day and a series of
visits to theatrical costumiers, opticians, a men's clothing store in the
West End specialising in garments of American type and mainly made in
New York to acquire a set of blue-tinted clear-vision contact lenses: two
pairs of spectacles, one with gold rims and the other with heavy black
frames, and both with clear lenses; a complete outfit consisting of a pair
of black leather sneakers, T-shirt and underpants, off-white slacks and a
sky-blue nylon windcheater with a zip-up front and collars and cuffs in
red and white wool, all made in New York; and a clergyman's white
shirt, starched dog-collar and black bib. From each of the last three the
maker's label was carefully removed.

His last visit of the day was to a men's wig and toupee emporium in
Chelsea run by two homosexuals. Here he acquired a preparation for
tinting the hair a medium grey and another for tinting it chestnut brown,
along with precise and coyly delivered instructions on how to apply the
tint to achieve the best and most natural-looking effect in the shortest
time. He also bought several small hair-brushes for applying the liquids.
Otherwise, apart from the complete set of American clothes, he did not
make more than one purchase at any one shop.

The following day, July 18th, there was a small paragraph at the bottom of an inside page of *Le Figaro*. It announced that in Paris the Deputy Chief of the Brigade Criminelle of the Police Judiciaire, Commissaire Hyppolite Dupuy, had suffered a severe stroke in his office at the Quai des Orfèvres and had died on his way to hospital. A successor had been named. He was Commissaire Claude Lebel, Chief of the Homicide Division, and in view of the pressure of work on all the departments of the Brigade during the summer months he would take up his new duties forthwith. The Jackal, who read every French newspaper available in London each day, read the paragraph after his eye had been caught by the word 'Criminelle' in the headline, but thought nothing of it.

Before starting his daily watch at London Airport he had decided to operate throughout the whole of the forthcoming assassination under a false identity. It is one of the easiest things in the world to acquire a false British passport. The Jackal followed the procedure used by most mercenaries, smugglers and others who wish to adopt an alias for passing national boundaries. First he took a car trip through the Home Counties of the Thames Valley looking for small villages. In the third cemetery he visited, the Jackal found a gravestone to suit his purpose, that of Alexander Duggan who died at the age of two and a half years in 1931. Had he lived, the Duggan child would have been a few months older than the Jackal in July 1963. The elderly vicar was courteous and helpful when the visitor presented himself at the vicarage to announce that he was an amateur genealogist engaged in attempting to trace the family tree of the Duggans. He had been informed that there had been a Duggan family that had settled in the village in years past. He wondered, somewhat diffidently, if the parish records might be able to help in his search.

The vicar was kindness itself, and on their way over to the church a compliment on the beauty of the little Norman building and a contribution to the donations box for the restoration fund improved the atmosphere yet more. The records showed both the Duggan parents had died over the past seven years, and, alas, their only son Alexander had been buried in this very churchyard over thirty years before. The Jackal idly turned over the pages in the parish register of births, marriages and deaths for 1929, and for the month of April the name of Duggan, written in a crabbed and clerkly hand, caught his eye.

Alexander James Quentin Duggan, born April 3rd, 1929, in the parish of St Mark's, Sambourne Fishley.

He noted the details, thanked the vicar profusely and left. Back in London he presented himself at the Central Registry of Births, Marriages and Deaths, where a helpful young assistant accepted without query his visiting card showing him to be a partner in a firm of solicitors of Market Drayton, Shropshire, and his explanation that he was engaged in trying to trace the whereabouts of the grandchildren of one of the firm's clients who had recently died and left her estate to her grandchildren. One of these grandchildren was Alexander James Quentin Duggan, born at Sambourne Fishley, in the parish of St Mark's, on April 3rd, 1929.

Most civil servants in Britain do their best to be helpful when confronted with a polite enquiry, and in this case the assistant was no exception. A search of the records showed that the child in question had been registered precisely according to the enquirer's information, but had died on November 8th, 1931, as the result of a road accident. For a few shillings the Jackal received a copy of both the birth and death certificates. Before returning home he stopped at a branch office of the Ministry of Labour and was issued with a passport application form, at a toyshop where for fifteen shillings he bought a child's printing set, and at a post office for a one-pound postal order.

Back in his flat he filled in the application form in Duggan's name, giving exactly the right age, date of birth, etc., but his own personal description. He wrote in his own height, colour of hair and eyes, and for profession put down simply 'business man'. The full names of Duggan's parents, taken from the child's birth certificate, were also filled in. For the referee he filled in the name of Rev. James Elderly, vicar of St Mark's, Sambourne Fishley, to whom he had spoken that morning, and whose full name and title of LL.D had obligingly been printed on a board outside the church gate. The vicar's signature was forged in a thin hand in thin ink with a thin nib, and from the printing set he made up a stamp reading: 'St Mark's Parish Church, Sambourne Fishley', which was placed firmly next to the vicar's name. The copy of the birth certificate, the application form, and the postal order were sent off to the Passport Office in Petty France. The death certificate he destroyed. The brand-new passport arrived at the accommodation address by post four days later as he was reading that morning's edition of *Le Figaro*. He picked it up after lunch. Late that afternoon he locked the flat, and drove to London Airport where he boarded the flight to Copenhagen, paying in cash again to avoid using a cheque-book. In the false bottom of his suitcase, in a compartment barely thicker than an ordinary magazine and almost undetectable except to the most thorough search, was two thousand pounds which he had drawn earlier that day from his private deed-box in the vaults of a firm of solicitors in Holborn.

The visit to Copenhagen was brisk and businesslike. Before leaving Kastrup Airport he booked himself on the next afternoon's Sabena flight to Brussels. In the Danish capital it was far too late to go shopping, so he booked in at the Hôtel d'Angleterre on Kongs Ny Torv, ate like a king at the Seven Nations, had a mild flirtation with two Danish blondes while strolling through the Tivoli Gardens and was in bed by one in the morning.

The next day he bought a lightweight clerical-grey suit at one of the best-known men's outfitters in central Copenhagen, a pair of sober black walking shoes, a pair of socks, a set of underwear and three white shirts with collars attached. In each case he bought only what had the Danish maker's name on a small cloth tab inside. In the case of the three white shirts, which he did not need, the point of the purchase was simply to acquire the tabs for transference to the clerical shirt, dog collar and bib that he had bought in London while claiming to be a theological student on the verge of ordination.

His last purchase was a book in Danish on the notable churches and cathedrals of France. He lunched off a large cold collation at a lakeside restaurant in the Tivoli Gardens and caught the 3.15 plane to Brussels.

4

Why a man of the undoubted talents of Paul Goossens should have gone wrong in middle age was something of a mystery even to his few friends, his rather more numerous customers and to the Belgian police. During his thirty years as a trusted employee of the Fabrique Nationale at Liége he had established a reputation for unfailing precision in a branch of engineering where precision is absolutely indispensable. Of his honesty also there had been no doubt. He had also during those thirty years become the company's foremost expert in the very wide range of weapons that the excellent company produces, from the tiniest lady's automatic to the heaviest of machine guns.

His war record had been remarkable. Although he had continued after the Occupation to work in the arms factory run by the Germans for the Nazi war effort, later examination of his career had established beyond doubt his undercover work for the Resistance, his participation in private in a chain of safe-houses for the escape of downed Allied airmen, and at work his leadership of a sabotage ring that ensured a fair proportion of the weapons turned out by Liége either never fired accurately or blew up at the fiftieth shell, killing the German crews. All this, so modest and unassuming was the man, had been wormed out of him later by his defence lawyers and triumphantly produced in court on his behalf. It had gone a long way to mitigating his sentence, and the jury had also been impressed by his own halting admission that he had never revealed his activities during the war because post-liberation honours and medals would have embarrassed him.

By the time in the early fifties that a large sum of money had been embezzled from a foreign customer in the course of a lucrative arms deal, and suspicion had fallen upon him, he was a departmental chief in the firm and his own superiors had been loudest in informing the police that their suspicions with regard to the trusted M. Goossens were ridiculous.

Even at the trial his managing director spoke for him. But the presiding judge took the view that to betray a position of trust in such a manner was all the more reprehensible, and he had been given ten years in prison. On appeal it was reduced to five. With good conduct he had been released after three and a half.

His wife had divorced him, and taken the children with her. The old life of the suburban dweller in a neat flower-rimmed detached house in one of the prettier outskirts of Liége (there are not many) was over, a thing of the past. So was his career with FN. He had taken a small flat in Brussels, later a house further out of town, as his fortunes prospered from his thriving business as the source of illegal arms to half the underworld in Western Europe.

By the early sixties he had the nickname L'Armurier, the Armourer. Any Belgian citizen can buy a lethal weapon, revolver, automatic or rifle, at any sports or gun shop in the country on production of a national identity card proving Belgian nationality. Goossens never used his own, for at each sale of the weapon and subsequent ammunition the sale is noted in the gunsmith's log-book, along with the name and ID card number of the purchaser. Goossens used other people's cards, either stolen or forged.

He had established close links with one of the city's top pickpockets, a man who, when not languishing in prison as a guest of the state, could abstract any wallet from any pocket at ease. These he bought outright for cash from the thief. He also had at his disposal the services of a master forger who, having come badly unstuck in the late forties over the production of a large amount of French francs in which he had inadvertently left the 'u' out of 'Banque de France' (he was young then), had finally gone into the false passport business with much greater success. Lastly, when he needed to acquire a firearm for a customer, the client who presented himself at the gunsmith's with a neatly forged ID card was never himself but always an out-of-work and out-of-jail petty crook or an actor resting between conquests of the stage.

Of his own 'staff' only the pickpocket and the forger knew his real identity. So also did some of his customers, notably the top men in the Belgian underworld, who not only left him alone to his devices but also offered him a certain amount of protection in refusing to reveal when captured where they had got their guns from, simply because he was so useful to them.

This did not stop the Belgian police being aware of a portion of his activities, but it did prevent them ever being able to catch him with the goods in his possession or of being able to get testimony that would stand up in court and convict him. They were aware of and highly suspicious of the small but superbly equipped forge and workshop in his converted garage, but repeated visits had revealed nothing more than the paraphernalia for the manufacture of wrought-metal medallions and souvenirs of the statues of Brussels. On their last visit he had solemnly presented the Chief Inspector with a figurine of Mannikin Piss as a token of his esteem for the forces of law and order.

He felt no qualms as he waited on the morning of July 21st, 1963, for the arrival of an Englishman who had been guaranteed to him over the phone by one of his best customers, a former mercenary in the service of Katanga from 1960 to 1962 and who had since masterminded a protection business among the whorehouses of the Belgian capital.

The visitor turned up at noon, as promised, and M. Goossens showed him into his little office off the hall.

'Would you please remove your glasses?' he asked when his visitor was seated, and, as the tall Englishman hesitated, added: 'You see, I think it is better that we trust each other in so far as we can while our business association lasts. A drink, perhaps?'

The man whose passport would have announced him as Alexander Duggan removed his dark glasses and stared quizzically at the little gunsmith as two beers were poured. M. Goossens seated himself behind his desk, sipped his beer and asked quietly,

'In what way may I be of service to you, monsieur?'

'I believe Louis rang you earlier about my coming?'

'Certainly,' M. Goossens nodded, 'otherwise you would not be here.'

'Did he tell you what is my business?'

'No. Simply that he knew you in Katanga, that he could vouch for your discretion, that you needed a firearm, and that you would be prepared to pay in cash, sterling.'

The Englishman nodded slowly. 'Well, since I know what your business is, there is little reason why you should not know mine. Besides which, the weapon I need will have to be a specialist gun with certain unusual attachments. I ... er ... specialise in the removal of men who have powerful and wealthy enemies. Evidently, such men are usually powerful and wealthy themselves. It is not always easy. They can afford specialist protection. Such a job needs planning and the right weapon. I have such a job on hand at the moment. I shall need a rifle.'

M. Goossens again sipped his beer, nodded benignly at his guest.

'Excellent, excellent. A specialist like myself. I think I sense a challenge. What kind of rifle had you in mind?'

'It is not so much the type of rifle that is important. It is more a question of the limitations that are imposed by the job, and of finding a rifle which will perform satisfactorily under those limitations.'

M. Goossens' eyes gleamed with pleasure.

'A one-off,' he purred delightedly. 'A gun that will be tailor-made for one man and one job under one set of circumstances, never to be repeated. You have come to the right man. I sense a challenge, my dear monsieur. I am glad that you came.'

The Englishman permitted himself a smile at the Belgian's professorial enthusiasm. 'So am I, monsieur.'

'Now tell me, what are these limitations?'

'The main limitation is of size, not in length but in the physical bulk of the working parts. The chamber and breech must be no bulkier than that ...' He held up his right hand, the tip of the middle finger touching the end of the thumb in the form of a letter O less than two and a half inches in diameter.

'That seems to mean it cannot be a repeater, since a gas chamber would be larger than that, and nor can it have a bulky spring mechanism for the same reason,' said the Englishman. 'It seems to me it must be a bolt-action rifle.'

M. Goossens was nodding at the ceiling, his mind taking in the details of what his visitor was saying, making a mental picture of a rifle of great slimness in the working parts.

'Go on, go on,' he murmured.

'On the other hand, it cannot have a bolt with a handle that sticks out sideways like the Mauser 7.92 or the Lee Enfield .303. The bolt must slide straight back towards the shoulder, gripped between forefinger and thumb for the fitting of the bullet into the breech. Also there must be no trigger guard and the trigger itself must be detachable so that it can be fitted just before firing.'

'Why?' asked the Belgian.

'Because the whole mechanism must pass into a tubular compartment for storage and carrying, and the compartment must not attract attention. For that it must not be larger in diameter than I have just shown, for reasons I shall explain. It is possible to have a detachable trigger?'

'Certainly, almost all is possible. Of course, one could design a single-shot rifle that breaks open at the back for loading like a shotgun. That would dispense with the bolt completely, but it would involve a hinge, which might be no saving. Also it would be necessary to design and manufacture such a rifle from scratch, milling a piece of metal to make the entire breech and chamber. Not an easy task in a small workshop, but possible.'

'How long would that take?' asked the Englishman.

The Belgian shrugged and spread his hands. 'Several months, I am afraid.'

'I do not have that amount of time.'

'In that case it will be necessary to take an existing rifle purchasable in a shop and make modifications. Please go on.'

'Right. The gun must also be light in weight. It need not be of heavy calibre, the bullet will do the work. It must have a short barrel, probably not longer than twelve inches. . . .'

'Over what range will you have to fire?'

'This is still not certain, but probably not more than a hundred and thirty metres.'

'Will you go for a head or chest shot?'

'It will probably have to be head. I may get a shot at the chest, but the head is surer.'

'Surer to kill, yes, if you get a good hit,' said the Belgian. 'But the chest is surer to get a good hit. At least, when one is using a light weapon with a short barrel over a hundred and thirty metres with possible obstructions. I assume,' he added, 'from your uncertainty on this point of the head or the chest that there may be someone passing in the way?'

'Yes, there may be.'

'Will you get the chance of a second shot, bearing in mind that it will take several seconds to extract the spent cartridge and insert a fresh one, close the breech and take aim again?'

'Almost certainly not. I just might get a second if I use a silencer and the first shot is a complete miss which is not noticed by anyone nearby. But even if I get a first hit through the temple, I need the silencer to effect my own escape. There must be several minutes of clear time before anyone nearby realises even roughly where the bullet has come from.'

The Belgian continued nodding, by now staring down at his desk pad.

'In that case you had better have explosive bullets. I shall prepare a handful along with the gun. You know what I mean?'

The Englishman nodded. 'Glycerine or mercury?'

'Oh, mercury I think. So much neater and cleaner. Are there any more points concerning this gun?'

'I'm afraid so. In the interests of slimness all the woodwork of the handgrip beneath the barrel should be removed. The entire stock must be removed. For firing it must have a frame-stock like a Sten gun, each of the three sections of which, upper and lower members and shoulder-rest, must unscrew into three separate rods. Lastly, there must be a completely effective silencer and a telescopic sight. Both of these too must be removable for storage and carrying.'

The Belgian thought for a long time, sipping his beer until it was drained. The Englishman became impatient.

'Well, can you do it?'

M. Goossens seemed to emerge from his reverie. He smiled apologetically.

'Do forgive me. It is a very complex order. But yes, I can do it. I have never failed yet to produce the required article. Really what you have described is a hunting expedition in which the equipment must be carried past certain checks in such a manner as to arouse no suspicion. A hunting expedition supposes a hunting rifle, and that is what you shall have. Not as small as a .22 calibre, for that is for rabbits and hares. Nor as big as a Remington .300 which would never conform to the limitations of size you have demanded.

'I think I have such a gun in mind, and easily available here in Brussels at some sports shops. An expensive gun, a high-precision instrument. Very accurate, beautifully tooled and yet light and slim. Used a lot for chamois and other small deer, but with explosive bullets just the thing for bigger game. Tell me, will the ... er ... gentleman be moving slowly, fast or not at all?'

'Stationary.'

'No problems, then. The fitting of a frame-stock of three separate steel rods and the screw-in trigger is mere mechanics. The tapping of the end of the barrel for the silencer and the shortening of the barrel by eight inches I can do myself. One loses accuracy as one loses eight inches of barrel. Pity, pity. Are you a marksman?'

The Englishman nodded.

'Then there will be no problem with a stationary human being at a hundred and thirty metres with a telescopic sight. As for the silencer, I shall make it myself. They are not complex, but difficult to obtain as a manufactured article, particularly long ones for rifles which are not usual in hunting. Now, monsieur, you mentioned earlier some tubular compartments for carrying the gun in its broken-down form. What had you in mind?'

The Englishman rose and crossed to the desk, towering over the little Belgian. He slipped his hand inside his jacket, and for a second there was a flicker of fear in the smaller man's eyes. For the first time he noticed that whatever expression was on the killer's face it never touched his eyes which appeared clouded by streaks of grey like wisps of smoke covering all expression that might have touched them. But the Englishman produced only a silver propelling pencil.

He spun round M. Goossens' note-pad and sketched rapidly for a few seconds.

'Do you recognise that?' he asked, turning the pad back to the gunsmith.

'Of course,' replied the Belgian, after giving the precisely drawn sketch a glance.

'Right. Well now, the whole thing is composed of a series of hollow aluminium tubes which screw together. This one ...' tapping with the point of the pencil at a place on the diagram ... 'contains one of the struts of the rifle stock. This here contains the other strut. Both are concealed within the tubes that make up this section. The shoulder-rest of the rifle is this ... here ... in its entirety. This is therefore the only part which doubles up with two purposes without changing in any way.

'Here ...' tapping at another point on the diagram as the Belgian's eyes widened in surprise ... 'at the thickest point is the largest diameter tube which contains the breech of the rifle with the bolt inside it. This tapers to the barrel without a break. Obviously with a telescopic sight being used there need be no foresight, so the whole thing slides out of this compartment when the assemblage is unscrewed. The last two sections ... here and here ... contain the telescopic sight itself and the silencer. Finally the bullets. They should be inserted into this little stump at the bottom. When the whole thing is assembled it must pass for precisely what it looks. When unscrewed into its seven component parts the bullets, silencer, telescope, rifle and the three struts that make up the triangular frame stock can be extracted for reassembly as a fully operational rifle. OK?'

For a few seconds longer the little Belgian looked at the diagram. Slowly he rose, then held out his hand.

'Monsieur,' he said with reverence, 'it is a conception of genius. Undetectable. And yet so simple. It shall be done.'

The Englishman was neither gratified nor displeased.

'Good,' he said. 'Now, the question of time. I shall need the gun in about fourteen days, can that be arranged?'

'Yes. I can acquire the gun within three. A week's work should see the modifications achieved. Buying the telescopic sight presents no problems. You may leave the choice of the sight to me, I know what will be required for the range of a hundred and thirty metres you have in mind. You had better calibrate and zero the settings yourself at your own discretion. Making the silencer, modifying the bullets and constructing the outer casing . . . yes, it can be done within the time allowed if I burn the candle at both ends. However, it would be better if you could arrive back here with a day or two in hand, just in case there are some last-minute details to talk over. Could you be back in twelve days?'

'Yes, any time between seven and fourteen days from now. But fourteen days is the deadline. I must be back in London by August the 4th.'

'You shall have the completed weapon with all last details arranged to your satisfaction on the morning of the 4th if you can be here yourself on August 1st for final discussions and collection, monsieur.'

'Good. Now for the question of your expenses and fee,' said the Englishman. 'Have you an idea how much they will be?'

The Belgian thought for a while. 'For this kind of job, with all the work it entails, for the facilities available here and my own specialised knowledge, I must ask a fee of one thousand English pounds. I concede that is above the rate for a simple rifle. But this is not a simple rifle. It must be a work of art. I believe I am the only man in Europe capable of doing it justice, of making a perfect job of it. Like yourself, monsieur, I am in my field the best. For the best one pays. Then on top there would be the purchasing price of the weapon, bullets, telescope and raw materials . . . say, the equivalent of another two hundred pounds.'

'Done,' replied the Englishman without argument. He reached into his breast pocket again and extracted a bundle of five-pound notes. They were bound in lots of twenty. He counted out five wads of twenty notes each.

'I would suggest,' he went on evenly, 'that in order to establish my bona fides I make you a down payment as an advance and to cover costs of five hundred pounds. I shall bring the remaining seven hundred pounds on my return in eleven days Is that agreeable to you?'

'Monsieur,' said the Belgian skilfully pocketing the notes, 'it is a pleasure to do business both with a professional and a gentleman.'

'There is a little more,' went on his visitor, as though he had not been interrupted. 'You will make no attempt further to contact Louis, nor to ask him or anyone else who I am, nor what is my true identity. Nor will you seek to enquire for whom I am working, nor against whom. In the event that you should try to do so it is certain I shall hear about the enquiries. In that eventuality you will die. On my return here, if there has been any attempt to contact the police or to lay a trap, you will die. Is that understood?'

M. Goossens was pained. Standing in the hallway he looked up at the Englishman, and an eel of fear wriggled in his bowels. He had faced many of the tough men of the Belgian underworld when they came to him to ask for special or unusual weapons, or simply a run-of-the-mill snub-nosed Colt Special. These were hard men. But there was something distant and implacable about the visitor from across the Channel who intended to kill an important and well-protected figure. Not another gangland boss, but a big man, perhaps a politician. He thought of protesting or expostulating, then decided better.

'Monsieur,' he said quietly, 'I do not want to know about you, anything about you. The gun you will receive will bear no serial number. You see, it is of more importance to me that nothing you do should ever be traced back to me than that I should seek to know more than I do about you. *Bonjour, monsieur.*'

The Jackal walked away into the bright sunshine and two streets away found a cruising taxi to take him back to the city centre and the Hôtel Amigo.

He suspected that in order to acquire guns Goossens would have to have a forger in his employ somewhere, but preferred to find and use one of his own. Again Louis, his contact from the old days in Katanga, helped him. Not that it was difficult. Brussels has a long tradition as the centre of the forged identity-card industry and many foreigners appreciate the lack of formalities with which assistance in this field can be obtained. In the early sixties Brussels had also become the operations base of the mercenary soldier, for this was before the emergence in the Congo of the French and South African/British units who later came to dominate the business. With Katanga gone, over three hundred out-of-work 'military advisers' from the old Tshombe regime were hanging around the bars of the red-light quarter, many of them in possession of several sets of identity papers.

The Jackal found his man in a bar off the Rue Neuve after Louis had arranged the appointment. He introduced himself and the pair retired to a corner alcove. The Jackal produced his driving licence, which was in his own name, issued by the London County Council two years earlier and with some months still to run.

'This,' he told the Belgian, 'belonged to a man now dead. As I am banned from driving in Britain, I need a new front page in my own name.'

He put the passport in the name of Duggan in front of the forger. The man opposite glanced at the passport first, took in the newness of the passport, the fact that it had been issued three days earlier, and glanced shrewdly at the Englishman.

'*En effet,*' he murmured, then flicked open the little red driving licence. After a few minutes he looked up.

'Not difficult, monsieur. The English authorities are gentlemen. They do not seem to expect that official documents might perhaps be forged, therefore they take few precautions. This paper ...' he flicked the small sheet gummed on to the first page of the licence, which carried the licence number and the full name of the holder ... 'could be printed by a child's printing set. The watermark is easy. This presents no problems. Was that all you wanted?'

'No, there are two other papers.'

'Ah. If you will permit my saying so, it appeared strange that you should wish to contact me for such a simple task. There must be men in your own London who could do this within a few hours. What are the other papers?'

The Jackal described them to the last detail. The Belgian's eyes nar-

rowed in thought. He took out a packet of Bastos, offered one to the
Englishman, who declined, and lit one for himself.

'That is not so easy. The French identity card, not too bad. There are
plenty about from which one can work. You understand, one must work
from an original to achieve the best results. But the other one. I do not
think I have seen such a one. It is a most unusual requirement.'

He paused while the Jackal ordered a passing waiter to refill their
glasses. When the waiter had gone he resumed.

'And then the photograph. That will not be easy. You say there must
be a difference in age, in hair colouring and length. Most of those wishing
for a false document intend that their own photograph shall be on the
document, but with the personal details falsified. But to devise a new
photograph which does not even look like you as you now appear, this
complicates things.'

He drank off half his beer, still eyeing the Englishman opposite him.
'To achieve this it will be necessary to seek out a man of the approximate age of the bearer of the cards, and who also bears a reasonable
similarity to yourself, at least as far as the head and face is concerned, and
cut his hair to the length you require. Then a photograph of this man
would be put on to the cards. From that point on it would be up to you
to model your subsequent disguise on this man's true appearance, rather
than the reverse. You follow me?'

'Yes,' replied the Jackal.

'This will take some time. How long can you stay in Brussels?'

'Not long,' said the Jackal. 'I must leave fairly soon, but I could be back
on August 1st. From then I could stay another three days. I have to be
returning to London on the fourth.'

The Belgian thought again for a while, staring at the photograph in the
passport in front of him. At last he folded it closed and passed it back to
the Englishman after copying on to a piece of paper from his pocket the
name Alexander James Quentin Duggan. He pocketed both the piece of
paper and the driving licence.

'All right. It can be done. But I have to have a good portrait photograph of yourself as you are now, full-face and profile. This will take
time. And money. There are extra expenses involved ... it may be
necessary to undertake an operation into France itself with a colleague
adept in picking pockets in order to acquire the second of these cards
you mention. Obviously, I shall ask around Brussels first, but it may be
necessary to go to these lengths. . . .'

'How much?' cut in the Englishman.

'Twenty thousand Belgian francs.'

The Jackal thought for a moment. 'About a hundred and fifty pounds
sterling. All right. I will pay you a hundred pounds deposit and the remainder on delivery.'

The Belgian rose. 'Then we had better get the portrait photos taken. I
have my own studio.'

They took a taxi to a small basement flat more than a mile away. It
turned out to be a seedy and run-down photographer's studio, with a sign

outside indicating that the premises were run as a commercial establishment specialising in passport photographs developed while the customer
waited. Inevitably stuck in the window were what a passer-by must have
presumed to be the high points of the studio owner's past work – two
portraits of simpering girls, hideously retouched, a marriage photo of a
couple sufficiently unprepossessing to deal a nasty blow to the whole
concept of wedlock, and two babies. The Belgian led the way down the
steps to the front door, unlocked it and ushered his guest inside.

The session took two hours, in which the Belgian showed a skill with
the camera that could never have been possessed by the author of the
portraits in the window. A large trunk in one corner, which he unlocked
with his own key, revealed a selection of expensive cameras and flash
equipment, besides a host of facial props including hair tints and dyes,
toupees, wigs, spectacles in great variety and a case of theatrical cosmetics.

It was halfway through the session that the Belgian hit on the idea that
obviated the necessity to seek out a substitute to pose for the real photograph. Studying the effect of thirty minutes working on the Jackal's face
with make-up, he suddenly dived into the chest and produced a wig.

'What do you think of this?' he asked.

The wig was of hair coloured iron-grey and cut *en brosse*.

'Do you think that your own hair, cut to this length and dyed this
colour, could look like this?'

The Jackal took the wig and examined it. 'We can give it a try and see
how it looks in the photo,' he suggested.

And it worked. The Belgian came out of the developing room half an
hour after taking six photos of his customer with a sheaf of prints in his
hand. Together they pored over the desk. Staring up was the face of an
old and tired man. The skin was an ashen grey and there were dark rings
of fatigue or pain beneath the eyes. The man wore neither beard nor
moustache, but the grey hair on his head gave the impression he must
have been in his fifties at least, and not a robust fifty at that.

'I think it will work,' said the Belgian at last.

'The problem is,' replied the Jackal, 'that you had to work on me with
cosmetics for half an hour to achieve this effect. Then there was the wig.
I cannot emulate all that by myself. And here we were under lights
whereas I shall be in the open air when I have to produce these papers I
have asked for.'

'But this is precisely not the point,' riposted the forger. 'It is not so
much that you will not be a dead image of the photograph, but that
the photograph will not be a dead likeness of you. This is the way
the mind of a man examining papers works. He looks at the face first,
the real face, then asks for the papers. Then he sees the photograph. He
already has the image of the man standing beside him in his mind's eye.
This affects his judgement. He looks for points of similarity, not the
opposite.

'Secondly, this photograph is twenty-five by twenty centimetres.
The photograph in the identity card will be three by four. Thirdly, a too

precise likeness should be avoided. If the card was issued several years previously, it is impossible that a man should not change a bit. In the photograph here we have you in open-necked striped shirt with collar attached. Try to avoid that shirt for example, or even avoid an open-necked shirt at all. Wear a tie or a scarf or a turtle-necked sweater.

'Lastly, nothing that I have done to you cannot be easily simulated. The main point, of course, is the hair. It must be cut *en brosse* before this photo is presented, and dyed grey, perhaps even greyer than the photograph, but not less so. To increase the impression of age and decrepitude, grow two or three days of beard stubble. Then shave with a cut-throat razor, but badly, nicking yourself in a couple of places. Elderly men tend to do this. As for the complexion, this is vital. To extract pity it must be grey and tired, rather waxy and ill-looking. Can you get hold of some pieces of cordite?'

The Jackal had listened to the exposé of the forger with admiration, though nothing showed on his face. For the second time in a day he had been able to contact a professional who knew his job thoroughly. He reminded himself to thank Louis appropriately – after the job was done.

'It might be arranged,' he said cautiously.

'Two or three small pieces of cordite, chewed and swallowed, produce within half an hour a feeling of nausea, uncomfortable but not disastrous. They also turn the skin a grey pallor and cause facial sweating. We used to use this trick in the Army to simulate illness and avoid fatigues and route marches.'

'Thank you for the information. Now for the rest, do you think you can produce the documents in time?'

'From the technical standpoint, there is no doubt of it. The only remaining problem is to acquire an original of the second French document. For that I may have to work fast. But if you come back in the first few days of August, I think I can have them all ready for you. You . . . er . . . had mentioned a down payment to cover expenses . . .'

The Jackal reached into his inside pocket and produced a single bundle of twenty five-pound notes which he handed the Belgian.

'How do I contact you?' he asked.

'I would suggest by the same way as tonight.'

'Too risky. My contact man may be missing, or out of town. Then I would have no way of finding you.'

The Belgian thought for a minute. 'Then I shall wait from six until seven each evening in the bar where we met tonight on each of the first three days of August. If you do not come, I shall presume the deal is off.'

The Englishman had removed the wig and was wiping his face with a towel soaked in removing spirit. In silence he slipped on his tie and jacket. When he was finished he turned to the Belgian.

'There are certain things I wish to make clear,' he said quietly. The friendliness was gone from the voice and the eyes stared at the Belgian as bleak as a Channel fog. 'When you have finished the job you will be present at the bar as promised. You will return to me the new licence and the page removed from the one you now have. Also the negatives and all prints of the photographs we have just taken. You will also forget the names of Duggan and of the original owner of that driving licence. The name on the two French documents you are going to produce you may select yourself, providing it is a simple and common French name. After handing them over to me you will forget that name also. You will never speak to anyone of this commission again. In the event that you infringe any of these conditions you will die. Is that understood?'

The Belgian stared back for a few moments. Over the past three hours he had come to think of the Englishman as a run-of-the-mill customer who simply wished to drive a car in Britain and masquerade for his own purposes as a middle-aged man in France. A smuggler, perhaps running dope or diamonds from a lonely Breton fishing port into England. But quite a nice sort of fellow, really. He changed his mind.

'It is understood, monsieur.'

A few seconds later the Englishman was gone into the night. He walked for five blocks before taking a taxi back to the Amigo and it was midnight when he arrived. He ordered cold chicken and a bottle of Moselle in his room, bathed thoroughly to get rid of the last traces of make-up, then slept.

The following morning he checked out of the hotel and took the Brabant Express to Paris. It was July 22nd.

The head of the Action Service of the SDECE sat at his desk on that same morning and surveyed the two pieces of paper before him. Each was a copy of a routine report filed by agents of other departments. At the head of each piece of blue flimsy was a list of department chiefs entitled to receive a copy of the report. Opposite his own designation was a small tick. Both reports had come in that morning and in the normal course of events Colonel Rolland would have glanced at each, taken in what they had to say, stored the knowledge somewhere in his fearsome memory, and had them filed under separate headings. But there was one word that cropped up in each of the reports, a word that intrigued him.

The first report that arrived was an interdepartmental memo from R.3 (Western Europe) containing a synopsis of a despatch from their permanent office in Rome. The despatch was a straightforward report to the effect that Rodin, Montclair and Casson were still holed up in their top floor suite and were still being guarded by their eight guards. They had not moved out of the building since they established themselves there on June 18th. Extra staff had been drafted from R.3 Paris to Rome to assist in keeping the hotel under round-the-clock surveillance. Instructions from Paris remained unchanged: not to make any approach but simply to keep watch. The men in the hotel had established a routine for keeping in touch with the outside world three weeks previously (see R.3 Rome report of June 30th), and this was being maintained. The courier remained Viktor Kowalski. End of message.

Colonel Rolland flicked open the buff file lying on the right of his desk next to the sawn-off 105 mm shell case that served for a copious ashtray and was even by then half-full of Disque Bleue stubs. His eyes strayed down the R.3 Rome report of June 30th till he found the paragraph he wanted.

Each day, it said, one of the guards left the hotel and walked to the head post office of Rome. Here a *poste restante* pigeon-hole was reserved in the name of one Poitiers. The OAS had not taken a postal box with a key, apparently for fear it might be burgled. All mail for the top men of the OAS was addressed to Poitiers, and was kept by the clerk on duty at the *poste restante* counter. An attempt to bribe the original such clerk to hand over the mail to an agent of R.3 had failed. The man had reported the approach to his superiors, and had been replaced by a senior clerk. It was possible that mail for Poitiers was now being screened by the Italian security police, but R.3 had instructions not to approach the Italians to ask for co-operation. The attempt to bribe the clerk had failed, but it was felt the initiative had had to be taken. Each day the mail arriving over-night in the post office was handed to the guard, who had been identified as one Viktor Kowalski, formerly a corporal of the Foreign Legion and a member of Rodin's original company in Indo-China. Kowalski seemingly had adequate false papers identifying him to the post office as Poitiers, or a letter of authority acceptable to the post office. If Kowalski had letters to post, he waited by the post box inside the main hall of the building until five minutes before collection time, dropped the mail through the slit, then waited until the entire boxful was collected and taken back into the heart of the building for sorting. Attempts to interfere with the process of either collection or despatch of the OAS chief's mail would entail a degree of violence, which had already been precluded by Paris. Occasionally Kowalski made a telephone call, long-distance, from the Overseas Calls telephone counter, but here again attempts either to learn the number asked for or overhear the conversation had failed. End of message.

Colonel Rolland let the cover of the file fall back on the contents and took up the second of the two reports that had come in that morning. It was a police report from the Police Judiciaire of Metz stating that a man had been questioned during a routine raid on a bar and had half-killed two policemen in the ensuing fight. Later at the police station he had been identified by his fingerprints as a deserter from the Foreign Legion by the name of Sandor Kovacs, Hungarian by birth and a refugee from Budapest in 1956. Kovacs, a note from PJ Paris added at the end of the information from Metz, was a notorious OAS thug long wanted for his connection with a series of terror murders of loyalist notables in the Bone and Constantine areas of Algeria during 1961. At that time he had operated as partner of another OAS gunman still at large, former Foreign Legion corporal Viktor Kowalski. End of message.

Rolland pondered the connection between the two men yet again, as he had done for the previous hour. At last he pressed a buzzer in front of him and replied to the 'Oui, mon colonel' that came out of it, 'Get me the personal file on Viktor Kowalski. At once.'

He had the file up from archives in ten minutes, and spent another hour reading it. Several times he ran his eye over one particular paragraph. As other Parisians in less stressing professions hurried past on the pavement below to their lunches, Colonel Rolland convened a small meeting consisting of himself, his personal secretary, a specialist in handwriting from the documentation department three floors down and two strong-arm men from his private Praetorian guard.

'Gentlemen,' he told them, 'with the unwilling but inevitable assistance of one not here present, we are going to compose, write and despatch a letter.'

5

The Jackal's train arrived at the Gare du Nord just before lunch and he took a taxi to a small but comfortable hotel in the Rue de Suresne, leading off the Place de la Madeleine. While it was not a hotel in the same class as the d'Angleterre of Copenhagen or the Amigo of Brussels, he had reasons for wishing to seek a more modest and less known place to stay while in Paris. For one thing his stay would be longer, and for another there was far more likelihood of running into somebody in Paris in late July who might have known him fleetingly in London under his real name than in either Copenhagen or Brussels. Out on the street he was confident that the wrap-around dark glasses he habitually wore, and which in the bright sunshine of the boulevards were completely natural, would protect his identity. The possible danger lay in being seen in a hotel corridor or foyer. The last thing he wished at this stage was to be halted by a cheery 'Well, fancy seeing you here', and then the mention of his name within the hearing of a desk clerk who knew him as Mr Duggan.

Not that his stay in Paris had anything about it to excite attention. He lived quietly, taking his breakfast of croissants and coffee in his room. From the delicatessen across the road from his hotel he bought a jar of English marmalade to replace the blackcurrant jam provided on the breakfast tray, and asked the hotel staff to include the jar of marmalade on his tray each morning in place of the jam.

He was quietly courteous to the staff, spoke only a few words of French with the Englishman's habitually atrocious pronunciation of the French language, and smiled politely when addressed. He replied to the management's solicitous enquiries by assuring them that he was extremely comfortable and thank you.

'M. Duggan,' the hotel proprietress told her desk clerk one day, 'est extrêmement gentil. Un vrai gentleman.' There was no dissent.

His days were spent out of the hotel in the pursuits of the tourist. On his first day he bought a street map of Paris, and from a small notebook marked off on the map the places of interest he most wanted to see.

These he visited and studied with remarkable devotion, even bearing in mind the architectural beauty of some of them or the historical associations of the others.

He spent three days roaming round the Arc de Triomphe or sitting on the terrace of the Café de l'Elysée scanning the monument and the roof-tops of the great buildings that surround the Place de l'Etoile. Anyone who had followed him in those days (and no one did) would have been surprised that even the architecture of the brilliant M. Haussmann should have attracted so devoted an admirer. Certainly no watcher could have divined that the quiet and elegant English tourist stirring his coffee and gazing at the buildings for so many hours was mentally working out angles of fire, distances from the upper storeys to the Eternal Flame flickering beneath the Arc, and the chances of a man escaping down a rear fire escape unnoticed into the milling crowds.

After three days he left the Etoile and visited the ossuary of the martyrs of the French Resistance at Montvalérien. Here he arrived with a bouquet of flowers, and a guide, touched by the gesture of the English-man to the guide's one-time fellow Résistants, gave him an exhaustive tour of the shrine and a running commentary. He was hardly to perceive that the visitor's eyes kept straying away from the entrance to the ossuary towards the high walls of the prison which cut off all direct vision into the courtyard from the roofs of the surrounding buildings. After two hours he left with a polite 'Thank you' and a generous but not extravagant *pourboire*.

He also visited the Place des Invalides, dominated on its southern side by the Hôtel des Invalides, home of Napoleon's tomb and shrine to the glories of the French Army. The western side of the enormous square, formed by the Rue Fabert, interested him most, and he sat for a morning at the corner café where the Rue Fabert adjoins the tiny triangular Place de Santiago du Chili. From the seventh or eighth floor of the building above his head, No. 146 Rue de Grenelle, where that street joins the Rue Fabert at an angle of ninety degrees, he estimated a gunman would be able to dominate the front gardens of the Invalides, the entrance to the inner courtyard, most of the Place des Invalides, and two or three streets. A good place for a last stand, but not for an assassination. For one thing the distance from the upper windows to the gravelled path leading from the Invalides to where cars would be drawn up at the base of the steps between the two tanks was over two hundred metres. For another the view downwards from the windows of No. 146 would be partly obscured by the topmost branches of the dense lime trees growing in the Place de Santiago and from which the pigeons dropped their off-white tributes on to the shoulders of the uncomplaining statue of Vauban. Regretfully, he paid for his Vittel Menthe and left.

A day was spent in the precincts of Notre Dame Cathedral. Here amid the rabbit warren of the Ile de la Cité were back stairways, alleys and passageways, but the distance from the entrance to the cathedral to the parked cars at the foot of the steps was only a few metres, and the roof-tops of the Place du Parvis were too far away, while those of the tiny abutting Square Charlemagne were too close and easy for security forces to infest with watchers.

His last visit was to the square at the southern end of the Rue de Rennes. He arrived on July 28th. Once called the Place de Rennes, the square had been renamed Place du 18 Juin 1940 when the Gaullists took power in the City Hall. The Jackal's eyes strayed to the shining new name plate on the wall of the building and remained there. Something of what he had read the previous month returned to him. June 18th, 1940, the days when the lonely but lofty exile in London had taken the microphone to tell the French that if they had lost a battle, they had not lost the war.

There was something about this square, with the crouching bulk of the Gare Montparnasse on its southern side, full of memories for the Parisians of the war generation, that caused the assassin to stop. Slowly he surveyed the expanse of tarmac, crisscrossed now by a maelstrom of traffic pounding down the Boulevard de Montparnasse and joined by other streams from the Rue d'Odessa and the Rue de Rennes. He looked round at the tall, narrow-fronted buildings on each side of the Rue de Rennes that also overlooked the square. Slowly he wended his way round the square to the southern side and peered through the railings into the courtyard of the station. It was a-buzz with cars and taxis bringing or taking away tens of thousands of commuter passengers a day, one of the great mainline stations of Paris. By that winter it would become a silent hulk, brooding on the events, human and historical, that had taken place in its steely, smoky shadow. The station was destined for demolition.*

The Jackal turned with his back to the railings and looked down the traffic artery of the Rue de Rennes. He was facing the Place du 18 Juin 1940, convinced that this was the place the President of France would come, one last time, on the appointed day. The other places he had examined during the past week were possibles; this one, he felt sure, was the certainty. Within a short time there would be no more Gare Montparnasse, the columns that had looked down on so much would be smelted for suburban fences and the forecourt that had seen Berlin humiliated and Paris preserved would be just another executives' cafeteria. But before that happened, he, the man with the kepi and two gold stars, would come once again. But in the meantime the distance from the top floor of the corner house on the western side of the Rue de Rennes and the centre of the forecourt was about a hundred and thirty metres.

The Jackal took in the landscape facing him with a practised eye. Both corner houses on the Rue de Rennes where it debouched into the square were obvious choices. The first three houses up the Rue de Rennes were possibles, presenting a narrow firing angle into the forecourt. Beyond them the angle became too narrow. Similarly, the first three houses that fronted the Boulevard de Montparnasse running straight through the

* Author's note: The old Gare Montparnasse façade was demolished in 1964 to make way for office-block development. The new station building has been erected five hundred yards further down the railway line.

square east to west were possibilities. Beyond them the angles became too narrow again, and the distances too great. There were no other buildings that dominated the forecourt that were not too far away, other than the station building itself. But this would be out of bounds, its upper office windows overlooking the forecourt crawling with security men. The Jackal decided to study the three corner houses on the western side of the Rue de Rennes first, and sauntered over to a café on the corner at the eastern side, the Café Duchesse Anne.

Here he sat on the terrace a few feet from the roaring traffic, ordered a coffee, and stared at the houses across the street. He stayed for three hours. Later he lunched at the Hansi Brasserie Alsacienne on the far side, and studied the eastern façades. For the afternoon he sauntered up and down, looking at closer quarters into the front doors of the blocks of apartments he had picked out as possibles.

He moved on eventually to the houses that fronted the Boulevard de Montparnasse itself, but here the buildings were offices, newer and more briskly busy.

The next day he was back again, sauntering past the façades, crossing the road to sit on a pavement bench under the trees and toying with a newspaper while he studied the upper floors. Five or six floors of stone façade, topped by a parapet, then the steeply sloping black-tiled roofs containing the attics, pierced by *mansarde* windows, once the quarters of the servants, now the homes of the poorer *pensionnaires*. The roofs, and possibly the *mansardes* themselves would certainly be watched on the day. There might even be watchers on the roofs, crouching among the chimney stacks, their field glasses on the opposite windows and roofs. But the topmost floor below the attics would be high enough, provided one could sit well back into the darkness of the room not to be visible from across the street. The open window on the sweltering heat of a Paris summer would be natural enough.

But the further back one sat inside the room, the narrower would be the angle of fire sideways down into the forecourt of the station. For this reason the Jackal ruled out the third house into the Rue de Rennes on each side of the street. The angle would be too narrow. That left him four houses to choose from. As the time of day he expected to fire would be the mid-afternoon, with the sun moving towards the west, but still high enough in the sky to shine over the top of the station roof into the windows of the houses on the east side of the street, he eventually chose those two on the west side. To prove it, he waited until four o'clock on July 29th, and noticed that on the west side the topmost windows were receiving only a slanting ray from the sun, while it still fiercely lit the houses on the east.

The next day he noticed the concierge. It was his third day sitting either at a café terrace or on a pavement bench, and he had chosen a bench a few feet from the doorways of the two blocks of flats that still interested him. Within a few feet, behind him and separated by the pavement down which pedestrians scurried endlessly, the concierge sat in her doorway and knitted. Once, from a nearby café, a waiter strolled over for a chat. He called the concierge Madame Berthe. It was a pleasant scene. The day was warm, the sun bright, reaching several feet into the dark doorway while it was still in the south-east and south, high in the sky over the station roof across the square.

She was a comfortable grandmotherly soul, and from the way she chirped *'Bonjour, monsieur'* to the people who occasionally entered or left her block, and from the cheerful *'Bonjour, Madame Berthe'* that she received each time in return, the watcher on the bench twenty feet away judged that she was well liked. A good-natured body, and with compassion for the unfortunate of this world. For shortly after two in the afternoon a cat presented itself and within a few minutes, after diving into the dark recesses of her *loge* at the rear of the ground floor, Madame Berthe was back with a saucer of milk for the creature she referred to as the little Minet.

Shortly before four she bundled up her knitting, put it into one of the capacious pockets of her pinafore and shuffled on slippered feet down the road to the bakery. The Jackal rose quietly from his bench and entered the apartment block. He chose the stairs rather than the lift and ran silently upwards.

The stairs ran round the lift shaft, and at each curve on the rear of the building the stairs halted to make room for a small half-landing. On each second floor this landing gave access through a door in the rear wall of the block to a steel fire-escape. At the sixth and top floor, apart from the attics, he opened the rear door and looked down. The fire-escape led to an inner courtyard, around which were the rear entrances to the other blocks that made up the corner of the square behind him. On the far side of the courtyard the hollow square of buildings was penetrated by a narrow covered alleyway leading towards the north.

The Jackal closed the door quietly, replaced the safety bar, and mounted the last half-flight to the sixth floor. From here, at the end of the passage, a humbler staircase led to the upper attics. There were two doors in the passage giving access to flats overlooking the inner courtyard and two others for flats on the front of the building. His sense of direction told him either of these front flats contained windows looking down into the Rue de Rennes, or half-sideways on to the square and beyond it the forecourt of the station. These were the windows he had been observing for so long from the street below.

One of the name plates next to the bell pushes of the two front flats he now confronted bore the inscription *'Mlle Béranger'*. The other bore the name *'M. et Mme Charrier'*. He listened for a moment but there was no sound from either of the flats. He examined the locks; both were embedded in the woodwork, which was thick and strong. The tongues of the locks on the far side were probably of the thick bar of steel type so favoured by the security-conscious French, and of the double-locking variety. He would need keys, he realised, of which Mme Berthe would certainly have one for each flat somewhere in her little *loge*.

A few minutes later he was running lightly down the stairs the way he had come. He had been in the block less than five minutes. The concierge was back. He caught a glimpse of her through the frosted glass pane in the door of her cubbyhole, then he had turned and was striding out of the arched entrance.

He turned left up the Rue de Rennes, passed two other blocks of apartments, then the façade of a post office. At the corner of the block was a narrow street, the Rue Littré. He turned into it, still following the wall of the post office. Where the building ended there was a narrow covered alleyway. The Jackal stopped to light a cigarette, and while the flame flickered glanced sideways down the alley. It gave access to a rear entrance into the post office for the telephone exchange switchboard night staff. At the end of the tunnel was a sunlit courtyard. On the far side he could make out in the shadows the last rungs of the fire-escape of the building he had just left. The assassin took a long draw on his cigarette and walked on. He had found his escape route.

At the end of the Rue Littré he turned left again into the Rue de Vaugirard and walked back to where it joined the Boulevard de Montparnasse. He had reached the corner and was looking up and down the main street for a free taxi, when a police motor-cyclist swept into the road junction, jerked his machine on to its stand, and in the centre of the junction began to halt the traffic. By shrill blasts on his whistle he stopped all the traffic coming out of the Rue de Vaugirard, as well as that heading down the Boulevard from the direction of the station. The cars coming up the Boulevard from Duroc were imperiously waved into the right-hand side of the road. He had barely got them all stopped when the distant wail of police sirens was heard from the direction of Duroc. Standing on the corner looking down the length of the Boulevard de Montparnasse, the Jackal saw five hundred yards away a motorcade sweep into the Duroc junction from the Boulevard des Invalides and start to head towards him.

In the lead were two black-leather-clad motards, white helmets gleaming in the sun, sirens blaring. Behind them appeared the shark-like snouts of two Citroën DS 19s in line astern. The policeman in front of the Jackal stood bolt upright facing away from him, left arm gesturing rigidly down towards the Avenue du Maine on the southern side of the junction, right arm bent across the chest, palm downwards, indicating priority passage for the approaching motorcade.

Heeling over to the right, the two motards swept into the Avenue du Maine, followed by the limousines. In the back of the first one, sitting upright behind the driver and the ADC, staring rigidly in front of himself, was a tall figure in a charcoal-grey suit. The Jackal had a fleeting glimpse of the uptilted head and the unmistakable nose before the convoy was gone. The next time I see your face, he silently told the departed image, it will be in closer focus through a telescopic sight. Then he found a taxi and was taken back to his hotel.

Further down the road near the exit from the Duroc Métro station from which she had just emerged, another figure had watched the passing of the President with more than usual interest. She had been about to cross the road when a policeman had waved her back. Seconds later the motor-cade swept out of the Boulevard des Invalides across the expanse of cobbles and into the Boulevard de Montparnasse. She too had seen the distinctive profile in the back of the first Citroën, and her eyes had glowed with a passionate fervour. Even when the cars had gone she stared after them, until she saw the policeman looking her up and down. Hastily she had resumed her crossing of the road.

Jacqueline Dumas was then twenty-six years old and of considerable beauty, which she knew how to show off to its best advantage for she worked as a beautician in an expensive salon behind the Champs Elysées. On the evening of July 30th she was hurrying home to her little flat off the Place de Breteuil to get ready for her evening's date. Within a few hours she knew she would be naked in the arms of the lover she hated, and she wanted to look her best.

A few years earlier the thing that mattered most in her life was her next date. Hers was a good family, a tight-knit group with her father working as a respectable clerk in a banking house, her mother being a typi-cal middle-class French housewife and Maman, she finishing her beauti-cian's course and Jean-Claude doing his National Service. The family lived in the outer suburb of Le Vezinet, not in the best part, but a nice house all the same.

The telegram from the Ministry of the Armed Forces had come one day at breakfast towards the end of 1959. It said that the Minister was required with infinite regret to inform Monsieur and Madame Armand Dumas of the death in Algeria of their son Jean-Claude, private soldier in the First Colonial Paratroops. His personal effects would be returned to the bereaved family as soon as possible.

For some time Jacqueline's private world disintegrated. Nothing seemed to make sense, not the quiet security of the family at Le Vezinet, nor the chatter of the other girls at the salon on the charms of Yves Montand or the latest dance craze imported from America, le Rock. The only thing that seemed to pound through her mind like a tape-recorded loop going eternally round the same bobbins was that little Jean-Claude, her darling baby brother, so vulnerable and gentle, hating war and vio-lence, wanting only to be alone with his books, scarcely more than a boy whom she loved to spoil, had been shot dead in a battle in some God-forsaken wadi in Algeria. She began to hate it. It was the Arabs, the loath-some, dirty, cowardly 'melons', who had done it.

Then François came. Quite suddenly one winter morning he turned up at the house on a Sunday when her parents were away visiting rela-tives. It was December, there was snow in the avenue and crusted on to the garden path. Other people were pale and pinched, and François looked tanned and fit. He asked if he could speak to Mademoiselle Jac-queline. She said, 'C'est moi-même' and what did he want? He replied he commanded the platoon in which one Jean-Claude Dumas, private soldier, had been killed, and he bore a letter. She asked him in.

The letter had been written some weeks before Jean-Claude died, and he had kept it in his inside pocket during the patrol in the djebel looking for a band of fellagha who had wiped out a settler family. They had not found the guerrillas, but had run into a battalion of the ALN, the trained troops of the Algerian national movement, the FLN. There had been a bitter skirmish in the half-light of dawn and Jean-Claude had taken a bullet through the lungs. He gave the letter to the platoon commander before he died.

Jacqueline read the letter and cried a little. It said nothing of the last weeks, just chatter about the barracks at Constantine, the assault courses and the discipline. The rest she learned from François: the pull-back through the scrub for four miles while the outflanking ALN closed in, the repeated calls on the radio for air support, and at eight o'clock the arrival of the fighter-bombers with their screaming engines and thundering rockets. And how her brother, who had volunteered for one of the toughest regiments to prove he was a man, had died like one, coughing blood over the knees of a corporal in the lee of a rock.

François had been very gentle with her. As a man he was hard as the earth of the colonial province in whose four years of war he had been forged as a professional soldier. But he was very gentle with the sister of one of his platoon. She liked him for that and accepted his offer to dine in Paris. Besides, she feared her parents would return and surprise them. She did not want them to hear how Jean-Claude had died, for both had managed to numb themselves to the loss in the intervening two months and somehow carry on as usual. Over dinner she swore the lieutenant to silence and he agreed.

But for her the curiosity became insatiable, to know about the Algerian war, what really happened, what it really stood for, what the politicians were really playing at. General de Gaulle had come to the presidency from the premiership the previous January, swept into the Elysée on a tide of patriotic fervour as the man who would finish the war and still keep Algeria French. It was from François that she first heard the man her father adored referred to as a traitor to France.

They spent François' leave together, she meeting him every evening after work in the salon to which she had gone in January 1960 from the training school. He told her of the betrayal of the French Army, of the Paris Government's secret negotiations with the imprisoned Ahmed Ben Bella, leader of the FLN, and of the pending handover of Algeria to the *melons*. He had returned to his war in the second half of January and she had snatched a brief time alone with him when he managed to get a week's leave in August in Marseilles. She had waited for him, building him in her private thoughts into the symbol of all that was good and clean and manly in French young manhood. She had waited throughout the autumn and winter of 1960, with his picture on her bedside table throughout the day and evening, pushed down her nightdress and clasped to her belly while she slept.

In his last leave in the spring of 1961 he had come again to Paris, and when they walked down the boulevards, he in uniform, she in her prettiest dress, she thought he was the strongest, broadest, handsomest man in the city. One of the other girls at work had seen them, and the next day the salon was a-buzz with news of Jacqui's beautiful 'para'. She was not there; she had taken her annual holiday to be with him all the time.

François was excited. There was something in the wind. The news of the talks with the FLN was public knowledge. The Army, the real Army, would not stand for it much longer, he promised. That Algeria should remain French was, for both of them, the combat-hardened twenty-seven-year-old officer and the adoring twenty-three-year-old mother-to-be, an article of faith.

François never knew about the baby. He returned to Algeria in March 1961 and on April 21st several units of the French Army mutinied against the Metropolitan government. The First Colonial Paras were in the mutiny almost to a man. Only a handful of conscripts scuttled out of barracks and made rendezvous at the Préfet's office. The professionals let them go. Fighting broke out between the mutineers and the loyal regiment within a week. Early in May François was shot in a skirmish with a loyalist Army unit.

Jacqueline, who had expected no letters from April onwards, suspected nothing until she was told the news in July. She quietly took a flat in a cheap suburb of Paris and tried to gas herself. She failed because the room had too many gas leaks, but lost the baby. Her parents took her away with them for their August annual holidays and she seemed to have recovered by the time they returned. In December she became an active underground worker for the OAS.

Her motives were simple: François, and after him Jean-Claude. They should be avenged, no matter by what means, no matter what the cost to herself or anyone else. Apart from this passion, she was without an ambition in the world. Her only complaint was that she could not do more than run errands, carry messages, occasionally a slab of plastic explosive stuffed into a loaf in her shopping bag. She was convinced she could do more. Did not the 'flics' on the corners, carrying out snap searches of passers-by after one of the regular bombings of cafés and cinemas, inevitably let her pass after one flutter of her long dark eyelashes, one pout of her lips?

After the Petit-Clamart affair one of the would-be killers had spent three nights at her flat off the Place de Breteuil while on the run. It had been her big moment, but then he had moved on. A month later he had been caught, but said nothing of his stay with her. Perhaps he had forgotten. But to be on the safe side, her cell leader instructed her to do no more for the OAS for a few months, until the heat wore off. It was January 1963 when she began carrying messages again.

And so it went on, until in July a man came to see her. He was accompanied by her cell leader, who showed him great deference. He had no name. Would she be prepared to undertake a special job for the Organisation? Of course. Perhaps dangerous, certainly distasteful? No matter.

Three days later she was shown a man emerging from a block of flats. They were sitting in a parked car. She was told who he was, and what was his position. And what she had to do.

By mid-July they had met, apparently by chance, when she sat next to the man in a restaurant and smiled shyly at him while asking for the loan of the salt cellar on his table. He had spoken, she had been reserved, modest. The reaction had been the right one. Her demureness interested him. Without seeming to, the conversation blossomed, the man leading, she docilely following. Within a fortnight they were having an affair.

She knew enough about men to be able to judge the basic types of appetites. Her new lover was accustomed to easy conquests, experienced women. She played shy, attentive but chaste, reserved on the outside with just a hint now and again that her superb body was one day not to be completely wasted. The bait worked. For the man the ultimate conquest became a matter of top priority.

In late-July her cell leader told her their cohabitation should begin soon. The snag was the man's wife and two children who lived with him. On July 29th they left for the family's country house in the Loire Valley, while the husband was required to stay on in Paris for his work. Within a few minutes of his family's departure he was on the phone to the salon to insist that Jacqueline and he should dine alone at his flat the following night.

Once inside her flat, Jacqueline Dumas glanced at her watch. She had three hours to get ready, and although she intended to be meticulous in her preparations, two hours would suffice. She stripped and showered, drying herself in front of the full-length mirror on the back of the wardrobe door, watching the towel run over her skin with unfeeling detachment, raising her arms high to lift the full, rose-nippled breasts with none of the feeling of anticipatory delight she used to feel when she knew they would soon be caressed in François' palms.

She thought dully of the coming night and her belly tightened with revulsion. She would, she vowed, she would go through with it, no matter what kind of loving he wanted. From a compartment in the back of the bureau she took her photo of François, looking out of the frame with the same old ironic half-smile he had always smiled when he saw her flying the length of the station platform to meet him. The picture's soft brown hair, the cool buff uniform with the hard-muscled pectorals beneath, against which she loved once long ago to rest her face, and the steel paratrooper's wings, so cool on the burning cheek. They were all still there – in celluloid. She lay on the bed and held François above her, looking down like he did when they made love, asking superfluously, '*Alors, petite, tu veux? ...*' She always whispered, '*Oui, tu sais bien ...*' and then it happened.

When she closed her eyes she could feel him inside her, hard and hot and throbbing strength, and hear the softly growled endearments in her ear, the final stifled command '*Viens, viens ...*' which she never disobeyed.

She opened her eyes and stared at the ceiling, holding the warmed glass of the portrait to her breasts. 'François,' she breathed, 'help me, please help me tonight.'

On the last day of the month the Jackal was busy. He spent the morning at the Flea Market, wandering from stall to stall with a cheap holdall by his side. He bought a greasy black beret, a pair of well-scuffed shoes, some not-too-clean trousers, and after much searching a long once-military greatcoat. He would have preferred one of the lighter material, but military greatcoats are seldom tailored for midsummer and in the French Army are made of duffel. But it was long enough, even on him, stretching to well below the knee, which was the important thing.

As he was on his way out, his eye was caught by a stall full of medals, mostly stained with age. He bought a collection, together with a booklet describing French military medals with faded colour pictures of the ribbons and captions telling the reader for which campaigns or for what kinds of acts of gallantry the various medals were awarded.

After lunching lightly at Queenie's on the Rue Royale he slipped round the corner to his hotel, paid his bill and packed. His new purchases went into the bottom of one of his two expensive suitcases. From the collection of medals and with the help of the guide-book he made up a bar of decorations starting with the Médaille Militaire for courage in the face of the enemy, and adding the Médaille de la Libération and five campaign medals awarded to those who fought in the Free French Forces during the Second World War. He awarded himself decorations for Bir Hakeim, Libya, Tunisia, D-Day and the Second Armoured Division of General Philippe Leclerc.

The rest of the medals, and the book, he dumped separately into two waste-paper baskets attached to lamp-posts up the Boulevard Malesherbes. The hotel desk clerk informed him there was the excellent Etoile du Nord express for Brussels leaving the Gare du Nord at 5.15. This he caught, and dined well, arriving in Brussels in the last hours of July.

6

The letter for Viktor Kowalski arrived in Rome the following morning. The giant corporal was crossing the foyer of the hotel on his return from picking up the daily mail from the post office when one of the bell-hops called after him, '*Signor, per favore . . .*'

He turned, as surly as ever. The Wop was one he did not recognise, but there was nothing unusual in that. He never noticed them as he bulled his way across the floor of the foyer towards the lift. The dark-eyed young man held a letter in his hand as he came to Kowalski's side.

'*E una lettera, signor. Per un Signor Kowalski . . . no cognosco questo signor . . . E forse un francese. . . .*'

Kowalski did not understand a word of the babble of Italian, but he got the sense and he recognised his own name, badly pronounced though it was. He snatched the letter from the man's hand and stared at the scrawled name and address. He was registered under another name, and not being a reading man had failed to notice that five days earlier a Paris newspaper had had a scoop announcing that three of the top men of the OAS were now holed up on the top floor of the hotel.

So far as he was concerned no one was supposed to know where he was. And yet the letter intrigued him. He did not often receive letters, and as with most simple people the arrival of one was an important event. He had cottoned from the Italian, now standing with spaniel eyes by his side staring up as if he, Kowalski, was the fount of human know-ledge who would solve the dilemma, that none of the desk staff had heard of a guest of that name and did not know what to do with the letter.

Kowalski looked down. '*Bon. Je vais demander,*' he said loftily. The Italian's brow did not uncrease.

'*Demander, demander,*' repeated Kowalski, pointing upwards through the ceiling. The Italian saw the light.

'*Ah, si. Domandare. Prego, Signor. Tante grazie . . .*'

Kowalski strode away, leaving the Italian gesticulating his gratitude. Taking the lift to the eighth floor, he emerged to find himself confronted by the desk duty man in the corridor, automatic drawn and cocked. For a second the two stared at each other. Then the other slipped on the safety catch and pocketed the gun. He could see only Kowalski, no one else in the lift. It was purely routine, happening every time the lights above the lift doors indicated that the ascending lift was coming beyond the seventh floor.

Apart from the desk duty man, there was another facing the fire-escape door at the end of the corridor and another at the head of the stairs. Both the stairs and the fire-escape were booby-trapped, although the management did not know this, and the booby-traps could only be rendered harmless when the current to the detonators was cut off from a switch under the desk in the corridor.

The fourth man on the day shift was on the roof above the ninth floor where the chiefs lived, but in case of attack there were three others now asleep in their rooms down the corridor who had been on night shift, but who would awake and be operational in a few seconds if anything happened. On the eighth floor the lift doors had been welded closed from the outside, but even if the light above the lift on the eighth floor indicated the lift was heading right for the top it was a sign for a general alert. It had only happened once and then by accident, when a bell-hop delivering a tray of drinks had pressed the button for 'Nine'. He had been quickly discouraged from this practice.

The desk man telephoned upstairs to announce the arrival of the mail, then signalled to Kowalski to go up. The ex-corporal had already stuffed the letter addressed to himself into his inside pocket while the mail for his chiefs was in a steel *étui* chained to his left wrist. Both the lock for the chain and for the flat case were spring-loaded and only Rodin had the keys. A few minutes later the OAS colonel had unlocked both, and Kowalski returned to his room to sleep before relieving the desk man in the later afternoon.

In his room back on the eighth floor he finally read his letter, starting with the signature. He was surprised that it should be from Kovacs, whom he had not seen for a year and who hardly knew how to write, as Kowalski had some difficulty in reading. But by dint of application he deciphered the letter. It was not long.

Kovacs began by saying that he had seen a newspaper story on the day of writing, which a friend had read aloud to him, saying that Rodin, Montclair and Casson were hiding at that hotel in Rome. He had supposed his old mate Kowalski would be with them, hence writing on the offchance of reaching him.

Several paragraphs followed to the effect that things were getting tough in France these days, with the 'flics' everywhere asking for papers, and orders still coming through for smash-and-grab raids on jewellers. He had personally been in four, said Kovacs, and it was no bloody joke, particularly when one had to hand over the proceeds. He had done better in Budapest in the good old days, even though these had only lasted for a fortnight.

The last paragraph recounted that Kovacs had met Michel some weeks before, and Michel had said that he had been talking to JoJo who had said little Sylvie was sick with Luke-something; anyway it was to do with her blood having gone wrong, but that he Kovacs hoped she would soon be all right and Viktor should not worry.

But Viktor did worry. It worried him badly to think that little Sylvie was ill. There was not a great deal that had ever penetrated into the heart of Viktor Kowalski in his thirty-six violent years. He had been twelve years old when the Germans invaded Poland and one year older when his parents were taken away in a dark van. Old enough to know what his sister was doing in the big hotel behind the cathedral that had been taken over by the Germans and was visited by so many of their officers, which so upset his parents that they protested to the military governor's office. Old enough to join the partisans, he had killed his first German at fifteen. He was seventeen when the Russians came, but his parents had always hated and feared them, and told him terrible tales about what they did to Poles, so he left the partisans who were later executed on orders of the commissar, and went westwards like a hunted animal towards Czecho-slovakia. Later it was Austria and a Displaced Persons camp for the tall raw-boned gangling youth who spoke only Polish and was weak from hunger. They thought he was another of the harmless flotsam of post-war Europe. On American food his strength returned. He broke out one spring night in 1946 and hitched south towards Italy, and thence into France in company with another Pole he had met in DP camp who spoke French. In Marseilles he broke into a shop one night, killed the proprietor who disturbed him, and was on the run again. His companion left him, advising Viktor there was only one place to go – the Foreign Legion. He signed on the next morning and was in Sidi-Bel-Abbes before the police investigation in war-torn Marseilles was really off the ground. The Medi-terranean city was still a big import-base for American foodstuffs and murders committed for these foodstuffs were not uncommon. The case was dropped in a few days when no immediate suspect came to light. By the time he learned this, however, Kowalski was a legionnaire.

He was nineteen and at first the old sweats called him 'petit bon-homme'. Then he showed them how he could kill, and they called him Kowalski.

Six years in Indo-China finished off what might have been left in him of a normally adjusted individual, and after that the giant corporal was sent to Algeria. But in between he had a posting to a weapons training course for six months outside Marseilles. There he met Julie, a tiny but vicious scrubber in a dockside bar, who had been having trouble with her mec. Kowalski knocked the man six metres across the bar and out cold for ten hours with one blow. The man enunciated oddly for years after-wards, so badly was the lower mandible shattered.

Julie liked the enormous legionnaire and for several months he became her 'protector' by night, escorting her home after work to the sleazy attic in the Vieux Port. There was a lot of lust, particularly on her side, but no love between them, and even less when she discovered she was pregnant. The child, she told him, was his, and he may have believed it because he wanted to. She also told him she did not want the baby, and knew an old woman who would get rid of it for her. Kowalski clouted her, and told her if she did that he would kill her. Three months later he had to return to Algeria. In the meantime he had become friendly with another Polish ex-legionnaire, Josef Grzybowski, known as JoJo the Pole, who had been invalided out of Indo-China and had settled with a jolly widow running a snack-stall on wheels up and down the platforms at the main station. Since their marriage in 1953 they had run it together, JoJo limping along behind his wife taking the money and giving out the change while his wife dispensed the snacks. On the evenings when he was not working, JoJo liked to frequent the bars haunted by the legionnaires from the nearby barracks to talk over old times. Most of them were youngsters, recruits since his own days at Tourane, Indo-China, but one evening he ran into Kowalski.

It was to JoJo that Kowalski had turned for advice about the baby. JoJo agreed with him. They had both been Catholics once.

'She wants to have the kid done in,' said Viktor.

'*Salope*,' said JoJo.

'Cow,' agreed Viktor. They drank some more, staring moodily into the mirror at the back of the bar.

'Not fair on the little bugger,' said Viktor.

'Not right,' agreed JoJo.

'Never had a kid before,' said Viktor after some thought.

'Nor me, even being married and all,' replied JoJo.

Somewhere in the small hours of the morning, very drunk, they agreed on their plan, and drank to it with the solemnity of the truly intoxicated. The next morning JoJo remembered his pledge, but could not think how to break the news to Madame. It took him three days. He skated warily round the subject once or twice, then blurted it out while he and the missis were in bed. To his amazement, Madame was delighted. And so it was arranged.

In due course Viktor returned to Algeria, to rejoin Major Rodin who now commanded the battalion, and to a new war. In Marseilles JoJo and his wife, by a mixture of threats and cajolement, supervised the pregnant Julie. By the time Viktor left Marseilles she was already four months gone and it was too late for an abortion, as JoJo menacingly pointed out to the pimp with the broken jaw who soon came hanging around. This individual had become wary of crossing legionnaires, even old veterans with gammy legs, so he obscenely forswore his former source of income and looked elsewhere.

Julie was brought to bed in late 1955 and produced a girl, blue-eyed and golden-haired. Adoption papers were duly filed by JoJo and his wife, with the concurrence of Julie. The adoption went through. Julie went back to her old life, and the JoJos had themselves a daughter whom they named Sylvie. They informed Viktor by letter and in his barrack bed he was strangely pleased. But he did not tell anyone. He had never actually owned anything within his memory that, if divulged, had not been taken away from him.

Nevertheless, three years later, before a long combat mission in the Algerian hills, the chaplain had proposed to him that he might like to make a will. The idea had never even occurred to him before. He had never had anything to leave behind for one thing, since he spent all his accumulated pay in the bars and whorehouses of the cities when given his rare periods of leave, and what he had belonged to the Legion. But the chaplain assured him that in the modern Legion a will was perfectly in order, so with considerable assistance he made one, leaving all his worldly goods and chattels to the daughter of one Josef Grzybowski, former legionnaire, presently of Marseilles. Eventually a copy of this document, along with the rest of his dossier, was filed with the archives of the Ministry of the Armed Forces in Paris. When Kowalski's name became known to the French security forces in connection with the Bone and Constantine terrorism in 1961, this dossier was unearthed along with many others, and came to the attention of Colonel Rolland's Action Service at the Porte des Lilas. A visit was paid to the Grzybowskis, and the story came out. But Kowalski never learned this.

He saw his daughter twice in his life, once in 1957 after taking a bullet in the thigh and being sent on convalescent leave to Marseilles, and again in 1960 when he came to the city when on escort duty for Lieutenant-Colonel Rodin who had to attend a court martial as a witness. The first time the little girl was two, the next time four and a half. Kowalski arrived laden with presents for the JoJos, and toys for Sylvie. They got on very well together, the small child and her bear-like Uncle Viktor. But he never mentioned it to anyone else, not even Rodin.

And now she was sick with Luke something and Kowalski worried a lot throughout the rest of the morning. After lunch he was upstairs to have the steel *étui* for the mail chained to his wrist. Rodin was expecting an important letter from France containing further details of the total sum of money amassed by the series of robberies Casson's underground of thugs had arranged throughout the previous month, and he wanted Kowalski to pay a second visit to the post office for the afternoon mail arrivals.

'What,' the corporal suddenly blurted out, 'is Luke something?'

Rodin, attaching the chain to his wrist, looked up in surprise.

'I've never heard of him,' he replied.

'It's a malady of the blood,' explained Kowalski.

From the other side of the room where he was reading a glossy magazine Casson laughed.

'Leukaemia, you mean,' he said.

'Well, what is it, monsieur?'

'It's cancer,' replied Casson, 'cancer of the blood.'

Kowalski looked at Rodin in front of him. He did not trust civilians.

'They can cure it, the *toubibs, mon colonel*?'

'No, Kowalski, it's fatal. There's no cure. Why?'

'Nothing,' mumbled Kowalski, 'just something I read.'

Then he left. If Rodin was surprised that his bodyguard who had never been known to read anything more complex than standing orders of the day had come across that word in a book he did not show it and the matter was soon swept from his mind. For the afternoon's mail brought the letter he was waiting for, to say that the combined OAS bank accounts in Switzerland now contained over two hundred and fifty thousand dollars.

Rodin was satisfied as he sat down to write and despatch the instructions to the bankers transferring that sum to the account of his hired assassin. For the balance he had no qualms. With President de Gaulle dead there would be no delay before the industrialists and bankers of the extreme right wing, who had financed the OAS in its earlier and more successful days, produced the other two hundred and fifty thousand. The same men who had replied to his approaches for a further advance of cash only a few weeks earlier with mealy-mouthed excuses that the 'lack of progress and initiative shown over recent months by the forces of patriotism' had decreased their chances of ever seeing a return on previous investments, would be clamouring for the honour of backing the soldiers who shortly afterwards would become the new rulers of a reborn France.

He finished the instructions to the bankers as darkness fell, but when he saw the orders Rodin had written instructing the Swiss bankers to pay over the money to the Jackal, Casson objected. He argued that one vitally important thing they had all three promised their Englishman was that he would have a contact in Paris capable of supplying him constantly with the latest accurate information about the movements of the French President, along with any changes in the security routines surrounding him that might occur. These could, indeed probably would, be of vital importance to the assassin. To inform him of the transfer of the money at this stage, Casson reasoned, would be to encourage him to go into action prematurely. Whenever the man intended to strike was obviously his own choice, but a few extra days would make no difference. What might very well make a difference between success and another, certainly the last, failure would be the question of information provided to the killer.

He, Casson, had received word that very morning in the mail that his chief representative in Paris had succeeded in placing an agent very close to one of the men in De Gaulle's immediate entourage. A few days more would be necessary before this agent was in a position to acquire consistently reliable information as to the General's whereabouts and above all his travelling intentions and his public appearances, neither of which were being publicly announced any more in advance. Would Rodin therefore please stay his hand for a few more days until Casson was in a position to supply the assassin with a telephone number in Paris from which he could receive the information that would be vital to his mission?

Rodin reflected long over Casson's argument, and eventually agreed that he was right. Neither man could be aware of the Jackal's intentions, and in fact the transmission of the instructions to the bankers, followed later by the letter to London containing the Paris telephone number, would not have caused the assassin to alter any detail of his schedule. Neither terrorist in Rome could know that the killer had already chosen his day and was proceeding with his planning and contingency precautions with clockwork precision.

Sitting up on the roof in the hot Roman night, his bulky form merging into the shadows of the air conditioner ventilation stack, the Colt .45 resting easily in a practised hand, Kowalski was worried about a little girl in a bed in Marseilles with Luke something in her blood. Shortly before dawn he had an idea. He remembered that the last time he had seen JoJo in 1960 the ex-legionnaire had talked of getting a telephone in his flat.

On the morning that Kowalski received his letter, the Jackal left the Amigo hotel in Brussels and took a taxi to a corner of the street where M. Goossens lived. He had rung the armourer over breakfast in the name of Duggan, which was how Goossens knew him, and the appointment was for 11 a.m. He arrived at the corner of the street at 10.30 and spent half an hour surveying the street from behind a newspaper on a kerbside bench in the little public gardens at the end of the street.

It seemed quiet enough. He presented himself at the door at eleven sharp and Goossens let him in and led him to the little office off the hallway. After the Jackal had passed M. Goossens carefully locked the front door and put it on the chain. Inside the office the Englishman turned to the armourer.

'Any problems?' he asked. The Belgian looked embarrassed.

'Well, yes, I am afraid so.'

The assassin surveyed him coldly, with no expression on his face, the eyes half closed and sullen.

'You told me that if I came back on August 1st I could have the gun by August 4th to take home with me,' he said.

'That's perfectly true, and I assure you the problem is not with the gun,' said the Belgian. 'Indeed the gun is ready, and frankly I regard it as one of my masterpieces, a beautiful specimen. The trouble has been with the other product, which evidently had to be made from scratch. Let me show you.'

On top of the desk lay a flat case about two feet long, eighteen inches broad and four inches deep. M. Goossens opened the case and the Jackal looked down on it as the upper half fell back to the table.

It was like a flat tray, divided into carefully shaped compartments, each exactly the shape of the component of the rifle that it contained.

'It was not the original case, you understand,' explained M. Goossens. 'That would have been much too long. I made the case myself. It all fits.'

It fitted very compactly. Along the top of the open tray was the barrel and breech, the whole no longer than eighteen inches. The Jackal lifted it out and examined it. It was very light, and looked rather like a sub-machine-gun barrel. The breech contained a narrow bolt which was closed shut. It ended at the back with a gnurled grip no larger than the breech into which the rest of the bolt was fitted.

The Englishman took the gnurled end of the bolt between forefinger and thumb of the right hand, gave it a sharp turn anti-clockwise. The bolt unlocked itself and rolled over in its groove. As he pulled, the bolt slid back to reveal the gleaming tray in which the bullet would lie, and the dark hole at the rear end of the barrel. He rammed the bolt back home and twisted it clockwise. Smoothly it locked into place.

Just below the rear end of the bolt an extra disc of steel had been expertly welded on to the mechanism. It was half an inch thick but less than an inch round and in the top part of the disc was a cut-out crescent to allow free passage backwards of the bolt. In the centre of the rear face of the disc was a single hole half an inch across; the inside of this hole had been threaded as if to take a screw.

'That's for the frame of the stock,' said the Belgian quietly.

The Jackal noticed that where the wooden stock of the original rifle had been removed no trace remained except the slight flanges running along the underside of the breech where the woodwork had once fitted. The two holes made by the retaining screws that had secured the wooden stock to the rifle had been expertly plugged and blued. He turned the rifle over and examined the underside. There was a narrow slit beneath the breech. Through it he could see the underside of the bolt that contained the firing pin which fired the bullet. Through both slits protruded the stump of the trigger. It had been sawn off flush with the surface of the steel breech.

Welded to the stump of the old trigger was a tiny knob of metal, also with a threaded hole in it. Silently M. Goossens handed him a small sliver of steel, an inch long, curved and with one end threaded. He fitted the threaded end into the hole and twiddled it quickly with forefinger and thumb. When it was tight the new trigger protruded below the breech.

By his side the Belgian reached back into the tray and held up a single narrow steel rod, one end of it threaded.

'The first part of the stock assembly,' he said.

The assassin fitted the end of the steel rod into a hole at the rear of the breech and wound it till it was firm. In profile the steel rod seemed to emerge from the back of the gun and cant downwards at thirty degrees. Two inches from the threaded end, up near the mechanism of the rifle, the steel rod had been lightly flattened, and in the centre of the flattened portion a hole had been drilled at an angle to the line of the rod. This hole now faced directly backwards. Goossens held up a second and shorter steel rod.

'The upper strut,' he said.

This too was fitted into place. The two rods stuck out backwards, the upper one at a much shallower angle to the line of the barrel so that the two rods separated from each other like two sides of a narrow triangle with no base. Goossens produced the base. It was curved, about five or six inches long and heavily padded with black leather. At each end of the shoulder guard, or butt of the rifle, was a small hole.

'There's nothing to screw here,' said the armourer, 'just press it on to the ends of the rods.'

The Englishman fitted the end of each steel rod into the appropriate hole and smacked the butt home. The rifle now, when seen in profile, looked more normal, with a trigger and a complete stock sketched in outline by the upper and lower strut and the base plate. The Jackal lifted the butt-plate into his shoulder, left hand gripping the underside of the barrel, right forefinger round the trigger, left eye closed and right eye squinting down the barrel. He aimed at the far wall and squeezed the trigger. There was a soft click from inside the breech.

He turned to the Belgian, who held what looked like a ten-inch long black tube in each hand.

'Silencer,' said the Englishman. He took the proffered tube and studied the end of the rifle barrel. It had been finely 'tapped' or threaded. He slipped the wider end of the silencer over the barrel and wound it quickly round and round until it would go no more. The silencer protruded off the end of the barrel like a long sausage. He held his hand out from his side and M. Goossens slipped the telescopic sight into it.

Along the top of the barrel were a series of pairs of grooves gouged into the metal. Into these the sprung clips on the underside of the tele-scope fitted, ensuring the telescopic sight and the barrel were exactly parallel. On the right hand side and on the top of the telescope were tiny grub screws for adjusting the crossed hairs inside the sight. Again the Englishman held up the rifle and squinted as he took aim. For a casual glance he might have been an elegant check-suited English gentleman in a Piccadilly gunshop trying out a new sporting gun. But what had been ten minutes before a handful of odd-looking components was no sporting gun any more; it was a high-velocity, long-range, fully-silenced assassin's rifle. The Jackal put it down. He turned to the Belgian and nodded, satisfied.

'Good,' he said. 'Very good. I congratulate you. A beautiful piece of work.'

M. Goossens beamed.

'There still remains the question of zeroing the sights and firing some practice shots. Do you have any shells?'

The Belgian reached into the drawer of the desk and pulled out a box of a hundred bullets. The seals of the packet had been broken, and six shells were missing.

'These are for practice,' said the armourer. 'I have taken six others out for converting them to explosive tips.'

The Jackal poured a handful of the shells into his hand and looked at them. They seemed terribly small for the job one of them would have to do, but he noticed they were the extra-long type of that calibre, the extra explosive charge giving the bullet a very high velocity, and consequently increased accuracy and killing power. The tips too were pointed, where most hunting bullets are snub-nosed, and where hunting bullets have a dull leaden head, these were tipped with cupro-nickel. They were com-petition rifle bullets of the same calibre as the hunting gun he held.

'Where are the real shells?' asked the assassin.

M. Goossens went to the desk again and produced a screw of tissue paper.

'Normally, of course, I keep these in a very safe place,' he explained, 'but since I knew you were coming, I got them out.'

He undid the screw of paper and poured the contents out on to the white blotter. At first glance the bullets looked the same as those the Englishman was pouring from his cupped hand back into the cardboard box. When he had finished he took one of the bullets off the blotter and examined it closely.

From a small area around the extreme tip of the bullet the cupro-nickel had been finely sanded away to expose the lead inside. The sharp tip of the bullet had been slightly blunted, and into the nose a tiny hole had been drilled down the length of the nose-cap for a quarter of an inch. Into this aperture a droplet of mercury was poured, then the hole was tamped with a drop of liquid lead. After the lead had hardened, it too was filed and papered until the original pointed shape of the bullet tip had been exactly re-created.

The Jackal knew about these bullets, although he had never had oc-casion to use one. Far too complex to be used en masse except if factory-produced, banned by the Geneva Convention, more vicious than the simple dum-dum, the explosive bullet would go off like a small grenade when it hit the human body. On firing, the droplet of mercury would be slammed back in its cavity by the forward rush of the bullet, as when a car passenger is pressed into his seat by a violent acceleration. As soon as the bullet struck flesh, gristle or bone, it would experience a sudden deceleration.

The effect on the mercury would be to hurl the droplet forwards towards the plugged front of the bullet. Here its onward rush would rip away the tip of the slug, splaying the lead outwards like the fingers of an open hand or the petals of a blossoming flower. In this shape the leaden projectile would tear through nerve and tissue, ripping, cutting, slicing, leaving fragments of itself over an area the size of a tea-saucer. Hitting the head, such a bullet would not emerge, but would demolish every-thing inside the cranium, forcing the bone-shell to fragment from the terrible pressure energy released inside.

The assassin put the bullet carefully back on the tissue paper. Beside him the mild little man who had designed it was looking up at him quizzically.

'They look all right to me. You are evidently a craftsman, M. Goossens. What then is the problem?'

'It is the other, monsieur. The tubes. These have been more difficult to fabricate than I had imagined. First I used aluminium as you suggested. But please understand I acquired and perfected the gun first. That is why I only got around to doing the other things a few days ago. I had hoped it would be relatively simple, with my skill and the machinery I have in my workshop.

'But in order to keep the tubes as narrow as possible, I bought very thin metal. It was too thin. When threaded on my machine for later assembly piece by piece, it was like tissue paper. It bent when the slightest pressure was put upon it. In order to keep the inside measurement big enough to accommodate the breech of the rifle at its widest part, and yet get thicker-metalled tubes, I had to produce something that simply would not have looked natural. So I decided on stainless steel.

'It was the only thing. It looks just like aluminium, but slightly heavier. Being stronger, it can be thinner. It can take the thread and still be tough enough not to bend. Of course, it is a harder metal to work, and it takes time. I began yesterday. . . .'

'All right. What you say is logical. The point is, I need it, and I need it perfect. When?'

The Belgian shrugged. 'It is difficult to say. I have all the basic components, unless other problems crop up. Which I doubt. I am certain the last technical problems are licked. Five days, six days. A week perhaps. . . .'

The Englishman showed no signs of his annoyance. The face remained impassive, studying the Belgian as he completed his explanations. When he had finished, the other was still thinking.

'All right,' he said at last. 'It will mean an alteration of my travelling plans. But perhaps not as serious as I thought the last time I was here. That depends to a certain degree on the results of a telephone call I shall have to make. In any event, it will be necessary for me to acclimatise myself to the gun, and that may as well be done in Belgium as anywhere else. But I shall need the gun and the undoctored shells, plus one of the doctored ones. Also, I shall need some peace and quiet in which to·practise. Where would one pick in this country to test a new rifle in conditions of complete secrecy? Over a hundred and thirty to a hundred and fifty metres in the open air?'

M. Goossens thought for a moment. 'In the forest of the Ardennes,' he said at length. 'There are great reaches of forest there where a man may be alone for several hours. You could be there and back in a day. Today is Thursday, the weekend starts tomorrow and the woods might be too full of people picnicking. I would suggest Monday the 5th. By Tuesday or Wednesday I hope to have the rest of the job finished.'

The Englishman nodded, satisfied.

'All right. I think I had better take the gun and the ammunition now. I shall contact you again on Tuesday or Wednesday next week.'

The Belgian was about to protest when the customer forestalled him.

'I believe I still owe you some seven hundred pounds. Here . . .' He dropped another few bundles of notes on to the blotter . . . 'is a further five hundred pounds. The outstanding two hundred pounds you will receive when I get the rest of the equipment.'

'Merci, monsieur,' said the armourer, scooping the five bundles of twenty five-pound notes into his pocket. Piece by piece he disassembled the rifle, placing each component carefully into its green baize-lined compartment in the carrying case. The single explosive bullet the assassin had asked for was wrapped in a separate piece of tissue paper and slotted into the case beside the cleaning rags and brushes. When the case was closed, he proffered it and the box of shells to the Englishman, who pocketed the shells and kept the neat attaché case in his hand.

M. Goossens showed him politely out.

The Jackal arrived back at his hotel in time for a late lunch. First he placed the case containing the gun carefully in the bottom of the wardrobe, locked it and pocketed the key.

In the afternoon he strolled unhurriedly into the main post office and asked for a call to a number in Zürich, Switzerland. It took half an hour for the call to be put through and another five minutes until Herr Meier came on the line. The Englishman introduced himself by quoting a number and then giving his name.

Herr Meier excused himself and came back two minutes later. His tone had lost the cautious reserve it had previously had. Customers whose accounts in dollars and Swiss francs grew steadily merited courteous treatment. The man in Brussels asked one question, and again the Swiss banker excused himself, this time to be back on the line in less than thirty seconds. He had evidently had the customer's file and statement brought out of the safe and was studying it.

'No, *mein Herr*,' the voice crackled into the Brussels phone booth. 'We have here your letter of instruction requiring us to inform you by letter express airmail the moment any fresh in-payments are made, but there have been none over the period you mention.'

'I only wondered, Herr Meier, because I have been away from London for two weeks and it might have come in my absence.'

'No, there has been nothing. The moment anything is paid in we shall inform you without delay.'

In a flurry of Herr Meier's good wishes the Jackal put the phone down, settled the amount charged, and left.

He met the forger in the bar off the Rue Neuve that evening, arriving shortly after six. The man was there already, and the Englishman spotted a corner seat still free, ordering the forger to join him with a jerk of his head. A few seconds after he had sat down and lit a cigarette the Belgian joined him.

'Finished?' asked the Englishman.

'Yes, all finished. And very good work, even if I do say so myself.'

The Englishman held out his hand.

'Show me,' he ordered. The Belgian lit one of his Bastos, and shook his head.

'Please understand, monsieur, this is a very public place. Also one needs a good light to examine them, particularly the French cards. They are at the studio.'

The Jackal studied him coldly for a moment, then nodded.

'All right. We'll go and have a look at them in private.'

They left the bar a few minutes later and took a taxi to the corner of the street where the basement studio was situated. It was still a warm, sunny evening, and as always when out of doors the Englishman wore his wrap-around dark glasses that masked the upper half of his face from possible recognition. But the street was narrow and no sun percolated.

One old man passed them coming the other way, but he was bent with arthritis and shuffled with his head to the ground.

The forger led the way down the steps and unlocked the door from a key on his ring. Inside the studio it was almost as dark as if it were night outside. A few shafts of dullish daylight filtered between the ghastly photographs stuck to the inside of the window beside the door, so that the Englishman could make out the shapes of the chair and table in the outer office. The forger led the way through the two velvet curtains into the studio and switched on the centre light.

From inside his pocket he drew a flat brown envelope, tipped it open and spread the contents on the small round mahogany table that stood to one side, a 'prop' for the taking of portrait photographs. The table he then lifted over to the centre of the room and placed it under the centre light. The twin arc lamps above the tiny stage at the far back of the studio remained unlit.

'Please, monsieur.' He smiled broadly and gestured towards the three cards lying on the table. The Englishman picked the first up and held it under the light. It was his driving licence, the first page covered by a stuck-on tab of paper. This informed the reader that 'Mr Alexander James Quentin Duggan of London WI is hereby licensed to drive motor vehicles of Group 1a, 1b, 2, 3, 11, 12 and 13 only from 10 DEC 1960 until 9 DEC 1963 inclusive.' Above this was the licence number (an imaginary one, of course) and the words 'London County Council' and 'Road Traffic Act 1960'. Then, 'DRIVING LICENCE', and 'Fee of 15/- received.' So far as the Jackal could tell, it was a perfect forgery, certainly enough for his purposes.

The second card was simply a French *carte d'identité* in the name of André Martin, aged fifty-three, born at Colmar and resident in Paris. His own photograph, aged by twenty years, with iron-grey hair cut *en brosse*, muzzy and embarrassed, stared out of a tiny corner of the card. The card itself was stained and dog-eared, a working man's card.

The third specimen interested him most. The photograph on it was slightly different from the one on the ID card, for the date of issue of each card was different by several months, since the renewal dates would probably not have coincided precisely, had they been real. The card bore another portrait of himself that had been taken nearly two weeks earlier, but the shirt seemed to be darker and there was a hint of stubble round the chin of the photo on the card he now held. This effect had been achieved by skilful retouching, giving the impression of two different photographs of the same man, taken at different times and in different clothes. In both cases the draughtsmanship of the forgery was excellent. The Jackal looked up and pocketed the cards.

'Very nice,' he said. 'Just what I wanted. I congratulate you. There is fifty pounds outstanding, I believe.'

'That is true, monsieur. *Merci*.' The forger waited expectantly for the money. The Englishman drew a single wad of ten five-pound notes from his pocket and handed them over.

Before he let go of the end of the wad that he held between forefinger and thumb he said, 'I believe there is something more, no?'

The Belgian tried unsuccessfully to look as if he did not comprehend. 'Monsieur?'

'The genuine front page of the driving licence. The one I said I wanted back.'

There could be no doubt now that the forger was playing theatre. He raised his eyebrows in extravagant surprise, as if the thought had just occurred to him, let go of the wad of bills, and turned away. He walked several paces one way, head bowed as if deep in thought, hands held behind his back. Then he turned and walked back.

'I thought we might be able to have a little chat about that piece of paper, monsieur.'

'Yes?' The Jackal's tone gave nothing away. It was flat, without expression, apart from a slight interrogative. The face said nothing either, and the eyes seemed half shrouded as if they stared only into their own private world.

'The fact is, monsieur, that the original front page of the driving licence, with, I imagine, your real name on it, is not here. Oh please, please ...' he made an elaborate gesture as if to reassure one seized by anxiety, which the Englishman gave no sense of being ... 'it is in a very safe place. In a private deed-box in a bank, which can be opened by no one but me. You see, monsieur, a man in my precarious line of business has to take precautions, take out, if you like, some form of insurance.'

'What do you want?'

'Now, my dear sir, I had hoped that you might be prepared to do business on the basis of an exchange of ownership of that piece of paper, business based on a sum somewhat above the last figure of a hundred and fifty pounds which we mentioned in this room.'

The Englishman sighed softly, as if slightly puzzled by the ability of Man to complicate unnecessarily his own existence on this earth. He gave no other sign that the proposal of the Belgian interested him.

'You are interested?' asked the forger, coyly. He was playing his part as if he had rehearsed it at length; the oblique approach, the supposedly subtle hints. It reminded the man in front of him of a bad B-picture.

'I have met blackmailers before,' said the Englishman, not an accusation, just a flat statement in a flat voice. The Belgian was shocked.

'Ah, monsieur, I beg you. Blackmail? Me? What I propose is not blackmail, since that is a process that repeats itself. I propose simply a trade. The whole package for a certain sum of money. After all, I have in my deed-box the original of your licence, the developed plates and all the negatives of the photographs I took of you, and, I am afraid ...' he made a regretful moue to show he was afraid ... 'one other picture taken of you very quickly while you were standing under the arc lights without your make-up. I am sure these documents, in the hands of the British and French authorities, could cause you some inconvenience. You are evidently a man accustomed to paying in order to avoid the inconveniences of life. ...'

'How much?'

'One thousand pounds, monsieur.'

The Englishman considered the proposition, nodding quietly as if it was of mild academic interest only.

'It would be worth that amount to me to recover those documents,' he conceded.

The Belgian grinned triumphantly. 'I am most glad to hear it, monsieur.'

'But the answer is no,' went on the Englishman, as if he were still thinking hard. The Belgian's eyes narrowed.

'But why? I do not understand. You say it is worth a thousand pounds to you to have them back. It is a straight deal. We are both used to dealing in desirable property and being paid for it.'

'There are two reasons,' said the other mildly. 'Firstly I have no evidence whatever that the original negatives of the photographs have not been copied, so that the first demand would not be succeeded by others. Nor have I any evidence that you have not given the documents to a friend, who when asked to produce them will suddenly decide that he no longer has them, unless he too is sweetened to the tune of another thousand pounds.'

The Belgian looked relieved. 'If that is all that worries you, your fears are groundless. Firstly, it would be in my interest not to entrust the documents to any partner, for fear that he might not produce them. I do not imagine you would part with a thousand pounds without receiving the documents. So there is no reason for me to part with them. I repeat, they are in a bank deposit box.

'From the point of view of repeated requests for money, that would not make sense. A photostat copy of the driving licence would not impress the British authorities, and even if you were caught with a false driving licence it would only cause you some inconvenience, but not enough to justify several payments of money to me. As for the French cards, if the French authorities were informed that a certain Englishman were masquerading as a non-existent Frenchman called André Martin they might indeed arrest you if you passed in France under that name. But if I were to make repeated requests for money it would become worth your while to throw the cards away and get another forger to make you a new set. Then you would no longer need to fear exposure while in France as André Martin, since Martin would have ceased to exist.'

'Then why cannot I do that now?' asked the Englishman. 'Since another complete set would cost me probably no more than an extra one hundred and fifty pounds?'

The Belgian gestured with hands apart, palms upwards.

'I am banking on the fact that convenience and the time element to you are worth money. I think you need those André Martin papers and my silence in not too long a time. To get another set made would involve a lot more time, and they would not be as good. Those you have are perfect. So you want the papers, and my silence, and both now. The papers you have. My silence costs a thousand pounds.'

'Very well, since you put it like that. But what makes you think I have a thousand pounds right here in Belgium?'

The forger smiled tolerantly as one who knows all the answers but has no rooted objections to exposing them to satisfy the whims of a close friend.

'Monsieur, you are an English gentleman. It is clear to all. Yet you wish to pass for a middle-aged French working man. Your French is fluent and almost without accent. That is why I put the birthplace of André Martin as Colmar. You know, Alsatians speak French with a trace of accent like your own. You pass through France disguised as André Martin. Perfect, a stroke of genius. Who would ever think of searching an old man like Martin? So whatever you are carrying on you must be valuable. Drugs perhaps? Very fashionable in certain smart English circles these days. And Marseilles is one of the main supply centres. Or diamonds? I do not know. But the business you are in is profitable. English milords do not waste their time with picking pockets on racecourses. Please, monsieur, we stop playing games, *hein*? You telephone your friends in London and ask them to cable a thousand pounds to you at the bank here. Then tomorrow night we exchange packages and – hop – you are on your way, not so?'

The Englishman nodded several times, as if in rueful contemplation of a past life full of errors. Suddenly he raised his head and smiled engagingly at the Belgian. It was the first time the forger had seen him smile, and he felt enormously relieved that this quiet Englishman had taken the matter so calmly. The usual twisting around to seek an outlet. But in the long run no problems. The man had come round. He felt the tension drain out of him.

'Very well,' said the Englishman. 'You win. I can have a thousand pounds here by noon tomorrow. But there is one condition.'

'Condition?' At once the Belgian was wary again.

'We do not meet here.'

The forger was baffled. 'There is nothing wrong with this place. It is quiet, private . . .'

'There is everything wrong with this place from my point of view. You have just told me that you took a clandestine picture of me here. I do not wish our little ceremony of handing over our respective packages to be interrupted by the quiet click of a camera from some concealed point where one of your friends has thoughtfully hidden himself. . . .'

The Belgian's relief was visible. He laughed aloud.

'You need have no fears of that, *cher ami*. This place is mine, very discreet, and nobody comes in here unless they are invited in by me. One has to be discreet, you understand, for I make a sideline from here in taking pictures for the tourists, you know; very popular but not quite the kind of work one does in a studio on the Grande Place. . . .'

He held up his left hand, the forefinger and thumb forming the letter O, and ran the extended forefinger of the right hand through the circular aperture several times to indicate the sex act in progress.

The Englishman's eyes twinkled. He grinned wide, then started to laugh. The Belgian laughed too at the joke. The Englishman clapped his hands against the Belgian's upper arms, and the fingers tightened on the biceps muscles, holding the forger steady, his hands still going through their erotic gestures. The Belgian was still laughing when he got the impression his private parts had been hit by an express train.

The head jerked forward, the hands discontinued their mime and dropped downwards to the crushed testicles from which the man who held him had withdrawn his right knee, and the laugh turned to a screech, and a gurgle, a retch. Half unconscious, he slithered to his knees, then tried to roll forwards and sideways to lie on the floor and nurse himself.

The Jackal let him slip quite gently to his knees. Then he stepped round and over the fallen figure, straddling the exposed back of the Belgian. His right hand slipped round the Belgian's neck and out the other side, and with it he gripped his own left bicep. The left hand was placed against the back of the forger's head. He gave one short vicious twist to the neck, backwards, upwards and sideways.

The crack as the cervical column snapped was probably not very loud, but in the quiet of the studio it sounded like a small pistol going off. The forger's body gave one last contraction, then slumped as limp as a rag doll. The Jackal held on for a moment longer before letting the body fall face down on the floor. The dead face twisted sideways, hands buried beneath the hips still clutching the privates, tongue protruding slightly between the clenched teeth, half bitten through, eyes open and staring at the faded pattern of the linoleum.

The Englishman walked quickly across to the curtains to make sure they were closed completely, then went back to the body. He turned it over and patted the pockets, finding the keys eventually in the left-hand side of the trousers. In the far corner of the studio stood the large trunk of 'props' and make-up trays. The fourth key he tried opened the lid, and he spent ten minutes removing the contents and piling them in untidy heaps on the floor.

When the trunk was quite empty, the killer lifted the body of the forger by the armpits and hefted it over to the trunk. It went in quite easily, the limp limbs buckling to conform with the contours of the interior of the trunk. Within a few hours rigor mortis would set in, jamming the corpse into its adopted position at the bottom of the case. The Jackal then started replacing the articles that had come out. Wigs, women's underwear, toupees and anything else that was small and soft were stuffed into the crevices between the limbs. On top went the several trays of make-up brushes and tubes of grease. Finally the jumble of remaining pots of cream, two negligées, some assorted sweaters and jeans, a dressing-gown and several pairs of black fishnet stockings were placed on top of the body, completely covering it and filling the trunk to the brim. It took a bit of pressure to make the lid close, but then the hasp went home and the padlock was shut.

Throughout the operation the Englishman had handled the pots and jars by wrapping his hand in a piece of cloth from inside the case. Using his own handkerchief he now wiped off the lock and all outer surfaces of the trunk, pocketed the bundle of five-pound notes that still lay on the table, wiped that too and replaced it against the wall where it had stood when he came in. Finally he put out the light, took a seat on one of the occasional chairs against the wall, and settled down to wait until darkness fell. After a few minutes he took out his box of cigarettes, emptied the remaining ten into one of the side pockets of his jacket, and smoked one of them, using the empty box as the ashtray and carefully preserving the used stub by putting it into the box when it was finished.

He had few illusions that the disappearance of the forger could remain undetected for ever, but thought there was a likelihood that a man like that would probably have to go underground or travel out of town at periodic intervals. If any of his friends remarked on his sudden failure to appear at his normal haunts they would probably put the fact down to that. After a while a search would start, first of all among the people connected with the forging or pornographic-photo business. Some of these might know about the studio and visit it, but most would be deterred by the locked door. Anyone who did penetrate into the studio would have to ransack the place, force the lock on the trunk and empty it before finding the body.

A member of the underworld, doing this, would probably not report the matter to the police, he reasoned, thinking the forger had fallen foul of a gangland boss. No maniac customer interested in pornography alone would have bothered to hide the body so meticulously after a killing in passion. But eventually the police would have to know. At that point a photograph would doubtless be published, and the barman would probably remember the departure of the forger from his bar on the evening of August 1st in company with a tall blond man in a check suit and dark glasses.

But it was an extremely long shot that anyone would for months to come examine the dead man's deed-box, even if he had registered it under his own name. He had exchanged no words with the barman, and the order for drinks he had given to the waiter in the same bar had been two weeks earlier. The waiter would have to have a phenomenal memory to recall the slight trace of foreign accent in the order for two beers. The police would launch a perfunctory search for a tall blond man, but even if the enquiry got as far as Alexander Duggan, the Belgian police would still have to go a long way to find the Jackal. On balance, he felt he had at least a month, which was what he needed. The killing of the forger was as mechanical as stamping on a cockroach. The Jackal relaxed, finished a second cigarette, and looked outside. It was 9.30 and a deep dusk had descended over the narrow street. He left the studio quietly, locking the outer door behind him. No one passed him as he went quietly down the street. Half a mile away he dropped the unidentifiable keys down a large drain set into the pavement and heard them splosh into the water several feet down in the sewer beneath the street. He returned to his hotel in time for a late supper.

The next day, Friday, he spent shopping in one of the working-class suburbs of Brussels. From a shop specialising in camping equipment he bought a pair of hiking boots, long woollen socks, denim trousers, check woollen shirt and a haversack. Among his other purchases were several sheets of thin foam rubber, a string shopping bag, a ball of twine, a hunting knife, two thin paint brushes, a tin of pink paint and another of brown. He thought of buying a large Honeydew melon from an open fruit stall, but decided not to until later.

Back at the hotel he used his new driving licence, now matching his passport in the name of Alexander Duggan, to order a self-drive hire car for the following morning, and prevailed on the head reception clerk to book him a single room with a shower/bath for the weekend at one of the resorts along the sea coast. Despite the lack of accommodation available in August, the clerk managed to find him a room in a small hotel overlooking the picturesque fishing harbour of Zeebrugge, and wished him a pleasant weekend by the sea.

7

While the Jackal was doing his shopping in Brussels, Viktor Kowalski was wrestling with the intricacies of international telephone enquiries from Rome's main post office.

Not speaking Italian, he had sought the aid of the counter clerks, and eventually one of them had agreed that he spoke a little French. Laboriously Kowalski explained to him that he wished to telephone a man in Marseilles, France, but that he did not know the man's telephone number.

Yes, he knew the name and address. The name was Grzybowski. That baffled the Italian, who asked Kowalski to write it down. This Kowalski did, but the Italian, unable to believe that any name could start 'Grzyb...' spelt it out to the operator at the international exchange as 'Grib...' thinking that Kowalski's written 'z' had to be an 'i'. No name Josef Gribowski existed in the Marseilles telephone directory, the operator informed the Italian at the other end of the phone. The clerk turned to Kowalski and explained that there was no such person.

Purely by chance, because he was a conscientious man anxious to please a foreigner, the clerk spelt the name out to underline that he had got it right.

'*Il n'existe pas, monsieur. Voyons ... jay, air, eee....*'

'*Non, jay, air, zed ...*' cut in Kowalski.

The clerk looked perplexed.

'*Excusez-moi, monsieur. Jay, air, Zed?? Jay, air, zed, i grec, bay?*'

'*Oui,*' insisted Kowalski, 'G.R.Z.Y.B.O.W.S.K.I.'

The Italian shrugged and presented himself to the switchboard operator once again.

'Get me international enquiries, please.'

Within ten minutes Kowalski had JoJo's telephone number and half an hour later he was through. At the end of the line the ex-legionnaire's voice was distorted by crackling and he seemed hesitant to confirm the bad news in Kovacs' letter. Yes, he was glad Kowalski had rung, he had been trying to trace him for three months.

Unfortunately, yes, it was true about the illness of little Sylvie. She had been getting weaker and thinner, and when finally a doctor had diagnosed the illness, it had already been time to put her to bed. She was in the next bedroom at the flat from which JoJo was speaking. No it was not the same flat, they had taken a newer and larger one. What? The address? JoJo gave it slowly, while Kowalski, tongue between pursed lips, slowly wrote it down.

'How long do the quacks give her?' he roared down the line. He got his meaning over to JoJo at the fourth time of trying. There was a long pause.

'*Allo? Allo?*' he shouted when there was no reply. JoJo's voice came back.

'It could be a week, maybe two or three,' said JoJo.

Disbelievingly, Kowalski stared at the mouthpiece in his hand. Without a word he replaced it on the cradle and blundered out of the cabin. After paying the cost of the call he collected the mail, snapped the steel case on his wrist tight shut, and walked back to the hotel. For the first time in many years his thoughts were in a turmoil and there was no one to whom he could turn for orders how to solve the problem by violence.

In his flat in Marseilles, the same one he had always lived in, JoJo also put down the receiver when he realised Kowalski had hung up. He turned to find the two men from the Action Service still where they had been, each with his Colt .45 Police Special in his hands. One was trained on JoJo, the other on his wife who sat ashen-faced in the corner of the sofa. 'Bastards,' said JoJo with venom. 'Shits.'

'Is he coming?' asked one of the men.

'He didn't say. He just hung up on me,' said the Pole.

The black flat eyes of the Corsican stared back at him.

'He must come. Those are the orders.'

'Well, you heard me, I said what you wanted. He must have been shocked. He just hung up. I couldn't prevent him doing that.'

'He had better come, for your sake, JoJo,' repeated the Corsican.

'He will come,' said JoJo resignedly. 'If he can, he will come. For the girl's sake.'

'Good. Then your part is done.'

'Then get out of here,' shouted JoJo. 'Leave us alone.'

The Corsican rose, the gun still in his hand. The other man remained seated, looking at the woman.

'We'll be going,' said the Corsican, 'but you two will come with us. We can't have you talking around the place, or ringing Rome, now can we, JoJo?'

'Where are you taking us?'

'A little holiday. A nice pleasant hotel in the mountains. Plenty of sun and fresh air. Good for you, JoJo.'

'For how long?' asked the Pole dully.

'For as long as it takes.'

The Pole stared out of the window at the tangle of alleys and fish stalls that crouch behind the picture postcard frontage of the Old Port.

'It is the height of the tourist season. The trains are full these days. In August we make more than all the winter. It will ruin us for several years.'

The Corsican laughed as if the idea amused him.

'You must consider it rather a gain than a loss, JoJo. After all, it is for France, your adopted country.'

The Pole spun round. 'I don't give a shit about politics. I don't care who is in power, what party wants to make a balls-up of everything. But I know people like you. I have been meeting them all my life. You would serve Hitler, your type. Or Mussolini, or the OAS if it suited you. Or anybody. Regimes may change, but bastards like you never change. . . .' He was shouting, limping towards the man with the gun whose snout had not quivered a millimetre in the hand that held it.

'JoJo,' screamed the woman from the sofa. 'JoJo, je t'en prie. Laisse-le.'

The Pole stopped and stared at his wife as if he had forgotten she were there. He looked round the room and at the figures in it one by one. They all looked back at him, his wife imploring, the two Secret Service toughs without noticeable expression. They were used to reproaches which had no effect on the inevitable. The leader of the pair nodded towards the bedroom.

'Get packed. You first, then the wife.'

'What about Sylvie? She will be home from school at four. There will be no one to meet her,' said the woman.

The Corsican still stared at her husband.

'She will be picked up by us on the way past the school. Arrangements have been made. The headmistress has been told her granny is dying and the whole family has been summoned to her death-bed. It's all very discreet. Now move.'

JoJo shrugged, gave a last glance at his wife and went into the bedroom to pack, followed by the Corsican. His wife continued to twist her handkerchief between her hands. After a while she looked up at the other agent on the end of the sofa. He was younger than the Corsican, a Gascon.

'What . . . what will they do to him?'

'Kowalski?'

'Viktor.'

'Some gentlemen want to talk to him. That is all.'

An hour later the family were in the back seat of a big Citroën, the two agents in the front, speeding towards a very private hotel high in the Vercors.

The Jackal spent the weekend at the seaside. He bought a pair of swimming trunks and spent the Saturday sunning himself on the beach at Zeebrugge, bathed several times in the North Sea, and wandered round the little harbour town and along the mole where British sailors and soldiers had once fought and died in a welter of blood and bullets. Some of the walrus-moustached old men who sat along the mole and threw for sea bass might have remembered forty-six years before, had he asked them, but he did not. The English present that day were a few families scattered along the beach enjoying the sunshine and watching their children play in the surf.

On Sunday morning he packed his bags and drove leisurely through the Flemish countryside, strolling through the narrow streets of Ghent and Bruges. He lunched off the unmatchable steaks broiled over a timber fire served by the Siphon restaurant at Damm and in the mid-afternoon turned the car back towards Brussels. Before turning in for the night he asked for an early call with breakfast in bed and a packed lunch, explaining that he wished to drive into the Ardennes the following day and visit the grave of his elder brother who had died in the Battle of the Bulge between Bastogne and Malmedy. The desk clerk was most solicitous, promising that he would be called without fail for his pilgrimage.

In Rome Viktor Kowalski spent a much less relaxed weekend. He turned up regularly on time for his periods of guard duty, either as the desk man on the landing of the eighth floor, or on the roof by night. He slept little in his periods off duty, mostly lying on his bed off the main passage of the eighth floor, smoking and drinking the rough red wine that was imported by the gallon flagon for the eight ex-legionnaires who made up the guard. The crude Italian *rosso* could not compare for bite with the Algerian *pinard* that sloshes inside every legionnaire's pannikin, he thought, but it was better than nothing.

It habitually took Kowalski a long time to make up his mind on anything where no orders from above were available to help him, nor standing orders to decide on his behalf. But by Monday morning he had come to his decision.

He would not be gone long, perhaps just a day, or maybe two days if the planes did not connect properly. In any event, it was something that had to be done. He would explain to the *patron* afterwards. He was sure the *patron* would understand, even though he would be bloody angry. It occurred to him to tell the Colonel of the problem and ask for forty-eight hours' leave. But he felt sure that the Colonel, although a good commanding officer who also stuck by his men when they got into trouble, would forbid him to go. He would not understand about Sylvie, and Kowalski knew he could never explain. He could never explain anything in words. He sighed heavily as he got up for the Monday morning shift. He was deeply troubled by the thought that for the first time in his life as a legionnaire he was going to go AWOL.

The Jackal rose at the same time and made his meticulous preparations. He showered and shaved first, then ate the excellent breakfast placed on the tray by his bedside. Taking the case containing the rifle from the locked wardrobe, he carefully wrapped each component in several layers of foam rubber, securing the bundles with twine. These he stuffed into the bottom of his rucksack. On top went the paint tins and brushes, the denim trousers and check shirt, the socks and the boots. The string shopping bag went into one of the outer pockets of the rucksack, the box of bullets into the other.

He dressed himself in one of his habitual striped shirts that were fashionable in 1963, a dove-grey lightweight suit as opposed to his usual check worsted ten-ounce, and a pair of light black leather sneakers from Gucci. A black silk knitted tie completed the ensemble. He took the rucksack in one hand and went down to his car, parked in the hotel lot. This he locked in the boot. Returning to the foyer he took delivery of his packed lunch, nodded a reply to the desk clerk's wishes for a *bon voyage*, and by nine was speeding out of Brussels along the old E. 40 highway towards Namur. The flat countryside was already basking in a warm sunshine that gave a hint of a scorching day to come. His road map told him it was ninety-four miles to Bastogne and he added a few more to find a quiet place in the hills and forests to the south of the little town. He estimated he would do the hundred miles by noon easily, and gunned the Simca Aronde into another long, flat straight across the Walloon plain.

Before the sun had reached zenith he was through Namur and Marche, following the signposts that indicated Bastogne was approaching. Passing through the little town that had been torn to pieces by the guns of Hasso von Manteuffel's King Tiger tanks in the winter of 1944, he took the road southwards into the hills. The forests grew thicker, the winding road more frequently darkened by great elms and beeches and less often sliced by a single beam of sunshine between the trees.

Five miles beyond the town the Jackal found a narrow track running off into the forest. He turned the car down it, and after another mile found a second trail leading away into the forest. He turned the car a few yards up this and hid it behind a clump of undergrowth. For a while he waited in the cool shade of the forest, smoking a cigarette and listening to the ticking of the engine block as it cooled, the whisper of wind through the upper branches, and the distant cooing of a pigeon.

Slowly he climbed out, unlocked the boot and laid the rucksack on the bonnet. Piece by piece he changed his clothes, folding the impeccable dove-grey suit along the back seat of the Aronde and slipping on the denim slacks. It was warm enough to do without a jacket, and he changed the collared and tied shirt for the lumberjack check shirt. Finally the expensive town sneakers gave way to the hiking boots and woollen socks, into which he tucked the bottoms of the denims.

One by one he unwrapped the component parts of the rifle, fitting it together piece by piece. The silencer he slipped into one trouser pocket, the telescopic sight into the other. He tipped twenty shells from the box into one breast pocket of his shirt, the single explosive shell, still in its tissue-paper wrapper, into the other.

When the rest of the rifle was assembled he laid it on the bonnet of the car and went round to the boot again and took from it the purchase he had made the previous evening from a market stall in Brussels before returning to the hotel, and which had lain in the boot all night. It was the Honeydew melon. He locked the boot, tipped the melon into the empty rucksack along with the paint brushes and hunting knife, locked the car and set off into the woods. It was just after noon.

Within ten minutes he had found a long, narrow clearing, a glade where from one end one could get a clear vision for a hundred and fifty yards. Placing the gun beside a tree, he paced out a hundred and fifty paces, then sought a tree from which the place where he had left the gun was visible. He tipped the contents of the rucksack out on to the ground, prised the lids off both tins of paint, and set to work on the melon. The upper and lower parts of the fruit were painted quickly brown over the dark green skin. The centre section was coloured pink. While both colours were still wet, he used his forefinger to draw crudely a pair of eyes, a nose, moustache and mouth.

Jabbing the knife into the top of the fruit to avoid smearing the paint by finger contact, the Jackal gingerly placed the melon inside the string shopping bag. The big mesh and fine string of the bag in no way concealed either the outline of the melon or the design sketched upon it.

Lastly he jabbed the knife hard into the trunk of the tree about seven feet from the ground, and hung the handles of the shopping bag over the hilt. Against the green bark of the tree the pink and brown melon hung suspended like a grotesque autonomous human head. He stood back and surveyed his handiwork. At a hundred and fifty yards it would serve its purpose.

He closed the two tins of paint and hurled them far into the forest where they crashed through the undergrowth and disappeared. The brushes he jabbed into the ground bristles foremost and stamped on them until they too were lost to view. Taking the rucksack he went back to the rifle.

The silencer went on easily, swivelling round the end of the barrel until it was tight. The telescopic sight fitted snugly along the top of the barrel. He slipped back the bolt and inserted the first cartridge into the breech. Squinting down the sight, he scoured the far end of the clearing for his hanging target. When he found it, he was surprised to find how large and clear it looked. To all appearances, had it been the head of a living man, it would have been no more than thirty yards away. He could make out the criss-cross lines of the string of the shopping bag where it restrained the melon, his own finger smears denoting the main features of the face.

He altered his stance slightly, leaned against a tree to steady his aim, and squinted again. The two crossed wires inside the telescopic sight did not appear to be quite centred, so he reached out with the right hand and twiddled the two adjusting screws until the cross in the sight appeared to be perfectly central. Satisfied, he took careful aim at the centre of the melon and fired.

The recoil was less than he had expected, and the restrained 'phut' of the silencer hardly loud enough to have carried across a quiet street. Carrying the gun under his arm, he walked back the length of the clearing and examined the melon. Near the upper right-hand edge the bullet had scored its path across the skin of the fruit, snapping part of the string of the shopping bag, and had buried itself in the tree. He walked back again and fired a second time, leaving the setting of the telescopic sight exactly where it had been before.

The result was the same, with half an inch of difference. He tried four shots without moving the screws of the telescopic sight until he was convinced his aim was true but the sight was firing high and slightly to the right. Then he adjusted the screws.

His next shot was low and to the left. To make quite sure he again walked the length of the clearing and examined the hole made by the bullet. It had penetrated the lower left corner of the mouth on the dummy head. He tried three more shots with the sights still adjusted to this new position, and the bullets all went in the same area. Finally he moved the sights back by a whisker.

The ninth shot went clean through the forehead, where he had aimed it. A third time he walked up to the target, and this time he took a piece of chalk from his pocket and chalked the existing area touched by the bullets – the small cluster to the top and right, the second cluster round the left-hand side of the mouth, and the neat hole through the centre of the forehead.

From then on he plugged in succession each eye, the bridge of the nose, the upper lip and the chin. Swinging the target into a profile position he used the last six shots through the temple, ear-hole, neck, cheek, jaw and cranium, only one of them being slightly off-target.

Satisfied with the gun, he noted the positioning of the grub-screws that adjusted the telescopic sight and, taking a tube of balsa-wood cement from his pocket, squirted the viscous liquid over the heads of both grub-screws and the surface of the bakelite adjacent to them. Half an hour and two cigarettes later the cement was hard, and the sights were set for his eyesight with that particular weapon at a hundred and thirty metres at spot-on accuracy.

From his other breast pocket he took the explosive bullet, unwrapped it and slid it into the breech of the rifle. He took particularly careful aim at the centre of the melon and fired.

As the last plume of blue smoke curled away from the end of the silencer, the Jackal laid the rifle against the tree and walked down the clearing towards the hanging shopping bag. It sagged, limp and almost empty against the scarred trunk of the tree. The melon that had absorbed twenty lead slugs without coming to pieces had disintegrated. Parts of it had been forced through the mesh of the bag and lay scattered on the grass. Pips and juice dribbled down the bark. The remaining fragments of the fruit's flesh lay broken in the lower end of the shopping bag which hung like a weary scrotum from the hunting knife.

He took the bag and tossed it into some nearby bushes. The target it had once contained was unrecognisable as anything but pulp. The knife he jerked out of the wood and put back in its sheath. He left the tree, retrieved his rifle and strolled back to the car.

There each component was carefully wrapped in its swaddling of foam rubber sheeting and replaced in the rucksack, along with his boots, socks, shirt and slacks. He dressed again in his city clothes, locked the rucksack in the boot, and quietly ate his lunch sandwiches.

When he had finished, he left the drive and drove back to the main road, turning left for Bastogne, Marche, Namur and Brussels. He was back in the hotel shortly after six, and after taking his rucksack up to his room, descended to settle the charge for the hire car with the desk clerk. Before bathing for dinner he spent an hour carefully cleaning every part of the rifle and oiling the moving parts, stacked it away in its carrying case, and locked it into the wardrobe. Later that night the rucksack, twine, and several strips of foam rubber were dumped into a corporation refuse bucket, and twenty-one used cartridge cases went spinning into the municipal canal.

On the same Monday morning, August 5th, Viktor Kowalski was again at the main post office in Rome seeking the help of someone who spoke French. This time he wanted the clerk to telephone the Alitalia flight enquiries office and ask the times of planes during that week from Rome to Marseilles and back. He learned that he had missed the Monday flight, for it was leaving Fiumicino in an hour and he would not have time to catch it. The next direct flight was on Wednesday. No, there were no other airlines doing a direct flight to Marseilles from Rome. There were indirect flights; would the Signor be interested in that idea? No? The Wednesday flight? Certainly, it left at 11.15 a.m. arriving at Marignane Airport, Marseilles, shortly after noon. The return flight would be the next day. One booking? Single or return? Certainly, and the name? Kowalski gave the name on the papers he carried in his pocket. With passports abolished within the Common Market, the national identity card would be good enough.

He was asked to be at the Alitalia desk at Fiumicino one hour before take-off on Wednesday. When the clerk put the phone down, Kowalski took the waiting letters, locked them into his *étui*, and left to walk back to the hotel.

The following morning the Jackal had his last meeting with M. Goossens. He rang him over breakfast, and the armourer announced that he was pleased to say the work was finished. If Monsieur Duggan would like to call at 11 a.m.? And please to bring the necessary items for a final fitting.

He arrived again with half an hour in hand, the small attaché case inside an otherwise empty fibre suitcase that he had bought at a second-hand shop earlier in the morning. For thirty minutes he surveyed the street in which the armourer lived before finally walking quietly to the front door. When M. Goossens let him in, he went on into the office without hesitating. Goossens joined him after locking the front door, and closed the office door behind him.

'No more problems?' asked the Englishman.

'No, this time I think we have it.' From behind his desk the Belgian produced several rolls of hessian sacking and laid them on the desk. As he undid them, he laid side by side a series of thin steel tubes, so polished they looked like aluminium. When the last one was laid on the desk he held out his hand for the attaché case containing the component parts of the rifle. The Jackal gave it to him.

One by one, the armourer started to slide the parts of the rifle into the tubes. Each one fitted perfectly.

'How was the target practice?' he enquired as he worked.

'Very satisfactory.'

Goossens noticed as he handled the telescopic sight that the adjusting screws had been fixed into place with a blob of balsa-wood cement.

'I am sorry the calibrating screws should have been so small,' he said. 'It is better to work off precise markings, but again it was the size of the original screw heads that got in the way. So I had to use these little grub-screws. Otherwise the sight would never have fitted into its tube.' He slipped the telescope into the steel tube designed for it, and like the other components it fitted exactly. When the last of the five components of the rifle had disappeared from view he held up the tiny needle of steel that was the trigger, and the five remaining explosive bullets.

'These you see I have had to accommodate elsewhere,' he explained. He took the black leather padded butt of the rifle and showed his customer how the leather had been slit with a razor. He pushed the trigger into the stuffing inside and closed the slit with a strip of black insulating tape. It looked quite natural. From the desk drawer he took a lump of circular black rubber about one and a half inches in diameter and two inches long.

From the centre of one circular face a steel stud protruded upwards, threaded like a screw.

'This fits on to the end of the last of the tubes,' he explained. Round the steel stud were five holes drilled downwards into the rubber. Into each one he carefully fitted a bullet, until only the brass percussion caps showed to view.

'When the, rubber is fitted the bullets become quite invisible, and the rubber gives a touch of verisimilitude,' he explained. The Englishman remained silent. 'What do you think?' asked the Belgian with a touch of anxiety.

Without a word the Englishman took the tubes and examined them one by one. He rattled them, but no sound came from inside, for the interiors were lined with two layers of pale-grey baize to absorb both shock and noise. The longest of the tubes was twenty inches; it accommodated the barrel and breech of the gun. The others were about a foot each, and contained the two struts, upper and lower, of the stock, the silencer and the telescope. The butt, with the trigger inside its padding, was separate, as also was the rubber knob containing the bullets. As a hunting rifle, let alone an assassin's rifle, it had vanished.

'Perfect,' said the Jackal, nodding quietly. 'Absolutely what I wanted.' The Belgian was pleased. As an expert in his trade, he enjoyed praise as much as the next man, and he was aware that in his field the customer in front of him was also in the top bracket.

The Jackal took the steel tubes, with the parts of the gun inside them, and wrapped each one carefully in the sacking, placing each piece into the fibre suitcase. When the five tubes, butt and rubber knob were wrapped and packed, he closed the fibre suitcase and handed the attaché case with its fitted compartments back to the armourer.

'I shall not be needing that any more. The gun will stay where it is until I have occasion to use it.' He took the remaining two hundred pounds he owed the Belgian from his inner pocket and put it on the table.

'I think our dealings are complete, M. Goossens.' The Belgian pocketed the money.

'Yes, monsieur, unless you have anything else in which I may be of service.'

'Only one,' replied the Englishman. 'You will please remember my little homily to you a fortnight ago on the wisdom of silence.'

'I have not forgotten, monsieur,' replied the Belgian quietly.

He was frightened again. Would this soft-spoken killer try to silence him now, to ensure his silence? Surely not. The enquiries into such a killing would expose to the police the visits of the tall Englishman to this house long before he ever had a chance to use the gun he now carried in a suitcase. The Englishman seemed to be reading his thoughts. He smiled briefly.

'You do not need to worry. I do not intend to harm you. Besides, I imagine a man of your intelligence has taken certain precautions against being killed by one of his customers. A telephone call expected within an hour perhaps? A friend who will arrive to find the body if the call does not come through? A letter deposited with a lawyer, to be opened in the event of your death. For me, killing you would create more problems than it would solve.'

M. Goossens was startled. He had indeed a letter permanently deposited with a lawyer, to be opened in the event of his death. It instructed the police to search under a certain stone in the back garden. Beneath the stone was a box containing a list of those expected to call at the house each day. It was replaced each day. For this day, the note described the only customer expected to call, a tall Englishman of well-to-do appearance who called himself Duggan. It was just a form of insurance.

The Englishman watched him calmly.

'I thought so,' he said. 'You are safe enough. But I shall kill you, without fail, if you ever mention my visits here or my purchase from you to anyone, anyone at all. So far as you are concerned the moment I leave this house I have ceased to exist.'

'That is perfectly clear, monsieur. It is the normal working arrangement with all my customers. I may say, I expect similar discretion from them. That is why the serial number of the gun you carry has been scorched with acid off the barrel. I too have myself to protect.'

The Englishman smiled again. 'Then we understand each other. Good day, Monsieur Goossens.'

A minute later the door closed behind him and the Belgian who knew so much about guns and gunmen but so little about the Jackal breathed a sigh of relief and withdrew to his office to count the money.

The Jackal did not wish to be seen by the staff of his hotel carrying a cheap fibre suitcase, so although he was late for lunch he took a taxi straight to the mainline station and deposited the case in the left-luggage office, tucking the ticket into the inner compartment of his slim lizard-skin wallet.

He lunched at the Cygne well and expensively to celebrate the end of the planning and preparation stage in France and Belgium, and walked back to the Amigo to pack and pay his bill. When he left, it was exactly as he had come, in a finely cut check suit, wrap-round dark glasses and with two Vuitton suitcases following him in the hands of the porter down to the waiting taxi. He was also one thousand six hundred pounds poorer, but his rifle reposed safely inside an unobtrusive suitcase in the luggage office of the station and three finely forged cards were tucked into an inside pocket of his suit.

The plane left Brussels for London shortly after four, and although there was a perfunctory search of one of his bags at London Airport, there was nothing to be found and by seven he was showering in his own flat before dining out in the West End.

8

Unfortunately for Kowalski there were no telephone calls to make at the post office on Wednesday morning; had there been he would have missed his plane. And the mail was waiting in the pigeon-hole for M. Poitiers. He collected the five envelopes, locked them into his steel carrier on the end of the chain, and set off hurriedly for the hotel. By half past nine he had been relieved of both by Colonel Rodin, and was free to go back to his room for sleep. His next turn of duty was on the roof, starting at seven that evening.

He paused in his room only to collect his Colt .45 (Rodin would never allow him to carry it in the street) and tucked it into his shoulder holster. If he had worn a well-fitting jacket the bulge of the gun and holster would have been evident at a hundred yards, but his suits were as ill-fitting as a thoroughly bad tailor could make them, and despite his bulk they hung on him like sacks. He took the roll of sticking plaster and the beret that he had bought the day before and stuffed them into his jacket, pocketed the roll of lire notes and French francs that represented his past six months' savings, and closed the door behind him.

At the desk on the landing the duty guard looked up.

'Now they want a telephone call made,' said Kowalski, jerking his thumb upwards in the direction of the ninth floor above. The guard said nothing, just watched him as the lift arrived and he stepped inside. Seconds later he was in the street, pulling on the big dark glasses.

At the café across the street the man with a copy of *Oggi* lowered the magazine a fraction and studied Kowalski through impenetrable sunglasses as the Pole looked up and down for a taxi. When none came he started to walk towards the corner of the block. The man with the magazine left the café terrace and walked to the kerb. A small Fiat cruised out of a line of parked cars further down the street and stopped opposite him. He climbed in and the Fiat crawled after Kowalski at a walking pace.

On the corner Kowalski found a cruising taxi and hailed it. 'Fiumicino,' he told the driver.

At the airport the SDECE man followed him quietly as he presented himself at the Alitalia desk, paid for his ticket in cash, assured the girl on the desk that he had no suitcases or hand luggage, and was told passengers for the 11.15 Marseilles flight would be called in an hour and five minutes.

With time to kill the ex-legionnaire lounged into the cafeteria, bought a coffee at the counter and took it over to the plate-glass windows from where he could watch the planes coming and going. He loved airports although he could not understand how they worked. Most of his life the sound of aero engines had meant German Messerschmitts, Russian Stormoviks, or American Flying Forts. Later they meant air support with B-26s or Skyraiders in Vietnam, Mystères or Fougas in the Algerian djebel. But at a civilian airport he liked to watch them cruising in to land like big silver birds, engines muted, hanging in the sky as if on threads just before the touch-down. Although socially a shy man, he liked watching the interminable bustle of an airport. Perhaps, he mused, if his life had been different, he would have worked in an airport. But he was what he was, and there was no going back now.

His thoughts turned to Sylvie and his beetle brows darkened with concentration. It wasn't right, he told himself soberly, it wasn't right that she should die and all those bastards sitting up in Paris should live. Colonel Rodin had told him about them, and the way they had let France down, and betrayed the Army, and destroyed the Legion, and abandoned the people in Indo-China and Algeria to the terrorists. Colonel Rodin was never wrong.

His flight was called, and he filed through the glass doors and out on to the burning white concrete of the apron for the hundred-yard walk to the plane. From the observation terrace the two agents of Colonel Rolland watched him climb the steps into the plane. He now wore the black beret and the piece of sticking plaster on one cheek. One of the agents turned to the other and raised a weary eyebrow. As the turbo-prop took off for Marseilles, the two men left the rail. On the way through the main hall they stopped at a public kiosk while one of them dialled a Rome local number. He identified himself to the person at the end with a Christian name and said slowly, 'He's gone. Alitalia Four-Five-One. Landing Marignane 12.10. Ciao.'

Ten minutes later the message was in Paris, and ten minutes after that it was being listened to in Marseilles.

The Alitalia Viscount swung out over the bay of impossibly blue water and turned on to final approach for Marignane Airport. The pretty Roman air hostess finished her smiling walk down the gangway, checking that all seat belts were fastened and sat down in her own corner seat at the back to fasten her own belt. She noticed the passenger in the seat ahead of her was staring fixedly out of the window at the glaring off-white desolation of the Rhône Delta as if he had never seen it before.

He was the big lumbering man who spoke no Italian, and whose French was heavily accented from some motherland in Eastern Europe. He wore a black beret over his cropped black hair, a dark and rumpled suit and a pair of dark glasses which he never took off. An enormous piece of sticking plaster obscured one half of his face; he must have cut himself jolly badly, she thought.

They touched down precisely on time, quite close to the terminal building, and the passengers walked across to the Customs hall. As they filed through the glass doors, a small balding man standing beside one of the passport police kicked him lightly against the ankle.

'Big fellow, black beret, sticking plaster.' Then he strolled quietly away and gave the other the same message. The passengers divided themselves into two lines to pass through the guichets. Behind their grilles the two policemen sat facing each other, ten feet apart, with the passengers filing between them. Each passenger presented his passport and disembarkation card. The officers were of the Security Police, the DST, responsible for all internal state security inside France, and for checking incoming aliens and returning Frenchmen.

When Kowalski presented himself the blue-jacketed figure behind the grille barely gave him a glance. He banged his stamp down on the yellow disembarkation card, gave the proffered identity card a short glance, nodded and waved the big man on. Relieved, Kowalski walked on towards the Customs benches. Several of the Customs officers had just listened quietly to the small balding man before he disappeared into a glass-fronted office behind them. The senior Customs officer called to Kowalski.

'Monsieur, votre bagage.'

He gestured to where the rest of the passengers were waiting by the mechanical conveyor belt for their suitcases to appear from the wire-frame barrow parked in the sunshine outside. Kowalski lumbered over to the Customs officer.

'J'ai pas de bagage,' he said.

The Customs officer raised his eyebrows.

'Pas de bagage? Eh bien, avez-vous quelque chose à declarer?'

'Non, rien,' said Kowalski.

The Customs man smiled amiably, almost as broadly as his sing-song Marseilles accent.

'Eh bien, passez, monsieur.' He gestured towards the exit into the taxi rank. Kowalski nodded and went out into the sunshine. Not being accustomed to spending freely, he looked up and down until he caught sight of the airport bus, and climbed into it.

As he disappeared from sight several of the other Customs men gathered round the senior staffer.

'Wonder what they want him for,' said one.

'He looked a surly bugger.'

'He won't be when those bastards have finished with him,' said a third jerking his head towards the offices at the back.

'Come on, back to work,' chipped in the older one. 'We've done our bit for France today.'

'For Big Charlie you mean,' replied the first as they split up, and muttered under his breath, 'God rot him.'

It was the lunch-hour when the bus stopped finally at the Air France offices in the heart of the city and it was even hotter than in Rome. August in Marseilles has several qualities, but the inspiration to great exertions is not one of them. The heat lay on the city like an illness, crawling into every fibre, sapping strength, energy, the will to do anything but lie in a cool room with the jalousies closed and the fan full on.

Even the Cannebière, usually the bustling bursting jugular vein of Marseilles, after dark a river of light and animation, was dead. The few people and cars on it seemed to be moving through waist-deep treacle. It took half an hour to find a taxi; most of the drivers had found a shady spot in a park to have their siesta.

The address JoJo had given Kowalski was on the main road out of town heading towards Cassis. At the Avenue de la Libération he told the driver to drop him, so that he could walk the rest. The driver's 'si vous voulez' indicated plainer than text what he thought of foreigners who considered covering distances of over a few yards in this heat when they had a car at their disposal.

Kowalski watched the taxi turn back into town until it was out of sight. He found the side street named on the piece of paper by asking a waiter at a terrace café on the sidewalk. The block of flats looked fairly new, and Kowalski thought the JoJos must have made a good thing of their station food trolley. Perhaps they had got the fixed kiosk that Madame JoJo had had her eye on for so many years. That at any rate would account for the increase in their prosperity. And it would be nicer for Sylvie to grow up in this neighbourhood than round the docks. At the thought of his daughter, and the idiotic thing he had just imagined for her, Kowalski stopped at the foot of the steps to the apartment block. What had JoJo said on the phone. A week? Perhaps a fortnight? It was not possible.

He took the steps at a run, and paused in front of the double row of letter-boxes along one side of the hall. 'Grzybowski' read one. 'Flat 23.' He decided to take the stairs since it was only on the second floor.

Flat 23 had a door like the others. It had a bell push with a little white card in a slot beside it, with the word Grzybowski typed on it. The door stood at the end of the corridor, flanked by the doors of flats 22 and 24. He pressed the bell. The door in front of him opened and the lunging pickaxe handle swung out of the gap and down towards his forehead.

The blow split the skin but bounced off the bone with a dull 'thunk'. On each side of the Pole the doors of flats 22 and 24 opened inwards and men surged out. It all happened in less than half a second. In the same time Kowalski went berserk. Although slow-thinking in most ways, the Pole knew one technique perfectly, that of fighting.

In the narrow confines of the corridor his size and strength were useless to him. Because of his height the pickaxe handle had not reached the full momentum of its downward swing before hitting his head. Through the blood spurting over his eyes he discerned there were two men in the door in front of him and two others on each side. He needed room to move, so he charged forward into flat 23.

The man directly in front of him staggered back under the impact;

those behind closed in, hands reaching for his collar and jacket. Inside the room he drew the Colt from under his armpit, turned once and fired back into the doorway. As he did so another stave slammed down on his wrist, jerking the aim downwards.

The bullet ripped the kneecap off one of his assailants who went down with a thin screech. Then the gun was out of his hand, the fingers rendered nerveless from another blow on the wrist. A second later he was overwhelmed as the five men hurled themselves at him. The fight lasted three minutes. A doctor later estimated he must have taken a score of blows to the head from the leather-wrapped coshes before he finally passed out. A part of one of his ears was slashed off by a glancing blow, the nose was broken and the face was a deep-red mask. Most of his fighting was by reflex action. Twice he almost reached his gun, until a flying foot sent it spinning to the other end of the sitting-room. When he did finally go down on to his face there were only three attackers left standing to put the boot in.

When they had done and the enormous body on the floor was insensible, only a trickle of blood from the slashed scalp indicating that it was still alive, the three survivors stood back swearing viciously, chests heaving. Of the others, the man shot in the leg was curled against the wall by the door, white-faced, glistening red hands clutching his wrecked knee, a long monotonous stream of obscenities coming through pain-grey lips. Another was on his knees, rocking slowly back and forwards, hands thrust deep into the torn groin. The last lay down on the carpet not far from the Pole, a dull bruise discolouring his left temple where one of Kowalski's haymakers had caught him at full force.

The leader of the group rolled Kowalski over on to his back and flicked up one of the closed eyelids. He crossed to the telephone near the window, dialled a local number and waited.

He was still breathing hard. When the phone was answered he told the person at the other end:

'We got him. . . . Fought? Of course he bloody fought. . . . He got off one bullet, Guerini's lost a kneecap. Capetti took one in the balls and Vissart is out cold. . . . What? Yes, the Pole's alive, those were the orders weren't they? Otherwise he wouldn't have done all this damage. . . . Well, he's hurt, all right. Dunno, he's unconscious. . . . Look, we don't want a salad basket [police van], we want a couple of ambulances. And make it quick.'

He slammed the receiver down and muttered 'Cons' to the world in general. Round the room the fragments of shattered furniture lay about like firewood, which was all they would be good for. They had all thought the Pole would go down in the passage outside. None of the furniture had been stacked in a neighbouring room, and it had got in the way. He himself had stopped an armchair thrown by Kowalski with one hand full in the chest, and it hurt. Bloody Pole, he thought, the sods at head office hadn't said what he was like.

Fifteen minutes later two Citroën ambulances slid into the road outside the block and the doctor came up. He spent five minutes examining

Kowalski. Finally he drew back the unconscious man's sleeve and gave him an injection. As the two stretcher-bearers staggered away towards the lift with the Pole, the doctor turned to the wounded Corsican who had been regarding him balefully from his pool of blood beside the wall.

He prised the man's hands away from his knee, took a look and whistled.

'Right. Morphine and the hospital. I'm going to give you a knock-out shot. There's nothing I can do here. Anyway, *mon petit*, your career in this line is over.'

Guerini answered him with a stream of obscenities as the needle went in.

Vissart was sitting up with his hands to his head, a dazed expression on his face. Capetti was upright by now, leaning against the wall, retching dry. Two of his colleagues gripped him under the armpits and led him hobbling from the flat into the corridor. The leader helped Vissart to his feet as the stretcher-bearers from the second ambulance carried the inert form of Guerini away.

Out in the corridor the leader of the six took a last look back into the desolated room. The doctor stood beside him.

'Quite a mess, *hein*?' said the doctor.

'The local office can clean it up,' said the leader. 'It's their bloody flat.'

With that he closed the door. The doors of flats 22 and 24 were also open, but the interiors were untouched. He pulled both doors closed.

'No neighbours?' asked the doctor.

'No neighbours,' said the Corsican, 'we took the whole floor.'

Preceded by the doctor, he helped the still dazed Vissart down the stairs to the waiting cars.

Twelve hours later, after a fast drive the length of France, Kowalski was lying on a cot in a cell beneath a fortress barracks outside Paris. The room had the inevitable whitewashed walls, stained and musty, of all prison cells, with here and there a scratched obscenity or prayer. It was hot and close, with an odour of carbolic acid, sweat and urine. The Pole lay face up on a narrow iron cot whose legs were embedded in the concrete floor. Apart from the biscuit mattress and a rolled-up blanket under his head, the cot contained no other linen. Two heavy leather straps secured his ankles, two more his thighs and wrists. A single strap pinned his chest down. He was still unconscious, but breathing deeply and irregularly.

The face had been bathed clean of blood, the ear and scalp sutured. A stick of plaster spanned the broken nose, and through the open mouth out of which the breath rasped could be seen the stumps of two broken front teeth. The rest of the face was badly bruised.

Beneath the thick mat of black hair covering the chest, shoulders and belly other livid bruises could just be discerned, the results of fists, boots and coshes. The right wrist was heavily bandaged and taped.

The man in the white coat finished his examination, straightened up and replaced his stethoscope in his bag. He turned and nodded at the man behind him, who tapped at the door. It swung open and the pair of them went outside. The door swung to, and the jailer slid home the two enormous steel bars.

'What did you hit him with, an express train?' asked the doctor as they walked down the passage.

'It took six men to do that,' replied Colonel Rolland.

'Well, they did a pretty good job. They damn nearly killed him. If he wasn't built like a bull they would have done.'

'It was the only way,' replied the Colonel. 'He ruined three of my men.'

'It must have been quite a fight.'

'It was. Now, what's the damage?'

'In layman's terms: possible fracture of the right wrist – I haven't been able to do an X-ray, remember – plus lacerated left ear, scalp and broken nose. Multiple cuts and bruising, slight internal haemorrhaging, which could get worse and kill him, or could clear up on its own. He enjoys what one might call a rude good health – or he did. What worries me is the head. There's concussion all right, whether mild or severe is not easy to say. No signs of a skull fracture, though that was not the fault of your men. He's just got a skull like solid ivory. But the concussion could get worse if he's not left alone.'

'I need to put certain questions to him,' observed the Colonel, studying the tip of his glowing cigarette. The doctor's prison clinic lay one way, the stairs leading to the ground floor the other. Both men stopped. The doctor glanced at the head of the Action Service with distaste.

'This is a prison,' he said quietly. 'All right, it's for offenders against the security of the state. But I am still the prison doctor. Elsewhere in this prison what I say, concerning prisoners' health, goes. That corridor ...' he jerked his head backwards in the direction from which they had come ... 'is your preserve. It has been most lucidly explained to me that what happens down there is none of my business, and I have no say in it. But I will say this: if you start "questioning" that man before he's recovered, with your methods, he'll either die or become a raving lunatic.'

Colonel Rolland listened to the doctor's bitter prediction without moving a muscle.

'How long?' he asked.

The doctor shrugged. 'Impossible to say. He may regain consciousness tomorrow, or not for days. Even if he does, he will not be fit for questioning – medically fit that is – for at least a fortnight. At the very least. That is, if the concussion is only mild.'

'There are certain drugs,' murmured the Colonel.

'Yes, there are. And I have no intention of prescribing them. You may be able to get them, you probably can. But not from me. In any case, nothing he could tell you now would make the slightest sense. It would probably be gibberish. His mind is scrambled. It may clear, it may not. But if it does, it must happen in its own time. Mind-bending drugs now would simply produce an idiot, no use to you or anyone else. It will probably be a week before he flickers an eyelid. You'll just have to wait.'

With that he turned on his heel and walked back to his clinic.

But the doctor was wrong. Kowalski opened his eyes three days later, on August 10th, and the same day had his first and only session with the interrogators.

The Jackal spent the three days after his return from Brussels putting the final touches to his preparations for his forthcoming mission into France.

With his new driving licence in the name of Alexander James Quentin Duggan in his pocket he went down to Fanum House, headquarters of the Automobile Association, and acquired an International Driving Licence in the same name.

He bought a matching series of leather suitcases from a second-hand shop specialising in travel goods. Into one he packed the clothes that would, if necessary, disguise him as Pastor Per Jensen of Copenhagen. Before the packing he transferred the Danish maker's labels from the three ordinary shirts he had bought in Copenhagen to the clerical shirt, dog collar and black bib that he had bought in London, removing the English maker's labels as he did so. These clothes joined the shoes, socks, underwear and charcoal-grey light suit that might one day make up the persona of Pastor Jensen. Into the same suitcase went the clothes of American student Marty Schulberg, sneakers, socks, jeans, sweat-shirts and windcheater.

Slitting the lining of the suitcase, he inserted between the two layers of leather that comprised the stiffened sides of the case the passport of the two foreigners he might one day wish to become. The last additions to this caseful of clothes were the Danish book on French cathedrals, the two sets of spectacles, one for the Dane, the other for the American, the two different sets of tinted contact lenses, carefully wrapped in tissue paper, and the preparations for hair tinting.

Into the second case went the shoes, socks, shirt and trousers of French make and design that he had bought in the Paris Flea Market, along with the ankle-length greatcoat and black beret. Into the lining of this case he inserted the false papers of the middle-aged Frenchman André Martin. This case remained partly empty, for it would soon also have to hold a series of narrow steel tubes containing a complete sniper's rifle and ammunition.

The third, slightly smaller, suitcase was packed with the effects of Alexander Duggan: shoes, socks, underwear, shirts, ties, handkerchiefs and three elegant suits. Into the lining of this suitcase went several thin wads of ten-pound notes to the value of a thousand pounds, which he had drawn from his private bank account on his return from Brussels.

Each of these cases was carefully locked and the keys transferred to his private key-ring. The dove-grey suit was cleaned and pressed, then left hanging in the wall cupboard of his flat. Inside the breast pocket were his passport, driving licence, international licence and a folder containing one hundred pounds in cash.

Into the last piece of his luggage, a neat hand case, went shaving tackle, pyjamas, sponge-bag and towel, and the final pieces of his purchases – a light harness of finely sewn webbing, a two-pound bag of plaster of Paris, several rolls of large-weave lint bandages, half a dozen rolls of sticky plaster, three packs of cotton wool and a pair of stout shears with blunt but powerful blades. The grip would travel as hand-luggage, for it was his experience that in passing Customs at whatever airport an attaché case was not usually the piece of luggage selected by the Customs officer for an arbitrary request to open up.

With his purchases and packing complete he had reached the end of his planning. The disguises of Pastor Jensen and Marty Schulberg, he hoped, were merely precautionary tactics which would probably never be used unless things went wrong and the identity of Alexander Duggan had to be abandoned. The identity of André Martin was vital to his plan, and it was possible that the other two would never be required. In that event the entire suitcase could be abandoned in a left-luggage office when the job was over. Even then, he reasoned, he might need either of them for his escape. André Martin and the gun could also be abandoned when the job was over, as he would have no further use for them. Entering France with three suitcases and an attaché case, he estimated he would leave with one suitcase and the hand luggage, certainly not more.

With this task finished he settled down to wait for the two pieces of paper that would set him on his way. One was the telephone number in Paris which could be used to feed him information concerning the exact state of readiness of the security forces surrounding the French President. The other was the written notification from Herr Meier in Zürich that two hundred and fifty thousand dollars had been deposited in his numbered bank account.

While he was waiting for them he passed the time by practising walking round his flat with a pronounced limp. Within two days he was satisfied that he had a sufficiently realistic limp to prevent any observer from being able to detect that he had not sustained a broken ankle or leg.

The first letter he awaited arrived on the morning of August 9th. It was an envelope postmarked in Rome and bore the message: 'Your friend can be contacted at MOLITOR 5901. Introduce yourself with the words "Ici Chacal". Reply will be "Ici Valmy". Good luck.'

It was not until the morning of the 11th that the letter from Zürich arrived. He grinned openly as he read the confirmation that, come what may, provided he remained alive, he was a wealthy man for the rest of his life. If his forthcoming operation was successful, he would be even richer. He had no doubts that he would succeed. Nothing had been left to chance.

He spent the rest of that morning on the telephone booking air passages, and fixed his departure for the following morning, August 12th.

The cellar was silent except for the sound of breathing, heavy but controlled from the five men behind the table, a rasping rattle from the man strapped to the heavy oaken chair in front of it. One could not tell how big the cellar was, nor what was the colour of the walls. There was only one pool of light in the whole place and it encircled the oak chair and the prisoner. It was a standard table lamp such as is often used for reading, but its bulb was of a great power and brightness, adding to the over-powering warmth of the cellar. The lamp was clipped to the left-hand edge of the table and the adjustable shade was turned so that it shone straight at the chair six feet away.

Part of the circle of light swept across the stained wood of the table, illuminating here and there the tips of a set of fingers, a hand and a wrist, a clipped cigarette sending a thin stream of blue smoke upwards.

So bright was the light that by contrast the rest of the cellar was in darkness. The torsos and shoulders of the five men behind the table in a row were invisible to the prisoner. The only way he could have seen his questioners would have been to leave his chair and move to the side, so that the indirect glow from the light picked out their silhouettes.

This he could not do. Padded straps pinned his ankles firmly against the legs of the chair. From each of these legs, front and back, an L-shaped steel bracket was bolted into the floor. The chair had arms, and the wrists of the prisoner were secured to these also by padded straps. Another strap ran round his waist and a third round his massive hairy chest. The padding of each was drenched with sweat.

Apart from the quiescent hands, the top of the table was almost bare. Its only other decoration was a slit bordered in brass and marked along one side with figures. Out of the slit protruded a narrow brass arm with a bakelite knob on the top which could be moved backwards and forwards up and down the slit. Beside this was a simple on/off switch. The right hand of the man on the end of the table rested negligently close to the controls. Little black hairs crawled along the back of the hand.

Two wires fell beneath the table, one from the switch, the other from the current control, towards a small electrical transformer lying on the floor near the end man's feet. From here a stouter rubber-clad black cable led to a large socket in the wall behind the group.

In the far corner of the cellar behind the questioners a single man sat at a wooden table, face to the wall. A tiny glow of green came from the 'on' light of the tape recorder in front of him, although the spools were still.

Apart from the breathing, the silence of the cellar was almost tangible. All the men were in shirt sleeves, rolled up high and damp with sweat. The odour was crushing, a stench of sweat, metal, stale smoke and human vomit. Even the latter, pungent enough, was overpowered by one even stronger, the unmistakable reek of fear and pain.

The man in the centre spoke at last. The voice was civilised, gentle, coaxing.

'Ecoute, mon p'tit Viktor. You are going to tell us. Not now perhaps. But eventually. You are a brave man. We know that. We salute you. But even you cannot hold out much longer. So why not tell us? You think Colonel Rodin would forbid you if he were here. He would order you to tell us. He knows about these things. He would tell us himself to spare you more discomfort. You yourself know, they always talk in the end. N'est-ce pas, Viktor? You have seen them talk, hein? No one can go on and on and on. So why not now, *hein*? Then back to bed. And sleep, and sleep and sleep. No one will disturb you. . . .'

The man in the chair raised a battered face, glistening with sweat, into the light. The eyes were closed, whether by the great blue bruises caused by the feet of the Corsicans in Marseilles or by the light, one could not tell. The face looked at the table and the blackness in front of it for a while, the mouth opened and tried to speak. A small gobbet of puke emerged and dribbled down the matted chest to the pool of vomit in his lap. The head sagged back until the chin touched the chest again. As it did so the shaggy hair shook from side to side in answer. The voice from behind the table began again.

'*Viktor, écoute-moi.* You're a hard man. We all know that. We all recognise that. You have beaten the record already. But even you can't go on. But we can, Viktor, we can. If we have to we can keep you alive and conscious for days, weeks. No merciful oblivion like in the old days. One is technical nowadays. There are drugs, *tu sais.* Third degree is finished now, probably gone for good. So why not talk? We understand, you see. We know about the pain. But the little crabs, they do not understand. They just don't understand, Viktor. They just go on and on. . . . You want to tell us, Viktor? What are they doing in that hotel in Rome? What are they waiting for?'

Lolling against the chest, the great head shook slowly from side to side. It was as if the closed eyes were examining first one and then the other of the little copper crabs that gripped the nipples, or the single larger one whose serrated teeth clipped each side of the head of the penis.

The hands of the man who had spoken lay in front of him in a pool of light, slim, white, full of peace. He waited for a few moments longer. One of the white hands separated itself from the other, the thumb tucked into the palm, the four fingers spread wide, and laid itself on the table.

At the far end the hand of the man by the electric switch moved the brass handle up the scale from figure two to figure four, then took the on/off switch between finger and thumb.

The hand further along the wooden top withdrew the splayed fingers, lifted the forefinger once into the air, then pointed the fingertip downwards in the world-wide signal for 'Go'. The electric switch went on.

The little metal crabs fixed to the man in the chair and linked by wires to the on/off switch appeared to come alive with a slight buzzing. In silence the huge form in the chair rose as if by levitation, propelled by an unseen hand in the small of the back. The legs and wrists bulged outwards against the straps until it seemed that even with the padding the leather must cut clean through the flesh and bone. The eyes, medically unable to see clearly through the puffed flesh around them, defied medicine and started outwards bulging into vision and staring at the ceiling above. The mouth was open as if in surprise and it was half a second before the demonic scream came out of the lungs. When it did come, it went on and on and on. . . .

Viktor Kowalski broke at 4.10 in the afternoon and the tape recorder went on.

As he started to talk, or rather ramble incoherently between whimpers and squeaks, the calm voice from the man in the centre cut across the maunderings with incisive clarity.

'Why are they there, Viktor ... in that hotel ... Rodin, Montclair and Casson ... what are they afraid of ... where have they been, Viktor ... who have they seen ... why do they see nobody, Viktor ... tell us, Viktor ... why Rome ... before Rome ... why Vienna, Viktor ... where in Vienna ... which hotel ... why were they there, Viktor. ...?'

Kowalski was finally silent after fifty minutes, his last ramblings as he went into relapse being recorded on tape until they stopped. The voice behind the table continued, more gently for another few minutes until it became clear there were going to be no more answers. Then the man in the centre gave an order to his subordinates and the session was over.

The tape recording was taken off the spool and rushed by a fast car from the cellar beneath the fortress into the outskirts of Paris and the offices of the Action Service.

The brilliant afternoon that had warmed the friendly pavements of Paris throughout the day faded to golden dusk, and at nine the street lights came on. Along the banks of the Seine the couples strolled as always on summer nights, hand in hand, slowly as if drinking in the wine of dusk and love and youth that will never, however hard they try, be quite the same again. The open-fronted cafés along the water's edge were alive with chatter and clink of glasses, greetings and mock protests, raillerie and compliments, apologies and passes, that make up the conversation of the French and the magic of the river Seine on an August evening. Even the tourists were almost forgiven for being there and bringing their dollars with them.

In a small office near the Porte des Lilas the insouciance did not penetrate. Three men sat round a tape recorder that turned slowly on a desk. Through the late afternoon and evening they worked. One man controlled the switches, continuously flicking the spools on to 'playback' or 're-wind' and then 'playback' again on the instruction of the second. This man had a pair of earphones over his head, brow furrowed in concentration as he tried to decipher meaningful words out of the jumble of sounds coming through the phones. A cigarette clipped between his lips, rising blue smoke making his eyes water, he signed with his fingers to the operator when he wanted to hear a passage again. Sometimes he listened to a ten-second passage half a dozen times before nodding to the operator to hold on. Then he would dictate the last passage of speech.

The third man, a younger blond, sat behind a typewriter and waited for dictation. The questions that had been asked in the cellar beneath the fortress were easy to understand, coming clear and precise through the earphones. The answers were more disjointed. The typist wrote the transcript like an interview, the questions always on a fresh line and beginning with the letter Q. The answers were on the next line, beginning with the letter R. These were disjointed, involving the use of plenty of spacing dots where the sense broke up completely.

It was nearly twelve midnight before they had finished. Despite the open window the air was blue with smoke and smelt like a powder magazine.

The three men rose stiff and weary. Each stretched in his own fashion to untwine the bunched and aching muscles. One of the three reached for the telephone, asked for an outside line and dialled a number. The man with the earphones took them off and re-wound the tape back on to the original spool. The typist took the last sheets out of the machine, extracted the carbons from between them and began to arrange the separate piles of paper into sets of the confession in order of pages. The top set would go to Colonel Rolland, the second to files, and the third to mimeograph for extra copies to be made for department heads, to be distributed if Rolland deemed fit.

The call reached Colonel Rolland at the restaurant where he had been dining with friends. As usual the elegant-looking bachelor civil servant had been his witty and gallant self, and his compliments to the ladies present had been much appreciated, by them if not by their husbands. When the waiter called him to the phone, he apologised and left. The phone was on the counter. The Colonel said simply 'Rolland' and waited while his operative at the other end identified himself.

Rolland then did the same by introducing into the first sentence of his conversation the correct prearranged word. A listener would have learned that he had received information that his car, which had been under repair, was mended, and could be collected at the Colonel's convenience. Colonel Rolland thanked his informant, and returned to the table. Within five minutes he was excusing himself with urbanity, explaining that he faced a hard day in the morning and ought to get his ration of sleep. Ten minutes later he was alone in his car, speeding through the still-crowded city streets towards the quieter faubourg of Porte des Lilas. He reached his office soon after one in the morning, took off his immaculate dark jacket, ordered coffee from the night staff, and rang for his assistant.

The top copy of Kowalski's confession came with the coffee. The first time he read the twenty-six pages of the dossier quickly, trying to grasp the gist of what the demented legionnaire had been saying. Something in the middle caught his eye, causing him to frown, but he read on to the end without a pause.

His second reading was slower, more cautious, giving greater concentration to each paragraph. The third time he took a black felt-nib pen from the tray in front of the blotter and read even more slowly, drawing the thick black line of ink through the words and passages relating to Sylvie, Luke something, Indo-China, Algeria, JoJo, Kovacs, Corsican, bastards, the Legion. All these he understood, and they did not interest him.

Much of the wandering concerned Sylvie, some of it a woman called Julie, which meant nothing to Rolland. When all this was deleted, the confession would not have covered more than six pages. Out of the remaining passages he tried to make some sense. There was Rome. The three leaders were in Rome. Well, he knew that anyway. But why? This question had been asked eight times. By and large the answer had been the same each time. They did not wish to be kidnapped like Argoud had been in February. Natural enough, thought Rolland. Had he then been wasting his time with the whole Kowalski operation? There was one word the legionnaire had mentioned twice, or rather mumbled twice, in answering these eight identical questions. The word was 'secret'. As an adjective? There was nothing secret about their presence in Rome. Or as a noun. What secret?

Rolland went through to the end for the tenth time, then back again to the beginning. The three OAS men were in Rome. They were there because they did not wish to be kidnapped. They did not wish to be kidnapped because they possessed a secret.

Rolland smiled ironically. He had known better than General Guibaud that Rodin would not run for cover because he was frightened.

So they knew a secret, did they? What secret? It all seemed to have stemmed from something in Vienna. Three times the word Vienna cropped up, but at first Rolland had thought it must be the town called Vienne that lies twenty miles south of Lyons. But perhaps it was the Austrian capital, not the French provincial town.

They had a meeting in Vienna. Then they went to Rome and took refuge against the possibility of being kidnapped and interrogated until they revealed a secret. The secret must stem from Vienna.

The hours passed, and so did innumerable cups of coffee. The pile of stubs in the shell-case ashtray grew. Before the thin line of paler grey started to tip the grisly industrial suburbs that lie east of the Boulevard Mortier Colonel Rolland knew he was on to something.

There were pieces missing. Were they really missing, gone for all time since the message by phone at three in the morning had told him Kowalski would never be questioned again because he was dead? Or were they hidden somewhere in the jumbled text that had come out of the deranged brain as the final reserves of strength failed?

With his right hand Rolland began to jot down pieces of the puzzle that had no seeming place to be there. Kleist, a man called Kleist. Kowalski, being a Pole, had pronounced the word correctly and Rolland, knowing some German still from his wartime days, wrote it down correctly although it had been spelt wrongly by the French transcriber. Or was it a person? A place perhaps? He rang the switchboard and asked them to seek out the Viennese telephone directory and search for a person or place called Kleist. The answer was back in ten minutes. There were two columns of Kleists in Vienna, all private individuals, and two places of that name: the Ewald Kleist Primary School for Boys, and the Pension Kleist in the Brucknerallee. Rolland noted both, but underlined the Pension Kleist. Then he read on.

There were several references to a foreigner over whom Kowalski seemed to have mixed feelings. Sometimes he used the word *bon*, meaning good, to refer to this man; at other times he called him a *fâcheur*, an annoying or irritating type. Shortly after 5 a.m. Colonel Rolland sent for the tape and tape recorder, and spent the next hour listening to it. When he finally switched off the machine he swore quietly and violently to himself. Taking a fine pen he made several alterations to the transcribed text.

Kowalski had not referred to the foreigner as *bon* but as 'blond'. And the word coming from the torn lips that had been written down as *fâcheur* had in reality been *faucheur*, meaning a killer.

From then on the task of piecing together Kowalski's hazy meaning was easy. The word for jackal, which had been crossed out wherever it occurred because Rolland had thought it was Kowalski's way of insulting the men who had hunted him down and were torturing him, took on a new meaning. It became the code name of the killer with the blond hair, who was a foreigner, and whom the three OAS chiefs had met at the Pension Kleist in Vienna days before they had gone into heavily protected hiding in Rome.

Rolland could work out for himself the reason now for the wave of bank and jewel robberies that had rocked France over the preceding eight weeks. The blond, whoever he was, wanted money to do a job for the OAS. There was only one job in the world that could command that kind of money. The blond had not been called in to settle a gang fight.

At seven in the morning Rolland called his communications room and ordered the night-duty operator to send off a blitz imperative to the SDECE office in Vienna, overriding inter-departmental protocol under which Vienna was within the manor of R.3 Western Europe. Then he called in every copy of the Kowalski confession and locked them all in his safe. Finally he sat down to write a report, which had only one listed recipient and was headed 'for your eyes only'.

He wrote carefully in longhand, describing briefly the operation which he had personally mounted on his own initiative to capture Kowalski; relating the return of the ex-legionnaire to Marseilles, lured by the ruse of a false belief that someone close to him was ill in hospital, the capture by Action Service agents, a brief mention for the record that the man had been interrogated by agents of the service, and had made a garbled confession. He felt bound to include a bald statement that in resisting arrest the ex-legionnaire had crippled two agents but had also done himself sufficient damage in an attempt at suicide that by the time he was overcome the only possible recourse was to hospitalise him. It was here, from his sick bed, that he had made his confession.

The rest of the report, which was the bulk, concerned the confession itself and Rolland's interpretation of it. When he had finished this he paused for a moment, scanning the roof-tops now gilded by the morning sun streaming in from the east. Rolland had a reputation as he was well aware for never overstating his case nor exaggerating an issue. He composed his final paragraph with care.

'Enquiries with the intention of establishing corroborative evidence of this plot are still under way at the hour of writing. However, in the event that these enquiries should indicate the above is the truth, the plot described above constitutes in my view the most dangerous single conception that the terrorists could possibly have devised to endanger the life of the President of France. If the plot exists as described, and if the foreign-born assassin known only by the code-name of The Jackal has been engaged for this attempt on the life of the President, and is even now preparing his plans to execute the deed, it is my duty to inform you that in my opinion we face a national emergency.'

Most unusually for him, Colonel Rolland typed the final fair copy of the report himself, sealed it in an envelope with his personal seal, addressed it and stamped it with the highest security classification in the secret service. Finally he burned the sheets of foolscap on which he had written in longhand and washed the ashes down the plug of the small hand basin in a cabinet in the corner of his office.

When he had finished he washed his hands and face. As he dried them he glanced in the mirror above the wash-stand. The face that stared back at him was, he ruefully admitted, losing its handsomeness. The lean face that had been so dashing in youth and so attractive to women in maturity was beginning to look tired and strained in middle age. Too many experiences, too much knowledge of the depths of bestiality to which Man could sink when he fought for his survival against his fellow men, and too much scheming and double-crossing, sending men out to die or to kill, to scream in cellars or to make other men scream in cellars, had aged the head of the Action Service far beyond his fifty-four years. There were two lines down the side of the nose and on down beyond the corners of the mouth that if they got much longer would no more be distinguished but simply agricultural. Two dark smudges seemed to have settled permanently under the eyes and the elegant grey of the sideburns was becoming white without turning silver.

'At the end of this year,' he told himself, 'I really am going to get out of this racket.' The face looked back at him haggard. Disbelief or simply resignation? Perhaps the face knew better than the mind did. After a certain number of years there was no getting out any more. One was what one was for the rest of one's days. From the Resistance to the security police, then the SDECE, and finally the Action Service. How many men, and how much blood in all those years? he asked the face in the mirror. And all for France. And what the hell does France care? And the face looked back out of the mirror and said nothing. For they both knew the answer.

Colonel Rolland summoned a motor-cycle despatch rider to report to him personally in his office. He also ordered fried eggs, rolls and butter, and more coffee, but this time a large cup of milky coffee, with aspirins for his headache. He handed over the package with his seal and gave the despatch rider his orders. Finishing his eggs and rolls, he took his coffee and drank it on the sill of the open window, the corner that faced towards Paris. He could make out across the miles of roofs the spires of Notre Dame and in the already hot morning haze that hung over the Seine the Eiffel Tower further on. It was already well after nine o'clock on the morning of August 11th, and the city was busily at work, probably cursing the motor-cyclist in the black leather jerkin and the wailing siren who slewed his machine through the traffic towards the eighth arrondissement.

Depending on whether the menace described in the despatch on that motor-cyclist's hip could be averted, thought Rolland, might hang whether or not at the end of the year he had a job to retire from.

The Minister of the Interior sat at his desk later that morning and stared sombrely out of the window into the sunlit circular courtyard beneath. At the far end of the courtyard were the beautiful wrought-iron gates, decorated on each half with the coat of arms of the Republic of France, and beyond them the Place Beauvau where streams of traffic from the Faubourg St Honoré and the Avenue de Marigny hooted and swirled around the hips of the policeman directing them from the centre of the square.

From the other two roads that led into the square, the Avenue de Miromesnil and the Rue des Saussaies, other streams of traffic would emerge on a whistled command from the policeman to cross the square and disappear on their way. He seemed to be playing the five streams of lethal Parisian traffic as a bullfighter plays a bull, calmly, with aplomb, with dignity and mastery. M. Roger Frey envied the ordered simplicity of his task, the assured confidence he brought to it.

At the gates of the ministry two other gendarmes watched their colleague's virtuosity in the centre of the square. They carried submachine guns slung across their backs, and looked out on the world through the wrought-iron grille of the double gates, protected from the furore of the world beyond, assured of their monthly salaries, their continuing careers, their places in the warm August sunshine. The Minister envied them too, for the uncomplicated simplicity of their lives and ambitions.

He heard a page rustle behind him and spun his swivel chair back to face his desk. The man across the desk closed the file and laid it reverently on the desk before the Minister. The two men eyed each other, the silence broken only by the ticking of the ormolu clock on the mantelpiece opposite the door and the subdued road traffic from the Place Beauvau.

'Well, what do you think?'

Commissaire Jean Ducret, head of President De Gaulle's personal security corps, was one of the foremost experts in France on all questions of security, and particularly as that subject relates to the protection of a single life against assassination. That was why he held his job, and that was why six known plots to kill the President of France had either failed in execution or been dismantled in preparation up till that date.

'Rolland is right,' he said at length. His voice was flat, unemotional, final. He might have been giving his judgement on the probable forth-coming result of a football match. 'If what he says is true, the plot is of an exceptional danger. The entire filing system of all the security agencies of France, the whole network of agents and infiltrators pre-sently maintained inside the OAS, are all reduced to impotence in the face of a foreigner, an outsider, working completely alone, without con-tacts or friends. And a professional into the bargain. As Rolland puts it, it is ...' he flicked over the last page of the Action Service chief's report and read aloud ... ' "the most dangerous single conception" that one can imagine.'

Roger Frey ran his fingers through the iron-grey short-cut hair and spun away towards the window again. He was not a man easily ruffled, but he was ruffled on the morning of August 11th. Throughout his many years as a devoted follower of the cause of Charles de Gaulle he had built up the reputation of a tough man behind the intelligence and urbanity that had brought him to a Minister's chair. The brilliant blue eyes that could be warmly attractive or chillingly cold, the virility of the compact chest and shoulders and the handsome, ruthless face that had brought admiring glances from not a few women who enjoy the companionship of men of power, these were not merely props for the electoral platform in Roger Frey.

In the old days, when the Gaullists had had to fight for survival against American enmity, British indifference, Giraudist ambition and Commu-nist ferocity, he had learned his in-fighting the hard way. Somehow they had won through, and twice in eighteen years the man they followed had returned from exile and repudiation to take the position of supreme power in France. And for the past two years the battle had been on again, this time against the very men who had twice restored the General to power – the Army. Until a few minutes before, the Minister had thought the last struggle was waning, their enemies once again sliding into im-potence and helpless wrath.

Now he knew it was not over yet. A lean and fanatical colonel in Rome had devised a plan that could still bring the whole edifice tumbling down by organising the death of a single man. Some countries have insti-tutions of sufficient stability to survive the death of a president or the abdication of a king, as Britain had shown twenty-eight years earlier and America would show before the year was out. But Roger Frey was well enough aware of the state of the institutions of France in 1963 to have no illusions that the death of his President could only be the prologue to putsch and civil war.

'Well,' he said finally, still looking out into the glaring courtyard, 'he must be told.'

The policeman did not answer. It was one of the advantages of being a technician that you did your job and left the top decisions to those who were paid to take them. He did not intend to volunteer to be the one who did the telling. The Minister turned back to face him.

'Bien. Merci, Commissaire. Then I shall seek an interview this afternoon and inform the President.' The voice was crisp and decisive. A thing had to be done. 'I need hardly ask you to maintain complete silence on this matter until I have had time to explain the position to the President and he has decided how he wishes this affair to be handled.'

Commissaire Ducret rose and left, to return across the square and a hundred yards down the road to the gates of the Elysée Palace. Left to himself the Minister of the Interior spun the buff file round to face him and again read it slowly through. He had no doubt Rolland's assessment was right, and Ducret's concurrence left him no room for manoeuvre. The danger was there, it was serious, it could not be avoided and the President had to know.

Reluctantly he threw down a switch on the intercom in front of him and told the plastic grille that immediately buzzed at him, 'Get me a call to the Secretary General of the Elysée.'

Within a minute the red telephone beside the intercom rang. He lifted it and listened for a second.

'M. Foccart, s'il vous plaît.' Another pause, then the deceptively soft voice of one of the most powerful men in France came on the line. Roger Frey explained briefly what he wanted and why.

'As soon as possible, Jacques. ... Yes, I know you have to check. I'll wait. Please call me back as soon as you can.'

The call back came within an hour. The appointment was fixed for four that afternoon, as soon as the President had finished his siesta. For a second it crossed the Minister's mind to protest that what he had on the blotter in front of him was more important than any siesta, but he stifled the protest. Like everybody in the entourage of the President, he was aware of the inadvisability of crossing the soft-voiced civil servant who had the ear of the President at all times and a private filing system of intimate information about which more was feared than was known.

At twenty to four that afternoon the Jackal emerged from Cunningham's in Curzon Street after one of the most delicious and expensive lunches that the London sea-food specialists could provide. It was after all, he mused as he swung into South Audley Street, probably his last lunch in London for some time to come, and he had reason to celebrate.

At the same moment a black DS 19 saloon swung out of the gates of the Interior Ministry of France into the Place Beauvau. The policeman in the centre of the square, forewarned by a shout from his colleagues on the iron gates, held up the traffic from all the surrounding streets, then snapped into a salute.

A hundred metres down the road the Citroën turned towards the grey stone portico in front of the Elysée Palace. Here too the gendarmes on duty, forewarned, had held up the traffic to give the saloon enough turning room to get through the surprisingly narrow archway. The two Gardes Républicains standing in front of their sentry-boxes on each side of the portico smacked their white-gloved hands across the magazines of their rifles in salute, and the Minister entered the forecourt of the palace.

A chain hanging in a low loop across the inner arch of the gate halted the car while the duty inspector of the day, one of Ducret's men, briefly glanced inside the car. He nodded towards the Minister, who nodded back. At a gesture from the inspector the chain was let fall to the ground and the Citroën crunched over it. Across a hundred feet of tan-coloured gravel lay the façade of the palace. Robert, the driver, pulled the car to the right and drove round the courtyard anti-clockwise, to deposit his master at the foot of the six granite steps that lead to the entrance.

The door was opened by one of the two silver-chained, black frock-coated ushers. The Minister stepped down and ran up the steps to be greeted at the plate-glass door by the chief usher. They greeted each other formally, and he followed the usher inside. They had to wait for a moment in the vestibule beneath the vast chandelier suspended on its long gilded chain from the vaulted ceiling far above while the usher telephoned briefly from the marble table to the left of the door. As he put the phone down, he turned to the Minister, smiled briefly, and proceeded at his usual majestic, unhurried pace up the carpeted granite stairs to the left.

At the first floor they went down the short wide landing that over-looked the hallway below, and stopped when the usher knocked softly on the door to the left of the landing. There was a muffled reply of '*Entrez*' from within, the usher smoothly opened the door and stood back to let the Minister pass into the Salon des Ordonnances. As the Minister entered, the door closed behind him without a sound and the usher made his stately way back down the stairs to the vestibule.

From the great south windows on the far side of the salon the sun streamed through, bathing the carpet in warmth. One of the floor-to-ceiling windows was open, and from the palace gardens came the sound of a wood pigeon cooing among the trees. The traffic of the Champs Elysées five hundred yards beyond the windows and completely shielded from view by the spreading limes and beeches, magnificent in the foliage of full summer, was simply another murmur, not even as loud as the pigeon. As usual when he was in the south-facing rooms of the Elysée Palace, M. Frey, a townsman born and bred, could imagine he was in some château buried in the heart of the country. The roar of the traffic down the Faubourg St Honoré on the other side of the building was just a memory. The President, as he knew, adored the countryside.

The ADC of the day was Colonel Tesseire. He rose from behind his desk.

'Monsieur le Ministre . . .'

'Colonel. . . .' M. Frey gestured with his head towards the closed double doors with the gilt handles on the left-hand side of the salon. 'I am expected?'

'Of course, M. le Ministre.' Tesseire crossed the room, knocked briefly on the doors, opened one half of them and stood in the entrance.

'The Minister of the Interior, Monsieur le Président.'

There was a muffled assent from inside. Tesseire stepped back, smiled at the Minister, and Roger Frey went past him into Charles de Gaulle's private study.

There was nothing about that room, he had always thought, that did not give a clue to the man who had ordered its decoration and furnishing. To the right were the three tall and elegant windows that gave access to the garden like those of the Salon des Ordonnances. In the study also one of them was open, and the murmuring of the pigeon, muted as one passed through the door between the two rooms, was heard again coming from the gardens.

Somewhere under those limes and beeches quiet men toting automatics with which they could pick the ace out of the ace of spades at twenty paces lurked. But woe betide the one of them who let himself be seen from the windows on the first floor. Around the palace the rage of the man they would fanatically protect if they had to had become legendary in the event that he learned of the measures taken for his own protection, or if those measures obtruded on his privacy. This was one of the heaviest crosses Ducret had to bear, and no one envied him the task of protecting a man for whom all forms of personal protection were an indignity he did not appreciate.

To the left, against the wall containing the glass-fronted bookshelves, was a Louis XV table on which reposed a Louis XIV clock. The floor was covered by a Savonnerie carpet made in the royal carpet factory at Challot in 1615. This factory, the President had once explained to him, had been a soap factory before its conversion to carpet making, and hence the name that had always applied to the carpets it produced.

There was nothing in the room that was not simple, nothing that was not dignified, nothing that was not tasteful, and above all nothing that did not exemplify the grandeur of France. And that, so far as Roger Frey was concerned, included the man behind the desk who now rose to greet him with his usual elaborate courtesy.

The Minister recalled that Harold King, doyen of British journalists in Paris and the only contemporary Anglo-Saxon who was a personal friend of Charles de Gaulle, had once remarked to him that in all of his personal mannerisms the President was not from the twentieth, but from the eighteenth century. Every time he had met his master since then Roger Frey had vainly tried to imagine a tall figure in silks and brocades making those same courteous gestures and greetings. He could see the connection, but the image escaped him. Nor could he forget the few occasions when the stately old man, really roused by something that had displeased him, had used barrack-room language of such forceful crudity as to leave his entourage or Cabinet members stunned and speechless.

As the Minister well knew, one subject likely to produce such a response was the question of the measures the Interior Minister, responsible for the security of the institutions of France, of which the President himself was the foremost, felt obliged to take. They had never seen eye to eye on that question, and much of what Frey did in that regard had to be done clandestinely. When he thought of the document he carried in his briefcase and the request he was going to have to make, he almost quaked.

'Mon cher Frey.'

The tall charcoal-grey-suited figure had come round the edge of the great desk behind which he normally sat, hand outstretched in greeting.

'Monsieur le Président, mes respects.' He shook the proffered hand. At least Le Vieux seemed to be in a good mood. He found himself ushered to one of the two upright chairs covered in First Empire Beauvais tapestry in front of the desk. Charles de Gaulle, his hostly duty done, returned to his side and sat down, back to the wall. He leaned back, placing the fingertips of both hands on the polished wood in front of him.

'I am told, my dear Frey, that you wished to see me on a matter of urgency. Well, what have you to say to me?'

Roger Frey breathed in deeply once and began. He explained briefly and succinctly what had brought him, aware that De Gaulle did not appreciate long-winded oratory except his own, and then only for public speaking. In private he appreciated brevity, as several of his more verbose subordinates had discovered to their embarrassment.

While he talked, the man across the desk from him stiffened perceptibly. Leaning back further and further, seeming to grow all the while, he gazed down the commanding promontory of his nose at the Minister as if an unpleasant substance had been introduced into his study by a hitherto trusted servant. Roger Frey, however, was aware that at five yards range his face could be no more than a blur to the President, whose short-sightedness he concealed on all public occasions by never wearing glasses except to read speeches.

The Interior Minister finished his monologue, which had lasted barely more than one minute, by mentioning the comments of Rolland and Ducret, and finishing, 'I have the Rolland report in my case.'

Without a word the presidential hand stretched out across the desk. M. Frey slid the report out of the briefcase and handed it over.

From the top pocket of his jacket Charles de Gaulle took his reading glasses, put them on, spread the folder on his desk and started to read. The pigeon had stopped cooing as if appreciating that this was not the moment. Roger Frey stared out at the trees, then at the brass reading lamp on the desk next to the blotter. It was a beautifully turned Flambeau de Vermeil from the Restoration, fitted with an electric light, and in the five years of the presidency it had spent thousands of hours illuminating the documents of state that passed during the night across the blotter over which it stood.

General de Gaulle was a quick reader. He finished the Rolland report in three minutes, folded it carefully on the blotter, crossed his hands over it and asked:

'Well, my dear Frey, what do you want of me?'

For the second time Roger Frey took a deep breath and launched into a succinct recitation of the steps he wished to take. Twice he used the phrase 'in my judgement, Monsieur le Président, it will be necessary if

we are to avert this menace. . . .' In the thirty-third second of his dis-
course he used the phrase 'The interest of France. . . .'

It was as far as he got. The President cut across him, the sonorous voice
rolling the word France into that of a deity in a way no other French
voice before or since has known how to do.

'The interest of France, my dear Frey, is that the President of France is
not seen to be cowering before the menace of a miserable hireling,
and . . .' he paused while the contempt for his unknown assailant hung
heavy in the room . . . 'of a foreigner.'

Roger Frey realised that he had lost. The General did not lose his
temper as the Interior Minister feared he might. He began to speak
clearly and precisely, as one who has no intention that his wishes shall be
in any way unclear to his listener. As he spoke some of the phrases
drifted through the window and were heard by Colonel Tesseire.

'*La France ne saurait accepter . . . la dignité et la grandeur assujetties
aux misérables menaces d'un . . . d'un CHACAL. . . .*'

Two minutes later Roger Frey left the President's presence. He nodded
soberly at Colonel Tesseire, walked out through the door of the Salon des
Ordonnances and down the stairs to the vestibule.

There, thought the chief usher as he escorted the Minister down the
stone steps to the waiting Citroën, and watched him drive away, goes a
man with one hell of a problem, if I ever saw one. Wonder what the Old
Man had to say to him. But being the chief usher, his face retained the
immobile calm of the façade of the palace he had served for twenty
years.

'No, it cannot be done that way. The President was absolutely formal on
that point.'

Roger Frey turned from the window of his office and surveyed the
man to whom he had addressed the remark. Within minutes of returning
from the Elysée he had summoned his chef de cabinet, or chief of personal staff. Alexandre Sanguinetti was a Corsican. As the man to whom
the Interior Minister had delegated over the past two years much of the
detailed work of master-minding the French state security forces, Sanguinetti had established a renown and a reputation that varied widely
according to the beholder's personal political affiliations or concept of
civil rights.

By the extreme left he was hated and feared for his unhesitating mobil-
isation of the CRS anti-riot squads and the no-nonsense tactics these
forty-five thousand para-military bruisers used when confronted with a
street demonstration from either the left or the right.

The Communists called him a Fascist, perhaps because some of his
methods of keeping public order were reminiscent of the means used in
the workers' paradises beyond the Iron Curtain. The extreme right, also
called Fascists by the Communists, loathed him equally, quoting the
same arguments of the suppression of democracy and civil rights, but
more probably because the ruthless efficiency of his public order
measures had gone a long way to preventing the complete breakdown of

order that would have helped precipitate a right-wing coup ostensibly aimed at restoring that very order.

And many ordinary people disliked him, because the draconian decrees that stemmed from his office affected them all, with barriers in the streets, examinations of identity cards at most major road junctions, roadblocks on all main roads, and the much-publicised photographs of young demonstrators being bludgeoned to the ground by the truncheons of the CRS. The Press had already dubbed him 'Monsieur Anti-OAS' and, apart from the relatively small Gaullist Press, reviled him roundly. If the odium of being the most criticised man in France affected him at all, he managed to hide it. The deity of his private religion was ensconced in an office in the Elysée Palace, and within that religion Alexandre Sanguinetti was the head of the Curia. He glowered at the blotter in front of him, on which lay the buff folder containing the Rolland report.

'It's impossible. Impossible. He is impossible. We have to protect his life, but he won't let us. I could have this man, this Jackal. But you say we are allowed to take no counter-measures. What do we do? Just wait for him to strike? Just sit around and wait?'

The Minister sighed. He had expected no less from his chef de cabinet, but it still made his task no easier. He seated himself behind his desk again.

'Alexandre, listen. Firstly, the position is that we are not yet absolutely certain that the Rolland report is true. It is his own analysis of the ramblings of this . . . Kowalski, who has since died. Perhaps Rolland is wrong. Enquiries in Vienna are still being conducted. I have been in touch with Guibaud and he expects to have the answer by this evening. But one must agree that, at this stage, to launch a nation-wide hunt for a foreigner only known to us by a code-name is hardly a realistic proposition. To that extent, I must agree with the President.

'Beyond that, these are his instructions . . . no, his absolutely formal orders. I repeat them so that there will be no mistake in any of our minds. There is to be no publicity, no nation-wide search, no indication to anyone outside a small circle around us that anything is amiss. The President feels that if the secret were out the Press would have a field day, the foreign nations would jeer, and any extra security precautions taken by us would be interpreted both here and abroad as the spectacle of the President of France hiding from a single man, a foreigner at that.

'This he will not, I repeat, will not tolerate. In fact . . .' the Minister emphasised his point with pointed forefinger . . . 'he made quite plain to me that if in our handling of the affair the details, or even the general impression, became public knowledge, heads would roll. Believe me, *cher ami*, I have never seen him so adamant.'

'But the public programme,' expostulated the Corsican civil servant, 'it must inevitably be changed. There must be no more public appearances until the man is caught. He must surely . . .'

'He will cancel nothing. There will be no changes, not by an hour or a minute. The whole thing has got to be done in complete secrecy.'

For the first time since the dismantlement of the Ecole Militaire assassination plot in February, with the arrest of the plotters, Alexandre Sanguinetti felt he was back where he started. In the past two months, battling against the wave of bank robberies and smash-and-grab raids, he had permitted himself to hope that the worst was over. With the OAS apparatus crumbling under the twin assaults of the Action Service from within and the hordes of police and CRS from without, he had interpreted the crime wave as the death throes of the Secret Army, the last handful of thugs on the rampage trying to acquire enough money to live well in exile.

But the last page of Rolland's report made plain that the scores of double agents Rolland had been able to infiltrate into even the highest ranks of the OAS had been outflanked by the anonymity of the assassin, except to three men who were unobtainable in a hotel in Rome, and he could see for himself that the enormous archives of dossiers on everyone who had ever been remotely connected with the OAS, on which the Interior Ministry could usually rely for the information, had been rendered useless by one simple fact. The Jackal was a foreigner.

'If we are not allowed to act, what can we do?'

'I did not say we were not allowed to act,' corrected Frey. 'I said we were not allowed to act publicly. The whole thing must be done secretly. That leaves us only one alternative. The identity of the assassin must be revealed by a secret enquiry, he must be traced wherever he is, in France or abroad, and then destroyed without hesitation.'

'. . . and destroyed without hesitation. That, gentlemen, is the only course left open to us.'

The Interior Minister surveyed the meeting seated round the table of the ministry conference room to let the impact of his words sink in. There were fourteen men in the room including himself.

The Minister stood at the head of the table. To his immediate right sat his chef de cabinet, and to his left the Prefect of Police, the political head of France's police forces.

From Sanguinetti's right hand down the length of the oblong table sat General Guibaud, head of the SDECE, Colonel Rolland, chief of the Action Service and the author of the report of which a copy lay in front of each man. Beyond Rolland were Commissaire Ducret of the Corps de Sécurité Présidentielle, and Colonel Saint-Clair de Villauban, an air force colonel of the Elysée staff, a fanatical Gaullist but equally renowned in the entourage of the President as being equally fanatical concerning his own ambition.

To the left of M. Maurice Papon, the Prefect of Police, were M. Maurice Grimaud, the Director-General of France's national crime force the Sûreté Nationale, and in a row the five heads of the departments that make up the Sûreté.

Although beloved of novelists as a crime-busting force, the Sûreté Nationale itself is simply the very small and meagrely staffed office that has control over the five crime branches that actually do the work. The task of the Sûreté is administrative, like that of the equally misdescribed Interpol, and the Sûreté does not have a detective on its staff.

The man with the national detective force of France under his personal orders sat next to Maurice Grimaud. He was Max Fernet, Director of the Police Judiciaire. Apart from its enormous headquarters on the Quai des Orfèvres, vastly bigger than the Sûreté's headquarters at 11 Rue des Saussaies, just round the corner from the Interior Ministry, the Police Judiciaire controls seventeen Services Régionaux headquarters, one for each of the seventeen police districts of Metropolitan France. Under these come the borough police forces, 453 in all, being comprised of seventy-four Central Commissariats, 253 Constituency Commissariats and 126 local Postes de Police. The whole network ranges through two thousand towns and villages of France. This is the crime force. In the rural areas and up and down the highways the more general task of maintaining law and order is carried out by the Gendarmerie Nationale and the traffic police, the Gendarmes Mobiles. In many areas, for reasons of efficiency, the gendarmes and the agents de police share the same accommodation and facilities. The total number of men under Max Fernet's command in the Police Judiciaire in 1963 was just over twenty thousand.

Running down the table from Fernet's left were the heads of the other four sections of the Sûreté: the Bureau de Sécurité Publique, the Renseignements Généraux, the Direction de la Surveillance du Territoire, and the Corps Républicain de Sécurité.

The first of these, the BSP, was concerned mainly with protection of buildings, communications, highways and anything else belonging to the state from sabotage or damage. The second, the RG or central records office was the memory of the other four; in its Panthéon headquarters archives were four and a half million personal dossiers on individuals who had come to the notice of the police forces of France since those forces were founded. They were cross-indexed along five and a half miles of shelves in categories of the names of the persons to whom they applied, or the type of crime for which the person had been convicted or merely suspected. Names of witnesses who had appeared in cases, or those who had been acquitted, were also listed. Although the system was not at that time computerised, the archivists prided themselves that within a few minutes they could unearth the details of arson committed in a small village ten years back, or the names of witnesses in an obscure trial that had hardly made the newspapers.

Added to these dossiers were the fingerprints of everyone who had ever had his fingerprints taken in France, including many sets that had never been identified. There were also ten and a half million cards, including the disembarkation card of every tourist at every border crossing point, and the hotel cards filled in by all who stayed at French hotels outside Paris. For reasons of space alone these cards had to be cleared out at fairly short intervals to make way for the vast number of fresh ones that came in each year.

The only cards regularly filled in within the area of France that did not go to the RG were those filled in at the hotels of Paris. These went to the Préfecture de Police in the Boulevard du Palais.

The DST, whose chief sat three places down from Fernet, was and is the counter-espionage force of France, responsible also for maintaining a constant watch on France's airports, docks and borders. Before going to the archives, the disembarkation cards of those entering France are examined by the DST officer at the point of entry, for screening to keep tabs on undesirables.

The last man in the row was the chief of the CRS, the forty-five thousand-man force of which Alexandre Sanguinetti had already made such a well publicised and heartily unpopular use over the previous two years.

For reasons of space, the head of the CRS was sitting at the foot of the table, facing down the length of the wood at the Minister. There was one last seat remaining, that between the head of the CRS and Colonel Saint-Clair, at the bottom right-hand corner. It was occupied by a large stolid man whose pipe fumes evidently annoyed the fastidious Colonel on his left. The Minister had made a point of asking Max Fernet to bring him along to the meeting. He was Commissaire Maurice Bouvier, head of the Brigade Criminelle of the PJ.

'So that is where we stand, gentlemen,' resumed the Minister. 'Now you have all read the report by Colonel Rolland which lies in front of each of you. And now you have heard from me the considerable limitations which the President, in the interests of the dignity of France, has felt obliged to impose on our efforts to avert this threat to his person. I will stress again, there must be absolute secrecy in the conduct of the investigation and in any subsequent action to be taken. Needless to say, you are all sworn to total silence and will discuss the matter with no one outside this room until and unless another person has been made privy to the secret.

'I have called you all here because it seems to me that whatever we are to do, the resources of all the departments here represented must sooner or later be called upon, and you, the departmental chiefs, should have no doubt as to the top priority that this affair demands. It must on all occasions require your immediate and personal attention. There will be no delegation to juniors, except for tasks which do not reveal the reason behind the requirement.'

He paused again. Down both sides of the table some heads nodded soberly. Others kept their eyes fixed on the speaker, or on the dossier in front of them. At the far end, Commissaire Bouvier gazed at the ceiling, emitting brief bursts of smoke from the corner of his mouth like a Red Indian sending up signals. The air force colonel next to him winced at each emission.

'Now,' resumed the Minister, 'I think I may ask for your ideas on the subject. Colonel Rolland, have you had any success with your enquiries in Vienna?'

The head of the Action Service glanced up from his own report, cast a sideways look at the general who led the SDECE, but received neither encouragement nor a frown.

General Guibaud, remembering that he had spent half the day sobering down the head of R.3 Section over Rolland's early-morning decision to use the Viennese office for his own enquiries, stared straight ahead of him.

'Yes,' said the Colonel. 'Enquiries were made this morning and afternoon by operatives in Vienna at the Pension Kleist, a small private hotel in the Brucknerallee. They carried with them photographs of Marc Rodin, René Montclair and André Casson. There was no time to transmit to them photographs of Viktor Kowalski, which were not on file in Vienna.

'The desk clerk at the hotel stated that he recognised at least two of the men. But he could not place them. Some money changed hands, and he was asked to search the hotel register for the days between June 12th and 18th, the latter being the day the three OAS chiefs took up residence together in Rome.

'Eventually he claimed to have remembered the face of Rodin as a man who booked a room in the name of Schulz on June 15th. The clerk said he had a form of business conference in the afternoon, spent the night in that room and left the next day.

'He remembered that Schulz had had a companion, a very big man with a surly manner, which was why he remembered Schulz. He was visited by two men in the morning and they had a conference. The two visitors could have been Casson and Montclair. He could not be sure, but he thought he had seen at least one of them before.

'The clerk said the men remained in their room all day, apart from one occasion in the late morning when Schulz and the giant, as he called Kowalski, left for half an hour. None of them had any lunch, nor did they come down to eat.'

'Were they visited at all by a fifth man?' asked Sanguinetti impatiently. Rolland continued his report as before, in flat tones.

'During the evening another man joined them for half an hour. The clerk said he remembered because the visitor entered the hotel so quickly and headed straight up the stairs, that the clerk did not get a chance to see him. He thought he must be one of the guests, who had retained his key. But he saw the tail of the man's coat going up the stairs. A few seconds later the man was back in the hall. The clerk was sure it was the same man because of the coat.

'The man used the desk phone and asked to be put through to Schulz's room, number 64. He spoke two sentences in French, then replaced the phone and went back up the stairs. He spent half an hour there, then left without saying another word. About an hour after that, the other two who had visited Schulz left separately. Schulz and the giant stayed for the night, then left after breakfast in the morning.

'The only description the clerk could give of the evening visitor was: tall, age uncertain, features apparently regular but he wore wrap-around dark glasses, spoke fluent French, and had blond hair left rather long and swept back from the forehead.'

'Is there any chance of getting the man to help make up an Identikit picture of the blond?' asked the Prefect of Police, Papon.

Rolland shook his head.

'My . . . our agents were posing as Viennese plain-clothes police. Fortunately one of them could pass for Viennese. But that is a masquerade that could not be sustained indefinitely. The man had to be interviewed at the hotel desk.'

'We must get a better description than that,' protested the head of the Records Office. 'Was any name mentioned?'

'No,' said Rolland. 'What you have just heard is the outcome of three hours spent interrogating the clerk. Every point was gone over time and time again. There is nothing else he can remember. Short of an Identikit picture, that's the best description he could give.'

'Could you not snatch him like Argoud, so that he could make up a picture of this assassin here in Paris?' queried Colonel Saint-Clair.

The Minister interjected.

'There can be no more snatches. We are still at daggers drawn with the German Foreign Ministry over the Argoud snatch. That kind of thing can work once, but not again.'

'Surely in a matter of this seriousness the disappearance of a desk clerk can be done more discreetly than the Argoud affair?' suggested the head of the DST.

'It is in any case doubtful,' said Max Fernet quietly, 'whether an Identikit picture of a man wearing wrap-around dark glasses would be very helpful. Very few Identikit pictures made up on the basis of an unremarkable incident lasting twenty seconds two months before ever seem to look like the criminal when he is eventually caught. Most such pictures could be of half a million people and some are actually misleading.'

'So apart from Kowalski, who is dead, and who told everything he knew, which was not much, there are only four men in the world who know the identity of this Jackal,' said Commissaire Ducret. 'One is the man himself, and the other three are in a hotel in Rome. How about trying to get one of them back here?'

Again the Minister shook his head.

'My instructions on that are formal. Kidnappings are out. The Italian Government would go out of its mind if this kind of thing happened a few yards from the Via Condotti. Besides there are some doubts as to its feasibility. General?'

General Guibaud lifted his eyes to the assembly.

'The extent and quality of the protective screen Rodin and his two henchmen have built round themselves, according to the reports of my agents who have them under permanent surveillance, rule this out from the practical standpoint also,' he said. 'There are eight top-class ex-Legion gunmen around them, or seven if Kowalski has not been replaced. All the lifts, stairs, fire-escape and roof are guarded. It would involve a major gun battle, probably with gas grenades and submachine guns to get one of them alive. Even then, the chances of getting the man out of the country and five hundred kilometres north to France, with the Italians on the rampage, would be very slight inded. We have men who are some of the world's top experts in this kind of thing, and they say it would be just about impossible short of a commando-style military operation.'

Silence descended on the room again.

'Well, gentlemen,' said the Minister, 'any more suggestions?'

'This Jackal must be found. That much is clear,' replied Colonel Saint-Clair. Several of the others round the table glanced at each other and an eyebrow or two was raised.

'That much certainly is clear,' murmured the Minister at the head of the table. 'What we are trying to devise is a way in which that can be done, within the limits imposed upon us, and on that basis perhaps we can best decide which of the departments here represented would be best suited for the job.'

'The protection of the President of the Republic,' announced Saint-Clair grandiosely, 'must depend on the last resort when all others have failed on the Presidential Security Corps and the President's personal staff. We, I can assure you, Minister, will do our duty.'

Some of the hard-core professions closed their eyes in unfeigned weariness. Commissaire Ducret shot the Colonel a glance which, if looks could kill, would have dropped Saint-Clair in his tracks.

'Doesn't he know the Old Man's not listening?' growled Guibaud under his breath to Rolland.

Roger Frey raised his eyes to meet those of the Elysée Palace courtier and demonstrated why he was a minister.

'The Colonel Saint-Clair is perfectly right, of course,' he purred. 'We shall all do our duty. And I am sure it has occurred to the Colonel that should a certain department undertake the responsibility for the destruction of this plot, and fail to achieve it, or even employ methods inadvertently capable of bringing publicity contrary to the wishes of the President, certain disapprobation would inevitably descend upon the head of him who had failed.'

The menace hung above the long table more tangible than the pall of blue smoke from Bouvier's pipe. Saint-Clair's thin pale face tightened perceptibly and the worry showed in his eyes.

'We are all aware here of the limited opportunities available to the Presidential Security Corps,' said Commissaire Ducret flatly. 'We spend our time in the immediate vicinity of the President's person. Evidently this investigation must be far more wide-ranging than my staff could undertake without neglecting its primary duties.'

No one contradicted him, for each department chief was aware that what the presidential security chief said was true. But neither did anyone else wish the ministerial eye to fall on him. Roger Frey looked round the table, and his gaze rested on the smoke-shrouded bulk of Commissaire Bouvier at the far end.

'What do you think, Bouvier? You have not spoken yet?'

The detective eased the pipe out of his mouth, managed to let a last squirt of odoriferous smoke waft straight into the face of Saint-Clair who had turned towards him, and spoke calmly as one stating a few simple facts that had just occurred to him.

'It seems to me, Minister, that the SDECE cannot disclose this man through their agents in the OAS, since not even the OAS know who he is;

that the Action Service cannot destroy him since they do not know who to destroy. The DST cannot pick him up at the border for they do not know whom to intercept, and the RG can give us no documentary information about him because they do not know what documents to search for. The police cannot arrest him, for they do not know whom to arrest, and the CRS cannot pursue him, since they are unaware whom they are pursuing. The entire structure of the security forces of France is powerless for want of a name. It seems to me therefore that the first task, without which all other proposals become meaningless, is to give this man a name. With a name we get a face, with a face a passport, with a passport an arrest. But to find the name, and do it in secret, is a job for pure detective work.'

He was silent again, and inserted the stem of his pipe between his teeth. What he had said was digested by each of the men round the table. No one could fault it. Sanguinetti nodded slowly by the Minister's side.

'And who, Commissaire, is the best detective in France?' asked the Minister quietly. Bouvier considered for a few seconds, before removing his pipe again.

'The best detective in France, messieurs, is my own deputy, Commissaire Claude Lebel.'

'Summon him,' said the Minister of the Interior.

PART TWO
Anatomy of a manhunt

10

An hour later Claude Lebel emerged from the conference room dazed and bewildered. For fifty minutes he had listened as the Minister of the Interior had briefed him on the task that lay ahead.

On entering the room he had been bidden to sit at the end of the table, sandwiched between the head of the CRS and his own chief, Bouvier. In silence from the other fourteen men he had read the Rolland report, while aware that curious eyes were assessing him from all sides.

When he put the report down the worry had started inside him. Why call him? Then the Minister started to speak. It was neither a consultation nor a request. It was a directive, followed by a copious briefing. He would set up his own office; he would have unlimited access to all necessary information; the entire resources of the organisations headed by the men seated round the table would be at his disposal. There were to be no limits to the costs incurred.

Several times the need for absolute secrecy, the imperative of the Head of State himself, had been impressed on him. While he listened his heart sank. They were asking – no, demanding – the impossible. He had nothing to go on. There was no crime – yet. There were no clues. There were no witnesses, except three whom he could not talk to. Just a name, a code-name, and the whole world to search in.

Claude Lebel was, as he knew, a good cop. He had always been a good cop, slow, precise, methodical, painstaking. Just occasionally he had shown the flash of inspiration that is needed to turn a good cop into a remarkable detective. But he had never lost sight of the fact that in police work ninety-nine per cent of the effort is routine, unspectacular enquiry, checking and double-checking, laboriously building up a web of parts until the parts become a whole, the whole becomes a net, and the net finally encloses the criminal with a case that will not just make headlines but stand up in court.

He was known in the PJ as a bit of a plodder, a methodical man who hated publicity and had never given the sort of press conferences on which some of his colleagues had built their reputations. And yet he had gone steadily up the ladder, solving his cases, seeing his criminals con-victed. When a vacancy had occurred at the head of the Homicide Division of the Brigade Criminelle three years ago, even the others in line for the job had agreed it was fair that Lebel should have got the job. He had a good steady record with Homicide and in three years had never failed to procure an arrest, although once the accused was acquitted on a technicality.

As head of Homicide he had come more closely to the notice of Maur-ice Bouvier, chief of the whole Brigade, and another old-style cop. So when Dupuy had died suddenly a few weeks back it was Bouvier who had asked that Lebel become his new deputy. There were some in the PJ who suspected that Bouvier, bogged down for a lot of the time with administrative details, appreciated a retiring subordinate who could handle the big, headline-making cases quietly, without stealing his superior's thunder. But perhaps they were just being uncharitable.

After the meeting at the Ministry the copies of the Rolland report were gathered up for storage in the Minister's safe. Lebel alone was allowed to keep Bouvier's copy. His only request had been that he be allowed to seek the co-operation, in confidence, of the heads of some of the criminal investigation forces of the major countries likely to have the identity of a professional assassin like the Jackal on their files. Without such co-oper-ation, he pointed out, it would be impossible even to start looking.

Sanguinetti had asked if such men could be relied on to keep their mouths shut. Lebel had replied that he knew personally the men he needed to contact, that his enquiries would not be official but would be along the personal-contact basis that exists between most of the Western world's top policemen. After some reflection the Minister had granted the request.

And now he stood in the hall waiting for Bouvier, and watching the chiefs of department file past him on their way out. Some nodded curtly and passed on; others ventured a sympathetic smile as they said good night. Almost the last to leave, while inside the conference room Bou-vier conferred quietly with Max Fernet, was the aristocratic Colonel from the Elysée staff. Lebel had briefly caught his name, as the men round the table were introduced, as Saint-Clair de Villauban. He stopped in front of the small and roly-poly commissaire and eyed him with ill-concealed distaste.

'I hope, Commissaire, that you will be successful in your enquiries, and rapidly so,' he said. 'We at the palace will be keeping a very close eye on your progress. In the event that you should fail to find this bandit, I can assure you that there will be . . . repercussions.'

He turned on his heel and stalked down the stairs towards the foyer. Lebel said nothing but blinked rapidly several times.

One of the factors in the make-up of Claude Lebel that had led to his successes when enquiring into crime over the previous twenty years since he had joined the police force of the Fourth Republic as a young detective in Normandy was his capacity to inspire people with the confidence to talk to him.

He lacked the imposing bulk of Bouvier, the traditional image of the authority of the law. Nor did he have the smartness with words that exemplified so many of the new breed of young detectives now coming into the force, who could bully and browbeat a witness into tears. He did not feel the lack.

He was aware that most crime in any society is either carried out against, or witnessed by, the little people, the shopkeeper, the sales assistant, the postman or the bank clerk. These people he could make talk to him, and he knew it.

It was partly because of his size; he was small, and resembled in many ways the cartoonist's image of a hen-pecked husband, which, although no one in the department knew it, was just what he was.

His dress was dowdy, a crumpled suit and a mackintosh. His manner was mild, almost apologetic, and in his request of a witness for information it contrasted so sharply with the attitude the witness had experienced from his first interview with the law, that the witness tended to warm towards the detective as to a refuge from the roughness of the subordinates.

But there was something more. He had been head of the Homicide Division of the most powerful criminal police force in Europe. He had been ten years a detective with the Brigade Criminelle of the renowned Police Judiciaire of France. Behind the mildness and the seeming simplicity was a combination of shrewd brain and a dogged refusal to be ruffled or intimidated by anyone when he was carrying out a job. He had been threatened by some of the most vicious gang bosses of France, who had thought from the rapid blinking with which Lebel greeted such approaches that their warnings had been duly taken. Only later, from a prison cell, had they had the leisure to realise they had underestimated the soft brown eyes and the toothbrush moustache.

Twice he had been subjected to intimidation by wealthy and powerful figures, once when an industrialist had wished to see one of his junior employees charged with embezzlement on the basis of a cursory glance at the auditor's evidence, and once when a society blade had wished investigations into the death by drugs of a young actress to be dropped.

In the first case the enquiry into the affairs of the industrialist had resulted in certain other and far bigger discrepancies being unearthed which had nothing to do with the junior accountant, but which had caused the industrialist to wish he had departed for Switzerland while he had the chance. The second time the society host had ended up with a lengthy period as a guest of the state in which to regret he had ever bothered to head a vice ring from his Avenue Victor Hugo penthouse.

Claude Lebel's reaction to the remarks of Colonel Saint-Clair was to blink like a rebuked schoolboy and say nothing. But it did not subsequently in any way affect his conduct of the job with which he had been saddled.

As the last man filed out of the conference room Maurice Bouvier joined him. Max Fernet wished him luck, shook hands briefly and headed down the stairs. Bouvier clapped a ham-like hand on Lebel's shoulder.

'*Eh bien, mon petit Claude.* So that's the way it is, *hein*? All right, it was me who suggested the PJ handle this business. It was the only thing to do. Those others would have talked round in circles for ever. Come, we'll talk in the car.' He led the way downstairs and the pair of them climbed into the back of the Citroën that waited in the courtyard.

It was past nine o'clock and a dark-purple weal lying over Neuilly was all that remained of the day. Bouvier's car swept down the Avenue de Marigny and over the Place Clemenceau. Lebel glanced out to the right and up the brilliant river of the Champs Elysées, whose grandeur on a summer night never ceased to surprise and excite him, despite the ten years that had passed since he came up from the provinces.

Bouvier spoke at last.

'You'll have to drop whatever you are doing. Everything. Clear the desk completely. I'll assign Favier and Malcoste to take over your outstanding cases. Do you want a new office for this job?'

'No, I prefer to stick to my present one.'

'OK, fine, but from now on it becomes the headquarters of Operation find-the-Jackal. Nothing else. Right? Is there anyone you want to help you?'

'Yes. Caron,' said Lebel, referring to one of the younger inspectors who had worked with him in Homicide and whom he had brought to his new job as assistant chief of the Brigade Criminelle.

'OK, you have Caron. Anyone else?'

'No thank you. But Caron will have to know.'

Bouvier thought for a few moments.

'It should be all right. They can't expect miracles. Obviously you must have an assistant. But don't tell him for an hour or two. I'll ring Frey when I get to the office and ask for formal clearance. Nobody else has to know, though. It would be in the Press inside two days if it got out.'

'Nobody else, just Caron,' said Lebel.

'*Bon.* There's one last thing. Before I left the meeting Sanguinetti suggested the whole group who were there tonight be kept informed at regular intervals of progress and developments. Frey agreed. Fernet and I tried to head it off, but we lost. There's to be a briefing by you every evening at the Ministry from now on. Ten o'clock sharp.'

'Oh God,' said Lebel.

'In theory,' continued Bouvier with heavy irony, 'we shall all be available to offer our best advice and suggestions. Don't worry, Claude, Fernet and I will be there too, in case the wolves start snapping.'

'This is until further notice?' asked Lebel.

' 'Fraid so. The bugger of it is, there's no time schedule for this operation. You've just got to find this assassin before he gets to Big Charles. We don't know whether the man himself has a timetable, or what it could be. It might be for a hit tomorrow morning, maybe not for a month yet. You have to assume you are working flat out until he has been caught, or at least identified and located. From then on I think the Action Service boys can take care of things.'

'Bunch of thugs,' murmured Lebel.

'Granted,' said Bouvier easily, 'but they have their uses. We live in hair-raising times, my dear Claude. Added to a vast increase in normal crime, we now have political crime. There are some things that just have to be done. They do them. Anyway, just try and find this blighter, huh.'

The car swept into the Quai des Orfèvres and turned through the gates of the PJ. Ten minutes later Claude Lebel was back in his office. He walked to the window, opened it and leant out, gazing across the river towards the Quai des Grands Augustins on the Left Bank in front of him. Although separated by a narrow strip of the Seine where it flowed round the Île de la Cité, he was close enough to see the diners in the pavement restaurants dotted along the quay and hear the laughter and the clink of bottles on glasses of wine.

Had he been a different kind of man it might have occurred to him to realise that the powers conferred on him in the last ninety minutes had made him, for a spell at least, the most powerful cop in Europe: that nobody short of the President or the Interior Minister could veto his request for facilities; that he could almost mobilise the Army, provided it could be done secretly. It might also have occurred to him that exalted though his powers were they were dependent upon success; that with success he could crown his career with honours, but that in failure he could be broken as Saint-Clair de Villauban had obliquely indicated.

But because he was what he was, he thought of none of these things. He was puzzling as to how he would explain over the phone to Amélie that he was not coming home until further notice. There was a knock on the door.

Inspectors Malcoste and Favier came in to collect the dossiers of the four cases on which Lebel had been working when he had been called away earlier that evening. He spent half an hour briefing Malcoste on the two cases he was assigning to him, and Favier on the other two.

When they had gone he sighed heavily. There was a knock on the door. It was Lucien Caron.

'I just got a call from Commissaire Bouvier's office,' he began. 'He told me to report to you.'

'Quite right. Until further notice I have been taken off all routine duties and given a rather special job. You've been assigned to be my assistant.'

He did not bother to flatter Caron by revealing that he had asked for the young inspector to be his right-hand man. The desk phone rang, he picked it up and listened briefly.

'Right,' he resumed, 'that was Bouvier to say you have been given security clearance to be told what it is all about. For a start you had better read this.'

While Caron sat on the chair in front of the desk and read the Rolland file, Lebel cleared all the remaining folders and notes off his desk and stacked them on the untidy shelves behind him. The office hardly looked like the nerve centre of the biggest manhunt in France. Police offices never do look much. Lebel's was no exception.

It was no more than twelve feet by fourteen, with two windows on the south face looking out over the river towards the lively honeycomb of the Latin Quarter clustering round the Boulevard St Michel. Through one of the windows the sounds of the night and the warm summer air drifted in. The office contained two desks, one for Lebel, which stood with its back to the window, another for a secretary, which stood along the east wall. The door was opposite the window.

Apart from the two desks and two chairs behind them, there was one other upright chair, an armchair next to the door, six large grey filing cabinets standing along almost the whole of the west wall and whose combined tops supported an array of reference and law books, and one set of bookshelves, situated between the windows and stuffed with almanacs and files.

Of signs of home there was only the framed photograph on Lebel's desk of an ample and determined-looking lady who was Madame Amélie Lebel, and two children, a plain girl with steel-rimmed glasses and pigtails, and a youth with an expression as mild and put-upon as his father's.

Caron finished reading and looked up.

'*Merde,*' he said.

'As you say, *une énorme merde,*' replied Lebel, who seldom permitted himself the use of strong language. Most of the top commissaires of the PJ were known to their immediate staff by nicknames like le Patron or le Vieux, but Claude Lebel, perhaps because he never drank more than a small aperitif, did not smoke or swear, and reminded younger detectives inevitably of one of their former schoolteachers, was known within Homicide and more lately in the corridors of the Brigade chief's administrative floor as *le Professeur.* Had he not been such a good thief-taker, he would have become something of a figure of fun.

'Nevertheless,' continued Lebel, 'listen while I fill you in on the details. It will be the last occasion I shall have time.'

For thirty minutes he briefed Caron on the events of the afternoon, from Roger Frey's meeting with the President to the meeting in the ministry conference room, to his own brusque summons on the recommendation of Maurice Bouvier, to the final setting up of the office in which they now sat as the headquarters of the manhunt for the Jackal. Caron listened in silence.

'Blimey,' he said at last when Lebel had finished, 'they *have* lumbered you.' He thought for a moment, then looked up at his chief with worry and concern. '*Mon Commissaire*, you know they have given you this because no one else wants it? You know what they will do to you if you fail to catch this man in time?'

Lebel nodded with a tinge of sadness.

'Yes, Lucien, I know. There's nothing I can do. I've been given the job. So from now we just have to do it.'

'But where on earth do we start?'

'We start by recognising that we have the widest powers ever granted to two cops in France,' replied Lebel cheerfully, 'so, we use them.

'To start with, get installed behind that desk. Take a pad and note the following. Get my normal secretary transferred or given paid leave until further notice. No one else can be let into the secret. You become my assistant and secretary rolled into one. Get a camp bed in here from emergency stores, linen and pillows, washing and shaving tackle. Get a percolator of coffee, some milk and sugar brought from the canteen and installed. We're going to need a lot of coffee.

'Get on to the switchboard and instruct them to leave ten outside lines and one operator permanently at the disposal of this office. If they quibble, refer them to Bouvier personally. As for any other requests from me for facilities, get straight on to the department chief and quote my name. Fortunately this office now gets top priority from every other ancillary service – by order. Prepare a circular memorandum, copy to every department chief who attended this evening's meeting, ready for my signature, announcing that you are now my sole assistant and empowered to require from them anything that I would ask them for personally if I were not engaged. Got it?'

Caron finished writing and looked up.

'Got it, chief. I can do that throughout the night. Which is the top priority?'

'The telephone switchboard. I want a good man on that, the best they've got. Get on to Chief of Admin at his home, and again quote Bouvier for authority.'

'Right. What do we want from them first?'

'I want, as soon as they can get it, a direct link personally to the head of the Homicide Division of the criminal police of seven countries. Fortunately, I know most of them personally from past meetings of Interpol. In some cases I know the Deputy Chief. If you can't get one, get the other.

'The countries are: United States, that means the Office of Domestic Intelligence in Washington. Britain, Assistant Commissioner (Crime) Scotland Yard. Belgium. Holland. Italy. West Germany. South Africa. Get them at home or in the office.

'When you get each of them one by one, arrange a series of telephone calls from Interpol Communications Room between me and them between seven and ten in the morning at twenty-minute intervals. Get on to Interpol Communications and book the calls as each Homicide chief at the other end agrees to be in his own communications room at the appointed time. The calls should be person-to-person on the UHF frequency and there is to be no listening in. Impress on each of them that what I have to say is for their ears only and of top priority not only for France but possibly for their own country. Prepare me a list by six in the morning of the schedule of the seven calls that have been booked, in order of sequence.

'In the meantime, I am going down to Homicide to see if a foreign killer has ever been suspected of operating in France and not been picked up. I confess, nothing in that line comes to mind, and in any case I suspect Rodin would have been more careful in his selection than that. Now, do you know what to do?'

Caron, looking slightly dazed, glanced up from his several pages of scribbled notes.

'Yes, chief, I've got it. *Bon*, I'd better get to work.' He reached out for the telephone.

Claude Lebel passed out of the office and headed for the stairs. As he did so the clock of Notre Dame further down the island chimed midnight, and the world passed into the morning of August 12th.

11

Colonel Raoul Saint-Clair de Villauban arrived home just before midnight. He had spent the previous three hours meticulously typing his report on the evening's meeting in the Interior Ministry, which would be on the desk of the Secretary-General of the Elysée first thing in the morning.

He had taken particular pains over the report, tearing up two rough copies before he was satisfied, then carefully typing out the third into a fair copy by himself. It was irritating to have to engage in the menial task of typing, and he was not used to it, but it had the advantage of keeping the secret from any secretary, a fact that he had not hesitated to point out in the body of the report, and also of enabling him to have the document ready for production first thing in the morning, which he hoped would not go unnoticed. With luck the report would be on the President's desk an hour after being read by the Secretary-General, and this also would do him no harm.

He had used extra care in selecting just the right phraseology to give a slight hint of the writer's disapproval of putting a matter so important as the security of the head of state into the sole hands of a commissaire of police, a man more accustomed by training and experience to uncovering petty criminals of little brains or talent.

It would not have done to go too far, for Lebel might even find his man. But in the event that he did not, it was as well that there was someone sufficiently on his toes to have had doubts about the wisdom of the choice of Lebel at the time.

Moreover, he had certainly not taken to Lebel. A common little man had been his private judgement. 'Possessed no doubt of a competent record' had been his phrasing in the report.

Musing over the first two copies he had written in longhand, he had come to the conclusion that the most advantageous position for him to take would be not to oppose outright the appointment of this promoted constable at the outset, since the appointment had been agreed by the meeting as a whole, and if he opposed the selection he would be asked for specific reasons; but, on the other hand, to keep a close watch on the whole operation, on behalf of the presidential secretariat, and to be the first to point out, with due sobriety, the inefficiencies in the conduct of the investigation as and when they occurred.

His musings on how he could best keep track of what Lebel was up to were interrupted by a telephone call from Sanguinetti to inform him that the Minister had made a last-minute decision to preside over nightly meetings at ten each evening to hear a progress report from Lebel. The news had delighted Saint-Clair. It solved his problem for him. With a little background homework during the daytime, he would be able to put forceful and pertinent questions to the detective, and reveal to the others that at least in the presidential secretariat they were keeping wide awake to the gravity and urgency of the situation.

Privately he did not put the assassin's chances very high, even if there were an assassin in the offing. The presidential security screen was the most efficient in the world, and part of his job in the secretariat was to devise the organisation of the President's public appearances and the routes he would follow. He had few qualms that this intensive and highly planned security screen could be penetrated by some foreign gunman.

He let himself in by the front door of his flat and heard his newly installed mistress call him from the bedroom.

'Is that you, darling?'

'Yes, chérie. Of course it's me. Have you been lonely?'

She came running through from the bedroom, dressed in a filmy black baby-doll nightie, trimmed at throat and hem with lace. The indirect light from the bedside lamp, shining through the open door of the bedroom, silhouetted the curves of her young woman's body. As usual when he saw his mistress, Raoul Saint-Clair felt a thrill of satisfaction that she was his, and so deeply in love with him. His character, however, was to congratulate himself for the fact, rather than any fortunate providence that might have brought them together.

She threw her bare arms round his neck and gave him a long open-mouthed kiss. He responded as best he could while still clutching his briefcase and the evening paper.

'Come,' he said when they separated, 'get into bed and I'll join you.' He gave her a slap on the bottom to speed her on her way. The girl skipped back into the bedroom, threw herself on the bed and spread out her limbs, hands crossed behind her neck, breasts upthrust.

Saint-Clair entered the room without his briefcase and glanced at her with satisfaction. She grinned back lasciviously.

During their fortnight together she had learned that only the most blatant suggestiveness coupled with an assumption of crude carnality could produce any lust from the juiceless loins of the career courtier. Privately Jacqueline hated him as much as on the first day they had met, but she had learned that what he lacked in virility he could be made to make up in loquacity, particularly about his importance in the scheme of things at the Elysée Palace.

'Hurry,' she whispered, 'I want you.'

Saint-Clair smiled with genuine pleasure and took off his shoes, laying them side by side at the foot of the dumb waiter. The jacket followed, its pockets carefully emptied on to the dressing-table top. The trousers came next, to be meticulously folded and laid over the protruding arm of the dumb waiter. His long thin legs protruded from beneath the shirt-tails like whiskery white knitting needles.

'What kept you so long?' asked Jacqueline. 'I've been waiting for ages.'

Saint-Clair shook his head sombrely.

'Certainly nothing that you should bother your head with, my dear.'

'Oh, you're mean.' She turned over abruptly on to her side in a mock-sulk facing away from him, knees bent. His fingers slipped on the tie-knot as he looked across the room at the chestnut hair tumbling over the shoulders and the full hips now uncovered by the shortie nightdress. Another five minutes and he was ready for bed, buttoning the mono-grammed silk pyjamas.

He stretched his length on the bed next to her and ran his hand down the dip of the waist and up to the summit of her hip, the fingers slipping down towards the sheet and round the swell of the warm buttock.

'What's the matter, then?'

'Nothing.'

'I thought you wanted to make love.'

'You just don't give me any explanation. I can't ring you at the office. I've been lying here for hours worrying that something might have hap-pened to you. You've never been this late before without ringing me.'

She rolled over on to her back and looked up at him. Propped on his elbow he slipped his free hand under the nightie and started to knead one of her breasts.

'Look, darling, I've been very busy. There was something of a crisis, something I had to sort out before I could get away. I'd have rung but there were people still working, popping in and out of the office the whole time. Several of them know my wife is away. It would have seemed odd for me to ring home through the switchboard.'

She slipped a hand through his pyjama fly to encircle the limp penis, and was rewarded with a light tremor.

'There couldn't have been anything so big you couldn't have let me know you'd be late, darling. I was worrying all night.'

'Well, there's no need to worry any more. Go down on me, you know I like that.'

She laughed, reached up with her other hand to pull his head down and bit him on the ear-lobe.

'No, he doesn't deserve it. Not yet anyway.' She squeezed the slowly hardening prick in rebuke. The Colonel's breathing was noticeably shal-lower. He started kissing her open-mouthed, his hand kneading first one and then the other nipple so hard that she wriggled.

'Go down on me,' he growled.

She shifted slightly and undid the pyjama cord. Raoul Saint-Clair watched the mane of brown hair fall forward from her head to shroud his belly, lay back and sighed with pleasure.

'It seems the OAS are still after the President,' he said. 'The plot was discovered this afternoon. It's being taken care of. That's what kept me.'

There was a soft 'plop' as the girl withdrew her head a few inches.

'Don't be silly, darling, they were finished long ago.' She went back to her task.

'They're bloody well not. Now they've hired a foreign assassin to try to kill him. Aeegh, don't bite.'

Half an hour later Colonel Raoul Saint-Clair de Villauban lay asleep, face half-buried in the pillow, snoring gently from his exertions. Beside him his mistress lay staring up through the darkness at the ceiling, dimly lit where the lights from the street outside filtered through a tiny crack where the curtains joined.

What she had learned had left her aghast. Although she had had no previous knowledge of any such plot she could work out for herself the importance of Kowalski's confession.

She waited in silence until the bedside clock with the luminous dial registered two in the morning. Easing herself out of the bed, she slid the plug of the bedroom telephone extension out of its socket.

Before walking to the door she bent over the Colonel, and was grateful he was not the sort of man who liked to sleep in embrace with his bedmate. He was still snoring.

Outside the bedroom she quietly closed the door, crossed the sitting-room towards the hall and closed that door after her. From the phone on the hall table she dialled a Molitor number. There was a wait of several minutes until a sleepy voice answered. She spoke rapidly for two minutes, received an acknowledgement and hung up. A minute later she was back in bed, trying to get to sleep.

Throughout the night crime chiefs of the police forces of five European countries, America and South Africa were being woken with long-distance calls from Paris. Most of them were irritated and sleepy. In Western Europe the time was the same as Paris, the small hours of the morning. In Washington the time was nine in the evening when the call from Paris came through, and the chief of FBI Homicide was at a dinner party. It was only at the third attempt that Caron could get him, and then their conversation was marred by the chatter of guests and the clink of glasses from the next room where the party was in progress. But he got the message and agreed to be in the communications room of the FBI headquarters at two in the morning, Washington time, to take a call from Commissaire Lebel who would be ringing him from Interpol at 8 a.m. Paris time.

The crime chiefs of the Belgian, Italian, German and Dutch police were all apparently good family men; each was awoken in turn and after listening to Caron for a few minutes agreed to be in their communications rooms at the times Caron suggested to take a person-to-person call from Lebel on a matter of great urgency.

THE DAY OF THE JACKAL

Van Ruys of South Africa was out of town and would not be able to get back to headquarters by sunrise, so Caron spoke to Anderson, his deputy. Lebel, when he heard, was not displeased for he knew Anderson fairly well, but Van Ruys not at all. Besides, he suspected Van Ruys was more of a political appointment while Anderson had once been a constable on the beat like himself.

The call reached Mr Anthony Mallinson, Assistant Commissioner Crime for Scotland Yard, in his home at Bexley shortly before four. He growled in protest at the insistent clanging of the bell beside his bed, reached out for the mouthpiece and muttered 'Mallinson'.

'Mr Anthony Mallinson?' asked a voice.

'Speaking.' He shrugged to clear the bedclothes from his shoulders, and glanced at his watch.

'My name is Inspector Lucien Caron, of the French Sûreté Nationale. I am ringing on behalf of Commissaire Claude Lebel.'

The voice, speaking good but strongly accented English, was coming over clearly. Obviously line traffic at that hour was light. Mallinson frowned. Why couldn't the blighters call at a civilised hour?

'Yes.'

'I believe you know Commissaire Lebel, perhaps, Mr Mallinson.'

Mallinson thought for a moment. Lebel? Oh, yes, little fellow, had been head of Homicide in the PJ. Didn't look much but he got results. Been damn helpful over that murdered English tourist two years back. Could have been nasty in the Press if they hadn't caught the killer in double-quick time.

'Yes, I know Commissaire Lebel,' he said down the phone. 'What's it about?'

Beside him his wife, Lily, disturbed by the talking, grumbled in her sleep.

'There is a matter of very considerable urgency, which also requires a great degree of discretion, that has cropped up. I am assisting Commissaire Lebel on the case. It is a most unusual case. The Commissaire would like to place a person-to-person call to you in your communications room at the Yard this morning at nine o'clock. Could you please be present to take the call?'

Mallinson thought for a moment.

'Is this a routine enquiry between co-operating police forces?' he asked. If it were they could use the routine Interpol network. Nine o'clock was a busy time at the Yard.

'No, Mr Mallinson, it is not. It is a question of a personal request by the Commissaire to you for a little discreet assistance. It may be there is nothing that affects Scotland Yard in the matter that has come up. Most probably so. If that is the case, it would be better if there were no formal request placed.'

Mallinson thought it over. He was by nature a cautious man and had no wish to be involved in clandestine enquiries from a foreign police force. If a crime had been committed, or a criminal had fled to Britain, that was another matter. In that case why the secrecy? Then he remembered a case years ago where he had been sent out to find and bring back the daughter of a Cabinet Minister who had gone astray with a handsome young devil. The girl had been a minor, so charges of removing the child from parental authority could have been brought. A bit marginal. But the Minister had wanted the whole thing done without a murmur reaching the Press. The Italian police had been very helpful when the couple was found at Verona playing Romeo and Juliet. All right, so Lebel wanted a bit of help on the Old Boy network. That was what Old Boy networks were for.

'All right, I'll take the call. Nine o'clock.'

'Thank you so much, Mr Mallinson.'

'Good night.' Mallinson replaced the receiver, re-set the alarm clock for six-thirty instead of seven, and went back to sleep.

In a small fusty bachelor flat, while Paris slept towards the dawn, a middle-aged schoolmaster paced up and down the floor of the cramped bedsitter. The scene around him was chaotic: books, newspapers, magazines and manuscripts lay scattered over the table, chairs and sofa, and even on the coverlet of the narrow bed set into its alcove on the far side of the room. In another alcove a sink overflowed with unwashed crockery.

What obsessed his thoughts in his nocturnal pacings was not the untidy state of his room, for since his removal from his post as headmaster of a Lycée at Sidi-bel-Abbes and the loss of the fine house with two manservants that went with it, he had learned to live as he now did. His problem lay elsewhere.

As dawn was breaking over the eastern suburbs, he sat down finally and picked up one of the papers. His eye ran yet again down the second lead story on the foreign news page. It was headlined: 'OAS Chiefs Holed Up in Rome Hotel.' After reading it for the last time he made up his mind, threw on a light mackintosh against the chill of the morning, and left the flat.

He caught a cruising taxi on the nearest boulevard and ordered the driver to take him to the Gare du Nord. Although the taxi dropped him in the forecourt, he walked away from the station as soon as the taxi had left, crossed the road and entered one of the all-night cafés of the area.

He ordered a coffee and a metal disc for the telephone, left the coffee on the counter and went into the back of the café to dial. Directory Enquiries put him on to the International Exchange and he asked them the number of a hotel in Rome. He got it within sixty seconds, replaced the receiver and left.

At a café a hundred metres down the street he again used the phone, this time to ask Enquiries for the location of the nearest all-night post office from which international calls could be placed. He was told, as he had expected, that there was one round the corner from the mainline station.

At the post office he placed a call to the Rome number he had been given, without naming the hotel represented by the number, and spent an anxious twenty minutes waiting until it came through.

'I wish to speak to Signor Poitiers,' he told the Italian voice that answered.

'*Signor Che?*' asked the voice.

'*Il signor francesi. Poitiers. Poitiers.* . . .'

'*Che?*' repeated the voice.

'*Francesi, francesi* . . .' said the man in Paris.

'*Ah si, il signor francesi. Momento, per favore* . . .'

There was a series of clicks, then a tired voice answered in French.

'*Ouay* . . .'

'Listen,' said the man in Paris urgently. 'I don't have much time. Take a pencil and note what I say. Begins. "Valmy to Poitiers. The Jackal is blown. Repeat. The Jackal is blown. Kowalski was taken. Sang before dying. Ends." Got that?'

'*Ouay,*' said the voice. 'I'll pass it on.'

Valmy replaced the receiver, hurriedly paid his bill and scurried out of the building. In a minute he was lost in the crowds of commuters streaming out of the main hall of the station. The sun was over the horizon, warming the pavements and the chill night air. Within half an hour the smell of morning and croissants and grinding coffee would vanish beneath the pall of exhaust fumes, body odour and stale tobacco. Two minutes after Valmy had disappeared a car drew up outside the post office and the two men from the DST hurried inside. They took a description from the switchboard operator, but it could have described anybody.

In Rome Marc Rodin was awakened at 7.55 when the man who had spent the night on the duty desk on the floor below shook him by the shoulder. He was awake in an instant, half out of bed, hand groping for the gun under his pillow. He relaxed and grunted when he saw the face of the ex-legionnaire above him. A glance at the bedside table told him he had overslept anyway. After years in the tropics his habitual waking hour was much earlier, and the August sun of Rome was already high above the roofs. But weeks of inactivity, passing the evening hours playing piquet with Montclair and Casson, drinking too much rough red wine, taking no exercise worth the name, all had combined to make him slack and sleepy.

'A message, *mon colonel*. Someone phoned just now, seemed in a hurry.'

The legionnaire proffered a sheet from a note pad on which were scribbled the disjointed phrases of Valmy. Rodin read through the message once, then leapt out of the thinly sheeted bed. He wrapped the cotton sarong he habitually wore, a habit from the East, round his waist, and read the message again.

'All right. Dismiss.' The legionnaire left the room and went back downstairs.

Rodin swore silently and intensely for several seconds, crumpling the piece of paper in his hands. Damn, damn, damn, damn Kowalski.

For the first two days after Kowalski's disappearance he had thought the man had simply deserted. There had been several defections of late from the cause, as the conviction set in among the rank and file that the OAS had failed and would fail in its aim of killing Charles de Gaulle and bringing down the present Government of France. But Kowalski he had always thought would remain loyal to the last.

And here was evidence that he had for some inexplicable reason returned to France, or perhaps been picked up inside Italy and abducted. Now it seemed he had talked, under pressure of course.

Rodin genuinely grieved his dead servitor. Part of the considerable reputation he had built up as a fighting soldier and commanding officer had been based on the enormous concern he showed for his men. These things are appreciated by fighting soldiers more than any military theorist can ever imagine. Now Kowalski was dead, and Rodin had few illusions of the manner of his passing.

Still, the important thing was to try to recollect just what Kowalski had had to tell. The meeting in Vienna, the name of the hotel. Of course, all of that. The three men who had been at the meeting. This would be no news to the SDECE. But what did he know about the Jackal? He had not been listening at the door, that was certain. He could tell them of a tall blond foreigner who had visited the three of them. That in itself meant nothing. Such a foreigner could have been an arms dealer, or a financial backer. There had been no names mentioned.

But Valmy's message mentioned the Jackal by his code-name. How? How could Kowalski have told them that?

With a start of horror Rodin recalled the scene as they had parted. He had stood in the doorway with the Englishman; Viktor had been a few feet down the corridor, annoyed at the way the Englishman had spotted him in the alcove, a professional outmanoeuvred by another professional, waiting for trouble, almost hoping for it. What had he, Rodin said? 'Bonsoir, Mr Jackal.' Of course, damn and blast it.

Thinking things over again, Rodin realised that Kowalski could never have got the killer's real name. Only he, Montclair and Casson knew that. All the same, Valmy was right. With Kowalski's confession in the hands of the SDECE, it was too far blown to be retrievable. They had the meeting, the hotel, probably they had already talked to the desk clerk; they had the face and figure of a man, a code-name. There could be no doubt they would guess what Kowalski had guessed – that the blond was a killer. From then on the net around De Gaulle would tighten; he would abandon all public engagements, all exits from his palace, all chances for an assassin to get him. It was over; the operation was blown. He would have to call off the Jackal, insist on the money back, minus all expenses and a retainer for the time and trouble involved.

There was one thing to be settled, and quickly. The Jackal himself must be warned urgently to halt operations. Rodin was still enough of a commanding officer not to send a man out on his orders on a mission for which success had become impossible.

He summoned the bodyguard to whom, since the departure of Kowalski, he had given the duties of going every day to the main post office to collect the mail and, if necessary, make telephone calls, and briefed him at length.

By nine o'clock the bodyguard was in the post office and asked for a telephone number in London. It took twenty minutes before the telephone at the other end began to ring. The switchboard operator gestured the Frenchman to a cabin to take the call. He picked up the receiver as the operator put hers down, and listened to the bzzz-bzzz ... pause ... bzzz-bzzz of an English telephone ringing.

The Jackal rose early that morning, for he had much to do. The three main suitcases he had checked and re-packed the previous evening. Only the hand-grip remained to be topped up with his sponge bag and shaving tackle. He drank his habitual two cups of coffee, washed, showered and shaved. After packing the remainder of the overnight toiletries he closed up the hand luggage and stored all four pieces by the door.

He made himself a quick breakfast of scrambled eggs, orange juice and more black coffee in the flat's small but compact kitchen, and ate it off the kitchen table. Being a tidy and methodical man he emptied the last of the milk down the sink, broke the two remaining eggs and poured them also down the sink. The remainder of the orange juice he drank off, junked the can in the trash basket and the remainder of the bread, egg shells and coffee grounds went down the disposal unit. Nothing left would be likely to go rotten during his absence.

Finally he dressed, choosing a thin silk polo-necked sweater, the dove-grey suit containing the private papers in the name of Duggan, and the hundred pounds in cash, dark grey socks and slim black moccasin shoes. The ensemble was completed by the inevitable dark glasses.

At nine-fifteen he took his luggage, two pieces in each hand, closed the self-locking flat door behind him, and went downstairs. It was a short walk to South Audley Street and he caught a taxi on the corner.

'London Airport, Number Two Building,' he told the driver.

As the taxi moved away, the phone in his flat began to ring.

It was ten o'clock when the legionnaire returned to the hotel off the Via Condotti and told Rodin he had tried for thirty minutes to get a reply from the London number he had been given, but had not succeeded.

'What's the matter?' asked Casson, who had heard the explanation given to Rodin and seen the legionnaire dismissed to return to his guard duties. The three OAS chiefs were sitting in the drawing-room of their suite. Rodin withdrew a piece of paper from his inside pocket and passed it over to Casson.

Casson read it and passed it to Montclair. Both men finally looked at their leader for an answer. There was none. Rodin sat staring out of the windows across the baking roofs of Rome, brow furrowed in thought.

'When did it come?' asked Casson eventually.

'This morning,' replied Rodin briefly.

'You've got to stop him,' protested Montclair. 'They'll have half of France on the lookout for him.'

'They'll have half of France on the lookout for a tall blond foreigner,' said Rodin quietly. 'In August there are over one million foreigners in France. So far as we know they have no name to go on, no face, no passport. Being a professional he is probably using a false passport. They still have a long way to go to get him yet. There's a good chance he will be forewarned if he rings Valmy, and then he'll be able to get out again.'

'If he rings Valmy he will, of course, be ordered to drop the operation,' said Montclair. 'Valmy will order him.'

Rodin shook his head.

'Valmy does not have the authority to do that. His orders are to receive information from the girl and pass it on to the Jackal when he is telephoned. He will do that, but nothing else.'

'But the Jackal must realise of his own accord that it is all over,' protested Montclair. 'He must get out of France as soon as he rings Valmy the first time.'

'In theory yes,' said Rodin thoughtfully. 'If he does he hands back the money. There's a lot at stake, for all of us, including him. It depends how confident he feels of his own planning.'

'Do you think he has a chance now ... now that this has happened?' asked Casson.

'Frankly, no,' said Rodin. 'But he is a professional. So am I, in my way. It is a frame of mind. One does not like to stand down an operation one has planned personally.'

'Then for God's sake recall him,' protested Casson.

'I can't. I would if I could, but I can't. He's gone. He's on his way. He wanted it this way and now he's got it. We don't know where he is or what he is going to do. He's completely on his own. I can't even call up Valmy and order him to instruct the Jackal to drop the whole thing. To do so would risk "blowing" Valmy. Nobody can stop the Jackal now. It's too late.'

Commissaire Claude Lebel arrived back in his office just before six in the morning to find Inspector Caron looking tired and strained, in shirt-sleeves at his desk.

He had several sheets of foolscap paper in front of him covered with handwritten notes. In the office some things had changed. On top of the filing cabinets an electric coffee percolator bubbled, sending out a delicious aroma of freshly brewed coffee. Next to it stood a pile of paper cups, a tin of unsweetened milk and a bag of sugar. These had come up from the basement canteen during the night.

In the corner between the two desks a single truckle bed had been set up, covered with a rough blanket. The waste-paper basket had been emptied and stored next to the armchair by the door.

The window was open still, a faint haze of blue smoke from Caron's cigarettes drifting out into the cool morning. Beyond the window the first flecks of the coming day mottled the spire of St Sulpice.

Lebel crossed to his desk and slumped into the chair. Although it was only twenty-four hours since he had woken from his last sleep he looked tired, like Caron.

'Nothing,' he said. 'I've been through the lot over the past ten years. The only foreign political killer who ever tried to operate here was Degueldre, and he's dead. Besides, he was OAS and we had him on file as such. Presumably Rodin has chosen a man who has nothing to do with the OAS, and he's quite right. There were only four contract-hire killers who tried it in France over the past ten years – apart from the home-grown variety – and we got three. The fourth is serving a lifer in Africa somewhere. Besides, they were all gangland killers, not of the calibre to shoot down a President of France.

'I got on to Bargeron of Central Records and they're doing a complete double-check, but I suspect already that we don't have this man on file. Rodin would in any case insist on that before hiring him.'

Caron lit up another Gauloises, blew out the smoke and sighed.

'So we have to start from the foreign end?'

'Precisely. A man of this type must have got his training and experience somewhere. He wouldn't be one of the world's tops unless he could prove it with a string of successful jobs behind him. Not presidents perhaps, but important men, bigger than mere underworld *caïds*. That means he must have come to someone's attention somewhere. Surely. What have you arranged?'

Caron picked up one of the sheets of paper, showing a list of names with, in the left-hand column, a series of timings.

'The seven are all fixed,' he said. 'You start with Head of the Office of Domestic Intelligence at ten past seven. That's ten past one in the morning Washington time. I fitted him in first because of the lateness of the hour in America.

'Then Brussels at half past seven, Amsterdam at quarter to eight and Bonn at eight-ten. The link is arranged with Johannesburg at eight-thirty and Scotland Yard at nine. Lastly there is Rome at nine-thirty.'

'The heads of Homicide in each case?' asked Lebel.

'Or the equivalent. With Scotland Yard it's Mr Anthony Mallinson, Assistant Commissioner Crime. It seems they don't have a homicide section in the Metropolitan Police. Apart from that, yes, except South Africa. I couldn't get Van Ruys at all, so you're talking to Assistant Commissioner Anderson.'

Lebel thought for a moment.

'That's fine. I'd prefer Anderson. We worked on a case once. There's the question of language. Three of them speak English. I suppose only the Belgian speaks French. The others almost certainly can speak English if they have to. . . .'

'The German, Dietrich, speaks French,' interjected Caron.

'Good, then I'll speak to those two in French personally. For the other five I'll have to have you on the extension as interpreter. We'd better go. Come on.'

It was ten to seven when the police car carrying the two detectives drew up outside the innocent green door in the tiny Rue Paul Valéry which housed the headquarters of Interpol at that time.

For the next three hours Lebel and Caron sat hunched over the telephone in the basement communications room talking to the world's top crime busters. From the seemingly tangled porcupine of aerials on the roof of the building the high-frequency signals beamed out across three continents, streaming high beyond the stratosphere to bounce off the ionic layer above and home back to earth thousands of miles away to another stick of aluminium jutting from a tiled rooftop.

The wavelengths and scramblers were uninterceptable. Detective spoke to detective while the world drank its morning coffee or final nightcap.

In each telephone conversation Lebel's appeal was much the same.

'No, Commissioner, I cannot yet put this request for your assistance on the level of an official enquiry between our two police forces . . . certainly I am acting in an official capacity. . . . It is simply that for the moment we are just not sure if even the intent to commit an offence has been formulated or put into the preparation stage. . . . It's a question of a tip-off, purely routine for the moment. . . . Well, we are looking for a man about whom we know extremely little. . . . not even a name, and only a poor description. . . .'

In each case he gave the description as best he knew it. The sting came in the tail, as each of his foreign colleagues asked why their help was being sought, and what clues they could possibly go on. It was at that point that the other end of the line became tensely silent.

'Simply this; that whoever this man is or may be, he must have one qualification that marks him out . . . he would have to be one of the world's top professional contract-hire assassins . . . no, not a gangland trigger, a political assassin with several successful kills behind him. We would be interested to know if you have anybody like that on your files, even if he has never operated in your own country. Or anybody that even springs to mind.'

Inevitably there was a long pause at the other end before the voice resumed. Then it was quieter, more concerned.

Lebel had no illusions that the heads of the Homicide departments of the major police forces of the Western world would fail to understand what he was hinting at but could not say. There was only one target in France that could interest a first-league political killer.

Without exception the reply was the same. 'Yes, of course. We'll go through all the files for you. I'll try and get back to you before the day is out. Oh, and Claude, good luck.'

When he put down the radio-telephone receiver for the last time, Lebel wondered how long it would be before the Foreign Ministers and even Prime Ministers of the seven countries would be aware of what was on. Probably not long. Even a policeman had to report to the politicians something of that size. He was fairly certain the Ministers would keep quiet about it. There was, after all, a strong bond over and above political differences between the men of power the world over. They were all members of the same club, the club of the potentates. They stuck together against common enemies, and what could be more inimical to any of them than the activities of a political assassin? He was aware all the same that if the enquiry did become public knowledge and reached the Press, it would be blasted across the world and he would be finished.

The only people who did worry him were the English. If it could only be kept between cops, he would have trusted Mallinson.

But he knew that before the day was out it would have to go higher than Mallinson. It was only seven months since Charles de Gaulle had brusquely rebuffed Britain from the Common Market, and in the wake of the General's January 14th press conference the London Foreign Office, as even so apolitical a creature as Lebel was aware, had become almost lyrical in its campaign of words planted through the political correspondents against the French President. Would they now use this to get their revenge on the old man?

Lebel stared for a moment at the now silent transmitter panel in front of him. Caron watched him quietly.

'Come on,' said the little Commissaire, rising from the stool and heading for the door, 'let's get some breakfast and try to get some sleep. There's not much more we can do now.'

Assistant Commissioner Anthony Mallinson put down the telephone with a thoughtful frown and left the communications room without acknowledging the salute of the young policeman who was entering to take up his morning shift. He was still frowning as he went back upstairs to his spacious but soberly appointed office overlooking the Thames.

There was no doubt in his mind what kind of enquiry Lebel had been making, nor of his motives for making it. The French police had got some kind of a tip-off that a top-class assassin was on the loose, and that it affected them. As Lebel had predicted to himself, it took very little acumen to work out who could be the only possible target in France in August 1963 for that kind of killer. He considered Lebel's predicament with the knowledge of a long-time policeman.

'Poor bastard,' he said aloud as he stared down at the warm and sluggish river flowing past the Embankment beneath his window.

'Sir?' asked his personal aide, who had followed him into the office to put the morning mail that needed his attention on the walnut desk.

'Nothing.' Mallinson continued to stare out of the window as the PA left. However much he might feel for Claude Lebel in his task of trying to protect his president without being able to launch an official manhunt, he too had masters. Sooner or later they would have to be told of Lebel's request to him that morning. There was the daily heads-of-department conference at ten, in half an hour's time. Should he mention it there?

On the balance he decided not to. It would be enough to write a formal but private memorandum to the Commissioner himself, outlining the nature of Lebel's request. The necessity for discretion would explain later, if necessary, why the matter had not been raised at the morning meeting. In the meantime it would do no harm to put through the enquiry without revealing why it was being made.

He took his seat behind the desk and pressed one of the buttons on the intercom.

'Sir?' His PA's voice came through from the adjoining office.

'Come in here a minute, would you, John?'

The charcoal-grey-suited young detective inspector came in, notebook in hand.

'John, I want you to get on to Central Records. Speak to Chief Superintendent Markham personally. Tell him the request is from me personally, and that I cannot explain for the moment why I am making it. Ask him to check every existing record of known living professional assassins in this country....'

'Assassins, sir?' The PA looked as if the Assistant Commissioner had asked for a routine check on all known Martians.

'Yes, assassins. Not, repeat not, run-of-the-mill gangland thugs who either have or are known to be capable of knocking off somebody in a feud in the underworld. Political killers, John, men or a man capable of assassinating a well-guarded politician or statesman for money.'

'That sounds more like Special Branch customers, sir.'

'Yes, I know. I want to pass the whole thing to Special Branch. But we had better do a routine check first. Oh, and I want an answer one way or the other by midday. OK?'

'Right, sir, I'll get on to it.'

Fifteen minutes later Assistant Commissioner Mallinson took his seat at the morning conference.

When he returned to his office he flicked through the mail, pushed it to one side of the desk and ordered the PA to bring him in a typewriter. Sitting alone, he typed out a brief report for the Commissioner of Metropolitan Police. It mentioned briefly the morning call to his home, the person-to-person call over the Interpol link at nine in the morning, and the nature of Lebel's enquiry. He left the bottom of the memorandum form empty, and locked it away in his desk to get on with the day's work.

Shortly before twelve the PA knocked and entered.

'Superintendent Markham's just been on from CRO,' he said. 'Apparently there's no one on Criminal Records who can fit that description. Seventeen known contract-hire killers from the underworld, sir; ten in jail and seven on the loose. But they all work for the big gangs, either here or in the main cities. The Super says none would fit for a job against a visiting politician. He suggested Special Branch too, sir.'

'Right, John, thank you. That's all I needed.'

With the PA dismissed, Mallinson took the half-finished memo from his drawer and re-inserted it into the typewriter. On the bottom he wrote:

'Criminal Records reported upon enquiry that no person fitting the description of type submitted by Commissaire Lebel could be traced in their files. The enquiry was then passed to the Assistant Commissioner, Special Branch.'

He signed the memorandum and took the top three copies. The remainder went into the waste-paper basket for classified waste, later to be shredded into millions of particles and destroyed.

One of the copies he folded into an envelope and addressed to the Commissioner. The second he filed in the 'Secret Correspondence' file and locked it into the wall-safe. The third he folded and placed in his inside pocket.

On his desk note-pad he scribbled a message.

'To: Commissaire Claude Lebel, Deputy Director-General, Police Judiciaire, Paris.

'From: Assistant Commissioner Anthony Mallinson, A.C. Crime, Scotland Yard, London.

Message: Following your enquiry this date fullest research criminal records reveals no such personage known to us. stop. request passed to

Special Branch for further checking. stop. any useful information will be passed to you soonest. stop. Mallinson.

'Time sent: . . . 12.8.63.'

It was just gone half past twelve. He picked up the phone, and when the operator answered, asked for Assistant Commissioner Dixon, head of Special Branch.

'Hallo, Alec? Tony Mallinson. Can you spare me a minute? I'd love to but I can't. I shall have to keep lunch down to a sandwich. It's going to be one of those days. No, I just want to see you for a few minutes before you go. Fine, good, I'll come right along.'

'I'm just going up to see Dixon of the SB. Get that along to the Commissioner's office would you, John? Personally. And get this message off to the addressee. Type it out yourself in the proper style.'

'Yessir.' Mallinson stood over the desk while the detective inspector's eyes ran through the message. They widened as they reached the end.

'John . . .'

'Sir?'

'And keep quiet about it, please.'

'Yes, sir.'

'Very quiet, John.'

'Not a word, sir.'

Mallinson gave him a brief smile and left the office. The PA read the message to Lebel a second time, thought back to the enquiries he had made with Records that morning for Mallinson, worked it out for himself, and whispered 'Bloody hell'.

Mallinson spent twenty minutes with Dixon and effectively ruined the other's forthcoming club lunch. He passed over to the Head of Special Branch the remaining copy of the memorandum to the Commissioner. As he rose to leave he turned at the door, hand on the knob.

'Sorry, Alec, but this really is more up your street. But if you ask me, there's probably nothing and nobody of that calibre in this country, so a good check of records and you should be able to telex Lebel to say we can't help. I must say I don't envy him his job this time.'

Assistant Commissioner Dixon, whose job among other things was to keep tabs on all the weird and crazy of Britain who might think of trying to assassinate a visiting politician, not to mention the scores of embittered and cranky foreigners domiciled in the country, felt even more keenly the impossibility of Lebel's position. To have to protect home and visiting politicians from unbalanced fanatics was bad enough, but at least they could usually be relied upon as amateurs to fail in the face of his own corps of case-hardened professionals.

To have one's own head of state the target for a native organisation of tough ex-soldiers was even worse. And yet the French had beaten the OAS. As a professional, Dixon admired them for it. But the hiring of a foreign professional was a different matter. Only one thing could be said in its favour, from Dixon's point of view; it cut the possibilities down to so few that he had no doubts there would prove to be no Englishman of the calibre of the man Lebel sought on the books of the Special Branch.

After Mallinson had left, Dixon read the carbon copy of the memorandum. Then he summoned his own PA.

'Please tell Detective Superintendent Thomas I would like to see him here at...' he glanced at his watch, estimated how long a much shortened lunch-hour would take him ... 'two o'clock sharp.'

The Jackal landed at Brussels National just after twelve. He left his three main pieces of luggage in an automatic locker in the main terminal building and took with him into town only the hand-grip containing his personal effects, the plaster of Paris, pads of cotton wool and bandages. At the main station he dismissed the taxi and went to the left-luggage office.

The fibre suitcase containing the gun was still on the shelf where he had seen the clerk deposit it a week earlier. He presented the reclamation slip and was given the case in return.

Not far from the station he found a small and squalid hotel, of the kind that seem to exist in proximity to all main line stations the world over, which ask no questions but get told a lot of lies.

He booked a single room for the night, paid cash in advance in Belgian money that he had changed at the airport, and took his case up to the room himself. With the door safely locked behind him, he ran a basin of cold water, emptied the plaster and bandages on to the bed, and set to work.

It took over two hours for the plaster to dry when he had finished. During this time he sat with his heavy foot and leg resting on a stool, smoking his filter cigarettes and looking out over the grimy array of rooftops that formed the vista from the bedroom window. Occasionally he would test the plaster with his thumb, each time deciding to let it harden a bit more before moving.

The fibre suitcase that had formerly contained the gun lay empty. The remainder of the bandages were re-packed in the hand-grip along with the few ounces of plaster that were left, in case he had to do some running repairs. When he was finally ready he slid the cheap fibre case under the bed, checked the room for any last telltale signs, emptied the ashtray out of the window, and prepared to leave.

He found that with the plaster on a realistic limp became obligatory. At the bottom of the stairs he was relieved to find the grubby and sleepy-looking desk clerk was in the back room behind the desk, where he had been when the Jackal arrived. Being lunchtime, he was eating, but the door with the frosted glass that gave him access to the front counter was open.

With a glance at the front door to make sure no one was coming in, the Jackal clutched his hand-case to his chest, bent on to all fours and scuttled quickly and silently across the tiled hall. Because of the heat of summer the front door was open and he was able to stand upright on the top of the three steps that led to the street, out of the line of sight of the desk clerk.

He limped painfully down the steps and along the street to the corner where the main road ran past. A taxi spotted him inside half a minute, and he was on his way back to the airport.

He presented himself at the Alitalia counter, passport in hand. The girl smiled at him.

'I believe you have a ticket for Milan reserved two days ago in the name of Duggan,' he said.

She checked the bookings for the afternoon flight to Milan. It was due to leave in an hour and a half.

'Yes indeed,' she beamed at him. 'Meester Duggan. The ticket was reserved but not paid for. You wish to pay for it?'

The Jackal paid in cash again, was issued with his ticket, and told he would be called in an hour. With the aid of a solicitous porter who tut-tutted over his plastered foot and pronounced limp, he withdrew his three suitcases from the locker, consigned them to Alitalia, passed through the Customs barrier which, seeing that he was an outgoing traveller, was merely a passport check, and spent the remaining hour enjoying a late but pleasant lunch in the restaurant attached to the passenger departure lounge.

Everybody concerned with the flight was very kind and considerate towards him because of the leg. He was assisted aboard the coach out to the aircraft and watched with concern as he made his painful way up the steps to the aircraft's door. The lovely Italian hostess gave him an extra wide smile of welcome and saw him comfortably seated in one of the group of seats in the centre of the aircraft that face towards each other. There was more leg-room there, she pointed out.

The other passengers took elaborate pains not to knock against the plastered foot as they took their seats, while the Jackal lay back in his seat and smiled bravely.

At 4.15 the airliner was on take-off, and soon speeding southwards bound for Milan.

Superintendent Bryn Thomas emerged from the Assistant Commissioner's office just before three, feeling thoroughly miserable. Not only was his summer cold one of the worst and most persistent he had ever been plagued with, but the new assignment with which he had just been saddled had ruined his day.

As Monday mornings went it had been rotten; first he had learned that one of his men had been slipped by a Soviet trade delegate whom he was supposed to be tailing, and by mid-morning he had received an inter-departmental complaint from MI-5 politely asking his department to lay off the Soviet delegation, an unmistakable suggestion that in the view of MI-5 the whole matter had better be left to them.

Monday afternoon looked like being worse. There are few things that any policeman, Special Branch or not, likes less than the spectre of the political assassin. But in the case of the request he had just received from his superior, he had not even been given a name to go on.

'No name, but I'm afraid plenty of pack-drill,' had been Dixon's *bon mot* on the subject. 'Try and get it out of the way by tomorrow.'

'Pack-drill,' snorted Thomas when he reached the office. Although the short-list of known suspects would be extremely short, it still presented him and his department with hours of checking of files, records for political trouble-making, convictions and, unlike the criminal branch, mere suspicions. All would have to be checked. There was only one ray of light in Dixon's briefing: the man would be a professional operator and not one of the numberless bee-in-the-bonnet merchants that made the Special Branch's life a misery before and during any foreign statesman's visit.

He summoned two detective inspectors whom he knew to be presently engaged on low-priority research work, told them to drop whatever they were doing, as he had done, and to report to his office. His briefing to them was shorter than Dixon's had been to him. He confined himself to telling them what they were looking for, but not why. The suspicions of the French police that such a man might be out to kill General de Gaulle need have nothing to do with the search through the archives and records of Scotland Yard's Special Branch.

The three of them cleared the desks of outstanding paper-work and settled down.

The Jackal's plane touched down at Linate Aiport, Milan, shortly after six. He was helped by the ever-attentive hostess down the steps to the tarmac, and escorted by one of the ground hostesses to the main terminal building. It was at Customs that his elaborate preparations in getting the component parts of the gun out of the suitcases and into a less suspicious means of carriage paid dividends. The passport check was a formality but as the suitcases from the hold came rumbling through on the conveyor belt and were deposited along the length of the Customs bench, the risks began to mount.

The Jackal secured a porter who assembled the three main suitcases into a line side by side. The Jackal put his hand-grip down beside them. Seeing him limp up to the bench, one of the Customs officers sauntered across.

'Signor? This is all your baggage?'

'Er, yes, these three suitcases and this little case.'

'You have anything to declare?'

'No, nothing.'

'You are on business, signor?'

'No, I've come on holiday, but it turns out it must also include a period of convalescence. I hope to go up to the lakes.'

The Customs man was not impressed.

'May I see your passport, signor?'

The Jackal handed it over. The Italian examined it closely, then handed it back without a word.

'Please, open this one.'

He gestured at one of the three larger suitcases. The Jackal took out his key-ring, selected one of the keys and opened the case. The porter had laid it flat on its side to help him. Fortunately it was the case containing the clothes of the fictitious Danish pastor and the American student. Riffling through the clothes, the Customs officer attached no importance

to a dark-grey suit, underwear, white shirt, sneakers, black walking
shoes, windcheater and socks. Nor did the book in Danish excite him.
The cover was a colour plate of Chartres Cathedral, and the title, although in Danish, was sufficiently like the equivalent English words not
to be remarkable. He did not examine the carefully re-sewn slit in the
side lining, nor find the false identity papers. A really thorough search
would have found them, but his was the usual perfunctory run-through
that would only have become intensive if he had found something suspicious. The component parts of a complete sniper's rifle were only three
feet away from him across the desk, but he suspected nothing. He closed
the case and gestured to the Jackal to lock it again. Then he chalked all
four cases in quick succession. His job done, the Italian's face broke into
a smile.

'Grazie, signor. A 'appy holiday.'

The porter found a taxi, was well tipped, and soon the Jackal was
speeding into Milan, its usually clamorous streets made even noisier by
the streams of commuter traffic trying to get home and the hooter-con-
scious behaviour of the drivers. He asked to be taken to the Central
Station.

Here another porter was summoned, and he hobbled after the man to
the left-luggage office. In the taxi he had slipped the steel shears out of
the overnight case into his trouser pocket. At the left-luggage office he
deposited the hand-grip and two suitcases, retaining the one containing
the long French military overcoat, which also had plenty of spare room.

Dismissing the porter he hobbled into the men's toilet, to find only one
of the washbasins in the long row on the left-hand side of the urinals was
in use. He dropped the case and laboriously washed his hands until the
other occupant was finished. When the toilet was empty for a second he
was across the room and locked into one of the cubicles.

With his foot up on the lavatory seat he clipped silently for ten
minutes at the plaster on his foot until it began to drop away, revealing
the cotton-wool pads beneath that had given the foot the bulk of a normally fractured ankle encased in plaster.

When the foot was finally clear of the last remnants of plaster he put
back on the silk sock and the slim leather moccasin which had been
taped to the inside of his calf while the foot had been in plaster. The
remainder of the plaster and cotton wool he gathered up and deposited
down the pan. At the first flushing half of it jammed, but it cleared at the
second.

Laying the suitcase on top of the toilet, he laid the series of circular
steel tubes containing the rifle side by side among the folds of the coat
until the case was full. When the inside straps were tight the contents of
the case were prevented from banging about. Then he closed the case and
cast a look outside the door. There were two people at the washbasins
and two more standing at the urinals. He left the cubicle, turned sharply
towards the door and was up the steps into the main hall of the station
before any had time to notice him, even if they had wished to.

He could not go back to the left-luggage office a fit and healthy man so soon after leaving it as a cripple, so he summoned a porter, explained that he was in a hurry, wished to change money, reclaim his baggage and get a taxi as soon as possible. The baggage check he thrust into the porter's hand, along with a thousand-lire note, pointing the man towards the left-luggage office. He himself, he indicated, would be in the bureau de change getting his English pounds changed into lire.

The Italian nodded happily and went off to get the luggage. The Jackal changed the last twenty pounds that remained to him into Italian currency, and was just finished when the porter returned with the other three pieces of luggage. Two minutes later he was in a taxi speeding dangerously across the Piazza Duca d'Aosta and heading for the Hotel Continentale.

At the reception desk in the splendid front hall he told the clerk:

'I believe you have a room for me in the name of Duggan. It was booked by telephone from London two days ago.'

Just before eight the Jackal was enjoying the luxury of a shower and shave in his room. Two of the suitcases were carefully locked into the wardrobe. The third, containing his own clothes, was open on the bed and the suit for the evening, a navy-blue wool-and-mohair summer lightweight, was hanging from the wardrobe door. The dove-grey suit was in the hands of the hotel's valet service for sponging and pressing. Ahead lay cocktails, dinner and an early night, for the next day, August 13th, would be extremely busy.

13

'Nothing.'

The second of the two young detective inspectors in Bryn Thomas's office closed the last of the folders he had been allotted to read and looked across at his superior.

His colleague had also finished, and his conclusion had been the same. Thomas himself had finished five minutes before and had walked over to the window, standing with his back to the room and staring at the traffic flowing past in the dusk. Unlike Assistant Commissioner Mallinson, he did not have a view of the river, just a first-floor vista of the cars churning down Horseferry Road. He felt like death. His throat was raw from cigarettes, which he knew he should not have been smoking with a heavy cold, but could not give up, particularly when under pressure.

His head ached from the fumes, the incessant calls that had been made throughout the afternoon checking on characters turned up in the records and files. Each call-back had been negative. Either the man was fully accounted for, or simply not of the calibre to undertake a mission like killing the French President.

'Right, that's it, then,' he said firmly, spinning round from the window. 'We've done all we can, and there just isn't anybody who could possibly fit the guide-lines laid down in the request we have been investigating.'

'It could be that there is an Englishman who does this kind of work,' suggested one of the inspectors. 'But he's not on our files.'

'They're all on our files, look you,' growled Thomas. It did not amuse him to think that as interesting a fish as a professional assassin existed in his 'manor' without being on file somewhere, and his temper was not improved by the cold or his headache. When ill-tempered his Welsh accent tended to intensify. Thirty years away from the valley had never quite eradicated the lilt.

'After all,' said the other inspector, 'a political killer is an extremely rare bird. There probably isn't such a thing in this country. It's not quite the English cup of tea, is it?'

Thomas glowered back. He preferred the word British to describe the inhabitants of the United Kingdom, and the inspector's inadvertent use of the word English he suspected might be a veiled suggestion that the Welsh, Scottish or Irish could well have produced such a man. But it wasn't.

'All right, pack up the files. Take them back to registry. I'll reply that a thorough search has revealed no such character known to us. That's all we can do.'

'Who was the enquiry from, Super?' asked one.

'Never you mind, boy. Someone's got problems by the look of it, but it isn't us.'

The two younger men had gathered up all the material and headed for the door. Both had families to get home to, and one was expecting to become a first-time father almost any day. He was the first to the door. The other turned back with a thoughtful frown.

'Super, there's one thing occurred to me while I was checking. If there is such a man, and he's got British nationality, it seems he probably wouldn't operate here anyway. I mean, even a man like this has to have a base somewhere. A refuge, sort of, a place to come back to. Chances are such a man is a respectable citizen in his own country.'

'What are you getting at, a sort of Jekyll and Hyde?'

'Well, something like that. I mean, if there is a professional killer about of the type we've been trying to track, and he's big enough for somebody to pull the kind of weight to get an investigation like this started, with a man of your rank leading it, well the man in question must be big. And if he's that, in his field, he must have a few jobs behind him. Otherwise he wouldn't be anything, would he?'

'Go on,' said Thomas, watching him carefully.

'Well, I just thought that a man like that would probably operate only outside his own country. So he wouldn't normally come to the attention of the internal security forces. Perhaps the Service might have got wind of him once....'

Thomas considered the idea, then slowly shook his head. 'Forget it, get on home, boy. I'll write the report. And just forget we ever made the enquiry.'

But when the inspector was gone the idea he had sown remained in Thomas's mind. He could sit down and write the report now. Completely negative. Drawn a blank. There could be no comebacks on the basis of the search of records that had been made. But supposing there was something behind the enquiry from France? Supposing the French had not, as Thomas suspected they had, simply lost their heads over a rumour concerning their precious President? If they really had as little to go on as they claimed, if there was no indication that the man was an Englishman, then they must be checking all over the world in a similar way. Chances were heavily odds-on there was no killer, and if there were, that he came from one of those nations with long histories of political assassinations. But what if the French suspicions were accurate? And if the man turned out to be English, even by birth alone?

Thomas was intensely proud of the record of Scotland Yard, and particularly of the Special Branch. They had never had trouble of this kind. They had never lost a visiting foreign dignitary, never even a smell of scandal. He personally had even had to look after that little Russian bastard, Ivan Serov, head of the KGB, when he came to prepare for Khrushchev's visit, and there had been scores of Balts and Poles who wanted to get Serov. Not even a shooting, and the place crawling with Serov's own security men, every one packing a gun and quite prepared to use it.

Superintendent Bryn Thomas had two years to go before retirement and the journey back to the little house he and Meg had bought looking out over the green turf to the Bristol Channel. Better be safe, check everything.

In his youth Thomas had been a very fine rugby player, and there were many who had played against Glamorgan who remembered clearly the inadvisability of making a blindside break when Bryn Thomas was wing forward. He was too old for it now, of course, but he still took a keen interest in the London Welsh when he could get away from work and go down to the Old Deer Park at Richmond to see them play. He knew all the players well, spending time in the club house chatting with them after a match, and his reputation was enough to ensure that he was always welcome.

One of the players was known to the rest of the members simply to be on the staff of the Foreign Office. Thomas knew he was a bit more than that; the department, under the auspices of the Foreign Secretary but not attached to the Foreign Office, for which Barrie Lloyd worked was the Secret Intelligence Service, sometimes called the SIS, sometimes simply 'The Service' and more usually among the public by its incorrect name of MI-6.

Thomas lifted the telephone on his desk and asked for a number....

The two men met for a drink in a quiet pub down by the river between eight and nine. They talked rugby for a while, as Thomas bought the drinks. But Lloyd guessed the man from Special Branch had not asked to see him at a riverside pub to talk about a game for which the season would not start for another two months. When they had both got their drinks, and given each other a perfunctory 'Cheers', Thomas gestured with his head outside on to the terrace that led down to the wharf. It was quieter outside, for most of the young couples from Chelsea and Fulham were drinking up and heading off for dinner.

'Got a bit of a problem, boyo,' began Thomas. 'Hoped you might be able to help.'

'Well ... if I can,' said Lloyd.

Thomas explained about the request from Paris, and the blank drawn by Criminal Records and the Special Branch.

'It occurred to me that if there ever was such a man, and a British one at that, he might be the kind who would never get his hands dirty inside this country, see. Might just stick to operations abroad. If he ever had left a trail, maybe he came to the attention of the Service?'

'Service?' asked Lloyd quietly.

'Come on, Barrie. We have to know a lot of things, from time to time.' Thomas's voice was hardly above a murmur. From the back they looked like two men in dark suits staring out over the dusky river at the lights of the south bank, talking of the day's dealings in the City. 'We had to turn over a lot of files during the Blake investigations. A lot of Foreign Office people got a peek taken at what they were really up to. Yours was one, see. You were in his section at the time he came under suss. So I know what department you work with.'

'I see,' said Lloyd.

'Now look, I may be Bryn Thomas down at the Park. But I'm also a superintendent of the SB, right? You can't all be anonymous from everyone, now can you?'

Lloyd stared into his glass.

'Is this an official enquiry for information?'

'No, I can't make it that yet. The French request was an unofficial request from Lebel to Mallinson. He could find nothing in Central Records, so he replied that he couldn't help, but he also had a word with Dixon. Who asked me to have a quick check. All on the quiet, see? Sometimes things have to be done that way. Very delicate, all this. Mustn't get out to the Press or anything. Chances are there's nothing here in Britain at all that might help Lebel. I just thought I'd cover all the angles, and you were the last.'

'This man is supposed to be after De Gaulle?'

'Must be, by the sound of the enquiry. But the French must be playing it very cagey. They obviously don't want any publicity.'

'Obviously. But why not contact us direct?'

'The request for suggestions as to a name has been put through on the old boy network. From Lebel to Mallinson, direct. Perhaps the French Secret Service doesn't have an old boy network with your section.'

If Lloyd had noticed the reference to the notoriously bad relations between the SDECE and the SIS, he gave no sign of it.

'What are you thinking?' asked Thomas after a while.

'Funny,' said Lloyd staring out over the river. 'You remember the Philby case?'

'Of course.'

'Still a very sore nerve in our section,' resumed Lloyd. 'He went over from Beirut in January '61. Of course, it didn't get out until later, but it caused a hell of a rumpus inside the Service. A lot of people got moved around. Had to be done, he had blown most of the Arab Section and some others as well. One of the men who had to be moved very fast was our top resident in the Caribbean. He had been with Philby in Beirut six months before, then transferred to Carib.

'About the same time the dictator of the Dominican Republic, Trujillo, was assassinated on a lonely road outside Ciudad Trujillo. According to the reports he was killed by partisans – he had a lot of enemies. Our man came back to London then, and we shared an office for a while until he was re-deployed. He mentioned a rumour that Trujillo's car was stopped, for the ambushers to blow it open and kill the man inside, by a single shot from a marksman with a rifle. It was a hell of a shot – from one hundred and fifty yards at a speeding car. Went through the little triangular window on the driver's side, the one that wasn't of bullet-proof glass. The whole car was armoured. Hit the driver through the throat and he crashed. That was when the partisans closed in. The odd thing was, rumour had it the shooter was an Englishman.'

There was a long pause as the two men, the empty beer mugs swinging from their fingers, stared across the now quite darkened waters of the Thames. Both had a mental picture of a harsh, arid landscape in a hot and distant island; of a car careering at seventy miles an hour off a bitumen strip and into the rocky verge; of an old man in fawn twill and gold braid, who had ruled his kingdom with an iron and ruthless hand for thirty years, being dragged from the wreck to be finished off with pistols in the dust by the roadside.

'This . . . man . . . in the rumour. Did he have a name?'

'I don't know. I don't remember. It was just talk in the office at the time. We had an awful lot on our plate then, and a Caribbean dictator was the last thing we needed to worry about.'

'This colleague, the one who talked to you. Did he write a report?'

'Must have done. Standard practice. But it was just a rumour, understand. Just a rumour. Nothing to go on. We deal in facts, solid information.'

'But it must have been filed, somewhere?'

'Suppose so,' said Lloyd. 'Very low priority, only a bar rumour in that area. Place abounds in rumours.'

'But you could just have a look back at the files, like? See if the man on the mountain had a name?'

Lloyd pulled himself off the rail.

'You get on home,' he said to the Superintendent. 'I'll ring you if there's anything that might help.'

They walked back into the rear bar of the pub, deposited the glasses, and made for the street door.

'I'd be grateful,' said Thomas as they shook hands. 'Probably nothing in it. But just on the off-chance.'

While Thomas and Lloyd were talking above the waters of the Thames, and the Jackal was scooping the last drops of his Zabaglione from the glass in a roof-top restaurant in Milan, Commissaire Claude Lebel attended the first of the progress report meetings in the conference room of the Interior Ministry in Paris.

The attendance was the same as it had been twenty-four hours earlier. The Interior Minister sat at the head of the table, with the department heads down each side. Claude Lebel sat at the other end with a small folder in front of him. The Minister nodded curtly for the meeting to begin.

His chef de cabinet spoke first. Over the previous day and night, he said, every Customs officer on every border post in France had received instructions to check through the luggage of tall blond male foreigners entering France. Passports particularly were to be checked, and were to be scrutinised by the DST official at the Customs post for possible forgeries. (The head of the DST inclined his head in acknowledgement.) Tourists and business men entering France might well remark a sudden increase in vigilance at Customs, but it was felt unlikely that any victim of such a baggage search would realise it was being applied across the country to tall blond men. If any enquiries were made by a sharp-eyed Press man, the explanation would be that they were nothing but routine snap searches. But it was felt no enquiry would ever be made.

He had one other thing to report. A proposal had been made that the possibility be considered of making a snatch on one of the three OAS chiefs in Rome. The Quai d'Orsay had come out strongly against such an idea for diplomatic reasons (they had not been told of the Jackal plot) and they were being backed in this by the President (who was aware of the reason). This must therefore be discounted as a way out of their difficulties.

General Guibaud for the SDECE said a complete check of their records had failed to reveal knowledge of the existence of a professional political killer outside the ranks of the OAS or its sympathisers, and who could not be completely accounted for.

The head of Renseignements Généraux said a search through France's criminal archives had revealed the same thing, not only among Frenchmen but also among foreigners who had ever tried to operate inside France.

The chief of the DST then made his report. At 7.30 that morning a call had been intercepted from a post office near the Gare du Nord to the number of the Rome hotel where the three OAS chiefs were staying. Since their appearance there eight weeks before, operators on the international switchboard had been instructed to report all calls placed to that number. The one on duty that morning had been slow on the uptake. The call had been placed before he had realised that the number was the one on his list. He had put the call through, and only then rung the DST. However, he had had the sense to listen in. The message had been: 'Valmy to Poitiers. The Jackal is blown. Repeat. The Jackal is blown. Kowalski was taken. Sang before dying. Ends.'

There was silence in the room for several seconds.

'How did they find out?' asked Lebel quietly from the far end of the table. All eyes turned on him, except those of Colonel Rolland who was staring at the opposite wall deep in thought.

'Damn,' he said clearly, still staring at the wall. The eyes swivelled back to the head of the Action Service.

The Colonel snapped out of his reverie.

'Marseilles,' he said shortly. 'To get Kowalski to come from Rome we used a bait. An old friend called JoJo Grzybowski. The man has a wife and daughter. We kept them all in protective custody until Kowalski was in our hands. Then we allowed them to return home. All I wanted from Kowalski was information about his chiefs. There was no reason to suspect this Jackal plot at the time. There was no reason why they should not know we had got Kowalski – then. Later of course things changed. It must have been the Pole JoJo who tipped off the agent Valmy. Sorry.'

'Did the DST pick Valmy up in the post office?' asked Lebel.

'No, we missed him by a couple of minutes, thanks to the stupidity of the operator,' replied the man from DST.

'A positive chapter of inefficiency,' snapped Colonel Saint-Clair suddenly. A number of unfriendly glances were levelled at him.

'We are feeling our way, largely in the dark, against an unknown adversary,' replied General Guibaud. 'If the Colonel would like to volunteer to take over the operation, and all the responsibility it implies . . .'

The Colonel from the Elysée Palace studiously examined his folders as if they were more important and of greater consequence than the veiled threat from the head of the SDECE. But he realised it had not been a wise remark.

'In a way,' mused the Minister, 'it might be as well they know their hired gun is blown. Surely they must call the operation off now?'

'Precisely,' said Saint-Clair, trying to recoup, 'the Minister is right. They would be crazy to go ahead now. They'll simply call the man off.'

'He isn't exactly blown,' said Lebel quietly. They had almost forgotten he was there. 'We still don't know the man's name. The forewarning might simply cause him to take extra contingency precautions. False papers, physical disguises . . .'

The optimism to which the Minister's remark had given birth round the table vanished. Roger Frey eyed the little Commissaire with respect.

'I think we had better have Commissaire Lebel's report, gentlemen. After all, he is heading this enquiry. We are here to assist him where we can.'

Thus prompted, Lebel outlined the measures he had taken since the previous evening; the growing belief, supported by the check through the French files, that the foreigner could only be on the files of some foreign police force, if at all. The request to make enquiries abroad; request granted. The series of person-to-person phone calls via Interpol to police chiefs of seven major countries.

'The replies came in during the course of today,' he concluded. 'Here they are: Holland, nothing. Italy, several known contract-hire killers, but all in the employ of the Mafia. Discreet enquiries between the Carabinieri and the Capo of Rome elicited a pledge that no Mafia killer would ever do a political killing except on orders, and the Mafia would not subscribe to killing a foreign statesman.' Lebel looked up. 'Personally, I am inclined to believe that is probably true.

'Britain. Nothing, but routine enquiries have been passed to another department, the Special Branch, for further checking.'

'Slow as always,' muttered Saint-Clair under his breath. Lebel caught the remark and looked up again.

'But very thorough, our English friends. Do not under-estimate Scotland Yard.' He resumed reading.

'America. Two possibles. One the right-hand man of a big international arms dealer based in Miami, Florida. This man was formerly a US Marine, later a CIA man in the Caribbean. Fired for killing a Cuban anti-Castroist in a fight just before the Bay of Pigs affair. The Cuban was to have commanded a section of that operation. The American then was taken on by the arms dealer, one of the men the CIA had unofficially used to supply arms to the Bay of Pigs invading force. Believed to have been responsible for two unexplained accidents that happened later to rivals of his employer in the arms business. Arms dealing, it seems, is a very cut-throat business. The man's name is Charles "Chuck" Arnold. The FBI is now checking for his whereabouts.

'The second man suggested by FBI as a possible. Marco Vitellino, formerly personal bodyguard to a New York gangland boss, Albert Anastasia. This Capo was shot to death in a barber's chair in October '57 and Vitellino fled America in fear of his own life. Settled in Caracas, Venezuela. Tried to go into the rackets there on his own account, but with little success. He was frozen out by the local underworld. FBI think that if he was completely broke he might be in the market for a contract killing job for a foreign organisation, if the price were right.'

There was complete silence in the room. The fourteen other men listened without a murmur.

'Belgium. One possibility. Psychopathic homicide, formerly on the staff of Tschombe in Katanga. Expelled by United Nations when captured in 1962. Unable to return to Belgium because of pending charges on two counts of murder. A hired gun, but a clever one. Name of Jules Bérenger. Believed also emigrated to Central America. Belgian police are still checking on his possible present whereabouts.

'Germany. One suggestion. Hans-Dieter Kassel, former SS-Major, wanted by two countries for war crimes. Lived after the war in West Germany under an assumed name, and was a contact-killer for ODESSA, the ex-SS members' underground organisation. Suspected of being implicated in the killing of two left-wing Socialists in post-war politics who were urging a government-sponsored intensification of enquiries into war crimes. Later unmasked as Kassel, but skipped to Spain after a tip-off for which a senior police official lost his job. Believed now living in retirement in Madrid. . . .'

Lebel looked up again. 'Incidentally, this man's age seems to be a bit advanced for this sort of job. He is now fifty-seven.

'Lastly, South Africa. One possible. Professional mercenary. Name: Piet Schuyper. Also one of Tschombe's top gunmen. Nothing officially against him in South Africa, but he's considered undesirable. A crack shot, and a definite penchant for individual killing. Last heard of when expelled from the Congo on the collapse of the Katangese secession early this year. Believed to be still in West Africa somewhere. The South African Special Branch is checking further.'

He stopped and looked up. The fourteen men round the table were looking back at him without expression.

'Of course,' said Lebel deprecatingly, 'it's very vague, I'm afraid. For one thing I only tried the seven most likely countries. The Jackal could be a Swiss, or Austrian, or something else. Then three countries out of seven replied that they have no suggestion to make. They could be wrong. The Jackal could be an Italian, or Dutchman or English. Or he could be South African, Belgian, German or American, but not among those listed. One doesn't know. One is feeling in the dark, hoping for a break.'

'Mere hoping isn't going to get us far,' snapped Saint-Clair.

'Perhaps the Colonel has a fresh suggestion?' enquired Lebel politely.

'Personally, I feel the man has certainly been warned off,' said Saint-Clair icily. 'He could never get near the President now that his plan has been exposed. However much Rodin and his henchmen have promised to pay this Jackal, they will ask for their money back and cancel the operation.'

'You *feel* the man has been warned off,' interposed Lebel softly, 'but feeling is not far from hoping. I would prefer to continue enquiries for the present.'

'What is the position of these enquiries now, Commissaire?' asked the Minister.

'Already, Minister, the police forces who have made these suggestions are beginning to send by telex the complete dossiers. I expect to have the last by noon tomorrow. Pictures will also come by wire. Some of the police forces are continuing enquiries to try and pin the whereabouts of the suspect down, so that we can take over.'

'Do you think they will keep their mouths shut?' asked Sanguinetti.

'There's no reason for them not to,' replied Lebel. 'Hundreds of highly confidential enquiries are made each year by senior policemen of the Interpol countries, some of them on an unofficial person-to-person basis. Fortunately all countries, whatever their political outlook, are opposed to crime. So we are not involved in the same rivalries as the more political branches of international relations. Co-operation among police forces is very good.'

'Even for political crime?' asked Frey.

'For policemen, Minister, it's all crime. That is why I preferred to contact my foreign colleagues rather than enquire through foreign ministries. Doubtless the superiors of these colleagues must learn that the enquiry was made, but there would be no good reason for them to make mischief. The political assassin is the world's outlaw.'

'But so long as they know the enquiry was made, they can work out the implications and still privately sneer at our President,' snapped Saint-Clair.

'I do not see why they should do that. It might be one of them, one day,' said Lebel.

'You do not know much about politics if you are not aware how some people would be delighted to know a killer is after the President of France,' replied Saint-Clair. 'This public knowledge is precisely what the President was so anxious to avoid.'

'It is not public knowledge,' corrected Lebel. 'It is extremely private knowledge, confined to a tiny handful of men who carry in their heads secrets that, if revealed, might well ruin half the politicians of their own countries. Some of these men know most of the inner details of installations that protect Western security. They have to, in order to protect them. If they were not discreet, they would not hold the jobs they do.'

'Better a few men should know we are looking for a killer than they should receive invitations to attend the President's funeral,' growled Bouvier. 'We've been fighting the OAS for two years. The President's instructions were that it must not become a press sensation and public talking point.'

'Gentlemen, gentlemen,' interposed the Minister. 'Enough of this. It was I who authorised Commissaire Lebel to make discreet enquiries among the heads of foreign police services, after . . .' he glanced at Saint-Clair . . . 'consulting with the President.'

The general amusement at the Colonel's discomfiture was ill-concealed.

'Is there anything else?' asked M. Frey.

Rolland raised a hand briefly.

'We have a permanent bureau in Madrid,' he said. 'There are a number of refugee OAS in Spain, that's why we keep it there. We could check on the Nazi, Kassel, without bothering the West Germans about it. I understand our relations with the Bonn Foreign Office are still not of the best.'

His reference to the Argoud snatch of February and the consequent anger of Bonn brought a few smiles. Frey raised his eyebrows at Lebel.

'Thank you,' said the detective, 'that would be most helpful, if you could pin the man down. For the rest there is nothing, except to ask that all departments continue to assist me as they have been doing over the past twenty-four hours.'

'Then until tomorrow, gentlemen,' said the Minister briskly and rose, gathering his papers. The meeting broke up.

Outside on the steps, Lebel gratefully drew in a lungful of the mild night air of Paris. The clocks struck twelve and ushered in Tuesday, August 13th.

It was just after twelve when Barrie Lloyd rang Superintendent Thomas at his home in Chiswick. Thomas was just about to put the bedside light out, thinking the SIS man would ring in the morning.

'I found the flimsy of the report we were talking about,' said Lloyd. 'I was right in a way. It was just a routine report of a rumour running round the island at the time. Marked "No action to be taken" almost as soon as it was filed. Like I said, we were pretty tied up with other things at that time.'

'Was any name mentioned?' asked Thomas quietly, so as not to disturb his wife who was asleep.

'Yes, a British business man on the island, who disappeared around that time. He might have had nothing to do with it, but his name was linked in the gossip. Name of Charles Calthrop.'

'Thanks, Barrie. I'll follow it in the morning.' He put the phone down and went to sleep.

Lloyd, being a meticulous young man, made a brief report of the request and his reply to it, and despatched it to Requirements. In the small hours the night duty man on requirements examined it quizzically for a moment, and as it concerned Paris, put it in the pouch for the Foreign Office's France Desk, the entire pouch to be delivered personally according to routine to Head of France when he came in later the same morning.

14

The Jackal rose at his habitual hour of 7.30, drank the tea placed by his bedside, washed, showered and shaved. Once dressed, he took the wad of one thousand pounds from inside the lining of his suitcase, slipped it into his breast pocket and went down for breakfast. At nine o'clock he was on the pavement of the Via Manzoni outside the hotel, and striding down the road looking for banks. For two hours he went from one to another, changing the English pounds. Two hundred were changed into Italian lire and the remaining eight hundred into French francs.

By mid-morning he was finished with his task, and broke for a cup of Espresso on a café terrace. After that he set out on his second search. After numerous enquiries he found himself in one of the back streets off the Porta Garibaldi, a working-class area near the Garibaldi Station. Here he found what he was looking for, a row of lock-up garages. One of these he hired from the proprietor who ran the garage on the corner of the street. The hire charge for two days was ten thousand lire, well above the odds but then it was a very short let.

In a local hardware store he bought a set of overalls, a pair of metal clippers, several yards of thin steel wire, a soldering iron and a foot of solder rod. These he packed into a canvas grip bought at the same store, and deposited the grip in the garage. Pocketing the key, he went off for lunch at a trattoria in the more fashionable centre of the city.

In the early afternoon, after making an appointment by phone from the trattoria, he arrived by taxi at a small and not-too-prosperous car-hire firm. Here he hired a second-hand 1962 vintage Alfa Romeo sports two-seater. He explained that he wished to tour Italy for the forthcoming fortnight, the length of his holiday in Italy, and return the car at the end of that time.

His passport and British and international driving licences were in order, and insurance was arranged within the hour from a nearby firm which habitually handled the business of the hire-car firm. The deposit was heavy, the equivalent to over a hundred pounds, but by the mid-afternoon the car was his, the keys in the ignition, and the proprietor of the firm wishing him a happy holiday.

Previous enquiries with the Automobile Association in London had assured him that as both France and Italy were members of the Common Market, there were no complicated formalities for driving an Italian-registered car into France, provided the driving licences, car registration hire documents and insurance cover were in order.

From a personal enquiry at the reception desk of the Automobil Club Italiano on the Corso Venezia he was given the name of a highly respectable insurance firm close by, which specialised in offering motor insurance cover for travel in foreign countries. Here he paid cash for extra insurance cover for an expedition into France. This firm, he was assured, enjoyed a mutual relationship with a large French insurance company, and their cover would be accepted without question.

From here he drove the Alfa back to the Continentale, parked it in the hotel car-park, went up to his room and retrieved the suitcase containing the component parts of the sniper's rifle. Shortly after teatime he was back in the mews street where he had hired the lock-up garage.

With the door safely shut behind him, the cable from the soldering iron plugged into the overhead light socket, and a high-powered torch lying on the floor beside him to illuminate the underside of the car, he went to work. For two hours he carefully welded the thin steel tubes that contained the rifle parts into the inner flange of the Alfa's chassis. One of the reasons for choosing an Alfa had been because a search through motor magazines in London had taught him that among Italian cars the Alfa possessed a stout steel chassis with a deep flange on the inner side.

The tubes themselves were each wrapped in a thin sock of sacking material. The steel wire lashed them tightly inside the flange, and the places where the wire touched the chassis' edge were spot-welded with the soldering iron.

By the time he was finished the overalls were smeared with grease from the garage floor and his hands ached from the exertions of heaving the wire tighter round the chassis. But the job was done. The tubes were almost undetectable except to a close search made from underneath the car, and would soon be coated with dust and mud.

He packed the overalls, soldering iron and the remains of the wire into the canvas grip and dumped it under a pile of old rags in the far corner of the garage. The metal clippers went into the glove compartment set in the dashboard.

Dusk was settling again over the city when he finally emerged at the wheel of the Alfa, the suitcase shut into the boot. He closed and locked the garage door, pocketed the key and drove back to the hotel.

Twenty-four hours after his arrival in Milan he was again in his room, showering away the exertions of the day, soaking his smarting hands in a bowl of cold water, before dressing for cocktails and dinner.

Stopping at the reception desk before going into the bar for his habitual Campari and soda, he asked for his bill to be made up for settlement after dinner, and for a morning call with a cup of tea at five-thirty the following morning.

After a second splendid dinner he settled the bill with the remainder of his lire and was in bed asleep by shortly after eleven.

Sir Jasper Quigley stood with his back to the office, hands clasped behind him, and stared down from the windows of the Foreign Office across the immaculate acres of Horse Guards Parade. A column of Household Cavalry in impeccable order trotted across the gravel towards the Annexe and the Mall and on in the direction of Buckingham Palace.

It was a scene to delight and to impress. On many mornings Sir Jasper had stood at his window and gazed down from the ministry at this most English of English spectacles. Often it seemed to him that just to stand at this window and see the Blues ride by, the sun shine and the tourists crane, to hear across the square the clink of harness and bit, the snort of a mettled horse and the oooohs and aahs of the hoi-polloi was worth all those years in embassies in other and lesser lands. It was rare for him that, watching this sight, he did not feel his shoulders square a little squarer, the stomach draw in a trifle under the striped trousers, and a touch of pride lift the chin to iron out the wrinkles of the neck. Sometimes, hearing the crunch of the hooves on gravel, he would rise from his desk just to stand at the neo-Gothic window and see them pass, before returning to the papers or the business of the state. And sometimes, thinking back on all those who had tried from across the sea to change this scene and supplant the jingle of the spurs with the tramp of brodequins from Paris or jackboots from Berlin, he felt a little pricking behind the eyes and would hurry back to his papers.

But not this morning. This morning he glowered down like an avenging acid drop and his lips were pressed so tightly together that, never full or rosy, they had disappeared completely. Sir Jasper Quigley was in a towering rage, and by a small sign here and there it showed. He was, of course, alone.

He was also the Head of France, not in the literal sense of possessing any jurisdiction over the country across the Channel towards friendship with whom so much lip-service had been paid and so little felt during his lifetime, but head of the bureau in the Foreign Office whose business it was to study the affairs, ambitions, activities and, often, conspiracies of that confounded place and then report upon them to the Permanent Under Secretary and, ultimately, to Her Majesty's Secretary of State for Foreign Affairs.

He possessed, or he would not have got the appointment, all the essential requirements: a long and distinguished record of service in diplomacy elsewhere than France, a history of soundness in his political judgements which, although frequently wrong, were inevitably in accord with those of his superiors of the given moment; a fine record and one of which to be justly proud. He had never been publicly wrong, nor inconveniently right, never supported an unfashionable viewpoint nor proffered opinions out of line with those prevailing at the highest levels of the Corps.

A marriage to the virtually unmarriageable daughter of the Head of Chancery in Berlin, who had later become an Assistant Deputy Under Secretary of State, had done no harm. It had enabled an unfortunate memorandum in 1937 from Berlin advising that German rearmament would have no real effect in political terms on the future of Western Europe to be overlooked.

During the war, back in London, he had been for a while on the Balkan Desk, and had forcefully counselled British support for the Yugoslav partisan Mikailovitch and his Cetniks. When the Prime Minister of the time had unaccountably preferred to listen to the advice of an obscure young Captain called Fitzroy MacLean who had parachuted into the place and who advised backing a wretched Communist called Tito, young Quigley had been transferred to France Desk.

Here he had distinguished himself by becoming a leading advocate of British support for General Giraud in Algiers. It was, or would have been, a jolly good policy too, had it not been out-manoeuvred by that other and less senior French general who had been living in London all the while trying to put together a force called the Free French. Why Winston ever bothered with the man was something none of the professionals could ever understand.

Not that any of the French were much use, of course. No one could ever say of Sir Jasper (knighted in '61 for his services to diplomacy) that he lacked the essential qualification for a good Head of France. He had a congenital dislike of France and everything to do with the place. These feelings had become, by the close of President de Gaulle's press conference of January 14th, 1963, in which he barred Britain from the Common Market and caused Sir Jasper to have an uncomfortable twenty minutes with the Minister, as nothing compared to his feelings towards the person of the French President.

There was a tap on his door. Sir Jasper swung away from the window. From the blotter in front of him he picked up a piece of blue flimsy paper and held it as though he had been reading it when the knock came.

'Enter.'

The younger man entered the office, closed the door behind him and approached the desk.

Sir Jasper glanced at him over the half-moon glasses.

'Ah, Lloyd. Just looking at this report you filed during the night. Interesting, interesting. An unofficial request lodged by a senior French police detective to a senior British police officer. Passed on to a senior superintendent of the Special Branch, who sees fit to consult, unofficially of course, a junior member of the Intelligence Service. Mmm?'

'Yes, Sir Jasper.'

Lloyd stared across at the spare figure of the diplomat standing by the window studying his report as if he had never seen it before. He had cottoned on at least that Sir Jasper was already well versed in the contents, and that the studied indifference was probably a pose.

'And this junior officer sees fit, off his own bat and without reference to higher authority, to assist the Special Branch officer by passing on to him a suggestion. A suggestion, moreover, that without a shred of proof indicates that a British citizen thought to be a business man may in fact be a cold-blooded killer. Mmmmm?'

What the hell's the old buzzard getting at? thought Lloyd.

He soon found out.

'What intrigues me, my dear Lloyd, is that although this request, unofficial of course, is lodged yesterday morning, it is not until twenty-four hours later that the head of the department of the ministry most closely concerned with what happens in France gets to be informed. Rather an odd state of affairs, wouldn't you say?'

Lloyd got the drift. Inter-departmental pique. But he was equally aware that Sir Jasper was a powerful man, versed over decades in the power struggle within the hierarchy into which its component members habitually put more effort than into state business.

'With the greatest respect, Sir Jasper, Superintendent Thomas' request to me, as you say an unofficial one, was made at nine last night. The report was filed at midnight.'

'True, true. But I notice his request was also complied with before midnight. Now can you tell me why that was?'

'I felt the request for guidance, or possible guidance as to a line of enquiry only, came within the scope of normal inter-departmental co-operation,' replied Lloyd.

'Did you now? Did you now?' Sir Jasper had dropped the pose of mild enquiry and some of his pique was coming through. 'But not apparently within the scope of inter-departmental co-operation between your service and the France Desk, mmm?'

'You have my report in your hand, Sir Jasper.'

'A bit late, sir. A bit late.'

Lloyd decided to riposte. He was aware that if he had committed any error in not consulting high authority before helping Thomas, it was his own chief he should have consulted, not Sir Jasper Quigley. And the head of the SIS was beloved by his staff and disliked by the mandarins of the FO for his refusal to allow anyone other than himself to rebuke his subordinates.

'Too late for what, Sir Jasper?'

Sir Jasper glanced up sharply. He was not going to fall into the trap of admitting it was too late to prevent the co-operation with Thomas' request from being fulfilled.

'You realise of course that a British citizen's name is concerned here. A man against whom there is not a shred of evidence, let alone proof. Don't you think it a rather odd procedure to bandy a man's name and, in view of the nature of the request, reputation about in this manner?'

'I hardly think divulging a man's name to a superintendent of the Special Branch simply as a possible line of enquiry can be described as bandying it about, Sir Jasper.'

The diplomat found his lips were pressed hard together as he sought to control his rage. Impertinent pup, but astute too. Needed watching very carefully. He took a grip on himself.

'I see, Lloyd. I see. In view of your evident desire to assist the Special Branch, a most laudable desire, of course, do you think it too much to expect you to consult a little before throwing yourself into the breach?'

'Are you asking, Sir Jasper, why you were not consulted?'

Sir Jasper saw red.

'Yes, sir, I am, sir. That is exactly what I am asking!'

'Sir Jasper, with the greatest of deference to your seniority, I feel I must draw your attention to the fact that I am on the staff of the Service. If you disagree with my course of conduct of last night I think it would be more seemly if your complaint went to my own superior officer rather than to me directly.'

Seemly? Seemly? Was this young upstart trying to tell a Head of France what was and was not seemly?

'And it shall, sir,' snapped Sir Jasper, 'and it shall. In the strongest terms.'

Without asking for permission, Lloyd turned and left the office. He had few doubts that he was in for a roasting from the Old Man, and all he could say in mitigation was that Bryn Thomas's request had seemed urgent, with time possibly a pressing matter. If the Old Man decided that the proper channels should have been gone through, then he, Lloyd, would have to take the rap. But at least he would take it from the OM and not from Quigley. Oh, damn Thomas.

However, Sir Jasper Quigley was very much in two minds whether to complain or not. Technically he was right, the information about Calthrop, although completely buried in long discarded files, should have been cleared with higher authority, but not necessarily with himself. As Head of France, he was one of the customers of SIS intelligence reporting, not one of the directors of it. He could complain to that cantankerous genius (not his choice of words) who ran the SIS and probably secure a good ticking off for Lloyd, possibly damage the brat's career. But he might also get a dose of the rough edge of the SIS chief's tongue for summoning an intelligence officer without asking *his* permission, and that thought did not amuse. Besides, the head of SIS was reputed to be extremely close to some of the men at the Very Top. Played cards with them at Blades; shot with them in Yorkshire. And the Glorious Twelfth was only a month away. He was still trying to get invited to some of those parties. Better leave it.

'The damage is done now, anyway,' he mused as he gazed out over Horse Guards Parade.

'The damage is done now anyway,' he remarked to his luncheon guest at his club just after one o'clock. 'I suppose they'll go right ahead and co-operate with the French. Hope they don't work too hard, what?'

It was a good joke and he enjoyed it very much. Unfortunately he had not fully estimated his lunch guest, who was also close to some of the men at the Very Top.

Almost simultaneously a personal report from the Commissioner of Metropolitan Police and news of Sir Jasper's little *bon mot* reached the Prime Minister's eyes and ears respectively just before four when he returned to 10 Downing Street after questions in the House.

At ten past four the phone in Superintendent Thomas's office rang.

Thomas had spent the morning and most of the afternoon trying to track down a man about whom he knew nothing but the name. As usual when enquiring into a man of whom it was definitely known that he had been abroad, the Passport Office in Petty France had been the starting point.

A personal visit there when they opened at nine in the morning had elicited from them photostat copies of application forms for passports from six separate Charles Calthrops. Unfortunately they all had middle names, and all were different. He had also secured the submitted photographs of each man, on a promise that they would be copied and returned to the Passport Office's archives.

One of the passports had been applied for since January 1961, but that did not necessarily mean anything, although it was significant that no records existed of a previous application by that Charles Calthrop before the one Thomas now possessed. If he had been using another name in Dominican Republic, how come the rumours that had later linked him with Trujillo's killing had mentioned him as Calthrop? Thomas was inclined to downgrade this late applicant for a passport.

Of the other five, one seemed too old; he was sixty-five by the August of 1963. The remaining four were possibles. It did not matter whether they tallied with Lebel's description of a tall blond, for Thomas's job was one of elimination. If all six could be eliminated from suspicion of being the Jackal, so much the better. He could advise Lebel accordingly with a clear conscience.

Each application form had an address, two in London and two in the provinces. It was not enough simply to ring up, ask for Mr Charles Calthrop and then ask if the man had been in Dominican Republic in 1961. Even if he had been there, he might well deny it now.

Nor were any of the four top-listed suspects marked down as 'business man' in the space for professional status. That too was not conclusive. Lloyd's report of a bar rumour at the time might call him a business man, but that could well be wrong.

During the morning the country and borough police, after a telephone request by Thomas, had traced the two provincial Calthrops. One was still at work, expecting to go on holiday with his family at the weekend. He was escorted home in the lunch-break and his passport was examined. It had no entry or exit visas or stamps for Dominican Republic in 1960 or 1961. It had only been used twice, once for Mallorca and once for the Costa Brava. Moreover, enquiries at his place of work had revealed that this particular Charles Calthrop had never left the accounts department of the soup factory where he worked during January 1961, and he had been on the staff for ten years.

The other outside London was traced to a hotel in Blackpool. Not having his passport on him, he was persuaded to authorise the police of his home town to borrow his house key off the next-door neighbour, go to the top drawer of his desk, and look at the passport. It too bore no Dominican police stamps, and at the man's place of work it was found he was a typewriter repair mechanic who also had not left his place of work in 1961 except for his summer holidays. His insurance cards and attendance records showed that.

Of the two Charles Calthrops in London one was discovered to be a greengrocer in Catford who was selling vegetables in his shop when the two quiet-spoken men in suits came to talk to him. As he lived above his own shop he was able to produce his passport within a few minutes. Like the others it gave no indication that the possessor had ever been to Dominican Republic. When asked, the greengrocer convinced the detectives that he did not even know where that island was.

The fourth and last Calthrop was proving more difficult. The address given in his application form for a passport four years previously was visited and turned out to be a block of flats in Highgate. The estate agents managing the block searched their records and revealed that he had left that address in December 1960. No forwarding address was known.

But at least Thomas knew his middle name. A search of the telephone directory revealed nothing, but using the authority of Special Branch Thomas learned from the General Post Office that one C. H. Calthrop had an ex-directory number in West London. The initials tallied with the names of the missing Calthrop – Charles Harold. From there Thomas checked with the registration department of the borough in which the telephone number was listed.

Yes, the voice from the borough hall told him, a Mr Charles Harold Calthrop was indeed the tenant of the flat at that address, and was listed on the electoral roll as a voter of that borough.

At this point a visit was made to the flat. It was locked and there was no reply to the repeated rings on the bell. Nobody else in the block seemed to know where Mr Calthrop was. When the squad car returned to Scotland Yard, Superintendent Thomas tried a new tack. The Inland Revenue was asked to check their records for the tax returns of one Charles Harold Calthrop, private address given. Particular point of interest – who employed him, and who had been employing him over the past three years?

It was at this point that the phone rang. Thomas picked it up, identified himself, and listened for a few seconds. His eyebrows lifted.

'Me?' he asked. 'What, personally? Yes, of course, I'll come over. Give me five minutes? Fine, see you.'

He left the building and walked across to Parliament Square, blowing his nose noisily to clear the blocked sinuses. Far from getting better, his cold seemed to be worse, despite the warm summer day.

From Parliament Square he headed up Whitehall and took the first left into Downing Street. As usual it was dark and gloomy, the sun never penetrating to the inconspicuous cul-de-sac that contains the residence of the Prime Ministers of Britain. There was a small crowd in front of the door of No. 10, kept on the far side of the road by two stolid policemen, perhaps just watching the stream of messengers arriving at the door with buff envelopes to deliver, perhaps hoping to catch a glimpse of an important visage at one of the windows.

Thomas left the roadway and cut to the right across a small courtyard enclosing a little lawn. His walk brought him to the back entrance of No. 10 where he pressed the buzzer beside the door. It opened immediately to reveal a large uniformed police sergeant, who recognised him at once and saluted.

' 'Afternoon, sir. Mr Harrowby asked me to show you to his room directly.'

James Harrowby, the man who had telephoned Thomas in his office a few minutes before, was the Prime Minister's personal security chief, a handsome man looking younger than his forty-one years. He wore a public-school tie, but had a brilliant career as a policeman behind him before he was transferred to Downing Street. Like Thomas, he had the rank of a superintendent. He rose as Thomas entered.

'Come in, Bryn. Nice to see you.' He nodded to the sergeant. 'Thank you, Chalmers.' The sergeant withdrew and closed the door.

'What's it all about?' asked Thomas. Harrowby looked at him with surprise.

'I was hoping you could tell me. He just rang fifteen minutes ago, mentioned you by name and said he wanted to see you personally and at once. Have you been up to something?'

Thomas could only think of one thing he had been up to, but he was surprised it had got so high in a short time. Still, if the PM did not wish to take his own security man into his confidence for once, that was his business.

'Not that I know of,' he said.

Harrowby lifted the telephone on his desk and asked for the Prime Minister's private office. The line crackled and a voice said 'Yes?'

'Harrowby here, Prime Minister. Superintendent Thomas is with me . . . yes, sir. Right away.' He replaced the receiver.

'Straight in. Almost on the double. You must have been up to something. There are two ministers waiting. Come on.'

Harrowby led the way out of his office and down a corridor towards a green baize door at the far end. A male secretary was coming out, saw the pair of them and stepped back, holding the door open. Harrowby ushered Thomas inside, said clearly, 'Superintendent Thomas, Prime Minister,' and withdrew, closing the door quietly behind him.

Thomas was aware of being in a very quiet room, high-ceilinged and elegantly furnished, untidy with books and papers, of a smell of pipe tobacco and wood-panelling, a room more like the study of a university don than the office of a Prime Minister.

The figure at the window turned round.

'Good afternoon, Superintendent. Please sit down.'

'Good afternoon, sir.' He chose an upright chair facing the desk and perched on the edge of it. He had never had occasion to see the Prime

Minister that close before, nor ever in private. He got the impression of a pair of sad, almost beaten, eyes, drooping lids, like a bloodhound who has run a long race and taken little joy from it.

There was silence in the room as the Prime Minister walked to his desk and sat behind it. Thomas had heard the rumours round Whitehall, of course, that the PM's health was not all it might be, and of the toll taken by the strain of bringing the Government through the rottenness of the Keeler/Ward affair, which had even then only just ended and was still number one talking point throughout the land. Even so, he was surprised at the look of exhaustion and sadness in the man opposite him.

'Superintendent Thomas, it has come to my attention that you are presently conducting an investigation based on a request for assistance telephoned from Paris yesterday morning by a senior detective of the French Police Judiciaire.'

'Yes, sir ... Prime Minister.'

'And that this request stems from a fear among the French security authorities that a man may be on the loose ... a professional assassin, hired, presumably by the OAS, to undertake a mission in France at some future time?'

'That was not actually explained to us, Prime Minister. The request was for suggestions as to the identity of any such professional assassin who might be known to us. There was no explanation as to why they wanted such suggestions.'

'Nevertheless, what do you deduce from the fact that such a request was made, Superintendent?'

Thomas shrugged slightly.

'The same as yourself, Prime Minister.'

'Precisely. One does not need to be a genius to be able to deduce the only possible reason for the French authorities wishing to identify such a ... specimen. And what would you deduce to be the eventual target of such a man, if indeed a man of this type has come to the attention of the French police?'

'Well, Prime Minister, I suppose they fear an assassin has been engaged to attempt to kill the President.'

'Precisely. Not the first time such an attempt would have been made?'

'No, sir. There have been six attempts already.'

The Prime Minister stared at the papers in front of him as if they might give him some clue as to what had happened to the world in the closing months of his premiership.

'Are you aware, Superintendent, that there apparently exist some persons in this country, persons occupying not obscure positions of authority, who would not be distressed if your investigations were to be less energetic than possible?'

Thomas was genuinely surprised.

'No, sir.' Where on earth had the PM got that titbit from?

'Would you please give me a résumé of the state of your enquiries up to the present time?'

Thomas began at the beginning, explained clearly and concisely the trail from Criminal Records to Special Branch, the conversation with Lloyd, the mention of a man called Calthrop, and the investigations that had taken place up to that moment.

When he had finished the Prime Minister rose and walked to the window, which gave on to the sunlit square of grass in the courtyard. For long minutes he stared down into the courtyard and there was a sag to the set of the shoulders. Thomas wondered what he was thinking.

Perhaps he was thinking of a beach outside Algiers where he had once walked and talked with the haughty Frenchman who now sat in another office three hundred miles away, governing the affairs of his own country. They had both been twenty years younger then, and a lot of things had not happened that were to come later, and a lot of things had not come between them.

Maybe he was thinking of the same Frenchman sitting in the gilded hall of the Elysée Palace eight months earlier destroying in measured and sonorous phrases the hopes of the British Premier of crowning his political career by bringing Britain into the European Community before retiring into the contentment of a man who has fulfilled his dream.

Or possibly he was just thinking of the past agonising months when the revelations of a pimp and a courtesan had almost brought down the Government of Britain. He was an old man, who had been born and brought up in a world that had its standards, for good or evil, and had believed in those standards and had followed them. Now the world was a different place, full of a new people with new ideas, and he was of the past. Did he understand that there were new standards now, which he could dimly recognise and did not like?

Probably he knew, looking down on to the sunny grass, what lay ahead. The surgical operation could not long be delayed, and with it retirement from the leadership. Before long the world would be handed over to the new people. Much of the world had already been handed over to them. But would it also be handed over to pimps and tarts, spies and . . . assassins?

From behind, Thomas saw the shoulders straighten, and the old man in front of him turned round.

'Superintendent Thomas, I wish you to know that General de Gaulle is my friend. If there is the remotest danger to his person, and if that danger could emanate from a citizen of these islands, then that person must be stopped. From now on you will conduct your investigations with unprecedented vigour. Within the hour your superiors will be authorised by me personally to accord you every facility within their powers. You will be subjected to no limits in either expenditure or manpower. You will have the authority to co-opt on to your team whomsoever you wish to assist you, and to have access to the official documentation of any department in the land which may be able to further your enquiries. You will, by my personal order, co-operate without any hint of reserve with the French authorities in this matter. Only when you are absolutely satisfied that whoever this man may be whom the French are seeking to identify and arrest, he is not a British subject, nor operating from these shores, may you desist from your enquiries. At that point you will report back to me in person.

'In the event that this man Calthrop, or any other man bearing a British passport, may reasonably be considered to be the man whom the French are seeking, you will detain this man. Whoever he is, he must be stopped. Do I make myself clear?'

It could not have been clearer. Thomas knew for certain that some piece of information had come to the PM's ears that had sparked off the instructions he had just given. Thomas suspected it had to do with the cryptic remark about certain persons who wished his investigations to make little progress. But he could not be sure.

'Yes, sir,' he said.

The PM inclined his head to indicate the interview was over. Thomas rose and went to the door.

'Er . . . Prime Minister.'

'Yes.'

'There is one point, sir. I am not certain whether you would wish me to tell the French yet about the enquiries into the rumour about this man Calthrop in Dominican Republic two years ago.'

'Do you have reasonable grounds to believe as of now that this man's past activities justify fitting him to the description of the man the French wish to identify?'

'No, Prime Minister. We have nothing against any Charles Calthrop in the world except the rumour of two years ago. We do not yet know whether the Calthrop we have spent the afternoon trying to trace is the one who was in the Caribbean in January 1961. If he is not, then we are back to square one.'

The Prime Minister thought for a few seconds.

'I would not wish you to waste your French colleague's time with suggestions based on unsubstantiated rumours two and a half years old. Note the word "unsubstantiated", Superintendent. Please continue your enquiries with energy. At the moment you feel there is enough information in your possession concerning this, or any other, Charles Calthrop, to add substance to the rumour that he was involved in the affair of General Trujillo, you will inform the French at once and at the same time track the man down, whatever he is.'

'Yes, Prime Minister.'

'And would you please ask Mr Harrowby to come to me. I shall issue the authorities you need at once.'

Back in Thomas's office things changed quickly through the rest of the afternoon. Round him he grouped a task force of six of the Special Branch's best detective inspectors. One was recalled from leave; two were taken off their duties watching the house of a man suspected to be passing classified information obtained from the Royal Ordnance Factory where he worked to an East European military attaché. Two of the others were the ones who had helped him the day before go through the records of the Special Branch looking for a killer who had no name. The last had been on his day off, and was gardening in his greenhouse when the call came through to report to the Branch headquarters immediately.

He briefed them all exhaustively, swore them to silence, and answered a continuous stream of phone calls. It was just after 6 p.m. when the Inland Revenue found the tax returns of Charles Harold Calthrop. One of the detectives was sent out to bring the whole file back. The rest went to work on the telephone, except one who was sent to Calthrop's address to seek out every neighbour and local tradesman for information as to where the man might be. Photographs taken from the one submitted by Calthrop on his application form for a passport four years previously were printed in the photographic laboratory, and every inspector had one in his pocket.

The tax returns of the wanted man showed that for the past year he had been unemployed, and before that had been abroad for a year. But for most of the financial year 1960–61 he had been in the employ of a firm whose name Thomas recognised as belonging to one of Britain's leading manufacturers and exporters of small arms. Within an hour he had the name of the firm's managing director, and found the man at home at his country house in the stockbroker belt of Surrey. By telephone Thomas made an appointment to see him immediately and as dusk descended on the Thames his police Jaguar roared over the river in the direction of the village of Virginia Water.

Patrick Monson hardly looked like a dealer in lethal weapons but then, Thomas reflected, they never do. From Monson, Thomas learned the arms firm had employed Calthrop for just under a year. More important, during December 1960 and January 1961 he had been sent by the firm to Ciudad Trujillo to try and sell a consignment of British Army surplus submachine guns to Trujillo's police chief.

Thomas eyed Monson with distaste.

And never mind what they later get used for, eh, boyo, he thought, but did not bother to voice his distaste. Why had Calthrop left Dominican Republic in such a hurry?

Monson seemed surprised by the question. Well, because Trujillo had been killed, of course. The whole regime fell within hours. What could be expected from the new regime by a man who had come to the island to sell the old regime a load of guns and ammunition? Of course he'd had to get out.

Thomas pondered. Certainly it made sense. Monson said Calthrop had later claimed he was actually sitting in the office of the dictator's police chief discussing the sale when the news came through that the General had been killed in an ambush outside the town. The Chief of Police had gone white, and left immediately for his private estate where his aircraft and pilot were permanently waiting for him. Within a few hours mobs were rampaging through the streets seeking adherents of the old regime. Calthrop had to bribe a fisherman to sail him out of the island.

Why, Thomas asked eventually, did Calthrop leave the firm? He was dismissed, was the answer. Why? Monson thought carefully for a few moments. Finally he said:

'Superintendent, the second-hand arms business is highly competitive. Cut-throat, you might say. To know what another man is offering for sale, and the price he is asking, can be vital for a rival wishing to clinch the same deal with the same buyer. Let us just say that we were not entirely satisfied with Calthrop's loyalty to the company.'

In the car back into town Thomas thought over what Monson had told him. Calthrop's explanation at the time as to why he had got out of Dominican Republic so fast was logical. It did not corroborate, indeed it tended to negate, the rumour subsequently reported by the Caribbean SIS resident that his name was linked with the killing.

On the other hand, according to Monson, Calthrop was a man who was not above playing a double cross. Could he have arrived as the accredited representative of a small-arms company wishing to make a sale, and at the same time have been in the pay of the revolutionaries?

There was one thing Monson had said that disturbed Thomas; he had mentioned that Calthrop did not know much about rifles when he joined the company. Surely a crack shot would be an expert? But then of course he could have learned that while with the company. But if he was a newcomer to rifle shooting, why did the anti-Trujillo partisans want to hire him to stop the General's car on a fast road with a single shot? Or did they not hire him at all? Was Calthrop's own story the literal truth?

Thomas shrugged. It didn't prove anything, nor disprove anything. Back to square one again, he thought bitterly.

But back at the office there was news that changed his mind. The inspector who had been enquiring at Calthrop's address had reported in. He had found a next-door neighbour who had been out at work all day. The woman said Mr Calthrop had left some days before and had mentioned he was going touring in Scotland. In the back of the car parked in the street outside the woman had seen what looked like a set of fishing rods.

Fishing rods? Superintendent Thomas felt suddenly chilly, although the office was warm. As the detective finished talking one of the others came in.

'Super?'

'Yes?'

'Something has just occurred to me.'

'Go on.'

'Do you speak French?'

'No, do you?'

'Yes, my mother was French. This assassin the PJ are looking for, he's got the code-name Jackal, right?'

'So what?'

'Well, Jackal in French is Chacal. C-H-A-C-A-L. See? It could just be a coincidence. He must be as thick as five posts to pick a name, even in French, that's made up of the first three letters of his Christian name and the first three letters of his . . .'

'Land of my bloody fathers,' said Thomas, and sneezed violently. Then he reached for the telephone.

15

The third meeting in the Interior Ministry in Paris began shortly after ten o'clock, due to the lateness of the Minister who had been held up in the traffic on his way back from a diplomatic reception. As soon as he was seated, he gestured for the meeting to start.

The first report was from General Guibaud of the SDECE. It was short and to the point. The ex-Nazi killer, Kassel, had been located by agents of the Madrid office of the Secret Service. He was living quietly in retirement at his roof-top flat in Madrid, had become a partner with another former SS-commando leader in a prosperous business in the city, and so far as could be determined was not involved with the OAS. The Madrid office had in any case had a file on the man by the time the request from Paris for a further check came through, and was of the view that he had never been involved with the OAS at all.

In view of his age, increasingly frequent bouts of rheumatism that were beginning to affect his legs, and a remarkably high alcohol intake, Kassel, in the general view, could be discounted as a possible Jackal.

As the General finished, eyes turned to Commissaire Lebel. His report was sombre. During the course of the day reports had come into the PJ from the other three countries who had originally suggested possible suspects twenty-four hours earlier.

From America had come news that Chuck Arnold, the gun salesman, was in Columbia trying to clinch a deal for his American employer to sell a consignment of ex-US Army surplus AR-10 assault rifles to the Chief of Staff. He was in any case under permanent CIA surveillance while in Bogota, and there was no indication that he was planning anything other than to put through his arms deal, despite official US disapproval.

The file on this man had, however, been telexed to Paris, as had also the file on Vitellino. This showed that although the former Cosa Nostra gunman had not yet been located, he was five feet four inches tall, immensely broad and squat, with jet-black hair and a swarthy complexion. In view of the radical difference in appearance from the Jackal as described by the hotel clerk in Vienna, Lebel felt he too could be discounted.

The South Africans had learned Piet Schuyper was now the head of a private army of a diamond-mining corporation in a West African country of the British Commonwealth. His duties were to patrol the borders of the vast mining concessions owned by the company and ensure a continuous disincentive to illicit diamond poachers from across the border. No inconvenient questions were asked of him as to the methods he used to discourage poaching, and his employers were pleased with his efforts. His presence was confirmed by his employers; he was definitely at his post in West Africa.

The Belgian police had checked on their ex-mercenary. A report in the files from one of their Caribbean embassies had been unearthed, which reported the former employee of Katanga had been killed in a bar fight in Guatemala three months previously.

Lebel finished reading the last of the reports from the file in front of him. When he looked up it was to find fourteen pairs of eyes on him, most of them cold and challenging.

'Alors, rien?'

The question from Colonel Rolland was that of everyone present.

'No, nothing, I'm afraid,' agreed Lebel. 'None of the suggestions seem to stand up.'

'Seem to stand up,' echoed Saint-Clair bitterly. 'Is that what we have come to with your "pure detective work"? Nothing seems to stand up?' He glared angrily at the two detectives, Bouvier and Lebel, quickly aware that the mood of the room was with him.

'It would seem, gentlemen,' the Minister quietly used the plural form to take in both the police commissaires, 'that we are back where we started. Square one, so to speak?'

'Yes, I'm afraid so,' replied Lebel. Bouvier took up the cudgels on his behalf.

'My colleague is searching, virtually without clues and without any sort of lead, for one of the most elusive types of men in the world. Such specimens do not advertise their professions or their whereabouts.'

'We are aware of that, my dear commissaire,' retorted the Minister, coldly, 'the question is . . .'

He was interrupted by a knock on the door. The Minister frowned; his instructions had been that they were not to be disturbed except in an emergency.

'Come in.'

One of the ministry's porters stood in the doorway, diffident and abashed.

'Mes excuses, Monsieur le Ministre. A telephone call for Commissaire Lebel. From London.' Feeling the hostility of the room, the man tried to cover himself. 'They say it is urgent. . . .'

Lebel rose.

'Would you excuse me, gentlemen?'

He returned in five minutes. The atmosphere was as cold as when he had left it, and evidently the wrangle over what to do next had continued in his absence. As he entered he interrupted a bitter denunciation from Colonel Saint-Clair, who tailed off as Lebel took his seat. The little commissaire had an envelope in his hand with scribbled writing on the back.

'I think, gentlemen, we have the name of the man we are looking for,' he began.

The meeting ended thirty minutes later almost in a mood of levity. When Lebel had finished his relation of the message from London, the men round the table had let out a collective sigh, like a train arriving at its platform after a long journey. Each man knew that at last there was something he could do. Within half an hour they had agreed that without a word of publicity it would be possible to scour France for a man in the name of Charles Calthrop, to find him and, if deemed necessary, to dispose of him.

The fullest known details of Calthrop, they knew, would not be available until the morning, when they would be telexed from London. But in the meantime Renseignements Généraux could check their miles of shelves for a disembarkation card filled in by this man, for a hotel card registering him at a hotel anywhere in France. The Prefecture of Police could check its own records to see if he was staying at any hotel within the confines of Paris.

The DST could put his name and description into the hands of every border post, port, harbour and airfield in France, with instructions that such a man was to be held immediately on his touching on French territory.

If he had not yet arrived in France, no matter. Complete silence would be maintained until he arrived, and when he did, they would have him.

'This odious creature, the man they call Calthrop, we have him already in the bag,' Colonel Raoul Saint-Clair de Villauban told his mistress that night as they lay in bed.

When Jacqueline finally coaxed a belated orgasm from the Colonel to send him to sleep the mantelpiece clock chimed twelve and it had become August 14th.

Superintendent Thomas sat back in his office chair and surveyed the six inspectors whom he had regrouped from their various tasks after putting down the phone following the call to Paris. Outside in the still summer night Big Ben tolled midnight.

His briefing took an hour. One man was allocated to examine Calthrop's youth, where his parents now lived, if indeed he had any; where he had been to school; shooting record, if any, in the cadet corps as a schoolboy. Noticeable characteristics, distinguishing marks, etc.

A second was designated to investigate his young manhood, from school leaving, through National Service, record of service and prowess at shooting, employment following discharge from the Army, right up to the time he left the employ of the arms dealers who had dismissed him for suspected double-dealing.

The third and fourth detectives were put on the trail of his activities since leaving his last known employers in October 1961. Where had he been, whom had he seen, what had been his income, from what sources; since there was no police record and therefore presumably no finger-prints, Thomas needed every known and latest photograph of the man, up to the present time.

The last two inspectors were to seek to establish the whereabouts of Calthrop at that moment. Go over the entire flat for fingerprints, find where he bought the car, check at County Hall, London, for records of issue of a driving licence, and if there were none start checking with the provincial county licensing departments. Trace the car, make, age and colour, registration number. Trace his local garage to see if he was plan-ning a long journey by car, check the cross-Channel ferries, go round all the airline companies for a booking on a plane, no matter what the destination.

All six men took extensive notes. Only when he had finished did they rise and file out of the office. In the corridor the last two eyed each other askance.

'Dry-clean and re-texture,' said one. 'The complete bloody works.'

'The funny thing is,' observed the other, 'that the old man won't tell us what he's supposed to have done, or be going to do.'

'One thing we can be sure of. To get this kind of action, it must have come down right from the top. You'd think the bugger was planning to shoot the King of Siam.'

It took a short while to wake up a magistrate and get him to sign a search warrant. By the small hours of the morning, while an exhausted Thomas dozed in the armchair of his office and an even more haggard Claude Lebel sipped strong black coffee in his office, two Special Branch men went through Calthrop's flat with a fine tooth comb.

Both were experts. They started with the drawers, emptying each one systematically into a bedsheet and sorting the contents diligently. When all the drawers were clean, they started on the woodwork of the draw-erless desk for secret panels. After the wooden furniture came the up-holstered pieces. When they had finished with these the flat looked like a turkey farm on Thanksgiving Day. One man was working over the draw-ing-room, the other the bedroom. After these two came the kitchen and bathroom.

With the furniture, cushions, pillows and coats and suits in the cup-boards dealt with, they started on the floors, ceilings and walls. By six in the morning the flat was as clean as a whistle. Most of the neighbours were grouped on the landing looking at each other and then the closed door of Calthrop's flat, conversing in whispers that hushed when the two inspectors emerged from the flat.

One was carrying a suitcase stuffed with Calthrop's personal papers, and private belongings. He went down to the street, jumped into the waiting squad car and drove back to Superintendent Thomas. The other started on the long round of interviews. He began with the neighbours, aware that most would have to head for their places of work within an hour or two. The local tradesmen could come later.

Thomas spent several minutes riffling through the collection of possessions spread all over his office floor. Out of the jumble the detective inspector grabbed a small blue book, walked to the window and started to flick through it by the light of the rising sun.

'Super, have a look at this.' His finger jabbed at one of the pages in the passport in front of him. 'See ... "*Republica de Dominica, Aeroporto Ciudad Trujillo, Decembre 1960, Entrada* ..." He was there all right. This is our man.'

Thomas took the passport from him, glanced at it for a moment, then stared out of the window.

'Oh yes, this is our man, boyo. But does it not occur to you that we're holding his passport in our hands?'

'Oh, the sod ...' breathed the inspector when he saw the point.

'As you say,' said Thomas, whose chapel upbringing caused him only very occasionally to use strong language. 'If he's not travelling on this passport, then what is he travelling on? Give me the phone, and get me Paris.'

By the same hour the Jackal had already been on the road for fifty minutes and the city of Milan lay far behind him. The hood of the Alfa was down and the morning sun already bathed the Autostrada 7 from Milan to Genoa. Along the wide straight road he pushed the car well over eighty miles an hour and kept the tachometer needle flickering just below the start of the red band. The cool wind lashed his pale hair into a frenzy around the forehead, but the eyes were protected by the dark glasses.

The road map said it was two hundred and ten kilometres to the French frontier at Ventimiglia, about a hundred and thirty miles, and he was well up on his estimated driving time of two hours. There was a slight hold-up among the lorry traffic of Genoa as it headed for the docks just after seven o'clock, but before 7.15 he was away on the A.10 to San Remo and the border.

The daily road traffic was already thick when he arrived at ten to eight at the sleepiest of France's frontier points, and the heat was rising.

After a thirty-minute wait in the queue he was beckoned up to the parking ramp for Customs examination. The policeman who took his passport examined it carefully, muttered a brief '*Un moment, monsieur*' and disappeared inside the Customs shed.

He emerged a few minutes later with a man in civilian clothes who held the passport.

'*Bonjour, monsieur.*'

'*Bonjour.*'

'This is your passport?'

'Yes.'

There was another searching examination of the passport.

'What is the purpose of your visit to France?'

'Tourism. I have never seen the Côte d'Azur.'

'I see. The car is yours?'

'No. It's a hired car. I had business in Italy, and it has unexpectedly occasioned a week with nothing to do before returning to Milan. So I hired a car to do a little touring.'

'I see. You have the papers for the car?'

The Jackal extended the international driving licence, the contract of hire, and the two insurance certificates. The plain-clothes man examined both.

'You have luggage, monsieur?'

'Yes, three pieces in the boot, and a hand-grip.'

'Please bring them all into the Customs hall.'

He walked away. The policeman helped the Jackal off-load the three suitcases and the hand-grip, and together they carried them to Customs.

Before leaving Milan he had taken the old greatcoat, scruffy trousers and shoes of André Martin, the non-existent Frenchman whose papers were sewn into the lining of the third suitcase, and rolled them in a ball at the back of the boot. The clothes from the other two suitcases had been divided between the three. The medals were in his pocket.

Two Customs officers examined each case. While they were doing so he filled in the standard form for tourists entering France. Nothing in the cases excited any attention. There was a brief moment of anxiety as the Customs men picked up the jars containing the hair-tinting dyes. He had taken the precaution of emptying them into after-shave flasks, previously emptied. At that time after-shave lotion was not in vogue in France, it was too new on the market and mainly confined to America. He saw the two Customs men exchange glances, but they replaced the flasks in the hand-grip.

Out of the corner of his eye he could see through the windows another man examining the boot and engine bonnet of the Alfa. Fortunately he did not look underneath. He unrolled the greatcoat and trousers in the boot and looked at them with distaste, but presumed the coat was for covering the bonnet on winter nights and old clothes were a contingency in case repairs had to be done on the car along the road. He replaced the clothes and closed the boot.

As the Jackal finished filling in his form, the two Customs men inside the shed closed the cases and nodded to the plain-clothes man. He in turn took the entry card, examined it, checked it again with the passport, and handed the passport back.

'Merci, monsieur. Bon voyage.'

Ten minutes later the Alfa was booming into the eastern outskirts of Menton. After a relaxed breakfast at a café overlooking the old port and yacht basin, the Jackal headed along the Corniche Littorale for Monaco, Nice and Cannes.

In his London office Superintendent Thomas stirred a cup of thick black coffee and ran a hand over his stubbled chin. Across the room the two inspectors saddled with the task of finding the whereabouts of Calthrop faced their chief. The three were waiting for the arrival of six extra men, all sergeants of the Special Branch released from their routine duties as the result of a string of telephone calls Thomas had been making over the previous hour.

Shortly after nine, as they reported to their offices and learned of their re-deployment to Thomas's force, the men started to trickle in. When the last had arrived he briefed them.

'All right, we're looking for a man. There's no need for me to tell you why we want him, it's not important that you should know. What is important is that we get him, and get him fast. Now we know, or think we know, that he's abroad at this moment. We are pretty certain he is travelling under a false passport.

'Here . . .' he passed out among them a set of photographs, blown-up copies of the portrait photo on Calthrop's passport application form . . . 'is what he looks like. The chances are he will have disguised himself and therefore not necessarily respond to that description. What you are going to have to do is go down to the Passport Office and get a complete list of every application for a passport made recently. Start by covering the last fifty days. If that yields nothing, go back another fifty days. It's going to be a hard grind.'

He continued by giving a rough description of the most common way of getting a false passport, which was in fact the method the Jackal had used.

'The important thing is,' he concluded, 'not to be content with birth certificates. Check the death certificates. So after you've got the list from Passport Office, take the whole operation down to Somerset House, get settled in, divide the list of names among yourselves, and get to work among those death certificates. If you can find one application for a passport submitted by a man who isn't alive any longer, the impostor will probably be our man. Off you go.'

The eight men filed out, while Thomas got on to the Passport Office by phone, then the Registry of Births, Marriages and Deaths at Somerset House, to ensure that his team would get the fullest co-operation.

It was two hours later as he was shaving on a borrowed electric razor plugged into his desk lamp that the senior of the two inspectors, who was the leader of the team, phoned back. There were, he said, eight thousand and forty-one applications for new passports submitted in the previous hundred days. It was the summer, he explained, holiday time. There were always more in holiday time.

Bryn Thomas hung up and snuffled into his handkerchief.

'Damn summer,' he said.

Just after eleven that morning the Jackal rolled into the centre of Cannes. As usual when he wanted something done, he looked for one of the best hotels, and after a few minutes' cruising swept into the fore-court of the Majestic. Running a comb through his hair, he strode into the foyer.

Being the middle of the morning, most of the guests were out and the hall was not busy. His elegant light suit and confident manner picked him out as an English gentleman and raised no eyebrows when he asked a bell-hop where the telephone booths were. The lady behind the counter that separated the switchboard from the entry to the cloakrooms looked up as he approached.

'Please get me Paris, MOLITOR 5901,' he asked.

A few minutes later she gestured him to a booth beside the switchboard and watched him close the sound-proof door behind him.

'Allo, ici Chacal.'

'Allo, ici Valmy. Thank God you've rung. We've been trying to get hold of you for two days.'

Anyone looking through the glass panel of the booth's door would have seen the Englishman inside stiffen and frown at the mouthpiece. For most of the ten-minute conversation he remained silent, listening. Occasionally his lips moved as he asked a short, terse question. But nobody was looking; the switchboard operator was busy in a romantic novel. The next thing she saw was the guest towering over her, the dark glasses staring down. From the meter on the switchboard she read off the charge for the call, and was paid.

The Jackal took a pot of coffee on the terrace looking over the Croisette and the glittering sea where brown bathers romped and screamed. Deep in thought, he drew heavily on a cigarette.

The bit about Kowalski he could follow; he remembered the hulking Pole from the hotel in Vienna. What he could not follow was how the bodyguard outside the door had known his code-name, or what he had been hired to do. Perhaps the French police had worked that out for themselves. Perhaps Kowalski had sensed what he was, for he also had been a killer, but oafish and clumsy.

The Jackal took stock. Valmy had advised him to quit and go home, but had admitted he had no direct authority from Rodin to cancel the operation. What had happened confirmed the Jackal's intense suspicions of the security slackness of the OAS. But he knew something that they did not; and something that the French police could not know. It was that he was travelling under an assumed name with a legitimate passport in that name, and three separate sets of false papers, including two foreign passports and disguises to match, up his sleeve.

Just what did the French police, this man Valmy had mentioned, Commissaire Lebel, have to go on? A rough description, tall, blond, foreign. There must be thousands of such men staying in France in August. They could not arrest every one.

The second advantage he had was that the French police were hunting for a man carrying the passport of Charles Calthrop. Then let them, and good luck. He was Alexander Duggan, and could prove it.

From here on, with Kowalski dead, nobody, not even Rodin and his henchmen, knew who he was or where. He was on his own at last, and that was the way he had always wanted it to be.

Nevertheless, the dangers had increased, there was no doubt of it. With the idea of an assassination once revealed, he would be attacking a fortress of security that was on its guard. The question was: could his plan for carrying out the killing beat the security screen? On balance, he was confident that it could.

The question still remained, and it had to be answered. To go back, or to go on? To go back would be to enter into dispute with Rodin and his bunch of thugs over the ownership of the quarter million dollars presently in his account in Zürich. If he refused to hand the bulk of it back they would not hesitate to track him down, torture him for the signed paper that would release the money from the account, then kill him. To stay ahead of them would cost money, a lot of it, probably the full extent of the money he possessed.

To go on would mean further dangers until the job was over. It would become ever harder to pull back at the last minute as the day approached.

The bill came, he glanced at it and winced. God, the prices these people charged! To live this kind of life a man needed to be rich, to have dollars, and dollars and even more dollars. He looked out at the jewelled sea and the lithe brown girls walking along the beach, the hissing Cadillacs and snarling Jaguars that crept along the Croisette, their bronzed young drivers keeping half an eye on the road and the other flicking across the pavements for a likely pick-up. This was what he had wanted for a long time, from the days when he had pressed his nose to the travel agent's windows and gazed at the posters showing another life, another world, far from the drudgery of the commuter train and the forms in triplicate, the paper clips and tepid tea. Over the past three years he had almost made it; a glimpse here, a touch there. He had got used to good clothes, expensive meals, a smart flat, a sports car, elegant women. To go back meant to give it all up.

The Jackal paid the bill and left a large tip. He climbed into the Alfa and headed away from the Majestic and into the heart of France.

Commissaire Lebel was sitting at his desk, feeling as though he had never slept in his life and probably never would again. In the corner Lucien Caron snored loudly on the camp-bed, having been up all night masterminding the search through the records for Charles Calthrop somewhere on the face of France. Lebel had taken over at dawn.

In front of him now was a growing pile of reports from the various agencies whose task it was to keep check on the presence and whereabouts of foreigners in France. Each one bore the same message. No man of that name had crossed any border point legally since the start of the year, the farthest back the checks had extended. No hotel in the country, either in the provinces or Paris, had taken in a guest of that name, at least, not under that name. He was not on any list of undesirable aliens, nor had he ever come to the notice of the French authorities in any way.

As each report came in, Lebel wearily told the informant to go on checking further and further back until any visit Calthrop had ever paid to France could be traced. From that, possibly, could be established whether he had a habitual place of residence, a friend's house, a favourite hotel, where he might even now be masquerading under an assumed name.

Superintendent Thomas's call of that morning had come as yet another blow to hopes of an early capture of the elusive killer. Once again the phrase 'back to square one' had been used, but fortunately this time it was only between Caron and himself. The members of the evening council had not yet been informed that the Calthrop lead was probably going to prove abortive. This was something he was going to have to tell them that evening at ten o'clock. If he could not produce an alternative name to Calthrop, he could imagine once again the scorn of Saint-Clair and the silent reproach of the rest.

Two things only could comfort him. One was that at least they now had a description of Calthrop and a photograph of his head and shoulders, full-face to the camera. He had probably changed his appearance considerably if he had taken a false passport, but still, it was better than nothing. The other thing was that no one else on the council could think of anything better to do than what he was doing – check everything.

Caron had put forward the idea that perhaps the British police had surprised Calthrop while he was away from his flat on an errand in the town; that he had no alternative passport; that he had gone to ground and cried off on the whole operation.

Lebel had sighed.

'That would indeed be lucky,' he told his adjutant, 'but don't count on it. The British Special Branch reported that all his washing things and shaving tackle were missing from the bathroom, and that he had mentioned to a neighbour that he was going away touring and fishing. If Calthrop left his passport behind, it was because he no longer needed it. Don't count on this man making too many errors; I'm beginning to get a feeling about the Jackal.'

The man the police of two countries were now searching for had decided to avoid the agonising congestion of the Grande Corniche on its murderous way from Cannes to Marseilles, and to stay away from the southern part of the RN7 when it turned north out of Marseilles for Paris. Both roads in August he knew to be a refined form of hell on earth.

Safe in his assumed and documented name of Duggan, he decided to drive leisurely up from the coast through the Alpes Maritimes where the air was cooler in the altitude, and on through the rolling hills of Burgundy. He was in no particular hurry, for the day he had set for his kill was not yet on him, and he knew he had arrived in France slightly ahead of schedule.

From Cannes he headed due north, taking the RN85 through the picturesque perfume town of Grasse and on towards Castellane where the turbulent Verdon river, tamed by the high dam a few miles upstream, flowed more obediently down from Savoy to join the Durance at Cadarache.

From here he pushed on to Barrême and the little spa town of Digne. The blazing heat of the Provençal plain had fallen away behind him, and the air of the hills was sweet and cool even in the heat. When he stopped he could feel the sun blazing down, but when motoring the wind was like a cooling shower and smelled of the pines and woodsmoke from the farms.

After Digne he crossed the Durance and ate lunch in a small but pretty hostelry looking down into the waters. In another hundred miles the Durance would become a a grey and slimy snake hissing shallow amid the sun-bleached shingle of its bed at Cavaillon and Plan d'Orgon. But here in the hills it was still a river, the way a river should look, a cool and fishful river with shade along its banks and grass growing all the greener for its presence.

In the afternoon he followed the long northward curving run of the RN85 through Sisteron, still following the Durance upstream on its left bank until the road forked and the RN85 headed towards the north. As dusk was falling he entered the little town of Gap. He could have gone on towards Grenoble, but decided that as there was no hurry and more chance of finding rooms in August in a small town, he should look around for a country-style hotel. Just out of town he found the brightly gabled Hôtel du Cerf, formerly a hunting lodge of one of the Dukes of Savoy, and still retaining an air of rustic comfort and good food.

There were several rooms still vacant. He had a leisurely bath, a break with his usual habit of showering, and dressed in his dove-grey suit with a silk shirt and knitted tie, while the room-maid, after receiving several winning smiles, had blushfully agreed to sponge and press the check suit he had worn all day so that he could have it back by morning.

The evening meal was taken in a panelled room overlooking a sweep of the wooded hillside, loud with the chatter of cicadas among the pinèdes. The air was warm and it was only halfway through the meal when one of the women diners, who wore a sleeveless dress and a de-colleté, commented to the maître d'hôtel that a chill had entered the air and asked that the windows be closed.

The Jackal turned round when he was asked if he objected to the window next to which he sat being closed, and glanced at the woman indicated by the maître as the person who had asked that they be shut. She was dining alone, a handsome woman in her late thirties with soft white arms and a deep bosom. The Jackal nodded to the maître to close the windows, and gave a slight inclination of the head to the woman behind him. She answered with a cool smile.

The meal was magnificent. He chose speckled river trout grilled on a wood fire, and tournedos broiled over charcoal with fennel and thyme. The wine was a local Côtes du Rhône, full, rich and in a bottle with no label. It had evidently come from the barrel in the cellar, the proprietor's personal choice for his vin de la maison. Most of the diners were having it, and with reason.

As he finished his sorbet he heard the low and authoritative voice of the woman behind him telling the maître that she would take her coffee in the residents' lounge, and the man bowed and addressed her as 'Madame la Baronne'. A few minutes later the Jackal had also ordered his coffee in the lounge, and headed that way.

The call from Somerset House came for Superintendent Thomas at a quarter past ten. He was sitting by the open window of the office staring down into the now silent street where no restaurants beckoned late diners and drivers into the area. The offices between Millbank and Smith Square were silent hulks, lightless, blind, uncaring. Only in the anonymous block that housed the offices of the Special Branch did the lights burn late as always.

A mile away, in the bustling Strand, the lights were also burning late in the section of Somerset House that housed the death certificates of millions of Britain's deceased citizens. Here Thomas's team of six detective sergeants and two inspectors were hunched over their piles of paper work, rising every few minutes to accompany one of the staff clerks, kept back at work long after the others had gone home, down the rows of gleaming files to check on yet another name.

It was the senior inspector in charge of the team who rang. His voice was tired, but with a touch of optimism, a man hoping that what he had to say would get them all released from the grind of checking hundreds of death certificates that did not exist because the passport holders were not dead.

'Alexander James Quentin Duggan,' he announced briefly, after Thomas had answered.

'What about him?' said Thomas.

'Born April 3rd, 1929, in Sambourne Fishley, in the parish of St Mark's. Applied for a passport in the normal way on the normal form on July 14th this year. Passport issued the following day and mailed July 17th to the address on the application form. It will probably turn out to be an accommodation address.'

'Why?' asked Thomas. He disliked being kept waiting.

'Because Alexander James Quentin Duggan was killed in a road accident in his home village at the age of two and a half, on November 8th, 1931.'

Thomas thought for a moment.

'How many more of the passports issued in the last hundred days remain to be checked?' he asked.

'About three hundred to go,' said the voice on the phone.

'Leave the others to continue checking the remainder, just in case there is another phoney among the bunch,' instructed Thomas. 'Hand over the team leadership to the other fellow. I want you to check out that address to which the passport was sent. Report back to me by phone the moment you have found it. If it's an occupied premises, interview the householder. Bring me back the full details on the phoney Duggan, and the file copy of the photograph he submitted with the application form. I want to have a look at this lad Calthrop in his new disguise.'

It was just before eleven that the senior inspector phoned back in. The address in question was a small tobacconist and newsagent shop in Paddington, the kind that had a window full of cards advertising the addresses of prostitutes. The owner, living above the shop, had been roused and had agreed he often took in mail for customers who had no fixed address. He made a charge for his services. He could not remember a regular customer named Duggan, but it could have been that Duggan only called twice, once to arrange for his mail to be received there, the second time to pick up the one envelope that he was waiting for. The inspector had showed the newsagent a photograph of Calthrop, but the man could not recognise him. He also showed him the photograph of Duggan on the application form, and the man said he thought he remembered the second man, but could not be sure. He felt the man might have worn dark glasses. Many of those who came into his shop to buy the erotic pin-up magazines displayed behind the counter wore dark glasses.

'Bring him in,' ordered Thomas, 'and get back here yourself.'

Then he picked up the phone and asked for Paris.

A second time, the call came halfway through the evening conference. Commissaire Lebel had explained that beyond a doubt Calthrop was not inside France under his own name, unless he had smuggled himself into the country in a fishing boat or across one of the land borders at an isolated spot. He personally did not think a professional would do that, because at any subsequent spot check by the police he could be caught for not having his papers in order, that is, having no entry stamp on his passport.

Nor had any Charles Calthrop checked into any French hotel in his own name.

These facts were corroborated by the head of the Central Records office, the head of the DST and the Prefect of Police of Paris, so they were not disputed.

The two alternatives, argued Lebel, were that the man had not made any provision for obtaining a false passport, and had thought he was unsuspected. In that case, the police raid on his flat in London must have caught him short. He explained that he did not believe this, as Superintendent Thomas's men had found gaps in the wardrobe and half-empty clothes drawers, and absence of washing accoutrements and shaving tackle, indicating that the man had left his London flat for planned absence elsewhere. This was borne out by a neighbour, who reported Calthrop as having said he was going touring by car in Scotland. Neither the British nor the French police had any reason to believe this was true.

The second alternative was that Calthrop had acquired a false passport, and this was what the British police were presently searching for. In that event, he might either still not be in France, but at some other place completing his preparations, or he might already have entered France unsuspected.

It was at this point that several of the conference members exploded.

'You mean he might be here, in France, even in the centre of Paris?' expostulated Alexandre Sanguinetti.

'The point is,' explained Lebel, 'that he has got his timetable, and only he knows it. We have been investigating for seventy-two hours. We have no way of knowing at which point in the man's timetable we have intervened. The one thing we can be sure of is, that apart from knowing we are aware of the existence of a plot to assassinate the President, the killer cannot know what progress we have made. Therefore we stand a reasonable chance of apprehending an unsuspecting man, as soon as we have him identified under his new name, and located under that name.'

But the meeting refused to be mollified. The thought that the killer might even then be within a mile of them, and that in that man's timetable the attempt on the life of the President might be for tomorrow, caused each of them acute anxiety.

'It could be, of course,' mused Colonel Rolland, 'that having learned from Rodin, through the unknown agent Valmy, that the plan was exposed in principle, that Calthrop then left his flat to dispose of the evidence of his preparations. His gun and ammunition, for example, could even now be tipped into a lake in Scotland, so that he can present himself to his own police on his return as clean as a whistle. In that event it would be very difficult to bring charges.'

The meeting thought over Rolland's suggestion, with increasing signs of agreement.

'Then tell us, Colonel,' said the Minister, 'if you had been hired for this job, and had learned that the plot was exposed, even if your own identity were still a secret, is that what you would do?'

'Certainly, Monsieur le Ministre,' replied Rolland. 'If I were an experienced assassin I would realise that I must be on some file somewhere, and with the plot exposed it could only be a matter of time before I received a visit from the police and a search of my premises. So I would want to get rid of the evidence, and what better place than an isolated Scottish lake.'

The round of smiles that greeted him from the table indicated how much those assembled approved of his speculation.

'However, that does not mean that we should just let him go. I still think we should . . . take care of this Monsieur Calthrop.'

The smiles vanished. There was silence for several seconds.

'I do not follow you, *mon colonel*,' said General Guibaud.

'Simply this,' explained Rolland. 'Our orders were to locate and destroy this man. He may have dismantled his plot for the moment. But he may not have destroyed his equipment, but merely hidden it, in order to pass the scrutiny of the British police. After that, he could simply take up again where he left off, but with a new set of preparations even more difficult to penetrate.'

'But surely, when the British police locate him, if he is still in Britain, they will detain him?' someone asked.

'Not necessarily. Indeed I doubt it. They will probably have no proof, only suspicions. And our friends the English are notoriously sensitive about what they are pleased to call "civil liberties". I suspect they may find him, interview him, and then let him go for lack of evidence.'

'Of course the Colonel is right,' interjected Saint-Clair. 'The British police have stumbled on this man by a fluke. They are incredibly foolish about things like leaving a dangerous man at liberty. Colonel Rolland's section should be authorised to render this man Calthrop harmless once and for all.'

The Minister noticed that Commissaire Lebel had remained silent and unsmiling through the interchange.

'Well, Commissaire, and what do you think? Do you agree with Colonel Rolland that Calthrop is even now dismantling and hiding, or destroying, his preparations and equipment?'

Lebel glanced up at the two rows of expectant faces on each side of him.

'I hope,' he said quietly, 'that the Colonel is right. But I fear he may not be.'

'Why?' The Minister's question cut like a knife.

'Because,' explained Lebel mildly, 'his theory, although logical if indeed Calthrop has decided to call off the operation, is based on the theory that he has indeed made that decision. Supposing he has not? Supposing he has either not received Rodin's message or received it but decided to press ahead nevertheless?'

There was a buzz of deprecatory consternation. Only Rolland did not join in. He gazed contemplatively down the table at Lebel. What he was thinking was that Lebel had a far better brain than anyone present seemed prepared to give him credit for. Lebel's ideas, he recognised, could well be as realistic as his own.

It was at this point that the call came through for Lebel. This time he was gone for over twenty minutes. When he came back he spoke to a completely silent assembly for a further ten minutes.

'What do we do now?' asked the Minister when he had finished. In his quiet way, without seeming to hurry, Lebel issued his orders like a general deploying his troops, and none of the men in the room, all senior to him in rank, disputed a word.

'So there we are,' he concluded, 'we will all conduct a quiet and discreet nation-wide search for Duggan in his new appearance, while the British police search the records of airline ticket offices, cross-Channel ferries, etc. If they locate him first, they pick him up if he is on British soil, or inform us if he has left it. If we locate him, inside France, we arrest him. If he is located in a third country, we can either wait for him to enter unsuspectingly and pick him up at the border, or ... take another course of action. At that moment, however, I think my task of finding him will have been achieved. However, until that moment, gentlemen, I would be grateful if you would agree to do this my way.'

The effrontery was so bold, the assurance so complete, that nobody would say a thing. They just nodded. Even Saint-Clair de Villauban was silent.

It was not until he was at home shortly after midnight that he found an audience to listen to his torrent of outrage at the thought of this ridiculous little bourgeois policeman having been right, while the top experts of the land had been wrong.

His mistress listened to him with sympathy and understanding, massaging the back of his neck as he lay face down on their bed. It was not until just before dawn, when he was sound asleep, that she could slip away to the hall and make a brief phone call.

Superintendent Thomas looked down at the two separate application forms for passports, and two photographs spread out on the blotter in the pool of light thrown by the reading lamp.

'Let's run through it again,' he ordered the senior inspector seated beside him. 'Ready?'

'Sir.'

'Calthrop: height, five feet eleven inches. Check?'

'Sir.'

'Duggan: height six feet.'

'Thickened heels, sir. You can raise your height up to two and a half inches with special shoes. A lot of short people in show business do it for vanity. Besides, at a passport counter no one looks at your feet.'

'All right, I'll wear that. Calthrop, colour of eyes, brown. Duggan, hair, brown. That doesn't mean much, it could vary from pale brown to chestnut brown. He looks to me here as if he had dark brown hair. Duggan also says, brown. But he looks like a pale blond.'

'That's true, sir. But hair habitually looks darker in photographs. It depends on the light, where it is placed and so forth. And then again, he could have tinted it paler to become Duggan.'

'All right, I'll wear that. Calthrop, colour of eyes, brown, Duggan, colour of eyes, grey.'

'Contact lenses, sir, it's a simple thing.'

'OK. Calthrop's age is thirty-seven, Duggan's is thirty-four last April.'

'He had to become thirty-four,' explained the inspector, 'because the real Duggan, the little boy who died at two and a half, was born in April 1929. That couldn't be changed. But nobody would query a man who happened to be thirty-seven but whose passport said he was thirty-four. One would believe the passport.'

Thomas looked at the two photographs. Calthrop looked heftier, fuller in the face, a more sturdily built man. But to become Duggan he could have changed his appearance. Indeed, he had probably changed it even for his first meeting with the OAS chiefs, and remained with changed appearance ever since, including the period when he applied for the false passport. Men like this evidently had to be able to live in a second identity for months at a time if they were to escape identification. It was probably by being this shrewd and painstaking that Calthrop had managed to stay off every police file in the world. If it had not been for that bar rumour in the Caribbean they would never have got him at all.

But from now on he had become Duggan, dyed hair, tinted contact lenses, slimmed-down figure, raised heels. It was the description of Duggan, with passport number and photograph, that he sent down to the telex room to be transmitted to Paris. Lebel, he estimated, glancing at his watch, should have them all by two in the morning.

'After that, it's up to them,' suggested the inspector.

'Oh, no, boyo, after that there's a lot more work to be done,' said Thomas maliciously. 'First thing in the morning we start checking the airline ticket offices, the cross-Channel ferries, the continental train ticket offices ... the whole lot. We not only have to find out who he is now, but where he is now.'

At that moment a call came through from Somerset House. The last of the passport applications had been checked, and all were in order.

'OK, thank the clerks and stand down. Eight-thirty sharp in my office, the lot of you,' said Thomas.

A sergeant entered with a copy of the statement of the newsagent, who had been taken to his local police station and interviewed there. Thomas glanced at the sworn statement, which said little more than he had told the Special Branch inspector on his own doorstep.

'There's nothing we can hold him on,' said Thomas. 'Tell them at Paddington nick they can let him go back to his bed and his dirty photos, will you?'

The sergeant said 'Sir,' and left.

Thomas settled back in the armchair to try to get some sleep.

While he had been talking it had quietly become August 15th.

16

Madame la Baronne de la Chalonnière paused at the door of her room and turned towards the young Englishman who had escorted her there. In the half-darkness of the corridor she could not make out the details of his face; it was just a blur in the gloom.

It had been a pleasant evening and she was still undecided whether she would or would not insist that it end at her doorway. The question had been at the back of her mind for the past hour.

On the one hand, although she had taken lovers before, she was a respectable married woman staying for a single night in a provincial hotel, and not in the habit of permitting herself to be seduced by total strangers. On the other hand she was at her most vulnerable, and was candid enough to admit it to herself.

She had spent the day at the military cadet academy at Barcelonette, high in the Alps, attending the passing-out parade of her son as a newly breveted second lieutenant in the Chasseurs Alpins, his father's old regiment. Although she had undoubtedly been the most attractive mother at the parade, the sight of her son receiving his officer's bars and commissioned into the French Army had brought home to her with something of a shock the full realisation that she was a few months short of forty, and the mother of a grown son.

Although she could pass for five years younger, and sometimes felt ten years less than her age, the knowledge that her son was twenty and probably screwing his own women by now, no more to come home for the school holidays and go shooting in the forests around the family château, had caused her to wonder what she was going to do now.

She had accepted the laborious gallantry of the creaking old colonel who was the academy commandant, and the admiring glances of the pink-cheeked class-mates of her own boy, and had felt suddenly very lonely. Her marriage, she had known for years, was finished in all but name, for the Baron was too busy chasing the teenage dollies of Paris between the Bilboquet and Castel's to come down to the château for the summer, or even to turn up at his son's commissioning.

It had occurred to her as she drove the family saloon back from the high Alps to stay overnight at a country hotel outside Gap that she was handsome, virile and alone. Nothing now seemed to lie in prospect but the attentions of elderly gallants like the colonel at the academy, or frivolous and unsatisfying flirtations with boys, and she was damned if she was going to devote herself to charitable works. Not yet, at any rate.

But Paris was an embarrassment and a humiliation, with Alfred constantly chasing his teenagers and half society laughing at him and the other half laughing at her.

She had been wondering about the future over coffee in the lounge, and feeling an urge to be told she was a woman and a beautiful one, and not simply Madame la Baronne, when the Englishman had walked across and asked if, as they were alone in the residents' salon, he might take his coffee with her. She had been caught unawares, and too surprised to say no.

She could have kicked herself a few seconds later, but after ten minutes she did not regret accepting his offer. He was, after all, between thirty-three and thirty-five, or so she estimated, and that was the best age for a man. Although he was English, he spoke fluent and rapid French; he was reasonably good-looking, and could be amusing. She had enjoyed the deft compliments, and had even encouraged him to pay them, so that it was close to midnight when she rose, explaining that she had to make an early start the following morning.

He had escorted her up the stairs and at the landing window had pointed outside at the wooded hill slopes bathed in bright moonlight. They had stayed for a few moments looking at the sleeping countryside, until she had glanced at him and seen that his eyes were not on the view beyond the window but on the deep divide between her breasts where the moonlight turned the skin to alabaster white.

He had smiled when detected, and leaned to her ear and murmured, 'Moonlight turns even the most civilised man into a primitive.' She had turned and walked on up the stairs, feigning annoyance, but inside her the unabashed admiration of the stranger caused a flutter of pleasure.

'It has been a most pleasant evening, monsieur.'

She had her hand on the handle of the door, and wondered vaguely whether the man would try to kiss her. In a way she hoped he would. Despite the triteness of the words she could feel the hunger beginning in her belly. Perhaps it was just the wine, or the fiery Calvados he had ordered with the coffee, or the scene in the moonlight, but she was aware that this was not how she had foreseen the evening ending.

She felt the stranger's arms slip round her back, without a word of warning, and his lips came down on to hers. They were warm and firm. 'This must stop,' said a voice inside her. A second later she had responded to the kiss, mouth closed. The wine made her head swim, it must have been the effect of the wine. She felt the arms round her tighten perceptibly and they were hard and strong.

Her thigh was pressed against him below the belly and through the satin of her dress she felt the rigid arrogance of his prick. For a second she withdrew her leg, then pushed it back again. There was no conscious moment of decision-taking; the realisation came without effort that she wanted him badly, between her thighs, her belly, all night.

She felt the door behind her open inwards, broke the embrace and stepped backwards into her room.

'Viens, primitif.'

He stepped into the room and closed the door.

Throughout the night every archive in the Panthéon was checked again, this time for the name of Duggan, and with more success. A card was unearthed showing that Alexander James Quentin Duggan entered France on the Brabant Express from Brussels on July 22nd. An hour later another report from the same frontier post, the Customs unit that regularly travels on the express trains from Brussels to Paris and back, doing its task while the train is in motion, was found with Duggan's name among those passengers on the Etoile du Nord Express from Paris to Brussels on July 31st.

From the Prefecture of Police came a hotel card filled out in the name of Duggan, and quoting a passport number that matched the one Duggan was carrying, as contained in the information from London, showing that he had stayed in a small hotel near the Place de la Madeleine between July 22nd and 30th inclusive.

Inspector Caron was all for raiding the hotel, but Lebel preferred to pay a quiet visit in the small hours of the morning and had a chat with the proprietor. He was satisfied the man he sought was not at the hotel by August 15th, and the proprietor was grateful for the Commissaire's discretion in not waking all his guests.

Lebel ordered a plain-clothes detective to check into the hotel as a guest until further notice, and to stay there without moving outside, in case Duggan turned up again. The proprietor was happy to co-operate.

'This July visit,' Lebel told Caron when he was back in his office at 4.30, 'was a reconnaissance trip. Whatever he has got planned, it's all laid on.'

Then he lay back in his chair, gazed at the ceiling, and thought. Why did he stay in a hotel? Why not in the house of one of the OAS sympathisers, like all the other OAS agents on the run? Because he does not trust the OAS sympathisers to keep their mouths shut. He's quite right. So he works alone, trusting nobody, plotting and planning his own operation in his own way, using a false passport, probably behaving normally, politely, raising no suspicion. The proprietor of the hotel whom he had just interviewed confirmed this. 'A real gentleman,' he had said. A real gentleman, thought Lebel, and dangerous as a snake. They are always the worst kind, for a policeman, the real gentlemen. Nobody ever suspected them.

He glanced at the two photographs that had come in from London, of Calthrop and Duggan. Calthrop become Duggan, with a change of height, hair and eyes, age and, probably, manner. He tried to build up a mental image of the man. What would he be like to meet? Confident, arrogant, assured of his immunity. Dangerous, devious, meticulous, leaving nothing to chance. Armed of course, but with what? An automatic under the left armpit? A throwing knife lashed against the ribs? A rifle? But where would he put it when he went through Customs? How would he get near to General de Gaulle carrying such a thing, when even women's handbags were suspect within twenty yards of the President, and men with long packages were hustled away without ceremony from anywhere near a public appearance by the President?

Mon Dieu, and that colonel from the Elysée thinks he's just another thug! Lebel was aware he had one advantage: he knew the killer's new name, and the killer did not know that he knew. That was his only ace; apart from that it all lay with the Jackal, and nobody at the evening conference could or would realise it.

If he ever gets wind of what you know before you catch him, and changes his identity again, Claude my boy, he thought, you are going to be up against it in a big way.

Aloud, he said 'Really up against it.'

Caron looked up.

'You're right, chief. He hasn't a chance.'

Lebel was short-tempered with him, which was unusual. The lack of sleep must be beginning to tell.

The finger of light from the waning moon beyond the window panes withdrew slowly across the rumpled coverlet and back towards the casement. It picked out the rumpled satin dress between the door and the foot of the bed, the discarded brassière and limp nylons scattered on the carpet. The two figures on the bed were muffled in shadow.

Colette lay on her back and gazed up at the ceiling, the fingers of one hand running idly through the blond hair of the head pillowed on her belly. Her lips parted in a half-smile as she thought over the night.

He had been good, this English primitive, hard but skilled, knowing how to use fingers and tongue and prick to bring her on five times and himself three. She could still feel the blazing heat going into her when he came, and she knew how badly she had needed a night like this for so long when she responded as she had not for years.

She glanced at the small travelling clock beside the bed. It said a quarter past five. She tightened her grip in the blond hair and pulled.

'Hey.'

The Englishman muttered, half asleep. They were both lying naked among the disordered sheets, but the central heating kept the room comfortably warm. The blond head disengaged itself from her hand and slid between her thighs. She could feel the tickle of the hot breath and the tongue flickering in search again.

'No, no more.'

She closed her thighs quickly, sat up and grabbed the hair, raising his face until she could look at him. He eased himself up the bed, plunged his face on to one of her full heavy breasts and started to kiss.

'I said no.'

He looked up at her.

'That's enough, lover. I have to get up in two hours, and you have to go back to your room. Now, my little English, now.'

He got the message and nodded, swinging off the bed to stand on the floor, looking round for his clothes. She slid under the bedclothes, sorted them out from the mess around her knees and pulled them up to the chin. When he was dressed, with jacket and tie slung over one arm, he looked down at her in the half-darkness and she saw the gleam of teeth as he grinned. He sat on the edge of the bed and ran his right hand round to the back of her neck. His face was a few inches from hers.

'It was good?'

'Mmmmmm. It was very good. And you?'

He grinned again. 'What do you think?'

She laughed. 'What is your name?'

He thought for a moment. 'Alex,' he lied.

'Well, Alex, it was very good. But it is also time you went back to your own room.'

He bent down and gave her a kiss on the lips.

'In that case, good night, Colette.'

A second later he was gone, and the door closed behind him.

At seven in the morning, as the sun was rising, a local gendarme cycled up to the Hôtel du Cerf, dismounted and entered the lobby. The proprietor who was already up and busy behind the reception desk organising the morning calls and *café complet* for the guests in their rooms, greeted him.

'*Alors*, bright and early?'

'As usual,' said the gendarme. 'It's a long ride out here on a bicycle, and I always leave you till the last.'

'Don't tell me,' grinned the proprietor, 'we do the best breakfast coffee in the neighbourhood. Marie-Louise, bring Monsieur a cup of coffee, and no doubt he'll take it laced with a little Trou Normand.'

The country constable grinned with pleasure.

'Here are the cards,' said the proprietor, handing over the little white cards filled in the previous evening by the newly arrived guests. 'There were only three new ones last night.'

The constable took the cards and put them in the leather pouch in his belt.

'Hardly worth turning up for,' he grinned, but sat on the foyer bench and waited for his coffee and Calvados, exchanging a few words of lustful banter with Marie-Louise when she brought it.

It was not until eight that he got back to the gendarmerie and commissariat of Gap with his pouchful of hotel registration cards. These were then taken by the station inspector who flicked through them idly and put them in the rack, to be taken later in the day to the regional headquarters at Lyons, and later to the archives of Central Records in Paris. Not that he could see the point of it all.

As the inspector was dropping the cards into the rack in the commissariat, Madame Colette de la Chalonnière settled her bill, climbed behind the wheel of her car and drove off towards the west. One floor above, the Jackal slept on until nine o'clock.

Superintendent Thomas had dozed off when the phone beside him gave a shrill buzz. It was the intercom phone linking his office with the room down the corridor where the six sergeants and two inspectors had been working on a battery of telephones since his briefing had ended.

He glanced at his watch. Ten o'clock. Damn, not like me to drop off. Then he remembered how many hours' sleep he had had, or rather had not had, since Dixon had summoned him on Monday afternoon. And now it was Thursday morning. The phone buzzed again.

'Hallo.'

The voice of the senior detective inspector answered.

'Friend Duggan,' he began without preliminary. 'He left London on a scheduled BEA flight on Monday morning. The booking was taken on Saturday. No doubt about the name. Alexander Duggan. Paid cash at the airport for the ticket.'

'Where to? Paris?'

'No, Super. Brussels.'

Thomas's head cleared quickly.

'All right, listen. He may have gone but come back. Keep checking airline bookings to see if there have been any other bookings in his name. Particularly if there is a booking for a flight that has not left London. Check with advance bookings. If he came back from Brussels, I want to know. But I doubt it. I think we've lost him, although of course he left London several hours before investigations were started, so it's not our fault. OK?'

'Right. What about the search in the UK for the real Calthrop? It's tying up a lot of the provincial police, and the Yard's just been on to say that they're complaining.'

Thomas thought for a moment.

'Call it off,' he said. 'I'm pretty certain he's gone.'

He picked up the outside phone and asked for the office of Commissaire Lebel at the Police Judiciaire.

Inspector Caron thought he was going to end up in a lunatic asylum before Thursday morning was out. First the British were on the phone at five past ten. He took the call himself, but when Superintendent Thomas insisted on speaking to Lebel he went over to the corner to rouse the sleeping form on the camp-bed. Lebel looked as if he had died a week before. But he took the call. As soon as he had identified himself to Thomas, Caron had to take the receiver back because of the language barrier. He translated what Thomas had to say, and Lebel's replies.

'Tell him,' said Lebel when he had digested the information, 'that we will handle the Belgians from here. Say that he has my very sincere thanks for his help, and that if the killer can be traced to a location on the Continent rather than in Britain, I will inform him immediately so that he can stand his men down.'

When the receiver was down both men settled back at their desks. 'Get me the Sûreté in Brussels,' said Lebel.

The Jackal rose when the sun was already high over the hills and gave promise of another beautiful summer day. He showered and dressed, taking his check suit, well pressed, from the hands of the maid, Marie-Louise, who blushed again when he thanked her.

Shortly after ten-thirty he drove the Alfa into town and went to the post office to use the long-distance telephone to Paris. When he emerged twenty minutes later he was tight-lipped and in a hurry. At a hardware store nearby he bought a quart of high-gloss lacquer in midnight blue, a half-pint tin in white, and two brushes, one a fine-tipped camel-hair for lettering, the other a two-inch soft bristle. He also bought a screwdriver. With these in the glove compartment of the car he drove back to the Hôtel du Cerf and asked for his bill.

While it was being prepared he went upstairs to pack, and carried the suitcases down to the car himself. When the three cases were in the boot and the hand-grip on the passenger seat, he re-entered the foyer and settled the bill. The day clerk who had taken over the reception desk would say later that he seemed hurried and nervous, and paid the bill with a new hundred-franc note.

What he did not say, because he had not seen it, was that while he was in the back room getting change for the note the blond Englishman turned over the pages of the hotel registry that the clerk had been making up for that day's list of coming clients. Flicking back one page, the Englishman had seen yesterday's inscriptions including one in the name of Mme la Baronne de la Chalonnière, Haute Chalonnière, Corrèze.

A few moments after settling the bill the roar of the Alfa was heard in the driveway, and the Englishman was gone.

Just before midday more messages came into the office of Claude Lebel. The Sûreté of Brussels rang to say Duggan had only spent five hours in the city on Monday. He had arrived by BEA from London, but had left on the afternoon Alitalia flight to Milan. He had paid cash at the desk for his ticket, although it had been booked on the previous Saturday by phone from London.

Lebel at once placed another call with the Milanese police.

As he put the phone down it rang again. This time it was the DST, to say that a report had been received as normal routine that the previous morning among those entering France from Italy over the Ventimiglia crossing point, and filling in cards as they did so, had been Alexander James Quentin Duggan.

Lebel had exploded.

'Nearly thirty hours,' he yelled. 'Over a day . . .' He slammed down the receiver. Caron raised an eyebrow.

'The card,' explained Lebel wearily, 'has been in transit between Venti-miglia and Paris. They are now sorting out yesterday morning's entry cards from all over France. They say there are twenty-five thousand of them. For one day, mark you. I suppose I shouldn't have yelled. At least we know one thing – he's here. Definitely. Inside France. If I don't have something for the meeting tonight they'll skin me. Oh, by the way, ring up Superintendent Thomas and thank him again. Tell him the Jackal is inside France, and we shall handle it from here.'

As Caron replaced the receiver after the London call, the Service Regional headquarters of the PJ at Lyons came on the phone. Lebel listened, then glanced up at Caron triumphantly. He covered the mouthpiece with his hand.

'We've got him. He's registered for two days at the Hôtel du Cerf in Gap, starting last night.' He uncovered the mouthpiece and spoke down it.

'Now listen, Commissaire, I am not in a position to explain to you why we want this man Duggan. Just take it from me it is important. This is what I want you to do . . .'

He spoke for ten minutes, and as he finished, the phone on Caron's desk rang. It was the DST again to say Duggan had entered France in a hired white Alfa Romeo sports two-seater, registration MI–61741.

'Shall I put out an all-stations alert for it?' asked Caron.

Lebel thought for a moment.

'No, not yet. If he's out motoring in the countryside somewhere he'll probably be picked up by a country cop who thinks he's just looking for a stolen sports car. He'll kill anybody who tries to intercept him. The gun must be in the car somewhere. The important thing is that he's booked into the hotel for two nights. I want an army round that hotel when he gets back. Nobody must get hurt if it can be avoided. Come on, if we want to get that helicopter, let's go.'

While he was speaking the entire police force at Gap was moving steel road blocks into position on all the exits from the town and the area of the hotel and posting men in the undergrowth round the barriers. Their orders came from Lyons. At Grenoble and Lyons men armed with submachine guns and rifles were clambering into two fleets of Black Marias. At Satory Camp outside Paris a helicopter was being made ready for Commissaire Lebel's flight to Gap.

Even in the shade of the trees the heat of early afternoon was sweltering. Stripped to the waist to avoid staining more of his clothes than was necessary, the Jackal worked on the car for two hours.

After leaving Gap he had headed due west through Veyne and Aspres-sur-Buech. It was downhill most of the way, the road winding between the mountains like a carelessly discarded ribbon. He had pushed the car to the limit, hurling it into the tight bends on squealing tyres, twice nearly sending another driver coming the other way over the edge into one of the chasms below. After Aspres he picked up the RN93 which followed the course of the Drôme river eastwards to join the Rhône.

For another eighteen miles the road had hunted back and forth across the river. Shortly after Luc-en-Diois he had thought it time to get the Alfa off the road. There were plenty of side roads leading away into the hills and the upland villages. He had taken one at random and after a mile and a half chosen a path to the right leading into the woods.

In the middle of the afternoon he had finished painting and stood back. The car was a deep gleaming blue, most of the paint already dry. Although by no means a professional painting job, it would pass muster except if given a close inspection, and particularly in the dusk. The two number plates had been unscrewed and lay face down on the grass. On the back of each had been painted in white an imaginary French number of which the last two letters were 75, the registration code for Paris. The Jackal knew this was the commonest type of car number on the roads of France.

The car's hiring and insurance papers evidently did not match the blue French Alfa as they had the white Italian one, and if he were stopped for a road check, without papers, he was done for. The only question in his mind as he dipped a rag in the petrol tank and wiped the paint stains off his hands was whether to start motoring now and risk the bright sunlight showing up the amateurishness of the paintwork on the car, or whether to wait until dusk.

He estimated that with his false name once discovered, his point of entry into France would follow not long behind, and with it a search for the car. He was days too early for the assassination, and he needed to find a place to lie low until he was ready. That meant getting to the department of Corrèze two hundred and fifty miles across country, and the quickest way was by using the car. It was a risk, but he decided it had to be taken. Very well, then, the sooner the better, before every speed cop in the country was looking for an Alfa Romeo with a blond Englishman at the wheel.

He screwed the new number plates on, threw away what remained of the paint and the two brushes, pulled back on his polo-necked silk sweater and jacket, and gunned the engine into life. As he swept back on to the RN93 he checked his watch. It was 3.41 in the afternoon.

High overhead he watched a helicopter clattering on its way towards the east. It was seven miles further to the village of Die. He knew well enough not to pronounce it in the English way, but the coincidence of the name occurred to him. He was not superstitious, but his eyes narrowed as he drove into the centre of the village. At the main square near the war memorial a huge black-leather-coated motor-cycle policeman was standing in the middle of the road waving him to stop and pull in to the extreme right-hand side of the road. His gun, he knew, was still in its tubes wired to the chassis of the car. He carried no automatic or knife. For a second he hesitated, unsure whether to hit the policeman a glancing blow with the wing of the car and keep driving, later to abandon the car a dozen miles further on and try without a mirror or a wash-basin to transform himself into Pastor Jensen, with four pieces of luggage to cope with, or whether to stop.

It was the policeman who made the decision for him. Ignoring him completely as the Alfa began to slow down, the policeman turned round and scanned the road in the other direction. The Jackal slid the car into the side of the road, watched and waited.

From the far side of the village he heard the wailing of sirens. Whatever happened, it was too late to get out now. Into the village came a convoy of four Citroën police cars and six Black Marias. As the traffic cop jumped to one side and swept his arm up in salute, the convoy raced past the parked Alfa and headed down the road from which he had come. Through the wired windows of the vans, which give them the French nickname of salad-baskets, he could see the rows of helmeted police, submachine guns across their knees.

Almost as soon as it had come, the convoy was gone. The speed cop brought his arm down from the salute, gave the Jackal an indolent gesture that he could now proceed, and stalked off to his motor-cycle parked against the war memorial. He was still kicking the starter when the blue Alfa disappeared round the corner heading west.

It was 5.50 p.m. when they hit the Hôtel du Cerf. Claude Lebel, who had landed a mile on the other side of the township and been driven to the driveway of the hotel in a police car, walked up to the front door accompanied by Caron who carried a loaded and cocked MAT 49 submachine carbine under the mackintosh slung over his right arm. The forefinger was on the trigger. Everyone in the town knew there was something afoot by this time, except the proprietor of the hotel. It had been isolated for five hours, and the only odd thing had been the non-arrival of the trout-seller with his day's catch of fresh fish.

Summoned by the desk clerk, the proprietor appeared from his labours over the accounts in the office. Lebel listened to him answer Caron's questions, glancing nervously at the odd-shaped bundle under Caron's arms, and his shoulders sagged.

Five minutes later the hotel was deluged with uniformed police. They interviewed the staff, examined the bedroom, chased through the grounds. Lebel walked alone out into the drive and stared up at the surrounding hills. Caron joined him.

'You think he's really gone, chief?' Lebel nodded.

'He's gone all right.'

'But he was booked in for two days. Do you think the proprietor's in this with him?'

'No. He and the staff aren't lying. He changed his mind sometime this morning. And he left. The question now is where the hell has he gone, and does he suspect yet that we know who he is?'

'But how could he? He couldn't know that. It must be coincidence. It must be.'

'My dear Lucien, let us hope so.'

'All we've got to go on now, then, is the car number.'

'Yes. That was my mistake. We should have put the alert out for the car. Get on to the police R/T to Lyons from one of the squad cars and make it an all-stations alert. Top priority. White Alfa Romeo, Italian, Number MI–61741. Approach with caution, occupant believed armed and dangerous. You know the drill. But one more thing, nobody is to mention it to the Press. Include in the message the instruction that the suspected man probably does not know he's suspected, and I'll skin anybody who lets him hear it on the radio or read it in the Press. I'm going to tell Commissaire Gaillard of Lyons to take over here. Then let's get back to Paris.'

It was nearly six o'clock when the blue Alfa coasted into the town of Valence where the steel torrent of the Route Nationale Seven, the main road from Lyons to Marseilles and the highway carrying most of the traffic from Paris to the Côte d'Azur, thunders along the banks of the Rhône. The Alfa crossed the great road running south and took the bridge over the river towards the RN533 to St Peray on the western bank. Below the bridge the mighty river smouldered in the afternoon sunlight, ignored the puny steel insects scurrying southwards and rolled at its own leisurely but certain pace towards the waiting Mediterranean.

After St Peray, as dusk settled on the valley behind him, the Jackal gunned the little sports car higher and higher into the mountains of the Massif Central and the province of Auvergne. After Le Puy the going got steeper, the mountains higher and every town seemed to be a watering spa where the life-giving streams flowing out from the rocks of the massif had attracted those with aches and eczemas developed in the cities and made fortunes for the cunning Auvergnat peasants who had gone into the spa business with a will.

After Brioude the valley of the Allier river dropped behind, and the smell in the night air was of heather and drying hay in the upland pastures. He stopped to fill the tank at Issoire, then sped on through the casino town of Mont Doré and the spa of La Bourdoule. It was nearly midnight when he rounded the headwaters of the Dordogne, where it rises among the Auvergne rocks to flow south and west through half a dozen dams and spend itself into the Atlantic at Bordeaux.

From La Bourdoule he took the RN89 towards Ussel, the county town of Corrèze.

"You are a fool, Monsieur le Commissaire, a fool. You had him within your grasp, and you let him slip.' Saint-Clair had half-risen to his feet to make his point, and glared down the polished mahogany table at the top of Lebel's head. The detective was studying the papers of his dossier, for all the world as if Saint-Clair did not exist.

He had decided that was the only way to treat the arrogant colonel from the Palace, and Saint-Clair for his part was not quite sure whether the bent head indicated an appropriate sense of shame or an insolent indifference. He preferred to believe it was the former. When he had finished and sank back into his seat, Claude Lebel looked up.

'If you will look at the mimeographed report in front of you, my dear Colonel, you will observe that we did not have him in our hands,' he observed mildly. 'The report from Lyons that a man in the name of Duggan had registered the previous evening at a hotel in Gap did not reach the PJ until 12.15 today. We now know that the Jackal left the hotel abruptly at 11.05. Whatever measures had been taken, he still had an hour's start.

'Moreover, I cannot accept your strictures on the efficiency of the police forces of this country in general. I would remind you that the orders of the President are that this affair will be managed in secret. It was therefore not possible to put out an alert to every rural gendarmerie for a man named Duggan for it would have started a hullabaloo in the Press. The card registering Duggan at the Hôtel du Cerf was collected in the normal way at the normal time, and sent with due despatch to Regional Headquarters at Lyons. Only there was it realised that Duggan was a wanted man. This delay was unavoidable, unless we wish to launch a nation-wide hue-and-cry for the man, and that is outside my brief.

'And, lastly, Duggan was registered at the hotel for two days. We do not know what made him change his mind at 11 a.m. today and decide to move elsewhere.'

'Probably your police gallivanting about the place,' snapped Saint-Clair.

'I have already made it plain, there was no gallivanting before 12.15 and the man was already seventy minutes gone,' said Lebel.

'All right, we have been unlucky, very unlucky,' cut in the Minister. 'However, there is still the question of why no immediate search for the car was instituted. Commissaire?'

'I agree it was a mistake, Minister, in the light of events. I had reason to believe the man was at the hotel and intended to spend the night there. If he had been motoring in the vicinity, and had been intercepted by a motor-patrol man for driving a wanted car, he would almost certainly have shot the unsuspecting policeman, and thus forewarned made his escape. . . .'

'Which is precisely what he has done,' said Saint-Clair.

'True, but we have no evidence to suggest that he has been forewarned, as he would have been if his car had been stopped by a single patrolman. It may well be he just decided to move on somewhere else. If so, and if he checks into another hotel tonight, he will be reported. Alternately, if his car is seen he will be reported.'

'When did the alert for the white Alfa go out?' asked the director of the PJ, Max Fernet.

'I issued the instructions at 5.15 p.m. from the courtyard of the hotel,' replied Lebel. 'It should have reached all major road-patrol units by seven, and the police on duty in the main towns should be informed throughout the night as they check in for night duty. In view of the danger of this man, I have listed the car as stolen, with instructions that its presence be reported immediately to the Regional HQ, but that no approach should be made to the occupant by a lone policeman. If this meeting decides to change these orders, then I must ask that the responsibility for what may ensue be taken by this meeting.'

There was a long silence.

'Regrettably, the life of a police officer cannot be allowed to stand in the way of protecting the President of France,' murmured Colonel Rolland. There were signs of assent from round the table.

'Perfectly true,' assented Lebel. 'Providing a single police officer can stop this man. But most town and country policemen, the ordinary men on the beat and the motor patrolmen, are not professional gunfighters. This Jackal is. If he is intercepted, shoots down one or two policemen, makes another getaway and disappears, we shall have two things to cope with: one will be a killer fully forewarned and perhaps able to adopt yet a new identity about which we know nothing, the other will be a nationwide headline story in every newspaper which we will not be able to play down. If the Jackal's real reason for being in France remains a secret for forty-eight hours after the killing story breaks, I will be most surprised. The Press will know within days that he is after the President. If anyone here would like to explain that to the General, I will willingly retire from this investigation and hand it over.'

No one volunteered. The meeting broke up as usual around midnight. Within thirty minutes it had become Friday, August 16th.

The blue Alfa Romeo cruised into the Place de la Gare at Ussel just before one in the morning. There was one café remaining open across the square from the station entrance, and a few late-night travellers waiting for a train were sipping coffee. The Jackal dragged a comb through his hair and walked past the stacked-up chairs and tables on the terrace and up to the bar counter. He was cold, for the mountain air was chill when driving at over sixty miles an hour; and stiff, with aching thighs and arms from hauling the Alfa through innumerable mountain curves; and hungry, for he had not eaten since dinner twenty-eight hours previously, apart from a buttered roll for breakfast.

He ordered two large buttered slices of a long thin loaf, sliced down the middle and known as a *tartine beurrée,* and four hard-boiled eggs from the stand on the counter. Also a large white coffee.

While the buttered bread was being prepared and the coffee was per-colating through the filter, he glanced round for the telephone booth. There was none, but a telephone stood at the end of the counter.

'Have you got the local telephone directory?' he asked the barman. Without a word, still busy, the barman gestured to a pile of directories on a rack behind the counter.

'Help yourself,' he said.

The Baron's name was listed under the words 'Chalonnière, M. le Baron de la ...' and the address was the château at La Haute Challon-nière. The Jackal knew this, but the village was not listed on his road map. However, the telephone number was given as Egletons, and he found this easily enough. It was another thirty kilometres beyond Ussel on the RN89. He settled down to eat his eggs and sandwiches.

It was just before two in the morning that he passed a stone by the roadside saying 'Egletons, 6 km' and decided to abandon the car in one of the forests that bordered the road. They were dense woods, probably the estate of some local noble, where once boars had been hunted with horse and hound. Perhaps they still were, for parts of Corrèze seem to have stepped straight from the days of Louis the Sun King.

Within a few hundred metres he had found a drive leading into the forest, separated from the road by a wooden pole slung across the entrance, adorned by a placard saying *'Chasse Privée'*. He removed the pole, drove the car into the wood and replaced the pole.

From there he drove half a mile into the forest, the headlamps lighting the gnarled shapes of the trees like ghosts reaching down with angry branches at the trespasser. Finally he stopped the car, switched off the headlights, and took the wire-cutters and torch from the glove compartment.

He spent an hour underneath the vehicle, his back getting damp from the dew on the forest floor. At last the steel tubes containing the sniper's rifle were free from their hiding place of the previous sixty hours, and he re-packed them in the suitcase with the old clothes and the army greatcoat. He had a last look round the car to make sure there was nothing left in it that could give anyone who found it a hint of who its driver had been, and drove it hard into the centre of a nearby clump of wild rhododendron.

Using the metal shears, he spent the next hour cutting rhododendron branches from nearby bushes and jabbing them into the ground in front of the hole in the shrubbery made by the Alfa, until it was completely hidden from view.

He knotted his tie with one end round the handle of one of the suitcases, the other end round the handle of the second case. Using the tie like a railway porter's strap, his shoulder under the loop so that one case hung down his chest and the other down his back, he was able to grab the remaining two pieces of baggage in his two free hands and start the march back to the road.

It was slow going. Every hundred yards he stopped, put the case down and went back over his tracks with a branch from a tree, sweeping away the light impressions made in the moss and twigs by the passage of the Alfa. It took another hour to reach the road, duck under the pole, and put half a mile between himself and the entrance to the forest.

His check suit was soiled and grimy, the polo sweater stuck to his back with greasy obstinacy, and he thought his muscles would never stop aching again. Lining the suitcases up in a row, he sat down to wait as the eastern sky grew a fraction paler than the surrounding night. Country buses, he reminded himself, tend to start early.

In fact he was lucky. A farm lorry towing a trailer of hay came by at 5.50 heading towards the market town.

'Car broken down?' bawled the driver as he slowed up.

'No. I've got a weekend pass from camp, so I'm hitch-hiking home. Got as far as Ussel last night and decided to push on to Tulle. I've got an uncle there who can fix me a lorry to Bordeaux. This was as far as I got.' He grinned at the driver, who laughed and shrugged.

'Crazy, walking through the night up here. No one comes this way after dark. Jump on the trailer, I'll take you in to Egletons, you can try from there.'

They rolled into the little town at quarter to seven. The Jackal thanked the farmer, gave him the slip round the back of the station and headed for a café.

'Is there a taxi in town?' he asked the barman over coffee.

The barman gave him the number and he rang to call up the taxi company. There was one car that would be available in half an hour, he was told. While he waited he used the fundamental conveniences of the cold-water tap offered by the café's lavatory to wash his face and hands, change into a fresh suit and brush his teeth which felt furry from cigarettes and coffee.

The taxi arrived at 7.30, an old rattletrap Renault.

'Do you know the village of Haute Chalonnière?' he asked the driver.

' 'Course.'

'How far?'

'Eighteen kilometres.' The man jerked his thumb up towards the mountains. 'In the hills.'

'Take me there,' said the Jackal, and hefted his luggage on to the roof rack, except for one case that went inside with him.

He insisted on being dropped in front of the Café de la Poste in the village square. There was no need for the taxi-driver from the nearby town to know he was going to the château. When the taxi had driven away he brought his luggage into the café. Already the square was blazing hot, and two oxen yoked to a hay-cart ruminated their cud reflectively outside while fat black flies promenaded round their gentle patient eyes.

Inside the café it was dark and cool. He heard rather than saw the customers shift at their tables to examine the newcomer, and there was a clacking of clogs on tiles as an old peasant woman in a black dress left one group of farm workers and went behind the bar.

'Monsieur?' she croaked.

He put down the luggage and leaned on the bar. The locals, he noticed, were drinking red wine.

'*Un gros rouge, s'il vous plaît, madame.*'

'How far is the Château, madame?' he asked when the wine was poured. She eyed him keenly from wily black marbles.

'Two kilometres, monsieur.'

He sighed wearily. 'That fool of a driver tried to tell me there was no château here. So he dropped me in the square.'

'He was from Egletons?' she asked. The Jackal nodded.

'They are fools at Egletons,' she said.

'I have to get to the château,' he said.

The ring of peasants watching from their tables made no move. No one suggested how he might get there. He pulled out a new hundred-franc note.

'How much is the wine, madame?'

She eyed the note sharply. There was a shifting among the blue cotton blouses and trousers behind him.

'I haven't got change for that,' said the old woman.

He sighed.

'If only there were someone with a van, he might have change,' he said.

Someone got up and approached from behind.

'There is a van in the village, monsieur,' growled a voice.

The Jackal turned with mock surprise.

'It belongs to you, *mon ami*?'

'No, monsieur, but I know the man who owns it. He might run you up there.'

The Jackal nodded as if considering the merits of the idea.

'In the meantime, what will you take?'

The peasant nodded at the crone, who poured another large glass of rough red wine.

'And your friends? It's a hot day. A thirsty day.'

The stubbled face split into a smile. The peasant nodded again to the woman who took two full bottles over to the group round the big table. 'Benoît, go and get the van,' ordered the peasant, and one of the men, gulping down his wine in one swallow, went outside.

The advantage of the peasantry of the Auvergne, it would seem, mused the Jackal, as he rattled and bumped the last two kilometres up to the château, is that they are so surly they keep their damn mouths shut – at least to outsiders.

Colette de la Chalonnière sat up in bed, sipped her coffee and read the letter again. The anger that had possessed her on the first reading had dissipated, to be replaced by a kind of weary disgust.

She wondered what on earth she could do with the rest of her life. She had been welcomed home the previous afternoon after a leisurely drive from Gap by old Ernestine, the maid who had been in service at the château since Alfred's father's day, and the gardener, Louison, a former peasant boy who had married Ernestine when she was still an under housemaid.

The pair were now virtually the curators of the château of which two thirds of the rooms were shut off and blanketed in dust covers.

She was, she realised, the mistress of an empty castle where there were no children playing in the park any more, nor a master of the household saddling his horse in the courtyard.

She looked back at the cutting from the Paris glossy society magazine that her friend had so thoughtfully mailed to her; at the face of her husband grinning inanely into the flash-bulb, eyes torn between the lens of the camera and the jutting bosom of the starlet over whose shoulder he was peering. A cabaret dancer, risen from bar hostess, quoted as saying she hoped 'one day' to be able to marry the Baron, who was her 'very good friend'.

Looking at the lined face and scrawny neck of the ageing Baron in the photograph, she wondered vaguely what had happened to the handsome young captain of the Resistance partisans with whom she had fallen in love in 1942 and married a year later when she was expecting her son.

She had been a teenage girl, running messages for the Resistance, when she met him in the mountains. He had been in his mid-thirties, known by the code-name of Pegasus, a lean, hawk-faced commanding man who had turned her heart. They had been married in a secret ceremony in a cellar chapel by a priest of the Resistance, and she had borne her son in her father's house.

Then after the war had come the restoration of all his lands and properties. His father had died of a heart attack when the Allied armies swept across France, and he had emerged from the heather to become the Baron of Chalonnière, cheered by the peasantry of the countryside as he brought his wife and son back to the château. Soon the estates had tired him, the lure of Paris and the lights of the cabarets, the urge to make up for the lost years of his manhood in the undergrowth had proved too strong to resist.

Now he was fifty-seven and could have passed for seventy.

The Baroness threw the cutting and its accompanying letter on the floor. She jumped out of bed and stood in front of the full-length mirror on the far wall, pulling open the laces that held the peignoir together down the front. She stood on tiptoe to tighten the muscles of her thighs as a pair of high-heeled shoes would do.

Not bad, she thought. Could be a lot worse. A full figure, the body of a mature woman. The hips were wide, but the waist had mercifully remained in proportion, firmed by hours in the saddle and long walks in the hills. She cupped her breasts one in each hand and measured their weight. Too big, too heavy for real beauty, but still enough to excite a man in bed.

Well, Alfred, two can play at that game, she thought. She shook her head, loosening the shoulder-length black hair so that a strand fell forward by her cheek and lay across one of her breasts. She took her hands away and ran them between her thighs, thinking of the man who had been there just over twenty-four hours before. He had been good. She wished now she had stayed on at Gap. Perhaps they could have holidayed together, driving round using a false name, like runaway lovers. What on earth had she come home for?

There was a clatter of an old van drawing up in the courtyard. Idly she drew the peignoir together and walked to the window that gave on to the front of the house. A van from the village was parked there, the rear doors open. Two men were at the back taking something down from the tailboard. Louison was walking across from where he had been weeding one of the ornamental lawns to help carry the load.

One of the men hidden behind the van walked round to the front, stuffing some paper into his trouser pocket, climbed into the driving seat and engaged the grinding clutch. Who was delivering things to the château? She had not ordered anything. The van started to pull away and she gave a start of surprise. There were three suitcases and a hand-grip on the gravel, beside them was a man. She recognised the gleam of the blond hair in the sun and smiled wide with pleasure.

'You animal. You beautiful primitive animal. You followed me.'

She hurried into the bathroom to dress.

When she came on to the landing she caught the sound of voices in the hall below. Ernestine was asking what Monsieur wanted.

'*Madame la Baronne, elle est là?*'

In a moment Ernestine came hurrying up the stairs as fast as her old legs would carry her. 'A gentleman has called, ma'am.'

The evening meeting in the Ministry that Friday was shorter than usual. The only thing to report was that there was nothing. For the past twenty-four hours the description of the wanted car had been circulated in a routine manner, so as not to arouse undue suspicion, throughout France. It had not been spotted. Similarly every Regional Headquarters of the Police Judiciaire had ordered its dependent local commissariats in town and country to get all hotel registration cards into HQ by eight in the morning at the latest. At the Regional HQs they were immediately scoured, tens of thousands of them, for the name of Duggan. Nothing had been spotted. Therefore, he had not stayed last night in a hotel, at least, not in the name of Duggan.

'We have to accept one of two premises,' explained Lebel to a silent gathering. 'Either he still believes he is unsuspected, in other words his departure from the Hôtel du Cerf was an unpremeditated action and a coincidence; in which case there is no reason for him not to use his Alfa Romeo openly and stay openly in hotels under the name of Duggan. In that case he must be spotted sooner or later. In the second case he has decided to ditch the car somewhere and abandon it, and rely on his own resources. In the latter case, there are a further two possibilities.

'Either he has no further false identities on which to rely; in which case he cannot get far without registering at a hotel or trying to pass a frontier point on his way out of France. Or he has another identity and has passed into it. In the latter case he is still extremely dangerous.'

'What makes you think he might have another identity?' asked Colonel Rolland.

'We have to assume,' said Lebel, 'that this man, having been offered evidently a very large sum by the OAS to carry out this assassination, must be one of the best professional killers in the world. That implies that he has had experience. And yet he has managed to stay clear of any official suspicion, and all official police dossiers. The only way he could do this would be by carrying out his assignments in a false name and with a false appearance. In other words, an expert in disguise as well.

'We know from the comparison of the two photographs that Calthrop was able to extend his height by high-heeled shoes, slim off several kilos in weight, change his eye colour by contact lenses and his hair colour with dye to become Duggan. If he can do that once, we cannot afford the luxury of assuming he cannot do it again.'

'But there's no reason to suppose he suspected he would be exposed before he got close to the President,' protested Saint-Clair. 'Why should he take such elaborate precautions as to have one or more false identities?'

'Because,' said Lebel, 'he apparently does take elaborate precautions. If he did not, we should have had him by now.'

'I note from Calthrop's dossier, as passed on by the British police, that he did his National Service just after the war in the parachute regiment. Perhaps he's using this experience to live rough, hiding out in the hills,' suggested Max Fernet.

'Perhaps,' agreed Lebel.

'In that case he is more or less finished as a potential danger.'

Lebel considered for a moment.

'Of this particular person, I would not like to say that until he is behind bars.'

'Or dead,' said Rolland.

'If he's got any sense, he'll be trying to get out of France while he's still alive,' said Saint-Clair.

On that note the meeting broke up.

'I wish I could count on that,' Lebel told Caron back in the office. 'But as far as I'm concerned he's alive, well, free and armed. We keep on looking for him and that car. He had three pieces of luggage, he can't have got far on foot with all that. Find that car and we start from there.'

The man they wanted was lying on fresh linen in a château in the heart of Corrèze. He was bathed and relaxed, filled with a meal of country pâté and jugged hare, washed down with rough red wine, black coffee and brandy. He stared up at the gilt curlicues that writhed across the ceiling and planned the course of the days that now separated him from his assignment in Paris. In a week, he thought, he would have to move, and getting away might prove difficult. But it could be done. He would have to think out a reason for going.

The door opened and the Baroness came in. Her hair had been let down around her shoulders and she wore a peignoir held together at the throat but open down the front. As she moved it swayed briefly open. She was quite naked beneath it, but had kept on the stockings she had worn at dinner and the high-heeled court shoes. The Jackal propped himself up on one elbow as she closed the door and walked over to the bed.

She looked down at him in silence. He reached up and slipped loose the bow of ribbon that held the nightdress closed at the throat. It swung open to reveal the breasts, and as he craned forward his hand slid the lace-edged material off her shoulders. It slid down to the floor without a sound.

She pushed his shoulder so that he rolled back on to the bed, then gripped his wrists and pinned them against the pillow as she climbed over him. He stared back up at her as she knelt above him, her thighs gripping his ribs hard. She smiled down at him, two curling strands of hair falling down to the nipples.

'*Bon*, my *primitif*, now let's see you perform.'

He eased his head forward as her bottom rose off his chest, and started.

For three days the trail went cold for Lebel, and at each evening meeting the volume of opinion that the Jackal had left France secretly with his tail between his legs increased. By the meeting on the evening of the 19th he was alone in maintaining his view that the killer was still somewhere in France, lying low and biding his time, waiting.

'Waiting for what?' shrilled Saint-Clair that evening. 'The only thing he can be waiting for, if he is still here, is an opportunity to make a dash for the border. The moment he breaks cover we have got him. He has every man's arm against him, nowhere to go, no one to take him in, if your supposition that he is completely cut off from the OAS and their sympathisers is correct.'

There was a murmur of assent from the table, most of whose members were beginning to harden in their opinion that the police had failed, and that Bouvier's original dictum that the location of the killer was a purely detective task had been wrong.

Lebel shook his head doggedly. He was tired, exhausted by lack of sleep, by strain and worry, by having to defend himself and his staff from the constant needling attacks of men who owed their exalted positions to politics rather than experience. He had enough sense to realise that if he was wrong, he was finished. Some of the men round the table would see to that. And if he was right? If the Jackal was still on the trail of the President? If he slipped through the net and closed with his victim? He knew those round the table would desperately seek for a scapegoat. And it would be him. Either way his long career as a policeman was ended. Unless ... unless he could find the man and stop him. Only then would they have to concede that he had been right. But he had no proof; only an odd faith, that he could certainly never divulge, that the man he was hunting was another professional who would carry out his job no matter what.

Over the eight days since this affair had landed on his lap he had come to a grudging respect for the silent unpredictable man with the gun who seemed to have everything planned down to the last detail, including the contingency planning. It was as much as his career was worth to admit his feelings amidst the gathering of political appointees around him. Only the massive bulk of Bouvier beside him, hunching his head into his shoulders and glaring at the table, gave him a small comfort. At least he was another detective.

'Waiting for I don't know what,' Lebel replied. 'But he's waiting for something, or some appointed day. I do not believe, gentlemen, that we have heard the last of the Jackal yet. All the same, I cannot explain why I feel this.'

'Feelings!' jeered Saint-Clair. 'Some appointed day!! Really, Commissaire, you seem to have been reading too many romantic thrillers. This is no romance, my dear sir, this is reality. The man has gone, that's all there is to it.' He sat back with a self-assured smile.

'I hope you are right,' said Lebel quietly. 'In that case, I must tender to you, Monsieur le Ministre, my willingness to withdraw from the enquiry and return to the investigation of crime.'

The Minister eyed him with indecision.

'Do you think the enquiry is worth pursuing, Commissaire?' he asked. 'Do you think a real danger still subsists?'

'As to the second question, sir, I do not know. For the former, I believe we should go on looking until we are absolutely certain.'

'Very well then. Gentlemen, it is my wish that the Commissaire continue his enquiries, and that we continue our evening meetings to hear his reports – for the moment.'

On the morning of August 20th Marcange Callet, a gamekeeper, was shooting vermin on the estates of his employer between Egletons and Ussel in the department of Corrèze when he pursued a wounded woodpigeon that had tumbled into a clump of wild rhododendron. In the centre of the clump he found the pigeon, fluttering madly on the driving seat of an open sports car that had evidently been abandoned.

At first he thought as he wrung the bird's neck that it must have been parked by a pair of lovers who had come into the forest for a picnic, despite the warning notice that he had nailed up on the pole at the entrance to the woods half a mile away. Then he noticed that some of the branches of shrubbery that concealed the car from view were not growing in the ground but had been jabbed into the earth. Further examination showed the cut stumps of the branches on other nearby bushes, the white cuts having been smeared over with earth to darken them.

From the bird droppings on the seats of the car he reckoned it had been there for several days at least. Taking his gun and bird he cycled back through the woods to his cottage, making a mental note to mention the car to the local village constable when he went into the village later that morning to buy some more rabbit snares.

It was nearly noon when the village policeman wound up the hand-cranked telephone in his house and filed a report to the commissariat at Ussel to the effect that a car had been found abandoned in the woods nearby. Was it a white car, he was asked. He consulted his notebook. No, it was a blue car. Was it Italian? No, it was French-registered, make unknown. Right, said the voice from Ussel, a towaway truck will be sent during the afternoon, and he had better be ready waiting to guide the crew to the spot, because there was a lot of work on and everyone was short-staffed, what with a search going on for a white Italian sports car that the bigwigs in Paris wanted to have a look at. The village constable promised to be ready and waiting when the towaway truck arrived.

It was not until after four that afternoon that the little car was towed into the pound at Ussel, and close to five before one of the motor maintenance staff, giving the car a check over for identification, noticed that the paintwork was appallingly badly done.

He took out a screwdriver and scratched at one of the wings. Under the blue, a streak of white appeared. Perplexed, he examined the number plates, and noticed that they seemed to have been reversed. A few minutes later the front plate was lying in the courtyard face up, exhibiting white lettering MI-61741, and the policeman was hurrying across the yard towards the office.

Claude Lebel got the news just before six. It came from Commissaire

Valentin of the Regional Headquarters of the PJ at Clermont Ferrand, capital of the Auvergne. Lebel jerked upright in his chair as Valentin's voice started talking.

'Right, listen, this is important. I can't explain why it's important, I can only say that it is. Yes, I know it's irregular, but that's the way it is. I know you're a full Commissaire, my dear chap, but if you want confirmation of my authority in this case I'll pass you right on to the Director-General of the PJ.

'I want you to get a team down to Ussel now. The best you can get, and as many men as you can get. Start enquiring from the spot where the car was found. Mark off the map with that spot in the centre and prepare for a square search. Ask at every farmhouse, every farmer who regularly drives along that road, every village store and café, every hotel and woodcutter's shack.

'You are looking for a tall blond, English by birth but speaking good French. He was carrying three suitcases and a hand-grip. He carried a lot of money in cash and is well dressed, but probably looking as if he had slept rough.

'Your men must ask where he was, where he went, what he tried to buy. Oh, and one other thing, the Press must be kept out at all costs. What do you mean, they can't? Well of course the local stringers will ask what goes on. Well, tell them there was a car crash and it's thought one of the occupants might be wandering in a dazed state. Yes, all right, a mission of mercy. Anything, just allay their suspicions. Tell them there's no story the national papers would bother to pay for, not in the holiday season with five hundred road accidents a day. Just play it down. And one last thing, if you locate the man holed up somewhere, don't get near him. Just surround him and keep him there. I'll be down as soon as I can.'

Lebel put the phone down and turned to Caron.

'Get on to the Minister. Ask him to bring the evening meeting forward to eight o'clock. I know that's supper time, but it will only be short. Then get on to Satory and get the helicopter again. A night flight, to Ussel, and they'd better tell us where they will be landing so we can get a car laid on to pick me up. You'll have to take over here.'

The police vans from Clermont Ferrand, backed up by others contributed by Ussel, set up their headquarters in the village square of the tiny hamlet nearest to where the car had been found, just as the sun was setting. From the radio van Valentin issued instructions to the scores of squad cars converging on the other villages of the area. He had decided to start with a five-mile radius of the spot where the car was found, and working through the night. People were more likely to be home in the hours of darkness. On the other hand, in the twisting valleys and hillsides of the region, there was more chance that in the darkness his men would get lost, or overlook some small woodcutter's shack where the fugitive might be hiding.

There was one other factor that he could not have explained to Paris over the phone, and which he dreaded having to explain to Lebel face to face. Unbeknown to him, some of his men came across this factor before midnight. A group of them were interviewing a farmer in his cottage two miles from the spot where the car was found.

He stood in the doorway in his nightshirt, pointedly refusing to invite the detectives in. From his hand the paraffin lamp cast flickering splashes of light over the group.

'Come on, Gaston, you drive along that road to market pretty often. Did you drive down that road towards Egletons on Friday morning?'

The peasant surveyed them through narrowed eyes.

'Might have done.'

'Well, did you or didn't you?'

'Can't remember.'

'Did you see a man on the road?'

'I mind my own business.'

'That's not what we're asking. Did you see a man?'

'I saw nobody, nothing.'

'A blond man, tall, athletic. Carrying three suitcases and a hand-grip?'

'I saw nothing. *J'ai rien vu, tu comprends.*'

It went on for twenty minutes. At last they went, one of the detectives making a meticulous note in his book. The dogs snarled on the ends of their chains and snapped at the policemen's legs, causing them to skip to one side and step in the compost heap. The peasant watched them until they were back on the road and jolting away in their car. Then he slammed the door, kicked an inquisitive goat out of the way and clambered back into bed with his wife.

'That was the fellow you gave a lift to, wasn't it?' she asked. 'What do they want with him?'

'Dunno,' said Gaston, 'but no one will ever say Gaston Grosjean helped give away another creature to them.' He hawked and spat into the embers of the fire. '*Sales flics.*'

He turned down the wick and blew out the light, swung his legs off the floor and pushed further into the cot against the ample form of his wife. 'Good luck to you, mate, wherever you are.'

Lebel faced the meeting and put down his papers.

'As soon as this meeting is over, gentlemen, I am flying down to Ussel to supervise the search myself.'

There was silence for nearly a minute.

'What do you think, Commissaire, can be deduced from this?'

'Two things, Monsieur le Ministre. We know he must have bought paint to transform the car, and I suspect enquiries will show that if the car was driven through the night from Thursday into Friday morning from Gap to Ussel, that it was already transformed. In that case, and enquiries along these lines are proceeding, it would appear he bought the paint in Gap. If that is so, then he was tipped off. Either somebody rang him, or he rang somebody, either here or in London, who told him of the discovery of his pseudonym of Duggan. From that he could work out that we would be on to him before noon, and on to his car. So he got out, and fast.'

He thought the elegant ceiling of the conference room was going to crack, so pressing was the silence.

'Are you seriously suggesting,' somebody asked from a million miles away, 'there is a leak from within this room?'

'I cannot say that, monsieur. There are switchboard operators, telex operators, middle and junior level executives to whom orders have to be passed. It could be that one of them is clandestinely an OAS agent. But one thing seems to emerge ever more clearly. He was tipped off about the unmasking of the overall plan to assassinate the President of France, and decided to go ahead regardless. And he was tipped off about his unmasking as Alexander Duggan. He has after all got one single contact. I suspect it might be the man known as Valmy whose message to Rome was intercepted by the DST.'

'Damn,' swore the head of the DST, 'we should have got the blighter in the post office.'

'And what is the second thing we may deduce, Commissaire?' asked the Minister.

'The second thing is that when he learned he was blown as Duggan, he did not seek to quit France. On the contrary, he headed right into the centre of France. In other words, he is still on the trail of the head of state. He has simply challenged the whole lot of us.'

The Minister rose and gathered his papers.

'We will not detain you, M. le Commissaire. Find him. Find him, and tonight. Dispose of him if you have to. Those are my orders, in the name of the President.'

With that he stalked from the room.

An hour later Lebel's helicopter lifted away from the take-off pad at Satory and headed through the purpling-black sky towards the south.

'Impertinent pig. How dare he? Suggesting that somehow we, the topmost officials of France, were at fault. I shall mention it, of course, in my next report.'

Jacqueline eased the thin straps of her slip from her shoulders and let the transparent material fall to settle in folds round her hips. Tightening her biceps to push the breasts together with a deep cleavage down the middle, she took her lover's head and pulled it towards her bosom.

'Tell me all about it,' she cooed.

18

The morning of August 21st was as bright and clear as the previous fourteen of that summer heat-wave had been. From the windows of the Château de la Haute Chalonnière, looking out over a rolling vista of heather-clad hills, it looked calm and peaceful, giving no hint of the tumult of police enquiries that was even then enveloping the town of Egletons eighteen kilometres away.

The Jackal, naked under his dressing-gown, stood at the windows of the Baron's study making his routine morning call to Paris. He had left his mistress asleep upstairs after another night of ferocious lovemaking.

When the connection came through he began as usual '*Ici Chacal*'.

'*Ici Valmy*,' said the husky voice at the other end. 'Things have started to move again. They have found the car. . . .'

He listened for another two minutes, interrupting only with a terse question. With a final '*merci*' he replaced the receiver and fumbled in his pockets for cigarettes and lighter. What he had just heard, he realised, changed his plans whether he liked it or not. He had wanted to stay on at the château for another two days, but now he had to leave, and the sooner the better. There was something else about the phone call that worried him, something that should not have been there.

He had thought nothing of it at the time, but as he drew on his cigarette it niggled at the back of his mind. It came to him without effort as he finished the cigarette and threw the stub through the open window on to the gravel. There had been a soft click on the line soon after he had picked up the receiver. That had not happened during the phone calls over the past three days. There was an extension phone in the bedroom, but surely Colette had been fast asleep when he left her. Surely. . . . He turned and strode briskly up the stairs on silent bare feet and burst into the bedroom.

The phone had been replaced on its cradle. The wardrobe was open and the three suitcases lay about the floor, all open. His own keyring with the keys that opened the suitcases lay nearby. The Baroness, on her knees amid the debris, looked up with wide staring eyes. Around her lay a series of slim steel tubes, from each of which the hessian caps that closed the open ends had been removed. From one emerged the end of a telescopic sight, from another the snout of the silencer. She held something in her hands, something she had been gazing at in horror when he entered. It was the barrel and breech of the gun.

For several seconds neither spoke. The Jackal recovered first.

'You were listening.'

'I . . . wondered who you were phoning each morning like that.'

'I thought you were asleep.'

'No. I always wake when you get out of bed. This . . . thing; it's a gun, a killer's gun.'

It was half question, half statement, but as if hoping he would explain that it was simply something else, something quite harmless. He looked down at her, and for the first time she noticed that the grey flecks in the eyes had spread and clouded over the whole expression, which had become dead and lifeless like a machine staring down at her.

She rose slowly to her feet, dropping the gun barrel with a clatter among the other components.

'You want to kill him,' she whispered. 'You are one of them, the OAS. You want to use this to kill de Gaulle.'

The lack of any answer from the Jackal gave her the answer. She made a rush for the door. He caught her easily and hurled her back across the room on to the bed, coming after her in three fast paces. As she bounced on the rumpled sheets her mouth opened to scream. The back-handed blow across the side of the neck into the carotid artery choked off the scream at source, then his left hand was tangled in her hair, dragging her face downwards over the edge of the bed. She caught a last glimpse of the pattern of the carpet when the forehanded chop with the edge of the palm came down on the back of the neck.

He went to the door to listen, but no sound came from below. Ernestine would be preparing the morning rolls and coffee in the kitchen at the back of the house and Louison should be on his way to market shortly. Fortunately both were rather deaf.

He re-packed the parts of the rifle in their tubes and the tubes in the third suitcase with the army greatcoat and soiled clothes of André Martin, patting the lining to make sure the papers had not been disturbed. Then he locked the case. The second case, containing the clothes of the Danish pastor Per Jensen, was unlocked but had not been searched.

He spent five minutes washing and shaving in the bathroom that adjoined the bedroom. Then he took his scissors and spent a further ten minutes carefully combing the long blond hair upwards and snipping off the last two inches. Next he brushed into it enough of the hair tint to turn it into a middle-aged man's iron-grey. The effect of the dye was to dampen the hair, enabling him finally to brush it into the type shown in Pastor Jensen's passport, which he had propped on top of the bathroom shelf. Finally he slipped on the blue-tinted contact lenses.

He wiped every trace of the hair tint and washing preparations off the washbasin, collected up the shaving things and returned to the bedroom. The naked body on the floor he ignored.

He dressed in the vest, pants, socks and shirt he had bought in Copenhagen, fixed the black bib round his neck and topped it with the parson's dog collar. Finally he slipped on the black suit and conventional walking shoes. He tucked the gold-rimmed glasses into his top pocket, re-packed the washing things in the hand-grip and put the Danish book on French cathedrals in there as well. Into the inside pocket of his suit he transferred the Dane's passport, and a wad of money.

The remainder of his English clothes went back into the suitcase from which they had come, and this too was finally locked.

It was nearly eight when he finished and Ernestine would be coming up shortly with the morning coffee. The Baroness had tried to keep their affair from the servants, for both had doted on the Baron when he had been a small boy and later the master of the house.

From the window he watched Louison cycle down the broad path that led towards the gates of the estate, his shopping pannier jolting along behind the bicycle. At that moment he heard Ernestine knock at the door. He made no sound. She knocked again.

'Ya vot' café, madame,' she shrilled through the closed door. Making up his mind, the Jackal called out in French, in a tone half asleep.

'Leave it there. We'll pick it up when we're ready.'

Outside the door Ernestine's mouth formed a perfect 'O'. Scandalous. Whatever were things coming to . . . and in the Master's bedroom. She hurried downstairs to find Louison, but as he had left had to content herself with giving a lengthy lecture to the kitchen sink on the depravity of people nowadays, not at all like what the old Baron had been used to. So she did not hear the soft thud as four cases, lowered from the bedroom window on a looped sheet, plumped into the flowerbed on the front of the house.

Nor did she hear the bedroom door locked from the inside, the limp body of her mistress arranged in a natural sleeping position on the bed with the clothes tucked up to the chin, the snap of the bedroom window as it shut behind the grey-haired man crouching outside on the sill, nor the thud as he dropped in a clean fall down to the lawn.

She did hear the roar as Madame's Renault was gunned into life in the converted stable at the side of the château and peering through the scullery window she caught a glimpse as it swung round in the driveway leading to the front courtyard and away down the drive.

'Now what is that young lady up to?' she muttered as she scuttled back upstairs.

In front of the bedroom door the tray of coffee was still lukewarm but untouched. After knocking several times, she tried the door but it would not open. The gentleman's bedroom door was also locked. Nobody would answer her. Ernestine decided there were goings-on, the sort of goings-on that had not happened since the Boche came to stay as guests of the unwilling Baron back in the old days and ask him silly questions about the Young Master.

She decided to consult Louison. He would be at market, and someone in the local café would go to fetch him. She did not understand the telephone, but believed that if you picked it up people spoke to you and went and found the person you really wanted to speak to. But it was all nonsense. She picked it up and held it for ten minutes but no one spoke to her. She failed to notice the neat slice through the cord where it joined the skirting board of the library.

Claude Lebel took the helicopter back to Paris shortly after breakfast. As he said later to Caron, Valentin had been doing a first-class job, despite the obstructions of those damned peasants. By breakfast time he had traced the Jackal to a café in Egletons where he had had breakfast, and was looking for a taxi-driver who had been summoned. Meanwhile he had arranged for road blocks to be erected in a twenty-kilometre radius around Egletons, and they should be in place by midday.

Because of the calibre of Valentin he had given him a hint of the importance of finding the Jackal, and Valentin had agreed to put a ring round Egletons, in his own words 'tighter than a mouse's arsehole'.

From Haute Chalonnière the little Renault sped off through the mountains heading south towards Tulle. The Jackal estimated that if the police had been enquiring since the previous evening in ever-widening circles from where the Alfa had been found they must have reached Egletons by dawn. The café barman would talk, the taxi-driver would talk, and they would be at the château by the afternoon, unless he had a lucky break.

But even then they would be looking for a blond Englishman, for he had taken good care that no one had seen him as a grey-haired priest. All the same, it was going to be a close-run thing. He whipped the little car through the mountain byways, finally emerging on to the RN8 eighteen kilometres south-west of Egletons on the road to Tulle, which lay another twenty kilometres ahead. He checked his watch: twenty to ten.

As he vanished round a bend at the end of a stretch of straight, a small convoy came buzzing down from Egletons. It comprised a police squad car and two closed vans. The convoy stopped in the middle of the straight, and six policemen started to erect a steel road block.

'What do you mean, he's out?' roared Valentin to the weeping wife of a taxi-driver in Egletons. 'Where did he go?'

'I don't know, monsieur. I don't know. He waits every morning at the station square when the morning train comes in from Ussel. If there are no passengers he comes back here to the garage and gets on with some repair work. If he does not come back it means he has picked up a fare.'

Valentin looked around gloomily. It was no use bawling out the woman. It was a one-man taxi business run by a fellow who also did a bit of repair work on cars.

'Did he take anyone anywhere on Friday morning?' he asked, more patiently.

'Yes, monsieur. He had come back from the station because there was no one there, and a call from the café that somebody there wanted a taxi. He had got one of the wheels off, and was worried in case the customer should leave and go in another taxi. So he was cussing all through the twenty minutes it took to put the wheel back on. Then he left. He got the fare, but he never said where he took him.' She snuffled. 'He doesn't talk to me much,' she added by way of explanation.

Valentin patted her on the shoulder.

'All right, madame. Don't upset yourself. We'll wait till he gets back.' He turned to one of the sergeants. 'Get a man to the main station, another to the square to the café. You know the number of that taxi. The moment he shows up I want to see him – fast.'

He left the garage and strode to his car.

'The commissariat,' he said. He had transferred the headquarters of the search to Egletons police station, which had not seen activity like it in years.

In a ravine six miles outside Tulle the Jackal dumped the suitcase containing all his English clothes and the passport of Alexander Duggan. It had served him well. The case plummeted over the parapet of the bridge and vanished with a crash into the dense undergrowth at the foot of the gorge.

After circling Tulle and finding the station, he parked the car unobtrusively three streets away and carried his two suitcases and grip the half-mile to the railway booking office.

'I would like a single ticket to Paris, second class please,' he told the clerk. 'How much is that?' he peered over his glasses and through the little grille into the cubbyhole where the clerk worked.

'Ninety-seven new francs, monsieur.'

'And what time is the next train please?'

'Eleven-fifty. You've got nearly an hour to wait. There's a restaurant down the platform. Platform One for Paris, *je vous en prie*.'

The Jackal picked up his luggage and headed for the barrier. The ticket was clipped, he picked up the cases again and walked through. His path was barred by a blue uniform.

'*Vos papiers, s'il vous plaît*.'

The CRS man was young, trying to look sterner than his years would allow. He carried a submachine carbine slung over his shoulder. The Jackal put down his luggage again and proffered his Danish passport. The CRS man flicked through it, not understanding a word.

'*Vous êtes Danois?*'

'*Pardon?*'

'*Vous ... Danois*.' He tapped the cover of the passport.

The Jackal beamed and nodded in delight.

'*Danske ... ja, ja*.'

The CRS man handed the passport back and jerked his head towards the platform. Without further interest he stepped forward to bar passage to another traveller coming through the barrier.

It was not until nearly one o'clock that Louison came back, and he had had a glass of wine or two. His distraught wife poured out her tale of woe. Louison took the matter in hand.

'I shall,' he announced, 'mount to the window and look in.'

He had trouble with the ladder to start with. It kept wanting to go its own way. But eventually it was propped against the brickwork beneath the window of the Baroness's bedroom and Louison made his unsteady way to the top. He came down five minutes later.

'Madame la Baronne is asleep,' he announced.

'But she never sleeps this late,' protested Ernestine.

'Well, she is doing today,' replied Louison, 'one must not disturb her.'

The Paris train was slightly late. It arrived at Tulle on the dot of twelve o'clock. Among the passengers who boarded it was a grey-haired Protestant pastor. He took a corner seat in a compartment inhabited only by two middle-aged women, put on a pair of gold-rimmed reading glasses, took a large book on churches and cathedrals from his hand-grip, and started to read. The arrival time at Paris, he learned, was ten past eight that evening.

Charles Bobet stood on the roadside next to his immobilised taxi, looked at his watch and swore. Half past one, time for lunch, and here he was stuck on a lonely stretch of road between Egletons and the hamlet of Lamazière. With a busted half-shaft. *Merde* and *merde* again. He could leave the car and try to walk to the next village, take a bus into Egletons and return in the evening with a repair truck. That alone would cost him a week's earnings. But then again the car doors had no locks, and his fortune was tied up in the rattletrap taxi. Better not leave it for those thieving village kids to ransack. Better to be a little patient and wait until a lorry came along that could (for a consideration) tow him back to Egletons. He had no lunch, but there was a bottle of wine in the glove-compartment. Well, it was almost empty now. Crawling around under taxis was thirsty work. He climbed into the back of the car to wait. It was extremely hot on the roadside, and no lorries would be moving until the day had cooled a little. The peasants would be taking their siesta. He made himself comfortable and fell fast asleep.

'What do you mean he's not back yet? Where's the bugger gone?' roared Commissaire Valentin down the telephone. He was sitting in the commissariat at Egletons, ringing the house of the taxi-driver and speaking to his own policeman. The babble of the voice on the other end was apologetic. Valentin slammed the phone down. All morning and through the lunch-hour radio reports had come in from the squad cars manning the road blocks. No one remotely resembling a tall blond Englishman had left the twenty-kilometre-radius circle round Egletons. Now the sleepy market town was silent in the summer heat, dozing blissfully as if the two hundred policemen from Ussel and Clermont Ferrand had never descended upon it.

It was not until four o'clock that Ernestine got her way.

'You must go up there again and wake Madame,' she urged Louison. 'It's not natural for anyone to sleep right through the day.'

Old Louison, who could think of nothing better than to be able to do just that, and whose mouth tasted like a vulture's crotch, disagreed, but knew there was no use in arguing with Ernestine when her mind was made up. He ascended the ladder again, this time more steadily than before, eased up the window and stepped inside. Ernestine watched from below.

After a few minutes the old man's head came out of the window.

'Ernestine,' he called hoarsely, 'Madame seems to be dead.'

He was about to climb back down again when Ernestine screamed at him to open the bedroom door from the inside. Together they peered over the edge of the coverlet at the eyes staring blankly at the pillow a few inches away from the face.

Ernestine took over.

'Louison.'

'Yes, my dear.'

'Hurry down to the village and fetch Dr Mathieu. Hurry now.'

A few minutes later Louison was pedalling down the drive with all the force his frightened legs could muster. He found Dr Mathieu, who had tended the ills of the people of Haute Chalonnière for over forty years, asleep under the apricot tree at the bottom of his garden, and the old man agreed to come at once. It was past four-thirty when his car clattered into the courtyard of the château and fifteen minutes later when he straightened up from the bed and turned round on the two retainers who stood in the doorway.

'Madame is dead. Her neck has been broken,' he quavered. 'We must fetch the constable.'

Gendarme Caillou was a methodical man. He knew how serious was the job of an officer of the law, and how important it was to get the facts straight. With much licking of his pencil he took statements from Ernestine, Louison and Dr Mathieu as they sat around the kitchen table.

'There is no doubt,' he said, when the doctor had signed his statement, 'that murder has been done. The first suspect is evidently the blond Englishman who has been staying here, and who has disappeared in Madame's car. I shall report the matter to the headquarters in Egletons.'

And he cycled back down the hill.

Claude Lebel rang Commissaire Valentin from Paris at six-thirty.

'Alors, Valentin?'

'Nothing yet,' replied Valentin. 'We've had road blocks up on every road and track leading out of the area since mid-morning. He must be inside the circle somewhere, unless he moved far away after ditching the car. That thrice-damned taxi-driver who drove him out of Egletons on Friday morning has not turned up yet. I've got patrols scouring the roads around here for him. . . . Hold it a minute, another report just coming in.'

There was a pause on the line and Lebel could hear Valentin conferring with someone who was speaking quickly. Then Valentin's voice came back on the line.

'Name of a dog, what's going on round here? There's been a murder.'

'Where?' asked Lebel with quickened interest.

'At a château in the neighbourhood. The report has just come in from the village constable.'

'Who's the dead person?'

'The owner of the château. A woman. Hold on a moment. ... The Baroness de la Chalonnière.'

Caron watched Lebel go pale.

'Valentin, listen to me. It's him. Has he got away from the château yet?'

There was another conference in the police station at Egletons.

'Yes,' said Valentin, 'he drove away this morning in the Baroness's car. A small Renault. The gardener discovered the body, but not until this afternoon. He thought she must have been sleeping. Then he climbed through the window and found her.'

'Have you got the number and description of the car?' asked Lebel.

'Yes.'

'Then put out a general alert. There's no need for secrecy any more. It's a straight murder hunt now. I'll put out a nation-wide alert for it, but try and pick up the trail near the scene of the crime if you can. Try to get his general direction of flight.'

'Right, will do. Now we can really get started.'

Lebel hung up.

'Dear God, I'm getting slow in my old age. The name of the Baroness de la Chalonnière was on the guest list at the Hôtel du Cerf the night the Jackal stayed there.'

The car was found in a back street in Tulle at 7.30 by a policeman on the beat. It was 7.45 before he was back in the police station at Tulle and 7.55 before Tulle had contacted Valentin. The Commissaire of Auvergne rang Lebel at 8.05.

'About five hundred metres from the railway station,' he told Lebel.

'Have you got a railway timetable there?'

'Yes, there should be one here somewhere.'

'What was the time of the morning train to Paris from Tulle, and what time is it due at the Gare d'Austerlitz? Hurry, for God's sake hurry.'

There was a murmured conversation at the Egletons end of the line.

'Only two a day,' said Valentin. 'The morning train left at eleven-fifty and is due in Paris at . . . here we are, ten past eight . . .'

Lebel left the phone hanging and was halfway out of the office yelling at Caron to follow him.

The eight-ten express steamed majestically into the Gare d'Austerlitz precisely on time. It had hardly stopped when the doors down its gleaming length were flung open and the passengers were spilling on to the platform, some to be greeted by waiting relatives, others to stride towards the series of arches that led from the main hall into the taxi-rank. One of these was a tall grey-haired person in a dog collar. He was one of the first at the taxi-rank, and humped his three bags into the back of a Mercedes diesel.

The driver slammed the meter over and eased away from the entrance to slide down the incline towards the street. The forecourt had a semi-circular driveway, with one gate for coming and one for going out. The taxi rolled down the slope towards the exit. Both driver and passenger became aware of a wailing sound rising over and above the clamour of passengers trying to attract the attention of taxi-drivers before their turn had arrived. As the taxi reached the level of the street and paused before entering the traffic, three squad cars and two Black Marias swept into the entrance and drew to a halt before the main arches leading to the station hall.

'Huh, they're busy tonight, the sods,' said the taxi-driver. 'Where to, Monsieur l'Abbé?'

The parson gave him the address of a small hotel on the Quai des Grands Augustins.

Claude Lebel was back in his office at nine o'clock, to find a message asking him to ring Commissaire Valentin at the commissariat in Tulle. He was through in five minutes. While Valentin talked, he took notes.

'Have you fingerprinted the car?' asked Lebel.

'Of course, and the room at the château. Hundreds of sets, all matching.'

'Get them up here as fast as you can.'

'Right, will do. Do you want me to send the CRS man from Tulle railway station as well?'

'No, thanks, he can't tell us more than he already has. Thanks for trying, Valentin. You can stand your boys down. He's in our territory now. We'll have to handle it from here.'

'You're sure it is the Danish pastor?' asked Valentin. 'It could be co-incidence.'

'No,' said Lebel, 'it's him all right. He's junked one of the suitcases, you'll probably find it somewhere between Haute Chalonnière and Tulle. Try the rivers and ravines. But the other three pieces of luggage match too closely. It's him all right.'

He hung up.

'A parson this time,' he said bitterly to Caron, 'a Danish parson. Name unknown, the CRS man couldn't remember the name on the passport. The human element, always the human element. A taxi-driver goes to sleep by the roadside, a gardener is too nervous to investigate his employer oversleeping by six hours, a policeman doesn't remember a name in a passport. One thing I can tell you, Lucien, this is my last case. I'm getting too old. Old and slow. Get my car ready, would you. Time for the evening roasting.'

The meeting at the Ministry was strained and tense. For forty minutes the group listened to a step by step account of the trail from the forest clearing to Egletons, the absence of the vital taxi-driver, the murder in the château, the tall grey Dane boarding the Paris express at Tulle.

'The long and short of it,' said Saint-Clair icily, when he had finished, 'is that the killer is now in Paris, with a new name and new face. You seem to have failed once again, my dear commissaire.'

'Let us save the recriminations for later,' interposed the Minister. 'How many Danes are there in Paris tonight?'

'Probably several hundreds, Monsieur le Ministre.'

'Can we check them?'

'Only in the morning, when the hotel registration cards come in to the Prefecture,' said Lebel.

'I will arrange to have every hotel visited at midnight, two o'clock and four o'clock,' proposed the Prefect of Police. 'Under the head of "profession" he will have to put "pastor" or the hotel clerk will be suspicious.'

The room brightened.

'He will probably wrap a scarf round his dog collar, or take it off, and register as "mister" whatever-his-name-is,' said Lebel. Several people glowered at him.

'At this point, gentlemen, there is only one thing left to do,' said the Minister. 'I shall ask for another interview with the President and ask him to cancel all public appearances until this man is found and disposed of. In the meantime every Dane registering in Paris tonight will be checked personally first thing in the morning. I can rely on you for that, Commissaire? Monsieur le Préfect de Police?'

Lebel and Papon nodded.

'Then that is all, gentlemen.'

'The thing that sticks in my craw,' said Lebel to Caron later in their office, 'is that they insist on thinking it's just his good luck and our stupidity. Well, he's had good luck, but he's also devilishly clever. And we've had bad luck, and we've made mistakes. I've made them. But there's another element. Twice we've missed him by hours. Once he gets out of Gap with a re-painted car in the nick of time. Now he leaves the château and kills his mistress into the bargain within hours of the Alfa Romeo being found. And each time it's the morning after I have told that meeting at the Ministry that we have him in the bag, and his capture can be expected within twelve hours. Lucien, my dear fellow, I think I'm going to use my limitless powers and organise a little wire-tapping.'

He was leaning against the window-ledge, looking out across the softly flowing Seine towards the Latin Quarter where the lights were bright and the sound of laughter floated over the floodlit water.

Three hundred yards away another man leaned over his window sill in the summer night and gazed pensively at the bulk of the Police Judiciaire lying to the left of the spotlit spires of Notre Dame. He was clad in black trousers and walking shoes, with a polo-necked silk sweater covering a white shirt and black bib. He smoked a king-size English filter cigarette, and the young face belied the shock of iron-grey hair above it.

As the two men looked towards each other unknowing above the waters of the Seine, the varied chimes of the churches of Paris ushered in August 22nd.

PART THREE
Anatomy of a kill

19

Claude Lebel had a bad night. It was half past one, and he had barely got to sleep when Caron shook him awake.

'Chief, I'm sorry about this, but I've had an idea. This chap, the Jackal. He's got a Danish passport, right?'

Lebel shook himself awake.

'Go on.'

'Well, he must have got it from somewhere. Either he had it forged or he stole it. But as carrying the passport has entailed a change of hair colouring, it looks as if he stole it.'

'Reasonable. Go on.'

'Well, apart from his reconnaissance trip to Paris in July, he has been based in London. So the chances are he stole it in one of those two cities. Now what would a Dane do when his passport was lost or stolen? He'd go to his consulate.'

Lebel struggled off the cot.

'Sometimes, my dear Lucien, I think you will go far. Get me Super-intendent Thomas at his home, then the Danish Consul-General in Paris. In that order.'

He spent another hour on the phone and persuaded both men to leave their beds and get back to their offices. Lebel went back to his cot at nearly three in the morning. At four he was woken by a call from the Préfecture de Police to say that over nine hundred and eighty hotel registration cards filled in by Danes staying in Paris hotels had been brought in by the collections at midnight and 2 a.m., and sorting of them into categories of 'probable', 'possible' and 'others' had already started.

At six he was still awake and drinking coffee when the call came from the engineers at the DST, to whom he had given his instructions just after midnight. There had been a catch. He took a car and drove down through the early-morning streets to their headquarters with Caron beside him. In a basement communications laboratory they listened to a tape-recording.

It started with a loud click, then a series of whirrs as if someone was

dialling seven figures. Then there was the long buzz of a telephone ringing, followed by another click as the receiver was lifted.

A husky voice said, '*Allo?*'

A woman's voice, '*Ici Jacqueline.*'

The man's voice replied, '*Ici Valmy.*'

The woman said quickly, 'They know he's a Danish parson. They're
checking through the night the hotel registration cards of all Danes in
Paris, with card collections at midnight, two and four o'clock. Then
they're going to visit every one.'

There was a pause, then the man's voice said, '*Merci.*' He hung up, and
the woman did the same.

Lebel stared at the slowly turning tape spool.

'You know the number she rang?' Lebel asked the engineer.

'Yup. We can work it out from the length of the delay while the
dialling spins back to zero. The number was MOLITAR 5901.'

'You have the address?'

The man passed him a slip of paper. Lebel glanced at it.

'Come on, Lucien. Let's go and pay a call on Monsieur Valmy.'

'What about the girl?'

'Oh, she'll have to be charged.'

The knock came at seven o'clock. The schoolmaster was brewing himself
a cup of breakfast food on the gas-ring. With a frown he turned down
the gas and crossed the sitting-room to open the door. Four men were
facing him. He knew who they were and what they were without being
told. The two in uniform looked as if they were going to lunge at him,
but the short, mild-looking man gestured for them to remain where they
were.

'We tapped the phone,' said the little man quietly. 'You're Valmy.'

The schoolmaster gave no sign of emotion. He stepped back and let
them enter the room.

'May I get dressed?' he asked.

'Yes, of course.'

It took him only a few minutes, as the two uniformed policemen stood
over him, to draw on trousers and shirt, without bothering to remove his
pyjamas. The younger man in plain clothes stood in the doorway. The
older man wandered round the flat, inspecting the piles of books and
papers.

'It'll take ages to sort through this little lot, Lucien,' he said and the
man in the doorway grunted.

'Not our department, thank God.'

'Are you ready?' the little man asked the schoolmaster.

'Yes.'

'Take him downstairs to the car.'

The Commissaire remained when the other four had left, riffling
through the papers on which the schoolmaster had apparently been
working the night before. But they were all ordinary school examination
papers being corrected. Apparently the man worked from his flat; he

would have to stay in the flat all day to remain on the end of the telephone in case the Jackal called. It was ten past seven when the telephone
rang. Lebel watched it for several seconds. Then his hand reached out
and picked it up.

'Allo?'

The voice on the other end was flat, toneless.

'Ici Chacal.'

Lebel thought furiously.

'Ici Valmy,' he said. There was a pause. He did not know what else to
say.

'What's new?' asked the voice at the other end.

'Nothing. They've lost the trail in Corrèze.'

There was a film of sweat on his forehead. It was vital the man stay
where he was for a few hours more. There was a click and the phone
went dead. Lebel replaced it and raced downstairs to the car at the kerbside.

'Back to the office,' he yelled at the driver.

In the telephone booth in the foyer of a small hotel by the banks of the
Seine the Jackal stared out through the glass perplexed. Nothing? There
must be more than nothing. This Commissaire Lebel was no fool. They
must have traced the taxi-driver in Egletons, and from there to Haute
Chalonnière. They must have found the body in the château, and the
missing Renault. They must have found the Renault in Tulle, and questioned the staff at the station. They must have ...

He strode out of the telephone booth and across the foyer.

'My bill, if you please,' he told the clerk. 'I shall be down in five
minutes.'

The call from Superintendent Thomas came in as Lebel entered his office
at seven-thirty.

'Sorry to have been so long,' said the British detective. 'It took ages to
wake the Danish consular staff and get them back to the office. You were
quite right. On July 14th a Danish parson reported the loss of his passport. He suspected it had been stolen from his room at a West End hotel,
but could not prove it. Did not file a complaint, to the relief of the hotel
manager. Name of Pastor Per Jensen, of Copenhagen. Description, six
feet tall, blue eyes, grey hair.'

'That's the one, thank you, Superintendent.' Lebel put the phone down.
'Get me the Prefecture,' he told Caron.

The four Black Marias arrived outside the hotel on the Quai des Grands
Augustins at 8.30. The police turned room 37 over until it looked as if a
tornado had hit it.

'I'm sorry, Monsieur le Commissaire,' the proprietor told the rumpled-
looking detective who led the raid, 'Pastor Jensen checked out an hour
ago.'

The Jackal had taken a cruising taxi back towards the Gare d'Austerlitz where he had arrived the previous evening, on the grounds that the search for him would have moved elsewhere. He deposited the suitcase containing the gun and the military greatcoat and clothes of the fictitious Frenchman André Martin in the left-luggage office, and retained only the suitcase in which he carried the clothes and papers of American student Marty Schulberg, and the hand-grip with the articles of make-up.

With these, still dressed in the black suit but with a polo sweater covering the dog-collar, he checked into a poky hotel round the corner from the station. The clerk let him fill in his own registration card, being too idle to check the card against the passport of the visitor as regulations required. As a result the registration card was not even in the name of Per Jensen.

Once up in his room, the Jackal set to work on his face and hair. The grey dye was washed out with the aid of a solvent, and the blond reappeared. This was tinted with the chestnut-brown colouring of Marty Schulberg. The blue contact lenses remained in place, but the gold-rimmed glasses were replaced by the American's heavy-rimmed executive spectacles. The black walking shoes, socks, shirt, bib and clerical suit were bundled into the suitcase, along with the passport of Pastor Jensen of Copenhagen. He dressed instead in the sneakers, socks, jeans, T-shirt and windcheater of the American college boy from Syracuse, New York State.

By mid-morning, with the American's passport in one breast pocket and a wad of French francs in the other, he was ready to move. The suitcase containing the last remains of Pastor Jensen went into the wardrobe, and the key of the wardrobe went down the flush of the bidet. He used the fire-escape to depart, and was no more heard of in that hotel. A few minutes later he deposited the hand-grip in the left-luggage office at the Gare d'Austerlitz, stuffed the docket for the second case into his back pocket to join the docket of the first suitcase, and went on his way. He took a taxi back to the Left Bank, got out at the corner of Boulevard Saint Michel and the Rue de la Huchette, and vanished into the maelstrom of students and young people who inhabit the rabbit warren of the Latin Quarter of Paris.

Sitting at the back of a smoky dive for a cheap lunch, he started to wonder where he was going to spend the night. He had few doubts that Lebel would have exposed Paster Per Jensen by this time, and he gave Marty Schulberg no more than twenty-four hours.

'Damn that man Lebel,' he thought savagely, but smiled broadly at the waitress and said, 'Thanks, honey.'

Lebel was back on to Thomas in London at ten o'clock. His request caused Thomas to give a low groan, but he replied courteously enough that he would do everything he could. When the phone went down Thomas summoned the senior inspector who had been on the investigation the previous week.

'All right, sit down,' he said. 'The Frenchies have been back on. It seems they've missed him again. Now he's in the centre of Paris, and they suspect he might have another false identity prepared. We can both start as of now ringing round every consulate in London and asking for a list of passports of visiting foreigners reported lost or stolen since July 1st. Forget Negroes and Asiatics. Just stick to Caucasians. In each case I want to know the height of the man. Everybody above five feet eight inches is suspect. Get to work.'

The daily meeting at the Ministry in Paris had been brought forward to two in the afternoon.

Lebel's report was delivered in his usual inoffensive monotone, but the reception was icy.

'Damn the man,' exclaimed the Minister halfway through, 'he has the luck of the devil!'

'No, Monsieur le Ministre, it hasn't been luck. At least, not all of it. He has been kept constantly informed of our progress at every stage. This is why he left Gap in such a hurry, and why he killed the woman at La Chalonnière and left just before the net closed. Every night I have reported my progress to this meeting. Three times we have been within hours of catching him. This morning it was the arrest of Valmy and my inability to impersonate Valmy on the telephone that caused him to leave where he was and change into another identity. But the first two occasions he was tipped off in the early morning after I had briefed this meeting.'

There was a frigid silence round the table.

'I seem to recall, Commissaire, that this suggestion of yours has been made before,' said the Minister coldly. 'I hope you can substantiate it.'

For answer Lebel lifted a small portable tape-recorder on to the table and pressed the starter button. In the silence of the conference room the conversation tapped from the telephone sounded metallic and harsh. When it finished the whole room stared at the machine on the table. Colonel Saint-Clair had gone ashen grey and his hands trembled slightly as he shuffled his papers together into his folder.

'Whose voice was that?' asked the Minister finally.

Lebel remained silent. Saint-Clair rose slowly, and the eyes of the room swivelled on him.

'I regret to have to inform you ... M. le Ministre ... that it was the voice of ... a friend of mine. She is staying with me at the present time ... Excuse me.'

He left the room to return to the palace and write his resignation. Those in the room stared at their hands in silence.

'Very well, Commissaire.' The Minister's voice was very quiet. 'You may continue.'

Lebel resumed his report, relating his request to Thomas in London to trace every missing passport over the previous fifty days.

'I hope,' he concluded, 'to have a short list by this evening of probably no more than one or two who fit the description we already have of the Jackal. As soon as I know, I shall ask the countries of origin of these tourists in London who lost their passports to provide photographs of those people, for we can be sure the Jackal will by now look more like his new identity than like either Calthrop or Duggan or Jensen. With luck I should have these photographs by noon tomorrow.'

'For my part,' said the Minister, 'I can report on my conversation with President de Gaulle. He has refused point blank to change an item of his itinerary for the future to shield himself from this killer. Frankly, it was to be expected. However, I was able to obtain one concession. The ban on publicity may now be lifted, at least in this respect. The Jackal is now a common murderer. He has slain the Baroness de la Chalonnière in her own home in the course of a burglary of which the objective was her jewellery. He is believed to have fled to Paris and to be hiding here. All right, gentlemen?

'That is what will be released for the afternoon papers, at least the last editions. As soon as you are quite certain as to the new identity, or choice of two or three alternative identities, under which he is now masquerading, Commissaire, you are authorised to release that name or those names to the Press. This will enable the morning papers to up-date the story with a new lead.

'When the photograph of the unfortunate tourist who lost his passport in London comes through tomorrow morning you can release it to the evening papers, radio and television for a second up-date to the murder-hunt story.

'Apart from that, the moment we get a name, every policeman and CRS man in Paris will be on the street stopping every soul in sight to examine their papers.'

The Prefect of Police, chief of the CRS and Director of the PJ were taking furious notes. The Minister resumed:

'The DST will check every sympathiser of the OAS known to them, with the assistance of the Central Records Office. Understood?'

The heads of the DST and the RG office nodded vigorously.

'The Police Judiciaire will take every one of its detectives off whatever he is on and transfer them to the murder hunt.'

Max Fernet of the PJ nodded.

'As regards the palace itself, evidently I shall need a complete list of every movement the President intends to take from now on, even if he himself has not been informed of the extra precautions being taken in his interest. This is one of those occasions when we must risk his wrath in his own interest. And, of course, I can rely on the Presidential Security Corps to tighten up the ring round the President as never before. Com-missaire Ducret?'

Jean Ducret, head of De Gaulle's personal bodyguard, inclined his head.

'The Brigade Criminelle ...' the Minister fixed Commissaire Bouvier with his eye, 'obviously has a lot of underworld contacts in its pay. I want every one mobilised to keep an eye out for this man, name and description to be supplied. Right?'

Maurice Bouvier nodded gruffly. Privately he was disquieted. He had seen a few manhunts in his time, but this was gigantic. The moment

Lebel provided a name and a passport number, not to mention a description, there would be nearly a hundred thousand men from the security forces to the underworld scanning the streets, hotels, bars and restaurants for one man.

'Is there any other source of information that I have overlooked?' asked the Minister.

Colonel Rolland glanced quickly at General Guibaud, then at Commissaire Bouvier. He coughed.

'There is always the Union Corse.'

General Guibaud studied his nails. Bouvier looked daggers. Most of the others looked embarrassed. The Union Corse, brotherhood of the Corsicans, descendants of the Brothers of Ajaccio, sons of the vendetta, was and still is the biggest organised crime syndicate in France. They already ran Marseilles and most of the south coast. Some experts believed them to be older and more dangerous than the Mafia. Never having emigrated like the Mafia to America in the early years of this century, they had avoided the publicity that had since then made the Mafia a household word.

Twice already Gaullism had allied itself with the Union, and both times found it valuable but embarrassing. For the Union always asked for a kickback, usually in a relaxation of police surveillance of their crime rackets. The Union had helped the Allies to invade the south of France in August 1944, and had owned Marseilles and Toulon ever since. It had helped again in the fight against the Algerian settlers and the OAS after April 1961, and for this had spread its tentacles far north and into Paris.

Maurice Bouvier, as a policeman, hated their guts, but he knew Rolland's Action Service used Corsicans heavily.

'You think they can help?' asked the Minister.

'If this Jackal is as astute as they say,' replied Rolland, 'then I would reckon that if anyone in Paris can find him the Union can.'

'How many of them are there in Paris?' asked the Minister dubiously.

'About eighty thousand. Some in the police, Customs officers, CRS, Secret Service, and, of course, the underworld. And they are organised.'

'Use your discretion,' said the Minister.

There were no more suggestions.

'Well, that's it then. Commissaire Lebel, all we want from you now is one name, one description, one photograph. After that I give this Jackal six hours of liberty.'

'Actually, we have three days,' said Lebel, who had been staring out of the window. His audience looked startled.

'How do you know that?' asked Max Fernet.

Lebel blinked rapidly several times.

'I must apologise. I have been very silly not to see it before. For a week now I have been certain that the Jackal had a plan, and that he had picked his day for killing the President. When he quit Gap, why did he not immediately become Pastor Jensen? Why did he not drive to Valence and pick up the express to Paris immediately? Why did he arrive in France and then spend a week killing time?'

'Well, why?' asked someone.

'Because he has picked his day,' said Lebel. 'He knows when he is going to strike. Commissaire Ducret, has the President got any engagements outside the palace today, or tomorrow, or Saturday?'

Ducret shook his head.

'And what is Sunday, August 25th?' asked Lebel.

There was a sigh round the table like wind blowing through corn.

'Of course,' breathed the Minister, 'Liberation Day. And the crazy thing is, most of us were here with him on that day, the Liberation of Paris, 1944.'

'Precisely,' said Lebel. 'He is a bit of a psychologist, our Jackal. He knows there is one day of the year that General de Gaulle will never spend elsewhere than here. It is, so to speak, his great day. That is what the assassin has been waiting for.'

'In that case,' said the Minister briskly, 'we have got him. With his source of information gone, there is no corner of Paris that he can hide, no single community of Parisians that will take him in, even unwittingly, and give him protection. We have him. Commissaire Lebel, give us that man's name.'

Claude Lebel rose and went to the door. The others were rising and preparing to leave for lunch.

'Oh, there is one thing,' the Minister called after Lebel, 'how did you know to tap the telephone line of Colonel Saint-Clair's private flat?'

Lebel turned in the doorway and shrugged.

'I didn't,' he said, 'so last night I tapped all your telephones. Good day, gentlemen.'

At five that afternoon, sitting over a beer at a café terrace just off the Place de l'Odéon, his face shielded from the sunlight by dark glasses such as everyone else was wearing, the Jackal got his idea. He got it from watching two men stroll by in the street. He paid for his beer, got up and left. A hundred yards down the street he found what he was looking for, a women's beauty shop. He went in and made a few purchases.

At six the evening papers changed their headlines. The late editions carried a screaming banner across the top. *Assassin de la Belle Baronne se réfugie a Paris*. There was a photo beneath it of the Baronne de la Chalonnière, taken from a society picture of her five years ago at a party in Paris. It had been found in the archives of a picture agency and the same photo was in every paper. At 6.30, with a copy of *France-Soir* under his arm, Colonel Rolland entered a small café off the Rue Washington. The dark-jowled barman glanced at him keenly and nodded towards another man in the back of the hall.

The second man came over and accosted Rolland.

'Colonel Rolland?'

The head of the Action Service nodded.

'Please follow me.'

He led the way through the door at the back of the café and up to a small sitting-room on the first floor, probably the owner's private dwelling. He knocked, and a voice inside said, '*Entrez.*'

As the door closed behind him, Rolland took the outstretched hand of the man who had risen from an armchair.

'Colonel Rolland? *Enchanté.* I am the Capu of the Union Corse. I understand you are looking for a certain man. . . .'

It was eight o'clock when Superintendent Thomas came through from London. He sounded tired. It had not been an easy day. Some consulates had co-operated willingly, others had been extremely difficult.

Apart from women, Negroes, Asiastics and shorties, eight foreign male tourists had lost their passports in London during the previous fifty days, he said. Carefully and succinctly he listed them all, with names, passport numbers and descriptions.

'Now let's start to deduct those whom it cannot be,' he suggested to Lebel. 'Three lost their passports during periods when we know that the Jackal, alias Duggan, was not in London. We've been checking airline bookings and ticket sales right back to July 1st as well. It seems on July 18th he took the evening flight to Copenhagen. According to BEA he bought a ticket at their counter in Brussels, paying cash, and flew back to England on the evening of August 6th.'

'Yes, that checks,' said Lebel. 'We have discovered that part of that journey out of London was spent in Paris. From July 22nd until July 31st.'

'Well,' said Thomas, his voice crackling on the London line, 'three of the passports were missed while he was not here. We can count them out, yes?'

'Right,' said Lebel.

'Of the remaining five, one is immensely tall, six feet six inches, that's over two metres in your language. Besides which, he's Italian, which means that his height on the flyleaf of his passport is given in metres and centimetres, which would be immediately understood by a French Customs officer who would notice the difference, unless the Jackal is walking on stilts.'

'I agree, the man must be a giant. Count him out. What of the other four?' asked Lebel.

'Well, one is immensely fat, two hundred and forty-two pounds, or well over a hundred kilos. The Jackal would have to be so padded he could hardly walk.'

'Count him out,' said Lebel. 'Who else?'

'Another is too old. He's the right height, but over seventy. The Jackal could hardly look that old unless a real expert in theatrical make-up went to work on his face.'

'Count him out too,' said Lebel. 'What about the last two?'

'One's Norwegian, the other American,' said Thomas. 'Both fit the bill. Tall, wide-shouldered, between twenty and fifty. There are two things that militate against the Norwegian being your man. For one thing he is blond; I don't think the Jackal, after being exposed as Duggan, would go back to his own hair-colouring, would he? He would look too much like Duggan. The other thing is, the Norwegian reported to his consul that he is certain his passport slipped out of his pocket when he fell fully clothed into the Serpentine while boating with a girl-friend. He swears the passport was in his breast pocket when he fell in, and was not there fifteen minutes later when he climbed out. On the other hand, the American made a sworn statement to the police at London Airport to the effect that his hand-grip with the passport inside it was stolen while he was looking the other way in the main hall of the airport building. What do you think?'

'Send me,' said Lebel, 'all the details of the American Marty Schulberg. I'll get his photograph from the Passport Office in Washington. And thank you again for all your efforts.'

There was a second meeting in the Ministry at ten that evening. It was the briefest so far. Already an hour previously every department of the apparatus of the security of state had received mimeographed copies of the details of Marty Schulberg, wanted for murder. A photograph was expected before morning, in time for the first editions of the evening papers that would be appearing on the streets by ten in the morning.

The Minister rose.

'Gentlemen, when we first met, we agreed to a suggestion by Commissaire Bouvier that the identification of the assassin known as the Jackal was basically a task for pure detective work. With hindsight, I would not disagree with that diagnosis. We have been fortunate in having had, for these past ten days, the services of Commissaire Lebel. Despite three changes of identity by the assassin, from Calthrop to Duggan, Duggan to Jensen, and Jensen to Schulberg, and despite a constant leak of information from within this room, he has managed both to identify and, within the limits of this city, to track down our man. We owe him our thanks.' He inclined his head towards Lebel, who looked embarrassed.

'However, from now on the task must devolve upon us all. We have a name, a description, a passport number, a nationality. Within hours we shall have a photograph. I am confident that with the forces at your disposal, within hours after that, we shall have our man. Already every policeman in Paris, every CRS man, every detective, has received his briefing. Before morning, or at the latest tomorrow noon, there will be no place to hide for this man.

'And now let me congratulate you again, Commissaire Lebel, and remove from your shoulders the burden and the strain of this enquiry. We shall not be needing your invaluable assistance in the hours to come. Your task is done, and well done. Thank you.'

He waited patiently. Lebel blinked rapidly several times, and rose from his seat. He bobbed his head at the assembly of powerful men who commanded thousands of underlings and millions of francs. They smiled back at him. He turned and left the room.

For the first time in ten days Commissaire Claude Lebel went home to bed. As he turned the key in the lock and caught the first shrill rebuke of his wife, the clock chimed midnight and it was August 23rd.

The Jackal entered the bar an hour before midnight. It was dark and for several seconds he could hardly make out the shape of the room. There was a long bar running down the left-hand wall, with an illuminated row of mirrors and bottles behind it. The barman stared at him as the door swung closed, with unveiled curiosity.

The shape of the room was long and narrow down the length of the bar, with small tables set on the right-hand wall. At the far end the room broadened into a saloon, and here there were larger tables where four or six could sit together. A row of bar-stools were against the bar counter. Most of the chairs and stools were occupied by the night's habitual clientele.

The conversation had stopped at the tables nearest the door while the customers examined him, and the hush spread down the room as others further away caught the glances of their companions and turned to study the tall athletic figure by the door. A few whispers were exchanged, and a giggle or two. He spotted a spare bar-stool at the far end and walked between the tables on the right and the bar on the left to reach it. He swung himself on to the bar-stool. Behind him he caught a quick whisper.

'Oh, *regarde-moi ça!* Those muscles, darling I'm going out of my mind.'

The barman slipped down the length of the bar to stand opposite him and get a better look. The carmined lips widened in a coquettish smile.

'Bonsoir ... *monsieur.*' There was a chorus of giggles from behind, most of them malicious.

'Donnez-moi un Scotch.'

The barman waltzed away delighted. A man, a man, a man. Oh there was going to be such a row tonight. He could see the *'petites folles'* on the far side of the corridor sharpening their claws. Most were waiting for their regular 'butches', but some were without a date and had turned up on spec. This new boy, he thought, was going to create an absolute sensation.

The client next to the Jackal turned towards him and gazed with unconcealed curiosity. The hair was a metallic gold, meticulously groomed down on to the forehead in a series of pointed spikes like a young Greek god on an ancient frieze. There the likeness ended. The eyes were mascaraed, the lips a delicate coral, the cheeks dusted with powder. But the makeup could not conceal the tired lines of an ageing degenerate, nor the mascara the arid hungry eyes.

'*Tu m'invites?*' The voice was a girlish lisp.

The Jackal slowly shook his head. The drag shrugged and turned back to his companion. They went on with their conversation in whispers and squeaks of mock dismay. The Jackal had taken off his windcheater, and as he reached for his drink proffered by the barman, the muscles down the shoulders and back rippled under the T-shirt.

The barman was delighted. A 'straight'? No, he couldn't be, he wouldn't be here. And not a butch looking for a nance, or why had he snubbed poor little Corinne when she asked for a drink. He must be ... how marvellous! A handsome young butch looking for an old queen to take him home. What fun there was going to be tonight.

The butches started homing in just before midnight, sitting at the back, surveying the crowd, occasionally beckoning the barman for a whispered conversation. The barman would return to the bar and signal to one of the 'girls'.

'Monsieur Pierre wants to have a word with you, darling. Try and look your best, and for God's sake don't cry like you did last time.'

The Jackal made his mark shortly after midnight. Two of the men at the back had been eyeing him for several minutes. They were at different tables and occasionally shot each other venomous glances. Both were in late middle age; one was fat, with tiny eyes buried in obese lids and rolls on the back of his neck that flowed over his collar. He looked gross and piggish. The other was slim, elegant, with a vulture's neck and balding pate across which the few strands of hair were elaborately plastered. He wore a beautifully tailored suit with narrow trousers and a jacket whose sleeves showed a hint of lace at the cuffs. There was a flowing silk foulard artfully knotted at the throat. Something to do with the world of the arts, fashion or hair-styling, the Jackal thought.

The fat one beckoned to the barman and whispered in his ear. A large note slipped into the barman's tight trousers. He returned across the bar floor.

'The monsieur wonders if you would care to join him for a glass of champagne,' whispered the barman, and regarded him archly.

The Jackal put down his whisky.

'Tell the monsieur,' he said clearly, so the pansies round the bar could hear, 'that he does not attract me.'

There were gasps of horror, and several of the flick-knife-thin young men slipped off their bar-stools to come nearer so that they would not miss a word. The barman's eyes opened wide with horror.

'He's offering you champagne, darling. We know him, he's absolutely loaded. You've made a hit.'

For reply the Jackal slid off his bar-stool, took his glass of whisky and sauntered over to the other old queen.

'Would you permit that I sit here?' he asked. 'One is embarrassing me.'

The arty one almost fainted with pleasure. A few minutes later the fat man, still glowering from the insult, left the bar, while his rival, his bony old hand indolently placed across that of the young American at his table, told his new-found friend what absolutely absolutely shocking manners some people had.

The Jackal and his escort left the bar after one o'clock. Several minutes before, the queer, whose name was Jules Bernard, had asked the Jackal where he was staying. With a show of shamefacedness the Jackal admitted that he had nowhere to stay, and that he was flat broke, a student down on his luck. As for Bernard, he could hardly believe his good fortune. As chance would have it, he told his young friend, he had a beautiful flat, very nicely decorated, and quite quiet. He lived alone, no one ever disturbed him and he never had anything to do with the neighbours in the block, because in the past they had been terribly, terribly rude. He would be delighted if young Martin would stay with him while he was in Paris. With another show, this time of intense gratitude, the Jackal had accepted. Just before they left the bar he had slipped into the lavatory (there was only one) and had emerged a few minutes later with his eyes heavily mascaraed, powder on his cheeks, and lipstick on his mouth. Bernard looked very put out, but concealed it while they were still in the bar.

Outside on the pavement he protested, 'I don't like you in that stuff. It makes you look like all those nasty pansies back in there. You're a very good-looking young boy. You don't need all that stuff.'

'Sorry, Jules, I thought it would improve things for you. I'll wipe it all off when we get home.'

Slightly mollified, Bernard led the way to his car. He agreed to drive his new friend first to the Gare d'Austerlitz to pick up his bags, before going home. At the first cross-roads a policeman stepped into the road and flagged them down. As the policeman's head came down to the driver's side window, the Jackal flicked the inside light on. The policeman stared for a minute, then his face drew back with an expression of revulsion.

'*Allez*,' he commanded without further ado. As the car rolled away he muttered, '*Sales pédés.*'

There was one more stop, just before the station, and the policeman asked for papers. The Jackal giggled seductively.

'Is that all you want?' he asked archly.

'Sod off,' said the policeman and withdrew.

'Don't annoy them like that,' protested Bernard *sotto voce*. 'You'll get us arrested.'

The Jackal withdrew his two suitcases from the left-luggage office without more than a disgusted glance from the clerk in charge, and hefted them into the back of Bernard's car.

There was one more stop on the way to Bernard's flat. This time it was by two CRS men, one a sergeant and the other a private, who flagged them down at a street junction a few hundred metres from where Bernard lived. The private came round to the passenger door and stared into the Jackal's face. Then he recoiled.

'Oh my God. Where are you two going?' he growled.

The Jackal pouted.

'Where do you think, duckie?'

The CRS man screwed up his face in disgust.

'You bloody pooves make me sick. Move on.'

'You should have asked to see their identity papers,' said the sergeant to the private as the tail-lights of Bernard's car disappeared down the street.

'Oh, come on, Sarge,' protested the private, 'we're looking for a fellow who screwed the arse off a baroness and did her in, not a couple of raving nances.'

Bernard and the Jackal were inside the flat by two o'clock. The Jackal insisted on spending the night on the studio couch in the drawing-room and Bernard quelled his objections, although he peeked through the bedroom door as the young American undressed. It was evidently going to be a delicate but exciting chase to seduce the iron-muscled student from New York.

In the night the Jackal checked the fridge in the well-appointed and effeminately decorated kitchen, and decided there was enough food for one person for three days, but not for two. In the morning Bernard wanted to go out for fresh milk, but the Jackal detained him, insisting that he preferred tinned milk in his coffee. So they spent the morning indoors talking. The Jackal insisted on seeing the midday television news.

The first item concerned the hunt for the killer of Madame la Baronne de la Chalonnière forty-eight hours earlier. Jules Bernard squealed with horror.

'Oooh, I can't stand violence,' he said.

The next second the screen was filled with a face: a good-looking young face, with chestnut-brown hair and heavy-rimmed glasses, belonging, so the announcer said, to the killer, an American student by the name of Marty Schulberg. Would anybody having seen this man or having any knowledge . . .

Bernard, who was sitting on the sofa, turned round and looked up. The last thing he thought was that the announcer had not been right, for he had said Schulberg's eyes were blue; but the eyes looking down at him from behind the steel fingers that gripped his throat were grey. . . .

A few minutes later the door of the hall coat-cupboard closed on the staring distorted features, hair awry and tongue protruding, of Jules Bernard. The Jackal took a magazine out of the rack in the drawing-room and settled down to wait for two days.

During those two days Paris was searched as it never had been before. Every hotel from the smartest and most expensive to the sleaziest whorehouse was visited and the guest-list checked; every pension, rooming house, doss-house and hostel was searched. Bars, restaurants, night-clubs, cabarets and cafés were haunted by plain-clothes men who showed the picture of the wanted man to waiters, barmen and bouncers. The house or flat of every known OAS sympathiser was raided and turned over. More than seventy young men bearing a passing resemblance to the killer were taken for questioning, later to be released with routine apologies, even these only because they were all foreigners, and foreigners have to be more courteously treated than indigenes.

Hundreds of thousands in the streets, in taxis and on buses were stopped and their papers examined. Road-blocks appeared on all the major access points for Paris, and late-night strollers were accosted several times within the space of a mile or two.

In the underworld the Corsicans were at work, silently slipping through the haunts of pimps, prostitutes, hustlers, pickpockets, hoodlums, thieves and conmen, warning that anyone withholding information would incur the wrath of the Union, with all that that could entail.

A hundred thousand men in the employ of the state, in various capacities from senior detectives to soldiers and gendarmes, were on the lookout. The estimated fifty thousand of the underworld and its fringe industries vetted the passing faces. Those making a living off the tourist industry by day or night were briefed to keep their eyes open. Students' cafés, bars and talking clubs, social groups and unions were infiltrated with youthful-looking detectives. Agencies specialising in placing foreign-exchange students with French families were visited and warned.

It was on the evening of August 24th that Commissaire Claude Lebel, who had spent the Saturday afternoon pottering about his garden in a cardigan and patched trousers, was summoned by telephone to report to the Minister in his private office. A car came for him at six.

When he saw the Minister he was surprised. The dynamic chief of the whole of France's internal security apparatus looked tired and strained. He seemed to have grown older inside forty-eight hours, and there were lines of sleeplessness round his eyes. He gestured Lebel to a chair opposite his desk, and seated himself in the swivel chair in which he liked to be able to spin round from the window with his view of the Place Beauvau back to the desk. This time he did not look out of the window.

'We can't find him,' he said briefly. 'He's vanished, just disappeared off the face of the earth. The OAS people, we are convinced, just don't know where he is any more than we do. The underworld hasn't had sight nor sound of him. The Union Corse reckons he can't be in town.'

He paused and sighed, contemplating the little detective across the desk, who blinked several times but said nothing.

'I don't think we ever really had any idea what kind of a man you have been pursuing these past two weeks. What do you think?'

'He's here, somewhere,' said Lebel. 'What are the arrangements like for tomorrow?'

The Minister looked as if he was in physical pain.

'The President won't change a thing or permit any of his planned itinerary to be altered. I spoke to him this morning. He was not pleased.

So tomorrow remains the same as published. He will re-kindle the Eternal Flame under the Arc de Triomphe at ten. High Mass in Notre Dame at eleven. Private meditation at the shrine of the martyred resistants at Montválerien at 12.30, then back to the palace for lunch, and siesta. One ceremony in the afternoon, presentation of Médailles de la Libération to a group of ten veterans of the Resistance whose services to the Resistance are being rather belatedly recognised.

'That's at four o'clock on the square in front of the Gare de Montparnasse. He chose the place himself. As you know work has already started on the foundations for the new station, which will be set back five hundred metres from the present site. Where the station buildings now stand is due to become an office block and shopping precinct. If construction goes ahead according to plan it may be the last Liberation Day that the old façade of the station remains untouched.'

'What about crowd control?' asked Lebel.

'Well, we've all been working on it. Crowds are to be kept back at every ceremony further than ever before. Steel crowd barriers go up several hours before each ceremony, then the area inside the barrier ring is searched from top to bottom, including the sewers. Every house and flat is to be searched. Before each ceremony and during it there will be watchers with guns on every nearby roof-top surveying the opposite roofs and windows. Nobody gets through the barriers except officials, and those taking part in the ceremonies.

'We've gone to some extraordinary lengths this time. Even the cornices of Notre Dame, inside and out, will be infiltrated by policemen, right up on the roof and among the spires. All the priests taking part in Mass will be searched for concealed weapons, and the acolytes and choirboys. Even the police and CRS are having special lapel badges issued tomorrow morning at dawn, in case he tries to masquerade as a security man.

'We've spent the past twenty-four hours secretly slipping bullet-proof windows into the Citroën the President will ride in. Incidentally, don't breathe a word of that; not even the President must know. He'd be furious. Marroux will drive him as usual, and he's been told to speed up the pace faster than usual, in case our friend tries for a snap snot at the car. Ducret has drafted in a posse of especially tall officers and officials to try and hedge the General round without him noticing.

'Apart from that, everybody who comes within two hundred metres of him is going to be frisked – no exceptions. It will create havoc with the Diplomatic Corps, and the Press is threatening a revolt. All press and diplomatic passes are going to be suddenly changed at dawn tomorrow in case the Jackal tries to slip in as one of them. Obviously, anyone with a package or a lengthy-looking object will be hustled away as soon as spotted. Well, have you any ideas?'

Lebel thought for a moment, twisting his hands between his knees like a schoolboy trying to explain himself to his headmaster. In truth he found some of the workings of the Fifth Republic rather overpowering for a cop who had started on the beat and had spent his life catching criminals by keeping his eyes open a bit wider than anyone else.

'I don't think,' he said at length, 'that he will risk getting killed himself. He is a mercenary, he kills for money. He wants to get away and spend his money. And he has worked out his plan in advance, during his reconnaissance trip here in the last eight days of July. If he had any doubts, either about the success of the operation or of his chances of getting away, he would have turned back before now.

'So he must have something up his sleeve. He could work out for himself that one day of the year, Liberation Day, General de Gaulle's pride would forbid him staying at home, no matter what the personal danger. He could probably have worked out that the security precautions, particularly after his presence had been discovered, would be as intensive as you describe, Monsieur le Ministre. And yet he didn't turn back.'

Lebel rose and, despite the breach of protocol, paced up and down the room.

'He didn't turn back. And he won't turn back. Why? Because he thinks he can do it, and get away. Therefore he must have hit on some idea that nobody else has ever thought of. It has to be a bomb triggered by remote control, or a rifle. But a bomb could well be discovered, and that would ruin everything. So it's a gun. That was why he needed to enter France by car. The gun was in the car, probably welded to the chassis or inside the panelling.'

'But he can't get a gun near De Gaulle!' cried the Minister. 'Nobody can get near him, except a few, and they are being searched. How can he get a gun inside the circle of crowd barriers?'

Lebel stopped pacing and faced the Minister. He shrugged.

'I don't know. But he thinks he can, and he's not failed yet, despite having some bad luck and some good. Despite being betrayed and tracked by two of the best police forces in the world, he's here. With a gun, in hiding, perhaps with yet another face and identity card. One thing is certain, Minister. Wherever he is, he must emerge tomorrow. When he does he must be spotted for what he is. And that comes down to one thing – the old detective's adage of keeping your eyes open.

'There's nothing more I can suggest as regards the security precautions, Minister. They seem perfect, indeed overwhelming. So may I just wander round each of the ceremonies and see if I can spot him? It's the only thing left to do.'

The Minister was disappointed. He had hoped for some flash of inspiration, some brilliant revelation from the detective whom Bouvier had described a fortnight earlier as the best in France. And the man had suggested he keep his eyes open. The Minister rose.

'Of course,' he said coldly. 'Please do just that, Monsieur le Commissaire.'

Later that evening the Jackal laid out his preparations in Jules Bernard's bedroom. On the bed were the pair of scuffed black shoes, grey woollen socks, trousers and open-necked shirt, long military greatcoat with a single row of campaign ribbons, and black beret of the French war veteran André Martin. He tossed on top the false papers, forged in Brussels, that gave the wearer of the clothes his new identity.

Beside these he laid out the light webbing harness he had had made in London, and the five steel tubes that looked like aluminium and which contained the stock, breech, barrel, silencer and telescopic sight of his rifle. Lying beside them was the black rubber stud into which were stuffed five explosive bullets.

He took two of the bullets out of the rubber, and using the pliers from the tool-box under the kitchen sink carefully prised the noses off them. From inside each he slid the small pencil of cordite they contained. These he kept; the cases of the now useless cartridges he threw in the ash-can. He still had three bullets left, and these would suffice.

He had not shaved for two days, and a light golden stubble covered his chin. This he would shave off badly with the cut-throat razor he had bought on his arrival in Paris. Also lying on the bathroom shelf were the flasks of after-shave that in fact contained the grey hair-tint he had once used already for Pastor Jensen, and the solvent spirit. He had already washed out the chestnut-brown tint of Marty Schulberg, and sitting in front of the bathroom mirror he cut his own blond hair shorter and shorter, until the tufts stuck up from the top of the head in an untidy brush-cut.

He made one last check to see that all the preparations for the morning were in order, then cooked himself an omelette, settled in front of the television and watched a variety show until it was time for bed.

Sunday, August 25th, 1963, was scorching hot. It was the height of the summer heatwave, as it had been just one year and three days previously when Lieutenant-Colonel Jean-Marie Bastien-Thiry and his men had tried to shoot Charles de Gaulle at the roundabout at Petit-Clamart. Although none of the plotters of that evening in 1962 realised it, their action had set off a chain of events that were only to terminate once and for all on the afternoon of the summer Sunday that now blazed down on a city on holiday.

But if Paris was on holiday to celebrate its own liberation from the Germans nineteen years earlier, there were seventy-five thousand among them who sweated in blue-serge blouses and two-piece suits trying to keep the rest in order. Heralded by ecstatic columns of press publicity, the ceremonies to mark the day of liberation were massively attended. Most of those who came, however, hardly had a glimpse of the Head of State as he stalked through solid phalanxes of guards and policemen to officiate at the commemorations.

Apart from being boxed in from public view by a cohort of officers and civil servants who, although delighted to be asked to be in attendance, failed to notice that their one common characteristic was their height, and that each in his way served as a human shield for the President, General de Gaulle was also surrounded by all four of his body-guards.

Fortunately his short-sightedness, accentuated by his refusal to wear glasses in public, prevented him from noting that behind each elbow and flanking him on each side were the huge bulks of Roger Tessier, Paul Comiti, Raymond Sasia and Henri d'Jouder.

They were known to the Press as 'gorillas' and many thought this was simply a tribute to their looks. In fact there was a practical reason for their manner of walking. Each man was an expert in combat of all forms, with heavily muscled chest and shoulders. With muscles tensed, the dorsals forced the arms out from the sides so that the hands swung well away from the body. To add to this, each man carried his favourite automatic under his left armpit, accentuating the gorilla-like stance. They walked with hands half-open, ready to sweep the gun out from its shoulder-holster and start firing at the first hint of trouble.

But there was none. The ceremony at the Arc de Triomphe went off exactly as planned, while all along the great amphitheatre of roofs that overlook the Place de l'Etoile hundreds of men with binoculars and rifles crouched behind chimney stacks, watched and guarded. As the presidential motorcade finally swept down the Champs Elysées towards Notre Dame, they all breathed a sigh of relief and started to come down again.

At the cathedral it was the same. The Cardinal Archbishop of Paris officiated, flanked by prelates and clergy, all of whom had been watched as they robed. In the organ loft two men perched with rifles (not even the Archbishop knew they were there) and watched the gathering below. The worshippers were heavily infiltrated by plain-clothes police, who did not kneel, nor close their eyes, but who prayed as fervently as the rest the old policeman's prayer: 'Please, dear Lord, not while I'm on duty.'

Outside, several bystanders, even though they were two hundred metres from the door of the cathedral, were hustled away when they reached inside their jackets. One had been scratching his armpit, the other going for a cigarette case.

And still nothing happened. There was no crack of a rifle from a roof-top, no muffled crump of a bomb. The police even scanned each other, making sure that their colleagues had the indispensable lapel badge issued that very morning so that the Jackal could not copy it and masquerade as a policeman. One CRS man who lost his badge was arrested on the spot and hustled to a waiting van. His submachine carbine was taken from him, and it was not until the evening that he was released. Even then it took twenty of his colleagues, who personally recognised the man and vouched for him, to convince the police that he was who he said he was.

At Montvalérien the atmosphere was electric, although if the President noticed it he gave no sign. In this working-class suburb the security men had estimated that while actually inside the ossuary the General would be safe. But while his car was wending its way through the narrow streets approaching the prison, slowing down for the corners, the assassin might make his attempt.

In fact, at that moment, the Jackal was elsewhere.

Pierre Valrémy was fed up. He was hot, his blouse was sticking to his back, the strap of his submachine carbine chafed his shoulder through the soaking material, he was thirsty and it was just on lunchtime, which he knew he was going to miss. He was beginning to regret joining the CRS at all.

It had been all very well when he was laid off redundant from his factory job at Rouen and the clerk at the Labour Exchange had pointed to the poster on the wall of a beaming young man in the uniform of the CRS who was telling the world that he had a job with a future and prospects of an interesting life. The uniform in the picture looked as if it had been tailored by Balenciaga himself. So Valrémy had enlisted.

No one had mentioned the life in the barracks that looked like a prison, which was just what it had once been. Nor the drill, nor the night exercises, nor the itchy serge blouse, nor the hours of waiting on street corners in bitter cold or blazing heat for the Great Arrest that never took place. People's papers were always in order, their missions inevitably mundane and harmless, and it was enough to drive anyone to drink.

And now Paris, the first trip out of Rouen he had ever made. He had thought he might see the City of Lights. Not a hope, not with Sergeant Barbichet in charge of the squad. Just more of the same. 'See that crowd barrier, Valrémy. Well, stand by it, watch it, see it don't move, and don't let nobody through it unless they're authorised, see? Yours is a responsible job, me lad.'

Responsible indeed! Mind you, they had gone a bit wild over this Paris Liberation Day, bringing in thousands from the provinces to supplement the Paris troops. There had been men from ten different cities in his billet last night, and the Paris men had a rumour someone was expecting something to happen, else why all the fuss. Rumours, there were always rumours. They never came to anything.

Valrémy turned round and looked back up the Rue de Rennes. The crowd barrier he was guarding was one of a chain stretched across the street from one building to the other, about two hundred and fifty metres up the street from the Place du 18 Juin. The façade of the railway station was another two hundred metres beyond the square, fronted by the forecourt in which the ceremony was to take place. In the distance he could see some men inside the forecourt, marking out the places where the old veterans would stand, and the officials, and the band of the Garde Républicaine. Three hours to go. Jesus, would it never end?

Along the line of barriers the first of the public were beginning to assemble. Some of them had fantastic patience, he thought. Fancy waiting in this heat for hours just to see a crowd of heads three hundred metres away and know that De Gaulle was in the middle of that lot, somewhere. Still, they always came when Old Charlie was about.

There were about a hundred or two hundred scattered along the barriers when he saw the old man. He was hobbling down the steet looking like he was never going to make it another half-mile. The black beret was stained with sweat and the long greatcoat swished below his knee. There was a row of medals dangling and clinking on his chest. Several of the crowd by the barrier cast him glances full of pity.

These old codgers always kept their medals, Valrémy thought, like it was the only thing they had in life. Well, maybe it *was* the only thing left for some of them. Especially when you had had one of your legs shot off. Maybe, thought Valrémy, watching the old man hobbling down the street, he had run around a bit when he was young, when he had two legs to run on. Now he looked like a smashed-up old seagull the CRS man had seen once on a visit to the seaside at Kermadec.

Christ, fancy having to spend the rest of your days limping about with one leg, propping yourself up on an aluminium crutch. The old man hobbled up to him.

'*Je peux passer?*' he asked timidly.

'Come on, Dad, let's have a look at your papers.'

The old war veteran fumbled inside his shirt, which could have done with a wash. He produced two cards which Valrémy took and looked at. André Martin, French citizen, aged fifty-three, born at Colmar, Alsace; resident in Paris. The other card was for the same man. Written across the top of it were the words: '*Mutilé de Guerre.*'

Well, you're mutilated all right, mate, thought Valrémy.

He studied the photographs on each card. They were of the same man, but taken at different times. He looked up.

'Take off your beret.'

The old man took it off and crumpled it in his hand. Valremy compared the face in front of him with those in the photograph. It was the same. The man in front of him looked sick. He had cut himself shaving, and small bits of toilet paper were stuck on the cuts where specks of blood still showed. The face was grey-coloured and greasy with a film of sweat. Above the forehead the tufts of grey hair stuck up at all angles, disarranged by the act of sweeping off the beret. Valrémy handed the cards back.

'What do you want to go down there for?'

'I live there,' said the old man. 'I'm retired on my pension. I have an attic.'

Valrémy snatched the cards back. The identity card gave his address as 154 Rue de Rennes, Paris 6 ème. The CRS man looked at the house above his head. Written over the door was the number 132. Fair enough, 154 must be further down the road. No orders against letting an old man go home.

'All right, pass through. But don't get into no mischief. Big Charlie's going to be along in a couple of hours.'

The old man smiled, putting away his cards and nearly stumbling on his one leg and crutch, so that Valremy reached out to steady him.

'I know. One of my old mates is getting his medal. I got mine two years ago . . .' he tapped the Médaille de la Liberation on his chest . . . 'but only from the Minister of the Armed Forces.'

Valrémy peered at the medal. So that's the Liberation Medal. Hell of a small thing to get a leg shot off for. He remembered his authority and nodded curtly. The old man hobbled away down the street. Valrémy turned to stop another chancer who was trying to slip through the barrier.

'All right, all right, that's enough of that. Stay back behind the barrier.'

The last thing he saw of the old soldier was the flash of the greatcoat disappearing into a doorway at the far end of the street next to the square.

Madame Berthe looked up startled as the shadow fell over her. It had been a trying day, what with policemen looking in all the rooms, and she didn't know what the tenants would have said if they had been there. Fortunately all but three were away for the August holidays.

When the police had gone she had been able to settle back in her usual place in the doorway for a bit of quiet knitting. The ceremony due to take place a hundred yards away across the square in the station forecourt in two hours interested her not in the slightest.

'Excusez-moi, madame ... I was wondering ... perhaps a glass of water. It is terribly hot waiting for the ceremony....'

She took in the face and form of an old man in a greatcoat such as her long-dead husband had once worn, with medals swinging below the lapel on the left breast. He leaned heavily on a crutch, one single leg protruding from beneath the greatcoat. His face looked haggard and sweaty. Madame Berthe bundled up her knitting and stuffed it into the pocket of her apron.

'Oh, mon pauv', monsieur. Walking around like that ... and in this heat. The ceremony is not for two hours yet. You are early ... Come in, come in ...'

She bustled off towards the glass-fronted door of her parlour at the back of the hall to get a glass of water. The war veteran hobbled after her.

Above the running of the water from the kitchen tap she did not hear the door close on the outer lobby; she hardly felt the fingers of the man's left hand slide round her jawbone from behind. And the crash of the bunched knuckles under the mastoid bone on the right side of her head just behind the ear was completely unexpected. The image of the running tap and the filling glass in front of her exploded into fragments of red and black, and her inert form slid soundlessly to the floor.

The Jackal opened the front of his coat, reached for the waist and unbuckled the harness that kept his right leg strapped up under his buttocks. As he straightened the leg and flexed the cramped knee his face tightened with pain. He spent several minutes allowing the blood to flow back into the calf and ankle of the leg before putting any weight on it.

Five minutes later Madame Berthe was trussed up hand and foot with the clothes line from beneath the sink, and her mouth was covered with a large square of sticking plaster. He put her in the scullery and shut the door.

A search of the parlour revealed the keys of the flat in the table drawer. Re-buttoning the coat, he took up the crutch, the same on which he had hobbled through the airports of Brussels and Milan twelve days earlier, and peered outside. The hall was empty. He left the parlour, locked the door after him, and loped up the stairs.

On the sixth floor he chose the flat of Mademoiselle Béranger and knocked. There was no sound. He waited and knocked again. From neither that flat nor the next-door one of M. and Mme Charrier came a sound. Taking the keys he searched for the name Béranger, found it and entered the flat, closing and locking the door after him.

He crossed to the window and looked out. Across the road, on the roof-tops of the blocks opposite, men in blue uniforms were moving into position. He was only just in time. At arm's length he unclipped the window lock and swung both halves of the frame quietly inwards until they came back against the inside of the living-room wall. Then he stepped well back. A square shaft of light fell through the window on to the carpet. By contrast the rest of the room appeared darker.

If he stayed away from that square of light, the watchers opposite would see nothing.

Stepping to the side of the window, keeping to the shadows of the withdrawn curtains, he found he could look downwards and sideways into the forecourt of the station a hundred and thirty metres away. Eight feet back from the window and well to one side, he set up the living-room table, removing the tablecloth and pot of plastic flowers and replacing them with a pair of cushions from the armchair. These would form his firing rest.

He stripped off his greatcoat and rolled up his sleeves. The crutch came to pieces section by section. The black rubber ferrule on the end was unscrewed and revealed the shining percussion caps of his three remaining shells. The nausea and sweating inspired by eating the cordite out of the other two was only beginning to leave him.

The next section of the crutch was unscrewed, and from it slid the silencer. The second section came away to disgorge the telescopic sight. The thickest part of the crutch, where the two upper supports merged into the main stem, revealed the breech and barrel of the rifle.

From the Y-shaped frame above the join, he slid the two steel rods which, when fitted together, would become the frame of the rifle's stock. Lastly the padded armpit support of the crutch; this alone concealed nothing except the trigger of the rifle embedded in the padding. Otherwise the armpit support slid on to the stock of the gun as it was, to become the shoulder-guard.

Lovingly and meticulously he assembled the rifle – breech and barrel, upper and lower component of the stock, shoulder-guard, silencer and trigger. Lastly he slid on the telescopic sight and clipped it fast.

Sitting on a chair behind the table, leaning slightly forward with the gun barrel resting on top of the upper cushion, he squinted through the telescope. The sunlit square beyond the windows and fifty feet down leapt into focus. The head of one of the men still marking out the standing positions for the forthcoming ceremony passed across the line of sight. He tracked the target with the gun. The head appeared large and clear, as large as a melon had looked in the forest glade in the Ardennes.

Satisfied at last, he lined the three cartridges up on the edge of the table like soldiers in a row. With finger and thumb he slid back the rifle's bolt and eased the first shell into the breech. One should be enough, but he had two spare. He pushed the bolt forward again until it closed on the base of the cartridge, gave a half-twist and locked it. Finally he laid the rifle carefully among the cushions and fumbled for cigarettes and matches.

Drawing hard on his first cigarette, he leant back to wait for another hour and three-quarters.

Commissaire Claude Lebel felt as if he had never had a drink in his life. His mouth was dry and the tongue stuck to the roof of it as though it were welded there. Nor was it just the heat that caused this feeling. For the first time in many many years he was really frightened. Something, he was sure, was going to happen during that afternoon, and he still could find no clue as to how or when.

He had been at the Arc de Triomphe that morning, and at Notre Dame and at Montvalérin. Nothing had happened. Over lunch with some of the men from the committee which had met for the last time at the Ministry that day at dawn he had heard the mood change from tenseness and anger to something almost of euphoria. There was only one more cere- mony to go, and the Place du 18 Juin, he was assured, had been scoured and sealed off.

'He's gone,' said Rolland, as the group who had lunched together at a brasserie not far from the Elysée Palace while General de Gaulle lunched inside it, emerged into the sunlight. 'He's gone, pissed off. And a very wise thing too. He'll surface somewhere, sometime, and my boys will get him.'

Now Lebel prowled disconsolately round the edge of the crowd held two hundred metres down the Boulevard de Montparnasse, so far away from the square that no one could see what was going on. Each police- man and CRS man he spoke to on the barriers had the same message. No one had passed through since the barriers went up at twelve.

The main roads were blocked, the side roads were blocked, the alleys were blocked. The roof-tops were watched and guarded, the station itself, honeycombed with offices and attics facing down on to the forecourt, was crawling with security men. They perched atop the great engine sheds, high above the silent platforms from which all trains had been diverted for the afternoon to the Gare Saint-Lazare.

Inside the perimeter every building had been scoured from basement to attic. Most of the flats were empty, their occupants away on holiday at the seaside or in the mountains.

In short, the area of the Place du 18 Juin was sealed off, as Valentin would say, 'tighter than a mouse's arsehole'. Lebel smiled at the memory of the language of the Auvergnat policeman. Suddenly the grin was wiped off. Valentin had not been able to stop the Jackal either.

He slipped through the side streets, showing his police pass to take a short cut, and emerged in the Rue de Rennes. It was the same story; the road was blocked off two hundred metres from the square, the crowds massed behind the barriers, the street empty except for the patrolling CRS men. He started asking again.

Seen anyone? No, sir. Anyone been past, anyone at all? No, sir. Down in the forecourt of the station he heard the band of the Garde Républicaine tuning their instruments. He glanced at his watch. The General would be arriving any time now. Seen anybody pass, anyone at all? No, sir. Not this way. All right, carry on.

Down in the square he heard a shouted order, and from one end of the Boulevard de Montparnasse a motorcade swept into the Place du 18 Juin. He watched it turn into the gates of the station forecourt, police erect and at the salute. All eyes down the street were watching the sleek black cars. The crowd behind the barrier a few yards from him strained to get through. He looked up at the roof-tops. Good boys. The watchers of the roofs ignored the spectacle below them; their eyes never stopped flickering across the roof-tops and windows across the road from where they crouched on the parapets, watching for a slight movement at a window.

He had reached the western side of the Rue de Rennes. A young CRS man stood with his feet planted squarely in the gap where the last steel crowd barrier abutted the wall of number 132. He flashed his card at the man, who stiffened.

'Anybody passed this way?'

'No, sir.'

'How long have you been here?'

'Since twelve o'clock, sir, when the street was closed.'

'Nobody been through that gap?'

'No, sir. Well . . . only the old cripple, and he lives down there.'

'What cripple?'

'Oldish chap, sir. Looked sick as a dog. He had his ID card, and *Mutilé de Guerre* card. Address given as 154 Rue de Rennes. Well, I had to let him through, sir. He looked all in, real sick. Not surprised with him in that greatcoat, and in this weather and all. Daft, really.'

'Greatcoat?'

'Yessir. Great long coat. Military like the old soldiers used to wear. Too hot for this weather, though.'

'What was wrong with him?'

'Well, he was too hot, wasn't he, sir?'

'You said he was a war-wounded. What was wrong with him?'

'One leg, sir. Only one leg. Hobbling along he was, on a crutch.'

From down in the square the first clear peals from the trumpets sounded. 'Come, children of the Motherland, the day of glory has ar-

rived. . . .' Several of the crowd took up the familiar chant of the Mar-
seillaise.

'Crutch?' To himself, Lebel's voice seemed a small thing, very far
away. The CRS man looked at him solicitously.

'Yessir. A crutch, like one-legged men always have. An aluminium
crutch. . . .'

Lebel was haring off down the street yelling at the CRS man to follow
him.

They were drawn up in the sunlight in a hollow square. The cars were
parked nose to tail along the wall of the station façade. Directly opposite the cars, along the railings that separated the forecourt from the
square, were the ten recipients of the medals to be distributed by the
Head of State. On the east side of the forecourt were the officials and
diplomatic corps, a solid mass of charcoal-grey suiting, with here and
there the red rosebud of the Legion of Honour.

The western side was occupied by the serried red plumes and bur-
nished casques of the Garde Républicaine, the bandsmen standing a little
out in front of the guard of honour itself.

Round one of the cars up against the station façade clustered a group
of protocol officials and palace staff. The band started to play the Mar-
seillaise.

The Jackal raised the rifle and squinted down into the forecourt. He
picked the war veteran nearest to him, the man who would be the first to
get his medal. He was a short, stocky man, standing very erect. His head
came clearly into the sight, almost a complete profile. In a few minutes,
facing this man, about one foot taller, would be another face, proud,
arrogant, topped by a khaki képi adorned with two gold stars on the
front.

'Marchons, marchons, à la Victoire . . .' Boom-a-boom. The last notes
of the National Anthem died away, replaced by a great silence. The roar
of the Commander of the Guard echoed across the station yard. 'General
Salute. . . . Pres-e-e-ent arms.' There were three precise crashes as white-
gloved hands smacked in unison across rifle-butts and magazines, and
heels came down together. The crowd around the car parted, falling back
in to halves. From the centre a single tall figure emerged and began to
stalk towards the line of war veterans. At fifty metres from them the rest
of the crowd stopped, except the Minister of Ancient Combatants, who
would introduce the veterans to their President, and an official carrying a
velvet cushion with a row of ten pieces of metal and ten coloured
ribbons on it. Apart from these two, Charles de Gaulle marched forward
alone.

'This one?'

Lebel stopped, panting, and gestured towards a doorway.

'I think so, sir. Yes, this was it, second from the end. This was where he
came in.'

The little detective was gone down the hallway, and Valrémy followed

him, not displeased to be out of the street, where their odd behaviour in
the middle of a serious occasion was attracting disapproving frowns
from the higher brass standing at attention against the railings of the
station yard. Well, if he was put on the carpet, he could always say that
the funny little man had posed as a Commissaire of Police, and that he
had been trying to detain him.

When he got into the hall the detective was shaking the door of the
concierge's parlour.

'Where's the concierge?' he yelled.

'I don't know, sir.'

Before he could protest, the little man had smashed the frosted-glass
panel with his elbow, reached inside and opened the door.

'Follow me,' he called, and dashed inside.

Too bloody right I'm going to follow you, thought Valrémy. You're off
your chump.

He found the little detective at the door or the scullery. Looking over
the man's shoulder he saw the concierge tied up on the floor, still unconscious.

'Blimey.' Suddenly it occured to him the little man was not joking. He
was a police commissaire, and they were after a criminal. This was the
big moment he had always dreamed of, and he wished he was back in
barracks.

'Top floor,' shouted the detective, and was gone up the stairs with a
speed that surprised Valrémy, who pounded after him, unslinging his
carbine as he ran.

The President of France paused before the first man in the line of veterans and stooped slightly to listen to the Minister explain who he was
and what was his citation for valour shown on that day nineteen years
before. When the Minister had finished he inclined his head towards the
veteran, turned towards the man with the cushion, and took the
proffered medal. As the band began a softly played rendering of 'La Marjolaine' the tall General pinned the medal on to the rounded chest of the
elderly man in front of them. Then he stepped back for the salute.

Six floors up and a hundred and thirty metres away the Jackal held
the rifle very steady and squinted down the telescopic sight. He could
see the features quite clearly, the brow shaded by the peak of the képi,
the peering eyes, the prow-like nose. He saw the raised saluting hand
come down from the peak of the cap, the crossed wires of the sight were
spot on the exposed temple. Softly, gently, he squeezed the trigger. . . .

A split second later he was staring down into the station forecourt as if
he could not believe his eyes. Before the bullet had passed out of the end
of the barrel, the President of France had snapped his head forward without warning. As the assassin watched in disbelief, he solemnly planted a
kiss on each cheek of the man in front of him. As he himself was a foot
taller, he had had to bend forward and down to give the traditional kiss
of congratulation that is habitual among the French and certain other
nations, but which baffles Anglo-Saxons.

It was later established the bullet had passed a fraction of an inch behind the moving head. Whether the President heard the whipcrack from the sound barrier, travelling on a narrow line down the flight path of the bullet, is not known. He gave no sign of it. The Minister and the official heard nothing: neither did those fifty metres away.

The slug tore into the sun-softened tarmacadam of the forecourt, its disintegration taking place harmlessly inside more than an inch of tar. 'La Marjolaine' played on. The President, after planting the second kiss, straightened up and moved sedately on towards the next man.

Behind his gun, the Jackal started to swear, softly, venomously. He had never missed a stationary target at a hundred and fifty yards in his life before. Then he calmed down; there was still time. He tore open the breech of the rifle, ejecting the spent cartridge to fall harmlessly on to the carpet. Taking the second one off the table he pushed it home and closed the breech.

Claude Lebel arrived panting on the sixth floor. He thought his heart was going to come out of his chest and roll all over the landing. There were two doors leading towards the front of the building. He looked from one to the other as the CRS man joined him, submachine carbine held on his hip, pointing forward. As Lebel hesitated in front of the two doors, from behind one of them came a low but distinct 'Phut'. Lebel pointed at the door lock with his forefinger.

'Shoot it off,' he ordered, and stepped back. The CRS man braced himself on both feet and fired. Bits of wood, metal and spent, flattened slugs flew in all directions. The door buckled and swung drunkenly inwards. Valrémy was first into the room, Lebel on his heels.

Valrémy could recognise the grey tufts of hair, but that was all. The man had two legs, the greatcoat was gone, and the forearms that gripped the rifle were on a strong young man. The gunman gave him no time; rising from his seat behind the table, swinging in one smooth motion at a half-crouch, he fired from the hip. The single bullet made no sound; the echoes of Valrémy's gun-burst were still ringing in his ears. The slug from the rifle tore into his chest, struck the sternum and exploded. There was a feeling of tearing and ripping and of great sudden stabs of pain; then even they were gone. The light faded as if summer had turned to winter.

A piece of carpet came up and smacked him on the cheek, except that it was his cheek that was lying on the carpet. The loss of feeling swept up through the thighs and belly, then the chest and neck. The last thing he remembered was a salty taste in the mouth, like he had had after bathing in the sea at Kermadec, and a one-legged old gull sitting on a post. Then it was all dark.

Above his body Claude Lebel stared into the eyes of the other man. He had no trouble with his heart; it did not seem to be pumping any more.

'Chacal,' he said. The other man said simply, 'Lebel.' He was fumbling with the gun, tearing open the breech. Lebel saw the glint as the cartridge case dropped to the floor. The man swept something off the table and stuffed it into the breech. His grey eyes were still staring at Lebel.

He's trying to fix me rigid, thought Lebel with a sense of unrealism. He's going to shoot. He's going to kill me.

With an effort he dropped his eyes to the floor. The boy from the CRS had fallen sideways: his carbine had slipped from his fingers and lay at Lebel's feet. Without conscious thought he dropped to his knees, grabbed the MAT 49, swinging it upwards with one hand, the other clawing for the trigger. He heard the Jackal snap home the breech of the rifle as he found the trigger of the carbine. He pulled it.

The roar of the exploding ammunition filled the small room and was heard in the square. Later press enquiries were met with the explanation that it had been a motor-cycle with a faulty silencer which some ass had kicked into life a few streets away at the height of the ceremony. Half a magazine full of nine-millimetre bullets hit the Jackal in the chest, picked him up, half-turned him in the air and slammed his body into an untidy heap in the far corner near the sofa. As he fell, he brought the standard lamp with him. Down below, the band struck up 'Mon Régiment et Ma Patrie'.

Superintendent Thomas had a phone call at six that evening from Paris. He sent for the senior inspector of his staff.

'They got him,' he said. 'In Paris. No problems, but you'd better get up to his flat and sort things out.'

It was eight o'clock when the inspector was having a last sort-through of Calthrop's belongings that he heard someone come into the open door-way. He turned. A man was standing there scowling at him. A big-built, burly man.

'What are you doing here?' asked the inspector.

'I might ask you just the same thing. What the hell do you think you're doing?'

'All right, that's enough,' said the inspector. 'Let's have your name.'

'Calthrop,' said the newcomer, 'Charles Calthrop. And this is my flat. Now what the hell are you doing to it?'

The inspector wished he carried a gun.

'All right,' he said quietly, warily. 'I think you'd better come down to the Yard for a little chat.'

'Too bloody right,' said Calthrop. 'You've got a bit of explaining to do.'

But in fact it was Calthrop who did the explaining. They held him for twenty-four hours, until three separate confirmations came through from Paris that the Jackal was dead, and five landlords of isolated taverns in the far north of Sunderland County, Scotland, had testified that Charles Calthrop had indeed spent the previous three weeks indulging his passion for climbing and fishing, and had stayed at their establishments.

'If the Jackal wasn't Calthrop,' asked Thomas of his inspector when Calthrop finally walked out of the door a free man, 'then who the hell was he?'

'There can be no question, of course,' said the Commissioner of Metro-politan Police the next day to Assistant Commissioner Dixon and Superintendent Thomas, 'of Her Majesty's Government ever conceding that this Jackal fellow was an Englishman at all. So far as one can see there was a period when a certain Englishman came under suspicion. He has now been cleared. We also know that for a period of his ... er ... assignment in France, the Jackal feller masqueraded as an Englishman under a falsely issued English passport. But he also masqueraded as a Dane, an American and a Frenchman, under two stolen passports and one set of forged French papers. As far as we are concerned, our enquiries established that the assassin was travelling in France under a false passport in the name of Duggan, and in this name he was traced to ... er ... this place Gap. That's all. Gentlemen, the case is closed.'

The following day the body of a man was buried in an unmarked grave at a suburban cemetery in Paris. The death certificate showed the body to be that of an unnamed foreign tourist, killed on Sunday, August 25th, 1963, in a hit-and-run accident on the motorway outside the city. Present were a priest, a policeman, a registrar and two grave-diggers. Nobody present showed any interest as the plain deal coffin was lowered into the grave, except the single other person who attended. When it was all over he turned round, declined to give his name, and walked back down the cemetery path, a solitary little figure, to return home to his wife and children.

The day of the Jackal was over.

THE
ODESSA
FILE

To all Press reporters

Author's note

It is customary for authors to thank those who have helped them to compile a book, particularly on a difficult subject, and in doing so to name them. All those who helped me, in however small a way, by assisting me to get the information I needed to write *The Odessa File* are entitled to my heartfelt thanks, and if I do not name them it is for three reasons.

Some, being former members of the SS, were not aware at the time either who they were talking to or that what they said would end up in a book. Others have specifically asked that their names never be mentioned as sources of information about the SS. In the case of others still, the decision not to mention their names is mine alone, and taken I hope for their sakes rather than for mine.

Foreword

The ODESSA of the title is neither the city in southern Russia nor the small town in America. It is a word composed of six initial letters, which in German stand for 'Organisation Der Ehemaligen SS-Angehörigen'. In English this means 'Organisation of Former Members of the SS'.

The SS, as most readers will know, was the army within an army, the state within a state, devised by Adolf Hitler, commanded by Heinrich Himmler, and charged with special tasks under the Nazis who ruled Germany from 1933 to 1945. These tasks were supposedly concerned with the security of the Third Reich; in effect they included the carrying out of Hitler's ambition to rid Germany and Europe of all elements he considered to be 'unworthy of life', to enslave in perpetuity the 'subhuman races of the Slavic lands', and to exterminate every Jew, man, woman and child, on the face of the continent.

In carrying out these tasks the SS organised and executed the murder of some fourteen million human beings, comprising roughly six million Jews, five million Russians, two million Poles, half a million gypsies and half a million mixed others, including, though it is seldom mentioned, close to two hundred thousand non-Jewish Germans and Austrians. These were either mentally or physically handicapped unfortunates or so-called enemies of the Reich, like Communists, Social Democrats, Liberals, editors, reporters and priests who spoke out too inconveniently, men of conscience and courage, and later army officers suspected of lack of loyalty to Hitler.

Before it had been destroyed the SS had made the two initials of its name, and the twin-lightning symbol of its standard, syonymous with inhumanity in a way that no other organisation before or since has been able to do.

Before the end of the war its most senior members, quite aware the war was lost and under no illusions as to how civilised men would regard their actions when the reckoning came, made secret provision to disappear to a new life, leaving the entire German people to carry and share the blame for the vanished culprits. To this end vast sums of SS gold were smuggled out and deposited in numbered bank accounts, false identity papers were prepared, escape channels opened up. When the Allies finally conquered Germany the bulk of the mass-murderers had gone.

The organisation which they formed to effect their escape was the Odessa. When the first task of ensuring the escape to more hospitable climes of the killers had been achieved the ambitions of these men developed. Many never left Germany at all, preferring to remain under cover with false names and papers while the Allies ruled; others came back, suitably protected by a new identity. The few very top men remained abroad to manipulate the organisation from the safety of a comfortable exile.

The aim of the Odessa was and remains five-fold: to rehabilitate former SS men into the professions of the new Federal Republic created in 1949 by the Allies, to infiltrate at least the lower echelons of political party activity, to pay for the very best legal defence for any SS killer hauled before a court and in every way possible to stultify the course of justice in West Germany when it operates against a former *Kamerad*, to ensure former SS men establish themselves in commerce and industry in time to take advantage of the economic miracle that has rebuilt the country since 1945, and finally to propagandise the German people to the viewpoint that the SS killers were in fact none other than ordinary patriotic soldiers doing their duty to the Fatherland, and in no way deserving of the persecution to which justice and conscience have ineffectually subjected them.

In all these tasks, backed by their considerable funds, they have been measurably successful, and in none more so than in reducing official retribution through the West German courts to a mockery. Changing its name several times, the Odessa has sought to deny its own existence as an organisation, with the result that many Germans are inclined to say the Odessa does not exist. The short answer is: it exists and the *Kameraden* of the Death's Head insignia are still linked within it.

Despite its successes in almost all its objectives, the Odessa does occasionally take a defeat. The worst it ever suffered occurred in the early spring of 1964 when a package of documents arrived unannounced and anonymously at the Ministry of Justice in Bonn. To the very few officials who ever saw the list of names on these sheets, the package became known as 'The Odessa File'.

1

Everyone seems to remember with great clarity what they were doing on November 22nd, 1963, at the precise moment they heard President Kennedy was dead. He was hit at 12.22 in the afternoon, Dallas time, and the announcement that he was dead came at half past one in the same time zone. It was 2.30 in New York, 7.30 in the evening in London and 8.30 on a chilly, sleet-swept night in Hamburg.

Peter Miller was driving back into the town centre after visiting his mother at her home in Osdorf, one of the outer suburbs of the city. He always visited her on Friday evenings, partly to see if she had everything she needed for the weekend and partly because he felt he had to visit her once a week. He would have telephoned her if she had a telephone, but as she had none, he drove out to see her. That was why she refused to have a telephone.

As usual he had the radio on, and was listening to a music show being broadcast by North West German Radio. At half past eight he was in the Osdorf Way, ten minutes from his mother's flat, when the music stopped in the middle of a bar and the voice of the announcer came through, taut with tension.

'*Achtung, Achtung.* Here is an announcement. President Kennedy is dead. I repeat, President Kennedy is dead.'

Miller took his eyes off the road and stared at the dimly illuminated band of frequencies along the upper edge of the radio, as if his eyes would be able to deny what his ears had heard, assure him he was tuned in to the wrong radio station, the one that broadcast nonsense.

'Jesus,' he breathed quietly, eased down on the brake pedal and swung into the right-hand side of the road. He glanced up. Right down the long, broad, straight highway through Altona towards the centre of Hamburg other drivers had heard the same broadcast and were pulling in to the side of the road as if driving and listening to the radio had suddenly become mutually exclusive, which in a way they had.

Along his own side he could see the brake lights glowing on as the drivers ahead swung to the right to park at the kerb and listen to the supplementary information pouring from their radios. On the left the headlights of the cars heading out of town wavered wildly as they too swung away towards the pavement. Two cars overtook him, the first hooting angrily and he caught a glimpse of the driver tapping his forehead in Miller's direction in the usual rude sign, indicating lunacy, that one German driver makes to another who has annoyed him.

He'll learn soon enough, thought Miller.

The light music on the radio had stopped, replaced by the Funeral March, which was evidently all the disc jockey had to hand. At intervals he read snippets of further information straight off the teleprinter as they were brought in from the newsroom. The details began to fill in: the open car ride into Dallas city, the rifleman in the window of the School Book Depository. No mention of an arrest.

The driver of the car ahead of Miller climbed out and walked back towards him. He approached the left-hand window, then realised that the driver's seat was inexplicably on the right and came round the car. He wore a nylon-fur collared jacket. Miller wound down his window.

'You heard it?' asked the man, bending down to the window.

'Yeah,' said Miller.

'Bloody fantastic,' said the man. All over Hamburg, Europe, the world, people were walking up to complete strangers to discuss the event.

'You reckon it was the Communists?' asked the man.

'I don't know.'

'It could mean war, you know, if it was them,' said the man.

'Maybe,' said Miller. He wished the man would go away. As a reporter he could imagine the chaos sweeping across the newspaper offices of the country as every staff man was called back to help put out a crash edition for the morning breakfast tables. There would be obituaries to prepare, the thousands of instant tributes to correlate and type-set, the telephone lines jammed with yelling men seeking more and ever more details because a man with his throat torn out lay on a slab in a town in Texas.

He wished in a way he were back on the staff of a daily newspaper, but since he became a freelance three years earlier he had specialised in news features inside Germany, mainly connected with crime, the police, the underworld. His mother hated the job, accusing him of mixing with 'nasty people', and his arguments that he was becoming one of the most sought-after reporter-investigators in the country availed nothing in persuading her that a reporter's job was worthy of her only son.

As the reports from the radio came through, his mind was racing, trying to think of another 'angle' that could be chased up inside Germany and might make a sidebar story to the main event. The reaction of the Bonn government would be covered out of Bonn by the staff men, the memories of Kennedy's visit to Berlin the previous June would be covered from there. There didn't seem to be a good pictorial feature he could ferret out to sell to any of the score of German picture magazines that were the best customers of his kind of journalism.

The man leaning on the window sensed that Miller's attention was

285 THE ODESSA FILE

elsewhere and assumed it was out of grief for the dead president. Quickly he dropped his talk of world war and adopted the same grave demeanour.

'Ja, ja, ja,' he murmured with sagacity, as if he had seen it coming all along. 'Violent people, these Americans, mark my words, violent people. There's a streak of violence in them that we over here will never understand.'

'Sure,' said Miller, his mind still miles away. The man took the hint at last.

'Well, I must be getting home,' he said straightening up. 'Grüss Gott.' He started to walk back to his own car. Miller became aware he was going.

'Ja, gute Nacht,' he called out of the open window, then wound it up against the sleet whipping in off the Elbe river. The music on the radio had been replaced by a slow march, and the announcer said there would be no more light music that night, just news bulletins interspersed with suitable music.

Miller leaned back in the comfortable leather upholstery of his Jaguar and lit up a Roth-Händl, a filterless black-tobacco cigarette with a foul smell, another thing that his mother complained about in her disappointing son.

It is always tempting to wonder what would have happened if ... or if not. Usually it is a futile exercise, for what might have been is the greatest of all the mysteries. But it is probably accurate to say that if Miller had not had his radio on that night he would not have pulled in to the side of the road for half an hour. He would not have seen the ambulance, nor heard of Salomon Tauber or Eduard Roschmann, and forty months later the republic of Israel would probably have ceased to exist.

He finished his cigarette, still listening to the radio, wound down the window and threw the stub away. At a touch of the button the 3.8 litre engine beneath the long sloping bonnet of the Jaguar XK 150 S thundered once and settled down to its habitual and comforting rumble like an angry animal trying to get out of a cage. Miller flicked on the two headlights, checked behind and swung out into the growing traffic stream along Osdorf Way.

He had got as far as the traffic lights on Stresemann Strasse and they were standing at red when he heard the clamour of the ambulance behind him. It came past him on the left, the wail of the siren rising and falling, slowed slightly before heading into the road junction against the red light, then swung across Miller's nose and down to the right into Daimler Strasse. Miller reacted on reflexes alone. He let in the clutch and the Jaguar surged after the ambulance twenty metres behind it.

As soon as he had done it he wished he had gone straight on home. It was probably nothing, but one never knew. Ambulances meant trouble and trouble could mean a story, particularly if one were first on the scene and the whole thing had been cleared up before the staff reporters arrived. It could be a major crash on the road, or a big wharf fire, a tenement building ablaze with children trapped inside. It could be anything. Miller always carried a small Yashica with flash attachment in the glove compartment of his car because one never knew what was going to happen right in front of one's eyes.

He knew a man who had been waiting for a plane at Munich airport on February 6th, 1958, and the plane carrying the Manchester United football team had crashed a few hundred metres from where he stood. The man was not even a professional photographer, but he had unslung the camera he was taking on a ski-ing holiday and snapped the first exclusive pictures of the burning aircraft. The pictorial magazines had paid over £5000 for them.

The ambulance twisted into the maze of small and mean streets of Altona, leaving the Altona railway station on the left and heading down towards the river. Whoever was driving the flat-snouted, high-roofed Mercedes ambulance knew his Hamburg and knew how to drive. Even with his great acceleration and hard suspension, Miller could feel the back wheels of the Jaguar skidding across the cobbles, slick with rain.

Miller watched Menck's auto-parts warehouse rush by and two streets later his original question was answered. The ambulance drew up in a poor and sleazy street, ill-lit and gloomy in the slanting sleet, bordered by crumbling tenements and rooming-houses. It stopped in front of one of these where a police car already stood, its blue roof-light twirling, the beam sending a ghostly glow across the faces of a knot of bystanders grouped round the door.

A burly police sergeant in a rain-cape roared at the crowd to stand back and make a gap in front of the door for the ambulance. Into this the Mercedes slid. Its driver and attendant climbed down, ran round to the back and eased out an empty stretcher. After a brief word with the sergeant the pair hastened upstairs.

Miller pulled the Jaguar to the opposite kerb twenty yards down the road and raised his eyebrows. No crash, no fire, no trapped children. Probably just a heart attack. He climbed out and strolled over to the crowd which the sergeant was holding back in a semicircle around the door of the rooming-house to clear a path from the door to the rear of the ambulance.

'Mind if I go up?' asked Miller.

'Certainly do. It's nothing to do with you.'

'I'm Press,' said Miller, proffering his Hamburg City press card.

'And I'm police,' said the sergeant. 'Nobody goes up. Those stairs are narrow enough as it is, and none too safe. The ambulance men will be down directly.'

He was a big man, as befits top sergeants of the police force in the rougher sections of Hamburg. Standing six feet three and in his rain-cape, with his arms spread wide to hold back the crowd, he looked as immovable as a barn door.

'What's up, then?' asked Miller.

'Can't make statements. Check at the station later on.'

A man in civilian clothes came down the stairs and emerged on to the pavement. The turning light on top of the Volkswagen patrol car swung across his face and Miller recognised him. They had been at school together at Hamburg Central High. The man was now a junior detective inspector in the Hamburg police, stationed at Altona Central.

'Hey, Karl.'

The young inspector turned at the call of his name and scanned the crowd behind the sergeant. In the next swirl of the police-car light he caught sight of Miller and his raised right hand. His face broke into a grin, part of pleasure, part exasperation. He nodded to the sergeant.

'It's all right, Sergeant. He's more or less harmless.'

The sergeant lowered his arm and Miller darted past. He shook hands with Karl Brandt.

'What are you doing here?'

'Followed the ambulance.'

'Bloody vulture. What are you up to these days?'

'Same as usual. Freelancing.'

'Making quite a packet out of it, by the look of it. I keep seeing your name in the picture magazines.'

'It's a living. Hear about Kennedy?'

'Yes. Hell of a thing. They must be turning Dallas inside out tonight. Glad it wasn't on my patch.'

Miller nodded towards the dimly lit hallway of the rooming-house where a low-watt naked bulb cast a yellow glare over peeling wallpaper.

'A suicide. Gas. Neighbours smelt it coming under the door and called us. Just as well no one struck a match, the place was reeking with it.'

'Not a film-star, by any chance?' asked Miller.

'Yeah. Sure. They always live in places like this. No, it was an old man. Looked as if he had been dead for years anyway. Someone does it every night.'

'Well, wherever he's gone now it can't be worse than this.'

The inspector gave a fleeting smile and turned as the two ambulance men negotiated the last seven steps of the creaking stairs and came down the hallway with their burden. Brandt turned round.

'Make a bit of room. Let them through.'

The sergeant promptly took up the cry and pushed the crowd back even further. The two ambulance men walked out on to the pavement and round to the open doors of the Mercedes. Brandt followed them, with Miller at his heels. Not that Miller wanted to look at the dead man, or even intended to. He was just following Brandt. As the ambulance men reached the door of the vehicle the first one hitched his end of the stretcher into the runners and the second prepared to shove it inside.

'Hold it,' said Brandt, and flicked back the corner of the blanket above the dead man's face. He remarked over his shoulder, 'Just a formality. My report has to say I accompanied the body to the ambulance and back to the morgue.'

The interior lights of the Mercedes ambulance were bright, and Miller caught a single two-second look at the face of the suicide. His first and only impression was that he had never seen anything so old and ugly. Even given the effects of gassing, the dull mottling of the skin, the bluish tinge at the lips, the man in life could have been no beauty. A few strands of lank hair were plastered over the otherwise naked scalp. The eyes were closed. The face was hollowed out to the point of emaciation and, with the man's false teeth missing, each cheek seemed to be sucked inwards till they almost touched inside the mouth, giving the effect of a ghoul in a horror film. The lips hardly existed and both upper and lower were lined with vertical creases, reminding Miller of the shrunken skull from the Amazon basin he had once seen, whose lips had been sewn together by the natives. To cap the effect the man seemed to have two pale and jagged scars running down his face, each from the temple or upper ear to the corner of the mouth.

After a quick glance, Brandt pulled the blanket back and nodded to the ambulance attendant behind him. He stepped back as the man rammed the stretcher into its berth, locked the doors and went round to the cab to join his mate. The ambulance surged away, the crowd started to disperse accompanied by the sergeant's muted growls, 'Come on, it's all over. There's nothing more to see. Haven't you got homes to go to?'.

Miller looked at Brandt and raised his eyebrows.

'Charming.'

'Yes. Poor old sod. Nothing in it for you, though?'

Miller looked pained.

'Not a chance. Like you say, there's one a night. People are dying all over the world tonight and nobody's taking a bit of notice. Not with Kennedy dead.'

Inspector Brandt laughed mockingly.

'You bloody journalists.'

'Let's face it. Kennedy's what people want to read about. They buy the newspapers.'

'Yeah. Well, I must get back to the station. See you, Peter.'

They shook hands again and parted. Miller drove back towards Altona station, picked up the main road back into the city centre and twenty minutes later swung the Jaguar into the underground car-park off the Hansa Square, 200 yards from the house where he had his roof-top flat.

Keeping the car in an underground car-park all winter was costly, but it was one of the extravagances he permitted himself. He liked his fairly expensive flat because it was high and he could look down on the bustling boulevard of the Steindamm. Of his clothes and food he thought nothing, and at twenty-nine, just under six feet, with the rumpled brown hair and brown eyes that women go for, he didn't need expensive clothes. An envious friend had once told him, 'You could pull birds in a monastery,' and he had laughed, but been pleased at the same time because he knew it was true.

The real passion of his life was sports cars, reporting and Sigrid, though he sometimes shamefacedly admitted that if it came to a choice between Sigi and the Jaguar, Sigi would have to find her loving somewhere else.

He stood and looked at the Jaguar in the lights of the garage after he had parked it. He could seldom get enough of looking at that car. Even approaching it in the street he would stop and admire it, occasionally joined by a passer-by who, not realising it was Miller's, would stop also and remark, 'Some motor, that.'

Normally a young freelance reporter does not drive a Jaguar XK 150 S. Spare parts were almost impossible to come by in Hamburg, the more so as the XK series, of which the S model was the last ever made, had gone out of production in 1960. He maintained it himself, spending hours on Sunday in overalls beneath the chassis or half buried in the engine. The petrol it used with its three SU carburetters was a major strain on his pocket, the more so with the price of petrol in Germany, but he paid it willingly. The reward was to hear the berserk snarl of the exhausts when he hit the accelerator on the open autobahn, to feel the surge of thrust as it rocketed out of a turn on a mountain road. He had even hardened up the independent suspension on the two front wheels and as the car had stiff suspension at the back it took corners steady as a rock, leaving other drivers rolling wildly on their cushion springs if they tried to keep up with him. Just after buying it he had had it re-sprayed black with a long wasp-yellow streak down each side. As it had been made in Coventry, England, and not as an export car, the driver's wheel was on the right, which caused the occasional problem for overtaking but allowed him to change gear with the left hand and hold the shuddering steering wheel in the right hand, which he had come to prefer.

Even thinking back how he had been able to buy it caused him to wonder at his luck. Earlier that summer he had idly opened a pop magazine while waiting in a barber's shop to have his hair cut. Normally he never read the gossip about pop-stars, but there was nothing else to read. The centre-page spread had been about the meteoric rise to fame and international stardom of four tousle-headed English youths. The face on the extreme right of the picture, the one with the big nose, meant nothing to him, but the other three faces rang a bell in his filing-cabinet of a memory.

The names of the two discs that had brought the quartet to stardom, 'Please Please Me' and 'Love Me Do', meant nothing either, but three of the faces puzzled him for two days. Then he remembered them, two years earlier in 1961, singing way down the bill at a small cabaret off the Reeperbahn. It took him another day to recall the name, for he had only once popped in for a drink to chat up an underworld figure from whom he needed information about the Sankt Pauli gang. The Star Club. He went down there and checked through the billings for 1961 and found them. They had been five then, the three he recognised and two others, Pete Best and Stuart Sutcliffe.

From there he went to the photographer who had done the publicity photographs for the impresario Bert Kaempfert, and had bought right and title to every one he had. His story 'How Hamburg Discovered the Beatles' had made almost every pop-music and picture magazine in Germany and a lot abroad. On the proceeds he had bought the Jaguar which he had been eyeing in a car showroom where it had been sold by a British

Army officer whose wife had grown too pregnant to fit into it. He even bought some Beatle records out of gratitude, but Sigi was the only one who ever played them.

He left the car and walked up the ramp to the street and back to his flat. It was nearly midnight and although his mother had fed him at six that evening with the usual enormous meal she provided when he called, he was hungry again. He made a plate of scrambled eggs and listened to the late night news. It was all about Kennedy and heavily accented on the German angles, since there was little more news coming through from Dallas. The police were still searching for the killer. The announcer went into great lengths about Kennedy's love of Germany, his visit to Berlin the previous summer, and his statement in German: 'Ich bin ein Berliner.'

There was then a recorded tribute from the Governing Mayor of West Berlin, Willy Brandt, his voice choked with emotion, and other tributes were read from Chancellor Ludwig Erhard and the former Chancellor Konrad Adenauer who had retired the previous October 15th.

Peter Miller switched off and went to bed. He wished Sigi was home because he always wanted to snuggle up to her when he felt depressed, and then he got hard and then they made love, after which he fell into a dreamless sleep, much to her annoyance because it was after love-making that she always wanted to talk about marriage and children. But the cabaret at which she danced did not close till nearly four in the morning, often later on Friday nights when the provincials and tourists were thick down the Reeperbahn, prepared to buy champagne at ten times its restaurant price for a girl with big tits and a low frock, and Sigi had the biggest and the lowest.

So he smoked another cigarette and fell asleep alone at quarter to two to dream of the hideous face of the old gassed man in the slums of Altona.

While Peter Miller was eating his scrambled eggs at midnight in Hamburg five men were sitting drinking in the comfortable lounge of a house attached to a riding school near the pyramids outside Cairo. The time there was one in the morning. The five men had dined well and were in a jovial mood, the cause being the news from Dallas they had heard four hours earlier.

Three of the men were Germans, the other two Egyptians. The wife of the host and proprietor of the riding school, a favourite meeting place of the cream of Cairo society and the several-thousand-strong German colony, had gone to bed, leaving the five men to talk into the small hours.

Sitting in the leather-backed easy chair by the shuttered window was Peter Bodden, formerly a Jewish expert in the Nazi Propaganda Ministry of Dr Joseph Goebbels. Having lived in Egypt since shortly after the end of the war, where he had been spirited by the Odessa, Bodden had taken the Egyptian name of El Gumra, and worked as an expert on Jews in the Egyptian Ministry of Orientation. He held a glass of whisky. On his left was another former expert from Goebbels' staff, Max Bachmann, also working in the Orientation Ministry. He had in the meantime adopted the Moslem faith, made a trip to Mecca and was called El Hadj. In deference to his new religion he held a glass of orange juice. Both men were fanatical Nazis.

The two Egyptians were Colonel Chams Edine Badrane, personal aide to Marshal Abdel Hakim Amer, later to become Egyptian Defence Minister before being sentenced to death for treason after the Six-Day War of 1967. Colonel Badrane was destined to pass into disgrace with him. The other was Colonel Ali Samir, head of the Moukhabarat, the Egyptian secret intelligence service.

There had been a sixth guest at dinner, the guest of honour, who had rushed back to Cairo when the news came through at nine-thirty, Cairo time, that President Kennedy was dead. He was the Speaker of the Egyptian National Assembly, Anwar el Sadat, a close collaborator of President Nasser and later to become his successor.

Peter Bodden raised his glass to the ceiling.

'So Kennedy the Jew-lover is dead. Gentlemen, I give you a toast.'

'But our glasses are empty,' protested Colonel Samir.

Their host hastened to remedy the matter, filling the empty glasses with a bottle of scotch from the sideboard.

The reference to Kennedy as a Jew-lover baffled none of the five men in the room. On March 14th, 1960, while Dwight Eisenhower was still President of the United States, the Premier of Israel, David Ben-Gurion, and the Chancellor of Germany, Konrad Adenauer, had met secretly at the Waldorf-Astoria Hotel in New York, a meeting that ten years earlier would have been deemed impossible. What was deemed impossible even in 1960 was what happened at that meeting, which was why details of it took years to leak out and why even at the end of 1963 President Nasser refused to take seriously the information that the Odessa and the Moukhabarat of Colonel Samir placed on his desk.

The two statesmen had signed an agreement whereby West Germany agreed to open a credit account for Israel to the tune of fifty million dollars a year without any strings attached. Ben Gurion, however, soon discovered that to have money was one thing, to have a secure and certain source of arms was quite another. Six months later the Waldorf agreement was topped off with another, signed between the defence ministers of Germany and Israel, Franz-Josef Strauss and Shimon Peres. Under its terms Israel would be able to use the money from Germany to buy weapons in Germany.

Adenauer, aware of the vastly more controversial nature of the second agreement, delayed for months, until in November 1961 he was in New York to meet the new President, John Fitzgerald Kennedy, Kennedy put the pressure on. He did not wish to have arms delivered directly from the USA to Israel, but he wanted them to arrive somehow. Israel needed fighters, transport planes, Howitzer 105 mm artillery pieces, armoured cars, armoured personnel carriers and tanks, but above all tanks.

Germany had all of them, mainly of American make, either bought from America to offset the cost of keeping American troops in Germany under the NATO agreement or made under licence in Germany.

Under Kennedy's pressure the Strauss-Peres deal was pushed through.

The first German tanks started to arrive at Haifa in late June 1963. It was difficult to keep the news secret for long; too many people were involved. The Odessa found out in late 1962 and promptly informed the Egyptians with whom their agents in Cairo had the closest links.

In late 1963 things started to change. On October 15th Konrad Adenauer, the Fox of Bonn, the Granite Chancellor, also resigned and went into retirement. Adenauer's place was taken by Ludwig Erhard, a good vote-catcher as the father of the German economic miracle, but in matters of foreign policy weak and vacillating.

Even when Adenauer was in power there had been a vociferous group inside the West German cabinet in favour of shelving the Israeli arms deal and halting the supplies before they had begun. The old Chancellor had silenced them with a few terse sentences and such was his power they stayed silenced.

Erhard was quite a different man and already had earned himself the nickname the Rubber Lion. As soon as he took the chair the anti-arms-deal group, based on the Foreign Ministry, ever mindful of its excellent and improving relations with the Arab world, opened up again. Erhard dithered. But behind them all was the determination of John Kennedy that Israel should get her arms via Germany.

And then he was shot. The big question in the small hours of the morning of November 23rd was simply: would President Lyndon Johnson take the American pressure off Germany and let the indecisive Chancellor in Bonn renege on the deal? In fact he did not, but there were high hopes in Cairo that he would.

The host at the convivial meeting outside Cairo that night, having filled his guests' glasses, turned back to the sideboard to top up his own. His name was Wolfgang Lutz, born at Mannheim in 1921, a former major in the German Army, a fanatical Jew-hater, who had emigrated to Cairo in 1961 and started his riding academy. Blond, blue-eyed, hawk-faced, he was a top favourite among both the influential political figures of Cairo and the expatriate German and mainly Nazi community along the banks of the Nile.

He turned to face the room and gave them a broad smile. If there was anything false about that smile no one noticed it. But it was false. He had been born, a Jew, in Mannheim but had emigrated to Palestine in 1933 at the age of twelve. His name was Ze'ev and he held the rank of Rav-Seren (major) in the Israeli Army. He was also the top agent of Israeli Intelligence in Egypt at that time. On February 28th, 1965, after a raid on his home, in which a radio transmitter was discovered in the bathroom scales, he was arrested. Tried on June 26th, 1965, he was sentenced to hard labour in perpetuity. Released after the end of the 1967 war as part of an exchange against thousands of Egyptian prisoners of war, he and his wife stepped back on to the soil of home at Lod Airport on February 4th, 1968.

But the night Kennedy died this was all in the future, the arrest, the tortures, the multiple rape of his wife. He raised his glass to the four smiling faces in front of him.

In fact, he could hardly wait for his guests to depart, for something one of them had said over dinner was of vital importance to his country, and he desperately wished to be alone, to go up to his bathroom, get the transmitter out of the bathroom scales and send a message to Tel Aviv. But he forced himself to keep smiling.

'Death to the Jew-lovers,' he toasted. '*Sieg Heil.*'

Peter Miller woke the next morning just before nine and shifted luxuriously under the enormous feather cushion that covered the double bed. Even half awake he could feel the warmth of the sleeping figure of Sigi seeping across the bed at him and by reflex he snuggled closer so that her buttocks pushed into the base of his stomach. Automatically be began to erect.

Sigi, still fast asleep, after only four hours in bed, grunted in annoyance and shifted away towards the edge of the bed.

'Go away,' she muttered without waking up.

Miller sighed, turned on to his back and held up his watch, squinting at the face of it in the half-light. Then he slipped out of bed on the other side, pulled a towelling bathrobe round him and padded through into the sitting-room to pull back the curtains. The steely November light washed across the room, making him blink. He focussed his eyes and looked down into the Steindamm. It was a Saturday morning and traffic was light down the wet black tarmac. He yawned and went into the kitchen to brew the innumerable cups of coffee. Both his mother and Sigi reproached him with living almost entirely on coffee and cigarettes.

Drinking his coffee and smoking the first cigarette of the day in the kitchen he considered if there was anything particular he ought to do that day and decided there was not. For one thing all the newspapers and the next issues of the magazines would be about President Kennedy, probably for days or weeks to come. And for another there was no particular story he was chasing up at the time. Besides which, Saturday and Sunday are bad days to get hold of people in their offices, and they seldom like being disturbed at home. He had recently finished a well-received series on the steady infiltration of Austrian, Parisian and Italian gangsters into the gold-mine of the Reeperbahn, Hamburg's half-mile of night-clubs, brothels and vice, and had not yet been paid for it. He thought he might chase up the magazine to which he had sold the series, then decided against it. They would pay in time, and he was not short of money for the moment. Indeed his bank statement, which had arrived three days earlier, showed he had over 5000 marks (£500) to his credit, which he reckoned would keep him going for a while.

'The trouble with you, mate,' he told his reflection in one of Sigi's brilliantly polished saucepans as he rinsed out the cup with his forefinger, 'is that you are lazy.'

He had once been asked by a civilian careers officer at the end of his military service ten years earlier what he wanted to be in life. He had replied, 'A rich layabout,' and at twenty-nine, although he had not achieved it and probably never would, he still thought it a perfectly reasonable ambition.

He carried the portable transistor radio into the bathroom, closed the door so Sigi would not hear it, and listened to the news while he showered and shaved. The main item was that a man had been arrested for the murder of President Kennedy. As he supposed, there were no other items of news on the entire programme but those connected with the Kennedy assassination.

After drying off he went back to the kitchen and made more coffee, this time two cups. He took them into the bedroom, placed them on the bedside table, slipped off his robe and clambered back under the cushion beside Sigi, whose fluffy blonde head was protruding on to the pillow.

She was twenty-two and at school had been a champion gymnast who, so she said, could have gone on to Olympic standard if her bust had not developed to the point where it got in the way and no leotard could safely contain it. On leaving school she became a teacher of physical training at a girls' school. The change to striptease dancer in Hamburg came a year later and for the very best and most simple of economic reasons. It earned her five times more than a teacher's salary.

Despite her willingness to take her clothes off to the buff in a night-club, she was remarkably embarrassed by any lewd remarks made about her body by anyone whom she could see when the remarks were made.

'The point is,' she once told an amused Peter Miller with great seriousness, 'when I'm on the stage I can't see anything behind the lights, so I don't get embarrassed. If I could see them I think I'd run off stage.'

This did not stop her later taking her place at one of the tables in the auditorium when she was dressed again, and waiting to be invited to a drink by one of the customers. The only drink allowed was champagne, in half-bottles or preferably whole bottles. On these she collected a fifteen per cent commission. Although almost without exception the customers who invited her to drink champagne with them hoped to get much more than an hour gazing in stunned admiration at the canyon between her breasts, they never did. She was a kindly and understanding girl and her attitude to the pawing attentions of the customers was one of gentle regret rather than the contemptuous loathing that the other girls hid behind their neon smiles.

'Poor little men,' she once said to Miller, 'they ought to have a nice woman to go home to.'

'What do you mean – poor little men?' protested Miller. 'They're dirty old sods with a pocketful of cash to spend.'

'Well, they wouldn't be if they had someone to take care of them,' retorted Sigi, and on this her feminine logic was unshakable.

Miller had seen her by chance on a visit to Madam Kokett's bar just below the Café Keese on the Reeperbahn when he had gone to have a chat and a drink with the owner, an old friend and contact. She was a big girl, five feet nine inches tall and with a figure to match, which on a shorter girl would have been out of proportion. She stripped to the music with the habitual supposedly sensual gestures, her face set in the usual bedroom pout of strippers. Miller had seen it all before and sipped his drink without batting an eyelid.

But when her brassière came off even he had to stop and stare, glass half-raised to his mouth. His host eyed him sardonically.

'She's built, eh?' he said.

Miller had to admit she made *Playboy*'s playmates of the month look like severe cases of undernourishment. But she was so firmly muscled that her bosom stood outwards and upwards without a vestige of support.

At the end of her turn, when the applause started, the girl dropped the bored poise of the professional dancer, bobbed a shy, half-embarrassed little bow to the audience and gave a big sloppy grin like a half-trained bird-dog which, against all the betting, has just brought back a downed partridge. It was the grin which got Miller, not the dance routine or the figure. He asked if she would like a drink, and she was sent for.

As Miller was in the company of the boss, she avoided a bottle of champagne and asked for a gin-fizz. To his surprise Miller found she was a very nice person to be around, and asked if he might take her home after the show. With obvious reservations she agreed. Playing his cards coolly, Miller made no pass at her that night. It was early spring, and she emerged from the cabaret when it closed clad in a most unglamorous duffel coat, which he presumed was intentional.

They just had a coffee together and talked, during which she unwound from her previous tension and chatted gaily. He learned she liked pop music, art, walking along the banks of the Alster, keeping house and children. After that they started going out on her one free night a week, taking in a dinner or a show, but not sleeping together.

After three months Miller took her to his bed and later suggested she might like to move in. With her single-minded attitude to the important things of life, Sigi had already decided she wanted to marry Peter Miller and the only problem was whether she should try to get him by not sleeping in his bed or the other way round. Noticing his ability to fill the other half of his mattress with other girls if the need arose, she decided to move in and make his life so comfortable that he would want to marry her. They had been together for six months by the end of November.

Even Miller, who was hardly house-trained, had to admit she kept a beautiful home, and she made love with a healthy and bouncing enjoyment. She never mentioned marriage directly but tried to get the message across in other ways. Miller feigned not to notice. Strolling in the sun by the Alster lake she would sometimes make friends with a toddler, under the benevolent eyes of its parent.

'Oh, Peter, isn't he an angel?'

Miller would grunt: 'Yeah. Marvellous.'

After that she would freeze him for an hour for having failed to take the hint. But they were happy together, especially Peter Miller, whom the arrangement of all the comforts of marriage, the delights of regular loving, without the ties of marriage, suited down to the ground.

Drinking half his coffee, Miller slithered down into the bed and put his arms round her from behind, gently caressing her crotch, which he knew would wake her up. After a few minutes she muttered with pleasure and rolled over on to her back. Still massaging, he leant over and started to kiss her breasts. Still half asleep, she gave vent to a series of long mmmms and her hands started to move drowsily over his back and buttocks. Ten minutes later they made love, squealing and shuddering with pleasure.

'That's a hell of a way to wake me up,' she grumbled afterwards.

'There are worse ways,' said Miller.

'What's the time?'

'Nearly twelve,' Miller lied, knowing she would throw something at him if she learned it was half past ten and she had only had five hours' sleep. 'Never mind, you go back to sleep if you feel like it.'

'Mmmm. Thank you, darling, you are good to me,' said Sigi, and fell asleep again.

Miller was halfway to the bathroom after drinking the rest of his coffee and Sigi's as well when the phone rang. He diverted into the sitting-room and answered it.

'Peter?'

'Yes, who's that?'

'Karl.'

His mind was still fuzzed and he did not recognise the voice.

'Karl?'

The voice was impatient.

'Karl Brandt. What's the matter? Are you still asleep?'

Miller recovered.

'Oh yes. Sure, Karl. Sorry, I just got up. What's the matter?'

'Look, it's about this dead Jew. I want to talk to you.'

Miller was baffled.

'What dead Jew?'

'The one who gassed himself last night in Altona. Can you remember that far back?'

'Yes, of course I remember last night,' said Miller. 'I didn't know he was Jewish. What about him?'

'I want to talk to you,' said the police inspector. 'But not on the phone. Can we meet?'

Miller's reporter's mind clicked into gear immediately. Anyone who has got something to say but does not wish to say it over the phone must think it important. In the case of Brandt, Miller could hardly suspect a police detective would be so cagey about something ridiculous.

'Sure,' he said down the phone. 'Are you free for lunch?'

'I can be,' said Brandt.

'Good. I'll stand you some if you think it's something worthwhile.' He named a small restaurant on the Goose Market for one o'clock and replaced the receiver. He was still puzzled, for he couldn't see a story in the suicide of an old man, Jewish or not, in a slum tenement in Altona.

Throughout the lunch the young detective seemed to wish to avoid the subject over which he had asked for the meeting, but when the coffee came he said simply, 'The man last night.'

'Yes,' said Miller. 'What about him?'

'You must have heard, like we all have, about what the Nazis did to the Jews during the war and even before it?'

'Of course. They rammed it down our throats at school, didn't they?'

Miller was puzzled and embarrassed. Like most young Germans he had been told at school when he was twelve or thirteen that he and the rest of his countrymen had been guilty of massive war crimes. At the time he had accepted it without even knowing what was being talked about.

Later it had been difficult to find out what the teachers had meant in the immediate post-war period. There was nobody to ask, nobody who wanted to talk, not the teachers, not the parents. Only with coming manhood had he been able to read a little about it, and although what he read disgusted him, he could not feel it concerned him. It was another time, another place, a long way away. He had not been there when it happened, his father had not been there, his mother had not been there. Something inside him had persuaded him it was nothing to do with Peter Miller, so he had asked for no names, dates, details. He wondered why Brandt should be bringing the subject up.

Brandt stirred his coffee, himself embarrassed, not knowing how to go on.

'That old man last night,' he said at length. 'He was a German Jew. He was in a concentration camp.'

Miller thought back to the death's head on the stretcher the previous evening. Was that what they ended up like? It was ridiculous. The man must have been liberated by the Allies eighteen years earlier and had lived on to die of old age. But the face kept coming back. He had never seen anyone who had been in a camp before, at least, not knowingly. For that matter he had never met one of the SS mass killers, he was sure of that. One would notice, after all. The man would be different.

His mind strayed back to the publicity surrounding the Eichmann trial in Jerusalem two years earlier. The papers had been full of it for weeks on end. He thought of the face in the glass booth, and remembered that his impression at the time had been how ordinary that face had been, so depressingly ordinary. It was reading the press coverage of the trial that for the first time he had gained an inkling of how the SS had done it, how they had got away with it. But it had all been about things in Poland, Russia, Hungary, Czechoslovakia, far away and a long time back. He could not make it personal.

He brought his thoughts back to the present and the sense of unease Brandt's line of talk aroused in him.

'What about it?' he asked the detective.

For answer Brandt took a brown-paper-wrapped parcel out of his attaché case and pushed it across the table.

'The old man left a diary. Actually, he wasn't so old. Fifty-six. It seems he wrote notes at the time and stored them in his foot-wrappings. After the war he transcribed them all. They make up the diary.'

Miller looked at the parcel with scant interest.

'Where did you find it?'

'It was lying next to the body. I picked it up and took it home. I read it last night.'

Miller looked at his former schoolfriend quizzically.

'It was bad?'

'Horrible. I had no idea it was that bad, the things they did to them.'

'Why bring it to me?'

Now Brandt was embarrassed. He shrugged.

'I thought it might make a story for you.'

'Who does it belong to now?'

'Technically, Tauber's heirs. But we'll never find them. So I suppose it belongs to the Police Department. But they'd just file it. You can have it, if you want it. Just don't let on that I gave it to you. I don't need any trouble in the Force.'

Miller paid the bill and the pair walked outside.

'All right, I'll read it. But I don't promise to get steamed up about it. It might make an article for a magazine.'

Brandt turned to him with a half smile.

'You're a cynical bastard,' he said.

'No,' said Miller. 'It's just that like most people I'm concerned with the here and now. What about you? After ten years in the Force I'd have thought you'd be a tough cop. This thing really upset you, didn't it?'

Brandt was serious again. He looked at the parcel under Miller's arm and nodded slowly.

'Yes. Yes, it did. I just never thought it was that bad. And by the way, it's not all past history. That story ended here in Hamburg last night. Good-bye Peter.'

The detective turned and walked away, not knowing how wrong he was.

Peter Miller took the brown paper parcel home and arrived there just after three. He threw the package on to the sitting-room table and went to make a large pot of coffee before sitting down to read it.

Settled in his favourite armchair, with a cup of coffee at his elbow and a cigarette going, he opened it. The diary was in the form of a loose-leaf folder with stiff covers of cardboard bound in a dull black vinyl material and a series of clips down the spine so that the leaves of the book could be extracted, or further leaves inserted, if necessary.

The contents consisted of a hundred and fifty pages of typewritten script, apparently banged out on an old machine, for some of the letters were above the line, others below it and some either distorted or faint. The bulk of the pages seemed to have been written years before, or over a period of years, for most of the pages, although neat and clean, bore the unmistakable tinting of white paper several years old. But at the front and back were a number of fresh sheets, evidently written barely a few days previously. There was a preface of some new pages at the front of the typescript and a sort of epilogue at the back. A check of the dates on the preface and the epilogue showed both to have been written on November 21st, two days previously. Miller supposed the dead man had written them after he had made the decision to end his life.

A quick glance at some of the paragraphs on the first page surprised him, for the language was clear and precise German, the writing of a well-educated and cultured man. On the outside front cover a square of white paper had been gummed, and over it a large square of cellophane to keep it clean. On the square of paper had been written in large block capitals in black ink THE DIARY OF SALOMON TAUBER.

Miller settled himself deeper in his chair, turned to the first page and began to read.

THE DIARY OF SALOMON TAUBER
Preface

My name is Salomon Tauber, I am a Jew and about to die. I have decided to end my own life because it has no more value, nor is there anything left for me to do. Those things that I have tried to do with my life have come to nothing, and my efforts have been unavailing. For the evil that I have seen has survived and flourished and only the good has departed in dust and mockery. The friends that I have known, the sufferers and the victims, are all dead and only the persecutors are all around me. I see their faces on the streets in the daytime, and in the night I see the face of my wife Esther who died long ago. I have stayed alive this long only because there was one more thing I wished to do, one thing I wanted to see, and now I know I never shall.

I bear no hatred nor bitterness towards the German people, for they are a good people. Peoples are not evil; only individuals are evil. The English philosopher Burke was right when he said, 'I do not know the means for drawing up the indictment of an entire nation'. There is no collective guilt, for the Bible relates how the Lord wished to destroy Sodom and Gomorrah for the evil of the men who lived in them, with their women and their children, but how there was living among them one righteous man, and because he was righteous he was spared. Therefore guilt is individual like salvation.

When I came out of the concentration camps of Riga and Stutthof, when I survived the Death March to Magdeburg, when the British soldiers liberated my body there in April 1945, leaving only my soul in chains, I hated the world. I hated the people, and the trees and the rocks, for they had conspired against me and made me suffer. And above all I hated the Germans. I asked then as I had asked many times over the previous four years why the Lord did not strike them down, every last man, woman and child, destroying their cities and their houses for ever from the face of the earth. And when He did not, I hated Him too, crying that he had deserted me and my people, whom he had led to believe were his chosen people, and even saying that He did not exist.

But with the passing of the years I have learned again to love; to love the rocks and the trees, the sky above and the river flowing past the city, the stray dogs and the cats, the weeds growing between the cobble stones, and the children who run away from me in the street because I am so ugly. They are not to blame. There is a French adage, 'To understand everything is to forgive everything'. When one can understand the people, their gullibility and their fear, their greed and their lust for power, their ignorance and their docility to the man who shouts the loudest, one can forgive. Yes, one can forgive even what they did. But one can never forget.

There are some men whose crimes surpass comprehension and therefore forgiveness, and here is the real failure. For they are still among us, walking through the cities, working in the offices, lunching in the canteens, smiling and shaking hands and calling decent men *Kamerad*. That they should live on, not as outcasts but as cherished citizens, to smear a whole nation in perpetuity with their individual evil, this is the true failure. And in this we have failed, you and I, we have all failed, and failed miserably.

Lastly, as time passed, I came again to love the Lord, and to ask his forgiveness for the things I have done against His Laws, and they are many.

SHEMA YISROEL, ADONAI ELOHENU, ADONAI EHAD. . . .

The diary began with twenty pages during which Tauber described his birth and boyhood in Hamburg, his working-class war-hero father, and the death of his parents shortly after Hitler came to power in 1933. By the late thirties he was married to a girl called Esther, working as an architect, and was spared being rounded up before 1941 due to the intervention of his employer. Finally he was taken in Berlin, on a journey to see a client. After a period in a transit camp he was packed with other Jews into a box-car on a cattle train bound for the east.

I cannot really remember the date the train finally rumbled to a halt in a railway station. I think it was six days and seven nights after we were shut up in the truck in Berlin. Suddenly the train was stationary, the slits of white light told me it was daytime outside, and my head reeled and swam from exhaustion and the stench.

There were shouts outside, the sound of bolts being drawn back, and the doors were flung open. It was just as well I could not see myself, who had once been dressed in a white shirt and well-pressed trousers. (The tie and jacket had long since been dropped to the floor.) The sight of the others was bad enough.

As brilliant daylight rushed into the car men threw arms over their eyes and screamed with the pain. Seeing the doors opening I had squeezed my eyes shut to protect them. Under the pressure of bodies half the truck emptied itself on to the platform in a tumbling mass of stinking humanity. As I had been standing at the rear of the car to one side of the centrally placed doors, I avoided this and risking a half-open eye despite the glare I stepped down upright to the platform.

The SS guards who had opened the gates, mean-faced, brutal men who jabbered and roared in a language I could not understand, stood back with expressions of disgust. Inside the box-car thirty-one men lay huddled and trampled on the floor. They would never get up again. The remainder, starved, half-blind, steaming and reeking from head to foot in their rags, struggled upright on the platform. From thirst our tongues were gummed to the roof of the mouth, blackened and swollen, and our lips were split and parched.

Down the platform forty other carriages from Berlin and eighteen from Vienna were disgorging their occupants, about half of them women and children. Many of the women and most of the children were naked, smeared with excrement and in much as bad shape as we were. Some women carried the lifeless bodies of their children in their arms as they stumbled out into the light.

The guards ran up and down the platform, clubbing the deportees into a sort of column, prior to marching us away into the town. But what town? And what was the language these men were speaking? Later I was to discover this town was Riga and the SS guards were locally recruited

Latvians, as fiercely anti-Semitic as the SS from Germany, but of a much lower intelligence, virtually animals in human form.

Standing behind the guards was a cowed group in soiled shirts and slacks, each bearing a black square patch with a big J on the chest and back. This was a special commando from the ghetto, brought down to empty the cattle cars of the dead and bury them outside the town. They too were guarded by half a dozen men who also had the J on their chests and backs, but who wore an armband and carried a pickaxe handle. These were Jewish Kapos, who got better food than the other internees for doing the job they did.

There were a few German SS officers standing in the shade of the station awning, distinguishable only when my eyes were accustomed to the light. One stood aloof on a packing crate, surveying the several thousand human skeletons who emptied themselves from the train with a thin but satisfied smile. He tapped a black riding quirt of plaited leather against one jack-boot. He wore the green uniform with black and silver flashes of the SS as if it were designed for him and carried the twin-lightning strikes of the Waffen SS on the right collar lapel. On the left his rank was indicated as captain.

He was tall and lanky, with pale blond hair and washed-out blue eyes. Later I was to learn he was a dedicated sadist, already known by the name that the Allies would also later use for him – The Butcher of Riga. It was my first sight of SS-Captain Eduard Roschmann. . . .

At 5 a.m. on the morning of June 22nd, 1941, Hitler's 130 divisions divided into three army groups, had rolled across the border to invade Russia. Behind each army group came the swarms of SS extermination squads, charged by Hitler, Himmler and Heydrich with wiping out the Communist commissars and the rural-dwelling Jewish communities of the vast tracts of land the army overran, and penning the large urban Jewish communities into the ghettos of each major town for later 'special treatment'.

The army took Riga, capital of Latvia, on July 1st, 1941, and in the middle of that month the first SS commandos moved in. The first on-site unit of the SD and SP sections of the SS established themselves in Riga on August 1st, 1941, and began the extermination programme that would make Ostland (as the three occupied Baltic states were renamed) Jew-free.

Then it was decided in Berlin to use Riga as the transit camp to death for the Jews of Germany and Austria. In 1938 there were 320,000 German Jews and 180,000 Austrians, a round half million. By July 1941 tens of thousands had been dealt with, mainly in the concentration camps within Germany and Austria, notably Sachsenhausen, Mauthausen, Ravensbrück, Dachau, Buchenwald, Belsen and Theresienstadt in Bohemia. But they were getting overcrowded, and the obscure lands of the east seemed an excellent place to finish off the rest. Work was begun to expand or begin the six extermination camps of Auschwitz, Treblinka, Belzec, Sobibor, Chelmno and Maidanek. Until they were ready, how-

*ever, a place had to be found to exterminate as many as possible and
'store' the rest. Riga was chosen.*

*Between August, 1941, and October 14th, 1944, almost 200,000 ex-
clusively German and Austrian Jews were shipped to Riga. Eighty thousand stayed there dead, 120,000 were shipped onwards to the six
extermination camps of southern Poland, mentioned above, and 400
came out alive, half of them to die at Sutthof or on the Death March back
to Magdeburg. Tauber's transport was the first into Riga from Reich Germany, and reached there at 3.45 in the afternoon of August 18, 1941.*

The Riga ghetto was an integral part of the city and had formerly been
the home of the Jews of Riga, of whom only a few hundred existed by
the time I got there. In less than three weeks Roschmann and his deputy
Krause, had overseen the extermination of most of them as per orders.

The ghetto lay at the northern edge of the city, with open countryside
to the north. There was a wall along the south face, the other three were
sealed off with rows of barbed wire. There was one gate, on the northern
face, through which all exits and entries had to pass. It was guarded by
two watch-towers manned by Latvian SS. From this gate running clear
down the centre of the ghetto to the south wall was Mase Kalnu Iela, or
Little Hill Street. To the right-hand side of this (looking from south to
north towards the main gate) was the Blech Platz, or Tin Square, where
selections for execution took place, along with roll-call selection of slave-
labour parties, floggings and hangings. The gallows with its eight steel
hooks and permanent nooses swinging in the wind stood in the centre of
this. It was occupied every night by at least six unfortunates and frequently several shifts had to be effected by the eight hanging hooks before
Roschmann was satisfied with his day's work.

The whole ghetto must have been just under two square miles, a
township that had once housed 12,000 to 15,000 people. Before our arrival the Riga Jews, at least the 2000 of them left, had done the bricking
off work, so the area left to our transport of just over 5000 men, women
and children, was spacious. But after we arrived transports continued to
come day after day until the population of our part of the ghetto soared
to 30,000 to 40,000 and with the arrival of each new transport a number
of the existing inhabitants equal to the number of the surviving new
arrivals had to be executed to make room for the newcomers. Otherwise
the overcrowding would have become a menace to the health of the
workers among us, and that Roschmann would not have.

So that first evening we settled ourselves in, taking the best-con-
structed houses, one room per person, using curtains and coats for blankets and sleeping on real beds. After drinking his fill from a water-butt,
my room neighbour remarked that perhaps it would not be too bad
after all. We had not yet met Roschmann. . . .

As summer merged into autumn and autumn into winter the conditions
in the ghetto grew worse. Each morning the entire population, mainly
men, for the women and children were exterminated on arrival in far

greater percentages than the work-fit males, was assembled on Tin Square, pushed and shoved by the rifle-butts of the Latvians and roll-call took place. No names were called, we were counted and divided into work groups. Almost the whole population, men, women and children, left the ghetto each day in columns to work twelve hours at forced labour in the growing host of workshops nearby.

I had said early on that I was a carpenter, which was not true, but as an architect I had seen carpenters at work and knew enough to get by. I guessed, correctly, that there would always be a need for carpenters, and I was sent to work in a nearby lumber mill where the local pines were sawn up and made into prefabricated hutments for the troops.

The work was back-breaking, enough to ruin the constitution of a healthy man, for we worked summer and winter mainly outside in the cold and damp of the low-lying regions near the coast of Latvia. . . .

Our food rations were a half-litre of so-called soup, mainly tinted water, sometimes with a knob of potato in it, before marching to work in the mornings, and another half-litre, with a slice of black bread and a mouldy potato on return to the ghetto at night.

Bringing food into the ghetto was punishable by immediate hanging before the assembled population at evening roll-call on Tin Square. Nevertheless, to take that risk was the only way to stay alive.

As the columns trudged back through the main gate each evening, Roschmann and a few of his cronies used to stand by the entrance, doing spot checks on those passing through. They would call to a man or a woman or a child at random, ordering the person out of the column to strip by the side of the gate. If a potato or a piece of bread was found the person would wait behind while the others marched through towards the Tin Square for evening roll-call.

When they were all assembled Roschmann would stalk down the road, followed by the other SS guards and the dozen or so condemned people. The males among them would mount the gallows platform and wait with the ropes round their neck while roll-call was completed. Then Roschmann would walk along the line, grinning up at the faces above him and kicking the chairs out from under, one by one. He liked to do this from the front, so the person about to die would see him. Sometimes he would pretend to kick the chair away, only to pull his foot back in time. He would laugh uproariously to see the man on the chair tremble, thinking he was already swinging at the rope's end, only to realise the chair was still beneath him.

Sometimes the condemned men would pray to the Lord, sometimes they would cry for mercy. Roschmann liked to hear this. He would pretend he was slightly deaf, cocking an ear and asking, 'Can you speak up a little. What was that you said?'

When he had kicked the chair away – it was more like a wooden box, really – he would turn to his cronies and say, 'Dear me, I really must get a hearing aid. . . .'

Within a few months Eduard Roschmann had become the Devil incarnate to us prisoners. There was little that he did not succeed in devising.

When a woman was caught bringing food into the camp she was made to watch the hangings of the men first, especially if one was her husband or brother. Then Roschmann made her kneel in front of the rest of us, drawn up round three sides of the square, while the camp barber shaved her bald.

After roll-call she would be taken to the cemetery outside the wire, made to dig a shallow grave, then kneel beside it while Roschmann or one of the others fired a bullet from his Lüger point-blank into the base of the skull. No one was allowed to watch these executions, but word seeped through from the Latvian guards that he would often fire past the ear of the woman to make her fall into the grave with shock, then climb out again and kneel in the same position. Other times he would fire on an empty chamber, so there was just a click when the woman thought she was about to die. The Latvians were brutes, but Roschmann managed to amaze them for all that. . . .

There was one certain girl at Riga who helped the prisoners at her own risk. She was Olli Adler, from Munich I believe. Her sister Gerda had already been shot in the cemetery for bringing in food. Olli was a girl of surpassing beauty, and took Roschmann's fancy. He made her his concubine – the official term was housemaid, because relations between an SS man and a Jewess were banned. She used to smuggle medicines into the ghetto when she was allowed to visit it, having stolen them from the SS stores. This, of course, was punishable by death. The last I saw of her was when we boarded the ship at Riga docks. . . .

By the end of that first winter I was certain I could not survive much longer. The hunger, the cold, the damp, the overwork and the constant brutalities had whittled my formerly strong frame down to a mass of skin and bones. Looking in the mirror, what I saw staring back at me was a haggard, stubbled old man with red-rimmed eyes and hollow cheeks. I was just turned thirty-five and I looked double that. But so did everyone else.

I had witnessed the departure of tens of thousands to the forest of the mass graves, the deaths of hundreds from cold, exposure and overwork, and of scores from hanging, shooting, flogging and clubbing. Even after surviving five months I had outlived my time. The will to live that I had begun to show in the train had dissipated, leaving nothing but a mechanical routine of going on living that sooner or later had to break. And then something happened in March that gave me another year of willpower.

I remember the date even now. It was March 3rd, 1942, the day of the second Dunamunde convoy. About a month earlier we had seen for the first time the arrival of a strange van. It was about the size of a long single-decker bus, painted steel grey and yet without windows. It parked just outside the ghetto gates, and at morning roll-call Roschmann said he had an announcement to make. He said there was a new fish-pickling factory just started at the town of Dunamunde, situated on the river

Duna, about eighty miles from Riga. It involved light work, he said, good food and good living conditions. Because the work was so light the opportunity was open only to old men and women, the frail, the sick and the small children.

Naturally, many were eager to go to such a comfortable kind of labour. Roschmann walked down the lines selecting those to go, and this time, instead of the old and sick hiding themselves at the back to be dragged screaming and protesting forward to join the forced marches to execution hill, they seemed eager to show themselves. Finally over a hundred were selected, and all climbed into the van. Then the doors were slammed shut, and the watchers noticed how tight they fitted together. The van rolled away, emitting no exhaust fumes. Later word filtered back what the van was. There was no fish-pickling factory at Dunamunde; the van was a gassing van. In the parlance of the ghetto the expression 'Dunamunde Convoy' henceforward came to mean death by gassing.

On March 3rd the whisper went round the ghetto that there was to be another Dunamunde convoy, and sure enough, at morning roll-call Roschmann announced it. But there was no pressing forward to volunteer, so with a wide grin Roschmann began to stroll along the ranks, tapping on the chest with his quirt those who were to go. Astutely, he started at the fourth and rear rank, where he expected to find the weak, the old and the unfit for work.

There was one old woman who had foreseen this and stood in the front rank. She must have been close to sixty-five, but in an effort to stay alive she had put on high-heeled shoes, a pair of black silk stockings, a short skirt even above her knees and a saucy hat. She had rouged her cheeks, powdered her face and painted her lips carmine. In fact she would have stood out among any group of ghetto prisoners, but she thought she might be able to pass for a young girl.

Reaching her as he walked by, Roschmann stopped, stared and looked again. Then a grin of joy spread over his face.

'Well, what have we here!' he cried, pointing to her with his quirt to draw the attention of his comrades in the centre of the square, guarding the hundred already chosen. 'Don't you want a little ride to Dunamunde, young lady?'

Trembling with fear, the old woman whispered, 'No, sir.'

'And how old are you then?' boomed Roschmann as his SS friends began to giggle. 'Seventeen, twenty?'

The old woman's knobbly knees began to tremble.

'Yes, sir,' she whispered.

'How marvellous,' cried Roschmann. 'Well, I always like a pretty girl. Come out into the centre so we can all admire your youth and beauty.'

So saying he grabbed her by the arm and hustled her towards the centre of Tin Square. Once there, he stood her out in the open and said, 'Well now, little lady, since you're so young and pretty, perhaps you'd like to dance for us, eh?'

She stood there, shivering in the bitter wind, shaking with fear as well. She whispered something we could not hear.

'What's that?' shouted Roschmann. 'You can't dance? Oh, I'm sure a nice young thing like you can dance, can't you?'

His cronies of the German SS were laughing fit to bust. The Latvians could not understand, but started to grin. The old woman shook her head. Roschmann's smile vanished.

'Dance,' he snarled.

She made a few little shuffling movements, then stopped. Roschmann drew his Lüger, eased back the hammer and fired it into the sand an inch from her feet. She jumped a foot in the air from fright.

'Dance ... dance ... dance for us, you hideous Jewish bitch,' he shouted, firing a bullet into the sand beneath her feet each time he said 'Dance'.

Smacking in one spare magazine after another until he had used up three in his pouch, he made her dance for half an hour, leaping ever higher and higher, her skirts flying round her hips with each jump, until at last she fell to the sand unable to rise whether she lived or died. Roschmann fired his last three slugs into the sand in front of her face, blasting the sand up into her eyes. Between the crash of each shot came the old woman's rattling wheeze that could be heard across the parade square.

When he had no more ammunition left he shouted 'Dance' again and slammed his jack-boot into her belly. All this had happened in complete silence from us, until the man next to me started to pray. He was a Hassid, small and bearded, still wearing the rags of his long black coat; despite the cold which forced most of us to wear ear-muffs on our caps, he had the broad-brimmed hat of his sect. He began to recite the Shema, over and over again, in a quavering voice that grew steadily louder. Knowing that Roschmann was in his most vicious mood, I too began to pray, silently, that the Hassid would be quiet. But he would not.

'Hear O Israel ...'

'Shut up,' I hissed out of the corner of my mouth.

'*Adonai elohenu* ... the Lord is our God ...'

'Will you be quiet. You'll get us all killed.'

'The Lord is One ... *Adonai Eha-a-ad.*'

Like a cantor he drew out the last syllable in the traditional way, as Rabbi Akiva had done as he died in the amphitheatre at Caesarea on the orders of Tinius Rufus. It was just at that moment that Roschmann stopped screaming at the old woman. He lifted his head like an animal scenting the wind and turned towards us. As I stood a head taller than the Hassid, he looked at me.

'Who was that talking?' he screamed, striding towards me across the sand. 'You ... step out of line.' There was no doubt he was pointing at me. I thought, This is the end then. So what? It doesn't matter, it had to happen, now or some other time. I stepped forward as he arrived in front of me.

He did not say anything, but his face was twitching like a maniac. Then it relaxed and he gave his quiet, wolfish smile that struck terror into everyone in the ghetto, even the Latvian SS men.

His hand moved so quickly no one could see it. I felt only a sort of

thump down the left side of my face, simultaneous with a tremendous
bang as if a bomb had gone off next to my ear-drums. Then the quite
distinct but detached feeling of my own skin splitting like rotten calico
from temple to mouth. Even before it had started to bleed, Roschmann's
hand moved again, the other way this time, and his quirt ripped open the
other side of my face with the same loud bang in the ear and the feeling
of something tearing. It was a two-foot quirt, sprung with whippy steel
core at the handle end, the remaining foot-length being of plaited leather
thongs without the core, and when drawn across and down the human
skin at the same time the plaiting could split the hide like tissue paper. I
had seen it done.

Within a matter of seconds I felt the trickle of warm blood beginning
to flow down the front of my jacket, dripping off my chin in two little
red fountains. Roschmann swung away from me, then back, pointing to
the old woman still sobbing in the centre of the square.

'Pick up that old hag and take her to the van,' he barked.

And so, a few minutes ahead of the arrival of the other hundred victims, I picked up the old woman and carried her down Little Hill Street
to the gate and the waiting van, pouring blood on to her from my chin.
I set her down in the back of the van and made to leave her there. As I
did so she gripped my wrist in withered fingers, with a strength I would
not have thought she possessed. She pulled me down towards her, squatting on the floor of the death-van, and with a small cambric handkerchief
that must have come from better days staunched some of the still
flowing blood.

She looked up at me from a face streaked with mascara, rouge, tears
and sand, but with dark eyes bright as stars.

'Jew, my son,' she hissed, 'you must live. Swear to me that you will
live. Swear to me you will get out of this place alive. You must live, so
that you can tell them, them outside in the other world, what happened
to our people here. Promise me, swear it by Sefer Torah.'

And so I swore that I would live, somehow, no matter what the cost.
Then she let me go. I stumbled back down the road into the ghetto, and
halfway down I fainted. . . .

Shortly after returning to work I made two decisions. One was to keep a
secret diary, nightly tattooing words and dates with a pin and black ink
into the skin of my feet and legs, so that one day I would be able to
transcribe all that had happened in Riga, and give precise evidence
against those responsible.

The second decision was to become a Kapo, a member of the Jewish
police.

The decision was hard, for these were men who herded their fellow
Jews to work and back, and often to the place of execution. Moreover,
they carried a pickaxe handle and occasionally, when under the eye of a
German SS officer, used them liberally to beat their fellow Jews to work
harder. Nevertheless, on April 1st, 1942, I went to the chief of the Kapos
and volunteered, thus becoming an outcast from the company of my

fellow Jews. There was always room for an extra Kapo, for despite the better rations, living conditions and release from slave labour, very few agreed to become one. . . .

I should here describe the method of execution of those unfit for labour, for in this manner between 70,000 and 80,000 Jews were exterminated under the orders of Eduard Roschmann at Riga. When the cattle train arrived at the station with a new consignment of prisoners, usually about 5000 strong, there were always close to a thousand already dead from the journey. Only occasionally was it as low as a few hundred, scattered between fifty cars.

When the new arrivals were lined up on Tin Square the selections for extermination took place, not merely among the new arrivals but among us all. That was the point of the head-count each morning and evening. Among the new arrivals those weak or frail, old or diseased, most of the women and almost all the children, were singled out as being unfit for work. These were set on one side. The remainder were then counted. If they totalled 2000, then 2000 of the existing inmates were also picked out, so that 5000 had arrived and 5000 went to execution hill. That way there was no overcrowding. A man might survive six months of slave labour, seldom more, then, when his health was reduced to ruins, Roschmann's quirt would tap him on the chest one day and he would go to join the ranks of the dead. . . .

At first these victims were marched in column to a forest outside the town. The Latvians called it Bickernicker Forest, and the Germans renamed it the Hochwald or High Forest. Here, in clearings between the pines, enormous open ditches had been dug by the Riga Jews before they died. And here the Latvian SS guards, under the eye and orders of Eduard Roschmann, mowed them down so that they fell into the ditches. The remaining Riga Jews then filled in enough earth to cover the bodies, adding one more layer of corpses to those underneath until the ditch was full. Then a new one was started.

From the ghetto we could hear the chattering of the machine guns when each new consignment was liquidated, and watch Roschmann riding back down the hill and through the ghetto gates in his open car when it was over. . . .

After I became a Kapo all social contact between me and the other internees ceased. There was no point in explaining why I had done it, that one Kapo more or less would make no difference, not increasing the death toll by a single digit; but that one single surviving witness might make all the difference, not to save the Jews of Germany, but to avenge them. This at least was the argument I repeated to myself, but was it the real reason? Or was I just afraid to die? Whatever it was, fear soon ceased to be a factor, for in August that year something happened that caused my soul to die inside my body, leaving only the husk struggling to survive. . . .

In July 1942 a big new transport of Austrian Jews came through from

Vienna. Apparently they were marked without exception for 'special treatment', for the entire shipment never came to the ghetto. We did not see them, for they were all marched from the station to High Forest and machine-gunned. Later that evening down the hill rolled four lorries full of clothes, which were brought to the Tin Square for sorting. They made a mound as big as a house until they were sorted out into piles of shoes, socks, underpants, trousers, dresses, jackets, shaving brushes, spectacles, dentures, wedding rings, signet rings, caps and so forth.

Of course, this was standard procedure for executed transports. All those killed on execution hill were stripped at the graveside and their effects brought down later. These were then sorted and sent back to the Reich. The gold, silver and jewellery was taken in charge by Roschmann personally. . . .

In August 1942 there was another transport from Theresienstadt, a camp in Bohemia where tens of thousands of German and Austrian Jews were held before being sent eastwards to extermination. I was standing to one side of the Tin Square, watching Roschmann as he went round making his selections. The new arrivals were already shaved bald, which had been done at their previous camp, and it was not easy to tell the men from the women, except for the shift dresses the women mainly wore. There was one woman across the other side of the square who caught my attention. There was something about her cast of features that rang a bell in my mind, although she was emaciated, thin as a rake and coughing continuously.

Arriving opposite her, Roschmann tapped her on the chest and passed on. The Latvians following him at once seized her arms and pushed her out of line to join the others in the centre of the square. There were many from that transport who were not work fit and the list of selections was long. That meant fewer of us would be selected to make up the numbers, though for me, the question was academic. As a Kapo I wore an armband and carried a club, and extra food rations had increased my strength a little. Although Roschmann had seen my face, he did not seem to remember it. He had slashed so many across the face that one more or less would not attract his attention.

Most of those selected that summer evening were formed into a column and marched to the ghetto gate by the Kapos. The column was then taken over by the Latvians for the last four miles to High Forest and death.

But as there was a gassing van standing by also at the gates, a group of about a hundred of the frailest of the selected ones was detached from the crowd. I was about to escort the other condemned men and women to the gates when SS Lieutenant Krause pointed to four or five of the Kapos. 'You lot,' he shouted, 'take these to the Dunamunde convoy.'

After the others had left we five escorted the last hundred, mainly limping, crawling or coughing, to the gates where the van waited. The thin woman was among them, her chest racked by tuberculosis. She knew where she was going, they all did, but like the rest she stumbled with resigned obedience to the rear of the van. She was too weak to get up, for the tailboard was high off the ground, so she turned to me for help. We stood and looked at each other in stunned amazement.

Behind me I heard somebody approach, and the other two Kapos at the tailboard straightened to attention, scraping their caps off with one hand. Realising it must be an SS officer, I did the same. The woman just stared at me unblinking. The man behind me came forward. It was Captain Roschmann. He nodded to the other two Kapos to carry on, and stared at me with those pale blue eyes. I thought it could only mean I would be flogged that evening for being slow to take my cap off.

'What's your name?' he asked softly.

'Tauber, Herr Captain,' I said, still ramrod at attention.

'Well, Tauber, you seem to be a bit slow. Do you think we ought to liven you up a little this evening?'

There was no point in saying anything. The sentence was passed. Roschmann's eyes flickered to the woman, narrowed as if suspecting something, then his slow wolfish smile spread across his face.

'Do you know this woman?' he asked.

'Yes, Herr Captain,' I answered.

'Who is she?' he asked. I could not reply. My mouth was gummed together as if by glue.

'Is she your wife?' he went on. I nodded dumbly. He grinned even wider.

'Well, now my dear Tauber, where are your manners? Help the lady up into the van.'

I still stood there, unable to move. He put his face closer to mine and whispered, 'You have ten seconds to pack her in. Then you go yourself.'

Slowly I held out my arm and Esther leaned upon it. With this assistance she climbed into the van. The other two Kapos waited to slam shut the doors. When she was up she looked down at me, and two tears came, one from each eye, and rolled down her cheeks. She did not say anything to me, we never spoke throughout. Then the doors were slammed shut and the van rolled away. The last thing I saw were her eyes looking at me.

I have spent twenty years trying to understand the look in her eyes. Was it love or hatred, contempt or pity, bewilderment or understanding? I shall never know.

When the van had gone Roschmann turned to me, still grinning. 'You may go on living, until it suits us to finish you off, Tauber,' he said, 'but you are dead as from now.'

And he was right. That was the day my soul died inside me. It was August 29th, 1942.

After August that year I became a robot. Nothing mattered any more. There was no feeling of cold nor of pain, no sensation of any kind at all. I watched the brutalities of Roschmann and his fellow SS without batting an eyelid. I was inured to everything that can touch the human spirit and most things that can touch the body. I just noted everything, each tiny detail, filing them away in my mind or pricking the dates into the skin of my legs. The transports came, marched to execution hill or to the vans, died and were buried. Sometimes I looked into their eyes as they went, walking beside them to the gates of the ghetto with my armband and club. It reminded me of a poem I had once read by an English poet, which described how an ancient mariner, condemned to live, had looked into the eyes of his crew-mates as they died of thirst, and read the curse in them. But for me there was no curse, for I was immune even to the feeling of guilt. That was to come years later. There was only the emptiness of a dead man still walking upright. . . .

Peter Miller read on late into the night. The effect of the narration of the atrocities on him was at once monotonous and mesmeric. Several times he sat back in his chair and breathed deeply for a few minutes to regain his calm. Then he read on.

Once, close to midnight, he laid the book down and made more coffee. He stood at the window before drawing the curtains, looking down into the street. Further down the road the brilliant neon lights of the Café Chérie blazed across the Steindamm, and he saw one of the part-time girls who frequent it to supplement their incomes emerge on the arm of a business man. They disappeared into a pension a little further down, where the business man would be relieved of a hundred marks for half an hour of copulation.

Miller pulled the curtains across, finished his coffee and returned to Salomon Tauber's diary.

In the autumn of 1943 the order came through from Berlin to dig up the tens of thousands of corpses in the High Forest and destroy them more permanently, either with fire or quicklime. The job was easier said than done, with winter coming on and the ground about to freeze hard. It put Roschmann in a foul temper for days, but the administrative details of carrying out the order kept him busy enough to stay away from us.

Day after day the newly formed labour squads were seen marching up the hill into the forest with their pickaxes and shovels, and day after day the columns of black smoke rose above the forest. For fuel they used the pines of the forest, but largely decomposed bodies do not burn easily, so the job was slow. Eventually they switched to quicklime, covered each layer of corpses with it and in the spring of 1944, when the earth softened, filled them in.*

The gangs who did the work were not from the ghetto. They were totally isolated from all other human contact. They were Jewish, but were kept imprisoned in one of the worst camps in the neighbourhood, Salas Pils, where they were later exterminated by being given no food at all until they died of starvation, despite the cannibalism to which many resorted. . . .

When the work was more or less completed in the spring of 1944 the

---

* This procedure badly burned the corpses but did not destroy the bones. The Russians later uncovered these 80,000 skeletons.

ghetto was finally liquidated. Most of its 30,000 inhabitants were marched towards the forest to become the last victims that pine wood was destined to receive. About 5,000 of us were transferred to the camp of Kaiserwald while behind us the ghetto was fired, then the ashes bull-dozed. Of what **had** once been there nothing was left but an area of flattened ashes covering hundreds of acres. . . .*

For a further twenty pages of typescript Tauber's diary described the struggle to survive in Kaiserwald concentration camp against the on-slaught of starvation, disease, overwork and the brutality of the camp guards. During this time no sign was seen of SS-Captain Eduard Rosch-mann. But apparently he was still in Riga. Tauber described how in the early October of 1944 the SS, by now panic-stricken at the thought they might be taken alive by the vengeful Russians, prepared for a desperate evacuation of Riga by sea, taking along a handful of the last surviving prisoners as their passage-ticket back to the Reich in the west.

It was in the afternoon of October 11th that we arrived, by now barely 4000 strong, at the town of Riga, and the column went straight down to the docks. In the distance we could hear a strange crump as if of thunder along the horizon. For a while it puzzled us, for we had never heard the sound of shells or bombs. Then it filtered through to our minds, dazed by hunger and cold – there were Russian mortars landing in the suburbs of Riga.

When we arrived at the dock area it was crawling with officers and men of the SS. I had never seen so many in one place at the same time. There must have been more of them than there were of us. We were lined up in rows against one of the warehouses and again most of us thought that this was where we would die under the machine guns. But this was not to be.

Apparently the SS were going to use us, the last remainder of the hundreds of thousands of Jews who had passed through Riga, as their alibi to escape from the Russian advance, their passage back to the Reich. The means of travel was berthed alongside Quay Six, a freighter, the last one out of the encircled enclave. As we watched, the loading began of some of the hundreds of German Army wounded who were lying on stretchers in two of the warehouses farther along the quay. . . .

* The Russian spring offensive of 1944 carried the tide of war so far westwards that the Soviet troops pushed south of the Baltic states and through the Baltic Sea to the west of them. This cut off the whole of Ostland from the Reich, and led to a blazing row between Hitler and his generals. They had seen it coming and had pleaded with Hitler to pull back the forty-five divisions inside the enclave. He had refused, reiterating his parrot-cry 'Death or Victory'. All he offered these 500,000 soldiers inside the enclave was death. Cut off from re-supply they fought with dwindling ammunition to delay a certain fate, and eventually surrendered. Of the majority, made prisoners and transported back in the winter of 1944–5 to Russia, few returned ten years later to Germany.

It was almost dark when Captain Roschmann arrived, and he stopped short when he saw how the ship was being loaded. When he had taken in the sight of the German Army wounded being taken on to the ship he turned round and shouted to the medical orderlies bearing the stretchers, 'Stop that.'

He strode towards them across the quay and slapped one of the orderlies in the face. He whirled round on the ranks of us prisoners and roared, 'You scum. Get up on that ship and get these men off. Bring them back down here. That ship is ours.'

Under the prodding of the gun barrels of the SS men who had come down with us, we started to move towards the gangplank. Hundreds of other SS men, privates and NCOs, who till then had been standing back watching the loading, surged forward and followed the prisoners up on to the ship. When we got on the deck we began picking up the stretchers and carrying them back to the quay. Rather, we were about to, when another shout stopped us.

I had reached the foot of the gangway and was about to start up when I heard the shout and turned to see what was happening.

An army captain was running down the quay and he came to a stop quite close to me by the gangway. Staring up at the men above, bearing stretchers they were about to unload, the captain shouted, 'Who ordered these men to be off-loaded?'

Roschmann walked up behind him and said, 'I did. This boat is ours.' The captain spun round on him. He delved in his pocket and produced a piece of paper. 'This ship was sent to pick up army wounded,' he said. 'And army wounded is what it will take.'

With that he turned to the army orderlies and shouted to them to resume the loading. I looked across at Roschmann. He was standing trembling, I thought with anger. Then I saw he was scared. He was frightened of being left to face the Russians. Unlike us, they were armed.

He began to scream at the orderlies, 'Leave them alone, I have commandeered this ship in the name of the Reich.' The orderlies ignored him and obeyed the captain of the Wehrmacht. I noticed his face, as he was only two metres away from me. It was grey with exhaustion, with dark smudges under the eyes. There were lines down each side of the nose and several weeks of stubble on his chin. Seeing the loading work begin again, he made to march past Roschmann to supervise his orderlies. From among the crowded stretchers in the snow of the quay I heard a voice shout in the Hamburg dialect, 'Good on you, Captain. You tell the swine.'

As he was abreast of Roschmann, the SS officer grabbed his arm, swung him round and slapped the army man across the face with his gloved hand. I had seen him slap men a thousand times, but never with the same result. The captain took the blow, shook his head, bunched his fist and landed a haymaker of a right-fisted punch on Roschmann's jaw. Roschmann flew back several feet and went flat on his back in the snow, a small trickle of blood coming from his mouth. The captain moved towards his orderlies.

As I watched, Roschmann drew his SS officer's Lüger from its holster, took careful aim and fired between the Captain's shoulders. Everything stopped at the crash from the pistol. The army captain staggered and turned. Roschmann fired again, and the bullet caught the captain in the throat. He spun over backwards and was dead before he hit the quay. Something he had been wearing round his neck flew off as the bullet struck, and when I passed it, after being ordered to carry the body and throw it into the dock, I saw that the object was a medal on a ribbon. I never knew the captain's name, but the medal was the Knight's Cross with Oak Leaf Cluster. . . .

Miller read this page of the diary with growing astonishment, gradually turning to disbelief, doubt, belief again and finally a deep anger. He read the page a dozen times to make sure there was no doubt, then resumed reading the diary.

After this we were ordered to start unloading the Wehrmacht wounded and told to lay them back in the gathering snow on the quayside. I found myself helping one young soldier back down the gangplank on to the quay. He had been blinded and round his eyes was wrapped a dirty bandage torn from a shirt-tail. He was half-delirious and kept asking for his mother. I suppose he must have been about eighteen.

Finally they were all taken off, and we prisoners were ordered on board. The whole lot of us were taken down into the two holds, one forward and one aft, until we were so cramped we could hardly move. Then the hatches were battened down and the SS began to come aboard. We sailed just before midnight, the captain evidently wishing to be well out into the Gulf of Latvia before dawn came to avoid the chance of being spotted and bombed by the patrolling Russian Stormoviks. . . .

It took three days to reach Danzig, well behind German lines. Three days in a pitching, tossing hell below decks, without food or water, during which a quarter of the 4000 prisoners died. There was no food to vomit, and yet everyone was retching dry from seasickness. Many died of the exhaustion of vomiting, others from hunger or cold, others because they simply lost the will to live, lay back and surrendered to Death. And then the ship was berthed again, the hatches were opened and gusts of ice-cold winter air came rushing into the foetid, stinking holds.

When we were unloaded on to the quay at Danzig the dead bodies were laid out in rows alongside the living, so that the numbers should tally with those that had been taken on board at Riga. The SS were always very precise about numbers.

We learned later that Riga had fallen to the Russians on October 14th, while we were still at sea. . . .

Tauber's pain-racked Odyssey was reaching its end. From Danzig the surviving inmates were taken by barge to the concentration camp of Stutthof, outside Danzig, and until the first weeks of 1945 he worked daily in the submarine works of Burggraben by day and lived in the camp by night. Thousands more at Stutthof died of malnutrition. He watched them all die, but somehow stayed alive.

In January 1945, as the advancing Russians closed on Danzig, the survivors of Stutthof camp were driven westward on the notorious Death March through the winter snow towards Berlin. All across eastern Germany these columns of wraiths, being used as a ticket to safety in Western hands by their SS guards, were being herded westward. Along the route, in snow and frost, they died like flies.

Tauber survived even this, and finally the remnant of his column reached Magdeburg, west of Berlin, where the SS finally abandoned them and sought their own safety. Tauber's group was lodged in Magdeburg prison, in the charge of the bewildered and helpless old men of the local Home Guard. Unable to feed their prisoners, terrified of what the advancing Allies would say when they found them, the Home Guard permitted the fittest of them to go scrounging for food in the surrounding countryside.

The last time I had seen Eduard Roschmann was when we were being counted on Danzig quayside. Warmly wrapped against the winter cold, he was climbing into a car. I thought it would be my last glimpse of him, but I was to see him one last time. It was April 3rd, 1945.

I had been out that day towards Gardelegen, a village east of the city, and had gathered a small sackful of potatoes with three others. We were trudging back with our booty when a car came up behind us heading west. It paused to negotiate a horse and cart on the road, and I glanced round with no particular interest to see the car pass. Inside were four SS officers, evidently making their escape towards the west. Sitting beside the driver, pulling on the uniform jacket of an army corporal, was Eduard Roschmann.

He did not see me, for my head was largely covered by a hood cut from an old potato sack, a protection against the cold spring wind. But I saw him. There was no doubt about it.

All four men in the car were apparently changing their uniforms even as the vehicle headed west. As it disappeared down the road a garment was thrown from one window and fluttered into the dust. We reached the spot where it lay a few minutes later and stooped to examine it. It was the jacket of an SS officer, bearing the silver twin-lightning symbols of the Waffen-SS and the rank of captain. Roschmann of the SS had disappeared. . . .

Twenty-four days after this came the liberation. We had ceased to go out at all, preferring to stay hungry in the prison than venture along the streets, where complete anarchy was loose. Then on the morning of April 27th all was quiet in the town. Towards mid-morning I was in the courtyard of the prison talking to one of the old guards, who seemed terrified and spent nearly an hour explaining that he and his colleagues had nothing to do with Adolf Hitler and certainly nothing to do with the persecution of the Jews.

I heard the sound of a vehicle drive up outside the locked gates, and there was a hammering on them. The old Home Guard went to open them. The man who stepped through, cautiously with a revolver in his hand, was a soldier in full battle uniform, one that I had never seen before.

He was evidently an officer, for he was accompanied by a soldier in a flat round tin hat who carried a rifle. They just stood there in silence, looking round at the courtyard of the prison. In one corner were stacked about fifty corpses, those who had died in the past two weeks and whom no one had the strength to bury. Others, half-alive, lay round the walls trying to soak up a little of the spring sunshine, their sores festering and stinking.

The two men looked at each other, then at the seventy-year-old Home Guard. He looked back, embarrassed. Then he said something he must have learned in the First World War. He said:

'Hello, Tommy.'

The officer looked back at him, looked again round the courtyard, and said quite clearly in English, 'You fucking Kraut pig.'

And suddenly I began to cry. . . .

I do not really know how I made it back to Hamburg, but I did. I think I wanted to see if there was anything left of the old life. There wasn't. The streets where I was born and grew up had vanished in the great Fire Storm of the Allied bombing raids, the office where I had worked was gone, my flat, everything.

The English put me in hospital in Magdeburg for a while, but I left of my own accord and hitch-hiked back home. But when I got there and saw there was nothing left, I finally, belatedly, collapsed completely. I spent a year in hospital as a patient, along with others who had come out of a place called Bergen-Belsen, and then another year working in the hospital as an orderly, looking after those who were worse than I had been.

When I left there I went to find a room in Hamburg, the place of my birth, to spend the rest of my days. . . .

The book ended with a further two clean, white sheets of paper, evidently recently typed, which formed the epilogue.

I have lived in this little room in Altona since 1947. Shortly after I came out of hospital I began to write the story of what happened to me and to the others at Riga.

But long before I had finished it, it became perfectly clear that others had survived also, others better informed and better able than I to bear witness to what was done. Hundreds of books have now appeared to describe the holocaust, so nobody would be interested in mine. I never took it to anyone else to read.

Looking back it was all a waste of time and energy, the battle to survive and to be able to write down the evidence, when others have already done it so much better. I wish now I had died in Riga with Esther.

Even the last wish, to see Eduard Roschmann stand before a court, and to give evidence to that court about what he did, will never be fulfilled. I know this now.

I walk through the streets sometimes and remember the old days here, but it can never be the same. The children laugh at me and run away when I try to be friends. Once I got talking to a little girl who did not run away, but her mother came up screaming and dragged her away. So I do not talk to many people.

Once a woman came to see me. She said she was from the Reparations Office and that I was entitled to money. I said I did not want any money. She was very put out, insisting that it was my right to be recompensed for what was done. I kept on refusing. They sent someone else to see me, and I refused again. He said it was very irregular to refuse to be recompensed. I sensed he meant it would upset their books. But I only take from them what is due to me.

When I was in the British hospital one of their doctors asked me why I did not emigrate to Israel, which was soon to have its independence. How could I explain to him? I could not tell him that I can never go up to the Land, not after what I did to Esther, my wife. I think about it often and dream about what it must be like, but I am not worthy to go.

But if ever these lines should be read in the land of Israel, which I shall never see, will someone there please say Kaddish for me?

SALOMON TAUBER,
Altona, Hamburg,
21st November 1963.

Peter Miller put the diary down and lay back in his chair for a long time, staring at the ceiling and smoking. Just before five in the morning he heard the flat door open and Sigi came in from work. She was startled to find him still awake.

'What are you doing up so late?' she asked.

'Been reading,' said Miller.

Later they lay in bed as the first glint of dawn picked out the spire of St Michaelis, Sigi drowsy and contented like a young woman who has just been loved, Miller staring up at the ceiling silent and preoccupied.

'Penny for them,' said Sigi after a while.

'Just thinking.'

'I know. I can tell that. What about?'

'The next story I'm going to cover.'

She shifted and looked across at him.

'What are you going to do?' she asked. Miller leaned over and stubbed out his cigarette.

'I'm going to track a man down,' he said.

3

While Peter Miller and Sigi were asleep in each other's arms in Hamburg a giant Coronado of Argentine Airlines swung over the darkened hills of Castile and entered final approach for a landing at Barjas airport, Madrid.

Sitting in a window seat in the third row back of the first-class passenger section was a man in his early sixties with iron-grey hair and a trim moustache.

Only one photograph had ever existed of the man showing him in his early forties, with close-cropped hair, no moustache to cover the rat-trap mouth, and a razor-straight parting along the left side of his head. Hardly anyone of the small group of men who had ever seen that photograph would recognise the man in the airliner, his hair now growing thickly back from the forehead, without a parting. The photograph in his passport matched his new appearance.

The name in that same passport identified him as Señor Ricardo Suertes, citizen of Argentina, and the name itself was his own grim joke against the world. For Suerte in Spanish means Luck, and Luck in German is Glueck. The airline passenger that January night had been born Richard Gluecks, later to become full general of the SS, head of the Reich Economic Administration Main Office and Hilter's Inspector-General of Concentration Camps. On the wanted list of West Germany and Israel, he was number three after Martin Bormann and the former chief of the Gestapo, Heinrich Müller. He ranked higher even than Dr Josef Mengele, the Devil Doctor of Auschwitz. In the Odessa he ranked number two, direct deputy of Martin Bormann on whom the mantle of the Fuehrer had fallen after 1945.

The role Richard Gluecks had played in the crimes of the SS was unique and matched only by the manner in which he managed to effect his own complete disappearance in May 1945. More even than Adolf Eichmann, Gluecks had been one of the most senior master-minds of the holocaust, and yet he had never pulled a trigger.

Had an uninformed passenger been told who the man sitting next to him was, he might well have wondered why the former head of an economic administration office should be so high on the wanted list.

Had he asked, he would have learned that of the crimes against humanity committed on the German side between 1933 and 1945 probably ninety-five per cent can accurately be laid at the door of the SS. Of these, probably eighty to ninety per cent can be attributed to two departments within the SS. These were the Reich Security Main Office and the Reich Economic Administration Main Office.

If the idea of an economic bureau being involved in mass-murder strikes a strange note, one must understand how it was intended that the job should be done. Not only was it intended to exterminate every Jew on the face of Europe, and most of the Slavic races with them, but it was intended that the victims should pay for the privilege. Before the gas chambers opened, the SS had already carried out the biggest robbery in history.

In the case of the Jews the payment was in three stages. First they were robbed of their businesses, houses, factories, bank accounts, furniture, cars and clothes. They were shipped eastwards to the slave-labour camps and the death camps, assured they were destined for re-settlement and mainly believing it, with what they could carry, usually two suitcases. On the camp square these were also taken off them, along with the clothes they wore.

Out of this luggage of six million people, thousands of millions of dollars worth of booty was extracted, for the European Jews of the time habitually travelled with their wealth upon them, particularly those from Poland and the eastern lands. From the camps entire trainloads of gold trinkets, diamonds, sapphires, rubies, silver ingots, louis d'ors, gold dollars, and bank-notes of every kind and description were shipped back to the SS headquarters inside Germany. Throughout its history the SS made a profit on its operations. A part of this profit in the form of gold bars stamped with the eagle of the Reich and the twin-lightning symbol of the SS was deposited towards the end of the war in the banks of Switzerland, Liechtenstein, Tangier and Beirut to form the fortune on which the Odessa was later based. Much of this gold still lies, beneath the streets of Zürich, guarded by the complacent and self-righteous bankers of that city.

The second stage of the exploitation lay in the living bodies of the victims. They had calories of energy in them, and these could profitably be used. At this point the Jews came on to the same level as the Russians and the Poles, who had been captured penniless in the first place. Those in all categories unfit for work were exterminated as useless. Those able to work were hired out, either to the SS's own factories or to German industrial concerns like Krupp, Thyssen, von Opel, and others at three marks a day for unskilled workers, four marks for artisans. The phrase 'per day' meant as much work as could be abstracted from the living body for as little food during a twenty-four-hour period. Hundreds of thousands died at their place of work in this manner.

The SS was a state within a state. It had its own factories, workshops, engineering division, construction section, repair and maintenance shops and clothing department. It made for itself almost everything it could ever need, and used the slave labourers, which by Hitler's decree were the property of the SS, to do the work.

The third stage of the exploitation lay in the corpses of the dead. These went naked to death, leaving behind waggon-loads of shoes, socks, shaving brushes, spectacles, jackets and trousers. They also left their hair, which was shipped back to the Reich to be turned into felt boots for the winter fighting, and their gold teeth fillings, which were yanked out of the corpses with pliers and later melted down to be deposited as gold bars in Zürich. Attempts were made to use the bones for fertilisers and render the body fats down for soap, but this was found to be un-economical.

In charge of the entire economic or profit-making side of the extermination of fourteen million people was the Reich Economic Administration Main Office of the SS, headed by the man in Seat 3-B on the airliner that night.

Gluecks was one who preferred not to chance his arm, or his lifelong liberty, by returning to Germany after his escape. He had no need to. Handsomely provided for out of the secret funds, he could live out his days comfortably in South America, and still does. His dedication to the Nazi ideal remained unshaken by the events of 1945 and this, coupled with his former eminence, secured him a high and honoured place among the fugitive Nazis of Argentina, whence the Odessa was ruled.

The plane landed uneventfully and the passengers cleared Customs with no problems. The fluent Spanish of the first-class passenger from Row Three caused no eyebrows to be raised, for he had long since been able to pass for a South American.

Outside the terminal building he took a cab, and from long habit gave an address a block away from Zurburan Hotel. Paying off the cab in the centre of Madrid, he took his grip, and walked the remaining 200 yards to the hotel.

His reservation had been made by telex, so he checked in and went up to his room to shower and shave. It was at nine o'clock on the dot that three soft knocks, followed by a pause and two more, sounded at his door.

He opened it himself and stood back when he recognised the visitor.

The new arrival closed the door behind him, snapped to attention and flashed up his right arm, palm downwards in the old salute.

'Sieg Heil,' said the man.

General Gluecks gave the younger man an approving nod and raised his own right hand.

'Sieg Heil,' he said more softly. He waved his visitor to a seat. The man facing him was another German, a former officer of the SS, and presently the chief of the Odessa network inside West Germany. He felt very keenly the honour of being summoned to Madrid for a personal conference with such a senior officer, and suspected it had something to do with the death of President Kennedy thirty-six hours earlier. He was not wrong.

General Gluecks poured himself a cup of coffee from the breakfast tray beside him and carefully lit a large Corona.

'You have probably guessed the reason for this sudden and somewhat hazardous visit by me to Europe,' he said. 'As I dislike remaining on this continent longer than necessary, I will get to the point and be brief.'

The subordinate from Germany sat forward expectantly.

'Kennedy is now dead, for us a remarkable stroke of good fortune,' the general went on. 'There must be no failure to extract the utmost advantage from this event. Do you follow me?'

'Certainly, in principle, Herr General,' the young man replied eagerly, 'but in what specific form?'

'I am referring to the secret arms deal between the rabble of traitors in Bonn and the pigs in Tel Aviv. You know about the arms deal? The tanks, guns and other weaponry even now flowing from Germany to Israel?'

'Yes, of course.'

'And you know also that our organisation is doing everything in its power to assist the Egyptian cause so that they may one day prove completely victorious in the coming struggle?'

'Certainly. We have already organised the recruiting of numerous German scientists to that end.'

General Gluecks nodded.

'I'll return to that later. What I was referring to was our policy of keeping our Arab friends as closely informed as possible about the details of this treacherous deal, so that they may make the strongest representations to Bonn through diplomatic channels. These Arab protests have led to the formation of a group in Germany strongly opposed to the arms deal on political grounds, because the deal upsets the Arabs. This group, mainly unwittingly, is playing our game for us, bringing pressure on the fool Erhard even as high as cabinet level to call off the arms deal.'

'Yes. I follow you, Herr General.'

'Good. So far Erhard has not called off the arms shipments, but he has wavered several times. For those who wish to see the German-Israeli arms deal completed, the main argument to date has been that the deal is supported by Kennedy and what Kennedy wants, Erhard gives him.'

'Yes. That's true.'

'But Kennedy is now dead.'

The younger man from Germany sat back, his eyes alight with enthusiasm, as the new state of affairs opened up its perspectives to his mind. The SS general flicked an inch of ash from the cigar into the coffee-cup, and jabbed the glowing tip at his subordinate.

'For the rest of this year, therefore, the main plank of political action within Germany that our friends and supporters must undertake, will be to whip up public opinion on as wide a scale as possible against this arms deal and in favour of Germany's true and traditional friends, the Arabs.'

'Yes, yes, that can be done.' The younger man was smiling broadly.

'Certain contacts we have in the government of Cairo will ensure a constant stream of diplomatic protests through their own and other embassies,' the general continued. 'Other Arab friends will ensure demonstrations by Arab students and German friends of the Arabs. Your job will be to co-ordinate press publicity through the various pamphlets and magazines we secretly support, advertisements taken in major newspapers and magazines, lobbying of civil servants close to government and politicans who must be persuaded to join the growing weight of opinion against the arms deal.'

The younger man's brow furrowed.

'It's very difficult to promote feelings against Israel in Germany today,' he murmured.

'There need be no question of that,' said the other tartly. 'The angle is simple: for practical reasons Germany must not alienate eighty million Arabs with these foolish supposedly secret arms shipments. Many Germans will listen to that argument, particularly diplomats. Known friends of ours in the Foreign Office can be enlisted. Such a practical viewpoint is wholly permissible. Funds, of course, will be made available. The main thing is, with Kennedy dead and Johnson unlikely to adopt the same internationalist, pro-Jewish outlook, Erhard must be subjected to constant pressure at every level, including his own cabinet, to shelve this arms deal. If we can show the Egyptians that we have caused foreign policy in Bonn to change course, our stock in Cairo must inevitably rise sharply.'

The man from Germany nodded several times, already seeing his plan of campaign taking shape before him.

'It shall be done,' he said.

'Excellent,' replied General Gluecks. The man in front of him looked up.

'Herr General, you mentioned the German scientists now working in Egypt ...'

'Ah yes, I said I would return to them later. They represent the second prong in our plan to destroy the Jews once and for all. You know about the rockets of Helwan, of course?'

'Yes, sir. At least, the broad details.'

'But not what they are really for?'

'Well, I assumed of course ...'

'That they would be used to throw a few tons of high explosive on to Israel?' General Gluecks smiled broadly. 'You could not be more wrong. However, I think the time is ripe to tell you why these rockets and the men who build them are in truth so vitally important.'

General Gluecks leaned back, gazed at the ceiling, and told his subordinate the *real* story behind the rockets of Helwan.

In the aftermath of the war, when King Farouk still ruled Egypt, thousands of Nazis and former members of the SS had fled from Europe and found a sure refuge along the sands of the Nile. Among those who came were a number of scientists. Even before the *coup d'état* that dislodged Farouk, two German scientists had been charged by Farouk with the first studies for the eventual setting-up of a factory to manufacture rockets. This was in 1952, and the two professors were Paul Goerke and Rolf Engel.

The project went into abeyance for a few years after Gamal Abdel Nasser took power, but after the military defeat of the Egyptian forces, in the 1956 Sinai campaign, the new dictator of Egypt swore an oath. He vowed that one day Israel would be totally destroyed.

In 1961, when he got Moscow's final 'No' to his requests for heavy rockets, the Goerke/Engel project for an Egyptian rocket factory was revitalised with a vengeance, and during this year, working against the clock and without rein on their expenditure of money, the German professors and the Egyptians built and opened Factory 333, at Helwan, north of Cairo.

To open a factory is one thing; to design and build rockets is another. Long since, the senior supporters of Nasser, mostly with pro-Nazi backgrounds stretching back to the Second World War, had been in close contact with the Odessa representatives in Egypt. From these came the answer to the Egyptians' main problem – the problem of acquiring the scientists necessary to make the rockets.

Neither Russia, America, Britain nor France would supply a single man to help. But the Odessa pointed out that the kind of rockets Nasser needed were remarkably similar in size and range to the V.2 rockets that Werner von Braun and his team had once built at Peenemunde to pulverise London. And many of his former team were still available.

In late 1961 the recruiting of German scientists started. Many of these were employed at the West German Institute for Aerospace Research at Stuttgart. But they were frustrated because the Paris Treaty of 1954 forbade Germany to indulge in research or manufacture in certain realms, notably nuclear physics and rocketry. They were also chronically short of research funds. To many of these scientists the offer of a place in the sun, plenty of research money and the chance to design real rockets, was too tempting.

The Odessa appointed a chief recruiting officer in Germany, and he in turn employed as his leg-man a former SS-sergeant, Heinz Krug. Together they scoured Germany looking for men prepared to go to Egypt and build Nasser's rockets for him.

With the salaries they could offer they were not short of choice recruits. Notable among them were Professor Wolfgang Pilz, who had been recuperated from post-war Germany by the French and had later become the father of the French Véronique rocket, itself the foundation of De Gaulle's aerospace programme. Professor Pilz left for Egypt in early 1962. Another was Dr Heinz Kleinwachter; Dr Eugen Saenger and his wife Irene, both formerly on the von Braun V.2 team, also went along, as did Doctors Josef Eisig and Kirmayer, all experts in propulsion fuels and techniques.

The world saw the first results of their labours at a parade through the streets of Cairo on 23rd July, 1962, to mark the eighth anniversary of the fall of Farouk. Two rockets, the El Kahira and the El Zafira, respectively with ranges of 500 and 300 kilometres, were trundled past the screaming crowds. Although these rockets were only the casings, without warheads or fuel, they were destined to be the first of 400 such weapons that would one day be launched against Israel.

General Gluecks paused, drew on his cigar and returned to the present.

'The problem is, that although we solved the matter of making the casings, the warheads and the fuel, the key of a guided missile lies in the tele-guidance system.'

He stabbed his cigar in the direction of the West German.

'And *that* was what we were unable to furnish to the Egyptians,' he went on.

'By ill-luck, although there were scientists and experts in guidance systems working at Stuttgart and elsewhere, we could not persuade one of them of any value to emigrate to Egypt. All the experts sent out there were specialists in aerodynamics, propulsion and the design of warheads.

'But we had promised Egypt that she would have her rockets and have them she will. President Nasser is determined there will one day be war between Egypt and Israel, and war there will be. He believes his tanks and soldiers alone will win for him. Our information is not so optimistic. They might not, despite their numerical superiority. But just think what our position would be if, when all the Soviet weaponry, bought at a cost of billions of dollars, had failed, it turned out to be the rockets provided by the scientists recruited through our network which won the war. Our position would be unassailable. We would have carried out the double coup of ensuring an eternally grateful Middle East, a safe and sure home for our people for all time, and of achieving the final and utter destruction of the Jew-pig State, thus fulfilling the last wish of the dying Fuehrer. It is a mighty challenge, and one in which we must not and will not fail.'

The subordinate watched his senior officer pacing the room, with awe and some puzzlement.

'Forgive me, Herr General, but will 400 medium warheads really finish off the Jews once and for all? A massive amount of damage, yes, but total destruction?'

Gluecks spun round and gazed down at the younger man with a triumphant smile.

'But what warheads,' he exclaimed. 'You do not think we are going to waste mere high explosive on these swine. We have proposed to President Nasser, and he has accepted with alacrity, that these warheads on the Kahiras and Zafiras be of a different type. Some will contain concentrated cultures of bubonic plague and the others will explode high above the ground, showering the entire territory of Israel with irradiated Strontium 90. Within hours they will all be dying of the pest or of gamma-ray sickness. *That* is what we have in store for them.'

The other gazed at him open-mouthed.

'Fantastic,' he breathed. 'Now I recall reading something about a trial in Switzerland last summer. Just summaries, so much of the evidence was in camera. Then it's true. But, General, it's brilliant.'

'Brilliant, yes, and inevitable, provided we of the Odessa can equip those rockets with the tele-guidance systems necessary to direct them not merely in the right direction but to the exact locations where they must explode. The man who controls the entire research operation aimed at devising a tele-guidance system for those rockets is now working in West Germany. His code-name is Vulkan. You may recall that in Greek mythology Vulkan was the smith who made the thunderbolts of the Gods.'

'He is a scientist?' asked the West German in bewilderment.

'No, certainly not. When he was forced to disappear in 1955 he would normally have returned to Argentina. But your predecessor was required by us to provide him immediately with a false passport to enable him to stay in Germany. He was then funded out of Zürich with one million US dollars with which to start a factory in Germany. The original purpose was to use the factory as a front for another type of research in which we were interested at the time, but which now has been shelved in favour of the guidance systems for the rockets of Helwan.

'The factory Vulkan now runs manufactures transistor radios. But this is a front. In the research department of the factory a group of scientists is even now in the process of devising the tele-guidance systems that will one day be fitted to the rockets of Helwan.'

'Why don't they simply go to Egypt?' asked the other.

Gluecks smiled again and continued pacing.

'That is the stroke of genius behind the whole operation. I told you there were men in Germany capable of producing such rocket-guidance systems, but none could be persuaded to emigrate. The group of them who now work in the research department of Vulkan's factory actually believe they are working on a contract, in conditions of top secrecy of course, for the Defence Ministry in Bonn.'

This time the subordinate got out of his chair, his coffee spilling on the carpet.

'God in heaven. How on earth was that arranged?'

'Basically quite simple. The Paris Treaty forbids Germany to do research into rockets. Then men under Vulkan were sworn to secrecy by a genuine official of the Defence Ministry in Bonn, who also happens to be one of us. He was accompanied by a general whose face the scientists could recognise from the last war. They are all men prepared to work for Germany, even against the terms of the Paris Treaty, but not necessarily prepared to work for Egypt. Now they believe they *are* working for Germany.

'Of course, the cost is stupendous. Normally research of this nature can only be undertaken by a major power. This entire programme has made enormous inroads into our secret funds. Now do you understand the importance of Vulkan?'

'Of course,' replied the Odessa chief from Germany. 'But if anything happened to him, could not the programme go on?'

'No. The factory and the company are owned and run by him alone. He is chairman and managing director, sole shareholder and paymaster. He alone can continue to pay the salaries of the scientists and the enormous research costs involved. None of the scientists ever has anything to do with anyone else in the firm, and no one else in the firm knows the true nature of the over-large research section. They believe the men in the closed-off section are working on micro-wave circuits with a view to making a breakthrough in the transistor market. The secrecy is explained as a precaution against industrial espionage. The only link man between the two sections is Vulkan. If he went, the entire project would collapse.'

'Can you tell me the name of the factory?'

General Gluecks considered for a moment, then mentioned a name. The other man stared at him in astonishment.

'But I know those radios,' he protested.

'Of course. It's a bona-fide firm and makes bona-fide radios.'

'And the managing director . . . he is?'

'Yes. He is Vulkan. Now you see the importance of this man and what he is doing. For that reason there is one other instruction to you. Here . . .'

General Gluecks took a photograph from his breast pocket and handed it to the man from Germany. After a long, perplexed gaze at the face, he turned it over and read the name on the back.

'Good God, I thought he was in South America.'

Gluecks shook his head.

'On the contrary. He is Vulkan. At the present time his work has reached a most crucial stage. If by any chance, therefore, you should get a whisper of anyone asking inconvenient questions about this man, that person should be . . . discouraged. One warning, and then a permanent solution. Do you follow me, *Kamerad*? No one, repeat, no one is to get anywhere near exposing Vulkan for who he really is.'

The SS general rose. His visitor did likewise.

'That will be all,' said Gluecks. 'You have your instructions.'

4

'But you don't even know if he's alive.'

Peter Miller and Karl Brandt were sitting side by side in Miller's car outside the house of the detective inspector, where Miller had traced him over Sunday lunch on his day off.

'No, I don't. So that's the first thing I have to find out. If Roschmann's dead, obviously that's the end of it. Can you help me?'

Brandt considered the request, then slowly shook his head.

'No, sorry, I can't.'

'Why not?'

'Look, I gave you that diary as a favour. Just between us. Because it shocked me, because I thought it might make a story for you. But I never thought you were going to try and track Roschmann down. Why can't you just make a story out of the finding of the diary?'

'Because there's no story in it,' said Miller. 'What am I supposed to say? "Surprise, surprise, I've found a loose-leaf folder in which an old man who just gassed himself describes what he went through during the war?" You think any editor's going to buy that? I happen to think it's a horrifying document, but that's just my opinion. There have been hundreds of memoirs written since the war. The world's getting tired of them. Just the diary alone won't sell to any editor in Germany.'

'So what are you going on about?' asked Brandt.

'Simply this. Get a major police hunt started for Roschmann on the basis of the diary, and I've got a story.'

Brandt tapped his ash slowly into the dashboard tray.

'There won't be a major police hunt,' he said. 'Look, Peter, you may know journalism, but I know the Hamburg police. Our job is to keep Hamburg crime-free now, in 1963. Nobody's going to start detaching overworked detectives to hunt a man for what he did in Riga twenty years ago. It's not on.'

'But you could at least raise the matter?' said Miller. Brandt shook his head.

'No. Not me.'

'Why not? What's the matter?'

'Because I don't want to get involved. You're all right. You're single, unattached. You can go off chasing will-o'-the-wisps if you want to. I've got a wife and two kids, and a good career, and I don't intend to jeopardise that career.'

'Why should this jeopardise your career with the police? Roschmann's a criminal, isn't he? Police forces are supposed to hunt criminals. Where's the problem?'

Brandt crushed out his stub.

'It's difficult to put one's finger on. But there's a sort of attitude in the police, nothing concrete, just a feeling. And that feeling is that to start probing too energetically into the war crimes of the SS can do a young policeman's career a power of no-good. Nothing comes of it anyway. The request would simply be denied. But the fact that it was made goes into a file. Then bang goes your chance of promotion. Nobody mentions it, but everyone knows it. So if you want to make a big issue out of this, you're on your own. Count me out.'

Miller sat and stared through the windscreen.

'All right. If that's the way it is,' he said at length. 'But I've got to start somewhere. Did Tauber leave anything else behind when he died?'

'Well, there was a brief note. I had to take it and include it in my report on the suicide. By now it will have been filed away. And the file's closed.'

'What did he say in it?' asked Miller.

'Not much,' said Brandt. 'He just said he was committing suicide. Oh, there was one thing; he said he left his effects to a friend of his, a Herr Marx.'

'Well, that's a start. Where's this Marx?'

'How the hell should I know?' said Brandt.

'You mean to say that's all the note said? Just Herr Marx? No address?'

'Nothing,' said Brandt. 'Just Marx. No indication where he lives.'

'Well, he must be around somewhere. Didn't you look for him?'

Brandt sighed.

'Will you get this through your head? We are very busy in the police force. Have you any idea how many Marxs there are in Hamburg? Hundreds in the telephone directory alone. We can't spend weeks looking for this particular Marx. Anyway what the old man left wasn't worth ten pfennigs.'

'That's all then?' asked Miller. 'Nothing else?'

'Not a thing. If you want to find Marx you're welcome to try.'

'Thanks. I will,' said Miller. The two men shook hands and Brandt returned to his family lunch table.

Miller started the next morning by visiting the house where Tauber had lived. The door was opened by a middle-aged man wearing a pair of stained trousers supported by string, a collarless shirt open at the neck and three days' stubble round his chin.

' 'Morning. Are you the landlord?'

The man looked Miller up and down and nodded. He smelled of cabbage.

'There was a man gassed himself here a few nights back,' said Miller.

'Are you from the police?'

'No. The Press.' Miller showed the man his press card.

'I ain't got nothing to say.'

Miller eased a ten-mark note without too much trouble into the man's hand.

'I only want to look at his room.'

'I've re-let it.'

'What did you do with his stuff?'

'It's in the backyard. Nothing else I could do with it.'

The pile of junk was lying in a heap under the thin rain. It still smelt of gas. There was a battered old typewriter, two scuffed pairs of shoes, an assortment of clothes, a pile of books and a fringed white-silk scarf that Miller assumed must be something to do with the Jewish religion. He went through everything in the pile, but there was no indication of an address book and nothing addressed to Marx.

'Is that the lot?' he asked.

'That's the lot,' said the man, regarding him sourly from the shelter of the back door.

'Do you have any tenant by the name of Marx?'

'Nope.'

'Do you know of any Marx?'

'Nope.'

'Did old Tauber have any friends?'

'Not that I knew of. Kept himself to himself. Came and went at all hours, shuffling about up there. Barmy if you ask me. But he paid his rent regular. Didn't cause no trouble.'

'Ever see him with anybody? Out in the street I mean.'

'No, never. Didn't seem to have any friends. Not surprised, the way he kept mumbling to himself. Barmy.'

Miller left, and started asking up and down the street. Most people remembered seeing the old man, shuffling along, head down, wrapped in an ankle-length greatcoat, head covered by a woollen cap, hands in woollen gloves from which the fingertips protruded.

For three days he quartered the area of streets where Tauber lived, checking through the dairy, the greengrocer, the butcher, the hardware store, the beer-bar, the tobacconist, intercepting the milkman and the postman. It was Wednesday afternoon when he found the group of urchins playing football up against the warehouse wall.

'What, that old Jew? Mad Solly?' said the leader of the group in answer to his question. The rest gathered round.

'That's the one,' said Miller. 'Mad Solly.'

'He was barmy,' said one of the crowd. 'He used to walk like this.'

The boy hunched his head into his shoulders, hands clutching his jacket round him, and shuffled forward a few paces, muttering to himself and casting his eyes about. The others dissolved in laughter, and one gave the impersonator a hefty shove which sent him sprawling.

'Anyone ever see him with anyone else?' asked Miller. 'Talking with anyone else. Another man.'

'Whatcher want to know for?' asked the leader, suspiciously.

'We didn't do him no harm.'

Miller flicked a five-mark coin idly up and down in one hand. Eight pairs of eyes watched the silver glitter of the spinning coin. Eight heads shook slowly. Miller turned and walked away.

'Mister.'

He stopped and turned round. The smallest of the group had caught up with him.

'I seen him once with a man. Talking they was. Sitting and talking.'

'Where was that?'

'Down by the river. On the grass bank along the river. There are some benches there. They was sitting on a bench talking.'

'How old was he, the other one?'

'Very old. Lot of white hair.'

Miller tossed him the coin, convinced it had been a wasted gesture. But he walked to the river and stared down the length of the grass bank in either direction. There were a dozen benches along the bank, each of them empty. In summer there would be plenty of people sitting along the Elbe Chaussee watching the great liners come in and out, but not at the end of November.

To his left along the near bank lay the fisher port, with half a dozen North Sea trawlers drawn up at the wharves, discharging their loads of fresh-caught herring and mackerel, or preparing for the sea again.

As a boy he had returned to the shattered city from a farm in the country where he had been evacuated during the bombing, and had grown up amid the rubble and the ruins. His favourite playing place had been this fisher port along the river Altona.

He liked the fishermen, gruff, kindly men who smelt of tar and salt and shag tobacco. He thought of Eduard Roschmann in Riga, and wondered how the same country could produce them both.

His mind came back to Tauber and went over the problem again. Where could he possibly have met his friend Marx? He knew there was something missing, but could not put his finger on it. It was not until he was back in his car and had stopped for petrol close to Altona railway station that the answer came. As so often, it was a chance remark. The pump attendant pointed out there had been a price increase in top-grade petrol and added, just to make conversation with his customer, that money went less and less far these days. He went to get the change and left Miller staring at the open wallet in his hand.

Money. Where did Tauber get his money? He didn't work, he refused to accept any compensation from the State of Germany. Yet he paid his rent regularly and must have had something left over with which to eat. He was fifty-six years old, so he could not have an old-age pension, but he could well have had a disability pension. Probably did.

Miller pocketed his change, gunned the Jaguar to life and drove round to Altona post office. He approached the grille marked 'Pensions'.

'Can you tell me when the pensioners collect their money?' he asked the fat lady behind the grille.

'Last day of the month, of course,' she said.

'That will be Saturday then?'

'Except at weekends. This month it will be Friday, the day after tomorrow.'

'Does that include those with disability pensions?' he asked.

'Everyone who's entitled to a pension collects it on the last day of the month.'

'Here, at this grille?'

'If the person lives in Altona, yes,' replied the woman.

'At what time?'

'From opening time onwards.'

'Thank you.'

Miller was back on Friday morning, watching the queue of old men and women begin to filter through the doors of the post office when it opened. He positioned himself against the wall opposite, watching the direction they took as they departed. Many had white hair, but most wore hats against the cold. The weather had turned dry again, sunny but chill. Just before eleven an old man with a shock of white hair like candy floss came out of the post office, counted his money to make sure it was all there, put it in his inside pocket and looked round as if searching for someone. After a few minutes he turned and began to walk slowly away. At the corner he looked up and down again, then turned down Museum Street in the direction of the river bank. Miller eased himself off the wall and followed him.

It took the old man twenty minutes to get the half-mile to the Elbe Chaussee, then he turned up the bank, crossed the grass and settled himself on a bench. Miller approached slowly from behind.

'Herr Marx?'

The old man turned as Miller came round the end of the bench. He showed no surprise, as though he was often recognised by complete strangers.

'Yes,' he said gravely, 'I am Marx.'

'My name is Miller.'

Marx inclined his head gravely in acceptance of this news.

'Are you . . . er . . . waiting for Herr Tauber?'

'Yes, I am,' said the old man without surprise.

'May I sit down?'

'Please.'

Miller sat beside him, so they both faced towards the river Elbe. A giant dry-cargo ship, the *Kota Maru* out of Yokohama, was easing down-river on the tide.

'I'm afraid Herr Tauber is dead.'

The old man stared at the passing ship. He showed neither grief nor surprise, as if such news was brought frequently. Perhaps it was.

'I see,' he said.

Miller told him briefly about the events of the previous Friday night.

'You don't seem surprised. That he killed himself.'

'No,' said Marx, 'he was a very unhappy man.'

'He left a diary, you know.'

'Yes, he told me once about that.'

'Did you ever read it?' asked Miller.

'No, he never let anybody read it. But he told me about it.'

'It described the time he spent in Riga during the war.'

'Yes, he told me he was in Riga.'

'Were you in Riga too?'

The man turned and looked at him with sad old eyes.

'No, I was in Dachau.'

'Look, Herr Marx, I need your help. In his diary your friend mentioned a man, an SS officer, called Roschmann. Captain Eduard Roschmann. Did he ever mention him to you?'

'Oh, yes. He told me about Roschmann. That was really what kept him alive. Hoping one day to give evidence against Roschmann.'

'That's what he said in his diary. I read it after his death. I'm a press reporter. I want to try and find Roschmann. Bring him to trial. Do you understand?'

'Yes.'

'But there's no point if Roschmann is already dead. Can you remember if Herr Tauber ever learned whether Roschmann was still alive and free?'

Marx stared out at the disappearing stern of the *Kota Maru* for several minutes.

'Captain Roschmann is alive,' he said simply. 'And free.'

Miller leaned forward earnestly.

'How do you know?'

'Because Tauber saw him.'

'Yes, I read that. It was in early April 1945.'

Marx shook his head slowly.

'No, it was last month.'

For several more minutes there was silence as Miller stared at the old man, and Marx stared out to the water.

'Last month?' repeated Miller at length. 'Did he say how he saw him?'

Marx sighed, then turned to Miller.

'Yes. He was walking late at night as he often used to do when he could not sleep. He was walking back home past the State Opera House just as a crowd of people started to come out. He stopped as they came to the pavement. He said they were wealthy people, the men in dinner-jackets, the women in furs and jewels. There were three taxis lined up at the kerb waiting for them. The commissionaire held the passers-by back so they could climb in. And then he saw Roschmann.'

'In the crowd of opera-goers?'

'Yes. He climbed into a taxi with two others and they drove off.'

'Now listen, Herr Marx, this is very important. Was he absolutely sure it was Roschmann?'

'Yes, he said he was.'

'But it was nineteen years since he last saw him. He must have changed a lot. How could he be so sure?'

'He said he smiled.'

'He what?'

'He smiled. Roschmann smiled.'

'That is significant?'

Marx nodded several times.

'He said once you had seen Roschmann smile that way you never forgot it. He could not describe the smile, but just said he would recognise it among a million others, anywhere in the world.'

'I see. Do you believe him?'

'Yes. Yes, I believe he saw Roschmann.'

'All right. Let's accept that I do too. Did he get the number of the taxi?'

'No. He said his mind was so stunned he just watched it drive away.'

'Damn,' said Miller. 'It probably drove to a hotel. If I had the number I could ask the driver where he took that party. When did Herr Tauber tell you all this?'

'Last month, when we picked up our pensions. Here, on this bench.'

Miller stood up and sighed.

'You must realise that nobody would ever believe his story?'

Marx shifted his gaze off the river and looked up at the reporter.

'Oh yes,' he said softly, 'he knew that. You see, that was why he killed himself.'

That evening Peter Miller paid his usual weekend visit to his mother, and as usual she fussed over whether he was eating enough, the number of cigarettes he smoked in a day and the state of his laundry.

She was a short, plump, matronly person in her early fifties who had never quite resigned herself to the idea that all her son wanted to be was a reporter.

During the course of the evening she asked him what he was doing at the moment. Briefly he told her, mentioning his intention to try to track down the missing Eduard Roschmann. She was aghast.

Peter ate away stolidly, letting the tide of reproach and recrimination flow over his head.

'It's bad enough you always having to go about covering the doings of those nasty criminals and people,' she was saying, 'without going and getting mixed up with those Nazi people. I don't know what your dear father would have thought, I really don't. . . .'

A thought struck him.

'Mother.'

'Yes dear?'

'During the war . . . those things that the SS did to people . . . in the camps. Did you ever suspect . . . did you ever think that it was going on?'

She busied herself furiously tidying up the table. After a few seconds she spoke.

'Horrible things. Terrible things. The British made us look at the films after the war. I don't want to hear any more about it.'

She bustled out. Peter rose and followed her into the kitchen.

'You remember in 1950 when I was sixteen and I went to Paris with a school party?'

She paused, filling the sink for the washing up.

'Yes, I remember.'

'And we were taken to see a church called the Sacré Coeur. And there was a service just finishing, a memorial service for a man called Jean Moulin. Some people came out, and they heard me speaking German to another boy. One of the group turned and spat at me. I remember the spittle running down my jacket. I remember I came home later and told you about it. Do you remember what you said?'

Mrs Miller was furiously scouring the dinner plates.

'You said the French were like that. Dirty habits, you said.'

'Well, they have. I never did like them.'

'Look, Mother, do you know what we did to Jean Moulin before he died? Not you, not father, not me. But us, the Germans, or rather the Gestapo, which for millions of foreigners seems to be the same thing.'

'I'm sure I don't want to hear. Now that's enough of that.'

'Well, I can't tell you, because I don't know. Doubtless it's recorded somewhere. But the point is, I was spat on not because I was in the Gestapo, but because I'm a German.'

'And you should be proud of it.'

'Oh, I am, believe me, I am. But that doesn't mean I've got to be proud of the Nazis, and the SS and the Gestapo.'

'Well, nobody is, but it won't get better for keeping talking about it.'

She was flustered, as always when he argued with her, drying her hands on the dish towel before bustling back into the sitting-room. He trailed after her.

'Look, Mother, try to understand. Until I read that diary I never even asked precisely what it was we were all supposed to have done. Now at least I'm beginning to understand. That's why I want to find this man, this monster, if he's still about. It's right that he should be brought to trial.'

She sat on the settee, close to tears.

'Please, Peterkin, leave them alone. Just don't keep probing into the past. It won't do any good. It's over now, over and done with. It's best forgotten.'

Peter Miller was facing the mantelpiece, dominated by the clock and the photograph of his dead father. He was wearing his captain's uniform of the Army, staring out of the frame with the kind, rather sad smile that Miller remembered of him. It was taken before he returned to the front after his last leave.

Peter remembered his father with startling clarity, looking at his photograph nineteen years later as his mother asked him to drop the Roschmann enquiry. He could remember before the war, when he was five years old, and his father had taken him to Hagenbeck's Zoo and pointed out all the animals to him, one by one, patiently reading the details off the little tin plaques in front of each cage to reply to the endless flow of questions from the boy.

He could remember how he came home after enlisting in 1940, and how his mother had cried and how he had thought how stupid women are to cry over such a wonderful thing as having a father in uniform. He recalled the day in 1944 when he was eleven years old, and an army officer had come to the door to tell his mother that her war-hero husband had been killed on the Eastern Front.

'Besides, nobody wants these awful exposures any more. Nor these terrible trials that we keep having, with everything dragged out into the open again. Nobody's going to thank you for it, even if you do find him. They'll just point to you in the street; I mean, they don't want any more trials. Not now, it's too late. Just drop it, Peter, please, for my sake.'

He remembered the black-edged column of names in the newspaper, the same length as every day, but different that day in late October, for halfway down was the entry:

'Fallen for Fuehrer and Fatherland. Miller, Erwin, Captain, on October 11th. In Ostland.'

And that was it. Nothing else. No hint of where, or when, or why. Just one of tens of thousands of names pouring back from the east to fill the ever-lengthening black-edged columns, until the government had ceased to print them because they destroyed morale.

'I mean,' said his mother behind him, 'you might at least think of your father's memory. You think he'd want his son digging around into the past, trying to drag up another war crimes trial? Do you think that's what he'd want?'

Miller spun round and walked across the room to his mother, placed both hands on her shoulders and looked down into her frightened, china-blue eyes. He stooped and kissed her lightly on the forehead.

'Yes, *Mutti*,' he said. 'I think that's exactly what he'd want.'

He let himself out, climbed into his car and headed back into Hamburg, his anger seething inside him.

Everyone who knew him and many who did not agreed Hans Hoffmann looked the part. He was in his late forties, boyishly handsome with carefully styled greying hair, cut in the latest trendy fashion, manicured fingers. His medium-grey suit was from Savile Row, his heavy silk tie was from Cardin. There was an air of expensive good taste of the kind money can buy about him.

If looks had been his only asset he would not have been one of West Germany's wealthiest and most successful magazine publishers. Starting after the war with a hand-operated press, turning out handbills for the British occupation authorities, he had founded in 1949 one of the first weekly picture magazines. His formula was simple – tell it in words and make it shocking, then back it up with pictures that made all competitors look like novices with their first box Brownie. It worked. His chain of eight magazines ranging from love stories for teenagers to the glossy chronicle of the doings of the rich and sexy had made him a multi-millionaire. But *Komet*, the news and current-affairs magazine, was still his favourite, his baby.

The money had brought him a luxurious ranch-style house at Oth-marschen, a chalet in the mountains, a villa by the sea, a Rolls-Royce and a Ferrari. Along the way, he had picked up a beautiful wife whom he dressed from Paris and two handsome children he seldom saw. The only millionaire in Germany whose succession of young mistresses, discreetly maintained and frequently exchanged, were never photographed in the gossip magazine was Hans Hoffmann. He was also very astute.

That Wednesday afternoon he closed the cover of the diary of Salomon Tauber after reading the preface, leaned back and looked at the young reporter opposite.

'All right. I can guess the rest. What do you want?'

'I think that's a great document,' said Miller. 'There's a man mentioned throughout the diary called Eduard Roschmann, Captain in the SS. Commandant of Riga ghetto throughout. Killed 80,000 men, women and children. I believe he's alive and here in West Germany. I want to find him.'

'How do you know he's alive?'

Miller told him briefly. Hoffmann pursed his lips.

'Pretty thin evidence.'

'True. But worth a second look. I've brought home stories that started on less.'

Hoffmann grinned, recalling Miller's talent for ferreting out stories that hurt the establishment. Hoffmann had been happy to print them, once they were checked out as accurate. They sent circulation soaring.

'Then presumably this man, what do you call him, Roschmann? Presumably he's already on the wanted list. If the police can't find him, what makes you think you can?'

'Are the police really looking?' asked Miller.

Hoffmann shrugged.

'They're supposed to. That's what we pay them for.'

'It wouldn't hurt to help a little, would it? Just check out whether he's really alive, whether he was ever picked up, if so, what happened to him.'

'So what do you want from me?' asked Hoffmann.

'A commission to give it a try. If nothing comes of it, I drop it.'

Hoffmann swung in his chair, spinning round to face the picture windows looking out over the sprawling docks, mile after mile of cranes and wharves, spread out twenty floors below and a mile away.

'It's a bit out of your line of country, Miller. Why the sudden interest?'

Miller thought hard. Trying to sell an idea was always the hardest part. A freelance reporter has to sell the story, or the idea of the story, to the publisher or the editor first. The public comes much later.

'It's a good human-interest story. If *Komet* could find the man where the police forces of the country had failed, it would be a beat. Something people want to know about.'

Hoffmann gazed out at the December skyline and slowly shook his head.

'You're wrong. That's why I'm not giving you a commission for it. I should think it's the last thing people want to know about.'

'But look, Herr Hoffmann, this is different. These people Roschmann killed, they weren't Poles and Russians. These were Germans, all right German Jews, but they *were* Germans. Why wouldn't people want to know about it?'

Hoffmann spun back from the window, put his elbows on the desk and rested his chin on his knuckles.

'Miller, you're a good reporter. I like the way you cover a story, you've got style. And you're a ferret. I can hire twenty, fifty, a hundred men in this city by picking up the phone, and they'll all do what they're told, cover the stories they're sent to cover. But they can't dig out a story for themselves. You can. That's why you get a lot of work from me, and will get a lot more in the future. But not this one.'

'But why? It's a good story.'

'Listen, you're young. I'll tell you something about journalism. Half of journalism is about writing good stories. The other half is about selling them. You can do the first, but I can do the second. That's why I'm here and you're there. You think this is a story everyone will want to read, because the victims of Riga were German Jews. I'm telling you, that's exactly why *no one* will want to read the story. It's the last story in the world they'll want to read. And until there's a law in this country forcing people to buy magazines and read what's good for them, they'll go on buying magazines to read what they want to read. And that's what I give them. What they want to read.'

'Then why not about Roschmann?'

'You still don't get it? Then I'll tell you. Before the war just about everyone in Germany knew one Jew. The fact is, before Hitler started, nobody hated the Jews in Germany. We had the best record of treatment of our Jewish minority of any country in Europe. Better than France, better than Spain, infinitely better than Poland and Russia where the pogroms were fiendish.

'Then Hitler started. Telling people the Jews were to blame for the first war, the unemployment, the poverty and everything else that was wrong. People didn't know what to believe. Almost everyone knew one Jew who was a nice guy. Or just harmless. People had Jewish friends, good friends; Jewish employers, good employers; Jewish employees, hard workers. They obeyed the laws, they didn't hurt anyone. And here was Hitler saying they were to blame for everything.

'So when the vans came and took them away, people didn't do anything. They stayed out of the way, they kept quiet. They even got to believing the voice that shouted the loudest. Because that's the way people are, particularly the Germans. We're a very obedient people. It's our greatest strength and our greatest weakness. It enables us to build an economic miracle while the British are on strike, and it enables us to follow a man like Hitler into a great big mass grave.

'For years people haven't asked what happened to the Jews of Germany. They just disappeared, nothing else. It's bad enough to read at every war-crimes trial what happened to the faceless, anonymous Jews of Warsaw, Lublin, Bialystok, nameless, unknown Jews from Poland and Russia. Now you want to tell them chapter and verse what happened to their next-door neighbours. Now can you understand it? These Jews' – he tapped the diary – 'these people they knew, they greeted them in the street, they bought in their shops, and they stood around while they were taken away for your Herr Roschmann to deal with. You think they want to read about that? You couldn't have picked a story that people in Germany want to read about less.'

Having finished, Hans Hoffmann leaned back, selected a fine panatella from a humidor on the desk, and lit it from a rolled-gold Dupont. Miller sat and digested what he had not been able to work out for himself.

'That must have been what my mother meant,' he said at length.

Hoffmann grunted.

'Probably.'

'I still want to find that bastard.'

'Leave it alone, Miller. Drop it. No one will thank you.'

'That's not the only reason, is it? The public reaction. There's another reason, isn't there?'

Hoffmann eyed him keenly through the cigar smoke.

'Yes,' he said shortly.

'Are you afraid of them – still?' asked Miller.

Hoffmann shook his head.

'No. I just don't go looking for trouble. That's all.'

'What kind of trouble?'

'Have you ever heard of a man called Hans Habe?' asked Hoffmann.

'The novelist? Yes, what about him?'

'He used to run a magazine in Munich once. Back in the early fifties. A good one too, he was a damn good reporter, like you. *Echo of the Week*, it was called. He hated the Nazis, so he ran a series of exposures of former SS men living in freedom in Munich.'

'What happened to him?'

'To him, nothing. One day he got more mail than usual. Half the letters were from his advertisers, withdrawing their custom. Another was from his bank asking him to drop round. When he did he was told the bank was foreclosing on the overdraft, as of that minute. Within a week the magazine was out of business. Now he writes novels, good ones too. But he doesn't run a magazine any more.'

'So what do the rest of us do? Keep running scared?'

Hoffmann jerked his cigar out of his mouth.

'I don't have to take that from you, Miller,' he said, his eyes snapping. 'I hated the bastards then and I hate them now. But I know my readers. And they don't want to know about Eduard Roschmann.'

'All right. I'm sorry. But I'm still going to cover it.'

'You know, Miller, if I didn't know you, I'd think there was something personal behind it. Never let journalism get personal. It's bad for reporting and it's bad for the reporter. Anyway, how are you going to finance yourself?'

'I've got some savings.' Miller rose to go.

'Best of luck,' said Hoffmann, rising and coming round the desk. 'I tell you what I'll do. The day Roschmann is arrested and imprisoned by the West German police, I'll commission you to cover the story. That's straight news, so it's public property. If I decide not to print, I'll buy it out of my pocket. That's as far as I'll go. But while you're digging for him you're not carrying the letterhead of my magazine around as your authority.'

Miller nodded.

'I'll be back,' he said.

5

That same Wednesday morning was also the time of the week when the heads of the five branches of the Israeli intelligence *apparat* met for their informal weekly discussion.

In most countries the rivalry between various separate intelligence services is legendary. In Russia the KGB hates the guts of the GRU; in America the FBI will not co-operate with the CIA. The British Security Service regards Scotland Yard's Special Branch as a crowd of flat-footed coppers, and there are so many crooks in the French SDECE that experts wonder whether that French intelligence service is part of the government or the underworld.

But Israel is fortunate. Once a week the chiefs of the five branches meet for a friendly chat without inter-departmental friction. It is one of the dividends of being a nation surrounded by enemies. At these meetings coffee and soft drinks are passed round, those present use first-name terms to each other, the atmosphere is relaxed and more work gets done than could be effected by a torrent of written memoranda.

It was to this meeting that the controller of Mossad, head of the joint five services of Israeli intelligence, General Meir Amit, was travelling on the morning of December 4th. Beyond the windows of his long, black chauffeur-driven limousine a fine dawn was beaming down to the whitewashed sprawl of Tel Aviv. But the general's mood failed to match it. He was a deeply worried man.

The cause of his worry was a piece of information that had reached him in the small hours of the morning. A small fragment of knowledge to be added to the immense file in the archives, but vital, for the file into which that despatch from one of his agents in Cairo would be added was the file of the rockets of Helwan.

The forty-two-year-old general's poker face betrayed nothing of his feelings as the car swung round the Zina Circus and headed towards the northern suburbs of the capital. He leaned back in the upholstery of his seat and considered the long history of those rockets being built north of

Cairo, which had already cost several men their lives and had cost his predecessor, General Isser Harel, his job. . . .

During the course of 1961, long before Nasser's two rockets went on public display in the streets of Cairo, the Israeli Mossad had learned of their existence. From the moment the first despatch came through from Egypt, they had kept Factory 333 under constant surveillance.

They were perfectly well aware of the large-scale recruitment by the Egyptians, through the good offices of the Odessa, of German scientists to work on the rockets of Helwan. It was a serious matter then; it became infinitely more serious in the spring of 1962.

In May that year Heinz Krug, the German recruiter of the scientists, made approaches to the Austrian physicist, Dr Otto Yoklek, in Vienna. Instead of allowing himself to be recruited, the Austrian professor made contact with the Israelis. What he had to say electrified Tel Aviv. He told the agent of the Mossad who was sent to interview him that the Egyptians intended to arm their rockets with warheads containing irradiated nuclear waste and cultures of bubonic plague.

So important was the news that the Controller of the Mossad, General Isser Harel, the man who had personally escorted the kidnapped Adolf Eichmann back from Buenos Aires to Tel Aviv, flew to Vienna to talk to Yoklek himself. He was convinced the professor was right, a conviction corroborated by the news that the Cairo government had just purchased through a firm in Zürich a quantity of radio-active cobalt equivalent to twenty-five times their possible requirement for medical purposes.

On his return from Vienna, Isser Harel went to see Premier David Ben-Gurion and urged that he be allowed to begin a campaign of reprisals against the German scientists who were either working in Egypt or about to go there. The old premier was in a quandary. On the one hand he realised the hideous danger the new rockets and their genocidal warheads presented to his people; on the other he recognised the value of the German tanks and guns due to arrive at any moment. Israeli reprisals on the streets of Germany might just be enough to persuade Chancellor Adenauer to listen to his Foreign Ministry faction and shut off the arms deal.

Inside the Tel Aviv cabinet there was a split developing similar to the split inside the Bonn cabinet over the arms sales. Isser Harel and the Foreign Minister, Madame Golda Meir, were in favour of a tough policy against the German scientists; Shimon Peres and the army were terrified by the thought they might lose their precious German tanks. Ben-Gurion was torn between the two.

He hit on a compromise: he authorised Harel to undertake a muted, discreet campaign to discourage German scientists from going to Cairo to help Nasser build his rockets. But Harel, with his burning gut-hatred of Germany and all things German, went beyond his brief.

On September 11th, 1962, Heinz Krug disappeared. He had dined the previous evening with Dr Kleinwachter, the rocket-propulsion expert he was trying to recruit, and an unidentified Egyptian. On the morning of the 11th Krug's car was found abandoned close to his home in a suburb of Munich. His wife immediately claimed he had been kidnapped by Israeli agents, but the Munich police found not a trace, either of Krug or of evidence as to his kidnappers. In fact, he had been abducted by a group of men led by a shadowy figure called Leon, and his body dumped in the Starnberg lake, assisted to the weed-bed by a corset of heavy-link chain.

The campaign then turned against the Germans in Egypt already. On November 27th a registered package, posted in Hamburg and addressed to Professor Wolfgang Pilz, the rocket scientist who had worked for the French, arrived in Cairo. It was opened by his secretary, Miss Hannelore Wenda. In the ensuing explosion the girl was maimed and blinded for life.

On November 28th another package, also posted in Hamburg, arrived at Factory 333. By this time the Egyptians had set up a security screen for arriving parcels. It was an Egyptian official in the mail-room who cut the cord. Five dead and ten wounded.

On the 29th a third package was defused without an explosion.

By February 20th, 1963, Harel's agents had turned their attention once again to Germany. Dr Kleinwachter, still undecided whether to go to Cairo or not, was driving back home from his laboratory at Loerrach, near the Swiss frontier, when a black Mercedes barred his route. He threw himself to the floor as a man emptied his automatic through the windscreen. Police subsequently discovered the black Mercedes abandoned. It had been stolen earlier in the day. In the glove compartment was an identity card, in the name of Colonel Ali Samir. Enquiries revealed this was the name of the chief of the Egyptian Secret Service. Isser Harel's agents had got their message across – with a touch of black humour for good measure.

By now the reprisal campaign was making headlines in Germany. It became a scandal with the Ben Gal affair. On March 2nd the young Heidi Goerke, daughter of Professor Paul Goerke, pioneer of Nasser's rockets, received a telephone call at her home in Freiburg, Germany. A voice suggested she meet the caller at the Three Kings Hotel in Basel, Switzerland, just over the border.

Heidi informed the German police, who tipped off the Swiss. They planted a bugging device in the room that had been booked for the meeting. During the meeting two men in dark glasses warned Heidi Goerke and her young brother to persuade their father to get out of Egypt if he valued his life. Tailed to Zürich and arrested the same night, the two men went on trial at Basel on June 10th, 1963. It was an international scandal. The chief of the two agents was Yossef Ben Gal, Israeli citizen.

The trial went well. Professor Yoklek testified as to the warheads of plague and radio-active waste, and the judges were scandalised. Making the best of a bad job, the Israeli government used the trial to expose the Egyptian intent to commit genocide. Shocked, the judges acquitted the two accused.

But back in Israel there was a reckoning. Although the German

Chancellor Adenauer had personally promised Ben-Gurion he would try to stop German scientists taking part in the Helwan rocket-building, Ben-Gurion was humiliated by the scandal. In a rage he rebuked General Isser Harel for the lengths to which he had gone in his campaign of intimidation. Harel riposted with vigour, and handed in his resignation. To his surprise Ben-Gurion accepted it, proving the point that no one in Israel is indispensable, not even the Controller of Intelligence.

That night, June 20th, 1963, Isser Harel had a long talk with his close friend, General Meir Amit, then the head of military intelligence. General Amit could remember the conversation clearly, the taut angry face of the Russian-born fighter, nicknamed Isser the Terrible.

'I have to inform you, my dear Meir, that as from now Israel is no longer in the retribution business. The politicians have taken over. I have tendered my resignation and it has been accepted. I have asked that you be named my successor, and I believe they will agree.'

The ministerial committee that presides in Israel over the activities of the intelligence networks agreed. At the end of June, General Meir Amit became Controller of Intelligence.

The knell had also sounded, however, for Ben-Gurion. The hawks of his cabinet, headed by Levi Eshkol and his own Foreign Minister, Golda Meir, forced his resignation, and on June 26th, 1963, Levi Eshkol was named Prime Minister. Ben-Gurion, shaking his snowy head in anger, went down to his kibbutz in the Negev in disgust. But he stayed on as a member of the Knesset.

Although the new government had ousted David Ben-Gurion, it did not reinstate Isser Harel. Perhaps it felt that Meir Amit was a general more likely to obey orders than the choleric Harel, who had become a legend in his own lifetime among the Israeli people, and relished it.

Nor were Ben-Gurion's last orders rescinded. General Amit's instructions remained the same, to avoid any more scandals in Germany over the rocket scientists. With no alternative, he turned the terror campaign against the scientists already inside Egypt.

These Germans lived in the suburb of Meadi, seven miles south of Cairo on the northern bank of the Nile. A pleasant suburb, except that it was ringed by Egyptian security troops, and its German inhabitants were almost prisoners in a gilded cage. To get at them Meir Amit used his top agent inside Egypt, the riding-school owner Wolfgang Lutz, who found himself from September 1963 onwards forced to take suicidal risks, which sixteen months later would lead to his undoing.

For the German scientists, already shaken badly by the series of bomb parcels sent from Germany, autumn 1963 became a nightmare. In the heart of Meadi, ringed by Egyptian security guards, they began to get letters threatening their lives, posted from inside Cairo.

Dr Josef Eisig received one which described his wife, two children and the type of work he was engaged on with remarkable precision, then told him to get out of Egypt and go back to Germany. All the other scientists got the same kind of letter. On September 27th a letter blew up in the face of Dr Kirmayer. For some of the scientists this was the last straw. At the end of September Dr Pilz left Cairo for Germany, taking the unfortunate Fräulein Wenda with him.

Others followed, and the furious Egyptians were unable to stop them, for they could not protect them from the threatening letters.

The man in the back of the limousine that bright winter morning in 1963 knew that his own agent, the supposedly pro-Nazi German, Lutz, was the writer of the letters and the sender of the explosives.

But he also knew the rocket programme was not being halted. The information he had just received proved it. He flicked his eye over the decoded message once again. It confirmed simply that a virulent strain of bubonic bacillus had been isolated in the contagious diseases laboratory of Cairo Medical Institute, and that the budget of the department involved had been increased tenfold. The information left no doubt that despite the adverse publicity Egypt had received over the Ben Gal trial in Basel the previous summer, they were going ahead with the genocide programme.

Had Hoffmann been watching he would have been forced to give Miller full marks for cheek. Leaving the penthouse office he took the lift down to the fifth floor and dropped in to see Max Dorn, the magazine's legal affairs correspondent.

'I've just been up to see Herr Hoffmann,' he said, dropping into a chair in front of Dorn's desk. 'Now I need some background. Mind if I pick your brains?'

'Go ahead,' said Dorn, assuming Miller had been commissioned to do a story for *Komet*.

'Who investigates war crimes in Germany?'

The question took Dorn aback.

'War crimes?'

'Yes. War crimes. Which authorities are responsible for investigating what happened in all the various countries we overran during the war and finding and prosecuting the individuals guilty of mass-murder?'

'Oh, I see what you mean. Well, basically it's the various Attorney Generals' offices of the provinces of West Germany.'

'You mean, they *all* do it?'

Dorn leaned back in his chair, at home in his own field of expertise.

'There are sixteen provinces in West Germany. Each has a state capital and a State Attorney General. Inside each SAG's office there is a department responsible for investigation to what are called "crimes of violence committed during the Nazi era". Each state capital is allocated an area of the former Reich or of the occupied territories as its special responsibility.'

'Such as?' asked Miller.

'Well, for example, all crimes committed by the Nazis and the SS in Italy, Greece and Polish Galicia are investigated by Stuttgart. The biggest extermination camp of all, Auschwitz, comes under Frankfurt. You may have heard there's a big trial coming up in Frankfurt next May of twenty-two former guards from Auschwitz. Then the extermination camps of Treblinka, Chelmno, Sobibor and Maidanek are investigated by Dusseldorf/Cologne. Munich is responsible for Belzec, Dachau, Buckenwald and Flossenburg. Most crimes in the Soviet Ukraine and the Lodz area of former Poland come under Hanover. And so on.'

Miller noted the information, nodding.

'Who is supposed to investigate what happened in the three Baltic states?' he asked.

'Hamburg,' said Dorn promptly, 'along with crimes in the areas of Danzig and the Warsaw sector of Poland.'

'Hamburg?' said Miller. 'You mean it's right here in Hamburg?'

'Yes. Why?'

'Well, it's Riga I'm interested in.'

Dorn made a move.

'Oh, I see. The German Jews. Well, that's the pigeon of the SAG's office right here.'

'If there had ever been a trial, or even an arrest, of anyone who had been guilty of crimes in Riga, it would have been here in Hamburg?'

'The trial would have been,' said Dorn. 'The arrest could have been made anywhere.'

'What's the procedure with arrests?'

'Well, there's a book called the Wanted Book. In it is the name of every wanted war criminal with surname, first names and date of birth. Usually the SAG's office covering the area where the man committed the crimes spend years preparing the case against him before arrest. Then when they are ready they request the police of the State in which the man is living to arrest him. A couple of detectives go there and bring him back. If a very much wanted man is discovered, he can be arrested wherever he's discovered, and the appropriate SAG's office informed that he's being held. Then they go and bring him back. The trouble is, most of the big SS men are not living under their own names.'

'Right,' said Miller. 'Has there ever been a trial in Hamburg of anyone guilty of crimes committed in Riga?'

'Not that I remember,' said Dorn.

'Would it be in the cuttings library?'

'Sure. If it happened since 1950 when we started the cuttings library, it'll be there.'

'Mind if we look?' asked Miller.

'No problem.'

The library was in the basement, tended by five archivists in grey smocks. It was almost half an acre in size, filled by row upon row of grey steel shelves on which reposed reference books of every kind and description. Round the walls, from floor to ceiling, were steel filing cabinets, the doors of each drawer indicating the contents of the files within.

'What do you want?' asked Dorn as the chief librarian approached.

'Roschmann, Eduard,' said Miller.

'Personal index section, this way,' said the librarian and led the way along one wall. He opened a cabinet door labelled ROA–ROZ, and flicked through it.

'Nothing on Roschmann, Eduard,' he said. Miller thought.

'Do you have anything on war crimes?' he asked.

'Yes,' said the librarian. 'War-crimes and war-trials section, this way.'

They went along another hundred yards of cabinets.

'Look under Riga,' said Miller.

The librarian mounted a step-ladder and foraged. He came back with a red folder. It bore the label 'Riga – War Crimes Trial'. Miller opened it. Two pieces of newsprint the size of large postage stamps fluttered out. Miller picked them up. Both were from the summer of 1950. One recorded that three SS privates went on trial for brutalities committed at Riga between 1941 and 1944. The other recorded they had all three been sentenced to long terms of imprisonment. Not long enough, they would all be free by late 1963.

'Is that it?' asked Miller.

'That's it,' said the librarian.

'Do you mean to say,' said Miller turning to Dorn, 'that a section of the State Attorney General's office has been beavering away for fifteen years on my tax money, and all they've got to show for it is two postage stamps?'

Dorn was a rather establishment figure.

'I'm sure they're doing their best,' he said huffily.

'I wonder,' said Miller.

They parted in the main hall two floors up and Miller went out into the rain.

The building in the northern suburbs of Tel Aviv that houses the headquarters of the Mossad excites no attention, even from its nearest neighbours. The entrance to the underground car-park of the office block is flanked by quite ordinary shops. On the ground floor is a bank, and in the entrance hall, before the plate-glass doors that lead into the bank, is a lift, a board stating the business of the firms on the floor above and a porter's desk for enquiries.

The board reveals that inside the block are the offices of several trading companies, two insurance firms, an architect, an engineering consultant and an import-export company on the top floor. Enquiries for any of the firms below the top floor will be met courteously. Questions asked about the top-floor company are politely declined. The company on the top floor is the front for the Mossad.

The room where the chiefs of Israeli intelligence meet is bare and cool, white-painted, with a long table and chairs round the walls. At the table sit the five men who control the branches of intelligence. Behind them on the chairs sit clerks and stenographers. Other non-members can be seconded for a hearing if required, but this is seldom done. The meetings are classified top secret, for all confidences may be aired.

At the head of the table sits the Controller of the Mossad. Founded in 1937, its full name Mossad Aliyah Beth, or Organisation for the Second

Immigration, the Mossad was the first Israeli intelligence organ. Its first job was to get Jews from Europe to a safe berth in the land of Palestine.

After the founding of the state of Israel in 1948 it became the senior of all intelligence organs, its Controller automatically the head of all the five.

To the controller's right sits the chief of the Aman, the military in-intelligence unit whose job is to keep Israel informed of the state of war-readiness of her enemies. The man who held the job at that time was General Aharon Yaariv.

To the left sits the chief of the Shabak, sometimes wrongly referred to as the Shin Beth. These letters stand for Sherut Bitachon, the Hebrew for security service. The full title of the organ that watches over Israel's internal security, and *only* internal security, is Sherut Bitachon Klali, and it is from these three words that the abbreviation Shabak is taken.

Beyond these two men sit the last two of the five. One is the director-general of the research division of the Foreign Ministry, charged specifically with the evaluation of the political situation in Arab capitals, a matter of vital importance to the security of Israel. The other is the director of a service solely occupied with the fate of Jews in the 'countries of persecution'. These countries include all the Arab countries and all the Communist countries. So that there shall be no overlapping of activities, the weekly meetings enable each chief to know what the other departments are doing.

Two other men are present as observers, the Inspector-General of Police, and the Head of the Special Branch, the executive arms of the Shabak in the fight against terrorism inside the country.

The meeting on that day was quite normal. Meir Amit took his place at the head of the table, and the discussion began. He saved his bombshell until last. When he had made his statement, there was silence, as the men present, including the aides scattered round the walls, had a mental vision of their country dying as the radio-active and plague warheads slammed home.

'The point surely is,' said the head of the Shabak at last, 'that those rockets must never fly. If we cannot prevent them making warheads, we have to prevent the warheads ever taking off.'

'Agreed,' said Amit, taciturn as ever, 'but how?'

'Hit them,' growled Yaariv. 'Hit them with everything we've got. Ezer Weizmann's jets can take out Factory 333 in one raid.'

'And start a war with nothing to fight with,' replied Amit. 'We need more planes, more tanks, more guns, before we can take Egypt. I think we all know, gentlemen, that war is inevitable. Nasser is determined on it, but he will not fight until he is ready. But if we force it on him now, the simple answer is that he, with his Russian weaponry, is more ready than we are.'

There was silence again. The head of the Foreign Ministry Arab section spoke.

'Our information from Cairo is they think they will be ready in early 1967, rockets and all.'

'We will have our tanks and guns by then, and our new French jets,' replied Yaariv.

'Yes, and they will have those rockets from Helwan. Four hundred of them. Gentlemen, there is only one answer. By the time we are ready for Nasser, those rockets will be in silos all over Egypt. They'll be unreachable. For once in their silos and ready to fire, we must not simply take out ninety per cent of them, but all of them. And not even Ezer Weizmann's fighter pilots can take them all, without exception.'

'Then we have to take them in the factory at Helwan,' said Yaariv with finality.

'Agreed,' said Amit, 'but without a military attack. We shall just have to try to force the German scientists to resign before they have finished their work. Remember, the research stage is almost at an end. We have six months. After that the Germans won't matter any more. The Egyptians can build the rockets, once they are designed down to the last nut and bolt. Therefore I shall step up the campaign against the scientists in Egypt and keep you informed.'

For several seconds there was silence again as the unspoken question ran through the minds of all those present. It was one of the men from the Foreign Ministry who finally voiced it.

'Couldn't we discourage them inside Germany again?'

General Amit shook his head.

'No. That remains out of the question in the prevailing political climate. The orders from our superiors remain the same; no more muscle tactics inside Germany. For us from henceforth the key to the rockets of Helwan lies inside Egypt.'

General Meir Amit, Controller of the Mossad, was not often wrong. But he was wrong that time. For the key to the rockets of Helwan lay in a factory inside West Germany.

6

It took Miller a week before he could get an interview with the chief of section in the department of the Hamburg Attorney General's office responsible for investigation into war crimes. He suspected Dorn had found out he was not working at Hoffmann's behest and had reacted accordingly.

The man he confronted was nervous, ill-at-ease.

'You must understand I have only agreed to see you as a result of your persistent enquiries,' he began.

'That's nice of you all the same,' said Miller ingratiatingly. 'I want to enquire about a man whom I assume your department must have under permanent investigation, called Eduard Roschmann.'

'Roschmann?' said the lawyer.

'Roschmann,' repeated Miller. 'Captain of the SS. Commandant of Riga ghetto from 1941 to 1944. I want to know if he's alive; if not, where he's buried. If you have found him, if he has ever been arrested and if he has ever been on trial. If not, where he is now.'

The lawyer was shaken.

'Good Lord, I can't tell you that,' he said.

'Why not? It's a matter of public interest. Enormous public interest.'

The lawyer had recovered his poise.

'I hardly think so,' he said smoothly. 'Otherwise we would be receiving constant enquiries of this nature. Actually so far as I can recall yours is the first enquiry we've ever had from . . . a member of the public.'

'Actually, I'm a member of the Press,' said Miller.

'Yes, that may be. But I'm afraid as regards this kind of information that only means you are entitled to as much as one would give a member of the public.'

'How much is that?' asked Miller.

'I'm afraid we are not empowered to give information regarding the progress of our enquiries.'

'Well, that's not right to start with,' said Miller.

'Oh, come now, Herr Miller, you would hardly expect the police to give you information about the progress of *their* enquiries in a criminal case.'

'I would. In fact that's just what I do. The police are customarily very helpful in issuing bulletins on whether an early arrest may be expected. Certainly they'd tell a press enquiry if their main suspect was to their knowledge alive or dead. It helps their relations with the public.'

The lawyer smiled thinly.

'I'm sure you perform a very valuable function in that regard,' he said. 'But from this department no information may be issued of the state of progress of our work.' He seemed to hit on a point of argument. 'Let's face it, if wanted criminals knew how close we were to completing the case against them, they'd disappear.'

'That may be so,' riposted Miller. 'But the records show your department has only put on trial three privates who were guards in Riga. And that was in 1950, so the men were probably in pre-trial detention when the British handed over to your department. So the wanted criminals don't seem to be in much danger of being forced to disappear.'

'Really, that's a most unwarranted suggestion.'

'All right. So your enquiries are progressing. It still wouldn't harm your case if you were to tell me quite simply whether Eduard Roschmann is under investigation, and where he now is.'

'All I can say is that all matters concerning the area of responsibility of my department are under constant enquiry. I repeat, constant enquiry. And now I really think, Herr Miller, there is nothing more I can do to help you.'

He rose, and Miller followed suit.

'Don't bust a gut,' he said as he walked out.

It was another week before Miller was ready to move. He spent it mainly at home, reading six books concerned in whole or in part with the war along the Eastern Front and things that had been done in the camps in the occupied eastern territories. It was the librarian at his local reading library who mentioned the Z-Commission.

'It's in Ludwigsburg,' he told Miller. 'I read about it in a magazine. Its full name is the Central Federal Agency for the Elucidation of Crimes of Violence committed during the Nazi Era. That's a bit of a mouthful, so people call it the Zentrale Stelle for short. Even shorter, the Z-Commission. It's the only organisation in the country that hunts Nazis on a nation-wide, even an international level.'

'Thanks,' said Miller as he left. 'I'll see if they can help me.'

Miller went to his bank the next morning, made out a cheque to his landlord for three months' rent to cover January–March and drew the rest of his bank balance in cash, leaving a ten-mark note to keep the account open.

He kissed Sigi before she went off to work at the club, telling her he would be gone for a week, maybe more. Then he took the Jaguar from its underground home and headed south towards the Rhineland.

The first snows had started, whistling in off the North Sea, slicing in flurries across the wide stretches of the autobahn as it swept south of Bremen and into the flat plain of Lower Saxony.

He paused once for coffee after two hours, then pressed on across North Rhine/Westphalia. Despite the wind he enjoyed driving down the autobahn in bad weather. Inside the XK 150 S he had the impression of being in the cockpit of a fast plane, the dashboard lights glowing dully under the facia, and, outside, the descending darkness of a winter's night, the icy cold, the slanting flurries of snow caught for a moment in the harsh beam of the headlights, whipping past the windscreen and back into nothingness again.

He stuck to the fast lane, as always, pushing the Jag to close to 100 miles an hour, watching the growling hulks of the heavy lorries swish past to his right as he overtook.

By six in the evening he was beyond the Hamm Junction and the glowing lights of the Ruhr began to be dimly discernible to his right through the darkness. He never ceased to be amazed by the Ruhr, mile after mile after mile of factories and chimneys, towns and cities so close as to be in effect one gigantic city a hundred miles long and fifty broad. When the autobahn went into an overpass he could look down to the right and see it stretching away into the December night, thousands of hectares of lights and mills, aglow from a thousand furnaces churning out the wealth of the economic miracle. Fourteen years ago, as he travelled through it by train towards his school holiday in Paris, it had been rubble, and the industrial heart of Germany was hardly even beating. Impossible not to feel proud of what his people had done since then.

'Just so long as I don't have to live in it,' he thought as the giant signs of the Cologne Ring began to come up in the light of the headlamps. From Cologne he ran south-east, past Wiesbaden and Frankfurt, Mannheim and Heilbronn, and it was late that evening when he cruised to a halt in front of a hotel in Stuttgart, the nearest city to Ludwigsburg, where he spent the night.

Ludwigsburg is a quiet and inoffensive little market town set in the rolling pleasant hills of Württemberg, fifteen miles north of the state capital of Stuttgart. Set in a quiet road off the High Street, to the extreme embarrassment of the town's upright inhabitants, is the home of the Z-Commission, a small, understaffed, underpaid, overworked group of men whose job and dedication in life is to hunt down the Nazis and the SS guilty during the war of the crime of mass-murder. Before the Statute of Limitations eliminated all SS crimes with the exception of murder and mass-murder, those being sought might have been guilty only of extortion, robbery, grievous bodily harm including torture, and a variety of other forms of unpleasantness.

Even with murder as the only remaining charge able to be brought, the Z-Commission still had 170,000 names in its files. Not unnaturally, the main effort had been and still is to trace down the worst few thousand of the mass-murderers, if and where possible.

Deprived of any powers of arrest, able only to request the police of the various states of Germany to make an arrest when positive identification has already been made, unable to squeeze more than a pittance each year out of the Federal Government in Bonn, the men of Ludwigsburg worked solely because they were dedicated to the task.

There were eighty detectives on the staff and fifty investigating attorneys. Of the former group all were young, below the age of thirty-five, so that none could possibly have had any implication in the matters under examination. The lawyers were mainly older, but vetted to ensure they too were uninvolved with events prior to 1945.

The lawyers were mainly taken from private practice, to which they would one day return. The detectives knew their careers were finished. No police force in Germany wanted to see on its staff a detective who had once served a term at Ludwigsburg. For detectives prepared to hunt the SS in West Germany, promotion was finished in any other police force in the country.

Quite accustomed to see their requests for co-operation ignored in over half the states, to see their loaned files go unaccountably missing, to see the quarry suddenly disappear after an anonymous tip-off, the Z-men worked on as best they might at a task they realised was not in accordance with the wishes of the majority of their fellow countrymen.

Even on the streets of the smiling town of Ludwigsburg the men on the staff of the Z-Commission went ungreeted and unacknowledged by the citizens to whom their presence brought an undesired notoriety.

Peter Miller found the Commission at 58, Schorndorfer Strasse, a large former private house set inside an eight-foot-high wall. Two massive steel gates barred the way up the drive. To one side was a bell handle which he pulled. A steel shutter slid back and a face appeared. The inevitable gatekeeper.

'Please?'

'I would like to speak to one of your investigating attorneys,' said Miller.

'Which one?' said the face.

'I don't know any names,' said Miller. 'Any one will do. Here is my card.'

He thrust his press card through the aperture, forcing the man to take it. Then at least he knew it would go inside the building. The man shut the hatch and went away. When he came back it was to open the gate. Miller was shown up the five stone steps to the front door, closed against the clear but icy winter air. Inside it was stuffily hot from the central heating. Another porter emerged from a glass-fronted booth to his right and showed him into a small waiting room.

'Someone will be with you directly,' he said, and shut the door.

The man who came three minutes later was in his early fifties, mild-mannered and courteous. He handed Miller back his press card and asked, 'What can I do for you?'

Miller started at the beginning, explaining briefly about Tauber, the diary, his enquiries into what happened to Eduard Roschmann. The lawyer listened intently.

'Fascinating,' he said at last.

'The point is, can you help me?'

'I wish I could,' said the man, and for the first time since he had started asking questions about Roschmann in Hamburg weeks before, Miller believed he had met an official who genuinely would like to help him. 'But the point is, although I am prepared to accept your enquiries as completely sincere, I am bound hand and foot by the rules that govern our continued existence here. Which are in effect that no information may be given out about any wanted SS criminal to anyone other than a person supported by the official backing of one of a specific number of authorities.'

'In other words, you can tell me nothing?' said Miller.

'Please understand,' said the lawyer, 'this office is under constant attack. Not openly, no one would dare. But privately, within the corridors of power, we are incessantly being sniped at, our budget, such powers as we have, our terms of reference. We are allowed no latitude where the rules are concerned. Personally, I would like to engage the alliance of the Press of Germany to help, but it's forbidden.'

'I see,' said Miller. 'Do you then have any newspaper-cuttings reference library?'

'No we don't.'

'Is there in Germany at all a newspaper-cuttings reference library that is open to an enquiry by a member of the public?'

'No. The only newspaper-cuttings libraries in the country are compiled and held by the various newspapers and magazines. The most comprehensive is reputed to be that of *Der Spiegel* magazine. After that, *Komet* has a very good one.'

'I find this rather odd,' said Miller. 'Where in Germany today does a citizen enquire about the progress of investigation into war crimes, and for background material on wanted SS criminals?'

The lawyer looked slightly uncomfortable.

'I'm afraid the ordinary citizen can't do that,' he said.

'All right,' said Miller, 'where are the archives in Germany that refer to the men of the SS?'

'There's one set here, in the basement,' said the lawyer. 'And ours is all composed of photostats. The originals of the entire card index of the SS were captured in 1945 by an American unit. At the last minute a small group of the SS stayed behind at the castle where they were stored in Bavaria and tried to burn the records. They got through about ten per cent before the American soldiers rushed in and stopped them. The rest were all mixed up. It took the Americans with some German help two years to sort out the rest.

'During those two years a number of the worst SS men escaped after being temporarily in Allied custody. Their dossiers could not be found in the muddle. Since the final classification the entire SS-Index has remained in Berlin, still under American ownership and direction. Even we have to apply to them if we want something more. Mind you, they're very good about it; no complaints at all about co-operation from that quarter.'

'And that's it?' asked Miller. 'Just two sets in the whole country?'

'That's it,' said the lawyer. 'I repeat, I wish I could help you. Incidentally, if you should get anything on Roschmann, we'd be delighted to have it.'

Miller thought.

'If I find anything, there are only two authorities that can do anything with it. The Attorney General's Office in Hamburg, and you. Right?'

'Yes, that's all,' said the lawyer.

'And you're more likely to do something positive with it than Hamburg.' Miller made it a flat statement. The lawyer gazed fixedly at the ceiling.

'Nothing that comes here that is of real value gathers dust on a shelf,' he observed.

'OK. Point taken,' said Miller and rose. 'One thing, between ourselves, are you still looking for Eduard Roschmann?'

'Between ourselves, yes, very much.'

'And if he were caught, there'd be no problems about getting a conviction?'

'None at all,' said the lawyer. 'The case against him is tied up solid. He'd get hard labour for life without the option.'

'Give me your phone number,' said Miller.

The lawyer wrote it down and handed Miller the piece of paper.

'There's my name and two phone numbers. Home and office. You can get me any time, day or night. If you get anything new, just call me from any phone box on direct-dial. In every state police force there are men I can call and know I'll get action if necessary. There are others to avoid. So call me first, right?'

Miller pocketed the paper.

'I'll remember that,' he said as he left.

'Good luck,' said the lawyer.

It's a long drive from Stuttgart to Berlin and it took Miller most of the following day. Fortunately it was dry and crisp and the tuned Jaguar ate the miles northwards past the sprawling carpet of Frankfurt, past Kassel and Göttingen to Hanover. Here he followed the branch-off to the right from autobahn E4 to E8 and the border with East Germany.

There was an hour delay at the Marienborn checkpoint while he filled out the inevitable currency declaration forms, transit visas to travel through 110 miles of East Germany to West Berlin; and while the blue-uniformed Customs men and the green-coated People's Police, fur-hatted against the cold, poked around in and under the Jaguar. The Customs man seemed torn between the frosty courtesy required of a servant of the German Democratic Republic towards a national of revanchist West Germany, and one young man's desire to examine another's sports car.

Twenty miles beyond the border the great motorway bridge reared up to cross the Elbe where in 1945 the British, honourably obeying the rules laid down at Yalta, had halted their advance on Berlin. To his right Miller looked down at the sprawl of Magdeburg and wondered if the old prison still stood. There was a further delay at the entry into West Berlin, where again the car was searched, his overnight case emptied on to the Customs bench and his wallet opened to see he had not given all his West marks away to the people of the workers' paradise on his progress down the road. Eventually he was through and the Jaguar roared past the Avus circuit towards the glittering ribbon of the Kurfurstendamm, brilliant with Christmas decorations. It was the evening of December 17th.

He decided not to go blundering into the American Document Center the same way he had the Attorney General's office in Hamburg or the Z-Commission in Ludwigsburg. Without official backing, he had come to realise, no one got anywhere with Nazi files in Germany.

The following morning he called Karl Brandt from the main post office. Brandt was aghast at his request.

'I can't,' he said down the phone. 'I don't know anyone in Berlin.'

'Well, think. You must have come across someone from the West Berlin force at one of the colleges you attended. I need him to vouch for me when I get there,' shouted Miller back.

'I told you I didn't want to get involved.'

'Well, you are involved.' Miller waited a few seconds before putting in the body blow. 'Either I get a look at that archive officially or I blow in and say you sent me.'

'You wouldn't do that,' said Brandt.

'I bloody well would. I'm fed up with being pushed from pillar to post round this damn country. So find somebody who'll get me in there officially. Let's face it, the request will be forgotten within the hour, once I've seen those files.'

'I'll have to think,' said Brandt, stalling for time.

'I'll give you an hour,' said Miller. 'Then I'm calling back.'

He slammed down the receiver. An hour later Brandt was as angry as ever, and more than a little frightened. He heartily wished he had kept the diary to himself and thrown it away.

'There's a man I was at detective college with,' he said down the phone. 'I didn't know him well, but he's now with Bureau One of the West Berlin force. That deals with the same subject.'

'What's his name?'

'Schiller. Volkmar Schiller, detective inspector.'

'I'll get in touch with him,' said Miller.

'No, leave him to me. I'll ring him today and introduce you to him. Then you can go and see him. If he doesn't agree to get you in, don't blame me. He's the only one I know in Berlin.'

Two hours later Miller rang Brandt back. Brandt sounded relieved.

'He's away on leave,' he said. 'They tell me he's doing Christmas duty, so he's away until Monday.'

'But it's only Wednesday,' said Miller. 'That gives me four days to kill.'

'I can't help it. He'll be back on Monday morning. I'll ring him then.'

Miller spent four boring days hanging round West Berlin waiting for Schiller to come back off leave. Berlin was completely involved as the Christmas of 1963 approached with the issue by the East Berlin authorities for the first time since the Wall had been built in August 1961 of passes enabling West Berliners to go through the Wall and visit relatives living in the eastern sector. The progress of the negotiations between the two sides of the city had held the headlines for days. Miller spent one of his days that weekend by going through the Hein Strasse checkpoint into the eastern half of the city (as a West German citizen was able to do on the strength of his passport alone) and dropped in on a slight acquaintance, the Reuter correspondent in East Berlin. But the man was up to his neck in work on the Wall-passes story, so after a cup of coffee he left and returned to the west.

On Monday morning he went to see Detective Inspector Volkmar Schiller. To his great relief the man was about his own age, and seemed, unusually for an official of any kind in Germany, to have his own cavalier attitude to red tape. Doubtless he would not get far, thought Miller, but that was his problem. He explained briefly what he wanted.

'I don't see why not,' said Schiller. 'The Americans are pretty helpful to us in Bureau One. Because we're charged by Willy Brandt with investigating Nazi crimes, we're in there almost every day.'

They took Miller's Jaguar and drove out to the suburbs of the city, to the forests and the lakes, and at the bank of one of the lakes arrived at Number One, Wasser Käfer Stieg, in the suburb of Zehlendorf, Berlin 37.

The building was a long, low, single-storey affair set amid the trees.

'Is that it?' said Miller incredulously.

'That's it,' said Schiller. 'Not much, is it? The point is, there are eight floors below ground level. That's where the archives are stored, in fireproof vaults.'

They went through the front door to find a small waiting room with the inevitable porter's lodge on the right. The detective approached it and proffered his police card. He was handed a form and the pair of them repaired to a table and filled it out. The detective filled in his name and rank, then asked, 'What was the chap's name again?'

'Roschmann,' said Miller. 'Eduard Roschmann.'

The detective filled it in and handed the form back to the clerk in the front office.

'It takes about ten minutes,' said the detective. They went into the larger room, set out with rows of tables and chairs. After a quarter of an hour another clerk quietly brought them a file and laid it on the desk. It was about an inch thick, stamped with the single title 'Roschmann, Eduard'.

Volkmar Schiller rose.

'If you don't mind I'll be on my way,' he said. 'I'll find my own way back. Mustn't stop away too long after a week's leave. If you want anything photostatted, ask the clerk.' He gestured to a clerk sitting on a dais at the other end of the reading room, no doubt to ensure no visitors tried to remove pages from the files. Miller rose and shook hands.

'Many thanks.'

'Not at all.'

Ignoring the other three or four readers hunched over their desks,

Miller put his head between his hands and started to peruse the SS's own dossier on Eduard Roschmann.

It was all there. Nazi Party number, SS number, application form for each, filled out and signed by the man himself, result of his medical check, appreciation of him after his training period, self-written curriculum vitae, transfer papers, officer's commission, promotion certificates, right up to April 1945. There were also two photographs, taken for the SS records, one full-face, one profile. They showed a man of six feet one inch, hair shorn close to the head with a parting on the left, staring at the camera with a grim expression, a pointed nose and a lipless slit of a mouth. Miller began to read . . .

Eduard Roschmann was born on August 25th, 1908, in the Austrian town of Graz, a citizen of Austria, son of a highly respectable and honest brewery worker. He attended kindergarten, junior and high school in Graz. He attended college to try to become a lawyer but failed. In 1931 at the age of twenty-three he began work in the brewery where his father had a job and in 1937 was transferred to the administrative department from the brewery floor. The same year he joined the Austrian Nazi Party and the SS, both at that time banned organisations in neutral Austria. A year later Hitler annexed Austria and rewarded the Austrian Nazis with swift promotions all round.

In 1939 at the outbreak of war he volunteered for the Waffen-SS, was sent to Germany, trained during the winter of 1939 and the spring of 1940 and served in a Waffen-SS unit in the overrunning of France. In December 1940 he was transferred back from France to Berlin – here somebody had handwritten in the margin the word 'Cowardice?' – and in January 1941 was seconded to the SD, Amt Three of the RSHA.

In July 1941 he set up the first SD post in Riga, and the following month became commandant of Riga ghetto. He returned to Germany by ship in October 1944 and after handing over the remainder of the Jews of Riga to the SD of Danzig, returned to Berlin to report. He returned to his desk in Berlin HQ of the SS and remained there awaiting reassignment.

The last SS document in the file was evidently never completed, presumably because the meticulous little clerk in Berlin SS headquarters reassigned himself rather quickly in May 1945.

Attached to the back of the bunch of documents was one last one apparently affixed by an American hand since the end of the war. It was a single sheet bearing the typewritten words:

'Enquiry made about this file by the British occupation authorities in December 1947.'

Beneath this was the scrawled signature of some GI clerk long since forgotten, and the date December 21st, 1947.

Miller gathered the file and eased out of it the self-written life story, the two photographs and the last sheet. With these he approached the clerk at the end of the room.

'Could I have these photo-copied please?'

'Certainly.' The man took the file back and placed it on his desk to await the return of the three missing sheets after copying. Another man also tendered a file and two sheets of its contents for copying. The clerk took these also and placed the lot in a tray behind him, from where the sheets were whisked away by an unseen hand.

'Please wait. It will take about ten minutes,' the clerk told Miller and the other man. The pair re-took their seats and waited, Miller wishing he could smoke a cigarette, which was forbidden, the other man, neat and grey in a charcoal winter coat, sitting with hands folded in his lap.

Ten minutes later there was a rustle behind the clerk and two envelopes slid through the aperture. He held them up. Both Miller and the middle-aged man rose and went forward to collect. The clerk glanced quickly inside one of the envelopes.

'The file on Eduard Roschmann?' he queried.

'For me,' said Miller, and extended his hand.

'These must be for you,' he said to the other man, who was glancing sideways at Miller. The grey-coated man took his own envelope and side by side they walked to the door. Outside Miller ran down the steps and climbed into the Jaguar, slipped away from the kerb and headed back towards the centre of the city. An hour later he rang Sigi.

'I'm coming home for Christmas,' he told her.

Two hours later he was on his way out of West Berlin. As his car headed towards the first checkpoint at Drei Linden, the man with the grey coat was sitting in his neat and tidy flat off Savigny Platz, dialling a number in West Germany. He introduced himself briefly to the man who answered.

'I was in the Document Center today. Just normal research, you know the sort I do. There was another man in there. He was reading through the file of Eduard Roschmann. Then he had three sheets photo-copied. After the message that went round recently I thought I'd better tell you.'

There was a burst of questions from the other end.

'No, I couldn't get his name. He drove away afterwards in a long black sports car. Yes, yes I did. It was a Hamburg number plate.'

He recited it slowly while the man at the other end took it down.

'Well, I thought I'd better. I mean, one never knows with these snoopers. Yes, thank you, very kind of you. ... Very well, I'll leave it with you. ... Happy Christmas, *Kamerad*.'

Christmas Day was on the Wednesday of that week and it was not until after the Christmas period that the man in West Germany who had received the news from Berlin about Miller passed it on. When he did so it was to his ultimate superior.

The man who took the call thanked his informant, put the office phone down, leaned back in his comfortable leather-padded executive chair and gazed out of the window at the snow-covered roof-tops of the Old Town.

'*Verdammt* and once again *verdammt*,' he whispered. 'Why now of all times? Why now?'

To all of the citizens of his city who knew him he was a clever and brilliantly successful lawyer in private practice. To the score of his senior executive officers scattered across West Germany and West Berlin he was the chief executive inside Germany of the Odessa. His telephone number was strictly ex-directory and his code-name was the Werwolf.

Unlike the monster figure of the mythology of Hollywood and the horror films of Britain and America, the German werwolf is not an odd man who grows hair on the backs of his hands during the full moon. In old Germanic mythology the werwolf is a patriotic figure who stays behind in the homeland when the Teuton warrior-heroes have been forced to flee into exile by the invading foreigner, and who leads the resistance against the invader from the shadows of the great forests, striking by night and disappearing, leaving only the spoor of the wolf in the snow.

At the end of the war a group of SS officers, convinced the destruction of the invading Allies was merely a matter of months, trained and briefed a score of groups of ultra-fanatical teenage boys to remain behind to sabotage the Allied occupiers. They were formed in Bavaria, then being overrun by the Americans. These were the original Werwolves. Fortunately for them, they never put their training into practice, for after discovering Dachau the GIs were just waiting for someone to start something.

When the Odessa began in the late forties to reinfiltrate West Germany their first chief executive had been one of those who had trained the teenage werwolves of 1945. He took the title. It had the advantage of being anonymous, symbolic, and sufficiently melodramatic to satisfy the eternal German lust for play-acting. But there was nothing theatrical about the ruthlessness with which the Odessa dealt with those who crossed their plans.

The Werwolf of late 1963 was the third to hold the title and position. Fanatic and astute, constantly in touch with his superiors in Argentina, the man watched over the interests of all former members of the SS inside West Germany, but particularly those formerly of high rank or those high on the wanted list.

He stared out of his office window and thought back to the image of SS-General Gluecks facing him in a Madrid hotel room thirty-five days earlier; and to the general's warning about the vital importance of maintaining at all costs the anonymity and security of the radio factory owner now preparing, under the code-name Vulkan, the guidance systems for the Egyptian rockets. Alone in Germany, he also knew that in an earlier part of his life Vulkan had been better known under his real name of Eduard Roschmann.

He glanced down the jotting pad on which he had scribbled the number of Miller's car and pressed a buzzer on his desk. His secretary's voice came through from the next room.

'Hilda, what was the name of that private investigator we employed last month on the divorce case?'

'One moment . . .' There was a sound of rustling paper as she looked up the file. 'It was Memmers, Heinz Memmers.'

'Give me the telephone number, will you? No, don't ring him, just give me the number.'

He noted it down beneath the number of Miller's car, then took his finger off the intercom key.

He rose and crossed the room to a wall-safe set in a block of concrete, a part of the wall of the office. From the safe he took a thick, heavy book and went back to his desk. Flicking through the pages he came to the entry he wanted. There were only two Memmers listed, Heinrich and Walter. He ran his finger along the page opposite Heinrich, usually shortened to Heinz. He noted the date of birth, worked out the age of the man in late 1963 and recalled the face of the private investigator. The ages fitted. He jotted down two other numbers listed against Heinz Memmers, picked up the telephone and asked Hilda for an outside line.

When the dialling tone came through he dialled the number she had given him. The telephone at the other end was picked up after a dozen rings. It was a woman's voice.

'Memmers Private Enquiries.'

'Pass me Herr Memmers personally,' said the lawyer.

'May I say who's calling?' asked the secretary brightly.

'No, just put him on the line. And hurry.'

There was a pause. The tone of voice took its effect.

'Yes, sir,' she said.

A minute later a gruff voice said, 'Memmers.'

'Is that Herr Heinz Memmers?'

'Yes, who is that speaking?'

'Never mind my name. It is not important. Just tell me, does the number 245.718 mean anything to you?'

There was a dead silence down the phone, broken only by a heavy sigh as Memmers digested the fact that his SS number had just been quoted at him. The book now lying open on the Werwolf's desk was a list of every former member of the SS. Memmers' voice came back, harsh with suspicion.

'Should it?'

'Would it mean anything to you if I said that my own corresponding number had only five figures in it ... *Kamerad*?'

The change was electric. Five figures meant a very senior officer.

'Yes, sir,' said Memmers down the line.

'Good,' said the Werwolf. 'There's a small job I want you to do. Some snooper has been enquiring into one of the *Kameraden*. I need to find out who he is.'

'*Zu Befehl*' ('At your command') came down the phone.

'Excellent. But between ourselves *Kamerad* will do. After all, we are all comrades-in-arms.'

Memmers' voice came back, evidently pleased by the flattery.

'Yes, *Kamerad*.'

'All I have about the man is his car number. A Hamburg registration.' The Werwolf read it slowly down the telephone.

'Got that?'

'Yes, *Kamerad*.'

'I'd like you to go to Hamburg personally. I want to know the name and address, profession, family and dependents, social standing ... you know, the normal run-down. How long would that take you?'

'About forty-eight hours,' said Memmers.

'Good, I'll ring you back forty-eight hours from now. One last thing. There is to be no approach made to the subject. If possible it is to be done in such a way that he does not know any enquiry has been made. Is that clear?'

'Certainly. It's no problem.'

'When you have finished, prepare your account and give it to me over the phone when I ring you. I will send you the cash by post.'

Memmers expostulated.

'There will be no account, *Kamerad*. Not for a matter concerning the Comradeship.'

'Very well then. I'll ring you back in two days.'

The Werwolf put the phone down.

Miller set off from Hamburg the same afternoon, taking the same autobahn he had travelled two weeks earlier past Bremen, Osnabrück and Münster towards Cologne and the Rhineland. This time his destination was Bonn, the small and boring town on the river's edge that Konrad

Adenauer had chosen as the capital of the Federal Republic, because he came from it.

Just south of Bremen his Jaguar crossed Memmers' Opel speeding north to Hamburg. Oblivious of each other the two men flashed past on their separate missions.

It was dark when he entered the single long main street of Bonn and seeing the white-topped peaked cap of a traffic policeman he drew up beside him.

'Can you tell me the way to the British Embassy?' he asked the policeman.

'It will be closed in an hour,' said the policeman, a true Rhinelander.

'Then I'd better get there all the quicker,' said Miller. 'Where is it?'

The policeman pointed straight down the road towards the south.

'Keep straight on down here, follow the tramlines. This street becomes Friedrich Ebert Allee. Just follow the tramlines. As you are about to leave Bonn and enter Bad Godesberg, you'll see it on your left. It's lit up and it's got the British flag flying outside it.'

Miller nodded his thanks and drove on. The British Embassy was where the policeman had said, sandwiched between a building site on the Bonn side and a football pitch on the other, both a sea of mud in the December fog rolling up off the river behind the embassy.

It was a long, low grey concrete building, built back to front, referred to by British newspaper correspondents in Bonn since it was built as 'The Hoover Factory'. Miller swung off the road and parked in one of the slots provided for visitors.

He walked through the wooden-framed glass doors and found himself in a small foyer with a desk on his left, behind which sat a middle-aged receptionist. Beyond her was a small room inhabited by two blue-serge-suited men who bore the unmistakable stamp of former army sergeants.

'I would like to speak with the press attaché, please,' said Miller, using his halting school English. The receptionist looked worried.

'I don't know if he's still here. It is Friday afternoon, you know.'

'Please try,' said Miller, and proffered his press card.

The receptionist looked at it and dialled a number on her house telephone. Miller was in luck. The press attaché was just about to leave. He evidently asked for a few minutes to get his hat and coat back off again. Miller was shown into a small waiting room adorned by several Rowland Hilder prints of the Cotswolds in Autumn. On a table lay several back copies of the *Tatler* and brochures depicting the onward march of British industry. Within seconds, however, he was summoned by one of the ex-sergeants and led upstairs, along a corridor and shown into a small office.

The press attaché, he was glad to see, was in his mid-thirties and seemed eager to help.

'What can I do for you?' he asked. Miller decided to go straight into the matter.

'I am investigating a story for a news magazine,' he lied. 'It's about a former SS captain, one of the worst, a man still sought by our own

authorities. I believe he was also on the wanted list of the British authorities when this part of Germany was under British administration. Can
you tell me how I can check whether the British ever captured him, and
if so what happened to him?'

The young diplomat was perplexed.

'Good Lord, I'm sure I don't know. I mean, we handed over all our
records and files to your government in 1949. They took over where our
chaps left off. I suppose they would have all these things now.'

Miller tried to avoid mentioning that the German authorities had all
declined to help.

'True,' he said. 'Very true. However, all my enquiries so far indicate he
has never been put on trial in the Federal Republic since 1949. That would
indicate he had not been caught since 1949. However, the American
Document Center in West Berlin reveals a copy of the man's file was
requested from them by the British in 1947. There must have been a
reason for that, surely?'

'Yes, one would indeed suppose so,' said the attaché. He had evidently
taken in the reference to Miller having procured the co-operation of the
American authorities in West Berlin, and furrowed his brow in thought.

'So who on the British side would be the investigating authority during
the occupation . . . I mean, the administration period?'

'Well, you see, it would have been the Provost Marshal's office of the
army at that time. Apart from Nuremberg, which were the major
war-crimes trials, the separate Allies were investigating individually,
although obviously we co-operated with each other. Except the Russians.
These investigations led to some Zonal War-Crimes Trials, do you follow
me?'

'Yes.'

'The investigations were carried out by the Provost Marshal's department, that's the military police, you know, and the trials were prepared
by the legal branch. But the files of both were handed over in 1949. Do
you see?'

'Well, yes,' said Miller, 'but surely copies must have been kept by the
British?'

'I suppose they were,' said the diplomat. 'But they'd be filed away in
the archives of the Army by now.'

'Would it be possible to look at them?'

The attaché appeared shocked.

'Oh, I very much doubt it. I don't think so. I suppose bona-fide research
scholars might be able to make an application to see them, but it would
take a long time. And I don't think a reporter would be allowed to see
them – no offence meant, you understand?'

'I understand,' said Miller.

'The point is,' resumed the diplomat earnestly, 'that, well, you're not
exactly *official*, are you? And one doesn't wish to upset the German
authorities, does one?'

'Perish the thought.'

The attaché rose.

'I don't think there's really much the Embassy can do to help you.'

'OK. One last thing. Was there anybody here then who is still here now?'

'On the Embassy staff? Oh dear me no. No, they've all changed many times.' He escorted Miller to the door. 'Wait a minute, there's Cadbury. I think he was here then. He's been here for ages, I do know that.'

'Cadbury?' said Miller.

'Anthony Cadbury. The foreign correspondent. He's the sort of senior British press chap here. Married a German girl. I think he was here after the war, just after. You might ask him.'

'Fine,' said Miller. 'I'll try him. Where do I find him?'

'Well, it's Friday now,' said the attaché. 'He'll probably be at his favourite place by the bar in the Cercle Français later on. Do you know it?'

'No, I've never been here before.'

'Ah yes, well, it's a restaurant, run by the French, you know. Jolly good food too. It's very popular. It's in Bad Godesberg, just down the road.'

Miller found it, a hundred yards from the bank of the Rhine on a road called Am Schwimmbad. The barman knew Cadbury well, but had not seen him that evening. He told Miller if the doyen of the British foreign correspondents' corps in Bonn was not in that evening he would almost certainly be there for pre-lunch drinks the following day.

Miller checked into the Dreesen Hotel down the road, a great turn-of-the-century edifice that had formerly been Adolf Hitler's favourite hotel in Germany, the place he had picked to meet Neville Chamberlain of Britain for their first meeting in 1938. He dined at the Cercle Français and dawdled over his coffee, hoping Cadbury would turn up. But by eleven the elderly Englishman had not put in an appearance, so he went back to the hotel to sleep.

Cadbury walked into the bar of the Cercle Français a few minutes before twelve the following morning, greeted a few acquaintances and seated himself at his favourite corner stool at the bar. When he had taken his first sip of his Ricard, Miller rose from his table by the window and came over.

'Mr Cadbury?'

The Englishman turned and surveyed him. He had smooth-brushed white hair coming back from what had evidently once been a very handsome face. The skin was still healthy, with a fine tracery of tiny veins on the surface of each cheek. The eyes were bright blue under shaggy grey eyebrows. He surveyed Miller warily.

'Yes.'

'My name is Miller. Peter Miller. I am a reporter from Hamburg. May I talk with you a moment, please?'

Anthony Cadbury gestured to the stool beside him.

'I think we had better talk in German, don't you?' he said, dropping into the language. Miller was relieved he could go back to his own language, and it must have showed. Cadbury grinned.

'What can I do for you?'

Miller glanced at the shrewd eyes and backed a hunch. Starting at the beginning he told Cadbury the story from the moment of Tauber's death. The London man was a good listener. He did not interrupt once. When Miller had finished he gestured to the barman to fill his own Ricard and another beer for Miller.

'*Spatenbräu*, wasn't it?' he asked.

Miller nodded and poured the fresh beer to a foaming head on top of the glass.

'Cheers,' said Cadbury. 'Well now, you've got quite a problem. I must say I admire your nerve.'

'Nerve?' said Miller.

'It's not quite the most popular story to investigate among your countrymen in their present state of mind,' said Cadbury, 'as you will doubtless find out in course of time.'

'I already have,' said Miller.

'Mmm. I thought so,' said the Englishman, and grinned suddenly. 'A spot of lunch? The wife's away for the day.'

Over lunch Miller asked Cadbury if he had been in Germany at the end of the war.

'Yes, I was a war correspondent. Much younger then, of course. About your age. I came in with Montgomery's army. Not to Bonn, of course. No one had heard of it then. The headquarters was at Luneberg. Then I just sort of stayed on. Covered the end of the war, signature of the surrender and all that, then the paper asked me to remain.'

'Did you cover the Zonal War-Crimes Trials?' asked Miller.

Cadbury transferred a mouthful of fillet steak and nodded while he chewed.

'Yes. All the ones held in the British Zone. We had a specialist come over for the Nuremberg Trials. That was the American Zone, of course. The star criminals in our zone were Josef Kramer and Irma Grese. Heard of them?'

'No, never.'

'Well, they were called the Beast and Beastess of Belsen. I invented the titles, actually. They caught on. Did you hear about Belsen?'

'Only vaguely,' said Miller. 'My generation wasn't told much about all that. Nobody wanted to tell us anything.'

Cadbury shot him a shrewd glance under his bushy eyebrows.

'But you want to know now?'

'We have to know sooner or later. May I ask you something? Do you hate the Germans?'

Cadbury chewed for a few minutes, considering the question seriously.

'Just after the discovery of Belsen a crowd of journalists attached to the British Army went up for a look. I've never been so sickened in my life, and in war you see a few terrible things. But nothing like Belsen. I think at that moment, yes, I hated them all.'

'And now?'

'No. Not any longer. Let's face it, I married a German girl in 1948. I still live here. I wouldn't if I still felt the way I did in 1945. I'd have gone back to England long ago.'

'What caused the change?'

'Time. The passage of time. And the realisation that not all Germans were Josef Kramers. Or, what was his name, Roschmann? Or Roschmanns. Mind you, I still can't get over a sneaking sense of mistrust for people of my own generation among your nation.'

'And my generation?' Miller twirled his wineglass and gazed at the light refracting through the red liquid.

'They're better,' said Cadbury. 'Let's face it, you have to be better.'

'Will you help me with the Roschmann enquiry? Nobody else will.'

'If I can,' said Cadbury. 'What do you want to know?'

'Do you recall him being put on trial in the British Zone?'

Cadbury shook his head.

'No. Anyway, you said he was Austrian by birth. Austria was also under four-power occupation at the time. But I'm certain there was no trial against Roschmann in the British Zone of Germany. I'd remember the name if there were.'

'But why would the British authorities request a photo-copy of his career from the Americans in Berlin?'

Cadbury thought for a moment.

'Roschmann must have come to the attention of the British in some way. At that time nobody knew about Riga. The Russians were at the height of their bloody-mindedness in the late forties. They didn't give us any information from the east. Yet that was where the overwhelming majority of the worst crimes of mass-murder took place. So we were in the odd position of having about eighty per cent of the crimes against humanity committed east of what is now the Iron Curtain, and the ones responsible for them were about ninety per cent in the three western zones. Hundreds of guilty men slipped through our hands because we knew nothing about what they had done a thousand miles to the east.'

'But if an enquiry was made about Roschmann in 1947 he must have come to our attention somehow.'

'That's what I thought,' said Miller. 'Where would one start to look, among the British records?'

'Well, we can start with my own files. They're back at my house. Come on, it's a short walk.'

Fortunately, Cadbury was a methodical man and had kept every one of his despatches from the end of the war onwards. His study was lined with box-files along two walls. Besides these, there were two grey filing cabinets in one corner.

'I run the office out of my home,' he told Miller as they entered the study. 'This is my own filing system, and I'm about the only one who understands it. Let me show you.'

He gestured to the filing cabinets.

'One of these is stuffed with files on people, listed under the names in alphabetical order. The other concerns subjects listed under subject headings, alphabetically. We'll start with the first one. Look under Roschmann.'

It was a brief search. There was no folder with Roschmann's name on it.

'All right,' said Cadbury. 'Now let's try subject headings. There are four that might help. There's one called Nazis, another labelled SS. Then there's a very large section headed Justice, which has subsections one of which contains cuttings about trials that have taken place. But they're mostly criminal trials that have taken place in West Germany, since 1949. The last one that might help is about War Crimes. Let's start going through them.'

Cadbury read faster than Miller, but it took them until nightfall to wade through the hundreds of cuttings and clippings in all four files. Eventually Cadbury rose with a sigh and closed the War Crimes file, replacing it in its proper place in the filing cabinet.

'I'm afraid I have to go out to dinner tonight,' he said. 'The only thing left to look through are these.' He gestured to the box-files on shelves along two of the walls.

Miller closed the file he had been searching.

'What are those?'

'Those,' said Cadbury, 'are nineteen years of despatches from me to the paper. That's the top row. Below them are nineteen years of cuttings from the paper of news stories and articles about Germany and Austria. Obviously a lot in the first set are reprinted in the second. Those are my pieces that were printed. But there are other pieces in the second set that were not from me. After all, other contributors have had pieces printed in the paper as well. And some of the stuff I sent was not used.

'There are about six boxes of cuttings per year. That's quite a lot to get through. Fortunately it's Sunday tomorrow, so we can use the whole day if you like.'

'It's very kind of you to take so much trouble,' said Miller.

Cadbury shrugged. 'I had nothing else to do this weekend. Anyway, weekends in late December in Bonn are hardly full of gaiety. The wife's not due back till tomorrow evening. Meet me for a drink in the Cercle Français about eleven-thirty.'

It was in the middle of Sunday afternoon that they found it. Anthony Cadbury was nearing the end of the box-file labelled November-December 1947 of the set that contained his own despatches. He suddenly shouted 'Eureka', eased back the spring-clip and took out a single sheet of paper, long since faded, typewritten and headed '23rd December 1947'.

'No wonder it wasn't used in the paper,' he said. 'No one would have wanted to know about a captured SS man just before Christmas. Anyway, with the shortage of newsprint in those days the Christmas Eve edition must have been tiny.'

He laid the sheet on the writing desk and shone the Anglepoise lamp on to it. Miller leaned over to read it.

'British Military Government, Hanover, 23rd Dec.—A former captain of the notorious SS has been arrested by British military authorities at Graz, Austria, and is being held pending further investigation, a spokesman at BMG headquarters said here today.

'The man, Eduard Roschmann, was recognised on the streets of the Austrian town by a former inmate of a concentration camp, who alleged Roschmann had been the commandant of the camp in Latvia. After identification at the house to which the former camp inmate followed him, Roschmann was arrested by members of the British Field Security Service in Graz.

'A request has been made to Soviet Zonal headquarters at Potsdam for further information about the concentration camp in Riga, Latvia, and a search for further witnesses is under way,' the spokesman said. 'Meanwhile the captured man has been positively identified as Eduard Roschmann from his personal file, stored by the American authorities in their SS Index in Berlin. endit. Cadbury.'

Miller read the brief despatch four or five times.

'Christ,' he breathed. 'You got him.'

'I think this calls for a drink,' said Cadbury.

When he had made the call to Memmers on Friday morning the Werwolf had overlooked that forty-eight hours later it would be Sunday. Despite this he tried to call Memmers' office from his home on Sunday, just as the two men in Bad Godesberg made their discovery. There was no reply.

But he was in the office the following morning at nine sharp. The call from the Werwolf came through at half past.

'So glad you called, *Kamerad*,' said Memmers. 'I got back from Hamburg late last night.'

'You have the information?'

'Certainly. If you would like to note it . . .?'

'Go ahead,' said the voice down the phone.

In his office Memmers cleared his throat and began to read from his notes.

'The owner of the car is a freelance reporter, one Peter Miller. Description: aged twenty-nine, just under six feet tall, brown hair, brown eyes. Has a widowed mother who lives in Osdorf, just outside Hamburg. He himself lives in a flat close to the Steindamm in central Hamburg.'

Memmers read off Miller's address and telephone number.

'He lives there with a girl, strip-tease dancer, Miss Sigrid Rahn. He works mainly for the picture magazines. Apparently does very well. Specialises in investigative journalism. Like you said, *Kamerad*, a snooper.'

'Any idea who commissioned him on his latest enquiry?' asked the Werwolf.

'No, that's the funny thing. Nobody seems to know what he is doing at the moment. Or for whom he is working. I checked with the girl, claiming to be from the editorial office of a big magazine. Only by phone, you understand. She said she did not know where he was, but she expected a call from him this afternoon, before she goes to work.'

'Anything else?'

'Just the car. It's very distinctive. A black Jaguar, British model with a yellow stripe down the side. A sports car, two-seater, fixed-head coupé, called the XK 150. I checked his local garage.'

The Werwolf digested this.

'I want to try and find out where he is now,' he said at length.

'He's not in Hamburg now,' said Memmers hastily. 'He left on Friday about lunchtime, just as I was arriving. He spent Christmas there. Before that he was somewhere else.'

'I know,' said the Werwolf.

'I could find out what story he is enquiring about,' said Memmers helpfully. 'I did not enquire too closely, because you said you did not want him to discover he was being asked about.'

'I know what story he is working on. Exposing one of our comrades.'

The Werwolf thought for a minute.

'Could you find out where he is now?' he asked.

'I think so,' said Memmers. 'I could ring the girl back this afternoon, pretend I was from a big magazine and needed to contact Miller urgently. She sounded a simple girl on the phone.'

'Yes, do that,' said the Werwolf. 'I'll ring you at four this afternoon.'

Cadbury was down in Bonn that Monday morning where a ministerial press conference was scheduled. He rang Miller at the Dreesen Hotel at ten-thirty.

'Glad to get you before you left,' he told the German. 'I've got an idea. It might help you. Meet me at the Cercle Français this afternoon around four.'

Just before lunch Miller rang Sigi and told her he was at the Dreesen.

When they met Cadbury ordered tea.

'I had an idea while not listening to that wretched conference this morning,' he told Miller. 'If Roschmann was captured and identified as a wanted criminal, his case would have come under the eyes of the British authorities in our zone of Germany at the time. All files were copied and passed between the British, French and Americans both in Germany and Austria at that time. Have you ever heard of a man called Lord Russell of Liverpool?'

'No, never,' said Miller.

'He was the legal adviser to the British Military Governor in all our war-crimes trials during the occupation. Later he wrote a book called *The Scourge of the Swastika*. You can imagine what it was about. Didn't make him terribly popular in Germany, but it was quite accurate. About atrocities.'

'He's a lawyer?' asked Miller.

'He was,' said Cadbury. 'A very brilliant one. That was why he was chosen. He's retired now, lives in Wimbledon. I don't know if he'd remember me, but I could give you a letter of introduction.'

'Would he remember so far back?'

'He might. He's not a young man any more, but he was reputed to have a memory like a filing cabinet. If the case of Roschmann was ever referred to him to prepare a prosecution, he'd remember every detail of it. I'm sure of that.'

Miller nodded and sipped his tea.

'Yes, I could fly to London to talk to him.'

Cadbury reached into his pocket and produced an envelope.

'I wrote the letter already.' He handed Miller the letter of introduction and stood up.

'Good luck.'

Memmers had the information for the Werwolf when the latter rang just after four.

'His girl-friend got a call from him,' said Memmers. 'He's in Bad Godesberg, staying at the Dreesen Hotel.'

The Werwolf put the phone down and thumbed through an address book. Eventually he fixed on a name, picked up the phone again and rang a number in the Bonn/Bad Godesberg area.

Miller went back to the hotel to ring Cologne Airport and book a flight to London for the following day, Tuesday, December 31st. As he reached the reception desk the girl behind the counter smiled brightly and pointed to the open seating area in the bay window overlooking the Rhine.

'There's a gentleman to see you, Herr Miller.'

He glanced towards the groups of tapestry-backed chairs set round various tables in the window alcove. In one of them a middle-aged man in a black winter coat, carrying a black Homberg and a rolled umbrella, sat waiting. He strolled over, puzzled as to who could have known he was there.

'You wanted to see me?' Miller asked him. The man sprang to his feet.

'Herr Miller?'

'Yes.'

'Herr Peter Miller?'

'Yes.'

The man inclined his head in the short, jerky bow of old-fashioned Germans.

'My name is Schmidt. Dr Schmidt.'

'What can I do for you?'

Dr Schmidt smiled deprecatingly and gazed out of the windows where the black bleak mass of the Rhine flowed under the fairy lights of the deserted terrace.

'I am told you are a journalist. Yes? A freelance journalist. A very good one.' He smiled brightly. 'You have a reputation for being very thorough, very tenacious.'

Miller remained silent, waiting for him to get to the point.

'Some friends of mine heard you are presently engaged on an enquiry into events that happened ... well, let us say ... a long time ago. A very long time ago.'

Miller stiffened and his mind raced, trying to work out who the 'friends' were and who could have told them. Then he realised he had been asking questions about Roschmann all over the country.

'An enquiry about a certain Eduard Roschmann,' and he said tersely, 'So?'

'Ah yes, about Captain Roschmann. I just thought I might be able to help you.' The man swivelled his eyes back from the river and fixed them kindly on Miller. 'Captain Roschmann is dead.'

'Indeed?' said Miller. 'I didn't know.'

Dr Schmidt seemed delighted.

'Of course not. There's no reason why you should. But it is true nevertheless. Really, you are wasting your time.'

Miller looked disappointed.

'Can you tell me when he died?' he asked the doctor.

'You have not discovered the circumstances of his death?' the man asked.

'No. The last trace of him I can find was in late April 1945. He was seen alive then.'

'Ah yes, of course.' Dr Schmidt seemed happy to oblige. 'He was killed, you know, shortly after that. He returned to his native Austria and was killed fighting against the Americans in early 1945. His body was identified by several people who had known him in life.'

'He must have been a remarkable man,' said Miller.

Dr Schmidt nodded in agreement. 'Well, yes, some thought so. Yes indeed, some of us thought so.'

'I mean,' continued Miller, as if the interruption had not occurred, 'he must have been remarkable to be the first man since Jesus Christ to have risen from the dead. He was captured alive by the British on December 20th, 1947, at Graz in Austria.'

The doctor's eyes reflected the glittering snow along the balustrade outside the window.

'Miller, you are being very foolish. Very foolish indeed. Permit me to give you a word of advice, from an older man to a much, much younger one. Drop this enquiry.'

Miller eyed him.

'I suppose I ought to thank you,' he said without gratitude.

'If you will take my advice, perhaps you ought,' said the doctor.

'You misunderstand me again,' said Miller. 'Roschmann was also seen alive in mid-October this year in Hamburg. The second sighting was not confirmed. Now it is. You just confirmed it.'

'I repeat, you are being very foolish if you do not drop this enquiry.' The doctor's eyes were as cold as ever, but there was a hint of anxiety in them. There had been a time when people did not reject his orders and he had never quite got used to the change.

Miller began to get angry, a slow glow of anger working up from his collar to his face.

'You make me sick, Herr Doktor,' he told the older man. 'You and your kind, your whole stinking gang. You have a respectable façade, but you are filth on the face of my country. So far as I am concerned I'll go on asking questions till I find him.'

He turned to go, but the elder man grabbed his arm. They stared at each other from a range of two inches.

'You're not Jewish, Miller. You're Aryan. You're one of us. What did we ever do to you, for God's sake, what did we ever do to you?'

Miller jerked his arm free.

'If you don't know yet, Herr Doktor, you'll never understand.'

'Ach, you people of the younger generation, you're all the same. Why can you never do what you're told?'

'Because that's the way we are. Or at least it's the way I am.'

The older man stared at him with narrowed eyes.

'You're not stupid, Miller. But you're behaving like you are. As if you were one of these ridiculous creatures constantly governed by what they call their conscience. But I'm beginning to doubt that. It's almost as if you had something personal in this matter.'

Miller turned to go.

'Perhaps I have,' he said, and walked away across the lobby.

8

Miller found the house in a quiet residential street off the main road of the London borough of Wimbledon without difficulty. Lord Russell himself answered the ring at the door, a man in his late sixties wearing a woollen cardigan and a bow tie. Miller introduced himself.

'I was in Bonn yesterday,' he told the British peer, 'lunching with Mr Anthony Cadbury. He gave me your name and a letter of introduction to you. I hoped I might have a talk with you, sir.'

Lord Russell gazed down at him from the step with perplexity.

'Cadbury? Anthony Cadbury? I can't seem to remember . . .'

'A British newspaper correspondent,' said Miller. 'He was in Germany just after the war. He covered the war-crimes trials at which you were Deputy Judge Advocate. Josef Kramer and the others from Belsen. You recall those trials . . .'

' 'Course I do. 'Course I do. Yes, Cadbury, yes, newspaper chap. I remember him now. Haven't seen him in years. Well, don't just stand here. It's cold and I'm not as young as I was. Come in, come in.'

Without waiting for an answer he turned and walked back down the hall. Miller followed, closing the door on the chill wind of the first day of 1964. He hung his coat on a hook in the hall at Lord Russell's bidding and followed him through into the back of the house where a welcoming fire burned in the sitting-room grate.

Miller held out the letter from Cadbury. Lord Russell took it, read it quickly and raised his eyebrows.

'Humph. Help in tracking down a Nazi? Is that what you came about?' He regarded Miller from under his eyebrows. Before the German could reply Lord Russell went on: 'Well, sit down, sit down. No good standing around.'

They sat in flower-print-covered armchairs on either side of the fire.

'How come a young German reporter is chasing Nazis?' asked Lord Russell without preamble. Miller found his gruff directness disconcerting.

'I'd better explain from the beginning,' said Miller.

'I think you better had,' said the peer, leaning forward to knock out the dottle of his pipe on the side of the grate. While Miller talked he refilled the pipe, lit it, and was puffing contentedly away when the German had finished.

'I hope my English is good enough,' said Miller at last, when no reaction seemed to be coming from the retired prosecutor.

Lord Russell seemed to wake from a private reverie.

'Oh, yes, yes, better than my German after all these years. One forgets, you know.'

'This Roschmann business . . .' began Miller.

'Yes, interesting, very interesting. And you want to try and find him. Why?'

The last question was shot at Miller and he found the old man's eyes gazing keenly from under the eyebrows.

'Well, I have my reasons,' he said stiffly. 'I believe the man should be found and brought to trial.'

'Humph. Don't we all. The question is, will he be? Will he ever be?'

Miller played it straight back.

'If I can find him, he will be. You can take my word on that.'

The British peer seemed unimpressed. Little smoke signals shot out of the pipe as he puffed, rising in perfect series towards the ceiling. The pause lengthened.

'The point is, my lord, do you remember him?'

Lord Russell seemed to start.

'Remember him? Oh yes, I remember him. Or at least the name. Wish I could put a face to the name. An old man's memory fades with the years, you know. And there were so many of them in those days.'

'Your Military Police picked him up on December 20th, 1947, in Graz,' Miller told him.

He took the two photo-copies of Roschmann's picture from his breast pocket and passed them over. Lord Russell gazed at the two pictures, full-face and profile, rose and began to pace the sitting-room, lost in thought.

'Yes,' he said at last, 'I've got him. I can see him now. Yes, the file was sent on from Graz Field Security to me in Hanover a few days later. That would be where Cadbury got his despatch from. Our office in Hanover.'

He paused and swung round on Miller.

'You say your man Tauber last saw him on April 3rd, 1945, driving west through Magdeburg in a car with several others?'

'That's what he said in his diary.'

'Mmmm. Two and a half years before we got him. And do you know where he was?'

'No,' said Miller.

'In a British prisoner-of-war camp. Cheeky. All right young man, I'll fill in what I can. . . .'

The car carrying Eduard Roschmann and his colleagues from the SS passed through Magdeburg and immediately turned south towards Bavaria and Austria. They made it as far as Munich before the end of

April, then split up. Roschmann by this time was in the uniform of a corporal of the German Army, with papers in his own name but describing him as an army man.

South of Munich the American Army columns were sweeping through Bavaria, mainly concerned not with the civilian population, which had merely become an administrative headache, but with rumours that the Nazi hierarchy intended to shut themselves up in a mountain fortress in the Bavarian Alps around Hitler's home at Berchtesgaden and fight it out to the last man. The hundreds of unarmed, wandering German soldiers were paid scant attention as Patton's columns rolled through Bavaria.

Travelling by night across country, hiding by day in woodsmen's huts and barns, Roschmann crossed the Austrian border that had not even existed since the annexation of 1938 and headed south and onwards for Graz, his home town. In and around Graz he knew people on whom he could count to shelter him.

He passed round Vienna and had almost made it when he was challenged by a British patrol on May 6th. Foolishly he tried to run for it. As he dived into the undergrowth by the roadside a hail of bullets cut through the brushwood, and one passed clean through his chest, piercing one lung. After a quick search in the darkness the British Tommies passed on, leaving him wounded and undiscovered in a thicket. From here he crawled to a farmer's house half a mile away.

Still conscious, he told the farmer the name of a doctor he knew in Graz, and the man cycled through the night and the curfew to fetch him. For three months he was tended by his friends, first at the farmer's house, later at another house in Graz itself. When he was fit enough to walk the war was three months over and Austria under four-power occupation. Graz was in the heart of the British Zone.

All German soldiers were required to do two years in a prisoner-of-war camp, and Roschmann deeming it the safest place to be, gave himself up. For two years from August 1945 to August 1947, while the hunt for the worst of the wanted SS murderers went on, Roschmann remained at ease in the camp. For on giving himself up he had used another name, that of a former friend who had gone into the Army and had been killed in North Africa.

There were so many tens of thousands of German soldiers wandering about without any identity papers at all that the name given by the man himself was accepted by the Allies as genuine. They had neither the time nor the facilities to conduct a probing examination of army corporals. In the summer of 1947 Roschmann was released and felt it safe to leave the custody of the camp. He was wrong.

One of the survivors of Riga camp, a native of Vienna, had sworn his own vendetta against Roschmann. This man haunted the streets of Graz, waiting for Roschmann to return to his home, the parents he had left in 1939 and the wife he had married while on leave in 1948, Hella Roschmann. The old man roamed from the house of the parents to the house of the wife, waiting for the SS man to return.

After release Roschmann remained in the countryside outside Graz, working as a labourer in the fields. Then on December 20th, 1947, he went home to spend Christmas with his family. The old man was waiting. He hid behind a pillar when he saw the tall, lanky figure with the pale blond hair and cold blue eyes approach his wife's house, glance round a few times, then knock and enter.

Within an hour, led by the former inmate of the camp at Riga, two hefty British sergeants of the Field Security Service, puzzled and sceptical, arrived at the house and knocked. After a quick search Roschmann was discovered under a bed. Had he tried to brazen it out, claiming mistaken identity, he might have made the sergeants believe the old man was wrong. But hiding under a bed was the giveaway. He was led off to be interviewed by Major Hardy of the FSS, who promptly had him locked up in a cell while a request went off to Berlin and the American index of the SS.

Confirmation arrived in forty-eight hours, and the balloon went up. Even while the request was in Potsdam asking for Russian help in establishing the dossier on Riga, the Americans asked for Roschmann to be transferred to Munich on a temporary basis, to give evidence at Dachau where the Americans were putting on trial other SS men who had been active in the complex of camps around Riga. The British agreed.

At six in the morning of January 8th, 1948, Roschmann, accompanied by a sergeant of the Royal Military Police and another from Field Security, was put on a train at Graz bound for Salzburg and Munich.

Lord Russell paused in his pacing, crossed to the fireplace and knocked out his pipe.

'Then what happened?' asked Miller.

'He escaped,' said Lord Russell.

'He *what*?'

'He escaped. He jumped from the lavatory window of the moving train, after complaining the prison diet had given him diarrhoea. By the time his two escorts had smashed in the lavatory door, he was gone into the snow. They never found him. A search was mounted, of course, but he had gone, evidently through the snowdrifts to make contact with one of the organisations prepared to help ex-Nazis escape. Sixteen months later, in May 1949, your new republic was founded and we handed over all our files to Bonn.'

Miller finished writing and laid his notebook down.

'Where does one go from here?' he asked.

Lord Russell blew out his cheeks.

'Well, now, your own people, I suppose. You have Roschmann's life from birth to January 8th, 1948. The rest is up to the German authorities.'

'Which ones?' asked Miller, fearing what the answer would be.

'As it concerns Riga, the Hamburg Attorney General's office, I suppose,' said Lord Russell.

'I've been there.'

'They didn't help much?'

'Not at all.'

Lord Russell grinned. 'Not surprised, not surprised. Have you tried Ludwigsburg?'

'Yes. They were nice, but not very helpful. Against the rules,' said Miller.

'Well, that exhausts the official lines of enquiry. There's only one other man. Have you ever heard of Simon Wiesenthal?'

'Wiesenthal? Yes, vaguely. The name rings a bell, but I can't place it.'

'He lives in Vienna. Jewish chap, came from Polish Galicia originally. Spent four years in a series of concentration camps, twelve in all. Decided to spend the rest of his days tracking down wanted Nazi criminals. No rough stuff, mind you. He just keeps collating all the information about them he can get, then when he's convinced he has found one, usually living under a false name, not always, he informs the police. If they don't act, he gives a press conference and puts them in a spot. Needless to say, he's not terribly popular with officialdom in either Germany or Austria. He reckons they are not doing enough to bring known Nazi murderers to book, let alone chase the hidden ones. The former SS hate his guts and have tried to kill him a couple of times; the bureaucrats wish he would leave them alone, and a lot of other people think he's a great chap, and help him where they can.'

'Yes, the name rings a bell now. Wasn't he the man who found Adolf Eichmann?' asked Miller.

Lord Russell nodded.

'He identified him as Ricardo Klement, living in Buenos Aires. The Israelis took over from there. He's also traced several hundred other Nazi criminals. If anything more is known about your Eduard Roschmann, he'll know it.'

'Do you know him?' asked Miller.

Lord Russell nodded.

'I'd better give you a letter. He gets a lot of visitors wanting information. An introduction would help.'

He went to the writing desk, swiftly wrote a few lines on a sheet of headed notepaper, folded the sheet into an envelope and sealed it.

'Good luck; you'll need it,' he said, as he showed Miller out.

The following morning Miller took the BEA flight back to Cologne, picked up his car and set off on the two-day run through Stuttgart, Munich, Salzburg and Linz to Vienna.

Miller spent the night at Munich, having made slow time along the snow-encrusted autobahns, frequently narrowed down to one lane while a snow-plough or gritting truck tried to cope with the steadily falling snow. The following day he set off early and would have made Vienna by lunchtime had it not been for the long delay at Bad Tolz just south of Munich.

The autobahn was passing through dense pine forests when a series of 'Slow' signs brought the traffic to a halt. A police car, blue light spinning a warning, was parked at the edge of the road and two white-coated patrolmen were standing across the road holding back the traffic. On the left-hand, north-bound lane the procedure was the same. To the right and left of the autobahn a drive cut into the pine forests, and two soldiers in winter clothing, each with a battery-powered illuminated baton, stood at the entrance to each, waiting to summon something hidden in the forests across the road.

Miller fumed with impatience and finally wound down his window to call to one of the policemen.

'What's the matter? What's the hold-up?'

The patrolman walked slowly over and grinned.

'The Army,' he said shortly. 'They're on manoeuvres. There's a column of tanks coming across in a minute.'

Fifteen minutes later the first one appeared, a long gun barrel poking out of the pine trees, like a pachyderm scenting the air for danger, then with a rumble the flat armoured bulk of the tank eased out of the trees and clattered down to the road.

Top Sergeant Ulrich Frank was a happy man. At the age of thirty he had already fulfilled his life's ambition, to command his own tank. He could remember to the day when his life's ambition had been born to him. It was January 10th, 1945, when as a small boy in the city of Mannheim he had been taken to the cinema. The screen during the newsreels was full of the spectacle of Hasso von Manteuffel's King Tiger tanks rolling forward to engage the Americans and British.

He stared in awe at the muffled figures of the commanders, steel-helmeted and goggled, gazing forward out of the turret. For Ulrich Frank, ten years old, it was a turning point. When he left the cinema he had made a vow, that one day he would command his own tank.

It took him nineteen years, but he made it. On those winter manoeuvres in the forests around Bad Tolz, Top Sergeant Ulrich Frank commanded his first tank, an American-built M-48 Patton.

It was his last manoeuvre with the Patton. Waiting for the troop back at camp was a row of shining, brand-new French AMX-13s with which the unit was being re-equipped. Faster, more heavily armed than the Patton, the AMX would become his in another week.

He glanced down at the black cross of the new German Army on the side of the turret, and the tank's personal name stencilled beneath it, and felt a touch of regret. Though he had only commanded it for six months, it would always be his first tank, his favourite. He had named it 'Drachenfels, the Dragon Rock, after the rock overlooking the Rhine where Martin Luther, translating the Bible into German, had seen the Devil and hurled his ink-pot at him. After the re-equipment he supposed the Patton would go for scrap.

With a last pause on the far side of the autobahn the Patton and its crew breasted the rise and vanished into the forest.

Miller finally made it to Vienna in the mid-afternoon of that day, January 4th. Without checking into a hotel he drove straight into the city centre and asked his way to Rudolf Square.

He found number seven easily enough and glanced at the list of tenants. Against the third floor was a card saying 'Documentation Centre'. He mounted and knocked at the cream-painted wooden door. From behind it someone looked through the peep-hole before he heard the lock being drawn back. A pretty blonde girl stood in the doorway.

'Please?'

'My name is Miller. Peter Miller. I would like to speak with Herr Wiesenthal. I have a letter of introduction.'

He produced his letter and gave it to the girl. She looked uncertainly at it, smiled briefly and asked him to wait.

Several minutes later she reappeared at the end of the corridor on to which the door gave access, and beckoned him.

'Please come this way.'

Miller closed the front door behind him and followed her down the passage, round a corner and to the end of the flat. On the right was an open door. As he entered a man rose to greet him.

'Please come in,' said Simon Wiesenthal.

He was bigger than Miller had expected, a burly man over six feet tall, wearing a thick tweed jacket, stooping as if permanently looking for a mislaid piece of paper. He held Lord Russell's letter in his hand.

The office was small to the point of being cramped. One wall was lined from end to end and ceiling to floor in shelves, each crammed with books. The wall facing was decorated with illuminated manuscripts and testimonials from a score of organisations of former victims of the SS. The back wall contained a long sofa, also stacked with books, and to the left of the door was a small window looking down on a courtyard. The desk stood away from the window, and Miller took the visitor's chair in front of it. The Nazi-hunter of Vienna seated himself behind it and re-read Lord Russell's letter.

'Lord Russell tells me you are trying to hunt down a former SS killer,' he began without preamble.

'Yes, that's true.'

'May I have his name?'

'Roschmann. Captain Eduard Roschmann.'

Simon Wiesenthal raised his eyebrows and exhaled his breath in a whistle.

'You've heard of him?' asked Miller.

'The Butcher of Riga? One of my top fifty wanted men,' said Wiesenthal. 'May I ask why you are interested in him?'

Miller started to explain, briefly.

'I think you'd better start at the beginning,' said Wiesenthal. 'What's all this about a diary?'

With the man in Ludwigsburg, Cadbury and Lord Russell this made the fourth time Miller had had to relate the story. Each time it grew a little longer, another period added to his knowledge of Roschmann's life-story. He began again and went through until he had described the help given by Lord Russell.

'What I have to know now,' he ended, 'is where did he go when he jumped from the train?'

Simon Wiesenthal was gazing out into the court of the block of flats, watching the snowflakes dropping down the narrow shaft to the ground three floors down.

'Have you got the diary?' he asked at length. Miller reached down, took it out of his brief-case and laid it on the desk. Wiesenthal eyed it appreciatively.

'Fascinating,' he said. He looked up and smiled.

'All right, I accept the story,' he said.

Miller raised his eyebrows.

'Was there any doubt?'

Simon Wiesenthal eyed him keenly.

'There is always a little doubt, Herr Miller,' he said. 'Yours is a very strange story. I still cannot follow your motive for wanting to track Roschmann down.'

Miller shrugged.

'I'm a reporter. It's a good story.'

'But not one you will ever sell to the Press, I fear. And hardly worth your life savings. Are you sure there's nothing personal in this?'

Miller ducked the question.

'You're the second person who has suggested that. Hoffmann suggested the same at *Komet*. Why should there be? I'm only twenty-nine years old. All this was before my time.'

'Of course.' Wiesenthal glanced at his watch and rose. 'It is five o'clock, and I like to get home to my wife these winter evenings. Would you let me read the diary overnight?'

'Yes. Of course,' said Miller.

'Good. Then please come back on Monday morning and I will fill in what I know of the Roschmann story.'

Miller arrived on Monday at ten and found Simon Wiesenthal attacking a pile of letters. He looked up as the German reporter came in and gestured him to a seat. There was silence for a while as the Nazi-hunter carefully snipped the edges off the sides of his envelopes before sliding the contents out.

'I collect the stamps,' he said. 'So I don't like to damage the envelope.'

He worked away for a few more minutes.

'I read the diary last night at home. Remarkable document.'

'Were you surprised?' asked Miller.

'Surprised? No, not by the contents. We all went through much the same sort of thing. With variations, of course. But so precise. Tauber would have made a perfect witness. He noticed everything, even the small details. And noted them – at the time. That is very important to get a conviction before German or Austrian courts. And now he's dead.'

Miller considered for a while. He looked up.

'Herr Wiesenthal, so far as I know you're the first Jew I have ever really had a long talk with who went through all that. One thing Tauber said in his diary surprised me – he said there was no such thing as col-

382 THE NOVELS OF FREDERICK FORSYTH

lective guilt. But we Germans have been told for twenty years that we are all guilty. Do you believe that?'

'No,' said the Nazi-hunter flatly. 'Tauber was right.'

'How can you say that if we killed millions of people?'

'Because you, personally, were not there. You did not kill anyone. As Tauber said, the tragedy is that the specific murderers have not been brought to justice.'

'Then who,' asked Miller, 'really did kill those people?'

Simon Wiesenthal regarded him intently.

'Do you know about the various branches of the SS? About the sections within the SS who really were responsible for killing those millions?' he asked.

'No.'

'Then I'd better tell you. You've heard about the Reich Economic Administration Main Office, charged with exploiting the victims before they died?'

'Yes, I read something about it.'

'Their job was in a sense the middle section of the operation,' said Herr Wiesenthal.

'That left the business of identifying the victims among the rest of the population, rounding them up, transporting them and, when the economic exploitation was over, finishing them off.

'This was the task of the RSHA, the Reich Security Main Office, which actually killed the millions already mentioned. The rather odd use of the word "Security" in the title of this office stems from the quaint Nazi idea that the victims posed a threat to the Reich which had to be made secure against them. Also in the functions of the RSHA were the tasks of rounding up, interrogating and incarcerating in concentration camps other enemies of the Reich like Communists, Social Democrats, Liberals, Quakers, reporters and priests who spoke out too inconveniently, resistance fighters in the occupied countries, and later army officers like Field Marshal Erwin Rommel and Admiral Wilhelm Canaris, both murdered for suspicion of harbouring anti-Hitler sentiments.

'The RSHA was divided into six departments, each called an Amt. Amt One was for administration and personnel; Amt Two was equipment and finance. Amt Three was the dreaded Security Service and Security Police, headed by Reinhard Heydrich, assassinated in Prague in 1942, and later by Ernst Kaltenbrunner, executed by the Allies. Theirs were the teams who devised the tortures used to make suspects talk, both inside Germany and in the occupied countries.

'Amt Four was the Gestapo, headed by Heinrich Müller (still missing) and whose Jewish Section, department B.4, was headed by Adolf Eichmann, executed by the Israelis in Jerusalem after being kidnapped from Argentina. Amt Five was the Criminal Police and Amt Six the Foreign Intelligence Service.

'The two successive heads of Amt Three, Heydrich and Kaltenbrunner, were also the overall chiefs of the whole RSHA, and throughout the reigns of both men the head of Amt One was their deputy. He is three-star general of the SS, Bruna Streckenbach, who today has a well-paid job with a department store in Hamburg and lives in Vogelweide.

'If one is going to specify guilt, therefore, most of it rests on these two departments of the SS, and the numbers involved are thousands, not the millions who made up contemporary Germany. The theory of the collective guilt of sixty million Germans, including millions of small children, women, old-age pensioners, soldiers, sailors and airmen, who had nothing to do with the holocaust, was originally conceived by the Allies, but has since suited the former members of the SS extremely well. The theory is the best ally they have, for they realise, as few Germans seem to do, that so long as the collective guilt theory remains unquestioned nobody will start to look for specific murderers, at least, not look hard enough. The specific murderers of the SS therefore hide even today behind the collective guilt theory.'

Miller digested what he had been told. Somehow the very size of the figures involved baffled him. It was not possible to consider fourteen million people as each and every one an individual. It was easier to think of one man, dead on a stretcher under the rain in a Hamburg street.

'The reason Tauber apparently had for killing himself,' Miller asked, 'do you believe it?'

Herr Wiesenthal studied a beautiful pair of African stamps on one of the envelopes.

'I believe he was right in thinking no one would believe him, that he saw Roschmann on the steps of the Opera. If that's what he believed then he was right.'

'But he didn't even go to the police,' said Miller.

Simon Wiesenthal snipped the edge off another envelope and scanned the letter inside. After a pause he replied.

'No. Technically he should have done. I don't think it would have done any good. Not in Hamburg at any rate.'

'What's wrong with Hamburg?'

'You went to the State Attorney General's office there?' asked Wiesenthal mildly.

'Yes, I did. They weren't terribly helpful.'

Wiesenthal looked up.

'I'm afraid the Attorney General's department in Hamburg has a certain reputation in this office,' he said. 'Take, for example, the man mentioned in Tauber's diary and by me just now, Gestapo chief and SS-General Bruno Streckenbach. Remember the name?'

'Of course,' said Miller. 'What about him?'

For answer Simon Wiesenthal riffled through a pile of papers on his desk, abstracted one and gazed at it.

'Here he is,' he said. 'Known to West German justice as Document 141 JS 747/61. Want to hear about him?'

'I have time,' said Miller.

'Right. Here goes. Before the war Gestapo chief in Hamburg. Climbed rapidly from then on to a top position in the SD and SP, the Security Service and Security Police sections of the RSHA. In 1939 he recruited extermination squads in Nazi-occupied Poland. At the end of 1940 he was head of the SD and SP sections of the SS for the whole of Poland, the so-called General Government, sitting in Cracow. Thousands were exterminated by SD and SP units in Poland during that period, mainly through Operation AB.

'At the start of 1941 he came back to Berlin, promoted to Chief of Personnel for the SD. That was Amt Three of the RSHA. His chief was Reinhard Heydrich, and he became his deputy. Just before the invasion of Russia he helped to organise the extermination squads that went in behind the Army. As head of staffing he picked the personnel himself, for they were all from the SD branch.

'Then he was promoted again, this time to head of personnel for the entire six branches of the RSHA and remained deputy chief of the RSHA under first Heydrich, who was killed by Czech partisans in Prague in 1942 – that was the killing that led to the reprisal at Lidice – and then deputy to Ernst Kaltenbrunner. As such he had all-embracing responsibility for the choice of personnel of the roving extermination squads and the fixed SD units throughout the Nazi-occupied eastern territories until the end of the war.'

'So where is he now?' asked Miller.

'Walking around Hamburg, free as air,' said Wiesenthal.

Miller looked stunned.

'They haven't arrested him?' he asked.

'Who?'

'The police of Hamburg, of course.'

For answer Simon Wiesenthal asked his secretary to bring him the bulging file labelled 'Justice – Hamburg', from which he extracted a sheet of paper. He folded it neatly down the centre from top to bottom, and laid it in front of Miller so that only the left side of the sheet was facing upwards.

'Do you recognise those names?' he asked.

Miller scanned the list of ten names with a frown.

'Of course. I've been a police reporter in Hamburg for years. These are all senior police officers of the Hamburg force. Why?'

'Spread the paper out,' said Wiesenthal.

Miller did so. Fully expanded, the sheet read:

NAME	NAZI PARTY NO.	SS-NO.	RANK	PROMOTION DATE
A.	—	455,336	Capt.	1.3.43
B.	5,451,195	429,339	1st. Lt.	9.11.42
C.	—	353,004	1st. Lt.	1.11.41
D.	7,039,564	421,176	Capt.	21.6.44
E.	—	421,445	1st. Lt.	9.11.42
F.	7,040,308	174,902	Major	21.6.44
G.	—	426,553	Capt.	1.9.42
H.	3,138,798	311,870	Capt.	30.1.42
I.	1,867,976	424,361	1st. Lt.	20.4.44
J.	5,063,331	309,825	Major	9.11.43

Miller looked up.

'Christ!' he said.

'Now, do you begin to understand why a lieutenant-general of the SS is walking around Hamburg today?'

Miller looked at the list in disbelief.

'That must have been what Brandt meant about the enquiries into the former SS not being very popular in the Hamburg police.'

'Probably,' said Wiesenthal. 'Nor is the Attorney General's office the most energetic in Germany. There's one lawyer on the staff at least who is keen, but certain interested parties have tried to have him dismissed several times.'

The pretty secretary poked her head round the door.

'Tea or coffee?' she asked.

It was after the lunchtime break that Miller returned to the office. Simon Wiesenthal had in front of him a number of sheets spread out, extracts from his own Roschmann file. Miller settled himself in front of the desk, got out his notebook and waited.

Simon Wiesenthal began to relate the Roschmann story from January 8th, 1948.

It had been agreed between the British and American authorities that after Roschmann had testified at Dachau he would be moved on to the British Zone of Germany, probably Hanover, to await his own trial and almost certain hanging. Even while in prison in Graz he had begun to plan his escape.

He had made contact with a Nazi escape organization working in Austria called the 'Six-point Star', nothing to do with the Jewish symbol of the six-pointed star, but so called because the Nazi organisation had its tentacles in six major Austrian provincial cities.

At 6 a.m. on the 8th Roschmann was woken and taken to the train waiting at Graz station. Once in the compartment, an argument started between the Military Police sergeant who wanted to keep the handcuffs on Roschmann throughout the journey and the Field Security sergeant who suggested taking them off.

Roschmann influenced the argument by claiming that he had diarrhoea from the prison diet and wished to go to the lavatory. He was taken, the handcuffs removed and one of the sergeants waited outside the door until he had finished. As the train chugged through the snowbound landscape Roschmann made three requests to go to the lavatory. Apparently during this time he prised the window in the lavatory open, so that it slid easily on its runners.

Roschmann knew he had to get out before the Americans took him over at Salzburg for the last run by car to their own prison at Munich, but station after station went by and still the train was going too fast. It stopped at Hallein, and one of the sergeants went to buy some food on the platform. Roschmann again said he wanted to go to the lavatory. It was the more easy-going FSS sergeant who accompanied him, warning him not to use the toilet while the train was stationary. As the train moved slowly out of Hallein Roschmann jumped from the window into the snowdrifts. It was ten minutes before the sergeants beat down the door, and by then the train was running fast down the mountains towards Salzburg.

Police enquiries later established that he staggered through the snow as far as a peasant's cottage and took refuge there. The following day he crossed the border from Upper Austria into Salzburg province and contacted the Six-point Star organisation. They brought him to a brick factory, where he passed as a labourer, while contact was made with the Odessa for a passage to the south and Italy.

At that time the Odessa was in close contact with the recruitment section of the French Foreign Legion, into which scores of former SS soldiers had fled. Four days after contact was made, a car with French number plates was waiting outside the village of Ostermieting, and took on board Roschmann and five other Nazi escapers. The Foreign Legion driver, equipped with papers that enabled the car to cross borders without being searched, brought the six SS men over the Italian border to Merano, being paid in cash by the Odessa representative there, a hefty sum per head of his passengers.

From Merano, Roschmann was taken down to an internment camp at Rimini. Here, in the camp hospital, he had the five toes of his right foot amputated, for they were rotten with frostbite he had picked up while wandering through the snow after escaping from the train. Since then he had worn an orthopaedic shoe.

His wife in Graz got a letter from him in October 1948 from the camp at Rimini. For the first time he used the new name he had been given, Fritz Bernd Wegener.

Shortly afterwards he was transferred to the Franciscan monastery in Rome, and when his papers were finalised he set sail from the harbour at Naples for Buenos Aires. Throughout his stay at the monastery in the Via Sicilia he had been among scores of comrades of the SS and the Nazi party, and under the personal supervision of Bishop Alois Hudal, who ensured that they lacked for nothing.

In the Argentinian capital he was received by the Odessa and lodged with a German family called Vidmar in the Calle Hippolito Irigoyen. Here he lived for months in a furnished room. Early in 1949 he was advanced the sum of 50,000 American dollars out of the Bormann funds, and went into business as an exporter of South American hardwood timber to Western Europe. The firm was called Stemmler and Wegener, for his false papers from the Vatican in Rome firmly established him as Fritz Bernd Wegener, born in the South Tyrol province of Italy.

He also engaged a German girl as his secretary, Irmtraud Sigrid Müller, and in early 1955 he married her, despite already having his first wife Hella living in Graz. In the spring of 1955 Eva Peron, wife of the dictator of Argentina and the power behind the throne, died of cancer. The writing was on the wall for the Peron regime, and Roschmann spotted it. If Peron fell, much of the protection accorded by him to ex-Nazis might be removed by his successors. With his new wife Roschmann left for Egypt.

He spent three months there in the summer of 1955, and came to West Germany in the autumn. Nobody would have known a thing but for the anger of a woman betrayed. His first wife, Hella Roschmann, wrote to him from Graz, care of the Vidmar family in Buenos Aires during that summer. The Vidmars, having no forwarding address for their former lodger, opened the letter and replied to the wife in Graz, telling her that he had gone back to Germany, but had married his secretary.

His wife then informed the police of his new identity. In consequence, the police started a search for Roschmann on a matter of bigamy. Immediately a look-out was posted for a man calling himself Fritz Bernd Wegener in West Germany.

'Did they get him?' asked Miller.

Wiesenthal looked up and shook his head.

'No, he disappeared again. Almost certainly under a new set of false papers, and almost certainly in Germany. You see, that's why I believe Tauber could have seen him. It all fits with the known facts.'

'Where's the first wife, Hella Roschmann?' asked Miller.

'She still lives in Graz.'

'Is it worth contacting her?'

Wiesenthal shook his head.

'I doubt it. Needless to say, after being "blown" Roschmann is not likely to reveal his whereabouts to her again. Or his new name. For him it must have been quite an emergency when his identity of Wegener was exposed. He must have acquired his new papers in a devil of a hurry.'

'Who would have got them for him?' asked Miller.

'The Odessa, certainly.'

'Just what is the Odessa? You've mentioned it several times in the course of the Roschmann story.'

'You've never heard of them?' asked Wiesenthal.

'No. Not until now.'

Simon Wiesenthal glanced at his watch.

'You'd better come back in the morning. I'll tell you all about them.'

9

Peter Miller returned to Simon Wiesenthal's office the following morning.

'You promised to tell me about the Odessa,' he said. 'I remembered something overnight that I forgot to tell you yesterday.'

He recounted the incident of Dr Schmidt who had accosted him at the Dreesen Hotel and warned him off the Roschmann enquiry.

Wiesenthal pursed his lips and nodded.

'You're up against them, all right,' he said. 'It's most unusual for them to take such a step as to warn a reporter in that way, particularly at such an early stage. I wonder what Roschmann is up to that could be so important.'

Then for two hours the Nazi-hunter told Miller about the Odessa, from its start as an organisation for getting wanted SS criminals to a place of safety, to its development into an all-embracing freemasonry among those who had once worn the black-and-silver collars, their aiders and abettors.

When the Allies stormed into Germany in 1945 and found the concentration camps with their hideous contents, they not unnaturally rounded on the German people to demand who had carried out the atrocities. The answer was 'The SS' – but the SS were nowhere to be found.

Where had they gone? They had either gone underground inside Germany and Austria, or fled abroad. In both cases their disappearance was no spur-of-the-moment flight. What the Allies failed to realise until much later was that each had meticulously prepared his disappearance beforehand.

It casts an interesting light on the so-called patriotism of the SS that, starting at the top with Heinrich Himmler, each tried to save his own skin at the expense of massive sufferings inevitably inflicted on the German people. As early as November 1944 Heinrich Himmler tried to negotiate his own safe conduct through the offices of Count Bernadotte of the Swedish Red Cross. The Allies refused to consider letting him off the hook. While the Nazis and the SS screamed at the German people to fight on until the wonder weapons waiting round the corner were delivered, they themselves prepared for their departure to a comfortable exile elsewhere. They at least knew there were no wonder weapons; the destruction of the Reich and, if Hitler had anything to do with it, of the entire German nation, was inevitable.

On the eastern front the German Army was bullied into battle against the Russians to take unbelievable casualties, not to produce victory but to produce a delay while the SS finalised their escape plans. Behind the Army stood the SS, shooting and hanging some of the Army men who took a step backwards after already taking more punishment than military flesh and blood is usually expected to stand. Thousands of officers and men of the Wehrmacht died at the end of the SS hanging ropes in this way.

Just before the final collapse, delayed six months after the chiefs of the SS knew defeat was inevitable, the leaders of the SS disappeared. From one end of the country to the other they quit their posts, changed into civilian clothes, stuffed their beautifully (and officially) forged personal papers into their pockets, and vanished into the swirling masses of chaotic people who made up Germany in May 1945. They left the granddads of the Home Guard to meet the British and the Americans at the gates of the concentration camps, the exhausted Wehrmacht to go into prisoner-of-war camps and the women and children to live or die under Allied rule in the coming bitter winter of 1945.

Those who knew they were too well known to escape detection for long fled abroad. This was where the Odessa came in. Formed just before the end of the war, its job was to get wanted SS men out of Germany to safety. Already it had established close and friendly links with Juan Peron's Argentina, which had issued seven thousand Argentinian passports 'in blank' so that the refugee merely had to fill in a false name, his own photograph, get it stamped by the ever-ready Argentine consul, and board ship for Buenos Aires or the Middle East.

Thousands of SS murderers poured southwards through Austria and into the South Tyrol province of Italy. They were shuttled from safe-house to safe-house along the route, thence mainly to the Italian port of Genoa or further south to Rimini and Rome. A number of organisations, some supposed to be concerned with charitable work among the truly dispossessed, took it upon themselves, for reasons best known to themselves, to decide on some evidence of their own imagining, that the SS refugees were being over-harshly persecuted by the Allies.

Among the chief Scarlet Pimpernels of Rome who spirited thousands away to safety was Bishop Alois Hudal, the German bishop in Rome. The main hiding-out station for the SS killers was the enormous Franciscan monastery in Rome, where they were hidden and boarded until papers could be arranged, along with a passage to South America. In some cases the SS men travelled on Red Cross travel documents, issued through the intervention of the Church, and in many cases the charitable organisation Caritas paid for their tickets.

This was the first task of Odessa, and it was largely successful. Just how many thousands of SS murderers who, had they been caught by the Allies, would have died for their crimes, passed to safety will never be known, but it was well over eighty per cent of those meriting the death sentence.

Having established itself comfortably on the proceeds of mass-murder, transferred from the Swiss banks, the Odessa sat back – and watched the deterioration of relations between the Allies of 1945. The early ideas of the quick establishment of a Fourth Reich were discarded in the course of time by the leaders of the Odessa in South America as impractical, but with the establishment in May 1949 of a new Republic of West Germany those leaders of the Odessa set themselves five new tasks.

The first was the reinfiltration of former Nazis into every facet of life in the new Germany. Throughout the late forties and fifties former members of the Nazis slipped into the civil service at every level, back into lawyers' offices, on to judges' benches, into the police forces, local government and doctors' surgeries. From these positions, however lowly, they were able to protect each other from investigation and arrest, advance each others' interests and generally ensure that investigation and prosecution of former comrades – they call each other 'Kamerad' – went forward as slowly as possible, if at all.

The second task was to infiltrate the mechanisms of political power. Avoiding the high levels, former Nazis slipped into the grass-roots organisation of the ruling party at ward and constituency level. Again, there was no law to forbid a former member of the Nazis from joining a political party. It may be a coincidence, but unlikely that no politician with a known record of calling for increased vigour in the investigation and prosecution of Nazis crimes has ever been elected in the CDU or the CSU, either at Federal level or at the equally important level of the very powerful Provincial Parliaments. One politican expressed it with crisp simplicity – 'It's a question of election mathematics. Six million dead Jews don't vote. Five million former Nazis can do, at every election.'

The main aim of both these programmes was simple. It was and is to slow down if not stop the investigation and prosecution of former members of the Nazis. In this the Odessa had one other great ally. This was the secret knowledge in the minds of hundreds of thousands that they had either helped in what was done, albeit in a small way, or had known at the time what was going on and had remained silent. Years later, established and respected in their communities and professions, they could hardly relish the idea of energetic investigation into past events, let alone the mention of their name in a faraway courtroom where a Nazi was on trial.

The third task the Odessa set itself in post-war Germany was to reinfiltrate business, commerce and industry. To this end certain former Nazis were established in businesses of their own in the early fifties, bankrolled by funds from the Zürich deposits. Any reasonably well administered concern founded with plenty of liquidity in the early fifties would take full advantage of the staggering Economic Miracle of the fifties and sixties, to become in turn a large and flourishing business. The point of this was to use funds out of the profits from these businesses to influence press coverage of the Nazi crimes through advertising revenue, to assist financially the crop of SS-oriented propaganda sheets that have come and gone in post-war Germany, to keep alive some of the ultra-right-wing publishing houses, and to provide jobs for former *Kameraden* fallen on hard times.

The fourth task was and still is to provide the best possible legal defence for any Nazi forced to stand trial. In later years a technique was developed whereby the accused at once engaged a brilliant and expensive lawyer, had a few sessions with him, and then announced they could not afford to pay him. The lawyer could then be appointed defence counsel by the court according to the provisions of the legal-aid laws. But in the early and mid-fifties, when hundreds of thousands of German POWs streamed home from Russia, unamnestied SS criminals were sifted out and taken to Camp Friedland. Here girls circulated among them, handing out to each a small white card. On it was the man's designated defence lawyer.

The fifth task is propaganda. This takes many forms, from encouraging the dissemination of right-wing pamphlets to lobbying for a final ratification of the Statute of Limitations, under whose terms an end would be put to all culpability in law of the Nazis. Efforts are made to assure the Germans of today that the death figures of the Jews, Russians, Poles and others were but a tiny fraction of those quoted by the Allies – a hundred thousand dead Jews is the usual figure mentioned – and to point out that the Cold War between the West and the Soviet Union in some way proves Hitler to have been right.

But the mainstay of the Odessa propaganda is to persuade the sixty million West Germans of today – and with a large degree of success – that the SS were in fact patriotic soldiers like the Wehrmacht and that solidarity between former comrades must be upheld. This is the weirdest ploy of them all.

During the war the Wehrmacht kept its distance from the SS, which it regarded with repugnance, while the SS treated the Wehrmacht with contempt. At the end millions of young Wehrmacht men were hurled into death or captivity at Russian hands, from which only a small proportion returned, and this so that the SS men could live prosperously elsewhere. Thousands more were executed by the SS, including 5000 in the aftermath of the July 1944 plot against Adolf Hitler, in which less than fifty men were implicated.

How former members of the German Army, Navy and Air Force can conceivably regard ex-SS men as meriting from them the title of *Kamerad*, let alone their protection and solidarity from prosecution, is a mystery. Yet herein lies the real success of the Odessa.

By and large Odessa has succeeded in its tasks of impeding West German efforts to hunt down and bring to trial the SS murderers. It has succeeded by virtue of its own ruthlessness, occasionally against its own kind if they look like making a full confession to the authorities, Allied mistakes between 1945 and 1949, the Cold War, and the usual German cowardice when faced with a moral problem, in stark contrast to their courage when faced with a military task or a technical issue like the reconstruction of post-war Germany.

When Simon Wiesenthal had finished, Miller laid down the pencil with which he had made copious notes and sat back.

'I hadn't the faintest idea,' he said.

'Very few Germans have,' conceded Wiesenthal. 'In fact very few people know much about the Odessa at all. The word is hardly ever mentioned in Germany and just as certain members of the American underworld will stoutly deny the existence of the Mafia, so any former member of the SS will deny the existence of the Odessa. To be perfectly frank, the term is not used as much nowadays as formerly. The new word is "The Comradeship" just as the Mafia in America is called the Cosa Nostra. But what's in a name? The Odessa is still there, and will be while there is an SS criminal to protect.'

'And you think these are the men I'm up against?' asked Miller.

'I'm sure of it. The warning you were given in Bad Godesberg could not have come from anyone else. Do be careful, these men can be dangerous.'

Miller's mind was on something else.

'When Roschmann disappeared in 1955, you said he would need a new passport?'

'Certainly.'

'Why the passport particularly?'

Simon Wiesenthal leaned back in his chair and nodded.

'I can understand why you are puzzled. Let me explain. After the war in Germany, and here in Austria, there were tens of thousands wandering about with no identification papers. Some had genuinely lost them, others had thrown them away for good reason.

'To obtain new ones, it would normally be necessary to produce a birth certificate. But millions had fled from the former German territories overrun by the Russians. Who was to say if a man was, or was not, born in a small village in East Prussia, now miles behind the Iron Curtain? In other cases the buildings in which the certificates were stored had been destroyed by bombing.

'So the process was very simple. All one needed were two witnesses to swear that one was who one said, and a fresh personal ID card was issued. In the case of prisoners-of-war, they often had no papers either. On their release from camp, the British and American camp authorities would sign a release paper to the effect that Corporal Johann Schumann was certified as released from prisoner-of-war camp. These chits were then taken by the soldier to the civilian authorities who issued an ID card in the same name. But often the man had only told the Allies his name was Johann Schumann. It could have been something else. No one checked. And so he got a new identity.

'That was all right in the immediate aftermath of the war, which was when most of the SS criminals were getting their new identities. But what happens to a man who is blown wide open in 1955, as was Roschmann? He can't go to the authorities and say he lost his papers during the war. They would be bound to ask how he had got by during the ten-year interim period. So he needs a passport.'

'I understand so far,' said Miller. 'But why a passport? Why not a driving licence, or an ID card?'

'Because shortly after the founding of the republic the German authorities realised there must be hundreds of thousands wandering about under false names. There was a need for one document that was so well researched that it could act as the yardstick for all the others. They hit on the passport. Before you get a passport in Germany, you have to produce the birth certificate, several references, and a host of other documentation. These are thoroughly checked before the passport is issued.

'By contrast, once you have a passport, you can get anything else on the strength of it. Such is bureaucracy. The production of the passport convinces the civil servant that, since previous bureaucrats must have checked out the passport holder thoroughly, no further checking is necessary. With a new passport, Roschmann could quickly build up the rest of the identity – driving licence, bank accounts, credit cards. The passport is the open sesame to every other piece of necessary documentation in present-day Germany.'

'Where would the passport come from?'

'From the Odessa. They must have a forger somewhere who can turn them out,' surmised Herr Wiesenthal.

Miller thought for a while.

'If one could find the passport forger, one might find the man who could identify Roschmann today?' he suggested.

Wiesenthal shrugged.

'One might. But it would be a long shot. And to do that one would have to penetrate the Odessa. Only an ex-SS man could do that.'

'Then where do I go from here?' said Miller.

'I should think your best bet would be to try and contact some of the survivors of Riga. I don't know whether they would be able to help you further, but they'd certainly be willing. We are all trying to find Roschmann. Look ...'

He flicked open the diary on his desk.

'There's reference here to a certain Olli Adler from Munich, who was in Roschmann's company during the war. It may be she survived and came home to Munich.'

Miller nodded.

'If she did, where would she register?'

'At the Jewish Community Centre. It still exists. It contains the archives of the Jewish community of Munich, since the war, that is. Everything else was destroyed. I should try there.'

'Do you have the address?'

Simon Wiesenthal checked through an address book.

'Reichenbach Strasse, Number Twenty-seven, Munich,' he said. 'I suppose you want the diary of Salomon Tauber back?'

'Yes, I'm afraid I do.'

'Pity. I'd like to have kept it. A remarkable diary.'

He rose and escorted Miller to the front door.

'Good luck,' he said, 'and let me know how you get on.'

Miller had dinner that evening in the House of the Golden Dragon, which had been in business as a beer-house and restaurant in the Steindelgasse without a break from 1566, and thought over the advice. He had little hope of finding more than a handful of survivors of Riga still in Germany or Austria, and even less hope that any might help him track Roschmann beyond November 1955. But it was a hope, a last hope.

He left the next morning for the drive back to Munich.

10

Miller drove into Munich at mid-morning of January 8th, and found 27, Reichenbach Strasse from a map of Munich bought at a newspaper kiosk in the outskirts. Parking down the road he surveyed the Jewish Community Centre before entering. It was a flat-fronted five-storey building. The façade of the ground floor was of uncovered stone blocks; above this the façade was of grey cement over brick. The fifth and top floor was marked by a row of mansard windows set in the red tile roof. At ground level there was a double door of glass panels, set at the extreme left end of the building.

The building contained a kosher restaurant, the only one in Munich, on the ground floor, the leisure rooms of the old people's home on the one above. The third floor contained the administration and records department, and the upper two housed the guest rooms and sleeping quarters of the inmates of the old people's home. At the back was a synagogue.

The whole building was destroyed on the night of Friday, February 15th, 1970, when petrol bombs were poured into it from the roof. Seven died, suffocated by smoke. Swastikas were daubed on the synagogue.

He went up to the third floor and presented himself at the enquiry desk. While he waited he glanced round the room. There were rows of books, all new, for the original library had long since been burnt by the Nazis. Between the library shelves were portraits of some of the leaders of the Jewish community stretching back hundreds of years, teachers and rabbis, gazing out of their frames above luxuriant beards, like the figures of the prophets he had seen in his scripture textbooks at school. Some wore phylacteries bound to their foreheads and all were hatted.

There was a rack of newspapers, some in German, others in Hebrew. He presumed the latter were flown in from Israel. A short dark man was scanning the front page of one of the latter.

'Can I help you?'

He looked round to the enquiry desk to find it now occupied by a dark-eyed woman in her mid-forties. There was a strand of hair falling over her eyes, which she nervously brushed back into place several times a minute.

Miller made his request: any trace of Olli Adler, who might have reported back to Munich after the war?

'Where would she have returned from?' asked the woman.

'From Magdeburg. Before that Stutthof. Before that from Riga.'

'Oh dear, Riga,' said the woman. 'I don't think we have anyone on the lists who came back here from Riga. They all disappeared, you know. But I'll look.'

She went into a back room and Miller could see her going steadily through an index of names. It was not a big index. She returned after five minutes.

'I'm sorry. Nobody of that name reported back here after the war. It's a common name. But there is nobody listed under it.'

Miller nodded.

'I see. That looks like it, then. Sorry to have troubled you.'

'You might try the International Tracing Service,' said the woman. 'It's really their job to find people who went missing. They have lists from all over Germany, whereas we only have the lists of those originating in Munich who came back.'

'Where is the Tracing Service?' asked Miller.

'It's at Arolsen-in-Waldeck. That's just outside Hanover, Lower Saxony. It's run by the Red Cross, really.'

Miller thought for a minute.

'Would there be anybody else left in Munich who was at Riga? The man I'm really trying to find is the former commandant.'

There was silence in the room. Miller sensed the man by the newspaper rack turn round to look at him. The woman seemed subdued.

'It might be possible there are a few left who were at Riga and now live in Munich. Before the war there were 25,000 Jews in Munich. About a tenth came back. Now we are about 5000 again, half of them children born since 1945. I might find someone who was at Riga. But I'd have to go through the whole list of survivors. The camps they were in are marked against the names. Could you come back tomorrow?'

Miller thought for a moment, debating whether to give up and go home. The chase was getting pointless.

'Yes,' he said at length. 'I'll come back tomorrow. Thank you.'

He was back in the street, reaching for his car keys, when he felt a step behind him.

'Excuse me,' said a voice. He turned. The man behind him was the one who had been reading the newspapers.

'You are enquiring about Riga?' asked the man. 'About the commandant of Riga? Would that be Captain Roschmann?'

'Yes, it would,' said Miller. 'Why?'

'I was at Riga,' said the man. 'I knew Roschmann. Perhaps I can help you.'

The man was short and wiry, somewhere in his mid-forties, with button-bright eyes and the rumpled air of a damp sparrow.

'My name is Mordecai,' he said. 'But people call me Motti. Shall we have a coffee and talk?'

They adjourned to a nearby coffee-shop. Miller, melted slightly by his companion's chirpy manner, explained his hunt so far from the back streets of Altona to the Community Centre of Munich. The man listened quietly, nodding occasionally.

'Mmmm. Quite a pilgrimage. Why should you, a German, want to track down Roschmann?'

'Does it matter? I've been asked that so many times I'm getting tired of it. What's so strange about a German being angry at what was done years ago?'

Motti shrugged.

'Nothing,' he said. 'It's unusual for a man to go to such lengths, that's all. About Roschmann's disappearance in 1955. You really think his new passport must have been provided by the Odessa?'

'That's what I've been told,' replied Miller. 'And it seems the only way to find the man who forged it would be to penetrate the Odessa.'

Motti considered the young German in front of him for some time.

'What hotel are you staying at?' he asked at length.

Miller told him he had not checked in to any hotel yet, as it was still early afternoon. But there was one he knew that he had stayed in before. At Motti's request he went to the coffee-shop telephone and called the hotel for a room.

When he got back to the table Motti had gone. There was a note under the coffee-cup. It said, 'Whether you get a room there or not, be in the residents' lounge at eight tonight.'

Miller paid for the coffees and left.

The same afternoon in his lawyer's office the Werwolf read once again the written report that had come in from his colleague in Bonn, the man who had introduced himself to Miller a week earlier as Dr Schmidt.

The Werwolf had had the report already for five days, but his natural caution had caused him to wait and reconsider before taking direct action.

The last words his superior General Gluecks had spoken to him in Madrid in late November virtually robbed him of any freedom of action, but like most desk-bound men he found comfort in delaying the inevitable. 'A permanent solution' had been the way his orders were expressed, and he knew what that meant. Nor did the phraseology of 'Dr Schmidt' leave him any more room for manoeuvre.

'A stubborn young man, truculent and headstrong, probably obstinate, and with an undercurrent of genuine and personal hatred in him for the *Kamerad* in question, Eduard Roschmann, for which no explanation seems to exist. Unlikely to listen to reason, even in the face of personal threat. . . .'

The Werwolf read the doctor's summing up again and sighed. He reached for the phone and asked his secretary Hilda for an outside line. When he had it he dialled a number in Düsseldorf.

After several rings it was answered, and a voice said simply, 'Yes.'

'There's a call for Herr Mackensen,' said the Werwolf.

The voice from the other end said simply, 'Who wants him?'

Instead of answering the question directly, the Werwolf gave the first part of the identification code.

'Who was greater than Frederick the Great?'

The voice from the other end replied:

'Barbarossa.' There was a pause, then:

'This is Mackensen,' said the voice.

'Werwolf,' replied the chief of the Odessa. 'The holiday is over, I'm afraid. There is work to be done. Get over here by tomorrow morning.'

'When?' replied Mackensen.

'Be here at ten,' said the Werwolf. 'Tell my secretary your name is Keller. I will ensure you have an appointment in that name.'

He put the phone down. In Düsseldorf, Mackensen rose and went into the bathroom of his flat to shower and shave. He was a big, powerful man, a former sergeant of the Das Reich division of the SS, who had learned his killing when hanging French hostages in Tulle and Limoges, back in 1944.

After the war he had driven a truck for the Odessa, running human cargoes south through Germany and Austria into the South Tyrol province of Italy. In 1946, stopped by an overly suspicious American patrol, he had slain all four occupants of the jeep, two of them with his bare hands. From then on he too was on the run.

Employed later as a bodyguard for senior men of the Odessa, he had been saddled with the nickname 'Mack the Knife', although oddly he never used a knife, preferring the strength of his butcher's hands to strangle or break the necks of his 'assignments'.

Rising in the esteem of his superiors, he had become in the mid-fifties the executioner of the Odessa, the man who could be relied on to cope quietly and discreetly with those who came too close to the top men of the organisation, or those from within who elected to squeal on their comrades. By January 1964 he had fulfilled twelve assignments of this kind.

The call came on the dot of eight. It was taken by the reception clerk who put his head round the corner of the residents' lounge, where Miller sat watching television.

He recognised the voice on the end of the phone.

'Herr Miller? It's me, Motti. I think I may be able to help you. Rather, some friends may be able to. Would you like to meet them?'

'I'll meet anybody who can help me,' said Miller, intrigued by the manoeuvres.

'Good,' said Motti. 'Leave your hotel and turn left down Schiller Strasse. Two blocks down on the same side is a cake-and-coffee shop called Lindemann. Meet me in there.'

'When, now?' asked Miller.

'Yes. Now. I would come to the hotel but I'm with my friends here. Come right away.'

He hung up. Miller took his coat and walked out through the doors. He turned left and headed down the pavement. Half a block from the hotel something hard was jabbed into his ribs from behind, and a car slid up to the kerb.

'Get into the back seat, Herr Miller,' said a voice in his ear.

The door beside him swung open and with a last dig in the ribs from the man behind, Miller ducked his head and entered the car. The driver was up front, the back seat contained another man who slid over to make room for him. He felt the man behind him enter the car also, then the door was slammed and the car slid from the kerb.

Miller's heart was thumping. He glanced at the three men in the car with him, but recognised none of them. The man to his right, who had opened the door for him to enter, spoke first.

'I am going to bind your eyes,' he said simply. 'We would not want you to see where you are going.'

Miller felt a sort of black sock pulled over his head until it covered his nose. He remembered the cold blue eyes of the man in the Dreesen Hotel and recalled what the man in Vienna had told him. 'Be careful, the men of Odessa can be dangerous.' Then he remembered Motti, and wondered how one of them could have been reading a Hebrew newspaper in the Jewish Community Centre.

The car drove for twenty-five minutes, then slowed and stopped. He heard some gates being opened, the car surged forward again and stopped finally. He was eased out of the back seat, and with a man on each side he was helped across a courtyard. For a moment he felt the cold night air on his face, then he was back inside again. A door slammed behind him, and he was led down some steps into what seemed to be a cellar. But the air was warm and the chair into which he was lowered was well upholstered.

He heard a voice say, 'Take off the bandage,' and the sock over his head was removed. He blinked as his eyes got used to the light.

The room he was in was evidently below ground, for it had no windows. But an air extractor hummed high on one wall. It was well decorated and comfortable, evidently a form of committee room, for there was a long table with eight chairs ranged close to the far wall. The remainder of the room was an open space, fringed by easy armchairs. In the centre was a circular carpet and a coffee table.

Motti was standing smiling quietly, almost apologetically, beside the committee table. The two men who had brought him, both well built and in early middle age, were perched on the arms of the armchairs to his left and right. Directly opposite him, across the coffee table, was the fourth man. He supposed the car driver had remained upstairs to lock up.

The fourth man was evidently in command. He sat at ease in his chair while his three lieutenants stood or perched around him. Miller judged him to be about sixty, lean and bony, with a hollow-cheeked hook-nosed face. The eyes worried Miller. They were brown and deep-sunk into the sockets, but bright and piercing, the eyes of a fanatic. It was he who spoke.

'Welcome, Herr Miller. I must apologise for the strange way in which you were brought to my home. The reason for it was that if you decide you wish to turn down my proposal to you you can be returned to your hotel and will never see any of us again.

'My friend here,' he gestured to Motti, 'informs me that for reasons of your own you are hunting a certain Eduard Roschmann. And that to get closer to him you might be prepared to attempt to penetrate the Odessa. To do that you would need help. A lot of help. However, it might suit our interests to have you inside the Odessa. Therefore we might be prepared to help you. Do you follow me?'

Miller stared at him in astonishment.

'Let me get one thing straight,' he said at length. 'Are you telling me you are not from the Odessa?'

The man raised his eyebrows.

'Good heavens, you *have* got hold of the wrong end of the stick.'

He leaned forward and drew back the sleeve of his left wrist. On the forearm was tattooed a number in blue ink.

'Auschwitz,' said the man. He pointed to the two men at Miller's sides. 'Buchenwald and Dachau.' He pointed at Motti. 'Riga and Treblinka.' He pulled back his sleeve.

'Herr Miller, there are some who think the murderers of our people should be brought to trial. We do not agree. Just after the war I was talking with a British officer, and he told me something that has guided my life ever since. He said to me, "If they had murdered six million of my people, I too would build a monument of skulls. Not the skulls of those who died in the concentration camps, but of those who put them there." Simple logic, Herr Miller, but persuasive. I and my group are men who decided to stay on inside Germany after 1945 with one object and one only in mind. Revenge, revenge pure and simple. We don't arrest them, Herr Miller, we kill them like the swine they are. My name is Leon.'

Leon interrogated Miller for four hours before he was satisfied of the reporter's genuineness. Like others before him he was puzzled for the motivation, but had to concede it was possible Miller's reason was the one he gave, indignation at what had been done by the SS during the war. When he had finished, Leon leant back in his chair and surveyed the younger man for a long time.

'Are you aware how risky it is to try and penetrate the Odessa, Herr Miller?' he asked.

'I can guess,' said Miller. 'For one thing I'm too young.'

Leon shook his head.

'There's no question of your trying to persuade former SS men you are one of them under your own name. For one thing they have lists of former SS men, and Peter Miller is not on that list. For another you have to age ten years at least. It can be done, but involves a complete new identity, and a real identity. The identity of a man who really existed and was in the SS. That alone means a lot of research by us, and the expenditure of a lot of time and trouble.'

'Do you think you can find such a man?' asked Miller.

Leon shrugged.

'It would have to be a man whose death cannot be checked out,' he said. 'Before the Odessa accept a man at all, they check him out. You have to pass all the tests. That also means you will have to live for five or six weeks with a genuine former SS man who can teach you the folklore, the technical terms, the phraseology, the behaviour patterns. Fortunately we know such a man.'

Miller was amazed.

'Why should he do such a thing?'

'The man I have in mind is an odd character. He is a genuine SS captain who sincerely regretted what was done. He experienced remorse. Later he was inside the Odessa, and passed information about wanted Nazis to the authorities. He would be doing so yet, but he was "shopped" and was lucky to escape with his life. Now he lives under a new name, in a house outside Bayreuth.'

'What else would I have to learn?'

'Everything about your new identity. Where he was born, his date of birth, how he got into the SS, where he trained, where he served, his unit, his commanding officer, his entire history from the end of the war onwards. You will also have to be vouched for by a guarantor. That will not be easy. A lot of time and trouble will have to be spent on you, Herr Miller. Once you are in, there will be no pulling back.'

'What's in this for you?' asked Miller suspiciously.

Leon rose and paced the carpet.

'Revenge,' he said simply. 'Like you, we want Roschmann. But we want more. The worst of the SS killers are living under false names. We want those names. That's what's in it for us. There's one other thing. We need to know who is the new recruiting officer of the Odessa for German scientists now being sent to Egypt to develop Nasser's rockets for him. The former one, Brandner, resigned and disappeared last year after we coped with his assistant Heinz Krug. Now they have a new one.'

'That sounds more like information of use to Israeli intelligence,' said Miller. Leon glanced at him shrewdly.

'It is,' he said shortly. 'We occasionally co-operate with them, though they do not own us.'

'Have you ever tried to get your own men inside the Odessa?' asked Miller.

Leon nodded.

'Twice,' he said.

'What happened?'

'The first was found floating in a canal without his fingernails. The second disappeared without trace. Do you still want to go ahead?'

Miller ignored the question.

'If your methods are so efficient, why were they caught?'

'They were both Jewish,' said Leon shortly. 'We tried to get the tattoos from the concentration camps off their arms, but they left scars. Besides, they were both circumcised. That was why, when Motti reported to me on a genuine Aryan German with a grudge against the SS, I was interested. By the way, are you circumcised?'

'Does it matter?' enquired Miller.

'Of course. If a man is circumcised it does not prove he's a Jew. Many Germans are circumcised as well. But if he is not, it more or less proves he is not a Jew.'

'I'm not,' said Miller shortly.

Leon breathed a long sigh.

'This time I think we may be able to get away with it,' he said.

It was long past midnight. Leon looked at his watch.

'Have you eaten?' he asked Miller. The reporter shook his head.

'Motti, I think a little food for our guest.'

Motti grinned and nodded. He disappeared through the door of the cellar room and went up into the house.

'You'll have to spend the night here,' said Leon to Miller. 'We'll bring a bedroll down to you. Don't try to leave, please. The door has three locks, and all will be shut on the far side. Give me your car keys and I'll have your car brought round here. It will be better out of sight for the next few weeks. Your hotel bill will be paid and your luggage brought round here too. In the morning you will write letters to your mother and girlfriend, explaining that you will be out of contact for several weeks, maybe months. Understood?'

Miller nodded and handed over his car keys. Leon gave them to one of the other two men, who quietly left.

'In the morning we will drive you to Bayreuth and you will meet our SS officer. His name is Alfred Oster. He's the man you will live with. I will arrange it. Meanwhile, excuse me. I have to start looking for a new name and identity for you.'

He rose and left. Motti soon returned with a plate of food and half a dozen blankets. As he ate the cold chicken and potato salad, Miller wondered what he had let himself in for.

Far away to the north, in the General Hospital of Bremen, a ward orderly was patrolling his ward in the small hours of the morning. Round a bed at the end of the room was a tall screen that shut off the occupant from the rest of the ward.

The orderly, a middle-aged man called Hartstein, peered round the screen at the man in the bed. He lay very still. Above his head a dim light was burning through the night. The orderly entered the screened-off area and checked the patient's pulse. There was none.

He looked down at the ravaged face of the cancer victim, and something the man had said in delirium three days earlier caused the orderly to lift the left arm of the dead man out of the blankets. Inside the man's armpit was tattooed a number. It was the dead man's blood group, a sure sign that the patient had once been in the SS. The reason for the tattoo was that SS men were regarded in the Reich as more valuable than ordinary soldiers, so when wounded they always had first share of any available plasma. Hence the tattooed blood group.

Orderly Hartstein covered the dead man's face and glanced into the drawer of the bedside table. He drew out the driving licence that had been placed there along with the other personal possessions when the man had been brought in after collapsing in the street. It showed a man of about thirty-nine, date of birth June 18th, 1925, and the name of Rolf Gunther Kolb.

The orderly slipped the driving licence into the pocket of his white coat and went off to report the decease to the night physician.

11

Peter Miller wrote his letters to his mother and Sigi under the watchful eye of Motti, and finished by mid-morning. His luggage had arrived from his hotel, the bill had been paid, and shortly before noon the two of them, accompanied by the same driver of the previous night, set off for Bayreuth.

With a reporter's instinct he flashed a glance at the number plates of the blue Opel which had taken the place of the Mercedes that had been used the night before. Motti, at his side, noticed the glance and smiled.

'Don't bother,' he said. 'It's a hired car, taken out in a false name.'

'Well, it's nice to know one is among professionals,' said Miller.

Motti shrugged.

'We have to be. It's one way of staying alive when you're up against the Odessa.'

The garage had two berths, and Miller noticed his own Jaguar in the second slot. Half-melted snow from the previous night had formed puddles beneath the wheels, and the sleek black bodywork gleamed in the electric light.

Once in the back of the Opel the black sock was again pulled over his head, and he was pushed down to the floor as the car eased out of the garage, through the gates of the courtyard and into the street. Motti kept the blindfold on him until they were well clear of Munich and heading north up Autobahn E6 towards Nuremberg and Bayreuth.

When Miller finally lost the blindfold he could see there had been another heavy snowfall overnight. The rolling forested countryside where Bavaria ran into Franconia was clothed in a heavy coat of unmarked white, giving a chunky roundness to the leafless trees of the beech forests along the road. The driver was slow and careful, the windscreen wipers working constantly to clear the glass of the fluttering flakes and the mush thrown up by the lorries they passed.

They lunched at a wayside inn at Ingolstadt, pressed on to skirt Nuremberg to the east and were at Bayreuth an hour later.

Set in the heart of one of the most beautiful areas of Germany, nick-

named the Bavarian Switzerland, the small country town of Bayreuth
has only one claim to fame, its annual festival of Wagner music. In
earlier years the town had been proud to play host to almost the whole
Nazi hierarchy as they descended in the wake of Adolf Hitler, a keen fan
of the composer who immortalised the heroes of Nordic mythology.

But in January it is a quiet little town, blanketed by snow, the holly
rings only a few days since removed from the door-knockers of its neat
and well-kept houses. They found the cottage of Alfred Oster on a quiet
by-road a mile beyond the town and there was not another car on the
road as the small party went to the front door.

The former SS officer was expecting them, a big bluff man with blue
eyes and a fuzz of ginger hair spreading over the top of his cranium.
Despite the season, he had the healthy ruddy tan of men who spend their
time in the mountains among wind and sun and unpolluted air.

Motti made the introductions and handed Oster a letter from Leon.
The Bavarian read it and nodded, glancing sharply at Miller.

'Well, we can always try,' he said. 'How long can I have him?'

'We don't know yet,' said Motti. 'Obviously, until he's ready. Also, it will
be necessary to devise a new identity for him. We will let you know.'

A few minutes later he was gone.

Oster led Miller into the sitting-room and drew the curtains against the
descending dusk before he put on the light.

'So, you want to be able to pass as a former SS man, do you?' he asked.
Miller nodded.

'That's right,' he said.

Oster turned on him.

'Well, we'll start by getting a few basic facts right. I don't know where
you did your military service, but I suspect it was in that ill-disciplined,
democratic, wet-nursing shambles that calls itself the new German
Army. Here's the first fact. The new German Army would have lasted
exactly ten seconds against any crack regiment of the British, American
or Russians during the last war. Whereas the Waffen-SS, man for man,
could beat the shit out of five times their own number of Allies of the last
war.

'Here's the second fact. The Waffen-SS were the toughest, best-trained,
best-disciplined, smartest, fittest bunch of soldiers who ever went into
battle in the history of this planet. Whatever they did can't change that.
SO SMARTEN UP, MILLER. So long as you are in this house this is the procedure.

'When I walk into a room you leap to attention. And I mean LEAP.
When I walk past, you smack those heels together and remain at attention until I am five paces beyond you. When I say something to you that
needs an answer, you reply:

' "*Jawohl*, Herr Hauptsturmfuehrer."

'And when I give an order or an instruction, you reply:

' "*Zu Befehl*, Herr Hauptsturmfuehrer."

'Is that clearly understood?'

Miller nodded in amazement.

'Heels together,' roared Oster. 'I want to hear the leather smack. All right, since we may not have much time, we'll press on, starting from tonight. Before supper we'll tackle the ranks, from private up to full general. You'll learn the titles, mode of address, and collar insignia of every SS rank that ever existed. Then we'll go on to the various types of uniform used, the differing branches of the SS and their different insignia, the occasions when gala uniform, full-dress uniform, walking-out uniform, combat uniform and fatigue dress would be worn.

'After that I'll put you through the full political-ideological course that you would have undergone at Dachau SS training camp, had you been there. Then you'll learn the marching songs, the drinking songs and the various unit songs.

'I can get you as far as your departure from training camp for your first posting. After that Leon has to tell me what unit you were supposed to have joined, where you worked, under which commanding officer, what happened to you at the end of the war, how you have passed your time since 1945. However, the first part of the training will take from two to three weeks, and that's a crash course.

'By the way, don't think this is a joke. If you are once inside the Odessa, knowing who the top men are, and you make one slip in procedure, you'll end up in a canal. Believe me, I'm no milksop, and after betraying the Odessa, even I'm running scared of them. That's why I live here under a new name.'

For the first time since he had set off on his one-man hunt for Eduard Roschmann, Miller wondered if he had not already gone too far.

Mackensen reported to the Werwolf on the dot of ten. When the door to the room where Hilda worked was safely shut, the Werwolf seated the executioner in the client's chair opposite the desk and lit a cigar.

'There is a certain person, a newspaper reporter, enquiring about the whereabouts and the new identity of one of our comrades,' he began. The liquidator nodded with understanding. Several times before he had heard one of his briefings begin in the same way.

'In the normal course of events,' resumed the Werwolf, 'we would be prepared to let the matter rest, convinced either that the reporter would eventually give up for lack of progress or because the man being sought was not worth our while making an expensive and hazardous effort to save.'

'But this time it's different?' asked Mackensen softly. The Werwolf nodded, with what might have been a genuine regret.

'Yes. Through bad luck, ours on the grounds of the inconvenience involved, his on the grounds it will cost him his life, the reporter has unwittingly touched a nerve. For one thing the man he is seeking is a man of vital, absolutely vital, importance to us and to our long-term planning. For another, the reporter himself seems to be an odd character – intelligent, tenacious, ingenious, and I regret wholly committed to extracting a sort of personal vengeance from the *Kamerad*.'

'Any motive?' asked Mackensen. The Werwolf's puzzlement showed in his frown. He tapped ash from his cigar before replying.

'We cannot understand why there should be, but evidently there is,' he murmured. 'The man he is looking for undoubtedly has a background which might excite certain dislike among such as the Jews and their friends. He commanded a ghetto in Ostland. Some, mainly foreigners, refuse to acknowledge our justification for what was done there. The odd thing about this reporter is that he is neither foreign, nor Jewish, not a noted left-winger, nor one of the well-known type of conscience cowboy, who in any case seldom get beyond giving vent to a lot of piss and wind, but nothing else.

'But this man seems different. He's a young German, Aryan, son of a war hero, nothing in his background to suggest such a depth of hatred towards us, nor such an obsession with tracing one of our *Kameraden*, despite a firm and clear warning to stay off the matter. It gives me some regret to order his death. Yet he leaves me no alternative. That is what I must do.'

'Kill him?' asked Mack the Knife.

'Kill him,' confirmed the Werwolf.

'Whereabouts?'

'Not known.' The Werwolf flicked two sheets of foolscap paper covered with typed words across the desk.

'That's the man. Peter Miller, reporter and investigator. He was last seen at the Dreesen Hotel in Bad Godesberg. He's certainly gone from there by now, but it's a good enough place to start. The other place would be his own flat, where his girl-friend lives with him. You should represent yourself as a man sent by one of the major magazines for which he normally works. That way, the girl will probably talk to you, if she knows his whereabouts. He drives a noticeable car. You'll find all the details of it there.'

'I'll need money,' said Mackensen. The Werwolf had foreseen the request. He pushed a wad of 10,000 marks across the desk.

'And the orders?' asked the killer.

'Locate and liquidate,' said the Werwolf.

It was January 13th before the news of the death in Bremen five days earlier of Rolf Gunther Kolb reached Leon in Munich. The letter from his north German representative included the dead man's driving licence.

Leon checked the man's rank and number in his list of former SS men, checked the West German wanted list and saw that Kolb was not on it, spent some time gazing at the face of the driving licence, and made his decision.

He called Motti, who was on duty at the telephone exchange where he worked, and his assistant reported to him when he had finished his shift. Leon laid the driving licence of Kolb in front of him.

'That's the man we need,' he said. 'He was a staff sergeant at the age of nineteen, promoted just before the war ended. They must have been very short of material. Kolb's face and Miller's don't match, even if Miller were made up, which is a procedure I don't like anyway. It's too easy to see through at close range.

'But the height and build fit with Miller. So we'll need a new photograph. That can wait. To cover the photograph we'll need a replica of the stamp of the Bremen Police Traffic Department. See to it.'

When Motti had gone, Leon dialled a number in Bremen and gave further orders.

'All right,' said Alfred Oster to his pupil. 'Now we'll start on the songs. You heard of the Horst Wessel song?'

'Of course,' said Miller. 'It was the Nazi marching song.'

Oster hummed the first few bars.

'Oh, yes, I remember hearing it now. But I can't remember the words.'

'OK,' said Oster. 'I'll have to teach you about a dozen songs. Just in case you are asked. But this is the most important. You may even have to join in a sing-song, when you're among the *Kameraden*. Not to know it would be a death sentence. Now, after me . . .

> 'The flags are high,
> The ranks are tightly closed . . .'

It was January 18th.

Mackensen sat and sipped a cocktail in the bar of the Schweizer Hof Hotel in Munich and considered the source of his puzzlement: Miller, the reporter whose personal details and face were etched in his mind. A thorough man, Mackensen had even contacted the main Jaguar agents for West Germany and obtained from them a series of publicity photographs of the Jaguar XK 150 sports car, so he knew what he was looking for. His trouble was, he could not find it.

The trail at Bad Godesberg had quickly led to Cologne Airport and the answer that Miller had flown to London and back within thirty-six hours over the New Year. Then he and his car had vanished.

Enquiries at his flat led to a conversation with his handsome and cheerful girl-friend, but she had only been able to produce a letter postmarked Munich, saying Miller would be staying there for a while.

For a week Munich had proved a dead lead. Mackensen had checked every hotel, public and private parking space, servicing garage and petrol station. There was nothing. The man he sought had disappeared as if from the face of the earth.

Finishing his drink Mackensen eased himself off his bar stool and went to the telephone to report to the Werwolf. Although he did not know it, he stood just twelve hundred metres from the black Jaguar with the yellow stripe, parked inside the walled courtyard of the antique shop and private house where Leon lived and ran his small and fanatic organisation.

In Bremen General Hospital a man in a white coat strolled into the registrar's office. He had a stethoscope round his neck, almost the badge of office of a new intern.

'I need a look at the medical file on one of our patients, Rolf Gunther Kolb,' he told the receptionist and filing clerk.

The woman did not recognise the intern, but it meant nothing. There were scores of them working in the hospital. She ran through the names in the filing cabinet, spotted the name of Kolb on the edge of a dossier, and handed it to the intern. The phone rang and she went to answer it.

The intern sat on one of the chairs and flicked through the dossier. It revealed simply that Kolb had collapsed in the street and been brought in by ambulance. An examination had diagnosed cancer of the stomach in a virulent and terminal form. A decision had later been made not to operate. The patient had been put on a series of drugs, without any hope, and later on pain-killers. The last sheet in the file stated simply:

'Patient deceased on the night of January 8th/9th. Cause of death: carcinoma of the main intestine. No next of kin. *Corpus delicti* delivered to the municipal mortuary January 10th.'

It was signed by the doctor in charge of the case.

The new intern eased the last sheet out of the file and inserted in its place one of his own. The new sheet read:

'Despite serious condition of patient on admission, the carcinoma responded to a treatment of drugs and went into recession. Patient was adjudged fit to be transferred on January 16th. At his own request he was transferred by ambulance for convalescence at the Arcadia Clinic, Delmenhorst.'

The signature was an illegible scrawl.

The intern gave the file back to the filing clerk, thanked her with a smile and left. It was January 22nd.

Three days later Leon received a piece of information that filled in the last section of his private jigsaw puzzle. A clerk in a ticket agency in North Germany sent a message to say a certain bakery proprietor in Bremerhaven had just confirmed bookings on a winter cruise for himself and his wife. The pair would be touring the Caribbean for four weeks, leaving from Bremerhaven on Sunday, February 16th. Leon knew the man to have been a colonel of the SS during the war, and a member of Odessa after it. He ordered Motti to go out and buy a book of instructions on the art of making bread.

The Werwolf was puzzled. For nearly three weeks he had had his representatives in the major cities of Germany on the lookout for a man called Miller and a black Jaguar sports car. The flat and the garage in Hamburg had been watched, a visit had been made to a middle-aged woman in Osdorf, who had only said she did not know where her son was. Several telephone calls had been made to a girl called Sigi, purporting to come from the editor of a major picture magazine with an urgent offer of very lucrative employment for Miller, but the girl had also said she did not know where her boy-friend was.

Enquiries had been made at his bank in Hamburg, but he had not cashed any cheques since November. In short, he had disappeared. It was already January 28th, and against his wishes the Werwolf felt obliged to make a phone call. With regret, he lifted his receiver and made it.

Far away, high in the mountains, a man put down his telephone half an hour later and swore softly and violently for several minutes. It was a Friday evening and he had barely returned to his weekend manor for two days of rest when the call had come through.

He walked to the window of his elegantly appointed study and looked out. The light from the window spread out across the thick carpet of snow on the lawn, the glow reaching away towards the pine trees that covered most of the estate.

He had always wanted to live like this, in a fine house on a private estate in the mountains since, as a boy, he had seen during the Christmas school holidays the houses of the rich in the mountains around Graz. Now he had it, and he liked it.

It was better than the house of a brewery worker, where he had been brought up; better than the house in Riga where he had lived for four years; better than a furnished room in Buenos Aires, or a hotel room in Cairo. It was what he had always wanted.

The call he had taken disturbed him. He had told the caller there had been no one spotted near his house, no one hanging around his factory, no one asking questions about him. But he was worried. Miller? Who the hell was Miller? The assurances down the phone that the reporter would be taken care of only partly assuaged his anxiety. The seriousness with which the caller and his colleagues took the threat posed by Miller was indicated by the decision to send him a personal bodyguard the next day, to act as his chauffeur and stay with him until further notice.

He drew the curtains of the study, shutting out the winter landscape. The thickly padded door cut out all sounds from the rest of the house. The only sound in the room was the crackle of fresh pine logs in the hearth, the cheerful glow framed by the great cast-iron fireplace with its wrought vine-leaves and curlicues, one of the fitments he had kept when he bought and modernised the house.

The door opened and his wife put her head round.

'Dinner's ready,' she called.

'Coming, dear,' said Eduard Roschmann.

The next morning, Saturday, Oster and Miller were disturbed by the arrival of a party from Munich. The car contained Leon and Motti, the driver and another man who carried a black bag.

When they reached the sitting-room Leon said to the man with the bag, 'You'd better get up to the bathroom and set out your gear.'

The man nodded and went upstairs. The driver had remained in the car.

Leon sat at the table and bade Oster and Miller take their places. Motti remained by the door, a camera with flash attachment in his hand.

Leon passed a driving licence over to Miller. Where the photograph had been was blank.

'That's who you are going to become,' said Leon. 'Rolf Gunther Kolb, born June 18th, 1925. That would make you nineteen at the end of the war, almost twenty. And thirty-eight years old now. You were born and brought up in Bremen. You joined the Hitler Youth at the age of ten in 1935, and the SS in January 1944 at the age of eighteen. Both your parents are dead. They were killed in an air raid on Bremen docks in 1944.'

Miller stared down at the driving licence in his hand.

'What about his career in the SS?' asked Oster. 'At the moment we have reached something of a dead end.'

'How is he so far?' asked Leon. Miller might as well not have existed.

'Pretty good,' said Oster. 'I gave him a two-hour interrogation yesterday and he could pass. Until someone starts asking for specific details of his career. Then he knows nothing.'

Leon nodded for a while, examining some papers he had taken from his attaché-case.

'We don't know Kolb's career with the SS,' he said. 'It couldn't have been very much, for he's not on any wanted list and nobody has ever heard of him. In a way that's just as well, for the chances are the Odessa have never heard of him either. But the disadvantage is, he has no reason to seek refuge and help from the Odessa unless he was being pursued. So we have invented a career for him. Here it is.'

He passed the sheets over to Oster who began to read them. When he had finished he nodded.

'It's good,' he said. 'It all fits with the known facts. And it would be enough to get him arrested if he were exposed.'

Leon grunted with satisfaction.

'That's what you have to teach him. Incidentally, we have found a guarantor for him. A man in Bremerhaven, a former SS colonel, is going on a sea cruise, starting February 16th. The man is now a bakery owner. When Miller presents himself, which must be after February 16th, he will have a letter from this man assuring the Odessa that Kolb, his employee, is genuinely a former SS man and genuinely in trouble. By that time the bakery owner will be on the high seas and uncontactable. By the way,' he turned to Miller and passed a book across to him, 'you can learn bakery as well. That's what you have been since 1945, an employee in a bakery.'

He did not mention that the bakery owner would be away only for four weeks, and that after that period Miller's life would hang by a thread.

'Now my friend the barber is going to change your appearance somewhat,' Leon told Miller. 'After that we'll take a new photograph for the driving licence.'

In the upstairs bathroom the barber gave Miller one of the shortest haircuts he had ever had. The white scalp gleamed through the stubble almost up to the crown of the head by the time he had finished. The rumpled look was gone, but he also looked older. A ruler-straight parting was scraped in the short hair on the left side of his head. His eyebrows were plucked until they almost ceased to exist.

'Bare eyebrows don't make a man look older,' said the barber chattily, 'but they make the age almost unguessable within six or seven years. There's one last thing. You're to grow a moustache. Just a thin one, the same width as your mouth. It adds years, you know. Can you do that in three weeks?'

Miller knew the way the hair on his upper lip grew.

'Sure,' he said. He gazed back at his reflection. He looked in his mid-thirties. The moustache would add another four years.

When they got downstairs Miller was stood up against a white sheet, held in place by Oster and Leon, and Motti took several full-face portraits of him.

'That'll do,' he said. 'I'll have the driving licence ready within three days.'

The party left and Oster turned to Miller.

'Right, Kolb,' he said, having long ceased to refer to him in any other way, 'you were trained at Dachau SS training camp, seconded to Flossenburg concentration camp in July 1944 and in April 1945 you commanded the squad that executed Admiral Canaris, chief of the Abwehr. You also helped kill a number of the other army officers suspected by the Gestapo of complicity in the July 1944 assassination attempt on Hitler. No wonder the authorities today would like to arrest you. Admiral Canaris and his men were not Jews. There can be no overlooking that. OK, let's get down to work, Staff Sergeant.'

The weekly meeting of the Mossad had reached its end when General Amit raised his hand and said, 'There is just one last matter, though I regard it as of comparatively low importance. Leon has reported from Munich that he has for some time had under training a young German, an Aryan, who for some reason of his own has a grudge against the SS and is being prepared to infiltrate the Odessa.'

'His motive?' asked one of the men suspiciously.

General Amit shrugged.

'For reasons of his own, he wants to track down a certain former SS captain called Roschmann.'

The head of the Office for the Countries of Persecution, a former Polish Jew, jerked his head up.

'Eduard Roschmann? The Butcher of Riga?'

'That's the man.'

'Phew. If we could get him, that would be an old score settled.'

General Amit shook his head.

'I have told you before, Israel is no longer in the retribution business. My orders are absolute. Even if the man finds Roschmann, there is to be no assassination. After the Ben Gal affair it would be the last straw on Adenauer's back. The trouble now is that if any ex-Nazi dies in Germany, Israeli agents get the blame.'

'So what about this young German?' asked the Shabak chief.

'I want to try and use him to identify any more Nazi scientists who might be sent out to Cairo this year. For us that is priority number one. I propose to send an agent over to Germany, simply to put the young man under surveillance. Just a watching brief, nothing else.'

'You have such a man in mind?'

'Yes,' said General Amit. 'He's a good man, reliable. He'll just follow the German and watch him, reporting back to me personally. He can pass for a German. He's a Yekke. He came from Karlsruhe.'

"What about Leon?' asked someone else. 'Will he not try to settle accounts on his own?'

'Leon will do what he's told,' said General Amit angrily. 'There are to be no more settlings of accounts.'

In Bayreuth that morning Miller was being given another grilling by Alfred Oster.

'OK,' said Oster. 'What are the words engraved on the hilt of the SS dagger?'

'My honour is loyalty,' replied Miller.

'Right. When is the dagger presented to an SS man?'

'At his passing-out parade from training camp,' replied Miller.

'Right. Repeat to me the oath of loyalty to the person of Adolf Hitler.'

Miller repeated it, word for word.

'Repeat the blood oath of the SS.'

Miller complied.

'What is the significance of the emblem of the Death's Head?'

Miller closed his eyes and repeated what he had been taught.

'The sign of the Death's Head comes from distant Germanic mythology. It is the emblem of those groups of Teuton warriors who have sworn fealty to their leader and to each other, unto the grave and even beyond into Valhalla. Hence the skull and crossed bones, signifying the world beyond the grave.'

'Right. Were all SS men automatically members of Death's Head units?'

'No. But the oath was the same.'

Oster rose and stretched.

'Not bad,' he said. I can't think of anything else you might be asked in general terms. Now let's get on to specifics. This is what you would have to know about Flossenburg concentration camp, your first and only posting. . . .'

The man who sat in the window seat of the Olympic Airways flight from Athens to Munich seemed quiet and withdrawn.

The German business man next to him, after several attempts at conversation, took the hint and confined himself to reading *Playboy* magazine. His next-door neighbour stared out of the window as the Aegean Sea passed beneath them and the airliner left the sunny spring of the eastern Mediterranean for the snow-capped peaks of the Dolomites and the Bavarian Alps.

The business man had at least elicited one thing from his companion. The traveller in the window seat was undoubtedly a German, his grasp of the language fluent and familiar, his knowledge of the country without fault. The business man travelling home after a sales mission to the Greek capital had not the slightest doubt that he was seated next to a fellow countryman.

He could hardly have been more wrong. The man next to him had
been born in Germany thirty-three years earlier, under the name of Josef
Kaplan, son of a Jewish tailor, in Karlsruhe. Three years old when Hitler
came to power, seven when his parents had been taken away in a black
van, he had been hidden in an attic for another three years until, at the
age of ten in 1940, he too had been discovered and taken away in a van.
His early teens had been spent using the resilience and the ingenuity of
youth to survive in a series of concentration camps until in 1945, with
the suspicion of a wild animal burning in his eyes, he had snatched a
thing called a Hershey bar from the outstretched hand of a man who
spoke to him in a foreign language through his nose, and had run away
to eat the offering in a corner of the camp before it was taken away
from him.

Two years later, weighing a few pounds more, aged seventeen and
hungry as a rat, with that creature's suspicion and mistrust of everyone
and everything, he had come on a ship called the *President Warfield*,
alias the *Exodus*, to a new shore many miles from Kalrsruhe and Dachau.

The passing years had mellowed him, matured him, taught him many
things, given him a wife and two children, a commission in the Army,
but never eliminated the hatred he felt for the country to which he was
travelling that day. He had agreed to go, to swallow his feelings, to take
up again as he had done twice before in the previous ten years, the
façade of amiability and bonhomie that was necessary to effect his
transformation back into a German.

The other requirements had been provided by the Service: the passport
in his breast pocket, the letters, cards, and documentary paraphernalia of
a citizen of a West European country, the underclothes, shoes, suits and
luggage of a German commercial traveller in textiles.

As the heavy and freezing clouds of Europe engulfed the plane he
reconsidered his mission, fed into him in days and nights of briefing by
the quiet-spoken colonel on the kibbutz that produced so little fruit and
so many Israeli agents. To follow a man, to keep an eye on him, a young
German four years his junior, while that man sought to do what several
had tried and failed, to infiltrate the Odessa. To observe him and measure
his success, to note the persons he contacted and was passed on to, check
on his findings, ascertain if the German could trace the recruiter of the
new wave of German scientists headed for Egypt to work on the rockets.
Never to expose himself, never to take matters into his own hands. Then
to report back with the sum total of what the young German had found
out before he was 'blown' or discovered, one of which was bound to
happen. He would do it: he did not have to enjoy doing it, that was not
part of the requirement. Fortunately, no one required that he liked becoming a German again. No one asked him to enjoy mixing with them,
talking their language, smiling and joking with them. Had it been asked,
he would have refused 't. For he hated them all, the young reporter he
was ordered to follow .1cluded. Nothing, he was certain, would ever
change that.

The following day Oster and Miller had their last visit from Leon. Apart from Leon and Motti, there was a new man, sun-tanned and fit looking, much younger than the others. Miller adjudged the new man to be in his mid-thirties. He was introduced simply as Josef. He said nothing throughout.

'By the way,' Motti told Miller, 'I drove your car up here today. I've left it on a public parking lot down in the town, by the market square.'

He tossed Miller the keys, adding, 'Don't use it when you go to meet the Odessa. For one thing it's too noticeable, for another you're supposed to be a bakery worker on the run after being spotted and identified as a former camp guard. Such a man would not have a Jaguar. When you go, travel by rail.'

Miller nodded his agreement, but privately he regretted being separated from his beloved Jaguar.

'Right. Here is your driving licence, complete with your photograph as you now look. You can tell anyone who asks that you drive a Volkswagen, but you have left it in Bremen, as the number could identify you to the police.'

Miller scanned the driving licence. It showed himself with his short hair but no moustache. The one he now had could simply be explained as a precaution, grown since he was identified.

'The man who, unbeknown to him, is your guarantor, left from Bremerhaven on a cruise ship on the morning tide. This is the former SS colonel, now a bakery-owner, and your former employer. His name is Joachim Eberhardt. Here is a letter from him to the man you are going to see. The paper is genuine, taken from his office. The signature is a perfect forgery. The letter tells its recipient that you are a good former SS man, reliable, now fallen on misfortune after being recognised, and it asks the recipient to help you acquire a new set of papers and a new identity.'

Leon passed the letter across to Miller. He read it and put it back in its envelope.

'Now seal it,' said Leon. Miller did so.

'Who's the man I have to present myself to?' he asked.

Leon took a sheet of paper with a name and address on it.

'This is the man,' he said. 'He lives in Nuremberg. We're not certain what he was in the war, for he almost certainly has a new name. However, of one thing we are quite certain. He is very high up in the Odessa. He may have met Eberhardt, who is a big wheel in the Odessa in North Germany. So here is a photograph of Eberhardt the baker. Study it, in case your man asks for a description of him from you. Got that?'

Miller looked at Eberhardt's photograph and nodded.

'When you are ready,' he said. 'I suggest a wait of a few days until Eberhardt's ship is beyond the reach of ship-to-shore radio-telephone. We don't want the man you will see to get through a telephone call to Eberhardt while the ship is still off the German coast. Wait till it's in mid-Atlantic. I think you should probably present yourself on Thursday morning next.'

Miller nodded.

'All right. Thursday it is.'

'Two last things,' said Leon. 'Apart from trying to trace Roschmann, which is your desire, we also would like some information. We want to know who is now recruiting scientists to go to Egypt and develop Nasser's rockets for him. The recruiting is being done by the Odessa, here in Germany. We need to know specifically who the new chief recruiting officer is. Secondly, stay in touch. Use public telephones and phone this number.'

He passed a piece of paper across to Miller.

'The number will always be manned, even if I am not there. Report in whenever you get anything.'

Twenty minutes later the group was gone.

In the back seat of the car on their way back to Munich Leon and Josef sat side by side, the Israeli agent hunched in his corner and silent. As they left the twinkling lights of Bayreuth behind them Leon nudged Josef with his elbow.

'Why so gloomy?' he asked. 'Everything is going fine.'

Josef glanced at him.

'How reliable do you reckon this man Miller?' he asked.

'Reliable? He's the best chance we have ever had for penetrating the Odessa. You heard Oster. He can pass for a former SS man in any company, provided he keeps his head.'

Josef retained his doubts.

'My brief was to watch him at all times,' he grumbled. 'I ought to be sticking to him when he moves, keeping an eye on him, reporting back on the men he is introduced to and their position in the Odessa. I wish I'd never agreed to let him go off alone and check in by phone when he thinks fit. Supposing he doesn't check in?'

Leon's anger was barely controlled. It was evident they had been through this argument before.

'Now listen one more time. This man is my discovery. His infiltration into Odessa was my idea. He's my agent. I've waited years to get someone where he is now – a non-Jew. I'm not having him exposed by someone tagging along behind him.'

'He's an amateur. I'm a pro,' growled the agent.

'He's also an Aryan,' riposted Leon. 'By the time he's outlived his usefulness I hope he'll have given us the names of the top ten Odessa men in Germany. Then we go to work on them one by one. Among them one must be the recruiter of the rocket scientists. Don't worry, we'll find him, and the names of the scientists he intends to send to Cairo.'

Back in Bayreuth Miller stared out of the window at the falling snow. Privately he had no intention of checking in by phone, for he had no interest in tracing recruited rocket scientists. He still had only one objective – Eduard Roschmann.

It was actually on the evening of Wednesday, February 19th, that Peter Miller finally bade farewell to Alfred Oster in his cottage in Bayreuth and headed for Nuremberg. The former SS officer shook him by the hand on the doorstep.

'Best of luck, Kolb. I've taught you everything I know. Let me give you a last word of advice. I don't know how long your cover can hold. Probably not long. If you ever spot anyone whom you think has seen through the cover, don't argue. Get out and revert to your real name.'

As the young reporter walked down the drive, Oster muttered to himself, 'Craziest idea I ever heard,' shut the door and went back to his hearth.

Miller walked the mile to the railway station, going steadily downhill and passing the public car park. At the small station, with its Bavarian eaves and gables, he bought a single ticket to Nuremberg. It was only as he passed through the ticket barrier towards the windswept platform that the collector told him:

'I'm afraid you'll have quite a wait, sir. The Nuremberg train will be late tonight.'

Miller was surprised. German railways make a point of honour of running to time.

'What's happened?' he asked. The ticket collector nodded up the line where the track disappeared into close folds of hills and valleys heavy-hung with fresh snow.

'There's been a large snowfall down the track. Now we've just heard the snow plough's gone on the blink. The engineers are working on it.'

Years in journalism had given Miller a deep loathing of waiting rooms. He had spent too long in them, cold, tired and uncomfortable. In the small station buffet he sipped a cup of coffee and looked at his ticket. It had already been clipped. His mind went back to his car parked up the hill.

Surely, if he parked it on the other side of Nuremberg, several miles from the address he had been given . . .? If, after the interview, they sent him on somewhere else by another means of transport, he would leave the Jaguar in Munich. He could even park it in a garage, out of sight. No one would ever find it. Not before the job was done. Besides, he reasoned, it wouldn't be a bad thing to have another way of getting out fast if the occasion required. There was no reason for him to think anyone in Bavaria had ever heard of him or his car.

He thought of Motti's warning about it being too noticeable, but then he recalled Oster's tip an hour earlier about getting out in a hurry. To use it was a risk, of course, but then so was to be stranded on foot. He gave the prospect another five minutes, then left his coffee, walked out of the station and back up the hill. Within ten minutes he was behind the wheel of the Jaguar and heading out of town.

It was a short trip back to Nuremberg. When he arrived Miller checked into a small hotel near the main station, parked his car in a side street two blocks away and walked through the King's Gate into the old walled medieval city of Albrecht Dürer.

It was already dark, but the lights from the streets and windows lit up the quaint pointed roofs and decorated gables of the walled town. It was almost possible to think oneself back in the Middle Ages, when the Kings of Franconia had ruled over Nuremberg, one of the richest merchant cities of the Germanic states. It was hard to recall that almost every brick and stone of what he saw around him had been built since 1945, meticulously reconstructed from the actual architects' plans of the original town, reduced with its cobbled streets and timbered houses to ashes and rubble by the Allied bombs of 1943.

He found the house he was looking for, two streets from the square of the Main Market, almost under the twin spires of St Sebald's Church. The name on the doorplate checked with the one typed on the letter he carried, the forged introduction supposedly from former SS colonel Joachim Eberhardt of Bremen. As he had never met Eberhardt he could only hope the man in the house in Nuremberg had not met him either.

He walked back to the market square, looking for a place to have supper. After strolling past two or three traditional Franconian eating-houses he noticed the smoke curling up into the frosty night sky from the red-tiled roof of the small sausage-house in the corner of the square, in front of the doors of St Sebald's. It was a pretty little place, fronted by a terrace fringed with boxes of purple heather from which a careful owner had brushed the morning's snow.

Inside, the warmth and good cheer hit him like a wave. The wooden tables were almost all occupied, but a couple from a corner table were leaving, so he took it, bobbing and smiling back at the couple on their way out, who wished him a good appetite. He took the speciality of the house, the small, spiced Nuremberg sausages, a dozen on one plate, and treated himself to a bottle of the local wine to wash them down.

After his meal he sat back and dawdled over his coffee and chased the black liquid home with two Asbachs. He didn't feel like bed and it was pleasant to sit and gaze at the logs flickering in the open fire, to listen to the crowd in the corner roaring out a Franconian drinking song, locking arms and swinging from side to side to the music, voices and wine tumblers raised high each time they reached the end of a stanza.

For a long time he wondered why he should bother to risk his life in the quest for a man who had committed his crimes twenty years before. He almost decided to let the matter drop, to shave off his moustache, grow his hair again, go back to Hamburg and the bed warmed by Sigi. The waiter come over, bobbed a bow and deposited the bill on the table with a cheerful '*Bitte Schön*'.

He reached into his pocket for his wallet and his fingers touched a photograph. He pulled it out and gazed at it for a while. The pale, red-rimmed eyes and the rat-trap mouth stared back at him above the collar with the black tabs and the silver lightning symbols. After a while he muttered, 'You shit,' and held the corner of the photograph above the candle on his table. When the picture had been reduced to ashes he crumpled them in the copper tray. He would not need it again. He could recognise the face when he saw it.

Peter Miller paid for his meal, buttoned his coat about him and walked back to his hotel.

Mackensen was confronting an angry and baffled Werwolf about the same time.

'How the hell can he be missing?' snapped the Odessa chief. 'He can't vanish off the face of the earth, he can't disappear into thin air. His car must be one of the most distinctive in Germany, visible half a mile off. Six weeks of searching and all you can tell me is that he hasn't been seen. . . .'

Mackensen waited until the outburst of frustration had spent itself.

'Nevertheless, it's true,' he pointed out at length. 'I've had his flat in Hamburg checked out, his girl-friend and mother interviewed by supposed friends of Miller, his colleagues contacted. They all know nothing. His car must have been in a garage somewhere all this time. He must have gone to ground. Since he was traced leaving the airport car park in Cologne after returning from London and driving south, he was gone.'

'We have to find him,' repeated the Werwolf. 'He must not get near to this comrade. It would be a disaster.'

'He'll show up,' said Mackensen with conviction. 'Sooner or later he has to break cover. Then we'll have him.'

The Werwolf considered the patience and logic of the professional hunter. He nodded slowly.

'Very well. Then I want you to stay close to me. Check into a hotel here in town and we'll wait it out. If you're nearby I can get you easily.'

'Right, sir. I'll get into a hotel down town and call you to let you know. You can get me there any time.'

He bade his superior good night and left.

It was just before nine the following morning that Miller presented himself at the house and rang the brilliantly polished bell. He wanted to get the man before he left for work. The door was opened by a maid, who showed him into the sitting-room and went to fetch her employer.

The man who entered the sitting-room ten minutes later was in his mid-fifties, with medium-brown hair and silver tushes at each temple, self-possessed and elegant. The furniture and décor of his room also spelled elegance and a substantial income.

He gazed at his unexpected visitor without curiosity assessing at a glance the inexpensive trousers and jacket of a working-class man.

'And what can I do for you?' he enquired calmly.

The visitor was plainly embarrassed and ill at ease among the opulent surroundings of the sitting-room.

'Well, Herr Doktor, I was hoping you might be able to help me.'

'Come now,' said the Odessa man, 'I'm sure you know my working chambers are not far from here. Perhaps you should go there and ask my secretary for an appointment.'

'Well, it's not actually professional help I need,' said Miller. He had dropped into the vernacular of the Hamburg and Bremen area, the language of working people. He was obviously embarrassed. At a loss for words he produced a letter from his inside pocket and held it out.

'I brought a letter of introduction from the man who suggested I come to you, sir.'

The Odessa man took the letter without a word, slit it open and cast his eyes quickly down it. He stiffened slightly and gazed narrowly across the sheet of paper at Miller.

'I see, Herr Kolb. Perhaps you had better sit down.'

He gestured Miller to an upright chair, while he himself took an easy armchair. He spent several minutes looking speculatively at his guest, a frown on his face. Suddenly he snapped, 'What did you say your name was?'

'Kolb, sir.'

'First names?'

'Rolf Gunther, sir.'

'Do you have any identification on you?'

Miller looked nonplussed.

'Only my driving licence.'

'Let me see it, please.'

The lawyer, for that was his profession, stretched out a hand, forcing Miller to rise from his seat and place the driving licence in the out-stretched palm. The man took it, flicked it open and digested the details inside. He glanced over it at Miller, comparing the photograph and the face. They matched.

'What is your date of birth?' he snapped suddenly.

'My birthday? Oh . . . er . . . June 18th, sir.'

'The year, Kolb.'

'Nineteen-twenty-five, sir.'

The lawyer considered the driving licence for another few minutes.

'Wait here,' he said suddenly, got up and left.

He left the room, traversed the house and entered the rear portion of it, an area that served as his lawyer's practice and was reached by clients from a street at the back. He went straight into the office and opened the wall safe. From it he took a thick book and thumbed through it.

By chance he knew the name of Joachim Eberhardt, but had never met the man. He was not completely certain of Eberhardt's last rank in the SS. The book confirmed the letter. Joachim Eberhardt, promoted colonel of the Waffen-SS on January 10th, 1945. He flicked over several more pages and checked against Kolb. There were seven such names, but only one Rolf Gunther. Staff sergeant as from April 1945. Date of birth 18.6.25. He closed the book, replaced it and locked the safe. Then he returned through the house to the sitting-room. His guest was still sitting awkwardly on the upright chair.

He settled himself again.

'It may not be possible for me to help you, you realise that, don't you?'

Miller bit his lip and nodded.

'I've nowhere else to go, sir. I went to Herr Eberhardt for help when they started looking for me, and he gave me the letter and suggested I come to you. He said if you couldn't help me no one could.'

The lawyer leaned back in his chair and gazed at the ceiling.

'I wonder why he didn't ring me, if he wanted to talk to me,' he mused. Then evidently he waited for an answer.

'Maybe he didn't want to use the phone . . . on a matter like this,' Miller suggested hopefully.

The lawyer shot him a scornful look.

'It's possible,' he said shortly. 'You'd better tell me how you got into this mess in the first place.'

'Oh, yes, well, sir, I mean I was recognised by this man, and then they said they were coming to arrest me. So I got out, didn't I? I mean I had to.'

The lawyer sighed.

'Start at the beginning,' he said wearily. 'Who recognised you, and as what?'

Miller drew a deep breath.

'Well, sir, I was in Bremen. I live there, and I work . . . well, I worked until this happened . . . for Herr Eberhardt. In the bakery. Well I was walking in the street one day about four months back, and I came over very queer. I felt terribly ill, with stomach pains. Anyway, I must have passed out. I fainted on the pavement. So they took me away to hospital.'

'Which hospital?'

'Bremen General, sir. They did some tests, and they said I'd got cancer. In the stomach. I thought that was my lot, see?'

'It usually is one's lot,' observed the lawyer drily.

'Well, that's what I thought, sir. Only apparently it was caught at an early stage. Anyway, they put me on a course of drugs, instead of operating, and after some time the cancer went into regress.'

'So far as I can see, you're a lucky man. What's all this about being recognised?'

'Yes, well, it was this hospital orderly, see? He was Jewish, and he kept staring at me. Every time he was on duty he kept staring at me. It was a funny sort of look, see? And it got me worried. The way he kept looking at me. With a sort of "I know you" look on his face. I didn't recognise him, but I got the impression he knew me.'

'Go on.' The lawyer was showing increasing interest.

'So about a month ago they said I was fit to be transferred, and I was taken away and put in a convalescent clinic. It was the employees' insurance scheme at the bakery that paid for it. Well, before I left the Bremen General I remembered him. The Jew-boy I mean. It took me weeks, then I got it. He was an inmate at Flossenburg.'

The lawyer jack-knifed upright.

'You were at Flossenburg?'

'Yes, well I was getting round to that, wasn't I— I mean, sir. And I remembered this hospital orderly from then. I got his name in the Bremen hospital. But at Flossenburg he had been in the party of Jewish inmates that we used to burn the bodies of Admiral Canaris and the other officers that we shot for their part in the assassination attempt on the Fuehrer.'

The lawyer stared at him again.

'You were one of those who executed Canaris and the others?' he asked.

Miller shrugged.

'I commanded the execution squad,' he said simply. 'Well, they were traitors, weren't they? They tried to kill the Fuehrer.'

The lawyer smiled.

'My dear fellow, I'm not reproaching you. Of course they were traitors. Canaris had even been passing information to the Allies. They were all traitors, those army swine, from the generals down. I just never thought to meet the man who killed them.'

Miller grinned weakly.

'The point is, the present lot would like to get their hands on me for that. I mean, knocking off the Jews is one thing, but now there's a lot of them saying Canaris and that lot, saying they were sort of heroes.'

The lawyer nodded.

'Yes, certainly that would get you into bad trouble with the present authorities in Germany. Go on with your story.'

'I was transferred to this clinic and I didn't see the Jewish orderly again. Then last Friday I got a telephone call at the convalescent clinic. I thought it must be the bakery calling, but the man wouldn't give his name. He just said he was in a position to know what was going on, and that a certain person had been and informed those swine at Ludwigsburg who I was and there was a warrant being prepared for my arrest. I didn't know who the man could be, but he sounded as if he knew what he was talking about. Sort of official-sounding voice, if you know what I mean, sir?'

The lawyer nodded understandingly.

'Probably a friend on the police force of Bremen. What did you do?'

Miller looked surprised.

'Well, I got out, didn't I? I discharged myself. I didn't know what to do. I didn't go home in case they were waiting for me there. I didn't even go and pick up my Volkswagen, which was still parked in front of my digs. I slept rough Friday night, then on Saturday I had an idea. I went to see the boss, Herr Eberhardt, at his house. He was in the telephone directory. He was real nice to me. He said he was leaving with Frau Eberhardt for a winter cruise the next morning, but he'd try and see me all right. So he gave me the letter and told me to come to you.'

'What made you suspect Herr Eberhardt would help you?'

'Ah, yes, well, you see, I didn't know what he had been in the war. But he was always real nice to me at the bakery. Then about two years back we was having the staff party. We all got a bit drunk, see? And I went to the men's room. There was Herr Eberhardt washing his hands. And singing. He was singing the Horst Wessel Song. So I joined in. There we was, singing it in the men's room. Then he clapped me on the back, and said, "Not a word, Kolb," and went out. I didn't think no more about it till I got into trouble. Then I thought, "Well, he might have been in the SS like me. So I went to him for help." '

'And he sent you to me?'

Miller nodded.

'What was the name of this Jewish orderly?'

'Hartstein, sir.'

'And the convalescent clinic you were sent to?'

'The Arcadia Clinic, at Delmenhorst, just outside Bremen.'

The lawyer nodded again, made a few notes on a sheet of paper taken from a writing bureau, and rose.

'Stay here,' he said, and left.

He crossed the passage and entered his study. From telephone directory enquiries he elicited the number of the Eberhardt Bakery, the Bremen General Hospital and the Arcadia Clinic at Delmenhorst. He rang the bakery first.

Eberhardt's secretary was most helpful.

'I'm afraid Herr Eberhardt is away on holiday, sir. No, he can't be contacted, he has taken his usual winter cruise to the Caribbean with Frau Eberhardt. He'll be back in four weeks. Can I be of any assistance?'

The lawyer assured her she could not, and hung up.

Next he dialled the Bremen General, and asked for Personnel and Staff.

'This is the Department of Social Security, Pensions Section here,' he said smoothly. 'I just wanted to confirm that you have a ward orderly on the staff by the name of Hartstein.'

There was a pause while the girl at the other end went through the staff file.

'Yes, we do,' she said. 'David Hartstein.'

'Thank you,' said the lawyer in Nuremberg and hung up. He dialled the same number again and asked for the Registrar's Office.

'This is the secretary of the Eberhardt Baking Company here,' he said. 'I just wanted to check on the progress of one of our staff who has been in your hospital with a tumour in the stomach. Can you tell me of his progress? Rolf Gunther Kolb.'

There was another pause. The girl filing clerk got out the file on Rolf Gunther Kolb and glanced at the last page.

'He's been discharged,' she told the caller. 'His condition improved to a point where he could be transferred to a convalescent clinic.'

'Excellent,' said the lawyer. 'I've been away on my annual ski-ing holiday, so I haven't caught up yet. Can you tell me which clinic?'

'The Arcadia, at Delmenhorst,' said the girl.

The lawyer hung up again and dialled the Arcadia Clinic. A girl answered. After listening to the request she turned to the doctor by her side. She covered the mouthpiece.

'There's an enquiry about that man you mentioned to me, Kolb,' she said. The doctor took the telephone.

'Yes,' he said. 'This is the chief of the clinic. I am Dr Braun. Can I help you?'

At the name of Braun, the secretary shot a puzzled glance at her employer. Without batting an eyelid he listened to the voice from Nuremberg and replied smoothly, 'I'm afraid Herr Kolb discharged himself last Friday afternoon. Most irregular, but there was nothing I could do to prevent him. Yes, that's right, he was transferred here from the Bremen General. A stomach tumour, well on the mend.'

He listened for a moment, then said, 'Not at all. Glad I could be of help to you.'

The doctor, whose real name was Rosemayer, hung up and then dialled a Munich number. Without preamble he said, 'Someone's been on the phone asking about Kolb. The checking up has started.'

Back in Nuremberg the lawyer replaced the phone and returned to the sitting-room.

'Right, Kolb, you evidently are who you say you are.'

Miller goggled at him in astonishment.

'However, I'd like to ask you a few more questions. You don't mind?'

Still amazed, the visitor shook his head.

'No, sir.'

'Good. Are you circumcised?'

Miller stared back blankly.

'No, I'm not,' he said dumbly.

'Show me,' said the lawyer calmly. Miller just sat in his chair and stared at him.

'Show me, Staff Sergeant,' snapped the lawyer.

Miller shot out of his chair, ramrodding to attention.

'Zu Befehl,' he responded, quivering at attention.

He held the attention position, thumbs down the seams of his trousers, for three seconds, then unzipped his fly. The lawyer glanced at him briefly, then nodded for him to do himself up again.

'Well, at least you're not Jewish,' he said amiably.

Back in his chair Miller goggled at him, open-mouthed.

'Of course I'm not Jewish,' he blurted.

The lawyer smiled.

'Nevertheless, there have been cases of Jews trying to pass themselves off as one of the *Kameraden*. They don't last long. Now you'd better tell me your story, and I'm going to shoot questions at you. Just checking up, you understand. Where were you born?'

'Bremen, sir.'

'Right, place of birth is in your SS records. I just checked. Were you in the Hitler Youth?'

'Yes, sir. Entered at the age of ten in 1935, sir.'

'Your parents were good National Socialists?'

'Yes, sir, both of them.'

'What happened to them?'

'They were killed in the great bombing of Bremen.'

'When were you inducted into the SS?'

'Spring 1944, sir. Age eighteen.'

'Where did you train?'

'Dachau SS training camp, sir.'

'You had your blood group tattooed under your right armpit?'

'No, sir. And it would have been the left armpit.'

'Why weren't you tattooed?'

'Well, sir, we were due to pass out of training camp in August 1944 and go to our first posting in a unit of the Waffen-SS. Then in July a large group of army officers involved in the plot against the Fuehrer were sent down to Flossenburg camp. Flossenburg asked for immediate draftings from Dachau training camp to increase the staff at Flossenburg. Me and about a dozen others were singled out as cases of special aptitude and posted straight there. We missed our tattooing and the formal passing-out parade of our draft. The commandant said the blood group was not necessary, as we would never get a posting to the front, sir.'

The lawyer nodded. No doubt the commandant had also been aware in July 1944 that with the Allies well into France the war was drawing to a close.

'Did you get your dagger?'

'Yes, sir. From the hands of the commandant.'

'What are the words on it?'

' "Blood and honour", sir.'

'What kind of training did you get at Dachau?'

'Complete military training, sir, and political-ideological training to supplement that of the Hitler Youth.'

'Did you learn the songs?'

'Yes, sir.'

'What was the book of marching songs from which the Horst Wessel Song was drawn?'

'The album *Time of Struggle for the Nation*, sir.'

'Where was Dachau training camp?'

'Ten miles north of Munich, sir. Three miles from the concentration camp of the same name.'

'What was your uniform?'

'Grey-green tunic and breeches, jackboots, black collar lapels, rank on the left one, black leather belt and gunmetal buckle.'

'The motto on the buckle?'

'A swastika in the centre, ringed with the words "My honour is loyalty", sir.'

The lawyer rose and stretched. He lit up a cigar and strolled to the window.

'Now you'll tell me about Flossenburg camp, Staff Sergeant Kolb. Where was it?'

'On the border of Bavaria and Thuringia, sir.'

'When was it opened?'

'In 1934, sir. One of the first for the pigs who opposed the Fuehrer.'

'How large was it?'

'When I was there, sir, 300 metres by 300. It was ringed by nineteen watch-towers with heavy and light machine guns mounted. It had a roll-call square 120 metres by 140. God, we had some fun there with them Yids. . . .'

'Stick to the point,' snapped the lawyer. 'What was the accommodation?'

'Twenty-four barracks, a kitchen for the inmates, a washhouse, a sanatorium and various workshops.'

'And for the SS guards?'

'Two barracks, a shop and a bordello.'

'How were the bodies of those who died disposed of?'

'There was a small crematorium outside the wire. It was reached from inside the camp by an underground passage.'

'What was the main kind of work done?'

'Stone-breaking in the quarry, sir. The quarry was also outside the wire, surrounded by barbed wire and watch-towers of its own.'

'What was the population in late 1944?'

'Oh, about 16,000 inmates, sir.'

'Where was the commandant's office?'

'Outside the wire, sir, halfway up a slope overlooking the camp.'

'Who were the successive commandants?'

'Two were before I got there, sir. The first was SS-Major Karl Kunstler. His successor was SS-Captain Karl Fritsch. The last one was SS-Lieutenant-Colonel Max Koegel.'

'Which was the number of the political department?'

'Department Two, sir.'

'Where was it?'

'In the commandant's block.'

'What were its duties?'

'To ensure that requirements from Berlin that certain prisoners received special treatment were carried out.'

'Canaris and the other plotters were so indicated?'

'Yes, sir. They were all designated for special treatment.'

'When was this carried out?'

'April 20th, 1945, sir. The Americans were moving up through Bavaria, so the orders came to finish them off. A group of us was designated to do the job. I was then a newly promoted staff sergeant, although I had arrived at the camp as a private. I headed the detail for Canaris and five others. Then we had a burial party of Jews bury the bodies. Hartstein was one of them, damn his eyes. After that we burned the camp documents. Two days later we were ordered to march the prisoners northwards. On the way we heard the Fuehrer had killed himself. Well, sir, the officers left us then. The prisoners started running off into the woods. We shot a few, us sergeants, but there didn't seem much point in marching on. I mean the Yanks were all over the place.'

'One last question about the camp, Staff Sergeant. When you look up, from anywhere in the camp, what did you see?'

Miller looked puzzled.

'The sky,' he said.

'Fool, I mean what dominated the horizon?'

'Oh, you mean the hill with the ruined castle keep on it?'

The lawyer nodded and smiled.

'Fourteenth-century, actually,' he said. 'All right, Kolb, you were at Flossenburg. Now, how did you get away?'

'Well, sir, it was on the march. We all broke up. I found an army private wandering around, so I hit him on the head and took his uniform. The Yanks caught me two days later. I did two years in a prisoner-of-war camp, but just told them I was an army private. Well, you know how it was, sir, there were rumours floating about the Yanks were shooting SS men out of hand. So I said I was in the Army.'

The lawyer exhaled a draught of cigar smoke.

'You weren't alone in that. Did you change your name?'

'No, sir. I threw my papers away because they identified me as SS. But I didn't think to change my name. I didn't think anyone would look for a staff sergeant. At the time the business with Canaris didn't seem very important. It was only much later people started to make a fuss of those army officers, and made a shrine out of the place in Berlin where they hanged the ringleaders. But then I had papers from the Federal Republic in the name of Kolb. Anyway, nothing would have happened if that orderly hadn't spotted me, and after that it wouldn't have mattered what I called myself.'

'True. Right, now we'll go on to a little of the things you were taught. Start by repeating to me the oath of loyalty to the Fuehrer,' said the lawyer.

It went on for another three hours. Miller was sweating, but was able to say he had left hospital prematurely and had not eaten all day. It was past lunchtime when at last the lawyer professed himself satisfied.

'Just what do you want?' he asked Miller.

'Well, the thing is, sir, with them all looking for me, I'm going to need a set of papers showing I am not Rolf Gunther Kolb. I can change my appearance, grow my hair, let the moustache grow longer, and get a job in Bavaria or somewhere. I mean, I'm a skilled baker, and people need bread, don't they?'

For the first time in the interview the lawyer threw back his head and laughed.

'Yes, my good Kolb, people need bread. Very well. Listen. Normally people of your standing in life hardly merit a lot of expensive time and trouble being spent on them. But as you are evidently in trouble through no fault of your own, obviously a good and loyal German, I'll do what I can. There's no point in your getting simply a new driving licence. That would not enable you to get a social security card without producing a birth certificate, which you haven't got. But a new passport would get you all these things. Have you got any money?'

'No, sir. I'm flush out. I've been hitch-hiking south for the past three days.'

The lawyer gave him a hundred-mark note.

'You can't stay here, and it will take at least a week before your new passport comes through. I'll send you to a friend of mine who will acquire the passport for you. He lives in Stuttgart. You'd better check into a commercial hotel and go and see him. I'll tell him you're coming and he'll be expecting you.'

The lawyer wrote on a piece of paper.

'He's called Franz Bayer and here's his address. You'd better take the train to Stuttgart, find a hotel and go straight to him. If you need a little more money, he'll help you out. But don't go spending madly. Stay under cover and wait until Bayer can fix you a new passport. Then we'll find you a job in southern Germany, and no one will ever trace you.'

Miller took the hundred marks and the address of Bayer with embarrassed thanks.

'Oh, thank you, Herr Doktor, you're a real gent.'

The maid showed him out and he walked back towards the station, his hotel and his parked car. An hour later he was speeding towards Stuttgart, while the lawyer rang Bayer and told him to expect Rolf Gunther Kolb, refugee from the police, in the early evening.

There was no autobahn between Nuremberg and Stuttgart in those days, and on a bright sunny day the road leading across the lush plain of Franconia and into the wooded hills and valleys of Württemberg would have been picturesque. On a bitter February afternoon, with ice glittering in the dips of the road surface and mist forming in the valleys, the twisting ribbon of tarmacadam between Ansbach and Crailsheim was murderous. Twice the heavy Jaguar almost slithered into a ditch, and twice Miller had to tell himself there was no hurry. Bayer, the man who knew how to get false passports, would still be there.

He arrived after dark and found a small hotel in the outer city that nevertheless had a night porter for those who preferred to stay out late, and a garage round the back for the car. From the hall porter he got a town plan and found Bayer's street in the suburb of Ostheim, a well-set-up area not far from the Villa Berg in whose gardens the Princes of Württemberg and their ladies had once disported themselves on summer nights.

Following the map he drove the car down into the bowl of hills that frames the centre of Stuttgart, along which the vineyards come up to the outskirts of the city, and parked his car a quarter of a mile from

Bayer's house. As he stooped to lock the driver's side door he failed to notice a middle-aged lady coming home from her weekly meeting of the Hospital Visitors Committee at the nearby Villa Hospital.

It was eight that evening that the lawyer in Nuremberg thought he had better ring Bayer and make sure the refugeee Kolb had arrived safely. It was Bayer's wife who answered.

'Oh, yes, the young man, he and my husband have gone out to dinner somewhere.'

'I just rang to make sure he had arrived safe and sound,' said the lawyer smoothly.

'Such a nice young man,' burbled Frau Bayer cheerfully. 'I passed him as he was parking his car. I was just on my way home from Hospital Visitors' committee meeting. But miles away from the house. He must have lost his way. It's very easy, you know, in Stuttgart ... so many road-ups and one-way streets ...'

'Excuse me, Frau Bayer,' the lawyer cut in. 'The man had not got his Volkswagen with him. He came by train.'

'No, no,' said Frau Bayer, happy to be able to show superior knowledge. 'He came by car. Such a nice young man, and such a lovely car. I'm sure he's a success with all the girls with a ...'

'Frau Bayer, listen to me. Carefully now. What kind of a car was it?'

'Well, I don't know the make of course. But a sports car. A long black one, with a yellow stripe down the side ...'

The lawyer slammed down the phone, then raised it and dialled a number in Nuremberg. He was sweating slightly. When he got the hotel he wanted he asked for a room number. The phone extension was lifted, and a familiar voice said, 'Hallo.'

'Mackensen,' barked the Werwolf, 'get over here fast. We've found Miller.'

13

Franz Bayer was as fat and round and jolly as his wife. Alerted by the Werwolf to expect the fugitive from the police, he welcomed Miller on his doorstep when he presented himself just after eight o'clock.

Miller was introduced briefly to his wife in the hallway before she bustled off to the kitchen.

'Well now,' said Bayer, 'have you ever been in Württemberg before, my dear Kolb?'

'No, I confess I haven't.'

'Ha, well, we pride ourselves here on being a very hospitable people. No doubt you'd like some food. Have you eaten yet today?'

Miller told him he had had neither breakfast nor lunch, having been on the train all afternoon. Bayer seemed most distressed.

'Good Lord, how awful. You must eat. Tell you what, we'll pop into town and have a slap-up dinner. Nonsense, dear boy, the least I can do for you.'

He waddled off into the back of the house to tell his wife he was taking their guest out for a meal in downtown Stuttgart, and ten minutes later they were heading in Bayer's car towards the city centre.

It is at least a two-hour drive from Nuremberg to Stuttgart along the old E12 high road, even if one pushes the car hard. And Mackensen pushed his car that night. Half an hour after he received the Werwolf's call, fully briefed and armed with Bayer's address, he was on the road. He arrived at half past ten and went straight to Bayer's house.

Frau Bayer, alerted by another call from the Werwolf that the man calling himself Kolb was not what he seemed to be, and might indeed be a police informer, was a trembling and frightened woman when Mackensen arrived. His terse manner was hardly calculated to put her at her ease.

'When did they leave?'

'About a quarter past eight,' she quavered.

'Did they say where they were going?'

'No. Franz just said the young man had not eaten all day and he was taking him into town for a meal at a restaurant. I said I could make something here at home, but Franz just loves dining out. Any excuse will do . . .'

'This man Kolb. You said you saw him parking his car. Where was this?'

She described the street where the Jaguar was parked, and how to get to it from her house. Mackensen thought deeply for a moment.

'Have you any idea which restaurant your husband might have taken him to?' he asked.

She thought for a while.

'Well, his favourite eating place is the Three Moors restaurant on Friedrich Strasse,' she said. 'He usually tries there first.'

Mackensen left the house and drove the half-mile to the parked Jaguar. He examined it closely, certain that he would recognise it again whenever he saw it. He was in two minds whether to stay with it and wait for Miller's return. But the Werwolf's orders were to trace Miller and Bayer, warn the Odessa man and send him home, then take care of Miller. For that reason he had not telephoned the Three Moors. To warn Bayer now would be to alert Miller to the fact that he had been uncovered, giving him the chance to disappear again.

Mackensen glanced at his watch. It was ten to eleven. He climbed back into his Mercedes and headed for the centre of town.

In a small and obscure hotel in the back streets of Munich, Josef was lying awake on his bed when a call came from the reception desk to say a cable had arrived for him. He went downstairs and brought it back to his room.

Seated at the rickety table he slit the buff envelope and scanned the lengthy contents. It began:

'Here are the prices we are able to accept for the commodities about which the customer has enquired.

Celery:	481 marks, 53 pfennigs.
Melons:	362 marks, 17 pfennigs.
Oranges:	627 marks, 24 pfennigs.
Grapefruit:	313 marks, 88 pfennigs . . .'

The list of fruit and vegetables was long, but all the articles were those habitually exported by Israel, and the cable read like the response to an enquiry by the German-based representative of an export company for price quotations. Using the public international cable network was not secure, but so many commercial cables pass through Western Europe in a day that checking them all would need an army of men.

Ignoring the words, Josef wrote down the figures in a long line. The five-figure groups into which the marks and pfennings were divided disappeared. When he had them all in a line he split them up into groups of six figures. From each six-figure group he subtracted the date, February 20th, 1964, which he wrote as 20264. In each case the result was another six-figure group.

It was a simple book code, based on the paper-back edition of Webster's *New World Dictionary* published by the popular Library of New York. The first three figures in the group represented the page in the dictionary; the fourth figure could be anything from one to nine. An odd number meant column one, an even number column two. The last two figures indicated the number of words down the column from the top. He worked steadily for half an hour, then read the message through and slowly held his head in his hands.

Thirty minutes later he was with Leon in the latter's house. The revenge-group leader read the message and swore.

'I'm sorry,' he said at last. 'I couldn't have known.'

Unknown to either man three tiny fragments of information had come into the possession of the Mossad in the previous six days. One was from the resident Israeli agent in Buenos Aires to the effect that someone had authorised the payment of a sum equivalent to one million German marks to a figure called Vulkan 'to enable him to complete the next stage of his research project'.

The second was from a Jewish employee of a Swiss bank known habitually to handle currency transfers from secret Nazi funds elsewhere to pay off Odessa men in Western Europe; it was to the effect that one million marks had been transferred to the bank from Beirut, and collected in cash by a man operating an account at the bank for the previous ten years in the name of Fritz Wegener.

The third was from an Egyptian colonel in a senior position in the security *apparat* around Factory 333, who, for a substantial consideration in money to help him prepare a comfortable retirement, had talked with a man from the Mossad for several hours in a Rome hotel. What the man had to say was that the rocket project was lacking only the provisions of a reliable tele-guidance system, which was being researched and constructed in a factory in West Germany and that the project was costing the Odessa millions of marks.

The three fragments, among thousands of others, had been processed in the computer banks of Professor Youvel Neeman, the Israeli genius who had first harnessed science in the form of the computer to intelligence analysis, and who later went on to become the father of the Israeli atomic bomb. Where a human memory might have failed, the whirring micro-circuits had linked the three items, recalled that up to his exposure by his wife in 1955 Roschmann had used the name of Fritz Wegener, and had reported accordingly.

Josef rounded on Leon in their underground headquarters.

'I'm staying here from now on. I'm not moving out of range of that telephone. Get me a powerful motor-cycle and protective clothing. Have both ready within the hour. If and when your precious Miller checks in, I'll have to get to him fast.'

'If he's exposed, you won't get there fast enough,' said Leon. 'No wonder they warned him to stay away. They'll kill him if he gets within a mile of his man.'

As Leon left the cellar Josef ran his eye over the cable from Tel Aviv once again. It said:

RED ALERT NEW INFORMATION INDICATES VITAL KEY ROCKET SUCCESS (GERMAN INDUSTRIALIST OPERATING) YOUR TERRITORY STOP CODE NAME VULCAN STOP PROBABLY IDENTIFICATION ROSH MAN STOP USE MILLER IN-STANTLY STOP TRACE AND ELIMINATE STOP CORMORANT

Josef sat at the table and meticulously began to clean and arm his Wal-ther PPK automatic. From time to time he glanced at the silent telephone.

Over dinner Bayer had been the genial host, roaring with laughter in great gusts as he told his own favourite jokes. Miller tried several times to get the talk round to the question of a new passport for himself.

Each time Bayer clapped him soundly on the back, told him not to worry and added:

'Leave it to me, old boy, leave it to old Franz Bayer.'

He tapped the right-hand side of his nose with his forefinger, winked broadly and dissolved into gales of merriment.

One thing Miller had inherited from eight years as a reporter was the ability to drink and keep a straight head. But he was not used to the white wine, of which copious draughts were used to wash down the meal. But white wine has one advantage if one is trying to get another man drunk. It comes in buckets of ice and cold water, to keep it chilled, and three times Miller was able to tip his entire glass into the ice bucket when Bayer was looking the other way.

By the dessert course they had demolished two bottles of excellent cold hock, and Bayer, squeezed into his tight horn-buttoned jacket, was perspiring in torrents. The effect was to enhance his thirst, and he called for a third bottle of wine.

Miller feigned to be worried that it would prove impossible to obtain a new passport for him, and that he would be arrested for his part in the events at Flossenburg in 1945.

'You'll need some photographs of me, won't you?' he asked with concern.

Bayer guffawed.

'Yes, a couple of photographs. No problem. You can get them taken in one of the automatic booths at the station. Wait till your hair's a bit longer, and the moustache a bit fuller, and no one will ever know it's the same man.'

'What happens then?' asked Miller agog.

Bayer leaned over and placed a fat arm round his shoulders. Miller felt the stench of wine on his face as the fat man chuckled in his ear.

'Then I send them away to a friend of mine, and a week later back comes the passport. With the passport we get you a driving licence – you'll have to pass the test, of course – and a social security card. So far as the authorities are concerned, you've just arrived back home after fifteen years abroad. No problem, old chap, stop worrying.'

Although Bayer was getting drunk, he was still in command of his tongue. He declined to say more, and Miller was afraid to push him too far in case he suspected something was amiss with his young guest and closed up completely.

Although he was dying for a coffee, Miller declined, in case the coffee should begin to sober up Franz Bayer. The fat man paid for the meal from a well-stuffed wallet and they headed for the coat-check counter. It was half past ten.

'It's been a marvellous evening, Herr Bayer. Thank you very much.'

'Franz, Franz,' wheezed the fat man as he struggled into his coat.

'I suppose that's the end of what Stuttgart has to offer in the way of night life,' observed Miller as he slipped into his own.

'Ha, silly boy. That's all you know. We have a great little city here, you know. Half a dozen good cabarets. You fancy going on to one?'

'You mean, there are cabarets, with strip-tease and everything?' asked Miller, pop-eyed.

Bayer wheezed with mirth.

'Are you talking? I wouldn't be against the idea of watching some of the little ladies take their clothes off.'

Bayer tipped the coat-check girl handsomely and waddled outside.

'What night-clubs are there in Stuttgart?' asked Miller innocently.

'Well now, let's see. There's the Moulin Rouge, the Balzac, the Imperial and the Sayonara. Then there's the Madeleine in Eberhardt Strasse . . .'

'Eberhardt? Good Lord, what a coincidence. That was my boss in Bremen, the man who got me out of this mess and passed me on to the lawyer in Nuremberg!' exclaimed Miller.

'Good. Good. Excellent. Let's go there then,' said Bayer and led the way to his car.

Mackensen reached the Three Moors at quarter past eleven. He enquired of the head waiter, supervising the departure of the last guests.

'Herr Bayer? Yes, he was here tonight. Left about half an hour ago.'

'He had a guest with him? A tall man with short brown hair and a moustache.'

'That's right. I remember them. Sitting at the corner table over there.'

Mackensen slipped a twenty-mark note into the man's hand without difficulty.

'It's vitally important that I find him. It's an emergency. His wife, you know, a sudden collapse . . .'

The head waiter's face puckered with concern.

'Oh dear, how terrible.'

'Do you know where they went from here?'

'I confess I don't,' said the head waiter. He called to one of the junior waiters. 'Hans, you served Herr Bayer and his guest at the corner table. Did they mention if they were going on anywhere?'

'No,' said Hans. 'I didn't hear them say anything about going on anywhere.'

'You could try the hat-check girl,' suggested the head waiter. 'She might have heard them say something.'

Mackensen asked the girl. Then he asked for a copy of the tourist booklet, 'What's on in Stuttgart'. In the section for cabarets were half a dozen names. In the middle pages of the booklet was a street map of the city centre. He walked back to his car and headed for the first name on the list of cabarets.

Miller and Bayer sat at a table for two in the Madeleine nightclub. Bayer, on his second large tumbler of whisky, stared with pop eyes at a generously endowed young woman gyrating her hips in the centre of the floor while her fingers unhooked the fasteners of her brassière. When it finally came off Bayer jabbed Miller in the ribs with his elbow.

He was quivering with mirth.

'What a pair, eh, lad, what a pair?' he chuckled.

It was well after midnight and he was becoming very drunk.

'Look, Herr Bayer, I'm worried,' whispered Miller. 'I mean it's me who's on the run. How soon can you make this passport for me?'

Bayer draped his arm round Miller's shoulders.

'Look, Rolf, my old buddy, I've told you. You don't have to worry, see? Just leave it to old Franz.' He winked broadly. 'Anyway, I don't make the passports. I just send off the photographs to the chap who makes them, and a week later back they come. No problem. Now, have a drink with old pal Franz.'

He raised a pudgy hand and flapped it in the air.

'Waiter, another round.'

Miller leaned back and considered. If he had to wait until his hair grew before the passport photographs could be taken he might wait weeks. Nor was he going to get the name and address of the Odessa passport-maker from Bayer by guile. Drunk he might be, but not so drunk he would give away his contact in the forging business by a slip of the tongue.

He could not get the fat Odessa man away from the club before the end of the first floor-show. When they finally made it back to the cold night air outside it was after one in the morning. Bayer was unsteady on his feet, one arm slung round Miller's shoulders, and the sudden shock of the cold air made him worse.

'I'd better drive you home,' he told Bayer as they approached the car parked by the kerb. He took the car keys from Bayer's coat pocket and helped the fat man unprotesting into the passenger seat. Slamming the door on him, he walked round to the driver's side and climbed in. At that moment a grey Mercedes slewed round the corner behind them and jammed on its brakes to stop twenty yards up the road.

Behind the windscreen Mackensen, who had already visited five night-clubs, stared at the number plate of the car moving away from the kerb outside the Madeleine. It was the number Frau Bayer had given him. Her husband's car. Letting in the clutch, he followed it.

Miller drove carefully, fighting his own alcohol level. The last thing he wanted was to be stopped by a patrol car and tested for drunkenness. He drove, not back to Bayer's house, but to his own hotel. On the way Bayer dozed, his head nodded forward, spreading out his multiple chins into an apron of fat over his collar and tie.

Outside the hotel Miller nudged him awake.

'Come on,' he said, 'come on, Franz old mate, let's have a night-cap.'

The fat man stared about him.

'Must get home,' he mumbled. 'Wife waiting.'

'Come on, just a little drink to finish the evening. We can have a noggin in my room and talk about the old times.'

Bayer grinned drunkenly.

'Talk about the old times. Great times we had in those days, Rolf.'

Miller climbed out and came round to the passenger door to help the fat man to the pavement.

'Great times,' he said, as he helped Bayer across the pavement and through the door. 'Come and have a chat about old times.'

Down the street the Mercedes had doused its lights and merged with the grey shadows of the street.

Miller had kept his room key in his pocket. Behind his desk the night porter dozed. Bayer started to mumble.

'Ssssh,' said Miller, 'got to be quiet.'

'Got to be quiet,' repeated Bayer, tiptoeing like an elephant towards the stairs. He giggled at his own play-acting. Fortunately for Miller his room was on the first floor or Bayer would never have made it. He eased open the door, flicked on the light, and helped Bayer into the only arm-chair in the room, a hard upright affair with wooden arms.

Outside in the street Mackensen stood across from the hotel and watched the blacked-out façade. At two in the morning there were no lights burning. When Miller's light came on he noted it was on the first floor, to the right of the hotel as he faced it.

He debated whether to go straight up and hit Miller as he opened his bedroom door. Two things decided him against it. Through the glass door of the lobby he could see that the night porter, woken by the heavy tread of Bayer past his desk, was pottering around the inside of the foyer. He would undoubtedly notice a non-resident heading up the stairs at two in the morning and later give a good description to the police. The other thing that dissuaded him was Bayer's condition. He had watched the fat man being helped across the pavement, and knew he could never get him out of the hotel in a hurry after killing Miller. If the police got Bayer there would be trouble with the Werwolf. Despite appearances, Bayer was a much-wanted man under his real name, and important inside the Odessa.

One last factor persuaded Mackensen to go for a window-shot. Across from the hotel was a building halfway through construction. The frame and the floors were in place, with a rough concrete stairway leading up to the first and second floors. He could wait, Miller was not going any-where. He walked purposefully back to his car and the hunting rifle locked in the boot.

Bayer was taken completely by surprise when the blow came. His reactions, slowed by drink, gave him no chance to react in time. Miller, pretending to search for his bottle of whisky, opened the wardrobe door and took out his spare tie. The only other one he had was round his neck. He took this off too.

He had never had occasion to use the blows he and his fellow rookies had practised in the gymnasium of their army training camp ten years before, and was not entirely certain how effective they were. The vast bulk of Bayer's neck, like a pink mountain when seen from behind as the man sat in the chair muttering, 'Good old times, great old times . . .' caused him to hit as hard as he could.

It was not even a knock-out blow, for the edge of his hand was soft and inexperienced, and Bayer's neck was insulated by layers of fat. But it was enough. By the time the Odessa contact man had cleared the dizziness from his brain both his wrists were lashed tightly to the arms of the wooden chair.

'What the shit . . .?' he growled thickly, shaking his head to clear the muzziness. His own tie came off and secured his left ankle to the foot of the chair, and the telephone flex secured the right one.

He looked up owlishly at Miller as a comprehension began to dawn in his button eyes. Like all of his kind, Bayer had one nightmare that never quite left him.

'You can't get me away from here,' he said. 'You'll never get me to Tel Aviv. You can't prove anything. I never touched you people . . .'

The words were cut off as a rolled-up pair of socks was stuffed in his mouth and a woollen scarf, a present to Miller from his ever-solicitous mother, was wound round his face. From above the patterned knitting his eyes glared balefully out.

Miller drew up the other chair in the room, reversed it and sat astride, his face two feet away from that of his prisoner.

'Listen, you fat slug. For one thing I'm not an Israeli agent. For another, you're not going anywhere. You're staying right here, and you're going to talk, right here. Understand?'

For answer Ludwig Bayer stared back above the scarf. The eyes no longer twinkled with merriment. They were red-tinged, like an angry boar in a thicket.

'What I want, and what I'm going to have before this night is through, is the name and address of the man who makes the passports for the Odessa.'

He looked round, spotted the lamp-stand on the bedside table, unhooked the wall socket and brought it over.

'Now, Bayer, or whatever your name is, I'm going to take the gag off. You are going to talk. If you attempt to yell, you get this right across the head. I don't really care if I crack your head or not. Got it?'

Miller was not telling the truth. He had never killed a man before and had no desire to start now.

Slowly he eased off the scarf and pulled the rolled socks out of Bayer's mouth, keeping the lamp poised in his right hand, high over the fat man's head.

'You bastard,' hissed Bayer. 'You're a spy. You'll get nothing out of me.'

He hardly got the words out before the socks went back into his bulging cheeks. The scarf was replaced.

'No?' said Miller. 'We'll see. I'll start on your fingers and see how you like it.'

He took the little finger and ring finger of Bayer's right hand and bent them backwards until they were almost vertical. Bayer threw himself about in the chair so that it almost fell over. Miller steadied it, and eased the pressure on the fingers.

He took off the gag again.

'I can break every finger on both your hands, Bayer,' he whispered. 'After that I'll take the bulb out of the table lamp, switch it on and stuff your prick down the socket.'

Bayer closed his eyes and sweat rolled in torrents off his face.

'No, not the electrodes. No, not the electrodes. Not there,' he mumbled.

'You know what it's like, don't you?' said Miller, his mouth a few inches from Bayer's ear.

Bayer opened his eyes and moaned softly. He knew what it was like. Twenty years before he had been one of the men who had pounded the 'White Rabbit', Wing Commander Yeo-Thomas, to a maimed pulp in the cellars beneath Fresnes jail in Paris. He knew too well what it was like, but not on the receiving end.

'Talk,' hissed Miller. 'The forger, his name and address.'

Bayer slowly shook his head.

'I can't,' he whispered. 'They'll kill me.'

Miller replaced the gag. He took Bayer's little finger, closed his eyes and jerked once. The bone snapped at the knuckle. Bayer heaved in his chair and vomited into the gag.

Miller whipped it off before he could drown. The fat man's head jerked forward and the evening's highly expensive meal, accompanied by two bottles of wine and several double Scotches, poured down his chest into his lap.

'Talk,' said Miller. 'You've got seven more fingers to go.'

Bayer swallowed, eyes closed.

'Winzer,' he said.

'Who?'

'Winzer. Klaus Winzer. He makes the passports.'

'He's a professional forger?'

'He's a printer.'

'Where? Which town?'

'They'll kill me.'

'I'll kill you if you don't tell me. Which town?'

'Osnabrück,' whispered Bayer.

Miller replaced the gag across Bayer's mouth and thought. Klaus Winzer, a printer in Osnabrück. He went to his attaché case, containing the diary of Salomon Tauber and various maps, and took out a road map of Germany.

The autobahn to Osnabrück, far away to the north in Nord Rhine/Westphalia, led through Mannheim, Frankfurt, Dortmund and Münster. It was a four- to five-hour drive, depending on road conditions. It was already nearly three in the morning of February 21st.

Across the road Mackensen shivered in his niche on the second floor of the half-completed building. The light still shone in the room over the road, the first-floor front. He flicked his eyes constantly from the illuminated window to the front door. If only Bayer would come out, he thought, he could take Miller alone. Or if Miller came out he could take him farther down the street. Or if someone opened the window for a breath of fresh air. He shivered again and clasped the heavy Remington .300. At a range of thirty yards there would be no problems with such a gun. Mackensen could wait, he was a patient man.

In his room Miller quietly packed his things. He needed Bayer to remain quiescent for at least six hours. Perhaps the man would be too terrified to warn his chiefs that he had given away the secret of the forger. But he couldn't count on it.

Miller spent a last few minutes tightening the bonds and the gags that held Bayer immobile and silent, then eased the chair on to its side so the fat man could not raise attention by rolling the chair over with a crash. The telephone cord was already ripped out. He took a last look round the room and left, locking the door behind him.

He was almost at the top of the stairs when a thought came to him. The night porter might have seen them both mount the stairs. What would he think if only one came down, paid his bill and left? Miller retreated and headed towards the back of the hotel. At the end of the corridor was a window looking out on to the fire-escape. He slipped the catch and stepped out on to the escape ladder. A few seconds later he was in the rear courtyard where the garage was situated. A back entrance led to a small alley behind the hotel.

Two minutes later he was striding the three miles to where he had parked his Jaguar, half a mile from Bayer's house. The effect of the drink and the night's activities combined to make him feel desperately tired. He needed sleep badly, but realised he had to reach Winzer before the alarm was raised.

It was almost four in the morning when he climbed into the Jaguar, and half past the hour before he had made his way back to the autobahn leading north for Heilbronn and Mannheim.

Almost as soon as he had gone Bayer, by now completely sober, began to struggle to get free. He tried to lean his head forward far enough to use his teeth, through the sock and the scarf, on the knots of the ties that bound his wrists to the chair. But his fatness prevented his head getting low enough, and the sock in his mouth forced his teeth apart. Every few minutes he had to pause to take deep breaths through his nose.

He tugged and pulled at his ankle bonds, but they held. Finally, despite the pain from his broken and swelling little finger, he decided to wriggle his wrists free.

When this did not work, he spotted the table lamp lying on the floor. The bulb was still in it, but a crushed light bulb leaves enough slivers of glass to cut a single necktie.

It took him an hour to inch the overturned chair across the floor and crush the light bulb.

It may sound easy, but it isn't, to use a piece of broken glass to cut wrist-bonds. It takes hours to get through a single strand of cloth. Bayer's wrists poured sweat, damping the cloth of the neckties and making them even tighter round his fat wrists. It was seven in the morning, and light was beginning to filter over the roofs of the town, before the first strands binding his left wrist parted from the effects of being rubbed on a piece of broken glass. It was nearly eight when his left wrist came free.

By that time Miller's Jaguar was boring round the Cologne Ring to the east of the city with another hundred miles before Osnabrück. It had started to rain, an evil sleet running in curtains across the slippery autobahn, and the mesmeric effect of the windscreen wipers almost sent him to sleep.

He slowed down to a steady cruise at 80 mph rather than risk running off the road into the muddy fields on either side.

With his left hand free, Bayer took only a few minutes to rip off his gag, then lay for several minutes whooping in great gulps of air. The smell in the room was appalling, a mixture of sweat, fear, vomit and whisky. He unpicked the knots on his right wrist, wincing as the pain from the snapped finger shot up his arm, then released his feet.

His first thought was the door, but it was locked. He tried the telephone, lumbering about on feet long since devoid of feeling from the tightness of the bindings. Finally he staggered to the window, ripped back the curtains and jerked the windows inwards and open.

In his shooting niche across the road Mackensen was almost dozing, despite the cold, when he saw the curtains of Miller's room pulled back. Snapping the Remington up into the aiming position, he waited until the figure behind the net curtains jerked the windows inwards, then fired straight into the face of the figure.

The bullet hit Bayer in the base of the throat and he was dead before his reeling bulk tumbled backwards to the floor. The crash of the rifle might be put down to a car back-firing for a minute, but not longer. Within less than a minute, even at that hour of the morning, Mackensen knew someone would investigate.

Without waiting to cast a second look into the room across the road, he was out of the second floor and running down the concrete steps of the building towards the ground. He left by the back, dodging two cement mixers and a pile of gravel in the rear yard. He regained his car within sixty seconds of firing, stowed the gun in the boot and drove off.

He knew as he sat at the wheel and inserted the ignition key that all was not right. He suspected he had made a mistake. The man the Werwolf had briefed him to kill was tall and lean. The mind's eye impression of the figure at the window was of a fat man. From what he had seen the previous evening, he was sure it was Bayer he had hit.

Not that it was too serious a problem. Seeing Bayer dead on his carpet, Miller would be bound to flee as fast as his legs would carry him. Therefore he would return to his Jaguar, parked three miles away. Mackensen headed the Mercedes back to where he had last seen the Jaguar. He only began to worry badly when he saw the space between the Opel and the

Benz truck where the Jaguar had stood the previous evening in the quiet residential street.

Mackensen would not have been the chief executioner for the Odessa if he had been the sort who panics easily. He had been in too many tight spots before. He sat at the wheel of his car for several minutes before he reacted to the prospect of Miller now being hundreds of miles away.

If Miller had left Bayer alive, he reasoned, it could only be because he had got nothing from him, or he had got something. In the first case there was no harm done; he could take Miller later. There was no hurry. If Miller had got something from Bayer it could only be information. The Werwolf alone would know what kind of information Miller had been seeking, that Bayer had to give. Therefore, despite his fear of the Werwolf's rage, he would ring him.

It took him twenty minutes to find a public telephone. He always kept a pocketful of one-mark pieces for long-distance calls.

When he took the call in Nuremberg and heard the news the Werwolf went into a transport of rage, mouthing abuse down the line at his hired killer. It took several seconds before he could calm down.

'You'd better find him, you oaf, and quickly. God knows where he's gone now.'

Mackensen explained to his chief he needed to know what kind of information Bayer could have supplied to Miller before he died.

At the other end of the line the Werwolf thought for a while.

'Dear God,' he breathed, 'the forger. He's got the name of the forger.'

'What forger, Chief?' asked Mackensen.

The Werwolf pulled himself together.

'I'll get on to the man and warn him,' he said crisply. 'This is where Miller has gone.'

He dictated an address to Mackensen and added, 'You get the hell up to Osnabrück like you've never moved before. You'll find Miller at that address, or somewhere in the town. If he's not at the house, keep searching the town for the Jaguar. And this time, don't leave the Jaguar. It's the one place he always returns.'

He slammed down the phone, then picked it up again and asked for directory enquiries. When he had the number he sought he dialled a number in Osnabrück.

In Stuttgart, Mackensen was left holding a buzzing receiver. With a shrug he replaced it and went back to his car, facing the prospect of a long, wearying drive followed by another 'job'. He was almost as tired as Miller, by then twenty miles short of Osnabrück. Neither man had slept for twenty-four hours, and Mackensen had not even eaten since the previous lunch.

Chilled to the marrow from his night's vigil, longing for a piping hot coffee and a Steinhäger to chase it, he got back into the Mercedes and headed it north on the road to Westphalia.

To look at him there was nothing about Klaus Winzer to suggest he had ever been in the SS. For one thing he was well below the required height of six feet, for another he was shortsighted. At the age of forty he was plump and pale, with fuzzy blond hair and a diffident manner.

In fact he had had one of the strangest careers of any man to have worn the uniform of the SS. Born in 1924, he was the son of a certain Johann Winzer, a pork butcher of Wiesbaden, a large, boisterous man who from the early twenties onwards was a trusting follower of Adolf Hitler and the Nazi Party. From his earliest days Klaus could remember his father coming home from street battles with the Communists and Socialists.

Klaus took after his mother, and to his father's disgust grew up small, weak, shortsighted and peaceful. He hated violence, sports and belonging to the Hitler Youth. At only one thing did he excel: from his early teens he fell completely in love with the art of handwriting and the preparation of illuminated manuscripts, an activity his disgusted father regarded as an occupation for cissies.

With the coming of the Nazis, the pork butcher flourished, obtaining as a reward for his earlier services to the Party the exclusive contract to supply meat to the local SS barracks. He mightily admired the strutting SS youths, and devoutly hoped he might one day see his own son wearing the black and silver of the Schütz Staffel.

Klaus showed no such inclination, preferring to spend his time poring over his manuscripts, experimenting with coloured inks and beautiful lettering.

The war came, and in the spring of 1942 Klaus turned eighteen years old, the age of call-up. In contrast to his ham-fisted, brawling, Jew-hating father, he was small, pallid and shy. Failing even to pass the medical then required for a desk job with the Army, Klaus was sent home from the recruiting board. For his father it was the last straw.

Johann Winzer took the train to Berlin to see an old friend from his street-fighting days, who had since risen high in the ranks of the SS, in the hopes the man might intercede for his son and obtain an entry into some branch of service to the Reich. The man was as helpful as he could be, which was not much, and asked if there was anything the young Klaus could do well. Shamefacedly, his father admitted he could write illuminated manuscripts.

The man promised he would do what he could, but to be getting on with, he asked if Klaus would prepare an illuminated address on parchment, in honour of a certain SS-Major Fritz Suhren.

Back in Wiesbaden, the young Klaus did as he was asked, and at a ceremony in Berlin a week later this manuscript was presented to Suhren by his colleagues. Suhren, then the Commandant of Sachsenhausen concentration camp, was being posted to take over command of the even more notorious Ravensbrück.

Suhren was executed by the French in 1945.

At the handing-over ceremony in the RSHA headquarters in Berlin everyone admired the beautifully prepared manuscript, and not least a certain SS-Lieutenant Alfred Naujocks. This was the man who had carried out the mock attack on Gleiwitz radio station on the German-Polish border in August 1939, leaving the bodies of concentration-camp inmates in German Army uniforms as 'proof' of the Polish attack on Germany, Hitler's excuse for invading Poland the following week.

Naujocks asked who had done the manuscript, and on being told, he requested the young Klaus Winzer be brought to Berlin.

Before he knew what was happening, Klaus Winzer was inducted into the SS, without any formal training period, made to swear the oath of loyalty, another oath of secrecy, and told he would be transferred to a top-secret Reich project. The butcher of Wiesbaden, bewildered, was in seventh heaven.

The project involved was then being carried out under the auspices of the RSHA, Amt Six, Section F, in a workshop in Dellbruck Strasse, Berlin. Basically it was quite simple. The SS was trying to forge hundreds of thousands of British five-pound notes and American 100-dollar bills. The paper was being made in the Reich banknote-paper factory at Spechthausen, outside Berlin, and the job of the workshop in Dellbruck Strasse was to try to get the right watermark for British and American currency. It was for his knowledge of papers and inks that they wanted Klaus Winzer.

The idea was to flood Britain and America with phoney money, thus ruining the economies of both countries. In early 1943, when the watermark for the British fivers had been achieved, the project of making the printing plates was transferred to Block 19, Sachsenhausen concentration camp, where Jewish and non-Jewish graphologists and graphic artists worked under the direction of the SS. The job of Winzer was quality control, for the SS did not trust their prisoners not to make a deliberate error in their work.

Within two years Klaus Winzer had been taught by his charges everything they knew, and that was enough to make him a forger extraordinary. Towards the end of 1944 the project in Block 19 was also being used to prepare forged identity cards for the SS officers to use after the collapse of Germany.

In the early spring of 1945 the private little world, happy in its way when contrasted with the devastation then overtaking Germany, was brought to an end.

The whole operation, commanded by a certain SS-Captain Bernhard Krueger, was ordered to leave Sachsenhausen and transfer itself into the remote mountains of Austria and continue the good work. They motored south and set up the forgery again in the deserted brewery of Redl-Zipf in Upper Austria. A few days before the end of the war a broken-hearted Klaus Winzer stood weeping on the edge of a lake as millions of pounds and billions of dollars in his beautiful forged currency were dumped in the lake.

He went back to Wiesbaden and home. To his astonishment, having never lacked for a meal in the SS, he found the German civilians almost starving in that summer of 1945. The Americans now occupied Wiesbaden, and although they had plenty to eat, the Germans were nibbling at crusts. His father, by now a lifelong anti-Nazi, had come down in the world. Where once his shop had been stocked with hams, only a single string of sausages hung from the rows of gleaming hooks.

Klaus' mother explained to him that all food had to be bought on ration cards, issued by the Americans. In amazement Klaus looked at the ration cards, noted they were locally printed on fairly cheap paper, took a handful and retired to his room for a few days. When he emerged it was to hand over to his astonished mother sheets of American ration cards, enough to feed them all for six months.

'But they're forged,' gasped his mother.

Klaus explained patiently what by then he sincerely believed: they were not forged, just printed on a different machine. His father backed Klaus.

'Are you saying, foolish woman, that our son's ration cards are inferior to the Yankee ration cards?'

The argument was unanswerable, the more so when they sat down to a four-course meal that night.

A month later Klaus Winzer met Otto Klops, flashy, self-assured, the king of the black market of Wiesbaden, and they were in business. Winzer turned out endless quantities of ration cards, petrol coupons, zonal border passes, driving licences, US military passes, PX cards; Klops used them to buy food, petrol, truck tyres, nylon stockings, soap, cosmetics, and clothing, using a part of the booty to enable him and the Winzers to live well, selling the rest at black-market prices. Within thirty months, by the summer of 1948, Klaus Winzer was a rich man. In his bank account reposed five million Reichsmarks.

To his horrified mother he explained his simple philosophy. 'A document is not either genuine or forged, it is either efficient or inefficent. If a pass is supposed to get you past a checkpoint, and if it gets you past the checkpoint, it is a good document.'

In October 1948 came the second dirty trick played on Klaus Winzer.

The authorities reformed the currency, substituting the new Deutsch-mark for the old Reichsmark. But instead of giving one for one, they simply abolished the Reichsmark and gave everyone the flat sum of 1000 new marks. He was ruined. Once again his fortune was mere useless paper.

The populace, no longer needing the black marketeers as goods came on the open market, denounced Klops, and Winzer had to flee. Taking one of his own zonal passes, he drove to the headquarters of the British Zone at Hanover and applied for a job in the passport office of the British Military Government.

His references from the US authorities at Wiesbaden, signed by a full colonel of the USAF, were excellent; they should be, he had written them himself. The British major who interviewed him for the job put down his cup of tea and told the applicant:

'I do hope you realise the importance of people having proper docu-mentation on them at all times.'

With complete sincerity Winzer assured the major that he did indeed. Two months later came his lucky break. He was alone in a beer-hall, sipping a beer, when a man got into conversation with him. The man's name was Herbert Molders. He confided to Winzer he was being sought by the British for war crimes and needed to get out of Germany. But only the British could supply passports to Germans, and he dared not apply. Winzer murmured that it might be arranged, but would cost money.

To his amazement, Molders produced a genuine diamond necklace. He explained that he had been in a concentration camp, and one of the Jewish inmates had tried to buy his freedom with the family jewellery. Molders had taken the jewellery, ensured the Jew was in the first party to the gas chambers, and against orders had kept the booty.

A week later, armed with a photograph of Molders, Winzer prepared the passport. He did not even forge it. He did not need to.

The system at the passport office was simple. In Section One, appli-cants turned up with all their documentation and filled out a form. Then they went away, leaving their documents for study. Section Two exam-ined the birth certificates, ID cards, driving licences, etc., for possible forgery, checked the war criminals wanted list, and if the applicaton was approved passed the documents to Section Three. Section Three, on re-ceipt of the note of approval from Section Two, took a blank passport from the safe where they were stored, filled it out, stuck in the appli-cant's photograph, and gave the passport to the applicant who presented himself a week later.

Winzer got himself transferred to Section Three. Quite simply, he filled out an application form for Molders in a new name, wrote out an 'Appli-cation Approved' slip from the head of Section Two and forged that British officer's signature.

He walked through into Section Two and picked up the nineteen appli-cation forms and approval slips waiting for collection, slipped the Molders application form and approval slip among them, and took the sheaf to Major Johnstone. Johnstone checked that there were twenty approval slips, went to his safe, took out twenty blank passports and handed them to Winzer. Winzer duly filled them out, gave them the official stamp, and handed nineteen to the waiting nineteen happy applicants. The twentieth went into his pocket. Into the filing-cabinet went twenty application forms to match the twenty issued passports.

That evening he handed Molders his new passport and took the diamond necklace. He had found his new métier.

In May 1949 West Germany was founded, and the passport office was handed over to the State Government of Lower Saxony, capital city Hanover. Winzer stayed on. He did not have any more clients. He did not need them. Each week, armed with a full-face portrait of some nonentity bought from a studio photographer, Winzer carefully filled out a passport application form, attached the photograph to the form, forged an approval slip with the signature of the head of Section Two (by now a German) and went to see the head of Section Three with a sheaf of application forms and approval slips. So long as the numbers tallied, he got a bunch of blank passports in return. All but one went to the genuine applicants. The last blank passport went into his pocket. Apart from that all he needed was the official stamp. To steal it would have been suspicious. He took it for one night, and by morning had a casting of the stamp of the Passport Office of the State Government of Lower Saxony.

In sixty weeks he had sixty blank passports. He resigned his job, blushingly acknowledged the praise of his superiors for his careful, meticulous work as a clerk in their employ, left Hanover, sold the diamond necklace in Antwerp, and started a nice little printing business in Osnabrück, at a time when gold and dollars could buy anything well below market price.

He would never have got involved with the Odessa if Molders had kept his mouth shut. But once arrived in Madrid and among friends, Molders boasted of his contact who could provide genuine West German passports in a false name to anyone who asked.

In late 1950 a 'friend' came to see Winzer, who had just started work as a printer in Osnabrück. There was nothing Winzer could do but agree. From then on, whenever an Odessa man was in trouble, Winzer supplied the new passport.

The system was perfectly safe. All Winzer needed was a photograph of the man and his age. He had kept a copy of the personal details written into each of the application forms by then reposing in the archive in Hanover. He would take a blank passport, and fill in the personal details already written on one of those application forms from 1949. The name was usually a common one, the place of birth usually by then far behind the Iron Curtain where no one would check, the date of birth would almost correspond to the real age of the SS applicant, and then he would stamp it with the stamp of Lower Saxony. The recipient would sign his new passport in his own handwriting with his new name when he received it.

Renewals were easy. After five years the wanted SS man would simply apply for renewal at the state capital of any state other than Lower

Saxony. The clerk in Bavaria, for example, would check with Hanover: 'Did you issue a passport Number So-and-So in 1950 to one Walter Schumann, place of birth such and date of birth such?' In Hanover another clerk would check the records in the files and reply, 'Yes.' The Bavarian clerk, reassured by his Hanoverian colleague that the original passport was genuine, would issue a new one, stamped by Bavaria.

So long as the face on the application form in Hanover was not compared with the face in the passport presented in Munich there could be no problem. But comparison of faces never took place. Clerks rely on forms correctly filled in, correctly approved and passport numbers, not faces.

Only after 1955, more than five years from the original issuing of the Hanover passport, would immediate renewal be necessary by the holder of a Winzer passport. Once the passport was obtained, the wanted SS man could acquire a fresh driving licence, social security card, bank account, credit card, in short an entire new identity.

By the spring of 1964 Winzer had supplied forty-two passports out of his stock of sixty originals.

But the cunning little man had taken one precaution. It occurred to him that one day the Odessa might wish to dispose of his services, and of him. So he kept a record. He never knew the real names of his clients; to make out a false passport in a new name it was not necessary. The point was immaterial. He took a copy of every photograph sent to him, pasted the original in the passport he was sending back, and kept the copy. Each photograph was pasted on to a sheet of cartridge paper. Beside it was typed the new name, the address (addresses are required on German passports) and the new passport number.

These sheets were kept in a file. The file was his life insurance. There was one in his house, and a copy with a lawyer in Zürich. If he were ever threatened for his life by the Odessa, he would tell them about the file, and warn them that if anything happened to him the lawyer in Zürich would send the copy to the German authorities.

The West Germans, armed with a photograph, would soon compare it with their 'Rogues Gallery' of wanted Nazis. The passport number alone, checked quickly with each of the sixteen state capitals, would reveal the domicile of the holder. Exposure would take no more than a week. It was a fool-proof scheme to ensure Klaus Winzer stayed alive and in good health.

This then was the man who sat quietly munching his toast and jam, sipping his coffee and glancing through the front page of the *Osnabrück Zeitung* over breakfast at half past eight that Friday morning when the phone rang. The voice at the other end was first peremptory, then reassuring.

'There is no question of your being in any trouble with us at all,' the Werwolf assured him. 'It's just this damn reporter. We have a tip that he's coming to see you. It's perfectly all right. We have one of our men coming up behind him and the whole affair will be taken care of within the day. But you must get out of there within ten minutes. Now here's what I want you to do . . .'

Thirty minutes later a very flustered Klaus Winzer had a small bag packed, cast an undecided glance in the direction of the safe where the file was kept, came to the conclusion he would not need it, and explained to a startled housemaid, Barbara, that he would not be going to the printing works that morning. On the contrary, he had decided to take a brief holiday in the Austrian Alps. A breath of fresh air, nothing like it to tone up the system.

Barbara stood on the doorstep open-mouthed as Winzer's Kadett shot backwards down the drive, swung out into the residential road in front of his house, and drove off. Ten minutes after nine o'clock he had reached the clover-leaf four miles west of the town where the road climbed up to join the autobahn. As the Kadett shot up the incline to the motorway on one side a black Jaguar was coming down the other side heading into Osnabrück.

Miller found a filling-station at the Saar Platz at the western entrance to the town. He pulled up by the pumps and climbed wearily out. His muscles ached and his neck felt as if it were locked solid. The wine he had drunk the evening before gave his mouth a taste like parrot-droppings.

'Fill her up. Super,' he told the attendant. 'Have you got a pay phone?'

'In the corner,' said the boy.

On the way over Miller noticed a coffee automat and took a steaming cup into the phone booth with him. He flicked through the phone book for Osnabrück town. There were several Winzers, but only one Klaus. The name was repeated twice. Against the first entry was the word 'Printer' and a number. The second Klaus Winzer had the abbreviation 'res.' for residence against it. It was 9.20. Working hours. He rang the printing works.

The man who answered was evidently the foreman.

'I'm sorry, he's not in yet,' said the voice. 'Usually he's here at nine sharp. He'll no doubt be along directly. Call back in half an hour.'

Miller thanked him and considered dialling the house. Better not. If he was at home, Miller wanted him personally. He noted the address and left the booth.

'Where's Westerberg?' he asked the pump attendant as he paid for the petrol, noting that he had only 500 marks left of his savings. The boy nodded across to the north side of the road.

'That's it. The posh suburb. Where all the well-off blokes live.'

Miller bought a town plan as well and traced the street he wanted. It was barely ten minutes away.

The house was obviously prosperous, and the whole area spoke of well-to-do professional people living in comfortable surroundings. He left the Jaguar at the end of the drive and walked to the front door.

The maid who answered it was in her late teens and very pretty. She smiled brightly at him.

'Good morning. I've come to see Herr Winzer,' he told her.

'Oooh, he's left, sir. You just missed him by about twenty minutes.'

Miller recovered. Doubtless Winzer was on his way to the printing works and had been held up.

'Oh, what a pity. I'd hoped to catch him before he went to work,' he said.

'He hasn't gone to work, sir. Not this morning. He's gone off on holiday,' replied the girl helpfully.

Miller fought down a rising feeling of panic.

'Holiday? That's odd at this time of year. Besides,' he invented quickly, 'we had an appointment this morning. He asked me to come here specially.'

'Oh, what a shame,' said the girl evidently distressed. 'And he went off so sudden. He got this phone call in the library, then upstairs he goes. Tells me, "Barbara" – that's my name, see? – "Barbara, I'm off on holiday in Austria. Just for a week," he says. Well, I'd never heard of him planning no holiday. Tells me to ring the works and say he's not coming in for a week, then off he goes. Not like Herr Winzer at all. Such a quiet gentleman.'

Inside Miller the hope began to die.

'Did he say where he was going?' he asked.

'No. Nothing. Just said he was going to the Austrian Alps.'

'No forwarding address? No way of getting in touch with him?'

'No, that's what's so strange. I mean, what about the printing works? I just rang them before you came. Very surprised they were, with all those orders to be completed.'

Miller calculated fast. Winzer had a half-hour start on him. Driving at 80 mph he would have covered forty miles. Miller could keep up a hundred, overtaking at twenty miles an hour. That would mean two hours before he saw the tail of Winzer's car. Too long. He could be anywhere in two hours. Besides, there was no proof he was heading south to Austria.

'Then could I speak to Frau Winzer please?' he asked.

Barbara giggled and looked at him archly.

'There ain't no Frau Winzer,' she said. 'Don't you know Herr Winzer at all?'

'No, I never met him.'

'Well, he's not the marrying kind, really. I mean very nice, but not really interested in women, if you know what I mean.'

'So he lives here alone, then?'

'Well, except for me. I mean, I live in. Mind you, it's quite safe. From that point of view.' She giggled.

'I see. Thank you,' said Miller, and turned to go.

'You're welcome,' said the girl, and watched him go down the drive and climb into the Jaguar, which had already caught her attention. What with Herr Winzer being away, she wondered if she might be able to ask a nice young man home for the night before her employer got back. She watched the Jaguar drive away with a roar of exhaust, sighed for what might have been and closed the door.

Miller felt the weariness creeping over him, accentuated by the last and, so far as he was concerned, final disappointment. He surmised Bayer had wriggled free from his bonds and used the hotel telephone in Stuttgart to ring Winzer and warn him. He had got so close, fifteen minutes from his target, and almost made it. Now he felt only the need for sleep.

He drove past the medieval wall of the old city, followed the map to the Theodor Heuss Platz, parked the Jaguar in front of the station and checked into the Hohenzollern Hotel across the square.

He was lucky, they had a room available at once, so he went upstairs, undressed and lay on the bed. There was something nagging in the back of his mind, some point he had not covered, some tiny detail of enquiry he had left unasked. It was still unsolved when he fell asleep at half past ten.

Mackensen made it to the centre of Osnabrück at half past one. On the way into town he had checked the house in Westerberg, but there was no sign of a Jaguar. He wanted to ring the Werwolf before he went there in case there was more news.

By chance the post office in Osnabrück flanks one side of the Theodor Heuss Platz. A whole corner and one side of the square is taken up by the main railway station, and a third side is occupied by the Hohenzollern Hotel. As Mackensen parked by the post office, his face split in a grin. The Jaguar he sought was in front of the town's main hotel.

The Werwolf was in a better mood.

'It's all right. Panic over for the moment,' he told the killer. 'I reached the forger in time and he got out of town. I just phoned his house again. It must have been the maid who answered. She told me her employer had left barely twenty minutes before a young man with a black sports car came enquiring after him.'

'I've got some news too,' said Mackensen. 'The Jaguar is parked right here on the square in front of me. Chances are he's sleeping it off in the hotel. I can take him right here in the hotel room. I'll use the silencer.'

'Hold it, don't be in too much of a hurry,' warned the Werwolf. 'I've been thinking. For one thing he must not get inside Osnabrück town. The maid has seen him and his car. She would probably report to the police. That would bring attention on our forger, and he's the panicking kind. I can't have him involved. The maid's testimony would cast a lot of suspicion on him. First he gets a phone call, then he dashes out and vanishes, then a young man calls to see him, then the man is shot in a hotel room. It's too much.'

Mackensen's brow was furrowed.

'You're right,' he said at length. 'I'll have to take him when he leaves.'

'He'll probably stick around for a few hours checking for a lead on the forger. He won't get one. There's one other thing. Does Miller carry a document case?'

'Yes,' said Mackensen. 'He had it with him as he left the cabaret last night. And he took it with him when he went back to his hotel room.'

'So why not leave it locked in the boot of his car? Why not in his hotel room? Because it's important to him. You follow me?'

'Yes,' said Mackensen.

'The point is,' said the Werwolf, 'he has now seen me and knows my name and address. He knows of the connection with Bayer and the forger. And reporters write things down. That document case is now vital. Even if Miller dies, the case must not fall into the hands of the police.'

'I've got you. You want the case as well?'

'Either get it or destroy it,' said the voice from Nuremberg. Mackensen thought for a moment.

'The best way to do both would be for me to plant a bomb in the car. Linked to the suspension, so it will detonate when he hits a bump at high speed on the autobahn.'

'Excellent,' said the Werwolf. 'Will the case be destroyed?'

'With the bomb I have in mind the car, Miller and the case will go up in flames and be completely gutted. Moreover at high speed it looks like an accident. The petrol tank exploded, the witnesses will say. What a pity.'

'Can you do it?' asked the Werwolf.

Mackensen grinned. The killing kit in the boot of his car was an assassin's dream. It included nearly a pound of plastic explosive and two electric detonators.

'Sure,' he growled, 'no problem. But to get at the car I'll have to wait until dark.'

He stopped talking, gazed out of the window of the post office and barked down the phone, 'Call you back.'

He called back in five minutes.

'Sorry about that. I just saw Miller, attaché case in hand, climbing into his car. He drove off. I checked the hotel and he's booked in there all right. He's left his travelling luggage, so he'll be back. No panic, I'll get on with the bomb and plant it tonight.'

Miller had woken up just before one feeling refreshed and somewhat elated. In sleeping he had remembered what was troubling him. He drove back to Winzer's house. The maid was plainly pleased to see him.

'Hallo, you again?' she beamed.

'I was just passing on my way back home,' said Miller, 'and I wondered, how long have you been in service here?'

'Oooh, about ten months. Why?'

'Well, with Herr Winzer not being the marrying kind, and you being so young, who looked after him before you came?'

'Oh, I see what you mean. His housekeeper, Fräulein Wendel.'

'Where is she now?'

'Oh, in hospital, sir. Dying, I'm afraid she is. Cancer of the breast, you know. Terrible thing. That's what makes it so funny Herr Winzer dashing off like that. He goes to visit her every day. Devoted to her, he is. Not that they ever, well, you know, *did* anything, but she was with him for ever such a long time, since 1950 I think, and he thinks the world of her. Always saying to me, 'Fräulein Wendel did it this way," and so on ...'

'What hospital is she in?' asked Miller.

'I forget now. No, hold on a minute. It's on the telephone note pad. I'll get it.'

She was back in two minutes and gave him the name of the clinic, an exclusive private sanatorium just behind the outskirts of the town.

Finding his way by the map, Miller presented himself at the clinic just after three in the afternoon.

Mackensen spent the early afternoon buying the ingredients for his bomb. 'The secret of sabotage,' his instructor had once told him, 'is to keep the requirements simple. The sort of thing you can buy in any shop.'

From a hardware shop he bought a soldering iron and a small stick of solder; a roll of black insulating tape; a card of thin wire and a pair of cutters; a one-foot hacksaw blade and a tube of instant glue. In an electrician's he acquired a nine-volt transistor battery; a small bulb one inch in diameter; and two lengths of fine, single-strand, five-amp plastic-coated wire each three yards long, one coloured red and the other blue. He was a neat man, and liked to keep positive and negative terminals distinct. A stationer's supplied him with five schoolboy's rubbers of the large kind, one inch wide, two inches long and a quarter of an inch thick. In a chemist's he bought two packets of condoms, each containing three rubber sheaths, and from a high-class grocer he got a tin of fine tea. It was a 250-gramme tin, with a tight-fitting lid. As a good workman he hated the idea of his explosives getting wet, and a tea tin has a lid designed to keep out the air, let alone the moisture.

With his purchases made, he took a room in the Hohenzollern Hotel overlooking the square, so that he could keep an eye on the parking area to which he was certain Miller would return, while he worked.

Before entering the hotel he took from his boot half a pound of the plastic explosive, squashy stuff like children's plasticine, and one of the electric detonators.

Seated at the table in front of the window, keeping half an eye on the square, with a pot of strong black coffee to stave off his tiredness, he went to work.

It was a simple bomb he made. First he emptied the tea down the lavatory and kept the tin only. In the lid he jabbed a hole with the handle of the wire clippers. He took the nine-foot-length of red wire and cut a ten-inch length off it.

One end of this short length of red-coated wire he spot-soldered to the positive terminal of the battery. To the negative terminal he soldered one end of the long, blue-coloured wire. To ensure that these wires never touched each other, he drew one down each side of the battery and whipped both wires and battery together with insulating tape.

The other end of the short red wire was twirled round the contact-point on the detonator. To the same contact point was fixed one end of the other, eight-foot, piece of red wire.

He deposited the battery and its wires in the base of the square tea tin, embedded the detonator deeply into the plastic explosive, and smoothed the explosive into the tin on top of the battery until the tin was full.

A near-circuit had now been set up. A wire went from the battery to the detonator. Another went from the detonator to nowhere, its bare end in space. From the battery another wire went to nowhere, its bare end in space. But when these two exposed ends, one of the eight-foot-long red wire, the other of the blue wire, touched each other the circuit would be complete. The charge from the battery would fire the detonator, which would explode with a sharp crack. But the crack would be lost in the roar as the plastic went off, enough to demolish two or three of the hotel's bedrooms.

The remaining device was the trigger mechanism. For this he wrapped his hands in handkerchiefs and bent the hacksaw blade until it snapped in the middle, leaving him with two six-inch lengths, each one perforated at one end by the small hole that usually fixes a hacksaw blade to its frame.

He piled the five rubbers one on top of the other so that together they made a block of rubber. Using this to separate the halves of the blade, he bound them along the upper and lower side of the block of rubber, so that the six-inch lengths of steel stuck out, parallel to each other and one and a quarter inches apart. In outline they looked rather like the jaws of a crocodile. The rubber block was at one end of the lengths of steel, so four inches of the blades were separated only by air. To make sure there was a little more resistance than air to prevent their touching, Mackensen lodged the light-bulb between the open jaws, fixing it in place with a generous blob of glue. Glass does not conduct electricity.

He was almost ready. He threaded the two lengths of wire, one red and one blue, which protruded from the tin of explosive, through the hole in the lid and replaced the lid on the tin, pushing it firmly back into place. Of the two pieces of wire, he soldered the end of one to the upper hacksaw blade, the other to the lower blade. The bomb was now live.

Should the trigger ever be trodden on, or subjected to sudden pressure the bulb would shatter, the two lengths of sprung steel would close together, and the electric circuit from the battery would be complete. There was one last precaution. To prevent the exposed hacksaw blades ever touching the same piece of metal at the same time, which would also complete the circuit, he smoothed all six condoms over the trigger, one on top of the other, until the device was protected from outside detonation by six layers of thin but insulating rubber. That at least would prevent accidental detonation.

His bomb complete, he stowed it in the bottom of the wardrobe, along with the binding wire, the clippers and the rest of the sticky tape, which he would need to fix it to Miller's car. Then he ordered more coffee to stay awake, and settled down at the window to wait for Miller's return to the parking lot in the centre of the square.

He did not know where Miller had gone, nor did he care. The Werwolf had assured him there were no leads he could pick up to give him the whereabouts of the forger, and that was that. As a good technician, Mackensen was prepared to do his job and leave the rest to those in charge. He was prepared to be patient. He knew Miller would return sooner or later.

15

The doctor glanced with little favour at the visitor. Miller, who hated collars and ties and avoided wearing them whenever he could, had a white nylon polo-necked sweater and over it a black pullover with a turtle neck. Over the two pullovers he wore a black blazer. For hospital visiting, the doctor's expression clearly said, a collar and tie would be more appropriate.

'Her nephew?' he repeated with surprise. 'Strange, I had no idea Fräulein Wendel had a nephew.'

'I believe I am her sole surviving relative,' said Miller. 'Obviously I would have come far sooner, had I known of my aunt's condition, but Herr Winzer only rang me this morning to inform me, and asked me to visit her.'

'Herr Winzer is usually here himself about this hour,' observed the doctor.

'I understand he's been called away,' said Miller blandly. 'At least, that was what he told me on the phone this morning. He said he would not be back for some days, and asked me to visit in his stead.'

'Gone away? How extraordinary. How very odd.' The doctor paused for a moment, irresolute, and then added, 'Would you excuse me?'

Miller saw him go back from the entrance hall where they had been talking to a small office to one side. From the open door he heard snatches of conversation as the clinic doctor rang Winzer's house.

'He has indeed gone away? ... This morning? ... Several days? ... Oh, no thank you, Fräulein, I just wanted to confirm that he will not be visiting this afternoon.'

The doctor hung up and came back to the hall.

'Strange,' he murmured. 'Herr Winzer has been here regular as clock-work since Fräulein Wendel was brought in. Evidently a most devoted man. Well, he had better be quick if he wishes to see her again. She is very far gone, you know.'

Miller looked sad.

'So he told me on the phone,' he lied. 'Poor Auntie.'

'As her relative, of course you may spend a short time with her. But I must warn you, she is hardly coherent, so I must ask you to be as brief as you can. Come this way.'

The doctor led Miller down several passages of what had evidently once been a large private house, now converted into a clinic, and stopped at a bedroom door.

'She's in here,' he said, and showed Miller in, closing the door after him. Miller heard his footsteps retreating down the passage.

The room was in semi-darkness and until his eyes had become accustomed to the dull light from the wintry afternoon that came through the gap in the slightly parted curtains, he failed to distinguish the shrivelled form of the woman in the bed. She was raised on several pillows under her head and shoulders, but so pale was her nightdress and the face above it that she almost merged with the bedclothes. Her eyes were closed. Miller had few hopes of obtaining from her the likely bolt-hole of the vanished forger.

He whispered, 'Fräulein Wendel,' and the eyelids fluttered and opened.

She stared at him without a trace of expression in the eyes, and Miller doubted if she could even see him. She closed her eyes again and began to mutter incoherently. He leaned closer to catch the phrases coming in a monotonous jumble from the grey lips.

They meant very little. There was something about Rosenheim, which he knew to be a small village in Bavaria, perhaps the place she had been born. Something else about 'all dressed in white, so pretty, so very pretty'. Then there was another jumble of words that meant nothing.

Miller leaned closer.

'Fräulein Wendel, can you hear me?'

The dying woman was still muttering. Miller caught the words 'each carrying a prayer book and a posy, all in white, so innocent then'.

Miller frowned in thought before he understood. In delirium she was trying to recall her first Communion. Like himself, she had once been a Roman Catholic.

'Can you hear me, Fräulein Wendel?' he repeated, without any hope of getting through. She opened her eyes again and stared at him, taking in the white band around his neck, the black material over his chest and the black jacket. To his astonishment she closed her eyes again and her flat torso heaved in spasm. Miller was worried. He thought he had better call the doctor. Then two tears, one from each closed eye, rolled down the parchment cheeks. She was crying.

On the coverlet one of her hands crawled slowly towards his wrist, where he had supported himself on the bed while leaning over her. With surprising strength, or simply desperation, her hand gripped his wrist possessively. Miller was about to detach himself and go, convinced she could tell him nothing about Klaus Winzer, when she said quite distinctly: 'Bless me, Father, for I have sinned.'

For a few seconds Miller failed to understand, then a glance at his own chest-front made him realise the mistake the woman had made in the dim light. He debated for two minutes whether to leave her and go back to Hamburg or whether to risk his soul and have one last try at locating Eduard Roschmann through the forger. He leaned forward again.

'My child, I am prepared to hear your confession.'

Then she began to talk. In a tired, dull monotone, her life story came out. Once she had been a girl, born and brought up amid the fields and forests of Bavaria. Born in 1910, she remembered her father going away to the first war, and returning three years later after the Armistice of 1918, angry and bitter against the men in Berlin who had capitulated.

She remembered the political turmoil of the early twenties and the attempted *putsch* in nearby Munich when a crowd of men headed by a street-corner rabble-rouser called Adolf Hitler had tried to overthrow the government. Her father had later joined the man and his party and by the time she was twenty-three the rabble-rouser and his party had become the government of Germany. There were the summer outings of the Union of German Maidens, the secretarial job with the Gauleiter of Bavaria and the dances with the handsome, blond young men in their black uniforms.

But she had grown up ugly, tall, bony and angular, with a face like a horse and hair along her upper lip. Her mousy hair tied back in a bun, in heavy clothes and sensible shoes, she had realised in her late twenties there would be no marriage for her, as for the other girls in the village. By 1939 she had been posted, an embittered and hate-filled woman, as a wardress in a camp called Ravensbrück.

She told of the people she had beaten and clubbed, the days of power and cruelty in the camp in Brandenburg, the tears rolling quietly down her cheeks, her fingers gripping Miller's wrist lest he should depart in disgust before she had done.

'And after the war?' he asked softly.

There had been years of wandering, abandoned by the SS, hunted by the Allies, working in kitchens as a scullery-maid, washing dishes and sleeping in Salvation Army hostels. Then in 1950 she met Winzer, staying in a hotel in Osnabrück while he looked for a house to buy. She had been a waitress. He bought his house, the little neuter man, and suggested she come and keep house for him.

'Is that all?' asked Miller when she stopped.

'Yes, Father.'

'My child, you know I cannot give you absolution if you have not confessed all your sins.'

'That is all, Father.'

Miller drew a deep breath.

'And what about the forged passports? The ones he made for the SS men on the run.'

She was silent for a while, and he feared she had passed into unconsciousness.

'You know about that, Father?'

'I know about it.'

'I did not make them,' she said.

'But you knew about them, about the work Klaus Winzer did.'

'Yes.' The word was a low whisper.

'He has gone now. He has gone away,' said Miller.

'No. Not gone. Not Klaus. He would not leave me. He will come back.'

'Do you know where he has gone?'

'No, Father.'

'Are you sure? Think, my child. He has been forced to run away. Where would he go?'

The emaciated head shook slowly against the pillow.

'I don't know, Father. If they threaten him, he will use the file. He told me he would.'

Miller started. He looked down at the woman, her eyes now closed as if in sleep.

'What file, my child?'

They talked for another five minutes, then there was a soft tap on the door. Miller eased the woman's hand off his wrist and rose to go.

'Father . . .'

The voice was plaintive, pleading. He turned. She was staring at him, her eyes wide open.

'Bless me, Father.'

The tone was imploring. Miller sighed. It was a mortal sin. He hoped somebody somewhere would understand. He raised his right hand and made the sign of the cross.

In nomine Patris, et Filii, et Spiritus Sancti, Ego te absolvo a peccatis tuis.

The woman sighed deeply, closed her eyes and passed into unconsciousness.

Outside in the passage the doctor was waiting.

'I really think that is long enough,' he said.

Miller nodded.

'Yes, she is sleeping,' he said, and after a glance round the door, the doctor escorted him back to the entrance hall.

'How long do you think she has?' asked Miller.

'Very difficult to say. Two days, maybe three. Not more. I'm very sorry.'

'Yes, well, thank you for letting me see her,' said Miller. The doctor held open the front door for him. 'Oh, there is one last thing, Doctor. We are all Catholics in our family. She asked me for a priest. The Last Rites, you understand?'

'Yes, of course.'

'Will you see to it?'

'Certainly,' said the doctor. 'I didn't know. I'll see to it this afternoon. Thank you for telling me. Good-bye.'

It was late afternoon and dusk was turning into night when Miller drove back into the Theodor Heuss Platz and parked the Jaguar twenty yards from the hotel. He crossed the road and went up to his room. Two floors above, Mackensen had watched his arrival. Taking his bomb in his hand-grip he descended to the foyer, paid his bill for the coming night, explaining that he would be leaving very early in the morning, and went out to his car. He manoeuvred it into a place where he could watch the hotel entrance and the Jaguar, and settled down to another wait.

There were still too many people in the area for him to go to work on the Jaguar, and Miller might come out of the hotel any second. If he drove off before the bomb could be planted, Mackensen would take him on the open highway several miles from Osnabrück, and steal the document case. If Miller slept in the hotel, Mackensen would plant the bomb in the small hours when no one was about.

In his room Miller was racking his brains for a name. He could see the man's face, but the name still escaped him.

It had been just before Christmas 1961. He had been in the press box in the Hamburg Provincial Court, waiting for a case to start in which he was interested. He had caught the tail end of the preceding case. There was a little ferret of a man standing in the dock, and defending counsel was asking for leniency, pointing out that it was just before the Christmas period, and his client had a wife and five children.

Miller remembered glancing at the well of the court, and noting the tired, harassed face of the convicted man's wife. She had covered her face with her hands in utter despair when the judge, explaining the sentence would have been longer but for the defending counsel's plea for leniency, sentenced the man to eighteen months in jail. The prosecution had described the prisoner as one of the most skilful safe-breakers in Hamburg.

A fortnight later Miller had been in a bar not 200 yards from the Reeperbahn, having a Christmas drink with some of his underworld contacts. He was flush with money, having been paid for a big picture feature that day. There was a woman scrubbing the floor at the far end. He had recognised the worried face of the wife of the cracksman who had been sentenced two weeks earlier. In a fit of generosity which he later regretted he had pushed a 100-mark note into her apron pocket and left.

In January he had got a letter from Hamburg jail. It was hardly literate. The woman must have asked the barman for his name and told her husband. The letter had been sent to a magazine for which he sometimes worked. They had passed it on to him.

'Dear Herr Miller, my wife wrote me what you done just before Christmas. I never met you, and I don't know why you done it, but I want to thank you very much. You are a real gent. The money helped Doris and the kids have a real good time over Christmas and the New Year. If ever I can do you a good turn back, just you let me know. Yours with respects ...'

But what was the name on the bottom of that letter? Koppel. That was it. Viktor Koppel. Praying that he had not got himself back inside prison again, Miller took out his little book of contacts' names and telephone numbers, dragged the hotel telephone on to his knees, and started ringing friends in the underworld of Hamburg.

He found Koppel at half past seven. Being a Friday evening he was in a bar with a crowd of friends, and down the line Miller could hear the juke-box in the background. It was playing the Beatles' 'I Want to Hold Your Hand', which had almost driven him mad that winter, so frequently had it been played.

With a bit of prompting Koppel remembered him, and the present he had given to Doris two years earlier. Koppel had evidently had a few drinks.

'Very nice of you, that was, Herr Miller, very nice thing to do.'

'Look, you wrote me from prison saying if there was ever anything you could do for me, you'd do it. Remember?'

Koppel's voice was wary.

'Yeah, I remember.'

'Well, I need a spot of help. Not much. Can you help me out?' said Miller.

The man in Hamburg was still wary.

'I ain't got much on me, Herr Miller.'

'I don't want a loan,' said Miller. 'I want to pay you for a job. Just a small one.'

Koppel's voice was full of relief.

'Oh, I see, yes, sure. Where are you?'

Miller gave him his instructions.

'Just get down to Hamburg station and grab the first train to Osnabrück. I'll meet you on the station. One last thing, bring your working tools with you.'

'Now look, Herr Miller, I don't never work outside my patch. I don't know about Osnabrück.'

Miller dropped into the Hamburg slang.

'It's a walkover, Koppel. Empty, owner gone away, and a load of gear inside. I've cased it, and there's no problem. You can be back in Hamburg for breakfast, with a bagful of boodle and no questions asked. The man will be away for a week, you can unload the stuff before he's back, and the cops down here will think it was a local job.'

'What about my train fare?' asked Koppel.

'I'll give it you when you get here. There's a train at nine out of Hamburg. You've got an hour. So get moving.'

Koppel sighed deeply.

'All right, I'll be on the train.'

Miller hung up, asked the hotel switchboard operator to call him at eleven, and dozed off.

Outside, Mackensen continued his lonely vigil. He decided to start on the Jaguar at midnight if Miller had not emerged.

But Miller walked out of the hotel at quarter past eleven, crossed the square and entered the station. Mackensen was surprised. He climbed out of the Mercedes and went to look through the entrance hall. Miller was on the platform, standing waiting for a train.

'What's the next train from this platform?' Mackensen asked a porter.

'Eleven-thirty-three to Münster,' said the porter.

Mackensen wondered idly why Miller should want to take a train when he had a car. Still puzzled, he returned to his Mercedes and resumed his wait.

At eleven-thirty-five his problem was solved. Miller came back out of the station accompanied by a small, shabby man carrying a black leather grip. They were in deep conversation. Mackensen swore. The last thing he wanted was for Miller to drive off in the Jaguar with company. That would complicate the killing to come. To his relief the pair approached a waiting taxi, climbed in and drove off. He decided to give them twenty minutes and then start on the Jaguar, still parked twenty yards away from him.

At midnight the square was almost empty. Mackensen slipped out of his car, carrying a pencil-torch and three small tools, crossed to the Jaguar, cast a glance around, and slid underneath it.

Among the mud and snow-slush of the square his suit, he knew, would be wet and filthy within seconds. That was the least of his worries. Using the pencil-torch beneath the front end of the Jaguar he located the locking switch for the bonnet. It took him twenty minutes to ease it free. The bonnet jumped upwards an inch when the catch was released. Simple pressure from on top would re-lock it when he had finished. At least he had no need to break into the car to release the bonnet catch from inside.

He went back to the Mercedes and brought the bomb over to the sports car. A man working under the bonnet of a car attracts little or no attention. Passers-by assume he is tinkering with his own car.

Using the binding wire and the pliers, he lashed the explosive charge to the inside of the engine bay, fixing it to the wall directly in front of the driving position. It would be barely three feet from Miller's chest when it went off. The trigger mechanism, connected to the main charge by two wires eight feet long, he lowered through the engine area to the ground beneath.

Sliding back under the car he examined the front suspension by the light of his torch. He found the place he needed within five minutes, and tightly wired the rear end of the trigger to a handy bracing-bar. The open jaws of the trigger, sheathed in rubber and held apart by the glass bulb, he jammed between two of the coils of the stout spring that formed the front nearside suspension.

When it was firmly in place, unable to be shaken free by normal jolting, he came back out from under. He estimated the first time the car hit a bump or a normal pot-hole at speed the retracting suspension on the front nearside wheel would force the open jaws of the trigger together, crushing the frail glass bulb that separated them, and make contact between the two lengths of electrically charged hacksaw blade. When that happened Miller and his incriminating documents would be blown to pieces.

Finally Mackensen gathered up the slack in the wires connecting the charge and the trigger, made a neat loop of them and taped them out of the way at the side of the engine bay, so they would not trail on the ground and be rubbed through by abrasion against the road surface. This done, he closed the bonnet and snapped it shut. Returning to the back seat of the Mercedes he curled up and dozed. He had done, he reckoned, a good night's work.

Miller ordered the taxi-driver to take them to the Saar Platz, paid him and dismissed him. Koppel had had the good sense to keep his mouth shut during the ride, and it was only when the taxi was disappearing back into town that he opened it again.

'I hope you know what you're doing, Herr Miller. I mean, it's odd you being on a caper like this, you being a reporter and that.'

'Koppel, there's no need to worry. What I'm after is a bunch of documents, kept in a safe inside the house. I'll take them, you get anything else there is to hand. OK?'

'Well, seeing it's you, all right. Let's get on with it.'

'There's one last thing. The place has a living-in maid,' said Miller.

'You said it was empty,' protested Koppel. 'If she comes down, I'll scarper. I don't want no part of violence.'

'We'll wait until two in the morning. She'll be fast asleep.'

They walked the mile to Winzer's house, cast a quick look up and down the road, and darted through the gate. To avoid the gravel both men walked up the grass edge along the driveway, then crossed the lawn to hide in the rhododendron bushes facing the windows of what looked like the study.

Koppel, moving like a furtive little animal through the undergrowth, made a tour of the house, leaving Miller to watch the bag of tools. When he came back he whispered, 'The maid's still got her light on. Window at the back under the eaves.'

Not daring to smoke, they sat for an hour, shivering beneath the fat, evergreen leaves of the bushes. At one in the morning Koppel made another tour, and reported the girl's bedroom light was out.

They sat for another ninety minutes before Koppel squeezed Miller's wrist, took his bag and padded across the stretch of moonlight on the lawn towards the study windows. Somewhere down the road a dog barked, and further away a car tyre squealed as a motorist headed home.

Fortunately for them, the area beneath the study windows was in shadow, the moon not having come round the side of the house. Koppel flicked on a pencil torch and ran it round the window frame, then along the bar dividing the upper and lower sections. There was a good burglar-proof window catch but no alarm system. He opened his bag and bent over it for a second, straightening up with a roll of sticky tape, a suction pad on a stick, a diamond-tipped glass cutter like a fountain pen, and a rubber hammer.

With remarkable skill he cut a perfect circle on the surface of the glass just below the window catch. For double insurance he taped two lengths of sticky tape across the disc with the ends of each tape pressed to the uncut section of window. Between the tapes he pressed the sucker, well licked, so that a small area of glass was visible either side of it.

Using the rubber hammer, holding the stick from the sucker in his left hand, he gave the exposed area of the cut circle of window-pane a sharp tap.

At the second tap there was a crack and the disc fell inwards towards the room. They both paused and waited for reaction, but no one had

462 THE NOVELS OF FREDERICK FORSYTH

heard the sound. Still gripping the end of the sucker, to which the glass disc was attached inside the window, Koppel ripped away the two pieces of sticky tape. Glancing through the window he spotted a thick rug five feet away, and with a flick of the wrist tossed the disc of glass and the sucker inwards, so it fell soundlessly on the rug.

Reaching through the hole he unscrewed the burglar catch and eased up the lower window. He was over it as nimble as a fly and Miller followed more cautiously. The room was pitch black by contrast with the moonlight on the lawn, but Koppel seemed to be able to see perfectly well.

He hissed, 'Keep still,' to Miller, who froze, while the burglar quietly closed the window and drew the curtains across it. He drifted through the room, avoiding the furniture by instinct, and closed the door that led to the passage, and only then flicked on his pencil torch.

It swept round the room, picking out a desk, telephone, a wall of bookshelves, a deep armchair, and finally settled on a handsome fireplace with a large surround of red brick.

He materialised at Miller's side.

'This must be the study, guv. There can't be two rooms like this, with two brick fireplaces, in one house. Where's the lever that opens the brickwork?'

'I don't know,' muttered Miller back, imitating the low murmur of the burglar, who had learned the hard way that a murmur is far more difficult to detect than a whisper. 'You'll have to find it.'

'Gor blimey. It could take ages,' said Koppel.

He sat Miller in the chair, warning him to keep his string-backed driving gloves on at all times. Taking his bag, Koppel went over to the fireplace, slipped a headband round his head and fixed the pencil torch into a bracket so that it pointed forward. Inch by inch, he went over the brickwork, feeling with sensitive fingers for bumps or lugs, indentations or hollow areas. Abandoning this when he had covered it all, he started again with a palette knife probing for cracks. He found it at half past three.

The knife blade slipped into a crack between two bricks and there was a low click. A section of bricks, two feet by two feet in size, swung an inch outwards. So skilfully had the work been done that no naked eye could spot the square area among the rest of the surround.

Koppel eased the door open, hinged on the left side by silent steel hinges. The four-square-foot area of brickwork was set in a steel tray that formed a door. Behind the door the thin beam of Koppel's headlamp picked out the front of a small wall-safe.

He kept the light on, but slipped a stethoscope round his neck and fitted the ear-pieces. After five minutes spent gazing at the four-disc combination lock, he held the listening end where he judged the tumblers would be, and began to ease the first ring through its combinations.

Miller, from his seat ten feet away, gazed at the work and became increasingly nervous. Koppel by contrast was completely calm, absorbed in his work. Apart from this, he knew that both men were unlikely to cause anyone to investigate the study so long as they remained completely immobile. The entry, the moving about and the exit were the danger period.

It took him forty minutes until the last tumbler fell over. Gently he eased the safe door back and turned to Miller, the beam from his head darting over a table containing a pair of silver candlesticks and a heavy old snuff-box.

Without a word Miller rose and went to join Koppel by the safe. He reached up, took the torch from Koppel's head bracket, and used it to probe the interior. There were several bundles of bank notes which he pulled out and passed to the grateful burglar, who uttered a low whistle that carried no more than several feet.

The upper shelf in the safe contained only one object, a buff manila folder. Miller pulled it out, flicked it open and riffled through the sheets inside. There were about forty of them. Each contained a photograph and several lines of type. At the eighteenth he paused and said out loud, 'Good God.'

'Quiet,' muttered Koppel with urgency.

Miller closed the file, handed the torch back to Koppel and said, 'Close it.'

Koppel slid the door back into place and twirled the dial not merely until the door was locked but until the figures were in the same order in which he had found them. When he was done he eased the brickwork across the area and pressed it firmly home. It gave another soft click and locked into place.

He had stuffed the bank notes in his pockets, the cash proceeds of Winzer's last four passports, and it remained only to lay the candle-sticks and snuff-box gently into his black leather holdall.

Switching off his light, he led Miller by the arm to the window, slipped the curtains back to right and left, and took a good look out through the glass. The lawn was deserted and the moon had gone behind cloud. Koppel eased up the window, hopped over it, bag and all, and waited for Miller to join him. He pulled the window down and headed for the shrubbery, followed by the reporter, who had stuffed the file inside his polo-necked sweater.

They kept to the bushes until close to the gate, then emerged on to the road. Miller had an urge to run.

'Walk slowly,' said Koppel in his normal talking voice. 'Just walk and talk like we was coming home from a party.'

It was three miles back to the railway station and already it was close to five o'clock. The streets were not wholly deserted, although it was Saturday, for the German working man rises early to go about his business. They made it to the station without being stopped and questioned.

There was no train to Hamburg before seven, but Koppel said he would be glad to wait in the buffet and warm himself with a coffee and a double corn liquor.

'A very nice little tickle, Herr Miller,' he said. 'I hope you got what you wanted.'

'Oh, yes, got it all right,' said Miller.

'Well, mum's the word. Bye-bye, Herr Miller.'

The little burglar nodded and strolled towards the station buffet. Miller turned back and crossed the square to the hotel, unaware of the red-rimmed eyes that watched him from the back of a parked Mercedes.

It was too early to make the enquiries Miller needed to make, so he allowed himself three hours of sleep and asked to be woken at nine-thirty.

The phone shrilled at the exact hour, and he ordered coffee and rolls, which arrived just as he had finished a piping hot shower. Over coffee he sat and studied the file papers, recognising about half a dozen of the faces but none of the names. The names, he had to tell himself, were meaningless.

Sheet eighteen was one he came back to. The man was older, the hair longer, a sporting moustache covered the upper lip. But the ears were the same, the part of a face that is more individual to each owner than any other feature, yet which are always overlooked. The narrow nostrils were the same, the tilt of the head, the pale eyes.

The name was a common one; what fixed his attention was the address. From the postal district it had to be the centre of the city, and that would probably mean an apartment block.

Just on ten o'clock he rang the telephone directory enquiries department of the city named on the sheet of paper. He asked for the number of the block manager for the apartment block at that address. It was a gamble, and it came off. It *was* a block of flats, and an expensive one.

He rang the block manager, really a glorified front hall porter, upgraded to manager by the German adoration of titles, and explained that he had repeatedly rung one of the tenants but could get no reply, which was odd because he had specifically been asked to ring the man at that hour. Could the block manager help him? Was the phone out of order?

The man at the other end was most helpful. The Herr Direktor would probably be at the factory, or perhaps at his weekend house in the country.

What factory was that? Why, his own, of course. The radio factory. Oh, yes, of course, how stupid of me, said Miller, and rang off. The directory enquiries gave him the number of the factory. The girl who answered passed him to the boss's secretary, who told the caller the Herr Direktor was spending the weekend at his country house and would be back on Monday morning. The private house number was not to be divulged from the factory. A question of privacy. Miller thanked her and hung up.

The man who finally gave him the private number and address of the owner of the radio factory was an old contact, industrial and business affairs correspondent of a large newspaper in Hamburg. He had the man's address in his private address book.

Miller sat and stared at the face of Roschmann, the new name and the private address scribbled in his notebook. Now he remembered hearing of the man before, an industrialist from the Ruhr; he had even seen the radios in the shops. He took out his map of Germany and located the country villa on its private estate, or at least the area of villages where it was situated.

It was past twelve o'clock when he packed his bags, descended to the hall and settled his bill. He was famished, so he went into the hotel dining-room, taking only his document case, and treated himself to a large steak.

Over his meal he decided to drive the last section of the chase that afternoon and confront his target the next morning. He still had the slip of paper with the private telephone number of the lawyer with the Z-Commission in Ludwigsburg. He could have rung him then, but he wanted, was determined, to face Roschmann first. He feared if he tried that evening the lawyer might not be at home when he called him to ask for a squad of policemen within thirty minutes. Sunday morning would be fine, just fine.

It was nearly two when he finally emerged, stowed his suitcase in the boot of the Jaguar, tossed the document case on to the passenger seat and climbed behind the wheel.

He failed to notice the Mercedes that tailed him to the edge of Osna-brück. The car behind him came on to the main autobahn after him, paused for a few seconds as the Jaguar accelerated fast down the south-bound lane, then left the main road twenty yards farther on and drove back into town.

From a telephone booth by the roadside Mackensen phoned the Wer-wolf in Nuremberg.

'He's on his way,' he told his superior. 'I just left him going down the south-bound lane like a bat out of hell.'

'Is your device accompanying him?'

Mackensen grinned.

'Too right. Fixed to the front nearside suspension. Within fifty miles he'll be in pieces you couldn't identify.'

'Excellent,' purred the man in Nuremberg. 'You must be tired, my dear *Kamerad*. Go back into town and get some sleep.'

Mackensen needed no second bidding. He had not slept a full night since Wednesday.

Miller made those fifty miles, and another hundred. For Mackensen had overlooked one thing. His trigger device would certainly have de-tonated quickly if it had been jammed into the cushion suspension system of a continental saloon car. But the Jaguar was a British sports car, with a far harder suspension system. As it tore down the autobahn towards Frankfurt the bumping caused the heavy springs above the front wheels to retract slightly, crushing the small bulb between the jaws of the bomb-trigger to fragments of glass. But the electrically charged lengths of steel failed to touch each other. In the hard bumps they flick-ered to within a millimetre of each other before springing apart.

Unaware of how close to death he was, Miller made the trip past Mün-ster, Dortmund, Wetzlar and Bad Homburg to Frankfurt in just under three hours, then turned off the ring road towards Königstein and the wild, snow-thick forests of the Taunus mountains.

It was already dark when the Jaguar slid into the small spa town in the eastern foothills of the mountain range. A glance at his map told Miller he was less than twenty miles from the private estate he sought. He decided to go no farther that night, but to seek a hotel and wait till morning.

To the north lay the mountains, straddled by the road to Limburg, lying quiet and white under the thick carpet of snow that muffled the rocks and shrouded the miles and miles of pine forest. There were lights twinkling down the main street of the small town and the glow of them picked out the skeletal frame of the ruined castle brooding on its hill, once the fortress home of the Lords of Falkenstein. The sky was clear, but an icy wind gave promise of more snow to come during the night.

At the corner of Haupt Strasse and Frankfurt Strasse he found a hotel, the Park, and asked for a room. In a spa town in February the cold-water cure has hardly the same charm as in the summer months. There was plenty of room.

The porter directed him to put his car in the small lot at the back of the hotel, fringed by trees and bushes. He had a bath and went out for supper, picking the Grüne Baum hostelry in the Haupt Strasse, one of the dozen old, beamed eating-houses the town had to offer.

It was over his meal that the nervousness set in. He noticed his hands were shaking as he raised his wineglass. Part of the condition was exhaustion, the lack of sleep in the past four days, the cat-napping for one and two hours at a time.

Part was delayed reaction from the tension of the break-in with Koppel, and part the sense of astonishment at the luck that had rewarded his instinct to go back to Winzer's house after the first visit and ask the maid who had looked after the bachelor forger all these years.

But most, he knew, was the sense of the impending end of the chase, the confrontation with the man he hated and had sought through so many unknown byways of enquiry, coupled with the fear that something might still go wrong.

He thought back to the anonymous doctor in the hotel in Bad Godes-berg who had warned him to stay away from the men of the Comrade-ship; and the Jewish Nazi-hunter of Vienna who had told him, 'Be careful; these men can be dangerous.' Thinking back, he wondered why they had not struck at him yet. They knew his name as Miller, the Dreesen Hotel visit proved that; and as Kolb, the beating of Bayer in Stuttgart would have blown that cover. Yet he had seen no one. One thing they could not know, he was sure, was that he had got as far as he had. Perhaps they had lost him, or decided to leave him alone, convinced, with the forger in hiding, he would end up by going in circles.

And yet he had the file, Winzer's secret and explosive evidence, and with it the greatest news story of the decade in West Germany. He grinned to himself, and the passing waitress thought it was for her. She swung her bottom as she passed his table next time, and he thought of Sigi. He had not called her since Vienna, and the letter he wrote in early January was the last she had had, six weeks back. He felt now he needed her like he never had before.

Funny, he thought, how men always need women more when they are frightened. He had to admit he *was* frightened, partly of what he had done, partly of the mass-murderer who waited unknowingly for him in the mountains.

He shook his head to shake off the mood, and ordered another half-bottle of wine. This was no time for melancholy. He had pulled off the greatest journalistic coup he had ever heard of, and was about to settle a score as well.

He ran over his plan as he drank the second portion of wine. A simple confrontation, a telephone call to the lawyer at Ludwigsburg, the arrival thirty minutes later of a police van to take the man away for impris-onment, trial, and a life sentence. If he had been a harder man, he would have wanted to kill the SS-captain himself.

He thought it over, and realised he was unarmed. Supposing Rosch-mann had a bodyguard? Would he really be alone, confident his new name would protect him from discovery? Or would there be a strong-arm retainer in case of trouble?

During his military service one of Miller's friends, spending a night in the guardroom for being late back into camp, had stolen a pair of handcuffs from the military police. Later he had become worried by the thought they might be found in his kit-bag, and had given them to Miller. The reporter had kept them, simply as a trophy of a wild night in the Army. They were at the bottom of a trunk in his Hamburg flat.

He also had a gun, a small Sauer automatic, bought quite legally when he had been covering an exposé of Hamburg's vice rackets in 1960, and had been threatened by Little Pauli's mobsters. That was locked in a desk drawer, also in Hamburg.

Feeling slightly dizzy from the effects of his wine, a double brandy and tiredness, he rose, paid his bill, and went back to the hotel. He was just about to enter to make his phone call when he saw two public booths almost at the hotel door. Safer to use these.

It was nearly ten o'clock, and he found Sigi at the club where she worked. Above the clamour of the band in the background he had to shout to make her hear him.

Miller cut short her stream of questions about where he had been, why he had not got in touch, where he was now, and told her what he wanted. She protested she couldn't get away, but something in his voice stopped her.

'Are you all right?' she shouted down the line.

'Yes. I'm fine. But I need your help. Please, darling, don't let me down. Not now, not tonight.'

There was a pause, then she said simply, 'I'll come. I'll tell them it's an emergency. Close family or something.'

'Do you have enough to hire a car?'

'I think so. I can borrow something off one of the girls.'

He told her the address of an all-night car-hire firm he had used before, and stressed she should mention his name as he knew the proprietor.

'How far is it?' she asked.

'From Hamburg, 500 kilometres. You can make it in five hours. Say six hours from now. You'll arrive about five in the morning. And don't forget to bring the things.'

'All right, you can expect me then.' There was a pause, then, 'Peter darling . . .'

'What?'

'Are you frightened of something?'

The pips started going and he had no more one-mark pieces.

'Yes,' he said, and put down the receiver as they were cut off.

In the foyer of the hotel he asked the night porter if he could have a large envelope, and after some hunting beneath the counter the man obligingly produced a stiff brown one large enough to take a quarto-sized sheet of paper. Miller also bought enough stamps to cover the cost of sending the envelope by first-class mail with a lot of contents, emptying the porter's stock of stamps, usually only needed when a guest wishes to send a postcard.

Back in his room he took his document case, which he had carried throughout the evening, laid it on the bed and took out Salomon Tauber's diary, the sheaf of papers from Winzer's safe, and two photographs. He read again the two pages in the diary that had originally sent him on this hunt for a man he had never heard of, and studied the two photographs side by side.

Finally he took a sheet of plain paper from his case and wrote on it a brief but clear message, explaining to any reader what the sheaf of documents enclosed really were. The note, along with the file from Winzer's safe and one of the photographs, he placed inside the envelope, addressed it and stuck on all the stamps he had bought.

The other photograph he put into the breast pocket of his jacket. The sealed envelope and the diary went back into his attaché case, which he slid under the bed.

He carried a small flask of brandy in his suitcase, and he poured a measure into the tooth-glass above the wash basin. He noticed his hands were trembling, but the fiery liquid relaxed him. He lay down on the bed, his head spinning slightly, and dozed off.

In the underground room in Munich, Josef paced the floor, angry and impatient. At the table Leon and Motti gazed at their hands. It was forty-eight hours since the cable had come from Tel Aviv.

Their own attempts to trace Miller had brought no result. At their request by telephone, Alfred Oster had been to the car park in Bayreuth and later called back to tell them the car was gone.

'If they spot that car, they'll know he can't be a bakery worker from Bremen,' growled Josef when he heard the news, 'even if they don't know the car owner is Peter Miller.'

Later a friend in Stuttgart had informed Leon the local police were looking for a young man in connection with the murder in a hotel room of a citizen called Bayer. The description fitted Miller in his disguise as Kolb too well for it to be any other man, but fortunately the name from the hotel register was neither Kolb nor Miller, and there was no mention of a black sports car.

'At least he had the sense to register in a false name,' said Leon.

'That would be in character with Kolb,' Mottie pointed out. 'Kolb was supposed to be on the run from the Bremen police for war crimes.'

But it was scant comfort. If the Stuttgart police could not find Miller, neither could the Leon group, and the latter could only fear the Odessa would by now be closer than either.

'He must have known after killing Bayer that he had blown his cover, and therefore reverted to the name of Miller,' reasoned Leon. 'So he has to abandon the search for Roschmann, unless he got something out of Bayer that took him to Roschmann.'

'Then why the hell doesn't he check in,' snapped Josef. 'Does the fool think he can take Roschmann on his own?'

Motti coughed quietly.

'He doesn't know Roschmann has any real importance to the Odessa,' he pointed out.

'Well, if he gets close enough, he'll find out,' said Leon.

'And by then he'll be a dead man, and we'll all be back to square one,' snapped Josef. 'Why doesn't the idiot ring in?'

But the phone lines were busy elsewhere that night, for Klaus Winzer had rung the Werwolf from a small mountain chalet in the Regensburg region. The news he got was reassuring.

'Yes, I think it's safer for you to return home,' the Odessa chief had answered in reply to the forger's question. 'The man who was trying to interview you has by now certainly been taken care of.'

The forger had thanked him, settled his overnight bill and set off through the darkness for the north and the familiar comfort of his large bed at home in Westerberg, Osnabrück. He expected to arrive in time for a hearty breakfast, a bath and a long sleep. By Monday morning he would be back in his printing works supervising the handling of the business.

Miller was awoken by a knock at the bedroom door. He blinked, realising the light was still on, and opened. The night porter stood there, Sigi behind him.

Miller quieted his fears by explaining the lady was his wife who had brought him some important papers from home for a business meeting the following morning. The porter, a simple country lad with an indecipherable Hessian accent, took his tip and left.

Sigi threw her arms round him as he kicked the door shut.

'Where have you been? What are you doing here?'

He shut off the questions in the simplest way and by the time they parted Sigi's cold cheeks were flushed and burning and Miller was feeling like a fighting rooster.

He took her coat and hung it on the hook behind the door. She started to ask more questions.

'First things first,' he said, and pulled her down on to the bed, still warm under the thick feather cushion from where he had lain dozing. She giggled.

'You haven't changed.'

She was still wearing her hostess dress from the cabaret, low-cut at the front, with a skimpy sling-bra beneath it. He unzipped the dress down the back and eased the thin shoulderstraps off.

'Have you?' he asked quietly.

She took a deep breath and lay back as he bent over her, pushing herself towards his face. She smiled.

'No,' she murmured, 'not at all. You know what I like.'

'And you know what I like,' muttered Miller indistinctly.

She squealed.

'Me first. I've missed you more than you've missed me.'

There was no reply, only silence disturbed by Sigi's rising sighs and groans.

It was an hour before they paused, panting and happy, and Miller filled the tooth-glass with brandy and water. Sigi sipped a little, for she was not a heavy drinker despite her job, and Miller took the rest.

'So,' said Sigi teasingly, 'first things having been dealt with ...'

'For a while,' interjected Miller. She giggled.

'For a while, would you mind telling me why the mysterious letter, why the six-week absence, why that awful skinhead haircut and why a small room in an obscure hotel in Hesse?'

Miller grew serious. At length he rose, still naked, crossed the room and came back with his document case. He seated himself on the edge of the bed.

'You're going to learn pretty soon what I've been up to,' he said, 'so I may as well tell you now.'

He talked for nearly an hour, starting with the discovery of the diary, which he showed her, and ending with the break-in to the forger's house. As he talked she grew more and more horrified.

'You're mad,' she said when he had finished. 'You're stark, staring, raving mad. You could have got yourself killed, or imprisoned or a hundred things.'

'I had to do it,' he said, bereft of an explanation for things that now seemed to him to have been crazy.

'All this for a rotten old Nazi? You're barmy. It's over, Peter, all that is over. What do you want to waste your time on them for?'

She was staring at him in bewilderment.

'Well, I have,' he said defiantly.

She sighed heavily and shook her head to indicate her failure to understand.

'All right,' she said, 'so now it's done. You know who he is and where he is. You must come back to Hamburg, pick up the phone and ring the police. They'll do the rest. That's what they're paid for.'

Miller did not know how to answer her.

'It's not that simple,' he said at last. 'I'm going up there later this morning.'

'Going up where?'

He jerked his thumb towards the window and the still-dark range of mountains beyond it.

'To his house.'

'To his house? What for?' Her eyes widened in horror. 'You're not going in to see him?'

'Yes. Don't ask me why, because I can't tell you. It's just something I have to do.'

Her reaction startled him. She sat up with a jerk, turned on to her knees and glared down at where he lay smoking, his head propped up by a pillow.

'That's what you wanted the gun for,' she threw at him, her breasts rising and falling in her growing anger. 'You're going to kill him . . .'

'I'm not going to kill him. . . .'

'Well then, he'll kill you. And you're going up there alone with a gun against him and his mob. You bastard, you rotten stinking horrible . . .'

Miller was staring at her in amazement.

'What have you got so het up for? Over Roschmann?'

'I'm not het up about that horrid old Nazi. I'm talking about me. About me and you, you stupid dumb oaf. You're going to risk getting yourself killed up there, all to prove some silly point and make a story for your idiotic magazine readers. You don't even think for a minute about me. . . .'

She had started crying as she talked, the tears making tracks of mascara down each cheek like black railway lines.

'Look at me, well, bloody well look at me. What do you think I am, just another good screw? You really think I want to give myself every night to some randy reporter so he can feel pleased with himself when he goes to chase some idiot story that could get him killed? You really think that? Listen, you great moron, I want to get married. I want to be Frau Miller. I want to have babies. And you're going to get yourself killed ... Oh God. ...'

She jumped off the bed and ran into the bathroom, slamming the door behind her and locking it.

Miller lay on the bed open-mouthed, the cigarette burning down to his fingers. He had never seen her so angry, and it had shocked him. He thought over what she had said as he listened to the tap running in the bathroom.

Stubbing out the cigarette he crossed the room to the bathroom door.
'Sigi.'
There was no answer.
'Sigi.'
The taps were turned off.
'Go away.'
'Sigi, please open the door. I want to talk to you.'
There was a pause, then the door was unlocked. She stood there, naked and looking sulky. She had washed the mascara streaks off her face.
'What do you want?' she asked.
'Come over to the bed. I want to talk to you. We'll freeze standing here.'
'No, you just want to start making love again.'
'I won't. Honestly. I promise you I won't. I just want to talk.'
He took her hand and led her back to the bed and the warmth it offered. Her face looked up warily from the pillow.
'What do you want to talk about?' she asked suspiciously.
He climbed in beside her and put his face close to her ear.
'Sigrid Rahn, will you marry me?'
She turned to face him.
'Do you mean it?' she asked.
'Yes, I do. I never really thought of it before. But then you never got angry before.'
'Gosh.' She sounded as if she couldn't believe her ears. 'I'll have to get angry more often.'
'Do I get an answer?' he asked.
'Oh yes, Peter, I will. We'll be so good together.'
He began caressing her again, becoming aroused as he did so.
'You said you weren't going to start that again,' she accused him.
'Well, just this once. After that I promise I'll leave you strictly alone for the rest of time.'
She swung her thigh across him and slid her hips on top of his lower belly. Looking down at him she said, 'Peter Miller, don't you dare.'
Miller reached up and pulled the toggle that extinguished the light as she started to make love to him.

Outside in the snow there was a dim light breaking over the eastern horizon. Had Miller glanced at his watch it would have told him the time was ten minutes before seven on the morning of Sunday, February 23rd. But he was already asleep.

Half an hour later Klaus Winzer rolled up the drive of his house, stopped before the closed garage door and climbed out. He was stiff and tired, but glad to be home.

Barbara was not yet up, taking advantage of her employer's absence to lie in longer than usual. When she did appear, after Winzer had let himself in and called from the hallway, it was in a nightie that would have set another man's pulses bounding. Instead, Winzer required fried eggs, toast and jam, a pot of coffee and a bath. He got none of them.

She told him instead of her discovery on the Saturday morning on entering the study to dust, of the broken window and the missing silverware. She had called the police, and they had been positive the neat, circular hole was the work of a professional burglar. She had had to tell them the house-owner was away, and they said they wanted to know when he returned, just for routine questions about the missing items.

Winzer listened in absolute quiet to the girl's chatter, his face paling, a single vein throbbing steadily in his temple. He dismissed her to the kitchen to prepare coffee, went into his study and locked the door. It took him thirty seconds and frantic scratching inside the empty safe to convince himself that the file of forty Odessa criminals was gone.

As he turned away from the safe the phone rang. It was the doctor from the clinic to infrom him Fräulein Wendel had died during the night.

For two hours Winzer sat in his chair before the unlit fire, oblivious of the cold seeping in through the newspaper-stuffed hole in the window, aware only of the cold fingers worming round inside himself as he tried to think what to do. Barbara's repeated calls from outside the locked door that breakfast was ready went unheeded. Through the keyhole she could hear him muttering occasionally, 'Not my fault, not my fault at all.'

Miller had forgotten to cancel the morning call he had ordered the previous evening before he rang Sigi in Hamburg. The bedside phone shrilled at nine. Bleary-eyed, he answered it, grunted his thanks and climbed out of bed. He knew if he did not he would fall asleep again. Sigi was still fast asleep, exhausted by her drive from Hamburg, their love-making and the contentment of being engaged at last.

Miller showered, finishing off with several minutes under the ice-cold spray, rubbed himself briskly with the towel he had left over the radiator all night, and felt like a million dollars. The depression and anxiety of the night before had vanished. He felt fit and confident.

He dressed in ankle-boots and slacks, a thick roll-neck pullover and his double-breasted blue duffel over-jacket, a German winter garment called a *Joppe*, halfway between a jacket and a coat. It had deep slit pockets at each side, capable of taking the gun and the handcuffs, and an inside breast pocket for the photograph. He took the handcuffs from Sigi's bag and examined them. There was no key and the manacles were self-locking, which made them useless for anything other than locking a man up until released by the police or a hacksaw blade.

The gun he opened and examined. He had never fired it, and it still had the maker's grease on the interior. The magazine was full, he kept it that way. To familiarise himself with it once again he worked the breech several times, made sure he knew which position of the safety-catch was the 'On' and 'Fire', smacked the magazine into the grip, pushed a round into the chamber and set the safety catch to 'On'. He stuffed the telephone number of the lawyer in Ludwigsburg into his trouser pocket.

He took his attaché case out from under the bed, and taking a plain sheet from it wrote a message for Sigi to read when she awoke. It said: 'My darling. I am going now to see the man I have been hunting. I have reason for wanting to look into his face, and be present when the police take him away in handcuffs. It is a good one, and by this afternoon I will be able to tell you. But just in case, here is what I want you to do. . . .'

The instructions were precise and to the point. He wrote down the telephone number in Munich she was to ring, and the message she was to give the man at the other end. He ended: 'Do not under any circumstances follow me up the mountain. You could only make matters worse, whatever the situation. So if I am not back by noon, or have not rung you in this room by then, call that number, give that message, check out of the hotel, post the envelope at any box in Frankfurt, then drive back to Hamburg. Don't get engaged to anyone else in the meantime. All my love, Peter.'

He propped the note on the bedside table by the telephone, along with the large envelope containing the Odessa file and three fifty-mark bills. Tucking Salomon Tauber's diary under his arm, he slipped out of the bedroom and headed downstairs. Passing the reception desk he ordered the porter to give his room another morning call at eleven-thirty.

He came out of the hotel doorway at nine-thirty and was surprised at the amount of snow that had fallen during the night.

Miller walked round to the back, climbed into the Jaguar, gave full choke and pressed the starter. It took several minutes before the engine caught. While it was warming up he took a hand-brush from the boot and brushed the thick carpet of snow off the bonnet, roof and windscreen.

Back behind the wheel he slipped into gear and drove out on to the main road. The thick layer of snow over everything acted as a sort of cushion and he could hear it crunching under the wheels. After a glance at the ordnance survey map he had bought the previous evening just before closing time, he set off down the road towards Limburg.

The morning had turned out grey and overcast after a brief and brilliant dawn which he had not seen. Beneath the clouds the snow glittered under the trees and a wind keened off the mountains.

The road led upwards, winding out of town and immediately becoming lost in the sea of trees that make up the Romberg Forest. After he had cleared town the carpet of snow along the road was almost virgin, only one set of tracks running parallel through it, where an early morning visitor to Königstein for church service had headed an hour before.

Miller took the branch-off towards Glashütten, skirted round the flanks of the towering Feldberg mountain and down a road signposted as leading to the village of Schmitten. On the flanks of the mountains the wind howled through the pines, its pitch rising to a near-scream among the snow-clogged boughs.

Although Miller had never bothered to think about it, it was once out of these and other oceans of pine and beech that the old Germanic tribes had swarmed to be checked by Caesar at the Rhine. Later, converted to Christianity, they had paid lip-service by day to the Prince of Peace, dreaming only in the dark hours of the ancient gods of strength and lust and power. It was this ancient atavism, the worship in the dark of the private gods of screaming endless trees, that Hitler had ignited with a magic touch.

In another twenty minutes of careful driving Miller checked his map again and began to look for a gateway off the road on to a private estate. When he found it, it was a barred gate held in place by a steel catch, with a notice board to one side saying 'Private Property, Keep Out'.

Leaving the engine running he climbed out and swung the gate inwards.

Miller entered the estate and headed up the driveway. The snow was untouched and he kept in bottom gear, for there was only frozen sand beneath the snow.

Two hundred yards up the track a branch from a massive oak tree had come down in the night, overladen with half a ton of snow. The branch had crashed into the undergrowth to the right, and some of its twigs lay on the track. It had also brought down a thin black pole that had stood beneath it, and this lay across the drive.

Rather than get out and move it, he drove carefully forward, feeling the bump as the pole passed under the front and then the rear wheels.

Clear of the obstruction he moved on towards the house and emerged into a clearing, which contained the villa and its gardens, fronted by a circular area of gravel. He halted the car in front of the main door, climbed out and rang the bell.

While Miller was climbing out of his car, Klaus Winzer made his decision and rang the Werwolf. The Odessa chief was brusque and irritable, for it was long past the time he should have heard on the news of a sports car being blown to pieces, apparently by an exploding petrol tank, on the autobahn south of Osnabrück. But as he listened to the man on the other end of the telephone his mouth tightened in a thin, hard line.

'You did what? You fool, you unbelievable, stupid little cretin. Do you know what's going to happen to you if that file is not recovered? . . .'

Alone in his study in Osnabrück Klaus Winzer replaced the receiver after the last sentences from the Werwolf came over the wire, and went back to his desk. He was quite calm. Twice already life had played him the worst of tricks, firstly over the destruction of his war-work in the lakes, then the ruin of his paper fortune in 1948, and now this. Taking an old but serviceable Lüger from the bottom drawer he placed the end in his mouth and shot himself. The lead slug that tore his head apart was not a forgery.

The Werwolf sat and gazed in something close to horror at the silent telephone. He thought of the men for whom it had been necessary to obtain passports through Klaus Winzer and the fact that each of them was a wanted man on the list of those destined for arrest and trial if caught. The exposure of the dossier would lead to a welter of prosecutions that could only jerk the population out of its growing apathy towards the question of continuing pursuit of wanted SS men, re-galvanise the hunting agencies. . . . The prospect was appalling.

But his first priority was the protection of Roschmann, one of those he knew to be on the list taken from Winzer. Three times he dialled the Frankfurt area number, followed by the private number of the house on the hill, and three times he got the 'unobtainable' signal. Finally he tried through the operator, who told him the line must be out of order.

Instead, he rang the Hohenzollern Hotel in Osnabrück and caught Mackensen about to leave. In a few sentences he told the killer of the latest disaster, and where Roschmann lived.

'It looks as if your bomb hasn't worked,' he told him. 'Get down there faster than you've ever driven,' he said. 'Hide your car and stick close to Roschmann. There's a bodyguard called Oskar as well. If Miller goes straight to the police with what he's got, we've all had it. But if he comes to Roschmann, take him alive and make him talk. We must know what he's done with those papers before he dies.'

Mackensen glanced at his road map inside the phone booth and estimated the distance.

'I'll be there at one o'clock,' he said.

The door opened at the second ring and a gust of warm air flowed out of the hall. The man who stood in front of him had evidently come from his study, the door of which Miller could see standing open and leading off the hallway.

Years of good living had put weight on the once-lanky SS officer. His face had a flush, either from drinking or from the country air, and his hair was grey at the sides. He looked the picture of middle-aged, upper-middle-class, prosperous good health. But although different in detail, the face was the same Tauber had seen and described. He surveyed Miller without enthusiasm.

'Yes?' he said.

It took Miller another ten seconds before he could speak. What he had rehearsed just went out of his head.

'My name is Miller,' he said, 'and yours is Eduard Roschmann.'

At the mention of both names something flickered through the eyes of the man in front of him, but iron control kept his face muscles straight.

'This is preposterous,' he said at length. 'I've never heard of the man you are talking about.'

Behind the façade of calm the former SS officer's mind was racing. Several times in his life since 1945 he had survived through sharp thinking in a crisis. He recognised the name of Miller well enough, and recalled his conversation with the Werwolf weeks before. His first instinct was to shut the door in Miller's face, but he overcame it.

'Are you alone in the house?' asked Miller.

'Yes,' said Roschmann, truthfully.

'We'll go into your study,' said Miller flatly.

Roschmann made no objection, for he realised he was now forced to keep Miller on the premises and stall for time, until . . .

He turned on his heel and strode back across the hallway. Miller slammed the front door after him and was at Roschmann's heels as they entered the study. It was a comfortable room, with a thick padded door which Miller closed behind him, and a log fire burning in the grate.

Roschmann stopped in the centre of the room and turned to face Miller.

'Is your wife here?' asked Miller. Roschmann shook his head.

'She has gone away for the weekend to visit relatives,' he said. This much was true. She had been called away the previous evening at a moment's notice and had taken the second car. The first car owned by the pair was by ill chance in the garage for repairs. She was due back that evening.

What Roschmann did not mention, but what occupied his racing mind, was that his bulky, shaven-headed chauffeur/bodyguard Oskar had cycled down to the village half an hour earlier to report the telephone being out of order. He knew he had to keep Miller talking until the man returned.

When he turned to face Miller the young reporter's right hand held an automatic pointed straight at his belly. Roschmann was frightened, but covered it with bluster.

'You threaten me with a gun in my own house?'

'Then call the police,' said Miller, nodding at the telephone on the writing desk. Roschmann made no move towards it.

'I see you still limp a little,' remarked Miller. 'The orthopaedic shoe almost disguises it, but not quite. The missing toes, lost in an operation in Rimini camp. The frostbite you got wandering through the fields of Austria caused that, didn't it?'

Roschmann's eyes narrowed slightly, but he said nothing.

'You see, if the police come, they'll identify you, Herr Direktor. The face is still the same, the bullet wound in the chest, the scar under the left armpit where you tried to remove the Waffen-SS blood-group tattoo, no doubt. Do you really want to call the police?'

Roschmann let out the air in his lungs in a long sigh.

'What do you want, Miller?'

'Sit down,' said the reporter. 'Not at the desk, there in the armchair where I can see you. And keep your hands on the arm-rests. Don't give me an excuse to shoot, because, believe me, I'd dearly love to.'

Roschmann sat in the armchair, his eyes on the gun. Miller perched on the edge of the desk facing him.

'So now we talk,' he said.

'About what?'

'About Riga. About eighty thousand people, men, women and children, whom you had slaughtered up there.'

Seeing he did not intend to use the gun, Roschmann began to regain his confidence. Some of the colour returned to his face. He switched his gaze to the face of the younger man in front of him.

'That's a lie. There were never eighty thousand disposed of in Riga.'

'Seventy thousand? Sixty?' asked Miller. 'Do you really think it matters precisely how many thousands you killed.'

'That's the point,' said Roschmann eagerly. 'It doesn't matter, not now, not then. Look, young man, I don't know why you've come after me. But I can guess. Someone's been filling your head with a lot of sentimental clap-trap about so-called war crimes and suchlike. It's all nonsense. Absolute nonsense. How old are you?'

'Twenty-nine.'

'Then you were in the Army military service?'

'Yes. One of the first national servicemen of the post-war army. Two years in uniform.'

'Well then, you know what the Army is like. A man's given orders, he obeys these orders. He doesn't ask whether they are right or wrong. You know that as well as I do. All I did was to obey my orders.'

'Firstly, you weren't a soldier,' said Miller quietly. 'You were an executioner. Put more bluntly, a murderer, and a mass-murderer. So don't compare yourself with a soldier.'

'Nonsense,' said Roschmann earnestly. 'It's all nonsense. We were soldiers just like the rest. We obeyed our orders just like the rest. You young Germans are all the same. You don't want to understand what it was like then.'

'So tell me, what was it like?'

Roschmann, who had leaned forward to make his point, leaned back in the chair, almost at ease, the immediate danger past.

'What was it like? It was like ruling the world. Because we did rule the world, we Germans. We had beaten every army they could throw at us. For years they had done us down, we poor Germans, and we had shown them, yes, all of them, that we were a great people. You youngsters today don't realise what it is to be proud of being a German.

'It lights a fire inside you. When the drums beat and the bands played, when the flags were waving and the whole nation was united behind one man, we could have marched to the ends of the world. That is greatness, young Miller, greatness your generation has never known and never will know. And we of the SS were the élite, still are the élite. Of course they hunt us down now, first the Allies and then the wishy-washy old women of Bonn. Of course they want to crush us. Because they want to crush the greatness of Germany, which we represented and still do.

'They say a lot of stupid things about what happened then in a few camps a sensible world would long since have forgotten about. They make a big cry because we had to clean up Europe from the pollution of this Jewish filth that impregnated every facet of German life and kept us down in the mud with them. We had to do it, I tell you. It was a mere sideshow in the great design of a Germany and a German people, pure in blood and ideals, ruling the world as is their right, *our* right, Miller, *our* right and our destiny, if those hell-damned Britishers and the eternally stupid Americans had not stuck their prissy noses in. For make no bones about it, you may point that thing at me, but we are on the same side, young man, a generation between us, but still on the same side. For we are Germans, the greatest people in the world. And you would let your judgement of all this, of the greatness that once was Germany's, and will be again one day, of the essential unity of us, all of us, the German people, you will let your judgement of all this be affected by what happened to a few miserable Jews? Can't you see, you poor misled young fool, that we are on the same side, you and me, the same side, the same people, the same destiny?'

Despite the gun, he rose from his chair and paced the carpet between the desk and the window.

'You want proof of our greatness? Look at Germany today. Smashed to rubble in 1945, utterly destroyed and at the prey of the barbarians from the east and the fools in the west. And now? Germany is rising again, slowly and surely, still lacking the essential discipline that we were able to give her, but increasing each year in her industrial and economic power. Yes and military power, one day, when the last vestiges of the influence of the Allies of 1945 have been shaken off, we will be as mighty again as we ever were. It will take time, and a new leader, but the ideals will be the same, and the glory, yes that will be the same too.

'And you know what brings this about? I will tell you, yes I will tell you, young man. It's discipline and management. Harsh discipline, the harsher the better, and management, our management, the most brilliant quality after courage that we possess. For we can manage things, we have shown that. Look at all this, you see all this? This house, this estate, the factory down in the Ruhr, mine and thousands like it, tens, hundreds of thousands, churning out power and strength each day, with each turn of the wheel another ounce of might to make Germany mighty once again.

'And who do you think did all this? You think people prepared to spend time mouthing platitudes over a few miserable Yids did all this? You think cowards and traitors trying to persecute good, honest patriotic German soldiers did all this? We did this, we brought this prosperity back to Germany, the same men as we had twenty, thirty years ago.'

He turned from the window and faced Miller, his eyes alight. But he also measured the distance from the farthest point of his pacing along the carpet to the heavy iron poker by the fire. Miller had noticed the glances.

'Now, you come here, a representative of the young generation, full of your idealism and your concern, and point a gun at me. Why not be idealistic for Germany, your own country, your own people? You think you represent the people, coming to hunt me down? You think that's what they want, the people of Germany?'

Miller shook his head.

'No, I don't,' he said shortly.

'Well, there you are then. If you call the police and turn me in to them, they might make a trial out of it, I say only "might" because even that is not certain, so long afterwards, with all the witnesses scattered or dead. So put your gun away and go home. Go home and read the true history of those days, learn that Germany's greatness then and her prosperity today stem from patriotic Germans like me.'

Miller had sat through the tirade mute, observing with bewilderment and rising disgust the man who paced the carpet in front of him, seeking to convert him to the old ideology. He had wanted to say a hundred, a thousand things, about the people he knew and the millions beyond them who did not want or see the necessity of purchasing glory at the price of slaughtering millions of other human beings. But the words did not come. They never do, when one needs them. So he just sat and stared, until Roschmann had finished.

After some seconds of silence Miller asked, 'Have you ever heard of a man called Tauber?'

'Who?'

'Salomon Tauber. He was a German too. Jewish. He was in Riga from the beginning to the end.'

Roschmann shrugged.

'I can't remember him. It was a long time ago. Who was he?'

'Sit down,' said Miller. 'And this time stay seated.'

Roschmann shrugged impatiently and went back to the armchair. With his rising conviction that Miller would not shoot, his mind was concerned with the problem of trapping him before he could get away, rather than with an obscure and long-dead Jew.

'Tauber died in Hamburg on November 22nd last year. He gassed himself. Are you listening?'

'Yes. If I must.'

'He left behind a diary. It was an account of his story, what happened to him, what you and others did to him, in Riga and elsewhere. But mainly in Riga. But he survived, he came back to Hamburg, and he lived there for eighteen years before he died, because he was convinced you were alive and would never stand trial. I got hold of his diary. It was my starting point in finding you, today, here, under your new name.'

'The diary of a dead man's not evidence,' growled Roschmann.

'Not for a court, but enough for me.'

'And you really came here to confront me over the diary of a dead Jew?'

'No, not at all. There's a page of that diary I want you to read.'

Miller opened the diary at a certain page and pushed it into Roschmann's lap.

'Pick it up,' he ordered, 'and read it – aloud.'

Roschmann unfolded the sheet and began to read it. It was the passage in which Tauber described the murder by Roschmann of an unnamed German Army officer wearing the Knight's Cross with Oak Leaf cluster.

Roschmann reached the end of the passage and looked up.

'So what?' he said, puzzled. 'The man struck me. He disobeyed orders. I had the right to commandeer that ship to bring the prisoners back.'

Miller tossed a photograph on to Roschmann's lap.

'Is that the man you killed?'

Roschmann looked at it and shrugged.

'How should I know? It was twenty years ago.'

There was a slow ker-lick as Miller thumbed the hammer back and pointed the gun at Roschmann's face.

'Was that the man?'

Roschmann looked at the photograph again.

'All right. So that was the man. So what?'

'That was my father,' said Miller.

The colour drained out of Roschmann's face as if a plug had been pulled. His mouth dropped open, his gaze dropped to the gun barrel two feet from his face and the steady hand behind it.

'Oh dear God,' he whispered, 'you didn't come about the Jews at all.'

'No. I'm sorry for them, but not that sorry.'

'But how could you know, how could you possibly know from that diary that the man was your father? I never knew his name, this Jew who wrote the diary never knew, how did you know?'

'My father was killed on October 11th, 1944, in Ostland,' said Miller. 'For twenty years that was all I knew. Then I read the diary. It was the same day, the same area, the two men had the same rank. Above all, both men wore the Knight's Cross with Oak Leaf cluster, the highest award for bravery in the field. There weren't all that many of those awarded, and very few to mere army captains. It would have been millions to one against two identical officers dying in the same area on the same day.'

Roschmann knew he was up against a man whom no argument could influence. He stared as if mesmerised at the gun.

'You're going to kill me. You mustn't do that, not in cold blood. You wouldn't do that. Please, Miller, I don't want to die.'

Miller leaned forward and began to talk.

'Listen to me, you repulsive piece of dog-shit. I've listened to you and your twisted mouthings till I'm sick to my guts. Now you're going to listen to me while I make up my mind whether you die here or rot in some jail for the rest of your days.

'You had the nerve, the crass bloody nerve, to tell me that you, you of all people, were a patriotic German. I'll tell you what you are. You and all your kind were and are the filthiest crap that was ever elevated from the gutters of this country to positions of power. And in twelve years you smeared my country with your dirt in a way that has never happened throughout our history.

'What you did sickened and revolted the whole of civilised mankind and left my generation a heritage of shame to live down that's going to take us all the rest of our lives. You spat on Germany throughout your lives. You bastards used Germany and the German people until they could not be used any more and then you quit while the going was good. You brought us so low it would have been inconceivable before your crew came along, and I don't mean in terms of bomb damage.

'You weren't even brave. You were the most sickening cowards ever produced in Germany or Austria. You murdered millions for your own profit and in the name of your maniac power-lust, and then you got out and left the rest of us in the shit. You ran away from the Russians, hanged and shot army men to keep them fighting, and then disappeared and left me to carry the can back.

'Even if there could be an oblivion of what you did to the Jews and the others, there can never be any forgetting that your lot ran and hid like the dogs you are. You talk of patriotism: you don't even know the meaning of the word. And as for daring to call army soldiers and others who fought, really fought, for Germany *Kamerad*, it's a bloody obscenity.

'I'll tell you one other thing, as a young German of the generation you so plainly despise. This prosperity we have today, it's got nothing to do with you. It's got a lot to do with millions who work a hard day and never murdered anyone in their lives. And as for murderers like you who may still be among us, as far as I and my generation are concerned we would put up with a little less prosperity if we could be sure scum like you were not still around. Which, incidentally, you are not going to be for very long.'

'You're going to kill me,' mumbled Roschmann.

'As a matter of fact I'm not.'

Miller reached behind him and pulled the telephone over towards where he sat on the desk. He kept his eyes on Roschmann and the gun pointed. He took the receiver off the cradle, slid it on the desk and dialled. When he had finished he picked up the receiver.

'There's a man in Ludwigsburg wants to have a chat with you,' he said, and put the telephone to his ear. It was dead.

He laid it back in the cradle, took it off again and listened for the dialling tone. There was none.

'Have you cut this off?' he asked.

Roschmann shook his head.

'Listen, if you've pulled the connection out I'll drill you here and now.'

'I haven't. I haven't touched the phone this morning. Honestly.'

Miller remembered the fallen branch of the oak tree and the telegraph pole lying across the track to the house. He swore softly. Roschmann gave a small smile.

'The lines must be down,' he said. 'You'll have to go into the village. What are you going to do now?'

'I'm going to put a bullet through you unless you do as you're told,' Miller snapped back. He dragged the handcuffs he had thought to use on a bodyguard out of his pocket.

He tossed the bracelets over to Roschmann.

'Walk over to the fireplace,' he ordered, and followed the man across the room.

'What are you going to do?'

'I'm going to lock you to the fireplace, then go and phone from the village,' said Miller.

He was scanning the wrought-iron scroll-work that composed the surround of the fireplace when Roschmann dropped the handcuffs at his feet. The SS man bent to pick them up, and Miller was almost caught unawares when Roschmann instead gripped a heavy fire-iron and swung it viciously at Miller's knee-caps. The reporter stepped back in time, the poker swished past and Roschmann was off his balance. Miller stepped in, whipped the barrel of the pistol across the bent head and stepped back.

'Try that again and I'll kill you,' he said.

Roschmann straightened up, wincing from the blow to the head.

'Clip one of the bracelets round your right wrist,' Miller commanded, and Roschmann did as he was told. 'You see that vine-leaf ornament in front of you? At head height. There's a branch next to it comes out of the metal-work and rejoins it again. Lock the other bracelet on to that.'

When Roschmann had snapped the second link home, Miller walked over and kicked the fire-tongs and poker out of reach. Keeping his gun against Roschmann's jacket, he frisked him and cleared the area around the chained man of all objects which he could throw to break the window.

Outside in the driveway the man called Oskar pedalled towards the door, his errand to report the broken phone line accomplished. He paused in surprise on seeing the Jaguar, for his employer had assured him before he went that no one was expected.

He leaned the bicycle against the side of the house and quietly let himself in by the front door. In the hallway he stood irresolute, hearing nothing through the padded door to the study, and not being heard himself by those inside.

Miller took a last look round and was satisfied.

'Incidentally,' he told the glaring Roschmann, 'it wouldn't have done you any good if you had managed to hit me. It's eleven o'clock now, and I left the complete dossier of evidence on you in the hands of my accomplice, to drop into the post-box, addressed to the right authorities, if I have not returned or phoned by midday. As it is I'm going to phone from the village. I'll be back in twenty minutes. You won't be out of there in twenty minutes, even with a hacksaw. When I get back the police will be thirty minutes behind me.'

As he talked Roschmann's hopes began to flicker. He knew he only had one chance left – for the returning Oskar to take Miller alive so that he could be forced to make the phone call from a phone in the village at their demand and keep the documents from reaching the post-box. He glanced at the clock on the mantelpiece close to his head. It read ten-forty.

Miller swung open the door at the other side of the room and walked through it. He found himself staring at the roll-neck of a pullover, worn by a man a full head taller than he was. From his place by the fire Roschmann recognised Oskar and screamed, 'HOLD HIM.'

Miller stepped back into the room and jerked up the gun he had been replacing in his pocket. He was too slow. A swinging left backhander from Oskar's paw swept the automatic out of his grasp and it flew across the room. At the same time Oskar thought his employer cried, 'HIT HIM!' He crashed a right hand into Miller's jaw. The reporter weighed 170 pounds, but the blow lifted him off his feet and threw him backwards. His feet caught in a low newspaper rack and as he went over his head slammed into the corner of a mahogany bookcase. Crumpling like a rag doll, his body slid to the carpet and rolled on to one side.

For several seconds there was silence as Oskar took in the spectacle of his employer manacled to the fireplace, and Roschmann stared at the inert figure of Miller, from the back of whose head a trickle of blood flowed on to the floor.

'You fool,' yelled Roschmann when he had taken in what had happened. Oskar looked baffled. 'Get over here.'

The giant lumbered across the room and stood waiting for orders. Roschmann thought fast.

'Try and get me out of these handcuffs,' he commanded, 'use the fire-irons.'

But the fireplace had been built in an age when craftsmen intended their handiwork to last for a long time. The result of Oskar's efforts was a curly poker and a pair of wriggly tongs.

'Bring him over here,' he told Oskar at last. While Oskar held Miller up, Roschmann looked under the reporter's eyelids and felt his pulse.

'He's still alive, but out cold,' he said. 'He'll need a doctor to come round in less than an hour. Bring me a pencil and paper.'

Writing with his left hand he scribbled two phone numbers on the paper while Oskar brought a hacksaw blade from the tool-chest under the stairs. When he returned Roschmann gave him the sheet of paper.

'Get down to the village as fast as you can,' he told Oskar. 'Ring this Nuremberg number and tell the man who answers it what has happened. Ring this local number and get the doctor up here immediately. You understand? Tell him it's an emergency. Now hurry.'

As Oskar ran from the room Roschmann glanced at the clock again. Ten-fifty. If Oskar could make the village by eleven, and he and the doctor could be back by eleven-fifteen, they might bring Miller round in time to get to a phone and delay the accomplice, even if the doctor would only work at gunpoint. Urgently, Roschmann began to saw at his handcuffs.

In front of the door Oskar grabbed his bicycle, then paused and glanced at the parked Jaguar. He peered through the driver's window and saw the key in the ignition. His master had told him to hurry, so dropping the bicycle he climbed behind the wheel of the car, gunned it into life, and spurted gravel in a wide arc as he slid the sports car out of the forecourt into the driveway.

He had got up into third gear and was boring down the slippery track as fast as he could take it when he hit the snow-covered telegraph pole lying across the road.

Roschmann was still sawing at the chain linking the two bracelets when the shattering roar in the pine forest stopped him. Straining to one side he could peer through the French windows and although the car and the driveway were out of sight, the plume of smoke drifting across the sky told him at least that the car had been destroyed by an explosion. He recalled the assurance he had been given that Miller would be taken care of. But Miller was on the carpet a few feet away from him, his bodyguard was certainly dead, and time was running out without hope of reprieve. He leaned his head against the chill metal of the fire-surround and closed his eyes.

'Then it's over,' he murmured quietly. After several minutes he continued sawing. It was over an hour before the specially hardened steel of the military handcuffs parted to the now blunt hacksaw. As he stepped free, with only a bracelet round his right wrist, the clock chimed midday.

If he had had time he might have paused to kick the body on the carpet, but he was a man in a hurry. From the wall safe he took a passport and several fat bundles of new, high-denomination bank notes. Twenty minutes later, with these and a few clothes in a hand-grip, he was cycling down the track, round the shattered hulk of the Jaguar and the still smouldering body lying face down in the snow, past the scorched and broken pines, towards the village.

From there he called a taxi and ordered it to take him to Frankfurt international airport. He walked to the Flight Information desk and enquired:

'What time is the next flight out of here for Argentina, preferably within an hour. Failing that . . .'

18

It was ten past one when Mackensen's Mercedes turned off the country road into the gate of the estate. Halfway up the drive to the house he found the way blocked.

The Jaguar had evidently been blown apart from inside, but its wheels had not left the road. It was still upright, slewed slantwise across the drive. The forward and rear sections were recognisable as those of a car, still held together by the tough steel girders that formed the chassis. But the centre section, including the cockpit, was missing from floor to roof. Bits of this section were scattered in an area round the wreckage.

Mackensen surveyed the skeleton with a grim smile and walked over to the bundle of scorched clothes and their contents on the ground twenty feet away. Something about the size of the corpse caught his attention and he stooped over it for several minutes. Then he straightened and ran at an easy lope up the rest of the drive towards the house.

He avoided ringing the front-door bell, but tried the handle. It opened and he went into the hallway. For several seconds he listened, poised like a carnivorous animal by a water-hole, sensing the atmosphere for danger. There was no sound. He reached under his left armpit and brought out a long-barrelled Lüger automatic, flicked off the safety-catch and started to open the doors leading off the hall.

The first was the dining-room, the second the study. Although he saw the body on the hearthrug at once, he did not move from the half-open door before he had covered the rest of the room. He had known two men fall for that trick – the obvious bait and the hidden ambush. Before entering he glanced through the crack between the door's hinges to make sure no one waited behind it, then entered.

Miller was lying on his back with his head turned to one side. For several seconds Mackensen stared down into the chalky white face, then bent to listen to the shallow breathing. The matted blood on the back of the head told him roughly what had happened.

He spent ten minutes scouring the house, noting the open drawers in the master bedroom, the missing shaving tackle from the bathroom. Back in the study, he glanced into the yawning and empty wall-safe, then sat himself at the desk and picked up the telephone.

He sat listening for several seconds, swore under his breath and replaced it. There was no difficulty finding the tool-chest under the stairs, for the cupboard door was still open. He took what he needed and went back down the drive, passing through the study to check on Miller and leaving by the French windows.

It took him almost an hour to find the parted strands of the telephone line, sort them out from the entangling undergrowth and splice them back together. When he was satisfied with his handiwork he walked back to the house, sat at the desk and tried the phone. He got the dialling tone and rang his chief in Nuremberg.

He had expected the Werwolf to be eager to hear from him, but the man's voice coming down the wire sounded tired and only half-interested. Like a good sergeant, he reported what he had found, the car, the corpse of the bodyguard, the half-handcuff still linked to the scroll-work by the fire, the blunt hacksaw blade on the carpet, Miller unconscious on the floor. He finished with the absent owner.

'He hasn't taken much, chief. Overnight things, probably money from the open safe. I can clear up here, he can come back if he wants to.'

'No, he won't come back,' the Werwolf told him. 'Just before you rang I put the phone down. He called me from Frankfurt Airport. He's booked on a flight to Madrid leaving in ten minutes. Connection this evening to Buenos Aires. . . .'

'But there's no need,' protested Mackensen. 'I'll make Miller talk, we can find where he left his papers. There was no document case in the wreckage of the car, and nothing on him, except a sort of diary lying on the study floor. But the rest of his stuff must be somewhere not far away.'

'Far enough,' replied the Werwolf. 'In a post-box.'

Wearily he told Mackensen what Miller had stolen from the forger, and what Roschmann had just told him on the phone from Frankfurt. 'Those papers will be in the hands of the authorities in the morning, or Tuesday at the latest. After that everyone on that list is on borrowed time. That includes Roschmann, the owner of the house you're in, and me. I've spent the whole morning trying to warn everyone concerned to get out of the country inside twenty-four hours.'

'So where do we go from here?' asked Mackensen.

'You get lost,' replied his chief. 'You're not on that list. I am, so I have to get out. Go back to your flat and wait until my successor contacts you. For the rest, it's over. Vulkan has fled and won't come back. With his departure his whole operation is going to fall apart unless someone new can come in and take over the project.'

'What Vulkan? What project?'

'Since it's over you might as well know. Vulkan was the name of Roschmann, the man you were supposed to protect from Miller. . . .' In a few sentences the Werwolf told the executioner why Roschmann had been so important, why his place in the project and the project itself were irreplaceable. When he had finished Mackensen uttered a low whistle and stared across the room at the form of Peter Miller.

'That little boy sure fucked things up for everyone,' he said.

The Werwolf seemed to pull himself together and some of his old authority returned to his voice.

'*Kamerad*, you must clear up the mess over there. You remember that disposal squad you used once before?'

'Yes, I know where to get them. They're not far from here.'

'Call them up, bring them over. Have them leave the place without a trace of what happened. The man's wife must be coming back late tonight, she must never know what happened. Understand?'

'It'll be done,' said Mackensen.

'Then make yourself scarce. One last thing. Before you go, finish off that bastard Miller. Once and for all.'

Mackensen looked across at the unconscious reporter with narrowed eyes.

'It'll be a pleasure,' he grated.

'Then good-bye and good luck.'

The phone went dead. Mackensen replaced it, took out an address book, thumbed through it and dialled a number. He introduced himself to the man who answered and reminded him of the previous favour the man had done for the Comradeship. He told him where to come, and what he would find.

'The car and the body inside it have to go into a deep gorge off a mountain road. Plenty of petrol over it, a real big blaze. Nothing identifiable about the man – go through his pockets and take everything, including his watch.'

'Got it,' said the voice on the phone. 'I'll bring a trailer and winch.'

'There's one last thing. In the study of the house you'll find another stiff on the floor and a bloodstained hearthrug. Get rid of it. Not in the car, a long cold drop to the bottom of a long cold lake. Well weighted. No traces. OK?'

'No problem. We'll be there by five and gone by seven. I don't like to move that kind of cargo in daylight.'

'Fine,' said Mackensen. 'I'll be gone before you get here. But you'll find things like I said.'

He hung up, slid off the desk and walked over to Miller. He pulled out his Lüger and automatically checked the breech, although he knew it was loaded.

'You little shit,' he told the body, and held the gun at arm's length, pointing downwards, lined up on the forehead.

Years of living like a predatory animal and surviving where others, victims and colleagues, had ended on a pathologist's slab had given Mackensen the senses of a leopard. He didn't see the shadow that fell on to the carpet from the open French window; he felt it and spun round, ready to fire. But the man was unarmed.

'Who the hell are you?' growled Mackensen, keeping him covered.

The man stood in the French window, dressed in the black leather leggings and jacket of a motor-cyclist. In his left hand he carried his crash helmet, gripped by the short peak and held across his stomach. The man flicked a glance at the body at Mackensen's feet and the gun in his hand.

'I was sent for,' he said innocently.

'Who by?' said Mackensen.

'Vulkan,' replied the man. 'My *Kamerad*, Roschmann.'

Mackensen grunted and lowered the gun.

'Well, he's gone.'

'Gone?'

'Pissed off. Heading for South America. The whole project's off. And all thanks to this little bastard reporter.'

He jerked the gun barrel towards Miller.

'You going to finish him?' asked the man.

'Sure. He screwed up the project. Identified Roschmann and posted the lot to the police, along with a pile of other stuff. If you're on that file, you'd better get out too.'

'What file?'

'The Odessa file.'

'I'm not on it,' said the man.

'Neither am I,' growled Mackensen. 'But the Werwolf is, and his orders are to finish this one off before we quit.'

'The Werwolf?'

Something began to sound a small alarm inside Mackensen. He had just been told that in Germany no one apart from the Werwolf and himself knew about the Vulkan project. The others were in South America, from where he assumed the new arrival had come. But such a man would know about the Werwolf. His eyes narrowed slightly.

'You're from Buenos Aires?' he asked.

'No.'

'Where from then?'

'Jerusalem.'

It took half a second before the meaning of the name made sense to Mackensen. Then he swung up his Lüger to fire. Half a second is a long time, long enough to die.

The foam rubber inside the crash helmet was scorched when the Walther went off. But the 7 mm parabellum slug came through the fibreglass without a pause and took Mackensen high in the breastbone with the force of a kicking mule. The helmet dropped to the ground to reveal the agent's right hand and from inside the cloud of blue smoke the PPK fired again.

Mackensen was a big man and a strong one. Despite the bullet in the chest he would have fired, but the second slug entering his head two finger widths above the right eyebrow spoilt his aim. It also killed him.

Miller awoke on Monday afternoon in a private ward in Frankfurt General Hospital. He lay for half an hour, becoming slowly aware that his head was swathed in bandages and contained a pair of energetic artillery units. He found a buzzer and pressed it, but the nurse who came told him to lie quietly because he had severe concussion.

So he lay, and piece by piece recollected the events of the previous day until the middle of the morning. After that there was nothing. He dozed off and when he woke it was dark outside and a man was sitting by his bed. The man smiled. Miller stared at him.

'I don't know you.'

'Well, I know you,' said the visitor.

Miller thought. 'I've seen you,' he said at length. 'You were in Oster's house. With Leon and Motti.'

'That's right. What else do you remember?'

'Almost everything. It's coming back.'

'Roschmann?'

'Yes. I talked with him. I was going for the police.'

'Roschmann's gone. Fled back to South America. The whole affair's over. Complete. Finished. Do you understand?'

Miller slowly shook his head.

'Not quite. I've got one hell of a story. And I'm going to write it.'

The visitor's smile faded. He leaned forward.

'Listen, Miller. You're a bloody amateur, and you're lucky to be alive. You're going to write nothing. For one thing you've got nothing to write. I've got Tauber's diary and it's going back home with me, where it belongs. I read it last night. There was a photograph of an army captain in your jacket pocket. Your father?'

Miller nodded.

'So that was what it was really about?' asked the agent.

'Yes.'

'Well, in a way I'm sorry. About your father, I mean. I never thought I'd say that to a German. Now about the file. What was it?'

Miller told him.

'Then why the hell couldn't you let us have it? You're an ungrateful little man. We took a lot of trouble getting you in there, and when you get something you hand it over to your own people. We could have used that information to best advantage.'

'I had to send it to someone, through Sigi. That meant by mail. You're so clever, you never let me have Leon's address.'

Josef nodded.

'All right. But either way you have no story to tell. You have no evidence. The diary's gone, the file is gone. All that remains is your personal word. If you insist on talking nobody will believe you except the Odessa, and they'll come for you. Or, rather, they'll probably hit Sigi or your mother. They play rough, remember?'

Miller thought for a while.

'What about my car?'

'You don't know about that. I forgot.'

Josef told Miller about the bomb in it, and the way it went off.

'I told you they play rough. The car has been found gutted by fire in a ravine. The body in it is unidentified, but not yours. Your story is that you were flagged down by a hitch-hiker, he hit you with an iron bar and went off in it.

'The hospital will confirm you were brought in by a passing motor-cyclist who called an ambulance when he saw you by the roadside. They won't recognise me again, I was in a helmet and goggles at the time. That's the official version and it will stay. To make sure, I rang the German Press Agency two hours ago, claiming to be the hospital, and gave them the same story. You were the victim of a hitch-hiker who later crashed and killed himself.'

Josef stood up and prepared to leave. He looked down at Miller.

'You're a lucky bastard, though you don't seem to realise it. I got the message your girl-friend passed me, presumably on your instructions, at midday yesterday, and by riding like a maniac I made it from Munich to the house on the hill in two and a half hours dead. Which was what you almost were – dead. They had a guy who was going to kill you. I man-aged to interrupt him in time.'

He turned, hand on the doorknob.

'Take a word of advice. Claim the insurance on your car, get a Volks-wagen, go back to Hamburg, marry Sigi, have kids and stick to reporting. Don't tangle with professionals again.'

Half an hour after he had gone the nurse came back.

'There's a phone call for you,' she said.

It was Sigi, crying and laughing down the line. She had received an anonymous call telling her Peter was in Frankfurt General.

'I'm on my way down, right this minute,' she said, and hung up. The phone rang again.

'Miller? This is Hoffmann. I just saw a piece on the agency tapes. You got a bang on the head. Are you all right?'

'I'm fine, Herr Hoffmann,' said Miller.

'Great. When are you going to be fit?'

'In a few days. Why?'

'I've got a story that's right up your street. A lot of daughters of wealthy papas in Germany are going down to the ski slopes and getting screwed by these handsome young ski-instructors. There's a clinic in Bavaria that gets them back out of trouble – for a fat fee and no word to Daddy about it. Seems some of the young studs take a rake-off from the clinic. A great little story. Sex amid the Snow, Orgies in Oberland. When can you start?'

Miller thought.

'Next week.'

'Excellent. By the way, that thing you were on. Nazi-hunting. Did you get the man? Is there a story at all?'

'No, Herr Hoffmann,' said Miller slowly. 'No story.'

'Didn't think so. Hurry up and get well. See you in Hamburg.'

Josef's plane from Frankfurt via London came into Lod Airport, Tel Aviv, as dusk was settling on Tuesday evening. He was met by two men in a car and taken to headquarters for debriefing by the colonel who had signed the cable from Cormorant. They talked until almost two in the morning, a stenographer noting it all down. When it was over the colonel leaned back, smiled and offered his agent a cigarette.

'Well done,' he said simply. 'We've checked on the factory and tipped off the authorities – anonymously of course. The research section will be dismantled. We'll see to that, even if the German authorities don't. But they will. The scientists apparently didn't know who they were working for. We'll approach them all privately and most will agree to destroy their records. They know if the story broke, the weight of opinion in Germany today is pro-Israeli. They'll get other jobs in industry and keep their mouths shut. So will Bonn, and so will we. What about Miller?'

'He'll do the same. What about those rockets?'

The colonel blew a column of smoke and gazed at the stars in the night sky outside.

'I have a feeling they'll never fly now. Nasser has to be ready by the summer of '67 at the latest, and if the research work in that Vulkan factory is destroyed, they'll never mount another operation in time to fit the guidance systems to the rockets before the summer of '67.'

'Then the danger's over,' said the agent. The colonel smiled.

'The danger's never over. It just changes shape. This particular danger may be over. The big one goes on. We're going to have to fight again, and maybe after that, before it's over. Anyway, you must be tired. You can go home now.'

He reached into a drawer and produced a polythene bag of personal effects, while the agent deposited on the desk his false German money, wallet, keys, and in a side room changed clothes, leaving the German clothes with his superior.

At the door the colonel looked the figure up and down with approval and shook hands.

'Welcome home, Major Uri Ben Shaul.'

The agent felt better back in his own identity, the one he had taken in 1947 when he first came to Israel and enlisted in the Palmach.

He took a taxi back home to his flat in the suburbs and let himself in with the key that had just been returned to him with his other effects.

In the darkened bedroom he could make out the sleeping form of Rivka, his wife, the light blanket rising and falling with her breathing. He peeked into the children's room and looked down at their two boys, Shlomo who was six, and the two-year-old baby, Dov.

He wanted badly to climb into bed beside his wife and sleep for several days, but there was one more job to be done. He set down his case and quietly undressed, taking off even the underclothes and socks. He dressed in fresh ones taken from the clothes chest, and Rivka slept on, undisturbed.

From the closet he took his uniform trousers, cleaned and pressed as they always were when he came home, and laced up the gleaming black calf-boots over them. His khaki shirts and ties were where they always were, with razor-sharp creases down the shirt where the hot iron had pressed. Over them he slipped his battle jacket, adorned only with the glinting steel wings of a paratroop officer and five campaign ribbons he had earned in Sinai and in raids across the borders.

The final article was his red beret. When he had dressed he took several articles and stuffed them into a small bag. There was already a dim glint in the east when he got back outside and found his small car still parked where he had left it a month before in front of the block of flats.

Although it was only February 26th, three days before the end of the last month of winter, the air was mild again and gave promise of a brilliant spring.

He drove eastwards out of Tel Aviv and took the road to Jerusalem. There was a stillness about the dawn that he loved, a peace and cleanness that never ceased to cause him wonder. He had seen it a thousand times on patrol in the desert, the phenomenon of a sunrise, cool and beautiful, before the onset of a day of blistering heat and sometimes of combat and death. It was the best time of the day.

The road led across the flat, fertile countryside of the littoral plain towards the ochre hills of Judea, through the waking village of Ramleh. After Ramleh there was in those days a detour round the Latroun Salient, five miles to skirt the front positions of the Jordanian forces. To his left he could see the morning breakfast fires of the Arab Legion sending up thin plumes of blue smoke.

There were a few Arabs awake in the village of Abu Gosh, and when he had climbed up the last hills to Jerusalem the sun had cleared the eastern horizon and glinted off the Dome of the Rock in the Arab section of the divided city.

He parked his car a quarter of a mile from his destination, the mausoleum of Yad Vashem, and walked the rest; down the avenue flanked by trees, planted to the memory of the Gentiles who had tried to help, and to the great bronze doors that guard the shrine to six million of his fellow Jews who died in the holocaust.

The old gatekeeper told him it was not open so early in the morning, but he explained what he wanted and the man let him in. He passed through into the hall of remembrance and glanced about him. He had been there before to pray for his own family, and still the massive grey granite blocks of which the hall was built overawed him.

He walked forward to the rail and gazed at the names written in black on the grey stone floor, in Hebrew and Roman letters. There was no light in the sepulchre but that from the Eternal Flame, flickering above the shallow black bowl from which it sprang.

By its light he could see the names across the floor, score upon score: Auschwitz, Treblinka, Belsen, Ravensbrück, Buchenwald. . . . There were too many to count, but he found the one he sought. Riga.

He did not need a yarmulka to cover himself, for he still wore his red beret which would suffice. From his bag he took a fringed silk shawl, the tallith, the same kind of shawl Miller had found among the effects of the old man in Altona, and not understood. This he draped round his shoulders.

He took a prayer-book from his bag and opened it at the right page. He advanced to the brass rail that separates the hall into two parts, gripped it with one hand and gazed across it at the flame in front of him. Because he was not a religious man he had to consult his prayer-book frequently, as he recited the prayer already five thousand years old.

'Yisgaddal,
Veyiskaddash,
Shemay rabbah ...'

And so it was that twenty-one years after it had died in Riga, a major of paratroops of the Army of Israel, standing on a hill in the Promised Land, finally said Kaddish for the soul of Salomon Tauber.

It would be agreeable if things in this world always finished with all the ends neatly tied up. That is very seldom the case. People go on, to live and die in their own appointed time and place. So far as it has been possible to establish, this is what happened to the main characters.

Peter Miller went home, married and stuck to reporting the sort of things that people want to read over breakfast and in the hairdresser's. By the summer of 1970 Sigi was carrying their third child.

The men of the Odessa scattered. Eduard Roschmann's wife returned home and later received a cable from her husband telling her he was in Argentina. She refused to follow him. In the summer of 1965 she wrote to him at their old address, the Villa Jerbal, to ask him for a divorce before the Argentinian courts.

The letter was forwarded to his new address, and she got a reply consenting to her request, but before the German courts, and enclosing a legal document agreeing to a divorce. She was awarded this in 1966. She still lives in Germany, but has retaken her maiden name of Müller, of which there are tens of thousands in Germany. The man's first wife, Hella, still lives in Austria.

The Werwolf finally made his peace with his furious superiors in Argentina, and settled on a small estate he bought from the money realised by the sale of his effects, on the Spanish island of Formenteria.

The radio factory went into liquidation. The scientists working on the guidance systems for the rockets of Helwan all found jobs in industry or the academic world. The project on which they had unwittingly been working for Roschmann, however, collapsed.

The rockets of Helwan never flew. The fuselages were ready, along with the rocket fuel. The warheads were under production. Those who may doubt the authenticity of those warheads should examine the evidence of Professor Otto Yoklek, given at the trial of Yossef Ben Gal, June 10th–26th, 1963, Basel Provincial Court, Switzerland. The forty pre-production rockets, helpless for want of the electronic systems necessary to guide them to their targets in Israel, were still standing in the deserted factory at Helwan when they were destroyed by bombers during the Six-Day War. Before that the German scientists had disconsolately returned to Germany.

The exposure to the authorities of Klaus Winzer's file upset a lot of Odessa apple-carts. The year which began so well ended for them disastrously. So much so that years later a lawyer and investigator of the Z-Commission in Ludswigsburg was able to say '1964 was a good year for us, yes, a very good year'.

At the end of 1964 Chancellor Erhard, shaken by the exposures, issued a nation-wide and international appeal for all those having knowledge of the whereabouts of wanted SS criminals to come forward and tell the authorities. The response was considerable and the work of the men of Ludwigsburg received an enormous fillip which continued for several more years.

Of the politicians behind the arms deal between Germany and Israel, Chancellor Adenauer of Germany lived in his villa at Rhöndorf, above his beloved Rhine and close to Bonn, and died there on April 19th, 1967. The Israeli Premier David Ben-Gurion stayed on as a member of the Knesset (Parliament) until 1970, then finally retired to his home on the kibbutz of Sede Boker, in the heart of the brown hills of the Negev, on the road from Beer Sheba to Eilat. He likes to receive visitors and talks with animation about many things, but not about the rockets of Helwan and the reprisal campaign against the German scientists who worked on them.

Of the secret service men in the story, General Amit remained Controller until September 1968, and on his shoulders fell the massive responsibility of ensuring his country was provided with pin-point information in time for the Six-Day War. As history records, he succeeded brilliantly.

On his retirement he became chairman and managing director of the labour-owned Koor Industries of Israel. He still lives very modestly, and his charming wife Yona refuses as ever to employ a maid, preferring to do all her own housework.

His successor, who still holds the post, is General Zvi Zamir.

Major Uri Ben Shaul was killed on Wednesday, June 7th, 1967, at the head of a company of paratroops fighting their way into Old Jerusalem. He took a bullet in the head from an Arab Legionary, and went down 400 yards east of the Mandelbaum Gate.

Simon Wiesenthal still lives and works in Vienna, gathering a fact here, a tip there, slowly tracking down the whereabouts of wanted SS murderers, and each month and year brings him a crop of successes.

Leon died in Munich in 1968 and after his death the group of men he had led on his personal crusade of vengeance lost heart and split up.

And last, Top Sergeant Ulrich Frank, the tank commander who crossed Miller's path on the road to Vienna. He was wrong about the fate of his tank, the Dragon Rock. It did not go to the scrap-heap. It was taken away on a low-loader, and he never saw it again. Forty months later he would not have recognised it anyway.

The steel-grey of its body had been painted out and covered with paint the colour of dust-brown to merge with the landscape of the desert. The black cross of the German Army was gone from the turret, and replaced by the pale-blue six-pointed star of David. The name he had given it was gone too, and it had been renamed 'The Spirit of Masada'.

It was still commanded by a top sergeant, a hawk-nosed, black-bearded man called Nathan Levy. On June 5th, 1967, the M-48 began its first and only week of combat since it had rolled from the workshops of Detroit, Michigan, ten years before. It was one of those tanks that General Israel Tal hurled into the battle for the Mitla Pass two days later, and at noon on Saturday, June 10th, caked with dust and oil, scored by bullets, its tracks worn to wafers by the rocks of Sinai, the old Patton rolled to a stop on the eastern bank of the Suez Canal.

THE DOGS OF WAR

For Giorgio, and Christian and Schlee
And Marc and Black Johnny,
And the others in the unmarked graves.
At least we tried.

Contents

'Cry "Havoc" and let slip the dogs of war.'

WILLIAM SHAKESPEARE

'That ... be not told of my death,
Or made to grieve on account of me,
And that I be not buried in consecrated ground,
And that no sexton be asked to toll the bell,
And that nobody is wished to see my dead body,
And that no mourners walk behind me at my funeral,
And that no flowers be planted on my grave,
And that no man remember me,
To this I put my name.'

THOMAS HARDY

Prologue

There were no stars that night on the bush airstrip, nor any moon; just the West African darkness wrapping round the scattered groups like warm, wet velvet. The cloud cover was lying hardly off the tops of the iroko trees and the waiting men prayed it would stay a while longer to shield them from the bombers.

At the end of the runway the battered old DC-4, which had just slipped in for a landing by runway lights that stayed alight for just the last fifteen seconds of final approach, turned and coughed its way blindly towards the palm-thatch huts.

A Federal MIG-17 night fighter, probably flown by one of the six East German pilots sent down over the past three months, to replace the Egyptians who had a horror of flying at night, moaned across the sky to the west. It was out of sight above the cloud layer, as was the runway also hidden from the pilot's eyes. He was seeking the tell-tale flicker of the landing lights going on to bring in a landing plane, but the lights were out.

The pilot of the taxiing DC-4, unable to hear the scream of the jet above him, flicked on his own lights to see where he was going, and from the darkness a voice cried uselessly, 'Kill de lights!' They went out anyway when the pilot had got his bearings, and the fighter above was miles away. To the south there was a rumble of artillery where the front had finally crumbled as men who had had neither food nor bullets for two months threw down their guns and headed for the protecting bush forest.

The pilot of the DC-4 brought his plane to a halt twenty yards from the Super Constellation already parked on the apron, killed the engines and climbed down to the concrete. An African ran over to him and there was a muttered conversation. The two men walked through the darkness towards one of the larger groups of men, a blob of darkness against the darkness of the palm forest. The group parted as the two from the tarmac approached, until the white man who had flown in the DC-4 was face to face with the one who stood in the centre. The white man had never seen him before, but he knew of him, and even in the darkness, dimly illumined by a few cigarettes, he could recognise the man he had come to see.

The pilot wore no cap, so instead of saluting he inclined his head slightly. He had never done that before, not to a black, and could not have explained why he did it.

'My name is Captain Van Cleef,' he said in English, accented in the Afrikaner manner.

The African nodded his acknowledgement, his bushy black beard brushing the front of his striped camouflage uniform as he did so.

'It's a hazardous night for flying, Captain Van Cleef,' he remarked dryly, 'and a little late for more supplies.'

His voice was deep and low, the accent more like that of an English public school man, which he was, than an African. Van Cleef felt uncomfortable and again, as a hundred times during his run through the cloud banks from the coast, asked himself why he had come.

'I didn't bring any supplies, sir. There weren't any more to bring.'

Another precedent set. He had sworn he would not call the man 'sir'. Not a Kaffir. It had just slipped out. But they were right, the other mercenary pilots in the hotel bar in Libreville, the ones who had met him. This one was different.

'Then why have you come?' asked the general softly. 'The children perhaps? There are a number here the nuns would like to fly out to safety, but no more Caritas planes will come in tonight.'

Van Cleef shook his head, then realised no one could see the gesture. He was embarrassed, and thankful that the darkness hid it. Around him the bodyguards clutched their submachine carbines and stared at him.

'No. I came to collect you. If you want to come, that is.'

There was a long silence. He could feel the African staring at him through the gloom, occasionally caught a flash of eye-white as one of the attendants raised his cigarette.

'I see. Did your government instruct you to come in here tonight?'

'No,' said Van Cleef. 'It was my idea.'

There was another long pause. The bearded head was nodding slowly in what could have been comprehension or bewilderment a few feet away from him.

'I am very grateful,' said the voice. 'It must have been quite a trip. Actually I have my own transport. The Constellation. Which I hope will be able to take me away to exile.'

Van Cleef felt relieved. He had no idea what the political repercussions would have been if he had flown back to Libreville with the general in his entourage.

'I'll wait till you're off the ground and gone,' he said, and nodded again. He felt like holding out his hand to shake, but did not know whether he ought. If he had but known it, the African general was in the same quandary. So he turned and walked back to his aircraft.

There was silence for a while in the group of black men after he had left.

'Why does a South African, and an Afrikaner, do a thing like that?' one of the cabinet asked the general. There was a flash of teeth as the leader of the group smiled briefly.

'I don't think we shall ever understand that,' he said.

Farther up the apron, also in the lee of a clump of palm, five men sat in a Landrover and watched the dim figures moving from the bush to the plane. The leader sat beside the African driver, and all five were smoking steadily.

'It must be the South African plane,' said the leader, and turned to one of the four other whites crouched in the Landrover behind him. 'Janni, go and ask the skipper if he'll make room for us.'

A tall, raw-boned, angular man climbed out of the rear of the vehicle. Like the others he was dressed from head to foot in predominantly green jungle camouflage uniform, slashed with streaks of brown. He wore green canvas jack-boots on his feet, the trousers tucked into them. From his belt hung a water bottle and a Bowie knife, three pouches for magazines for the FAL carbine over his shoulder, and they were all empty. As he came round to the front of the Landrover the leader called him again.

'Leave the FAL,' he said, stretching out an arm to take the carbine, 'and Janni, make it good, huh? Because if we don't get out of here in that crate, we could get chopped up in a few days.'

The man called Janni nodded, adjusted the beret on his head and ambled towards the DC-4. Captain Van Cleef did not hear the rubber soles moving up behind him.

'Naand, meneer.'

Van Cleef spun round at the sound of the Afrikaans and took in the shape and size of the man beside him. Even in the darkness he could pick out the black and white skull and crossbones motif on the man's left shoulder. He nodded warily.

'Naand. Jy Afrikaans?'

The tall man nodded.

'Jan Dupree,' he said and held out his hand.

'Kobus Van Cleef,' said the airman and shook.

'Waar gaan-jy nou?' asked Dupree.

'To Libreville. As soon as they finish loading. And you?'

Janni Dupree grinned.

'I'm a bit stuck, me and my mates. We'll get the chop for sure if the Federals find us. Can you help us out?'

'How many of you?' asked Van Cleef.

'Five in all.'

As another mercenary, albeit of the air, Van Cleef did not hesitate. Outlaws sometimes need each other.

'All right, get aboard. But hurry up. As soon as that Connie is off, so are we.'

Dupree nodded his thanks and jog-trotted back to the Landrover. The four other whites were standing in a group round the bonnet.

'It's OK, but we have to get aboard,' the South African told them.

'Right, dump the hardware in the back and let's get moving,' said the group leader. As the rifles and ammunition pouches thumped into the back of the vehicle, he leaned over to the black officer with the Second Lieutenant's tabs who sat at the wheel.

'G'bye, Patrick,' he said. 'I'm afraid it's over now. Take the Landrover and dump it. Bury the guns and mark the spot. Leave your uniform and go for bush. Understand?'

The lieutenant, who a year ago had been a recruit with the rank of private and had been promoted for his ability to fight rather than eat with a knife and fork, nodded sombrely, taking in the instructions.

'Good-bye, sah.'

The four other mercenaries called good-bye and walked towards the DC-4.

The leader was about to follow them when two nuns fluttered up to him from the darkness of the bush behind the parking apron.

'Major.'

The mercenary turned and recognised the first of them as a sister he had first met months earlier, when fighting had raged in the zone where she ran a hospital, and he had been forced to evacuate the whole complex.

'Sister Mary Joseph? What are you doing here?'

The elderly Irish nun began talking earnestly, holding the stained uniform sleeve of his jacket. He nodded.

'I'll try, I can do no more than that,' he said when she had finished.

He walked across the apron to where the South African pilot was standing under the wing of his DC-4 and a watcher could have seen the two mercenaries in discussion for several minutes. Finally the man in uniform came back to the waiting nuns.

'He says yes, but you must hurry, Sister. He wants to get this crate off the ground as soon as he can.'

'God bless you,' said the figure in the white habit, and gave hurried orders to her companion. The latter ran to the rear of the aircraft and began to climb the short ladder to the passenger door. The other scurried back to the shade of a patch of palm behind the parking apron, from which soon emerged a file of men. Each carried a bundle in his arms. On reaching the DC-4 the bundles were passed up to the waiting nun at the top of the steps. Behind her the co-pilot watched her lay the first three side by side in the beginning of a row down the aircraft's hull, then began gruffly to help, taking the bundles from the stretching hands beneath the aircraft's tail and passing them inside.

'God bless you,' whispered the Irishwoman. One of the bundles deposited a few ounces of liquid green excrement on to the co-pilot's sleeve.

'Bloody hell,' he hissed, and went on working.

Left alone the leader of the group of mercenaries glanced towards the

Super Constellation, up whose rear steps a file of refugees, mainly the relations of the leaders of the defeated people, was climbing. In the dim light emanating from the aeroplane's door he caught sight of the man he wanted to see. As he approached, the man was about to mount the steps in turn, while others, destined to stay and go into the bush to hide, waited to pull away the steps. One of them called to the man about to go up.

'Sah. Major Shannon come.'

The general turned as Shannon approached and even at this hour he managed a grin.

'So, Shannon, do you want to come along?'

Shannon arrived in front of him and brought up a salute. The general acknowledged.

'No, thank you, sir. We have transport to Libreville. I just wanted to say good-bye.'

'Yes. It was a long fight. Now it's over, I'm afraid. For some years at any rate. I find it hard to believe my people will continue to live in servitude for ever. By the way, have you and your colleagues been paid up to the contract?'

'Yes, thank you, sir. We're all up to date,' replied the mercenary. The African nodded sombrely.

'Well, good-bye then. And thank you for all you were able to do.'

He held out his hand and the two men shook.

'There's one more thing, sir,' said Shannon. 'Me and the boys, we were talking things over, sitting in the jeep. If there's ever any time . . . well, if you should ever need us, you only have to let us know. We'll all come. You only have to call. The boys want you to know that.'

The general stared at him for several seconds.

'This night is full of surprises,' he said slowly. 'You may not know it yet, but half my senior advisers and all of the wealthy ones are crossing the lines tonight to ingratiate themselves with the enemy. Most of the others will follow suit within a month. Thank you for your offer, Mr Shannon. I will remember it. Good-bye again, and good luck.'

He turned and walked up the steps into the dimly lit interior of the Super Constellation just as the first of the four engines coughed into life. Shannon stepped back and gave the man who had employed his services for a year and a half a last salute.

'Good luck to you,' he said, half to himself. 'You'll need it.'

He turned and walked back to the waiting DC-4. When the door had closed Van Cleef kept the aircraft on the apron, engines turning, as he watched through the gloom the dim droop-nosed shape of the Super Connie rumble down the runway, past his nose, and finally lift off. Neither plane carried any lights, but from the cockpit of the Douglas, the Afrikaner made out the three fins of the Constellation vanishing over the palm trees to the south and into the welcoming clouds. Only then did he ease the DC-4 with its wailing and whimpering cargo forward to the take-off point.

It was close to an hour before Van Cleef ordered his co-pilot to switch on the cabin lights, an hour of jinking from cloud-bank to cloud-bank, breaking cover and scooting across low racks of altostratus to find cover again with another denser bank, always seeking to avoid being caught out in the moonlit white plains by a roving MIG. Only when he knew he was far out over the Gulf, with the coast many miles astern, did he allow the lights on.

Behind him they lit up a weird spectacle which could have been drawn by Doré in one of his blacker moods. The floor of the aircraft was carpeted with sodden and fouled blankets, which an hour earlier had been the wrappings of their contents. These contents of the bundles lay writhing in rows down both sides of the cargo space, forty small children, shrunken, wizened, deformed by malnutrition. Sister Mary Joseph rose from her crouch behind the cabin door and began to move among the starvelings, each of whom had a piece of sticking plaster stuck to his or her forehead, just below the line of the hair, long since turned to an ochre red by anaemia. The plaster bore in ball-point letters the relevant information for the orphanage outside Libreville. Name and number, if not rank. They don't give rank to losers.

In the tail of the plane the five mercenaries blinked in the light and glanced at their fellow passengers. They had seen it all before, many times, over the past months. Each man felt some disgust, but none showed it. You can get used to anything eventually. In the Congo, Yemen, Katanga, Sudan. Always the same story, always the kids. And always nothing you can do about it. So they reasoned, and pulled out their cigarettes.

The cabin lights allowed them to see each other properly for the first time since sundown the previous evening. The uniforms were stained with sweat and the red earth and the faces drawn with fatigue. The leader sat with his back to the lavatory door, feet straight out, facing up the fuselage towards the pilot's cabin. Carlo Alfred Thomas Shannon, thirty-three, blond hair cropped to a ragged crew-cut. Very short hair is more convenient in the tropics because the sweat runs out easier and the bugs can't get in. Nicknamed Cat Shannon from his initials, he came originally from County Tyrone in the province of Ulster. Sent by his father to be educated at a minor English public school, he no longer carried the distinctive accent of Northern Ireland in his speech. After five years in the Royal Marines, he had left to try his hand at civilian life, and six years ago he had found himself working for a London-based trading company in Uganda. One sunny morning he quietly closed his accounts ledgers, climbed into his Landrover and drove westwards to the Congolese border. A week later he signed on as a mercenary in Mike Hoare's Fifth Commando at Stanleyville.

He had seen Hoare depart and John-John Peters take over, had quarrelled with Peters and driven north to join Denard at Paulis, had been in the Stanleyville mutiny two years later and, after the Frenchman's evacuation to Rhodesia with head wounds, had joined Black Jacques Schramme, the Belgian planter-turned-mercenary, on the long march to Bukavu and thence to Kigali. After repatriation by the Red Cross, he had promptly volunteered for another African war and had finally taken command of his own battalion. But too late to win, always too late to win.

To his immediate left sat what was arguably the best mortarman north of the Zambezi. Big Jan Dupree was aged twenty-eight and came from Paarl in Cape Province, a son of the impoverished stock of Huguenot extraction, whose ancestors had fled to the Cape of Good Hope from the wrath of Mazarin after the destruction of religious liberty in France. His hatchet face, dominated by a curved beak of a nose above a thin-lipped mouth, looked even more haggard than usual, his exhaustion furrowing deep lines down each cheek. The eyelids were down over the pale blue eyes, the sandy eyebrows and hair were smudged with dirt. After glancing down at the children lying down the aisle of the plane, he muttered '*Bliksems*' (bastards) at the world of possession and privilege he held responsible for the ills of this planet, and tried to get to sleep.

By his side sprawled Marc Vlaminck, Tiny Marc, so called because of his vast bulk. A Fleming from Ostend, he stood six feet and three inches in his socks, when he wore any, and weighed eighteen stone. Some people thought it might be fat. It was not. He was regarded with trepidation by the police of Ostend, for the most part peaceable men who prefer to avoid problems rather than seek them out, and was viewed with kindly appreciation by the glaziers and carpenters of that city for the work he provided them. They said you could tell a bar where Tiny Marc had become playful by the number of artisans it needed to put it back together again.

An orphan, he had been brought up in an institution run by the priests, who had tried to beat some sense of respect into the overgrown boy, and so repeatedly that even Marc had finally lost patience and at the age of thirteen laid one of the cane-wielding holy fathers cold along the flagstones with a single punch.

After that it had been a series of reformatories, then approved school, a dose of juvenile prison and an almost communal sigh of relief when he enlisted in the paratroops. He had been one of the 500 men who dropped on to Stanleyville with Colonel Laurent to rescue the missionaries whom the local Simba chief, Christophe Gbenye, theatened to roast alive in the main square.

Within forty minutes of hitting the airfield, Tiny Marc had found his vocation in life. After a week he went AWOL to avoid being repatriated to barracks in Belgium and joined the mercenaries. Apart from his fists and shoulders, Tiny Marc was extremely useful with a bazooka, his favourite weapon, which he handled with the easy nonchalance of a boy with a pea-shooter.

The night he flew out of the enclave towards Libreville he was just thirty.

Across the fuselage from the Belgian sat Jean-Baptiste Langarotti, engaged in his habitual occupation to while away the hours of waiting. Short, compact, lean and olive-skinned, he was a Corsican, born and raised in the town of Calvi. At the age of eighteen he had been called up by France to go and fight as one of the hundred thousand *appelés* in the Algerian war. Halfway through his eighteen months he had signed on as a regular and later had transferred to the 10th Colonial Paratroops, the dreaded red berets commanded by General Massu and known simply as '*les paras*'. He was twenty-one when the crunch came and some units of the professional French colonial army rallied to the cause of an eternally French Algeria, a cause embodied for the moment in the organisation of the OAS. Langarotti went with the OAS, deserted and, after the failure of the April 1961 *putsch*, went underground. He was caught in France three years later living under a false name and spent four years in prison, eating his heart out in the dark and sunless cells of first the Santé in Paris, then Tours, and finally the Île de Ré. He was a bad prisoner, and two guards would carry marks to prove it until they died.

Beaten half to death several times for attacks on guards, he had served his full time without remission, and emerged in 1968 with only one fear in the world, the fear of small enclosed spaces, cells and holes. He had long since vowed never to return to one, even if staying out cost him his life, and to take half a dozen with him if 'they' ever came for him again. Within three months of release he had flown down to Africa by paying his own way, talked himself into a war and joined Shannon as a professional mercenary. He was thirty-one when he flew out that night. Since being released from prison he had practised steadily with the weapon he had learned to use first as a boy in Corsica and with which he had later made himself a reputation in the back streets of Algiers. Round his left wrist he carried a broad leather strap, resembling for all the world the kind of strop used by old-fashioned barbers for honing their razors. It was held in place by two press-studs. In moments of idleness he would take it off, turn it over to the side unmarked by the studs, and wrap it round his left fist. That was where it was as he whiled away the time to Libreville. In his right hand was the knife, the six-inch-bladed bone-handled weapon that he could use so fast it was back in its sleeve-sheath before the victim had realised he was dead. In steady rhythm the blade moved backwards and forwards across the tense leather of the strop, already razor sharp, becoming with each stroke a mite sharper. The movement soothed his nerves. It also annoyed everybody else, but they never complained. Nor did those who knew him ever quarrel with the soft voice or the sad half-smile of the little man.

Sandwiched between Langarotti and Shannon was the oldest man in the party, the German. Kurt Semmler was forty, and it was he who, in the early days back in the enclave, had devised the skull-and-crossbones motif that the mercenaries and their African trainees wore. It was also he who had cleared a five-mile sector of Federal soldiers by marking out the front line with stakes, each bearing the head of one of the previous day's Federal casualties. For a month after that his was the quietest sector of the campaign. Born in 1930, he had been brought up in Germany through the Hitler period, the son of a Munich engineer who had later died on the Russian front with the Todt Organisation. At the age of fifteen, a fervent Hitler Youth graduate, as indeed was almost the entire youth of the country after twelve years of Hitler, he had commanded a small unit of children younger than himself and old men over seventy. His mission had been to stop the columns of tanks of General George Patton, armed with one Panzerfaust and three bolt-action rifles. Not surprisingly he had failed, and spent his adolescence in a Bavaria under American occupation, which he hated. He also had little time for his mother, a religious maniac who wanted him to become a priest. At seventeen, he ran away, crossed the French frontier at Strasbourg, and signed on in the Foreign Legion at the recruiting office sited in Strasbourg for the purpose of picking up runaway Germans and Belgians. After a year in Sidi-bel-Abbès, he went with the expeditionary force to Indo-China. Eight years and Dien Bien Phu later, with a lung removed by surgeons at Tourane (Danang), unable fortunately to watch the final humiliation in Hanoi, he was flown back to France. After recuperation he was sent to Algeria in 1958 as a top sergeant in the élite of the élite of the French colonial army, the 1st Regiment Étranger Parachutiste. He was one of a handful who had already survived the utter destruction of the 1st REP twice in Indo-China, when it was at battalion size and later at regiment size. He revered only two men, Colonel Roger Faulques, who had been in the original Compagnie Étrangère Parachutiste when, at company strength, it had been wiped out the first time, and Commandant Le Bras, another veteran, who now commanded the Garde Républicaine of the Republic of Gabon, and kept that uranium-rich state safe for France. Even Colonel Marc Rodin, who had once commanded him, had lost his respect when the OAS finally crumbled.

Semmler had been in the 1st REP when it marched to a man into perdition in the *putsch* of Algiers and was later disbanded permanently by Charles de Gaulle. He had followed where his French officers had led, and later, picked up just after Algerian independence in Marseilles in September 1962, had served two years in prison. His four rows of campaign ribbons had saved him worse. Out in Civvy Street for the first time in twenty years in 1964, he had been contacted by a former cell mate with a proposition – to join him in a smuggling operation in the Mediterranean. For three years, apart from one spent in an Italian jail, he had run spirits, gold, and occasionally arms, from one end of the Mediterranean to the other. Finally he had been making a fortune on the Italy–Yugoslavia cigarette run when his partner had double-crossed the buyers and the sellers at the same time, pointed the finger at Semmler and vanished with the money. Wanted by a lot of belligerent gentlemen, Semmler had hitched a lift by sea to Spain, ridden a series of buses to Lisbon, contacted an arms dealer friend and taken passage to the African war about which he had read in the papers. Shannon had taken him like a shot, for with sixteen years of combat he was more experienced than them all in jungle warfare. He too dozed on the flight to Libreville.

It was two hours before dawn when the DC-4 began to approach the airport. Above the mewling of the children another sound could be made out, the sound of a man whistling. It was Shannon. His colleagues knew he always whistled when he was going into action or coming out of it. They also knew the name of the tune, because he had told them once. It was called 'Spanish Harlem'.

The DC-4 circled the airport at Libreville twice while Van Cleef talked to ground control. As the old cargo plane rolled to a halt at the end of a runway a military jeep carrying two French officers swerved up in front of the nose and they beckoned Van Cleef to follow them round the taxi track.

They led away from the main airport buildings to a cluster of huts on the far side of the airport and it was here that the DC-4 was signalled to halt but keep its engines running. Within seconds a set of steps was up against the rear of the aeroplane and from the inside the co-pilot heaved open the door. A képi poked inside and surveyed the interior, the nose beneath it wrinkling in distaste at the smell. The French officer's eyes came to rest on the five mercenaries, and he beckoned them to follow him down the tarmac. When they were on the ground the officer gestured to the co-pilot to close the door, and without more ado the DC-4 moved forward again to roll round the airport to the main buildings where a team of French Red Cross nurses and doctors was waiting to receive the children and take them away to the paediatric clinic. As the aircraft swung past them the five mercenaries waved their thanks at Van Cleef up in his flight deck, and turned to follow the French officer.

They had to wait an hour in one of the huts, perched uncomfortably on upright wooden chairs, while several other young French servicemen peeked in through the door to take a look at *'les affreux'*, the terrible ones, as they were called in French slang. Finally they heard a jeep squeal to a halt outside and the smack of feet coming to attention in the corridor. When the door finally opened, it was to admit a tanned, hard-faced senior officer in tropical fawn uniform and a képi with gold braid ringing the peak. Shannon noticed the keen, darting eyes, the iron-grey hair cropped short beneath the képi, the parachutist's wings pinned above the five rows of campaign ribbons and the sight of Semmler leaping to ramrod attention, chin up, five fingers pointing straight down what had once been the seams of his combat trousers. Shannon needed no more to tell him who the visitor was, the legendary Le Bras.

The Indo-China/Algeria veteran shook hands with each, pausing in front of Semmler longer.

'*Alors*, Semmler?' he said softly, with a slow smile. 'Still fighting. But not an adjutant any more. A captain now, I see.'

Semmler was embarrassed.

'*Oui, mon commandant, pardon, colonel.* Just temporary.'

Le Bras nodded pensively several times. Then he addressed them all.

'I will have you quartered comfortably. No doubt you will appreciate a bath, a shave and some food. Apparently you have no other clothes; these will be provided. I am afraid for the time being you will have to remain confined to your quarters. This is solely a precaution. There are a lot of Press men in town, and all forms of contact with them must be avoided. As soon as it is feasible we will arrange to fly you back to Europe.'

He had said all he came to say, so he stopped. Raising his right hand to his képi brim at the five rigid figures, he left.

An hour later, after a journey in a closed van and entrance by the back door, the men were in their quarters, the five bedrooms of the top floor of the Gamba Hotel, a new construction situated only five hundred yards from the airport building across the road, and therefore miles from the centre of town. The young officer who came with them told them they would have to take their meals on the same floor, and remain there until further notice. Within an hour he was back with towels, razors, toothpaste and brushes, soap and sponges. A tray of coffee had already arrived, and each man sank gratefully into a deep, steaming, soap-smelling bath, the first in over six months.

At noon an Army barber came, and a corporal with piles of slacks and shirts, vests, pants and socks, pyjamas and canvas shoes. They tried them on, selected the ones they wanted and the corporal retired with the surplus. The officer was back at one with four waiters bearing lunch, and told them they must stay away from the balconies. If they wanted to exercise in their confinement they would have to do it in their rooms. He would return that evening with a selection of books and magazines, though he could not promise English or Afrikaans.

After eating as never in the previous six months, since their last leave period from the fighting, the five men rolled into bed and slept. While they snored on unaccustomed mattresses between unbelievable sheets, Van Cleef lifted his DC-4 off the tarmac in the dusk, flew a mile away past the windows of the Gamba Hotel and headed south for Caprivi and Johannesburg. His job too was over.

In fact the five mercenaries spent four weeks on the top floor of the hotel, while Press interest in them died down and the reporters were all called back to their head offices by editors who saw no point in keeping men in a city where there was no news to be had.

One evening, without warning, a French captain on the staff of Commandant Le Bras came to see them. He grinned broadly.

'Messieurs, I have news for you. You are flying out tonight. To Paris. You are all booked on the Air Afrique flight at 23.30 hours.'

The five men, bored to distraction by their prolonged confinement, cheered.

The flight to Paris took ten hours, with stops at Douala and Nice. Just before ten the following day they emerged into the blustery cold of Le Bourget airport on a mid-February morning. In the airport coffee lounge they made their good-byes. Dupree elected to take the transit coach to Orly and buy himself a single ticket on the next SAA flight to Johannesburg and Cape Town. Semmler opted to go with him and return to Munich for a visit at least. Vlaminck said he would head for the Gare du Nord and take the first express to Brussels and connect for Ostend. Langarotti was going to the Gare de Lyon to take the train to Marseilles.

'Let's stay in touch,' they said, and looked at Shannon. He was their leader, it would be up to him to look for work, another contract, another war. Similarly, if any of them heard anything that involved a group, he would want to contact one of the group, and Shannon was the obvious one.

'I'll stay in Paris for a while,' said Shannon. 'There's more chance of an interim job here than in London.'

So they exchanged addresses, *poste restante* addresses, or bars where the barman would pass on a message or keep a letter until the addressee dropped in for a drink. And then they parted and went their separate ways.

The security surrounding their flight back from Africa had been tight, for there were no waiting Press men. But someone had heard of their arrival, and he was waiting for Shannon when, after the others had left, the group's leader came out of the terminal building.

'Shannon.'

The voice pronounced the name in the French way, and the tone was not friendly. Shannon turned and his eyes narrowed fractionally as he saw the figure standing ten yards from him. The man was burly, with a down-turned moustache. He wore a heavy coat against the winter cold, and walked forward until the two men faced each other from two feet. To judge by the way they surveyed each other, there was no love lost between them.

'Roux,' said Shannon.

'So, you're back.'

'Yes. We're back.'

The Frenchman sneered. 'And you lost.'

'We didn't have much choice,' said Shannon.

'A word of advice, my friend,' snapped Roux. 'Go back to your own country. Do not stay here. It would be unwise. This is my city. If there is any contract to be found here, I will hear first news of it, I will conclude it. And I will select those who share in it.'

For answer Shannon walked to the first taxi waiting at the kerb and humped his grip into the back. Roux walked after him, his face mottling with anger.

'Listen to me, Shannon. I'm warning you . . .'

The Irishman turned to face him again.

'No, you listen to me, Roux. I'll stay in Paris just as long as I want. I was never impressed by you in the Congo, and I'm not now. So get stuffed.'

As the taxi moved away, Roux stared after it angrily. He was muttering to himself as he strode towards the car park and his own automobile.

He switched on, engaged gear and sat for a few moments staring through the windscreen.

'One day I'll kill that bastard,' he murmured to himself. But the thought hardly put him in a better mood.

PART ONE
The Crystal Mountain

1

Jack Mulrooney shifted his bulk on the canvas and frame cot beneath the mosquito netting and watched the slow lightening of the darkness above the trees to the east. A faint paling, enough to make out the trees towering over the clearing. He drew on his cigarette and cursed the primeval jungle which surrounded him, and like all old Africa hands asked himself once again why he ever returned to the pestiferous continent.

If he had really tried to analyse it, he would have admitted he could not live anywhere else, certainly not in London or even Britain. He couldn't take the cities, the rules and regulations, the taxes, the cold. Like all old hands, he alternately loved and hated Africa, but conceded it had got into his blood over the past quarter century, along with the malaria, the whisky and the million insect stings and bites.

He had come out from England in 1945 at the age of twenty-five, after five years as a fitter in the Royal Air Force, part of them at Takoradi where he had assembled crated Spitfires for onward flight to East Africa and the Middle East the long way round. That was his first sight of Africa, and on demobilisation he had taken his gratuity, bid good-bye to frozen, rationed London in December 1945 and taken ship for West Africa. Someone had told him there were fortunes to be made in Africa.

He had found no fortunes but after wandering the continent had got himself a small tin concession in the Benue Plateau, eighty miles from Jos in Nigeria. Prices had been good while the Malay emergency was on, and tin was expensive. He had worked alongside his Tiv labourers, and at the English club where the colonial ladies gossiped away the last days of empire they said he had 'gone native' and it was a 'damned bad show'. The truth was, Mulrooney really preferred the African way of life. He liked the bush, he liked the Africans who did not seem to mind that he swore and roared and cuffed them to get more work done. He also sat and took palm wine with them and observed the tribal taboos. He did not patronise them. His tin concession ran out in 1960 around the time of independence and he went to work as a chargehand for a company running a larger and more efficient concession nearby. It was called Manson

Consolidated, and when that concession was also exhausted in 1962 he was signed on the staff.

At fifty he was still a big, powerful man, large-boned and strong as an ox. His hands were enormous, chipped and scarred by years in the mines. He ran one of them through his wild, crinkly grey hair and with the other stubbed out the cigarette in the damp red earth beneath the cot. It was lighter now, soon it would be dawn. He could hear his cook blowing on the beginnings of a fire on the other side of the clearing.

Mulrooney called himself a mining engineer, although he had no degree in mining or engineering. He had done a course in both and added what no university could ever teach – twenty-five years of hard experience. He had burrowed for gold on the Rand and copper outside Ndola; drilled for precious water in Somaliland, grubbed for diamonds in Sierra Leone. He could tell an unsafe mine shaft by instinct and the presence of an ore deposit by the smell. At least, that was his claim and after he had taken his habitual twenty bottles of beer in the shanty town of an evening no one was going to argue the toss. In reality he was one of the last of the old prospectors. He knew that ManCon, as the company was known for short, gave him the little jobs, the ones in the deep bush, the wild hinterlands that were miles from civilisation and still had to be checked out. But he liked it that way. He preferred to work alone; it was his way of life.

The latest job had certainly fulfilled these conditions. For three months he had been prospecting in the foothills of the range called the Crystal Mountains in the hinterland of the republic of Zangaro, a tiny enclave on the coast of West Africa.

He had been told where to concentrate his survey, around the Crystal Mountain itself. The chain of large hills, curved hummocks rising to two or three thousand feet, ran in a line from one side of the republic to the other, parallel to the coast and forty miles from it. The range divided the coastal plain from the hinterland. There was only one gap in the chain and through it ran the only road into the interior, and that was a narrow dirt road, baked like concrete in summer, a quagmire in winter. Beyond the mountains the natives were the Vindu, a tribe of almost Iron Age development, except that their implements were of wood. He had been in some wild places but vowed he had never seen anything as backward as the hinterland of Zangaro.

Set on the farther side of the range of hills was the single mountain that gave its name to the rest. It was not even the biggest of them. Forty years earlier a lone missionary, penetrating the hills into the interior, branched to the south after following the gap in the range, and after twenty miles glimpsed a hill set aside from the rest. It had rained the previous night, a torrential downpour, one of the many that gave the area its annual rainfall of 300 inches during five soaking months. As the priest looked he saw that the mountain seemed to be glittering in the morning sun, and he called it the Crystal Mountain. He noted this in his diary. Two days later he was clubbed and eaten. The diary was found by a patrol of colonial soldiers a year later, used as a juju by a local village.

The soldiers did their duty and wiped out the village, then returned to the coast and handed the diary to the mission society. Thus the name the priest had given to the mountain lived on, even if nothing else he did for an ungrateful world was remembered. Later the same name was given to the entire range of hills.

What the man had seen in the morning light was not crystal but a myriad of streams caused by the water of the night's rain cascading off the mountain. Rain was also cascading off all the other mountains, but the sight of it was hidden by the dense jungle vegetation that covered them all like a chunky green blanket when seen from afar and proved to be a steaming hell when penetrated. The one that glittered with a thousand rivulets did so because the vegetation was substantially thinner on the flanks of this hill. It never occurred to him, or to any of the other dozen white men who had ever seen it, to wonder why.

After three months living in the steaming hell of the jungles that surrounded Crystal Mountain, Mulrooney knew why.

He had started by encircling the entire mountain and had discovered that there was effectively a gap between the seaward flank and the rest of the chain. This set the Crystal Mountain eastwards of the main chain, standing on its own. Because it was lower than the highest peaks to seaward, it was invisible from the other side. Nor was it particularly noticeable in any other way, except that it had more streams running off it per mile of hillside than the other hills to north and south.

Mulrooney counted them all, both on the Crystal Mountain and its companions. There was no doubt of it. The water ran off the other mountains after rain, but a lot of water was soaked up in the soil. The other mountains had twenty feet of topsoil over the basic rock structure beneath, the Crystal Mountain hardly any. He had his native workers, locally recruited Vindu, bore a series of holes with the auger he had with him, and confirmed the difference in depth of the topsoil in twenty places. From these he would work out why.

Over millions of years the earth had been formed by the decomposition of the rock and by dust carried on the wind, and although each rainfall had eroded some of it down the slopes into the streams, and from the streams to the rivers and thence to the shallow, silted estuary, some earth had also remained, lodged in little crannies, left alone by the running water which had bored its own holes in the soft rock. And these holes had become drains, so that part of the rainfall ran off the mountain, finding its own channels and wearing them deeper and deeper, and some had sunk into the mountain, both having the effect of leaving part of the topsoil intact. Thus the earth layer had built up and up, a little thicker each century or millennium. The birds and the wind had brought seeds, which had found the niches of earth and flourished there, their roots contributing to the process of retaining the earth on the hill slopes. When Mulrooney saw the hills, there was enough rich earth to sustain mighty trees and tangled vines which covered the slopes and the summits of all the hills. All except one.

On this one the water could not burrow channels that became streams nor could it sink into the rock face, especially on the steepest face which was to the east, towards the hinterland. Here the earth had collected in pockets and the pockets had produced clumps of bush, grass and fern. From niche to niche the vegetation had reached out to itself, linking vines and tendrils in a thin screen across bare patches of rock, regularly washed clean by the falling water of the rain season. It was these patches of shimmering water amid the green that the missionary had seen before he died. The reason for the change was simple; the separate hill was of a different rock from the main range, an ancient rock hard as granite as compared to the soft more recent rocks of the main chain of hills.

Mulrooney had completed his circle of the mountain and established this beyond a doubt. It took him a fortnight to do it, and to establish that no less than seventy streams ran off the Crystal Mountain. Most of them joined up into three main streams that flowed away eastwards out of the foothills into the deeper valley. He noticed something else. Along the banks of the streams that came off this mountain the soil colour was different, as was also the vegetation. Some plants appeared unaffected, others were non-existent although they flourished on the other mountains and beside the other streams. In general the vegetation was thinner beside the streams flowing off the Crystal Mountain than beside the others. This could not be explained by lack of soil, for there was plenty.

So there was something different about that earth, something that stunted plant life along the banks of the streams.

Mulrooney set about charting the seventy streams that took his interest, drawing his map as he went. He also took samples of the sand and gravel along the beds of the streams, starting with the surface gravel, then working down to bedrock.

In each case he took two buckets full of gravel, pouring them out on to a tarpaulin and coning and quartering. This is a process of sample-taking. He piled the gravel into a cone, then quartered it with a shovel blade, took the two opposite quarters of his choice, re-mixed them and made another one. Then quartered that one, working down till he had a cross-section of the sample weighing two to three pounds. This went into a polythene-lined canvas bag after drying, the bag sealed and carefully labelled. In a month he had 1500 pounds of sand and gravel in six hundred bags from the beds of the seventy streams. Then he started on the mountain itself.

He already believed his sacks of gravel would prove to contain, under laboratory examination, quantities of alluvial tin, minute particles washed down from the mountain over tens of thousands of years, showing that there was cassiterite, or tin ore, buried in the Crystal Mountain.

He divided the mountain faces into sections, seeking to identify the birthplaces of the streams and the rock faces that fed them in the wet season. By the end of the week he knew there was no mother lode of tin inside the rock, but suspected what geologists call a disseminated deposit. The signs of mineralisation were everywhere. Beneath the trailing tendrils of vegetation he found faces of rock shot through with stringers, half-inch wide veins like the capillaries in a drinker's nose, of milky white quartz, lacing yard after yard of bare rock face.

Everything he saw about him said 'Tin'. He went right round the mountain again three times, and his observations confirmed the disseminated deposit, the ever present stringers of white in the dark grey rock. With hammer and chisel he smashed holes deep in the rock and the picture was still the same. Sometimes he thought he saw dark blurs in the quartz, confirming the presence of tin.

Then he began chipping in earnest, marking his progress as he went. He took samples of the pure white stringers of quartz, and to be on the safe side he also took samples of the country rock, the rock between the veins. Three months after he had entered the primeval forest east of the mountains he was finished. He had another 1500 pounds of rock to carry back to the coast with him. The whole ton and a half of rock and alluvial samples had been carried in portions every three days back from his working camp to the main camp, where he now lay waiting for dawn, and stacked in cones under tarpaulins.

After coffee and breakfast the bearers, whose terms he had negotiated the previous day, would come from the village and carry his trophies back to the track that called itself a road and linked the hinterland with the coast. There, in a roadside village, lay his two-ton truck, immobilised by the lack of the key and distributor rotor that lay in his knapsack. It should still work, if the natives had not hacked it to bits. He had paid the village chief enough to look after it. With his samples aboard the lorry and twenty porters walking ahead to pull the lurching vehicle up the gradients and out of the ditches, he would be back in the capital in three days. After a cable to London he would have to wait several days for the company's chartered ship to come and take him off. He would have preferred to turn north at the coast highway and drive the extra hundred miles into the neighbouring republic where there was a proper airport, and freight his samples home. But the agreement between ManCon and the Zangaran government specified he would take it back to the capital.

Jack Mulrooney heaved himself out of his cot, swung aside the netting and roared at his cook, 'Hey, Dingaling, where's my bloody coffee?'

The Vindu cook who did not understand a word except 'coffee' grinned from beside the fire and waved happily. Mulrooney strode across the clearing towards his canvas wash bucket and began scratching as the mosquitoes descended on the sweating torso.

'Bloody Africa,' he muttered as he doused his face. But he was content that morning. He was convinced he had found both alluvial tin and tin-bearing rock. The only question was how much tin per rock-ton. With tin standing at about 3300 dollars per ton it would be up to the analysts and mining economists to work out if the quantity of tin per ton of rock merited establishing a mining camp with its complex machinery and teams of workers, not to mention improved access to the coast by a narrow-gauge railway that would have to be built from scratch. And it was certainly a God-forsaken and inaccessible place. As usual, everything would be worked out, taken up or thrown away, on the basis of pounds, shilling and pence. That was the way of the world. He slapped another mosquito off his upper arm and pulled on his tee-shirt.

Six days later Jack Mulrooney leaned over the rail of a small coaster, chartered by his company, and spat over the side as the coast of Sangaro slid away.

'Bloody bastards,' he muttered savagely. He carried a series of livid bruises about his chest and back, and a raw graze down one cheek, the outcome of swinging rifle butts when the troops had raided the hotel.

It had taken him two days to bring his samples from the deep bush to the track, and another grunting, sweating day and night to haul the truck along the pitted and rutted earth road from the interior to the coast. In the wet he would never have made it, and in the dry season which had another month to run the concrete-hard mud ridges had nearly smashed the Mercedes to pieces. Three days earlier he had paid and dismissed his Vindu workers and trundled the creaking truck down the last stretch to the tarmac road which started only fourteen miles from the capital. From there it had been an hour to the city and the hotel.

Not that 'hotel' was the right word. Since independence the town's main hostelry had degenerated into a flop-house, but it had a car park, and here he had parked and locked the truck, then sent his cable. He had only just been in time. Six hours after he sent it, all hell broke loose, and the port, airport and all other communications had been closed by order of the president.

The first he had known about it was when a group of soldiers, dressed like tramps and wielding rifles by the barrels, had burst into the hotel and started to ransack the rooms. There was no point in asking what they wanted, for they only screamed back in a lingo that meant nothing to him, though he thought he recognised the Vindu dialect he had heard his workers using over the past three months.

Being Mulrooney, he had taken two clubbings from rifle butts, then swung a fist. The blow carried the nearest soldier halfway down the hotel corridor on his back, and the rest of the pack had gone wild. It was only by the grace of God no shots were fired, and also due to the fact that the soldiers preferred to use their guns as clubs rather than search for complicated mechanisms like triggers and safety catches.

He had been dragged to the police barracks which were the nearest, and had been alternately screamed at and ignored in a subterranean cell for two days. If he did but know it, he had been lucky. A Swiss businessman, one of the rare foreign visitors to the republic, had witnessed his departure and feared for his life. The man had contacted the Swiss embassy, one of the only six European and North American embassies in the town, and they had contacted ManCon, whose name they had learned from the businessman, who in turn had looked through Mulrooney's belongings.

Two days later the called-for coaster had arrived from farther up the coast and the Swiss consul had negotiated Mulrooney's release. No doubt

a bribe had been paid, and no doubt ManCon would foot the bill. Jack
Mulrooney was still aggrieved. On release he had found his lorry broken
open and his samples strewn all over the car park. The rocks had all been
marked and could be reassembled but the sand, gravel and chippings
were mixed up. Fortunately each of the split bags, about fifty in all, had
half their contents intact, so he had re-sealed them and taken them to the
boat. Even here the customs men, police and soldiers had searched the
boat from stem to stern, screamed and shouted at the crew, and all without saying what they were looking for.

The terrified official from the Swiss consulate who had taken Mulrooney back from the barracks to his hotel had told him there had been
rumours of an attempt on the president's life and the troops were looking
for a missing senior officer who was presumed to be responsible.

Four days after leaving the port of Clarence, Jack Mulrooney, still nurse-
maiding his rock samples, arrived back at Luton, England, aboard a chartered aircraft. A truck had taken his samples away for analysis at
Watford, and after a checkout by the company doctor he had been allowed to start his three weeks' leave. He had gone to spend it with his
sister in Dulwich, and within a week was thoroughly bored.

Exactly three weeks later to the day, Sir James Manson, Knight Commander of the British Empire, chairman and managing director of
Manson Consolidated Mining Company Limited, leaned back in his
leather armchair in the penthouse office suite on the tenth floor of this
company's London headquarters, glanced once more at the report in
front of him and breathed, 'Jesus Christ'. No one answered.

He rose from behind the broad desk, crossed the room to the picture
windows on the south face, and gazed down at the sprawl of the City of
London, the inner square mile of the ancient capital and heart of a financial empire that was still worldwide, despite what its detractors said. To
some of the scuttling beetles in sombre grey, topped by black bowler
hats, it was perhaps a place of employment only, boring, wearisome,
exacting its toll of a man, his youth, his manhood, his middle age, until
final retirement. For others, young and hopeful, it was a palace of opportunity, where merit and hard work were rewarded with the prizes of
advancement and security. To romantics it was no doubt the home of the
houses of the great merchant-adventurers, to a pragmatist the biggest
market in the world, and to a left-wing trade unionist a place where the
idle and worthless rich, born to wealth and privilege, lolled at ease in
luxury. James Manson was a cynic and a realist. He knew what the
City was; it was a jungle pure and simple, and in it he was one of the
panthers.

A born predator, he had nevertheless realised early that there were
certain rules that needed to be publicly revered and privately ripped to
shreds; that, as in politics, there was only one commandment, the
eleventh, 'Thou shalt not be found out.' It was by obeying the first requirement that he had acquired his knighthood in the New Year's

Honours List a month before. This had been proposed by the Conservative Party (ostensibly for services to industry, but in reality for secret contributions to party funds for the general election), and accepted by the Wilson government because of his support for their policy on Nigeria. And it was by fulfilling the second requirement that he had made his fortune and why, holding twenty-five per cent of the stock of his own mining corporation, and occupying the penthouse floor, he was a millionaire several times over.

He was sixty-one, short, aggressive, built like a tank, with a thrusting vigour and a piratical ruthlessness that women found attractive and competitors feared. He had enough cunning to pretend to show respect for the establishments of both the City and the Realm, of commercial and political life, even though he was aware that both organs were riven through with men of almost complete moral unscrupulousness behind the public image. He had collected a few on his board of directors, including two former ministers in previous Conservative administrations. Neither was averse to a fat supplementary fee over and above director's salary, payable in the Cayman Islands or Grand Bahama, and one to his knowledge enjoyed the private diversion of waiting at table upon three or four leather-clad tarts, himself dressed in a maid's cap, a pinafore and a bright smile. Manson regarded both men as useful, possessing the advantage of considerable influence and superb connections without the inconvenience of integrity. The rest of the public knew both men as distinguished public servants. So James Manson was respectable within the set of rules of the City, a set of rules that had nothing whatever to do with the rest of humanity.

It had not always been so, which was why enquirers into his background found themselves up against one blank wall after another. Very little was known of his first start in life, and he knew enough to keep it that way. He would let it be known that he was the son of a Rhodesian train driver, brought up not far from the sprawling copper mines of Ndola, Northern Rhodesia, now Zambia. He would even let it be known that he had started work at the minehead as a boy, and later had made his first fortune in copper. But never how he had made it.

In fact he had quit the mines quite early, before he was twenty, and had realised that the men who risked their lives below ground amid roaring machinery would never make money, not big money. That lay above ground, and not even in mine management. As a teenager he had studied finance, the using and manipulating of money, and his nightly studies had taught him that more was made in shares in copper in a week than a miner made in his whole life.

He had started as a share-pusher on the Rand, had peddled a few illicit diamonds in his time, started a few rumours that set the punters reaching into their pockets, and sold a few worked-out claims to the gullible. That was where the first fortune came from. Just after the Second World War, at thirty-five, he was in London with the right connections for a copper-hungry Britain trying to get its industries back to work, and in 1948 had founded his own mining company. It had gone public in the mid-fifties and in fifteen years had developed worldwide interests. He was one of the first to see Harold Macmillian's wind of change blowing through Africa as independence for the black republics approached, and he took the trouble to meet and know most of the new power-hungry African politicians while most City businessmen were still deploring independence in the former colonies.

When he met the new men, it was a good match. They could see through his success story and he could see through their professed concern for their fellow blacks. They knew what he wanted and he knew what they wanted. So he fed their Swiss bank accounts and they gave Manson Consolidated mining concessions at prices below par for the course. ManCon prospered.

James Manson had also made several fortunes on the side. His latest was in the shares of the nickel-mining company in Australia called Poseidon. When Poseidon shares in late summer 1969 had been standing at four shillings, he had got a whisper that a survey team in central Australia might have found something on a stretch of land whose mining rights were owned by Poseidon. He had taken a gamble and paid out a very hefty sum to have a sneak preview of the first reports coming out of the interior. These reports said nickel, and lots of it. In fact nickel was not in shortage on the world market, but that never deterred the punters, and it was they who sent share prices spiralling, not investors.

He contacted his Swiss bank, an establishment so discreet that its only way of announcing its presence to the world was a small gold plate no larger than a visiting card, set into the wall beside a solid oak door in a small street in Zürich. Switzerland has no stockbrokers; the banks do all the investments. Manson instructed Dr Martin Steinhofer, the head of the Investments section of the Zwingli Bank, to buy on his behalf 5000 Poseidon shares. The Swiss banker contacted the prestigious London firm of Joseph Sebag & Co., in the name of Zwingli, and placed the order. Poseidon stood at five shillings a share when the deal was concluded.

The storm broke in late September when the size of the Australian nickel deposit became known. The shares began to rise, and, assisted by helpful rumours, the rising spiral became a rush. Sir James Manson had intended to start to sell when they reached £50 a share, but so vast was the rise that he held on. Finally he estimated the peak would be £115, and ordered Dr Steinhofer to start selling at £100 a share. This the discreet Swiss banker did, and had cleared the lot at an average of £103 for each share. In fact the peak was reached at £120 a share, before commonsense began to prevail and the shares slid back to £10. Manson did not mind the extra £20, for he knew the time to sell was just before the peak when buyers are still plentiful. With all fees paid, he netted a cool £500,000, which was still stashed in the Zwingli Bank.

It happens to be illegal for a British citizen and resident to have a foreign bank account without informing the Treasury, and also to make half a million sterling profit in sixty days without paying capital gains tax on it. But Dr Steinhofer was a Swiss resident, and Dr Steinhofer would keep his mouth shut. That was what Swiss banks were for.

On that mid-February afternoon Sir James Manson strolled back to his desk, sat back in the lush leather chair behind the desk and glanced again at the report that lay on the blotter. It had arrived in a large envelope, sealed with wax and marked for his eyes only. It was signed at the bottom by Dr Gordon Chalmers, the head of ManCon's Department of Study, Research, Geo-Mapping and Sample Analysis, situated outside London. It was the analyst's report on tests conducted on the samples a man called Mulrooney had apparently brought back from a place called Zangaro three weeks earlier.

Dr Chalmers did not waste words. The summary of the report was brief and to the point. Mulrooney had found a mountain, or a hill with a peak some 1800 feet high above ground level and close to 100 yards across the base. It was set slightly apart from a range of such mountains in the hinterland of Zangaro. The hill contained a widely disseminated deposit of mineral in apparently evenly consistent presence throughout the rock, which was of igneous type and millions of years older than the sandstone and ragstone of the mountains that surrounded it.

Mulrooney had found numerous and ubiquitous stringers of quartz and had predicated the presence of tin. He had returned with samples of the quartz, the country rock surrounding it, and shingle from the beds of the streams surrounding the hill. The quartz stringers did indeed contain small quantities of tin. But it was the country rock that was interesting. Repeated and varied tests showed that this country rock, and the gravel samples, contained minor quantities of low-grade nickel. They also contained remarkable quantities of platinum. It was present in all the samples and was fairly evenly distributed. The richest rock in platinum known in this world was in the Rustenberg mines in South Africa, where concentrations of 'grades' ran as high as Point Two Five of a Troy ounce per rock ton. The average concentration in the Mulrooney samples was Point Eight One. 'I have the honour to remain, Sir, Yours etc. . . .'

Sir James Manson knew as well as anyone in mining that platinum was the third most precious metal in the world, and stood at a market price of 130 dollars a Troy ounce as he sat in his chair. He was also aware that with the growing world hunger for the stuff it had to rise to at least 150 dollars an ounce over the next three years, probably to 200 dollars within five years. It would be unlikely to rise to the 1968 peak price of 300 dollars again, because that was ridiculous.

He did some calculations on a scratch pad. Two hundred and fifty million cubic yards of rock at two tons per cubic yard was five hundred million tons. At even half an ounce per rock ton that was two hundred and fifty million ounces. If the revelation of a new world source dragged the price down to ninety dollars an ounce, and even if the inaccessibility of the place meant a cost of fifty dollars an ounce to get it out and refined, that still meant . . .

Sir James Manson leaned back in his chair again and whistled softly.

'Jesus Christ. A ten-billion-dollar mountain.'

Platinum is a metal and like all metals it has its price. The price is basically controlled by two factors. These are the indispensability of the metal in certain processes that the industries of the world would like to complete, and the rarity of the metal. Platinum is very rare. Total world production each year, apart from stockpiled production which is kept secret by the producers, is a shade over one and a half million Troy ounces.

The overwhelming majority of it, probably over ninety-five per cent, comes from three sources: South Africa, Canada and Russia. Russia as usual is the uncooperative member of the group. The producers would like to keep the world price fairly steady so as to be able to make long-term investment planning in new mining equipment and development of new mines in the confidence that the bottom will not suddenly drop out of the market should a large quantity of stockpiled platinum suddenly be released. The Russians, by stockpiling unknown quantities and being able to release large quantities any time they feel like it, keep tremors running through the market whenever they can.

Russia releases each year about 350,000 Troy ounces on the world out of the 1,500,000 that reach the same market. This gives her between twenty-three and twenty-four per cent of the market, enough to ensure her a considerable degree of influence. Her supplies are marketed through Soyuss Prom Export. Canada puts on the market some 200,000 ounces a year, the whole production coming from the nickel mines of International Nickel, and just about the whole of this supply is bought up each year by the Engelhardt Industries of the USA. But should the US need for platinum suddenly rise sharply, Canada might well not be able to furnish the extra quantity.

The third source is South Africa, turning out close to 950,000 ounces a year and dominating the market. Apart from the Impala mines, which were just opening when Sir James Manson sat considering the world position of platinum, and have since become very important, the giants of platinum are the Rustenberg mines, which account for well over half the world's production. These are controlled by Johannesburg Consolidated, who have a big enough slice of the stock to be sole managers of the mines. The world refiners and marketers of Rustenberg's supply was and is the London-based firm of Johnson-Matthey.

James Manson knew this as well as anyone else. Although he was not into platinum when Chalmers's report hit his desk, he knew the position as well as a brain surgeon knows how a heart works. He also knew why, even at that time, the boss of Engelhardt Industries of America, the colourful Charlie Engelhardt, better known to the populace as the owner of the fabulous racehorse Nijinsky, was buying into South African platinum. It was because America would need much more than Canada could supply by the mid-seventies. Manson was certain of it.

And the reason why American consumption of platinum was bound to rise, even treble, by the mid- to late seventies lay in a piece of metal known as the motor car exhaust.

By the late 1960s the American smog problem had started to become a national issue. Words like 'air pollution', 'ecology', 'the environment', unheard ten years earlier, had jumped to every politician's lips and become the trendy, fashionable thing to be concerned about. The pressure was steadily mounting for legislation to limit, control and then reduce pollution, and thanks to Mr Ralph Nader the motor-car became target number one. Manson was certain that the move would gain strength through the early seventies and that by 1975 or 1976 at the latest every American motor-car would be fitted by law with a device for cleaning the exhaust fumes of their noxious gases. He also surmised that sooner or later cities like Tokyo, Madrid and Rome would have to follow suit. But California was the big one.

Motor-car exhausts are composed of three ingredients, and each can be rendered harmless, two of them by a chemical process called oxidation and the third by another process called reduction. The process of reduction needs a substance called a catalyst, and that of oxidation can be achieved by either burning the gases at very high temperatures in excess air, or by burning them at low temperatures, such as exist in a car exhaust. Low-temperature burning also needs a catalyst, the same one as the reduction process. The only viable known catalyst is called platinum.

Sir James Manson could work out two things for himself. Although work was going on and would continue throughout the seventies on a car exhaust control device that relied on a catalyst of non-precious metal, no one was likely to come up with one that really worked before 1980. Thus a platinum-based catalytic exhaust control device would remain the only workable solution for a decade, and each device would need one tenth of an ounce of pure platinum.

The second was that when the United States passed legislation, as he felt it would have to do by 1975, requiring a control device that passed stringent tests to be fitted to all new cars from that year onwards, there would be a need for another one and a half million ounces of platinum every year. That was equivalent to doubling world production, and the Americans would not know where to get it.

James Manson thought he had an idea where. They could always buy it from him. And with the absolute indispensability of platinum in every fume control device established for a decade, and world demand far outstripping supply, the price would be nice, very nice indeed.

There was only one problem. He had to be absolutely certain that he, and no one else, would control all mining rights to the Crystal Mountain. The question was, how?

The normal way would be to visit the republic where the mountain was situated, seek an interview with the president, show him the survey report, and propose to him a deal whereby ManCon secured the mining rights, the government secured a profit-participation clause that would fill the coffers of their treasury, and the president would secure a fat and regular payment into his Swiss account. That would be the normal way.

But apart from the fact that any other mining company in the world, if advised of what lay inside the Crystal Mountain, would counter-bid for the same mining rights, sending the government's share up and Manson's down, there were three parties who more than any other would want to take control, either to begin production or stop it for ever. These were the South Africans, the Canadians and most of all the Russians. For the advent on the world market of a new massive supply source would cut the Soviet slice of the market back to the level of the unnecessary, removing from them their power, influence and money-making capacity in the platinum field.

Manson had a vague recollection of having heard the name of Zangaro, but it was such an obscure place he realised he knew nothing about it. The first requirement was evidently to learn more. He leaned forward and depressed the intercom switch.

'Miss Cooke, would you come in, please.'

He had called her Miss Cooke throughout the seven years she had been his personal and private secretary, and even in the ten years before that, when she had been an ordinary company secretary, rising from the typing pool to the tenth floor, no one had ever suggested she might have a first name. In fact she had. It was Marjory. But she just did not seem the sort of person one called Marjory.

Certainly men had once called her Marjory, long ago, before the war, when she was a young girl. Perhaps they had even tried to flirt with her, pinch her bottom, those long thirty-five years ago. But that was then. Five years of war, hauling an ambulance through burning rubble-strewn streets, trying to forget a Guardsman who never came back from Dunkirk, and twenty years nursing a crippled and whining mother, a bedridden tyrant using tears for weapons, had taken away the youth and the pinchable qualities of Miss Marjory Cooke. At fifty-four, tailored, efficient and severe, her work at ManCon was almost all her life, the tenth floor her fulfilment, and the terrier who shared her neat apartment in suburban Chigwell and slept on her bed, her child and lover.

So no one ever called her Marjory. The young executives called her a shrivelled apple, and the secretary birds 'that old bat'. The others, including her employer Sir James Manson, about whom she knew more than she would ever tell him or anyone else, called her Miss Cooke. She entered through the door set in the beech-panelled wall which, when closed, looked like part of the wall.

'Miss Cooke, it has come to my attention that we have had, during the past few months, a small survey – one man I believe – in the republic of Zangaro.'

'Yes, Sir James. That's right.'

'Oh, you know about it.'

Of course she knew about it. Miss Cooke never forgot anything that had crossed her desk.

'Yes, Sir James.'

'Good. Then please find out for me who secured that government's permission for us to conduct the survey.'

'It will be on file, Sir James. I'll go and look.'

She was back in ten minutes, having first checked in her daily diary appointments book, cross indexed into two indices, one under personal names and the other under subject headings, and then confirmed with Personnel.

'It was Mr Bryant, Sir James.' She consulted a card in her hand. 'Michael Bryant, of Overseas Contracts.'

'He submitted a report, I suppose?' asked Sir James.

'He must have done, under normal company procedure.'

'Send me in his report, would you, Miss Cooke?'

She was gone again, and the head of ManCon stared out through the plate-glass windows across the room from his desk at the mid-afternoon dusk settling over the City of London. The lights were coming on in the middle level floors – they had been on all day in the lowest ones – but at skyline level there was still enough winter daylight to see by. But not to read by. Sir James Manson flicked on the reading lamp on his desk as Miss Cooke returned, laid the report he wanted on his blotter and receded back against the wall.

The report Richard Bryant had submitted was dated six months earlier and was written in the terse style favoured by the company. It recorded that according to instructions from the head of Overseas Contracts, he had flown to Clarence, the capital of Zangaro, and there, after a frustrating week in a hotel, had secured an interview with the Minister of Natural Resources. There were three separate interviews spaced over six days, and at length, an agreement had been reached that a single representative of ManCon might enter the republic to conduct a survey for minerals in the hinterland beyond the Crystal Mountains. The area to be surveyed was deliberately left vague by the company, so that the survey team could travel more or less where it wished. After further haggling during which it was made plain to the Minister that he could forget any idea that the company was prepared to pay the sort of fee he seemed to expect, and that there were no indications of mineral presence to work on, a sum had been agreed between Bryant and the Minister. Inevitably, the sum on the contract was just over half the total that changed hands, the balance being paid into the Minister's private account.

That was all. The only indication about the character of the place was in the reference to a corrupt minister. So what, thought Sir James Manson, nowadays Bryant might have been in Washington. Only the going rate was different.

He leaned forward to the intercom again.

'Tell Mr Bryant of Overseas Contracts to come up and see me, would you, Miss Cooke?'

He lifted the switch and pressed another one.

'Martin, come in a minute, please.'

It took Martin Thorpe two minutes to come from his office on the ninth floor. He did not look the part of a financial whizz-kid and protégé of one of the most ruthless go-getters in a traditionally ruthless and go-getting industry. He looked more like the captain of the athletics team from a good public school, charming, boyish, clean-cut, with dark wavy hair and deep blue eyes. The secretaries called him dishy and the directors who had seen stock options they were certain of whisked out from under their noses or found their companies slipping into control of a series of nominee shareholders fronting for Martin Thorpe called him something not quite so nice.

Despite the looks, Thorpe had never been either a public school man, or an athlete and certainly not captain of the team. He could not differentiate between a batting average and the ambient air temperature, but he could retain the hourly movement of share prices across the range of ManCon's subsidiary companies in his head throughout the day. At twenty-nine he had ambitions and the intent to carry them out. ManCon and Sir James Manson might provide the means, so far as he was concerned, and his loyalty depended on his exceptionally high salary, the contacts throughout the City that his job under Manson could bring him, and the knowledge that where he was constituted a good vantage point for spotting what he called 'the big one'.

By the time he entered Sir James had slipped the Zangaro report into a drawer and the Bryant report alone lay on his blotter.

He gave his protégé a friendly smile.

'Martin, I've got a job I need doing with some discretion. I need it done in a hurry and it might take half the night.'

It was not Sir James' way to ask if Thorpe had got any engagements that evening. Thorpe knew that, it went with the high salary.

'That's OK, Sir James. I had nothing on that a phone call can't kill.'

'Good. Look, I've been going over some old reports and come across this one. Six months ago one of our men from Overseas Contracts was sent out to a place called Zangaro. I don't know why, but I'd like to. The man secured that government's go-ahead for a small team from here to conduct a survey for any possible mineral deposits in uncharted land beyond the mountain range called the Crystal Mountains. Now, what I want to know is this: was it ever mentioned in advance or at the time, or since that visit six months ago, to the Board?'

'To the Board?'

'That's right. Was it ever mentioned to the Board of directors that we were doing any such survey? That's what I want to know. It may not necessarily be on the agenda. You'll have to look at the minutes. And in case it got a passing mention under "any other business", check through the documents of all Board meetings over the past twelve months. Secondly, find out who authorised the visit by Bryant six months ago and why, and who sent the survey engineer down there and why. The man who did the survey is called Mulrooney. I also want to know something about him, which you can get from his file in Personnel. Got it?'

Thorpe was surprised. This was way out of his line of country.

'Yes, Sir James, but Miss Cooke could do that in half the time, or get somebody to do it...'

'Yes, she could. But I want you to do it. If you look at a file from Personnel, or board-room documents, it will be assumed it has something to do with finance. Therefore it will remain discreet.'

The light began to dawn on Martin Thorpe.

'You mean ... they found something down there, Sir James?'

Manson stared out at the now inky sky and the blazing sea of lights below him as the brokers and traders, clerks and merchants, bankers and assessors, insurers and jobbers, buyers and sellers, lawyers and, in some offices no doubt, law-breakers, worked on through the winter afternoon towards the witching hour of five-thirty.

'Never mind,' he said gruffly to the young man behind him. 'Just do it.'

Martin Thorpe was grinning as he slipped through the back entrance of the office and down the stairs to his own premises.

'Cunning bastard,' he said to himself on the stairs.

Sir James Manson turned as the intercom broke the double-glazed, sound-proofed calm of the inner sanctum.

'Mr Bryant is here, Sir James.'

Manson crossed the room, switching on the main lights as he passed near the wall switch. Reaching his desk he depressed the switch.

'Send him in, Miss Cooke.'

There were three reasons why middle-level executives had occasion to be summoned to the sanctum on the tenth floor. One was to hear instructions or deliver a report that Sir James wanted to issue or hear personally, which was business. One was to be chewed into a sweat-soaked rag, which was hell. The third was when the chief executive decided he wanted to play favourite uncle to his cherished employees, which was reassuring.

On the threshold Michael Bryant, at thirty-nine a middle-level executive who did his work competently and well, but needed his job, was plainly aware the first reason of the three could not be the one that brought him here. He suspected the second and was immensely relieved to see it had to be the third.

From the centre of the office Sir James walked towards him with a smile of welcome.

'Ah, come in, Bryant. Come in.'

As Bryant entered Miss Cooke closed the door behind him and retired to her desk.

Sir James Manson gestured his employee to one of the easy chairs set well away from the desk in the conference area of the spacious office. Bryant, still wondering what it was all about, took the indicated chair and sank into its brushed suède cushions. Manson advanced towards the wall and opened two doors, revealing a well-stocked bar cabinet.

'Take a drink, Bryant? Sun's well down, I think.'

'Thank you, sir, er . . . Scotch, please.'

'Good man. My own favourite poison. I'll join you.'

Bryant glanced at his watch. It was quarter to five, and the tropical maxim about taking a drink after the sun has gone down was hardly coined for London winter afternoons. But he recalled an office party at which Sir James had snorted his derision of sherry drinkers and the like and spent the evening on Scotch. It pays to watch things like that, Bryant reflected, as his chief poured two fine old crystal glasses of his special Glenlivet. Of course he left the ice bucket strictly alone.

'Water? Dash of soda?' he called from the bar. Bryant craned round and spotted the bottle.

'Is that a single malt, Sir James? No thank you, straight as it comes.'

Manson nodded several times in approval, and brought the glasses over. They 'Cheersed' each other and savoured the whisky. Bryant was still waiting for the conversation to start. Manson noted this and gave him the gruff uncle look.

'No need to worry about me having you up here like this,' he began. 'I was just going through a sheaf of old reports in my desk drawers, and came across yours, or one of them. Must have read it at the time and forgotten to give it back to Miss Cooke for filing . . .'

'My report?' queried Bryant.

'Eh? Yes, yes, the one you filed after your return from that place, what's it called again? Zangaro? Was that it?'

'Oh, yes, sir. Zangaro. That was six months ago.'

'Yes, quite so. Six months, of course. Noticed as I re-read it that you'd had a bit of a rough time with the Minister fellow.'

Bryant began to relax. The room was warm, the chair extremely comfortable, and the whisky like an old friend. He smiled at the memory.

'But I got the contract for survey permission.'

'Damn right you did,' congratulated Sir James. He smiled as if at fond memories. 'I used to do that in the old days, y'know. Went on some rough missions to bring home the bacon. Never went to West Africa, though. Not in those days. Went later of course. But after all this started.'

To indicate 'all this' he waved his hand at the luxurious office.

'So nowadays I spend too much time up here buried in paperwork,' Sir James continued. 'I even envy you younger chaps going off to clinch deals in the old way. So tell me about your Zangaro trip.'

'Well, that really was doing things the old way. After a few hours in the place I half expected to find people running around with bones through their noses,' said Bryant.

'Really? Good Lord. Rough place is it, this Zangaro?'

Sir James Manson's head had tilted back into the shadows, and Bryant was sufficiently comfortable not to catch the gleam of concentration in the eye that belied the encouraging tone of voice.

'Too right, Sir James. It's a bloody shambles of a place, moving steadily backwards into the middle ages since independence five years ago.'

He recalled something else he had heard his chief say once in an aside remark to a group of executives.

'It's a classic example of the concept that most of the African republics today have thrown up power groups whose performance in power simply cannot justify their entitlement to leadership of a corporation garbage depot. As a result, of course, it's the ordinary people who suffer.'

Sir James, who was as capable as the next man of recognising his own words when he heard them played back at him, smiled, rose and walked to the window to look down at the teeming streets below.

'So who does run the show out there?' he asked quietly.

'The president. Or rather the dictator,' said Bryant from his chair. His glass was empty. 'A man called Jean Kimba. He won the first and only election just before independence five years ago against the wishes of the colonial power, some said by the use of terrorism and voodoo on the voters. They're pretty backward, you know. Most of them didn't know what a vote was. Now they don't need to know.'

'Tough guy, is he, this Kimba?' asked Sir James.

'It's not that he's tough, sir. He's just downright mad. A raving megalomaniac, and probably a paranoid to boot. He rules completely alone, surrounded by a small coterie of political yes-men. If they fall out with him, or arouse his suspicions in any way, they go into the cells of the old colonial police barracks. Rumour has it Kimba goes down there himself to supervise the torture sessions. No one has ever come out alive.'

'H'm, what a world we live in, Bryant. And they've got the same number of votes at the United Nations as Britain or America. Whose advice does he listen to in government?'

'No one of his own people. Of course, he has his voices. So the few local whites say, those who've stuck it out by staying on.'

'Voices?' queried Sir James.

'Yes, sir. He claims to the people he is guided by divine voices. He says he talks to God. He's told the people and the assembled diplomatic corps that in so many words.'

'Oh dear, not another,' mused Manson, still gazing down at the streets below. 'I sometimes think it was a mistake to introduce the Africans to God. Half their leaders now seem to be on first name terms with him.'

'Apart from that he rules by a sort of mesmeric fear. The people think he has a powerful juju, or voodoo, or magic or whatever. He holds them in the most abject terror of him personally.'

'What about the foreign embassies?' queried the man by the window.

'Well, sir, they keep themselves to themselves. It seems they are just as terrified of the excesses of this maniac as the natives. He's a bit like a cross between Sheikh Abeid Karume in Zanzibar, Papa Doc Duvalier in Haiti, and Sekou Touré in Guinea.'

Sir James turned smoothly from the window and asked with deceptive softness, 'Why Sekou Touré?'

Bryant was in his own element, expounding his carefully acquired knowledge of political Africa, glad to be able to show his employer he did long hours of homework.

'Well, he's next best thing to a Communist, Sir James. The man he really worshipped all his political life was Lumumba. That's why the Russians are so strong. They have an enormous embassy, for the size of the place. To earn foreign currency, now that the plantations have all failed through maladministration, they sell most of their produce to the Russian trawlers that call. Of course the trawlers are electronic spy ships or victualling ships for submarines they meet offshore and re-victual with fresh produce. Again, the money they get from the sale doesn't go to the people, it goes into Kimba's bank account.'

'It doesn't sound like Marxism to me,' joked Manson.

Bryant grinned widely.

'Money and bribes are where the Marxism stops,' he replied. 'As usual.'

'But the Russians are strong, are they? Influential? Another whisky, Bryant?'

While Bryant replied, the head of ManCon poured two more glasses of Glenlivet.

'Yes, Sir James. Kimba has virtually no understanding of matters outside his immediate experience, which has been exclusively inside his own country and maybe a couple of visits to other African states nearby. So he sometimes consults on matters when dealing with outside concerns. Then he uses any one of three advisers, black ones, who come from his own tribe. Two Moscow-trained, and one Peking-trained. Or he contacts the Russians direct. I spoke to a trader in the bar of the hotel one night, a Frenchman. He said the Russian ambassador or one of his counsellors was at the palace almost every day.'

Bryant stayed for another ten minutes, but Manson had learned most of what he needed to know. At five-twenty he ushered Bryant out as smoothly as he had welcomed him. As the younger man left, Manson beckoned Miss Cooke in.

'We employ an engineer in mineral exploration work called Jack Mulrooney,' he said. 'He returned from a three-month sortie into Africa, living in rough bush conditions, three months ago, so he may be on leave still. Try and get him at home. I'd like to see him at ten tomorrow morning. Secondly, Dr Gordon Chalmers, the chief survey analyst. You may catch him at Watford before he leaves the laboratory. If not, reach him at home. I'd like him here at twelve tomorrow. Cancel any other morning appointments and leave me time to take Chalmers out for a spot of lunch. And you'd better book me a table at Wilton's in Bury Street. That's all, thank you. I'll be on my way in a few minutes. Have a car round at the front in ten minutes.'

When Miss Cooke withdrew, Manson pressed one of the switches on his intercom and murmured, 'Come up for a minute, would you, Simon.'

Simon Endean was as deceptive as Martin Thorpe but in a different

way. He came from an impeccable background, and behind the veneer
had the morals of an East End thug. Going with the polish and the ruthlessness was a certain cleverness. He needed a James Manson to serve,
just as James Manson would sooner or later on his way to the top, or his
struggle to stay there in big-time capitalism, need the services of a Simon
Endean.

Endean was the sort to be found by the score in the very smartest and
smoothest of London's West End gambling clubs, beautifully spoken
hatchet men who never leave a millionaire unbowed to, or a showgirl
unbruised. The difference was that Endean's intelligence had brought
him to an executive position as an aide to the chief of a very superior
gambling club.

Unlike Thorpe he had no ambitions to become a multi-millionaire. He
thought one million would do, and until then the shadow of Manson
would suffice. It paid for the six-room pad, the Corvette, the girls. He too
came from the floor below and entered from the interior stair-well
through the beech-panelled door across the office from the one Miss
Cooke came and left by.

'Sir James?'

'Simon, tomorrow I'm having lunch with a fellow called Gordon Chalmers. One of the back-room boys. The chief scientist and head of the
laboratory out at Watford. He'll be here at twelve. Before then I want a
run-down on him. The personnel file of course, but anything else you can
find. The private man, what his home life is like, any failings; above all, if
he has any pressing need of money over and above his salary. His politics, if any. Most of these scientific people are Left. Not all though. You
might have a chat with Errington in Personnel tonight before he leaves.
Go through the file tonight and leave it for me to look at in the morning.
Sharp tomorrow start on his home environment. Phone me not later than
11.45. Got it? I know it's a short-notice job, but it could be important.'

Endean took in the instructions without moving a muscle, filing the lot.
He knew the score; Sir James Manson often needed information, for he
never faced any man, friend or foe, without a personal run-down on the
man including the private life. Several times he had beaten opponents
into submission by being better prepared. Endean nodded and left,
making his way straight to Personnel, an office which by chance Martin
Thorpe had only just left. But they did not cross paths.

As his chauffeur-driven Rolls-Royce slid away from the front of
ManCon House, taking its occupant back to his third-floor apartment in
Arlington House behind the Ritz, a long hot bath, and a dinner sent up
from the Caprice, Sir James Manson leaned back and lit his first cigar of
the evening. The chauffeur handed him a late *Evening Standard* and they
were abreast of Charing Cross station when a small paragraph in the Stop
Press caught his eye. It was in among the racing results. He glanced back
at it, then read it several times. He stared out at the swirling traffic and
huddled pedestrians, shuffling towards the station, or plodding to the
buses through the February drizzle, bound for their homes in Edenbridge
and Sevenoaks, after another exciting day in the City.

As he stared a small germ of an idea began to form in his mind. Another man would have laughed and dismissed it out of hand. Sir James Manson was not another man. He was a twentieth-century pirate and proud of it. The 9-point type headline above the obscure paragraph in the evening paper referred to an African republic. It was not Zangaro, but another one. He had hardly heard of the other one either. It had no known mineral wealth. The headline said:

'New *Coup d'État* in African State.'

3

Martin Thorpe was waiting in his chief's outer office when Sir James arrived at five past nine, and followed him straight in.

'What have you got?' demanded Sir James Manson, even while he was taking off his vicuña topcoat and hanging it in the built-in wardrobe. Thorpe flicked open a notebook he had pulled from his pocket and recited the result of his investigations of the night before.

'One year ago we had a survey team in the republic lying to the north and east of Zangaro. It was accompanied by an aerial reconnaissance unit hired from a French firm. The area to be surveyed was close to, and partly on the border with, Zangaro. Unfortunately there are few topographical maps of that area, and no aerial maps at all. Without Decca or any other form of beacon to give him cross-bearings, the pilot used speed and time of flight to assess the ground he had covered.

'One day when there was a following wind stronger than forecast he flew up and down the entire strip to be covered by aerial survey to his own satisfaction and returned to base. What he did not know was that on each downwind leg he had flown over the border and forty miles into Zangaro. When the aerial film was developed it showed that he had overshot the survey area by a large margin.'

'Who first realised it? The French company?' asked Manson.

'No, sir. They developed the film and passed it to us without comment, as per our contract with them. It was up to the men in our own aerial survey department to identify the areas on the ground represented by the pictures they had. Then they realised that at the end of each run was a stretch of territory not in the survey area. So they discarded the pictures, or at any rate put them on one side. They had realised that in one section of pictures a range of hills was featured that could not be in our survey area because there were no hills in that part of the area.

'Then one bright spark had a second look at the surplus photographs and noticed a part of the hilly area, slightly to the east of the main range, had a variation in the density and type of the plant life. The sort of thing you can't see down on the ground but an aerial picture from three miles up will show it up like a beermat on a billiard table.'

'I know how it's done,' growled Sir James. 'Go on.'

'Sorry, sir, I didn't know this. It was new to me. So anyway half a dozen photos were passed to someone in the Photo-Geology section, and he confirmed from a blow-up that the plant life was different over quite a small area involving a small hill about 1800 feet high and roughly conical in shape. Both sections prepared a report, and that went to the head of Topographic section. He identified the range as the Crystal Mountains and the hill as probably the original Crystal Mountain. He sent the file to Overseas Contracts and Willoughby, the head of OC, sent Bryant down there to get permission to survey.'

'He didn't tell me,' said Manson, now seated behind his desk.

'He sent a memo, Sir James. I have it here. You were in Canada at the time and were not due back for a month. He makes plain he felt the survey of that area was only an off-chance, but since a free aerial survey had been presented to us, and since Photo-Geology felt there had to be some reason for the different vegetation, the expense could be justified. Willoughby also suggested it might serve to give his man Bryant a bit of experience to go it alone for the first time. Up till then he had always accompanied Willoughby.'

'Is that it?'

'Almost. Bryant got visa-ed up and went in six months ago. He got permission and arrived back after three weeks. Four months ago Ground Survey agreed to detach an unqualified prospector-cum-surveyor called Jack Mulrooney from the diggings in Ghana and send him to look over the Crystal Mountains provided that the cost would be kept low. It was. He got back three weeks ago with a ton and a half of samples, which have been at the Watford laboratory ever since.'

'Fair enough,' said Sir James Manson after a pause. 'Now, did the Board ever hear about all this?'

'No, sir.' Thorpe was adamant. 'It would have been considered much too small. I've been through every Board meeting for twelve months, and every document presented, including every memo and letter sent to the Board members over the same period. Not a mention of it. The budget for the whole thing would simply have been lost in the petty cash anyway. And it didn't originate with Projects, because the aerial photos were a gift from the French firm and their ropy old navigator. It was just an *ad hoc* affair throughout, and never reached Board level.'

James Manson nodded in evident satisfaction.

'Right. Now Mulrooney. How bright is he?'

For answer Thorpe tendered Jack Mulrooney's file from Personnel.

'No qualifications, but a lot of practical experience, sir. An old sweat. A good Africa hand.'

Manson flicked through the file on Jack Mulrooney, scanned the biography notes and the career sheet since the man had joined the company.

'He's experienced all right,' grunted Manson. 'Don't underestimate the old Africa hands. I started out in the Rand, on a mining camp. Mulrooney just stayed at that level. So don't mock, lad, such people are very useful. And they can be perceptive.'

He dismissed Martin Thorpe and muttered to himself, 'Now let's see how perceptive Mr Mulrooney can be.'

He depressed the intercom switch and spoke to Miss Cooke.

'Is Mr Mulrooney there yet, Miss Cooke?'

'Yes, Sir James, he's here waiting.'

'Show him in, please.'

Manson was halfway to the door when his employee was ushered in. He greeted him warmly and led him to the chairs where he had sat with Bryant the previous evening. Before she left Miss Cooke was asked to produce coffee for them both. Mulrooney's coffee habit was on his file.

Jack Mulrooney in the penthouse suite of a London office block looked as out of place as Thorpe would have done in the dense bush. His hands hung way out of his coat sleeves and he did not seem to know where to put them. His grey hair was plastered down with water and he had cut himself shaving. It was the first time he had ever met the man he called the gaffer. Sir James used all his efforts to put the man at ease.

When Miss Cooke entered with a tray of porcelain cups, matching coffee pot, cream jug and sugar bowl, and an array of Fortnum and Mason biscuits, she heard her employer telling the Irishman,   '. . . that's just the point, man. You've got what I or anyone else can't teach these boys fresh out of college. Twenty-five years' hard-won experience getting the bloody stuff out of the ground and into the skips.'

It is always nice to be appreciated, and Jack Mulrooney was no exception. He beamed and nodded. When Miss Cooke had gone Sir James Manson gestured at the cups.

'Look at these poofy things. Used to drink out of a good mug. Now they give me thimbles. I remember back on the Rand in the late thirties, and that would be before your time, even . . .'

Mulrooney stayed for an hour. When he left he felt the gaffer was a damn good man despite all they said about him. Sir James Manson thought Mulrooney was a damn good man – at his job at any rate, and that was and would always be chipping bits of rock off hills and asking no questions.

Just before he left Mulrooney had reiterated his view.

'There's tin down there, Sir James. Stake my life on it. The only thing is, whether it can be got out at an economic figure.'

Sir James had slapped him on the shoulder.

'Don't you worry about that. We'll know as soon as the report comes through from Watford. And don't worry, if there's an ounce of it that I can get to the coast below market value, we'll have the stuff. Now how about you? What's your next adventure?'

'I don't know, sir. I have three more days leave yet, then I report back to the office.'

'Like to go abroad again?' beamed Sir James.

'Yes, sir. Frankly, I can't take this city and the weather and all.'

'Back to the sun, eh? You like the wild places, I hear.'

'Yes, I do. You can be your own man out there.'

'You can indeed,' smiled Manson. 'You can indeed. I almost envy you. No, dammit, I *do* envy you. Anyway, we'll see what we can do.'

Two minutes later Jack Mulrooney was gone. Manson ordered Miss Cooke to send his file back to Personnel, rang Accounts and instructed them to send Mulrooney a £1000 merit bonus and make sure he got it before the following Monday, and rang the head of Ground Survey.

'What surveys have you got pending in the next few days or just started?' he asked without preamble.

There were three, one of them in a remote stretch of the extreme north of Kenya, close to the Somaliland border, where the midday sun fries the brain like an egg in a pan, the nights freeze the bone marrow like Blackpool rock, and the shifta bandits prowl. It would be a long job, close to a year. He had nearly had two resignations trying to get a man to go there for so long.

'Send Mulrooney,' said Sir James and hung up.

He glanced at the clock. It was eleven. He picked up the personnel report on Dr Gordon Chalmers, which Endean had left on his desk the previous evening.

Chalmers was a graduate with honours from the London School of Mining, which is probably the best of its kind in the world, even if Witwatersrand likes to dispute that claim. He had taken his degree in geology and later chemistry and gone on to a doctorate in his mid-twenties. After five years of fellowship work at the college he had joined Rio Tinto Zinc in their scientific section and six years earlier ManCon had evidently poached him from RTZ for a better salary. For the last four years he had been head of the company's scientific department situated on the outskirts of Watford in Hertfordshire. The passport-size photograph in the file showed a man in his late thirties glowering at the camera over a bushy ginger beard. He wore a tweed jacket and a purple shirt. The tie was of knitted wool and askew.

At 11.35 the private phone rang and Sir James Manson heard the regular pips of a public coin box at the other end of the line. A coin clunked into the slot and Endean's voice came on the line. He spoke concisely for two minutes from Watford station. When he had finished, Manson grunted his approval.

'That's useful to know,' he said. 'Now get back to London. There's another job I want you to do. I want a complete run-down on the republic of Zangaro. I want the lot. Yes, Zangaro.' He spelt it out.

'Start back in the days when it was discovered, and work forwards. I want the history, geography, lie of the land, economy, crops, mineralogy if any, politics and state of development. Concentrate on the ten years prior to independence, and especially the period since. I want to know everything there is to know about the president, his cabinet, parliament if any, administration, executive, judiciary and political parties. There are three things that are more important than all else. One is the question of Russian or Chinese involvement and influence, or local Communist influence on the president. The second is that no one remotely connected with the place is to know any questions are being asked, so don't go there yourself, and thirdly under no circumstances are you to announce you come from ManCon. So use a different name. Got it? Good, well, report back as soon as you can and not later than twenty days. Draw cash from Accounts on my signature alone, and be discreet. For the record, consider yourself on leave; I'll let you make it up later.'

Manson hung up and called down to Thorpe to give further instructions. Within three minutes Thorpe came up to the tenth floor and laid the piece of paper his chief wanted on the desk. It was the carbon copy of a letter.

Ten floors down Dr Gordon Chalmers stepped out of his taxi at the corner of Moorgate and paid it off. He felt uncomfortable in a dark suit and topcoat, but Peggy had told him it was necessary for an interview and lunch with the Chairman of the Board.

As he walked the last few yards towards the steps and doorway of ManCon House his eye caught a poster fronting the kiosk of a seller of the *Evening News* and *Evening Standard*. What was written on the poster caused him to curl his lip in a bitter sneer but he bought both papers. The news was not the headline, but was on an inside page. The poster said simply: 'Thalidomide Parents Urge Settlement.'

The story backed up the headline in greater detail, though it was not long. It recorded that after another marathon round of talks between representatives of the parents of the 400-odd children in Britain who had been born deformed because of the thalidomide drug ten years earlier, and the company that had marketed the drug, a further impasse had been reached. So talks would be resumed 'at a later date'.

Gordon Chalmers's thoughts went back to the house outside Watford that he had left earlier the same morning, to Peggy his wife, just turned thirty and looking forty, and to Margaret, legless, one-armed Margaret, coming up to nine years, in need of a special pair of legs, a specially built house which they now lived in at long last, the mortgage on which was costing him a fortune.

'At a later date,' he snapped to no one in particular and stuffed the newspapers into a wall-basket. He seldom read the evening papers anyway. He preferred the *Guardian*, *Private Eye* and the left-wing *Tribune*. After nearly ten years of watching a group of almost unmoneyed parents try to face down the giant Distillers for their compensation, Gordon Chalmers harboured bitter thoughts about big-time capitalists. Ten minutes later he was facing one of the biggest.

Sir James Manson could not put Chalmers off his guard as he had Bryant and Mulrooney. The scientist clutched his glass of beer firmly and stared right back. Manson grasped the situation quickly and when Miss Cooke had handed him his whisky and retired, he came to the point.

'I suppose you can guess what I asked you to come and see me about, Dr Chalmers.'

'I can guess, Sir James. The report on Crystal Mountain.'

'That's it. Incidentally, you were quite right to send it to me personally in a sealed envelope. Quite right.'

Chalmers shrugged. He had done it because he realised that all important analysis results had to go direct to the chairman according to company policy. It was routine, as soon as he had realised what the samples contained.

'Let me ask you two things, and I need specific answers,' said Sir James. 'Are you absolutely certain of these results? There could be no other possible explanation of the tests on the samples?'

Chalmers was neither shocked nor affronted. He knew the work of scientists was seldom accepted by laymen as being far removed from black magic, and therefore imprecise. He had long since ceased trying to explain the precision of his craft.

'Absolutely certain. For one thing there are a variety of tests to establish the presence of platinum and these samples passed them all with unvarying regularity. For another, I not only did all the known tests on every one of the samples, I did the whole thing twice. Theoretically it is possible someone could have interfered with the alluvial samples, but not with the internal structures of the rocks themselves. The summary of my report is accurate beyond scientific dispute.'

Sir James Manson listened to the lecture with head-bowed respect, and nodded in admiration.

'And the second thing is, how many other people in your laboratory know of the results of the analysis of the Crystal Mountain samples?'

'No one,' said Chalmers with finality.

'No one?' echoed Manson. 'Come now, surely one of your assistants . . .'

Chalmers downed a swig of his beer and shook his head.

'Sir James, when the samples came in they were crated as usual and put in store. Mulrooney's accompanying report predicated the presence of tin in unknown quantities. As it was a very minor survey, I put a junior assistant on to it. Being inexperienced he assumed tin or nothing, and did the appropriate tests. When they failed to show up positive, he called me over and pointed this out. I offered to show him how, and again the tests were negative. So I gave him a lecture on not being mesmerised by the prospector's opinion and showed him some more tests. These too were negative. The laboratory closed for the night, but I stayed on late, so I was alone in the place when the first tests came up positive. By midnight I knew the shingle sample from the stream bed, of which I was using less than half a pound, contained small quantities of platinum. After that I locked up for the night.

'The next day I took the junior off that assignment and put him on another. Then I went on with it myself. There were 600 bags of shingle and gravel, and 1500 pounds weight of rocks, over 300 separate rocks taken from different places on the mountain. From Mulrooney's photographs I could picture the mountain. The disseminated deposit is present in all parts of the formation. As I said in my report.'

With a touch of defiance he drained his beer.

Sir James Manson continued nodding, staring at the scientist with well-feigned awe.

'It's incredible,' he said at length. 'I know you scientists like to remain detached, impartial, but I think even you must have become excited. This could form a whole new world source of platinum. You know how often that happens with a rare metal? Once in a decade, maybe once in a lifetime...'

In fact Chalmers had been excited by his discovery, and had worked late into the night for three weeks to cover every single bag and rock from the Crystal Mountain, but he would not admit it. Instead he shrugged and said:

'Well, it'll certainly be very profitable for ManCon.'

'Not necessarily,' said James Manson quietly. This was the first time he shook Chalmers.

'No?' queried the analyst. 'But surely it's a fortune?'

'A fortune in the ground, yes,' replied Sir James, rising and walking to the window. 'But it depends very much who gets it, if anyone at all. You see, there is a danger it could be kept unmined for years, or mined and stockpiled. Let me put you in the picture, my dear Doctor...'

He put Dr Chalmers in the picture for thirty minutes, talking finance and politics, neither of which was the analyst's forte.

'So there you are,' he finished. 'The chances are it will be handed on a plate to the Russian government if we announce it immediately.'

Dr Chalmers, who had nothing particular against the Russian government, shrugged slightly.

'I can't change the facts, Sir James.'

Manson's eyebrows shot up in horror.

'Good gracious, Doctor, of course you can't.' He glanced at his watch in surprise. 'Close to one,' he exclaimed, 'you must be hungry. I know I am. Let's go and have a spot of lunch.'

He had thought of taking the Rolls, but after Endean's phone call from Watford that morning and the information from the local newsagent about the regular subscription to *Tribune*, he opted for an ordinary taxi.

A spot of lunch proved to be pâté, truffled omelette, jugged hare in red wine sauce and trifle. As Manson had suspected Chalmers disapproved of such indulgence but at the same time had a healthy appetite. And even he could not reverse the simple laws of nature, which are that a good meal produces a sense of repletion, contentment, euphoria and a lowering of moral resistance. Manson had also counted on a beer drinker being unused to the fuller red wines, and two bottles of Côte du Rhône had encouraged Chalmers to talk about the subjects that interested him, his work, his family and his views on the world.

It was when he touched on his family and their new house that Sir James Manson, looking suitably sorrowful, mentioned that he recalled having seen Chalmers in a television interview in the street a year back.

'Do forgive me,' he said, 'I hadn't realised before ... I mean, about your little girl ... what a tragedy.'

Chalmers nodded and gazed at the tablecloth. Slowly at first, and then with more confidence, he began to tell his superior about Margaret.

'You wouldn't understand,' he said at one point.

'I can try,' replied Sir James quietly. 'I have a daughter myself, you know. Of course, she's older.'

Ten minutes later there was a pause in the talking. Sir James Manson drew a folded piece of paper from his inside pocket.

'I don't really know how to put this,' he said with some embarrassment, 'but ... well, I am as aware as any man how much time and trouble you put in for the company. I am aware you work long hours, and the strain of this personal matter must have its effect on you, and no doubt on Mrs Chalmers. So I issued this instruction to my personal bank this morning.'

He passed the carbon copy of the letter across to Chalmers who read it. It was brief and to the point. It instructed the manager of Coutts Bank to remit by registered mail each month on the first day fifteen banknotes, each of value £10, to Dr Gordon Chalmers at his home address. The remittances were to run for ten years unless further instructions were received.

Chalmers looked up. His employer's face was all concern, tinged with embarrassment.

'Thank you,' said Chalmers softly.

Sir James's hand rested on his forearm and shook it.

'Now come on, that's enough of this matter. Have a brandy.'

In the taxi on the way back to the office Manson suggested he drop Chalmers off at the station where he could take his train for Watford.

'I have to get back to the office and get on with this Zangaro business and your report,' he said.

Chalmers was staring out of the cab window at the traffic moving out of London that Friday afternoon.

'What *are* you going to do about it?' he asked.

'Don't know really. Of course I'd like not to send it. Pity to see all that going into foreign hands, which is what must happen when your report gets to Zangaro. But I've got to send them something, sooner or later.'

There was another long pause as the taxi swung into the station forecourt.

'Is there anything I can do?' asked the scientist.

Sir James Manson breathed a long sigh.

'Yes,' he said in measured tones. 'Junk the Mulrooney samples in the same way as you would junk any other rocks and bags of sand. Destroy your analysis notes completely. Take your copy of the report and make an exact copy, with one difference – let it show the tests prove conclusively there exist marginal quantities of low-grade tin which could not be economically mined. Burn your own copy of the original report. And then never mention a word of it.'

The taxi came to a halt, and as neither of his passengers moved the cabby poked his nose through the screen into the rear compartment.

'This is it, guv.'

'You have my solemn word,' murmured Sir James Manson. 'Sooner or later the political situation may well change, and when that happens ManCon will put in a tender for the mining concession exactly as usual and in accordance with normal business procedures.'

Dr Chalmers climbed out of the taxi and looked back at his employer in the corner seat.

'I'm not sure I can do that, sir,' he said. 'I'll have to think it over.'

Manson nodded.

'Of course you will. I know it's asking a lot. Look, why don't you talk it over with your wife. I'm sure she'll understand.'

Then he pulled the door to, and told the cabby to take him to the City.

Sir James dined with an official of the Foreign Office that evening and took him to his club. It was not one of the very uppercrust clubs of London, for Manson had no intention of putting up for one of the bastions of the old Establishment and finding himself blackballed. Besides, he had no time for social climbing and little patience with the posturing idiots one found at the top when one got there. He left the social side of things to his wife. The knighthood was useful, but that was an end to it.

He despised Adrian Goole, whom he reckoned for a pedantic fool. That was why he had invited him to dinner. That, and the fact that the man was in the Economic Intelligence section of the FO.

Years ago, when his company's activities in Ghana and Nigeria had reached a certain level, he had accepted a place on the inner circle of the City's West Africa Committee. This organ was and still is a sort of trade union of all major firms based in London and carrying on operations in West Africa. Concerned far more with trade and therefore money than, for example, the East Africa Committee, the WAC periodically reviewed events of both commercial and political interest in West Africa, and usually the two were bound to become connected in the long term, and tendered advice to the Foreign and Commonwealth Office on what would in their view constitute an advisable policy for British interests.

Sir James Manson would not have put it that way. He would have said they were in existence to suggest to the government what to do in that part of the world to improve profits. He would have been right, too. He had been on the committee during the Nigerian civil war and heard the various representatives of banks, mines, oil and trade advocate a quick end to the war, which seemed to be synonymous with a Federal victory in double time.

Predictably the committee had proposed to the government that the Federal side be supported provided they could show they were going to win and win quickly, and provided corroborative evidence from British sources on the spot confirmed this. They then sat back and watched the government on Foreign Office advice make another monumental African cock-up. Instead of lasting six months it had lasted thirty. And Harold Wilson, once committed to a policy, was no more going to concede his minions might have made a mistake on his behalf than fly to the moon.

Manson had lost a lot in revenue from his disrupted mining interests and the impossibility of shipping the stuff to the coast on crazily-running railways throughout the period, but MacFazdean of Shell-BP had lost a lot more in oil production.

Adrian Goole had been the FO's liaison officer on the committee for most of the time. Now he sat opposite James Manson in the alcove dining-recess, his cuffs showing the right inch and a quarter, his face registering earnest intent.

Manson told him some of the truth, but kept the reference to platinum out of it. He stuck to a tale of tin, but increased the quantities. It would have been viable to mine it, of course, but quite frankly he'd been scared off by the close dependence of the president on the Russian advisers. The profit-participation of the Zangaran government could well have made them a tidy sum and therefore more powerful, and since the despot was almost a puppet of the Russkies, who wanted to increase the republic's power and influence through wealth? Goole took it all in. His face was a solemn expression of deep concern.

'Damnably difficult decision,' he said with sympathy. 'Mind you, I have to admire your political sense. At the moment Zangaro is bankrupt and obscure. But if it became rich ... yes, you're quite right. A real dilemma. When do you have to send them the survey report and analysis?'

'Sooner or later,' grunted Manson. 'The question is, what do I do about it? If they show it to the Russians at the embassy, the trade counsellor is bound to realise the tin deposits are viable. Then it will go out for tender. So someone else will get it, still help to make the dictator rich, and then who knows what problems he'll make for the West? One is back to square one.'

Goole thought it over for a while.

'I just thought I ought to let you chaps know,' said Manson.

'Yes, yes, thank you.' Goole was absorbed. 'Tell me,' he said at length, 'what would happen if you halved the figures showing the quantity of tin per rock-ton in the report?'

'Halved them?'

'Yes. Halved the figures, showing a purity figure of tin per rock-ton of fifty per cent the figures shown by your rock samples?'

'Well, the quantity of tin present would be shown to be economically unviable.'

'And the rock samples could have come from another area a mile away, for example?' asked Goole.

'Yes, I suppose they could. But my surveyor found the richest rock samples.'

'But if he had not done so,' pursued Goole. 'If he had taken his samples from a mile from where he actually operated. The content could be down by fifty per cent?'

'Yes, they could. They probably would, probably would show even less than fifty per cent. But he operated where he did.'

'Under supervision?' asked Goole.

'No. Alone.'

'And there are no real traces of where he worked?'

'No,' replied Manson. 'Just a few rock chippings, long since overgrown. Besides, no one goes up there. It's miles from anywhere.'

He paused for a few instances to light a cigar.

'You know, Goole, you're a damnably clever fellow. Steward, another brandy if you please.'

They parted with mutual jocularity on the steps of the club. The doorman hailed a taxi for Goole to go back to Mrs Goole in Holland Park.

'One last thing,' said the FO man by the taxi door, 'not a word to anyone else about this. I'll have to file it, well classified, at the department, but otherwise it remains just between you and us at the FO.'

'Of course,' said Manson.

'I'm very grateful you saw fit to tell me all this. You have no idea how much easier it makes our job on the economic side to know what's going on. I'll keep a quiet eye on Zangaro and if there should be a change in the political scene there, you'll be the first to know. Good night.'

Sir James Manson watched the taxi head down the road and signalled to his Rolls-Royce waiting up the street.

'You'll be the first to know,' he mimicked. 'Too bloody right I will, boy. 'Cause I'm going to start it.'

He leaned through the passenger side window to see Craddock, his chauffeur, behind the wheel.

'If pisswilly little buggers like that had been in charge of building our empire, Craddock, we might by now just about have colonised the Isle of Wight.'

'You're absolutely right, Sir James,' said Craddock.

When his employer had climbed into the rear, the chauffeur slid open the communicating panel.

'Gloucestershire, Sir James?'

'Gloucestershire, Craddock.'

It was starting to drizzle again as the sleek limousine swished down Piccadilly and up Park Lane heading for the A40 and the West Country, carrying Sir James Manson towards his ten-bedroomed mansion bought three years earlier for him by a grateful company for £250,000. It also contained his wife and nineteen-year-old daughter, but these he had won himself.

An hour later Gordon Chalmers lay beside his wife, tired and angry from the row they had had for the past two hours. Peggy Chalmers lay on her back looking up at the ceiling.

'I can't do it,' Chalmers said for the umpteenth time. 'I can't just go and falsify a mining report to help James Bloody Manson make more money.'

There was a long silence. They had been over it all a score of times since Peggy had read Manson's letter to his banker and heard from her husband the conditions of future financial security.

'What does it matter?' she said in a low voice from the darkness beside him. 'When all's said and done, what does it matter? Whether he gets the concession, or the Russians, or no one. Whether the price rises or falls. What does it matter? It's all pieces of rock and grains of metal.'

Peggy Chalmers swung herself across her husband's torso and stared at the dim outline of his face. Outside, the night wind rattled the branches of the old elm close to which they had built the new house with the special fitments for their crippled daughter.

When Peggy Chalmers spoke again it was with passionate urgency.

'But Margaret is not a piece of rock, and I am not a few grains of metal. We need that money, Gordon, we need it now and for the next ten years. Please, darling, please, just one time forget the idea of a nice letter to *Tribune* or *Private Eye*, and do what he wants.'

Gordon Chalmers continued to stare at the slit of window between the curtains, half-open to let in a breath of air.

'All right,' he said at length.

'You'll do it?' she asked.

'Yes, I'll bloody do it.'

'You swear it, darling? You give me your word?'

There was another long pause.

'You have my word,' said the low voice from the face above her. She pillowed her head in the hair of his chest.

'Thank you, darling. Don't worry about it. Please don't worry. You'll forget it in a month. You'll see.'

Ten minutes later she was asleep, exhausted by the nightly struggle to get Margaret bathed and into bed, and by the unaccustomed row with her husband. Gordon Chalmers continued to stare into the darkness.

'They always win,' he said softly and bitterly after a while. 'The bastards, they always bloody win.'

The following day, Saturday, he drove the five miles to the laboratory and wrote out a completely new report for the republic of Zangaro. Then he burned his notes and the original report, and trundled the core samples over to the scrap-heap where a local builder would remove it for concrete and garden paths. He posted the fresh report, registered post, to Sir James Manson at head office, went home and tried to forget it.

On Monday the report was received in London and the instructions to the banker in Chalmers's favour were posted. The report was sent down to Overseas Contracts for Willoughby and Bryant to read, and Bryant was told to leave the next day and take it to the Minister of Natural Resources in Clarence. A letter from the company would be attached, expressing the appropriate regret.

On Tuesday evening, Richard Bryant found himself in Number One Building at London's Heathrow airport waiting for a BEA flight to Paris where he could get the appropriate visa and make a connecting flight by Air Afrique. Five hundred yards away in Three Building Jack Mulrooney humped his grip through passport control to catch the BOAC overnight

Jumbo to Nairobi. He was not unhappy. He had had enough of London. Ahead lay Kenya, sun, bush and the chance of a lion.

By the end of the week only two men had in their heads the knowledge of what really lay inside the Crystal Mountain. One had given his word to his wife to remain silent for ever, and the other was plotting his next move.

4

Simon Endean entered Sir James Manson's office with a bulky file containing his hundred-page report on the republic of Zangaro, a dossier of large photographs and several maps. He told his chief what he had brought. Manson nodded in approval.

'No one learned while you were putting all this together who you were or who you worked for?' he asked.

'No, Sir James. I used a pseudonym, and no one questioned it.'

'And no one in Zangaro could have learned that a file of data could have been put together about them?'

'No. I used existing archives, sparse though they are, some university libraries here and in Europe, standard works of reference, and the one tourist guide published by Zangaro itself, although in fact this is a left-over from colonial days and five years out of date. I always claimed I was simply seeking information for a graduate thesis on the entire African colonial and post-colonial situation. There will be no comebacks.'

'All right,' said Manson. 'I'll read the report later. Give me the main facts.'

For answer Endean took one of the maps from the file and spread it across the desk. It showed that section of the African coastline with Zangaro marked.

'As you see, Sir James, it's stuck like an enclave on the coast here, bordered on the north and east by this republic and on the short southern border by this one. The fourth side is the sea, here.

'It's shaped like a match-box, the short edge along the sea coast, the longer sides stretching inland. The borders were completely arbitrarily drawn in the old colonial days during the scramble for Africa, and merely represent lines on a map. On the ground there are no effective borders, and due to the almost complete non-existence of roads there is only one border crossing point – here, on the road leading north to the neighbour country. All land traffic enters and leaves by this road.'

Sir James Manson studied the enclave on the map and grunted.

'What about the eastern and southern borders?'

'No road, sir. No way in or out at all, unless you cut straight through the jungle, and in most places it is impenetrable bush.

'Now, in size it has 7000 square miles, being seventy miles along the coast and 100 miles deep into the hinterland. The capital, Clarence, named after the sea captain who first put in there for fresh water two hundred years ago, is here – in the centre of the coast, thirty-five miles from the northern and southern borders.

'Behind the capital lies a narrow coastal plain which is the only cultivated area in the country, apart from the bush natives' tiny clearings in the jungle. Behind the plain lies the river Zangaro, then the foothills of the Crystal Mountains, the mountains themselves and, beyond that, miles and miles of jungle up to the eastern border.'

'How about other communications?' asked Manson.

'There are virtually no roads at all,' said Endean. 'The river Zangaro flows from the northern border fairly close to the coast across most of the republic until it reaches the sea just short of the southern border. On the estuary there are a few jetties and a shanty or two which constitute a small port for the exporting of timber. But there are no wharves, and the timber businesses have virtually ceased since independence. The fact that the Zangaro river flows almost parallel to the coast, slanting in towards it, for sixty miles, in effect cuts the republic in two; there is this strip of coastal plain seawards side of the river, ending in mangrove swamps which make the whole coast unapproachable by shipping or small boats, and the hinterland beyond the river. East of the river are the mountains and beyond them the hinterland. The river could be used for barge traffic, but no one is interested. The republic to the north has a modern capital on the coast with a deep-water harbour, and the Zangaro river itself ends in a silted-up estuary.'

'What about the timber-exporting operations? How were they carried out?'

Endean took a larger-scale map of the republic out of the file and laid it on the table. With a pencil he tapped the Zangaro estuary in the south of Zangaro.

'The timber used to be cut upcountry, either along the banks or in the western foothills of the mountains. There's still quite good timber there, but since independence no one is interested. The logs were floated down-river to the estuary and parked there. When the ships came they would anchor offshore and the log rafts were towed out to them by powered boats. Then they hoisted the logs aboard by using their own derricks. It always was a tiny operation.'

Manson stared intently at the large-scale map, taking in the seventy miles of coast, the river running almost parallel to it, twenty miles inland, the strip of impenetrable mangrove swamp between the coast and the sea, and the mountains behind the river. He could identify the Crystal Mountain, but made no mention of it.

'What about the main roads? There must be some.'

Endean warmed to his explanation.

'The capital is stuck on the seaward end of a short, stubby peninsula here, midway down the coast. It faces towards the open sea. There's a small port, the only real one in the country, and behind the town the peninsula runs back to join the main land mass. There is one road which runs down the spine of the peninsula and six miles inland, going straight east. Then there is the junction – here. A road runs to the right, heading south. It is laterite for seven miles, then becomes an earth road for the next twenty. Then it peters out on the banks of the Zangaro estuary.

'The other branch turns left and runs north, through the plain west of the river and onwards to the northern border. Here there is a crossing point, manned by a dozen sleepy and corrupt soldiers. A couple of travellers told me they can't read a passport anyway, so they don't know whether there is a visa in it or not. You just bribe them a couple of quid to get through.'

'What about the road into the hinterland?' asked Sir James.

Endean pointed with his finger. 'It's not even marked, it's so small. Actually, if you follow the north-running road after the junction, go along it for ten miles, there is a turn-off to the right, towards the hinterland. It's an earth road. It crosses the remainder of the plain and then the Zangaro river, on a rickety wooden bridge . . .'

'So that bridge is the only communication between the two parts of the country either side of the river?' asked Manson in wonderment.

Endean shrugged. 'It's the only crossing for wheeled traffic. But there is hardly any wheeled traffic. The natives cross the Zangaro by canoe.'

Manson changed the subject, though his eyes never left the map.

'What about the tribes who live there?' he asked.

'There are two,' said Endean. 'East of the river and right back to the end of the hinterland is the country of the Vindu. For that matter, more Vindu live over the eastern border. I said the borders were arbitrary. The Vindu are practically in the Stone Age. They seldom if ever cross the river and leave their bush country. The plain to the west of the river and down to the sea, including the peninsula on which the capital stands, is the country of the Caja. They hate the Vindu and vice versa.'

'Population?'

'Almost uncountable in the interior. Officially put at 220,000 in the entire country. That is, 30,000 Caja and an estimated 190,000 Vindu. But the numbers are a total guess, except probably the Caja can be counted accurately.'

'Then how the hell did they ever hold an election?' asked Manson.

'That remains one of the mysteries of creation,' said Endean. 'It was a shambles anyway. Half of them didn't know what a vote was or what they were voting for.'

'What about the economy?'

'There is hardly any left,' replied Endean. 'The Vindu country produces nothing. The lot of them just about subsist on what they can grow in yam and cassava plots cut out of the bush by the women, who do any work there is to be done, which is precious little. Unless you pay them well, then they will carry things. The men hunt. The children are a mass of malaria, trachoma, bilharzia and malnutrition.

'In the coastal plain there were in colonial days plantations of low-grade cocoa, coffee, cotton and bananas. These were run and owned by whites, using native labour. It wasn't high quality stuff, but it made enough with a guaranteed European buyer, the colonial power, to make a bit of hard currency and pay for the minimal imports. Since independence these were nationalised by the president, who expelled the whites, and given to his party hacks. Now they're about finished, overgrown with weeds.'

'Got any figures?'

'Yes, sir. In the last year before independence total cocoa output, that was the main crop, was 30,000 tons. Last year it was 1000 tons, and there were no buyers. It's still rotting on the ground.'

'And the others, coffee, cotton, bananas?'

'Bananas and coffee virtually ground to a halt through lack of attention. Cotton got hit by a blight and there were no insecticides.'

'What's the economic situation now?'

'Total disaster. Bankrupt, money worthless paper, exports down to almost nothing, and nobody letting them have any imports. There have been gifts from the UN, the Russians and the former colonial power, but as the government always sells the stuff elsewhere and pockets the cash, even these three have given up.'

'A real banana republic, eh?' murmured Sir James.

'In every sense. Corrupt, vicious, brutal. They have seas off the coast rich in fish, but they can't fish. The two fishing boats they had were skippered by whites. One got beaten up by the army thugs, and both quit. Then the engines rusted up and they were abandoned. So the locals have protein deficiency. There aren't enough goats and chickens to go around.'

'What about medicines?'

'There's one hospital in Clarence which is run by the United Nations. That's the only one in the country.'

'Doctors?'

'There were two Zangarans who were qualified doctors. One was arrested and died in prison. The other fled into exile. The missionaries were expelled by the president as imperialist influences. They were mainly medical missionaries as well as preachers and priests. The nuns used to train up nurses, but they got expelled as well.'

'How many Europeans?'

'In the hinterland, probably none. In the coastal plain, a couple of agronomists, technicians sent by United Nations. In the capital, about forty diplomats, twenty of them in the Russian embassy, the rest spread between the French, Swiss, American, West German, East German, Czech and Chinese embassies, if you call the Chinese white. Apart from that, about five United Nations hospital staff, another five technicians manning the electrical generator, the airport control tower, the waterworks and so on. Then there must be fifty others, traders, managers, businessmen who have hung on hoping for an improvement.

'Actually, there was a ruckus six weeks ago and one of the UN men was beaten half to death. The five non-medical technicians threatened to quit and sought refuge in their respective embassies. They may be gone by now, in which case the water, electricity and airport will soon be out of commission.'

'Where is the airport?'

'Here, on the base of the peninsula behind the capital. It's not of international standard, so if you want to fly in you have to take Air Afrique to here, in the republic to the north, and take a connecting flight by a small two-engined plane that goes down to Clarence three times a week. It's a French firm that has the concession, though nowadays it's hardly economic.'

'Who are the country's friends, diplomatically speaking?'

Endean shook his head.

'They don't have any. No one is interested, it's such a shambles. Even the Organisation of African Unity is embarrassed by the whole place. It's so obscure no one ever mentions it. No Pressmen ever go, so it never gets publicised. The government is rabidly anti-white, so no one wants to send staff men down there to run anything. No one invests anything, because nothing is safe from confiscation by any Tom, Dick or Harry wearing a party badge. There's a party youth organisation that beats up anyone it wants to, and everyone lives in terror.'

'What about the Russians?'

'They have the biggest mission and probably a bit of say over the president in matters of foreign policy about which he knows nothing. His advisers are mainly Moscow-trained Zangarans, though he wasn't schooled in Moscow personally.'

'Is there any potential at all down there?' asked Sir James. Endean nodded slowly.

'I suppose there is enough potential, well managed and worked, to sustain the population at a reasonable degree of prosperity. The population is small, the needs few, they could be self-sufficient in food, clothing, the basics of a good local economy, with a little hard currency to the necessary extras. It could be done, but, in any case, the needs are so few the relief and charitable agencies could provide the total necessary, if it wasn't that their staff are always molested, their equipment smashed or looted, and their gifts stolen and sold for the government's private profit.'

'You say the Vindu won't work hard. What about the Caja?'

'Nor they either,' said Endean. 'They just sit about all day, or fade into the bush if anyone looks threatening. Their fertile plain has always grown enough to sustain them, so they are happy the way they are.'

'Then who worked the estates in the colonial days?'

'Ah, the colonial power brought in about 20,000 black workers from elsewhere. They settled and live there still. With their families they are about 50,000. But they were never enfranchised by the colonial power, so they never voted in the election at independence. If there is any work done, they still do it.'

'Where do they live?' asked Manson.

'About 15,000 still live in their huts on the estates, even though there is no more work worth doing, with all the machinery broken down. The rest have drifted towards Clarence and grub a living as best they can. They live in a series of shanty towns scattered down the road at the back of the capital, on the road to the airport.'

For five minutes Sir James Manson stared at the map in front of him, thinking deeply about a mountain, a mad president, a coterie of Moscow-trained advisers and a Russian embassy. Finally he sighed.

'What a bloody shambles of a place.'

'That's putting it mildly,' said Endean. 'They still have ritual public executions before the assembled populace in the main square. Death by being chopped to pieces with a matchet. Quite a bunch.'

'And who precisely has produced this paradise on earth?'

For answer Endean produced a photograph and placed it on the map.

Sir James Manson found himself looking at a middle-aged African in a silk top-hat, black frock-coat and sponge-bag trousers. It was evidently inauguration day, for several colonial officials stood in the background, by the steps of a large mansion. The face beneath the shining black silk was not round, but long and gaunt, with deep lines each side of the nose. The mouth was twisted downwards at each corner so that the effect was of deep disapproval of something. But the eyes held the attention. There was glazed fixity about them, as one sees in the eyes of fanatics.

'That's the man,' said Endean. 'Mad as a hatter, and nasty as a rattle-snake. West Africa's own Papa Doc. Visionary, communicant with spirits, liberator from the white man's yoke, redeemer of his people, swindler, robber, police chief and torturer of the suspicious, extractor of confessions, hearer of voices from the Almighty, seer of visions, Lord High Everything Else, His Excellency President Jean Kimba.'

Sir James Manson stared longer at the face of the man who, unknown to himself, was sitting in control of ten billion dollars-worth of platinum.

I wonder, he thought to himself, if the world would really notice his passing on?'

He said nothing, but after listening to Endean, that event was what he had decided to arrange.

Six years earlier the colonial power ruling the enclave now called Zangaro, increasingly conscious of world opinion, had decided to grant independence. Over-hasty preparations were made among a population wholly inexperienced in self-government, and the events of a general election and independence were fixed for the following year.

In the confusion five political parties came into being. Two were wholly tribal, one claiming to look after the interests of the Vindu, the other of the Caja. The other three parties devised their own political platforms and pretended to make appeal through the tribal division of the people. One of these parties was the conservative group, led by a man holding office under the colonialists and heavily favoured by them. He pledged he would continue the close links with the mother country which, apart from anything else, guaranteed the local paper money and bought the exportable produce. The second party was centrist, small and weak, led by an intellectual, a professor who had qualified in Europe. The third was radical, and led by a man who had served several terms in prison under a security classification. This was Jean Kimba.

Long before the elections two of his aides, men who during their time as students in Europe had been contacted by the Russians who had noticed their presence in anti-colonial street demonstrations, and who had accepted bursaries to finish their schooling at the Patrice Lumumba University outside Moscow, left Zangaro secretly and flew to Europe. There they met emissaries from Moscow, and as a result of their conversations received a sum of money and considerable advice of a very practical nature.

Using the money, Kimba and his men formed squads of political thugs from among the Vindu, and completely ignored the small minority of Caja. In the unpoliced hinterland the political squads went to work. Several agents of the rival parties came to very sticky ends, and the squads visited all the clan chiefs of the Vindu.

After several public burnings and eye-gougings, the clan chiefs got the message. When the elections came, acting on the simple and effective logic that you do what the man with the power to exact painful retribution tells you, and ignore or mock the weak and the powerless, the chiefs ordered their people to vote for Kimba. He won the Vindu by a clear majority, and the total votes cast for him swamped the combined opposition and the Caja votes. This was aided by the fact the numbers of the Vindu had been almost doubled by the persuasion of every village chief to increase the number of people he claimed lived in his village. The rudimentary census taken by the colonial officials was based on affidavits from each village chief as to the population of his village.

The colonial power had made a mess of it. Instead of taking a leaf from the French book, and ensuring that the colonial protégé won the first, vital election, and then signed a mutual defence treaty to ensure a company of white paratroops kept the pro-Western president in power in perpetuity, the colonists had allowed their worst enemy to win. A month after the election Jean Kimba was inaugurated as first president of Zangaro.

What followed was along traditional lines. The four other parties were banned as 'divisive influences', and later the four party leaders arrested on trumped-up charges. They died under torture in prison, after making over the party funds to the liberator, Kimba. The colonial army and police officers were dismissed as soon as a semblance of an exclusively Vindu army had been brought into being. The Caja soldiers, who had constituted most of the gendarmerie under the colonists, were dismissed at the same time, and trucks were provided to take them home. After leaving the capital the six trucks headed for a quiet spot on the Zangaro river, and here the machine guns opened up. That was the end of the trained Caja.

In the capital, the police and customs men, mainly Caja, were allowed to stay on, but their guns were emptied and all their ammunition was taken away. Power passed to the Vindu army and the reign of terror started. It had taken eighteen months to achieve this. The confiscation of the estates, assets and businesses of the colonists began, and the economy ran steadily down. There were no Vindu trained to take over who could run the republic's few enterprises with even moderate efficiency, and the estates were in any case given to Kimba's party supporters. As the colonists left, a few UN technicians came in to run the basic essentials, but the excesses they witnessed caused most sooner or later to write home to their governments insisting they be removed.

After a few short, sharp examples of terror, the timorous Caja were subdued into absolute submission, and even across the river in Vindu country several savage examples were made of chiefs who mumbled something about the pre-election promises. After that the Vindu simply shrugged and went back to their bush. What happened in the capital had never affected them anyway in living memory, so they could afford to shrug. Kimba and his group of supporters, backed by the Vindu army and the unstable and highly dangerous teenagers who made up the party's youth movement, continued to rule from Clarence entirely for their own benefit and profit.

Some of the methods used to obtain the latter were mind-boggling. Simon Endean's report contained documentation of an instance where Kimba, frustrated over the non-arrival of his share of a business deal, arrested the European businessman involved and imprisoned him, sending an emissary to his wife with the pledge that she would receive her husband's toes, fingers and ears by post unless a ransom was paid. A letter from her imprisoned husband confirmed this, and the woman raised the necessary half a million dollars from his business partners and paid. The man was released, but his government, terrified of black African opinion at United Nations, urged him to remain silent. The Press never heard about it. On another occasion two nationals of the colonial power were arrested and beaten in the former colonial police barracks, since converted into the army barracks. They were released after a handsome bribe was paid to the Minister of Justice, of which evidently a part went to Kimba. Their offence was failing to bow as Kimba's car drove past.

In the previous five years since independence all conceivable opposition to Kimba had been wiped out or driven into exile, and the latter were the lucky ones. As a result there were no doctors, engineers or other qualified people left in the republic. There had been few enough in the first place, and Kimba suspected all educated men as possible opponents.

Over the years he had developed a psychotic fear of assassination, and never left the country. He seldom left the palace, and when he did it was under a massive escort. Firearms of every kind and description had been rounded up and impounded, including hunting rifles and shotguns, which added to the lack of protein food. Import of cartridges and black powder was halted, so eventually the Vindu hunters of the interior, coming to the coast to buy the powder they needed to hunt game, were sent back empty-handed and hung up their useless dane-guns in their huts. Even the carrying of matchets within the city limits was forbidden. The carrying of any of these items was punishable by death.

When he had finally digested the lengthy report, studied the photographs of the capital, the palace and Kimba, and pored over the maps, Sir James Manson sent again for Simon Endean. The latter was becoming highly curious about his chief's interest in this obscure republic, and had asked Martin Thorpe in their adjoining offices on the ninth floor what it was about. Thorpe had just grinned and tapped the side of his nose with a rigid forefinger.

Thorpe was not completely certain either, but he suspected he knew. Both men knew well enough not to ask questions when their employer had got an idea in his head and needed information.

When Endean reported to Manson the following morning, the latter was standing in his favourite position by the plate-glass windows of his penthouse, looking down into the street, where pygmies hurried about their business.

'There are two things I need to know more about, Simon,' Sir James Manson said without preamble, and walked back to his desk where the Endean report was lying.

'You mention here a ruckus in the capital, about six to seven weeks ago. I heard another report about the same upset from a man who was there. He mentioned a rumour of an attempted assassination of Kimba. What was it all about?'

Endean was relieved. He had heard the same story from his own sources, but had thought it too small to include in the report.

'Every time the president has a bad dream there are arrests and rumours of an attempt on his life,' said Endean. 'Normally it just means he wants justification to arrest and execute somebody. In this case, in late January, it was the commander of the Army, Colonel Bobi. I was told on the quiet the quarrel between the two men was really about Kimba's not getting a big enough cut in the rake-off from a deal Bobi put through. A shipment of drugs and medicines had arrived for the UN hospital. The Army impounded them at the quayside and stole half. Bobi was responsible and the stolen portion of the cargo was sold elsewhere on the black market. The proceeds of the sale should have passed to Kimba. Anyway, the head of the UN hospital, when making his protest to Kimba and tendering his resignation, mentioned the true value of the missing stuff. It was a lot more than Bobi had admitted to Kimba.

'The president went mad and sent some of his own guards out looking for Bobi. They ransacked the town looking for him, and arrested anyone who got in the way or took their fancy.'

'What happened to Bobi?' asked Manson.

'He fled. He got away in a jeep and made for the border. He got across by abandoning his jeep and walking through the bush round the border control point.'

'What tribe is he?'

'Oddly enough, a half-breed. Half Vindu and half Caja, probably the outcome of a Vindu raid on a Caja village forty years ago.'

'Was he one of Kimba's new army, or the old colonial one?' asked Manson.

'He was a corporal in the colonial gendarmerie, so presumably he had some form of rudimentary training. Then he was busted, before independence, for drunkenness and insubordination. When Kimba came to power he took him back in the early days because he needed at least one man who could tell one end of a gun from the other. In the colonial days, Bobi styled himself a Caja, but as soon as Kimba came to power he swore he was a true Vindu.'

'Why did Kimba keep him on? Was he one of his original supporters?'

'From the time Bobi saw which way the wind was blowing, he went to Kimba and swore loyalty to him. Which was smarter than the colonial governor, who couldn't believe Kimba had won the election until the figures proved it. Kimba kept Bobi on, and even promoted him to command the Army, because it looked better for a half-Caja to carry out the reprisals against the Caja opponents of Kimba.'

'What's he like?' asked Manson pensively.

'A big thug,' said Endean. 'A human gorilla. No brains as such, but a certain low animal cunning. The quarrel between the two men was only a question of thieves falling out.'

'But Western-trained? Not Communist?' insisted Manson.

'No, sir. Not a Communist. Not anything politically.'

'Bribable? Co-operate for money?'

'Certainly. He must be living pretty humbly now. He couldn't have stashed much away outside Zangaro. Only the president could get the big money.'

'Where is he now?' asked Manson.

'I don't know, sir. Living somewhere in exile.'

'Right,' said Manson. 'Find him, wherever he is.'

Endean nodded.

'Am I to visit him?'

'Not yet,' said Manson. 'There was one other matter. The report is fine, very comprehensive, except in one detail. The military side. I want a complete breakdown of the military security situation in and around the president's palace, and the capital. How many troops, police, any special presidential bodyguards, where they are quartered, how good they are, level of training and experience, the amount of fight they would put up if under attack, what weapons they carry, can they use them, what reserves are there, where the arsenal is situated, whether they have guards posted overall, if there are armoured cars or artillery, if the Russians train the Army, if there are strike-force camps away from Clarence, in fact, the whole lot.'

Endean stared at his chief in amazement. The phrase 'if under attack' stuck in his mind. What on earth was the old man up to, he wondered, but his face remained impassive.

'That would mean a personal visit, Sir James.'

'Yes, I concede that. Do you have a passport in another name?'

'No, sir. In any case, I couldn't furnish that information. It requires a sound judgement of military matters, and a knowledge of African troops as well. I was too late for National Service. I don't know a thing about armies or weapons.'

Manson was back at the window, staring across the City.

'I know,' he said softly. 'It would need a soldier to produce that report.'

'Well, Sir James, you would hardly get any army man to go and do that sort of a mission. Not for any money. Besides, a soldier's passport would have his profession on it. Where could I find a military man who would go down to Clarence and find that sort of information?'

'There is a kind,' said Manson. 'They are called mercenaries. They fight for whoever pays them, and pays them well. I'm prepared to do that. So go and find me a mercenary with initiative and brains. The best in Europe.'

Cat Shannon lay on his bed in the small hotel in Montmartre and watched the smoke from his cigarette drifting up towards the ceiling. He was bored. In the weeks that had passed since his return from Africa he had spent most of his saved pay travelling round Europe trying to set up another job.

In Rome he had seen an order of Catholic priests he knew with a view to going to South Sudan on their behalf to set up an airstrip in the interior into which medical supplies and goods could be ferried. He knew there were three separate groups of mercenaries operating in South Sudan, helping the Negroes in their civil war against the Arab North. In Bahr-el-Gazar two other British mercenaries, Ron Gregory and Rip Kirby, were leading a small operation of Dinak tribesmen, laying mines along the roads used by the Sudanese Army in an attempt to knock out their British Saladin armoured cars. In the south, in Equatoria province, Rolf Steiner had a camp that was supposed to be training the locals in the arts of war, but nothing had been heard of him for months. In Upper Nile to the east there was a much more efficient camp, where four Israelis were training the tribesmen and equipping them with Soviet weaponry from the cast stocks the Israelis had taken off the Egyptians in 1967. The warfare in the three provinces of South Sudan kept the bulk of the Sudanese Army and Air Force pinned down there, so that five squadrons of Egyptian fighters were based around Khartoum, and thus not available to confront the Israelis on the Suez Canal.

Shannon had visited the Israeli embassy in Paris and talked for forty minutes to the military attaché. The latter had listened politely, thanked him politely and just as politely ushered him out. The only thing the officer would say was that there were no Israeli advisers on the rebel side in South Sudan, and therefore he could not help. Shannon had no doubts the conversation had been tape-recorded and sent to Tel Aviv, but doubted he would hear any more. He conceded the Israelis were first rate as fighters and good at intelligence, but he thought they knew nothing about Black Africa and were heading for a fall in Uganda and probably elsewhere.

Apart from Sudan, there was little else on offer. Rumours abounded that the CIA were hiring mercenaries for training anti-Communist Meos in Cambodia, and that some Persian Gulf sheikhs were getting fed up with their dependence on British military advisers and were looking for mercenaries who would be entirely their own dependants. The story was that there were jobs going for men prepared to fight for the sheikhs in the hinterland, or take charge of palace security. Shannon doubted all of these stories; for one thing he would trust the CIA like a hole in the head, and the Arabs were not much better when it came to making up their minds.

Outside the Gulf, Cambodia and Sudan, there was little scope, and no good wars. In fact he foresaw in the offing a very nasty outbreak of peace. That left the chance of working as a bodyguard for a European arms dealer, and he had had one approach from such a man in Paris who felt himself threatened and needed someone good to give him cover.

Hearing Shannon was in town and knowing his skill and speed, the arms dealer had sent an emissary with the proposition. Without actually turning it down, the Cat was not keen. The dealer was in trouble through his own stupidity; a small matter of sending a shipment of arms to the Provisional IRA and then tipping off the British as to where it would be landed. There had been a number of arrests and the Provos were angry. Then there had been a leak in Belfast's apology for security organs, and the Provos were furious. The aim of having a bodyguard is primarily to scare off the opposition until tempers have cooled and the matter has been forgotten. Having Shannon giving gun-cover would have sent most professionals back home while still alive, but the Provos were mad dogs and probably did not know enough to stay clear. So there would be a gunfight, and the French police would take a dim view of one of their streets littered with bleeding Fenians. Moreover, as he was an Ulster Protestant, they would never believe Shannon had just been doing his job. But, the offer was still open.

The month of March had opened and was ten days through, but the weather remained dank and chill, with daily drizzle and rain, and Paris was unwelcoming. Outdoors meant fine weather in Paris, and indoors cost a lot of money. Shannon was husbanding his remaining resources of dollars as best he could. So he left his telephone number with the dozen or so people he thought might hear something to interest him and read several paperback novels in his hotel room.

He lay staring at the ceiling and thinking of home. Not that he really had a home any more, but for want of a better word he still thought of the wild sweep of turf and stunted trees that sprawls across the border of Tyrone and Donegal as the place that he came from.

He had been born and brought up close to the small village of Castlederg, situated inside County Tyrone but lying on the border with Donegal. His parents' house had been set a mile from the village on a slope looking out to the west across Donegal.

They called Donegal the county God forgot to finish, and the few trees were bent towards the east, curved over by the constant beating of the winds from the North Atlantic.

His father had owned a flax mill that turned out fine Irish linen, and had been in a small way the squire of the area. He was Protestant and almost all the workers and local farmers were Catholic, and in Ulster ne'er the twain shall meet, so the young Carlo had had no other boys to play with. He made his friends among the horses instead, and this was horse country. He could ride before he could mount a bicycle, and had a pony of his own when he was five, and he could still remember riding the pony into the village to buy a half-pennyworth of sherbet powder from the sweetshop of old Mr Sam Gailey.

At eight he had been sent to boarding school in England at the urging of his mother, who was English and came from moneyed people. So for the next ten years he had learned to be an Englishman and to all intents and purposes lost the stamp of Ulster, both in speech and attitudes. During the holidays he had gone home to the moors and the horses, but he knew no contemporaries near Castlederg, so the vacations were lonely if healthy, consisting of long fast gallops in the wind.

It was while he was a sergeant in the Royal Marines at twenty-two that his parents had died in a car crash on the Belfast road. He had come home for the funeral, smart in his black belt and gaiters, topped by the green beret of the Commandos. Then he had accepted an offer for the run-down, nearly bankrupt mill, closed up the house and returned to Portsmouth.

That was eleven years ago. He had served the remainder of his five-year contract in the Marines, and on returning to civilian life had pottered from job to job until taken on as a clerk by a London merchant house with widespread African interests. Working his probationary year in London, he had learned the intricacies of company structure, trading and banking the profits, setting up holding companies and the value of a discreet Swiss account. After a year in London he had been posted as assistant manager of the Uganda branch office, from which he had walked out without a word and driven into the Congo. So for the last six years he had lived as a mercenary, often an outlaw, at best regarded as a soldier for hire, at worst a paid killer. The trouble was, once he was known as a mercenary there was no going back. It was not a question of being unable to get a job in a business house; that could be done, at a pinch, or even by giving a different name. Even without going to these lengths, one could always get hired as a truck driver, security guard or for some manual job if the worst came to the worst. The real problem was being able to stick it; to sit in an office under the orders of a wee man in a dark grey suit, and look out of the window and recall the bush country, the waving palms, the smell of sweat and cordite, the grunts of the men hauling the jeeps over the river crossings, the copper-tasting fear just before the attack and the wild cruel joy of being alive afterwards. To remember, and then to go back to the ledgers and the commuter train, that was what was impossible. He knew he would eat his heart out if it ever came to that. For Africa bites like a tsetse fly, and once the drug is in the blood it can never be wholly exorcised.

So he lay on his bed and smoked some more and wondered where the next job was coming from.

5

Simon Endean was aware that somewhere in London there has to exist the wherewithal to discover just about any piece of knowledge known to man, including the name and address of a first-class mercenary. The only problem sometimes is to know where to start looking and whom to start asking.

After a reflective hour drinking coffee in his office, he left and took a taxi down to Fleet Street. Through a friend on the City desk of one of London's biggest daily papers he got access to the paper's cuttings library and gave the archivist his request for the folders he wanted to study. For the next two hours he pored over the file in the agency archives that dealt with every newspaper cutting in Britain over the previous ten years concerning mercenaries. There were articles about Katanga, the Congo, Yemen, Vietnam, Cambodia, Laos, Sudan, Nigeria and Rwanda; news items, commentaries, editorials, feature articles and photographs. He read them all, and paid special attention to the names of the writers.

At this stage he was not looking for the name of a mercenary. There were in any case too many names, pseudonyms, *noms de guerre*, nicknames, and he had little doubt some of them were false. He was looking for the name of an expert on mercenaries, a writer or reporter whose articles seemed to be authoritative enough to indicate the journalist knew his subject well, who could find his way round the bewildering labyrinth of rival claims and alleged exploits, and give a balanced judgement. At the end of two hours he had secured the name he was looking for, although he had never heard of the man before.

There were three articles over the previous three years carrying the same by-line, apparently that of an Englishman or American. The writer seemed to know what he was talking about and he mentioned mercenaries from half a dozen different nationalities, neither over-praising them nor sensationalising their careers to set spines a-tingling. Endean noted the name and the three newspapers in which the articles had appeared, a fact which seemed to indicate that the writer was freelancing.

A second phone call to his newspaper friend eventually produced the writer's address. It was a small flat in North London.

Darkness had already fallen when Endean left ManCon House, and taking his Corvette from the underground car park, he drove northwards to find the journalist's flat. The lights were off when he got there, and there was no answer to the door bell. Endean hoped the man was not away abroad, and this was confirmed by the woman in the basement flat. He was glad to see the house was not large or smart, and hoped the reporter might be hard up for a little extra cash, as freelances usually are. He decided to come back in the morning.

Simon Endean pressed the bell next to the writer's name just after eight the following morning and half a minute later a voice tinkled 'Yes' at him from the meal grille set in the woodwork.

'Good morning,' said Endean into the grille, 'my name is Harris. Walter Harris. I'm a businessman. I wonder if I might have a word with you?'

The door opened and he mounted to the fourth floor where a door stood open onto the landing. Framed in it was the man he had come to see. When they were seated in the sitting-room, Endean came straight to the point.

'I am a businessman in the City,' he lied smoothly. 'I am here in a sense representing a consortium of friends, all of whom have this in common: that we all have business interests in a state in West Africa.'

The writer nodded wearily and sipped his coffee.

'Recently there have been increasing reports of the possibility of a *coup d'état*. The president is a moderate and reasonably good man, as things go down there, and very popular with his people. One of my business friends was told by one of his workers that the coup, if and when it came, could well be Communist-backed. Do you follow me?'

'Yes. Go on.'

'Well now, it is felt that no more than a small portion of the Army would support a coup unless the speed of it threw them into confusion and left them leaderless. In other words, if it were a *fait accompli*, the bulk of the Army might agree to go along in any case once they realised the coup had succeeded. But if it came, and half-failed, the bulk of the Army would, we all feel sure, support the president. As you may know, experience shows the twenty hours following the strike are the vital ones.'

'What has this to do with me?' asked the writer.

'I'm coming to that,' said Endean. 'The general feeling is that, for the coup to succeed, it would be necessary for the plotters first to assassinate the president. If he remained alive, the coup would fail, or might not even be tried, and all would be well. Therefore the question of palace security is vital, and becoming more so. We have been in touch with some friends in the Foreign Office, and they feel it is out of the question to second a professional British officer to advise on security in and around the palace.'

'So?' The writer sipped more coffee and lit a cigarette. He reckoned his visitor was too smooth, too smooth by half.

'So the president would be prepared to accept the services of a professional soldier to advise, on the basis of a contract, on all security matters regarding the person of the president. What he is seeking is a man who could go down there, make a complete and thorough survey of the palace and all its security arrangements, and plug any loopholes in the existing security measures surrounding the president. I believe such men, good soldiers who do not necessarily fight under the flag of their own country, are called mercenaries.'

The freelance nodded several times. He had few doubts the story of the man who called himself Harris was some way from true. For one thing, if palace security was really what was sought, the British government would not be against providing the expert to advise on its improvement. For another, there was a perfectly capable firm at 22 Sloane Street, London, called Watchguard International, whose speciality was precisely that.

In a few sentences he pointed this out to Harris. It did not faze him in the slightest.

'Ah,' he said, 'evidently I have to be a little more candid.'

'It would help,' said the writer.

'The point is, you see, that HMG might agree to send an expert merely to advise, but if the advice was that the palace security troops needed extensive further training, and a crash course at that, politically speaking a Britisher sent by the government could not do that. And if the president wished to offer the man a longer-term post on his staff, the same would apply. As for Watchguard, one of their ex-Special Air Service men would be fine, but if he were on the staff of the palace guard and a coup were tried, despite his presence, there might be a question of combat. Now you know what the rest of Africa would think about a staffman from Watchguard, which most of these blacks regard as being linked to the Foreign Office in some way, doing that. But a pure outsider, although not respectable, would at least be understandable, without exposing the president to the sneer of being a tool of the dirty old imperialists.'

'So what do you want?' asked the writer.

'The name of a good mercenary soldier,' said Endean. 'One with brains and initiative, who'll do a workmanlike job for his money.'

'Why come to me?'

'Your name was recalled by one of our group from an article you wrote several months ago. It seemed very authoritative.'

'I write for my living,' said the freelance.

Endean gently withdrew £200 in ten-pound notes from his pocket and laid them on the table.

'Then write for me,' he said.

'What? An article?'

'No, a memorandum. A list of names and track records. Or you can talk if you like.'

'I'll write,' said the freelance. He walked to a corner where his desk, a typewriter and a stack of white paper comprised the working area of the open-plan flat. Running a sheet into his machine, consulting occasionally from a set of files beside his desk, he wrote steadily for fifty minutes. When he rose he walked over to the waiting Endean with three sheets of quarto paper and held them out.

'These are the best around today, the older generation of the Congo six years ago, and the new up-and-comers. I haven't bothered with men who couldn't command a platoon well. Mere heavies would be no use to you.'

Endean took the sheets and studied them intently.

The contents were:

COLONEL LAMOULINE. Belgian, probably government man. Came into Congo in 1964 under Moise Tshombe, Probably with full approval of Belgian Govt. First-class soldier, not really a mercenary in full sense of the word. Set up Sixth Commando (French-speaking) and commanded until 1965, when he handed over command to Denard and left.

ROBERT DENARD. Frenchman. Police background, not army. Was in Katanga secession in 1961/62, probably as gendarmerie adviser. Left after failure of secession and exile of Tshombe. Commanded French mercenary operation in Yemen for Jacques Foccart. Returned Congo 1964, joined Lamouline. Commanded Sixth after Lamouline and up till 1967. Took part, half-heartedly, in second Stanleyville revolt (the mercenaries' mutiny) in 1967. Wounded badly in head by ricocheting bullet from own side. Flown out to Rhodesia for treatment. Tried to return by mounting November 1967 mercenary invasion of Congo from the south of Dilolo. Operation delayed, some said as a result of CIA bribes, was a fiasco when it happened. Since lived in Paris.

JACQUES SCHRAMME. Belgian. Planter-turned-mercenary. Nicknamed Black Jack. Formed own unit of Katangese, early in 1961, and was prominent in Katangese secession attempt. One of the last to flee into Angola on defeat of the secession. Took his Katangese with him. Waited in Angola until return of Tshombe, then marched back into Katanga. Through the 1964/65 war against the Simba rebels, his 10th Codo was more or less independent. Sat out the first Stanleyville revolt of 1966 (the Katangese mutiny) and his mixed mercenary/Katangese force was left intact. Launched 1967 Stanleyville mutiny in which Denard later joined. Took joint command after wounding of Denard and led the march to Bukavu. Repatriated 1968, no further mercenary work since then.

ROGER FAULQUES. Much decorated French professional officer. Sent, probably by French Govt, into Katanga during secession. Later commanded Denard who ran the French operation in the Yemen. Was not involved in Congolese mercenary operations. Mounted small operation at French behest in Nigerian civil war. Ferociously brave but now nearly crippled by combat wounds.

MIKE HOARE. British-turned-South African. Acted as mercenary adviser in Katanga secession, became a close personal friend of Tshombe. Invited back to Congo in 1964 when Tshombe returned to power and formed English-speaking Fifth Commando. Commanded through bulk of anti-Simba war, retired in December 1965 and handed over to Peters. Well-off and semi-retired.

JOHN PETERS. Joined Hoare in 1964 on first mercenary war. Rose to become deputy commander. Fearless and totally ruthless. Several officers under Hoare refused to serve under Peters and transferred or left 5th Codo. Retired wealthy late 1966.

N.B. The above six count as 'the older generation' inasmuch as they were the originals who came to prominence in the Katanga and Congolese wars. The following are younger in age, except Roux who is now in his mid-forties, but may be considered the 'younger' generation because they had junior commands in the Congo, or came to prominence since the Congo.

ROLF STEINER. German. Began first mercenary operation under Faulques-organised group that went into Nigerian civil war. Stayed on and led the remnants of the group for nine months. Dismissed. Signed on for South Sudan.

GEORGE SCHROEDER. South African. Served under Hoare and Peters in 5th Codo in the Congo. Prominent in the South African contingent in that unit. Their choice as leader after Peters. Peters conceded and gave him the command. 5th Codo disbanded and sent home a few months later. Not heard of since. Living in South Africa.

CHARLES ROUX. French. Very junior in Katangese secession. Quit early and went to South Africa via Angola. Stayed there and returned with South Africans to fight under Hoare in 1964. Quarrelled with Hoare and went to join Denard. Promoted and transferred to 6th Codo subsidiary unit, the 14th Codo, as second in command. Took part in 1966 Katangese revolt in Stanleyville in which his unit was nearly wiped out. Was smuggled out of the Congo by Peters. Returned by air with several South Africans and joined Schramme, May 1967. Took part in 1967 Stanleyville revolt as well. After wounding of Denard, proposed for overall command of 10th and 6th Commandos, now merged. Failed. Wounded at Bukavu in a shoot-out, quit and returned home via Kigali. Not in action since. Lives in Paris.

CARLO SHANNON. British. Served under Hoare in 5th, 1964. Declined to serve under Peters. Transferred to Denard 1966, joined the 6th. Served under Schramme on march to Bukavu. Fought throughout the siege. Repatriated among the last in April 1968. Volunteered for Nigerian civil war, served under Steiner. Took over remnants after Steiner's dismissal November 1968. Commanded till the end. Believed staying in Paris.

LUCIEN BRUN. Alias Paul Leroy. French, speaks fluent English. Served as enlisted officer French Army Algerian war. Normal discharge. Was in South Africa 1964, volunteered for Congo. Arrived 1964 with South African unit, joined Hoare's 5th Commando. Fought well, wounded late 1964. Returned 1965. Refused to serve under Peters, transferred to Denard and the 6th in early 1966. Left Congo May 1966 sensing forthcoming revolt. Served under Faulques in Nigerian civil war. Wounded and repatriated. Returned and tried for his own command. Failed. Repatriated 1968. Lives in Paris. Highly intelligent, also very politically minded.

When he had finished, Endean looked up.

'These men would all be available for such a job?' he asked. The writer shook his head.

'I doubt it,' he said. 'I included all those who could do such a job. Whether they would want to is another matter. It would depend on the size of the job, the number of men they would command. For the older ones there is a question of prestige involved. There is also the question of how much they need the work. Some of the older ones are more or less retired and comfortably off.'

'Point them out to me,' invited Endean.

The writer leaned over and ran his finger down the list.

'First the older generation. Lamouline you'll never get. He was always virtually an extension of Belgian government policy, a tough veteran and revered by his men. He's retired now. The other Belgian, Black Jacques Schramme, is now retired and runs a chicken farm in Portugal. Of the French, Roger Faulques is perhaps the most decorated ex-officer of the French Army. He also is revered by the men who fought under him, in and out of the Foreign Legion, and regarded as a gentleman by others. But he's also crippled with wounds and the last contract he got was a failure because he delegated the command to a subordinate who failed. If the colonel had been there himself it would probably not have done.

'Denard was good in the Congo, but got a very bad head wound at Stanleyville. Now he's past it. The French mercenaries still stay in contact with him, looking for a bite, but he hasn't been given a command or a project to set up since the fiasco at Dilolo. And little wonder.

'Of the Anglo-Saxons, Mike Hoare is retired and comfortably off. He might be tempted by a million-pound project, but even that's not certain. His last foray was into Nigeria where he proposed a project to each side, costed at half a million pounds. They both turned him down. John Peters is also retired and runs a factory in Singapore. All six made a lot of money in the hey-day, but none has adapted to the smaller, more technical mission that might be called for nowadays, some because they don't wish to, or because they can't!'

'What about the other five?' asked Endean.

'Steiner was good once, but deteriorated. The Press publicity got to

him, and that's always bad for a mercenary. They begin to believe they
are as fearsome as the Sunday papers say they are. Roux became bitter
when he failed to get the Stanleyville command after Denard's wounding, and claims leadership over all French mercenaries, but he hasn't
been employed since Bukavu. The last two are better; both in their
thirties, intelligent, educated and with enough guts in combat to be able
to command other mercs. Incidentally, mercs only fight under a leader
they choose themselves. So hiring a bad mercenary to recruit others
serves no purpose, because no one else wants to know about serving
under a guy who once ran out. So the combat record is important.

'Lucien Brun, alias Paul Leroy, could do this job. Trouble is, you would
never be quite sure if he was not passing stuff to French intelligence, the
SDECE. Does that matter?'

'Yes, very much,' said Endean shortly. 'You left out Schroeder, the
South African. What about him? You say he commanded Fifth Commando in the Congo?'

'Yes,' said the writer. 'At the end, the very end. It also broke up under
his command. He's a first-class soldier within his limitations. For
example, he would command a battalion of mercenaries excellently, providing it were within the framework of a brigade with a good staff. He's a
good combat man, but conventional. Very little imagination, not the sort
who could set up his own operation starting from scratch. He'd need staff
officers to take care of the admin.'

'And Shannon? He's British?'

'Anglo-Irish. He's new; he got his first command only a year ago, but
he did well. He can think unconventionally and has a lot of audacity. He
can also organise down to the last detail.'

Endean rose to go.

'Tell me something,' he said at the door. 'If you were mounting an ...
seeking a man to go on a mission and assess a situation, which would you
choose?'

The writer picked up the notes on the breakfast table.

'Cat Shannon,' he said without hesitation. 'If I were doing that, or
mounting an operation, I'd pick the Cat.'

'Where is he?' asked Endean.

The writer mentioned a hotel and a bar in Paris.

'You could try either of those,' he said.

'And if this man Shannon was not available, or for some other reason
could not be employed, who would be second on the list?'

The writer thought for a while.

'If not Lucien Brun, then the only other one who would almost certainly be available and has the experience would be Roux,' he said.

'You have his address?' asked Endean.

The writer flicked through a small notebook that he took from a
drawer in his desk.

'Roux has a flat in Paris,' he said, and gave Endean the address. A few
seconds later he heard the clump of Endean's feet descending the stairs.
He picked up the phone and dialled a number.

'Carrie? Hi, it's me. We're going out tonight. Somewhere expensive. I just got paid for a feature article.'

Cat Shannon walked slowly and pensively up the Rue Blanche towards the Place Clichy. The little bars were already open on both sides of the street, and from the doorways the hustlers tried to persuade him to step inside and see the most beautiful girls in Paris. The latter, who, whatever else they were, most certainly were not that, peered through the lace curtains at the darkened street. It was just after five o'clock on a mid-March evening, with a cold wind blowing. The weather matched Shannon's mood.

He crossed the square and ducked up another side street towards his hotel which had few advantages but a fine view from its top floors, since it was close to the summit of Montmartre. He was thinking about Dr Dunois, whom he had visited for a general check-up a week earlier. A former paratrooper and army doctor, Dunois had become a mountaineer and gone on two French expeditions to the Himalayas and the Andes as the team medico.

He had later volunteered for several tough medical missions in Africa, on a temporary basis and for the duration of the emergency, working for the French Red Cross. There he had met the mercenaries and had patched up several of them after combat. He had become known as the mercenaries' doctor, even in Paris, and had sewn up a lot of bullet holes, removed many splinters of mortar casing from their bodies. If they had a medical problem or needed a check-up, they usually went to him at his Paris surgery. If they were well off, flush with money, they paid on the nail in dollars. If not, he forgot to send his bill, which is unusual in French doctors.

Shannon turned in to the door of his hotel and crossed to the desk for his key. The old man was on duty behind the desk.

'Ah, monsieur, one has been calling you from London. All day. He left a message.'

The old man handed Shannon the slip of paper in the key aperture. It was written in the old man's scrawl, evidently dictated letter by letter. It said simply 'Careful Harris', and was signed with the name of a freelance writer he knew from his African wars and who he knew lived in London.

'There is another, m'sieu. He is waiting in the salon.'

The old man gestured towards the small room set aside from the lobby and through the archway Shannon could see a man about his own age dressed in the sober grey of a London businessman watching him as he stood by the desk. There was little of the London businessman in the ease with which the visitor came to his feet as Shannon entered the salon, nor about the build of the shoulders. Shannon had seen men like him before. They always represented older, richer men.

'Mr Shannon?'

'Yes.'

'My name is Harris, Walter Harris.'

'You wanted to see me?'

'I've been waiting a couple of hours for just that. Can we talk here, or in your room?'

'Here will do. The old man understands no English.'

The two men seated themselves facing each other. Endean relaxed and crossed his legs. He reached for a packet of cigarettes and gestured to Shannon with the packet. Shannon shook his head and reached for his own brand in his jacket pocket, then thought better of it.

'I understand you are a mercenary, Mr Shannon?'

'Yes.'

'In fact you have been recommended to me. I represent a group of London businessmen. We need a job done. A sort of mission. It needs a man who has some knowledge of military matters, and who can travel to a foreign country without exciting any suspicions. Also a man who can make an intelligent report on what he sees there, analyse a military situation, and then keep his mouth shut.'

'I don't kill on contract,' said Shannon briefly.

'We don't want you to,' said Endean.

'All right, what's the mission? And what's the fee?' asked Shannon. He saw no time in wasting words. The man in front of him was unlikely to be shocked by a spade being called a spade. Endean smiled briefly.

'First, you would have to come to London for briefing. We would pay for your trip and expenses, even if you decided not to accept.'

'Why London? Why not here?' asked Shannon.

Endean exhaled a long stream of smoke.

'There are some maps and other papers involved,' he said. 'I didn't want to bring them with me. Also, I have to consult my partners, report to them that you have accepted or not as the case may be.'

There was silence as Endean drew a wad of French 100-franc notes from his pocket.

'Fifteen hundred francs,' he said. 'About £120. That's for your air ticket to London, single or return, whichever you wish to buy. And your overnight stay. If you decline the proposition after hearing it, you get another £100 for your trouble in coming. If you accept, we discuss the further salary.'

Shannon nodded.

'All right. I'll listen – in London. When?'

'Tomorrow,' said Endean, and rose to leave.

'Arrive any time during the course of the day, and stay at the Post House Hotel on Haverstock Hill. I'll book your room when I get back tonight. At nine the day after tomorrow I'll phone you in your room and make a rendezvous for later that morning. Clear?'

Shannon nodded and picked up the francs.

'Book the room in the name of Brown, Keith Brown,' he said. The man who called himself Harris left the hotel and headed downhill looking for a taxi.

He had not seen any reason to mention to Shannon that he had spent three hours earlier that afternoon talking with another mercenary, a man by the name of Charles Roux. Nor did he mention that he had decided, despite the Frenchman's evident eagerness, that Roux was not the man for the job: he had left the man's flat with a vague promise to get in touch again with his decision.

Twenty-four hours later Shannon stood at his bedroom window in the Post House Hotel, and stared out at the rain and the commuter traffic swishing up Haverstock Hill from Camden Town towards Hampstead and the commuter suburbs.

He had arrived that morning on the first plane, using his passport in the name of Keith Brown. Long since, he had had to acquire a false passport by the normal method used in mercenary circles. At the end of 1967 he had been with Black Jacques Schramme at Bukavu, surrounded and besieged for months by the Congolese Army. Finally, undefeated but running out of ammunition, the mercenaries had vacated the Congolese lakeside city, walked across the bridge into neighbouring Rwanda and allowed themselves, with Red Cross guarantees which the Red Cross could not possibly fulfil, to be disarmed.

From then on, for nearly six months, they had sat idle in an internment camp at Kigali while the Red Cross and the Rwanda government hassled over their repatriation to Europe. President Mobutu of the Congo wanted them sent back to him for execution, but the mercenaries had threatened if that was the decision they would take the Rwanda Army barehanded, recover their guns and find their own way home. The Rwandan government had believed, rightly, that they might do it.

When finally the decision was made to fly them back to Europe, the British consul had visited the camp and soberly told the six British mercenaries present that he would have to impound their passports. They had soberly told him they had lost everything across the lake in Bukavu. On being flown home to London Shannon and the others had been told by the Foreign Office that each man owed £350 for the air fare, and would receive no new passport ever again.

Before leaving the camp, the men had been photographed, fingerprinted, and had their names taken. They also had to sign a document pledging never to set foot on the continent of Africa. These documents would be sent in copy to every African government.

The reaction cf the mercenaries was predictable. Every one had a lush beard and moustache, and hair left uncut after months in the camp, where no scissors were allowed in case they went on the warpath with them. The photographs were therefore unrecognisable. They then submitted their own fingerprints for another man's prints, and exchanged names. The result was that every identity document contained one man's name, another man's fingerprints and a third man's photograph. Finally they signed the pledge to leave Africa for ever with names like Sebastian Weetabix and Neddy Seagoon.

Shannon's reaction to the Foreign Office demand was no less unhelpful. As he still had his 'lost' passport he kept it, and travelled where he wished, until it expired. Then he took the necessary steps to secure another one, issued by the Passport Office but based on a birth certificate, secured from the Registry of Births in Somerset House for the standard fee of five shillings, which referred to a baby who had died of meningitis in Yarmouth about the time Shannon was born.*

On arrival in London that morning he had contacted the writer he had first met in Africa, and learned how Walter Harris had contacted him. He thanked the man for recommending him, and asked if he knew the name of a good agency of private enquirers. Later that afternoon he visited the agency and paid a deposit of twenty pounds, promising to phone them the next morning with further instructions.

Endean rang as he had promised on the dot of nine the following morning, and was put through to Mr Brown's room.

'There's a block of flats in Sloane Avenue called Chelsea Cloisters,' he said without preamble. 'I have booked flat 317 for us to talk. Please be there at eleven sharp. Wait in the lobby until I arrive, as I have the key.'

Then he rang off. Shannon noted the address from the telephone book under the bedside table, and rang the detective agency.

'I want your man in the lobby of Chelsea Cloisters in Sloane Avenue at ten-fifteen,' he said. 'He had better have his own transport.'

'He'll have a scooter,' said the head of the agency.

An hour later Shannon met the man from the agency in the lobby of the block of service flats. Rather to his surprise the man was a youth in his late teens, with long hair. Shannon surveyed him suspiciously.

'Do you know your job?' he asked. The boy nodded. He seemed full of enthusiasm, and Shannon only hoped it was matched by a bit of skill.

'Well, park that crash helmet outside on the scooter,' he said.'People who come in here don't carry crash helmets. Sit over there and read a newspaper.'

The youth had not got one, so Shannon gave him his own.

'I'll sit on the other side of the lobby. At about eleven a man will come in, nod to me, and we'll go into the lift together. Note that man, so you will recognise him again. He should come out about an hour later. By then you must be across the road, astride the scooter, with the helmet on and pretending to be busy with a breakdown. Got it?'

'Yes. I've got it.'

'The man will either take his own car from nearby, in which case grab the number of it, or he'll take a taxi. In either case, follow him and note where he goes. Keep on his tail until he arrives at what looks like his final destination.'

The youth drank in the instructions and took his place in the far corner of the lobby behind his newspaper.

The lobby porter frowned but left him alone. He had seen quite a few meetings take place in front of his reception desk.

Forty minutes later Simon Endean walked in. Shannon noticed that he

---

* For a more detailed explanation of this procedure, which was used by a would-be assassin of General de Gaulle, see *The Day of the Jackal*.

dismissed a taxi at the door, and hoped the youth had noticed it as well. He stood up and nodded to the newcomer, but Endean strolled past him and pressed the summons button for the lift. Shannon joined him, and remarked the youth peering over his newspaper.

For God's sake, thought Shannon, and mentioned something about the foul weather lest the man who called himself Harris should glance round the lobby.

Settled into an easy chair in flat 317, Endean opened his briefcase and took out a map. Spreading it out on the bed he told Shannon to look at it. Shannon gave it three minutes and had taken in all the details the map had to give. Then Endean began his briefing.

It was a judicious mixture of fact and fiction. He still claimed he represented a consortium of British businessmen, all of whom did some form of business with Zangaro and all of whose businesses, including some which were virtually out of business, had suffered as a result of President Kimba.

Then he went into the background of the republic from independence onwards, and what he said was truthful, most of it out of his own report to Sir James Manson. The punchline came at the end.

'A group of officers in the Army has got in touch with a group of local businessmen, who are incidentally a dying breed. They have mentioned that they are considering toppling Kimba in a coup. One of the local businessmen mentioned it to one of my group, and put their problem to us. It is basically that they are virtually untrained in military terms, despite their officer status, and do not know how to topple the man, because he spends too much time hidden inside the walls of his palace, surrounded by his guards.

'Frankly, we would not be sorry to see this Kimba go, and neither would his people. A new government would be good for the economy of the place, and good for the country. We need a man to go down there and make a complete assessment of the military and security situation in and around the palace and the important institutions. We want a complete report on Kimba's military strength.'

'So you can pass it on to your officers?' asked Shannon.

'They are not our officers. They are Zangaran officers. The fact is, if they are going to strike at all, they had better know what they are doing.'

Shannon believed half of the briefing, but not the second half. If the officers, who were on the spot, could not assess the situation, they would be incompetent to carry out a coup. But he kept silent.

'I'd have to go in as a tourist,' he said. 'There's no other cover that would work.'

'That's right.'

'There must be precious few tourists go there. Why cannot I go in as a company visitor to one of your friends' business houses?'

'That will not be possible,' said Endean. 'If anything went wrong, there would be all hell to pay.'

If I get caught, you mean, thought Shannon, but kept silent. He was being paid, so he would take risks. That, and his knowledge, was what was being paid for.

'There's the question of pay,' he said shortly.

'Then you'll do it?'

'If the money's right, yes.'

Endean nodded approvingly. 'Tomorrow morning a return ticket from London to the capital of the neighbouring republic will be at your hotel,' he said. 'You have to fly back to Paris and get a visa for this republic. Zangaro is so poor there is only one embassy in Europe, and that's in Paris also. But getting a Zangaran visa there takes a month. In the next-door republic's capital there is a Zangaran consulate. There you can get a visa for cash, and within an hour if you tip the consul. You understand the procedure.'

Shannon nodded. He understood it very well.

'So get visa-ed up in Paris, then fly down by Air Afrique. Get your Zangaran visa on the spot and take the connecting plane service from there to Clarence, paying cash. With the tickets at your hotel tomorrow will be £300 in French francs as expenses.'

'I'll need five,' said Shannon. 'It'll be ten days at least, possibly more depending on connections and how long the visas take to get. Three hundred leaves no margin for the occasional bribe or any delay.'

'All right, five hundred in French francs. Plus five hundred for yourself,' said Endean.

'A thousand,' said Shannon.

'Dollars? I understand you people deal in US dollars.'

'Pounds,' said Shannon. 'That's 2500 dollars, or two months at flat salary if I were on a normal contract.'

'But you'll only be away ten days,' protested Endean.

'Ten days of high risk,' countered Shannon. 'If this place is half what you say it is, anyone getting caught on this kind of job is going to be very dead, and very painfully. You want me to take the risks, rather than go yourself, you pay.'

'OK, a thousand pounds. Five hundred down, and five hundred when you return.'

'How do I know you'll contact me when I return?' said Shannon.

'How do I know you'll even go there at all?' countered Endean. Shannon considered the point. Then he nodded.

'All right, half now, half later.'

Ten minutes later Endean was gone, after instructing Shannon to wait five minutes before leaving himself.

At three that afternoon the head of the detective agency was back from his lunch. Shannon rang at three-fifteen.

'Ah, yes, Mr Brown,' said the voice on the phone. 'I have spoken to my man. He waited as you instructed, and when the subject left the building, he recognised him and followed. The subject hailed a taxi from the kerbside and my man followed him to the City. There he dismissed the taxi and entered a building.'

'What building?'

'ManCon House. That's the headquarters of Manson Consolidated Mining.'

'Do you know if he works there?' asked Shannon.

'It would seem he does,' said the agency chief. 'My man could not follow him into the building, but he noticed the commissionaire touched his cap to the subject and held the door open for him. He did not do that for a stream of secretaries and evidently junior executives who were emerging for lunch.'

'He's brighter than he looks,' conceded Shannon. The youth had done a good job. Shannon gave several further instructions and that afternoon mailed £50 by registered post to the detective agency. He also opened a bank account and put down £10 deposit in it. The following morning he banked a further £500 and that evening flew to Paris.

Dr Gordon Chalmers was not a drinking man. He seldom touched anything stronger than beer and when he did, he became talkative, as his employer Sir James Manson had found out for himself over their luncheon at Wilton's. The evening that Cat Shannon was changing planes at Le Bourget to catch the Air Afrique DC-8 to West Africa, Dr Chalmers was having dinner with an old college friend, now also a scientist and working in industrial research.

There was nothing special about their meal. He had run into his former classmate in one of those coincidental meetings on the street a few days earlier, and they had agreed to have dinner together.

Fifteen years earlier they had been young undergraduates, single and working hard on their respective degrees, earnest and concerned as so many young scientists feel obliged to be. In the mid-fifties the concern had been the Bomb and colonialism, and they had joined thousands of others marching for the Campaign for Nuclear Disarmament and the various movements that sought an instant end to empire, and world freedom now. Both had been indignant, serious, committed, and both had changed nothing. But in their indignation over the state of the world they had dabbled with the Young Communist movement. Chalmers had grown out of it, married, started his family, secured a mortgage for his house, and slowly merged into the salaried middle class.

The combination of worries that had come his way over the previous fortnight caused him to take more than his usual single glass of wine with dinner, considerably more. His friend, a kindly man with soft brown eyes, noticed his worry and asked if he could help.

It was over the brandy that Dr Chalmers felt he had to confide his worries to someone, someone who, unlike his wife, was a fellow scientist and would understand the problem. Of course it was highly confidential, and his friend was solicitous and sympathetic.

When he heard about the crippled daughter and the need for the money to pay for her expensive equipment, the man's eyes clouded over with sympathy, and he reached across the table to grip Dr Chalmers's forearm.

'Don't worry about it, Gordon. It's completely understandable. Anyone else would have done the same thing,' he told him. Chalmers felt better when they left the restaurant and made their separate ways home. He was easier in his mind, his problem somehow shared.

Though he had asked his old friend how he had fared in the intervening years since their undergraduate days together, the man had been slightly evasive. Chalmers, bowed under his own worries and his observation blunted by wine, had not pressed for details. Even had he done so, it was unlikely the friend would have told him that, far from merging into the bourgeoisie, he had remained a fully committed member of the Party.

6

The Convair 440 that ran the connecting air service into Clarence banked steeply over the bay and began its descent towards the airfield. Being intentionally on the left side of the plane, Shannon could look down towards the town as the aircraft overflew it. From a thousand feet he could see the capital of Zangaro occupying the end of the peninsula, surrounded on three sides by the palm-fringed waters of the Gulf, and on the fourth side by the land, where the stubby peninsula, just eight miles long, ran back to join the main coastline.

The spit of land was three miles wide at its base, set in the mangrove swamps of the coastline, and a mile wide at the tip, where the town was situated. The flanks along each side were also composed of mangrove, and only at the end did the mangroves give way to some shingly beaches.

The town spanned the end of the peninsula from side to side and stretched about a mile back down the length of it. Beyond the fringes of the town at this end, a single road ran between cultivated patches the remaining seven miles to the main coast.

Evidently all the best buildings were set towards the seaward tip of the land, where the breezes would blow, for the aerial view showed the buildings to be set in their own plots of land, one to an acre. The land-ward side of the town was evidently the poorer section, where thousands of tin-roofed shanties intersected with narrow muddy alleys. He concentrated on the richer section of Clarence, where the colonial masters once lived, for here would be the important buildings, and he would only ever have a few seconds to see them from this angle.

At the very end was a small port, formed where, for no geological reason, two long curving spits of shingle ran out into the sea like the antlers of a stag beetle or the pincers of an earwig. The port was set along the landward side of this bay. Outside the arms of the bay, Shannon could see the water ruffled by the breeze, while inside the three-quarter-circle enclosed within the arms, the water was a flat calm. No doubt it was this anchorage, tacked on to the end of the peninsula in one of nature's afterthoughts, which had attracted the first mariners.

The centre of the port, directly opposite the opening to the high seas, was dominated by a single concrete quay without any ship tied up to it, and a warehouse of sorts. To the left of the concrete quay was evidently the natives' fishing area, a shingly beach littered with long canoes and nets laid out to dry, and to the right of the quay was the old port, a series of decrepit wooden jetties pointing towards the water.

Behind the warehouse there were perhaps two hundred yards of rough grass ending with a road along the shore, and behind the road the buildings started. Shannon caught a glimpse of a white colonial-style church, and what could have been the governor's palace in bygone days, surrounded by a wall. Inside the wall, apart from the main buildings, was a large courtyard surrounded by lean-to hutments of evidently recent addition.

At this point the Corvair straightened up, the town disappeared from view, and they were on final approach.

Shannon had already had his first experience of Zangaro the previous day when he had applied for his visa for a tourist visit. The consul in the neighbouring capital had received him with some surprise, being unused to such applications. He had to fill out a five-page form giving everything from his parents' first names (as he had no idea of Keith Brown's parents' names, he invented them) and every other conceivable piece of information.

His passport, when he handed it over, had a handsome banknote idly lying between the first and second pages. This went into the consul's pocket. Then the man examined the passport from every angle, read every page, held it up to the light, turned it over, checked the currency allowances at the back. After five minutes of this Shannon began to wonder if there was something wrong. Had the British Foreign Office made an error in this particular passport? Then the consul looked at him and said:

'You are an American.'

With a sense of relief Shannon realised the man was illiterate.

He had had his visa in five minutes more. But at Clarence airport the fun stopped.

He had no luggage in the aircraft hold, just a hand grip. Inside the main (and only) passenger building the heat was overpowering and the place buzzed with flies. About a dozen soldiers lounged about, and ten policemen. They were evidently of different tribes. The policemen were self-effacing, hardly speaking even to each other, leaning against the walls. It was the soldiers who attracted Shannon's attention. He kept half an eye on them as he filled in another immensely long form (the same one he had filled the previous day in the consulate) and penetrated health and passport control, both manned by officials whom he took to be Caja, like the policemen.

It was when he got to customs that the trouble started. A civilian was waiting for him, and instructed him with a curt gesture to go into a side-room. As he did so, taking his grip with him, four soldiers swaggered in after him. Then he realised what it was about them that rang a bell in his memory.

Long ago in the Congo he had seen the same attitude, the blank-eyed sense of menace conveyed by an African of almost primeval cultural level, armed with a weapon, in a state of power, wholly unpredictable, with reactions to a situation that were utterly illogical, ticking away like a moving time bomb. Just before the worst of the massacres he had seen launched by Congolese on Katangese, Simbas on missionaries and Congolese Army on Simbas, he had noticed this same menacing mindlessness, the sense of power without reason, that can suddenly and for no recollected explanation, turn to frenetic violence. The Vindu soldiers of President Kimba had it.

The civilian customs officer ordered Shannon to put his grip on the rickety table, and then began to go through it. The search looked thorough, as if for concealed weapons, until he spotted the electric shaver, took it from its case, examined it, tried the 'on' switch. Being a Remington Lektronic and fully charged, it buzzed furiously. Without a trace of expression the customs man put it in his pocket.

Finishing with the grip, he gestured to Shannon to empty his pockets on to the table. Out came the keys, handkerchief, coins, wallet and passport. The customs man went for the wallet, extracted the travellers cheques, looked at them, grunted and handed them back. The coins he swept into his hands and pocketed them. Of the banknotes, there were two 5000 French-African franc-notes and several 100s. The soldiers had crowded nearer, still making no sound but for their breathing in the roasting atmosphere, gripping guns like clubs, but overcome with curiosity. The civilian behind the table pocketed the two 5000-franc notes, and one of the soldiers picked up the smaller denominations.

Shannon looked at the customs man. The man looked back. Then he lifted his singlet and showed the butt of a Browning 9mm short, or perhaps a 765, jammed into his trouser band. He tapped it.

'Police,' he said, and kept staring. Shannon's fingers itched to smash the man in the face. Inside his head he kept telling himself 'Keep cool, baby, absolutely cool.'

He gestured slowly, very slowly, to what remained of his belongings on the table and raised his eyebrows. The civilian nodded, and Shannon began to pick them up and put them back. Behind him he felt the soldiers back off, though they still gripped their rifles in both hands, able to swing or butt-jab as the mood took them.

It seemed an age before the civilian nodded towards the door, and Shannon left. He could feel the sweat running in a stream down the spine towards the waistband of his pants.

Outside in the main hall the only other white tourist on the flight, an American girl, had been met by a Catholic priest who, with his voluble explanations to the soldiers in Coast pidgin, was having less trouble. He looked up and caught Shannon's eye. Shannon raised his eyebrows slightly. The father looked beyond Shannon at the room he had come from and nodded imperceptibly.

Outside in the heat of the small square before the airport building there was no transport. Shannon waited. Five minutes later he heard a soft Irish-American voice behind him.

'Can I give you a lift into town, my son?'

They travelled in the priest's car, a Volkswagen Beetle, which he had hidden for safety in the shade of a palm grove several yards outside the gate. The American girl was shrill and outraged; someone had opened her handbag and gone through it. Shannon was silent, knowing how close they all had come to a beating. The priest was with the UN hospital, combining the roles of chaplain, almoner and doctor of medicine. He glanced across at Shannon with understanding.

'They shook you down.'

'The lot,' said Shannon. The loss of £15 was nothing, but both the men had recognised the mood of the soldiery.

'One has to be very careful here, very careful indeed,' said the priest softly. 'Have you a hotel?'

When Shannon told him he had not, the priest drove him to the Independence, the only hotel in Clarence where Europeans were permitted to stay.

'Gomez is the manager, he's a good enough sort,' said the priest.

Usually when a new face arrives in an African city there are invitations from the other Europeans to visit the club, come back to the bungalow, have a drink, come to a party that evening. The priest, for all his helpfulness, did no such thing. That was another thing Shannon learned quickly about Zangaro. The mood affected the whites as well. He would learn more in the days to come, much of it from Gomez.

It was that same evening that he came to know Jules Gomez, formerly proprietor and latterly manager of the Independence Hotel. Gomez was fifty and a *pied noir*, a Frenchman from Algeria. In the last days of French Algeria almost ten years earlier, he had sold his flourishing business in agricultural machinery just before the final collapse when one could not give a business away. With what he had made, he returned to France, but after a year found he could not live in the atmosphere of Europe any longer, and looked around for another place to go. He had settled on Zangaro, five years before independence and before it was even in the offing. Taking his savings he had bought the hotel and steadily improved it over the years.

After independence, things had changed. Three years before Shannon arrived, Gomez had been brusquely informed that the hotel was to be nationalised, and he would be paid in local currency. He never was, and it was worthless paper in any case. But he hung on as manager, hoping against hope that one day things might improve again, to secure him in old age. As manager, he ran the reception desk and the bar. Shannon found him at the bar.

It would have been easy to win Gomez's friendship by mentioning the friends and contacts Shannon had who were former OAS men, fighters in the Legion and the paras, who had turned up in the Congo. But that would have blown his cover as a simple English tourist who, with five days to kill, had flown down from the north, impelled only by curiosity to see the obscure republic of Zangaro. So he stuck to his role of tourist.

But later, after the bar closed, he suggested Gomez join him for a drink in his room. For no explicable reason the soldiers at the airport had left him a bottle of whisky he had been carrying in his case. Gomez's eyes opened wide at the sight of it. Whisky was another import the country could not afford. Shannon made sure Gomez drank more than he. When he mentioned that he had come to Zangaro out of curiosity, Gomez snorted.

'Curiosity? Huh, it's curious, all right. It's bloody weird.'

Although they were talking French, and alone in the room, Gomez lowered his voice and leaned forward as he said it. Once again Shannon got an impression of the extraordinary sense of fear present in everyone he had seen, except the bully-boy army thugs and the secret policeman who posed as a customs officer at the airport. By the time Gomez had sunk half the bottle, he had become slightly garrulous, and Shannon probed gently for information. Gomez confirmed much of the briefing Shannon had been given by the man he knew as Walter Harris, and added more anecdotal details of his own, some of them highly gruesome.

He confirmed that President Kimba was in town, that he hardly ever left it these days, except for the occasional trip to his home village across the river in Vindu country, and that he was in his presidential palace, the large, walled building Shannon had seen from the air.

By the time Gomez bade him good night and weaved his way back to his own room at two in the morning, further nuggets of information had been culled. The three units known as the civilian police force, the gendarmerie and the customs force, although all carried sidearms, had, Gomez swore, no ammunition in their weapons. Being Caja, they were not trusted to have any, and Kimba, with his paranoia about an uprising, kept them without one round of ammunition between the lot of them. He knew they would never fight for him, and must not have the opportunity of fighting against him. The sidearms were just for show.

Gomez had also vouchsafed that the power in the city was exclusively in the hands of Kimba's Vindu. The dreaded secret police usually wore civilian clothes and carried automatics, the soldiers of the army had bolt-action rifles such as Shannon had seen at the airport, and the president's own praetorian guards had submachine guns. The latter lived exclusively in the palace grounds, were ultra-loyal to Kimba, and he never moved without at least a squad of them hemming him round.

The next morning Shannon went out for a walk. Within seconds he found a small boy of ten or eleven scampering by his side, sent after him by Gomez. Only later did he learn why. He thought Gomez must have sent the boy as a guide, though as they could not exchange a word, there was not much point in that. The real purpose was different, a service Gomez offered to all his guests whether they asked or not. If the tourist was arrested for whatever reason, and carted off, the small boy would speed away through the bushes and tell Gomez. He would slip the information to the Swiss or West German embassy so that someone could begin to negotiate the tourist's release before he was beaten half-dead. The boy's name was Boniface.

Shannon spent the morning walking, mile after mile, while the small boy trotted at his heels. They were stopped by no one. There was hardly a vehicle to be seen, and the streets in the residential area were mainly deserted. From Gomez Shannon had obtained a small map of the town, a leftover from colonial days, and with this he tracked down the main buildings of Clarence. At the only bank, the only post office, half a dozen ministries, the port and the UN hospital there were groups of six or seven soldiers lounging about the steps. Inside the bank, where he went to cash a travellers cheque, he noticed bed-rolls in the lobby, and in the lunch hour he twice saw pots of food being carried by a soldier to his colleagues. Shannon judged that the guard details lived on the premises at each building. Gomez confirmed this later the same evening.

He noticed a soldier in front of each of six embassies he passed, three of them asleep in the dust. By the lunch hour he estimated there were about a hundred soldiers scattered in twelve groups, around the main area of the town. He noted what they were armed with. Each carried an old Mauser 7.92 bolt-action rifle, most of them looking rusted and dirty. The soldiers wore drab-green trousers and shirts, canvas boots, webbing belts and peaked caps, rather like American baseball caps. Without exception they were shabby, unpressed, unwashed and unprepossessing. He estimated their level of training, weapons familiarisation, leadership and fighting capacity at nil. They were a rabble, undisciplined thugs who could terrify the timorous Caja by their arms and their brutishness, but had probably never fired a shot in anger and certainly had never been fired at by people who knew what they were doing. Their purpose on guard duty seemed to be preventive of a civilian riot, but he estimated that in a real firefight they would quit and run.

The most interesting thing about them was the state of their ammunition pouches. They were pressed flat, empty of magazines. Each Mauser had its fixed magazine of course, but Mausers only hold five shells.

That afternoon Shannon patrolled the port. Seen from the ground, it looked different. The two spits of sand running out across the water and forming the natural harbour were about twenty feet high at the base and six feet above the water at the tip. He walked down both until he reached the end. Each one was covered in knee- to waist-high scrub vegetation, burned brown at the end of the long dry season, and invisible from the air. Each spit was about forty feet wide at the tip, forty yards wide at the base, where it left the shoreline. From the tip of each, looking back towards the port area, one had a panoramic view of the waterfront.

The concreted area was at dead centre, backed by the warehouse. To the north of this stood the old wooden jetties, some long crumbled away, their supports sticking up like broken teeth above or below the water. To the south of the warehouse was the shingly beach where the fishing canoes lay. From the tip of one sand-spit the president's palace was invisible, hidden behind the warehouse, but from the other spit the uppermost storey of the palace was plainly visible. Shannon walked back to the port and examined the fishing beach. It was a good place for a landing, he thought idly, a gentle slope to the water's edge.

Behind the warehouse the concrete ended and a sloping bank of waist-high scrub, dissected by numerous footpaths and one laterite ride for lorries, ran back towards the palace. Shannon took the road. As he breasted the top of the rise the full façade of the old colonial governor's mansion came into view, two hundred yards away. He continued another hundred yards and reached the lateral road running along the sea shore. At the junction a group of soldiers waited, four in all, smarter, better dressed than the Army, armed with Kalashnikov AK 47 assault rifles. They watched him in silence as he turned right along the road towards his hotel. He nodded, but they just stared back. The palace guards.

He glanced to his left as he walked and took in the details of the palace. Thirty yards wide, its ground-floor windows now bricked up and painted over the same off-white wash as the rest of the building, the building was dominated at ground level by a tall, wide, bolt-studded timber door, almost certainly another new addition. In front of the bricked-up windows ran a terrace, now useless because there was no access from the building to it. On the first floor a row of seven windows ran from side to side of the façade, three left, three right, and one above the main entrance. The topmost floor had ten windows, all much smaller. Above these was the gutter and the red-tiled roof sloping away towards the apex.

He noticed more guards lounging around the front door, and that the first-floor windows had shutters which might have been of steel (he was too far away to tell) and were drawn down. Evidently no closer access to the front of the building than the road junction was permitted, except on official business.

He completed the afternoon just before the sun went down by making a tour of the palace from afar. At each side he saw that a new wall, eight feet high, ran from the main mansion towards the land for a distance of eighty yards, and the fourth wall joined them together at the rear. Interestingly, there were no other gates to the entire compound. The wall was uniformly eight feet high – he could tell by the height of a guard he saw walking near the wall – and topped by broken bottles. He knew he would never see inside, but he could retain the image from the air. It almost made him laugh.

He grinned at Boniface.

'You know, kid, that bloody fool thinks he has protected himself with a big wall topped with glass and only one entrance. All he has really done is pin himself inside a brick trap, a great big, closed-in killing ground.'

The boy grinned widely, not understanding a word, and indicated he wanted to go home and eat. Shannon nodded, and they went back to the hotel, feet burning and legs aching.

Shannon made no notes or maps, but retained every detail in his head. He returned Gomez his map, and after dinner joined the Frenchman at the bar.

Two Chinese from the embassy sat quietly drinking beer at the back tables, so conversation between the Europeans was minimal. Besides, the windows were open. Later, however, Gomez, longing for company, took a dozen bottles of beer and invited Shannon up to his room on the top floor, where they sat on the balcony and looked out through the night at the sleeping town, mainly in darkness due to an electricity breakdown.

Shannon was in two minds whether to take Gomez into his confidence, but decided not to. He mentioned that he had found the bank and there had been a job to change a fifty-pound cheque. Gomez snorted.

'There always is,' he said. 'They don't see travellers cheques here, nor much foreign currency for very long.'

'They must see it at the bank, surely.'

'Not for long. The entire treasure of the republic Kimba keeps locked up inside the palace.'

Shannon was at once interested. It took two hours to learn, in dribs and drabs, that Kimba also kept the national armoury of ammunition in the old wine cellar of the governor's palace, under his own lock and key, and had also transferred the national radio broadcasting station there, so that he could broadcast direct from his communications room to the nation and the world, and no one else could take control of it from outside the palace. National radio stations always play a vital role in *coups d'état.* Shannon also learned he had no armoured cars and no artillery, and that apart from the hundred soldiers scattered around the capital, there were another hundred outside the town, a score in the native township on the airport road and the rest dotted in the Caja villages beyond the peninsula towards the Zangaro river bridge. These two hundred were half the army. The other half were in the army barracks, which were not barracks in truth but the old colonial police lines four hundred yards from the palace, rows of low tin shanties inside a reed fence enclosure. The four hundred men constituted the entire army, and the personal palace guards numbered from forty to sixty, living in the lean-to sheds inside the palace courtyard walls.

On his third day in Zangaro Shannon checked out the police lines, where the two hundred army men not on guard duty lived. It was, as Gomez had said, surrounded by a reed fence, but a visit to the nearby church enabled Shannon to slip unnoticed into the bell-tower, run up the circular brick staircase and sneak a view from the belfry. The lines were two rows of shanties, adorned with some clothes hung out to dry. At one end was a row of low brick kilns over which pots of stew bubbled. Two score of men lounged around in various stages of boredom, and all were unarmed. Their guns might be in the hutments, but Shannon guessed they were more probably in the armoury, a small stone pillbox set aside from the huts. The other facilities of the camp were primitive in the extreme.

It was that evening, when he had gone out without Boniface, that he met his soldier. He spent an hour circling the darkened streets, which fortunately for him had never seen lamp lighting, trying to get closer to the palace.

He had managed a good look at the back and sides, and had assured himself there were no patrolling guards on these sides. Trying the front of the palace, he had been intercepted by two of the palace guards, who had brusquely ordered him on his way home. He had established that there were three of them sitting at the road junction half-way between the top of the rise from the port and the front gate of the palace. More importantly, he had also established that they could not see the harbour from where they stood. From the road junction the soldiers' eyeline, passing over the top of the rise, would meet the sea beyond the tips of the arms of the harbour, and without a brilliant moon they would not even see the water five hundred yards away, though undoubtedly they would see a light out there, if there were one.

In the darkness on the road junction, Shannon could not see the front gate of the palace a hundred yards inland, but assumed there were two other guards there as usual. He offered packets of cigarettes to the soldiers who had accosted him, and left.

On the road back to the Independence he passed several bars, lit inside by paraffin lamps, and then moved on down the darkened road. A hundred yards farther on the soldier stopped him. The man was evidently drunk and had been urinating in a rain ditch by the roadside. He swayed up to Shannon, gripping his Mauser two-handed by the butt and barrel. In the light from the rising moon Shannon could now see him quite clearly as he moved towards him. The soldier grunted something. Shannon failed to understand, though assumed it was a demand for money.

He heard the soldier mutter 'Beer' several times, and added some more indistinguishable words. Then before Shannon could reach for money, or pass on, the man snarled and jabbed the barrel of the gun towards Shannon. From then on it was quick and silent. He took the barrel in one hand and moved it away from his stomach, jerking hard and pulling the soldier off balance. The man was evidently surprised at the reaction, not what he was accustomed to. Recovering, he squealed with rage, reversed the gun, gripped by the barrel and swung it club-wise. Shannon stepped in close, blocked the swing by gripping the soldier by both biceps, and brought up his knee.

It was too late to go back after that. As the gun dropped he brought up his right hand, crooked into a 90-degree angle, stiff-armed, and slammed the base of the hand under the soldier's jawbone. A stab of pain went up his arm and shoulder as he heard the neck crack, and later found he had torn a shoulder muscle with the effort. The Zangaran went down like a sack.

Shannon looked up and down the road, but no one was coming. He rolled the body into the rain ditch and examined the rifle. One by one he pumped the cartridges out of the magazine. At three they stopped coming. There had been nothing in the breech. He removed the bolt and held the gun to the moon, looking down the barrel. Several months of grit, dirt, dust, grime, rust and earth particles met his eye. He slipped the bolt back home, replaced the three cartridges where they had been, tossed the rifle on to the corpse and walked home.

'Better and better,' he murmured as he slipped into the darkened hotel and went to bed. He had few doubts there would be no effective police enquiry. The broken neck would be put down to a fall into the rain ditch, and tests for fingerprints were, he was sure, unheard of.

Nevertheless, the next day he pleaded a headache, stayed in and talked to Gomez. On the following morning he left for the airport and took the Convair 440 back to the north. As he sat in the plane and watched the republic disappear beneath the port wing, something Gomez had mentioned in passing ran like a current through his head.

There were not, and never had been, any mining operations in Zangaro.

Forty hours later he was back in London.

Ambassador Leonid Dobrovolsky always felt slightly uneasy when he had his weekly interview with President Kimba. Like others who had met the dictator, he had few doubts about the man's insanity. Unlike most of the others, Leonid Dobrovolsky had orders from his superiors in Moscow to make his utmost efforts to establish a working relationship with the unpredictable African. He stood in front of the broad mahogany desk in the president's study on the first floor of the palace and waited for Kimba to show some sort of reaction.

Seen close to, President Kimba was neither as large nor as handsome as his official portraits indicated. Behind the enormous desk he seemed almost dwarfish, the more so as he held himself hunched in his chair in a state of total immobility. Dobrovolsky waited for the period of immobility to end. He knew it could end one of two ways. Either the man who ruled Zangaro would speak carefully and lucidly, in every sense like a perfectly sane man, or the almost catatonic stillness would give way to a screaming rage during which the man would rant like someone possessed, which was in any case what he believed himself to be.

Kimba nodded slowly.

'Please proceed,' he said.

Dobrovolsky breathed a sigh of relief. Evidently the president was prepared to listen. But he knew the bad news was yet to come and he had to give it. That could change things.

'I am informed by my government, Mr President, that they have received information that a mining survey report recently sent to Zangaro by a British company may not be accurate. I am referring to the survey carried out several weeks ago by a firm called Manson Consolidated of London.'

The president's eyes, slightly bulging, still stared at the Russian ambassador without a flicker of expression. Nor was there any word from Kimba to indicate that he recalled the subject that had brought Dobrovolsky to his palace.

The ambassador continued to describe the mining survey that had been carried out by ManCon, and the report that had been delivered by a Mr Bryant into the hands of the Minister for Natural Resources.

'In essence then, Your Excellency, I am instructed to inform you that the government believes the report was not a true representation of what was really discovered in the area that was then under survey, specifically the Crystal Mountain range.'

He waited, aware that he could say little more. When Kimba finally spoke, it was calmly and cogently, and Dobrovolsky breathed again.

'In what way was this survey report inaccurate?' whispered Kimba.

'We are not sure of the details, but it is fair to assume that since the British company has apparently not made any effort to secure from you a mining concession, the report they submitted must have indicated there were no mineral deposits worth exploiting in that region. If the report was inaccurate, then it was probably in this respect. In other words, whatever the mining engineer's samples contained it would appear there was more than the British were prepared to inform you.'

There was another long silence, during which the ambassador waited for the explosion of rage. It did not come.

'They cheated me,' whispered Kimba.

'Of course, Your Excellency,' cut in Dobrovolsky hurriedly, 'the only way of being completely sure is for another survey party to examine the same area and take further samples of the rocks and the soil. To this end I am instructed by my government most humbly to ask Your Excellency to grant permission for a survey team from the Institute of Mining of Sverdlovsk to come to Zangaro and examine the same area as that covered by the British engineer.'

Kimba took a long time digesting the proposal. Finally he nodded.

'Granted,' he said. Dobrovolsky bowed. By his side Volkov, ostensibly Second Secretary at the embassy but more pertinently the Resident of the KGB detachment, shot him a glance.

'The second matter is that of your personal security,' said Dobrovolsky. At last he secured some reaction from the dictator. It was a subject that Kimba took extremely seriously. His head jerked up and he shot suspicious glances round the room. Three Zangaran aides standing behind the two Russians quaked.

'My security?' said Kimba in his usual whisper.

'We would respectfully seek once again to reiterate the Soviet government's view of the paramount importance of Your Excellency's being able to continue to lead Zangaro on the path of peace and progress Your Excellency has already so magnificently established,' said the Russian. The ocean of flattery caused no incongruous note; it was Kimba's habitual due and a regular part of any words addressed to him.

'To guarantee the continued security of the invaluable person of Your Excellency and in view of the recent most dangerous treason by one of your army officers, we would respectfully once again propose that a member of my embassy staff be permitted to reside inside the palace and lend his assistance to Your Excellency's own personal security corps.'

The reference to the 'treason' of Colonel Bobi brought Kimba out of his trance. He trembled violently, though whether from fear or rage the Russians could not make out. Then he began to talk, slowly at first, in his usual whisper, then faster, his voice rising as he glared at the Zangarans across the room. After a few sentences he lapsed back into the Vindu dialect, which only the Zangarans understood, but the Russians already knew the gist; the ever-present danger of treason and treachery that Kimba knew himself to be in, the warnings he had received from the spirits telling him of plots in all corners, his complete awareness of the identity of all those who were not loyal and who harboured evil thoughts in their minds, his intention to root them out, all of them, and what would happen to them when he did. He went on for half an hour in this vein, before finally calming down and reverting to a European language the Russians could understand.

When they emerged into the sunlight and climbed into the embassy car, both men were sweating, partly from the heat, for the air conditioning in the palace was broken yet again, partly because that was the effect Kimba usually had on them.

'I'm glad that's over,' muttered Volkov to his colleague as they drove back towards the embassy. 'Anyway, we got permission. I'll install my man tomorrow.'

'And I'll get the mining engineers sent in as soon as possible,' said Dobrovolsky. 'Let's hope there really is something fishy about that British survey report. If there isn't, I don't know how I'll explain that to the president.'

Volkov grunted.

'Rather you than me,' he said.

Shannon checked into the Lowndes Hotel off Knightsbridge as he had agreed with 'Walter Harris' to do before he left London. The agreement was that he would be away about ten days, and each morning at nine Harris would phone that hotel and ask for Mr Keith Brown. Shannon arrived at noon to find the first call for him had been three hours earlier that morning. The news meant he had till the next day to himself.

One of his first calls after a long bath, a change and lunch, was to the detective agency. The head of it recognised the name of Keith Brown after a few moments' thought, and Shannon heard him sorting out some files on his desk. Eventually he found the right one.

'Yes, Mr Brown, I have it here. Would you like me to mail it to you?'

'Rather not,' said Shannon. 'Is it long?'

'No, about a page. Shall I read it over the phone?'

'Yes please.'

The man cleared his throat and began.

'On the morning following the client's request, my operative waited close to the entrance of the underground car park beneath ManCon House. He was lucky, in that the subject, whom he had noticed the day before arriving back there by taxi from his interview at Sloane Avenue with our client, arrived by car. The operative got a clear view of him as he swung into the car-park tunnel entrance. It was beyond doubt the subject. He was at the wheel of a Chevrolet Corvette. The operative took the number as the car went down the ramp. Enquiries were later made with a contact at the Licensing Department at County Hall. The vehicle is registered in the name of Simon John Endean, resident in South Kensington.' The man paused. 'Do you want the address, Mr Brown?'

'Not necessarily,' said Shannon. 'Do you know what this man Endean does at ManCon House?'

'Yes,' said the private agent. 'I checked up with a friend who's a City journalist. He is the personal aide and right-hand man of Sir James Manson, chairman and managing director of Manson Consolidated.'

'Thank you,' said Shannon and put the phone down.

'Curiouser and curiouser,' he murmured as he left the hotel lobby and strolled down to Jermyn Street to cash a cheque and buy some shirts. It was the first of April, All Fools' Day, the sun was shining and daffodils covered the grass around Hyde Park Corner.

Simon Endean had also been busy while Shannon was away. The results of his labours he imparted to Sir James Manson that afternoon in the penthouse over Moorgate.

'Colonel Bobi,' he told his chief, as he entered the office. The mining boss furrowed his brow.

'Who?'

'Colonel Bobi. The former commander of the army of Zangaro. Now in exile, banished forever by President Jean Kimba. Who, incidentally, has sentenced him to death by presidential decree for high treason. You wanted to know where he was.'

Manson was at his desk by this time, nodding in recollection. He had still not forgotten the Crystal Mountain.

'All right, where is he?' he asked.

'In exile in Dahomey,' said Endean. 'It took a hell of a job to trace him without being too obvious about it. But he's taken up residence in the capital of Dahomey. Place called Cotonou. He must have a little money, but probably not much, or he'd be in a walled villa outside Geneva with all the other rich exiles. He has a small rented villa, and lives very quietly, probably because it is the safest way of ensuring the Dahomey government doesn't ask him to leave. It's believed Kimba has asked for his extradition back home, but no one has done anything about it. Besides, he's far enough away for Kimba to assume he'll never present a threat.'

'And Shannon, the mercenary?' asked Manson.

'Due back sometime today or tomorrow,' said Endean. 'I booked him into the Lowndes from yesterday onwards to be on the safe side. He hadn't arrived this morning at nine. I'm due to try again tomorrow at the same time.'

'Try now,' said Manson.

The hotel confirmed to Endean that Mr Brown had indeed arrived, but that he was out. Sir James Manson listened on the extension.

'Leave a message,' he growled at Endean. 'Ring him tonight at seven.'

THE DOGS OF WAR 589

Endean left the message and the two men put the phones down.

'I want his report as soon as possible,' said Manson. 'He should finish it at noon tomorrow. You meet him first and read the report. Make sure it covers every point I told you I wanted answered. Then bring it to me. Put Shannon on ice for two days to give me time to digest it.'

Shannon got Endean's message just after five, and was in his room to take the call at seven. He spent the rest of the evening between supper and bed making up his notes and the memorabilia he had brought back from Zangaro – a series of sketches done freehand on a pad of cartridge paper he had bought in the airport in Paris to while away the time, some scale-drawings done from measurements between fixed points in Clarence that he had paced out stride by stride, a local guide-book showing 'points of interest' of which the only interesting one was titled 'The residence of His Excellency the Governor of the Colony' and dated from 1959, and an official and highly flattering portrait of Kimba, one of the few items not in short supply in the republic.

The next day he strolled down Knightsbridge just as the shops opened, bought himself a typewriter and a block of paper, and spent the morning writing his report. It covered three subjects: a straight narrative of his visit, a detailed description of the capital, building by building and accompanied by the diagrams, and an equally detailed description of the military situation. He mentioned the fact that he had seen no signs of either an air force or a navy, and Gomez's confirmation that neither existed. He did not mention his stroll down the peninsula to the native shanty towns where he had seen the clustered shacks of the poorer Caja and beyond them the shanties of the thousands of immigrant workers and their families, chattering to each other in their native tongue, brought with them from many miles away.

He finished the report with a summary:

'The essence of the problem of toppling Kimba has been simplified by the man himself. In all respects the majority of the republic's land area, the Vindu country beyond the river, is of nil political or economic value. If Kimba should ever lose control of the coastal plain producing the bulk of the nation's few resources he must lose the country. To go one step further, he and his men could not hold this plain in the face of the hostility and hatred of the entire Caja population, which, although muted by fear, exists beneath the surface, if he had once lost the peninsula. Again, the peninsula is untenable by Vindu forces if once the town of Clarence is lost. And lastly, he has no strength within the town of Clarence if he and his forces have lost the palace. In short, his policy of total centralisation has reduced the number of targets necessary to be subdued for a takeover of the state to one – his palace complex, containing himself, his guards, the armoury, treasury and radio station.

'As to means of taking and reducing this palace and compound, they have been reduced to one, by virtue of the wall surrounding the entire place. It has to be stormed.

'The main gate could perhaps be rammed down by a very heavy truck or bulldozer driven straight at it by a man prepared to die in the attempt.

I saw no evidence of any such spirit present among the citizenry or the Army, nor signs of a suitable truck. Alternatively, self-sacrificing courage by hundreds of men with scaling ladders could overwhelm the palace walls and take the place. I saw no signs of such spirit either. More realistically, the palace and grounds could be taken with little life loss after being first pulverised with mortar fire. Against a weapon like this the encircling wall, far from being a protection, becomes a death-trap to those inside. The door could be taken apart by a bazooka rocket. I saw no signs of either of these weapons, nor any sign of one single person capable of using them. The unavoidable conclusion reached from the above has to be as follows:

'Any section or faction within the republic, seeking to topple Kimba and take over, must destroy him and his Praetorian guards inside the palace compound. To achieve this they would require expert assistance at a technical level which they have not achieved, and such assistance would have to arrive, complete with all necessary equipment, from outside the country. With these conditions fulfilled, Kimba could be destroyed and toppled in a firefight lasting no longer than one hour.'

'Is Shannon aware that there is no faction inside Zangaro that has indicated it wants to topple Kimba?' asked Sir James Manson the following morning when he read the report.

'I haven't told him so,' said Endean. 'I briefed him as you told me. Just said there was an army faction inside, and that the group I represented, as interested businessmen, were prepared to pay for a military assessment of their chances of success. But he's no fool. He must have seen for himself there's no one there capable of doing the job anyway.'

'I like the sound of this Shannon,' said Manson, closing the military report. 'He's obviously got nerve, to judge by the way he dealt with the soldier. He writes quite well, he's short and to the point. Question is, could he do the whole of this job himself?'

'He did mention something significant,' interjected Endean. 'He said when I was questioning him that the calibre of the Zangaran Army was so low that any assisting force of technicians would have to do practically the whole job anyway, then hand over to the new men when it was done.'

'Did he now? Did he?' mused Manson. 'Then he suspects already the reason for his going down there was not the stated one.'

He was still musing when Endean asked,

'May I put a question, Sir James?'

'What is it?' asked Manson.

'Just this: what did he go down there for? Why do you need a military report on how Kimba could be toppled and killed?'

Sir James Manson stared out of the window for some time. Finally he said, 'Get Martin Thorpe up here.' While Thorpe was being summoned, Manson walked to the window and gazed down, as he usually did when he wanted to think hard.

He knew he had personally taken Endean and Thorpe as young men and promoted them to salaries and positions beyond their years. It was not simply because of their intelligence, although they had plenty of it. It was because he recognised an unscrupulousness in each of them that matched his own, a preparedness to ignore so-called moral principles in pursuit of the goal – success. Like Shannon, like himself, they too were mercenaries. Only the degree of success and the question of public respectability separated the four of them. He had made them his team, his hatchet-men, paid by the company, but serving him personally in all things. The problem was: could he trust them with this one, the big one? As Thorpe entered the office, he decided he had to. He thought he knew how to guarantee their loyalty.

He bade them sit down, and, remaining standing with his back to the window, he told them:

'I want you two to think this one over very carefully, then give me your reply. How far would you be prepared to go to be assured of a personal fortune in a Swiss bank of five million pounds each?'

The hum of the traffic ten floors down was like a buzzing bee, accentuating the silence in the room. Endean stared back at his chief and nodded slowly.

'A very, very long way,' he said softly.

Thorpe made no reply. He knew this was what he had come to the City for, joined Manson for, absorbed his encyclopaedic knowledge of company business for. The big one, the once-in-a-decade grand slam. He nodded assent.

'How?' breathed Endean. For answer Manson walked to his wall safe and extracted two reports. The third, Shannon's, lay on his desk as he seated himself behind it.

Manson talked steadily for an hour. He started at the beginning, and soon read the final six paragraphs of Dr Chalmers's report on the samples from the Crystal Mountain. Thorpe whistled softly, and muttered 'Jesus.'

Endean required a ten-minute lecture on platinum to catch the point, then he too breathed a long sigh.

Manson went on to relate the exiling of Mulrooney to northern Kenya, ·the suborning of Chalmers, the second visit of Bryant to Clarence, the acceptance of the dummy report by Kimba's Minister. He stressed the Russian influence on Kimba, and the recent exiling of Colonel Bobi, who, given the right circumstances, could return as a plausible alternative in the seat of power.

For Thorpe's benefit he read much of Endean's general report on Zangaro and finished with the conclusion of Shannon's report.

'If it is to work at all, it must be a question of mounting two parallel, highly secret operations,' Manson said finally. 'In one, Shannon, stage-managed throughout by Simon, mounts a project to take and destroy that palace and all its contents, and for Bobi, accompanied by Simon, to take over powers of state the following morning and become the new president. In the other, Martin would have to buy a shell company without revealing who had gained control or why.'

Endean furrowed his brow.

'I can see the first operation, but why the second?' he asked.

'Tell him, Martin,' said Manson. Thorpe was grinning, for his astute mind had caught Manson's drift.

'A shell company, Simon, is a company, usually very old and without assets worth talking about, which has virtually ceased trading and whose shares are very cheap, say, a shilling each.'

'So why buy one?' asked Endean, still puzzled.

'Say Sir James has control of a company, bought secretly through un-named nominees, hiding behind a Swiss bank, all nice and legal, and the company has a million shares valued at one shilling each. Unknown to the other shareholders or the Board of Directors or the Stock Exchange, Sir James, via the Swiss bank, owns 600,000 of these million shares. Then Colonel – beg his pardon – President Bobi sells that company an exclusive ten-year mining franchise for an area of land in the hinterland of Zang-aro. A new mining survey team from a highly reputable company specialising in mining goes out and discovers the Crystal Mountain. What happens to the shares of Company X when the news hits the stock market?'

Endean got the message.

'They go up,' he said with a grin.

'Right up,' said Thorpe. 'With a bit of help they go from a shilling to well over £100 a share. Now do your arithmetic. Six hundred thou-sand shares at a shilling each cost £30,000 to buy. Sell 600,000 shares at £100 each – and that's the minimum you'd get – and what do you bring home? A cool sixty million pounds in a Swiss bank. Right, Sir James?'

'That's right,' nodded Manson grimly. 'Of course, if you sold half the shares in small packets to a wide variety of people, the control of the company owning the concession would stay in the same hands as before. But a bigger company might put in a bid for the whole block of 600,000 shares in one flat deal.'

Thorpe nodded thoughtfully.

'Yes, control of such a company bought at £60 million would be a good market deal. But whose bid would you acept?'

'My own,' said Manson. Thorpe's mouth opened.

'Your own?'

'ManCon's bid would be the only acceptable one. That way the con-cession would remain firmly British, and ManCon would have gained a fine asset.'

'But,' queried Endean, 'surely you would be paying yourself sixty million quid?'

'No,' said Thorpe quietly, 'ManCon's shareholders would be paying Sir James sixty million quid, without knowing it.'

'What's that called, in financial terms of course?' asked Endean.

'There *is* a word for it, on the Stock Exchange,' Thorpe admitted.

Sir James Manson tendered them each a glass of whisky. He reached round and took his own.

'Are you on, gentlemen?' he asked softly. Both younger men looked at each other and nodded.

'Then here's to the Crystal Mountain.'

They drank.

'Report to me here tomorrow morning at nine sharp,' Manson told them, and they rose to go. At the door to the back stairs Thorpe turned.

'You know, Sir James, it's going to be bloody dangerous. If one word gets out . . .'

Sir James Manson stood again with his back to the window, the westering sun slanting on to the carpet by his side. His legs were astride, his fists on his hips.

'Knocking off a bank or an armoured truck,' he said, 'is merely crude. Knocking off an entire republic has, I feel, a certain style.'

7

'What you are saying in effect is that there is no dissatisfied faction within the Army, that, so far as you know, has ever thought of toppling President Kimba?'

Cat Shannon and Simon Endean were sitting in Shannon's room at the hotel taking mid-morning coffee. Endean had phoned Shannon by agreement at nine, and told him to wait for a second call. He had been briefed by Sir James Manson and had called Shannon back, to make the eleven o'clock appointment.

Endean nodded. 'That's right. The information has changed in that one detail. I can't see what difference it makes. You yourself said the calibre of the Army was so low that the technical assistants would have to do all the work themselves in any case.'

'It makes a hell of a difference,' said Shannon. 'Attacking the palace and capturing it is one thing. Keeping it is quite another. Destroying the palace and Kimba simply creates a vacuum at the seat of power. Someone has to step in and take over that power. The mercenaries must not even be seen by daylight. So who takes over?'

Endean nodded again. He had not expected a mercenary to have any political sense at all.

'We have a man in view,' he said cautiously.

'He's in the republic now, or in exile?'

'In exile.'

'Well, he would have to be installed in the palace and broadcasting on the radio that he has conducted an internal *coup d'état* and taken over the country, by midday of the day following the night attack on the palace.'

'That could be arranged.'

'There's one more thing.'

'What's that?' asked Endean.

'There must be troops loyal to the new régime, the same troops who ostensibly carried out the coup of the night before, visibly present and mounting the guard by sunrise of the day after the attack. If they don't show up, we would be stuck – a group of white mercenaries holed up inside the palace, unable to show themselves for political reasons, and cut off from retreat in the event of a counter-attack. Now your man, the exile, does he have such a back-up force he could bring in with him when the coup comes? Or could he assemble them quickly once inside the capital?'

'I think you have to let us take care of that,' said Endean stiffly. 'What we are asking from you is a plan in military terms to mount the attack and carry it through.'

'That I can do,' said Shannon without hesitation. 'But what about the preparations, the organisation of the plan, getting the men, the arms, the ammo?'

'You must include that as well. Start from scratch and go right through to the capture of the palace and the death of Kimba.'

'Kimba has to get the chop?'

'Of course,' said Endean. 'Fortunately he has long since destroyed anyone with enough initiative or brains to become a rival. Consequently, he is the only man who might re-group his forces and counter-attack. With him dead, his ability to mesmerise the people into submission will also end.'

'Yeah. The juju dies with the man.'

'The what?'

'Nothing. You wouldn't understand.'

'Try me,' said Endean coldly.

'The man has a juju,' said Shannon, 'or at least the people believe he has. That's a powerful protection, given him by the spirits, protecting him against his enemies, guaranteeing him invincibility, guarding him from attack, ensuring him against death. In the Congo the Simbas believed their leader, Pierre Mulele, had a similar juju. He told them he could pass it on to his supporters and make them immortal. They believed him. They thought bullets would run off them like water. So they came at us in waves, bombed out of their minds on dagga and whisky, died like flies and still kept coming. It's the same with Kimba. So long as they think he's immortal, he is. Because they'll never lift a finger against him. Once they see his corpse, the man who killed him becomes the leader. He has the stronger juju.'

Endean stared in surprise. 'It's really that backward?'

'It's not so backward. We do the same with lucky charms, holy relics, the assumption of divine protection for our own particular cause. But we call it religion in us, savage superstition in them.'

'Never mind,' snapped Endean. 'If that's the way it is, all the more reason why Kimba has to die.'

'Which means he must be in that palace when we strike. If he's up-country it's no good. No one will support your man if Kimba is still alive.'

'He usually is in the palace, so I'm told.'

'Yes,' said Shannon, 'but we have to guarantee it. There's one day he never misses. Independence Day. On the eve of Independence Day he will be sleeping in the palace, sure as eggs is eggs.'

'When's that?'

'Three and a half months away.'

'Could a project be mounted in that time?' asked Endean.

'Yes, with a bit of luck. I'd like at least a couple of weeks longer.'

'The project has not been accepted yet,' observed Endean.

'No, but if you want to install a new man in that palace, an attack from outside is the only way of doing it. Do you want me to prepare the whole project from start to finish, with estimated costings and time schedule?'

'Yes. The costing is very important. My ... er ... associates will want to know how much they are letting themselves in for.'

'All right,' said Shannon. 'It will cost you £500.'

'You've already been paid,' said Endean coldly.

'I've been paid for a mission into Zangaro and a report on the military situation there,' replied Shannon. 'What you're asking for is a new report outside the original briefing you gave me.'

'Five hundred is a bit steep for a few sheets of paper with writing on them.'

'Rubbish. You know perfectly well if your firm consults a lawyer, architect, accountant or any other technical expert, you pay him a fee. I'm a technical expert in war. What you pay for is the knowledge and the experience – where to get the best men, the best arms, how to ship them, etc. That's what costs £500, and the same knowledge would cost you double if you tried to research it yourself in twelve months, which you couldn't anyway because you haven't the contacts.'

Endean rose. 'All right. It will be here this afternoon by special messenger. Tomorrow is Friday. My partners would like to read your report over the weekend. Please have it prepared by tomorrow afternoon at three. I'll collect it here.'

He left and as the door closed behind him Shannon raised his coffee cup in mock toast. 'Be seeing you, Mr Walter Harris oblique stroke Simon Endean,' he said softly.

Not for the first time he thanked his stars for the amiable and garrulous hotel-keeper Gomez. During one of their long nightly conversations Gomez had mentioned the affair of Colonel Bobi, now in exile. He had also mentioned that without Kimba, Bobi was nothing, being hated by the Caja for his army's cruelties against them on the orders of Kimba, and not able to command Vindu troops either. Which left Shannon with the problem of a back-up force with black faces to take over on the morning after.

Endean's brown manilla envelope containing fifty £10 notes arrived just after three in a taxi cab and was delivered to the reception desk of the Lowndes Hotel. Shannon counted the notes, stuffed them into the inside pocket of his jacket and began work. It took him the rest of the afternoon and most of that night.

He worked at the writing desk in his room, poring over his own diagrams and maps of the city of Clarence, its harbour, port area and the residential section that included the presidential palace and the army lines.

The classical military approach would have been to land a force on the othe side of the peninsula near the base with the main coastline, march the short distance inland and take the road from Clarence to the interior, with guns covering the T-junction. That would have sealed off the peninsula and the capital from reinforcement. It would also have lost the element of surprise.

Shannon's talent was that he understood Africa and the African soldier, and his thinking was unconventional, the same kind of thinking that had branded Hoare with the nickname of Mad Mike, although the Congo mercenary's tactics were exactly suited to African terrain and opposition, which are almost the exact opposite of the European situation.

Had Shannon's plans ever been seen by a European military mind, thinking in conventional terms, they would have been styled as reckless and without hope of success. He was banking on Sir James Manson's not having been in the British Army – there was no reference in *Who's Who* to indicate that he had – and accepting the plan. Shannon knew it was workable, and the only one that was.

He based his plan on three facts about war in Africa that he had learned the hard way. One was that the European soldier fights well and with precision in the dark, provided he has been well briefed on the terrain he can expect, while the African soldier, even on his own terrain, is sometimes reduced to near helplessness by his fear of the hidden enemy in the surrounding darkness. The second was that the speed of reaction of the African soldier, once wholly disoriented, his ability to recover, re-group and counter-attack, is longer than the European soldier's speed, exaggerating the normal effects of surprise. The third was that firepower and hence noise are the qualities that can bring African soldiers to fear, panic and headlong flight, without consideration of the smallness of the actual numbers of their opponents.

So Shannon based his plan on a night attack of total surprise in conditions of deafening noise and concentrated firepower.

He worked slowly and methodically, and, being a poor writer with a machine, tapped out the words with two forefingers. At two in the morning the occupant of the bedroom next door could stand no more of it, and banged on the wall to ask plaintively for a bit of peace so that he could get to sleep. Shannon concluded what he was doing five minutes later and packed up for the night. There was one other sound that disturbed the man next door, apart from the clacking of the typewriter. As he worked, and later as he lay in bed, the writer kept whistling a plaintive little tune. Had the insomniac next door known more of music he would have recognised 'Spanish Harlem'.

Martin Thorpe was also lying awake that night. He knew he had a long weekend ahead, two and a half days of monotonous and time-consuming poring over cards, each bearing the basic details of one of the 4500 public companies registered at Companies House in the City of London.

There are two agencies in London who provide their subscribers with such an information service about British companies. These are Moodies and the Exchange Telegraph, known as Extel. In his office in ManCon House Thorpe had the set of cards provided by Extel, the agency whose service ManCon took as a necessary part of its commercial activities. But for the business of searching for a shell company, Thorpe had decided to buy the Moodies service and have it sent to his home, partly because he thought Moodies did a better information job on the smaller companies registered in the United Kingdom, and partly for security reasons.

That Thursday he had heard his briefing from Sir James Manson and gone straight to a firm of lawyers. Acting for him, and keeping his name to themselves, the law practice had ordered a complete set of Moodies cards. He had paid the lawyer the £260 for the cards, plus £50 for the three grey filing cabinets in which they would arrive, plus the lawyer's fee for doing it. He had also engaged a small removers' firm to send a van round to Moodies after being told the set of cards would be ready for pick-up on Friday afternoon.

As he lay in bed in his elegant detached house in Hampstead Garden Suburb, he too was planning his campaign; not in detail like Shannon, for he had too little information, but in general terms, using nominee shareholders and parcels of voting stock as Shannon used submachine guns and mortars.

Shannon handed his completed project to Endean at three on the Friday afternoon. It contained fourteen pages, four of them diagrams and two of them lists of equipment. He had finished it after breakfast, confident that the sleepless one in the next bedroom would be gone, and had enclosed it in a brown folder. He was tempted to put 'For Sir James Manson's Eyes Only' on the cover, but had resisted. There was no need to blow the affair wantonly, and he could sniff a good contract in the offing if the mining baron offered the job to him.

So he continued to call Endean Harris, and to refer to 'your associates' instead of 'your boss'. After taking the folder, Endean told him to stay in town over the weekend and to be available from Sunday midnight onwards.

Shannon went shopping during the rest of the afternoon, but his mind was on the references he had already seen in *Who's Who* to the man he now knew employed him, Sir James Manson, self-made millionaire and tycoon.

He had an urge, partly from curiosity, partly from the feeling that one day he might need the information, to learn more about Sir James Manson, about the man himself, and about why he had hired a mercenary to make war in Zangaro on his behalf.

The reference from *Who's Who* that stuck in his mind was the mention of a daughter Manson had, a girl who would now be in her late teens or just turned twenty. In the middle of the afternoon he stepped into a phone box off Jermyn Street and called the private enquiry agents who had traced Endean from their first meeting in Chelsea and identified him as Manson's aide.

The head of the agency was cordial when he heard his former client on the phone. Previously, he knew, Mr Brown had paid promptly and in cash. Such customers were valuable. If he wished to remain on the end of a telephone, that was his affair.

'Do you have access to a fairly comprehensive newspaper cuttings library?' Shannon asked.

'I could have,' the agency chief admitted.

'I wish to get a brief description of a young lady of whom there has probably at one time been a reference in society gossip columns somewhere in the London Press. I need very little, simply what she does and where she lives. But I need it quickly.'

There was a pause on the other end.

'If there are such references, I could probably do it by phone,' said the enquiry agent. 'What is the name?'

'Miss Julia Manson, daughter of Sir James Manson.'

The enquiry agent thought it over. He recalled that this client's previous assignment had concerned a man who turned out to be Sir James Manson's aide. He also knew he could find out what Mr Brown wanted to know within an hour.

The two men agreed the fee, a modest one, and Shannon promised to mail it in cash by registered post within the hour. The enquiry agent decided to accept the promise, and asked his client to call him back just before five.

Shannon completed his shopping and called back on the dot of five. Within a few seconds Shannon had what he wanted. He was deep in thought as he walked back to his hotel and phoned the writer who had originally introduced him to 'Mr Harris'.

'Hi,' he said gruffly down the phone, 'it's me, Cat Shannon.'

'Oh hallo, Cat,' came the surprised reply. 'Where have you been?'

'Around,' said Shannon. 'I just wanted to say thanks again for recommending me to that fellow Harris.'

'Not at all. Did he offer you a job?'

Shannon was cautious. 'Yeah, a few days' worth. It's over now. But I'm in funds. How about a spot of dinner?'

'Why not?' said the writer.

'Tell me,' said Shannon, 'are you still going out with that girl you used to be with when we met last?'

'Yeah. The same one. Why?'

'She's a model, isn't she?'

'Yes.'

'Look,' said Shannon, 'you may think this crazy, but I very much want to meet a girl who's also a model but I can't get an introduction to. Name of Julie Manson. Could you ask your girl if she ever met her in the modelling world?'

The writer thought it over.

'Sure. I'll call Carrie and ask her. Where are you now?'

'In a call box. I'll call you back in half an hour.'

Shannon was lucky. His friend told him the two girls knew each other, and had been at model school together. They were also handled by the same agency. It took another hour before Shannon, by then speaking directly to the writer's girl-friend, learned that Julie Manson had agreed to a dinner date, provided it was a foursome with Carrie and her boy-friend. They agreed to meet at Carrie's flat just after eight, and that she would have Julie Manson there.

Shannon and the writer turned up within a few minutes of each other at Carrie's flat off Maida Vale, and the four of them went off to dinner. The writer had booked a table at a small cellar restaurant called the Baker and Oven in Marylebone, and the meal was the kind Shannon liked, enormous portions of English roast meats and vegetables, washed down with two bottles of Piat de Beaujolais. He liked the food and he liked Julie.

She was quite short, a little over five feet, and to give herself the im-pression of more height she wore high heels and carried herself well. She said she was nineteen, and she had a pert round face that could be inno-cently angelic when she wanted, or extremely sexy when she thought no one else was looking.

She was evidently spoiled and too accustomed to getting things her own way, probably, Shannon estimated, the result of an over-indulgent upbringing. But she was amusing and pretty, and Shannon had never asked more of a girl. She wore her dark brown hair loose so that it fell to her waist, and beneath her dress she evidently had a very curved figure. She also seemed to be intrigued by her blind date.

Although Shannon had asked his friend not to mention what he did for a living, Carrie had nevertheless let it slip that he was a mercenary. But the conversation managed to avoid the question during dinner. As usual Shannon did less talking then anyone, which was not difficult because Julie and the tall auburn-haired Carrie did enough for four between them.

As they left the restaurant and climbed back into the cool night air of the streets, the writer mentioned that he and his girlfriend were taking the car back to his flat. He hailed a taxi for Shannon, asking him if he would take Julie home before going on to his hotel. As the mercenary climbed in, the writer gave him a slow wink. 'I think you're on,' he whispered. Shannon grunted.

Outside her Mayfair flat Julie suggested he might like to come in for a coffee, so he paid off the taxi and accompanied her up to the evidently expensive apartment. Only when they were seated on the settee drinking the appalling coffee Julie had prepared did she refer to the way he earned his living.

He was leaning back in the corner of the settee, she was perched on the edge of the seat, turned towards him.

'Have you killed people?' she asked.

'Yes.'

'In battle?'

'Sometimes. Mostly.'

'How many?'

'I don't know. I never counted.'

She savoured the information and swallowed several times.

'I've never known a man who had killed people.'

'You don't know that,' countered Shannon. 'Anyone who has been in a war has probably killed people.'

'Have you got any scars from wounds?' It was another of the usual questions. In fact Shannon carried over a score of marks on his back and chest, legacies of bullets, fragments of mortar and shards of grenade. He nodded.

'Some.'

'Show me,' she said.

'No.'

'Go on, show me. Prove it.'

She stood up. He grinned up at her.

'I'll show you mine, if you'll show me yours,' he taunted, mimicking the old kindergarten challenge.

'I haven't got any,' Julie said indignantly.

'Prove it,' said Shannon shortly, and turned to place his empty coffee cup on the table behind the sofa. He heard a rustle of cloth. When he turned he nearly choked on the last mouthful of coffee. It had taken her less than a second to unzip her dress at the back and let the whole lot slip to a pool of crumpled cloth round her ankles. Beneath it she wore a pair of grip-top stockings and a thin gold waist-chain.

'See,' she said softly, 'not a mark anywhere.'

She was right. Her small, nubile teenager's body was an unblemished milky white from the floor to the mane of dark hair that hung round her shoulders and almost touched the waist-chain. Shannon swallowed.

'I thought you were supposed to be Daddy's sweet little girl,' he said.

She giggled. 'That's what they all think, especially Daddy,' she said. 'Now it's your turn.'

Sir James Manson sat at the same hour in the library of his country mansion not far from the village of Notgrove in the rolling Gloucestershire countryside, Shannon's file on his knee and a brandy and soda at his elbow. It was close to midnight and Lady Manson had long since gone to bed. He had saved the Shannon project to read alone in his library, resisting the temptation to open it in the car on the way down, or to slip away early from dinner. When he wanted to concentrate hard he preferred the night hours, and on this document he wanted to concentrate hard.

He flicked the cover open and set on one side the maps and sketches. Then he started on the narrative. It read:

PREAMBLE. The following plan has been prepared on the basis of the report of the republic of Zangaro written by Mr Walter Harris, my own visit to Zangaro and my own report on that visit, and the briefing given by Mr Harris on what it is desired to achieve. It cannot take into account elements known to Mr Harris but undisclosed by him to me. Notable among these must be the aftermath of the attack and the installation of the successor government. Nevertheless, this aftermath may well require preparations built in to the planning of the attack, and these I have obviously not been able to make.

OBJECT OF THE EXERCISE. To prepare, launch and carry out an attack on the presidential palace at Clarence, capital of Zangaro, to storm and capture that palace, and to liquidate the president and his personal guards living inside. Also, to take possession of the bulk of the weapons and armoury of the republic, its national treasury and broadcasting radio station, also inside the palace. Lastly to create such conditions that any armed survivors of the guard unit or the army are scattered outside the town and in no position to mount a viable counter-attack.

METHOD OF ATTACK. After studying the military situation of Clarence there is no doubt the attack must be from the sea, and launched directly from the sea at the palace itself. I have studied the idea of an airborne landing at the airport. It is not feasible. Firstly, the authorities at the airport of takeoff would not permit the necessary quantity of arms and men to board a charter aircraft without suspecting the nature of the flight. Such authorities, even if a set could be found to permit such a takeoff, would constitute a serious risk of arrest, or a breach of security.

Secondly, a land attack offers no extra advantages, and many disadvantages. To arrive in an armed column over the northern border would only mean the men and arms would have to be smuggled into the neighbouring republic, which has an efficient police and security system. The risk of premature discovery and arrest would be extremely high, unacceptably so. To land elsewhere on the coast of Zangaro and march to Clarence would be no more realistic. For one thing most of the coast is of tangled mangrove swamp impenetrable by boats, and such tiny coves as there are would be unfindable in darkness. For another, being without motor transport, the attacking force would have a long march to the capital, and the defenders would be forewarned. For a third, the paucity of the numbers of the attacking force would be visible in daylight, and would hearten the defenders to put up a stiff resistance.

Lastly, the idea was examined to smuggle the arms and the men into the republic clandestinely and hide them out until the night of the attack. This too is unreal, partly because the quantity of weapons would be too great in weight terms, partly because such quantities and so many unaccustomed visitors would inevitably be spotted and betrayed, and partly because such a plan would require an assisting organisation on the ground inside Zangaro, which does not exist.

In consequence it is felt the only realistic plan must be for an attack by light boats, departing from a large vessel moored out at sea, straight into the harbour of Clarence, and an attack on the palace immediately on landing.

REQUIREMENTS FOR THE ATTACK. The force should be not less than a dozen men, armed with mortars, bazookas and grenades, and all carrying as well submachine carbines for close quarters use. The men should come off the sea between two and three in the morning, giving ample time for all in Clarence to be asleep, but sufficiently before dawn for no visible traces of white mercenaries to be available by sunrise the same day.

The report continued for six more pages to describe exactly how Shannon proposed to plan the project, engage the necessary personnel, the arms and ammunition he would need, the ancillary equipment of radio sets, assault craft, outboard engines, flares, uniforms, webbing, food and victuals; how each item could be costed, and how he would destroy the palace and scatter the Army.

On the question of the ship to carry the attacking force he said: 'Apart from the arms, the acquisition of the ship will prove the most difficult part. On reflection I would be against chartering a vessel, since this involves crew who may turn out to be unreliable, a captain who could at any time change his mind, and the security hazard that vessels of a kind likely to undertake such a charter are probably notorious to the authorities of the countries bordering on the Mediterranean. I advocate spending more money to buy outright a small freighter, crew it with men paid by and loyal to the patrons, and with a legal reputation in shipping circles. Such a boat would in any case be a returnable asset and might work out cheaper in the long run.'

Shannon had also stressed the necessity of security at all times. He pointed out: 'Since I am unaware of the identity of the patrons, with the exception of Mr Harris, it is recommended that in the event of the project being accepted, Mr Harris remain the sole link between the patrons and me. Payments of the necessary money should be made to me by Mr Harris, and my accounting of expenditure returned the same way. Similarly, although I would need four subordinate operatives, none would know the nature of the project, and certainly not the destination, until all are well out to sea. Even the coastal charts should only be handed over to the captain after sailing. The above plan takes in the security angle, since wherever possible the purchases may be made legally on the open market, and only the arms an illegal purchase. At each stage there is a cut-out at which any investigator comes up against a blank wall, and also at each stage the equipment is being brought separately in different countries by different operatives. Only myself, Mr Harris and the patrons would know the whole plan, and in the worst event I could not identify the patrons, nor, probably, Mr Harris.'

Sir James Manson nodded and grunted in approval several times as he read. At one a.m. he poured himself another brandy and turned to the costings and timings, which were on separate sheets. These read:

Reconnaissance visit to Zangaro.		
Two reports	*Completed*	£2500
Project commander's fee		£10,000
Engagement all other personnel		
and their salaries		£10,000
Total administrative costs,		
travelling, hotels, etc., for		
CO and all subordinates		£10,000
Purchase of arms		£25,000
Purchase of vessel		£30,000
Purchase of ancillary equipment		£5000
Reserve		£7500
	Total	£100,000

The second sheet bore the estimated timings.

Preparatory Stage:	Recruitment and assembly of personnel. Setting up of bank account. Purchase of foreign based company.	20 days
Purchasing Stage:	Period to cover purchase of all items in sections	40 days
Assembly Stage:	Assembly of equipment and personnel onto the vessel, culminating in sailing day.	20 days
Shipment Stage:	Transporting entire project by sea from embarkation port to point off coast of Clarence.	20 days

Strike day would take place on Zangaran Independence Day, which in the above calendar, if set in motion not later than next Wednesday, would be Day 100.

Sir James Manson read the report twice, and spent a long hour steadily smoking one of his Upman Coronas while he stared at the rich panelling and Moroccan-bound books that lined his walls. Finally he locked the project file in his wall safe and went upstairs to bed.

Cat Shannon lay on his back in the darkened bedroom and ran his hand idly over the girl's body that lay half across his own. It was a small but highly erotic body, as he had discovered during the previous hour, and whatever Julie had spent her time learning in the two years since she left school it had not had much to do with shorthand-typing. Her appetite and taste for sexual variety were equalled only by her energy and almost constant stream of chatter between meals.

As he stroked her she stirred and began to play with him.

'Funny,' he said reflectively, 'it must be a sign of the times. We've been screwing half the night, and I don't know a thing about you.'

She paused for a second, said 'Like what?' and resumed.

'Where your home is,' he said. 'Apart from this pad.'

'Gloucestershire,' she mumbled.

'What does your old man do?' he asked softly. There was no answer. He took a handful of her hair and pulled her face round to him.

'Ow, you're hurting. He's in the City. Why?'

'Stockbroker?'

'No, he runs some company to do with mining. That's his speciality, and this is mine. Now, watch.'

Half an hour later she rolled off him and asked, 'Did you like that, darling?'

Shannon laughed and she caught a flash of teeth in the darkness as he grinned.

'Oh yes,' he said softly, 'I enjoyed that enormously. Tell me about your old man.'

'Daddy? Oh he's a boring old businessman. Spends all his day in a stuffy office in the City.'

'Some businessmen interest me. So tell me what he's like . . .'

Sir James Manson was enjoying his mid-morning coffee in the sun lounge on the south side of his country mansion that Saturday morning when the call came through from Adrian Goole. The Foreign Office official was speaking from his own home in Kent.

'I hope you won't mind my calling you over the weekend,' he said.

'Not at all, my dear fellow,' said Manson quite untruthfully. 'Any time.'

'I would have called at the office last night but I got held up at a meeting. Recalling our conversation some time ago about the results of your mining survey down in that African place. You remember?'

Manson supposed Goole felt obliged to go through the security rigmarole on an open line.

'Yes indeed,' he said. 'I took up your suggestion made at that dinner. The figures concerned were slightly changed, so that the quantities revealed were quite unviable from a business standpoint. The report went off, was received, and I've heard no more about it.'

Goole's next words jerked Sir James Manson out of his weekend relaxation.

'Actually, we have,' said the voice down the line. 'Nothing really disturbing, but odd all the same. Our ambassador in the area, although accredited to that country and three other small republics, doesn't live there, as you know. But he sends in regular reports, gleaned from a variety of sources, including normal liaison with our friendly diplomats. A copy of a section of his latest report, concerned with the economic side of things out there, landed on my desk yesterday at the office. It seems there's a rumour out there that the Soviet government has secured permission to send in a mining survey team of their own. Of course, they may not be concerned with the same area as your chaps . . .'

Sir James Manson stared at the telephone as Goole's voice twittered on. In his head a pulse began to hammer close to his left temple.

'I was only thinking, Sir James, that if these Russian chaps go over the same area as your man went over, their findings might be somewhat different. Fortunately, it's only a question of minor quantities of tin. Still, I thought you ought to know. Hello? Hello? Are you there . . .?'

Manson jerked himself out of his reverie. With a massive effort he made his voice appear normal.

'Yes indeed. Sorry, I was just thinking. Very good of you to call me, Goole. I don't suppose they'll be in the same area as my man. But damn useful to know, all the same.'

He went through the usual pleasantries before hanging up, and walked slowly back to the sun terrace, his mind racing. Coincidence? Could be, it just could be. If the Soviet survey team were going to cover an area miles away from the Crystal Mountain range, it would be purely a coincidence. On the other hand, if they went straight towards the Crystal Mountain without having done any aerial survey work to notice the difference in vegetation in that area, then that would be no coincidence. That would be bloody sabotage. And there was no way he could find out, no way of being absolutely certain, without betraying his own continuing interest. And that would be fatal.

He thought of Chalmers, the man he was convinced he had silenced with money. His teeth ground. Had he talked? Wittingly? Unwittingly? He had half a mind to let Endean, or one of Endean's friends, take care of Dr Chalmers. But that would change nothing. And there was no proof of a security leak.

He could shelve his plans at once, and think no more of them. He considered this, then considered again the pot of pure gold at the end of this particular rainbow. James Manson was no softy: he was not where he was because he had the habit of backing down on account of an increased element of risk, most of all an unproven one.

He sat down in the deck chair next to the now cold coffee pot and thought hard. He intended to go forward as planned, but he had to assume the Russian mining team would touch on the area Mulrooney had visited, and he had to assume they too would notice the vegetation changes. Therefore there was now a new element, a time limit. He did some mental calculation and came up with the figure of three months. If the Russians learned the content of the Crystal Mountain, there would be a 'technical aid' team in there like a dose of salts, and a big one at that. Over half the members, he knew, would be hard men from the KGB.

Shannon's shortest schedule had been a hundred days, but he had originally told Endean that another fortnight added to the timetable would make the whole project that much more feasible. Now they did not have that fortnight. In fact, if the Russians moved faster than usual, they might not even have a hundred days.

He returned to the telephone and called Simon Endean. His own weekend had been disturbed; there was no reason why Endean should not start doing a bit of work.

Endean called Shannon at the hotel on Monday morning and set up a rendezvous for two p.m. at a small block of flats in St John's Wood. He had hired the flat on the instructions of Sir James Manson that morning, after having had a long briefing at the country mansion on the Sunday afternoon. He had taken the flat for a month in the name of Harris, paying cash and giving a fictitious reference which no one checked. The reason for the hiring was simple: the flat had a telephone that did not go through a switchboard.

Shannon was there on time and found the man he still called Harris already installed. The telephone was hung in a desk microphone set that would enable a telephone conference between one or more people in the room and the person on the other end of the line to be held.

'The chief of the consortium has read your report,' he told Shannon, 'and wants to have a word with you.'

At two-thirty the phone rang. Endean threw the 'speak' switch on the machine and Sir James Manson's voice came on the line. Shannon already knew who it would be, but gave no sign.

'Are you there, Mr Shannon?' asked the voice.

'Yes, sir.'

'Now, I have read your report, and I approve your judgement and conclusions. If offered this contract, would you be prepared to go through with it?'

'Yes, sir, I would,' said Shannon.

'There are a couple of points I want to discuss. I notice in the budget you award yourself the sum of ten thousand pounds.'

'Yes, sir. Frankly, I don't think anyone would do the job for less, and most would ask more. Even if a budget were prepared by another person which quoted a lower sum, I think that person would still pass a minimum of ten per cent to himself, simply by hiding the sum in the prices of purchases that could not be checked out.'

There was a pause, then the voice said:

'All right, I accept it. What does this salary buy me?'

'It buys you my knowledge, my contacts, my acquaintanceship with the world of arms dealers, smugglers, gun-runners and mercenaries. It also buys my silence in the event of anything going wrong. It pays me for three months' damned hard work, and the constant risk of arrest and imprisonment. Lastly, it buys the risk of my getting killed in the attack.'

There was a grunt.

'Fair enough. Now as regards financing. The sum of £100,000 will be transferred into a Swiss account which Mr Harris will open this week. He will pay you the necessary money in slices, as and when you need it over the forthcoming two months. For that purpose you will have to set up your own communications system with him. When the money is spent, he will either have to be present or to receive receipts.'

'That will not always be possible, sir. There are no receipts in the arms business, least of all in black market deals, and most of the men I shall be dealing with would not have Mr Harris present. He is not in their world. I would suggest the extensive use of travellers cheques and credit transfers by banks. At the same time, if Mr Harris has to be present to counter-sign every banker's draft or cheque for £1000, he must either follow me around everywhere, which I would not accept on grounds of my own security, or we could never do it all inside a hundred days.'

There was another long pause.

'What do you mean by your own security?' asked the voice.

'I mean, sir, that I don't know Mr Harris. I could not accept that he be in a position to know enough to get me arrested in a European city. You have taken your security precautions. I have to take mine. These are that I travel and work alone and unsupervised.'

'You're a cautious man, Mr Shannon.'

'I have to be. I'm still alive.'

There was a grim chuckle.

'And how do I know you can be trusted with large sums of money to handle on your own?'

'You don't, sir. Up to a point Mr Harris can keep the sums low at each stage. But the payments for the arms have to be made in cash and by the buyer alone. The only alternatives are to ask Mr Harris to mount the operation personally, or hire another professional. And you would not know if you could trust him either.'

'Fair enough, Mr Shannon. Mr Harris . . .'

'Sir?' answered Endean immediately.

'Please return to see me at once after leaving where you are now. Mr Shannon, you have the job. You have one hundred days, Mr Shannon, to steal a republic. One hundred days.'

PART TWO
The Hundred Days

8
_____

For several minutes after Sir James Manson had rung off, Simon Endean and Cat Shannon sat and stared at one another. It was Shannon who recovered first.

'Since we're going to have to work together,' he told Endean, 'let's get this clear. If anyone, anyone at all, gets to hear about this project, it will eventually get back to one or other of the secret services of one of the main powers. Probably the CIA, or at least the British SIS or maybe the French SDECE. And they will screw, but good. There'll be nothing you or I could do to prevent them ending the affair stone dead. So we keep security absolute.'

'Speak for yourself,' snapped Endean. 'I've got a lot more tied up in this than you.'

'OK. First thing has to be money. I'll fly to Brussels tomorrow and open a bank account somewhere in Belgium. I'll be back by tomorrow night. Contact me then, and I'll tell you where, in which bank and in what name. Then I shall need a transfer of credit to the tune of at least £10,000. By tomorrow night I'll have a complete list of where it has to be spent. Mainly, it will be in salary cheques for my assistants, deposits, etc.'

'Where do I contact you?' asked Endean.

'That's point number two,' said Shannon. 'I'm going to need a permanent base, secure for telephone calls and letters. What about this flat? Is it traceable to you?'

Endean had not thought of that. He considered the problem.

'It's hired in my name. Cash in advance for one month,' he said.

'Does it matter if the name Harris is on the tenancy agreement?' asked Shannon.

'No.'

'Then I'll take it over. That gives me a month's tenancy – seems a pity to waste it – and I'll take up the payments at the end of that time. Do you have a key?'

'Yes, of course. I let myself in by it.'

'How many keys are there?'

For answer Endean reached into his pocket and brought out a ring with four keys on it. Two were evidently for the front door of the block and two for the flat door. Shannon took them from his hand.

'Now for communications,' he said. 'You can contact me by phoning here any time. I may be in, I may not. I may be away abroad. Since I assume you will not want to give me your phone number, set up a *poste restante* mailing address in London somewhere convenient either to your home or office, and check twice daily for telegrams. If I need you urgently I'll telegram with the phone number of where I am, and a time to phone. Understood?'

'Yes. I'll have it by tomorrow night. Anything else?'

'Only that I'll be using the name of Keith Brown throughout the operation. Anything signed as coming from Keith is from me. When ringing a hotel ask for me as Keith Brown. If ever I reply by saying "This is Mister Brown", get off the line fast. It means trouble. Explain that you have the wrong number, or the wrong Brown. That's all for the moment. You'd better get back to the office. Ring me here at eight tonight and I'll give you the progress to date.'

A few minutes later Endean found himself on the pavements of St John's Wood looking for a taxi.

Luckily Shannon had not banked the £500 he had received before the weekend for his attack project, and he still had £450 of it left. There was his hotel bill in Knightsbridge to settle, but that could come later.

He rang BEA and booked an economy class return on the morning flight to Brussels, returning at 1600 hours, which would get him back in his flat by six. Following that he telephoned four telegrams abroad, one to Paarl, Cape Province, South Africa, one to Ostend, one to Marseilles and one to Munich. Each said simply, 'URGENT YOU PHONE ME LONDON 507–0041 ANY MIDNIGHT OVER NEXT THREE DAYS STOP SHANNON'. Finally he summoned a taxi and had it take him back to the Lowndes Hotel. He checked out, paid his bill and left as he had come, anonymously.

At eight Endean rang him as agreed and he told Manson's aide what he had done so far. They agreed Endean would ring again at ten the following evening.

Shannon spent a couple of hours exploring the block he was now living in, and the surrounding area. He spotted several small restaurants including a couple not far away in St John's Wood High Street, and ate a leisurely supper at one of them. He was back home by eleven.

He counted his money – there was over £400 left – put £300 on one side for the air fare and expenses the following day, and checked over his effects. The clothes were unremarkable, all of them less than three months old, most bought in the last ten days in London. He had no gun to bother about, and for safety destroyed the typewriter ribbon he had used to type his reports, replacing it with one of his spares.

Though it was dark early in London that evening, it was still light on a warm, sunny summer evening in Cape Province as Janni Dupree gunned his car past Seapoint and on towards Cape Town. He too had a Chevrolet,

THE DOGS OF WAR 611

older than Endean's, but bigger and flashier, bought second-hand with some of the dollars with which he had returned from Paris four weeks earlier. After spending the day swimming and fishing from a friend's boat at Simonstown, he was driving back to his home in Paarl. He always liked to come home to Paarl after a contract, but inevitably it bored him quickly, just as it had when he left it ten years before.

As a boy he had been raised in the Paarl Valley and had spent his pre-school years scampering through the thin and poor vineyards owned by people like his parents. He had learned to stalk birds and shoot in the valley with Pieter, his klonkie, the coloured playmate white boys are allowed to play with until they grow too old and learn what skin colour is all about.

Pieter, with his enormous brown eyes, tangled mass of black curls and mahogany skin, had been two years older then he, and supposed to look after him. In fact they had been the same size, for Janni was physically precocious and had quickly taken the leadership of the pair. On summer days like this one, twenty years ago, the two barefoot boys used to take the bus along the coast to Cape Agulhas, where the Atlantic and the Indian oceans finally meet, and fish for yellowtail, galjoen and red steenbras off the point.

After Paarl Boys' High, Janni had been a problem, too big, aggressive, restless, getting into fights with those big, scything fists and ending up twice in front of the magistrates. He could have taken over his parents' farm, tending with his father the stubby little vines that produced such thin wine. The prospect appalled him, of becoming old and bent trying to make a living from the smallholding with only four coloured boys working with him. At eighteen he volunteered for the Army, did his basic training at Potchefstroom and transferring to the paratroops at Bloemfontein. It was here he had found the thing he wanted to do most in life, here and in the counter-insurgency training in the harsh bushveld around Pietersburg. The Army had agreed with him about his suitability, except on one point, his propensity for going to war while pointing in the wrong direction. In one fist-fight too many, Corporal Dupree had beaten a sergeant senseless and the commanding officer had busted him down to private.

Bitter, he went AWOL, was taken in a bar in East London, battered two MPs before they held him down, and did six months in the stockade. On release he saw an advertisement in an evening newspaper, reported to a small office in Durban, and two days later was flown out of South Africa to Kamina base in Katanga. He had become a mercenary at twenty-two, and that had been six years ago.

As he drove along the winding road through Franshoek towards the Paarl Valley, he wondered if there would be a letter from Shannon or one of the boys with news of a contract. But when he got there, there was nothing waiting at the post office. Clouds were blowing up from the sea, and there was a hint of thunder in the air.

It would rain that evening, a nice cooling shower, and he glanced up towards the Paarl Rock, the phenomenon that had given the valley and the town its name long ago when his ancestors first came into the valley. As a boy he stared in wonderment at the rock, a dull grey when dry, but which after rain glistened like an enormous pearl in the moonlight. Then it became a great, glistening, gleaming thing, dominating the tiny town beneath it. Although the town of his boyhood could never offer him the kind of life he wanted, it was still home; and when he saw the Pearl Rock glistening in the light, he always knew he was back home again. That evening he wished he was somewhere else, heading towards another war.

What he did not know was that by the following morning Shannon's telegram, summoning him to another war, would be in Paarl post office.

Tiny Marc Vlaminck leaned on the bar counter and downed another foaming schooner of Flemish ale. Outside the front windows of the place his girl-friend managed, the streets of Ostend's red-light district were almost empty. A chill wind was blowing off the sea and the summer tourists had not started to arrive yet. He was bored already.

For the first month since his return from the tropics it had been good to be back, good to take hot baths again, to chat with his mates who had dropped in to see him. Even the local press had taken an interest, but he had told them to get lost. The last thing he needed was trouble from the authorities, and he knew they would leave him alone if he did or said nothing to embarrass them with the African embassies in Brussels.

But after weeks the inactivity had palled. A few nights back it had been enlivened when he thumped a seaman who had tried to fondle Anna's bottom, an area he regarded as entirely his own preserve. The memory had started a thought running through his mind. He could hear a low thump-thump from upstairs where Anna was doing the housework in the small flat that they shared above the bar. He heaved himself off his bar-stool, drained the tankard and called, 'If anyone comes in, serve 'em yourself.'

Then he lumbered up the back stairs. As he did so the door opened and a telegram boy came in.

It was a clear spring evening with just a touch of chill in the air and the water of the Old Port of Marseilles was like glass. Across its centre, a few moments ago a mirror for the surrounding bars and cafés, a single home-coming trawler cut a swathe of ripples that wandered across the harbour and died chuckling under the hulls of the fisher boats already moored. The cars were locked solid along the Canebière, smells of cooking fish emanated from a thousand windows, the old men sipped their anisette and the heroin sellers scuttled through the alleys on their lucrative missions. It was an ordinary evening.

In the multi-national, multi-lingual cauldron of seething humanity that called itself Le Panier, where only a policeman is illegal, Jean-Baptiste Langarotti sat at a corner table in a small bar and sipped a long cool Ricard.

He was not as bored as Janni Dupree or Marc Vlaminck. Years in prison had taught him the ability to keep himself interested in even the smallest things, and long periods of inactivity he could survive better than most.

Moreover, he had been able to get himself a job of work and earn a living, so that his savings were still intact. He saved steadily, his economies mounting up in a bank in Switzerland that no one knew about. One day it would buy him the little bar in Calvi that he wanted.

A month earlier a good friend of his from the Algerian days had been picked up for a small matter of a suitcase containing twelve former French Army Colt Forty-fives and from Les Baumettes had sent Jean-Baptiste a message asking him to 'mind' the girl off whose earnings the imprisoned friend normally lived. He knew he could trust the Corsican not to cheat him. She was a good girl, a broad-beamed hoyden called Marie-Claire who went under the name of Lola and did her nightly stint in a bar in the Tubano district. She had taken quite a fancy to Langarotti, perhaps because of his size, and her only complaint was that he did not knock her about the way her boy-friend in prison had done. Being small was no hindrance to being a minder, because the rest of the underworld, who might have made a claim for Lola, needed no education about Langarotti.

So Lola was happy to be the best-minded girl in town, and Jean-Baptiste content to while away the days until another contract to fight came up. He was in contact with a few people in the mercenary business, but being new to it was relying more on Shannon to hear of something first. He was more the sort clients would come to.

Shortly after returning to France, Langarotti had been contacted by Charles Roux from Paris, who had proposed that the Corsican sign on with him in exclusivity, in exchange for first choice if and when a contract turned up. Roux had talked largely of the half-dozen projects he had brewing at the time, and the Corsican had remained non-committal. Later he had checked up and found Roux was mostly talk, for he had set up no projects of his own since his return from Bukavu in the autumn of '67 with a hole through his arm.

With a sigh Langarotti glanced at his watch, finished his drink and rose to go. It was time to fetch Lola from their apartment and escort her to the bar for work, and then drop in at the all-night post office to see if there was a telegram from Shannon offering a prospect of a new war.

In Munich it was even colder than in Marc Vlaming's Ostend, and Kurt Semmler, his blood thinned by years in the Far East, Algeria and Africa, shivered in his knee-length black leather coat as he headed towards the all-night post office. He made a regular check-call at the counter every morning and evening, and each time hoped for some letter or telegram bearing news of an invitation to meet someone for an interview for possible selection for a mercenary assignment.

The period from his return from Africa had been one of idleness and boredom. Like most army veterans he disliked civilian life, wore the clothes badly, despised the politics and longed again for some form of routine combined with action. The return to his birth-city had not been encouraging. Everywhere he saw long-haired youths, sloppy and ill-disciplined, waving their banners and screaming their slogans. There seemed to be none of the sense of purpose, of commitment to the ideal of the greatness of the Fatherland and its leader that had so completely absorbed his own childhood and youth, nor the sense of order that characterised the army life.

Even the smuggling life in the Mediterranean, although it had been free and easy, at least could offer the sense of activity, the scent of danger, the feeling of a mission planned, executed and accomplished. Easing a fast launch in towards the Italian coast with two tons of American cigarettes on board, he had at least been able to imagine himself back on the Mekong, going into action with the Legion against the Xoa Binh river pirates.

Munich offered him nothing. He had drunk too much, smoked too much, whored a bit and become thoroughly disgruntled.

At the post office there was nothing for him that evening. But the next morning it would be a different story, for Shannon's telegram was on its way across a darkened Europe.

At midnight Marc Vlaminck phoned in from Ostend. The Belgian telegram delivery services are excellent and deliver up to ten at night. Shannon told Vlaminck simply to meet him in front of Brussels National airport the following morning with a car and gave him his flight number.

Belgium has, from the point of view of those wishing to operate a discreet but legal bank account, many advantages that outweigh those offered by the much better publicised Swiss banking system. Not nearly as rich or powerful as Germany, nor neutral like Switzerland, Belgium nevertheless offers the facility of permitting unlimited quantities of money to pass in and out without government control or interference. The banks are also just as discreet as those of Switzerland, which is why they and the banks of Luxembourg and Leichtenstein have been steadily increasing their volume of business at the expense of the Swiss.

It was to the Kredietbank in Brugge, seventy minutes' driving time from Brussels airport, that Shannon had himself driven by Marc Vlaminck the following morning.

The big Belgian was evidently full of curiosity, but he kept it to himself. When they were on the road to Brugge Shannon mentioned briefly that he had been given a contract, and there was room for four helpers. Was Vlaminck interested?

Tiny Marc indicated that of course he was. Shannon told him he could not say what the operation was, other than that it was a job that not merely had to be fought, but set up from scratch. He was prepared to offer normal rates of 1250 dollars a month plus expenses for the next three months, and that the job, although not requiring absence from home until the third month, would require a few hours' risk inside Europe. That, of course, was not strictly mercenary work, but it had to be done. Marc grunted.

'I'm not knocking off banks,' he said. 'Not for that kind of money.'

'It's nothing like that. I need some guns taken on board a boat. We have to do it ourselves. After we sail, it's all set for Africa and a nice little firefight.'

Marc grinned.

'A long campaign, or a quick in-and-out job?'

'An attack,' said Shannon. 'Mind you, if it works, there could be a long contract in the offing. Can't promise, but it looks like that. And a fat success bonus.'

'OK, I'm on,' said Marc, and they drove into the main square at Brugge.

The Kredietbank head office is situated at Number 25 in the Vlamingstraat, a narrow thoroughfare flanked by house after house in the distinctive style of eighteenth-century Flemish architecture, and all in a perfect state of preservation. Most of the ground floors have been converted into shops, but upwards from the ground floors the façades resemble something from a painting by one of the old masters.

Inside the bank Shannon introduced himself to the head of the foreign accounts section, Mr Goossens, and proved his identity as Keith Brown by tendering his passport. Within forty minutes he had opened a current account with a deposit of £100 sterling in cash, informed Mr Goossens that a sum of £10,000 in the form of a transfer from Switzerland could be expected any day, and left instructions that of this sum £5000 was to be transferred at once to his account in London. He left several examples of his Keith Brown signature and agreed on a method of establishing his identity over the phone by reeling off the twelve numbers of his account in reverse order followed by yesterday's date. On this basis verbal instructions for transfers and withdrawals could be made without coming to Brugge again. He signed an indemnity form protecting the bank from any risks of using this method of communication, and agreed to write his account number in red ink under his signature on any written instruction to the bank again to prove authenticity.

By half past twelve he was finished, and joined Vlaminck outside. They ate a lunch of solid food accompanied by the inevitable chips at the Café des Arts on the main square before the Town Hall, and then Vlaminck drove him back to Brussels airport. Before parting from the Fleming, Shannon gave him £50 in cash and told him to take the Ostend-Dover ferry the next day and be at the London flat at six in the evening. He had to wait an hour for his plane and was back in London by tea-time.

Simon Endean had also had a busy day. He had caught the earliest flight of the day to Zürich and had landed at Kloten airport by just after ten. Within an hour he was standing at the counter of the Handelsbank of Zürich's head office at 58, Talstrasse, and opened a current account in his own name. He too left several specimen signatures, and agreed with the bank official who interviewed him on a method of signing all written communications to the bank simply by writing the account number at the bottom of the letter and under the number the day of the week on which the letter had been written. The day would be written in green ink, while the account number would inevitably be in black. He deposited the £500 in cash that he had brought and informed the bank the sum of £100,000 would be transferred into the account within the week. Lastly he instructed the Union Bank that as soon as the credit had been received, they were to remit £10,000 to an account in Belgium which he would give them later by letter. He signed a long contract which exonerated the bank from anything and everything including culpable negligence and left him no protection whatever in law. Not that there was any point in contesting a Swiss bank before a Swiss court, as he well knew.

Taking a taxi from Talstrasse he dropped a wax-sealed letter through the door of the Zwingli Bank and headed back to the airport.

The letter, which Dr Martin Steinhofer had in his hand within thirty minutes, was from Sir James Manson. It was signed in the approved manner by which Manson signed all his correspondence with his Zürich bank. It requested Dr Steinhofer to transfer £100,000 to the account of Mr Simon Endean at the Union Bank forthwith, and informed him that Sir James would be calling on him at his office the following day, Wednesday.

Endean was in London airport just before six.

Martin Thorpe was exhausted when he came into the office that Tuesday afternoon. He had spent the two days of the weekend and Monday going methodically through the 4500 cards in the Moodies index of companies quoted on the London Stock Exchange.

He had been concentrating on finding a suitable shell company, and had sought out the small companies, preferably founded many years ago, largely run-down and with few assets, companies which over the past three years had traded at a loss, or broken even, or made a profit below £10,000. He also wanted companies with a market capitalisation of under £200,000.

Martin Thorpe had come up with two dozen companies that fitted the bill, and these he showed to Sir James Manson. He had listed them provisionally in order from One to Twenty-Four on the basis of their apparent suitability.

He still had more to do, and by mid-afternoon he was at Companies House, in City Road, EC2.

He sent up to the archivists the list of his first eight companies and paid his statutory fee for each name on the list, giving him, as any other member of the public, the right to examine the full company documents. As he waited for the eight bulky folders to come back to the reading room, he glanced through the latest Stock Exchange Official List and noted with satisfaction that none of the eight was quoted at over three shillings a share.

When the files arrived he started with the first on his list and began to pore over the records. He was looking for three things not given in the

Moodies cards, which are simply a synopsis. He wanted to study the distribution of the ownership of the shares, to ensure that the company he sought was not controlled by the combined board of directors, and to be certain there had not been a recent build-up of shareholdings by another person or associated group, which would have indicated that another City predator was looking for a meal.

By the time Companies House closed for the evening, he had been through seven of the eight files. He would cover the remaining seventeen the following day. But already he was intrigued by the third on his list and mildly excited. On paper it looked great, from his point of view, even too good, and that was the rub. It looked so good, he was surprised no one had snapped it up ages ago. There had to be a flaw somewhere, but with Martin Thorpe's ingenuity there might even be a way of over-coming it. If there was such a way . . . it was perfect.

Simon Endean phoned Cat Shannon at the latter's flat at ten that evening. Shannon reported what he had done, and Endean gave a resumé of his own day. He told Shannon the necessary £100,000 should have been transferred to his new Swiss account before closing time that afternoon, and Shannon told Endean to have the first £10,000 sent to him under the name of Keith Brown at the Kredietbank in Brugge, Belgium.

Within a few minutes of hanging up, Endean had written his letter of instruction to the Handelsbank, stressing that the transferred sum should be sent at once but that under no condition was the name of the Swiss account holder to become known to the Belgian bank. The account number alone should be quoted on the transfer, which should be by telex. He mailed the letter express rate from the all-night post office in Trafalgar Square just before midnight.

At eleven-forty-five the phone rang again in Shannon's flat. It was Semmler on the line from Munich. Shannon told him he had work for all of them if they wanted it, but that he could not come to Munich. Semmler should take a single ticket by air to London the following day and be there by six. He gave his address and promised to repay the German his expenses in any case, and pay his fare back to Munich if he declined the job. Semmler agreed to come, and Shannon hung up.

The next on the line was Langarotti from Marseilles. He had checked his *poste restante* box and found Shannon's cable waiting for him. He would be in London by six and would report to the flat.

Janni Dupree's call was late, coming through at half past midnight. He too agreed to pack his bags and fly the 8000 miles to London, though he could not be there for a day and a half. He would be at Shannon's flat on the Friday evening instead.

With the last call taken, Shannon read for an hour and switched off the light. It was the end of Day One.

Sir James Manson did not fly economy class; he went first, and on the businessman's Trident Three to Zürich ate a hearty breakfast that Wednesday morning. Shortly before noon he was ushered respectfully into the panelled office of Dr Martin Steinhofer.

The two men had known each other for ten years and during this time the Zwingli Bank had several times carried out business on Manson's behalf in situations where he had needed a nominee to buy shares which, had it become known that the name of Manson was behind the purchase, would have trebled in value. Dr Steinhofer valued his client, and rose to shake hands and usher the English knight into a comfortable armchair.

The Swiss offered cigars, and coffee was brought, along with small glasses of Kirschwasser. Only when the male secretary had gone did Sir James broach his business.

'Over the forthcoming weeks I shall be seeking to acquire a controlling interest in a small British company, a public company. At the moment I cannot give the name of it, because a suitable vehicle for my particular operation has not yet come to light. I hope to know it fairly soon.'

Dr Steinhofer nodded silently and sipped his coffee.

'At the start it will be quite a small operation, involving relatively little money. Later, I have reason to believe news will hit the Stock Exchange that will have quite an interesting effect on the share value of that company,' he went on.

There was no need for him to explain to the Swiss banker the rules that apply in share dealings on the London Stock Exchange, for he was as familiar with them as Manson, as he was also with the rules of all the main exchanges and markets throughout the world.

Under British company law, any person acquiring ten per cent or more of the shares of a public quoted company must identify himself to the directors within fourteen days. The aim of the law is to permit the public to know who owns what, and how much, of any public company.

For this reason, a reputable London stockbroking house, buying on behalf of a client, will also abide by the law and inform the directors of their client's name, unless the purchase is less than ten per cent of the company's stock, in which case the buyer may remain anonymous.

One way round this rule is for a tycoon seeking to gain secret control of a company to use nominee buyers. But again, a reputable firm on the Stock Exchange will soon spot if the real buyer of the big block of shares is in fact one man operating through nominees, and will obey the law.

But a Swiss bank, not bound by the laws of Britain, abiding by its own laws of secrecy, simply refuses to answer questions about who stands behind the names they present as their clients, nor will they reveal anything else, even if they privately suspect that the front-men do not exist at all.

Both of the men in Dr Steinhofer's office that morning were well aware of all the finer points involved.

'In order to make the necessary acquisition of shares,' Sir James went on, 'I have entered into association with six partners. They will purchase the shares on my behalf. They have all agreed they would wish to open small accounts with the Zwingli Bank and to ask you to be so kind as to make the purchases on their behalf.'

Dr Steinhofer put down his coffee cup and nodded. As a good Swiss he agreed there was no point in breaking rules where they could be legally bent, with the obvious proviso that they were not Swiss rules, and he could also see the point in not wantonly sending the share price upwards, even in a small operation. One started by saving pfennigs, and one became rich after a lifetime of application.

'That presents no problem,' he said carefully. 'These gentlemen will be coming here to open their accounts?'

Sir James exhaled a stream of aromatic smoke.

'It may well be they will find themselves too busy to come personally. I have myself appointed my financial assistant to stand in for me. To save time and trouble, you understand. It may well be the other six partners will wish to avail themselves of the same procedure. You have no objection to that?'

'Of course not,' murmured Dr Steinhofer. 'Your financial assistant is who, please?'

'Mr Martin Thorpe.' Sir James Manson drew a slim envelope from his pocket and handed it to the banker.

'This is my power of attorney, duly notarised and witnessed, and signed by me. You have my signature for comparison of course. In it you will find Mr Thorpe's full name and the number of his passport, by which he will identify himself. He will be visiting Zürich in the next week or ten days to finalise arrangements. From then on he will act in all matters on my behalf and his signature will be as good as mine. Is that acceptable?'

Dr Steinhofer scanned the single sheet in the envelope and nodded.

'Certainly, Sir James. I see no problems.'

Manson rose and stubbed out his cigar.

'Then I'll bid you good-bye, Dr Steinhofer, and leave further dealings in the hands of Mr Thorpe, who of course will consult with me on all steps to be taken.'

They shook hands and Sir James Manson was ushered down to the street. As the solid oak door clicked quietly shut behind him he pulled up his coat collar against the still chilly air of the north Swiss town, stepped into the waiting hired limousine and gave instructions for the Baur au Lac for lunch. One ate well there, he reflected, but otherwise Zürich was a dreary place. It did not even have a good brothel.

Assistant Under-Secretary Sergei Golon was not in a good humour that morning. The mail had brought a letter to his breakfast table to notify him that his son had failed the entrance examination for the Civil Service Academy, and there had been a general family row. In consequence his perennial problem of acid indigestion had elected to ensure him a day of unrelenting misery and his secretary was away sick.

Beyond the windows of his small office in the West Africa section of the Foreign Ministry the canyons of Moscow's windswept boulevards were still covered with snow slush, a grimy grey in the dim morning light, waiting tiredly for the thaw of spring.

'Neither one thing nor the other,' the attendant had remarked as he had berthed his Moskvitch in the car park beneath the ministry building.

Golon had grunted agreement as he took the lift to his eighth floor to begin the morning's work. Devoid of a secretary, he had taken the pile of files brought for his attention from various parts of the building, and started to go through them, an antacid tablet revolving slowly in his mouth.

The third file had been marked for his attention by the office of the Under-Secretary, and the same clerkish hand had written on the cover-sheet 'Assess and Instigate Necessary Action'. Golon perused it gloomily. He noted that the file had been started on the basis of an inter-departmental memorandum from Foreign Intelligence, and that his Ministry had, on reflection, given Ambassador Dobrovolsky certain instructions which, according to the latest cable from Dobrovolsky, had been carried out. The request had been granted, the ambassador reported, and he urged prompt action.

Golon snorted. Passed over for an ambassadorship, he held firmly to the view that men in diplomatic posts abroad were far too prone to believe their own parishes were of consummate importance.

'As if we have nothing else to bother about,' he grunted. Already his eye had caught the folder beneath the one he was reading. He knew it concerned the Republic of Guinea, where a constant stream of telegrams from the Soviet ambassador reported the growth of Chinese influence in Conakry. Now that, he mused, was something of concern. Compared to this, he could not see the importance of whether there was, or was not, tin in commercial quantities in the hinterland of Zangaro. Besides, the Soviet Union had enough tin.

Nevertheless, action had been authorised from above, and as a good civil servant he took it. To a secretary borrowed from the typing pool he dictated a letter to the Director of the Sverdlovsk Institute of Mining requiring him to select a small team of survey geologists and engineers to carry out an examination of a suspected mineral deposit in West Africa, and to inform him in due course that the team and its equipment were ready to depart.

Privately he thought he would have to tackle the question of their transportation to West Africa through the appropriate directorate, but pushed the thought to the back of his mind. The painful burning in the back of his throat subsided, and he observed that the scribbling sten-ographer had rather pretty knees.

Cat Shannon had a quiet day. He rose late and went into the West End to his bank, where he withdrew most of the £1000 his account contained. He was confident the money would be replaced and more when the transfer came through from Belgium.

After lunch he rang his friend the writer, who seemed surprised to hear from him.

'I thought you'd left town,' said the scribe.

'Why should I?' asked Shannon.

'Well, little Julie has been looking for you. You must have made an impression. Carrie says she has not stopped talking. But she rang the Lowndes, and they said you had left, address unknown.'

Shannon promised he'd ring. He gave his own phone number, but not his address. With the small talk over, he requested the information he wanted.

'I suppose I could,' said the friend dubiously. 'But honestly, I ought to ring him first and see if it's OK.'

'Well, do that,' said Shannon. 'Tell him it's me, that I need to see him, and am prepared to go down there for a few hours with him. Tell him I wouldn't trouble him if it wasn't important in my opinion.'

The writer agreed to put through the call and ring Shannon back with the telephone number and address of the man Shannon wished to talk to, if the man agreed to speak to Shannon.

In the afternoon he wrote a letter to Mr Goossens at the Kredietbank to tell him that he would in the future give two or three business partners the Kredietbank as his mailing address, and would keep in contact by phone with the bank to check whether any mail was waiting for collection. He would also be sending some letters to business associates via the Kredietbank, in which case he would mail an envelope to Mr Goossens from wherever he happened to be. He requested Mr Goossens to take the enclosed envelope which would be inside, addressed but not stamped, and forward it from Brugge to its destination. Lastly he bade Mr Goossens deduct all postal and bank charges from his account.

At five p.m. Endean rang him at the flat and Shannon gave him a progress report, omitting to mention his contact with his writer friend, whom he had never mentioned to Endean. He told him however that he expected three of his four chosen associates to be in London for their separate briefings that evening, and the fourth to arrive on Friday evening at the latest.

Martin Thorpe had his fifth tiring day, but at least his search was over. He had perused the documents of another seventeen companies in the City Road, and had drawn up a second short list, this time of five companies. Top of the list was the company that had caught his eye the previous day. He finished his reading by the mid-afternoon and as Sir James Manson had not returned from Zürich, Thorpe decided to take the rest of the day off. He could brief his chief in the morning and later begin his private enquiries into the set-up of his chosen company, a series of enquiries to determine why such a prize was still available. By the late afternoon he was back in Hampstead Garden Suburb and mowing the lawn.

9

The first of the mercenaries to arrive at London's Heathrow airport was Kurt Semmler, on the Lufthansa flight from Munich. He tried to reach Shannon by phone soon after clearing customs, but there was no reply. He was early for his check-in call, so he decided to wait at the airport, took a seat in the restaurant window overlooking the apron of Number Two Building. He chain-smoked nervously as he sat over coffee and watched the jets leaving for Europe.

Marc Vlaminck phoned to check in with Shannon just after five. The Cat glanced down the list of three hotels in the neighbourhood of his apartment and read out the name of one. The Belgian took it down in his Victoria Station phone booth, letter by letter. A few minutes later he hailed a taxi outside the station and showed the paper to the driver.

Semmler was ten minutes after Vlaminck. He too received from Shannon the name of a hotel, wrote it down and took a mini-cab from the front of the airport building.

Langarotti was the last, checking in just before six from the Air Terminal in Cromwell Road. He too hired a taxi to take him to his hotel.

At seven Shannon rang them all, one after the other, and bade them assemble at his flat within thirty minutes.

When they greeted each other, it was the first indication any of them had that the others had been invited. The broad grins with which they learned the others were also present came partly from the pleasure of meeting friends, partly from the knowledge that Shannon's investment in bringing them all to London with a guarantee of a reimbursed air fare could only mean he had money. If they wondered who the patron might be, they knew better than to ask.

Their first impression was strengthened when Shannon told them that he had instructed Dupree to fly in from South Africa on the same terms. A £500 air ticket meant Shannon was not playing games. They settled down to listen.

'The job I've been given,' he told them, 'is a project that has to be organised from scratch. It has not been laid on, and the only way to set it up is to do it ourselves. The object is to mount an attack, a short, sharp attack, commando-style, on a town on the coast of Africa. We have to shoot the shits out of one building, storm it, capture it, knock off everyone in it, and pull back out again.'

The reaction was what he had confidently expected. The men exchanged glances of approval. Vlaminck gave a wide grin and scratched his chest; Semmler muttered '*Klasse*' and lit a fresh cigarette from the stub of the old one. He offered one to Shannon, who regretfully shook his head. Langarotti remained deadpan, his eyes on Shannon, the knife blade slipping smoothly across the black leather round his left fist.

Shannon spread a map out on the floor in the centre of the circle and the men eyed it keenly. It was a hand-drawn map, depicting a section of seashore and a series of buildings on the landward side. It was not even accurate, for it excluded the two curving spits of shingle that were the identifying marks of the harbour of Clarence. But it sufficed to indicate the kind of operation required.

The mercenary leader talked for twenty minutes, outlining the kind of attack he had already proposed to his patron as the only feasible way of taking the objective, and the three men concurred. None of them asked the name of the destination. They knew he would not tell them, and that they did not need to know. It was not a question of lack of trust, simply of security. If a leak was sprung in the secret, they did not want to be among the possible suspects.

Shannon spoke in French, his own strongly accented grasp of the language, which he had picked up in the Sixth Commando in the Congo. He knew Vlaminck had a reasonable grasp of English, as a barman in Ostend must have, and that Semmler commanded a vocabulary of about two hundred words. But Langarotti knew very little indeed, so French was the common language, except when Dupree was present, when everything had to be translated.

'So that's it,' said Shannon as he finished. 'The terms are that you all go on salary of 1250 dollars a month from tomorrow morning, plus expenses for living and travelling while in Europe. The budget is ample for the job. Only two of the tasks that have to be done in the preparation stages are illegal, because I've planned to keep the maximum of the preparations strictly legal. Of these tasks one is a border crossing from Belgium to France, the other a problem of loading some cases on to a ship somewhere in southern Europe. We'll all be involved in both jobs.

'You get three months' guaranteed salary, plus 5000 dollars each bonus for success. So what do you say?'

The three men looked at each other. Vlaminck nodded.

'I'm on,' he said. 'Like I said yesterday. It looks good.'

Langarotti stropped his knife.

'Is it against French interests?' he asked. 'I don't want to be an exile.'

'You have my word it is not against the French in Africa.'

'*D'accord*,' said the Corsican simply.

'Kurt?' asked Shannon.

'What about insurance?' asked the German. 'It doesn't matter for me, I have no relatives, but what about Marc?'

The Belgian nodded.

'Yes, I don't want to leave Anna with nothing,' he said.

Mercenaries on contract are usually insured by the contractor for 20,000 dollars for loss of life and 6000 for loss of a major limb.

'You have to take out your own, but it can be as high as you want to go. If anything happens to anyone, the rest swear blind he was lost overboard at sea by accident. If anyone gets badly hurt and survives we all swear the injury was caused by shifting machinery on board. You all take out insurance for a sea trip from Europe to South Africa as passengers on a small freighter. OK?'

The three men nodded.

'I'm on,' said Semmler.

They shook on it, and that was enough. Then Shannon went into the jobs he wanted each man to do.

'Kurt, you'll get your first salary cheque and £1000 expenses on Friday. I want you go go down to the Mediterranean and start looking for a boat. I need a small freighter with a clean record. Get that, it must be clean. Papers in order, ship for sale. One hundred to two hundred tons, coaster or converted trawler, possibly converted Navy vessel if needs be, but not looking like an MTB. I don't want speed, but reliability. The sort that can pick up a cargo in a Mediterranean port without exciting attention, even an arms cargo. Registered as a general freighter, owned by a small company or its own skipper. Price not over £25,000 including the cost of any work that needs any doing on it. Absolute latest sailing date, fully fuelled and victualled for a trip to Cape Town, not later than sixty days from now. Got it?'

Semmler nodded, and began to think at once of his contacts in the shipping world.

'Jean-Baptiste. Which city do you know best in the Mediterranean?'

'Marseilles,' said Langarotti without hesitation.

'OK. You get salary and £500 on Friday. Get to Marseilles, set up in a small hotel, and start looking. Find me three large inflatable semi-rigid craft of the same kind as Zodiac make. The sort developed for water sports from the basic design of the Marine Commando assault craft. Buy them at separate suppliers, then book them into the bonded warehouse of a respectable shipping agent for export to Morocco. Purpose – waterskiing and sub-aqua diving at a holiday resort. Colour black. Also three powerful outboard engines, battery-started. The boats should take up to a ton of payload. The engines should move such a craft and that weight at not less than ten knots, with a big reserve. You'll need about 60 horsepower. Very important – make sure they are fitted with underwater exhausts for silent running. If they can't be got in that condition, get a mechanic to make you three exhaust-pipe extensions with the necessary outlet valves, to fit the engines. Store them at the same export agent's bonded warehouse, for the same purpose as the dinghies. Water-sports in

Morocco. You won't have enough money in the £500. Open a bank account and send me the name and number, by mail, to this address. I'll send the money by credit transfer. Buy everything separately, and submit me the price lists, by mail, here. OK?'

Langarotti nodded and resumed his knife-stropping.

'Marc. You remember you mentioned once that you knew a man in Belgium had knocked off a German store of a thousand brand-new Schmeisser submachine pistols in 1945 and still had half of them in store? I want you to go back to Ostend on Friday with your salary and £500 and locate that man. See if he'll sell. I want a hundred, and in first-class working order. I'll pay 100 dollars each, which is way over the rate. Contact me by letter only here at this flat, when you have found the man and can set up a meeting between him and me. Got it?'

By nine-thirty they were through, the instructions memorised, noted and understood.

'Right, what about a spot of dinner?' Shannon asked his colleagues. The suggestion was met with noisy agreement, for the men had had little but airline lunches and snacks, and all were hungry. Shannon took them round the corner to the Paprika for a meal. They still spoke in French, but no one else took much notice, except to glance over when a loud burst of laughter came from the group of four. Evidently they were excited at something, though none of the diners could have surmised that what elated the group in the corner was the prospect of going once again to war under the leadership of Cat Shannon.

Across the Channel another man was thinking hard about Carlo Alfred Thomas Shannon, and his thoughts were not charitable. He paced the sitting room of his apartment in one of the residential boulevards near the Place de la Bastille, and considered the information he had been gathering for the previous week, and the snippet from Marseilles that had reached him several hours earlier.

If the writer who had originally recommended Charles Roux to Simon Endean as a second possible mercenary for Endean's project had known more about the Frenchman, his description would not have been so complimentary. But he knew only the basic facts of the man's background, and little about his character. Nor did he know, and thus was unable to tell Endean, of the vitriolic hatred that Roux bore for the other man he had recommended, Cat Shannon.

After Endean had left Roux, the Frenchman had waited a full fortnight for a second contact to be made. When it never came, he was forced to the conclusion either that the project in the mind of the visitor who had called himself Walter Harris had been abandoned or that someone else had got the job.

Pursuing the latter line of enquiry, he had looked for any one among the other possible selections that the English businessman could have made. It was while he was making these enquiries, or having them made for him, that he had learned Cat Shannon had been in Paris, staying under his own name at a small hotel in Montmartre. This had shaken him, for he had lost trace of Shannon after their parting at Le Bourget airport, and had thought the man had left Paris.

At this point, over a week earlier, he had briefed one of the men he knew to be loyal to him to make intensive enquiries about Shannon. The man was called Henri Alain, and was a former mercenary.

Alain had reported back within twenty-four hours that Shannon had left his Montmartre hotel and not reappeared. He had also been able to tell Roux two other things: that Shannon's disappearance had taken place the morning after Roux had received the London businessman in his own apartment, and secondly that Shannon had also received a visitor the same afternoon. The hotel clerk, with a little currency persuasion, had been able to describe Shannon's visitor, and privately Roux had no doubt the visitor in Montmartre had been the same man who came to him.

So Mr Harris from London had seen two mercenaries in Paris although he needed only one. As a result Shannon had disappeared while he, Roux, had been left on the shelf. That it was Shannon of all people who seemed to have got the contract made his rage even worse, for there was no one the man in the flat in the 11th arrondissement hated more.

He had had Henri Alain stake out the hotel for four days, but Shannon had not come back. Then he tried another tack. He recalled that newspaper reports had linked Shannon with the Corsican Langarotti in the fighting in the last days of the enclave. Presumably if Shannon was back in circulation, so was Langarotti. So he had sent Henri Alain to Marseilles to find the Corsican and discover where Shannon might be. Alain had just arrived back, bearing the news that Langarotti had left Marseilles that same afternoon. Destination, London.

Roux turned to his informant. '*Bon*, Henri. That's all. I'll contact you when I need you. Meantime, the clerk in the Montmartre place will let you know if Shannon returns?'

'Sure,' said Alain as he rose to go.

'Then ring me immediately if you hear.'

When Alain had gone, Roux thought things over. For him the disappearance of Langarotti to London of all places meant the Corsican had gone to join Shannon there. That in turn meant Shannon was recruiting, and that could only mean he had got the contract. Roux had no doubt it was Walter Harris's contract, one he felt he personally should have had. It was an impertinence, compounded by the recruiting of a Frenchman and on French territory, which Roux regarded as being his own exclusive preserve.

There was another reason why he wanted the Harris contract. He had not worked since the Bukavu affair, and his ability to keep his hold over the French mercenary community was likely to slip unless he could produce some form of work for them. If Shannon were unable to continue, if for instance he were to disappear permanently, Mr Harris would presumably have to come back to Roux, and engage him as he should have done in the first place.

Without further delay he made a local Paris phone call.

Back in London the dinner was nearing its end. The men had drunk a lot of carafe wine, for like most mercenaries they preferred it the rougher the better. Tiny Marc raised his glass and proposed the often-heard toast of the Congo.

'Vive la Mort, vive la guerre,
Vive le sacré mercenaire.'

Sitting back in his chair, clear-headed while the rest got drunk, Cat Shannon wondered idly how much havoc would be wreaked when he let slip this group of dogs on Kimba's palace. Silently he raised his own glass and drank to the dogs of war.

Charles Roux was forty-eight and several parts mad, although the two facts were quite unconnected. He could never have been certified insane, but most psychiatrists would at least have held him to be mentally unstable. The basis for such a diagnosis would have been the presence of a fair degree of megalomania, but this is present in many people outside lunatic asylums and is usually more kindly interpreted, at least when present in the rich and famous, as merely exaggerated egocentricity.

The same psychiatrists would probably have detected a tinge of paranoia and a severe examiner might have gone so far as to suggest there was a streak of the psychopath in the French mercenary. But as Roux had never been examined by a skilled psychiatrist and as his instability was usually well camouflaged beneath an exterior of some intelligence and considerable cunning, these questions were never raised.

The only exterior clues to his make-up lay in his capacity to impute a status and importance to himself that was wholly illusory, a quality for self-pity that insisted he had never once been at fault but that all others who disagreed with him were wholly in the wrong, and the capacity for vicious hatreds towards those he felt had wronged him.

Often the victims of his hatreds had done little or nothing beyond frustrating Roux, but in Shannon's case there were at least grounds for the dislike.

Roux had been a top sergeant in the French Army until his late thirties when he was dismissed after an affair involving certain missing funds.

In 1961, at a loose end, he had paid his own fare to Katanga and proposed himself as a well-qualified adviser to the secessionist movement of the then Katangese leader, Moise Tshombe. That year was the height of the struggle to tear the mineral-rich province of Katanga out of the union with the sprawling, anarchic and newly independent Congo. Several of the men who later became mercenary chieftains began their freelance careers in the imbroglio in Katanga. Hoare, Denard, and Schramme were among them. Despite his claims to greater things, Roux was permitted only a small role in the Katangese events, and when the mighty United Nations finally managed to vanquish the small bands of freebooting pistoleros, which had to be done politically since it could not be done militarily, Roux was among those who got out.

That was in 1962. Two years later, with the Congo falling like a set of skittles to the Communist-backed Simbas, Tshombe was recalled from exile to take over not Katanga but the whole Congo. He in turn sent for Hoare, and Roux was among those who flew back to enter service under Hoare. As a Frenchman, his natural unit would have been the French-speaking Sixth Commando, but as he had been in South Africa at the time, it was to the Fifth that he went. Here he was put in charge of a company, and one of his section commanders six months later was a young Anglo-Irishman called Shannon.

Roux's break with Hoare came three months later. Already becoming convinced of his own superiority as a military commander, Roux was entrusted with the job of knocking out a Simba road-block. He devised his own plan of attack and it was a total disaster. Four white mercenaries were killed and over a score of his Katangese levies. Part of the reason was the plan of attack, part the fact that Roux had been blind drunk. Behind the drunkenness was the secret certainty that, for all his bombast, Roux did not like combat.

Colonel Hoare called for a report from Roux and got it. Parts of it did not tally with the known facts. Hoare sent for the only surviving section commander, Carlo Shannon, and questioned him closely. From what emerged, he sent for Roux and dismissed him on the spot.

Roux went north and joined the Sixth Commando under Denard at Paulis, explaining his defection from the Fifth as being due to racial dislike of a superb French commander by the inferior British, a reason Denard found little difficulty in believing. He posted Roux as second-in-command of a smaller commando, nominally dependent on the Sixth but in fact almost independent. This was the Fourteenth Commando at Watsa, ruled by Commandant Tavernier.

By 1966 Hoare had retired and gone home, and Tavernier had left. The Fourteenth was commanded by Commandant Wautier, like Tavernier a Belgian. Roux was still second-in-command and hated Wautier. Not that the Belgian had done anything; the reason for the loathing was that Roux had expected the command after Tavernier's departure. He had not got it. So he hated Wautier.

The Fourteenth, heavily staffed by Katangese levies, was the spearpoint of the 1966 mutiny against the Congolese government. It had been planned, and well so, by Wautier, and would probably have succeeded. Black Jack Schramme was holding his own predominantly Katangese Tenth Commando in check only to see how things went. Had Wautier led the revolt, it might well have succeeded; Black Jack would probably have brought his Tenth into the affair had it been successful, and the Congolese government might well have fallen. To launch the revolt, Wautier had brought his Fourteenth to Stanleyville, where on the left bank of the Congo river the vast arsenal stood, containing enough munitions to enable anyone holding it to rule the central and eastern Congo for years.

Two hours before the attack, Commandant Wautier was shot dead. His death was never fully proved, but in fact it was Roux who murdered him with a shot in the back of the head. A wiser man might have called off the attack. Roux insisted on taking command, and the mutiny was a disaster. His forces never got across the river to the left bank, the Congolese Army rallied on learning the armoury was still theirs, and Roux's unit was wiped out to the last man. Schramme thanked his stars he had kept his own men out of the fiasco. On the run and terrified, Roux sought refuge with John Peters, new commander of the English-speaking Fifth, who were also not involved. Peters smuggled the desperate Roux out of the country, swathed in bandages and masquerading as an Englishman.

The only plane out was heading for South Africa, and that was where Roux went. Ten months later, Roux flew back into the Congo, this time accompanied by five South Africans. He had heard wind of the coming July 1967 revolt, and came to join Schramme at the headquarters of the Tenth Commando near Kindu. He was in Stanleyville again when mutiny broke out, this time with Schramme and Denard participating. Within hours Denard was out of action, hit in the head by a ricochet bullet loosed off in error by one of his own men. At a crucial point the leader of the joint forces of the Sixth and Tenth was out of the fight. Roux, claiming that as a Frenchman he should take precedence over the Belgian Schramme, maintaining he was the best commander present and the only one who could command the mercenaries, put himself forward for overall command.

The choice fell on Schramme, not because he was the best man to command the whites, but because he was the only man who could command the Katangese, and without these levies the small band of Europeans would have been too badly outnumbered.

Roux's claim failed on two fronts. The Katangese loathed and distrusted him, remembering the unit of their own people he had led to annihilation the previous year. And at the mercenaries' council, held the night Denard was flown out on a stretcher to Rhodesia, one of those who spoke against Roux's nomination was one of Denard's company commanders, Shannon, who had left the Fifth eighteen months earlier and joined the Sixth rather than serve under Peters.

A second time the mercenaries failed to take the arsenal, and Schramme opted for the long march from Stanleyville to Bukavu, a resort town on Lake Bukavu, abutting the neighbouring republic of Rwanda and offering some form of retreat if things went wrong.

By this time Roux was gunning for Shannon, and to keep them apart Schramme gave Shannon's company the hazardous job of point unit, breaking trail up front as the column of mercenaries, Katangese and thousands of camp followers fought their way through the Congolese towards the lake. Roux was given a job at the rear of the convoy, so the two never met.

They finally met in Bukavu town after the mercenaries had settled in, and the Congolese had surrounded them on all sides except the lake behind the town. It was September 1967 and Roux was drunk. Over a game of cards he lost through lack of concentration he accused Shannon of cheating. Shannon replied that Roux made a big mess of his poker as he had of attacks on Simba road-blocks and for the same reason – he had no nerve. There was dead silence among the group round the table, as the other mercenaries edged back towards the walls. But Roux backed down. Glaring at Shannon he let the younger man get up and walk towards the door. Only when the Irishman had his back turned did Roux reach for the Colt .45 they all carried and take aim.

Shannon reacted first. He turned, pulled his own automatic and fired down the length of the long hall. The slug was a lucky one for a shot from the hip on a half-turn. It took Roux high in the right arm, tore a hole through the biceps and left his arm hanging limp from his side, the fingers dripping blood on to the useless Colt on the floor by his side.

'There's one other thing I remember,' Shannon called down the room. 'I remember what happened to Wautier.'

Roux was finished after the shoot-out. He evacuated himself across the bridge into Rwanda, had himself driven to Kigali, the capital, and flew back to France. Thus he missed the fall of Bukavu when finally the ammunition ran out in November, and the five months in an internment camp in Kigali. He also missed a chance to settle scores with Shannon.

Being the first back into Paris from Bukavu, Roux had given several interviews in which he spoke glowingly of himself, his battle wound and his desire to get back and lead his men. The fiasco at Dilolo when a recuperated Denard tried a badly planned invasion of the Congo from Angola in the south, as a diversion to take the strain off his men in Bukavu, and the virtual retirement of the former leader of the Sixth, gave Roux the impression he had every right to claim leadership over the French mercenaries. He had made quite a lot of money from looting in the Congo, and had salted it away.

With the money, he was able to make a splash among the barflies and street-corner bums who like to style themselves mercenaries, and from them he still retained a certain degree of loyalty, but of the bought kind.

Henri Alain was one such, and so was Roux's next visitor, who came in answer to his telephoned summons. He was another mercenary, but of a different type.

Raymond Thomard was a killer by instinct and profession. He too had been in the Congo once, when on the run from the police, and Roux had used him as a hatchet man. For a few small handouts and in the mistaken view that Roux was a bigshot, Thomard was as loyal as a paid man can ever be.

'I've got a job for you,' Roux told him. 'A contract worth five thousand dollars. Are you interested?'

Thomard grinned.

'Sure, Patron. Who's the bugger you want knocked off?'

'Cat Shannon.'

Thomard's face dropped. Roux went on before he could reply.

'I know he's good. But you're better. Besides, he knows nothing. You'll be given his address when he checks into Paris next time. You just have to wait till he leaves, then take him at your own convenience. Does he know you by sight?'

Thomard shook his head.

'We never met,' he said.

'Then you've got nothing to worry about. Stay in touch, I'll let you know when and where you'll find him.'

10

Simon Endean's letter sent on the Tuesday night arrived at ten on Thursday morning at the Handelsbank in Zürich. According to the instructions in it, they telexed £10,000 to the account of Mr Keith Brown at the Kredietbank in Brugge.

By noon Mr Goossens had seen the telex, and wired £5000 to Mr Brown's account in the West End of London. Shortly before four that afternoon, Shannon made a check call to his bank and learned the credit was there waiting for him. He asked the manager personally to give him drawing facilities in cash up to £3500 the following morning. He was told it would be available for collection by eleven-thirty.

Shortly after nine the same morning Martin Thorpe presented himself in Sir James Manson's office with the file containing his findings since the previous Saturday.

The two men went over the short list together, studying the pages of photostat documents acquired at Companies House on Tuesday and Wednesday. When they finished, Manson sat back in his chair and gazed at the ceiling.

'There's no doubt you are right about Bormac, Martin,' he said, 'but why the hell hasn't the major stockholder been bought out long ago?'

It was the question Martin Thorpe had been asking himself all the previous night and day.

The Bormac Trading Company Limited had been founded in 1904 to exploit the output of a series of vast rubber plantations that had been created during the last years of the previous century on the basis of slave labour by Chinese coolies.

The founder of the estates had been an enterprising and ruthless Scot by the name of Ian Macallister, later created Sir Ian Macallister in 1921, and the estates were situated in Borneo, hence the name of the company.

More of a builder than a businessman, Macallister had agreed in 1903 to enter into partnership with a group of London businessmen and the following year Bormac was created and floated with an issue of half a million ordinary shares. Macallister, who had married a 17-year-old girl the previous year, received 150,000 shares, a place on the Board, and managership during his lifetime of the rubber estates.

Ten years after the company's founding, the London businessmen had clinched a series of lucrative contracts with companies supplying the British war effort with rubber, and the share price had climbed from its issue price of four shillings to over £2. The war profiteers' boom lasted until 1918. There was a slump for the company just after the First World War, until the motor-car craze of the twenties boosted the need for rubber tyres, and again shares rose. This time there was a one-for-one new issue, raising the total amount of the company's shares on the market to a million and Sir Ian's block to 300,000. There had been no more share issues after that.

The slump of the Depression sent prices and shares down again, and they were recovering by 1937. In that year one of the Chinese coolies finally ran amok and performed an unpleasantness on the sleeping Sir Ian with a heavy-bladed parang. Ironically he died of blood poisoning. The under-manager took over, but lacked the drive of his dead master, and production fell as prices rose. The Second World War could have been a boon to the company, but the Japanese invasion of 1941 disrupted supplies.

The death knell of the company was finally sounded by the Indonesian nationalist movement which wrested control of the Dutch Indies and Borneo from Holland in 1948. When the border between Indonesian Borneo and British North Borneo was finally drawn, the estates were on the Indonesian side, and were promptly nationalised without compensation.

For over twenty years the company had staggered on, its assets unrecoverable, fruitless lawsuits with President Soekarno's régime eating away at the cash, the prices falling. By the time Martin Thorpe went over the company's books, the shares stood at a shilling each, and their highest price over the previous year had been one shilling and threepence.

The Board was composed of five directors, and the company rules stipulated that two of them made a quorum for the purpose of passing a resolution. The company office's address was given and turned out to be the premises of an old-established firm of City solicitors, one of whose partners acted as company secretary and was also on the Board. The original offices had long since been given up due to rising costs. Board meetings were rare, and usually consisted of the chairman, an elderly man living in Sussex, who was the younger brother of Sir Ian's former under-manager. He had died in Japanese hands during the war, and his shares had passed to the younger brother. Sitting with the chairman was the company secretary, the City solicitor, and occasionally one of the other three, who all lived a long way from London. There was seldom any business to discuss, and the company income consisted mainly of the occasional belated compensation payments now being made by the Indonesian government under General Suharto.

The combined five directors controlled no more than eighteen per cent of the million shares, and fifty-two per cent were distributed between six and a half thousand shareholders scattered across the country. There seemed to be a fair proportion of married women and widows. No doubt portfolios of long-forgotten shares sat in deed boxes in banks and solicitors' offices up and down the land, and had done for years.

But that was not what interested Thorpe and Manson. If they had tried to acquire a controlling interest by buying through the market, it would firstly have taken years and secondly have become quickly plain to other City watchers that someone was at work on Bormac. Their interest was held by the one single block of 300,000 shares held by the widowed Lady Macallister.

The puzzle was why no one had not long since bought the entire block from her and taken over the shell of the once-flourishing rubber company. In every other sense it was ideal for the purpose, for its memorandum of association was widely drawn, permitting the company to operate in any field of exploitation of any country's natural assets outside the United Kingdom.

'She must be eighty-five if she's a day,' said Thorpe at last. 'Lives in a vast dreary old block of flats in Kensington, guarded by a long-serving lady companion, or whatever they are called.'

'She must have been approached,' mused Sir James, 'so why does she cling to them?'

'Perhaps she just doesn't want to sell,' said Thorpe, 'or didn't like the people who came to ask her to let them buy. Old people can be funny.'

It is not simply old people who are illogical about buying and selling stocks and shares. Most stockbrokers have long since had the experience of seeing a client refuse to do business when proposed a sensible advantageous offer, solely and simply for the reason that they did not like the stockbroker.

Sir James Manson shot forward in his chair and planted his elbows on the desk.

'Martin, find out about that old woman. Find out who she is, what she thinks, what she likes and hates, what are her tastes, and, above all, find out where her weak spot is. She has to have one, some little thing that would be too big a temptation for her, and for which she would sell her holding. It may not be money, probably isn't, for she's been offered money before now. But there has to be something. Find it.'

Thorpe rose to go. Manson waved him back to his chair. From his desk drawer he drew six printed forms, all identical and all application forms for a numbered account at the Zwingli Bank in Zürich.

He explained briefly and concisely what he wanted done, and Thorpe nodded.

'Book yourself on the morning flight, and you can be back tomorrow night,' said Manson as his aide left.

Simon Endean rang Shannon at his flat just after two, and was given an up-to-date report on the arrangements the mercenary was making. Manson's assistant was pleased by the precision of Shannon's reporting, and he noted the details on a scratch pad, so that he could later make up his own report for Sir James.

When he had finished, Shannon put forward his next requirements.

'I want £5000 telexed direct from your Swiss bank to my credit as Keith Brown at the head office of the Banque de Luxembourg in Luxembourg by next Monday noon,' he told Endean, 'and another £5000 telexed direct to my credit at the head office of the Landesbank in Hamburg by Wednesday morning.'

He explained tersely how the bulk of the £5000 he had imported to London was already spoken for, and the other £5000 was needed as a reserve in Brugge. The two identical sums required in Luxembourg and Hamburg were mainly so that he could show his contacts there a certified cheque to prove his credit before entering into purchasing negotiations. Later most of the money would be remitted to Brugge, and the balance fully accounted for.

'In any case, I can write you out a complete accounting of money spent to date or committed for spending,' he told Endean, 'but I have to have your mailing address.'

Endean gave him the name of a professional accommodation address where he had opened a box that morning in the name of Walter Harris, and promised to get the instructions off to Zürich within the hour to have both sums of £5000 awaiting collection by Keith Brown in Luxembourg and Hamburg.

Big Janni Dupree checked in from London airport at five. His had been the longest journey; from Cape Town to Johannesburg the previous day, an overnight stop at the Holiday Inn and then the long SAA flight through Luanda in Portuguese Angola and the Isla do Sol stopover which avoided overflying the territory of any black African country. Shannon ordered him to take a taxi straight to the flat.

While he was on his way, Shannon called up the other three mercenaries from their hotels and had them come round to his place.

At six there was a second reunion when they all greeted the South African and listened in silence as Shannon gave Dupree the same briefing they had received the night before. When he heard the terms Janni's face cracked into a grin.

'We going to go fighting again, Cat? Count me in.'

'Good man. So here's what I want from you. Stay here in London, find yourself a small bedsitter flat. I'll help you do that tomorrow. We'll go through the *Evening Standard* and get you fixed up by nightfall.

'I want you to buy all our clothing. We need fifty sets of tee-shirts, fifty sets of underpants, fifty pairs of light nylon socks. Then a spare set for each man, making a hundred. I'll give you the list later. After that, fifty sets of combat trousers, preferably in jungle camouflage and preferably matching the jackets. Next, fifty combat blouses, zip-fronted and in the same jungle camouflage.

'You can get all these quite openly at camping shops, sports shops and army surplus stores. Even the hippies are beginning to wear combat jackets about town, and so do people who go shooting in the country.

'You can get all the vests, socks and underpants at the same stockist, but get the trousers and blouses at different ones. Then fifty green berets, and fifty pairs of boots. Get the trousers on the large size, we can shorten them later; get the blouses half in large size, half in medium. Get the boots from a camping shop. I don't want heavy British Army boots, I want the green canvas jackboots with front-lacing and water-proofed.

'Now for the webbing. I need fifty webbing belts, ammo pouches, knapsacks and campers' haversacks, the ones with the light tubular frame to support them. These will carry the bazooka rockets with a bit of reshaping. Lastly, fifty light nylon sleeping bags. OK? I'll give you the full written list later.'

Dupree nodded.

'OK. How much will that lot cost?'

'About a thousand pounds. This is how you buy it. Take the Yellow Pages telephone directory and under Surplus Stores you'll find over a dozen shops and stockists. Get the jackets, blouses, belts, berets, webbing harnesses, knapsacks, haversacks and boots at different shops, placing one order at each. Pay cash and take the purchase away with you. Don't give your real name – not that anyone should ask for it – and don't leave a real address.

'When you have bought the stuff, store it in a normal storage ware-house, have it crated for export, and contact four separate freight agents accustomed to handling export shipments. Pay them to send it in four separate consignments in bond to a shipping freight agent in Marseilles for collection by Mr Jean-Baptiste Langarotti.'

'Which agent in Marseilles?' asked Dupree.

'We don't know yet,' said Shannon. He turned to the Corsican.

'Jean, when you have the name of the shipping agent you intend to use for the export of the boats and engines, send the full name and address by mail to London, one copy to me here at the flat, and a second copy to Jan Dupree, Poste Restante, Trafalgar Square Post Office, London. Got it?'

Langarotti noted the address while Shannon translated the instructions for Dupree.

'Janni, go down there in the next few days and get yourself *poste restante* facilities. Then check in every week or so until Jean's letter arrives. Then instruct the freight agents to send the crates to the Marseilles agent in a bonded shipment for export by sea from Marseilles onwards, in the ownership of Langarotti. Now for the question of money. I just heard the credit came through from Brussels.'

The three Europeans produced slips of paper from their pockets while Shannon took Dupree's airline ticket stub. From his desk Shannon took four letters, each of them from him to Mr Goossens at the Kredietbank. Each letter was roughly the same. It required the Kredietbank to transmit a sum of money in US dollars from Mr Keith Brown's account to another account for the credit of Mr X.

In the gaps Shannon filled in the sum equivalent to the return air fare to and from London, starting at Ostend, Marseilles, Munich and Cape

Town. The letters also bade Mr Goossens transmit 1250 dollars to each of the named men in the named banks on the day of receipt of the letter, and again on the 5th of May and again on the 5th of June. Each mercenary dictated to Shannon the name of his bank, usually in Switzerland, and Shannon typed in the gaps.

When he had finished, each man read his own letter, and Shannon signed them at his desk, sealed them in separate envelopes, and gave each man his own envelope for posting.

Lastly he gave them each £50 in cash to cover their 48-hour stay in London, and told them to meet him outside the door of his London bank at eleven the following morning.

When they had gone he sat down and wrote a long letter to a man in Africa. He rang the writer who, having checked by phone that it was in order to do so, gave him the African's mailing address. That evening Shannon mailed his letter, express rate, and dined alone.

Martin Thorpe got his interview with Dr Steinhofer at the Zwingli Bank just before lunch. Being previously announced by Sir James Manson, Thorpe received the same red carpet treatment. He presented the banker with six application forms for numbered accounts. Each had been filled out in the required manner and signed. Separate cards carried the required two specimen signatures of the men seeking to open the accounts. They were in the names of Messrs Adams, Ball, Carter, Davies, Edwards and Frost.

Attached to each form were two other letters. One was signed power of attorney, in which Messrs Adams, Ball, Carter, Davies, Edwards and Frost separately gave power of attorney to Mr Martin Thorpe to operate the accounts in their names. The other was a letter signed by Sir James Manson requesting Dr Steinhofer to transfer to the account of each of his associates the sum of £50,000 from Sir James's account.

Dr Steinhofer was neither as gullible nor as new to the business of banking as not to suspect that the fact the names of the six 'business associates' all began with the first six letters of the alphabet was a remarkable coincidence. But he was quite able to believe that the possible non-existence of the six nominees was not his business. If a wealthy British businessman chose to get round the tiresome rules of his own Companies Act, that was his own business. Besides, Dr Steinhofer knew certain things about quite a number of City businessmen that would have created enough Department of Trade enquiries to keep that London ministry occupied for the rest of the century.

There was another good reason why he should stretch out his hand and take the application forms from Thorpe. If the shares of the company Sir James was going to try and buy secretly shot up from their present level to astronomic heights – and Dr Steinhofer could see no other reason for the operation – there was nothing to prevent the Swiss banker from buying a few of those shares for himself.

'The company we have our eye on is called Bormac Trading Company,' Thorpe told him quietly. He outlined the position of the company, and the fact that old Lady Macallister held 300,000 shares, or thirty per cent of the company.

'We have reason to believe attempts may already have been made to persuade this old lady to sell her holding,' he went on. 'They appear to have been unsuccessful. We are going to have another try. Even should we fail, we will still go ahead and choose another shell company.'

Dr Steinhofer listened quietly as he smoked his cigar.

'As you know, Dr Steinhofer, it would not be possible for one purchaser to buy these shares without declaring his identity. Therefore the four buyers will be Mr Adams, Mr Ball, Mr Carter and Mr Davies, who will each acquire seven and a half per cent of the company. We would wish you to act on behalf of all four of them.'

Dr Steinhofer nodded. It was standard practice.

'Of course, Mr Thorpe.'

'I shall attempt to persuade the old lady to sign the share transfer certificates with the name of the buyer left out. This is simply because some people in England, especially old ladies, find Swiss banks rather, how shall I say? – secretive organisations.'

'I am sure you mean sinister,' said Dr Steinhofer smoothly. 'I completely understand. Let us leave it like this then. When you have had an interview with this lady, we will see how best it can be arranged. But tell Sir James to have no fear. The purchase will be by four separate buyers, and the rules of the Companies Act will not be affronted.'

As Sir James Manson had predicted, Thorpe was back in London by nightfall to begin his weekend.

The four mercenaries were waiting on the pavement when Shannon came out of his bank just before twelve. He had in his hand four brown envelopes.

'Marc, here's yours. There's £500 in it. Since you'll be living at home, your expenses will be the smallest. So within that £500 you have to buy a van and rent a lock-up garage. There are other items to be bought. You'll find the list inside the envelope. Trace the man who has the Schmeissers for sale and set up a meeting between me and him. I'll be in touch with you by phone at your bar in about ten days.'

The giant Belgian nodded and hailed a taxi at the kerbside to take him to Victoria Station and the boat train back to the Ostend ferry.

'Kurt, this is your envelope. There's £1000 inside it, because you'll have to do much more travelling. Find that ship, and inside forty days. Keep in touch by phone and cable, but be very discreet and brief when using either. You can be frank in writing letters to my flat. If my mail is on intercept we're finished anyway.

'Jean-Baptiste, here's £500 for you. It has to keep you for forty days. Stay out of trouble and avoid your old haunts. Find the boats and engines and let me know by letter. Open a bank account and tell me where it is. When I approve the type and price of the stuff, I'll transmit you the money. And don't forget the shipping agent. Keep it nice and legal all down the line.'

The Frenchman and the German took their money and instructions and looked for a second taxi to get them to London airport, Semmler bound for Naples and Langarotti for Marseilles.

Shannon took Dupree's arm and they strolled down Piccadilly together. Shannon passed Dupree his envelope.

'I've put £1500 in there for you, Janni. The £1000 should cover all the purchases and the storage, crating and shipping costs to Marseilles, with something to spare. The £500 should keep you easily for the next month to six weeks. I want you to get straight into the buying first thing Monday morning. Make your list of shops and warehouses with the Yellow Pages and a map over the weekend. You have to finish the buying in thirty days, because I want the stuff in Marseilles in forty-five.'

He stopped and bought an evening paper, opened it at the 'Properties to Let' page and showed Dupree the columns of adverts for flats and flatlets for rent, funished and unfurnished.

'Find yourself a small flat by tonight and let me know the address tomorrow.'

They parted just short of Hyde Park Corner.

Shannon spent the evening writing out a complete statement of accounts for Endean. He pointed out that the total had eaten up the bulk of the £5000 transferred from Brugge, and that he would leave the few hundreds left over from that sum in the London account as a reserve.

Lastly, he pointed out that he had not taken any part of his own £10,000 fee for the job, and proposed either that Endean transfer it straight from Endean's Swiss account into Shannon's Swiss account, or remit the money to the Belgian bank for credit to Keith Brown.

He mailed his letter that Friday evening.

The weekend was free, so he called Julie Manson and suggested taking her out to dinner. She had been about to set off for a weekend at her parents' country house, but rang up and told them she was not coming. As it was late by the time she was ready, she came to collect Shannon, looking pert and spoilt at the wheel of her pillar-box red MGB.

'Have you booked anywhere?' she asked.

'Yes. Why?'

'Let's go and eat at one of my places,' she suggested. 'Then I can introduce you to some of my friends.'

Shannon shook his head.

'Forget it,' he said. 'That's happened to me before. I am not spending the whole evening being stared at like a zoo animal and asked damn-fool questions about killing people. It's sick.'

She pouted.

'Please, Cat darling.'

'Nope.'

'Look, I won't say what you are and what you do. I'll just keep it a secret. Come on. No one will know you by your face.'

Shannon weakened.

'One condition,' he said. 'My name is Keith Brown. Got it? Keith

Brown. That's all. Nothing else do you say about me or where I come from. Nor about what I do. Understood?'

She giggled.

'Great, 'she said. 'Great idea. Mystery Man himself. Come on then, Mr Keith Brown.'

She took him to Tramps where she was evidently well known. Johnny Gold rose from his doorside table as they entered and greeted her effusively with a kiss on both cheeks. He shook hands with Shannon as she introduced him.

'Nice to see you, Keith. Have a good time.'

They dined at the long row of tables running parallel to the bar, and started by ordering the house lobster cocktail from a hollowed-out pine-apple. Seated facing the room, Shannon glanced round at the diners; most, from their long hair and casual dress, could be placed in show business or on its fringes. Others were evidently young generation businessmen trying to be trendy or make a model girl or small actress. Among the latter he spotted someone he knew, seated, across the room with a group, out of vision by Julie.

After the lobster Shannon ordered 'bangers and mash', and excusing himself got up. He strolled slowly out of the door and into the centre lobby as if on his way to the men's room. Within seconds a hand fell on his shoulder and he turned to face Simon Endean.

'Are you out of your mind?' grated the City hard boy.

Shannon looked at him in mock surprise, a wide-eyed innocent.

'No. I don't think so. Why?' he asked.

Endean was about to tell him, but checked himself in time. His face was white with anger. He knew his boss well enough to know how Manson doted on his supposedly innocent little girl, and knew roughly what his reaction would be should he ever hear about Shannon taking her out, let alone climbing into bed with her.

But he was check-mated. He assumed Shannon was still unaware of his own real name, and certainly of Manson's existence. To bawl him out for going dining with a girl called Julie Manson would 'blow' both his own concern, and Manson's name, together with both their roles as Shannon's employer. Nor could he tell Shannon to leave her alone, for fear Shannon would consult the girl and she would tell him who Endean was. He choked back his anger.

'What are you doing here?' he asked lamely.

'Having dinner,' said Shannon, appearing puzzled. 'Look, Harris, if I want to go out and have dinner, that's my affair. There's nothing to be done over the weekend. I have to wait till Monday to fly to Luxembourg.'

Endean was even angrier. He could not explain that Shannon slacking on the job was not what concerned him.

'Who's the girl?' he said.

Shannon shrugged.

'Name's Julie. Met her in a café two days ago.'

'Picked her up?' asked Endean in horror.

'Yes, you might say that. Why?'

'Oh, nothing. But be careful about girls. It would be better if you left them alone for a while, that's all.'

'Harris, don't worry about my security. There won't be any indiscretions, in bed or out. Besides, I told her my name was Keith Brown; I'm on leave in London and I'm in the oil business.'

For answer Endean spun round, snapped at Paolo to tell the group he was with that he had been called away, and headed for the stairs to the street before Julie Manson could recognise him. Shannon watched him leave.

'Up yours,' he said quietly, 'with Sir Bloody James Manson's biggest drill.'

On the pavement outside, Endean swore quietly. Apart from that he could only pray that Shannon had been telling the truth about the Keith Brown business, and that Julie Manson would not tell her father about her new boy-friend.

Shannon and his girl danced until shortly before three and had their first row on the way back to Shannon's flat. He had told her it would be better if she did not tell her father she was going out with a mercenary, or even mention his name.

'From what you have already told me about him, he seems to dote on you. He'd probably send you away somewhere, or have you made a ward of court.'

Her response had been to start teasing, keeping a straight face and saying she would be able to handle her father, as she always had, and in any case being made a ward of court would be fun, and would get her name in all the papers. Besides, she argued, Shannon could always come and get her, fight his way out, and elope with her.

Shannon was not sure how serious she was, and thought he might have gone too far in provoking Endean that evening, although he had not planned on meeting him anyway. They were still arguing when they reached the sitting room of the flat.

'Anyway, I'm not being told what I'll do and what I won't do,' said the girl as she dropped her coat over the armchair.

'You will by me,' growled Shannon. 'You'll just keep damn silent about me when you're with your father. And that's flat.'

'I'll do what I damn well like,' she insisted, and to emphasise her words, stamped her foot. Shannon got angry. He picked her up, spun her round, marched her to the armchair, sat down and pulled her over his knee. For five minutes there were two conflicting sounds in the sitting room, the girl's protesting squeals and the crack of Shannon's hand. When he let her up she scuttled into the bedroom sobbing loudly and slammed the door.

Shannon shrugged. The die was cast one way or the other, and there was nothing he could do about it. He went into the kitchen, made coffee and drank it slowly by the window, looking out at the backs of the houses across the gardens, almost all darkened as the respectable folk of St John's Wood slept.

When he entered the bedroom it was in darkness. In the far corner of

642 THE NOVELS OF FREDERICK FORSYTH

the double bed was a small hump, but no sound, as if she were holding
her breath. Halfway across the floor his foot scuffed her fallen dress and
two paces further he kicked one of her discarded shoes. He sat on the
edge of the bed and as his eyes grew accustomed to the darkness he made
out her face on the pillow, eyes watching him.

'You're rotten,' she whispered.

He leaned forward and slipped a hand into the angle of her neck and
jaw, stroking slowly and firmly.

'No one's ever hit me before.'

'That's why you've turned out the way you have,' he murmured.

'How is that?'

'A spoiled little girl.'

'I'm not.' There was a pause. 'Yes I am.'

He continued caressing her.

'Cat.'

'Yes.'

'Did you really think Daddy might take me away from you if I told
him?'

'Yes. I still do.'

'And do you think I'd really tell him?'

'I thought you might.'

'Is that why you got angry?'

'Yes.'

'Then you only smacked me because you love me?'

'I suppose so.'

She turned her head and he felt her tongue busily licking the inside of
his palm.

'Get into bed, Cat, darling. I'm so randy I can't wait any more.'

He was only half out of his clothes when she threw the bed-sheets
back and knelt on the mattress, running her hands over his chest and
muttering 'Hurry, hurry' between kisses.

You're a lying bastard, Shannon, he thought as he lay on his back
feeling this avid and infatuated young girl go to work on him.

There was a light grey glow in the east over Camden Town when they
lay still two hours later and he wished he had a cigarette. Julie was
curled up in the crook of his arm, her varied appetites for the moment
satisfied.

'Tell me something,' she said.

'What?'

'Why do you live the way you do? Why be a mercenary and go around
making wars on people?'

'I don't make wars. The world we live in makes wars, led and governed
by men who pretend they are creatures of morality and integrity,
whereas most of them are self-seeking bastards. They make the wars, for
increased profits or increased power. I just fight the wars, because it's the
way I like to live.'

'But why for money? Mercenaries fight for money, don't they?'

'Not only the money. The bums do, but when it comes to a crunch the bums who style themselves mercenaries usually don't fight. They scarper. Most of the best ones fight for the same reason I do; they enjoy the life, the hard living, the combat.'

'But why do there have to be wars? Why can't they all live in peace?'

He stirred and in the darkness scowled at the ceiling.

'Because there are only two kinds of people in this world: the predators and the grazers. And the predators always get to the top, because they're prepared to fight to get there and consume people and things that get in their way. The others haven't the nerve, or the courage, or the hunger or the ruthlessness. So the world is governed by the predators, who become the potentates. And the potentates are never satisfied. They must go on and on seeking more of the currency they worship.

'In the Communist world – and don't ever kid yourself into thinking the Communist leaders are peace-loving – the currency is power. Power, power and more power, no matter how many people have to die so they can get it. In the capitalist world the currency is money. More and more money. Oil, gold, stocks and shares, more and more, are the goals, even if they have to lie, steal, bribe and cheat to get it. These make the money, and the money buys the power. So really it all comes back to the lust for power. If they think there's enough of it to be taken, and it needs a war to grab it, you get a war. The rest, the so-called idealism, is a load of cock.'

'Some people fight for idealism. The Vietcong do. I've read it in the papers.'

'Yeah, some people fight for idealism, and ninety-nine out of a hundred of them are being conned. So are the ones back home who cheer for war. We're always right and they're always wrong. In Washington and Peking, London and Moscow. And you know what? They're being conned. Those GIs in Vietnam, do you think they died for life, liberty and the pursuit of happiness? They died for the Dow Jones Index in Wall Street, and always have done. And the British soldiers who died in Kenya, Cyprus, Aden. You really think they rushed into battle shouting for God, King and Country? They were in those lands because their colonel ordered them there, and he was ordered by the War Office, and that was ordered by the Cabinet, to keep British control over the economies. So what? They went back to the people who owned them in the first place, and who cared about the bodies the British Army left behind? It's a big con, Julie Manson, a big con. The difference with me is that no one tells me to go and fight, or where to fight, or which side to fight on. That's why the politicians, the establishments, hate mercenaries. It's not that we are more lethal than they are; in fact we're a damn sight less so. It's because they can't control us; we don't take their orders. We don't shoot the ones they tell us to shoot, and we don't start when they say "start" or stop when they say "stop". That's why we're outlaws; we fight on contract and we pick our own contracts.'

Julie sat up and ran her hands over the hard, scarred muscles of his chest and shoulders. She was a conventionally raised girl and could not, like so many of her generation, understand even a tiny fraction of the world she saw about her.

'What about the wars when people fight for what they know is right?' she asked. 'I mean, what about fighting against Hitler? That was right, wasn't it?'

Shannon sighed and nodded.

'Yes, that was right. He was a bastard all right. Except that they, the bigshots in the Western world, sold him steel up to the outbreak of war and then made more fortunes making more steel to crush Hitler's steel. And the Communists were no better. Stalin signed a pact with him and waited for capitalism and Nazism to destroy each other so he could take over the rubble. Only when Hitler struck Russia did the world's so-idealistic Communists decide Nazism was naughty. Besides, it cost thirty million lives to kill Hitler. A mercenary could have done it with one bullet costing less than a shilling.'

'But we won, didn't we? It was the right thing to do, and we won.'

'We won, my little darling, because the Russians, British and Americans had more guns, tanks, planes and ships than Adolf. That's why, and that's the only reason why. If he had had more, he'd have won, and you know what? History would have written that he was right and we were wrong. Victors are always right. There's a nice little adage I heard once: "God is on the side of the big battalions." It's the gospel of the rich and powerful, the cynical and the gullible. Politicians believe in it, the so-called quality newspapers preach it. The truth is, the Establishment is on the side of the big battalions, because it created and armed them in the first place. It never seems to occur to the millions of readers of that garbage that maybe God, if there is one, has something to do with truth, justice and compassion rather than sheer brute force, and that truth and justice might possibly be on the side of the little platoons. Not that it matters. The big battalions always win, and the "serious" Press always approves, and the grazers always believe it.'

'You're a rebel, Cat,' she murmured.

'Sure. Always have been. No, not always. Since I buried six of my mates in Cyprus. That was when I began to question the wisdom and integrity of all our leaders.'

'But apart from killing people, you could die yourself. You could get killed in one of these futile wars.'

'Yes, and I could live on, like a battery hen in one of these futile cities. Filling in futile forms, paying futile taxes to enable futile politicians and state managers to fritter it away on electorally useful white elephants. I could earn a futile salary in a futile office and commute futilely on a train, morning and evening, until a futile retirement. I prefer to do it my way, live my way and die my way.'

'Do you ever think of death?' she asked him.

'Of course. Often. Don't you?'

'Yes. But I don't want to die. I don't want you to die.'

'Death's not so bad. You get used to the idea when it has come very close, and passed by, many times. Let me tell you something. The other day I was clearing out the drawers in this place. There was some news-paper, a year old, at the bottom of one. I saw a piece of news and began to read it. It dated from the winter before last. There was this old man, see? He lived alone in a basement. They found him dead one day. A week or so after he died, the coroner was told no one ever came to see him, and he couldn't get out much. The pathologist said he had been under-nourished for at least a year. You know what they found in his throat? Bits of cardboard. He had been nibbling bits of cardboard from a cereal packet to try and get nourishment. Well, not me, baby. When I go, I'll go my way. I'd prefer to go with a bullet in my chest, and blood in my mouth, and a gun in my hand; with defiance in my heart and shouting "Sod the lot of you", than to flicker out in a damp basement with a mouth full of cardboard.

'Now go to sleep, love, it's dawn already.'

Shannon arrived in Luxembourg just after one p.m. on the following Monday and from the airport took a taxi to the Banque de Crédit. He identified himself as Keith Brown by using his passport, and asked for the £5000 that should be waiting for collection by him.

After delay while the telex room was checked, the credit was discovered. It had just come through from Zürich. Instead of drawing the whole sum in cash, Shannon took the equivalent in Luxembourg francs of £1000 and signed a form making over the balance of £4000 to the bank. In exchange for this he was given a certified bank cheque for the equivalent of £4000.

He had time for a quick lunch before making his way to the Hougstraat where he had an appointment with the firm of accountants Lang & Stein.

Luxembourg, like Belgium and Liechtenstein, maintains a system of offering to the investor a highly discreet and even secretive service in banking and the operation of companies, into whose affairs a foreign police force has the greatest difficulty in trying to pry. By and large, unless a company registered in Luxembourg can be shown to have broken the laws of the Archduchy, or can be proved beyond doubt to have been involved in international illegal activities of a highly unpleasant nature, foreign police enquiries as to who owns or controls such a company will be met with a stoic refusal to co-operate. It was this kind of facility that Shannon sought.

His interview, arranged by phone three days earlier, was with Mr Emil Stein, one of the partners in the highly respectable firm. For the occasion Shannon wore a newly acquired charcoal-grey suit, white shirt and school tie. He carried a briefcase and *The Times* under one arm. For some reason, the carrying of this newspaper always seems to impress Europeans that the bearer is a respectable Englishman.

'Over the forthcoming few months,' he told the grey-haired Luxembourger, 'a group of British associates, of whom I am one, wish to engage in commercial activities in the Mediterranean area, possibly

Spain, France and Italy. For this purpose we would like to establish a holding company in Luxembourg. As you may imagine, being British citizens, and residents, and doing business in several European countries with differing financial laws could prove very complicated. From a tax standpoint alone a holding company in Luxembourg seems to be advisable.'

Mr Stein nodded, for the request was no surprise. Many such holding companies were already registered in his tiny country, and his firm received such requests every day.

'That should present no problem, Mr Brown,' he told his visitor. 'You are aware of course that all the procedures required by the Archduchy of Luxembourg must be complied with. Once that is done, the holding company may hold the majority of shares in an array of other companies registered elsewhere, and after that the company affairs remain entirely private from foreign tax investigations.'

'That's very kind of you. Perhaps you would outline the essentials of starting such a company in Luxembourg,' said Shannon.

The accountant could reel off the requisites in a few seconds.

'Unlike in Britain, all limited liability companies in Luxembourg must have a minimum of seven shareholders and a minimum of three directors. However, quite often the accountant asked to help in setting the company up takes the chairmanship of the directors, his junior partners form the other two, and his staff become shareholders, each with a purely nominal number of shares. In this manner the person wishing to establish the company is merely the seventh shareholder although by virtue of his greater number of shares he controls the company.

'Shares will normally be registered and the names of the shareholders also, but there is the provision for the issue of bearer shares, in which case no registration of the identity of the majority holder is necessary. The snag to that is that the bearer shares are exactly what they mean, and the bearer of the majority controls the company. Should one man lose them, or have them stolen, the new owner would automatically become the controller without needing a vestige of proof as to how he acquired them. Do you follow me, Mr Brown?'

Shannon nodded. This was the arrangement he hoped to establish, in order to have Semmler buy the boat behind the cover of an uncheckable company.

'A holding company,' said Mr Stein, 'as its name implies, may not trade in any form. It may only hold stock in other companies. Does your group of associates hold shares in other companies which it would like to have taken over and held in Luxembourg?'

'No, not yet,' said Shannon. 'We hope to acquire existing companies in the area of chosen operations, or found other limited liability companies and transfer the majority shareholdings to Luxembourg for safe keeping.'

By the end of an hour the agreement had been reached. Shannon had shown Mr Stein his £4000 banker's cheque to prove his solvency, and had paid a deposit of £500 in cash.

Mr Stein had agreed to proceed at once with the foundation and registration of a holding company to be called Tyrone Holdings SA, after searching through the bulky list of already registered companies to ensure that no such name existed on the register. The total share capital would be £40,000 of which only £1000 would be issued immediately, and this would be issued in 1000 bearer shares of £1 each. Mr Stein would accept one share and the chairmanship of the board. One share each would go to his partner Mr Lang and a junior partner in the firm. These three men would form the board. Three other staff members of the firm – they turned out later to be secretaries – would be issued with one bearer share each, and the remaining 994 shares would be held by Mr Brown, who would thus control the company and whose wishes the board would have to implement.

A general meeting to float the company was fixed for twelve days thence, or any time after that if Mr Brown would let them know in writing when he could be in Luxembourg to attend it. On that note Shannon left.

Before closing time he was back at the bank, returned the cheque and had the £4000 transferred to the account at Brugge. He checked into the Excelsior and spent the night in Luxembourg. He already had his onward booking the next morning for Hamburg, and he had the hotel ring up to confirm it. It was to Hamburg that he flew the following morning. This time, he was looking for arms.

The trade in lethal weapons is the world's most lucrative after narcotics, and not surprisingly the governments of the world are deeply involved in it. Since 1945 it has become almost a point of national prestige to have one's own native arms industry, and they have flourished and multiplied to the point where by the early seventies it was estimated there existed one military firearm for every man, woman and child on the face of the planet. Arms manufacture simply cannot be kept down to arms consumption except in case of war, and the logical response has to be either to export the surplus or encourage war or both. As few governments want to be involved in a war themselves, but also do not wish to run down their arms industry just in case, the accent has for years been on the exporting of arms. To this end, all the major powers operate highly paid teams of salesmen to trot the globe persuading any potentate with whom they can secure an interview that he does not have enough weapons, or that those he does possess are not modern enough and should be replaced.

It is of no concern to the sellers that ninety-five per cent of all the hardware on the face of, for example, Africa is not used to protect the owner-country from external aggression but to keep the populace in subjection to the dictator. Arms sales having logically started as a product of the profits rivalry between competing Western nations, the entry of Russia and China into the arms manufacturing and exporting business has equally logically transferred the salesmanship into an extension of the power rivalry.

The interaction of profit desirability and political desirability has produced a tangled web of calculations that continue daily in the capitals of the major world powers. One power will sell arms to republic A, but not to B. At which a rival power will rush to sell weapons to B but not to A. This is called establishing a power balance and therefore keeping the peace. The profit desirability of selling arms is permanent; it is always profitable. The only constraints are imposed by political desirability in this or that country having certain arms in its possession at all, and from this shifting quicksand of expediency versus profit has evolved the intimate link between Foreign Affairs departments and Defence departments all over the world.

To establish an indigenous arms industry is not difficult, provided it is kept basic. It is relatively simple to manufacture rifles and submachine guns, ammunition for both, along with hand grenades and hand guns. The level of technology, industrial development and the variety of the raw materials is not large, but the smaller countries usually buy their weaponry ready-made from the larger ones, because their internal requirements are too small to justify the necessary industrialisation, and they know their technical level would not put them into the export market with a chance.

Nevertheless, a very large and growing number of medium-sized countries have in the past two decades gone ahead and established their own native, if basic, arms factories. The difficulties increase, and therefore the number of participating nations decreases, with the complexity of the weapon to be made. It is easy to make small arms, harder to make artillery, armoured cars and tanks, very difficult to create an entire shipbuilding industry to build modern warships, and hardest of all to turn out modern jet fighters and bombers. The level of development of a local arms industry can be judged by the point at which local weaponry reaches its technical limits, and imports have to be made for anything above those limits.

The main world arms makers and exporters are the United States, Canada, Britain, France, Italy, West Germany (with certain banned manufactures under the 1954 Paris treaty), Sweden, Switzerland, Spain, Belgium, Israel and South Africa in the Western world. Sweden and Switzerland are neutral but still make and export very fine weaponry, while Israel and South Africa built up their arms industries because of their peculiar situations, because they did not wish to be dependent on anyone in the event of a crisis, and both export very little indeed. The others are all NATO countries and linked by a common defence policy. They also operate an ill-defined degree of co-operation on foreign policy as it relates to arms sales, and an application for an arms purchase made to any of them habitually undergoes a close scrutiny before it is granted and the arms are sold. In the same vein, the small buyer country always has to sign a written undertaking not to pass weaponry sold to itself to another party without express written permission from the supplier. In other words, a lot of questions are asked before a sale is agreed by the Foreign Affairs office rather than the Weapons Sales office, and sales thus made are almost inevitably deals made government-to-government.

Communist arms are largely standardised and come mainly from Russia and Czechoslovakia. The newcomer, China, now also produces weaponry up to a sufficiently high level of sophistication for Mao's guerrilla war theory's requirements. For Communists the sales policy is different. Political influence, not money, is the overriding factor, and many Soviet arms shipments are made as gifts to curry favour, not as commercial deals. Being committed to the adage that power grows out of the barrel of a gun, and obsessed with power, the Communist nations will not merely sell weapons to other sovereign governments, but also to 'liberation' organisations that they politically favour. In most cases these are not sales, but gifts. Thus a Communist, Marxist, extreme left-wing or revolutionary movement almost anywhere in the world can be reasonably assured of not running short of the necessary hardware for guerrilla war.

In the middle, the neutral Swiss and Swedes operate their own self-imposed inhibitions on whom they will sell to, and thus curtail their arms export by their own volition on moral grounds. No one else does.

With the Russians selling or giving their hardware from governmental source to non-governmental recipients, and the West being too shy to do so, the private arms dealer enters into the picture. The Russians have no private arms dealers, so this creature fills the gap for the West. He is a businessman who may be used as a source of weaponry by someone seeking to buy, but in order to stay in business he must liaise closely with the defence department of his own country or the department will see that he goes out of business. It is in his interest to abide by his native country's wishes anyway; that country may be the source of his own purchases, which could be cut off if he causes displeasure, apart from his fear of being put out of business by other less pleasant means.

Thus the licensed arms dealer, usually a national and resident of his native country, sells arms to buyers after consulting his own government that the sale is acceptable to them. Such dealers are usually large companies, and hold stocks.

This is at the highest level of the private enterprise arms business. Lower in the pond are more dubious fish. Next down the scale is the licensed dealer who does not hold a stock of weapons in a warehouse but is licensed to hold a franchise by one of the large, often government-owned or -controlled arms manufacturing companies. He will negotiate a deal on behalf of a client, and take his cut. His licence depends on his toeing the line with the government whose franchise to operate he holds. This does not prevent some licensed arms dealers occasionally pulling a fast one, though two well-established arms dealers have been put out of business by their governments when discovered doing it.

Down in the mud at the bottom sit the black market arms dealers. These are self-styled, since they hold no licence. They may not therefore legally hold any stocks of weapons at all. They remain in business by being of value to the secret buyer, a man or organisation who, not being a government or representing one, cannot clinch an inter-governmental deal;

who would not be tacitly approved of by a Western government as desirable to receive arms; who cannot persuade a Communist government to support his cause on the grounds of political ideology; but who needs arms.

The vital document in an arms deal is called the end user certificate. This certifies that the weapons purchase is being made by, or on behalf of, the End User, who almost without exception in the Western world has to be a sovereign government. Only in the case of a flat gift by a secret service organisation to an irregular army or of a pure black market deal does the question of an end user certificate not apply. Examples of the former were the arming, without payment, by the CIA of the anti-Castro forces of the Bay of Pigs, and the arming of the Congo mercenaries also by the CIA. An example of the latter is the shipment to Ireland from various European and US private sources of arms for the Provisional IRA.

The end user certificate, being an international document, has no specific form, shape or size, or specific wording. It is a written affirmation from a certified representative of a national government that either he the bearer or Mr X the dealer is authorised to apply to the supplier government for permission to purchase *and export* a quantity of arms.

The vital point about the end user certificate is that some countries carry out the most rigorous checks to ensure the authenticity of this document, while others come under the heading of 'no questions asked' suppliers. Needless to say, end user certificates, like anything else, can be forged. It was into this world that Shannon carefully entered when he flew to Hamburg.

He was aware that he could certainly not make a direct application for permission to buy arms to any European government with a chance of success. Nor would Communist governments be kind enough to donate the weapons; indeed their reaction would be totally opposed to the toppling of Kimba. By the same token, any direct application would firstly 'blow' the entire operation, and thus lead to its being frustrated.

He was also not in a position, for the same reasons, to approach one of the leading government-owned arms makers, such as Fabrique Nationale of Belgium, for any request put to a government-owned combine in the arms-making and -selling business would be passed on to the government; similarly, he could not approach a large private arms dealer, like Cogswell and Harrison of London or Parker Hale of Birmingham. In the same category Bofors of Sweden, Oerlikon of Switzerland, CETME of Spain, Werner and the others in Germany, Omnipol of Czechoslovakia and Fiat of Italy were ruled out.

He also had his own peculiar buying circumstances to consider. The amount he had to spend was too small to interest the big legitimate licensed dealers who habitually dealt in millions. He could not have interested the erstwhile king of the private arms dealers, Sam Cummings of Interarmco, who for two decades after the war ran a private arms empire from his penthouse suite in Monaco and had retired to enjoy his wealth; nor Dr Strakaty of Vienna, the licensee franchise holder for

Omnipol across the border at Washington Street 11, Prague; nor Dr Langenstein in Munich; nor Dr Peretti in Rome; nor M Cammermundt in Brussels.

He had to go further down the scale to the men who dealt in smaller sums and quantities. He knew the names of Günther Leinhauser, the German, former associate of Cummings; in Paris, of Pierre Lorez, Maurice Herscu and Paul Favier. But on consideration he had decided to go and see two men in Hamburg.

The trouble with the packet of arms he sought was that it looked like what it was: a single packet of arms for a single job, and it would not need a keen military mind to realise that job had to be the taking of one building within a short period. There was not enough leeway in the quantities to kid any professional soldier that a defence ministry, even a small one, was behind the order.

Shannon had therefore decided to split the packet even smaller, so that at least the items sought from each dealer were consistent. A mixed package would be a giveaway.

From one of the men he was going to see he wanted 400,000 rounds of standard 9 mm ammunition, the sort that fits into automatic pistols and also submachine carbines. Such a consignment was too large and too heavy to be bought on the black market and shipped without a large amount of complicated smuggling to get it on board. But it could well be the kind of consignment needed by the police force of any small country, and was not suspicious in that there were no matching guns in the same packet and it could therefore pass under scrutiny as an order designed simply to replenish stocks.

To get it, he needed a licensed arms dealer who could slip such a small order through the procedures among a batch of bigger orders. Although licensed to trade in arms, the dealer must nevertheless be prepared to do a bent deal with a forged end user certificate. This was where an intimate knowledge of the no-questions-asked countries came in useful.

Ten years earlier there had been vast quantities of superfluous weaponry lying about Europe in private hands, 'black', i.e., illegally held, arms, leftovers from colonial wars like those of the French in Algeria and the Belgians in the Congo.

But a series of small irregular operations and wars throughout the sixties had used them up, notably in the Yemen and Nigeria. So he would have to find a man who would use a bent end user certificate and present it to a supplier government that asked no or few questions. Only four years earlier the most noted of these was the Czech government, which, although Communist, had continued the old Czech tradition of selling arms to all comers. Four years earlier one could have walked into Prague with a suitcase full of dollars, gone to the Omnipol headquarters, selected one's hardware and a few hours later have taken off from the airport in one's chartered plane with the stuff on board. It was that simple. But since the Soviet takeover of 1968, the KGB had taken to vetting all such applications, and far too many questions were being asked.

Two other countries had earned a reputation of asking few questions about where the presented end user certificates really came from. One was Spain, traditionally interested in earning foreign currency, and whose CETME factories produced a wide range of weapons which were then sold by the Spanish Army ministry to almost all comers. The other, a newcomer, was Yugoslavia.

Yugoslavia had only begun manufacturing her own arms a few years earlier, and inevitably had reached a point where her own armed forces were equipped with domestic arms. The next step was over-production (because factories cannot be run down a few years after they have been most expensively started), and hence the desire to export. Being a newcomer to the arms market, with weapons of unknown quality, and eager for foreign currency, the Yugoslavs had adopted the 'ask no questions and you'll get told no lies' attitude to applicants for her weaponry. She produced a good light company mortar and a useful bazooka, the latter based heavily on the Czech RPG-7.

Because her goods were new, Shannon estimated a dealer could persuade Belgrade to sell a tiny quantity of these arms, consisting of two 60 mm mortar tubes and 100 bombs, plus two bazooka tubes and forty rockets. The excuse could well be that the customer was a new one, wishing to make some tests with the new weaponry, and then come back with a far larger order.

For the first of his orders, Shannon intended to go to a dealer licensed to trade with CETME in Madrid, but known also not to be above putting through a phoney end user certificate. For the second, Shannon had heard the name of aonther man in Hamburg who had skilfully cultivated the baby Yugoslav arms makers at an early stage and had established a good relationship with them, although he was unlicensed.

Normally there is no point in going to an unlicensed dealer. Unless he can fulfil the order out of illegally held stocks of his own, which means no export licence, his only use can be in securing a bent but plausible end user certificate for those who cannot find their own, and then persuading a licensed dealer to accept this piece of paper. The licensed dealer can then fulfil it, with government approval, from his own legally held stocks and secure an export licence, or put the phoney certificate to a government with his name and guarantee backing it up. But occasionally he has one other use which makes him employable; his intimate knowledge of the state of the market, and where to go at any given moment with any given requirement to have the best chance of success. It was for this quality that Shannon was visiting the second man on his Hamburg list.

When he arrived in the Hansa city Shannon stopped by the Landesbank to find his £5000 was there already. He took the lot in the form of a banker's cheque made out to himself, and went on to the Atlantic Hotel where his room was booked. Deciding to give the Reeperbahn a miss, and being tired, he dined early and went to bed.

Johann Schlinker, when Shannon confronted him in his small and modest office the next morning, was short, round and jovial. His eyes sparkled with bonhomie and welcome, so much so that it took Shannon ten seconds to realise the man could be trusted as far as the door. The pair of them spoke in English, but talked of dollars, the twin languages of the arms market place.

Shannon thanked the arms dealer for agreeing to see him, and offered his passport in the name of Keith Brown as identification. The German flicked through it and handed it back.

'And what brings you here?' he asked.

'You were recommended to me, Herr Schlinker, as a businessman with a high reputation for reliability in the business of military and police hardware.'

Schlinker smiled and nodded, but the flattery made no impression.

'By whom, may I ask?'

Shannon mentioned the name of a man in Paris, closely associated with African affairs on behalf of a certain French governmental but clandestine service. The two had met during one of Shannon's previous African wars, and a month earlier Shannon had looked him up in Paris for old times' sake. A week ago Shannon had rung the man again, and he had indeed recommended Shannon to Schlinker for the kind of merchandise he wanted. Shannon had told the man he would be using the name Brown.

Schlinker raised his eyebrows.

'Would you excuse me a minute?' he asked, and left the room. In an adjoining booth Shannon could hear the chatter of a telex. It was thirty minutes before he came back. He was smiling.

'I had to call a friend of mine in Paris on a business matter,' he said brightly. 'Please go on.'

Shannon knew perfectly well he had telexed to another arms dealer in Paris, asking the man to contact the French agent and get a confirmation that Keith Brown was all right. Apparently the confirmation had just come back.

'I want to buy a quantity of 9 mm ammunition,' he said bluntly. 'I know it is a small order, but I have been approached by a group of people in Africa who need this ammunition for their own affairs, and I believe if those affairs go well, there would be further and much larger shipments in the future.'

'How much would the order be?' asked the German.

'Four hundred thousand rounds.'

Schlinker made a moue.

'That is not very much,' he said simply.

'Certainly. For the moment the budget is not large. One is hoping a small investment now might lead to greater things later on.'

The German nodded. It had happened in the past. The first order was usually a small one.

'Why did they come to you? You are not a dealer in arms or ammunition.'

'They happened to have retained me as a technical adviser on military matters of all kinds. When the question of seeking a fresh supplier for their needs arose, they asked me to come to Europe for them,' said Shannon.

'And you have no end user certificate?' the German asked.

'No, I'm afraid not. I hoped that sort of thing could be arranged.'

'Oh, yes, it can,' said Schlinker. 'No problem there. It takes longer, and costs more. But it can be done. One could supply this order from stocks, but they are held in my Vienna office. That way there would be no requirement for an end user certificate. Or one could obtain such a document and make the application normally through legal channels.'

'I would prefer the latter,' said Shannon. 'The delivery has to be by ship, and to bring that sort of quantity through Austria and into Italy, then on board a boat, would be hazardous. It enters an area I am not familiar with. Moreover, interception could mean long terms in prison for those found in possession. Apart from that, the cargo might be identified as coming from your stocks.'

Schlinker smiled. Privately he knew there would be no danger of that, but Shannon was right about the border controls. The newly emergent menace of the Black September terrorists had made Austria, Germany and Italy highly nervous about strange cargoes passing through the borders.

Shannon for his part did not trust Schlinker not to sell them the ammunition one day and betray them the next. With a phoney end user certificate, the German would have to keep his side of the bargain; it would be he who presented the bent certificate to the authorities.

'I think you are perhaps right,' Schlinker said at last. 'Very well. I can offer you 9 mm standard ball at sixty-five dollars per thousand. There would be a surcharge of ten per cent for the certificate, and another ten per cent free on board.'

Shannon calculated hastily. Free on board meant a cargo complete with export licence, cleared through customs and loaded on to the ship, with the ship itself clearing the harbour mouth. The price would be 26,000 dollars for the ammunition, plus 5200 dollars surcharge.

'How would payment be made?' he asked.

'I would need the 5200 dollars before starting work,' said Schlinker. 'That has to cover the certificate, which has to be paid for, plus all personal travelling and administrative costs. The full purchase price would have to be paid here in this office when I am able to show you the certificate; but before purchase. As a licensed dealer I would be buying on behalf of my client, the government named on the certificate. Once the stuff had been bought, the selling government would be extremely unlikely to take it back and repay the money. Therefore I would need total payment in advance. I would also need the name of the exporting vessel, to fill in the application for export permit. The vessel would have to be a scheduled liner or freighter, or a general freighter owned by a registered shipping company.'

Shannon nodded. The terms were steep, but beggars cannot be choosers. If he had really represented a sovereign government he would not be here in the first place.

'How long from the time I give you the money until shipment?' he asked.

'Madrid is quite slow in these matters. About forty days at the outside,' said the German.

Shannon rose. He showed Schlinker the banker's cheque to prove his solvency, and promised to be back in an hour with 5200 US dollars in cash, or the equivalent in German marks. Schlinker opted for German marks, and when Shannon returned gave him a standard receipt for the money.

While Schlinker had been writing out the receipt, Shannon glanced through a series of brochures on the coffee table. They covered the items put on sale by another company, which evidently specialised in non-military pyrotechnic goods of the kind that are not covered by the classification of 'arms', and a wide variety of items used by security companies, including riot sticks, truncheons, walkie-talkies, riot-gas canisters and launchers, flares, rockets and the like.

As Schlinker handed him his receipt, Shannon asked, 'Are you associated with this company, Herr Schlinker?'

Schlinker smiled broadly.

'I own it,' he said. 'It is what I am best known for to the general public.'

And a damn good cover for holding a warehouse full of crates labelled 'Danger of Explosion', thought Shannon. But he was interested. Quickly he wrote out a list of items and showed them to Schlinker.

'Could you fulfil this order, for export, out of your stocks?' he asked.

Schlinker glanced at the list. It included two rocket-launching tubes of the type used by coastguards to send up distress flares, ten rockets containing magnesium flares of maximum intensity and duration attached to parachutes, two penetrating fog-horns powered by compressed gas canisters, four sets of night-binoculars, three fixed-crystal walkie-talkie sets with a range of not less than five miles, and five wrist compasses.

'Certainly,' he said. 'I stock all of these things.'

'I'd like to place an order for the list. Being off the classification of arms, I assume there would be no problems with exporting them?'

'None at all. I can send them anywhere I want, particularly to a ship.'

'Good,' said Shannon. 'How much would that lot cost, with freight in bond to an exporting agent in Marseilles?'

Schlinker went through his catalogue and priced the list, adding on ten per cent for freight.

'Four thousand eight hundred dollars,' he said.

'I'll be in touch with you in twelve days,' said Shannon. 'Please have the whole lot ready crated for freighting. I will give you the name of the exporting agent in Marseilles, and mail you a banker's cheque in your favour for 4800 dollars. Within thirty days I expect to be able to give you the remaining 26,000 dollars for the ammunition deal, and the name of the ship.'

He met his second contact for dinner that night at the Atlantic. Alan Baker was an expatriate, a Canadian who had settled in Germany after the war and married a German girl. A former Royal Engineer during the war, he had got himself involved during the early post-war years in a series of border-crossing operations into and out of the Soviet Zone, running nylons, watches and refugees. From there he had drifted into arms running to the scores of tiny nationalist or anti-Communist bands of maquis who, left over from the war, still ran their resistance movements in Central and Eastern Europe – with the sole difference that during the war they had been resisting the Germans, while after it they were resisting the Communists.

Most of them had been paid for by the Americans, but Baker was content to use his knowledge of German and commando tactics to slip quantities of arms to them, and take a hefty salary cheque from the Americans for doing so. When these groups finally petered out, he found himself in Tangier in the early fifties, using the smuggling talents he had learned in the war and after it to bring cargoes of perfume and cigarettes into Italy and Spain from the then international and free port on the north coast of Morocco. Finally put out of business by the bombing and sinking of his ship in a gangland feud, he had returned to Germany and gone into the business of wheeler-dealing in any commodity that had a buyer and a supplier. His most recent feat had been to negotiate a deal in Yugoslav arms on behalf of the Basques in northern Spain.

He and Shannon had met when Baker was running guns into Ethiopia, and Shannon had been at a loose end after returning from Bukavu in April 1968. He knew Shannon under his real name.

He listened quietly while Shannon explained what he wanted, a short wiry man, his eyes flickering from his food to the other mercenary.

'Yes, it can be done,' he said when Shannon had finished. 'The Yugoslavs would accept the idea that a new customer wanted a sample set of two mortars and two bazookas for test purposes before placing a larger order if they were satisfied. It's plausible. There's no problem from my side in getting the stuff from them. My relations with the men in Belgrade are excellent. And they are quick. Just at the moment I have to admit I have one other problem though.'

'What's that?'

'End user certificate,' said Baker. 'I used to have a man in Bonn, diplomat for a certain East African country, who would sign anything for a price, and a few nice big German girls laid on at a party, the sort he liked. He was transferred back to his own country two weeks ago. I'm a bit stuck for a replacement at the moment.'

'Are the Yugoslavs particular about end users?'

Baker shook his head.

'Nope. So long as the documentation is in order, they don't check further. But there has to be a certificate, and it must have the right governmental stamp on it. They can't afford to be too slack, after all.'

Shannon thought for a moment. He knew of a man in Paris who had once boasted he had a contact in an embassy there who could make out end user certificates.

'If I could get you one, a good one, from an African country? Would that work?' he asked.

Baker inhaled on his cigar.

'No problem at all,' he said. 'As for the price, a 60 mm mortar tube would run you 1100 dollars each. Say, 2200 for the pair. The bombs are twenty-four dollars each. The only problem with your order is that the sums are really too small. Couldn't you up the number of mortar bombs from a hundred to three hundred? It would make things much easier. No one throws off just a hundred bombs, not even for test purposes.'

'All right,' said Shannon, 'I'll take three hundred, but no more. Otherwise I'll go over budget, and that comes off my cut.'

It did not come off his cut, for he had allowed a margin for over-expenditure, and his own salary was secure. But he knew Baker would accept the argument as final.

'Good,' said Baker. 'So that's 7200 dollars for the bombs. The bazookas cost 1000 dollars each, two thousand for the pair. The rockets are forty-two dollars and fifty cents each. The forty you want come out at ... let's see ...'

'Seventeen hundred dollars,' said Shannon. 'The whole packet comes out at 13,100 dollars.'

'Plus ten per cent for getting the stuff free on board your ship, Cat. Without the end user certificate. If I could have got one for you, it would have been twenty per cent. Let's face it, it's a tiny order, but the travelling and out-of-pocket expenses for me are constants. I ought to charge you fifteen per cent for such a small order. So the total is 14,400 dollars. Let's say fourteen and a half, eh?'

'We'll say 14,400,' said Shannon. 'I'll get the certificate and mail it to you, along with a fifty per cent deposit. I'll pay another twenty-five per cent when I see the stuff in Yugoslavia crated and ready to go, and twenty-five per cent as the ship leaves the quay. Travellers cheques in dollars, OK?'

Baker would have liked the lot in advance, but not being a licensed dealer he had no offices, warehouses, or business address as Schlinker had. He would act as broker, using another dealer he knew to make the actual purchase on his behalf. But being a black market man, he had to accept these terms, the lower cut and less in advance.

One of the oldest tricks in the book is to promise to fulfil an arms order, show plenty of confidence, assure the customer of the broker's absolute integrity, take the maximum in advance and disappear. Many a black and brown seeker after arms in Europe has had that happen to them. He knew Shannon would never fall for the trick; besides, fifty per cent of 14,400 dollars was too small a sum to disappear for.

'OK. The moment I get your end user certificate I'll get straight on to it.'

They rose to leave.

'How long from the time you make your first approach until shipping date?' asked Shannon.

'About thirty to thirty-five days,' said Baker. 'By the way, have you got a ship?'

'Not yet. You'll need the name, I suppose. I'll let you have it with the certificate.'

'If you haven't, I know a very good one for charter. Two thousand German marks a day and all found. Crew, victuals, the lot. Take you and the cargo anywhere and discreet as you like.'

Shannon thought it over. Twenty days in the Mediterranean, twenty days out to target and twenty days back. A hundred and twenty thousand marks, or £15,000. Cheaper than buying one's own ship. Tempting. But he objected to the idea of one man outside the operation controlling part of the arms deal, the ship, and being aware of the target as well. It would involve making Baker, or the man he would have to go to for the charter, virtually a partner.

'Yes,' he said cautiously. 'What's she called?'

'The *San Andrea*,' said Baker.

Shannon froze. He had heard Semmler mention that name.

'Registered in Cyprus?' asked Shannon.

'That's right.'

'Forget it,' he said shortly.

As they left the dining-room Shannon caught a swift glimpse of Johann Schlinker, dining in an alcove. For a moment he thought the German dealer might have followed him, but the man was dining with a second man, evidently a valued customer. Shannon averted his head and strode past.

On the doorstep of the hotel he shook hands with Baker.

'You'll be hearing from me,' he said. 'And don't let me down.'

'Don't worry, Cat. You can trust me,' said Baker.'

He turned and hurried off down the street. 'In a pig's ear I can,' muttered Shannon, and went back into the hotel.

On the way up to his room the face of the man he had seen dining with the German arms merchant stayed in his memory. He had seen the face somewhere, but could not place it. As he was falling asleep it came to him. The man was the chief of staff of the IRA.

The next morning, Wednesday, he flew back to London. It was the start of Day Nine.

Martin Thorpe stepped into Sir James Manson's office about the time Cat Shannon was taking off from Hamburg.

'Lady Macallister,' he said by way of introduction, and Sir James waved him to a seat.

'I've been into her with a fine toothcomb,' Thorpe went on. 'As I suspected, she has twice been approached by people interested in buying her thirty per cent holding in Bormac Trading. It would seem each person used the wrong approach, and got turned down. She's eighty-six, halfway senile, and very tetchy. At least, that's her reputation. She's also broad Scottish and has all her affairs handled by a solicitor up in Dundee. Here's my full report on her.'

He handed Sir James a buff folder, and the head of Manson Consolidated read it within a few minutes. He grunted several times, and muttered 'Bloody hell' once. When he had finished, he looked up.

'I still want those 300,000 shares in Bormac,' he said. 'You say the others went about it the wrong way. Why?'

'She would appear to have one obsession in life, and it's not money. She's rich in her own right. When she married she was the daughter of a Scottish laird with more land than ready cash. The marriage was no doubt arranged between the families. After her father died she inherited the lot, mile after mile of desolate moorland. But over the past twenty years the fishing and hunting rights have brought in a small fortune from city-dwelling sportsmen, and parcels of land sold off for industry have made even more. It's been invested by her broker, or whatever they call them up there. She has a nice income to live on. I suspect the other bidders offered a lot of money but nothing else. That would not interest her.'

'Then what the hell would?' asked Sir James.

'Look at paragraph two on the second page, Sir James. See what I mean? The notices in *The Times* every anniversary, the attempt to have a statue erected, which was refused by the London County Council. The memorial she had put up in his home town. I think that's her obsession – the memory of the old slave-driver she married.'

'Yes, yes, you may be right. So what do you propose?'

Thorpe outlined his idea and Manson listened thoughtfully.

'It might work,' he said eventually. 'Stranger things have happened. The trouble is, if you try it and she still refuses, you can hardly go back again with another offer couched in a different vein. But then I suppose a pure cash offer would in any case get the same reaction the previous two proposals met. All right, play it your way. Just get her to sell those shares.'

With that, Thorpe was on his way.

Shannon was back in his London flat shortly after twelve. Lying on the mat was a cable from Langarotti in Marseilles. It was signed simply 'Jean' and addressed to Keith Brown. Its message was simply an address, a hotel in a street a little way out of the centre of the town where the Corsican had checked in under the name of Lavallon. Shannon approved the precaution. Checking into a French hotel requires the filling out of a form which is later collected by the police. They might have wondered why their old friend Langarotti was staying so far out of town from his usual haunts.

Shannon spent ten minutes extracting the number of the hotel from Continental Directory Enquiries, and placed a call. When he asked the hotel for M. Lavallon, he was told the monsieur was out. He left a message asking M. Lavallon to call Mr Brown in London on his return. He had already given each of the four his own telephone number and made them commit it to memory.

Still using the telephone he sent a telegram to the *poste restante* address of Endean under the name of Walter Harris, advising the project manager that he was back in London and would like to discuss something. Another telegram went to Janni Dupree at his bedsitter instructing him to report to Shannon as soon as he received the cable.

He rang his own Swiss bank and learned that of the salary for himself of £10,000, half that amount had been transferred to him, the credit having come from an unnamed account holder at the Handelsbank. This he knew to be Endean. He shrugged. It was normal for half the salary only to be paid at this early date. He was confident from the sheer size of ManCon, and their evident eagerness to see Kimba fall from power, that the other £5000 would be his as the operation progressed.

Through the afternoon he typed out a full report of his Luxembourg and Hamburg trip, excluding the names of the firm of accountants in Luxembourg, and the two arms dealers. To these sheets he attached a full statement of expenditure.

It was past four when he finished, and he had not eaten since the mid-morning snack provided by Lufthansa on the flight from Hamburg. He found half a dozen eggs in the fridge, made a complete mess of an omelette, threw it away and had a nap.

The arrival of Janni Dupree at the door just after six woke him, and five minutes later the phone rang. It was Endean who had picked up the telegram in the post office.

Endean soon noticed that Shannon was not in a position to talk freely. 'Is there someone with you?' asked Endean down the phone.

'Yes.'

'Is it connected with business?'

'Yes.'

'Do you want to meet?'

'I think we ought,' said Shannon. 'What about tomorrow morning?'

'OK. About eleven suit you?'

'Sure,' said Shannon.

'Your place?'

'Suits me fine.'

'I'll be there at eleven,' said Endean and hung up.

Shannon turned to the South African.

'How are you getting on, Janni?' he asked.

Dupree had made a little progress in the three days he had been working. The hundred pairs of socks, singlets and underpants were on order and would be ready for collection by Friday. He had found a supplier for the fifty combat tunics, and had placed the order. The same firm could have provided trousers to match, but according to his orders Dupree was seeking another firm to supply the trousers, so that no one supplier would realise he was providing complete sets of uniforms. Dupree mentioned that no one seemed suspicious in any case, but Shannon decided nevertheless to stick to the original idea.

Janni said he had tried several footwear stores, but had not found the canvas boots he was looking for. He would go on trying for the rest of the week, and start searching for berets, haversacks, knapsacks, a variety of webbing and sleeping bags next week. Shannon advised him to contact his first export agent and get the first consignment of underwear and tunics off to Marseilles as soon as possible. He promised Dupree to get from Langarotti the name and address of a consignee agent in Marseilles within the next forty-eight hours.

Before the South African left, Shannon typed out a letter to Langarotti and addressed it to him under his real name at the main post office of Marseilles. In the letter he reminded the Corsican of a conversation they had had six months earlier beneath the palm trees when the talk had turned to the buying of arms. The Corsican had mentioned that he knew a man in Paris who could get end user certificates from a diplomat in one of the Paris embassies of an African republic. Shannon needed to know the name of the man and where he could be contacted.

When he had finished he gave Dupree the letter and ordered him to post it express rate that same evening from Trafalgar Square. He explained he would have done it himself but he had to wait in the flat for Langarotti himself to ring from Marseilles.

He was getting very hungry by eight when Langarotti finally called, his voice crackling down a telephone line that must have been created personally by the inventor of that antique masterpiece, the French telephone network.

Shannon asked him, in guarded terms, how he had been getting on. Before any of the mercenaries had left him he had warned them all that under no circumstances was a telephone line to be used to talk openly about what they were doing.

'I checked into a hotel and sent you a telegram with my address on it,' said Langarotti.

'I know. I got it,' shouted Shannon.

'I hired a scooter and toured all the shops that deal in the kind of merchandise we are looking for,' came the voice. 'There are three manufacturers in each category. I got the addresses and names of the three boatmakers and wrote off to each for their brochures. I should get them in a week or so. Then I can order the best-suited from the local dealers, quoting the maker's name and brand name of the article,' said Langarotti.

'Good idea,' said Shannon. 'What about the second articles?'

'They depend on the kind we pick from the brochures I shall get. One depends on the other. But don't worry. Of the second thing we need there are thousands of every kind and description in the shops along this coast. With spring coming, every shop in every port is stocking up with the latest models.'

'OK. Fine,' Shannon shouted. 'Now listen. I need the name of a good export agent for shipping. I need it earlier than I thought. There will be a few crates to be sent from here in the near future, and another from Hamburg.'

'I can get that easy enough,' said Langarotti from the other end. 'But I think it will be better in Toulon. You can guess why.'

Shannon could guess. Langarotti could use another name at his hotel, but for exporting goods from the port on a small freighter, he would have to identify himself with his identity card. Moreover, in the past year or so Marseilles police had tightened up considerably in their watch on the port and a new Customs chief had been drafted in, who was believed to be a holy terror. The aim of both operations was to clamp down on the heroin traffic that made Marseilles the start of the French connection with New York, but a search of a boat for drugs could just as easily turn up arms instead. It would be the worst irony to be caught because of something one was not even involved in.

'Fair enough, you know that area best,' said Shannon. 'Cable me the name and address as soon as you have it. There is one other thing. I have sent a letter, by express rate tonight, to you personally at the main post office in Marseilles. You'll see what I want when you read it. Cable me the man's name at once, when you get the letter, which should be Friday morning.'

'OK,' said Langarotti. 'Is that all?'

'Yes, for the moment. Send me those brochures as soon as you get them, with your own comments and the prices. We must stay in budget.'

'Right. Bye-bye,' called Langarotti, and Shannon hung up. He had a dinner alone at the Bois de St Jean and slept early.

Endean called at eleven the next morning and spent an hour reading the report and accounts, and discussing both with Shannon.

'Fair enough,' he said at length. 'How are things going?'

'Well,' said Shannon. 'It's early days yet, of course. I've only been on the job for ten days, but a lot of ground has been covered. I want to get all the orders placed by Day Twenty, which will leave forty days for them to be fulfilled. After that there must be an allowance of twenty days to collect all the component parts and get them safely and discreetly aboard the ship. Sailing date should be Day Eighty, if we are to strike on schedule. By the way, I shall need more money soon.'

'You have three and a half thousand in London, and seven thousand in Belgium,' objected Endean.

'Yes, I know. But there is going to be a spate of payments soon.'

He explained he would have to pay 'Johann', the Hamburg arms dealer, the outstanding 26,000 dollars within twelve days to allow him forty days to get the consignment through the formalities in Madrid and ready for shipment; then there would be 4800 dollars also to Johann for the ancillary gear he needed for the attack. When he had the end user certificate in Paris, he would have to send it to 'Alan', along with a credit transfer of 7200 dollars, being fifty per cent of the Yugoslav arms price.

'It all mounts up,' he said. 'The big payments, of course, are the arms and the boat. They form over half the total budget.'

'All right,' said Endean. 'I'll consult and prepare a draft to your Belgian account for another £20,000. Then the transfer can be made on a telephone call from me to Switzerland. In that way it will only take a matter of hours, when you need it.'

He rose to go.

'Anything else?'

'No,' said Shannon. 'I'll have to go away again at the weekend for another trip. I should be away most of next week. I want to check on the search for the boat, the choice of dinghies and outboards in Marseilles and the submachine guns in Belgium.'

'Cable me at the usual address when you leave and when you get back,' said Endean.

The drawing-room in the sprawling apartment above Cottesmore Gardens, not far from Kensington High Street, was gloomy in the extreme, with heavy drapes across the windows to shut out the spring sunshine. A gap a few inches wide between them allowed a little daylight to filter in through thick net curtains. Between the four formally placed and overstuffed chairs, each of them late Victorian pieces, a myriad small tables bore assorted bric-à-brac. There were buttons from long-punctured uniforms, medals won in long-past skirmishes with long-liquidated heathen tribes. Glass paperweights nudged Dresden china dolls, cameos of once-demure Highland beauties and fans that had cooled faces at balls whose music was no longer played.

Round the walls of discoloured brocades hung portraits of ancestors, Montroses and Monteaths, Farquhars and Frasers, Murrays and Mintos.

Surely such a gathering could not all be the ancestors of one old woman? Still, you never knew with the Scots.

Bigger than them all, in a vast frame above the fire that, clearly, was never lit, stood a man in a kilt, a painting evidently much more recent than the other blackened antiques, but still discoloured by age. The face, framed by two bristling ginger mutton-chop whiskers, glared down into the room, as if its owner had just spotted a coolie impudently collapsing from overwork at the other end of the plantation. Sir Ian Macallister, KBE, read the motto beneath the portrait.

Martin Thorpe dragged his eyes back to Lady Macallister, slumped in a chair and fiddling as she constantly did with the hearing aid that hung on her chest. He tried to make out from the mumblings and ramblings, sudden digressions and difficult accent, what she was saying.

'People have come before, Mr Martin,' she was saying; she insisted on calling him Mr Martin, although he had introduced himself twice. 'But I don't see why I should sell. It was my husband's company, don't you see. He founded all these estates that they make their money from. It was all his work. Now people come and say they want to take the company away and do other things with it ... build houses and play around with other things. I don't understand it all, not at all, and I will not sell ...'

'But Lady Macallister ...'

She went on as if she had not heard him, which indeed she had not, for her hearing aid was up to its usual tricks through her constant fiddling with it. Thorpe began to understand why other suitors had eventually gone elsewhere for their shell companies.

'You see, my dear husband, God rest his poor soul, was not able to leave me very much, Mr Martin. When those dreadful Chinese killed him, I was in Scotland on furlough, and I never went back. I was advised not to go. But they told me the estates belonged to the company, and he had left me a large part of the company. So that was his legacy to me, don't you see. I could not sell his own legacy to me ...'

Thorpe was about to say that the company was worthless, but realised that would not have been the right thing to say.

'Lady Macallister ...' he began again.

'You'll have to speak directly into the hearing aid. She's deaf as a post,' said Lady Macallister's companion.

Thorpe nodded his thanks at her, and noticed her properly for the first time. In her late sixties, she had the care-worn look of those who once had their own independence, but who, through the strange turns of fortune, have fallen on harder times and to survive have to put themselves in bond to others, often to cantankerous, troublesome, exhausting employers, whose money enables them to hire others to serve them.

Thorpe rose and approached the senile old woman in the armchair. He spoke closer to the hearing aid.

'Lady Macallister, the people I represent do not want to change the company. On the contrary, they want to put a lot of money into it and make it rich and famous again. We want to start up the Macallister estates, just like when your husband ran them ...'

For the first time since the interview had started an hour before, some-thing like a glimmer of light awoke in the old woman's eyes.

'Like when my husband ran them . . .?' she queried.

'Yes, Lady Macallister,' bawled Thorpe. He pointed up at the figure of the tyrant on the wall. 'We want to create all his life's work again just the way he would have wanted it, and make the Macallister estates a memorial to him and his work.'

But she was gone again.

'They never put up a memorial to him,' she quavered. 'I tried, you know. I wrote to the authorities. I said I would pay for the statue, but they said there was no room. No room. They put up lots of statues, but not to my Ian.'

'They will put up a memorial to him if the estates and the company become rich again,' Thorpe shouted into the hearing aid. 'They'll have to. If the company was rich, it could insist on a memorial. It could found a scholarship, or a foundation, called the Sir Ian Macallister Trust, so that people would remember him . . .'

He had already tried that ploy once, but no doubt she had not heard him, or not grasped what he was saying. But she heard him this time.

'It would cost a lot of money,' she quavered. 'I am not a rich woman . . .'

She was in fact extremely rich, but probably unaware of it.

'You don't have to pay for it, Lady Macallister,' he said. 'The company would pay for it. But the company would have to expand again. And that means money. The money would be put into the company by my friends . . .'

'I don't know, I don't know,' she wailed and began to sniff, reaching for a cambric handkerchief in her sleeve. 'I don't understand these things. If only my dear Ian were here. Or Mr Dalgleish. I always ask him what would be for the best. He always signs the papers for me. Mrs Barton, I'd like to go back to my room.'

'It's time enough,' said the housekeeper-companion brusquely. 'Now come along, it's time for your nap. And your medicine.'

She helped the old woman to her feet and assisted her out of the sitting-room and down the corridor. Through the open door Thorpe could hear her businesslike voice commanding her charge to get on to the bed, and the old woman's protests as she took her medicine.

After a while Mrs Barton came back to the sitting-room.

'She's on the bed, she'll rest for a while,' she said.

Thorpe smiled his most rueful smile.

'It looks as if I've failed,' he said sadly. 'And yet, you know, the stock she holds is quite valueless unless the company is rejuvenated with fresh management and some hard cash, quite a lot of it, which my partners would be prepared to put in.'

He prepared to leave for the door.

'I'm sorry if I put you to inconvenience,' he said.

'I'm quite used to inconvenience,' said Mrs Barton, but her face soft-ened. It had been a long time since anyone apologised for putting her to trouble. 'Would you care for a cup of tea? I usually make one at this hour.'

Some instinct at the back of Thorpe's mind prompted him to accept. As they sat over a pot of tea in the back kitchen which was the house-keeper-companion's domain, Martin Thorpe felt almost at home. His mother's kitchen in Battersea had not been dissimilar. Mrs Barton told him about Lady Macallister, her whining and her tantrums, her all-too-convenient deafness.

'She can't see all your fine arguments, Mr Thorpe, not even when you offered to put up a memorial to that old ogre in the sitting-room.'

Thorpe was surprised. Evidently the tart Mrs Barton had a mind of her own when her employer was not listening.

'She does what you tell her,' he said.

'Would you like another cup of tea?' she asked. As she poured it, she said quietly, 'Oh yes, she does what I tell her. She depends on me, and she knows it. If I went, she'd never get another companion. You can't nowa-days. People aren't prepared to put up with that sort of thing these days.'

'It can't be much of a life for you, Mrs Barton?'

'It's not,' she said shortly, 'but I have a roof over my head, and food and some clothes. I get by. It's the price one pays.'

'For being a widow?' asked Thorpe gently.

'Yes.'

There was a picture of a young man in the uniform of a pilot of the Royal Air Force, propped on the mantelpiece next to the clock. He wore a sheepskin jacket, a polka-dotted scarf and a broad grin. Seen at one angle, he looked not unlike Martin Thorpe.

'Your son?' said the financier, with a nod.

Mrs Barton nodded and gazed at the picture.

'Yes. Shot down over France in 1943.'

'I'm sorry.'

'It was a long time ago. One becomes accustomed.'

'So he won't be able to look after you when she's dead and gone.'

'No.'

'Then who will?'

'I'll get by. She'll no doubt leave me something in her will. I've looked after her for sixteen years.'

'Yes, of course she will. She'll see you all right – no doubt of it.'

He spent another hour in the back kitchen, and when he left he was a much happier man. It was nearly closing time for shops and offices, but from a corner phone booth he made a call to the head office of ManCon, and within ten minutes Endean had done what his colleague asked.

In the West End an insurance broker agreed to stay late in his office that night and receive Mr Thorpe at ten the next morning.

That Thursday evening Johann Schlinker flew into London from Ham-burg. He had arranged his evening appointment by telephone from Ham-burg the same morning, phoning his contact at his home rather than the office.

He met the diplomat from the Iraqui embassy for dinner at nine. It was an expensive dinner, even more so when the German arms dealer handed over an envelope containing the equivalent in German marks of £1000. In return he took an envelope from the Arab and checked the contents. They took the form of a letter on crested embassy notepaper. The letter was addressed to whom it might concern, and stated that the undersigned, being a diplomat on the staff of the London embassy of the Republic of Iraq, had been required and requested by the Interior and Police Ministry of his country to authorise Herr Johann Schlinker to negotiate the purchase of 400,000 rounds of standard 9 mm ball for shipment to Iraq to replenish the stocks of the police forces of the country. It was signed by the diplomat, and bore the stamp and seal of the Republic of Iraq, which would normally be on the desk of the ambassador.

The letter further stated that the purchase would be wholly and exclusively for the use of the Republic of Iraq and would under no circumstances be passed, in whole or in part, to any other party. It was an end user certificate.

When they parted, it was too late for the German to return home, so he spent the night in London and left the following morning.

At eleven on the Friday morning Cat Shannon phoned Marc Vlaminck at his flat above the bar in Ostend.

'Did you find that man I asked you to trace?' he enquired after introducing himself. He had already warned the Belgian to talk very carefully on the telephone.

'Yes, I found him,' replied Tiny Marc. He was sitting up in bed, while Anna snored gently beside him. The bar usually closed between three and four in the morning, so midday was the habitual rising time for both of them.

'Is he prepared to talk business about the merchandise?' asked Shannon.

'I think so,' said Vlaminck. 'I haven't raised the matter with him yet, but a business friend here says he will normally do business after a suitable introduction through a mutual acquaintance.'

'He still has the goods I mentioned to you at our last meeting?'

'Yes,' said the voice from Belgium. 'He still has them.'

'Fine,' said Shannon. 'Get a meeting and introduction with him yourself first, and tell him you have a customer who has approached you and would like to talk business. Ask him to be available for a meeting next weekend with the customer. Tell him the customer is good and reliable, and is an Englishman called Brown. You know what to say. Just get him interested in a business deal. Tell him the customer would wish to examine one example of the goods at the meeting, and if it is up to standard, discuss terms and delivery. I'll ring you towards the weekend and let you know where I am, and when I could come to see you and him together. Understand?'

'Sure,' said Marc, 'I'll get on with it over the next couple of days and set the meeting up for some time to be confirmed later, but during next weekend.'

They exchanged the usual good wishes and hung up.

At half past two, a cable arrived at the flat from Marseilles. It bore the name of a Frenchman and an address. Langarotti said he would telephone the man and introduce Shannon with a personal recommendation. The cable concluded by saying enquiries regarding the shipping agent were under way, and he expected to be able to give Shannon a name and address within five days.

Shannon picked up the phone and rang the offices of UTA Airlines in Piccadilly, to book himself a seat on the flight of the following Sunday midnight to Africa from Le Bourget, Paris. From BEA he reserved a ticket to Paris on the first flight the next morning, Saturday. By the late afternoon he had paid for both of them in cash.

He put £2000 of the money he had brought back from Germany into an envelope and slipped it into the lining at the bottom of his handgrip, for London airport representatives of the Treasury by and large disapprove of British citizens strolling out of the country with more than the permitted £25 in cash and £300 in travellers cheques.

Just after lunch Sir James Manson summoned Simon Endean to his office. He had finished reading Shannon's report and was agreeably surprised at the speed with which the mercenary's proposed plan of twelve days earlier was being carried out. He had checked the accounts and approved the expenditure. What pleased him even more was the long telephone call he had had from Martin Thorpe, who had spent half the night and most of the morning with an insurance broker.

'You say Shannon will be abroad for most of next week,' he told Endean when his aide entered the office.

'Yes, Sir James.'

'Good. There's a job that has to be done sooner or later, and it might as well be now. Get one of our standard contracts of employment, the kind we use for the engagement of African representatives. Paste over the name of ManCon with a strip of white paper and fill in the name of Bormac in its place. Make it out for a one-year's engagement for the services as West African representative of Antoine Bobi at a salary of £500 a month. When you've got it done, show it to me.'

'Bobi?' queried Endean. 'You mean Colonel Bobi?'

'That's the one. I don't want the future president of Zangaro running off anywhere. Next week, starting Monday, you are going down to Cotonou to interview the colonel and persuade him that Bormac Trading Company, whose representative you are, has been so impressed by his mental and business acumen that it would like to engage his services as a West African consultant. Don't worry, he'll never check to see who or what Bormac is, or that you are its representative. If I know anything about these lads, the hefty salary will be what interests him. If he's short of the ready, it ought to be manna from heaven.

'You are to tell him his duties will be communicated to him later, but the sole condition of employment for the moment is that he remain where he is at his house in Dahomey for the next three months or until you visit him again. Persuade him there will be a bonus in salary if he waits where he is. Tell him the money will be transferred to his local account in Dahomean francs. On no account is he to receive any hard currency. He might vamoose. One last thing. When the contract is ready, have it photo-copied to hide the traces of the change of name of the employing company, and only take with you photo-copies. As for the date on it, make sure the last figure for the year is blurred. Smudge it yourself.'

Endean absorbed the instructions and left to begin setting up the employment under false pretences of Colonel Antoine Bobi.

That Friday afternoon, just after four, Thorpe emerged from the gloomy Kensington apartment with the four share transfer deeds he needed, duly signed by Lady Macallister and witnessed by Mrs Barton. He also bore a letter of authority signed by the old woman instructing Mr Dalgleish, her attorney in Dundee, to hand over to Mr Thorpe the share certificates upon the presentation of the letter and proof of identity, and the necessary cheque.

The name of the recipient of the shares had been left blank on the transfer deeds, but Lady Macallister had not noticed. She had been too distraught at the thought of Mrs Barton packing her bags and leaving. Before nightfall the name of the Zwingli Bank's nominee company, acting on behalf of Messrs Adams, Ball, Carter and Davies, would be written into the vacant space. After a visit to Zürich the following Monday the bank stamp and counter-signature of Dr Steinhofer would complete the form, and four certified cheques, one drawn against the account of each of the four nominees buying seven and a half per cent of the stock of Bormac, would be brought back from Switzerland.

It had cost Sir James Manson two shillings to buy each of the 300,000 shares, then quoted at one shilling and one penny on the Stock Exchange, or a total of £30,000. It had also cost him another £30,000, shunted that morning through three bank accounts, withdrawn once in cash and re-paid into a fresh account an hour later to purchase a life annuity which would assure a comfortable and worry-free end to her days to an elderly housekeeper-companion.

All in all, Thorpe reckoned it was cheap at the price. Even more important, it was untraceable. Thorpe's name appeared nowhere on any document, the annuity had been paid for by a solicitor and solicitors are paid to keep their mouths shut; Thorpe was confident Mrs Barton would have enough sense to do the same. And to cap it all, it was even legal.

13

Benoît Lambert, known to friends and police as Benny, was a small-fry member of the underworld and self-styled mercenary. In point of fact, his sole appearance in the mercenary-soldier field had occurred when, with the police looking for him in the Paris area, he had taken a plane for Africa and signed on in the Sixth Commando in the Congo under the leadership of Denard.

For some strange reason the mercenary leader had taken a liking to the timorous little man and had given him a job at headquarters, which kept him well away from combat. He had been useful in his job, because it enabled him to exercise to good effect the one talent he really did possess. He was a wizard at obtaining things. He seemed to be able to conjure up eggs where there were no chickens and whisky where there was no still. In the headquarters of any military unit, such a man is always useful, and most units have one. He had stayed with the Sixth Commando for nearly a year, until May 1967 when he spotted trouble brewing in the form of a pending revolt by Schramme's Tenth Commando against the Congolese government. He felt, rightly as it turned out, that Denard and the Sixth might be drawn into this fracas, and there would be an opportunity for all, including headquarters staff, to see some real combat. For Benny Lambert this was the moment to move briskly in the other direction.

To his surprise he had been allowed to go.

Back in France he had cultivated the notion of himself as a mercenary and later called himself an arms dealer. The first he certainly was not, but as for arms, with his variety of contacts he had occasionally been able to provide an item of weaponry here and there, usually hand guns for the underworld, occasionally a case of rifles. He had also come to know an African diplomat who was prepared, for a price, to provide a moderately serviceable end user certificate in the form of a letter from the ambassador's personal desk, complete with embassy stamp. Eighteen months earlier, he had mentioned this in a bar to a Corsican called Langarotti.

Nevertheless, he was surprised on the Friday evening to hear the Corsican on the phone, calling long distance, to tell him he would be visited at his home the next day or Sunday by Cat Shannon. He had heard of Shannon, but even more so he was aware of the vitriolic hatred Charles Roux bore for the Irish mercenary, and he had long since heard on the grapevine that circulated among the mercenaries of Paris that Roux was prepared to pay money to anyone who would tip him off as to Shannon's whereabouts, should the Irishman ever turn up in Paris. After consideration, Lambert agreed to be at home to see Shannon.

'Yes, I think I can get that certificate,' he said when Shannon had finished explaining what he wanted. 'My contact is still in Paris. I deal with him fairly frequently, you know.'

It was a lie, for his dealings were very infrequent, but he was sure he could swing the deal.

'How much?' asked Shannon shortly.

'Fifteen thousand francs,' said Benny Lambert.

'Bollocks,' said Shannon, and he said it in French. It was one of the numerous phrases he had picked up in the Congo, even though it was not to be found in the best of Larousse's French dictionaries. 'I'll pay you a thousand pounds, and that's over the rate.'

Lambert calculated. The sum was just over eleven thousand francs at the current rate.

'OK,' he said.

'You let out one word of this, and I'll slit your gizzard like a chicken,' said Shannon. 'Even better, I'll get the Corsican to do it, and he'll start at the knee.'

'Not a word, honest,' protested Benny. 'A thousand pounds, and I'll get you the letter in four days. And not a word to anyone.'

Shannon put down five hundred pounds.

'You'll take it in sterling,' he said. 'Half now, half when I pick it up.'

Lambert was about to protest, but realised it would be no good. The Irishman did not trust him.

'I'll call you here on Wednesday,' said Shannon. 'Have the letter here, and I'll hand over the other five hundred.'

When he had gone Benny Lambert thought over what he would do. Finally he decided to get the letter, collect the remainder of his fee, and tell Roux later.

The following evening Shannon flew to Africa on the midnight flight, arriving at dawn on Monday morning.

It was a long drive upcountry. The taxi was hot and rattled abominably. It was still the height of the dry season, and the sky above the oil-palm plantations was robin's-egg blue, without a cloud. Shannon did not mind. It was good to be back in Africa again for a day and a half, even after a six-hour flight without sleep.

It was familiar to him, more so than the cities of western Europe. Familiar were the sounds and the smells, the villagers walking along the edge of the road to market, columns of women in Indian file, their gourds and bundles of wares balanced on their heads, unwaveringly steady.

At each village they passed, the usual morning market was set out beneath the shade of the palm-thatch roofs of the rickety stalls, the villagers bargaining and chattering, buying and selling, the women tending the stalls while the men sat in the shade and talked of important matters that only they could understand, and the naked brown children scampering through the dust between the legs of their parents and the stalls.

Shannon had both windows open. He sat back and sniffed the moisture and the palms, the woodsmoke and the brown stagnant rivers they crossed. From the airport he had already telephoned the number the writer had given him, and knew he was expected. He arrived at the villa set back from the road in a private, if small, park just before noon.

The guards checked him at the gate, frisking him from ankles to armpits, before letting him pay off the taxi and enter the gate. Inside, he recognised a face, one of the personal attendants of the man he had come to see. The servant grinned broadly and bobbed his head. He led Shannon to one of the three houses in the grounds of the park and ushered him into an empty sitting-room. He waited alone for half an hour.

Shannon was staring out of the windows, feeling the cool of the air conditioner dry out his clothes, when he heard the creak of a door and the soft sound of a sandal on tiles behind him. He turned round.

The general was much the same as when they had last met on the darkened airstrip, the same luxuriant beard, the same deep bass voice.

'Well, Major Shannon, so soon. Couldn't you stay away?'

He was bantering, as he usually did. Shannon grinned as they shook hands.

'I've come down because I need something, sir. And because there is something I think we ought to talk over. An idea in the back of my head.'

'There's not much that an impoverished exile can offer you,' said the general, 'but I'll always listen to your ideas. If I remember rightly, you used to have some fairly good ones.'

Shannon said, 'There's one thing you have, even in exile, that I could use. You still have your people's loyalty. And what I need is men.'

The two men talked through the lunch hour and through the afternoon. They were still discussing when darkness fell, Shannon's freshly drawn diagrams spread out on the table. He had brought nothing with him but clean white paper and a variety of coloured felt-nib pens. Just in case of a skin-search at Customs.

They reached agreement on the basic points by sundown and elaborated the plan through the night. Only at three in the morning was the car summoned to drive Shannon back to the coast and the airport for takeoff on the dawn plane to Paris.

As they parted on the terrace above the waiting car and its sleepy chauffeur, they shook hands again.

'I'll be in touch, sir,' said Shannon.

'And I'll have to send my emissaries immediately,' replied the general. 'But in sixty days the men will be there.'

Shannon was dead tired. The strain of the constant travelling was beginning to tell, the nights without sleep, the endless succession of airports and hotels, negotiations and meetings, had left him drained. In the car to the south he slept for the first time in two days, and dozed again on the plane trip back to Paris. The flight stopped too many times to enable a proper sleep, an hour at Ouagadougou, another at a God-forsaken strip in Mauretania, and again at Marseilles. He reached Le Bourget just before six in the afternoon. It was the end of Day Fifteen.

While he was landing in Paris, Martin Thorpe was boarding the over-night sleeper train to Glasgow, Stirling and Perth. From there he could make a connecting train to Dundee, where were situated the old-estab-lished offices of Dalgleish and Dalgleish, attorneys-at-law. He carried in his briefcase the document signed before the weekend by Lady Mac-allister and witnessed by Mrs Barton, along with the cheques issued by the Zwingli Bank of Zürich, four of them, each in the sum of £7500 and each enough to purchase 75,000 of Lady Macallister's shares in Bormac.

Twenty-four hours, he thought as he drew down the blinds of his first-class sleeper compartment, blotting out the sights of the scurrying platform of Euston station. Twenty-four hours should see it through, and they would be home and dry, and three weeks later a new director on the board, a nominee responding to the strings pulled by him and Sir James Manson. Settling himself on the bunk, his briefcase under the pillow, Martin Thorpe enjoyed the feel of it and gazed up at the ceiling.

Later that Tuesday evening Shannon was settled into a hotel not far from the Madeleine in the heart of Paris's 8th arrondissement. He had had to forsake his regular Montmartre hideout, where he was known as Carlo Shannon, because he was now using the name of Keith Brown. But the Plaza-Surene was a good substitute. He had bathed and shaved and was about to go out for dinner. He had telephoned to book a table at his favourite eating place in the quarter, the Restaurant Mazagran, and Madame Michelle had promised him a filet mignon the way he liked it, with a tossed lettuce salad by the side and a Pot de Chirouble to wash it down.

The two person-to-person calls he had booked came through almost together. First on the line was a certain M. Lavallon from Marseilles, whom he knew better as Jean-Baptiste Langarotti.

'Do you have that shipping agent yet?' asked Shannon when they had exchanged greetings.

'Yes,' said the Corsican. 'It's in Toulon. A very good one, very respect-able and efficient. They have their own bonded warehouse on the port.'

'Spell it out,' said Shannon. He had pencil and paper ready.

'Agence Maritime Duphot,' spelled Langarotti, and dictated the address. 'Send the consignments to the agency, clearly marked as the property of Monsieur Langarotti.'

Shannon hung up, and the hotel operator came on the line immedi-ately to say a Mr Dupree was calling from London.

'I just got your cable,' bawled Janni Dupree.

Shannon dictated the name and address of the Toulon agents to him, letter by letter, and Dupree took it down.

'Fine,' he said at length. 'I've got the first of the four crates ready and bonded over here. I'll tell the London agents to get the stuff on its way as soon as possible. Oh, by the way, I've found the boots.'

'Good,' said Shannon, 'well done.'

He placed one more call, this time to a bar in Ostend. There was a fifteen-minute delay before Marc's voice came through.

'I'm in Paris,' said Shannon. 'That man with the sample of merchandise I wanted to examine . . .'

'Yes,' said Marc. 'I've been in touch. He's prepared to meet you and discuss prices and terms.'

'Good. I'll be in Belgium Thursday night or Friday morning. Tell him I propose Friday morning over breakfast in my room at the Holiday Inn Hotel near the airport.'

'I know it,' said Marc. 'All right, I'll put it to him and call you back.'

'Call me tomorrow between ten and eleven,' said Shannon and hung up.

Only then did he slip on his jacket and head for a long-awaited dinner and a long-desired full night's sleep.

While Shannon slept, Simon Endean was also winging his way southwards to Africa on the overnight flight. He had arrived in Paris by the first flight on Monday and taken a taxi immediately to the embassy of Dahomey in the Avenue Victor Hugo. Here he had filled out a lengthy pink form requesting a six-day tourist visa. It was ready for collection just before the closure of the consular office on the Tuesday afternoon, and he had caught the midnight flight to Cotonou via Niamey. Shannon would not have been particularly surprised to know that Endean was going to Africa, for he assumed the exiled Colonel Bobi had to play some part in Sir James Manson's scheme of things, and that the former commander of the Zangaran Army was cooling his heels somewhere along the mangrove coast. But if Endean had known Shannon had just returned from a secret visit to the general in the same area of Africa, it would have quite ruined his sleep aboard the UTA DC-8 that night, despite the pill he had taken to ensure an uninterrupted slumber.

Marc Vlaminck rang Shannon at his hotel at ten-fifteen the next day.

'He agrees to the meeting, and he'll bring the sample,' said the Belgian. 'Do you want me to come too?'

'Certainly,' said Shannon. 'When you get to the hotel ask at reception for the room of Mr Brown. One other thing. Have you bought that van I asked you to get?'

'Yes, why?'

'Has this gentleman seen it yet?'

There was a pause while Vlaminck thought.

'No.'

'Then don't bring it to Brussels. Hire a car and drive yourself. Pick him up on the way. Understood?'

'Yes,' said Vlaminck, still perplexed. 'Anything you say.'

Shannon, who was still in bed but feeling a sight better, rang for breakfast and had his habitual five minutes under the shower, four of them in steaming hot water and sixty seconds under a stream of ice-cold. The coffee and rolls were on the side table when he emerged. He placed two calls from the bedside phone, to Benny Lambert in Paris and Mr Stein of Lang & Stein in Luxembourg.

'Have you got that letter for me?' he asked Lambert.

The little crook's voice sounded strained.

'Yes. I got it yesterday. Luckily my contact was on duty on Monday and I saw him that night. He produced the letter of introduction yesterday evening. When do you want it?'

'This afternoon,' said Shannon.

'All right. Have you got my fee?'

'Don't worry, I've got it right here.'

'Then come to my place about three,' said Lambert.

Shannon thought for a moment.

'No, I'll meet you here,' he said, and gave Lambert the name of his hotel. He preferred to meet the little man in a public place. Rather to his surprise Lambert agreed to come round to the hotel, with what sounded like elation in his voice. There was something not quite right about this deal, but Shannon could not put his finger on it. What he did not realise was that he had given the Paris crook the information he would later sell to Roux.

Mr Stein was engaged on the other phone when the call came, so rather than wait Shannon said he would ring back. This he did an hour later.

'About the meeting to launch my holding company, Tyrone Holdings,' he began.

'Ah yes, Mr Brown,' said Stein's voice down the line. 'Everything is in order. When would you suggest?'

'Tomorrow afternoon,' replied Shannon. It was agreed the meeting would be in Stein's office at three. Shannon got the hotel to book him a reserved place on the express from Paris to Luxembourg just after nine the next morning.

'I must say, I find it all very strange, very strange indeed.'

Mr Duncan Dalgleish Senior in appearance and manner matched his office, and his office looked as if it had been the scene for the reading of the will of Sir Walter Scott.

He examined the four share transfer deeds, signed by Lady Macallister and witnessed by Mrs Barton, carefully and at length. He had muttered 'Aye' in sorrowful tones several times, and the glances he shot at the younger man from London were disapproving. He was evidently quite unused to handling certified cheques from a bank in Zürich, and he had held them between forefinger and thumb, as he read them. He was examining the four deeds again as he spoke.

'Ye'll understand, Lady Macallister has been approached before, concerning the sale of these shares. In the past she has always seen fit to consult the firm of Dalgleish, and I have always seen fit to advise her against selling the stock,' he went on.

Thorpe thought privately that no doubt other of Mr Duncan Dalgleish's clients were holding on to piles of valueless stock on the basis of his advice, but he kept his face polite.

'Mr Dalgleish, you must agree the gentlemen whom I represent have paid Lady Macallister close to twice the face value of the stock. She for her part has freely signed the deeds and empowered me to collect the shares on presentation of cheque or cheques totalling £30,000. Which you now hold in your hand.'

The old man sighed again.

'It's just so strange that she should not have consulted me first,' he said sadly. 'I usually advise her on all her financial matters. For this I hold her general power of attorney.'

'But her own signature is still perfectly valid,' insisted Thorpe.

'Yes, yes, my power of attorney in no way invalidates her own power to sign on her behalf.'

'Then I would be grateful if you would let me have the share certificates so that I can return to London,' said Thorpe.

The old man rose slowly.

'Would you excuse me, Mr Thorpe,' he said with dignity, and withdrew into an inner sanctum. Thorpe knew he was going to telephone London, and prayed Lady Macallister's hearing aid would make it necessary for Mrs Barton to interpret for the pair of them on the telephone. It was half an hour before the old attorney came back. He held a large wad of old and discoloured share certificates in his hand.

'Lady Macallister has confirmed what you say, Mr Thorpe. Not, of course, that I doubted your word, ye understand. I felt obliged to speak with my client before completing such a large transaction.'

'Of course,' said Thorpe, rose and held out his hand. Dalgleish parted with the shares as if they had been his own.

An hour later Thorpe was in his train, rolling through the spring-lit countryside of Angus County on his way back to London.

Six thousand miles away from the heather-clad hills of Scotland Simon Endean was seated with the hulking form of Colonel Bobi in a small rented villa in the residential district of Cotonou. He had arrived on the morning plane and checked into the Hotel du Port, whose Israeli manager had helped him trace the house where the exiled Zangaran army officer lived in the straitened circumstances of exile.

Bobi was a lumbering giant of a man with a brooding brutishness and massive hands. The combination pleased Endean. It was of no consequence to him with what disastrous effects Bobi might rule Zangaro in succession to the equally disastrous Jean Kimba. What he had come to find was a man who would sign away the mineral rights of the Crystal Mountain range to Bormac Trading Company for a pittance and a hefty bribe to his personal account. He had found what he sought.

In exchange for a salary of £500 a month the colonel would be delighted to accept the post of West Africa consultant to Bormac. He had pretended to study the contract Endean had brought, but the Englishman noted with pleasure that when he turned to the second page, which Endean had stapled upside down between the first and third pages, Bobi's expression did not flicker. He was illiterate, or the next best thing to it.

Endean explained the terms of the contract slowly in the mishmash of language they had been using, a mixture of basic French and Coast-Pidgin English. Bobi nodded soberly, his small eyes, much flecked with blood-shot vessels around the whites, studying the contract intently. Endean stressed that Bobi was to remain in his villa or near it for the next two to three months, and that Endean would return to see him again in that time.

The Englishman elicited that Bobi had still got a valid Zangaran diplomatic passport, a legacy of a visit he had once made outside Zangaro at the side of the Defence Minister, Kimba's cousin.

Shortly before sundown he scrawled what could pass for a signature on the bottom of the document. Not that a signature really mattered. Only later would Bobi be told that Bormac was putting him back into power in exchange for mining rights. Endean surmised that if the price was right, Bobi would not quibble.

The following morning at dawn Endean was on another plane heading back to Paris and London.

The meeting with Benny Lambert took place as agreed in the hotel. It was short and to the point. Lambert handed over an envelope, which Shannon flicked open. From it he took two pieces of paper, both identical and both bearing the printed crest and letterhead of the stationery of the ambassador in Paris of the republic of Togo.

One of the sheets was blank, except for a signature on the bottom and an embassy seal. The other sheet was a letter, in which the author stated that he had been authorised by his government to engage the services of ... to apply to the government of ... for the purchase of the military weapons listed on the attached sheet. The letter concluded with the usual assurance that the weapons were intended solely for use by the armed forces of the republic of Togo, and would not be given or sold to any third party. This too was signed and decorated with the seal of the republic.

Shannon nodded. He was confident Alan Baker would be able to insert his own name as the authorised agent and the Federal Republic of Yugoslavia as the vendor government in such a way as to leave no trace of the insertion. He handed to Lambert the £500 he owed him and left the café.

THE DOGS OF WAR 679

Like most weak men, Lambert was indecisive. He had for three days been on the verge of ringing Charles Roux and telling him that Shannon was in town and seeking an end user certificate. He knew the French mercenary would be more than interested in the news, but he did not know why. He assumed it was because Roux regarded Paris and its resident mercenaries as his private preserve. He would not take kindly to a foreigner coming there to set up an operation in either arms or men without cutting Roux in on the deal as equal partner, or, more desirably, as the 'patron', the boss of the project. It would never occur to Roux that no one would want to finance him to set up an operation because he had blown far too many already, taken too many bribes to kill a project and cheated too many men of their salary.

But Lambert was afraid of Roux and felt he ought to tell him. He had been on the verge of doing so that afternoon, and would have done if Shannon had not had the balance of £500 with him. But to have warned Roux in those circumstances would have cost the little crook that £500 and he was sure Roux would not have made up such a large sum to him, simply for a tip-off. What Lambert did not know was that Roux had placed a killing contract on the Irishman. So in his state of ignorance he worked out another idea.

He was not very bright, was Benny Lambert, but he felt he had hit on the perfect solution. He could collect his full thousand pounds from Shannon, and tell Roux the Irishman had approached him with a request for an end user certificate, which he had promptly refused. There was just one snag. He had heard enough of Shannon to be afraid of him also, and he feared that if Roux was in contact with the Irishman too soon after Lambert's own meeting at the hotel, Shannon would guess from whom the tip-off came. He decided to wait until the following morning.

When he finally gave Roux the tip-off, it was too late. Roux telephoned the hotel at once under another name, and asked if a Mr Shannon was staying there. The chief desk clerk replied quite truthfully that there was no one of that name at the hotel.

Cross-examined, a thoroughly frightened Lambert claimed he had not actually visited the hotel, but had simply received a call from Shannon who had given that hotel as the place where he was staying.

Shortly after nine, Roux's man Henri Alain was at the reception desk of the Plaza-Surene, and established that the only Englishman or Irishman who had stayed in the hotel the previous night exactly corresponded in description to Cat Shannon; that his name and passport had been that of Keith Brown, and that he had booked through the reception desk a ticket on the nine a.m. express train to Luxembourg. Henri Alain learned one more thing; of a meeting that M. Brown had had in the residents' lounge the previous afternoon, and a description of the Frenchman with whom he had been seen speaking. All this he reported back to Roux at midday.

In the French mercenary leader's flat Roux, Henri Alain and Raymond Thomard held a conference of war. Roux made the final decision.

'Henri, we've missed him this time, but the chances are that he still knows nothing about it. So he may well return to that hotel next time he has to overnight in Paris. I want you to get friendly, real friendly, with someone on the staff there. The next time that man checks in there, I want to know, but at once. Understand?'

Alain nodded.

'Sure, *patron*. I'll have it staked out from the inside, and if he even rings to make a booking, we'll know.'

Roux turned to Thomard.

'When he comes again, Raymond, you take the bastard. In the meantime, there's one other little job. That shit Lambert lied his head off. He could have tipped me off last night and we'd have been finished with this affair. So he probably took money off Shannon, then tried to take some more off me for out-of-date information. Just make sure Benny Lambert doesn't do any walking for the next six months.'

The floating of the company to be known as Tyrone Holdings was shorter than Shannon could have thought possible. It was so quick it was over almost before it had begun. He was invited into Mr Stein's private office, where Mr Lang and a junior partner were already seated. Along one wall were three secretaries, as it turned out the secretaries of the three accountants present. With the required seven stockholders on hand, Mr Stein set up the company within five minutes. Shannon handed over the balance of £500 and the thousand shares were issued. Each person present received one and signed for it, then passed them to Mr Stein who agreed to keep them in the company safe. Shannon received 994 shares in a block constituted by one sheet of paper and signed for them. His own shares he pocketed. The articles and memorandum of association were signed by the chairman and company secretary, and copies of each would later be filed with the Registrar of Companies for the Archduchy of Luxembourg. The three secretaries were then sent back to their duties, the board of three directors met and approved the aims of the company, the minutes were noted on one sheet of paper, read out by the secretary and signed by the chairman. That was it. Tyrone Holdings SA existed in law.

The other two directors shook hands with Shannon, calling him Mister Brown as they did so and left. Mr Stein escorted him to the door.

'When you and your associates wish to buy a company in the chosen field of operations, to be owned by Tyrone Holdings,' he told Shannon, 'you will then need to come here, present us with a cheque for the appropriate amount, and buy the new issue at £1 per share. The formalities you can leave to us.'

Shannon understood. Any enquiries would stop at Mr Stein as company chairman. Two hours later he caught the evening plane for Brussels and checked into the Holiday Inn just before eight.

The man who accompanied Tiny Marc Vlaminck when they knocked at Shannon's room the following morning just after ten was introduced as M. Boucher. The pair of them, standing on the threshold when he opened the door, looked like a comic turn. Marc was bulky, towering over his companion, and he was beefy in every place. The other man was fat, extremely fat, the sort of fatness associated with vaudeville funny men and fairground sideshows. He seemed almost circular, balanced like one of those children's plastic toys that cannot be overturned because they are spherical. Only on closer examination was it apparent there were two tiny feet in brilliantly polished shoes beneath the mass, and that the bulk constituting the lower half was divided into two legs. In repose it looked like one single unit.

M. Boucher's head appeared to be the only object to mar the contour of the otherwise uniformly globular mass. It was small at the top and flowed downwards to engulf his collar and hide it from view, the flesh of the jowls resting thankfully on the shoulders. After several seconds Shannon conceded that he also had arms, one each side, and that one held a sleek document case some five inches thick.

'Please come in,' said Shannon and stepped back.

Boucher entered first, turning slightly sideways to slip through the door, like a large ball of grey worsted suiting on castors. Marc followed, giving Shannon a wink as he caught his eye. Introductions followed and they all shook hands. Shannon gestured to an armchair, but Boucher chose the edge of the bed. He was wise, and experienced. He might never have got out of the armchair.

Shannon poured them all coffee, and went straight into business, Tiny Marc sat and stayed silent.

M. Boucher, my associate and friend may have told you that my name is Brown, I am English by nationality, and I am here representing a group of friends who would be interested in acquiring a quantity of sub-machine carbines or machine pistols. M. Vlaminck kindly mentioned to me that he was in a position to introduce me to someone who might have a quantity of machine pistols for sale. I understand from him that these are Schmeisser 9 mm machine pistols, of wartime manufacture, but never used. I also understand and accept that there can be no question of obtaining an export licence for them, but this is accepted by my people and they are prepared to accept all responsibility in this regard. Is that a fair assessment?'

Boucher nodded slowly. He could not nod fast.

'I am in a position to make available a quantity of these pieces,' he said carefully. 'You are right about the impossibility of an export licence. For that reason the identity of my own people has to be protected. Any business arrangement we might come to would have to be on a cash basis, and with security arrangements for my own people.'

He's lying, thought Shannon. There are no people behind Boucher. He is the owner of this stuff, and works alone.

In fact M. Boucher in his younger and slimmer days had been a Belgian SS man, and had worked as a cook in the SS barracks at Namur. His extreme fondness, not to mention obsession, with food had taken him into cooking, and before the war he had lost several jobs because he tasted more than he served through the hatch. In the starving conditions of wartime Belgium he had opted for the cookhouse of the Belgian SS unit, one of the several local SS groups the Nazis recruited in the occupied countries. In the SS, surmised the younger Boucher, one could eat. In 1944, when the Germans pulled back from Namur towards the frontier, a lorry-load of unused Schmeissers from the armoury had been on their way east when the lorry broke down. There was no time to repair the lorry, so the cargo was shifted into a nearby bunker and the entrance dynamited. Boucher watched it happen. Years later he had returned, shovelled away the rubble and removed the thousand weapons.

Since then they had reposed beneath a trap-door built into the floor of the garage of his country cottage, a building left him by his parents who died in the mid-fifties. He had sold job lots of Schmeissers at various times, and had 'unloaded' half of his reserve.

'If these guns are in good working order, I would be interested in buying a hundred of them,' said Shannon. 'Of course, payment would be by cash, in any currency. All reasonable conditions imposed by you would be adhered to in the handing over of the cargo. We also would expect complete discretion.'

'As for the condition, monsieur, they are all brand new. Still in their maker's grease and each still wrapped in its sachet of greaseproof paper with seals unbroken. As they came from the factory thirty years ago and, despite their age, still possibly the finest machine pistol ever made.'

Shannon needed no lectures about the Schmeisser 9 mm. Personally he would have said the Israeli Uzi was better, but it was heavy. The Schmeisser was way ahead better than the Sten, and certainly as good as the much more modern British Sterling. He thought nothing of the American grease-gun, nor the Soviet and Chinese burp-guns. However, Uzis and Sterlings are almost unobtainable and never in mint condition.

'May I see?' he asked.

Wheezing heavily, Boucher pulled the black case he carried on to his knees and flicked open the catches after twirling the wheels of the combination lock. He lifted the lid and held the case forward without attempting to get up.

Shannon rose, crossed the room and took the case from him. He laid it on the bedside table and lifted out the Schmeisser.

It was a beautiful piece of weaponry. Shannon slid his hands over the smooth blue-black metal, gripped the pistol-grip and felt the lightness of it. He pulled back and locked the folding stock and operated the breech mechanism several times and squinted down the barrel from the foresight end. The inside was untouched, unmarked.

'That is the sample model,' wheezed Boucher. 'Of course it has had the maker's grease removed and carries only a light film of oil. But the others are identical. Unused.'

Shannon put it down.

'It takes standard 9 mm ammunition, which is easy to come by,' said Boucher helpfully.

'Thank you, I know,' said Shannon. 'What about magazines? They can't be picked up just anywhere, you know.'

'I can supply five with each weapon,' said Boucher.

'Five?' Shannon queried in feigned amazement. 'I need more than five. Ten at least.'

The bargaining had begun, Shannon complaining about the arms dealer's inability to provide enough magazines, the Belgian protesting that was the limit he could provide for each weapon without beggaring himself. Shannon proposed 75 dollars for each Schmeisser on a deal for 100 guns; Boucher claiming he could only allow that price for a deal of not less than 250 weapons, and that for 100 he would have to demand 125 dollars each. Two hours later they settled for a hundred Schmeissers at a 100 dollars each. They fixed time and place for the following Wednesday evening after dark, and agreed the method for the handover. When it was finished Shannon offered Boucher a lift back in Vlaminck's car to where he had come from, but the fat man chose to call a taxi and be taken to Brussels city centre to make his own way home. He was not prepared to assume that the Irishman, who he was certain was from the IRA, would not take him somewhere quiet and work on him until he had learned the location of the secret hoard. Boucher was quite right. Trust is a silly and superfluous weakness in the black market arms business.

Vlaminck escorted the fat man with his lethal briefcase down to the lobby and saw him away in his taxi. When he returned Shannon was packing.

'Do you see what I mean about the van you bought?' he asked Tiny.

'No,' said the other.

'We will have to use that van for the pick-up on Wednesday,' Shannon pointed out. 'I saw no reason why Boucher should see the real number plates. Have a spare set ready for Wednesday night, will you? It's only for an hour, but if Boucher does want to tip off anyone, they'll have the wrong van.'

'OK, Cat, I'll be ready. I got the lock-up garage two days ago. And the other stuff is on order. Is there anywhere I can take you? I have the hire car for the rest of the day.'

Shannon had Vlaminck drive him westwards to Brugge and wait in a café while Shannon went to the bank. M. Goossens was at lunch, so the pair ate their own lunch in the small restaurant on the main square and Shannon returned to the bank at two-thirty.

There was still £7000 in the Keith Brown account, but a debit of £2000 for the four mercenaries' salaries was due in nine days. He drew a banker's cheque in favour of Johann Schlinker and placed it in an envelope containing a letter from him to Schlinker that he had written in his hotel room late the previous night. It informed Schlinker that the enclosed cheque for 4800 dollars was in full payment for the assorted marine and life-saving articles he had ordered a week earlier, and gave the German the name and address of the Toulon shipping agent to whom the entire consignment should be sent in bond for export, for collection by M. Jean-Baptiste Langarotti. Lastly he informed Schlinker he would be telephoning him the coming week to enquire if the end user certificate for the ordered 9 mm ammunition was in order.

The other letter was to Alan Baker, addressed to his home in Hamburg. The cheque it contained was in Baker's favour for 7200 dollars, and Shannon's letter stated that the sum was in full settlement of the required fifty per cent advance for the purchase of the goods they had discussed over dinner at the Atlantic a week earlier. He included the end user certificate from the government of Togo and the spare sheet from the same source. Lastly he instructed Baker to get straight on with the purchase, and promised he would be in touch by phone regularly to check on progresss.

Both letters were mailed from Brugge post office, express rate and registered.

When they were in the posting box, Shannon had Vlaminck drive him onwards to Ostend, had a couple of beers with the Belgian in a local bar near the seaport, and bought himself a single fare on the evening ferry to Dover.

The boat train deposited him at Victoria station at midnight and he was in bed and asleep by one in the morning of that Saturday. The last thing he did before sleeping was to send a telegram to Endean's *poste restante* address to say he was back and he felt they ought to meet.

The Saturday morning post brought a letter mailed at express rate from Málaga in the south of Spain. It was addressed to Keith Brown but began 'Dear Cat'. It came from Kurt Semmler and stated briefly that he had found a boat, a converted motor fishing vessel built twenty years earlier in a British shipyard, owned by a British citizen and registered in London. It flew a British flag, was ninety feet overall and eighty tons deadweight, with a large central hold amidships and a smaller one aft. It was classed as a private yacht, but could be re-registered as a coaster.

Semmler went on to say the vessel was for sale at a price of £20,000 and that two of the crew would be worth engaging under the new management. He was certain he could find good replacements for the other two crew members.

He finished by saying he was staying at the Málaga Palacio Hotel and asked Shannon to contact him there with his own date of arrival to inspect the boat.

The boat was called the M.Y. *Albatross*.

Shannon checked with BEA and booked himself a flight to Málaga on Monday morning, an open-dated return for which he would pay in cash at the airport. Then he cabled Semmler at his hotel to advise him of his arrival time and flight number.

Endean phoned Shannon that afternoon after checking his mail and receiving the telegram. They met around dinner time that evening at the flat, and Shannon presented Endean with his third lengthy progress report and statement of accounts and expenditure.

'You'll have to make further transfers of money if we are to move ahead in the forthcoming weeks,' Shannon told him. 'We are entering the areas of major expenditure now – the arms and the ship.'

'How much do you need at once?' Endean asked.

Shannon said: 'Two thousand for salaries, four thousand for boats and engines, four thousand for submachine guns and over ten thousand for 9 mm ammunition. That's over twenty thousand. Better make it thirty thousand, or I'll be back next week.'

Endean shook his head.

'I'll make it twenty thousand,' he said. 'You can always contact me if you need more. By the way, I would like to see some of this stuff. That will be £50,000 you'll have gone through inside a month.'

'You can't,' said Shannon. 'The ammunition is not yet bought, nor the boats, engines and so forth. Nor are the mortars and bazookas, nor the submachine pistols. All these deals have to be put through cash on the barrelhead or in advance. I explained that in my first report to your associates.'

Endean eyed him coldly.

'There had better be some purchases being made with all this money,' he grated.

Shannon stared him out.

'Don't threaten me, Harris. A lot of people have tried it; it costs a fortune in flowers. By the way, what about the boat?'

Endean rose.

'Let me know which boat and from whom it is being bought. I'll make the credit transfer direct from my Swiss account.'

'Please yourself,' said Shannon.

He dined alone and well that evening, and had an early night. Sunday would be a free day and he had found Julie Manson was already at home with her parents in Gloucestershire. As he sat over his brandy and coffee he was lost in thought, planning the weeks ahead and trying to visualise the attack on the palace of Zangaro.

It was in the middle of Sunday morning that Julie Manson decided to ring her new lover's flat in London and see if he was there. Outside, the spring rain fell in a steady curtain on the Gloucestershire countryside. She had hoped to be able to saddle up the handsome new gelding her father had given her a month earlier and gallop through the parkland surrounding the family mansion. She had hoped it would be a tonic to the feeling that flooded through her when she thought of the man she had fallen for. But the rain had washed out the idea of riding. Instead she was confined to wandering round the old house, listening to her mother's chit-chat about charity bazaars and orphan relief committees, or staring at the rain falling on the garden.

Her father had been working in his study, but she had seen him go out to the stables to talk to the chauffeur a few minutes earlier. As her mother was within earshot of the telephone in the hallway, she decided to use the extension in the study.

She had lifted the telephone beside the desk in the empty room when her eye caught the sprawl of papers lying across the blotter. On top of them was a single folder. She noted the title and idly lifted the cover to glance at the first page. A name on it caused her to freeze, the telephone still buzzing furiously in her ear. The name was Shannon.

Like most young girls she had had her fantasies, seeing herself as she lay in the darkness of the dormitory at boarding school in the role of heroine of a hundred hazardous exploits, usually saving the man she loved from a terrible fate, to be rewarded by his undying devotion. Unlike most girls she had never completely grown up. From Shannon's persistent questioning about her father, she had already half managed to translate herself into the role of a girl agent on her lover's behalf. The trouble was, most of what she knew about her father was either personal, in his role of indulgent daddy, or very boring. Of his business affairs she knew nothing. And then here, on a rainy Sunday morning, lay her chance.

She flicked her eyes down the first page of the folder, and understood nothing. There were figures, costings, a second reference to the name Shannon, a mention of several banks by name and two references to a man called Clarence. She got no further. The turning of the door handle interrupted her.

With a start she dropped the cover of the folder, stood back a yard and began to babble into the unhearing telephone. Her father stood in the doorway.

'All right, Christine, that will be marvellous, darling. I'll see you on Monday then. 'Bye now,' she chattered into the telephone and hung up.

Her father's set expression had softened as he saw the person in the room was his daughter, and he walked across the carpet to sit behind his desk.

'Now, what are you up to?' he said with mock gruffness.

For answer she twined her soft arms round his neck from behind and kissed him on the cheek.

'Just phoning a friend in London, Daddy,' she said in her small, little-girl voice. 'Mummy was fussing about in the hall, so I came in here.'

'Humph. Well, you've got a phone in your own room. So please use that for private calls.'

'All right, Daddikins.' She cast her glance over the papers lying under the folder on the desk, but the print was too small to read, and was mostly columns of figures. She could make out the headings only. They concerned mining prices. Then her father turned to look up.

'Why don't you stop all this boring old work and come and help me saddle up Tamerlane?' she asked him. 'The rain will stop soon, and I can go riding.'

He smiled up at the girl who was the apple of his eye.

'Because this boring old work happens to be what keeps us all clothed and fed,' he said. 'But I will anyway. Give me a few more minutes and I'll join you in the stable.'

Outside the door, Julie Manson stopped and breathed deeply. Mata Hari, she was sure, could not have done better.

14

The Spanish authorities are far more tolerant to tourists than is generally thought. Bearing in mind the millions of Scandinavians, Germans, French and British who pour into Spain each spring and summer, and given that the law of averages must provide that a certain percentage of them are up to no good, the authorities have quite a lot to put up with. Irrelevant breaches of regulations such as importing two cartons of cigarettes rather than the permitted one carton, which would be pounced on at London airport, are shrugged off in Spain.

The attitude of the Spanish authorities has always tended to be that a tourist really has to work at it to get into trouble in Spain, but once he has made the effort the Spaniards will oblige and make it extremely unpleasant for him. The four items they object to finding in passenger luggage are arms and/or explosives, drugs, pornography and Communist propaganda. Other countries may object to two bottles of duty-free brandy but permit *Penthouse* magazine. Not Spain. Other countries have different priorities, but as any Spaniard will cheerfully admit, Spain is different.

The customs officer at Málaga airport that brilliant Monday afternoon cast a casual eye over the bundle of £1000 in used £20 notes he found in Shannon's travel bag and shrugged. If he was aware that to get it to Málaga Shannon must have carried it with him through London airport customs, which is forbidden, he gave no sign. In any case, that was London's problem. He found no copies of *Sexy Girls* or *Soviet News*, and waved the traveller on.

Kurt Semmler looked fit and tanned from his three weeks orbiting the Mediterranean looking for ships for sale. He was still rake-thin and chain-smoked nervously, a habit that belied his cold nerve when in action. But the suntan gave him an air of health and set off with startling clarity his close-cropped pale hair and icy blue eyes.

As they drove from the airport into Málaga town in the taxi Semmler had had waiting, he told Shannon he had been in Naples, Genoa, Valletta, Marseilles, Barcelona and Gibraltar, looking up old contacts in the world of small ships, checking the lists of perfectly respectable shipping brokers and agents for ships for sale, and looking some of them over as they lay at anchor. He had seen a score, but none of them suitable. He had heard of another dozen in ports he had not visited, and had rejected them because he knew from the names of their skippers they must have suspect backgrounds. From all his enquiries he had drawn up a list of seven, and the *Albatross* was the third. Of her qualities, all he would say was that she looked all right.

He had reserved Shannon a room in the Málaga Palacio in the name of Brown, and Shannon checked in there first. It was just after four when they strolled through the wide gates on the south face of the Acera de la Marina square and into the docks.

The *Albatross* was drawn up alongside a quay at the far end of the port. She was as Semmler had described her, and her white paint glistened in the sun and heat. They went aboard and Semmler introduced Shannon to the owner and captain, George Allen, who showed him over the vessel. Before very long Shannon had come to the conclusion it was too small for his purposes. There was a master cabin to sleep two, a pair of single cabins, and a saloon where mattresses and sleeping bags could be laid on the floor.

The after hold could, at a pinch, be converted into a sleeping area for another six men, but with the crew of four and Shannon's five, they would be cramped. He cursed himself for not warning Semmler there were six more men expected, who would also have to be fitted in.

Shannon checked the ship's papers, which appeared to be in order. She was registered in Britain and her Board of Trade paper confirmed it. Shannon spent an hour with Captain Allen, discussing methods of payment, examining invoices and receipts showing the amount of work that had been done on the Albatross over recent months and checking the ship's log.

He left with Semmler just before six and strolled back to the hotel, deep in thought.

'What's the matter?' asked Semmler. 'She's clean.'

'It's not that,' said Shannon. 'She's too small. She's registered as a private yacht. She doesn't belong to a shipping company. The thing that bugs me is that she might not be accepted by the exporting authorities as a fit vessel to take on board a load of arms.'

It was too late back at the hotel to make the calls he wanted to make, so they waited till the following morning. Shortly after nine Shannon called Lloyd's of London and asked for a check of the Yacht List. The *Albatross* was there all right, listed as an auxiliary ketch of 74 tons NRT, with her home port given as Milford and port of residence as Hooe, both of them in Britain.

'Then what the hell's she doing here?' he wondered, and then recalled the method of payment that had been demanded. His second call, to Hamburg, clinched it.

'*Nein*, not a private yacht, please,' said Johann Schlinker down the telephone. 'There would be too great a possibility she would not be accepted to carry freight on a commercial basis.'

'OK. When do you need to know the name of the ship?' asked Shannon.

'As soon as possible. By the way, I have received your credit transfer for the articles you ordered in my office. These will now be crated and sent in bond to the address in France you supplied. Secondly, I have the paperwork necessary for the other consignment, and as soon as I receive the balance of the money owing, I will go ahead and place the order.'

'When is the latest you need to know the name of the carrying vessel?' Shannon bawled into the phone.

There was a pause while Schlinker thought.

'If I receive your cheque within five days, I can make immediate application for permission to buy. The ship's name is needed for the export licence. In about fifteen days after that.'

'You will have it,' said Shannon and replaced the receiver. He turned to Semmler and explained what had happened.

'Sorry, Kurt. It has to be a registered company in the maritime freighting business, and it has to be a licensed freighter, not a private yacht. You'll have to keep on searching. But I want the name within twelve days and no later. I have to provide the man in Hamburg with the ship's name in twenty days or less.'

The two men parted that evening at the airport, Shannon to return to London and Semmler to fly to Madrid and thence to Rome and Genoa, his next port of call.

It was late when Shannon reached his flat again. Before turning in he called BEA and booked a flight on the noon plane to Brussels. Then he called Marc Vlaminck and asked him to be present at the airport to pick him up on arrival, to take him first to Brugge for a visit to the bank and then to the rendevous with Boucher for the handover of the equipment.

It was the end of Day Twenty-Two.

Mr Harold Roberts was a useful man. Born sixty-two years earlier of a British father and a Swiss mother, he had been brought up in Switzerland after the premature death of his father, and retained dual nationality. Entering banking at an early age, he had spent twenty years in the Zürich head office of one of Switzerland's largest banks, before being sent to their London branch as an assistant manager.

That had been just after the war, and over the second twenty-year period of his career he had risen to become the manager of the investment accounts section and later overall manager of the London branch, retiring at the age of sixty. By then he had decided to take his retirement and his pension in Swiss francs in Britain.

Since retirement he had been available for several delicate tasks on behalf not only of his former employers, but also of other Swiss banks. He was engaged on such a task that Wednesday afternoon.

It had taken a formal letter from the Zwingli Bank to the chairman and the secretary of Bormac to achieve the introduction to them of Mr Roberts, and he had been able to present letters corroborating his engagement as agent of the Zwingli Bank in London.

Two further meetings had taken place between Mr Roberts and the secretary of the company, the second one attended by the chairman, Major Luton, younger brother of the deceased under-manager to Sir Ian Macallister in the Far East.

The extraordinary Board meeting had been agreed on, and was called in the City offices of the secretary of Bormac. Apart from the solicitor and Major Luton, one other director had agreed to come to London for the meeting, and was present. Although two directors made up a working board, three gave an outright majority. They considered the resolution put by the company secretary and the documents he placed before them. The four unseen shareholders whose interests were being looked after by the Zwingli Bank undoubtedly did now own between them thirty per cent of the stock of the company. They certainly had empowered the Zwingli Bank to act on their behalf, and the bank had incontrovertibly appointed Mr Roberts to represent it.

The argument that clinched the discussion was the simple one that if a consortium of businessmen had agreed together to buy up such a large amount of Bormac stock, they could be believed when their bank said on their behalf that their intention was to inject fresh capital into the company and rejuvenate it. Such a course of action could not be bad for the share price, and all three directors were shareholders. The resolution was proposed, seconded and passed. Mr Roberts was taken on to the Board as a nominee director representing the interests of the Zwingli Bank. No one bothered to change the company rule stipulating that two directors constituted a quorum with power to pass resolutions, although there were now six and no longer five directors.

Mr Keith Brown was becoming a fairly regular visitor to Brugge and a valued customer at the Kredietbank. He was received with the usual friendliness by M. Goossens and the latter confirmed that a credit of £20,000 had arrived that morning from Switzerland. Shannon drew 10,000 dollars in cash and a certified bank cheque for 26,000 dollars in favour of Johann Schlinker of Hamburg.

From the nearby post office he mailed the cheque to Schlinker by registered post, accompanied by a letter from himself asking the arms dealer to go ahead with the Spanish purchase.

He and Marc Vlaminck had nearly four hours to kill before the rendezvous with Boucher, and they spent two of them taking a leisurely pot of tea in a café in Brugge before setting off just before dusk.

There is a lonely stretch of road between Brugge and Ghent, which lies forty-four kilometres to the east. Because the road twists and winds through flat farmland, most motorists prefer to take the new motorway E5 which also links the two Flemish towns as it runs from Ostend to Brussels. Halfway along the old road the two mercenaries found the abandoned farm that Boucher had described, or rather they found the faded notice-board pointing down the track to the farm, which was hidden from view by a clump of trees.

Shannon drove on past the spot and parked, while Marc got out and went to check the farm over. He came back twenty minutes later to confirm the farm was indeed deserted, and there were no signs anyone had been there for quite a time. Nor were there any preparations in progress to provide an unpleasant reception committee for the two buyers.

'Anyone in the house or outbuildings?' asked Shannon.

'The house is locked front and back. No signs of interference. I checked out the barns and stables. No one there.'

Shannon glanced at his watch. It was dark already and there was still an hour to go.

'Get back there and keep a watch from cover,' he ordered. 'I'll watch the front entrance from here.'

When Marc had gone Shannon checked the van once again. It was old and rattled, but it was serviceable and the engine had been looked over by a good mechanic. Shannon took the two false number plates from the facia and whipped them on to the real number plates with sticky insulating tape. They could be ripped off easily enough once the van was well away from the farm, but he saw no reason why Boucher should be able to note the real number plates. On each side of the van was a large publicity sticker that gave the vehicle a distinctive air, but which could also come off in a hurry. In the back were the six large sacks of potatoes he had ordered Vlaminck to bring with him, and the broad wooden board, sawn to make an internal tailgate when slotted into place. Satisfied, he resumed his vigil by the roadside.

The van he was expecting turned up at five to eight. As it slowed and swung down the track to the farm, Shannon could make out the form of the driver hunched over the wheel and beside him the blob surmounted by a pimple of a head that could only be M. Boucher. The red tail-lights of the vehicle disappeared down the track and went out of sight behind the trees. Apparently Boucher was playing it straight.

Shannon gave him three minutes, then he too pulled his van off the hard road and on to the track. When he got to the farmyard Boucher's van was standing with side-lights on in the centre. He cut his engine and climbed down, leaving his own side-lights on, the nose of his van parked ten feet from the rear of Boucher's.

'Monsieur Boucher,' he called into the gloom. He stood in darkness himself, well to one side of the glow of his own lights.

'Monsieur Brown,' he heard Boucher wheeze, and the fat man waddled into view. He had evidently brought his 'helper' along with him, a big beefy-looking type, whom Shannon assessed as being good at lifting things but slow-moving. Marc, he knew, could move like a ballet dancer when he wished. He saw no problems if it came to trouble.

'You have the money?' asked Boucher as he came close. Shannon gestured to the driving seat of his van.

'In there. You have the Schmeissers?'

Boucher waved a pudgy hand at his own van.

'In the back.'

'I suggest we get both our consignments out on to the ground between the vans,' said Shannon. Boucher turned and said something to his helper in Flemish, which Shannon could not follow. The man moved to the back of his own van and opened it. Shannon tensed. If there were to be any surprises, they would come when the doors opened. There were none. The dull glim from his own van's lights showed ten flat, square crates and an open-topped carton.

'Your friend is not here?' asked Boucher. Shannon whistled. Tiny Marc joined them from behind a nearby barn. There was silence. Shannon cleared his throat.

'Let's get the handover done,' he said. He reached into the driving compartment and pulled out the fat brown envelope. 'Cash, as you asked for. Twenty-dollar bills. Bundles of fifty. Ten bundles.'

He stayed close to Boucher as the fat man flicked through each bundle, counting with surprising speed for such plump hands and stuffing the bundles into his side pockets. When he had reached the last he pulled all the bundles back out and selected a note at random from each. By the light of a pencil torch he scanned them closely, the samples, checking for forgeries. There were none. At last he nodded.

'All in order,' he said, and called something to his helper. The man moved aside from the van doors. Shannon nodded at Marc, who went to the van and heaved the first crate on to the grass. From his pocket he produced a tyre lever and prised up the lid. By the light of his own torch he checked the ten Schmeissers lying side by side in the crate. One of them he took out and checked for firing mechanism, pin and breech movement. He replaced the machine pistol and smacked the loose lid back down tight.

It took him twenty minutes to check all ten cases. While he did so the big helper brought by M. Boucher stood nearby. Shannon stood at Boucher's elbow twelve feet away. Finally Marc looked into the open-topped crate. It contained 500 magazines for the Schmeissers. He tested one sample magazine to ensure it fitted, and that the magazines were not for a different model of pistol. Then he turned to Shannon and nodded.

'All in order,' he called.

'Would you ask your friend to help mine load them up?' asked Shannon of Boucher. The fat man passed the instruction to his assistant. Within another five minutes the ten flat crates and the cargo of magazines were loaded in Marc's van. Before loading, the two beefy Flemings removed the potato sacks and Shannon heard them discussing something in Flemish. Then Boucher's helper laughed.

When the crates of arms were loaded, Marc placed the board of wood in position as a tailgate which came halfway up the back of the van. Taking a knife he slit the first sack, hefted it on to his shoulder and emptied the contents into the back of the van. The loose potatoes rolled about furiously, finding the cracks between the edges of the crates and the sides of the van and filling them up. With a laugh the other Belgian started to help him.

The quantity of potatoes they had brought more than covered every trace of the ten crates of guns and the carton of magazines. Anyone looking in the back would be confronted with a sea of loose potatoes. The sacks were thrown in the hedge.

When they were finished both men came round from the back of the van together.

'OK, let's go,' said Marc.

'If you don't mind, we'll leave first,' said Shannon to Boucher. 'After all, we now have the incriminating evidence.'

He waited till Marc had started the engine and turned the van round so that it was facing the drive back to the road before he left Boucher's side and leaped aboard. Halfway down the track there was a particularly deep pothole, over which the van had to move with great care and very slowly. At this point Shannon muttered something to Marc, borrowed his knife and jumped from the van to hide in the bushes by the side of the lane.

Two minutes later Boucher's van came along. It too slowed almost to a halt to negotiate the pothole. Shannon slipped from the bushes as the van went past, caught it up, stooped low and jammed the knife point into the rear offside tyre. He heard it hiss madly as it deflated, then he was back in the bushes. He rejoined Tiny Marc on the main road, where the Belgian had just ripped the stickers from the sides of their vehicle and the false number plates off front and back. Shannon had nothing against Boucher; he just wanted a clear half-hour's start.

By ten-thirty the pair were back in Ostend, the van loaded with spring potatoes was garaged in the lock-up Vlaminck had hired on Shannon's instructions, and the pair were in Marc's bar on the Kleinstraat toasting each other in foaming steins of ale while Anna prepared a meal. It was the first time he had met the well-built woman who was his friend's mistress, and as is the tradition with mercenaries when meeting each other's womenfolk, he treated her with elaborate courtesy.

Vlaminck had booked him a room at a hotel in the town centre, but they drank until late, talking about old battles and skirmishes, recalling incidents and people, fights and narrow escapes, alternately laughing at the things that seemed hilarious in retrospect and nodding glumly at the memories that still rankled. The bar stayed open as long as Tiny Marc drank, and the lesser mortals sat around and listened.

It was almost dawn when they got to bed.

Tiny Marc called for him at his hotel in the middle of the morning and they had a late breakfast together. He explained to the Belgian that he wanted the Schmeissers packaged in such a way that they could be smuggled over the Belgian border into France for loading on to the ship in a southern French port.

'We could send them in crates of spring potatoes,' suggested Marc. Shannon shook his head.

'Potatoes are in sacks, not crates,' he said. 'The last thing we need is for a crate to be tipped over in transit or loading, so that the whole lot falls out. I've got a better idea.'

For half an hour he told Vlaminck what he wanted done with the submachine pistols and the Belgian nodded.

'All right,' he said when he understood exactly what was wanted. 'I can work mornings in the garage before the bar opens. When do we run them south?'

'About May 15th,' said Shannon. 'We'll use the champagne route. I'll bring Jean-Baptiste up here to help, and we'll change to a French-registered van at Paris. I want you to have everything packed and ready for shipment by May 15th.'

Marc accompanied him down to the port in a taxi, for the van would not be used again until it made its last run from Ostend to Paris with its cargo of illegal arms. There was no problem buying a single ticket on the car ferry to Dover, even though Shannon was on foot. He was back in London by early evening.

He spent what remained of the day writing a full report for Endean, omitting to mention from whom he had bought the guns or where they were stored. He attached to the report a statement of expenditure and a tally of what was left in the Brugge account. This he mailed to the *poste restante* address through which he communicated with Sir James Manson's organiser.

The first morning post of that Friday brought a large packet from Jean-Baptiste Langarotti. It contained a sheaf of brochures from three European firms who manufactured the rubberised inflatable semi-rigid boats of the kind he wanted. They were variously advertised as being capable of use as sea-rescue launches, power-boats, speed-craft for towing water-skiers, pleasure boats, launching vessels for sub-aqua diving, runabout and fast tenders for yachts and such like. No mention was made of the fact that they had all been developed from an original design produced to give marine commandos a fast and manoeuvrable type of assault craft.

Shannon read each brochure with interest. Of the three firms, one was Italian, one British and one French. The Italian firm, with six stockists along the Côte d'Azur, semed to be the best-suited for Shannon's purpose and to have the best delivery capability. Of their largest model, a five-and-a-half-metre launch, there were two available for immediate delivery. One was in Marseilles and the other in Cannes. The brochure from the French manufacturer showed a picture of their largest example, a five-metre craft, speeding through a blue sea, tail-down, nose-up.

Langarotti said in his letter there was one of these available at a shop for marine equipment in Nice. He added that all the British-made models needed to be ordered specially, and lastly that although there were several more of each type available in a brilliant orange colour, he was only concerning himself with those in black. He added that each could be powered by any outboard engine above fifty horse-power, and there were seven different makes of engine available locally and immediately which would suit.

Shannon replied with a long letter instructing Langarotti to buy the two models made by the Italian firm that were available for immediate delivery, and the third of French manufacture. He stressed that on receipt of the letter the Corsican should ring the stockists at once and place a firm order, sending each shopkeeper a ten per cent deposit by registered mail. He should also buy three engines of the best make, but at separate shops.

He noted the prices of each item and that the total came to just over £4000. This meant he would overrun on his estimated budget of £5000 for ancillary equipment, but he was not worried by that. He would be under budget on the arms and, he hoped, the ship. He told Langarotti he was transferring to the Corsican's account the equivalent of £4500, and with the balance he should buy a serviceable second-hand 20-hundredweight van, making sure it was licensed and insured.

With this he should motor along the coast and buy his three crated inflatable assault craft and his three outboard engines, delivering them himself to his freight agent in Toulon to be bonded for export. The whole consignment had to be in the warehouse and ready for shipment by May 15th. On the morning of that day Langarotti was to rendezvous with Shannon in Paris at the hotel Shannon usually used. He was to bring the van with him.

The mercenary leader sent another letter that day. It was to the Kredietbank in Brugge requiring the transfer of £4500 in French francs to the account of M. Jean-Baptiste Langarotti at the head office of the Société Générale bank in Marseilles. Both letters were posted express rate the same afternoon.

When he got back to his flat Cat Shannon lay on his bed and stared at the ceiling. He felt tired and flat; the strain of the past thirty days was taking its toll. On the credit side things seemed to be going according to plan. Alan Baker should be setting up the purchase of the mortars and bazookas from Yugoslavia for pick-up during the early days of June; Schlinker should be in Madrid buying enough nine-millimetre ammunition to keep the Schmeissers firing for a year. The only reason he had ordered such an excessive amount of rounds was to make the purchase plausible to the Spanish authorities. Clearance for their export should be obtained for mid to late June, provided he could let the German have the name of the carrier by the middle of May, and provided the ship and its company were acceptable to the officials in Madrid.

Vlaminck should already have the machine pistols stowed for transporting across Belgium and France to Marseilles, and loaded by June 1st. The assault craft and engines should be loaded at the same time in Toulon, along with the other ancillary gear he had ordered from Schlinker.

Apart from smuggling the Schmeissers, everything was legal and above board. That did not mean things could not still go wrong. Perhaps one of the two governments would make problems by taking over-long or refusing to sell on the basis of the provided documentation.

Then there were the uniforms, which Dupree was presumably still buying in London. They too should be in a warehouse in Toulon by the end of May at the latest.

But the big problem still to be solved was the ship. Semmler had to find the right ship, and he had been searching in vain for almost a month.

Shannon rolled off his bed and telephoned a telegram to Dupree's bed-sitter in Bayswater ordering him to check in. As he put the phone down it rang again.

'Hi, it's me.'

'Hallo, Julie,' he said.

'Where have you been, Cat?'

'Away. Abroad.'

'Are you going to be in town this weekend?' she asked.

'Yes. Should be.' In fact there was nothing more he could do and nowhere he could go until Semmler contacted him with news of a ship for sale. He did not even know where the German was by this time.

'Good,' said the girl on the phone. 'Let's spend the weekend doing things.'

It must have been tiredness. He was getting slow on the uptake.

'What things?' he asked.

She began to tell him in precise and clinical detail until he interrupted her and told her to come straight round and prove it.

Although she had been bubbling with her news a week earlier, in the thrill of seeing her lover again Julie had forgotten the news she had for him. It was not until nearly midnight that she remembered. She bent her head low over the face of the half-asleep mercenary and said, 'Oh, by the way, I saw your name the other day.'

Shannon grunted.

'On a piece of paper,' she insisted. Still he showed no interest, his face buried in the pillow between crossed forearms.

'Shall I tell you where?'

His reaction was disappointing. He grunted again.

'In a folder on my Daddy's desk.'

If she had meant to surprise him, she succeeded. He came off the sheet like in one movement, facing her, gripping both her upper arms hard. There was an intensity about his stare that frightened her.

'You're hurting me,' she said irrelevantly.

'What folder on your father's desk?'

'A folder,' she sniffed, on the verge of tears. 'I only wanted to help you.'

He relaxed visibly and his expression softened.

'Why did you go looking?' he asked.

'Well, you're always asking about him, and when I saw this folder, I just sort of looked. Then I saw your name.'

'Tell me about it, from the beginning,' he said gently.

When she had finished she reached forward and coiled her arms round his neck.

'I love you, Mister Cat,' she whispered. 'I only did it for that. Was it wrong?'

Shannon thought for a moment. She already knew far too much and there were only two ways of ensuring her silence.

'Do you really love me?' he asked.

'Yes. Really.'

'Would you want anything bad to happen to me, because of something you did or said?'

She pulled herself back from him, staring deep into his face. This was much more like the scenes in her schoolgirl dreams.

'Never,' she said soulfully. 'I'd never talk. Whatever they did to me.'

Shannon blinked several times in amazement.

'Nobody's going to do anything to you,' he said. 'Just don't tell your father that you know me, or went through his papers. You see, he employs me to gather information for him about the prospects of mining in Africa. If he learned we knew each other, he'd fire me. Then I'd have to find another job. There is one that's been offered to me, miles away in Africa. So you see, I'd have to go and leave you if he ever found out about us.'

That struck home, hard. She did not want him to go. Privately he knew one day soon he would have to go, but there was no need to tell her yet.

'I won't say anything,' she promised.

'A couple of points,' said Shannon. 'You said you saw the title on the sheets with mineral prices on them. What was the title?'

She furrowed her brow, trying to recall the word.

'That stuff they put in fountain pens. They mention it in the adverts for the expensive ones.'

'Ink?' asked Shannon.

'Platignum,' she said.

'Platinum,' he corrected, his eyes pensive. 'Lastly, what was the title on the folder?'

'Oh, I remember that,' she said happily. 'Like something out of a fairy tale. The Crystal Mountain.'

Shannon sighed deeply.

'Go and make me a coffee, there's a love.'

When he heard her clattering cups in the kitchen he leaned back against the bedhead and stared out over London.

'You cunning bastard,' he breathed. 'But it won't be that cheap, Sir James, not that cheap at all.'

Then he laughed into the darkness.

That same Saturday night Benny Lambert was ambling home towards his lodgings after an evening drinking with friends in one of his favourite cafés. He had been buying a lot of rounds for his cronies, using the money, now changed into francs, that Shannon had paid him. It made him feel good to be able to talk of the 'big deal' he had just pulled off, and buy the admiring bar girls champagne. He had had enough, more than enough, himself, and took no notice of the car that cruised slowly behind him, two hundred yards back. Nor did he think much of it when the car swept up to him as he came abreast of a plot of waste ground half a mile short of his home.

By the time he took notice and started to protest, the giant figure who had emerged from the car was hustling him across the lot and behind a hoarding that stood ten yards from the road.

His protests were silenced when the figure spun him round and, still holding him by the scruff, slammed a fist into the solar plexus. Benny Lambert sagged, and when the grip on his collar was removed, slumped to the ground. Standing above him, face shadowed in the obscurity behind the hoarding, the figure drew a two-foot iron bar from his belt. Stooping down the big man grabbed the writhing Lambert by the left thigh and jerked it upwards. The iron bar made a dull 'whumph' as it crashed down with all the assailant's force into the exposed kneecap, shattering it instantly. Lambert screamed once, shrilly, like a skewered rat and fainted. He never felt the second kneecap broken at all.

Twenty minutes later Thomard was phoning his employer from the booth in a late-night café a mile away. At the other end Roux listened and nodded.

'Good,' he said. 'Now I have some news for you. The hotel where Shannon usually stays. Henri Alain has just informed me they have received a letter from Mr Keith Brown. It reserves a room for him on the night of the 15th. Got it?'

'The 15th,' he said. 'Yes. He will be there then.'

'And so will you,' said the voice down the phone. 'Henri will keep in touch with his contact inside the hotel, and you will remain on stand-by not far from the hotel from noon of that day onwards.'

'Until when?' asked Thomard.

'Until he comes out, alone,' said Roux. 'And then you will take him. For five thousand dollars.'

Thomard was smiling slightly when he came out of the booth. As he stood at the bar sipping his beer, he could feel the pressure of the gun under his left armpit. It made him smile even more. In a few more days it would earn him a small fortune. He was quite sure of it. It would, he told himself, be simple and straightforward to take a man, even Cat Shannon, who had never even seen him and did not know he was there.

It was in the middle of Sunday morning that Kurt Semmler phoned. Shannon was lying naked on his back on the bed while Julie pottered round the kitchen making breakfast.

'Mr Keith Brown?' asked the operator.

'Yes. Speaking.'

'I have a personal call for you from a Mr Semolina in Genoa.'

Shannon swung himself off the bed and crouched on the edge, the telephone up to his ear.

'Put him on the line,' he ordered.

The German's voice was faint but reception was reasonably clear.

'Carlo?'

'Yes. Kurt?'

'I'm in Genoa.'

'I know. What news?'

'I have it. This time I am sure. She is just what you wanted. But there is someone else would like to buy her also. We may have to outbid them if we want the boat. But she is good. For us very good. Can you come out and see her?'

'You're quite sure, Kurt?'

'Yes. Quite sure. Registered freighter, property of a Genoa-based shipping company. Made to order.'

Shannon considered.

'I'll come tomorrow. What hotel are you staying at?'

Semmler told him.

'I'll be there on the first available plane. I don't know when that will be. Stay at the hotel in the afternoon and I'll contact you when I get there. Book me a room.'

A few minutes later he was speaking to BEA reservations and learned the first plane would be the Alitalia flight to Milan at 0905 the following morning, making a connection from Milan to Genoa and arriving at the port just after one in the afternoon. He booked himself a single ticket on the flight.

He was grinning when Julie returned with the coffee. If the ship was the right one he could conclude the deal over the next twelve days and be in Paris on the 15th for his rendezvous with Langarotti, secure in the knowledge that Semmler would prepare the ship ready for sea with a good crew and fully fuelled and victualled by the first of June.

'Who was that?' asked the girl.

'A friend.'

'Which friend?'

'A business friend.'

'What did he want?'

'I have to go and see him.'

'When?'

'Tomorrow morning. In Italy.'

'How long will you be gone?'

'I don't know. A fortnight. Maybe more.'

She pouted over her coffee cup.

'So what am I supposed to do all that time?' she asked.

Shannon grinned.

'You'll find something. There's a lot of it about.'

'You're a shit,' she said conversationally. 'But if you have to go, I suppose you must. It only leaves us till tomorrow morning, so I, my dear Tom Cat, am going to make the best of it.'

As his coffee was spilled over the pillow Shannon reflected that the fight for Kimba's palace was going to be a holiday compared with trying to satisfy Sir James Manson's sweet little daughter.

The port of Genoa was bathed in late afternoon sunshine when Cat Shannon and Kurt Semmler paid off their taxi and the German led his employer along the quays to where the Motor Vessel *Toscana* was moored. The old coaster was dwarfed by the two 3000-ton freighters that lay either side of her, but that was no problem. To Shannon's eye she was big enough for his purposes.

There was a tiny forepeak and a four-foot drop to the main deck, in the centre of which was the large square hatch to the only cargo hold set amidships. Aft was the tiny bridge and below it evidently the crew quarters and captain's cabin. She had a short stubby mast from which a single loading derrick was attached, rigged almost vertical. Right aft, above the stern, the ship's single lifeboat was slung.

She was rusty, her paint blistered by the sun in many places, flayed off by salt spray in others. Small and old and dowdy, she had the quality Shannon looked for – she was anonymous. There are thousands of such small freighters plying the coastal inshore trade from Haifa to Gibraltar, Tangier to Dakar, Monrovia to Simonstown. They all look much the same, attract no attention and are seldom suspected of being up to anything beyond carrying small cargoes from port to port.

Semmler took Shannon on board. They found their way aft to where a companionway led down into the darkness of the crew quarters, and Semmler called. Then they went on down. They were met at the bottom by a muscular, hard-faced man in his mid-forties who nodded at Semmler and stared at Shannon.

Semmler shook hands with him and introduced him to Shannon.

'Carl Waldenberg, the first mate.'

Waldenberg nodded abruptly and shook hands.

'You have come to look her over, our old *Toscana*?' he asked.

Shannon was pleased to note he spoke good if accented English and looked as if he might be prepared to run a cargo that did not appear on the manifest, if the price was right. He could understand the German seaman's interest in him. Semmler had already briefed him on the background that he had told the crew his employer would be coming to look the ship over, with a view to buying. For the first mate the new owner was an interesting person. Apart from anything else, Waldenberg had to be concerned about his own future.

The Yugoslav engineer was ashore somewhere, but they met the deckhand, a teenage Italian boy reading a girlie magazine on his bunk. Without waiting for the Italian captain's return, the first mate showed them both over the *Toscana*.

Shannon was interested in the three things: the ability of the boat to accommodate another twelve men somewhere, even if they had to sleep out on deck in the open, the main hold and the possibility of secreting a few crates below the flooring down in the bilges, and the trustworthiness of the engines to get them as far as South Africa.

Waldenberg's eyes narrowed slightly as Shannon asked his questions, but he answered them civilly. He could work out for himself that no fare-paying passengers were coming on board the *Toscana* for the privilege of sleeping wrapped in blankets on the hold-cover under the summer stars; nor was the *Toscana* going to pick up much freight for a run to the other end of Africa. Cargo sent that distance will be shipped in a bigger vessel. The advantage of a small coaster is that she can often load a cargo at very short notice and deliver it two days later a couple of hundred miles way. Big ships spend longer in port while turning round. But on a long run like that from the Mediterranean to South Africa, a bigger ship makes up in extra speed what she spent in port before setting out. For the exporter the *Toscana*s of the sea have little attraction over 500 miles.

After seeing the boat they went topsides and Waldenberg offered them bottles of beer, which they drank in the shade of the canvas awning set up behind the bridge. That was when the negotiations really started. The two Germans rattled away in their own language, the seaman evidently putting the questions and Semmler answering. At last Waldenberg looked keenly at Shannon, looked back at Semmler and nodded slowly.

'Possibly,' he said in English.

Semmler turned to Shannon and explained.

'Waldenberg is interested why a man like yourself who evidently does not know the charter cargo business wants to buy a freighter for general cargo. I said you were a businessman and not a seaman. He feels the general cargo business is too risky for a rich man to want to hazard money on it, unless he has something specific in mind.'

Shannon nodded.

'Fair enough. Kurt, I want a word with you alone.'

They went aft and leaned over the rail while Waldenberg drank his beer.

'How do you reckon this guy?' muttered Shannon.

'He's good,' said Semmler without hesitation.

'The captain is the owner also, and he is an old man and wants to retire. For this he has to sell the boat and retire on the money. That leaves a place vacant as captain. I think Waldenberg would like it, and I agree with that. He has his master's ticket and he knows this boat inside out. He also knows the sea. That leaves the question of whether he would run a cargo with a risk attached. I think he would, if the price is right.'

'He suspects something already?' asked Shannon.

'Sure. Actually he thinks you are in the business of running illegal immigrants into Britain. He would not want to get arrested, but if the price is right I think he would take the risk.'

'Surely, the first thing is to buy the ship. He can decide whether to stay on later. If he wants to quit, we can find another captain.'

Semmler shook his head.

'No. For one thing we would have to tell him enough beforehand for him to know roughly what the job was. If he quit then, it would be a breach of security.'

'If he learns what the job is, and then quits, he only goes out one way,' said Shannon, and pointed his forefinger down at the oil-slicked water beneath the stern.

'There's one other point, Cat. It would be an advantage to have him on our side. He knows the ship, and if he decides to stay on, he will try to persuade the captain to let us have the *Toscana*, rather than the local shipping company that is sniffing around. His opinion counts with the captain, because the old boy wants the *Toscana* to be in good hands, and he trusts Waldenberg.'

Shannon considered the logic. It appealed to him. Time was running short and he wanted the *Toscana*. The first mate might help him get it, and could certainly run it. He could also recruit his own first mate and make sure he was a kindred spirit. Apart from that, there is one useful precept about bribing people. Never try to bribe them all; just buy the man who controls his own subordinates, and let him keep the rest in line. Shannon decided to make an ally of Waldenberg if he could. They strolled back to the awning.

'I'll be straight with you, Mister,' he told the German. 'It's true if I bought the *Toscana* she would not be used for carrying peanuts. It's also true there would be a slight element of risk as the cargo went on board. There would be no risk as the cargo went ashore, because the ship would be outside territorial waters. I need a good skipper, and Kurt Semmler tells me you're good. So let's get down to basics. If I get the *Toscana* I'll offer you the post of captain. You get a six-month guaranteed salary at double your present one, plus a 5000-dollar bonus for the first shipment, which is due ten weeks from now.'

Waldenberg listened without saying a word. Then he grinned and uncoiled himself from where he sat. He held out his hand.

'Mister, you just got yourself a captain.'

'Fine,' said Shannon. 'Except the first thing is to buy the boat.'

'No problem,' said Waldenberg. 'How much would you spend for her?'

'What's she worth?' countered Shannon.

'What the market will take,' answered Waldenberg. 'The opposition has fixed its own ceiling at £25,000 and not a penny more.'

'I'll go to £26,000,' said Shannon. 'Will the captain take that?'

'Sure. Do you speak Italian?'

'No.'

'Spinetti speaks no English. So let me interpret for you. I'll fix it with the old man. With the price, and me as captain, he'll let you have her. When can you meet him?'

'Tomorrow morning?' asked Shannon.

'Right. Tomorrow at ten, here on board.'

They shook hands again and the two mercenaries left.

Tiny Marc Vlaminck was contentedly at work on the garage he had rented, while the locked van stood outside the door in the mews alley. Marc had closed and locked the garage door also, in case he be disturbed while he worked. It was his second afternoon alone in the garage and he had almost finished the first part of the job.

Along the rear wall of the garage he had erected a work bench of solid timber baulks, and equipped it with what he needed, the tools bought with Shannon's £500, as was also the van and the rest of the necessary items. Along one wall stood five large drums. They were bright green and bore the trading mark of the Castrol oil company. They were empty, which was the way Marc had bought them, quite cheaply, from one of the big shipping firms in the port and they had once contained heavy lubricating oil, which was also plainly marked on each barrel.

From the first in the line, Marc had cut a circular disc out of the bottom, and the barrel stood upended with the gaping hole showing upwards and the screw-cap at the top of the barrel on the floor. Round the hole was a one-and-a-half-inch flange, all that was left of the original base of the drum.

From the van Marc had taken two crates of Schmeissers, and the twenty machine pistols were almost ready to enter their new hiding place. Each gun had been carefully mummified from end to end in sticky masking tape, and each had five magazines taped to the weapon itself. Following the wrapping process, each machine pistol had been slipped into a stout polythene envelope, which Marc had then sucked empty of air and tied securely at the neck with twine. After that each had gone into a second and outer envelope of polythene, which was again tied at the neck. Such wrapping, he reckoned, should keep each weapon dry until it was next brought out into the air.

He took the twenty stubby packages and with two stout webbing straps rolled them into one large bundle. This he inserted into the hole at the top of the drum and lowered it to the bottom. The drums were the usual forty-four-gallon or two-hundred-litre type, and there was enough room in each for twenty Schmeissers and their accompanying magazines, with a little room to spare round the walls.

When the first bundle was secreted, Marc began the process of re-sealing the barrel. He had had fresh tinplate discs cut at a machine-shop in the port, and the first of these he fitted on to the top of the opened drum. It took half an hour of filing and rasping before the disc finally settled tight and neatly on to the drum-head, running right up to the rim

in all places, and nicely covering the inch-and-a-half overlap that remained of the previous end of the drum. Turning on his steam jet,
powered by a gas bottle and burner, and taking a stick of soft solder, he
began to 'sweat' the tinplate to tinplate.

Metal can be welded to metal, and to get the hardest join, it usually is.
But a barrel that has once contained oil or ignitable fuel always retains a
residue film on the inner surface of the metal. When heated, as it must
be by welding, the film turns to fumes, and can easily explode very
dangerously. 'Sweating' a piece of tinplate on to another piece does not
give the same strength of join, but can be done with steam heat at a
lower temperature. Provided the drums were not laid on their sides and
juggled about, which would have produced a powerful surge inside, they
would hold together against a fair amount of handling.

When he had finished, Marc packed any remaining crevices with
solder, and when all was cool spray-painted the whole area with a
colour the exact replica of Castrol oil drums the world over. Leaving the
paint to dry, he later eased the drum gently on to its new base, and
removing the screw-cap at the top, he took one of several large jerry-cans
standing ready and began to pour in the lubricating oil.

The emerald-green liquid, thick, sticky, viscous, flowed into the open
aperture and gurgled its way to the bottom of the drum. Slowly it filled
up the air spaces between the sides of the drum and the bundle of
machine pistols inside, slid noiseless into every nook and cranny between
the individual weapons and impregnated the webbing and twine. Despite
Marc's sucking before twisting the ends of each polythene bag tight shut,
there were still bubbles of air inside the bags, trapped in magazines,
barrels and breeches. These offset the weight of the metal, so that as the
barrel filled, the cumbersome bundle of guns became almost weightless,
bobbing in the heavy oil like a body on the tide and finally sinking slowly
below the surface

The Belgian used two jerry-cans, and when the drum was full to the
brim he estimated seven-tenths of the interior was taken up by the
bundle, three-tenths by oil. He had poured sixty litres into the two-hundred-litre drum. Finally he took a pencil torch and scanned the surface of
the liquid. It gleamed back at him in the light, slick and green, with hints
of gold. Of what lay at the bottom of the drum there was not a sign. He
waited another hour before he checked round the base. Nothing had
leaked, the new base of the barrel was sealed tight.

There was a jauntiness to him as he rolled open the garage doors and
ran the van back inside. He still had the wood of two flat crates with
German markings to destroy, and a disc of now useless tinplate to
throw away. The latter would go into the harbour, the former on to a
bonfire. He knew now that the system worked, and that he could convert
one barrel every two days. He would be ready for Shannon by May 15th
as promised. It was good to be back at work.

Doctor Ivanov was incensed, not for the first time and doubtless not for
the last.

'The bureaucracy,' he snapped at his wife across the breakfast table, 'the sheer, incompetent, stultifying bureaucracy in this country is bloody unbelievable.'

'I'm sure you're right, Mikhail Mikhailovich,' his wife said soothingly, pouring two more cups of tea, strong, dark and bitter as she knew her husband liked it. A placid and contented woman, she wished her volatile scientist husband would be careful with his outbursts, or at least confine them to the house.

'If the capitalist world knew how long it takes to get a couple of nuts and bolts in this country, they'd fall about laughing.'

'Shush, dear,' she told him, stirring in the sugar for herself. 'You must be patient.'

It had been weeks since the Director had summoned him to the pine-panelled office in the heart of the vast complex of laboratories and living quarters that made up the Institute in the heart of the Siberian New Lands to inform him that he would be in charge of a survey team being sent to West Africa, and that he should take charge of the details himself.

It had meant forsaking a project that interested him deeply, and doing the same to two of his junior colleagues. He had indented for the neces-sary equipment for an African climate, sending off his requirements to the half-dozen different supply directorates concerned, answering the petty queries as politely as he could, and waiting, always waiting, for the equipment to arrive and be crated. He knew from his membership of a survey team in Ghana while Nkrumah was in power there what working in the deep bush could entail.

'Give me the snow any time,' he had told his team leader at the time. 'I'm a cold-weather man.'

But he had done it, on orders and on time. His team was ready, his equipment prepared and crated, down to the last water-purification tablet and camp-bed. With luck, he had thought, he could be there, do the survey, and be back with his rock samples before the brief and glor-ious days of the Siberian summer had been eaten by the bitter autumn. The letter in his hand told him it was not to be.

It came from his Director personally, and he bore the man no ani-mosity, for he knew he was only passing on instructions from Moscow. Unfortunately the Transport Directorate there had ruled that the confidential nature of the survey forbade the use of public transport, but the Foreign Ministry did not feel able to instruct Aeroflot to put an air-liner at the team's disposal. In view of continuing Middle East develop-ments, neither would it be possible to use one of the military's Antonov freighters.

In consequence, ran the instructions from Moscow, it had been felt necessary, in view of the volume of equipment required for the survey, and the even greater volumes of samples that would have to be brought back from West Africa, to use maritime transport. It was decided that the team could be best transported by a Soviet freighter heading past the coast of West Africa towards the Far East. On their return, they would simply notify Ambassador Dobrovolsky that they had completed their survey, and on instructions from him a freighter heading back towards home would divert to take the three-man team and its crates of samples on board. Notification would be made in due course of the date and port of departure, and vouchers authorising the use of state transport to the port of embarkation would be provided.

'The whole summer,' shouted Ivanov as his wife helped him into his fur-collared coat and fur hat. 'I'm going to miss the whole bloody summer. And it'll be in the rainy season down there.'

Cat Shannon and Kurt Semmler were at the ship again the following morning and met Captain Alessandro Spinetti for the first time. He was a gnarled old man with a face like a walnut, a tee-shirt over what was still a barrel of a chest, and a white-topped peaked cap aslant on his head.

The negotiating started then and there, before they adjourned to the office of the captain's lawyer, a certain Guilio Ponti, who ran his practice from one of the narrow side streets that lead backwards and upwards from the brawling, riotous Via Gramschi. To be fair to the Signor, he was at least at the better end of the Via Gramschi and the tarts in the bars they passed became progressively more presentable and expensive as they neared the lawyer's office.

Nothing to do with the business of the law moves at faster than a snail's pace in Italy, and usually that of an arthritic snail.

The terms had been agreed already. With Carl Waldenberg translating, Captain Spinetti had accepted the package deal Shannon offered; £26,000 cash for the ship, to be paid in any currency or country the captain cared to name; his own first mate to be offered a minimum six-month contract as the new skipper, at a salary double that he had received as first mate; the chance for the other two men, the engineer and the deckhand, to stay on for six months at existing salary, or part company with severance pay of £500 for the deckhand and £1000 for the engineer.

Privately Shannon had already decided to persuade the deckhand to leave, but to do all he could to keep the engineer, a surly Serbian who Waldenberg said could coax those engines to hell and back, who said nothing and asked less, and best of all whose papers were probably not in order and who therefore needed the job.

For taxation reasons the captain had long ago invested £100 in forming a small private company, Spinetti Maritimo Shipping Company. It had 100 ordinary shares of which he held ninety-nine and his lawyer, Signor Ponti, held one, plus the post of company secretary. The sale of the ship MV *Toscana*, the company's only asset, was therefore linked to the sale of the shipping company Spinetti Maritimo which suited Shannon perfectly.

What did not suit him so well was that it took five days of meetings with the lawyer before the details were in order. And that was only for the first stage.

It was a week into May and Day Thirty-One of Shannon's private calendar of 100 days before Ponti could start drawing up the contracts. As the deal was going through in Italy, and the *Toscana* was an Italian registered and resident vessel, the contract had to comply with Italian law, which is complex. There were three contracts, that for the sale of Spinetti Maritimo and all her assets to Tyrone Holdings of Luxembourg, that which contracted Tyrone Holdings to offer Carl Waldenberg the post of captain for six months at the agreed salary, and the third guaranteeing the two other crewmen their existing salaries or severance pay. This process took four days, and Ponti's attitude was evidently that he was breaking all speed records, although all participant parties were anxious to complete the sale as soon as possible.

Big Janni Dupree was content with life that bright May morning when he emerged from the camping goods store, having placed the last of his orders. He had put down a deposit for the required number of haversacks and sleeping bags. Delivery had been promised for the next day, and that same afternoon he intended to pick up two large cardboard boxes full of military style knapsacks and berets from a warehouse in the east end of London.

Three bulky consignments of miscellaneous equipment were already on their way to Toulon. The first should have arrived, he estimated, and the other two should be in transit. The fourth would be crated and put in the hands of the shipping agent the following afternoon, which left him a week in hand. The day before, he had received a letter from Shannon telling him to vacate his London flatlet and fly to Marseilles on May 15th. He was to check into a given hotel in the French port and wait there to be contacted. He liked precise instructions; they left little room for errors and if anything did go wrong it could not be his fault. He had booked his ticket and was eager for the remaining week to pass so that he could be off. It was good to be going into action again.

When Signor Ponti had finally drawn up the necessary paperwork, Cat Shannon despatched a series of letters from his Genoa hotel. The first was to Johann Schlinker to tell him that the ship that would be engaged to carry the ammunition from Spain would be the MV *Toscana*, owned by Spinetti Maritimo Shipping Company of Genoa. He himself would need from Schlinker details of where the arms shipment was supposed to be heading, so that the captain could draw up the appropriate manifest.

He included in his letter full details of the *Toscana*, and had already checked with Lloyd's Shipping List, a copy of which he was able to study in the office of the British vice-consul in Genoa, to ensure the *Toscana* was listed there. He told Schlinker he would be contacting him within the next fifteen days.

Another letter went to Alan Baker, so that he too could inform the Yugoslav authorities of the name and details of the carrying vessel for the export licence to be granted. He already knew what the manifest would have to read. It would say the vessel was proceeding with her cargo from the Yugoslav port of embarkation to Lome, the capital of Togo.

He wrote a long letter to Mr Stein as chairman of Tyrone Holdings instructing him to prepare the papers for a board meeting of the company in his office four days hence, with two resolutions on the agenda. One would be for the company to buy Spinetti Maritimo and all its assets for £26,000 and the other would be to issue a further 26,000 £1 bearer shares to Mr Keith Brown in exchange for a certified cheque for £26,000.

He dashed off a line to Marc Vlaminck telling him the pick-up of the cargo in Ostend would have to be delayed until May 20th and another to Langarotti putting back the Paris rendezvous to the 19th.

Lastly he sent Simon Endean a letter in London asking him to meet Shannon in Luxembourg four days hence and to have at his disposal funds amounting to £26,000 for the purchase of the ship to carry the whole operation to the target area.

The evening of the 13th was soft and cool, and several hundred miles along the same coastline Jean-Baptiste Langarotti was driving his van westwards from Hyères on the last stretch into Toulon. He had the window down and sniffed the smell of conifer and maquis coming off the hills to his right. Like Dupree in London, preparing that evening to fly to Marseilles, like Vlaminck in Ostend putting the final touches to his fifth and last oil drum of guns, Langarotti was content with life.

He had in the back of the van the last two outboard engines, bought for cash, and equipped with underwater exhaust attachments for silent running. He was on his way back to Toulon to deliver them to the bonded warehouse. Already in the warehouse of Maritime Duphot were three black inflatable dinghies, each crated and unopened, and the third engine. Also there were four large crates of assorted clothing that had arrived over the past fortnight from London in his own name. He too would be ready on time.

It was a pity he had had to move from his hotel. A chance encounter with an old underworld friend as he left the doorway three days ago had forced him to make a quick excuse and move out the following morning. He was now in a new hotel, and would have informed Shannon of this except he did not know where Shannon was. It made no matter. In forty-eight hours, on the 15th, he would keep his rendezvous with his chief at the Plaza Surene hotel in Paris.

The meeting in Luxembourg on May 14th was surprisingly short. Shannon was not present. He had met Mr Stein earlier in his office and handed over to him the documents for the sale of the Spinetti Shipping Company and its vessel the *Toscana*, along with a certified cheque for £26,000, payable to Tyrone Holdings SA.

Thirty minutes later Mr Stein emerged from the board meeting and handed Shannon 26,000 ordinary bearer shares in Tyrone Holdings. He also showed him an envelope which contained the documents concerning the sale of the ship to Tyrone, and Tyrone Holdings' cheque in favour of Signor Alessandro Spinetti. He sealed the envelope, which was addressed to Signor Giulio Ponti at his Genoa office, and gave it to Shannon. The last document he handed over was a board decision to appoint Herr Kurt Semmler managing director of Spinetti Maritimo Shipping Company.

Two days later in the Italian lawyer's office the deal was finalised. The cheque for the purchase of the *Toscana* had been cleared and Tyrone Holdings legally owned one hundred per cent of Spinetti Maritimo. In respect of this, Signor Ponti despatched by registered post the one hundred ordinary shares in Spinetti Maritimo to the company office of Tyrone in Luxembourg. As a separate matter Signor Ponti accepted a package from Shannon and locked it in his vault for safe-keeping. He took two sample signatures from Shannon, in the name of Keith Brown, to be able to certify the authenticity of any letter from Shannon regarding disposal of the package. Unknown to Ponti the package contained the 26,994 controlling shares of Tyrone.

Carl Waldenberg received his captaincy and his six-month contract, as did the Serbian engineer. One month's salary was paid to each man in cash and the remaining five months' for each was placed in escrow in the hands of Signor Ponti.

The Italian deckhand was persuaded without difficulty to take his £500 severance pay, plus a bonus of £100, and left the crew. Semmler was installed as managing director.

Shannon had had a further £5000 transferred from Brugge to his credit in Genoa, and with this he had covered the two salaries of the crewmen who were remaining with the *Toscana*. Before he left Genoa on the 18th, he handed the rest over to Semmler and gave him his briefing.

'How about the two replacement crew?'

'Waldenberg is seeing to it already,' Semmler told him. 'He reckons this port is crawling with men available for recruitment. He knows the place inside out. He also knows what we need. Good hard men, the sort who ask no questions and do what they are told, particularly if they know there is a bonus at the end of it. Don't worry, he'll get a good pair before the end of the week.'

'Right. Fine. This is what I want. Get the *Toscana* ready for sea. A complete engine overhaul and servicing. Port dues paid up, papers in order with the new captain's name. Manifest prepared for Toulon to pick up general cargo for Morocco. Get her fuelled and victualled. Take on enough stores for the crew plus a further dozen men. Extra fresh water, beer, wine, cigarettes. When she's ready, take her to Toulon. You have to be there by June 1st, at the latest. I'll be there with Marc, Jean-Baptiste and Janni. Contact me through the shipping agent, Agence Maritime Duphot. They're in the port area. I'll see you then. Good luck.'

16

Jean-Baptiste Langarotti was alive in part at least due to his ability to sense danger before it came looking for him. The first day he reported to the Paris hotel he just sat quietly at the appointed hour in the residents' lounge and read a magazine. He gave Shannon two hours, but the mercenary leader did not show up.

On the off-chance, the Corsican enquired at the reception desk, for although Shannon had said nothing about staying the night, it might be he had arrived early and taken a room. The reception clerk checked the register and informed Langarotti there was no Monsieur Brown from London in the hotel. Langarotti assumed Shannon had been delayed, and would make the rendezvous at the same hour on the next day.

So the Corsican was there, sitting in the residents' lounge at the same hour on the 16th. There was still no Shannon, but there was something else. Twice the same staff member of the hotel peeked into the room and vanished as soon as Langarotti looked up. After another two hours, Shannon still not having come, he left the hotel again. As he passed down the street he had a glimpse of a man in the corner doorway showing a bizarre interest in the window into which he was staring with such fixed intensity. The shop window was full of women's corsets. Langarotti had the feeling the man was one component that did not fit into the pattern of that quiet back street on a spring morning.

Over the next twenty-four hours the Corsican began to sniff the wind in the bars of Paris where mercenaries forgather, using his old contacts of the Corsican Union in the Paris underworld. He continued to go to the hotel each morning, and on the fifth morning, that of the 19th, Shannon was there.

He had arrived the previous evening by plane from Genoa and Milan, and had stayed the night at the hotel. He seemed in good spirits, and told his colleague over coffee in the lounge that he had bought a ship for their operation.

'No problem?' asked Langarotti. Shannon shook his head.

'No problems.'

'But here in Paris we have a problem.'

Unable to strop his knife in such a public place, the small Corsican sat with his hands idle in his lap. Shannon put down his coffee cup. He knew if Langarotti referred to problems that meant trouble.

'Such as?' he asked softly.

'There's a contract on you,' said Langarotti.

The two men sat in silence for a while, as Shannon considered the news. His friend did not interrupt. He usually answered questions only when they were asked.

'Do you know who placed it?' asked Shannon.

'No. Nor who has taken it up. But it's expensive, about 5000 dollars.'

'Recently?'

'The word is, the contract was placed sometime in the past six weeks. It seems uncertain whether the contractor, who must be Paris-based, is the one who placed it, or whether he is acting for someone behind the scenes. The word is, only a good hit-man would take a contract on you, or a stupid one. But someone has taken it. Enquiries are being made about you.'

Shannon cursed silently. He had little doubt the Corsican was right. He was too careful a man to go bandying unchecked information like that around. He tried to think back to any incident that might give rise to the placing of a contract on his head. The trouble was, there were so many possible reasons, some of which he knew he could not even guess.

Methodically he began to go over the possibilities he could envisage. Either the contract stemmed from something to do with the present operation, or it came from a motive that lay further back. He considered the first option first.

Had there been a leak? Had some government agency received a whiff of intelligence that he was mounting a coup in Africa and decided to stop it permanently by snuffing out the operations commander? The thought even crossed his mind that Sir James Manson had learned of the multiple deflowering – if that was the word for such an experienced Lolita – of his daughter. He rejected them all. It could be that he had offended someone in the murky world of the black market arms dealers who had decided to settle the score the hard way while remaining in the background. But such a move would have been preceded by an argument over a deal, a squabble over money, a stand-up row, or threats. There had been none.

He turned his memory further back, to the wars and the fights gone by. The trouble was, one never knew if one might, at some time, have angered a big organisation without meaning to. Perhaps one of the men he had gunned down had secretly been an agent of the CIA or the KGB. Both organisations bore long grudges, and being peopled by the world's most savagely unprincipled men, insisted on settling scores even when there was no pragmatic motive, but simply revenge. He was aware the CIA still had an open-ended hit contract out on Bruce Rossiter who had shot an American in a bar in Leopoldville because the man was staring at him. The American, it had later turned out, was one of the horde of local

CIA men, though Rossiter had not known this. It did not help him. The contract still went out, and Rossiter was still running.

The KGB were as bad. They sent assassins across the world to liquidate fugitives, foreign agents who had hurt them and been blown for all to see, and were thus unprotectable by their own former employers; and the Russians needed no practical motive, like the information in the man's head that he had not yet spilled. They did it just for revenge.

That left the French SDECE, and the British SIS. The French could have taken him a hundred times over the past two years, and made sure it happened in the jungles of Africa. Moreover, they would not place the deal with a Paris contractor and risk a leak. They had their own men, good ones, on the staff. The British were even less likely. Legalistic to the end, they would have to get permission from almost Cabinet level for a hit, and only used the method in the direst emergency, to prevent a vital leak, to create a nasty example to encourage others to have confidence in the service, or occasionally to even a score where one of their own men had been knowingly knocked over by an identifiable killer. Shannon was sure he had never hit a blue-carded Britisher, and that left the motive of preventing an embarrassment. The Russians and French would kill for that reason, but not the British. They had left Stephen Ward alive to stand trial and nearly ruin the Macmillan government; they had left Philby alive after he was blown, and Blake too; in France or Russia both traitors would have entered the road accident statistics.

That left a private firm. The Corsican Union? No, Langarotti could not have stuck by him if it had been the Union. So far as he knew he had never upset the Mafia in Italy or the Syndicate in America. That took the matter back to a private individual with a private grudge. If it was not a government agency, and not a big private firm, it had to be an individual. But who, for God's sake?

Langarotti was still watching him, waiting for his reaction. Shannon kept his face still, his air bored.

'Do they know I'm here in Paris?'

'I think so. I believe they know about this hotel. You always stay here. It's a mistake. I was here four days ago, as you said . . .'

'Didn't you get my letter, putting the meeting back to today?'

'No. I had to move from my Marseilles hotel a week ago.'

'Oh. Go on.'

'There was someone watching the hotel the second time I came. I had already asked for you by the name of Brown. So I think the leak came from inside this hotel. The man was watching yesterday and today.'

'So I move hotels,' said Shannon.

'You might shake him. You might not. Someone knows the name of Keith Brown. They could find you elsewhere. How much do you have to be in Paris over the next few weeks?'

'Quite a bit,' admitted Shannon. 'I have to stage through several times, and we have to bring Marc's stuff down from Belgium to Toulon through Paris in two days.'

Langarotti shrugged.

'They might not find you. We don't know how good they are, or how many of them. Or who. But they might find you a second time. Then there would be problems, perhaps with the police.'

'I can't afford that. Not now. Not with Marc's consignment sitting in the van,' said Shannon.

He was a reasonable man, and would much prefer to have negotiated with one who had placed the contract on him. But whoever it was, he had chosen to do it the other way.

Shannon would still have tried to talk to the man, but first he had to identify him. There was only one man who could do that for him. The man who had taken the contract to kill him. He put this to the Corsican, who nodded sombrely.

'Yes, *mon ami*, I think you're right. We have to take the hit-man. But first he must be lured out.'

'Will you help me, Jean-Baptiste?'

'Of course,' said Langarotti. 'Whoever it is, it is not the Union. It is not my people, so I am your man.'

They spent close to an hour with a street map of Paris on the table in front of them. Then Langarotti left.

During the day he parked his Marseilles-registered van at a pre-arranged spot. In the late afternoon Shannon went to reception and asked the way to a well-known restaurant a mile away. He was within earshot of the hotel clerk who had been described to him by Langarotti. The chief receptionist told him where the restaurant was.

'Within walking distance?' asked Shannon.

'But certainly, m'sieu. About fifteen minutes, maybe twenty.'

Shannon thanked him and used the desk telephone to make a reservation in the name of Brown for ten o'clock that night. He did not leave the hotel all day.

At nine-forty exactly, carrying his overnight grip in one hand and a light raincoat over the other arm, he left the hotel and turned up the street in the direction for the restaurant. The route he took was not direct. It led down two streets even smaller than the one in which the hotel was situated. As he walked, he left the other pedestrians behind and entered streets in the First Arrondissement which were dimly lit and where no passers-by came his way. He dawdled, passing the time staring into lighted shop windows, killing time until the hour of his restaurant reservation was long past. He never looked back. Sometimes, in the quiet, he thought he could hear the soft slap of a moccasin somewhere up the dim-lit streets behind him. Whoever was there, it was not Langarotti. The Corsican could move without disturbing the dust.

It was past eleven when he reached the dark, black alley he had been told was there. It led to his left and had no lights on it at all. The far end was blocked by a row of bollards, making it into a cul-de-sac. On each side the walls were blank and tall. Any light that might have entered the alley from the other end was muted by the bulk of the French van that stood parked there, empty but with its rear doors open. Shannon walked towards the van's gaping back and when he reached it, turned.

Like most fighting men he always preferred to face danger than know it was somewhere behind. He knew from past experience that even when moving backwards, it is safer always to face the danger source. At least, then, you can watch it. Moving up the alley with his back to the entrance he had felt the hairs on his neck prickling. If the psychology was wrong, he could be very dead. But the psychology had been right. Keeping to empty streets the man behind him had stayed well back, hoping for just such an opportunity as now presented itself.

Shannon tossed his bag and raincoat to the ground and stared at the bulking shadow that blocked the vertical streak of lamplight from the end of the alley. He waited patiently. He hoped there would be no sound, not in the centre of Paris. The shadow paused, assessed the situation, and evidently checked Shannon for a gun. But the sight of the open van reassured the hit-man. He assumed Shannon had simply parked it there for discretion's sake, and had been all this time returning to it.

The shadow in the alley moved softly forward. Shannon could make out the right arm, out of the raincoat pocket now, held forward, holding something. The face was in shadow, the whole man was a silhouette, but he was big. His form stood dead centre of the cobbled cul de-sac, stopped now, raising his gun. He paused for several seconds as he aimed, then slowly lowered it again, straight-armed, down to his side. It was almost as if he had changed his mind.

Still staring at Shannon from the shadow-black face, the man slowly leaned forward and went on to his knees. Some shots do this to steady themselves. The gunman cleared his throat, leaned forward again and placed both his hands, knuckles down, on the cobbles in front of him. The metal of the Colt .45 clattered on the stones. Slowly, like a Moslem facing Mecca at the hour of prayer, the gunman bowed his head, staring for the first time in twenty seconds not at Shannon but at the cobbles. There was a light splashing sound as of liquid running fast on to cobbles, and finally the man's arms and thighs gave out. He slumped forward into the puddle of his own aortic blood and went to sleep, quite gently, like a child.

Shannon was still standing against the doors of the van. With the man down, a shaft of lamplight came from the lit end of the alley. It glistened on the polished black sheen of the four-inch bone knife-handle that protruded upwards from the mackintoshed back of the man on the pavement, slightly left of centre, between the fourth and fifth rib.

The Cat looked up. There was another figure against the lamplight, small, spare, motionless, still standing fifteen yards from the body at the point where he had made his throw. Shannon hissed and Langarotti padded noiselessly down the cobbles.

'I thought you'd left it too late,' grunted Shannon.

'*Non*. Never too late. He could not have squeezed the trigger of the Colt at any time since you emerged from the hotel.'

The rear of the van was already laid with a large sheet of tough industrial polythene over a canvas tarpaulin. The tarpaulin had loopholes all round the edge for easy lashing into a bundle, and plenty of cord and bricks were stacked at the far end. Each taking an arm and a leg, the two men slung the body up and inwards. Langarotti climbed in to retrieve his knife, while Shannon shut the doors. He heard them securely locked from the inside.

Langarotti climbed into the front seat and started up. Slowly he backed out, down the alley and into the street. As he swung the van round before driving off, Shannon approached the driver's window.

'Have you had a good look at him?'

'Sure.'

'You know him?'

'Yes. Name of Thomard, Raymond. In the Congo once for a short period, more of a city type. Professional hit-man. But not quality. Not the sort one of the big contractors would use. More likely to work for his own boss.'

'Who's that?' asked Shannon.

'Roux,' said Langarotti. 'Charles Roux.'

Shannon swore quietly and viciously.

'That bastard, that stupid, ignorant, incompetent fool. He could have fouled up a whole operation just because he wasn't invited to come in on it.'

He fell silent and thought for a while. Roux had to be discouraged, but in a way that would keep him out of the Zangaro affair once and for all.

'Hurry up,' said the Corsican, the engine still running. 'I want to get this customer put to bed before anyone comes along.'

Shannon made up his mind and spoke urgently and rapidly for several seconds. Langarotti nodded.

'All right. Actually, I like it. It should fix that bugger for a long time. But it will cost extra. Five thousand francs.'

'Done,' said Shannon. 'Get moving, and meet me outside the Porte de la Chapelle métro station in three hours.'

They met Marc Vlaminck for lunch in the small south Belgian town of Dinant by agreement. Shannon had called him the previous day and given him the instructions and the rendezvous. Tiny Marc had kissed Anna goodbye that morning and she had given him his lovingly packed suitcase of clothes and his snack box with half a loaf, some butter and a hunk of cheese for mid-morning break. As usual she had told him to take care of himself.

He had driven the van, carrying in the back five 200-litre drums of engine oil by Castrol, across Belgium without being stopped. There was no reason why he should be. His licence was in order, as was the permit for the van and the insurance.

As the three men sat over lunch at a main-street café, Shannon asked the Belgian:

'When do we go over?'

'Tomorrow morning, just before sun-up. It's the quietest time. Did you two sleep last night?'

'Nope.'

'You'd better get some rest,' said Marc. 'I'll watch over both vans. You can have till midnight.'

Charles Roux was another one who was tired that day. All the previous evening, since he had received his telephone call from Henri Alain about Shannon walking to his restaurant meal, he had waited for news. There had been none by midnight, when there should have been a call from Thomard to say it was all over. There had been none by three in the morning and none by sunrise.

Roux was unshaven and puzzled. He knew Thomard was no match for Shannon on equal terms, but he was sure the Irishman would be taken in the back as he walked through one of the quieter streets on his way to the evening meal.

At mid-morning, as Langarotti and Shannon in their empty van were passing without trouble into Belgium north of Valenciennes, Roux finally slipped on a pair of trousers and a shirt and took the lift the five floors down to the lobby to check his mailbox.

There did not seem to be anything wrong with the lock of his mailbox, a container some twelve inches tall, nine wide and nine deep, screwed to the wall of the lobby along with a score more for the other tenants.

There was no indication that it had been opened, and if so, the burglar must have picked the lock. But opened it most certainly had been.

Roux used his personal key to unlock the door and swung it open.

He stood for about ten seconds without moving. Nothing changed about him except the normal ruddy colour of his face, which slid into a chalky grey. Still staring mesmerised, he began to mutter, 'Mon Dieu, O mon Dieu ...' over and over again like an incantation. His stomach turned over, he felt like the moment in the Congo when he had heard the Congolese soldiers questioning his identity inside the bandages as he lay on a stretcher while John Peters smuggled him out from certain death. He felt he wanted to urinate, run, but could only sweat with fear. With an air of almost sleepy sadness, eyes half-closed, lips gummed together, the head of Raymond Thomard gazed back at him from inside the mailbox.

Roux was not squeamish, but he was no lion heart either. He closed the box, went back to his flat, and started into the brandy bottle, for medicinal purposes only. He needed a lot of medicine.

Alan Baker emerged from the office of the Yugoslav State arms company into the bright sunshine of Belgrade feeling well pleased with the way things were going. On receiving Shannon's down payment of 7200 dollars and the end user certificate, he had gone to a licensed arms dealer for whom he had occasionally done work in the past on a sub-contractual level. As in the case of Schlinker, the man had felt the amount of weaponry and money involved in the proposed deal to be derisory, but he had yielded to Baker's argument that if the buyers were satisfied with the first consignment they might well return for more, a lot more.

So he had given Baker his Fiat to fly to Belgrade and make application for the purchase, using the certificate from Togo, duly filled out with the appropriate names, and with a letter of authority from the dealer appointing Baker his representative.

It meant Baker would lose a part of his cut, but it was the only way he could be received in Belgrade, and for such a small deal he had in any case allowed a mark-up of a hundred per cent on the buying price of the arms.

His five days of talks with Mr Pavlovic had been fruitful and had included a visit to the state warehouse in which he had selected the two mortar tubes and two bazookas. The ammunition for both was standard and supplied in crates of twenty bazooka rockets and ten mortar bombs.

The Yugoslavs had accepted the Togolese end user certificate without demur, and although Baker, the licensed dealer, and probably Mr Pavlovic must be aware the certificate was just a piece of paper, the air was maintained that the government of Togo was eagerly awaiting the chance to buy Yugoslavia's weaponry for testing. Mr Pavlovic had also required full payment in advance, and Baker had needed to pay over what remained of the 7200 dollars Shannon had given him, after his travel costs, plus a thousand dollars of his own. He was confident Shannon's balance of another 7200 dollars would reimburse him, and even after the licensed dealer had taken his cut, leave 4000 dollars for Baker's pocket.

His morning's talks had confirmed that the goods would be granted an export licence and sent by army lorries to a bonded warehouse at the port of Ploce in the north-west, close to the holiday resorts of Dubrovnik and Split.

It was here that the *Toscana* should dock to take the shipment aboard, any time after June 10th. With a light heart Baker took the next flight for Munich and Hamburg.

Johann Schlinker was in Madrid that morning, May 20th. He had telexed the full details of the deal in 9 mm ammunition that he wanted to put through to his Madrid partner, a Spanish national, a full month earlier, and had later flown to the Spanish capital himself with his Iraqi end user certificate as soon as he had received Shannon's 26,000 dollars in full payment.

The Spanish formalities were more complicated than those Alan Baker had discovered in Belgrade. Two applications were necesary, the first to buy the hardware, the second to export it. The application to buy had been made three weeks earlier, and over the past twenty days had been vetted by the three departments of state in Madrid who concern themselves with such matters. First the Finance Ministry had been needed to confirm that the full purchase price of 18,000 dollars had been received into the appropriate bank in hard currency. A few years earlier only US dollars had been acceptable, but more recently Madrid was more than happy to take German marks.

The second department was the Foreign Ministry. Their job had been to confirm that the buyer country was not a state to whom Spain was opposed. There was no problem with Iraq, since the great bulk of Spanish arms exports habitually go to the Arabs, with whom Spain has always maintained close and friendly relations. The Foreign Ministry had no hesitation in confirming its approval of Iraq as a recipient of Spanish 9 mm ball ammunition.

Lastly the Defence Ministry had been required to confirm that nothing in the proposed sale was on the secret list, or among the categories of arms not for export. With simple small-arms ammunition, this too had been no problem.

Although there had been no sticky problems with such a consignment, it had taken eighteen days for the papers to pass through the three departments, accumulating more paperwork as they went, until the final dossier emerged with the stamp of approval. At this point the crates of ammunition were taken from the CETME factory and stored in a warehouse of the Spanish Army on the outskirts of Madrid. From this point the Army Ministry took over, and notably the head of its arms export section, Colonel Antonio Salazar.

Schlinker had come to Madrid to present personally the application for export licence. He had been in possession of the full details of the MV *Toscana* on his arrival, and the seven-page questionnaire had been filled out and presented. Back in his room in the Hotel Mindanao, the German expected no problems here either. The *Toscana* was a clean ship, small but belonging to a registered shipping company, Spinetti Maritimo, as Lloyd's Shipping List confirmed. According to the application form, she would wish to berth in Valencia between June 16th and June 20th, take the shipment on board, and proceed straight to Latakia on the coast of Syria, where the consignment would be handed over to the Iraqis for trucking to Baghdad. The export licence should take no longer than another two weeks, and then application would be made for a movement order, permitting the crates to be taken from the army warehouse and detailing an army officer to mount escort with ten soldiers as far as Valencia quayside. The latter precaution, brought into force over the previous three years, was to prevent any risk of hi-jacking by the Basque terrorists. The last thing the government of the Caudillo wanted was to see Madrid's bullets being used against the Guardia Civil in Corunna.

As Schlinker prepared to leave for Hamburg, he reflected that his Madrid partner was perfectly capable of ensuring the liaison with the Army Ministry remained at a cordial level and the crates were waiting in Valencia for the arrival of the *Toscana* on time.

In London a third and seemingly unconnected meeting took place. Over the past three weeks Mr Harold Roberts, the nominee director of Bormac Trading Company, controlling thirty per cent of the company stock, had been cultivating the chairman, Major Luton. He had several times taken him to lunch and once visited him at his Guildford home. They had become quite friendly.

Throughout their talks Roberts had made it clear that if the company were to get off the ground and go back into business, whether in rubber or some other area of trading, a large injection of fresh capital would be needed. Major Luton could well see that. When the time was ripe, Mr Roberts proposed to the chairman that the company should make a new one-for-two issue of shares, a total therefore of half a million of new stock.

At first the major was aghast at the boldness of the move, but Mr Roberts assured him that the bank, whose nominee he was, would find the necessary fresh finance. Mr Roberts added that in the event of any of the new shares not being taken up by existing shareholders or new share-holders, the Zwingli Bank would take up the rest at full value on behalf of its customers.

The clinching argument was that when news of the fresh share issue broke on the market, the price of Bormac ordinaries would be bound to rise, perhaps by as much again as their present value, which then stood at one shilling and threepence. Major Luton thought of his own 100,000 shares and agreed. As is so often the case when a man has once weakened, he then went along with Mr Robert's proposal without further demur.

The new director pointed out that the pair of them could form a quorum and hold a directors' meeting able to pass a resolution binding on the company. At the major's insistence a letter was still sent to the other four directors, simply stating that it was intended to hold a board meeting to discuss company business including the possibility of making a share issue.

In the event only the company secretary, the City solicitor, turned up. The resolution was passed, and the announcement of the new share issue posted. There was no need for a meeting of shareholders as in the long-distant past an increase in capital had been authorised but never carried out.

Existing shareholders were given the first choice to buy the stock and were sent allotment letters for the appropriate number of new shares. They were also given the right to apply for any shares not subscribed by those to whom they were originally offered.

Within a week papers and cheques signed by Messrs Adams, Ball, Carter and Davies, forwarded by the Zwingli Bank, were in the company secretary's hands. Each man opted to buy 50,000 of the new shares, in-cluding those originally allotted to them because of their existing hold-ings.

The shares had to be issued at par, which was four shillings each, and with the existing shares standing at less than a third of that price it was an unattractive offer. Two City speculators noticed the press announce-ment and tried to offer to underwrite the issue, assuming there had to be something in the wind. They would have succeeded, but for Mr Roberts. His own bid on behalf of the Zwingli Bank was already in, wishing to buy any shares remaining at the closure of the offer that had not been bought by existing shareholders of Bormac.

Some idiot in Wales agreed to buy a thousand shares, even at the too-high price, and another three thousand were bought by eighteen other shareholders scattered round the country, who apparently could not do basic arithmetic or were clairvoyant. Mr Roberts, as a nominee director, was not in a position to buy for himself, since he owned no stock. But for the remaining unsold shares at three in the afternoon of May 20th, the closing date of the offer, he subscribed for all the 296,000 in the name of the Zwingli Bank, who in turn was buying these on behalf of two of its customers. Their names happened to be Edwards and Frost. Again the bank used designated accounts of its nominee company.

In no case were the rules of the Companies Act regarding disclosure broken. Messrs Adams, Ball, Carter and Davies each owned 75,000 of the shares from their first purchase, and 50,000 from their second. But as the number of shares now in circulation had risen from a million to one and a half million, each man held less than ten per cent and was able to remain anonymous. Messrs Edwards and Frost each owned 148,000 shares, just under the ten per cent limit.

What did not appear in public or even to the directors was that Sir James Manson owned 796,000 shares in Bormac, an overwhelming majority. He controlled, through Martin Thorpe, the six non-existent shareholders who had bought so heavily. They could, through Martin Thorpe, direct the Zwingli Bank in its dealings with the company, and the bank controlled his contracted servant Mr Roberts. Using their proxies, the six invisible men behind the Zwingli Bank, operating through Harold Roberts, could make the company do anything they wished.

It had cost Sir James Manson £60,000 to buy the original 300,000 shares, and £100,000 to buy up the bulk of the new issue of half a million. But when the shares reached the predicted £100 each, which he was sure they would do after the chance 'discovery' of the Crystal Mountain in the heart of Bormac's Zangaran franchise, he stood to make £80 million.

Mr Roberts was a contented man when he left the Bormac offices after hearing how many shares his six Swiss-based stockholders had been allotted. He knew that when he placed the share certificates in the hands of Dr Martin Steinhofer, there would be a handsome bonus for him. Although not a poor man, his retirement in comfort was secured.

In Dinant Shannon and Langarotti woke from their slumbers shortly after dark had fallen to find Marc shaking them. Both were stretched out in the back of the empty French van.

'Time to be going,' said the Belgian.

Shannon looked at his watch.

'I thought you said before sunrise,' he grumbled.

'That's when we go over,' said Marc. 'We ought to get these vans out of town before they become too noticeable. We can park by the roadside for the rest of the night.'

They did park, but none of the men slept any more. Instead they smoked and played cards with the pack Vlaminck kept in the glove compartment of his van. Sitting under the trees by the Belgian roadside in the darkness, waiting for the dawn, feeling the night air on their faces, each could almost think he was back in the African bush again, about to go into action, except for the flashing lights through the trees where cars headed south on the road to France.

As they sat through the wee small hours, tired of playing cards, too tensed to sleep, each fell back into his old habits. Tiny Marc munched the remnants of the bread and cheese his girl Anna had made for him. Langarotti stropped his knife blade a little sharper. Shannon gazed at the stars and whistled softly.

There is no great technical difficulty in running an illegal consignment across the Belgian–French border in either direction, and that includes a quantity of black market arms.

Between the sea at La Panne and the junction with Luxembourg near Longwy, this border sprawls for miles, and most of it in the south-east corner is through heavily wooded hunting country. Here the border is crossed by scores of side roads and tracks through the forest, and by no means all of them are manned.

Both governments seek to establish some kind of control, using what they call '*douanes volantes*', or flying Customs. These are units of Customs men who pick a track or side road at random and set up a border post. By using the existing Customs points, one may reasonably assume that one vehicle in ten is likely to be stopped and examined. On the unmanned roads, if the flying Customs of either side happen to be sitting there for the day, every vehicle going through gets a check. One can take one's choice.

The third alternative is to pick a road where there is definitely no Customs post set up, and drive straight through. This method of running cargoes through the frontier is particularly favoured by the smugglers of French champagne, who see no reason why this drink connected with mirth and gaiety should receive the attentions of the very unhumorous Belgian import duty. As a bar owner, Marc Vlaminck knew about this route. It is called the Champagne Run.

Running south from Namur, the old fortress town of Belgium, following the line of the river Meuse, one comes first to Dinant, and from here the road runs almost due south over the border to the first French town, called Givet. Along this road there is a finger of French territory that juts upwards into Belgium's underbelly, and this corridor of France is surrounded on three sides by Belgian territory. It is also a hunting forest and intersected by scores of tracks and paths. The main road from Dinat to Givet has a Customs post on it – in fact, one Belgian post and one French, set four hundred yards apart but in sight of each other.

Shortly before dawn Marc got out his maps and briefed Shannon and Jean-Baptiste on what he needed to be sure of getting across the border unspotted. When both men understood exactly what was required, they set off in convoy, the Belgian van in front driven by Marc, the other two in the French van two hundred yards behind.

South from Dinant the road is fairly well built up, with a series of villages whose outskirts almost connect with each other. In the pre-dawn darkness these hamlets were quiet and obscure. At kilometre six, south of Dinant, there is a side road leading to the right, and this Marc took. It was the last they saw of the river Meuse. For four and a half kilometres they ran through undulating country of even-sized, rounded hills, thickly wooded and covered in the lush leafage of late May. The run was parallel to the border and into the heart of hunting country. Without warning Vlaminck swung his van off to the left, heading again towards the frontier, and after three to four hundred yards he pulled to the side. He climbed down and walked back to the French van.

'Make it snappy,' he said, 'I don't want to wait here for long. It's too obvious where I'm heading for, with Ostend number plates.' He pointed down the road.

'The border is down there at one and a half kilometres exactly. I'll give you twenty minutes while I pretend to change a tyre. Then I get back to Dinant and we meet at the café.'

The Corsican nodded and let in the clutch. The drill is, if either the Belgian or French Customs men have set up a flying barricade, the first vehicle stops and allows itself to be searched. Being clean, it then proceeds south to rejoin the main road, heads into Givet, turns north again and returns via the fixed Customs post to Dinant. If either Customs post is in operation, it cannot return back up the road within twenty minutes.

At kilometre one and a half Shannon and Langarotti saw the Belgian post. At each side of the road a vertical steel upright had been placed, embedded in concrete. Beside the right-hand one was a small glass and wooden booth, where the Customs men could shelter while drivers passed their papers through the window. If in occupation, there would be a red and white striped pole supported by both uprights, blocking the road. There was none.

Langarotti cruised slowly past, while Shannon scanned the booth. Not a sign. The French side was trickier. For half a kilometre the road wound between the flanks of the hills, lost to sight from the Belgian posts. Then came the French border. No posts, no booth. Just a lay-by on the left, where the French Customs van always parked. There was nothing there. They had been gone five minutes. Shannon gestured to the Corsican to go round two more corners, but there was nothing in sight. A glimmer of light showed in the east over the trees.

'Turn her round,' snapped Shannon. '*Allez.*'

Langarotti pulled the van into a tight turn, almost made it, backed up, and was off towards Belgium like a cork from a bottle of the very best champagne. From then on time was precious. They shot past the French lay-by, through the Belgian posts, and 1500 metres later saw the bulk of

Marc's waiting van. Langarotti flashed his lights, two short, one long, and Marc gunned his engine into life. A second later he was past them, racing through to France.

Jean-Baptiste turned round more leisurely and followed. If Marc drove fast, he could be through the danger area within four minutes, even heavily laden with a ton of cargo. If any Customs men hove in sight in those vital five minutes, it was bad luck. Marc would try to bluff it out, say he had got lost, hope the oil barrels stood up to a thorough checking.

There were no officials there, even on the second run. South of the French lay-by is a five-kilometre stretch with no turnings. Even here the French gendarmerie sometimes patrol, but there was nothing that morning. Langarotti caught up with the Belgian van and followed it at two hundred metres. After five kilometres Marc turned off to the right at another lay-by, and for six more kilometres wended his way through more back-roads until he finally emerged on to a sizable main road. There was a signpost by the roadside. Shannon saw Marc Vlaminck wave his arm out of the window and point to it. The sign said 'Givet' in the direction from which they had come, and pointed the way they were going with the word 'Reims'. A muted cheer came wafting back from the van in front.

They did the swap-over on a hard concrete car park next to a transport café just south of Soissons. The vans, open-doored, were backed up tight against each other, and Marc eased the five barrels from the Belgian van to the French one. It would have taken Shannon and Langarotti together all their strength, the more so as the loaded van was squashed on its springs so the floors of the two vehicles were not at the same height. There was a six-inch step-up to get into the empty van. Marc managed it on his own, gripping each barrel at the top in huge hands and swinging it in arcs while balanced on its lower rim.

Jean-Baptiste went to the café and returned with a breakfast of long, crisp baguette loaves, cheese, fruit and coffee. Shannon had no knife, so they all used Marc's. Langarotti would never use his knife for eating. He had his finer feelings. It would dishonour the knife to use it on orange peel.

Just after ten they set off again. The drill was different. The Belgian van, being old and slow, was soon driven into a gravel pit and abandoned, the licence plates and windscreen sticker being taken off and thrown into a stream. The van was originally of French make anyway. After that the three proceeded together. Langarotti drove. It was legally his van. He was licensed. If stopped he would say he was driving five barrels of lubricating oil south to his friend who owned a farm and three tractors outside Toulon. The other two were hitchhikers he had picked up.

They left the A1 autoroute, took the peripheral road round Paris, and picked up the A6 south to Lyons, Avignon, Aix and Toulon.

Just south of Paris they saw the sign to the right pointing to Orly airport.

Shannon climbed out and they shook hands.

'You know what to do?' he asked.

They both nodded.

'Keep her under cover and safe till you get to Toulon. Don't worry, no one will find this little baby when I've hidden her,' said Langarotti.

'The *Toscana* is due in by June 1st at the latest, maybe before. I'll be with you before then. You know the rendezvous? Then good luck.'

He hefted his grip and walked away as the van headed south. At the nearby garage he used the telephone, called a cab from the airport and was driven there an hour later. Paying cash he bought his single ticket to London and was home in St John's Wood by sundown. Of his hundred days, he had used up forty-six.

Although he sent Endean a telegram on his arrival home, it was a Sunday, and twenty-four hours before Endean rang him at the flat. They agreed to meet on the Tuesday morning.

It took him an hour to explain to Endean all that had happened since they last met. He also explained that he had used up all the money both in the cash sum he had retained in London, and the Belgian account.

'What's the next stage?' asked Endean.

'I have to return to France within five days at the latest and supervise the loading of the first section of the cargo on to the *Toscana*,' said Shannon. 'Everything about the shipment is legal except what's in those oil barrels. The four separate crates of assorted uniforms and webbing should pass without any problem on board, even if examined by Customs. The same goes for the non-military stuff bought in Hamburg. Everything in that section is the sort of stuff a ship might normally take on as ship's stores; distress flares, night glasses and so forth.

'The inflatable dinghies and outboard engines are for shipping to Morocco, at least that's what the manifest will say. Again, it's perfectly legal. The five oil drums have to go aboard as ship's stores. The quantity is rather excessive, but there shouldn't be any problem despite that.'

'And if there is?' asked Endean. 'If Toulon Customs men examine those barrels too closely?'

'We're busted,' said Shannon simply. 'The ship impounded unless the captain can show he hadn't a clue what was going on. The exporter arrested. The operation wrecked.'

'Bloody expensively,' observed Endean.

'What do you expect? The guns have got to go on board somehow. The oil barrels are about the best way possible. There was always that risk involved.'

'You could have bought the submachine guns legally, through Spain,' said Endean.

'I could,' Shannon conceded, 'but there would then have been a good chance the order would have been refused. The guns and the ammo together make a matching pair. That would have looked like a special order to outfit one company of men; in other words, a small operation. Madrid might have turned it down on those grounds, or examined the end user certificate too thoroughly. I could have ordered the guns from Spain and bought the ammunition on the "black". Then I would have had to smuggle the ammo on board, and it would have been a much bigger consignment . Either way, there has to be an element of smuggling, and hence of risk. So if it all goes wrong, it'll be me and my men who go down, not you. You're protected by a series of cut-outs.'

'I still don't like it,' snapped Endean.

'What's the matter?' Shannon mocked. 'Losing your nerve?'

'No.'

'So cool it. All you have to lose is a bit of money.'

Endean was on the verge of telling Shannon just how much he and his employer stood to lose, but thought better of it. Logic dictated that if the mercenary was going to face prison, he would be as careful as possible.

They talked finance for another hour. Shannon explained that the payment of Johann Schlinker in full, and half to Alan Baker, along with the mercenaries' second month's salary, the £5000 he had transferred to Genoa to fit out the *Toscana*, and his own travelling, had emptied the Brugge account.

'Also,' he added, 'I want my second half of salary.'

'Why now?' asked Endean.

'Because the risks of arrest start next Monday and I shall not be returning to London after. If the ship is loaded without fuss, she sails for Brindisi while I arrange the pick-up of the Yugoslav arms. After that, Valencia and the Spanish ammunition. Then we head for the target. If I'm ahead of schedule, I'd prefer to kill the extra time on the high seas rather than wait in a port. From the moment that ship has hardware on board, I want her in port as little as possible.'

Endean digested the argument.

'I'll put it to my associates,' he said.

'I want the stuff in my Swiss account before the weekend,' countered Shannon, 'and the rest of the agreed budget transferred to Brugge.'

They worked out that with Shannon's salary paid in full, there would be £20,000 left in Switzerland of the original money.

Shannon explained why he needed the lot.

'From now on I need a wad of big-denomination travellers cheques in US dollars on me all the time. If anything goes wrong from now, it can only be of a nature where a fat bribe on the spot might sort out the problem. I want to tidy up all the remaining traces, so that if we all get the chop, there are no clues left. Also, I may need to make cash bonuses on the spot to the ship's crewmen to persuade them to go ahead when they find out what the job really is, as they must when we are at sea. With the last half-payment for the Yugoslav arms still to come, I could need up to £20,000.'

Endean agreed to report all this to 'his associates' and let Shannon know.

The following day he rang back to say that both transfers of the money had been authorised and the letters instructing the Swiss bank had been sent.

Shannon booked his ticket from London to Brussels for the following Friday and a Saturday-morning flight from Brussels to Paris to Marseilles.

He spent that night with Julie, and Thursday as well and Thursday night. Then he packed his bags, mailed the flat keys with an explanatory letter to the estate agents and left. Julie drove him to the airport in her red MGB.

'When are you coming back?' she asked him as they stood outside the 'Departing Passengers Only' entrance to the Customs area of Number Two Building.

'I won't be coming back,' he said, and gave her a kiss.

'Then let me come with you.'

'No.'

'You will come back. I haven't asked where you are going, but I know it has to be dangerous. It's not just business, not ordinary business. But you will come back. You must.'

'I won't be coming back,' he said quietly. 'Go find someone else, Julie.'

She began to sniffle.

'I don't want anybody else. I love you. You don't love me. That's why you're saying you won't see me again. You've got another woman, that's what it is. You're going to see another woman . . .'

'There's no other woman,' he said, stroking her hair. An airport policeman looked discreetly away. Tears in the departure lounge are not uncommon anywhere. There would be, Shannon knew, no other woman in his arms. Just a gun, the cool comforting caress of the blued steel against his chest in the night. She was still crying when he kissed her on the forehead and walked through into passport control.

Thirty minutes later the Sabena jet made its last turn over south London and headed for its home in Brussels. Below the starboard wing the county of Kent was spread out in the sunshine. Weatherwise, it had been a beautiful month of May. From the portholes one could see the acres of blossom where the apple, pear and cherry orchards covered the land in pink and white.

Along the lanes that trickle through the heart of the Weald, the Maythorn would be out, the horse-chestnut trees glowing with green and white, the pigeons clattering among the oaks. He knew the country well from the time years ago when he had been stationed at Chatham and had bought an old motor-cycle to explore the ancient country pubs between Lamberhurst and Smarden. Good country, good country to settle down in, if you were the settling type.

Ten minutes later one of the passengers further back summoned the stewardess to complain about someone up front who was whistling a monotonous little tune.

It took Cat Shannon two hours on Friday afternoon to withdraw the money transferred from Switzerland and closed his account. He took two certified bank cheques, each for £5000, which could be converted into a bank account somewhere else, and from that into more travellers cheques; and the other £10,000 in fifty 500-dollar cheques that needed only counter-signature to be used as cash.

He spent that night in Brussels and flew the next morning to Paris and Marseilles.

A taxi from the airport brought him to the small hotel in the outskirts where Langarotti had once lived under the name of Lavallon, and where Janni Dupree, still following orders, was in residence. He was out at the time, so Shannon waited until he returned that evening, and together they drove in a hire-car Shannon had engaged to Toulon. It was the end of Day Fifty-two, and the sprawling French naval port was bathed in warm sunshine.

During Sunday the shipping agent's office was not open, but it made no matter. The rendezvous spot was the pavement in front of it, and here Shannon and Dupree met Marc Vlaminck and Langarotti on the dot of nine o'clock. It was the first time they had been together for weeks, and only Semmler was missing. He should be a hundred miles or so along the coast, steaming offshore in the *Toscana* towards Toulon.

At Shannon's suggestion Langarotti telephoned the harbour-master's office from a nearby café and ascertained that the *Toscana*'s agents in Genoa had cabled that she was due in on Monday morning and that her berth was reserved.

There was nothing more to do that day, so they went in Shannon's car along the coast road towards Marseilles and spent the day swimming at the cobbled fishing port of Sanary. Despite the heat and the holiday atmosphere of the picturesque little town, Shannon could not relax. Only Dupree bought himself a pair of swimming trunks and dived off the end of the mole of the yacht harbour. He said later the water was still damn cold. It would warm up later, through June and July when the tourists began to pour south from Paris. By then they would all be preparing to strike at another harbour town, not much larger and many miles away.

Shannon sat for most of the day with the Belgian and Corsican on the terrace of Charley's bar, the Pot d'Etain, soaking up the sunshine and thinking of the morning. The Yugoslav or the Spanish shipment might not turn up, or might be late, or might be blocked for some as yet unknown bureaucratic reason, but there would be no reason for them to be arrested in Yugoslavia or Spain. They might be held for a few days while the boat was searched, but that would be all. The following morning was different. If anyone insisted on peering deep into those oil barrels, there would be months, maybe years, spent sweating in Les Baumettes, the great forbidding fortress prison he had passed on Saturday as he drove from Marseilles to Toulon.

The waiting was always the worst, he reflected, as he settled the bill and called his three colleagues to the car.

It turned out to be smoother than they thought. Toulon is known as an enormous navy base, and the skyline at the harbour is dominated by the superstructures of the French Navy warships lying at anchor. The centre of attraction for the tourists and the strollers of Toulon that Monday was the battle cruiser *Jean Bart*, home from a voyage to the French Caribbean territories, full of sailors with back-pay to spend and looking for girls.

Along the broad sweep of esplanade fronting the leisure harbour the cafés were full of people indulging the favourite pastime of every Mediterranean country – watching life go by. They sat in brightly coloured hordes gazing from the shaded awnings across the half-mile of bobbing yachts, from little outboard-powered runabouts to the sleek sea greyhounds of the very rich.

Up against the eastward quay were the dozen fisher boats that had elected not to go to sea, and behind these were the long, low Customs sheds, warehouses and harbour offices.

It was beyond these, in the small and hardly observed commercial port, that the *Toscana* slipped into her berth just before noon.

Shannon waited till she was tied up, and from his seat on a bollard fifty metres away he could see Semmler and Waldenberg moving about the decks. There was no sign of the Serbian engineer, probably still in his beloved engine room, but two other figures were also on deck, making fast the coiling ropes. These had to be the two new crewmen recruited by Waldenberg.

A small Renault buzzed along the quay and came to a halt by the gangway. A rotund Frenchman in a dark suit emerged and went aboard the *Toscana*. The representative of Agence Maritime Duphot. Before long he came back down, followed by Waldenberg, and the two strolled over to the Customs shed. It was nearly an hour before the two men emerged, the shipping agent to return to his car and drive away into the town, the German captain to get back to his ship.

Shannon gave them another thirty minutes, then he too strolled up the gangway and on to the *Toscana*. Semmler beckoned him into the companionway that led down to the crew's saloon.

'So, what's been going on?' Shannon asked, when he and Semmler were seated below. Semmler grinned.

'All smooth and easy,' he said. 'I got the papers changed to show the new captain, had a complete engine service done, bought an unnecessarily large amount of blankets and a dozen foam-rubber mattresses. No one asked any questions and the captain still thinks we are going to run immigrants into Britain.

'I used the *Toscana*'s usual shipping agent in Genoa to book us in here and the manifest says we are taking on a mixed cargo of sporting goods and leisure equipment for a holiday camp on the coast of Morocco.'

'What about the engine lubricating oil?'

Semmler grinned.

'It was all ordered, then I called and cancelled it. When it didn't arrive, Waldenberg wanted to delay for a day and wait for it. I vetoed that and said we would get it here in Toulon.'

'Fine,' said Shannon, 'don't let Waldenberg order it. Tell him you've done it yourself. Then when it arrives he'll be expecting it. That man who came on board. . .'

'The shipping agent. He has all the stuff still in bond, and the papers prepared. He's sending it down this afternoon in a couple of vans. The crates are so small we can load them ourselves with the derrick.'

'Good. Let him and Waldenberg sort out the paperwork. An hour after the stuff is all aboard, the fuel company van will arrive with the oil. Driven by Langarotti. You have enough money left to pay for it?'

'Yes.'

'Then pay for it in full, cash, and get a signed receipt. Just make sure no one bangs it about too hard as it goes aboard. The last thing we need is for the bottom of one of the barrels to fall out. The quay will be waist-deep in Schmeissers.'

'When do the men come aboard?'

'Tonight after dark. One by one. Just Marc and Janni. I'm leaving Jean-Baptiste here for a while. He has the van, and there's one more job to be done at this end. When can you sail?'

'Any time. Tonight. I can fix it. Actually, it's rather nice being the managing director.'

'Don't get too accustomed to it. It's only a front.'

'OK, Cat. Incidentally, where are we going when we leave?'

'Brindisi. Know it?'

'Sure I know it. I've run more cigarettes into Italy from Yugoslavia than you've had hot dinners. What do we pick up there?'

'Nothing. You wait for my telegram. I'll be in Germany. I'll cable you through the port office at Brindisi with the next destination and the day you have to arrive. Then you must get a local agent to cable the Yugoslav port in question and reserve a berth. Are you OK to go to Yugoslavia?'

'I think so. Anyway, I won't get off the ship. We pick up more arms?'

'Yes. At least, that's the plan. I just have to hope my arms dealer and the Yugoslav officials have not cocked it up. Do you have all the charts you need?'

'Yes, bought them all in Genoa as you told me. You know, Waldenberg will have to realise what we are taking on board in Yugoslavia. Then he'll know we aren't running illegal immigrants. He accepts the speedboats and the engines, the walkie-talkies and the clothing as quite normal, but arms are something else again.'

'I know,' said Shannon. 'It will cost a bit of money. But I think he'll get the message. There'll be you and me, Janni and Marc, on board. Besides, by then we can tell him what's in the oil drums. He'll be so far in by then, he'll have to go along. What are the two new crewmen like?'

Semmler nodded and stubbed out his fifth cigarette. The air was a blue haze in the small saloon.

'Good. Two Italians. Hard boys, but obedient. I think they're both wanted by the carabinieri for something. They were so pleased to get on board and under cover. They couldn't wait to get to sea.'

'Fine. Then they won't want to be put ashore in a foreign country. That would mean they'd be picked up without papers and repatriated, straight into the hands of their own police.'

Waldenberg had done well. Shannon met both men briefly and short nods were exchanged. Semmler simply introduced him as a man from head office, and Waldenberg translated. The men, Norbiatto the first mate and Cipriani the deckhand, evinced no further interest. Shannon exchanged a few instructions with Waldenberg and left.

In mid-afternoon the two vans from Agence Maritime Duphot rolled to a stop by the *Toscana*, accompanied by the same man who had appeared that morning. A French Customs officer, clipboard in hand, emerged from the Customs house and stood by as the crates were swung inboard by the ship's derrick. Four crates of assorted rough clothing, belts, boots and caps, for the Moroccan workers at the holiday village; three crated large-size inflatable dinghies for sporting and leisure purposes – three outboard engines for same; two crates assorted flares, binoculars, ship's gas-powered foghorn, radio parts and magnetic compasses. The last crates were listed under ship's stores.

The Customs officer ticked them off as they went aboard and confirmed with the shipping agent that they were either bonded for re-export, having arrived from Germany or Britain, or they were locally bought and carried no export duty. The Customs man did not even want to look inside the crates. He knew the agency well, dealing with them every day.

When it was all aboard, the Customs man stamped the ship's cargo manifest. Waldenberg said something to Semmler in German, and the latter translated. He explained to the agency that Waldenberg needed lubricating oil for his engines. It had been ordered in Genoa, but had not been delivered in time

The agency man noted in his book.

'How much do you need?'

'Five drums,' said Semmler. Waldenberg did not understand the French.

'That's a lot,' said the agent.

Semmler laughed. 'This old bucket uses as much oil as diesel. Besides, we might as well get it here and have enough for a long time to come.'

'When do you need it?' asked the agent.

'Five this afternoon be all right?' asked Semmler.

'Make it six,' said the agency man, noting the type and quantity in his notebook, along with the hour of delivery. He looked up at the Customs man. The official nodded. He was uninterested, and strolled away. Shortly after, the agency man left in his car, followed by the two vans.

At five o'clock Semmler left the *Toscana*, went to a phone in a café on the waterfront, rang the agency and cancelled the oil order. The skipper, he said, had discovered a full barrel at the rear of the stores locker and would not be needing any more for several weeks. The agency man was disgruntled but agreed.

At six a van drove carefully along the quay and stopped opposite the *Toscana*. It was driven by Jean-Baptiste Langarotti in a bright green overall suit with the word Castrol on the back.

Opening the back of the van, he carefully rolled five large oil drums down the plank he had fitted to the rear step. From the window of the Customs house the duty officer peered out.

Waldenberg caught his eye and waved. He pointed to the barrels and back to his ship.

'OK?' he called, adding with a thick accent, 'Ça va?'

From the window the Customs man nodded and withdrew to make a note on his clipboard. At Waldenberg's orders the two Italian crewmen slipped cradles under the barrels and one by one winched them aboard. Semmler was uncommonly eager to help, steadying the drums as they swung over the ship's rail, shouting in German to Waldenberg on the winch to let them down easily. They slid out of sight into the dark, cool hold of the Toscana and soon the hatch was back in place and clamped down.

Langarotti, having made his despatch, had long since left in his van. A few minutes later the overall suit was at the bottom of a waste bin in the heart of the town. From his bollard at the other end of the quay Shannon had watched the loading with bated breath. He would have preferred to be involved, like Semmler, for the waiting was almost physically painful, worse than going into action.

When it was over, things quietened down on the Toscana. The captain and his three men were below decks, the engineer having taken one turn of the ship to sniff the salt air and then having gone back to his diesel fumes. Semmler gave them half an hour, then slipped down to the quay and came to join Shannon. They met up round three corners and out of sight of the harbour.

Semmler was grinning.

'I told you. No problems.'

Shannon nodded, and grinned back with the relief. He knew better than Semmler what was at stake, and unlike the German he was not familiar with port procedures.

'When can you take the men aboard?'

'The Customs office closes at nine. They should come between twelve and one in the morning. We sail at five. It's fixed.'

'Good,' said Shannon, 'let's go and find them and have a drink. I want you back there quickly in case there are any enquiries still to come.'

'There won't be.'

'Never mind. We'll play safe. I want you to watch that cargo like a mother hen. Don't let anyone near those barrels till I say so, and that will be in a harbour in Yugoslavia. Then we tell Waldenberg what he's carrying.'

They met the other three mercenaries at a prearranged café and had several beers to cool down. The sun was setting and the sea within the vast bowl of land that forms the anchorage and roads of Toulon was ruffled by only a slight breeze. A few yachts pirouetted like ballerinas far out on the stage as their crews brought them about, to catch the next gust. Semmler left them at eight and returned to the Toscana.

Janni Dupree and Marc Vlaminck slipped quietly aboard between mid-

night and one, and at five, watched from the quay by Shannon and Langarotti, the *Toscana* slipped back to the sea.

Langarotti ran Shannon to the airport in the mid-morning to catch his
plane. Over breakfast Shannon had given the Corsican his last set of
instructions and enough money to carry them out.

'I'd prefer to be going with you,' Jean-Baptiste said, 'or with the ship.'

'I know,' said Shannon. 'But I need someone good to do this part of it.
It's vital. Without it we can't go through. I need someone reliable, and
you have the added advantage of being French. Besides, you know two of
the men well, and one speaks a smattering of French. Janni couldn't go in
there with a South African passport. Marc I need to intimidate the crew
if they cut up rough. I know you're better with a knife than he is with
his hands, but I don't want a fight, just enough to persuade the crew to
do what they're told. And I need Kurt to check the navigation, in case
Waldenberg chickens out. In fact, if the worst comes to the worst, and
Waldenberg goes over the side, Kurt has to skipper the ship. So it has to
be you.'

Langarotti agreed to go on the mission.

'They're good boys,' he said with a little more enthusiasm. 'It will be
good to see them again.'

When they parted at the airport, Shannon reminded him, 'It can all
fall through if we get there and we have no back-up force. So it depends
on you to do it right. It's all set up. Just do what I said and cope with the
small problems as they arise. I'll see you in a month.'

He left the Corsican, walked through Customs and boarded his plane
for Paris and Hamburg.

18

'My information is that you can pick up the mortars and bazookas any time after June 10th, and that was re-confirmed yesterday by telex,' Alan Baker told him.

It was the day after Shannon's arrival in Hamburg, and they had met in a restaurant for lunch after a mid-morning telephone call to fix a rendezvous.

'What port?' asked Shannon.

'Ploce.'

'Where?'

'Ploce. Spelt P–l–o–c–e, pronounced Plochay. It's a small port almost exactly halfway between Split and Dubrovnik.'

Shannon thought. He had ordered Semmler while in Genoa to pick up the necessary sea charts to cover the whole Yugoslav coast, but he had supposed the pick-up would be at one of the larger ports. He hoped the German had got a chart covering the sea approaches to Ploce, or could get one at Brindisi.

'How small?'

'Quite small. Very discreet. Half a dozen wharves and two large ware-houses. The Yugoslavs usually use it for their arms exports. The last shipment out of Yugoslavia I did by plane, but I was told at that time if it was to be by sea, it would be from Ploce. It's better if it's a small port. There's usually a berth, and loading facilities are quicker. Moreover, the Customs there must be a very small unit, probably with one lowly man in charge, and if he gets his present, he'll see everything on board within a few hours.'

'OK, Ploce. On June 11th,' said Shannon. Baker noted the date.

'The *Toscana* is OK?' he asked. He still wished he could have clinched the deal for his friends who ran the *San Andrea*, but decided to bear the *Toscana* in mind for later use. Shannon, he was sure, would have little use for her after whatever operation he was mounting was finished, and Baker was always on the lookout for a good boat for running his cargoes into deserted coves.

'She's fine,' said Shannon. 'She's running for an Italian port now, where I have to let her know by telex or letter where to head for. Any problems at your end?'

Baker shifted slightly.

'One,' he said. 'The price.'

'What about it?'

'I know I quoted you fixed prices, totalling 14,400 dollars. But the system inside Yugoslavia has changed over the past six months. To get the paperwork through on time, I had to engage a Yugoslav partner. At least, that's what he is called, though in fact he's another middleman.'

'So?' asked Shannon.

'So he has to get a fee or salary for getting the paperwork through the Belgrade office. On balance, I supposed it was worth it to you to have the shipment ready on time, and no bureaucratic hang-ups. So I agreed to engage him. He's the brother-in-law of the official in the Trade Ministry. It's another way of taking a kickback. But what can you expect these days? The Balkans are still the Balkans, and they've got wised up.'

'How much extra will he cost?'

'A thousand pounds sterling.'

'In dinars or dollars?'

'In dollars.'

Shannon thought it over. It might be the truth, or it might be that Baker was trying to squeeze a bit more out of him. If it was the truth, refusing to pay would simply force Baker to pay the Yugoslav out of his own cut. That would reduce Baker's margin to such a small amount, he might lose interest in the deal, not caring whether it went through or not. And he still needed Baker, and would need him until he saw the white wake of the *Toscana* heading out of Ploce harbour on her way to Spain.

'All right,' he said. 'Who is this partner?'

'Fellow called Ziljak. He's out there now, taking care of the shipment right up to Ploce and into the warehouse there. When the ship comes in, he'll get the stuff from the warehouse, through Customs and on to the boat.'

'I thought that was your job.'

'It is, but now I have to engage a Yugoslav as partner. Honestly, Cat, they left me no alternative.'

'Then I'll pay him personally, in travellers cheques.'

'I wouldn't,' said Baker.

'Why not?'

'The buyers of this shipment are supposed to be the government of Togo, right? Black men. Another white turns up, obviously the pay-master, and they might begin to smell a rat. We can go to Ploce if you like, or I can go alone. But if you want to come with me, you'll have to come ostensibly as my assistant. Besides, travellers cheques have to be cashed at a bank, and in Yugoslavia that means they take the man's name and identity card number. If someone cashing them in is a Yugoslav, there are questions asked. It would be better if Ziljak got cash as he has asked.'

'All right. I'll cash some cheques here in Hamburg and I'll pay him in dollar bills,' said Shannon. 'But you get yours in cheques. I'm not carrying vast sums of dollars in cash around. Not to Yugoslavia. They get sensitive about that sort of thing. Security gets interested. They think you're funding a spy operation. So we go as tourists with travellers cheques.'

'Fine by me,' said Baker. 'When do you want to go?'

Shannon glanced at his watch. The next day would be the first of June.

'Day after tomorrow,' he said. 'We'll fly to Dubrovnik and have a week in the sun. I could do with a rest anyway. Or you can join me on the 8th or 9th, but not a day later. I'll hire a car and we can motor up the coast to Ploce on the 10th. I'll have the *Toscana* come in that night or early on the morning of the 11th.'

'You go on alone,' said Baker. 'I have work to do in Hamburg. I'll join you on the 8th.'

'Without fail,' said Shannon. 'If you don't turn up, I'll come looking. And I'll be hopping mad.'

'I'll come,' said Baker. 'I still want the balance of my money, don't forget. So far, I'm out of pocket on this deal. I want it to go through just as much as you.'

That was the way Shannon wanted him to feel.

'You do have the money, I suppose,' asked Baker, fingering a lump of sugar.

Shannon flicked through a booklet of large-denomination dollar cheques under Baker's nose. The arms dealer smiled.

They left the table and on the way out used the restaurant telephone to ring a Hamburg charter company specialising in package tours for the thousands of Germans who holiday along the Adriatic coast. From this company they learned the names of the three best hotels in the Yugoslav resort. Baker was told he would find Shannon in one of them under the name of Keith Brown.

Johann Schlinker was as confident as Baker that he could fulfil his arms deal, though he had no idea that Baker was also doing business with Shannon. No doubt the men knew of each other, might even be acquainted, but there would not be a question of discussing each other's business together.

'The port should be Valencia, though this has yet to be fixed and is in any case the choice of the Spanish authorities,' he told Shannon. 'Madrid tells me the dates have to be between the 16th and 20th of June.'

'I'd prefer the 20th for loading,' said Shannon. 'The *Toscana* should be permitted to berth on or during the night of the 19th and load in the morning.'

'Good,' said Schlinker. 'I'll inform my Madrid partner. He habitually handles the transporting and loading side of things, and employs a first-class freight agent in Valencia who knows all the Customs personnel very well. There should be no problem.'

'There must be no problem,' growled Shannon. 'The ship has been delayed already once, and by loading on the 20th I have enough sailing time but no margin to fulfil my own contract.'

It was not true, but he saw no reason why Schlinker should not believe it was true.

'I shall want to watch the loading also,' he told the arms dealer.

Schlinker pursed his lips. 'You may watch it from afar, of course,' he said. 'I cannot stop you. But as the customers are supposed to be an Arab government, you cannot propose yourself as the buyer of the merchandise.'

'I also want to board the ship at Valencia,' said Shannon.

'That will be even harder. The whole port area is sealed off inside a chain-link fence. Entry is by authority only. To board the ship you would have to go through passport control. Also, as she will be carrying ammunition, there will be a Guardia Civil at the bottom of the gangplank.'

'Supposing the captain needed another crewman. Could he engage a seaman locally?'

Schlinker thought it over.

'I suppose so. Are you connected with the company owning the vessel?'

'Not on paper,' said Shannon.

'If the captain informed the agent on arrival that he had permitted one of his crewmen to leave the vessel at its last port of call to fly home and attend his mother's funeral, and that the crewman would be rejoining the vessel at Valencia, I suppose there would be no objection. But you would need a merchant seaman's card to prove you were a seaman. And in the same name as yourself, Mr Brown.'

Shannon thought for a few minutes.

'OK. I'll fix it,' he said.

Schlinker consulted his diary.

'As it happens I shall be in Madrid on the 19th and 20th,' he said. 'I have another business deal to attend to. I shall be at the Mindanao Hotel. If you want to contact me, you can find me there. If loading is for the 20th, the chances are the convoy and escort from the Spanish Army will run the shipment down to the coast during the night of the 19th to arrive at crack of dawn. If you are going to board the ship at all, I think you should do so before the military convoy arrives at the docks.'

'I could be in Madrid on the 19th,' said Shannon. 'Then I could check with you that the convoy had indeed left on time. By driving fast to Valencia, I could be there ahead of it, and board the *Toscana* as the rejoining seaman before the convoy arrives.'

'That is entirely up to you,' said Schlinker. 'For my part, I will have my agents arrange the freighting, transportation and loading, according to all the normal procedures, for dawn of the 20th. That is what I contracted to do. If there is any risk attached to your boarding the vessel in harbour, that must be your affair. I cannot take responsibility for that. I can only point out that ships carrying arms out of Spain are subjected to scrutiny by the Army and Customs authorities. If anything goes wrong with the loading and clearance of the ship to sail, because of you, that is not my responsibility. One other thing. After loading arms a ship must leave a Spanish port within six hours, and may not re-enter Spanish waters until the cargo has been off-loaded. Also, the manifest must be in perfect order.'

'It will be,' said Shannon. 'I'll be with you in Madrid on the morning of the 19th.'

Before leaving Toulon Kurt Semmler had given Shannon a letter to post. It was from Semmler to the *Toscana*'s shipping agents in Genoa. It informed them there had been a slight change of plan, and that the *Toscana* would be proceeding from Toulon not directly to Morocco but first to Brindisi to pick up further cargo. The order, Semmler informed the agents, had been secured locally by him in Toulon and was lucrative, since it was a rush order, whereas the consignment of mixed cargo from Toulon to Morocco was in no hurry. As managing director of Spinetti Maritimo, Semmler's instructions were those of the boss. He required the Genoa agents to cable Brindisi reserving a berth for June 7th and 8th, and to instruct the port office to hold any mail addressed to the *Toscana* for collection when she berthed.

Such a letter was what Shannon wrote and despatched from Hamburg. It was to Signor Kurt Semmler, MV *Toscana*, c/o The Port Office, Brindisi, Italy.

In it he told Semmler that from Brindisi he should proceed to Ploce on the Adriatic coast of Yugoslavia, and that if he had no charts to negotiate the tricky straits north of Korcula Island, he should get them locally. He had to get the *Toscana* there on the evening of June 10th, and his berth would be reserved. There was no need to inform the agents in Genoa of the extra leg from Brindisi to Ploce.

His last instruction to Semmler was important. He told the German ex-smuggler he wanted him to acquire a merchant seaman's card for a deckhand called Keith Brown, stamped and up to date, and issued by the Italian authorities. The second thing the ship would need was a cargo manifest showing the *Toscana* had proceeded straight from Brindisi to Valencia without a halt, and would be heading from Valencia to Latakia, Syria, after taking cargo aboard in Valencia. Semmler would have to use his old Brindisi contacts to obtain these documents.

Before leaving Hamburg for Yugoslavia, Shannon's last letter was to Simon Endean in London. It required Endean to meet Shannon at a rendezvous in Rome on June 16th, and to bring certain maritime charts with him.

About the same time the MV *Toscana* was chugging steadily through the Bight of Bonifacio, the narrow channel of limpid blue water that separates the southern tip of Corsica from the northern end of Sardinia. The sun was blistering, but mellowed by a light wind. Marc Vlaminck was stretched out, stripped to the waist, on the hatch cover of the main hold, a wet towel beneath him, his torso like a pink hippopotamus covered in suntan oil. Janni Dupree, who always went a brick red in the sun, was propped up against the wall of the after structure, under the awning, swigging from his tenth bottle of beer of the morning. Cipriani, the deckhand, was painting part of the rail round the forepeak white, and the first mate, Norbiatto, was snoozing on his bunk down below after taking the night watch.

Also down below, in the stinking heat of the engine room, was the engineer, Grubic, oiling some piece of machinery that only he could understand but which no doubt was vital to keep the *Toscana* steady on her eight knots through the Mediterranean. In the wheelhouse Kurt Semmler and Carl Waldenberg were sipping cold beer and exchanging reminiscences of their respective careers.

Jean-Baptiste Langarotti would have liked to be there. From the port rail he could have watched the grey-white, sun-bleached coast of his homeland slipping past barely four miles across the water. But he was many miles away, in West Africa, where the rain season was already begun and where, despite the fever heat, the clouds were leaden grey.

Alan Baker came into Shannon's hotel in Dubrovnik just as the mercenary was returning from the beach on the evening of June 8th. He looked tired and dusty.

Cat Shannon by contrast was looking and feeling better. He had spent his week in the Yugoslav holiday resort behaving like any other tourist, sun-bathing and swimming several miles each day. He looked thinner, but fit and tanned. He was also optimistic.

After settling into his hotel he had sent Semmler a cable at Brindisi requesting confirmation of the arrival of the vessel and receipt of the waiting letter mailed from Hamburg. That morning he had got Semmler's telegrammed reply. The *Toscana* had arrived safely in Brindisi, the letter had been received and acted on, and they would depart on the morning of the 9th to make destination by midnight of the 12th.

Over drinks on the terrace of their hotel where Shannon had booked Baker a room for the night, he told the dealer from Hamburg the news. Baker nodded and smiled.

'Fine. I got a cable forty-eight hours ago from Ziljak in Belgrade. The crates have arrived in Ploce and are in the government warehouse near the quay under guard.'

They spent the night in Dubrovnik and the following morning hired a taxi to take them the hundred kilometres up the coast to Ploce. It was a boneshaker of a car, that appeared to have square wheels and cast-iron suspension, but the drive along the coast road was agreeable, mile upon mile of unspoilt coastline, with the small town of Slano at the halfway mark, where they stopped for a cup of coffee and to stretch their limbs.

They were established in their hotel by lunchtime, and waited in the shade of the terrace until the port office opened again at four in the afternoon.

The port was set on a broad sweep of deep blue water, shielded to its seaward side by a long peninsula of land called Peliesac, which curved out of the main coast to the south of Ploce and ran northwards parallel to the coast. Up to the north the gap between the tip of the peninsula and the coast was almost blocked by the rocky island of Hvar, and only a narrow gap gave access to the sea lagoon on which Ploce stood. This lagoon, nearly thirty miles long, surrounded on nine-tenths of its perimeter by land, was a paradise for swimming, fishing and sailing.

As they approached the port office a small and battered Volkswagen squealed to a halt a few yards away and hooted noisily. Shannon froze. His first instinct said trouble, something he had been fearing all along, some slip-up in the paperwork, a sudden block put on the whole deal by the authorities, and an extended stay under questioning in the local police station.

The man who climbed out of the small car and waved cheerily might have been a policeman, except that police in most totalitarian states of East or West seemed to be banned from smiling by Standing Orders. Shannon glanced at Baker and saw his shoulders sag in relief.

'Ziljak,' he muttered through closed mouth, and went to meet the Yugoslav. He was a big, shaggy man, like an amiable black-haired bear, and he embraced Baker with both arms. When he was introduced, his first name turned out to be Kemal, and Shannon supposed there was more than a touch of Turk in the man. That suited Shannon fine; he liked the type, normally good fighters and comrades, with a healthy dislike of bureaucracy.

'My assistant,' said Baker, and Ziljak shook hands and muttered something in what Shannon assumed to be Serbo-Croat. Baker and Ziljak communicated in German, which many Yugoslavs speak a little. He spoke no English.

With Ziljak's assistance, they knocked up the head of the Customs office and were taken off to inspect the warehouse. The Customs man jabbered a few words at the guard on the door, and in the corner of the building they found the crates. There were thirteen of them; one apparently contained the two bazookas, and two others contained one mortar including the base-plates and sighting mechanisms in each. The rest were of ammunition, four of them with ten bazooka rockets in each, and the other six containing the ordered three hundred mortar bombs. The crates were in new timber, unmarked with any description of contents, but stencilled with serial numbers and the word *Toscana*.

Ziljak and the Customs chief babbled away in their own dialect, and it appeared they were using the same one, which was helpful because there are dozens in Yugoslavia including seven major languages, and difficulties have been known to occur.

Eventually Ziljak turned to Baker and said several sentences in his halting German. Baker replied and Ziljak translated for the Customs man. He smiled and they all shook hands and parted. Outside the sunshine struck like a sledgehammer.

'What was all that about?' asked Shannon.

'Kemal was asked by the Customs man if there was a little present in it for him,' explained Baker. 'Kemal told him there would be a nice one if the paperwork could be kept trouble-free and the ship was loaded on time tomorrow morning.'

Shannon had already given Baker the first half of Ziljak's £1000 bonus for helping the deal go through, and Baker drew the Yugoslav to one side to slip it to him. The man's all-embracing bonhomie became even more embracing for both of them, and they adjourned to the hotel to celebrate with a little slivovits. A little was the word Baker had used. Ziljak may have used the same word. He did not mean it. Happy Yugoslavs never drink a little slivovits. With £500 under his belt, Ziljak ordered a bottle of the fiery plum liquor and bowl after bowl of almonds and olives. As the sun went down and the Adriatic evening slipped through the streets, he relived again his years in the war, hunting and hiding in the Bosnian hills to the north with Tito's partisans.

Baker was hard put to it to translate as the exuberant Kemal related his forays behind Dubrovnik in Montenegro, in the mountains behind where they sat, the coast of Herzogovina, and among the cooler, richer, wooded countryside north of Split in Bosnia. He relished the thought that he would once have been shot out of hand for venturing into any of the towns where now he drove on behalf of his brother-in-law who was in the government. Shannon asked if he was a committed Communist, having been a partisan, and Ziljak listened while Baker translated, using the word 'good' for 'committed'. Ziljak thumped his chest with his fist.

'Guter Kommunist,' he exclaimed, eyes wide, pointing at himself. Then he ruined the effect by giving a broad wink, throwing back his head and roaring with laughter as he tossed another glass of slivovits down the hatch. The folded notes of his first £500 bonus made a bulge under his waistband, and Shannon laughed too, and wished the giant was coming along to Zangaro with them. He was that kind of man.

They had no supper, but at midnight wandered unsteadily back to the quay to watch the Toscana come in. She was rounding the harbour wall, and an hour later was tied up alongside the single quay of hewn local stone. From the forepeak Semmler looked down in the half-light cast by the dock lamps. Each nodded slowly at the other and Waldenberg stood at the top of the gangplank consulting with his first mate. He had already been instructed, following Shannon's letter, that he should leave the talking to Semmler.

After Baker had headed back to the hotel with Ziljak, Shannon slipped up the gangplank and into the captain's tiny cabin. No one on the quay took any notice. Semmler brought Waldenberg in and they locked the door.

Slowly and carefully Shannon told Waldenberg why he had really brought the Toscana to Ploce. The German captain took it well. He kept his face expressionless until Shannon had finished.

'I never carried arms before,' he said. 'You say this cargo is legal. How legal?'

'Perfectly legal,' said Shannon. 'It has been bought in Belgrade, trucked up here, and the authorities are of course aware what the crates contain. Otherwise there would be no export licence. The licence has not been forged, nor has anyone been bribed. It's a perfectly legal shipment under the laws of Yugoslavia.'

'And the laws of the country it's going to?' asked Waldenberg.

'The *Toscana* never enters the waters of the country where these arms are due to be used,' said Shannon. 'After Ploce, there are two more ports of call. In each case only to take on board cargoes. You know ships are never searched for what they are carrying when they arrive in a port to take on more cargo only, unless the authorities have been tipped off.'

'It has happened all the same,' said Waldenberg. 'If I have these things on board and the manifest doesn't mention them, and there is a search, and they are discovered, the ship gets impounded and I get imprisoned. I didn't bargain on arms. With the Black September and the IRA about these days, everyone's looking for arms shipments.'

'Not at the port of embarkation of fresh cargo,' said Shannon.

'I didn't bargain for arms,' repeated Waldenberg.

'You bargained for illegal immigrants to Britain,' Shannon pointed out.

'They're not illegal until their feet touch British soil,' the captain pointed out. 'And the *Toscana* would be outside territorial waters. They could go inshore in fast boats. Arms are different. They are illegal on this ship if the manifest says there aren't any. Why not put it on the manifest? Just say these arms are being legally transported from Ploce to Togo. No one can prove we later deviate from course.'

'Because if there are arms already on board, the Spanish authorities will not allow the ship to stay in Valencia, or any other Spanish port. Even in transit. Certainly not to take on more arms. So they have to remain unmentioned on the manifest.'

'So where did we come from to reach Spain?' asked Waldenberg.

'From Brindisi,' replied Shannon. 'We went there to take on cargo, but it was not ready in time. Then the owners ordered you to Valencia to pick up a new cargo for Latakia. Of course, you obeyed.'

'Supposing the Spanish police search the boat?'

'There's not the slightest reason why they should,' said Shannon. 'But if they do, the crates have to be below decks in the bilges.'

'If they find them there, there's not a hope for us,' Waldenberg pointed out. 'They'd think we were bringing the stuff to the Basque terrorists. We'd be inside for ever.'

The talk went on till three in the morning. It cost Shannon a flat bonus of £5000, half before loading and half after sailing from Valencia. There was no extra charge for the stopover in the African port. That would present no problem.

'You'll take care of the crew?' Shannon asked.

'I'll take care of the crew,' said Waldenberg with finality. Shannon knew he would, too.

Back in his hotel Shannon paid Baker the third quarter of his bill for the arms, 3600 dollars, and tried to get some sleep. It was not easy. The sweat rolled off him in the heat of the night, and he had an image of the *Toscana* lying down there in the port, the arms in the Customs shed, and prayed there would be no problems. He felt he was so close now, just three short ceremonies away from the point where no one could stop him whatever they tried.

The loading started at seven, and the sun was already well up. With a Customs man, armed with a rifle, walking beside the crates, they were wheeled on trolleys down to the dockside and the *Toscana* hoisted them aboard with her own jumbo derrick. None of the crates were very large, and down in the hold Vlaminck and Cipriani swung them easily into position before they were roped down across the floor of the hold. By nine in the morning it was over, and the hatches went on.

Waldenberg had ordered the engineer to make steam and the latter needed no second bidding. Shannon learned later he had suddenly become very voluble when he learned three hours out from Brindisi that they were heading for his native country. Apparently he was wanted there for something or other. He stayed well hidden in his engine room, and no one went looking for him.

As he watched the *Toscana* chugging out of the port, Shannon slipped Baker the remaining 3600 dollars and the second £500 for Ziljak. Unbeknown to either, he had had Vlaminck quietly prise up the lids on five of the crates, taken at random, as they came aboard. Vlaminck had verified the contents, waved up to Semmler on the deck above him, and Semmler had blown his nose, the signal Shannon wanted. Just in case the crates contained scrap iron. It has been known, quite frequently, in the arms world.

Baker, having received his money, gave the £500 to Ziljak as if it came from himself, and the Yugoslav saw the Customs chief did not go without supper. Then Alan Baker and his British 'assistant' quietly left town.

On Shannon's calendar of a hundred days, given him by Sir James Manson to bring off his coup, it was Day Sixty-Seven.

No sooner was the *Toscana* out to sea than Captain Waldenberg began to organise his ship. One by one the three other crewmen were brought into his cabin for a quiet interview. Although none of them knew it, had they refused to continue to serve aboard the *Toscana* there would have been some unfortunate accidents on board. Few places are quite as well suited for a complete disappearing act as a ship on a dark night at sea, and Vlaminck and Dupree between them could have pitched anyone else on board a long way from the ship's side before he touched the water. Perhaps their presence did the trick. In any case, no one objected.

Waldenberg dispensed a thousand pounds of the two and a half he had received in travellers cheques from Shannon. The Yugoslav engineer, delighted to be out of his own country again, took his £250, stuffed it into his pocket and went back to his engines. He made no comment one way or the other. The first mate, Norbiatto, became quite excitable at the thought of a Spanish jail, but pocketed his £600 in dollars and thought of the difference that could make to his chances of his own ship one day. The crewman, Cipriani, seemed almost happy at the prospect of being on a vessel full of contraband, took his £150, said an ecstatic 'Thank you', and left muttering 'This is the life.' He had little imagination and knew nothing about Spanish jails.

With this done, the crates were broken open and all afternoon the contents were examined, wrapped in polythene and stowed deep in the bilges, below the floor of the hold and inside the curvature of the ship's hull. The planks which had been removed to make this possible were replaced and covered with the innocent cargo of clothing, dinghies and outboard engines.

Finally Semmler told Waldenberg he had better put the Castrol oil drums to the back of the stores locker, and when he told his fellow countryman why, Waldenberg finally did lose his composure. He lost his temper as well, and used some expressions that could best be described as regrettable.

Semmler calmed him down and they sat having beer as the *Toscana* ploughed her way south for the Otranto Channel and the Ionian Sea. Finally Waldenberg began to laugh.

'Schmeissers,' he said. 'Bloody Schmeissers. *Mensch*, it's a long time since they've been heard in the world.'

'Well, they're going to be heard again,' said Semmler. Waldenberg looked wistful.

'You know,' he said at length, 'I wish I was going ashore with you.'

When Shannon arrived, Simon Endean was reading a copy of *The Times*, bought that morning in London before he left for Rome. The lounge of the Excelsior Hotel was almost empty, for most of those taking late morning coffee were on the outside terrace watching the chaotic traffic of Rome inch past and trying to make themselves heard above the noise.

Shannon had only picked the place because it was in easy reach of Dubrovnik to the east and in line with Madrid to the west. It was the first time he had ever been to Rome, and he wondered what the ecstatic guide books were talking about. There were at least seven separate strikes in progress, one of them being among the garbage workers, and the city stank in the sun from the uncleared fruit and other rubbish on the pavements and down every back alley.

He eased himself into a seat beside the man from London and savoured the cool of the inner room after the heat and frustration of the taxi in which he had been stuck for the past hour. Endean eyed him.

'You've been out of touch for a long time,' he said coldly. 'My associates were beginning to think you had scarpered. That was unwise.'

'There was no point in my making contact until I had something to say. That ship doesn't exactly fly across the water. It takes time to get her from Toulon to Yugoslavia, and during that time there was nothing to report,' said Shannon. 'By the way, did you bring the charts?'

'Of course.'

Endean pointed to his bulging attaché case beside his chair.

On receiving Shannon's letter from Hamburg, he had spent several days visiting three of the top maritime chart companies in Leadenhall Street, London, and in separate lots had acquired inshore charts for the entire African coast from Casablanca to Cape Town.

'Why the hell do you need so many?' he asked in annoyance. 'One or two would suffice.'

'Security,' said Shannon briefly. 'If you or I were searched at Customs, or if the ship were boarded and searched in port, one single chart showing the area of the ship's destination would be a give-away. As it is, no one, including the captain and crew, can discover which section of the coast really interests me. Until the last moment, when I have to tell them. Then it's too late. Do you have the slides as well?'

'Yes, of course.'

Another of Endean's jobs had been to make up slides of all the photographs Shannon had brought back from Zangaro, along with others of the maps and sketches of Clarence and the rest of Zangaro's coastline.

Shannon himself had already sent a slide projector, bought duty-free at London airport, on to the *Toscana* in Toulon.

He gave Endean a complete progress report from the moment he had left London, mentioning the stay in Brussels, the loading of the Schmeissers and other equipment on to the *Toscana* in Toulon, the talks with Schlinker and Baker in Hamburg and the Yugoslav shipment a few days earlier in Ploce.

Endean listened in silence, making a few notes for the report he would later have to give to Sir James Manson.

'Where's the *Toscana* now?' he asked at length.

'She should be south and slightly west of Sardinia, en route for Valencia.'

Shannon went on to tell him what was planned in three day's time, the loading of the 400,000 rounds of 9 mm ammunition for the machine pistols in Valencia, and then departure for the target. He made no mention of the fact that one of his men was already in Africa.

'Now there's something I need to know from you,' he told Endean. 'What happens after the attack? What happens at dawn? We can't hold on for very long before some kind of new régime takes over, establishes itself in the palace, and broadcasts news of the coup and the new government.'

'That's all been thought of,' said Endean smoothly. 'In fact, the new government is the whole point of the exercise.'

From the briefcase he withdrew three foolscap sheets of paper covered with close typing.

'These are your instructions, starting the moment you have possession of the palace and the Army and guards have been destroyed or scattered. Read, memorise, and destroy these sheets before we part company, here in Rome. You have to carry the lot in your head.'

Shannon ran his eye quickly over the first page. There were few surprises for him. He had already suspected the man Manson was boosting into the presidency had to be Colonel Bobi, and although the new president was referred to simply as X, he did not doubt Bobi was the man in question. The rest of the plan was simple, from his point of view.

He glanced up at Endean.

'Where will you be?' he asked.

'A hundred miles north of you,' said Endean.

Shannon knew Endean meant he would be waiting in the capital of the republic next door to Zangaro on its northern side, the one with a road route straight along the coast to the border and thence to Clarence.

'Are you sure you'll pick up my message?' he asked.

'I shall have a portable radio set of considerable range and power. The Braun, the best they make. It will pick up anything within that range, provided it's broadcast on the right channel and frequency. A ship's radio should be powerful enough to send in clear over at least twice that distance.'

Shannon nodded and read on. When he had finished he put the sheets on the table.

'Sounds all right,' he said. 'But let's get one thing clear. I'll broadcast on that frequency at those hours from the *Toscana*, and she'll be hove-to somewhere off the coast, probably at five or six miles. But if you don't hear me, if there's too much static, I can't be responsible for that. It's up to you to hear me.'

'It's up to you to broadcast,' said Endean. 'The frequency is one that has been tested before by practical use. From the *Toscana*'s radio it must be picked up by my radio set at a hundred miles. Not first time, perhaps, but if you repeat for thirty minutes, I have to hear it.'

'All right,' said Shannon. 'One last thing. The news of what has happened in Clarence should not have reached the Zangaran border post. That means it'll be manned by Vindu. It's your business to get past them. After the border, and particularly nearer Clarence, there may be scattered Vindu, on the roads, running for the bush but still dangerous. Supposing you don't get through?'

'We'll get through,' said Endean. 'We'll have help.'

Shannon supposed, rightly, that this would be provided by the small operation in mining that he knew Manson had going for him in that republic. For a senior company executive they could provide a truck or jeep and maybe a couple of repeater hunting rifles. For the first time he supposed Endean might have some guts to back up his nastiness.

Shannon memorised the code-words and the radio frequency he needed and burned the sheets with Endean in the men's lavatory. They parted an hour later. There was nothing else to say.

Five floors above the streets of Madrid, Colonel Antonio Salazar, head of the exporting office of the Spanish Army Ministry (Foreign Arms Sales) sat at his desk and perused the file of papers in front of him. He was a grey-haired, grizzled man, a simple man, whose loyalties were uncomplicated and uncompromising. His fidelity was towards Spain, his beloved Spain, and for him all that was right and proper, and all that was truly Spanish, was embodied in one man, the short and aged generalissimo who sat in the Pardo. Antonio Salazar was a Franquist to his boot-heels.

Two years from retirement at the age of fifty-eight, he had been one of those who stepped ashore on the sand of Fuengirola with Francisco Franco many years ago when the Caudillo of modern Spain had been a rebel and outcast, returning against orders to launch war against the Republican government in Madrid. They had been few then, and condemned to death by Madrid, and they had nearly died.

Sergeant Salazar was a good soldier. He carried out his orders, whatever they were, went to mass between the battles and the executions, and believed, deeply, in God, the Virgin, Spain and Franco.

In another army, at another time, he would have retired as a sergeant-major. He emerged from the civil war a full captain, one of the ultras, the inner circle. His background was solid working class, peasant, his education next to nil. But he had made full colonel, and he was grateful. He was also trusted with one of the jobs that in Spain is unmentionable and top secret. No Spaniard ever, under any circumstances, learns that Spain exports arms, in large quantities, to almost all comers. Publicly, Spain regrets the international arms trade as unethical and conducive to further warfare in a world already torn by war. Privately, she makes a lot of money out of it. Antonio Salazar could be trusted to check the paperwork, decide whether to grant or refuse permission for export licences, and keep his mouth shut.

The dossier in front of him had been in his hands for four weeks. Individual papers from the dossier had been checked out by the Defence Ministry, who had confirmed, without knowing why the question was being asked, that 9 mm bullets were not on the secret list; by the Foreign Ministry, who had confirmed, without knowing why, that the possession by the Republic of Iraq of 9 mm ammunition was not contrary to established foreign policy; and by the Finance Ministry, which had confirmed simply that a sum of money in dollars, paid into a certain account in the Banco Popular, had been received and cleared.

The top paper on the file was an application for movement order, to shift a quantity of crates from Madrid to Valencia and export them on a vessel called the MV *Toscana*. Beneath this sheet was the export licence, granted by his own signature.

He glanced up at the civil servant in front of him.

'Why the change?' he asked.

'Colonel, it is simply that there is no berth available in Valencia port for two weeks. The place is crowded to capacity.'

Colonel Salazar grunted. The explanation was feasible. In the summer months Valencia was always crowded, with millions of oranges from the nearby Gancia area being exported. But he did not like changes. He liked to play things by the book. Nor did he like this order. It was small, too small, for an entire national police force. Target practice alone for a thousand policemen would use it up in an hour. Nor did he trust Schlinker, whom he knew well and who had slipped the order through his ministry with a batch of other orders, including over 10,000 artillery shells for Syria.

He glanced through the papers again. Outside, a church bell struck the hour of one. The hour of lunch. There was still nothing wrong with the papers, including the end user certificate. Everything bore the right stamp. If only he could have found one discrepancy, in the certificate, in the carrying ship of the company that owned it. But everything was clean. Making a final decision he scrawled his signature across the bottom of the movement order, and handed the file back to the civil servant.

'All right,' he growled. 'Castellon.'

'We've had to change the port of embarkation from Valencia to Castellon,' said Johann Schlinker two nights later. 'There was no choice if the loading date of the 20th was to be adhered to. Valencia was full up for weeks.'

Cat Shannon was sitting on the bed in the German arms dealer's room in the Mindanao Hotel.

'Where's Castellon?' asked Shannon.

'Forty miles up the coast. It's a smaller port, and quieter. Probably better than Valencia for you. The turnaround of your ship is likely to be quicker. The cargo agent in Valencia has been informed and will personally go north to Castellon to supervise the loading. As soon as the *Toscana* checks in with Valencia harbour authorities by radio, she will be advised of the change of port. She will only have a couple of hours' extra steaming if she diverts at once.'

'What about my going aboard?'

'Well, that's your business,' said Schlinker. 'However, I have informed the agent that a seaman from the *Toscana* who was left behind ten days ago in Brindisi is due to rejoin, and given him the name of Keith Brown. How are your papers?'

'Fine,' said Shannon. 'They're in order, passport and merchant seaman's card.'

'You'll find the agent at the Customs office in Castellon as soon as it opens on the morning of the 20th,' Schlinker told him. 'His name is Señor Moscar.'

'What about the Madrid end of things?'

'The movement order provides for the lorry to be loaded under Army supervision between eight and midnight on the 19th, tomorrow. It will set off with escort at midnight, timing its arrival at Castellon harbour gates at six a.m., the hour they open. If the *Toscana* is on time, she should have docked during the night. The lorry carrying the crates is a civilian one, from the same freight firm I always employ. They're very good and very experienced. I have given the transport manager instructions to see the convoy depart from the warehouse and to phone me here immediately.'

Shannon nodded. There was nothing he could think of that might go wrong.

'I'll be here,' he said, and left.

That afternoon he hired a powerful Mercedes from one of the internationally known hire-car agencies who have offices in Madrid.

At half past ten the following evening he was back in the Mindanao with Schlinker while they waited for the telephone call. Both men were nervous, as men must be when a carefully laid plan rests for its success or catastrophic failure in the hands of others. Schlinker was as concerned as Shannon but for different reasons. He knew that if anything went badly wrong, a complete investigation into the end user certificate he had supplied could be ordered, and that certificate would not stand up to a complete investigation, which must include a check with the Interior Ministry in Baghdad. If he were exposed on that one, other, and for him far more lucrative, deals with Madrid would be forfeit. Not for the first time he wished he had not taken the order in the first place, but like most arms dealers he was a man so greedy that no offer of money could be turned down. It would almost be physical pain to do it.

Midnight came, and still there was no call. Then half past midnight. Shannon paced the room, snarling his anger and frustration at the fat German who sat drinking whisky. At twelve-forty the phone rang. Schlinker leapt at it. He spoke several words in Spanish, and waited.

'What is it?' snapped Shannon.

'Moment,' replied Schlinker and waved his hand for silence. Then someone else came on the phone and there was more Spanish, which Shannon could not understand. Finally Schlinker grinned and said 'Gracias' down the phone several times.

'It's on its way,' he said when he put the phone down. 'The convoy left the depot fifteen minutes ago under escort for Castellon.'

But Shannon was gone.

The Mercedes was more than a match for the convoy, even though on the long motorway from Madrid to Valencia the convoy could keep up a steady 100 kilometres per hour. It took Shannon forty minutes to find his way out of the sprawling suburbs of Madrid, and he supposed the convoy would know the way much better. But on the motorway he could take the Mercedes to 180 kph. He kept a careful eye open as he sped past hundreds of lorries roaring through the night towards the coast, and found what he was looking for just past the town of Reuquena, forty miles west of Valencia.

His lights picked up the army jeep keeping station to a covered eight-ton truck and as he swept past he noted the name on the lorry's side. It was the name of the trucking company Schlinker had given him. Driving ahead of the lorry was another army vehicle, a four-door saloon, evidently with an officer sitting alone in the back. He touched the accelerator and the Mercedes sped past towards the coast.

At Valencia he took the ring road round the sleeping city, following the pointing to the E26 highway to Barcelona. The motorway ran out just north of Valencia, and he was back to crawling behind orange lorries and early farm vehicles, past the miraculous Roman fortress of Sagunto, hacked by the legionaries out of the living rock and later converted by the Moors into a citadel of Islam. He drove into Castellon just after four, and followed the signs labelled 'Puerto'.

The port of Castellon lies five kilometres from the main town, down a narrow, arrow-straight road that leads from the city to the sea. At the end of the road it is impossible to miss the port and harbour, for there is nothing else there.

As usual with Mediterranean ports, there are three separate harbours, one for freighters, one for yachts and pleasure craft and one for fishing vessels. In Castellon the commercial port lies to the left as one faces the sea, and like all Spanish ports is ringed by a fence and the gates are manned day and night by armed Guardia Civil. In the centre lies the harbourmaster's office and beside it the splendid yacht club, with a dining-room looking out over the commercial port on one side, and the yacht basin and fish harbour on the other. Landward side of the harbour office is a row of warehouses.

Shannon turned to the left and parked the car by the roadside, climbed out and started walking. Halfway round the perimeter fence of the port area he found the main gate, with a sentry dozing in a box inside it. The gate was locked. Further on he peered through the chain-links and with a surge of relief spotted the *Toscana* berthed against the far side of the basin. He settled to wait till six o'clock.

He was at the main gate at quarter to six, smiled and nodded at the Guardia Civil sentry, who stared coldly back. In the rising sunlight he could see the army staff car, lorry and jeep, with seven or eight soldiers milling round them, parked a hundred yards away. At six-ten a civilian car arrived, parked next to the gate and sounded its horn. A small, dapper Spaniard climbed out. Shannon approached him.

'Señor Moscar?'

'*Si.*'

'My name's Brown. I'm the seaman who's got to join his ship here.'

The Spaniard puckered his brow.

'*Por favor? Que?*'

'Brown,' insisted Shannon. '*Toscana.*'

The Spaniard's face lightened.

'*Ah, si. El marinero.* Come, please.'

The gate had been opened, and Moscar showed his pass. He babbled for several seconds at the guard and the Customs man who had opened the gate, and pointed at Shannon. Cat caught the word 'marinero' several times, and his passport and merchant seaman's card were examined. Then he followed Moscar to the Customs office. An hour later he was on board the *Toscana*.

The search started at nine. There was no warning. The captain's manifest had been present and checked out. It was perfectly in order. Down on the quay the truck from Madrid was parked, along with the car and the jeep. The army escort captain, a thin, sallow man with a face like a Moor and a lipless mouth, consulted with two Customs officers. Then the latter came aboard. Moscar followed. They checked the cargo to make sure it was what the manifest said, and no more. They peered in nooks and crannies, but not under the floorboards of the main hold. They looked in the store locker, gazed at the tangle of chains, oil drums and paint cans, and closed the door. It took an hour. The main thing that interested them was why Captain Waldenberg needed seven men on such a small ship. It was explained that Dupree and Vlaminck were company employees who had missed their ship in Brindisi and were being dropped off at Malta on the way to Latakia. They had no seaman's cards with them because they had left their gear on board their own ship. Asked for a name, Waldenberg gave the name of a ship he had seen in Brindisi harbour. There was silence from the Spaniards, who looked at their chief for advice. He glanced down at the army captain, shrugged and left the ship. Twenty minutes later, loading began.

At half past noon the *Toscana* slipped out of Castellon harbour and turned her helm south to Cape San Antonio. Cat Shannon, feeling sick now that it was all over, knowing that from then on he was virtually unstoppable, was leaning against the after rail, watching the flat green orange groves south of Castellon slip away as they headed for the sea. Carl Waldenberg came up behind him.

'That's the last stop?' he asked.

'The last where we have to open our hatches,' said Shannon. 'We have to pick up some men on the coast of Africa, but we'll moor in the roads. The men will come out by launch. Deck cargo native workers. At least, that's what they'll be shipped as.'

'I've only got charts as far as the Straits of Gibraltar,' objected Waldenberg.

Shannon reached into his zip-up windbreaker and pulled out a sheaf of charts, half of the number Endean had handed him in Rome.

'These,' he said, handing them to the skipper, 'will get you as far as Freetown, Sierra Leone. That's where we anchor and pick up the men. Please give me an arrival time at noon on July 2nd. That is the rendezvous.'

As the captain left to return to his cabin and start to plot his course and speed, Shannon was left alone at the rail. Seagulls wheeled around the stern, seeking morsels dropped from the galley where Cipriani was preparing lunch, squealing and cawing as they dipped towards the foaming wake to snatch up a scrap of bread or vegetable.

Anyone listening would have heard another sound amid their screaming, the sound of a man whistling 'Spanish Harlem'.

Far away to the north another ship slipped her moorings and under the guidance of a port pilot eased her way out of the harbour of Archangel. The Motor Vessel *Komarov* was only ten years old and something over 5000 tons.

Inside her bridge the atmosphere was warm and cosy. The captain and the pilot stood side by side staring forrard as the quays and warehouses slipped past to her port side and watched the channel ahead to the open sea. Each man held a cup of steaming coffee. The helmsman kept the vessel on the heading given him by the pilot and to his left the radar screen gleamed and died endlessly, its iridescent sweep arm picking up on each turn the dotted ocean ahead and beyond it the fringe of the ice that would never melt, even in high summer.

In the stern two men leaned over the rail beneath the flag with the hammer and sickle emblem and watched the Russian arctic port slip past. Dr Ivanov clipped the crushed cardboard filter of his black cigarette between his teeth and sniffed the crisp, salt-caked air. Both men were wrapped against the cold, for even in June the wind off the White Sea is no invitation to shirt sleeves. By his side one of the technicians, younger, eager for his first trip abroad, turned to him.

'Comrade Doctor,' he began.

Ivanov took the stump of the *papiross* from his teeth and flicked it into the foaming wake.

'My friend,' he said, 'I think as we are now aboard you can call me Mikhail Mikhailovich.'

'But at the Institute . . .'

'We are not at the Institute. We are on board a ship. And we will be in fairly close confinement either here or in the jungle for months to come.'

'I see,' said the younger man, but he was not to be repressed. 'Have you ever been to Zangaro before?'

'No,' said his superior.

'But to Africa,' insisted the younger man.

'To Ghana, yes.'

'What is it like?'

'Full of jungle, swamps, mosquitoes, snakes and people who don't understand a damn thing you say.'

'But they understand English,' said the assistant. 'We both speak English.'

'Not in Zangaro, they don't.'

'Oh.' The junior technician had read all he could find about Zangaro, which was not much, in the encyclopaedia borrowed from the vast library at the Institute.

'The captain told me if we make good time, we should arrive at Clarence in twenty-two days. That will be their Independence Day.'

'Bully for them,' said Ivanov, and walked away.

Past Cape Spartel, nosing her way from the Mediterranean into the Atlantic, the MV *Toscana* radioed a ship-to-shore telegram to Gibraltar for on-passing to London. It was to Mr Walter Harris at a London address. It said simply, 'Pleased announce your brother completely recovered.' It was the sign meaning the *Toscana* was on her way and on schedule. Slight variations of the message about Mr Harris's brother's health could have meant she was on course but late, or in some kind of trouble. No telegram of any kind meant she had been cleared from Spanish territorial waters.

That afternoon there was a conference in Sir James Manson's office.

'Good,' said the tycoon, when Endean broke the news. 'How much time has she got to reach target?'

'Twenty-two days, Sir James. It is now Day Seventy-Eight of the hundred estimated for the project. Shannon had allowed Day Eighty for his departure from Europe, and that would have left him twenty days. He estimated the time at sea between sixteen and eighteen days, allowing for adverse weather or a two-day breakdown. He had four days in hand, even on his own estimate.'

'Will he strike early?'

'No, sir. Strike day is still Day One Hundred. He'll kill time hove-to at sea if he has to.'

Sir James Manson paced up and down his office.

'How about the rented villa?' he asked.

'It has been arranged, Sir James.'

'Then I don't see any point in your waiting around London any longer. Get over to Paris again, get a visa for Cotonou, fly down there and get our new employee, Colonel Bobi, to accompany you to this place next to Zangaro. If he seems shifty, offer him more money.

'Get settled in, get the truck and the hunting guns ready, and when you receive Shannon's signal that he is going in for the attack that evening, break the news to Bobi. Get him to sign that mining concession as President Bobi, date it one month later, and send all three copies by registered post in three envelopes to me here.

'Keep Bobi virtually under lock and key until Shannon's second signal to say he has succeeded. Then in you go. By the way, that bodyguard you are taking with you. Is he ready?'

'Yes, Sir James. For the kind of money he's getting, he's good and ready.'

'What's he like?'

'As nasty as they come. Which is what I was looking for.'

'You could still have problems, you know. Shannon will have all his men round him, at least those who survive the battle. He could prove troublesome.'

Endean grinned.

'Shannon's men will follow Shannon,' he said. 'And I can handle him. Like all mercenaries, he's got his price. I'll just offer it to him – but in Switzerland and out of Zangaro.'

When he had gone Sir James Manson stared down at the City below him and wondered if any man had not got his price. Either in money, or in the inspiration of fear. He had never met one. 'They can all be bought, and if they can't they can be broken,' one of his mentors had once said to him. And after years as a tycoon, watching politicians, generals, journalists, editors, businessmen, ministers, entrepreneurs and aristocrats and union leaders, blacks and whites at work and play, he was still of that view.

Many years ago a Spanish seafarer, looking from the sea towards the land, had seen a mountain, which, with the sun behind it in the east, appeared to him to have the shape of a lion's head. He called the land Lion Mountain, and passed on. The name stuck, and the country became known as Sierra Leone. Later another man, seeing the same mountain in a different light, or through different eyes, called it Mount Aureole. That name also stuck. Even later, and in a more whimsical bout of fantasy, a white man named the town founded in its shadow Freetown, and it still bears the name today. It was just after noon on July 2nd, Day Eighty-Eight in Shannon's private calendar, that the Motor Vessel *Toscana* dropped anchor a third of a mile out from the shore off Freetown, Sierra Leone.

On the voyage from Spain, Shannon had insisted that the cargo remain just where it was, untouched and unopened. This was just in case there was a search at Freetown, although, with nothing to discharge and no cargo to take on board, that would have been most unusual. The ammunition crates had been scrubbed clean of their Spanish markings and sanded down with a disc sander to the bright white wood. Stencilled markings showing the crates contained drilling bits for oil rigs off the Cameroon coast had been painted on.

Only one job had he allowed to be done on the way south. The bundles of mixed clothing had been sorted and the one containing the haversacks and webbing had been opened. With canvas needle and palm, Cipriani, Vlaminck and Dupree had passed the days cutting the haversacks to pieces and transforming them into back-packs fitted with a score of long, narrow pouches, each capable of taking one bazooka rocket. These now shapeless and inexplicable bundles were stored in the paint locker among the cleaning rags.

The smaller knapsacks had also been altered. The packs had been cut away so that only the shoulder straps remained, with braces across the chest and round the waist. Dog-clips had been fastened atop each shoulder strap, with others at the belt, and later these frames would accommodate an entire crate of mortar bombs, enabling up to twenty to be carried at one time.

The *Toscana* had announced her presence while six miles off-shore to the harbourmaster's office of Freetown, and had been given permission to enter port and anchor out in the bay. As she had no cargo to load or unload, there was no need for her to take up room at the port's precious Queen Elizabeth II Quay. She had only come to take on deck crew.

Freetown is one of the favourite ports along the West African coast for taking aboard these brawny labourers who, trained in the use of tackle and winches, are used by the tramp steamers frequenting the smaller timber ports along the coast. They board at Freetown on the outward voyage and are discharged with their pay on the way back. In a hundred coves and creeks along the coast, where cranes and jetties are at a premium, ships have to use their own jumbo derricks to load cargo. It is grindingly hard work, sweating in the tropical fever heat, and white seamen are paid to be seamen, not stevedores. Locally recruited labour might not be available, and probably would not know how to handle cargo, so Sierra Leonians are brought along. They sleep in the open on the ship's deck for the voyage, brewing up their food and performing their ablutions over the stern. It caused no surprise in Freetown when the *Toscana* gave this as her reason for calling.

When the anchor cable rattled down, Shannon scanned the shoreline right round the bay, almost all of it taken up by the outer shanty town of the country's capital.

The sky was overcast, no rain fell, but beneath the clouds the heat was like a greenhouse, and he felt the sweat clamping his shirt to his torso. It would be like this from here on. His eyes riveted on the central area of the city's waterfront, where a large hotel stood looking out over the bay. If anywhere, this was where Langarotti would be waiting, staring out to sea. Perhaps he had not arrived yet. But they could not wait for ever. If he was not there by sundown, they would have to invent a reason for staying on, like a broken refrigerator. It would be unthinkable to sail without the cold store working. He took his eyes away from the hotel and watched the tenders plying round the big Elder Dempster ship tied up at the quay.

On shore the Corsican had already seen the *Toscana* before she dropped anchor, and was heading back into the town. He had been there for a week, and had all the men Shannon wanted. They were not the same tribal group as the Leonians, but no one minded. Men of mixed tribes were available as stevedores and deck cargo.

Just after two, a small pinnace came out from the Customs House with a uniformed man standing in the back. When he came aboard, he was the assistant chief Customs officer, white socks a-gleam, khaki shorts and tunic pressed, epaulettes sparkling and stiff peaked cap set dead straight. Between the regalia a pair of ebony knees and a beaming face could be distinguished. Shannon met him, introduced himself as the owner's representative, shook hands profusely, and led the Customs man to the captain's cabin.

The three bottles of whisky and two cartons of cigarettes were waiting. The officer fanned himself, sighed gustily with pleasure at the cool of the air conditioning, and sipped his beer. He cast an incurious eye over the new manifest, which said the *Toscana* had picked up machine parts at Brindisi and was taking them to the AGIP oil company's offshore concessions near the Cameroon coast. There was no mention of Yugoslavia or Spain. Other cargo was listed as powerboats (inflatables), engines (outboard) and tropical clothing (assorted), also for the oil drillers. On the way back, she would wish to load cocoa and some coffee at San Pedro, Ivory Coast, and return to Europe. He exhaled on his official stamp to moisten it, and placed his approval on the manifest. An hour later he was gone, his presents in his tucker bag.

Just after six, as the evening cooled, Shannon made out the longshore boat moving away from the beach. Amidships the two local men who ran passengers out to the waiting vessels in the bay heaved at their oars. Aft sat seven other Africans, clutching bundles on their knees. In the prow sat a lone European. As the craft swung expertly into the side of the *Toscana*, Jean-Baptiste Langarotti came nimbly up the ladder that hung to the water.

One by one the bundles were heaved from the bobbing rowing boat up to the rail of the freighter, then the seven Africans followed. Although it was indiscreet to do so in sight of land, Vlaminck, Dupree and Semmler started to clap them on the back and shake hands. The Africans, grinning from ear to ear, seemed as happy as the mercenaries. Waldenberg and his mate looked on in surprise. Shannon signed to the captain to take the *Toscana* back to sea.

After dark, sitting in groups on the main deck, taking with gratitude the cooling breeze off the sea as the *Toscana* rolled on to the south, Shannon introduced his recruits to Waldenberg. The mercenaries knew them all, as they did the mercenaries. Six of the Africans were young men, called Johnny, Patrick, Jinja (nicknamed Ginger), Sunday, Bartholomew and Timothy.

Each of them had fought with the mercenaries before, each of them had been personally trained by one of the European soldiers, each of them had been tried and tested in battle many times, and would stick it out however hard the firefight. And each of them was loyal to his leader. The seventh was an older man, who smiled less, bore himself with a confident dignity and was addressed by Shannon as 'Doctor'. He too was loyal to his leader and his people.

'How are things at home?' Shannon asked him.

Doctor Okoye shook his head sadly. 'Not well,' he said.

'Tomorrow we start work,' Shannon told him. 'We start preparing tomorrow.'

PART THREE
The Big Killing

20

For the remainder of the sea voyage, Cat Shannon worked his men without pause. Only the middle-aged African whom he called 'Doctor' was exempt. The rest were divided into parties, each with a separate job to do.

Marc Vlaminck and Kurt Semmler broke open the five green Castrol oil drums by hammering off the false bottoms, and from each plucked the bulky package of twenty Schmeissers and a hundred magazines that were inside. The superfluous lubricating oil was poured into smaller containers and saved for the ship's use.

Aided by the six African soldiers, the pair stripped the masking tape from each of the hundred submachine guns, which were then individually wiped clean of oil and grease. By the time they had finished, the six Africans had already learned the operating mechanisms of the Schmeisser in a way that was as good if not better than any weapon-familiarisation course that they could have undergone.

Breaking open the first ten boxes of 9 mm ammunition, the eight of them sat around the decks slotting the shells into the magazines, thirty to each, until the first 15,000 rounds from their store had gone into the 500 magazines at their disposal. Eighty of the Schmeissers were then set aside while Jean-Baptiste Langarotti prepared sets of uniforms from the bales stored in the hold. These sets consisted of two tee-vests, two pairs of pants, two pairs of socks, one pair of boots, one set of trousers, one beret, one combat blouse, and one sleeping bag. When these were ready, the bundle was wrapped up, one Schmeisser and five full magazines were wrapped in an oily cloth, slipped into a polythene bag, and the whole lot stuffed into the sleeping bag. Tied at the top and ready for handling like a sack, each sleeping bag comprised the necessary clothing and weaponry for one future soldier.

Twenty sets of uniforms and twenty Schmeissers with five magazines per carbine were set aside. These were for the attack force itself, although the force only numbered eleven, with spares for the crew if necessary. Langarotti, who had learned while in the Army and in prison to handle a needle and thread, altered and sewed eleven sets of uniform for the members of the attack party until each man was fitted out.

Dupree and Cipriani, the deckhand, who turned out to be a useful carpenter, stripped down several of the packing crates that had once contained ammunition and turned their attention to the outboard engines. All three were Johnson sixty-horsepower units. The two men built wooden boxes to fit neatly over the top of each engine, and lined the boxes with foam rubber from the mattresses they had brought along. With the exhaust noise of the engines muffled by the underwater exhausts, the mechanical noise emanating from the engine casings could also be reduced to a low murmur by the muffling boxes they thus prepared.

When Vlaminck and Dupree had finished these tasks, each turned his attention to the weapon he would be using on the night of the strike. Dupree uncrated his two mortar tubes and familiarised himself with the aiming mechanisms. He had not used the Yugoslav model of mortar before, but was relieved to see it was helpfully simple. He prepared seventy mortar bombs, checking and arming the primers in the nose-cone of each bomb.

Re-packing the prepared bombs into their boxes, he clipped two boxes, one above the other, to the webbing harness that had already been prepared from the army-style knapsacks he had bought in London two months earlier.

Vlaminck concentrated on his two bazookas, of which only one would be used on the night of the attack. Again, the main limitation on what he could take with him was the weight factor. Everything had to be carried on a human back. Standing on the forepeak, using the tip of the flag-pole sticking above the stern as a fixed point, his aiming disc slotted to the end of the bazooka, he carefully adjusted the sights to the weapon until he was certain he could take a barrel at two hundred metres with no more than two shots. He had already picked Patrick as his back-up man, for they had been together before and knew each other well enough to make a good team. With his back-pack, the African would be carrying ten bazooka rockets as well as his own Schmeisser. Vlaminck added another two rockets as his personal load, and Cipriani sewed him two pouches to hang from his belt, which could contain the extra rockets.

Shannon concentrated on the ancillary gear, examining the magnesium-flare rockets and explaining to Dupree how they worked. He distributed one compass to each mercenary, tested the gas-powered foghorn and checked the portable radio sets.

Having time in hand, Shannon had the *Toscana* heave-to for two days well out at sea in an area where the ship's radar told them there was no other shipping within twenty miles. As the ship lay almost stationary, heaving slightly on the swell, each man tested his personal Schmeisser. The whites had no problems; they had each in their time used half a dozen different submachine guns, and these weapons vary but slightly. The Africans took longer to get used to them, for most of their experience had been with bolt-action 7.92 mm Mausers or the standard 7.62

NATO self-loading rifle. One of the German carbines jammed repeatedly, so Shannon threw it overboard and gave the man another. Each African fired off nine hundred rounds, until he was accustomed to the feel of the Schmeisser in his hands, and each man had been cured of the annoying habit African soldiers tend to adopt, of closing their eyes while they fire.

The five empty and open-topped oil barrels had been stored for later use, and these were now streamed astern of the *Toscana* for target practice. At a hundred metres all of the men, black and white, could riddle a barrel before they had ceased their practice. Four barrels were destroyed and sunk in this manner, and the fifth was used by Marc Vlaminck. He let it stream to two hundred metres, then planted himself in the stern of the *Toscana*, feet apart and braced, the bazooka across his right shoulder, right eye applied to the sight. Judging the gentle heave of the deck, he waited until he was sure, and fired off his first rocket. It screamed over the top of the barrel and exploded with a spout of spray into the ocean. His second rocket took the barrel in the centre. There was a crash and the boom of the explosion echoed back over the water to the watching mercenaries and crew. Fragments of tinplate spattered the water close to where the barrel had been and a cheer came from the watchers. Grinning widely, Vlaminck turned to Shannon, ripped off the glasses he had used to protect his eyes and wiped the specks of smut from his face.

'You said you wanted a door taken off, Cat?'

'That's right, a bloody great wooden gate, Tiny.'

'I'll give it to you in matchsticks, and that's a promise,' said the Belgian.

Because of the noise they had made, Shannon ordered the *Toscana* to move on the next day, and two days later he called his second halt. In the period under way, the men had hauled out the three assault craft and inflated them. They lay side by side along the main deck. Each, despite being a deep, dark grey in colour, had a brilliant orange nose and the name of the manufacturer in the same luminous colour down each side. These were painted out with black paint from the ship's store.

When they were hove-to for the second time, they tested all three. Without the muffling boxes placed over the top of each engine, the Johnsons made an audible mutter even when four hundred yards away from the *Toscana*. With the boxes in place and the engines throttled back to less than quarter-power, there was hardly a sound at thirty yards. They tended to overheat after twenty minutes at half-power, but this could be stretched to thirty minutes if power was reduced. Shannon took one of the craft out for two hours, checking throttle settings for speed-against-noise, to get the best combination. As the powerful outboards gave him a large reserve, he elected never to push them beyond one-third of full power, and advised his men to close down to less than one-quarter power for the last two hundred yards as they approached the landing beaches of the target area.

The walkie-talkies were also tested at up to four miles, and despite the heavy atmospherics and the hint of thunder in the stifling air, messages could still be heard if read over clearly and slowly. To get them used to the notion, the Africans were also given trips in the power-craft, at a varying range of speeds, in daylight and at night.

The night exercises were the most important. For one of them Shannon took the other four whites and the six Africans three miles out from the *Toscana*, which burned one small light at her masthead. On the journey away from the ship, the ten men had their eyes bandaged. When the masks were taken off, each was given ten minutes to accustom his vision to the blackness of the sky and the ocean, before the move back to the boat began. With the engine throttled down and dead silence maintained aboard, the assault craft moved quietly back towards the light that represented the *Toscana*. Sitting with the tiller bar in his hand, holding the power setting steady at one third, then cutting back to less than a quarter for the final run-in, Shannon could feel the tension of the men in front of him. They knew this was what it would be like when they struck, and there would be no second chances.

Back on board, Carl Waldenberg came up to Shannon as the two men watched the crew winch the vessel inboard by torchlight.

'I hardly heard a sound,' he said. 'Not until you were a couple of hundred metres away, and I was listening hard. Unless they have very alert guards posted, you should be able to make the beach, wherever you are going. Incidentally, where are you going? I need more charts if I have to proceed much further.'

'I think you'd all better know,' said Shannon. 'We'll spend the rest of the night going through the briefing.'

Until dawn, the crew (with the exception of the engineer who still slept with his engines), the seven Africans and the four mercenaries listened to Shannon in the main saloon while he went through the entire plan of attack. He had prepared and set up his projector and slide transparencies, some of which were pictures he had taken while in Zangaro, others of which were the maps and charts he had bought or drawn for himself.

When he finished, there was dead silence in the stifling cabin, the blue wreaths of cigarette smoke trickling out through the open portholes into the equally clammy night outside.

Finally Waldenberg said, '*Gott in Himmel!*' Then they all started. It took an hour before the questions were answered. Waldenberg wanted reassurance that if anything went wrong the survivors would be back on board and the *Toscana* well over the horizon before sunrise. Shannon gave it to him.

'We only have your word for it they have no navy, no gunboats,' he said.

'Then my word will have to do,' said Shannon. 'They have none.'

'Just because you did not see any . . .'

'They have none,' snapped Shannon. 'I spent hours talking with people who have been there for years. There are no gunboats, no navy.'

The six Africans had no questions. They would each stick close to the mercenary who would lead them, and trust that he knew what he was doing. The seventh, the doctor, asked briefly where he would be, and accepted that he would remain on board the *Toscana*. The four mercenaries had a few purely technical questions, which Shannon answered in technical terms.

When they came back up on deck the Africans stretched themselves out on their sleeping bags and went to sleep. Shannon had often envied their ability to sleep at any time, in any place, in almost any circumstances. The doctor retired to his cabin, as did Norbiatto who would take the next watch. Waldenberg went into his wheelhouse and the *Toscana* began to move again towards her destination, just three days away.

The five mercenaries grouped themselves on the after deck behind the crew quarters and talked until the sun was high. They all approved of the plan of attack and accepted that Shannon's reconnaissance had been accurate and precise. If anything had changed since then, if there had been an unforeseen addition to the town's defences or improvements to the palace, they knew they could all die. They would be very few, dangerously few, for such a job, and there was no margin for things going wrong. But they accepted that either they had to win within twenty minutes or they would have to get back to their boats and leave in a hurry, those that could leave. They knew that no one was going to come looking for wounded, and that anyone finding one of his colleagues badly hurt, and unmovable would be expected to give him one mercenary's last gift to another, the quick clean way out, preferable to capture and the slow death. It was part of the rules, and they had all had to do it before.

Just before noon they parted company and turned in.

They all woke early on the morning of Day Ninety-Nine. Shannon had been up half the night, watching beside Waldenberg as the coastline loomed out of the perimeter of the tiny radar screen at the rear of the wheelhouse.

'I want you to come within visual range of the coast to the south of the capital,' he had told the captain, 'and spend the morning steaming northwards, parallel to the shore, so that at noon we are off the coast here.'

His finger jabbed the sea off the coast of the country to Zangaro's northern side. During the twenty days at sea he had come to trust the German captain. Waldenberg, having taken his money in Ploce port, had stuck by his side of the bargain, giving himself completely to making the operation as successful as he could. Shannon was confident the seaman would hold his ship at readiness four miles off the coast, a bit to the south of Clarence, while the firefight went on, and if the distress call came over the walkie-talkie, that he would wait until the men who had managed to escape rejoined the *Toscana* in their speedboats, before making at full power for the open sea. There was no spare man Shannon could leave behind to ensure this, so he had to trust Waldenberg.

He had already found the frequency on the ship's radio on which Endean wanted him to transmit his first message, and this was timed for noon.

The morning passed slowly. Through the ship's telescope Shannon watched the estuary of the Zangaro River move past, a long, low line of mangrove trees along the horizon. At mid-morning he could make out the break in the green line where the town of Clarence lay, and passed the telescope to Vlaminck, Langarotti, Dupree and Semmler. Each studied the off-white blur in silence and handed the glass to the next man. They smoked more than usual and mooched around the deck, tense and bored with the waiting, wishing, now they were so close, that they could go straight into action.

At noon Shannon began to transmit his message. He read it in clear into the radio speaker. It was just one word, 'Plantain'. He gave it every ten seconds for five minutes, then broke for five minutes, then gave it again. Three times within thirty minutes, each time over a five-minute period, he broadcast the word, and hoped that Endean would hear it somewhere on the mainland. It meant that Shannon and his men were on time and in position, and that they would strike Clarence and Kimba's palace in the small hours of the following morning.

Twenty-two miles away across the water, Simon Endean heard the word on his Braun transistor radio, folded the long wasp-antenna, left the hotel balcony and withdrew into the bedroom. Then he began, slowly and carefully, to explain to the former colonel of the Zangaran Army that within twenty-four hours he, Antoine Bobi, would be President of Zangaro. At four in the afternoon the colonel, grinning and chuckling at the thought of the reprisals he would take against those who had assisted in his ousting, struck his deal with Endean. He signed the document granting Bormac Trading Company a ten-year exclusive mining concession in the Crystal Mountains for a flat annual fee, a tiny profits-participation by the Zangaran government, and watched Endean place in an envelope and seal a cheque certified by a Swiss bank for half a million dollars in favour of Antoine Bobi.

In Clarence preparations went ahead through the afternoon for the following day's independence celebrations. Six prisoners, lying badly beaten in the cells beneath the former colonial police station, listened to the cries of the Kimba Patriotic Youth marching through the streets above them, and knew that they would be battered to death in the main square as part of the celebrations Kimba had prepared. Photographs of the president were prominently hung on every public building and the diplomatic wives prepared their migraines so they would be excused attendance at the ceremonies.

In the shuttered palace, surrounded by his guards, President Jean Kimba sat alone at his desk contemplating the advent of his sixth year of office.

During the afternoon the *Toscana* and her lethal cargo put about and began to cruise slowly back down the coast from the north.

In the wheelhouse Shannon sipped his coffee and explained to Waldenberg how he wanted the *Toscana* placed.

'Hold her just north of the border until sundown,' he told his captain.

'After nine p.m., start her again and move diagonally towards the coast. Between sundown and nine, we will have streamed the three assault craft astern of the ship, each loaded with its complement. That will have to be done by torchlight, but well away from the land, at least ten miles out.

'When you start to move, around nine, keep her really slow, so you end up here, four miles out from the shore and one mile north of the peninsula at 2 a.m. You'll be out of sight of the city in that position. With all lights doused, no one should see you. So far as I know there's no radar on the peninsula, unless a ship is in port.'

'Even if there is, she should not have a radar on,' growled Waldenberg. He was bent over his inshore chart of the coast, measuring his distances with dividers and parallel rule. 'When does the first craft set free and move inshore?'

'At two. That will be Dupree and his mortar crew. The other two boats cast adrift and head for the beach one hour later, OK?'

'OK,' said Waldenberg, 'I'll have you there.'

'It has to be accurate,' insisted Shannon. 'We'll see no lights in Clarence, even if there are any, until we round the headland. So we'll be on compass heading only, calculating by speed and heading, until we see the outline of the shore, which might be no more than a hundred metres. It depends on the sky; cloud, moon and stars.'

Waldenberg nodded. He knew the rest. After he heard the firefight begin, he was to ease the *Toscana* across the mouth of the harbour, four miles out, and heave-to again two miles to the south of Clarence, four miles out from the tip of the peninsula. From then on he would listen on his walkie-talkie. If all went well, he would stay where he was until sun-up. If things went badly he would turn on the lights at the masthead, the forepeak and the stern, to guide the returning force back to the *Toscana*.

Darkness that evening came early, for the sky was overcast and the moon would not rise until the small hours of the morning. The rains had already started, and twice in the previous three days they had weathered drenching downpours as the skies opened. The weather report, listened to avidly on the radio, indicated there would be scattered squalls along the coast that night, but no tornadoes, and they could only pray there would be no torrential rains while the men were in their open boats or while the battle for the palace was on.

Before sundown the tarpaulins were hauled off the equipment, piled in rows along the main deck, and when darkness fell Shannon and Norbiatto began organising the departure of the assault craft. The first over the side was the one Dupree would use. There was no point in using the derrick; the sea was only eight feet beneath the deck at the lowest point. The men lowered the fully-inflated craft into the water manually, and Semmler and Dupree went down into it as it bobbed against the *Toscana*'s side in the slow swell.

The two of them hoisted the heavy outboard engine into place over the stern and screwed it tight to the backboard. Before placing the muffler on top of it, Semmler started the Johnson up and ran her for two minutes. The Serbian engineer had already given all three engines a thorough check-over, and it ran like a sewing machine. With the muffling box on top, the noise died to a low hum.

Semmler climbed out and the equipment was lowered to Dupree's waiting hands. There were the base plates and sighting gear for both mortars, then the two mortar tubes. Dupree was taking forty mortar bombs for the palace and twelve for the barracks. To be on the safe side, he took sixty bombs, all primed and fused for detonation on impact.

He also took both flare-launching rockets and the ten flares, one of the gas-powered foghorns, one walkie-talkie and his night glasses. Slung over his shoulder he had his personal Schmeisser and stuck in his belt were five full magazines. The two Africans who were going with him, Timothy and Sunday, were the last into the assault craft.

When it was ready, Shannon stared down at the three faces that looked back up at him in the dim torchlight.

'Good luck,' he called softly. For answer Dupree raised one thumb and nodded. Holding the painter of the assault craft, Semmler moved back along the rail while Dupree fended off from down below. When the craft was streamed astern of the *Toscana* in complete drakness, Semmler tied her painter to the after-rail, leaving the three men to bob up and down on the swell.

The second boat took less time to let into the water, for the men had got the hang of it. Marc Vlaminck went down with Semmler to set the outboard engine in position, for this was their boat. Vlaminck was taking one bazooka and twelve rockets, two on his own body, the other ten carried by his back-up man, who was Patrick. Semmler had his personal Schmeisser and five magazines, each in easy-extraction pouches hung round his belt. He had a set of night glasses round his neck and the second walkie-talkie strapped to one thigh. As he was the only man who could speak German, French and reasonable English, he would double as the main attack party's radio operator. When the two whites were ensconced in their craft, Patrick and Jinja, who would be Semmler's back-up man, slid down the jacob's ladder from the *Toscana* and took their places.

The two were streamed astern of the ship, and Dupree's painter was passed to Semmler, who made it fast to his own assault craft. The two inflatable vessels bobbed behind the *Toscana* in line astern, separated by the length of rope, but none of their occupants said a word.

Langarotti and Shannon took the third and last boat. They were accompanied by Bartholomew and Johnny, the latter a big, grinning fighter who had been promoted to captain at Shannon's insistence when they last fought together, but who had refused to take his own company as his new rank entitled him, preferring to stick close to Shannon and look after him.

Just before Shannon, who was the last man into the boats, descended the ladder, Captain Waldenberg appeared from the direction of the bridge and tugged at his sleeve. The German pulled the mercenary to one side and muttered quietly, 'We may have a problem.'

Shannon was immobile, frozen by the thought that something had gone seriously wrong.

'What is it?' he asked.

'There's a ship. Lying off Clarence, further out than us.'

'How long since you saw it?'

'Some time,' said Waldenberg, 'but I thought it must be cruising south down the coast, like us, or moving northwards. But it's not, it's riding-to.'

'You're sure? There's no doubt about it?'

'None at all. When we came down the coast we were moving so slowly that if the other had been steaming in the same direction, she'd be well away by now. If northwards, she'd have passed us by now. She's immobile.'

'Any indication of what she is, who she belongs to?' The German shook his head.

'The size of a freighter. No indication who she is, unless we contact her.'

Shannon thought for several minutes.

'If she were a freighter, bringing cargo to Zangaro, would she anchor till morning before entering harbour?' he asked.

Waldenberg nodded.

'Quite possible. Entry by night is frequently not allowed in some of the smaller ports along this coast. She's probably riding out until the morning before asking permission to enter port.'

'If you've seen her, presumably she's seen you?' Shannon suggested.

'Bound to,' said Waldenberg. 'We're on her radar all right.'

'Could her radar pick up the dinghies?'

'Unlikely,' said the captain, 'too low in the water most probably.'

'We go ahead,' said Shannon. 'It's too late now. We have to assume she's just a freighter waiting out the night.'

'She's bound to hear the firefight,' said Waldenberg.

'What can she do about it?'

The German grinned.

'Not much. If you fail, and we're not out of here before sunrise, she'll recognise the *Toscana* through binoculars.'

'We mustn't fail then. Carry on as ordered.'

Waldenberg went back to his bridge. The middle-aged African doctor, who had watched the proceedings in silence, stepped forward.

'Good luck, Major,' he said in perfectly modulated English. 'God go with you.'

Shannon felt like saying that he would have preferred a Wombat recoil-less rifle, but held his tongue. He knew these people took religion very seriously. He nodded, said 'Sure' and went over the side.

Out of the darkness, looking up at the dim blob of the *Toscana*'s stern above him, there was complete silence but for the slop of the water against the rubberised hulls of the boats. Occasionally it gurgled behind the ship's rudder. From the landward side there was not a sound, for they were well out of earshot of the shore, and by the time they came close enough to hear shouts and laughter, it would be well past midnight, and with luck everyone would be asleep. Not that there was much laughter in Clarence, but Shannon was aware how far a single, sharp sound can travel over water at night, and everyone in his party, in the boats and on the *Toscana*, was sworn to silence and no smoking.

He glanced at his watch. It was quarter to nine. He sat back to wait.

At nine the hull of the *Toscana* emitted a low rumble, and the water beneath her stern began to churn and bubble, the phosphorescent white wake running back to slap against the snub nose of Shannon's assault craft. Then they were under way, and by dipping his fingers over the side he could feel the caress of the passing water. Five hours to cover twenty-eight nautical miles.

The sky was still overcast and the air was like that inside an old greenhouse, but a hole in the cloud cover let a little dim starlight through. Astern he could make out the craft of Vlaminck and Semmler at the end of twenty feet of rope, and somewhere behind them Janni Dupree was moving along in the wake of the *Toscana*.

The five hours went by like a nightmare. Nothing to do but watch and listen, nothing to see but the darkness and the glitter of the sea, nothing to hear but the low thump of the *Toscana*'s old pistons moving inside her rusted hull. No one could sleep, despite the mesmeric rocking of the light craft, for the tensions were building up in every man in the operation.

But they did pass, somehow. Shannon's watch said five past two when the noise of the *Toscana*'s engines died, and she slowed to idle in the water. From above the after-rail a low whistle came through the darkness; Waldenberg letting him know they were in position for cast-off. Shannon turned his head to signal Semmler, but Dupree must have heard the whistle, for a few seconds later they heard his engine cough into life and begin to move away towards the shore. They never saw him go, just heard the low buzz of the engine under its muffler vanishing into the darkness.

At the helm of his assault craft Big Janni checked his power setting on the twist-grip he held in his right hand and held his left arm, with the compass as steady as he could under his eyes. He knew he should have four and a half miles to cover, angling in towards the coast, trying to make landfall on the outer side of the northern arm that curved round the harbour of Clarence. At that power setting, on that course, he should make it in thirty minutes. At twenty-five minutes he would shut the engine almost closed and try to make out his landfall by eyesight. If the others gave him one hour to set up his mortars and flare-rockets, they should move past the tip of the point towards their own beach landing just about the time he was ready. But for that hour, he and his two Africans would be the only ones on the shore of Zangaro. That was all the more reason why they should be completely silent as they set up their battery.

Twenty-two minutes after he left the *Toscana*, Dupree heard a low 'pssst' from the bow of his dinghy. It was Timothy, whom he had posted as a lookout. Dupree glanced up from his compass and what he saw caused him to throttle back quickly. They were already close to a shoreline, little more than three hundred yards, and the dim starlight from the hole in the clouds above them made out a line of deeper darkness right ahead. Dupree squinted hard, easing the craft another two hundred yards inshore. It was mangrove, he could hear the water chuckling among the roots. Far out to his right he could discern the line of vegetation end and the single line of the horizon between sea and night sky run away to the end of vision. He had made landfall three miles into the northern coast of the peninsula.

He brought his boat about, still keeping the throttle very low and virtually silent, and headed back out towards the sea. He set the tiller to keep the shoreline of the peninsula in vision at half a mile until he reached the limit of the strip of land at whose end the town of Clarence stood, then again headed slowly inshore. At two hundred metres he could make out the long, low spit of gravel that he was seeking, and in the thirty-eighth minute after leaving the *Toscana*, he cut the engine and let the assault craft drift on its own momentum towards the spit. It grounded with a soft grating of fabric on gravel.

Dupree stepped lightly down the boat, avoiding the piles of equipment, swung a leg over the prow and dropped on to the sand. He felt for the painter and kept it in his hand to prevent the boat drifting away. For five minutes all three men remained immobile, listening for the slightest sound from the town they knew lay over the low hummock of gravel and scrub in front of them, and four hundred yards to the left. But there was no sound. They had arrived without causing any alarm.

When he was certain, Dupree slipped a marlin spike out of his belt and rammed it deep into the shingle of the shore, tying the painter securely to it. Then he rose to a crouch and ran lightly up the hummock ahead of him. It was barely fifteen feet above sea level at its top, and covered in knee-high scrub that rustled against his boots. The rustling was no problem; it was drowned by the slap of the sea on the shingle and far too soft to be heard away in the town. Crouching at the spine of the strip of land that formed one arm of the harbour, Dupree looked over the top. To his left he could make out the spit running away into the darkness, and straight ahead lay more water, the flat, mirror-calm of the protected harbour. The end of the spit of gravel was ten yards to his right.

Returning to the assault craft he whispered to the two Africans to begin unloading the equipment in complete silence. As the bundles came on to the shore he picked them up, and carried them one by one up to the top of the rise. Each metallic piece was covered in sacking to prevent noise if two should knock together.

When the whole of his weaponry was assembled, Dupree began to set it up. He worked fast and quietly. At the far end of the spit, where Shannon had told him there was a round, flat area, he set up his main mortar. He knew, if Shannon's measurements were accurate, and he trusted they would be, that the range from the tip of the land to the centre of the palace courtyard was 721 metres. Using his compass he pointed the mortar on the exact compass bearing Shannon had given him from the point he stood to the presidential palace and carefully adjusted his mortar's elevation to drop his first range-finding bomb as near to the centre of the palace courtyard as possible.

He knew when the flares went up that he would not see the whole palace, but just the top storey, so he could not watch the bomb hit the ground. But he would see the upward flash of the explosion over the brow of the ground behind the warehouse at the other end of the harbour, and that would be enough.

When he was finished with the first, he set up the second mortar. This was pointing at the barracks, and he put the base-plate ten yards away from the first, down the spine of the land on which he stood. He knew both range and bearing from this mortar to the barracks, and that the accuracy of the second mortar was not vital, since its intent was to drop bombs at random into the acreage of the former police lines and scatter the Zangaran army men through panic. Timothy, who had been his sergeant on mortars the last time they fought, would handle the second mortar on his own.

He established a pile of a dozen mortar bombs next to the second tube, settled Timothy beside it and whispered a few last instructions into his ear.

Between the two mortars he established the two flare-launching rockets and jammed one rocket down each launcher, leaving the other eight lying handy. Each flare was reputed to have a life of twenty seconds, so if he was to operate both his own mortar and the illuminations, he knew he would have to work fast and skilfully. He needed Sunday to pass him his mortar bombs from the stack he had built beside the emplacement.

When he was finished he looked at his watch. Three twenty-two in the morning. Shannon and the other two boys must be off the shore somewhere, heading for the harbour. He took his walkie-talkie, extended the aerial to its full length, switched on and waited the prescribed thirty seconds for it to warm up. From then on, it would not be switched off again. When he was ready he pressed the 'blip' button three times at one-second intervals.

A mile off the shore, Shannon was at the helm of the leading assault craft, eyes straining into the darkness ahead. To his left-hand side Semmler kept the second craft in formation order, and it was he who heard the three buzzes from the walkie-talkie on his knee. He steered his boat softly into the side of Shannon's, so the two rounded sides scuffed each other. Shannon looked towards the other boat. Semmler hissed and pulled his boat away again, to maintain station at two metres. Shannon was relieved. He knew Semmler had heard Dupree's signal across the water, and that the rangy Afrikaner was set up and waiting for them. Two minutes later, a thousand metres off the shore, Shannon caught the quick flash from Dupree's torch, heavily masked and blinkered to a pin-point of light. It was off to his right, so he knew that he was heading too far north. In unison the two craft swung to starboard, Shannon trying to recall the exact point from which the light had come, and to head for a point a hundred metres to the right of it. That would be the harbour entrance. The light came again when Dupree caught the low buzz of the two outboard engines as they were three hundred metres from the tip of the point. Shannon spotted the light and changed course a few degrees.

Two minutes later, shut down to less than a quarter power and making no noise louder than a bumble-bee, the two assault craft went by the tip of the spit where Dupree was crouching, fifty metres out. The South African caught the glitter of the wake, the bubbles from the exhausts rising to the surface, then they were gone into the harbour entrance and across the still water towards the warehouse on the other side.

There was still no sound from the shore when Shannon's straining eyes made out the bulk of the warehouse against the marginally lighter sky-line, steered to the right and grounded on the shingle of the fishing beach among the natives' dug-out canoes and hanging fish-nets.

Semmler brought his own boat to the shore a few feet away, and both engines died together. Like Dupree, all the men remained motionless for several minutes waiting for an alarm to be called. They tried to make out the difference between the humped backs of the fishing canoes and the shape of an awaiting ambush party. There was no ambush. Shannon and Semmler stepped over the side, each jabbed a marlin spike into the sand and tethered the boats to it. The rest followed. With a low, muttered, 'Come on, let's go,' Shannon led the way across the beach and up the sloping incline of the two-hundred-yard-wide plateau between the harbour and the sleeping palace of President Jean Kimba.

21

The eight men ran in a low crouch, up through the scrubland of the hillside and out on to the plain at the top. It was after half past three, and no lights were burning in the palace. Shannon knew that halfway between the top of the rise and the palace two hundred yards away they would meet the coast road, and standing at the junction would be at least two palace guards. He expected he would not be able to take them both silently, and that after the firing started they would have to crawl the last hundred yards to the palace wall. He was right.

Out across the water, waiting in his lonely vigil, Big Janni Dupree waited for the shot that would send him into action. He had been briefed that whoever fired the shot, or however many there were, the first one would be his signal. He crouched close to the flare-rocket launchers, waiting to let the first one go. In his spare hand was his first mortar bomb.

Shannon and Langarotti were out ahead of the other six when they made the road junction in front of the palace, and already both were wet with sweat. Their faces, blackened with sepia-dye, were streaked by the running perspiration. The rent in the clouds above them was larger, and more stars showed through, so that although the moon was still hidden, there was a dim light across the open area in front of the palace. At a hundred yards Shannon could make out the line of the roof against the sky, though he missed the guards until he stumbled over one. The man was seated on the ground, snoozing.

He was too slow and clumsy with the Commando knife in his right hand. After stumbling he recovered, but the Vindu guard rose with equal speed and emitted a brief yell of surprise. The call attracted his partner, also hidden in the uncut grass a few feet away. The second man rose, gurgled once as the Corsican's knife opened his throat from carotid artery to jugular vein, and went back down again, choking out his last seconds. Shannon's man took the swipe with the Bowie knife in the shoulder, let out another scream and ran.

A hundred yards in front, close to the palace gate, there was a second cry, and the sound of a bolt operating in the breech of a rifle. It was never quite certain who fired first. The wild shot from the palace gate and the snarling rip of Shannon's half-second burst that sliced the running man almost in two, blended with each other. From far behind them there was a whoosh and a scream in the sky; two seconds later the sky above them exploded in blistering white light. Shannon caught a brief impression of the palace in front of him, two figures in front of its gate, and the feeling of his other six men fanning out to right and left of him. Then the eight of them were face-down in the grass and crawling forward.

Janni Dupree stepped away from the rocket-launcher the instant he had torn the lanyard off the first rocket, and was slipping his mortar bomb down the tube as the rocket screamed upwards. The smack-thump of the mortar bomb departing on its parabola towards the palace blended with the crash of the magnesium flare exploding away towards the land, over the spot he hoped his colleagues would have reached. He took his second bomb and, squinting into the light from the palace, waited to watch the first one fall. He had given himself four sighting shots, on an estimate of fifteen seconds for each bomb in flight. After that he knew he could keep up a fire-rate of one every two seconds, with Sunday feeding him the ammunition singly but fast and in rhythm.

His first sighting bomb hit the front right-hand cornice of the palace roof, high enough for him to see the impact. It did not penetrate, but blew tiles off the roof just above the gutter. Stooping, he twirled the traverse knob of the directional aiming mechanism a few mills to the left, and slipped in his second bomb just as the flare fizzled out. He had stepped across to the other rocket-launcher, ripped off the firing lanyard of the rocket, sent it on its way and stuffed a fresh pair into the two launchers before he needed to look up again. The second flare burst into light above the palace and four seconds later the second bomb landed. It was dead centre, but short, for it fell on to the tiles directly above the main door.

Dupree was also pouring sweat and the grub-screw was slick between his fingers. He brought the angle of elevation slightly down, lowering the nose of the mortar a whisker towards the ground for extra range. Working the opposite way to artillery, mortars have to be lowered for extra range. Dupree's third mortar was on its way before the flare fizzled out, and he had a full fifteen seconds to send up the third flare, trot down the spit a short way to actuate the foghorn and be back in time to watch the mortar explode. It went clean over the palace roof and into the courtyard behind. He saw the red glow for a split second, then it was gone. Not that it mattered. He knew he had got his range and direction exactly right. There would be no shortfalls to endanger his own men in front of the palace.

Shannon and his men were face down in the grass as the three flares lit up the scene around them and Janni's ranging shots went in. No one was prepared to raise his head until the Afrikaner was sending the hardware over the top of the palace and into the rear courtyard.

Between the second and third explosions Shannon risked putting his head up. He knew he had fifteen seconds until the third mortar went home. He saw the palace in the glare of the third magnesium flare, and two lights had gone on in the upper rooms. After the reverberations of the second mortar bomb died away, he heard a variety of screams and shouts from inside the fortress. These were the first and last sounds the defenders made before the roar of explosives blotted out all else.

Within five seconds the foghorn had gone on, the long maniacal scream, howling across the water from the harbour spit, filling the African night with a wail like a thousand released banshees. The crash of the mortar going into the palace courtyard was almost drowned out, and he heard no more screams. When he raised his head again he could see no further damage to the front of the palace, and assumed Janni had dropped the bomb over the top. By agreement, Janni would use no more testing shots after his first on target, but go straight into the faster rhythm. From the sea behind him, Shannon heard the thud of mortars begin, steady, pulsing like a heartbeat in the ears, backed by the now monotonous wail of the foghorn that had a life of seventy seconds on its gas canister.

To get rid of forty bombs, Janni would need eighty seconds, and it was agreed that if there were a ten-second pause at any point after halfway, he would cease the bombardment so his colleagues would not run forward and be blown apart by a late-comer. Shannon had few doubts Janni would not muff it.

When the main barrage began to hit the palace fifteen seconds after the thumps of their firing were heard, the eight men in the grass had a grand-stand view. There was no more need for flares; the roaring crash of the mortar bombs going into the flagstone-covered courtyard behind the palace threw up gobbets of red light every two seconds. Only Tiny Marc Vlaminck had anything to do.

He was out to the left of the line of men, almost exactly in front of the main gate. Standing foresquare to the palace he took careful aim and sent off his first rocket. A twenty-foot-long tongue of flame whirled out of the rear of the bazooka, and the pineapple-sized warhead sped for the main gate. It exploded high to the right-hand edge of the double-doors, ripping a hinge out of the masonry and leaving a yard-square hole in the wood-work.

Kneeling by his side, Patrick slipped the rockets out of his back-pack, spread on the ground, and passed them upwards. The second shot began to topple in mid-air and exploded against the stonework of the arch above the door. The third hit the centre lock. Both doors seemed to erupt upwards under the impact, then they sagged on the twisted hinges, fell apart and swung inwards.

Janni Dupree was halfway through his barrage and the red glare from behind the roof of the palace had become constant. Something was burning in the courtyard, and Shannon supposed it was the guard houses. When the doors swung open, the men crouching in the grass could see the red glare through the archway, and two figures swayed in front of it and fell down before they could emerge.

Marc sent four more rockets straight through the open gate into the furnace beyond the archway, which apparently was a through-passage to the courtyard behind. It was Shannon's first glimpse of what lay beyond the gate.

The mercenary leader screamed to Vlaminck to stop firing, for he had used seven of his dozen rockets, and for all Shannon knew there might be an armoured vehicle somewhere in the town, despite what Gomez had said. But the Belgian was enjoying himself. He sent another four rockets through the front wall of the palace at ground level and the first floor, finally standing exultantly waving both his bazooka and his last rocket at the palace in front, while Dupree's mortar bombs whirred overhead.

At that moment the foghorn whined away to a whisper and died. Ignoring Vlaminck, Shannon shouted to the others to move forward, and he, Semmler and Langarotti began to run at a crouch through the grass, Schmeissers held forward, safety catches off, fingers tense on the triggers.

They were followed by Johnny, Jinja, Bartholomew and Patrick, who having no more bazooka rockets to carry, unslung his submachine gun and joined the others.

At twenty metres, Shannon stopped and waited for Dupree's last bombs to fall. He had lost count of how many were still to come, but the sudden silence after the last bomb fell told him it was over. For a second or two the silence itself was deafening. After the foghorn and the mortars, the roar and crash of Tiny's bazooka rockets, the absence of sound was almost uncanny. So much so, that it was almost impossible to realise the entire operation had lasted less than five minutes.

He wondered for a second if Timothy had sent off his dozen mortar bombs to the army barracks, if the soldiers had scattered as he surmised they would, and what the other citizens of the town had thought of the inferno that must have nearly deafened them. He was jerked into wakefulness when the next two magnesium flares exploded over him, one after the other, and without waiting longer he leapt to his feet, screamed 'Come on!' and ran the last twenty metres to the smouldering main gate.

He was firing as he went through, sensing more than seeing the figure of Jean-Baptiste Langarotti to his left and Kurt Semmler closing up on his right. Through the gate and inside the archway the scene was enough to stop anybody in their tracks. The arch went straight through the main building and into the courtyard. Above the courtyard the flares still burned with a stark brilliance that lit the scene behind the palace like something from the Inferno.

Kimba's guards had been caught asleep by the first sighting shots, which had brought them out of their lean-to barracks huts and into the centre of the paved area. That was where the third shot, and the succeeding forty quick-succession bombs, had found them. Up one wall ran a ladder, and four mangled men hung from its rungs, caught in the back as they tried to run to the top of the enclosing wall. The rest had taken the full force of the mortars, exploding on stone flags and scattering lethal shards of steel in all directions.

There were piles of bodies, some still half alive, most very dead. Two army trucks and three civilian vehicles, one the presidential Mercedes, were standing shredded from end to end against the rear wall. Several palace servants, about to flee the horror in the rear, had apparently been grouped behind the main gate when Vlaminck's mortars came through. They were strewn all over the undercover area beneath the archway.

To right and left were further arches, each leading to what seemed to be a set of stairs to the upper floors. Without waiting to be asked, Semmler took the right-hand set, Langarotti the left. Soon there were bursts of submachine carbine fire from each side as the two mercenaries laundered the upper floor.

Just beyond the stairs to the upper floors were doors at ground level, two on each side. Shouting to make himself heard above the screams of the maimed Vindu and the chattering of Semmler's Schmeisser upstairs, Shannon ordered the four Africans to take the ground floor. He did not have to tell them to shoot everything that moved. They were waiting to go, eyes rolling, chests heaving.

Slowly, cautiously, Shannon moved through the archway, into the threshold to the courtyard at the rear. If there was any opposition left in the palace guards, it would come from there. As he stepped outside, a figure with a rifle ran screaming at him from his left. It could be a panic-stricken Vindu was making a break for safety, but there was no time to find out. Shannon whirled and fired, the man jack-knifed and blew a froth of blood from an already dead mouth on to Shannon's blouse front. The whole area and palace smelt of blood and fear, sweat and death, and over it all the greatest intoxicant smell in the world for mercenaries, the reek of cordite.

He sensed rather than felt the scuff of footsteps in the archway behind him and swung round. From one of the side doors into which Johnny had run to start mopping up the remaining Vindu alive inside the palace, a man had emerged. What happened when he reached the centre of the flagstones, under the arch, Shannon could only recall later as a kaleidoscope of images. The man saw Shannon the same time Shannon saw him, and snapped off a shot from the gun he clenched in his right hand at hip level.

Shannon felt the slug blow softly on his cheek as it passed. He fired half a second later, but the man was agile. After firing he went to the ground, rolled and came up in the fire position a second time. Shannon's Schmeisser had let off five shots but they went above the gunman's body as he went to the flagstones, then the magazine ran out. Before the man in the hallway could take another shot, Shannon stepped aside and out of sight behind a stone pillar, snapped out the old magazine and slapped in a new one. Then he came round the corner firing. The man was gone.

It was only then he became fully conscious that the gunman, stripped to the waist and barefoot, had not been an African. The skin of his torso, even in the dim light beneath the arch, had been white, and the hair dark and straight.

Shannon swore and ran back towards the embers of the gate on their hinges. He was too late.

As the gunman ran out of the shattered palace, Tiny Marc Vlaminck was walking towards the archway. He had his bazooka cradled in both hands across his chest, the last rocket fitted into the end. The gunman never even stopped. Still running flat out, he loosed off two fast shots that emptied his magazine. They found the gun later in the long grass. It was a Makarov 9 mm, and it was empty.

The Belgian took both shots in the chest, one of them in the lungs. Then the gunman was past him, dashing across the grass for safety beyond the reach of the light cast by the flares Dupree was still sending up. Shannon watched as Vlaminck, moving in a kind of slow motion, turned to face the running man, raised his bazooka and slotted it carefully across his right shoulder, took steady aim and fired.

Not often does one see a bazooka the size of the warhead on the Yugoslav RPG-7 hit a man in the small of the back. Afterwards, they could not even find more than a few pieces of cloth from his trousers.

Shannon had to throw himself flat again to avoid being broiled by the backlash of flame from the Belgian's last shot. He was still on the ground, eight yards away, when Tiny Marc dropped his weapon and crashed forward, arms outspread, across the hard earth before the gateway.

Then the last of the flares went out.

Big Janni Dupree straightened up after sending off the last of his ten magnesium flares and yelled 'Sunday.'

He had to shout three times before the African standing ten yards away could hear him. All three men were partly deaf from the pounding their ears had taken from the mortar and the foghorn. He shouted to Sunday to stay behind and keep watch over the mortars and the boat, then signalling to Timothy to follow him, he began to jog-trot through the scrub and bushes along the spit of sand towards the mainland. Although he had loosed off more firepower than the other four mercenaries put together, he saw no reason why he should be denied all the action.

Besides, his job was still to silence the army barracks and he knew from his memory of the maps on board the *Toscana* roughly where it was. It took the pair of them ten minutes to reach the road that ran across the end of the peninsula from side to side, and instead of turning right towards the palace, Dupree led the way left towards the barracks. Janni and Timothy had slowed to a walk, one on each side of the laterite road, their Schmeissers pointing forward, ready to fire the moment trouble showed itself.

The trouble was round the first bend in the road. Scattered twenty minutes earlier by the first of the mortar bombs despatched by Timothy falling between the hutments that made up the barracks lines, the two hundred encamped men of Kimba's army had fled into the night. But about a dozen of them had re-grouped in the darkness, and were standing at the edge of the road muttering in low whispers among themselves. If they had not been so deaf, Dupree and Timothy would have heard them sooner. As it was, they were almost on the group before they saw them, shadows in the shadows of the palm trees. Ten of the men were naked, having been roused from sleep. The other two had been on guard duty, and were clothed and armed.

The previous night's torrential rain had left the ground so soft that most of Timothy's dozen mortar bombs had embedded themselves too deeply in the earth to have their full intended impact. The Vindu soliders they found waiting round that corner still had something of their wits about them. One of them also had a hand grenade.

It was the sudden movement of the soldiers when they saw the white gleam of Dupree's face, from which the dye had long since run away with his sweat, that alerted the South African. He screamed 'Fire' and opened up at the group. Four of them were cut apart by the stream of slugs from the Schmeisser. The other eight ran, two more falling as Dupree's fire pursued them into the trees. As he ran, one of them turned and hurled the thing he carried in his hand. He had never used one before, nor ever seen one used. But it was his pride and joy, and he had always hoped to use it one day.

The grenade went high in the air, out of sight, and when it fell it hit Timothy full in the chest. In instinctive reaction the African veteran clutched at the object as he went over backwards, and sitting on the ground recognised it for what it was. He also saw that the fool who had thrown it had forgotten to take the pin out. Timothy had seen a mercenary catch a grenade once. He had watched as the man hurled it straight back at the enemy. Rising to his feet Timothy whipped the pin out of the grenade and threw it as far as he could after the retreating Vindu soldiers.

It went high into the air a second time, but this time it hit a tree. There was a dull clunk and the grenade fell short of where it was intended to go. At that moment Janni Dupree started in pursuit, a fresh magazine in his carbine. Timothy shouted a warning, but Dupree must have thought it was a scream of elation. He ran eight paces forward into the trees, still firing from the hip, and was two yards from the grenade when it exploded.

He did not remember much more. He remembered the flash and the boom, the sensation of being picked up and tossed aside like a rag doll. Then he must have passed out. He came to, lying out on the laterite road, and there was someone kneeling in the road beside him, cradling his head. He could feel that his throat was very warm, like the time he had had a fever as a boy, a comfortable, drowsy feeling, half awake and half asleep. He could hear a voice talking to him, saying something repeatedly and urgently, but he could not make out the words, 'Sorry, Janni, so sorry, sorry . . .'

He could understand his own name, but that was all. This language was different, not his own language, but something else. He swivelled his eyes round to the person who was holding him and made out a dark face in the half-light beneath the trees. He smiled and said quite clearly in Afrikaans 'Hallo, Pieter.'

He was staring up at the gap between the palm fronds when finally the clouds shifted to one side and the moon came out. It looked enormous, as it always does in Africa, brilliant white and shining. He could smell the rain in the vegetation beside the road, and see the moon sitting up there glistening like a giant pearl, like the Paarl rock after the rain. It was good to be back home again, he thought. Janni Dupree was quite content when he closed his eyes again and died.

It was half past five when enough natural daylight filtered over the horizon for the men at the palace to be able to switch off their torches. Not that the daylight made the scene in the courtyard look any better. But the job was done.

They had brought Vlaminck's body inside and laid it out straight in one of the side rooms off the ground floor hallway. Beside him lay Janni Dupree, brought up from the seashore road by three of the Africans. Johnny was also dead, evidently surprised and shot by the white body-guard who had seconds later stopped Vlaminck's last bazooka rocket. The three of them were side by side.

Semmler had summoned Shannon to the main bedroom on the first floor and showed him by torchlight the figure he had gunned down as he tried to clamber out of the window.

'That's him,' said Shannon.

There were six survivors from among the dead president's domestic staff. They had been found cowering in one of the cellars, which they had found, more by instinct than logic, to be the best security from the rain of fire from the skies. These were being used as forced labour to tidy up. Every room in the main part of the palace was examined, and the bodies of all the other friends of Kimba and palace servants who had been lying around the rooms were carried down and dumped in the courtyard at the back. The remnants of the door could not be replaced, so a large carpet taken from one of the staterooms was hung over the entrance to mask the view inside.

At five o'clock Semmler had gone back to the *Toscana* in one of the speedboats, towing the other two behind him. Before leaving he had contacted the *Toscana* on his walkie-talkie to give them the code-word meaning all was in order.

He was back by six-thirty with the African doctor and the same three boats, this time loaded with stores, the remaining mortar bombs, the eighty bundles containing the remaining Schmeissers, and nearly a ton of 9 mm ammunition.

At six, according to a letter of instruction Shannon had sent to Captain Waldenberg, the *Toscana* had begun to broadcast three words on the frequency to which Endean was listening. The words, Paw-paw, Cassava and Mango, meant respectively: The operation went ahead as planned, it was completely successful, and Kimba is dead.

When the African doctor had viewed the scene of carnage at the palace, he sighed and said, 'I suppose it was necessary.'

'It was necessary,' affirmed Shannon, and asked the older man to set about the task he had been brought to do.

By nine nothing had stirred in the town and the clearing-up process was almost complete. The burial of the Vindu would have to be done later. Two of the speedboats were back at the *Toscana*, slung aboard and stowed below, while the third was hidden in a creek not far from the harbour. All traces of the mortars on the point had been removed, the tubes and the baseplates brought inside, the rocket-launchers and packing crates dropped out at sea. Everything and everyone else had been brought inside the palace, which although battered to hell from the inside, bore only two areas of shattered tiles, three broken windows in the front and the destroyed door to indicate from the outside that it had taken a beating.

At ten Semmler and Langarotti joined Shannon in the main diningroom, where the mercenary leader was finishing off some jam and bread that he had found in the presidential kitchen. Both men reported on the result of their searches. Semmler told Shannon the radio room was intact, apart from several bullet-holes in the wall, but the transmitter would still send. Kimba's private cellar in the basement had yielded at last to the persuasion of several magazines of ammunition. The national treasury was apparently in a safe at the rear of the cellar, and the national armoury was stacked round the walls – enough guns and ammunition to keep an army of two or three hundred men going for several months in action.

'So now what?' asked Semmler when Shannon had heard him out.

'So now we wait,' said Shannon.

'Wait for what?'

Shannon picked his teeth with a spent match. He thought of Janni Dupree and Tiny Marc lying below on the floor, and of Johnny who would not liberate another farmer's goat for his evening supper. Langarotti was slowly stropping his knife on the leather band round his left fist.

'We wait for the new government,' said Shannon.

The American-built one-ton truck carrying Simon Endean arrived just after one in the afternoon. There was another European at the wheel, and Endean sat beside him clutching a large-bore hunting rifle. Shannon heard the growl of the engine as the truck left the shore road and came slowly up to the front entrance of the palace, where the carpet hung lifeless in the humid air, covering the gaping hole where the main gate had been.

He watched from an upper window as Endean climbed suspiciously down, looked at the carpet and the other pock marks on the front of the building and examined the eight black guards at attention before the gate.

Endean's trip had not been completely without incident. After hearing the *Toscana*'s radio call that morning, it had taken him two hours to persuade Colonel Bobi that he was actually going back into his own country within hours of the coup. The man had evidently not won his colonelcy by personal courage. Endean himself had a private motive for his bravado, the pot of gold that awaited him when the platinum in the Crystal Mountain was 'discovered' in two or three months' time.

They had set off from the neighbouring capital by road at nine-thirty on the hundred-mile drive to Clarence. In Europe that distance may take two hours; in Africa it is more. They arrived at the border in the mid-morning, and the haggle began to bribe their way past the Vindu guards, who had still not heard of the night's coup in the capital. Colonel Bobi, hiding behind a pair of large and very dark glasses, and dressed in a white flowing robe, in aspect like a nightshirt, posed as their car-boy, a personal servant who, in Africa, never requires papers to cross a border. Endean's papers were in order, like those of the man he brought with him, a hulking strong-arm from London's East End, who had been recommended to Endean as one of the most feared protectors in Whitechapel and a former enforcer for the Kray Gang. Ernie Locke was being paid a very handsome fee to keep Endean alive and well, and was carrying a gun under his shirt, acquired locally through the offices of ManCon's mining enterprise in the republic. Tempted by the money offered, he had already made the mistake of thinking, like Endean, that a good hard-man in the East End will automatically make a good hard-man in Africa.

After crossing the frontier the truck had made good time until it blew a tyre ten miles short of Clarence. With Endean mounting guard with his rifle, Locke had changed the tyre while Bobi cowered under the canvas in the back. That was when the trouble started. A handful of Vindu troops, fleeing from Clarence, had spotted them and loosed off half a dozen shots. They all went wide except one, which hit the tyre Locke had just replaced. The journey was finished in first gear on a flat tyre.

Shannon leaned out of the window and called down to Endean. The latter looked up.

'Everything OK?' he called.

'Sure,' said Shannon. 'But get out of sight. No one seems to have moved yet, but someone is bound to start snooping soon.'

Endean led Colonel Bobi and Locke through the curtain and they mounted to the first floor where Shannon was waiting. When they were seated in the presidential dining-room Endean asked for a full report on the previous night's battle. Shannon gave it to him.

'Kimba's palace guard?' asked Endean.

For answer Shannon led him to the rear window whose shutters were closed, pushed one open and pointed down into the courtyard from which a ferocious buzzing of flies mounted. Endean looked out and drew back.

'The lot?' he asked.

'The lot,' said Shannon. 'Wiped out.'

'And the army?'

'Twenty dead, the rest scattered. All left their arms behind except perhaps a couple of dozen with bolt-action Mausers. No problem. The arms have been gathered up and brought inside.'

'The presidential armoury?'

'In the cellar, under our control.'

'And the national radio transmitter?'

'Downstairs on the ground floor. Intact. We haven't tried the electricity circuits yet, but the radio seems to have a separate diesel-powered generator.'

Endean nodded, satisfied.

'Then there's nothing for it but for the new president to announce the success of his coup last night, the formation of a new government, and to take over control,' he said.

'What about security?' asked Shannon. 'There's no army left intact until they filter back, and not all the Vindu may want to serve under the new man.'

Endean grinned.

'They'll come back when the word spreads that the new man has taken over, and they'll serve under him just so long as they know who is in charge. And they will. In the meantime, this group you seem to have recruited will suffice. After all, they're black, and no European diplomats here are likely to recognise the difference between one black and another.'

'Do you?' asked Shannon.

Endean shrugged.

'No,' he said, 'but it doesn't matter. By the way, let me introduce the new president of Zangaro.'

He gestured towards the Zangaran colonel, who had been surveying the room he already knew well, a broad grin on his face.

'Former commander of the Zangaran Army, successful operator of a *coup d'état* as far as the world knows, and new president of Zangaro. Colonel Antoine Bobi.'

Shannon rose, faced the colonel and bowed. Bobi's grin grew even wider. Shannon gestured to the door at the end of the dining-room.

'Perhaps the president would like to examine the presidential office,' he said. Endean translated.

Bobi nodded and lumbered across the tiled floor and through the door. It closed behind him. Five seconds later there came the crash of a single shot.

After Shannon reappeared, Endean sat for a moment staring at him.

'What was that?' he asked unnecessarily.

'A shot,' said Shannon.

Endean was on his feet, across the room and standing in the open doorway to the study. He turned round, ashen-faced, hardly able to speak.

'You shot him,' he whispered. 'All this bloody way, and you shot him. You're mad, Shannon, you're fucking crazy.'

His voice rose with his rage and bafflement.

'You don't know what you've done, you stupid, blundering maniac, you bloody mercenary idiot . . .'

Shannon sat back in the armed chair behind the dining table gazing at Endean with scant interest. From the corner of his eye he saw the body-guard's hand move under his floppy shirt. The second crash seemed louder to Endean for it was nearer. Ernie Locke went back out of his chair in a complete somersault and sprawled across the tiles, varying the pattern of the old colonial marquetry with a thin filament of blood that came from his midriff. He was quite dead, for the soft bullet had gone through to shatter his spine. Shannon brought his hand out from under the oak table and laid the Makarov 9 mm automatic on the table. A wisp of blue smoke wriggled out of the end of the barrel.

Endean seemed to sag at the shoulders, as if the knowledge of the certain loss of his personal fortune, promised by Sir James Manson when Bobi was installed, had suddenly been compounded by the realisation that Shannon was the most completely dangerous man he had ever met. But it was a bit late to realise that.

Semmler appeared in the doorway of the study behind Endean, and Langarotti slipped quietly through the dining-room door from the corridor. Both held Schmeissers, catch off, very steady, pointing at Endean. Shannon rose.

'Come on,' he said, 'I'll drive you back to the border. From there you can walk.'

The single unpunctured tyre from the two Zangaran trucks in the courtyard had been fitted to the vehicle that had brought Endean into the country. The canvas behind the cab had been taken away and three African soldiers crouched in the back with submachine carbines. Another twenty, fully uniformed and equipped, were being marshalled into a line outside the palace.

In the hallway close to the shattered door they met a middle-aged African in civilian clothes. Shannon nodded to him and exchanged a few words.

'Everything OK, Doctor?'

'Yes. So far. I have arranged with my people to send a hundred volunteer workers to clean up. Also another fifty will be here this afternoon for fitting out and equipping. Seven of the Zangaran men on the list of notables have been contacted at their homes and have agreed to serve. They will meet this evening.'

'Good. Perhaps you had better take time off to draft the first bulletin from the new government. It should be broadcast as soon as possible. Ask Mr Semmler to try to get the radio working. If it can't be done, we'll use the ship. Anything else?'

'One more thing,' said the Doctor. 'Mr Semmler reports that the ship lying off the shore is a Russian vessel, the *Komarov*, which has been making repeated requests for permission to enter harbour.'

Shannon thought for several moments.

'Ask Mr Semmler to have conveyed from the shore to the *Komarov*, the following: "REQUEST DECLINED STOP INDEFINITELY STOP",' he said.

They parted and Shannon took Endean back to his lorry. He took the wheel himself and swung the truck back on the road to the hinterland and the border.

'Who was that?' asked Endean sourly as the truck sped along the peninsula, past the shanty town of the immigrant workers, where all seemed to be bustle and activity. With amazement Endean noticed that each crossroads had an armed soldier with a submachine carbine standing on point duty.

'The man in the hallway?' asked Shannon.

'Yes.'

'That was Dr Okoye.'

'A witch doctor, I suppose.'

'Actually he's a PhD of Oxford.'

'Friend of yours?'

'Yes.'

There was no more conversation until they were on the highway towards the north.

'All right,' said Endean at last, 'I know what you've done. You've ruined one of the biggest and richest coups that has ever been attempted. You don't know that, of course. You're too bloody thick. What I'd like to know is, why? In God's name, why?'

Shannon thought for a moment, keeping the truck steady on the bumpy road that had deteriorated to a dirt track.

'You made two mistakes, Endean,' he said carefully. Endean started at the sound of his real name.

'You assumed that because I'm a mercenary, I'm automatically stupid. It never seemed to occur to you that we are both mercenaries, along with Sir James Manson and most of the people who have power in this world. The second mistake was that you assumed all black people were the same, because to you they look the same.'

'I don't follow you.'

'You did a lot of research on Zangaro, you even found out about the tens of thousands of immigrant workers who virtually keep this place running. It never occurred to you that those workers form a community of their own. They're a third tribe, the most intelligent and hard-working one in the country. Given half a chance they can play a part in the political life of the country. What's more you failed to recognise that the new army of Zangaro and therefore the power in the country might be recruited from among that third community. In fact, it just has been. Those soldiers you saw were neither Vindu nor Caja. There were fifty in uniform and armed when you were in the palace, and by tonight there'll be another fifty. In five days there will be over four hundred new soldiers in Clarence, untrained of course, but looking efficient enough to keep law and order. They'll be the real power in this country from now on. There was a *coup d'état* last night, all right, but it wasn't conducted for or on behalf of Colonel Bobi.'

'For whom then?'

'For the general.'

'Which general?'

Shannon told him the name. Endean faced him, mouth open in horror.

'Not *him*. He was defeated, exiled.'

'For the moment, yes. Not necessarily for ever. Those immigrant workers are his people. They call them the Jews of Africa. There are one and a half million of them scattered over this continent. In many areas they do most of the work and have most of the brains. Here in Zangaro, they live in the shanty town behind Clarence.'

'That stupid great idealistic bastard . . .'

'Careful,' warned Shannon.

'Why?'

Shannon jerked his head over his shoulder.

'They're the general's soldiers too.'

Endean turned and looked at the three impassive faces above the three Schmeisser barrels.

'They don't speak English all that well, do they?'

'The one in the middle,' said Shannon mildly, 'was a chemist once. Then he became a soldier, then his wife and four children were wiped out by a Saladin armoured car. They're made by Alvis in Coventry, you know. He doesn't like the people who were behind that.'

Endean was silent for a few more miles.

'What happens now?' he asked.

'The Committee of National Reconciliation takes over,' said Shannon. 'Four Vindu members, four Caja and two from the immigrant community. But the army will be made up of the people behind you. And this country will be used as a base and a headquarters. From here the newly trained men will go back one day to avenge what was done to them. Maybe the general will come and set up residence here, in effect to rule it.'

'You expect to get away with that?'

'You expected to impose that slobbering ape, Bobi, and get away with it. At least the new government will be moderately fair. That mineral deposit, which I happen to know is platinum, buried somewhere in the Crystal Mountain. No doubt the new government will find it, eventually. And no doubt it will be exploited. But if you want it you will have to pay for it. A fair price, a market price. Tell Sir James that when you get back home.'

Round the corner they came within view of the border post. News travels fast in Africa, even without telephones, and the Vindu soldiers on the border post had gone. Shannon stopped the truck and pointed ahead.

'You can walk the rest,' he said.

Endean climbed down. He looked back at Shannon in the cab with undiluted hatred.

'You still haven't explained why,' he said. 'You've explained what and how, but not why.'

Shannon stared ahead up the road.

'For nearly two years,' he said musingly, 'I watched between half a million and a million small kids starved to death because of people like you and Manson. It was done basically so that you and your kind can make bigger profits through a vicious and totally corrupt dictatorship, and it was done in the name of law and order, of legality and constitutional justification. I may be a fighter, I may be a killer, but I am not a bloody sadist. I worked out for myself how it was done and why it was done, and who were the men behind it. Visible up front were a bunch of politicians and Foreign Office men, but they are just a cage full of posturing apes, neither seeing nor caring past their inter-departmental squabbles and their re-election. Invisible behind them were profiteers like your precious James Manson. That's why I did it. Tell Manson when you get back home. I'd like him to know. Personally. From me. Now get walking.'

Ten yards on, Endean turned round.

'Don't ever come back to London, Shannon,' he called. 'We can deal with people like you there.'

'I won't,' yelled Shannon. Under his breath he murmured, 'I won't ever have to.' Then he turned the truck round and headed for the peninsula and Clarence.

Epilogue

The new government was duly installed, and at the last count was ruling humanely and well. There was hardly a mention of the coup in the European newspapers, just a brief piece in *Le Monde* to say that dissident units of the Zangaran Army had toppled the president on the eve of Independence Day and that a governing council had taken over the administration pending national elections. But there was nothing in the newspaper to report that the Soviet mining survey team would not be permitted to land in the republic and that new arrangements for surveying the area would be made in due course.

Big Janni Dupree and Tiny Marc Vlaminck were buried down on the point, beneath the palm trees where the wind blows off the Gulf. The graves were left unmarked at Shannon's request. The body of Johnny was taken by his own people who keened over him and buried him according to their own ways.

Simon Endean and Sir James Manson kept quiet about their parts in the affair. There was really nothing they could say publicly.

Shannon gave Jean-Baptiste Langarotti the £5000 remaining in his money belt from the operation's budget, and the Corsican went back to Europe. He was last heard of heading for Burundi where he wanted to train the Hutu partisans who were trying to oppose the Tutsi-dominated dictatorship of Miscombero. As he told Shannon when they parted on the shore, 'It's not really the money. It was never for the money.'

Shannon wrote out letters to Signor Ponti in Genoa in the name of Keith Brown ordering him to hand over the bearer shares controlling the ownership of the *Toscana* in equal parts to Captain Waldenberg and Kurt Semmler. A year later Semmler sold out his share to Waldenberg, who raised a mortgage to pay for it. Then he went off to another war. He died in South Sudan, when he, Ron Gregory and Rip Kirby were laying a mine to knock out a Sudanese Saladin armoured car. The mine went off, killing Kirby instantly and badly injuring Semmler and Gregory. Gregory got home via the British Embassy in Ethiopia, but Semmler died in the bush.

The last thing Shannon did was to send letters to his bank in

Switzerland through Langarotti, ordering the bank to make a credit transfer of £5000 to the parents of Janni Dupree in Paarl, Cape Province, and another in the same sum to a woman called Anna who ran a bar in the Kleinstraat in Ostend's red-light quarter.

He died a month after the coup, the way he had told Julie he wanted to go, with a gun in his hand, and blood in his mouth and a bullet in the chest. But it was his own gun and his own bullet. It was not the risks or the danger or the fighting that destroyed him, but the little white sticks with the filter tips. That was what he had learned from Dr Dunois in the Paris surgery. Up to a year if he took things easy, less than six months if he pushed himself, and the last month would be bad. So he went out alone when the coughing got worse and walked into the jungle with his gun and a fat envelope full of typescript, which was sent to a friend in London some weeks later.

The natives who saw him walking alone, and later brought him back to the town for burial, said he was whistling when he went. Being simple peasants, growers of yams and cassava, they did not know what the whistling was. It was a tune called 'Spanish Harlem'.

THE DEVIL'S
ALTERNATIVE

For Frederick Stuart,
who does not know yet

Prologue

The castaway would have been dead before sundown but for the sharp eyes of an Italian seaman called Mario. Even when he was spotted he had lapsed into unconsciousness, the exposed parts of his near-naked body grilled to second-degree burns by the relentless sun, and those parts submerged in sea water soft and white between the salt-sores like the limbs of a rotting goose.

Mario Curcio was the cook-steward on the *Garibaldi*, an amiable old rust-bucket out of Brindisi, thumping her way eastward towards Cape Ince and on to Trabzon in the far eastern corner of the north shore of Turkey. She was on her way to pick up a cargo of almonds from Anatolia.

Just why Mario decided that morning in the last ten days of April 1982 to empty his bucket of potato peelings over the weather rail instead of through the rubbish chute at the poop he could never explain, nor was he ever asked to. But perhaps to take a breath of fresh Black Sea air and break the monotony of the steam-heat in the cramped galley, he stepped out on deck, strolled to the starboard rail, and hurled his rubbish to an indifferent but patient ocean. He turned away and started to lumber back to his duties. After two steps he stopped, frowned, turned and walked back to the rail, puzzled and uncertain.

The ship was heading east-northeast to clear Cape Ince, so that as he shielded his eyes and gazed abaft the beam the noon sun was almost straight in his face. But he was sure he had seen something out there on the blue-green rolling swell between the ship and the coast of Turkey twenty miles to the south. Unable to see it again, he trotted up the after deck, mounted the outside ladders to the wing of the bridge and peered again. Then he saw it, quite clearly, for half a second between the softly moving hills of water. He turned to the open door behind him, leading into the wheelhouse, and shouted, '*Capitano.*'

Captain Vittorio Ingrao took some persuading, for Mario was a simple lad, but he was enough of a sailor to know that if a man might be out there on the water he was duty-bound to turn his ship around and have a closer look, and his radar had indeed revealed an echo. It took the captain half an hour to bring the *Garibaldi* around and back to the spot Mario had pointed at, and then he too saw it.

The skiff was barely twelve feet long, and not very wide. A light craft, of the type that could have been a ship's jolly boat. Forward of amidships there was a single thwart across the boat with a hole in it for the stepping of a mast. But either there had never been a mast, or it had been ill-secured and had gone overboard. With the *Garibaldi* stopped and wallowing in the swell, Captain Ingrao leaned on the bridge wing rail and watched Mario and the bo'sun Paolo Longhi set off in the motor lifeboat to bring the skiff alongside. From his elevation he could look down into the skiff as it was towed closer.

The man in it was lying on his back in several inches of sea water. He was gaunt and emaciated, bearded and unconscious, his head to one side, breathing in short gasps. He moaned a few times as he was lifted aboard and the sailors' hands touched his flayed shoulders and chest.

There was one permanently spare cabin in the *Garibaldi*, kept free as a sort of sick-bay, and the castaway was taken to it. Mario, at his own request, was given time off to tend the man, whom he soon came to regard as his personal property, as a boy will take especial care of a puppy he has personally rescued from death. Longhi, the bo'sun, gave the man a shot of morphine from the first-aid chest to spare him the pain, and the pair of them set to work on the sunburn.

Being Calabrians they knew a bit about sunburn and prepared the best sunburn salve in the world. Mario brought from his galley a fifty-fifty mixture of fresh lemon juice and wine vinegar in a basin, a light cotton cloth torn from his pillow case and a bowl of ice cubes. Soaking the cloth in the mixture and wrapping it round a dozen ice cubes, he gently pressed the pad to the worst areas, where the ultra-violet rays had bitten through almost to the bone. Plumes of steam rose from the unconscious man as the freezing astringent drew the heat out of the scorched flesh. The man shuddered.

'Better a fever than death by burn-shock,' Mario told him in Italian. The man could not hear, and if he did he could not have understood.

Longhi joined his skipper on the after deck where the skiff had been stowed.

'Anything?' he asked.

Captain Ingrao shook his head.

'Nothing on the man either. No watch, no name tag. A pair of cheap underpants with no label. And his beard looks about ten days old.'

'There's nothing here either,' said Ingrao. 'No mast, no sail, no oars. No food and no water container. No name on the boat even. But it could have peeled off.'

'A tourist from a beach resort, blown out to sea?' asked Longhi.

Ingrao shrugged. 'Or a survivor from a small freighter,' he said. 'We'll be at Trabzon in two days. The Turkish authorities can solve that one when he wakes up and talks. Meanwhile let's get under way. Oh, and we must cable our agent there and tell him what's happened. We'll need an ambulance on the quay when we dock.'

Two days later the castaway, still barely conscious and unable to speak, was tucked up between white sheets in a sick ward, in the small municipal hospital of Trabzon.

Mario the sailor had accompanied his castaway in the ambulance from the quay to the hospital, along with the ship's agent and the port's medical officer of health who had insisted on checking the delirious man for communicable diseases. After waiting an hour by the bedside, he had bade his unconscious friend farewell and returned to the *Garibaldi* to prepare the crew's lunch. That had been the previous day, and the old Italian tramp steamer had sailed during the evening.

Now another man stood by the bedside, accompanied by a police officer and the short-coated doctor. All three were Turkish, but the short, broad man in the civilian suit spoke passable English.

'He'll pull through,' said the doctor, 'but he's very sick for the moment. Heat-stroke, second-degree sunburns, exposure, and by the look of it he hasn't eaten for days. Generally weak.'

'What are these?' asked the civilian, gesturing at the drip-feed tubes that entered both the man's arms.

'Concentrated glucose drip for nourishment, saline drip to offset shock,' said the doctor. 'The sailors probably saved his life by taking the heat out of the burns, but we've bathed him in calamine to help the healing process. Now it's between him and Allah.'

Umit Erdal, partner in the shipping and trading company of Erdal and Sermit, was the Lloyd's sub-agent for the port of Trabzon, and the *Garibaldi*'s agent had thankfully passed the matter of the castaway over to him. The sick man's eyelids fluttered in the nut-brown, bearded face. Mr Erdal cleared his throat, bent over the figure and spoke in his best English.

'What . . . is . . . you . . . name?' he asked slowly and clearly.

The man groaned and moved his head from side to side several times. The Lloyd's man bent his head closer to listen. '*Zradzhenyi*,' the sick man murmured. '*Zradzhenyi*.'

Erdal straightened up. 'He's not Turkish,' he said with finality, 'but he seems to be called Zradzhenyi. What kind of country would that name come from?'

Both his companions shrugged. 'I'll inform Lloyd's in London,' said Erdal. 'Maybe they'll have news of a missing vessel somewhere in the Black Sea.' The daily bible of the world's merchant marine fraternity is *Lloyd's List*, which is published Monday to Saturday and contains editorials, features and news on one topic only – shipping. Its partner in harness, *Lloyd's Shipping Index*, gives the movements of the world's 30,000 active merchant vessels: name of ship, owner, flag of registry, year of build, tonnage, where last reported coming from, and where bound.

Both organs are published out of a building complex at Sheepen Place, Colchester, in Essex. It was to this building that Umit Erdal telexed the shipping movements into and out of the port of Trabzon, and added a small extra for the attention of the Lloyd's Shipping Intelligence unit in the same building.

The SI unit checked their maritime casualty records to confirm that there were no recent reports of missing, sunk or simply overdue vessels in the Black Sea, and passed the paragraph over to the editorial desk of the list. Here a sub-editor gave it a mention as a news brief on the front page, including the name the castaway had given as his own. It appeared the following morning.

Most of those who read the *Lloyd's List* that day in late April flipped past the paragraph about the unidentified man in Trabzon.

But the piece caught and held the sharp eyes and the attention of a man in his early thirties who worked as senior clerk and trusted employee in a firm of chartered shipbrokers situated in a small street called Crutched Friars in the centre of the City of London. His colleagues in the firm knew him as Andrew Drake.

Having absorbed the content of the paragraph, Drake left his desk and went to the company boardroom where he consulted a framed chart of the world which showed prevailing wind and ocean current circulation. The winds in the Black Sea during spring and summer are predominantly from the north, and the currents screw anti-clockwise round this small ocean from the southern coast of the Ukraine in the far northwest of the sea, down past the coasts of Romania and Bulgaria, then swing eastwards again into the shipping lanes between Istanbul and Cape Ince.

Drake did some calculations on a scratch pad. A small skiff, setting off from the marshes of the delta of the River Dniester just south of Odessa could make four or five knots with a following wind and favourable current, southwards past Romania and Bulgaria towards Turkey. But after three days it would tend to be carried eastwards, away from the Bosphorus towards the eastern end of the Black Sea.

The 'Weather and Navigation' section of *Lloyd's List* confirmed there had been bad weather nine days earlier in that area. The sort, Drake mused, that could cause a skiff in the hands of an unskilled seaman to capsize, lose its mast and all its contents and leave its occupant, even if he could climb back into it again, at the mercy of the sun and the wind.

Two hours later Andrew Drake asked for a week of his owed holidays, and it was agreed that he would take it, but only starting the following Monday, 3rd May.

He was mildly excited as he waited out the week and bought himself from a nearby agency a return ticket from London to Istanbul. He decided to buy the connecting ticket from Istanbul to Trabzon for cash in Istanbul. He also checked to confirm that a British passport holder needs no visa for Turkey, but after work he secured for himself the needed smallpox vaccination certificate at the British Airways medical centre at Victoria.

He was excited because he thought there just might be a chance that, after years of waiting, he had found the man he was looking for. Unlike the three men by the castaway's bed-side two days earlier, he *did* know what country the word *zradzhenyi* came from. He also knew it was not the man's name. The man in the bed had been muttering the word 'betrayed' in his native tongue, and that language was Ukrainian. Which could mean that the man was a refugee Ukrainian partisan.

Andrew Drake, despite his anglicized name, was also a Ukrainian, and a fanatic.

★

Drake's first call after arriving in Trabzon was at the office of Mr Erdal, whose name he had obtained from a friend at Lloyd's on the grounds that he was taking a holiday on the Turkish coast and, speaking not a word of Turkish, might need some assistance. Umit Erdal, seeing the letter of introduction that Drake was able to produce, was happily unquestioning as to why his visitor should want to see the castaway in the local hospital. He wrote a personal letter of introduction to the hospital administrator, and shortly after lunch Drake was shown into the small one-bed ward where the man lay.

The local Lloyd's agent had already told him that the man, while conscious again, spent much of the time sleeping, and during his periods of wakefulness had so far said absolutely nothing. When Drake entered the room the invalid was lying on his back, eyes closed. Drake drew up a chair and sat by the bedside. For a time he stared at the man's haggard face. After several minutes the man's eyelids flickered, half opened and closed again. Whether he had seen the visitor staring at him intently, Drake did not know. But he knew the man was on the fringe of wakefulness.

Slowly he leaned forward and said clearly in the sick man's ear: '*Shche ne vmerla Ukraina.*'

The words mean, literally, 'Ukraine is not dead', but a looser translation would be, 'Ukraine lives on'. They are the first words of the Ukrainian national anthem, banned by the Russian masters, and would be instantly recognizable by a nationally conscious Ukrainian.

The sick man's eyes flicked open and he regarded Drake intently. After several seconds he asked in Ukrainian, 'Who are you?'

'A Ukrainian, like yourself,' said Drake.

The other man's eyes clouded with suspicion. 'Quisling,' he said.

Drake shook his head. 'No,' he said calmly. 'I am British by nationality, born and bred there, son of a Ukrainian father and an English mother. But in my heart I'm as Ukrainian as you are.'

The man in the bed stared stubbornly at the ceiling.

'I could show you my passport, issued in London, but that would prove nothing. A Chekisti could produce one if he wanted, to try and trick you.' Drake had used the slang term for a Soviet secret policeman and KGB member.

'But you are not in the Ukraine any more, and there are no Chekisti here,' Drake went on. 'You were not washed up on the shores of the Crimea, nor of South Russia or Georgia. You did not land in Romania or Bulgaria either. You were picked up by an Italian ship and landed here at Trabzon. You are in Turkey. You are in the West. You made it.'

The man's eyes were on his face now, alert, lucid, wanting to believe.

'Can you move?' asked Drake.

'I don't know,' said the man.

Drake nodded across the small room to the window, beyond which the sounds of traffic could be heard. 'The KGB can dress up hospital staff to look like Turks,' he said, 'but they cannot change a whole city for one man whom they could torture for a confession if they wanted. Can you make the window?'

Helped by Drake, the castaway hobbled painfully to the window and looked out at the street scene.

'The cars are Austins and Morrises, imported from England,' said Drake. 'Peugeots from France and Volkswagens from West Germany. The words on the billboards are in Turkish. That advertisement over there is for Coca-Cola.'

The man put the back of one hand against his mouth and chewed at the knuckles. He blinked rapidly several times.

'I made it,' he said.

'Yes,' said Drake, 'by a miracle you made it.'

'My name,' said the castaway when he was back in bed, 'is Miroslav Kaminsky. I come from Ternopol. I was the leader of a group of seven Ukrainian partisans.'

Over the next hour the story came out. Kaminsky and six others like him, all from the Ternopol area, once a hotbed of Ukrainian nationalism and where some of the embers still glow, had decided to strike back at the programme of ruthless Russification of their land that had intensified in the sixties and become a 'final solution' in the seventies and early eighties for the whole area of Ukrainian national art, poetry, literature, language and consciousness. In six months of operations they had ambushed and killed two low-level Party secretaries – Russians imposed by Moscow on Ternopol – and a plain-clothes KGB agent. Then had come the betrayal.

Whoever had talked, he too had died in the hail of fire as the green insignia of the KGB special troops had closed in on the country cottage where the group was meeting to plan its next operation. Only Kaminsky had escaped, running like an animal through the undergrowth, hiding by day in barns and woodland, moving by night, heading south towards the coast with a vague idea of jumping a Western ship.

It had been impossible to get near the docks of Odessa. Living off potatoes and swedes from the fields, he had sought refuge in the swampy country of the Dniester estuary southwest of Odessa, towards the Romanian border. Finally, coming by night on a small fishing hamlet on a creek, he had stolen a skiff with a stepped mast and a small sail. He had never been in a sailing boat before, and knew nothing of the sea. Trying to manage the sail and the rudder, just holding on and praying, he had let the skiff run before the wind, southwards by the stars and the sun.

By pure luck he had avoided the patrol boats that cruise the offshore waters of the Soviet Union, and the fishing fleets. The tiny sliver of wood which contained him had slipped past the coastal radar sweeps until he was out of range. Then he was lost, somewhere between Romania and Crimea, heading south but far from the nearest shipping lanes, if he did but know where they were anyway. The storm caught him unawares. Not knowing how to shorten sail in time, he had capsized, spending the night using his last reserves of strength clinging to the upturned hull. By morning he had righted the skiff and crawled inside. His clothes, which he had taken off to let the night wind cool his skin, were gone. So also were his few raw potatoes, the open lemonade bottle of fresh water, the sail and the rudder. The pain came shortly after sunrise as the heat of the day increased. Oblivion came on the third day after the storm. When he regained consciousness he was in a bed, taking the pain of the burns in silence, listening to the voices he thought were Bulgarian. For six days he had kept his eyes closed and his mouth shut.

Andrew Drake heard him out with a song in his heart. He had found the man he had waited years for.

'I'll go and see the Swiss consul in Istanbul and try to obtain temporary travel documents for you from the Red Cross,' he said when Kaminsky showed signs of tiring. 'If I do, I can probably get you to England, at least on a temporary visa. Then we can try for asylum. I'll return in a few days.'

By the door he paused.

'You can't go back, you know,' he told Kaminsky. 'But with your help, I can. It's what I want. It's what I've always wanted.'

Andrew Drake took longer than he had thought in Istanbul, and it was not until 16th May that he was able to fly back to Trabzon with travel papers for Kaminsky. He had extended his leave after a long telephone call to London and a row with the broking firm's junior partner, but it was worth it. For through Kaminsky he was certain he could fulfil the single burning ambition of his life.

The tsarist and later Soviet empire, despite its monolithic appearance from outside, has two Achilles heels. One is the problem of feeding its 250 millions. The other is euphemistically called 'the nationalities question'. In the fourteen republics ruled by the Russian Republic are several score identifiable non-Russian nations, and the biggest and perhaps the most nationally conscious is the Ukraine. By 1982 the Great Russian state numbered only 120 millions out of the 250; the next most populous and richest with 70 millions was Ukraine, which was one reason why under tsars and Politburo the Ukraine had always been singled out for special attention and particularly ruthless Russification.

The second reason lay in its history. Ukraine has always traditionally been divided into two, which has been its downfall: Western and Eastern Ukraine. Western Ukraine stretches from Kiev westwards to the Polish border. The eastern part is more Russified, having dwelt under the tsars for centuries; during those same centuries Western Ukraine was part of the old Austro-Hungarian empire. Its spiritual and cultural orientation was and remains more western that the rest, except possibly the three Baltic states which are too small to resist. Ukrainians read and write with Roman letters, not Cyrillic script; they are overwhelmingly Uniate Catholics, not Russian Orthodox Christians. Their language, poetry, literature, arts and traditions pre-date the rise of the Rus conquerors who swept down from the north.

In 1918 with the break-up of Austro-Hungary, Western Ukrainians tried desperately for a separate republic out of the empire's ruins; unlike the Czechs, Slovaks and Magyars, they failed and were annexed in 1919 by Poland as the province of Galicia. When Hitler swept into western Poland in 1939, Stalin came in from the east with the Red Army and took Galicia. In 1941 the Germans took it. What followed was a violent and vicious confusion of hopes, fears and loyalties. Some hoped for concessions from Moscow if they fought the Germans; others mistakenly thought Free Ukraine lay through the defeat of Moscow by Berlin and joined the Ukrainian Division, which fought against the Red Army, in German uniform. Others, like Kaminsky's father, took to the Carpathian Mountains as guerrillas and fought first one invader then the next, then the first again. They all lost; Stalin won and pushed his empire westwards to the Bug River, the new border for Poland. West Ukraine came under the new tsars, the Politburo, but the old dreams lived on. Apart from one glimmer in the last days of Khrushchev, the programme to crush them once and for all had steadily intensified.

Stepan Drach, a student from Rovno, joined up with the Ukrainian Division. He was one of the lucky ones; he survived the war and was captured by the British in Austria in 1945. Sent to work as a farm labourer in Norfolk, he would certainly have been sent back for execution by the NKVD in 1946 as the British Foreign Office and American State Department quietly conspired to return the two million 'victims of Yalta' to the mercies of Stalin. But he was lucky again. Behind a Norfolk haystack he tumbled a Land Army girl and she became pregnant. Marriage was the answer, and six months later, on compassionate grounds, he was excused repatriation and allowed to stay. Freed from farm labour, he used the knowledge he had gained as a radio operator to set up a small repair shop in Bradford, a centre for Britain's 30,000 Ukrainians. The first baby died in infancy; a second son, christened Andriy, was born in 1950.

Andriy learned Ukrainian at his father's knee, and that was not all. He learned too of his father's land, of the great sweeping vista of the Carpathians and Ruthenia. He imbibed his father's loathing of Russians. But the father died in a road crash when the boy was twelve; his mother, tired of her husband's endless evenings with fellow exiles round the sitting room fire, talking of the past in a language she could never understand, anglicized both their names to Drake, and Andriy's given name to Andrew. It was as Andrew Drake that the boy went to grammar school and university; as Andrew Drake that he received his first passport.

The re-birth came in his late teens at university. There were other Ukrainians there, and he became fluent again in his father's language. This was the late sixties, and the brief renaissance of Ukrainian literature and poetry back in the Ukraine had come and gone, its leading lights mostly by then doing slave labour in the camps of Gulag. So he absorbed these events with hindsight and knowledge of what had befallen the writers. He read everything he could get his hands on as the first years of the seventh decade dawned: the classics of Taras Shevchenko and those who wrote in the brief flowering under Lenin, suppressed and liquidated under Stalin. But most of all he read the works of those called 'the Sixtiers', because they flourished for a brief few years until Brezhnev struck yet again to stamp out the national pride they called for. He read and grieved for Osdachy, Chornovil, Moroz and Dzyuba; and when he read the poems and secret diary of Pavel Symonenko, the young firebrand dead of cancer at twenty-eight, the cult figure of the Ukrainian students inside the USSR, his heart broke for a land he had never even seen.

With his love for this land of his dead father came a matching loathing of

those he saw as its persecutors; avidly he devoured the underground pamphlets that came out, smuggled from the resistance movement inside: the
Ukrainian Herald, with its accounts of what befell the hundreds of unknowns
who did not receive the publicity accorded to the great Moscow trials of
Daniel, Sinyavsky, Orlov, Scharansky, the miserable, forgotten ones. With
each detail his hatred grew until for Andrew Drake, once Andriy Drach, the
personification of all evil in the world was simply called KGB.

He had enough sense of reality to eschew the crude, raw nationalism of the
older exiles, and their divisions between West and East Ukrainians. He
rejected too their implanted anti-Semitism, preferring to accept the works of
Gluzman, both a Zionist and a Ukrainian nationalist, as the words of a
fellow-Ukrainian. He analysed the exile community in Britain and Europe
and perceived there were four levels: the language nationalists for whom
simply speaking and writing in the tongue of their fathers was enough; the
debating nationalists who would talk for ever and a day, but do nothing; the
slogan-daubers who irritated their adopted countrymen but left the Soviet
behemoth untouched; and the activists who demonstrated before visiting
Moscow dignitaries, were carefully photographed and filed by the Special
Branch and achieved a passing publicity.

Drake rejected them all. He remained quiet, well-behaved and aloof. He
came south to London and took a clerking job. There are many in such work
who have one secret passion, unknown to all their colleagues, which absorbs
all their savings, their spare time and their annual holidays. Drake was such a
man. He quietly put together a small group of men who felt just as he did; he
traced them, met them, befriended them, swore a common oath with them,
and bade them be patient. For Andriy Drach had a secret dream and, as T. E.
Lawrence said, he was dangerous because 'he dreamed with his eyes open'.
His dream was that one day he would strike one single gigantic blow against
the men of Moscow that would shake them as they had never been shaken
before. He would penetrate the walls of their power and hurt them right
inside the fortress.

His dream was alive and one step nearer fulfilment for the finding of
Kaminsky, and he was a determined and excited man as his plane slipped
once more out of a warm blue sky towards Trabzon.

Miroslav Kaminsky looked across at Drake with indecision on his face.

'I don't know, Andriy,' he said, 'I just don't know. Despite everything you
have done, I just don't know if I can trust you that much. I'm sorry, it's the
way I've had to live all my life.'

'Miroslav, you could know me for the next twenty years and not know
more about me than you do already. Everything I've told you about me is the
truth. If you cannot go back then let me go in your place. But I must have
contacts there. If you know of any, anybody at all. . . .'

Kaminsky finally agreed.

'There are two men,' he said at last. 'They were not blown away when my
group was destroyed, and no one knew of them. I had met them only a few
months earlier.'

'But they are Ukrainians, and partisans?' asked Drake eagerly.

'Yes, they are Ukrainians. But that is not their primary motivation. Their people too have suffered. Their fathers, like mine, have been for ten years in the labour camps, but for a different reason. They are Jews.'

'But do they hate Moscow?' asked Drake. 'Do they too want to strike against the Kremlin?'

'Yes, they hate Moscow,' replied Kaminsky. 'As much as you or I. Their inspiration seems to be a thing called the Jewish Defense League. They heard about it on the radio. It seems their philosophy, like ours, is to begin to strike back; not to take any more persecution lying down.'

'Then let me make contact with them,' urged Drake.

The following morning Drake flew back to London with the names and addresses in Lvov of the two young Jewish partisans. Within a fortnight he had subscribed to a package tour run by Intourist for early July, visiting Kiev, Ternopol and Lvov. He also quit his job and withdrew his life savings in cash.

Unnoticed by anyone, Andrew Drake, alias Andriy Drach, was going to his private war – against the Kremlin.

1

A gentle warming sun shone down on Washington that middle of May, bringing the first shirtsleeves to the street and the first rich, red roses to the garden outside the french windows of the Oval Office in the White House. But though the windows were open and the fresh smells of grass and flowers wafted into the private sanctum of the most powerful ruler in the world, the attention of the four men present was focused upon other plants in a far and foreign country.

President William Matthews sat where American presidents have always sat: back to the south wall of the room, facing northward across a wide antique desk towards the classical marble fireplace that dominates the north wall. His chair, unlike that of most of his predecessors, who had favoured personalized, made-to-measure seating, was a factory-made, high-backed swivel chair of the kind any senior corporate executive might have. For 'Bill' Matthews, as he insisted his publicity posters called him, had always through his successive and successful election campaigns stressed his ordinary, old-folks-at-home personal tastes in clothing, food and creature comforts. The chair, therefore, which could be seen by the scores of delegates he liked to welcome personally into the Oval Office, was not luxurious. The fine antique desk, he was at pains to point out, he had inherited and it had become part of the precious tradition of the White House. That went down well.

But there Bill Matthews drew the line. When he was in conclave with his senior advisers, the 'Bill' which his humblest constituent could call him to his face was out of court. He also dropped the nice-guy tones of voice and the rumpled bird-dog grin that had originally gulled the voters into putting the boy next door into the White House. He was not the boy next door, and his advisers knew it; he was the man at the top.

Seated in upright armchairs across the desk from the President were the three men who had asked to see him alone that morning. Closest to him in personal terms was the chairman of the National Security Council, his own adviser on security matters and confidant on foreign affairs. Variously referred to in the environs of the West Wing and the Executive Office Buildings as 'the doc' or 'that damned Polack', the sharp-faced Stanislav Poklewski was sometimes disliked but never underestimated.

They made a strange pair, to be so close; the blond, white, Anglo-Saxon Protestant from the deep South, and the dark, taciturn devout Roman Catholic who had come over from Cracow as a small boy. But what Bill Matthews lacked in understanding of the tortuous psychologies of Europeans in general and Slavs in particular could be made up by the Jesuit-educated calculating machine who always had his ear. There were two other reasons why Poklewski appealed to him: he was ferociously loyal and had no political ambitions outside the shadow of Bill Matthews. But there was one reservation: Matthews always had to balance the doctor's suspicious dislike of the men of Moscow with the more urbane assessments of his Bostonian secretary of state.

The secretary was not present that morning at the meeting asked for personally by Poklewski. The other two men on the chairs in front of the desk were Robert Benson, director of the Central Intelligence Agency, and Carl Taylor.

It has frequently been written that America's National Security Agency is the body responsible for all electronic espionage. It is a popular idea but not true. The NSA is responsible for that portion of electronic surveillance and espionage conducted outside the United States on her behalf that has to do with listening: wire-tapping, radio-monitoring and above all the plucking out of the ether of literally billions of words a day in hundreds of dialects and languages, for recording, de-coding, translating and analysing. But not spy satellites. The *visual* surveillance of the globe by cameras mounted in aeroplanes and, more importantly, in space satellites has always been the preserve of the National Reconnaissance Office, a joint US Air Force/CIA operation. Carl Taylor was its director and he was a two-star general of Air Force Intelligence.

The President shuffled together the pile of high-definition photographs on his desk and handed them back to Taylor, who rose to accept them and placed them back in his briefcase.

'All right, gentlemen,' he said slowly, 'so you have shown me that the wheat crop in a small portion of the Soviet Union, maybe even only in the few acres shown in these pictures, is coming up defective. What does it prove?'

Poklewski glanced across at Taylor and nodded. Taylor cleared his throat.

'Mr President, I've taken the liberty of setting up a screening of what is coming in right now from one of our Condor satellites. Would you care to see it?'

Matthews nodded and watched Taylor cross to one of the bank of television sets placed in the curving west wall below the bookcases, which had been specially shortened to accept the console of TV sets. When civilian deputations were in the room, the new row of TV screens was covered by sliding teak doors. Taylor turned on the extreme left-hand set and returned to the President's desk. He detached one of the six telephones from its cradle, dialled a number and said simply, 'Screen it.'

President Matthews knew about the Condor range of satellites. Flying higher than anything before, using cameras of a sophistication that could show close-up a human fingernail from two hundred miles, through fog, rain, hail, snow, cloud and night, the Condors were the latest and the best.

Back in the 1970s photographic surveillance though good had been slow, mainly because each cartridge of exposed film had to be ejected from the satellite at specific positions, free-fall to Earth in protective coverings, be retrieved with the aid of bleepers and tracing devices, air-freighted to the NRO's central laboratories, developed and screened. Only when the satellite was within that arc of flight which permitted a direct line from it to the USA or one of the American-controlled tracking stations, could simultaneous TV transmissions take place. But when the satellite passed close over the Soviet Union the curve of the Earth's surface baffled direct reception, so that the watchers had to wait until it came round again.

Then in the summer of 1978 the scientists cracked the problem with the 'Parabola Game'. Their computers devised a cat's cradle of infinite complexity for the flight tracks of half a dozen space cameras around the globe's surface to this end: whichever spy-in-the-sky the White House wanted to tap into could be ordered by signal to begin transmitting what it was seeing, and throw the images in a low parabola arc to another satellite which was out of vision. The second bird would throw the image on again, to a third satellite, and so on, like basketball players tossing the ball from fingertip to fingertip while they ran. When the needed images were fielded by a satellite of the USA they could be beamed back down to the NRO headquarters, and from there by patch-through to the Oval Office.

The satellites were travelling at over 40,000 land miles per hour; the globe was spinning with the hours, tilting with the seasons. The computations and permutations were astronomical, but the computers solved them. By 1980 the US President had twenty-four-hour access to every square inch of the world's surface at the touch of a button by simultaneous transmission. Sometimes it bothered him. It never bothered Poklewski: he had been brought up to the idea of the exposition of all private thoughts and actions in the confessional. The Condors were like confessionals, with himself as the priest he had once nearly become.

As the screen flickered into life, General Taylor spread a map of the Soviet Union on the President's desk and pointed with a forefinger.

'What you are seeing, Mr President, is coming to you from Condor Five, tracking here, northeast, between Saratov and Perm, across the Virgin Lands and the Black Earth country.'

Matthews raised his gaze to the screen. Great tracts of land were unrolling slowly down the screen from top to bottom, a swathe about twenty miles broad. The land looked bare, as in autumn after the harvest. Taylor muttered a few instructions into the telephone. Seconds later the view concentrated, closing to a band barely five miles wide. A small group of peasant shacks, wooden plank *izbas* no doubt, lost in the infinity of the steppe, drifted past on the left of the screen. The line of a road entered the picture, stayed centre for a few uncertain moments, then drifted off screen. Taylor muttered again; the picture closed to a track a hundred yards wide. Definition was better. A man leading a horse across the vast expanse of steppe came and went.

'Slow it down,' instructed Taylor into the telephone. The ground beneath the camera passed less quickly. High in space the satellite Condor was still on track at the same height and speed; inside the NRO's laboratories the images were being narrowed and slowed. The picture came closer, slower. Against the bole of a lone tree a Russian peasant slowly unbuttoned his fly. President Matthews was not a technical man and never ceased to be amazed. He was, he reminded himself, sitting in a warm office on an early summer morning in Washington, watching a man urinate somewhere in the shadow of the Urals mountain range. The peasant passed slowly out of vision towards the bottom of the screen. The image coming up was of a wheat field many hundreds of acres broad.

'And freeze,' instructed Taylor into the telephone. The picture slowly stopped moving and held.

'Close up,' said Taylor.

The picture came closer and closer until the entire square-yard screen was filled with twenty separate stalks of young wheat. Each looked frail, listless, bedraggled. Matthews had seen them like this in the dustbowls of the Middle West he had known in his boyhood fifty years before.

'Stan,' said the President. Poklewski, who had asked for the meeting and the screening, chose his words carefully.

'Mr President, the Soviet Union has a total grain target this year of two hundred and forty million metric tons. Now this breaks down into goal targets of one hundred and twenty million tons of wheat, sixty million of barley, and fourteen of oats, fourteen of maize or corn, twelve of rye and the remaining twenty of a mixture of rice, millet, buckwheat and leguminous grains. The giants of the crop are wheat and barley.'

He rose and came round the desk to where the map of the Soviet Union was still spread. Taylor flicked off the television and resumed his seat.

'About forty per cent of the annual Soviet grain crop or approximately one hundred million tons comes from here in the Ukraine and the Kuban area of southern Russian Republic,' Poklewski continued, indicating the areas on the map. 'And it is all winter wheat. That is, it's planted in September and October. It has reached the stage of young shoots by November when the first snows come. The snows cover the shoots and protect them from the bitter frosts of December and January.'

Poklewski turned and paced away from the desk to the curved ceiling-to-floor windows behind the presidential chair. He had this habit of pacing when he talked.

The Pennsylvania Avenue observer cannot actually see the Oval Office tucked away at the back of the tiny West Wing building, but because the tops of these south-facing tall windows to the office can just be observed from the Washington Monument a thousand yards away they have long been fitted with six-inch-thick, green-tinted bulletproof glass just in case a sniper near the monument might care to try a long shot. As Poklewski reached the windows the aquamarine tinted light coming through them cast a deeper pallor across his already pale face.

He turned and walked back, just as Matthews was preparing to swing his chair round to keep him in vision.

'Last December the whole of Ukraine and Kuban was covered by a freak thaw during the early days. They've had them before, but never as warm. A great wave of warm southern air swept in off the Black Sea and the Bosphorus and rolled northeastward over Ukraine and Kuban. It lasted a week and melted the first coverings of snow, about six inches deep, to water. The young wheat and barley stems were exposed. Ten days later, as if to make up, the same freak weather patterns hammered the whole area with frosts going fifteen, even twenty degrees, below zero.'

'Which did the wheat a power of no good,' suggested the President.

'Mr President,' interjected Robert Benson of the CIA, 'our best agricultural experts have estimated the Soviets will be lucky if they salvage fifty per cent of that Ukrainian and Kuban crop. The damage was massive and irreparable.'

'So that is what you have been showing me?' asked Matthews.

'No, sir,' said Poklewski, 'that is the point of this meeting. The other sixty per cent of the Soviet crop, nigh on one hundred and forty million tons, comes from the great tracts of the Virgin Lands, first put under the plough by Khrushchev in the early sixties, and the Black Earth country, butting up against the Urals. A small portion comes from across the mountains in Siberia. That is what we have been showing you.'

'What is happening there?' asked Matthews.

'Something odd, sir. Something strange is happening to the Soviet grain crop. All this remaining sixty per cent is spring wheat, put down as seed in March/April after the thaw. It should be coming up sweet and green by now. It's coming up stunted, sparse, sporadic, like it was hit by some kind of blight.'

'Weather again?' asked Matthews.

'No. They had a damp winter and spring over this area, but nothing serious. Now the sun has come out, the weather is perfect, warm and dry.'

'How widespread is this . . . blight?'

Benson came in again. 'We don't know, Mr President. We have maybe fifty samples of film of this particular problem. We tend to concentrate on military concentrations, of course: troop movements, new rocket bases, arms factories. But what we have indicates it must be pretty widespread.'

'So what are you after?'

'What we'd like,' resumed Poklewski, 'is your go-ahead to spend a lot more on this problem, find out just how big it is for the Soviets. It will mean trying to send in delegations, businessmen. Diverting a lot of space surveillance from non-priority tasks. We believe it is in America's vital interest to find out just exactly what it is that Moscow is going to have to handle here.'

Matthews considered and glanced at his watch. He had a troop of ecologists due to greet him and present him with yet another plaque in ten minutes. Then there was the attorney general before lunch about the new labour legislation. He rose.

'Very well, gentlemen, you have it. By my authority. This is one I think we need to know. But I want an answer within thirty days.'

General Carl Taylor sat in the seventh-floor office of Robert Benson, the director of central intelligence, or DCI, ten days later and gazed down at his own report, clipped to a large sheaf of photo stills, that lay on the low coffee table in front of him.

'It's a funny one, Bob. I can't figure it out,' he said.

Benson turned away from the great sweeping picture windows that form one entire wall of the DCI's office at Langley and face out north by northwest across vistas of trees towards the invisible Potomac River. Like his predecessors, he loved that view, particularly in late spring and early summer, when the woodlands were a wash of tender green. He took his seat on the low settee across the coffee table from Taylor.

'Neither can my grain experts, Carl. And I don't want to go to the Department of Agriculture. Whatever is going on over there in Russia, publicity is the last thing we need, and if I bring in outsiders it'll be in the press within a week. So what have you got?'

'Well, the photos show the blight, or whatever it is, is not pandemic,' said Taylor. 'It's not even regional. That's the twister. If the cause was climatic, there'd be weather phenomena to explain it. There are none. If it was a straight disease of the crop, it would be at least regional. If it was parasite-caused, same applies. But it's haphazard. There are stands of strong, healthy, growing wheat right alongside the affected acreage. The Condor reconnaissance shows no logical pattern at all. How about you?'

Benson nodded in agreement.

'It's illogical all right. I've put a couple of assets in on the ground, but they haven't reported back yet. The Soviet press has said nothing. My own agronomy boys have been over your photos backwards and forwards. All they can come up with is some blight of the seed or in the earth. But they too cannot figure the haphazard nature of it all. It fits no known pattern. But the important thing is I have to produce some kind of estimate for the President for the total probable Soviet grain harvest next September/October. And I have to produce it soon.'

'There's no way I can photograph every damn stand of wheat and barley in the Soviet Union, even with Condor,' said Taylor. 'It would take months. Can you give me that?'

'Not a chance,' said Benson. 'I need information about the troop movements along the China border, the build-up opposite Turkey and Iran. I need a constant watch on the Red Army deployments in East Germany and the locations of the new SS Twenties behind the Urals.'

'Then I can only come up with a percentage figure based on what we have photographed to date, and extrapolate for a Soviet-wide figure,' said Taylor.

'It's got to be accurate,' said Benson. 'I don't want a repeat of 1977.'

Taylor winced at the memory, even though he had not been director of the NRO in that year. In 1977 the American intelligence machine had been fooled by a gigantic Soviet confidence trick. Throughout the summer all the experts of the CIA and Department of Agriculture had been telling the President the Soviet grain crop would reach around 215 million metric tons. Agriculture delegates visiting Russia had been shown fields of fine healthy wheat; in fact these had been the exceptions. Photo-reconnaissance analysis had been faulty. In the autumn the then Soviet President, Leonid Brezhnev, had calmly announced the Soviet crop would be only 149 million tons.

As a result the price of US wheat surplus to domestic requirements had shot up, in the certainty the Russians would after all have to buy in close on 20,000,000 tons. Too late. Through the summer, acting through French-based front companies, Moscow had already bought up futures for enough wheat to cover the deficit – and at the old, low price. They had even chartered dry-cargo shipping space through front-men, then re-directed the ships, which were en route for Western Europe, into Soviet ports. The affair was known in Langley as 'the Sting'.

Carl Taylor rose. 'OK, Bob, I'll go on taking happy snap-shots.'

'Carl.' The DCI's voice stopped him in the doorway. 'Nice pictures are not enough. By 1st July I want the Condors back on military deployment. Give me the best grain figure estimates you have by the end of the month. Err, if you must, on the side of caution. And if there's *anything* your boys spot that could explain the phenomenon, go back and re-shoot it. Somehow we have to find out what the hell is happening to the Soviet wheat.'

President Matthews' Condor satellites could see most things in the Soviet Union but they could not observe Harold Lessing, one of the three first secretaries in the Commercial Section of the British embassy in Moscow, at his desk the following morning. It was probably just as well, for he would have been the first to agree he was not an edifying sight. He was pale as a sheet and feeling extremely sick.

The main embassy building of the British mission in the Soviet capital is a fine old, pre-Revolution mansion facing north on Maurice Thorez Embankment, staring straight across the Moscow River at the south façade of the Kremlin wall. It once belonged to a millionaire sugar merchant in tsarist days, and was snapped up by the British soon after the revolution. The Soviet government has been trying to get the British out of there ever since. Stalin hated the place; every morning as he rose he had to see, across the river from his private apartments, the Union Jack fluttering in the morning breeze, and it made him very angry.

But the Commercial Section does not have the fortune to dwell in this elegant cream and gold mansion. It functions in a drab complex of post-war jerry-built office blocks two miles away on Kutuzovsky Prospekt, almost opposite the wedding-cake-styled Ukraina Hotel. The same compound, guarded at its single gate by several watchful militia men, contains more drab apartment buildings set aside for the flats of diplomatic personnel from a score or more of foreign embassies, and called collectively the 'Korpus Diplomatik' or Diplomats' Compound.

Harold Lessing's office was on the top floor of the commercial office block. When he finally fainted at ten-thirty that bright May morning it was the sound of the telephone he brought crashing to the carpet with him that alerted his secretary in the neighbouring office. Quietly and efficiently she summoned the commercial counsellor, who had two young attachés assist Lessing, by this time groggily conscious again, out of the building, across the parking lot and up to his own sixth-floor apartment in Korpus 6, a hundred yards away.

Simultaneously the counsellor telephoned the main embassy on Maurice Thorez Embankment, informed the head of chancery and asked for the embassy doctor to be sent over. By noon, having examined Lessing in his own bed in his own flat, the doctor was conferring with the commercial counsellor. To his surprise the senior man cut him short and suggested they drive over to the main embassy to consult jointly with the head of chancery. Only later did the doctor, an ordinary British general practitioner doing a three-year stint on attachment to the embassy with the rank of first secretary, realize why the move was necessary. The head of chancery took them all to a special room in the embassy building which is secure from wire-tapping; something the Commercial Section was definitely not.

'It's a bleeding ulcer,' the medico told the two diplomats. 'He seemingly has been suffering from what he thought was an excess of acid indigestion for some weeks, even months. Put it down to strain of work and bunged down loads of antacid tablets. Foolish, really; he should have come to me.'

'Will it require hospitalization?' asked the head of chancery, gazing at the ceiling.

'Oh, yes indeed,' said the doctor. 'I think I can get him admitted here within a few hours. The local Soviet medical men are quite up to that sort of treatment.'

There was a brief silence as the two diplomats exchanged glances. The commercial counsellor shook his head. Both men had the same thought; because of their need to know, both of them were aware of Lessing's real function in the embassy. The doctor was not. The counsellor deferred to Chancery.

'That will not be possible,' said Chancery smoothly. 'Not in Lessing's case. He'll have to be flown to Helsinki on the afternoon shuttle. Will you ensure that he can make it?'

'But surely . . .' began the doctor. Then he stopped. He realized why they had had to drive two miles to have this conversation. Lessing must be the head of the Secret Intelligence Service operation in Moscow. 'Ah, yes. Well, now. He's shocked and has lost probably a pint of blood. I've given him a hundred milligrams of pethidine as a tranquilliser. I could give him another shot at three this afternoon. If he's chauffeur-driven to the airport and escorted all the way, yes, he can make Helsinki. But he'll need immediate entry into hospital when he gets there. I'd prefer to go with him myself just to be sure. I could be back tomorrow.'

The head of chancery rose. 'Splendid,' he pronounced. 'Give yourself two days. And my wife has a list of little items she's run short of, if you'd be so kind. Yes? Thank you so much. I'll make all the arrangements from here.'

For years it has been customary in newspapers, magazines and books to refer to the headquarters of Britain's Secret Intelligence Service, or the SIS, or M16, as being at a certain office block in the Borough of Lambeth in London. It is a custom that causes quiet amusement to the staff members of the firm for the Lambeth address is a sedulously maintained front.

In much the same way a front is maintained at Leconfield House in Curzon Street, still supposed to be the home of the counter-intelligence arm, M15, to decoy the unneeded enquirer. In reality those indefatigable spy-catchers have not dwelt near the Playboy Club for years.

The real home of the world's most secret Secret Intelligence Service is a modern-design, steel and concrete block allocated by the Department of the Environment a stone's throw from one of the capital's principal Southern Region railway stations, and it was taken over in the early 1970s.

It was in his top-floor suite with its tinted windows looking out towards the spire of Big Ben and the Houses of Parliament across the river that the director-general of the SIS received the news of Lessing's illness just after lunch. The call came on one of the internal lines from the head of personnel who had received the message from the basement cipher room. He listened carefully.

'How long will he be off?' he asked at length.

'Several months at least,' said Personnel. 'There'll be a couple of weeks in hospital in Helsinki, then home for a bit more. Probably several more weeks' convalescence.'

'Pity,' mused the director-general. 'We shall have to replace him rather fast.' His capacious memory recalled that Lessing had been running two Russian agents, low-level staffers in the Red Army and the Soviet Foreign Ministry respectively, not world-beating, but useful. Finally he said, 'Let me know when Lessing is safely tucked up in Helsinki. And get me a short list of possibles for his replacement. By close of play tonight, please.'

Sir Nigel Irvine was the third successive professional intelligence man to rise to the post of director-general of the SIS, or 'the firm' as it is more colloquially known in the community of such organizations.

The vastly bigger American CIA, which had been founded and brought back to the peak of its power by Allen Dulles, had as a result of abusing its strength with go-it-alone antics in the early seventies finally been brought under the control of an outsider, Admiral Stansfield Turner. It was ironic that, at exactly the same period, a British government had finally done the opposite, breaking the tradition of putting the firm under a senior diplomat from the Foreign Office and letting a professional take over.

The risk had worked well. The firm had paid a long penance for the Burgess, MacLean and Philby affairs, and Sir Nigel Irvine was determined that the tradition of a professional at the head of the firm would continue after him. That was why he intended to be as strict as any of his immediate predecessors in preventing the emergence of any Lone Rangers.

'This is a service, not a trapeze act,' he used to tell the novices at Beaconsfield. 'We're not here for the applause.'

It was already dark by the time the three files arrived on Sir Nigel Irvine's desk, but he wanted to get the selection finished and was prepared to stay on. He spent an hour poring over the files, but the selection seemed fairly obvious. Finally he used the telephone to ask the head of personnel, who was still in the building, to stop by. His secretary showed the staffer in two minutes later.

Sir Nigel hospitably poured the man a whisky and soda to match his own. He saw no reason not to permit himself a few of the gracious things of life, and he had arranged a well-appointed office, perhaps to compensate for the stink of combat in 1944 and 1945, and the dingy hotels of Vienna in the late forties when he was a junior agent in the firm suborning Soviet personnel in the

Russian-occupied areas of Austria. Two of his recruits of that period, sleepers for years, were still being run, he was able to congratulate himself.

Although the building housing the SIS was of modern steel, concrete and chrome, the top-floor office of its director-general was decorated to an older and more elegant motif. The wallpaper was a restful *café au lait*, the wall-to-wall carpet a burnt orange. The desk, the high chair behind it, the two uprights in front of it and the button-back leather Chesterfield were all genuine antiques.

From the Department of the Environment store of pictures, to which the mandarins of Britain's Civil Service have access for the decoration of their office walls, Sir Nigel had collared a Dufy, a Vlaminck and a slightly suspect Breughel. He had had his eye on a small but exquisite Fragonard, but a shifty grandee in Treasury had got there first.

Unlike the Foreign and Commonwealth Office whose walls were hung with oils of past foreign ministers like Canning and Grey, the firm had always eschewed ancestral portraits. In any case, who ever heard of such self-effacing men as Britain's successive spymasters enjoying having their likeness put on record in the first place? Nor were portraits of the Queen in full regalia much in favour, as the White House and Langley were plastered with signed photos of the latest president.

'One's commitment to service of Queen and country in this building needs no further advertisement,' a dumbfounded visitor from the CIA at Langley had once been told. 'If it did, one wouldn't be working here anyway.'

Sir Nigel turned from the window and his study of the lights of the West End across the water.

'It looks like Munro, wouldn't you say?' he asked.

'I would have thought so,' answered Personnel.

'What's he like? I've read the file, I know him slightly. Give me the personal touch.'

'Secretive.'

'Good.'

'A bit of a loner.'

'Blast.'

'It's a question of his Russian,' said Personnel. 'The other two have good, working Russian. Munro can pass for one. He doesn't normally. Speaks to them in strongly accented moderate Russian. When he drops that he can blend right in. It's just that, well, to run Mallard and Merganser at such short notice, brilliant Russian would be an asset.'

Mallard and Merganser were the code-names for the two low-level agents recruited and run by Lessing. Russians being run inside the Soviet Union by the firm tend to have bird names, in alphabetical order according to the date of recruitment. The two Ms were recent acquisitions. Sir Nigel grunted.

'Very well. Munro it is. Where is he now?'

'On training. At Beaconsfield. Tradecraft.'

'Have him here tomorrow afternoon. Since he's not married, he can probably leave quite quickly. No need to hang about. I'll have the Foreign Office agree the appointment in the morning as Lessing's replacement in the Commercial Section.'

*

Beaconsfield, being within easy reach of central London, was years ago a favoured area for the elegant country homes of those who enjoyed high and wealthy status in the capital. By the early 1970s most of them played host to seminars, retreats, executive courses in management and marketing or even religious observation. One of them housed the Joint Services School of Russian and was quite open about it; another smaller house contained the training school of the SIS and was not open about it at all.

Adam Munro's course in tradecraft was popular, not the least because it broke the wearisome routine of enciphering and deciphering. He had his class's attention and he knew it.

'Right,' said Munro that morning in the last week of the month. 'Now for some snags, and how to get out of them.'

The class was still with expectancy. Routine procedures were one thing; a sniff of some real opposition was more interesting.

'You have to pick up a package from a contract,' said Munro, 'but you are being tailed by the local fuzz. You have diplomatic cover in case of arrest, but your contact does not. He's right out in the cold, a local man. He's coming to a meet and you can't stop him. He knows that if he hangs about too long he could attract attention, so he'll wait ten minutes. What do you do?'

'Shake the tail,' suggested someone. Munro shook his head.

'For one thing you're supposed to be an innocent diplomat, not a Houdini. Lose the tail and you give yourself away as a trained agent. Secondly, you might not succeed. If it's the KGB and they're using the first team, you won't do it, short of dodging back into the embassy. Try again.'

'Abort,' said another trainee. 'Don't show. The safety of the unprotected contributor is paramount.'

'Right,' said Munro. 'But that leaves your man with a package he can't hold on to for ever, and no procedure for an alternative meet.' He paused for several seconds. 'Or does he . . . ?'

'There's a second procedure established in the event of an abort,' suggested a third student.

'Good,' said Munro. 'When you had him alone in the good old days before the routine surveillance was switched to yourself, you briefed him on a whole range of alternative meets in the event of an abort. So he waits ten minutes, you don't show up, he goes off nice and innocently to the second meeting point. What is this procedure called?'

'Fall-back,' ventured the bright spark who wanted to shake off the tail.

'First fall-back,' corrected Munro. 'We'll be doing all this on the streets of London in a couple of months, so get it right.' They scribbled hard. 'OK. You have a second location in the city, but you're still tailed. You haven't got anywhere. What happens at the first fall-back location?'

There was a general silence. Munro gave them thirty seconds.

'You don't meet at this location,' he instructed. 'Under the procedures you have taught your contact, the second location is always a place where he can observe you but you can stay well away from him. When you know he is watching you from a terrace perhaps, from a café, but always well away from you, you give him a signal. Can be anything: scratch an ear, blow your nose, drop a newspaper and pick it up again. What does that mean to the contact?'

'That you're setting up the third meet, according to your pre-arranged procedures,' said Bright Spark.

'Precisely. But you're *still* being tailed. Where does the third meet happen? What kind of place?'

This time there were no takers.

'It's any building – a bar, club, restaurant or what you like – that has a closed front so that once the door is closed no one can see through any plate-glass windows from the street inside the ground floor. Now, why is that the place for the exchange?'

There was a brief knock on the door and the head of student programme put his face round the door. He beckoned to Munro, who left his desk and went across to the door. His superior officer drew him outside into the corridor.

'You've been summoned,' he said quietly. 'The Master wants to see you. In his office at three. Leave here at the lunchbreak. Bailey will take over afternoon classes.'

Munro returned to his desk somewhat puzzled. The Master was the half affectionate and half respectful nickname for any holder of the post of director-general of the firm.

One of the class had a suggestion to make. 'So that you can walk to the contact's table and pick up the package unobserved?'

Munro shook his head. 'Not quite. When you leave the place the tailing opposition might leave one man behind to question the waiters. If you approached your man directly the face of the contact could be observed and the contributor identified, even by description. Anyone else?'

'Use a drop [dead-letter box] inside the restaurant,' proposed Bright Spark. Another shake from Munro.

'You won't have time,' he advised. 'The tails will be tumbling into the place a few seconds after you. Maybe the contact, who by arrangement was there before you, will not have found the right toilet cubicle free. Or the right table unoccupied. It's too hit-or-miss. No, this time we'll use the brush-pass. Note it; it goes like this.

'When your contact received your signal at the first fall-back location that you were under surveillance, he moved into the agreed procedure. He synchronized his watch to the nearest second with a reliable public clock, or, better still, the speaking clock operated by the telephone service. In another place, you did exactly the same.

'At an agreed hour he is already sitting in the agreed bar, or whatever. Outside the door, you are approaching at exactly the same time, to the nearest second. If you're ahead of time, delay a bit by adjusting your shoelace, pausing at a shop window. Do not consult your watch in an obvious manner.

'To the second, you enter the bar and the door closes behind you. At the same second, the contact is on his feet, bill paid, moving towards the door. At a minimum, five seconds will elapse before the door opens again and the fuzz come in. You brush past your contact a couple of feet inside the door, making sure it is closed to block off vision. As you brush past, you pass the package, or collect it, then part company and proceed to a vacant table or bar stool. The opposition will come in seconds later. As they move past him, the contact steps out and vanishes. Later the bar staff will confirm you spoke to nobody, contacted nobody. You paused at nobody's table, nor anyone at yours. You have the package in an outside pocket and you finish your drink and go back to the embassy. The opposition will hopefully report that you contacted nobody throughout the entire stroll.

'That is the brush-pass . . . and *that* is the lunch bell. All right, we'll scrub it for now.'

By mid-afternoon Adam Munro was closeted in the secure library beneath the firm's HQ building beginning to bore through a pile of buff folders. He had just five days to master and commit to memory enough background material to enable him to take over from Harold Lessing as the firm's 'legal resident' in Moscow.

On 31st May he flew from London to Moscow to take up his new appointment.

Munro spent the first week settling in. To all the embassy staff but an informed few he was just a professional diplomat and the hurried replacement for Harold Lessing. The ambassador, head of chancery, chief cipher clerk and commercial counsellor knew what his real job was. The fact of his relatively advanced age of forty-six years to be only a first secretary in the Commercial Section was explained by his late entrance into the diplomatic corps.

The commercial counsellor ensured that the commercial files placed before him were as unburdensome as possible. Munro had a brief and formal reception by the ambassador in the latter's private office, and a more informal drink with the head of chancery. He met most of the staff and was taken to a round of diplomatic parties to meet many of the other diplomats from Western embassies. He also had a face-to-face and more businesslike conference with his opposite number at the American embassy. 'Business', as the CIA man confirmed to him, was quiet.

Though it would have made any staffer at the British embassy in Moscow stand out like a sore thumb to speak no Russian, Munro kept his use of the language to a formal and accented version both in front of his colleagues and when talking to official Russians during the introduction process. At one party two Soviet foreign ministry personnel had had a brief exchange in rapid, colloquial Russian a few feet away. He had understood it completely, and as it was mildly interesting he had filed it to London.

On his tenth day he sat alone on a park bench in the sprawling Soviet Exhibition of Economic Achievements in the extreme northern outskirts of the Russian capital. He was waiting to make first contact with the agent from the Red Army whom he had taken over from Lessing.

Munro had been born in 1936, the son of an Edinburgh doctor, and his boyhood through the war years had been conventional, middle class, untroubled and happy. He had attended a local school up to the age of thirteen years and then spent five years at Fettes College, one of Scotland's best schools. It was during his period here that his senior languages master had detected in the lad an unusually acute ear for foreign languages.

In 1954, with national service then obligatory, he had gone into the army and after basic training secured a posting to his father's old regiment, the First Gordon Highlanders. Transferred to Cyprus, he had been on operations against EOKA partisans in the Troodos Mountains that late summer.

Sitting in a park in Moscow he could see the farmhouse still, in his mind's eye. They had spent half the night crawling through the heather to surround the place, following a tip-off from an informant. When dawn came, Munro was posted alone at the bottom of a steep escarpment behind the hill-top house. The main body of his platoon stormed the front of the farm just as dawn broke, coming up the shallower slope with the sun behind them.

From above him, on the other side of the hill, he could hear the chattering of the Stens in the quiet dawn. By the first rays of the sun he could see the two figures that came tumbling out of the rear windows, in shadow until their headlong flight down the escarpment took them clear of the lee of the house. They came straight at him, crouched behind his fallen olive tree in the shadow of the grove, their legs flying as they sought to keep their balance on the shale. They came nearer and one of them had what looked like a short, black stick in his right hand. Even if he had shouted, he told himself later, they could not have stopped their momentum. But he did not say that to himself at the time. Training took over; he just stood up as they reached a point fifty feet from him and loosed off two short, lethal bursts.

The force of the bullets lifted them both, one after the other, stopped their momentum and slammed them on to the shale at the foot of the slope. As a blue plume of cordite smoke drifted away from the muzzle of his Sten, he moved forward to look down at them. He thought he might feel sick, or faint. There was nothing; just a dead curiosity. He looked at the faces. They were boys, younger than himself, and he was eighteen.

His sergeant came crashing through the olive grove.

'Well done, laddie,' he shouted. 'You got 'em.'

Munro looked down at the bodies of the boys who would never marry or have children, never dance to a bouzouki or feel the warmth of sun and wine again. One of them was still clutching the black stick; it was a sausage. A piece of it hung out of the body's mouth. He had been having breakfast. Munro turned on the sergeant.

'You don't own me,' he shouted, 'you don't bloody own me. Nobody owns me but me.'

The sergeant put the outburst down to first-kill nerves and failed to report it. Perhaps that was a mistake. For authority failed to notice that Adam Munro was not completely, not one hundred per cent, obedient. Not ever again.

Six months later he was urged to consider himself as potential officer material and extend his time in the army to three years so as to qualify for a short-service commission. Tired of Cyprus, he did so and was posted back to England, to the Officer Cadet Training Unit at Eaton Hall. Three months later he got his 'pip' as a second lieutenant.

While form-filling at Eaton Hall, he had mentioned that he was fluent in

French and German. One day he was casually tested in both languages and his claim proved to be correct. Just after his commissioning it was suggested he might like to apply for the Joint Services Russian language course, which in those days was situated at a camp called Little Russia at Bodmin in Cornwall. The alternative was regimental duties at the barracks in Scotland, so he agreed. Within six months he emerged not merely fluent in Russian but virtually able to pass for a Russian.

In 1957, despite considerable pressure from the regiment to stay on, he left the army, for he had decided he wanted to be a foreign correspondent. He had seen a few of them in Cyprus and thought he would prefer the job to office work. At the age of twenty-one he joined the *Scotsman* in his native Edinburgh as a cub reporter, and two years later he moved to London where he was taken on by Reuters, the international news agency with its head-quarters at 85 Fleet Street. In the summer of 1960 his languages again came to his rescue: at twenty-four he was posted to the Reuters office in West Berlin as second man to the bureau chief, the late Alfred Kluehs. That was the summer before the Wall went up, and within three months he had met Valentina, the woman who he now realized was the only one he had ever really loved in his life.

A man sat down beside him and coughed. Munro jerked himself out of his reverie. Teaching tradecraft to sprogs one week, he told himself, and forgetting the basic rules a fortnight later. Never slacken attention before a meet.

The Russian looked at him uncomprehendingly, but Munro wore the necessary polka-dot tie. Slowly the Russian put a cigarette in his mouth, eyes on Munro. Corny, but it still worked; Munro took out his lighter and held the flame to the cigarette tip.

'Ronald collapsed at his desk two weeks ago,' he said softly and calmly. 'Ulcers, I'm afraid. I am Michael. I've been asked to take over from him. Oh, and perhaps you can help me; is it true that the Ostankino TV tower is the highest structure in Moscow?'

The Russian officer in plain clothes exhaled smoke and relaxed. The words were exactly the ones established by Lessing, whom he had known only as Ronald.

'Yes,' he replied. 'It is five hundred and forty metres high.'

He had a folded newspaper in his hand, which he laid on the seat between them. Munro's folded raincoat slipped off his knees to the ground. He retrieved it, re-folded it and placed it on top of the newspaper. The two men ignored each other for ten minutes, while the Russian smoked. Finally he rose and stubbed the butt into the ground, bending as he did so.

'A fortnight's time,' muttered Munro. 'The men's toilet under G block at the New State Circus. During the clown Popov's act. The show starts at seven-thirty.'

The Russian moved away and continued strolling. Munro surveyed the scene calmly for ten minutes. No one showed interest. He scooped up the mackintosh, newspaper and buff envelope inside it and returned by metro to Kutuzovsky Prospekt. The envelope contained an up-to-date list of Red Army officer postings.

2

While Adam Munro was changing trains at Revolution Square shortly before 11 a.m. that morning of 10th June, a convoy of a dozen sleek, black Zil limousines was sweeping through the Borovitsky Gate in the Kremlin wall a hundred feet above his head and one thousand three hundred feet southwest of him. The Soviet Politburo was about to begin a meeting that would change history.

The Kremlin is a triangular compound with its apex, dominated by the Sobakin Tower, pointing due north. On all sides it is protected by a fifty-foot wall studded by eighteen towers and penetrated by four gates.

The southern two-thirds of this triangle is the tourist area where docile parties troop along to admire the cathedrals, halls and palaces of the long-dead tsars. At the mid-section is a cleared swathe of tarmacadam, patrolled by guards, an invisible dividing line across which tourists may not step. But the cavalcade of hand-built limousines that morning purred across this open space towards the three buildings in the northern part of the Kremlin.

The smallest of these is the Kremlin Theatre to the east. Half exposed and half hidden behind the theatre stands the building of the Council of Ministers, seemingly the home of the government, in as much as the ministers meet here. But the real government of the USSR lies not in the Cabinet of Ministers, but in the Politburo, the tiny, exclusive group who constitute the pinnacle of the Central Committee of the Communist Party of the Soviet Union, or CPSU.

The third building is the biggest. It lies along the western façade, just behind the wall's crenellations, overlooking the Alexandrovsky Gardens down below. In shape it is a long, slim rectangle running north. The southern end is the old Arsenal, a museum for antique weaponry. But just behind the Arsenal the interior walls are blocked off. To reach the upper section, one must arrive from outside and penetrate a high, wrought-iron barrier that spans the gap between the ministers' building and the Arsenal. The limousines that morning swept through the wrought-iron gates and came to rest beside the upper entrance to the secret building.

In shape the upper Arsenal is a hollow rectangle; inside is a narrow courtyard running north/south and dividing the complex into two even narrower blocks of apartments and offices. There are four storeys including the attics. Halfway up the inner, eastern office block, on the third floor, overlooking the courtyard only and screened from prying eyes, is the room where the Politburo meets every Thursday morning to hold sway over 250 million Soviet citizens and scores of millions more who like to think they dwell outside the boundaries of the Russian empire.

For an empire it is. Although in theory the Russian Republic is one of fifteen republics that make up the Soviet Union, in effect the Russia of the tsars, ancient or modern, rules the other fourteen non-Russian republics with a rod of iron. The three arms Russia uses and needs to implement this rule are: the Red Army, including as it always does the navy and air force; the Committee of State Security, or KGB, with its 100,000 staffers, 300,000 armed troops and 600,000 informers; and the Party Organizations Section of the General Secretariat of the Central Committee, controlling the Party cadres in every place of work, thought, abode, study and leisure from the Arctic to the hills of Persia, from the fringes of Brunswick to the shores of the Sea of Japan. And that is just inside the empire.

The room in which the Politburo meets in the Arsenal of the Kremlin is about fifty feet long and twenty-five feet wide, not enormous for the power enclosed in it. It is decorated in the heavy, marbled decor favoured by the Party bosses, but dominated by a long, T-shaped table topped in green baize.

That 10th of June morning, 1982, was unusual, for they had received no agenda, just a summons. And the men who grouped at the table to take their places sensed with the perceptive collective nose for danger that had brought them all to this pinnacle of power that something of importance was afoot.

Seated in his usual chair at the centre point of the head of the T was the chief of them all, Maxim Rudin. Ostensibly his superiority lay in his title of president of the USSR. But nothing except the weather is ever quite what it appears in Russia. His real power came to him through his title of general secretary of the Communist Party of the USSR. As such, he was also chairman of the Central Committee, and chairman of the Politburo.

At the age of seventy-one he was craggy, brooding and immensely cunning; had he not been the latter he would never have occupied the chair that had once supported Stalin (who rarely called Politburo meetings), Malenkov, Khrushchev and Brezhnev. To his left and right he was flanked by four secretaries from his own personal secretariat, men loyal to him personally above all else. Behind him, at each corner of the north wall of the chamber, was a small table. At one sat two stenographers, a man and a woman, taking down every word in shorthand. At the other, as a counter-check, two men hunched over the slowly turning spools of a tape recorder. There was a spare recorder to take over during spool changes.

The other twelve members of the Politburo ranged themselves, six a side, down the stem of the T-shaped table, facing jotting pads, carafes of water, ashtrays. At the far end of this arm of the table was one single chair. The Politburo men checked numbers to make sure no one was missing. For the empty seat was the penal chair, sat in only by a man on his last appearance in that room, a man forced to listen to his own denunciation by his former colleagues, a man facing disgrace, ruin, and once, not long ago, death at the Black Wall of the Lubyanka. The custom has always been to delay the condemned man until, on entering, he finds all seats taken and only the penal chair free. Then he knows. But this morning it was empty. And all were present.

Rudin leaned back and surveyed the twelve through half-closed eyes, the smoke from his inevitable cigarette drifting past his face. He still favoured the old-style Russian papyross, half tobacco and half thin cardboard tube, the tube nipped twice between finger and thumb to filter the smoke. His aides had been taught to pass them to him one after the other, and his doctors to shut up.

To his left on the stem of the table was Vassili Petrov, aged forty-nine, Rudin's own protégé and young for the job he held, head of the Party Organizations Section of the General Secretariat of the Central Committee. Rudin could count on Petrov in the trouble that lay ahead. Beside Petrov was the veteran foreign minister, Dmitri Rykov, who would side with Rudin because he had nowhere else to go. Beyond him was Yuri Ivanenko, slim and ruthless at fifty-three, standing out like a sore thumb in his elegant London-tailored suit as if flaunting his sophistication to a group of men who hated all forms of Western-ness. Picked personally by Rudin to be chairman of the KGB, Ivanenko would side with him simply because the opposition would come from quarters who hated Ivanenko and wanted him destroyed.

On the other side of the table sat Yefrem Vishnayev, also young for the job, like half the post-Brezhnev Politburo. At fifty-five he was the Party theoretician, spare, ascetic, disapproving, the scourge of dissidents and deviationists, guardian of the Marxist purity and consumed by a pathological loathing of the capitalist West. The opposition would come here, Rudin knew. By his side was Marshal Nikolai Kerensky, aged sixty-three, defence minister and chief of the Red Army. He would go where the interests of the Red Army led him.

That left seven, including Komarov, responsible for agriculture. He was sitting white-faced because he, like Rudin and Ivanenko alone, knew roughly what was to come. The KGB chief betrayed no emotion, the rest did not know.

'It' came when Rudin gestured to one of the Kremlin praetorian guards at the door at the far end of the room to admit the person waiting in fear and trembling outside.

'Let me present Professor Ivan Ivanovich Yakovlev, comrades,' Rudin growled as the man advanced timorously to the end of the table and stood waiting, his sweat-damp report in his hands. 'The professor is our senior agronomist and grain specialist from the Ministry of Agriculture and member of the Academy of Sciences. He has a report for our attention. Proceed, professor.'

Rudin, who had read the report several days earlier in the privacy of his study, leaned back and gazed above the man's head at the far ceiling. Ivanenko carefully lit a Western filter kingsize. Komarov wiped his brow and studied his hands. The professor cleared his throat.

'Comrades,' he began hesitantly. No one disagreed that they were comrades. With a deep breath the scientist stared down at his papers and plunged straight into his report. 'Last December and January our long-range weather forecast satellites predicted an unusually damp winter and early spring. As a result and in accordance with habitual scientific practice it was decided at the Ministry of Agriculture that our seed grain for the spring planting should be dressed with a prophylactic dressing to inhibit fungoid infections that would probably be prevalent as a result of the dampness. This has been done many times before.

'The dressing selected was a dual-purpose seed dressing: an organo-mercury compound to inhibit fungoid attack on the germinating grain and a pesticide and bird-repellant called Lindane. It was agreed in scientific committee that because the USSR, following the unfortunate damage through frost to the winter wheat crop, would need at least a hundred and forty million tons of crop from the spring wheat plantings, it would be necessary to sow six and a quarter million tons of seed grain.'

All eyes were on him now, the fidgeting stilled. The Politburo members could smell danger a mile off. Only Komarov, the one responsible for agriculture, stared at the table in misery. Several eyes swivelled to him, sensing blood.

The professor swallowed hard and went on. 'At the rate of two ounces of organo-mercury seed dressing per ton of grain, the requirement was for three hundred and fifty tons of dressing. There were only seventy tons in stock. An immediate order was sent to the manufacturing plant for this dressing at Kuibyshev to get into immediate production to make up the required two hundred and eighty tons.'

'Is there only one such factory?' asked Petrov.

'Yes, comrade. The tonnages required do not justify more factories. The Kuibyshev factory is a major chemical plant, making many insecticides, weed-killers, fertilizers and so forth. The production of the two hundred and eighty tons of this chemical would take less than forty hours.'

'Continue,' ordered Rudin.

'Due to a confusion in communication, the factory was undergoing annual maintenance, and time was running short if the dressing was to be distributed to the one hundred and twenty-seven dressing stations for seed grain scattered across the union, the grain treated, and then taken back to the thousands of state and collective farms in time for planting. So an energetic young official and Party cadre was sent from Moscow to hurry things along. It appears he ordered the workmen to terminate what they were doing, restore the plant to operating order and start it functioning again.'

'He failed to do it in time?' rasped Marshal Kerensky.

'No, comrade marshal, the factory started work again, although the maintenance engineers had not quite finished. But something malfunctioned. A hopper valve. Lindane is a very powerful chemical, and the dosage of the Lindane to the remainder of the organo-mercury compound has to be strictly regulated.

'The valve on the Lindane hopper, although registering one-third open on the control panel, was in fact stuck at full-open. The whole two hundred and eighty tons of dressing was affected.'

'What about quality control?' asked one of the members who had been born on a farm. The professor swallowed again, and wished he could quietly go into exile in Siberia without any more of this torture.

'There was a conjunction of coincidence and error,' he confessed. 'The chief analytical and quality-control chemist was away on holiday at Sochi during the plant close-down. He was summoned back by cable. But because of fog in the Kuibyshev area, he had to divert and continue his return by train. When he arrived, production was complete.'

'The dressing was not tested?' asked Petrov in incredulity. The professor looked more sick than ever.

'The chemist insisted on making quality-control tests. The young functionary from Moscow wanted the entire production shipped at once. An argument ensued. In the event a compromise was reached. The chemist wanted to test every tenth bag of dressing, twenty-eight in all. The functionary insisted he could only have one. That was when the third error occurred.

'The new bags had been stacked along with the reserve of seventy tons left over from last year. In the warehouse one of the loaders, receiving a report to send one single bag to the laboratory for testing, selected one of the old bags. Tests proved it was perfectly in order and the entire consignment was shipped.'

He ended his report. There was nothing more to say. He could have tried to explain that a conjunction of three mistakes – a mechanical malfunction, an error of judgement between two men under pressure and a piece of carelessness by a warehouseman – had combined to produce the catastrophe. But that was not his job, and he did not intend to make lame excuses for other men. The silence in the room was murderous.

Vishnayev came in with icy clarity.

'What exactly is the effect of an excessive component of Lindane in this organo-mercury compound?' he asked.

'Comrade, it causes a toxic effect against the germinating seed in the ground, rather than a protective effect. The seedlings come up, if at all, stunted, sparse and mottled brown. There is virtually no grain yield from such affected stems.'

'And how much of the spring planting has been affected?' asked Vishnayev coldly.

'Just about four-fifths, comrade. The seventy tons of reserve compound was perfectly all right. The two-hundred and eighty tons of new compound was all affected by the jammed hopper valve.'

'And the toxic dressing was all mixed in with seed grain and planted?'

'Yes, comrade.'

Two minutes later the professor was dismissed, to his privacy and his oblivion. Vishnayev turned to Komarov.

'Forgive my ignorance, comrade, but it would appear you had some foreknowledge of this affair. What has happened to the functionary who produced this . . . cock-up?' He used a crude Russian expression that refers to a pile of dog-mess on the pavement.

Ivanenko cut in. 'He is in our hands,' he said, 'along with the analytic chemist who deserted his function, the warehouseman, who is simply of exceptionally low intelligence, and the maintenance team of engineers who claim they demanded and received written instructions to wind up their work before they had finished.'

'This functionary; has he talked?' asked Vishnayev.

Ivanenko considered a mental image of the broken man in the cellars beneath the Lubyanka.

'Extensively,' he said.

'Is he a saboteur, a fascist agent?'

'No,' said Ivanenko with a sigh. 'Just an idiot; an ambitious apparatchik trying to over-fulfil his orders. You can believe me on that one. We do know by now the inside of that man's skull.'

'Then one last question, just so that we can all be sure of the dimensions of this affair.' Vishnayev swung back to the unhappy Komarov. 'We already know we will only save fifty million tons of the expected hundred million from the winter wheat. How much will we now get from the spring wheat this coming October?'

Komarov glanced at Rudin who nodded imperceptibly.

'Out of the hundred-and-forty-million-ton target for the spring-sown wheat and other grains, we cannot reasonably expect more than fifty million tons,' he said quietly.

The meeting sat in stunned horror.

'That means a total yield over both crops of one hundred million tons,' breathed Petrov. 'A national shortfall of a hundred and forty million tons. We could have taken a shortfall of fifty, even seventy million tons. We've done it before, endured the shortages and bought what we could from elsewhere. But this. . . .'

Rudin closed the meeting.

'We have as big a problem here as we have ever confronted, Chinese and American imperialism included. I propose we adjourn and separately seek some suggestions. It goes without saying that this news does not pass outside those present in this room. Our next meeting will be today week.'

As the thirteen men and the four aides at the top table came to their feet, Petrov turned to the impassive Ivanenko.

'This doesn't mean shortages,' he muttered. 'This means famine.'

The Soviet Politburo descended to their chauffeur-driven Zil limousines still absorbing the knowledge that a weedy professor of agronomy had just placed a time-bomb under one of the world's two super-powers.

Adam Munro's thoughts a week later as he sat in the circle at the Bolshoi Theatre on Karl Marx Prospekt were not on crops, but on love; and not for the excited embassy secretary beside him who had prevailed on him to take her to the ballet.

He was not a great fan of ballet, though he conceded he liked some of the music. But the grace of the *entrechats* and *fouettés*, or, as he called it, the jumping-about, left him cold. By the second act of 'Giselle', the evening's offering, his thoughts were straying back again to Berlin.

It had been a beautiful affair, a once-in-a-lifetime love. He was twenty-four, turning twenty-five, and she nineteen, dark and lovely. Because of her job they had had to conduct their affair in secret, furtively meeting in darkened streets so that he could pick her up in his car and take her back to his small flat at the western end of Charlottenburg without anyone seeing. They had loved and talked, she had made him suppers and they had loved again.

At first the clandestine nature of their affair, like married people slipping away from the world and each other's partners, had added spice, piquancy to the loving. But by the summer of '61 when the forests of Berlin were ablaze with leaves and flowers, when there was boating on the lakes and swimming from the shores, it had become cramped, frustrating. That was when he had asked her to marry him, and she had almost agreed. She might still have agreed, but then came the Wall. It was completed on 14th August 1961, but it was obvious for a week that it was going up.

That was when she made her decision, and they loved for the last time. She could not, she told him, abandon her parents to what would happen to them; to the disgrace, the loss of her father's trusted job, her mother's beloved apartment for which she had waited so many years through the dark times. She could not destroy her young brother's chances of a good education and prospects; and finally she could not bear to know that she would never see her beloved homeland again.

So she left, and he watched from the shadows as she slipped back into the East through the last uncompleted section in the Wall, sad and lonely and heart-broken – and very, very beautiful.

He had never seen her again, and he had never mentioned her to anyone, guarding her memory with his quiet Scottish secretiveness. He never let on that he had loved and still loved a Russian girl called Valentina who had been a secretary/stenographer with the Soviet delegation to the Four-Power Conference in Berlin. And that, as he well knew, was far out against the rules.

After Valentina, Berlin had palled. A year later he was transferred by Reuters to Paris, and it was two years after that, when he was back in London, kicking his heels in head office in Fleet Street, that a civilian he had known in Berlin, a man who had worked at the British headquarters there – Hitler's old Olympic stadium – had made a point of looking him up and renewing acquaintance. There had been a dinner and another man had joined them. The acquaintance from the stadium had excused himself and left during coffee. The newcomer was friendly and non-committal. But by the second brandy he made his point.

'Some of my associates in the firm,' he said with disarming diffidence, 'were wondering if you could do us a little favour.'

That was the first time Munro had heard the term 'the firm'. Later he would learn the terminology. To those in the Anglo-American alliance of intelligence services, a strange and guarded, but ultimately vital, alliance, the SIS was always called 'the firm'. To its employees those in the counter-intelligence arm, the M15, were 'the colleagues'. The CIA at Langley, Virginia, was 'the company' and its staff 'the cousins'. On the opposite side worked 'the opposition' whose headquarters was at Number 2, Dzerzhinsky Square, Moscow, named after the founder of the old Cheka, Feliks

THE DEVIL'S ALTERNATIVE 823

Dzerzhinsky, Lenin's secret police boss. This building would always be known as 'the centre' and the territory east of the Iron Curtain as 'the bloc'.

The meeting in the London restaurant was in December 1964, and the proposal, confirmed later in a small flat in Chelsea, was for a 'little run into the bloc'. He made it in the spring of 1965 while ostensibly covering the Leipzig Fair in East Germany. It was a pig of a run.

He left Leipzig at the right time and drove to the meet in Dresden, close by the Albertinium Museum. The package in his inner pocket felt like five Bibles, and everyone seemed to be looking at him. The East German army officer who knew where the Russians were locating their tactical rockets in the Saxon hillsides showed up half an hour late, by which time two People's Policemen undoubtedly *were* watching him. The swap of packages went off all right, somewhere in the bushes of the nearby park. Then he returned to his car and set off southwest for the Gera crossroads and the Bavarian border checkpoint. On the outskirts of Dresden a local driver rammed him from the front offside, although Munro had right of way. He had not even had time to transfer the package to the hiding place between the boot and the back seat: it was still in the breast pocket of his blazer.

There were two gut-wrenching hours in a local police station, every moment dreading the command, 'Turn out your pockets, please, *mein herr*.' There was enough up against his breastbone to collect him twenty-five years in Potma labour camp. Eventually he was allowed to go. Then the battery went flat and four People's Policemen had to push-start him.

The front offside wheel was screaming from a fractured roller-bearing inside the hub, and it was suggested he might like to stay overnight and get it mended. He pleaded that his visa time expired at midnight – which it did – and set off again. He made the checkpoint on the Saale River between Plauen in East Germany and Hof in the West ten minutes before midnight, having driven at twenty miles per hour all the way, rending the night air with the screaming at the front wheel. When he chugged past the Bavarian guards on the other side, he was wet with sweat.

A year later he left Reuters and accepted a suggestion to sit for the Civil Service entrance examination as a late entrant. He was twenty-nine.

The CSE examinations are unavoidable for anyone trying to join the Civil Service. Based on the results, the Treasury has first choice of the cream, which enables that department to foul up the British economy with impeccable academic references. The Foreign and Commonwealth Office gets next choice, and as Munro had a first-class pass he had no trouble entering the foreign service, usually the cover for staffers of the firm.

In the next sixteen years he had specialized in economic intelligence matters and the Soviet Union, though he had never been there before. He had foreign postings in Turkey, Austria and Mexico. In 1967 he had married, just turned thirty-one. But after the honeymoon it had been an increasingly loveless union, a mistake, and it was quietly ended six years later. Since then there had been affairs, of course, and they were all known to the firm, but he had stayed single.

There was one affair he had never mentioned to the firm, and had the fact of it, and his covering up of it, leaked out he would have been fired on the spot. On joining the service, like everyone else, he had to write a complete life story of himself, followed by a *viva voce* examination by a senior officer.

This procedure is repeated every five years of service. Among the matters of interest are inevitably any emotional or social involvement with personnel from behind the Iron Curtain – or anywhere else, for that matter.

The first time he was asked, something inside him rebelled, as it had in the olive grove in Cyprus. He knew he was loyal, that he would never be suborned over the matter of Valentina, even if the opposition knew about it, which he was certain they did not. If an attempt were ever made to blackmail him over it, he would admit it and resign, but never accede. He just did not want the fingers of other men, not to mention filing clerks, rummaging through a part of the most private inside of him. Nobody owns me but me. So he said no to the question, and broke the rules. Once trapped by the lie, he had to stick with it. He repeated it three times in sixteen years. Nothing had ever happened because of it, and nothing ever would happen. He was certain of it. The affair was a secret, dead and buried. It would always be so.

Had he been less deep in his reverie, and not spellbound by the ballet like the girl beside him, he might have noticed something. From a private box high in the left-hand wall of the theatre, he was being observed. Before the lights went up for the *entr'acte*, the watcher had vanished.

The thirteen men who grouped around the Politburo table in the Kremlin the following day were subdued and watchful, sensing that the report of the professor of agronomy could trigger a faction fight such as there had not been since Khrushchev fell.

Rudin as usual surveyed them all through his drifting spire of cigarette smoke. Petrov of Party Organizations was in his customary seat to his left, with Ivanenko of the KGB beyond him. Rykov of Foreign Affairs shuffled his papers, Vishnayev the theoretician and Kerensky of the Red Army sat in stony silence. Rudin surveyed the other seven, calculating which way they would jump if it came to a fight.

There were the three non-Russians: Vitautas the Balt, from Vilnius, Lithuania; Chavadze the Georgian, from Tbilisi; and Mukhamed the Tadjik, an oriental and born a Moslem. The presence of each was a sop to the minorities, but in fact each had paid the price to be there. Each, Rudin knew, was completely Russified; the price had been high, higher than a Great Russian would have to pay. Each had been first party secretary for his republic, and two still were. Each had overlorded programmes of vigorous repression against their fellow nationals, crushing dissidents, nationalists, poets, writers, artists, intelligentsia and workers who had even hinted at a less than one hundred per cent acceptance of the rule of Great Russia over them. Each would not go back without the protection of Moscow, and each would side, if it came to it, with the faction which would ensure their survival; that is, the winning one. Rudin did not relish the prospect of a faction fight, but he had held it in mind since he had first read Professor Yakovlev's report in the privacy of his study.

That left four, all Russians. There was Komarov of agriculture, still extremely ill at ease; Stepanov, head of the trade unions; Shushkin, responsible for liaison with foreign Communist parties worldwide; and Petryanov with special responsibilities for economics and the industrial plan.

'Comrades,' began Rudin slowly, 'you have all studied the Yakovlev report at your leisure. You have all observed Comrade Komarov's separate report to the effect that next September/October our aggregate grain yield will fall short of target by close to one hundred and forty million tons of grain?'

The discussion lasted an hour. It was bitter, acrimonious but virtually unanimous. Such a shortage of grain would lead to privations that had not been seen since the Second World War. If the state bought in even an irreducible minimum to make bread for the cities, the countryside would be left with almost nothing. The slaughter of livestock, as the winter snows covered the grazing lands and the beasts were left without forage or feed grains, would strip the Soviet Union of every four-footed animal. It would take a generation to recover the livestock herds. To leave even the minimum of grain on the land would starve the cities.

At last Rudin cut them short.

'Very well. If we insist on accepting the famine, both in grains and, as a consequence, in meat several months later, what will be the outcome in terms of national discipline?'

Petrov broke the ensuing silence. He admitted that there existed a ground-swell of restiveness already among the broad masses of the people, evidenced by a recent rash of small outbreaks of disorder and resignations from the Party, all reported back to him in the Central Committee through the million tendrils of the Party machine. In the face of a true famine, many Party cadres could side with the proletariat.

The non-Russians nodded in agreement. In their republics the grip of the centre was always likely to be less total than inside Russia itself.

'We could strip the six East European satellites,' suggested Petryanov, not even bothering to refer to the East Europeans as fraternal comrades.

'Poland and Romania would burst into flame for a start,' countered Shushkin, the liaison man with Eastern Europe. 'Probably Hungary to follow suit.'

'The Red Army could deal with them,' snarled Marshal Kerensky.

'Not three at a time, not nowadays,' said Rudin.

'We are still only talking of a total acquisition of ten million tons,' said Komarov. 'It's not enough.'

'Comrade Stepanov?' asked Rudin.

The head of the state-controlled trade unions chose his words carefully.

'In the event of genuine famine this winter and next spring through summer,' he said, studying his pencil, 'it would not be possible to guarantee the absence of the outbreak of acts of disorder, perhaps on a wide scale.'

Ivanenko, sitting quietly gazing at the Western kingsize filter between his right forefinger and thumb, smelled more than smoke in his nostrils. He had smelled fear many times; in the arrest procedure, in the interrogation rooms, in the corridors of his craft. He smelled it now. He and the men around him were powerful, privileged, protected. But he knew them all well; he had the files. And he, who knew no fear for himself as the soul-dead know no fear, knew also that they all feared one thing more than war itself. If the Soviet proletariat, long-suffering, patient, ox-like in the face of deprivation, ever went berserk. . . .

All eyes were on him. Public 'acts of disorder', and the repression of them, were his country.

'I could,' he said evenly, 'cope with one Novocherkassk.' There was a hiss of indrawn breath down the table. 'I could cope with ten, or even twenty. But the combined resources of the KGB could not cope with fifty.'

The mention of Novocherkassk brought the spectre right out of the wallpaper as he knew it would. On 2nd June 1962, almost exactly twenty years earlier, the great industrial city of Novocherkassk erupted in worker riots. But twenty years had not dimmed the memory.

It had started when by a stupid coincidence one ministry raised the price of meat and butter, while another cut wages at the giant NEVZ locomotive works by thirty per cent. In the resulting riots the shouting workers took over the city for three days, an unheard-of phenomenon in the Soviet Union. Equally unheard of, they booed the local Party leaders into trembling self-imprisonment in their own headquarters, shouted down a full Soviet general, charged ranks of armed soldiers and pelted the tanks with mud until the vision-slits clogged up and the tanks ground to a halt.

The response of Moscow was massive. Every single line, every road, every telephone, every track in and out of Novocherkassk was sealed. The city became a vacuum, so the news should not leak out. Two divisions of KGB special troops had to be drafted to finish off the affair and mop up the rioters. There were eighty-six civilians shot down in the streets, over three hundred wounded. None ever returned home, none were buried locally. Not only the wounded, but every single member of every family of a dead or wounded man, woman or child, was deported to the camps of Gulag, lest they persist in asking after their relatives and thus keeping memory of the affair alive. Every trace was wiped out, but two decades later it was still well-remembered inside the Kremlin.

When Ivanenko dropped his bombshell there was silence again round the table. Rudin broke it.

'Very well then, the conclusion seems unescapable. We will have to buy in from abroad as never before. Comrade Komarov, what is the minimum we would need to buy abroad to avoid disaster?'

'Secretary-General, if we leave the irreducible minimum on the country-side, and use every scrap of our thirty million tons of national reserve, we will need fifty-five million tons of grain from outside. That would mean the entire surplus, in a year of bumper crops, from both the USA and Canada,' Komarov answered.

'They'll never sell it to us,' shouted Kerensky.

'They are not fools, Comrade Marshal,' Ivanenko cut in quietly. 'Their Condor satellites must have warned them already that something is wrong with our spring wheat. But they cannot know what, or how much. Not yet, but by the autumn they will have a pretty fair idea. And they are greedy, endlessly greedy for more money. I can raise the production levels in the gold mines of Siberia and Kolyma, ship more labour there from the camps of Mordovia. The money for such a purchase we can raise.'

'I agree with you on one point,' said Rudin, 'but not on the other, Comrade Ivanenko. They may have the wheat, we may have the gold, but there is a chance, just a chance, that this time they will require concessions.'

At the word 'concession' everyone stiffened.

'What kind of concession?' asked Marshal Kerensky suspiciously.

'One never knows until one negotiates,' said Rudin, 'but it's a possibility we have to face. They might require concessions in military areas. . . .'

'Never,' shouted Kerensky, on his feet and red-faced.

'Our options are somewhat closed,' countered Rudin. 'We appear to have agreed that a severe and nationwide famine is not tolerable. It would set back the progress of the Soviet Union and thence the global rule of Marxist-Leninism by a decade, maybe more. We need the grain; there are no more options. If the imperialists exact concessions in the military field, we may have to accept a drawback lasting two or three years; but only in order all the better to advance after the recovery.'

There was a general murmur of assent. Rudin was on the threshold of carrying his meeting.

Then Vishnayev struck. He rose slowly as the buzz subsided.

'The issues before us, comrades,' he began with silky reasonableness, 'are massive, with incalcuable consequences. I propose that this is too early to reach any binding conclusion. I propose an adjournment until this day fortnight while we all think over what has been said and suggested.'

His ploy worked. He had bought his time, as Rudin privately feared he would. The meeting agreed, ten against three, to adjourn without a resolution.

Yuri Ivanenko had reached the ground floor and was about to step into his waiting limousine when he felt a touch at his elbow. Standing beside him was a tall, beautifully tailored major of the Kremlin Guard.

'The Comrade Secretary-General would like a word with you in his private suite, Comrade Chairman,' he said quietly. Without another word he turned and headed down a corridor leading along the building away from the main doorway. Ivanenko followed. As he tailed the major's perfectly fitting barathea jacket, fawn whipcord trousers and gleaming boots, it occurred to him that if any one of the men of the Politburo came to sit one day in the penal chair, the subsequent arrest would be carried out by his own KGB special troops, called border guards, with their bright green cap bands and shoulder-flashes, the sword-and-shield insignia of the KGB above their peaks.

But if he, Ivanenko alone, were to be arrested, the KGB would not be given the job, as they could not be trusted almost thirty years earlier to arrest Lavrenti Beria. It would be these elegant, disdainful Kremlin elite guards, the praetorians round the seat of ultimate power, who would do the job. Perhaps the self-assured major walking before him, and he would have no qualms at all.

They reached a private lift, ascended to the third floor again, and Ivanenko was shown into the private apartment of Maxim Rudin.

Stalin had used to live in seclusion right in the heart of the Kremlin, but Malenkov and Khrushchev had ended the practice, preferring to establish themselves and most of their cronies in luxury apartments in a nondescript (from the outside) complex of apartment blocks, at the far end of

Kutuzovsky Prospekt. But when Rudin's wife had died two years earlier, he had moved back to the Kremlin.

It was a comparatively modest apartment for this most powerful of men: six rooms including a fitted kitchen, marbled bathroom, private study, sitting room, dining room and bedroom. Rudin lived alone, ate sparingly, dispensed with most luxuries and was cared for by an elderly cleaning woman and the ever-present Misha, a hulking but silent-moving ex-soldier, who never spoke but was never far away. When Ivanenko entered the study at Misha's silent gesture, he found Maxim Rudin and Vassili Petrov already there.

Rudin waved him to a vacant chair and began without preamble. 'I've asked you both here because there is trouble brewing and we all know it,' he rumbled. 'I'm old and I smoke too much. Two weeks ago I went out to see the quacks at Kuntsevo. They took some tests. Now they want me back again.'

Petrov shot Ivanenko a sharp look. The KGB chief was still impassive. He knew about the visit to the super-exclusive clinic in the woods southwest of Moscow; one of the doctors there reported back to him.

'The question of the succession hangs in the air, and we all know it,' Rudin continued. 'We all also know, or should, that Vishnayev wants it.'

Rudin turned to Ivanenko.

'If he gets it, Yuri Aleksandrovich, and he's young enough, that will be the end of you. He never approved of a professional taking over the KGB. He'll put his own man, Krivoi, in your place.'

Ivanenko steepled his hands and gazed back at Rudin. Three years earlier Rudin had broken a long tradition in Soviet Russia of imposing a political Party luminary as chairman and chief of the KGB. Shelepin, Semichastny, Andropov – they had all been Party men placed over the KGB from outside the service. Only the professional Ivan Serov had nearly made it to the top through a tide of blood. Then Rudin had plucked Ivanenko from among the senior deputies to Andropov and favoured him as the new chief.

That was not the only break with tradition. Ivanenko was young for the job of the world's most powerful policeman and spymaster. Then again, he had served as an agent in Washington twenty years earlier, always a base for suspicion among the xenophobes of the Politburo. He had a taste for Western elegance in his private life. And he was reputed, though none dared mention it, to have certain private reservations about dogma. That, for Vishnayev at least, was absolutely unforgivable.

'If he takes over, now or ever, that will also mark your cards, Vassili Alexeivitch,' Rudin told Petrov. In private he was prepared to call both his protégés by their familiar patronymics; never in public session.

Petrov nodded that he understood. He and Anatoly Krivoi had worked together in the Party Organizations section of the General Secretariat of the Central Committee. Krivoi had been older and senior. He had expected the top job, but when it fell vacant Rudin had preferred Petrov for the post that sooner or later carried the ultimate accolade, a seat on the all-powerful Politburo. Krivoi, embittered, had accepted the courtship of Vishnayev and had taken a post as the Party theoretician's chief of staff and right-hand man. But Krivoi still wanted Petrov's job.

Neither Ivanenko nor Petrov had forgotten that it was Vishnayev's predecessor as Party theoretician, Mikhail Suslov, who had put together the
majority that toppled Khrushchev in 1964.

Rudin let his words sink in. 'Yuri, you know my successor cannot be you,
not with your background.' Ivanenko inclined his head; he had no illusions
on that score. 'But,' Rudin resumed, 'you and Vassili together can keep this
country on a steady course, if you stick together and behind me. Next year,
I'm going, one way or the other. And when I go, I want you, Vassili, in this
chair.'

The silence between the two younger men was electric. Neither could
recall any predecessor of Rudin ever having been so forthcoming. Stalin had
suffered a heart attack and been finished off by his own Politburo as he
prepared to liquidate them all; Beria had tried for power and been arrested
and shot by his fearful colleagues; Malenkov had fallen in disgrace, likewise
Khrushchev; Brezhnev had kept them all guessing till the last minute.

Rudin stood up to signal the reception was at an end.

'One last thing,' he said. 'Vishnayev is up to something. He's going to try
and do a Suslov on me over this wheat foul-up. If he succeeds, we're finished,
perhaps Russia, too. Because he's an extremist; he's impeccable on theory
but impossible on practicalities. Now I have to know what he's doing, what
he's going to spring, who he's trying to enlist. Find out for me. Find out in
fourteen days.'

The headquarters of the KGB, the Centre, is a huge stone complex of office
blocks taking up the whole northeastern façade of Dzerzhinsky Square at the
top end of Karl Marx Prospekt. The complex is actually a hollow square, the
front and both wings being devoted to the KGB, the rear block being
Lubyanka interrogation centre and prison. The proximity of the one to the
other, with only the inner courtyard separating them, enables the interrogators to stay well on top of their work.

The chairman's office is on the third floor, left of the main doorway. But he
always comes by limousine with chauffeur and bodyguard through the side
gateway. The office is a big, ornate room with mahogany-panelled walls and
luxurious oriental carpets. One wall carries the required portrait of Lenin,
another a picture of Feliks Dzerzhinsky himself. Through the four, tall,
draped, bulletproof windows overlooking the square, the observer must look
at yet another representation of the Cheka's founder, standing twenty feet
tall in bronze in the centre of the square, sightless eyes staring down Marx
Prospekt to Revolution Square.

Ivanenko disliked the heavy, fustian, over-stuffed and brocaded decor of
Soviet officialdom, but there was little he could do about the office. The desk
alone, of the decor inherited from his predessor Andropov, he appreciated. It
was immense and adorned with seven telephones. The most important was
the Kremlevka, linking him directly with the Kremlin and Rudin. Next was
the Vertushka, in KGB green, which linked him with other Politburo
members and the Central Committee. Others linked him through high-
frequency circuits to the principal KGB representatives throughout the
Soviet Union and the East European satellites. Still others went direct to

Ministry of Defence and its intelligence arm, the GRU. All through separate exchanges. It was on this last one that he took the call for which he had been waiting ten days, that afternoon three days before the end of June.

If was a brief call, from a man who called himself Arkady. Ivanenko had instructed the exchange to accept Arkady and put him straight through. The conversation was short.

'Better face to face,' said Ivanenko shortly. 'Not now, not here. At my house this evening.' He put the phone down.

Most senior Soviet leaders never take their work home with them. In fact almost all Russians have two distinct personae: they have their official life and their private life, and never if possible shall the twain meet. The higher one gets, the greater the divide. As with the Mafia dons, whom the Politburo chiefs remarkably resemble, wives and families are simply not to be involved, even by listening to business talk, in the usually less-than-noble affairs that make up official life.

Ivanenko was different, the main reason why he was distrusted by the risen apparatchiks of the Politburo. For the oldest reason in the world he had no wife and family. Nor did he choose to live near the others, most of them content to dwell cheek by jowl with each other in the apartments on the western end of Kutuzovsky Prospekt on weekdays, and in neighbouring villas grouped around Zhukovka and Usovo at weekends. Members of the Soviet elite never like to be too far from each other.

Soon after·taking over the KGB Yuri Ivanenko had found a handsome old house in the Arbat, the once fine residential town quarter of central Moscow favoured before the revolution by merchants. Within six months teams of KGB builders, painters and decorators had restored it – an impossible feat in Soviet Russia save for a Politburo member.

Having restored the building to its former elegance, albeit with the most modern security and alarm devices, Ivanenko had no trouble either in furnishing it with the ultimate in Soviet status symbols – Western furniture. The kitchen was the last cry in California-convenience, the entire room flown to Moscow from Sears Roebuck in packing crates. The living room and bedroom were panelled in Swedish pine via Finland, and the bathroom was sleek in marble and tile. Ivanenko himself occupied only the upper floor, which was a self-contained suite of rooms and also included his study/music room with its wall-to-wall stereo deck by Philips, and a library of foreign and forbidden books, in English, French and German, all of which he spoke. There was a dining room off the living room, and a sauna off the bedroom to complete the floor area of the upper storey.

The staff of chauffeur, bodyguard and personal valet, all KGB men, lived on the ground floor which also housed the drive-in garage. Such was the house to which he returned after work and awaited his caller.

Arkady, when he came, was a thick-set, ruddy-faced man in civilian clothes, though he would have felt more at home in his usual uniform of a brigadier on the Red Army staff. He was one of Ivanenko's agents inside the army. He hunched forward on his chair in Ivanenko's sitting room, perched on the edge as he talked. The spare KGB chief leaned back at ease, asking a few questions, making the occasional note on a jotting pad. When the brigadier had finished, Ivanenko thanked him and rose to press a wall-button. In seconds the door opened as the valet, a young blond guard of startling good looks, arrived to show the visitor out by the door in the side wall.

Ivanenko considered the news for a long time, feeling increasingly tired and dispirited. So that was what Vishnayev was up to. He would tell Maxim Rudin in the morning.

He had a lengthy bath, redolent with an expensive London bath oil, wrapped himself in a silky robe and sipped an old French brandy. Finally he returned to the bedroom, turned out the lights barring only a small lamp in the corner and stretched himself on the wide coverlet. Picking up the telephone by the bedside he pressed one of the call buttons. It was answered instantly.

'Valodya,' he said quietly, using the affectionate diminutive of Vladimir, 'come up here, will you, please.'

3

The Polish Airlines twin-jet dipped a wing over the wide sweep of the Dnieper River and settled into its final approach to Borispil Airport outside Kiev, capital of the Ukraine. From his window seat Andrew Drake looked down eagerly at the sprawling city beneath him. He was tense with excitement.

Along with the other hundred-plus package tourists from London who had staged through Warsaw earlier in the day, he queued nearly an hour for passport control and customs. At the immigration control he passed his passport under the plate-glass window and waited. The man in the booth was in uniform, border guard uniform, with the green band around his cap and the sword-and-shield emblem of the KGB above its peak.

He looked at the photo in the passport, then stared hard at Drake. 'An-drev . . . Drak?' he asked.

Drake smiled and bobbed his head. 'Andrew Drake,' he corrected gently.

The immigration man glowered back. He examined the visa, issued in London, tore off the incoming half and clipped the exit visa to the passport. Then he handed it back. Drake was in.

On the Intourist coach from the airport to the seventeen-storey Lybid Hotel he took stock again of his fellow travellers. About half were of Ukrainian extraction, visiting the land of their fathers, excited and innocent. The other half were of British stock, just curious tourists. All seemed to have British passports. Drake with his English name was among the second group. He had given no indication he spoke Ukrainian fluently and passable Russian.

During the coach ride they met Ludmilla, their Intourist guide for the tour. She was a Russian, and spoke Russian to the driver who, though a Ukrainian, replied in Russian. As the coach left the airport she smiled brightly and in reasonable English began to describe the tour ahead of them.

Drake glanced at his itinerary: two days in Kiev, trotting round St Sophia's Cathedral ('A wonderful example of Kievan-Rus architecture where Prince Yaroslav the Wise is buried,' warbled Ludmilla from up front); the tenth-century Golden Gate and Vladimir Hill, not to mention the state university, the Academy of Sciences and the Botanical Gardens. No doubt, thought

Drake bitterly, no mention would be made of the 1964 fire at the academy library in which priceless manuscripts, books and archives devoted to Ukrainian national literature, poetry and culture had been destroyed; no mention of the fire brigade failing to arrive for three hours; no mention of the fire-setting by the KGB itself as their answer to the nationalistic writings of the Sixtiers.

After Kiev, there would be a day-trip by hydrofoil to Kaniv, then a day in Ternopol where a man called Miroslav Kaminsky would certainly not be a subject for discussion, and finally on to Lvov. As he had expected, he heard only Russian on the streets of the intensively Russified capital city of Kiev. It was not until Kaniv and Ternopol that he heard Ukrainian spoken extensively. His heart sang to hear it spoken so widely by so many people, and his only regret was that he had to keep saying, 'I'm sorry, do you speak English?' But he would wait, until he could visit the two addresses that he had memorized so well he could say them backwards.

Five thousand miles away the United States President was in conclave with his security adviser Poklewski, Robert Benson of the CIA, and a third man, Myron Fletcher, chief analyst of Soviet grain affairs in the Department of Agriculture.

'Bob, are you sure beyond any reasonable doubt that General Taylor's Condor reconnaissance and your ground reports point to these figures?' he asked, his eye running once again down the columns of numbers in front of him.

The report that his intelligence chief had presented to him via Stanislaw Poklewski five days earlier consisted of a breakdown of the entire Soviet Union into one hundred grain-producing zones. From each zone a sample square, ten miles by ten, had been seen in close-up and its grain problems analysed. From the hundred portraits, his experts and drawn up the nation-wide grain forecast.

'Mr President, if we err, it is on the side of caution, of giving the Soviets a better grain crop than they have any right to expect,' replied Benson.

The President looked across at the man from Agriculture.

'Dr Fletcher, how does this break down in layman's terms?'

'Well, sir, Mr President, for a start one has to deduct at a very minimum ten per cent of the gross harvest to produce a figure of usable grain. Some would say we should deduct twenty per cent. This modest, ten per cent figure is to account for moisture content, foreign matter like stones and grit, dust and earth, losses in transport and wastage through inadequate storage facilities, from which we know they badly suffer.

'Starting from there, one then has to deduct the tonnages the Soviets have to keep on the land itself, right in the countryside, before any state procurements can be made to feed the industrial masses. You will find my table for this on the second page of my separate report.'

President Matthews flicked over the sheets before him and examined the table. It read:

1. *Seed grain*. The tonnage the Soviets must put by for re-planting next year, both for winter wheat and spring-sown wheat .... 10 million tons

2. *Human feeding*. The tonnage that must be set aside to feed the masses who inhabit the rural areas, the state and collective farms and all sub-urban units from hamlets through villages up to townlets of population less than 5000 head ... 28 million tons

3. *Animal feedstuffs*. The tonnage that must be set aside for the feeding of the livestock through the winter months until the spring thaw .... 52 million tons

4. *Irreducible total* .... 90 million tons

5. Representing a gross total, prior to a ten per cent unavoidable wastage deduction, of .... 100 million tons

'I would point out, Mr President,' went on Fletcher, 'that these are not generous figures. They are the absolute minima required before they start feeding the cities. If they cut down on the human rations, the peasants will simply consume the livestock, with or without permission. If they cut back on the animal feedstuff the livestock slaughter will be wholesale; they'll have a meat glut in the winter, then a meat famine for three to four years.'

'Okay, doctor, I'll buy that. Now what about their reserves?'

'We estimate they have a national reserve of thirty million tons. It is unheard of to use up the whole of it, but if they did, that would give them an extra thirty million tons. And they *should* have twenty million tons left over from this year's crop available for the cities – a grand total for their cities of fifty million.'

The President swung back to Benson.

'Bob, what do they have to have by way of state procurements to feed the urban millions?'

'Mr President, 1977 was their worst year for a long time, the year they perpetrated "the Sting" on us. They had a total crop of a hundred and ninety-four million tons. They bought from their own farms sixty-eight million. They *still* needed to buy twenty million from us by subterfuge. Even in 1975, their worst year for a decade and a half, they needed seventy million tons for the cities. And that led to savage shortages. They cannot do nowadays, with a greater population than at that time, with less than eighty-five million tons of state buy-in.'

'Then,' concluded the President, 'by your figures even if they use the total of their national reserve, they are going to need thirty to thirty-five million tons of foreign grain?'

'Right, Mr President,' cut in Poklewski. 'Maybe even more. And we and the Canadians are the only people who are going to have it. Dr Fletcher?'

The man from Agriculture nodded. 'It appears North America is going to have a bumper crop this year. Maybe fifty million tons over domestic requirements for both us and Canada considered together.'

Minutes later Dr Fletcher was escorted out. The debate resumed. Poklewski pressed his point.

'Mr President, this time we have to act. We have to require a *quid pro quo* from them this time around.'

'Linkage?' asked the President suspiciously. 'I know your thoughts on that, Stan. Last time it didn't work; it made things worse. I will not have another repeat of the Jackson Amendment.'

All three men recalled the fate of that piece of legislation with little joy. At the end of 1974 the Americans had introduced the Jackson Amendment which specified in effect that unless the Soviets went easier on the question of Russian–Jewish emigration to Israel, there would be no US trade credits for the purchase of technology and industrial goods. The Politburo under Brezhnev contemptuously rejected the pressure, launched a series of predominantly anti-Jewish show trials, and bought their requirements, with trade credits, from Britain, Germany and Japan.

'The point about a nice little spot of blackmail,' Sir Nigel Irvine, who was in Washington in 1975, had remarked to Bob Benson, 'is that you must be sure the victim simply cannot do without something that you have, and cannot acquire it anywhere else.'

Poklewski had learned this remark from Benson and repeated it to President Matthews, avoiding the word blackmail.

'Mr President, this time around they cannot get their wheat elsewhere. Our wheat surplus is no longer a trading matter. It is a strategic weapon. It is worth ten squadrons of nuclear bombers. There is no way we would sell nuclear technology to Moscow for money. I urge you to invoke the Shannon Act.'

In the wake of 'the Sting' of 1977, the US administration had finally and belatedly in 1980 passed the Shannon Act. This said simply that in any year the Federal Government had the right to buy the option for the US grain surplus at the going rate per ton at the time of the announcement that Washington wished to exercise its option.

The grain speculators had hated it, but the farmers went along. The act smoothed out some of the wilder fluctuations in the world grain prices. In years of glut the farmers had got a too-low price for their grain; in years of shortages the prices had been exceptionally high. If operated, the Shannon Act ensured that the farmers would get a fair price, but the speculators would be out of business. The act also gave the administration a gigantic new weapon in dealing with customer countries, both the aggressive and the humble and poor.

'Very well,' said President Matthews, 'I will activate the Shannon Act. I will authorize the use of Federal funds to buy the futures for the expected surplus of fifty million tons of grain.'

Poklewski was jubilant.

'You won't regret it, Mr President. This time the Soviets will have to deal direct with your presidency, not with middlemen. We have them over a barrel. There is nothing else they can do.'

Yefrem Vishnayev thought differently. At the outset of the Politburo meeting he asked for the floor and got it.

'No one here, comrades, denies that the famine that faces us is not acceptable. No one denies that the surplus foods lie in the decadent capitalist West. It has been suggested that the only thing we can do is to humble ourselves, possibly accept concessions in our military might and therefore in the onward march of Marxism-Leninism in order to buy these surpluses to tide us over.

'Comrades, I disagree and I ask you to join me in rejection of the course of yielding to blackmail and betraying our great inspirator, Lenin. There is one other way; one other way in which we can secure acceptance by the entire Soviet people of rigid rationing at the minimum level, a nationwide upsurge of patriotism and self-sacrifice, and an imposition of that discipline without which we cannot get through the hunger that has to come.

'There is a way in which we can use what little harvest grain we shall cull this autumn, spin out the national reserve until the spring next year, use the meat from our herds and flocks in place of grain, and then, when all is used, turn to Western Europe where the milk lakes are, where the beef and butter mountains are, where the national reserves of ten wealthy nations are.'

'And buy them?' asked Foreign Minister Rykov ironically.

'No, comrade,' replied Vishnayev softly, 'take them. I yield the floor to Comrade Marshal Kerensky. He has a file he would wish each of us to examine.'

Twelve thick files were passed round. Kerensky kept his own and began reading from it. Rudin left his unopened in front of him and smoked steadily. Ivanenko also left his on the table and contemplated Kerensky. He and Rudin had known for four days what the file would be. In collaboration with Vishnayev, Kerensky had brought out of the general staff safe the Plan Boris file, named after Boris Goudonov, the great Russian conqueror. Now it had been brought right up to date.

And it was impressive, as Kerensky spent the next two hours reading it. During the following May the usual massive spring manoeuvres of the Red Army in East Germany would be bigger than ever, but with a difference. These would be no manoeuvres, but the real thing. On the command, all 30,000 tanks and armoured personnel carriers, mobile guns and amphibious craft would swing westwards, hammer across the Elbe and plough into West Germany, heading for France and the Channel ports.

Ahead of them, 50,000 paratroops would drop in over fifty locations to take out the principal tactical nuclear airfields of the French inside France and the Americans and British on German soil. Another 100,000 would drop on the four countries of Scandinavia to possess the capital cities and main arteries, with massive naval back-up from offshore.

The military thrust would avoid the Italian and Iberian peninsulas, whose governments, all partners with the Euro-Communists in office, would be ordered by the Soviet ambassador to stay out of the fight or perish by joining in. Within half a decade later, they would fall like ripe plums anyway. Likewise Greece, Turkey and Yugoslavia. Switzerland would be avoided, Austria used only as a through-route. Both would later be islands in a Soviet sea, and would not last long.

The primary zone of attack and occupation would be the three Benelux countries, France and West Germany. Britain, as a prelude, would be crippled by strikes and confused by the extreme Left which, on instructions, would mount an immediate clamour for non-intervention. London would be informed that if the nuclear Strike Command was used east of the Elbe, Britain would be wiped off the face of the map.

Throughout the entire operation the Soviet Union would be stridently demanding an immediate ceasefire in every capital in the world and the

United Nations, claiming the hostilities were local to West Germany, temporary and caused entirely by a West German pre-emptive strike towards Berlin, a claim that most of the non-German European Left would believe and support.

'And the United States, all this time?' Petrov interrupted. Kerensky looked irritated at being stopped in full flow after ninety minutes.

'The use of tactical nuclear weapons right across the face of Germany cannot be excluded,' pursued Kerensky, 'but the overwhelming majority of them will destroy West Germany, East Germany and Poland, no loss of course for the Soviet Union. Thanks to the weakness of Washington there is no deployment of either Cruise missiles or neutron bombs. Soviet military casualties are estimated at between one hundred and two hundred thousand, at the maximum. But as two million men in all three services will be involved, such percentages will be acceptable.'

'Duration?' asked Ivanenko.

'The point units of the forward mechanized armies will enter the French Channel ports one hundred hours after crossing the Elbe. At that point the ceasefire may be allowed to operate. The mopping up can take place under the ceasefire.'

'Is that time-scale feasible?' asked Petryanov.

This time Rudin cut in.

'Oh, yes, it's feasible,' he said mildly. Vishnayev shot him a suspicious look.

'I still have not had an answer to my question,' Petrov pointed out. 'What about the USA? What about their nuclear strike forces – not tactical nukes, strategic nukes? The hydrogen-bomb warheads in their intercontinental ballistic missile force, their bombers and their submarines.'

The eyes of the table riveted on Vishnayev. He rose again.

'The American President must, at the outset, be given three solemn assurances in absolute credible form,' he said. 'One, that for her part the USSR will never be the first to use thermo-nuclear weapons. Two, that if the three hundred thousand American troops in Western Europe are committed to the fight, they must take their chances in conventional or tactical nuclear warfare with ours. Three, that in the event the USA resorts to ballistic missiles aimed at the Soviet Union, the top hundred cities of the USA will cease to exist.

'President Matthews, comrades, will not trade New York for the decadence of Paris, nor Los Angeles for Frankfurt. There will be *no* American thermo-nuclear riposte.'

The silence was heavy as the perspectives sank in. The vast storehouse of food, including grain, of consumer goods, and of technology that was contained in Western Europe. The fall within a few years of Italy, Spain, Portugal, Austria, Greece and Yugoslavia. The treasure trove of gold beneath the streets of Switzerland. The utter isolation of Britain and Ireland off the new Soviet coast. The domination without a shot fired of the entire Arab and Third World. It was a heady mixture.

'It's a fine scenario,' said Rudin at last, 'but it all seems to be based on one assumption. That the USA will not rain her nuclear warheads on the Soviet

Union if we promise not to let ours loose on her. I would be grateful to hear if Comrade Vishnayev has any corroboration for that confident declaration. In short, is it a proven fact, or a fond hope?'

'More than a hope,' snapped Vishnayev. 'A realistic calculation. As capitalists and bourgeois nationalists, the Americans will always think of themselves first. They are paper tigers, weak and indecisive. Above all, when the prospect of losing their own lives faces them, they are cowards.'

'Are they indeed?' mused Rudin. 'Well, now, comrades, let me attempt to sum up. Comrade Vishnayev's scenario is realistic in every sense, but it all hangs on his hope – I beg his pardon – on his calculation that the Americans will not respond with their heavy thermo-nuclear weapons. Had we ever believed this before, we would surely already have completed the process of liberating the captive masses of Western Europe from Fascism-Capitalism to Marxism-Leninism. Personally, I perceive no new element to justify the calculation of Comrade Vishnayev.

'However, neither he nor the Comrade Marshal have ever had any dealings with the Americans, or ever been in the West. Personally, I have, and I disagree. Let us hear from Comrade Rykov.'

The elderly and veteran foreign minister was white-faced.

'All this smacks of Khrushchevism, as in the case of Cuba. I have spent thirty years in foreign affairs. Ambassadors around the world report to me, not Comrade Vishnayev. None of them, not one, not one single analyst in my department, nor I, have a single doubt that the US President would use the thermo-nuclear response on the Soviet Union. It is not a question of exchanging cities. He too can see that the outcome of such a war would be domination by the Soviet Union of almost the whole world. It would be the end of America as a super-power, as a power, as anything other than a nonentity. They will devastate the Soviet Union before they yield Western Europe and thence the world.'

'I would point out that if they do,' said Rudin, 'we cannot as yet stop them. Our high-energy-particle laser beams from space satellites are not fully functional yet. One day we will no doubt be able to vaporize incoming rockets in inner space before they can reach us. But not yet. The latest assessments of our experts – our experts, Comrade Vishnayev, not our optimists – suggest a full-blown Anglo-American thermo-nuclear strike would take out one hundred million of our citizens, mostly Great Russians, and devastate sixty per cent of the union from Poland to the Urals. But, to continue, Comrade Ivanenko, you have experience of the West. What do you say?'

'Unlike Comrades Vishnayev and Kerensky,' observed Ivanenko, 'I control hundreds of agents throughout the capitalist West. Their reports are constant. I too have no doubt at all the Americans would respond.'

'Then let me put it in a nutshell,' said Rudin brusquely. The time for sparring was over. 'If we negotiate with the Americans for wheat, we may have to accede to demands that could set us back by five years. If we tolerate the famine, we would probably be set back by ten years. If we launch a European war, we could be wiped out, certainly set back by twenty to forty years.

'I am not the theoretician that Comrade Vishnayev undoubtedly is. But I seem to recall the teachings of Marx and Lenin are very firm on one point: that while the triumph of the world rule of Marxism must be pursued at every stage by every means, the progress should not be endangered by the incurring of foolish risks. I estimate this plan as being based on a foolish risk. Therefore I propose that we – '

'I propose a vote,' said Vishnayev softly.

So that was it. Not a vote of no confidence in him, thought Rudin; that would come later, if he lost this round. The faction fight was out in the open now. He had not had the feeling so clearly in years that he was now fighting for his life. If he lost there would be no graceful retirement, no retaining the villas and the privileges like Mikoyan had done. It would be ruin, exile, perhaps the bullet in the nape of the neck. But he kept his composure. He put his own motion first. One by one the hands went up.

Rykov, Ivanenko, Petrov, all voted for him and the negotiation policy. There was hesitancy down the table. Who had Vishnayev got to? What had he promised them?'

Stepanov and Shushkin raised their hands. Last, slowly, came Chavadze the Georgian. Rudin put the counter-motion, for war in the spring. Vishnayev and Kerensky of course were for it. Komarov of Agriculture joined them. Bastard, thought Rudin, it was your bloody ministry that got us into this mess. Vishnayev must have persuaded the man that Rudin was going to ruin him in any case, so he thought he had nothing to lose. You're wrong, my friend, thought Rudin, face impassive; I'm going to have your entrails for this. Petryanov raised his hand. He's been promised the prime ministership, thought Rudin. Vitautas the Balt and Mukhamed the Tadjik also went with Vishnayev for war. The Tadjik would know that if nuclear war came, the orientals would rule over the ruins. The Lithuanian had been bought.

'Six for each proposal,' he said quietly. 'And my own vote for the negotiations.'

'Too close,' he thought, 'much too close.'

It was sundown when the meeting dissolved. But the faction fight, all knew, would now go on until it was resolved; no one could back away now, no one could stay neutral any more.

It was not until the fifth day of the tour that the party arrived in Lvov and stayed at the Intourist hotel. Up to this point Drake had gone with all the guided tours on the agenda, but this time he made an excuse that he had a headache and wished to stay in his room. As soon as the party left by coach for St Nicholas Church, he changed into more casual clothes and slipped out of the hotel.

Kaminsky had told him the sort of clothes that would pass without attracting attention: socks with sandals, light trousers, not too smart, and an open-necked shirt of the cheaper variety. With a street map he set off on foot for the seedy, poor, working-class suburb of Levandivka. He had not the slightest doubt that the two men he sought would treat him with the profoundest suspicion, once he found them. And this was hardly surprising when one considered the family backgrounds and circumstances that had forged them. He recalled what Miroslav Kaminsky in his Turkish hospital bed had told him.

On 29th September 1966 near Kiev, at the gorge of Babi Yar where over 50,000 Jews were slaughtered by the SS in Nazi-occupied Ukraine in 1941/42, the Ukraine's foremost contemporary poet, Ivan Dzuba, gave an address which was remarkable in as much as a Ukrainian Catholic was speaking out powerfully against anti-Semitism. Anti-Semitism has always flourished in the Ukraine, and successive rulers – tsars, Stalinists, Nazis, Stalinists again, and their successors – have vigorously encouraged it to flourish.

Dzuba's long speech began as a seeming plea for remembrance of the slaughtered Jews of Babi Yar, a straight condemnation of Nazism and Fascism. But as it developed, his theme began to encompass all those despotisms which, despite their technological triumphs, brutalize the human spirit and seek to persuade even the brutalized that this is normal.

'We should therefore judge each society,' he said, 'not by its external technical achievements but by the position and meaning it gives to man, by the value it puts on human dignity and human conscience.'

By the time he had reached this point the Chekisti who had infiltrated the silent crowd realized the poet was not talking about Hitler's Germany at all; he was talking about the Politburo's Soviet Union. Shortly after the speech he was arrested.

In the cellars of the local KGB barracks the chief interrogator, the man who had at his beck and call the two hulks in the corners of the room, the ones gripping the metre-long heavy hosepipes, was a fast-rising young colonel of the Second Chief Directorate, sent in from Moscow. His name was Yuri Ivanenko.

But at the address at Babi Yar there had been, in the front row, standing next to their fathers, two small ten-year-old boys. They did not know each other then, and would only meet and become firm friends six years later on a building site. One was called Lev Mishkin, the other was David Lazareff.

The presence of both the fathers of Mishkin and Lazareff at the meeting had also been noted, and when years later they had applied for permission to emigrate to Israel, both had been accused of anti-Soviet activities and drawn long sentences in labour camps.

Their families had lost their apartments, the sons any hope of university. Though highly intelligent, they were destined for pick-and-shovel work. Now both aged twenty-six, these were the young men Drake sought among the hot and dusty byways of Levandivka.

It was at the second address that he found David Lazareff who, after the introductions, treated him with extreme suspicion. But he agreed to bring his friend Mishkin to a rendezvous, since Drake knew both their names anyway.

That evening he met Lev Mishkin, and the pair regarded him with something close to hostility. He told them the whole story of the escape and rescue of Miroslav Kaminsky, and the background to himself. The only proof he could produce was the photograph of himself and Kaminsky together, taken in the hospital room at Trabzon on a Polaroid instant camera by a nursing orderly. Held up in front of them was that day's edition of the local

Turkish newspaper. Drake had brought the same newspaper as suitcase-lining and showed it to them as proof of his story.

'Look,' he said finally, 'if Miroslav had been washed up in Soviet territory and been taken by the KGB, if he had talked and revealed your names, and if I was from the KGB, I'd hardly be asking for your help.'

The two Jewish workers agreed to consider his request overnight. Unknown to Drake, both Mishkin and Lazareff had long shared an ideal close to his own – that of striking one single powerful blow of revenge against the Kremlin hierarchy in their midst. But they were near to giving up, weighed down by the hopelessness of trying to do anything without outside help.

Impelled by their desire for an ally beyond the borders of the USSR, the two shook hands in the small hours of the morning and agreed to take the Anglo-Ukrainian into their confidence. The second meeting was that afternoon, Drake having skipped another guided tour. For safety they strolled through wide, unpaved lanes near the outskirts of the city, talking quietly in Ukrainian. They told Drake of their desire also to strike at Moscow in a single, deadly act.

'The question is, what?' said Drake. Lazareff, who was the more silent and more dominant of the pair, spoke.

'Ivanenko,' he said, 'the most hated man in the Ukraine.'

'What about him?' asked Drake.

'Kill him.'

Drake stopped in his tracks and stared at the dark, intense young man.

'You'd never get near him,' he said finally.

'Last year,' said Lazareff, 'I was working on a job here in Lvov. I'm a house painter, right? We were redecorating the apartment of a Party big-wig. There was a little old woman staying with them. From Kiev. After she'd gone, the Party man's wife mentioned who she was. Later I saw a letter postmarked Kiev in the letter box. I took it, and it was from the old bird. It had her address on it.'

'So who was she?' asked Drake.

'His mother.'

Drake considered the information. 'You wouldn't think people like that have mothers,' he said. 'But you'd have to watch her flat for a long time before he might come to visit her.'

Lazareff shook his head. 'She's the bait,' he said, and outlined his idea. Drake considered the enormity of it.

Before coming to the Ukraine, he had envisaged the great single blow he had dreamed of delivering against the might of the Kremlin in many terms, but never this. To assassinate the head of the KGB would be to strike into the very centre of the Politburo, to send hairline cracks running through every corner of the power structure.

'It might work,' he conceded.

If it did, he thought, it would be hushed up at once. But if the news ever got out, the effect on popular opinion, especially in the Ukraine, would be traumatic.

'It could trigger the biggest uprising there has ever been here,' he said.

Lazareff nodded. Alone with his partner Mishkin, far away from outside help, he had evidently given the project a lot of thought.

'True,' he said.

'What equipment would you need?' asked Drake.

Lazareff told him.

Drake nodded. 'It can all be acquired in the West,' he said, 'but how to get it in?'

'Odessa,' cut in Mishkin. 'I was on the docks there for a while. The place is completely corrupt. The black market is thriving. Every Western ship brings seamen who do a vigorous trade with the local spivs in Turkish leather jackets, suede coats and denim jeans. We would meet you there. It is inside the Ukraine; we would not need inter-state passports.'

Before they parted the plan was agreed. Drake would acquire the equipment and bring it to Odessa by sea. He would alert Mishkin and Lazareff by a letter, posted inside the Soviet Union, well in advance of his own arrival. The wording would be innocent. The rendezvous in Odessa was to be a café that Mishkin knew from his days as a teenage labourer there.

'Two more things,' said Drake. 'When it is over, the publicity for it, the worldwide announcement that it has been done, is vital; almost as important as the act itself. And that means that you personally must tell the world. Only you will have the details to convince the world of the truth. But that means you must escape from here to the West.'

'It goes without saying,' murmured Lazareff. 'We are both Refuseniks. We have tried to emigrate to Israel like our fathers before us, and have been refused. This time we will go, with or without permission. When this is over, we have to get to Israel. It is the only place we will ever be safe, ever again. Once there, we will tell the world what we have done and leave those bastards in the Kremlin and the KGB discredited in the eyes of their own people.'

'The other point follows from the first,' said Drake. 'When it is done, you must let me know by coded letter or postcard – in case anything goes wrong with the escape. So that I can try to help get the news to the world.'

They agreed that an innocently worded postcard would be sent from Lvov to a *poste restante* address in London. With the details memorized, they parted, and Drake rejoined his tour group.

Two days later Drake was back in London. The first thing he did was to buy the most comprehensive book he could find on small arms. The second was to send a telegram to a friend in Canada, one of the best of that elite private list he had built up over the years of emigrés who thought as he did of carrying their hatred to the enemy. The third was to begin preparations for a long-dormant plan to raise the needed funds by robbing a bank.

At the far end of Kutuzovsky Prospekt on the southeastern outskirts of Moscow, a driver pulling to the right off the main boulevard on the Rublevo Road will arrive twenty kilometres later at the little village of Uspenskoye, in the heart of the weekend-villa country. In the great pine and birch forests around Uspenskoye lie the hamlets like Usovo and Zhukovka where stand the country mansions of the Soviet elite. Just beyond Uspenskoye bridge over the Moscow River is a beach where in summer the lesser-privileged but nevertheless very well-off (they have their own cars) come from Moscow to bathe from the sandy shore.

The Western diplomats come here too, and it is one of the rare places where a Westerner can be cheek by jowl with ordinary Muscovite families. Even the routine KGB tailing of Western diplomats seems to let up on Sunday afternoons in high summer.

Adam Munro came here with a party of British embassy staffers that Sunday afternoon, 11th July 1982. Some of them were married couples, some single and younger than he. Shortly before three the whole party of them left their towels and picnic baskets among the trees, ran down the low bluff towards the sandy beach and swam. When he came back, Munro picked up his rolled towel and began to dry himself. Something fell out of it.

He stopped to pick it up. It was a small pasteboard card, half the size of a postcard, white on both sides. On one side was typed, in Russian, the words: 'Three kilometres north of here is an abandoned chapel in the woods. Meet me there in thirty minutes. Please. It is urgent.'

He maintained his smile as one of the embassy secretaries came over, laughing, to ask for a cigarette. While he lit it for her, his mind was working out all the angles he could think of. A dissident wanting to pass over the underground literature? A load of trouble, that. A religious group wanting asylum in the embassy? The Americans had that in 1978, and it had caused untold problems. A trap, set by the KGB to identify the SIS man inside the embassy? Always possible. No ordinary commercial secretary would accept such an invitation, slipped into a rolled towel by someone who had evidently tailed him and watched from the surrounding woods. And yet it was crude for the KGB. They would have set up a pretended defector in central Moscow with information to pass, arranged for secret photographs at the handover point. So who was the secret writer?

He dressed quickly, still undecided. Finally, he pulled on his shoes and made up his mind. If it was a trap, then he had received no message and was simply walking in the forest. To the disappointment of his hopeful secretary he set off alone. After ninety metres he paused, took out his lighter and burnt the card, grinding the ash into the carpet of pine needles.

The sun and his watch gave him due north, away from the river bank which faced south. After ten minutes he emerged on the side of a slope and saw the onion-shaped dome of a chapel two kilometres further on across the valley. Seconds later he was back in the trees.

The forests around Moscow have dozens of such small chapels, once the worshipping places of the villagers, now mainly derelict, boarded up, deserted. The one he was approaching stood in its own clearing among the trees. At the edge of the clearing he stopped and surveyed the tiny church. He could see no one. Carefully he advanced into the open. He was a few metres from the sealed front door when he saw the figure standing in deep shadow under an archway. He stopped, and for minutes on end the two stared at each other.

There was really nothing to say, so he just said her name, 'Valentina.'

She moved out of the shadow and replied, 'Adam.'

'Twenty-one years,' he thought in wonderment. 'She must be turned forty.' She looked like thirty, still raven-haired, beautiful and ineffably sad.

They sat on one of the tombstones and talked quietly of the old times. She told him she had returned from Berlin to Moscow a few months after their parting, and had continued to be a stenographer for the Party machine. At twenty-three she had married a young army officer with good prospects. After seven years there had been a baby, and they had been happy, all three of them. Her husband's career had flourished, for he had an uncle high in the Red Army, and patronage is no different in the Soviet Union than anywhere else. The boy was now ten.

Five years ago her husband, having reached the rank of colonel at a young age, had been killed in a helicopter crash while surveying Red Chinese troop deployments along the Ussuri River in the Far East. To kill the grief she had gone back to work. Her husband's uncle had used his influence to secure her good, highly placed work, bringing with it privileges in the form of special food shops, special restaurants, better apartments, a private car – all the things that go with high rank in the Party machine.

Finally, two years ago, after special clearance, she had been offered a post in the tiny, closed group of stenographers and typists, a sub-section of the General Secretariat of the Central Committee, that is called the Politburo Secretariat.

Munro breathed deeply. That was high, very high, and very trusted.

'Who,' he asked, 'is the uncle of your late husband?'

'Kerensky,' she murmured.

'Marshal Kerensky?' he asked. She nodded. Munro exhaled slowly. Kerensky, the ultra-hawk. When he looked again at her face, the eyes were wet. She was blinking rapidly, on the verge of tears. On an impulse he put his arm round her shoulders and she leaned against him. He smelt her hair, the same sweet odour that had made him feel both tender and excited two decades ago in his youth.

'What's the matter?' he asked gently.

'Oh, Adam, I'm so unhappy.'

'In God's name, why?' In your society you have everything.'

She shook her head, slowly, then pulled away from him. She avoided his eyes, gazing across the clearing into the woods.

'Adam, all my life, since I was a small girl, I believed. I truly believed. Even when we loved, I believed in the goodness, the rightness, of socialism. Even in the hard times, the times of deprivation in my country, when the West had all the consumer riches and we had none, I believed in the justice of the Communist ideal that we in Russia would one day bring to the world. It was an ideal that would give us all a world without Fascism, without money-lust, without exploitation, without war.

'I was taught it, and I really believed it. It was more important than you, than our love, than my husband and child. As much at least as this country, Russia, which is part of my soul.'

Munro knew about the patriotism of the Russians towards their country, a fierce flame that would make them endure any suffering, any privation, make any sacrifice and which, when manipulated, would make them obey their Kremlin overlords without demur.

'What happened?' he asked quietly.

'They have betrayed it. Are betraying it. My ideal, my people and my country.'

'They?' he asked. She was twisting her fingers till they looked as if they would come off.

'The Party chiefs,' she said bitterly. She spat out the Russian slang word meaning 'the fat cats'. 'The *nachalstvo*.'

Munro had twice witnessed a recantation. When a true believer loses the faith, the reversed fanaticism goes to strange extremes.

'I worshipped them, Adam. I respected them. I revered them. Now, for years, I have lived close to them all. I have lived in their shadow, taken their gifts, been showered with their privileges. I have seen them close up, in private, heard them talk, about the people, whom they despise. They are rotten, Adam, corrupt and cruel. Everything they touch they turn to ashes.'

Munro swung one leg across the tombstone so he could face her, took her in his arms. She was crying softly. 'I can't go on, Adam, I can't go on,' she murmured into his shoulder.

'All right, my darling, do you want me to try to get you out?'

He knew it would cost him his career, but this time he was not going to let her go. It would be worth it, everything would be worth it.

She pulled away, her face tear-streaked. 'I cannot leave. I have Sasha to think about.'

He held her quietly for a while longer. His mind was racing.

'How did you know I was in Moscow?' he asked carefully.

She gave no hint of surprise at the question. It was in any case natural enough for him to ask it.

'Last month,' she said between sniffs, 'I was taken to the ballet by a colleague from the office. We were in a box. When the lights were low, I thought I must be mistaken. But when they went up in the interval, I knew it was really you. I could not stay after then. I pleaded a headache and left quickly.'

She dabbed her eyes, the crying spell over.

'Adam,' she asked eventually, 'did you marry?'

'Yes,' he said. 'Long after Berlin. It didn't work. We were divorced years ago.'

She managed a little smile. 'I'm glad,' she said. 'I'm glad there is no one else. That is not very logical, is it?'

He grinned back at her.

'No,' he said, 'it is not. But it is nice to hear. Can we see each other? In the future.'

Her smile faded; there was a hunted look in her eyes. She shook her dark head.

'No, not very often, Adam,' she said. 'I am trusted, privileged, but if a foreigner came to my apartment, it would soon be noticed and reported. The same applies to your apartment. Diplomats are watched – you know that. Hotels are watched also; no apartments are for rent here, without any formalities. It is not possible, Adam, it is just not possible.'

'Valentina, you started this meeting. You took the initiative. Was it just for old times' sake? If you do not like your life, here, if you do not like the men you work for. . . . But if you cannot leave because of Sasha, then what is it you want?'

She composed herself and thought for a while. When she spoke it was quite calmly.

'Adam, I want to try and stop them. I want to try and stop what they are doing. I suppose I have for several years now, but since I saw you at the Bolshoi, and remembered all the freedoms we had in Berlin, I began thinking about it more and more. Now I am certain. Tell me if you can; is there an intelligence officer in your embassy?'

Munro was shaken. He had handled two defectors-in-place, one from the Soviet embassy in Mexico City, the other in Vienna. One had been motivated by a conversation from respect to hatred for his own regime, like Valentina; the other by bitterness at lack of promotion. The former had been the trickier to handle.

'I suppose so,' he said slowly. 'I suppose there must be.'

Valentina rummaged in the shoulder-bag on the pine needles by her feet. Having made up her mind she was apparently determined to go through with her betrayal. She withdrew a thick padded envelope.

'I want you to give this to him, Adam. Promise me you will never tell him who it came from. Please, Adam, I am frightened by what I am doing. I cannot trust anyone, not anyone but you.'

'I promise,' he said. 'But I have to see you again. I can't just see you walk away through the gap in the wall as I did last time.'

'No, I cannot do that again either. But do not try to contact me at my apartment. It is in a walled compound for senior functionaries, with a single gate in the wall and a policeman on it. Do not try to telephone me. The calls are monitored. And I will never meet anyone else from your embassy, not even the intelligence chief.'

'I agree,' said Munro. 'But when can we meet again?'

She considered for a moment. 'It is not always easy for me to get away. Sasha takes up most of my spare time. But I have my own car and I am not followed. Tomorrow I must go away for two weeks, but we can meet here, four Sundays from today.' She looked at her watch. 'I must go, Adam. I am one of a house party at a *dacha* a few miles from here.'

He kissed her, on the lips, the way it used to be. And it was as sweet as it had ever been. She rose and walked away across the clearing. At the fringe of the trees he called after her.

'Valentina, what is in this?' He held up the package.

She paused and turned. 'My job,' she said, 'is to prepare the verbatim transcripts of the Politburo meetings, one for each member. And the digests for the candidate members. From the tape recordings. That is a copy of the recording of the meeting of 10th June.'

Then she was gone into the trees. Munro sat on the tombstone and looked down at the package.

'Bloody hell,' he said.

4

Adam Munro sat in a locked room in the main building of the British embassy on Maurice Thorez Embankment and listened to the last sentences of the tape recording on the machine in front of him. The room was safe from any chance of electronic surveillance by the Russians, which was why he had borrowed it for a few hours from head of chancery.

'. . . goes without saying that this news does not pass outside those present in this room. Our next meeting will be today week.'

The voice of Maxim Rudin died away and the tape hissed on the machine, then stopped. Munro switched off. He leaned back and let out a long, low whistle.

If it was true, it was bigger than anything Oleg Penkovsky had brought over, twenty years before. The story of Penkovsky was folklore in the SIS, CIA and most of all in the bitterest memories of the KGB. He was the full brigadier-general of the GRU, with access to the highest information, who, disenchanted with the Kremlin hierarchy, had approached first the Americans and then the British with an offer to provide information.

The Americans had turned him down, suspecting a trap. The British had accepted him, and for two and a half years 'run' him until he was trapped by the KGB, exposed, tried and shot. In his time he had brought over a golden harvest of secret information, but most important of all it was at the time of the October 1962 Cuban missile crisis. In that month the world had applauded the exceptionally skilful handling by President Kennedy of the eyeball-to-eyeball confrontation with Nikita Khrushchev over the matter of the planting of Soviet missiles in Cuba. What the world had not known was that the exact strengths and weaknesses of the Russian leader were already in the Americans' hands, thanks to Penkovsky.

When it was finally over, the Soviet missiles were out of Cuba, Khrushchev was humbled, Kennedy was a hero, and Penkovsky was under suspicion. He was arrested in November. Within a year, after a show trial, he was dead. Within a year also, Khrushchev had fallen, toppled by his own colleagues; ostensibly because of his failure in the grain policy, in fact because his adventurism had scared the daylights out of them. And that same winter of

1963 Kennedy too had died, just thirteen months after his triumph. The democrat, the despot and the spy had all left the stage. But even Penkovsky had never got right inside the Politburo.

Munro took the spool off the machine and carefully rewrapped it. The voice of Professor Yakovlev was of course unknown to him, and most of the tape was of him reading his report. But in the discussion following the professor there were ten voices and three at least were identifiable. The low growl of Rudin was well enough known, the high tones of Vishnayev he had heard before, when watching televised speeches by the man to Party congresses; and the bark of Marshal Kerensky he had heard at May Day celebrations, also on film and tape.

His problem, when he took the tape back to London for voice-print analysis, as he knew he must, was how to cover his source. He knew if he admitted to the secret rendezvous in the forest, following the typed note in the bathing towel, the question would be asked: 'Why you, Munro? How did she know you?' It would be impossible to avoid that question, and equally impossible to answer it. The only solution was to devise an alternative source, credible and uncheckable.

He had only been in Moscow six weeks, but his unsuspected mastery of even slang Russian had paid a couple of dividends. At a diplomatic reception in the Czech embassy a fortnight earlier he had been in conversation with an Indian attaché when he heard two Russians in muttered conversation behind him. One of them had said: 'He's a bitter bastard. Thinks he should have had the top slot.'

He had followed the gaze of the two who had spoken and noted they were observing and presumably talking about a Russian across the room. The guest list later confirmed the man was Anatoly Krivoi, personal aide and right-hand man to the Party theoretician, Vishnayev. So what had he got to be bitter about? Munro checked his files and came up with Krivoi's history. He had worked in the Party Organizations section of the Central Committee; shortly after the nomination of Petrov to the top job, Krivoi had appeared on Vishnayev's staff. Quit in disgust? Personality conflict with Petrov? Bitter at being passed over? They were all perfectly possible, and all interesting to an intelligence chief in a foreign capital.

Krivoi, he mused. Maybe. Just maybe. He too would have access, at least to Vishnayev's copy of the transcript, maybe even of the tape. And he was probably in Moscow; certainly his boss was. Vishnayev had been present when the East German premier had arrived a week before.

'Sorry, Anatoly, you've just changed sides,' he said as he slipped the fat envelope into an inside pocket and took the stairs to see the head of chancery.

'I'm afraid I have to go back to London with the Wednesday bag,' he told the diplomat. 'It's unavoidable, and it can't wait.'

Chancery asked no questions. He knew Munro's job and promised to arrange it. The diplomatic bag, which actually *is* a bag or at least a series of canvas sacks, goes from Moscow to London every Wednesday and always on the British Airways flight, never Aeroflot. A Queen's messenger, one of that team of men who constantly fly around the world from London picking up embassy bags and protected by the insignia of the crown and greyhound, comes out from London for it. The very secret material is carried in a hard-frame despatch box chained to the man's left wrist; the more routine stuff in the canvas sacks the messenger personally checks into the aircraft hold. Once there it is on British territory. But in the case of Moscow the messenger is accompanied by an embassy staffer.

The escort job is sought after, since it permits a quick trip home to London, a bit of shopping and a chance of a good night out. The second secretary who lost his place in the rota that week was annoyed, but asked no questions.

The following Wednesday the British Airways airbus-300B lifted out of the new, post-1980-Olympics Sheremetyevo Airport and turned its nose towards London. By Munro's side the messenger, a short, dapper ex-army major, withdrew straight into his hobby, composing crossword puzzles for a major newspaper.

'You have to do something to while away these endless aeroplane flights,' he told Munro. 'We all have our in-flight hobbies.'

Munro grunted and looked back over the wingtip at the receding city of Moscow. Somewhere down there in the sundrenched streets the woman he loved was working and moving among people she was going to betray. She was on her own and right out in the cold.

The country of Norway, seen in isolation from its eastern neighbour Sweden, looks like a great, pre-historic, fossilized human hand stretching down from the Arctic towards Denmark and Britain. It is a right hand, palm downwards to the ocean, a stubby thumb towards the east clenched into the forefinger. Up the crack between thumb and forefinger lies Oslo, its capital.

To the north the fractured forearm bones stretch up to Tromso and Hammerfest, deep in the Arctic, so narrow that in places there are only forty miles from the sea to the Swedish border. On a relief map the hand looks as if it has been smashed by some gigantic hammer of the gods, splintering bones and knuckles into thousands of particles. Nowhere is this breakage more marked than along the west coast, where the chopping edge of the hand would be.

Here the land is shattered into a thousand fragments and between the shards the sea has flowed in to form a million creeks, gullies, bays and gorges; winding narrow defiles where the mountains fall sheer to glittering water. These are the fjords, and it was from the headwaters of these that a race of men came out 1500 years ago who were the best sailors ever to set keel to the water or sail to the wind. Before their age was over they had sailed to Greenland and America, conquered Ireland, settled Britain and Normandy, hunted to Spain and Morocco and navigated from the Mediterranean to Iceland. They were the Vikings, and their descendants still live and fish along the fjords of Norway.

Such a man was Thor Larsen, sea captain and ship's master, who strode that mid-July afternoon past the royal palace in the Swedish capital of Stockholm from his company's head office back to his hotel. People tended to step aside for him; he was six feet three inches tall, wide as the pavements of the old quarter of the city, blue-eyed and bearded. Being shorebound, he was in civilian clothes, but he was happy because he had reason to think, after visiting the head office of the Nordia Line, that now lay behind him along the Ship Quay, that he might soon have a new command.

After six months attending a course at the company's expense in the intricacies of radar, computer navigation and supertanker technology, he was dying to get back to sea again. The summons to head office had been to receive from the hands of the personal secretary to the proprietor, chairman and managing director of Nordia Line his invitation to dinner that evening. The invitation also included Larsen's wife, who had been informed by telephone and was flying in from Norway on a company ticket. The Old Man was splashing out a bit, thought Larsen. There must be something in the wind.

He took his rented car from the hotel car park across the bridge on Nybroviken and drove the thirty-seven kilometres to the airport. When Lisa Larsen arrived in the concourse with her overnight bag, he greeted her with the delicacy of an excited St Bernard, swinging her off her feet like a girl. She was small and petite, with dark bright eyes, soft chestnut curls and a trim figure that belied her thirty-eight years. And he adored her.

Twenty years earlier, when he had been a gangling second mate of twenty-five, he had met her one freezing winter day in Oslo. She had slipped on the ice, he had picked her up like a doll and set her back on her feet. She was wearing a fur-trimmed hood that almost hid her tiny, red-nosed face, and when she thanked him he could only see her eyes, looking out of the mass of snow and fur like the bright eyes of a snow-mouse in the forests of winter. Ever since, through their courtship and marriage and the years in between, he had called her snow-mouse.

He drove her back into central Stockholm, asking all the way about their home in Alesund far away on Norway's western coast, and of the progress of their two teenage children. To the south a British Airways airbus passed by on its great circle route from Moscow to London. Thor Larsen neither knew nor cared.

The dinner that evening was to be in the famous Aurora Cellar, built below ground in the cellar-storerooms of an old palace in the city's medieval quarter. When Thor and Lisa Larsen arrived and were shown down the narrow steps to the cellar, the proprietor Leonard was waiting for them at the bottom.

'Mr Wennerstrom is already here,' he said, and showed them into one of the private rooms, a small, intimate cavern, arched in 500-year-old brick, spanned by a thick table of glittering ancient timber and lit by candles in cast-iron holders. As they entered, Larsen's employer, Harald Wennerstrom, lumbered to his feet, embraced Lisa and shook hands with her husband.

Harald 'Harry' Wennerstrom was something of a legend in his own lifetime among the seafaring people of Scandinavia. He was now seventy-five, grizzled and craggy with bristling eyebrows. Just after the Second World War, returning to his native Stockholm, he had inherited from his father half a dozen small cargo ships. In thirty-five years he had built up the biggest independently owned fleet of tankers outside the hands of the Greeks and the

Hong Kong Chinese. The Nordia Line was his creation, diversifying from dry-cargo ships to tankers in the mid-fifties, laying out the money, building the ships for the oil boom of the sixties, backing his own judgement, often going against the grain.

They sat and ate, and Wennerstrom talked only of small things, asking after the family. His own forty-year marriage had ended with the death of his wife four years earlier; they had had no children. But if he had had a son, he would have liked him to be like the big Norwegian across the table from him, a sailor's sailor, and he was particularly fond of Lisa.

The salmon, cured in brine and dill, Scandinavian way, was delicious, the tender duck from the Stockholm salt marshes excellent. It was only when they sat finishing their wine – Wennerstrom unhappily sipping at his balloon glass of water, 'all the bloody doctors will allow me nowadays' – that he came to business.

'Three years ago, Thor, back in 1979, I made three forecasts to myself. One was that by the end of 1982 the solidarity of the Organization of Petroleum Exporting Countries, OPEC, would have broken down. The second was that the American president's policy to curb the United States' consumption of oil energy and by-products would have failed. The third was that the Soviet Union would have changed from a net oil exporter to a net oil importer. I was told I was crazy, but I was right.'

Thor Larsen nodded. The formation of OPEC and its quadrupling of oil prices in the winter of 1973 had produced a world slump that had nearly broken the economies of the Western world. It had also sent the oil tanker business into a seven-year decline, with millions of tons of partially built tankers laid up, useless, uneconomic, loss-making. It was a bold spirit who could have seen three years earlier the events between 1979 and 1982: the break-up of OPEC as the Arab world split into feuding factions, the second revolution in Iran, the disintegration of Nigeria, the rush by the radical oil-producing nations to sell oil at any price to finance arms-buying sprees; the spiralling increase in US oil consumption based on the ordinary American's conviction of his God-given right to rape the globe's resources for his own comforts; and the Soviet native oil industry peaking at such a low production figure through poor technology and forcing Russia to become once again an oil importer. The three factors had produced the tanker boom into which they were now, in the summer of 1982, beginning to move.

'As you know,' Wennerstrom resumed, 'last September I signed a contract with the Japanese for a new supertanker. Down in the market place they all said I was mad; half my fleet laid up in Stromstad Sound, and I order a new one. But I'm not mad. You know the story of the East Shore Oil Company?'

Larsen nodded again. A small, Louisiana-based oil company in America ten years ago, it had passed into the hands of the dynamic Clint Blake. In ten years it had grown and expanded until it was on the verge of joining the Seven Sisters, the mastodons of the world oil cartels.

'Well, in the summer of next year, 1983, Clint Blake is invading Europe. It's a tough, crowded market, but he thinks he can crack it. He's putting several thousand service stations across the motorways of Europe, marketing his own brand of gasoline and oil. And for that he'll need tanker tonnage. And I've got it: a seven-year contract to bring crude from the Middle East to Western Europe. He's already building his own refinery at Rotterdam, alongside Esso, Mobil and Chevron. That is what the new tanker is for. She's big and she's ultra-modern and she's expensive, but she'll pay. She'll make five or six runs a year from the Arabian Gulf to Rotterdam, and in five years she'll amortize the investment. But that's not the reason I'm building her. She's going to be the biggest and the best; my flagship, my memorial. And you're going to be her skipper.'

Thor Larsen sat in silence. Lisa's hand stole across the table and laid itself on top of his, squeezing gently. Two years ago, Larsen knew, he could never have skippered a Swedish-flag vessel, being himself a Norwegian. But since the Gothenburg Agreement of the previous year, which Wennerstrom had helped to push through, a Swedish shipowner could apply for honorary citizenship of Sweden for exceptional Scandinavian but non-Swedish officers in his employ so that they could be offered a captaincy. He had applied successfully on behalf of Larsen.

The coffee came and they sipped in appreciation.

'I'm having her built at the Ishikawajima-Harima yard in Japan,' said Wennerstrom. 'It's the only yard in the world that can take her. They have the dry dock.'

Both men knew the days of ships being built on slipways and then allowed to slide into the water were long past. The size and weight factors were too great. The giants were now built in enormous dry docks, so that when ready for launching the sea was let in through dock sluices and the ship simply floated off her blocks and rode water inside the dock.

'Work began on her last 4th November,' Wennerstrom told them. 'The keel was laid 30th January. She's taking shape now. She'll float on 1st November next, and after three months at the fitting-out berth and sea trials, she'll sail on 2nd February. And you'll be on her bridge, Thor.'

'Thank you,' said Larsen. 'What are you calling her?'

'Ah, yes. I've thought of that. Do you remember the Sagas? We'll name her to please Niorn, the god of the sea,' said Wennerstrom quietly. He was gripping his glass of water, staring at the flame of the candle in its cast-iron holder before him. 'For Niorn controls the fire and the water, the twin enemies of a tanker captain; the explosion and the sea herself.'

The water in his glass and the flame of the candle reflected in the old man's eyes, as once fire and water had reflected in his eyes as he sat helpless in a lifeboat in the mid-Atlantic in 1942 four cables from his blazing tanker, his first command, watching his crew fry in the sea around him.

Thor Larsen stared at his patron, doubting that the old man could really believe this mythology; Lisa, being a woman, knew he meant every word of it. At last Wennerstrom sat back, pushed the glass aside with an impatient gesture, and filled his spare glass with red wine.

'So we will call her after the daughter of Niorn, Freya, the most beautiful of all the goddesses. We will call her the *Freya*.' He raised his glass. 'To the *Freya*.'

They all drank.

'When she sails,' said Wennerstrom, 'the world will never have seen the like of her. And when she is past sailing, the world will never see the like of her again.'

Larsen was aware that the two biggest tankers in the world were the French Shell tankers *Bellamya* and *Batillus*, both just over 500,000 tons.

'What will be her deadweight, the *Freya?*' asked Larsen. 'How much crude will she carry?'

'Ah, yes, I forgot to mention that,' said the old shipowner mischievously. 'She'll be carrying one million tons of crude oil.'

Thor Larsen heard a hiss of indrawn breath from his wife beside him.

'That's big,' he said at last. 'That's very big.'

'The biggest the world has ever seen,' said Wennerstrom.

Two days later a jumbo jet arrived at Heathrow Airport from Toronto. Amongst its passengers it carried one Azamat Krim, Canadian-born son of an emigré, who like Andrew Drake had anglicized his name to Arthur Crimmins. He was one of those whom Drake had noted years before as a man who shared his beliefs completely.

Drake was waiting to meet him as he came out of the customs area, and together they drove to Drake's flat off the Bayswater Road.

Azamat Krim was a Crimean Tatar, short, dark and wiry. His father, unlike Drake's, had fought in the Second World War *with* the Red Army rather than against it. His loyalty to Russia had availed him nothing. Captured by the Germans in combat, he and all his race had been accused by Stalin of collaboration with the Germans, a patently unfounded charge, but one which sufficed to allow Stalin to deport the entire Tatar nation to the wilds of the orient. Tens of thousands had died in the unheated cattle trucks, thousands more in the frozen wastes of Kazakhstan and Siberia without food or clothing.

In a German forced labour camp Chinghis Krim had heard of the death of his entire family. Liberated by the Canadians in 1945, he had been lucky not to be sent back to Stalin for execution or the slave camps. He had been befriended by a Canadian officer, a former rodeo rider from Calgary, who one day on an Austrian horse farm had admired the Tatar soldier's mastery of horses and brilliant riding. The Canadian had secured Krim's authorized emigration to Canada, where he had married and borne a son. Azamat was the boy, now aged thirty and like Drake bitter against the Kremlin for the sufferings of his father's people.

In his flat Andrew Drake explained his plan and the Tatar agreed to join him in it. Together they put the final touches to the scheme for securing the needed funds by taking out a bank in Northern England.

The man Adam Munro reported to at head office was his controller, Barry Ferndale, the head of the Soviet section. Years before, Ferndale had done his time in the field, and assisted in the exhaustive de-briefings of Oleg Penkovsky when the Russian defector had visited Britain while accompanying Soviet trade delegations.

He was short and rotund, pink-cheeked and jolly. He hid his keen brain and a profound knowledge of Soviet affairs behind mannerisms of great cheerfulness and seeming naïveté.

In his office on the fourth floor of the firm's headquarters, he listened to the tape from Moscow from end to end. When it was over he began furiously polishing his glasses, hopping with excitement.

'Good gracious me, my dear fellow. My dear Adam. What an extraordinary affair. This really is quite priceless.'

'If it's true,' said Munro carefully. Ferndale started, as if the thought had not occurred to him.

'Ah, yes, of course. If it's true. Now, you simply must tell me how you got hold of it.'

Munro told his story carefully. It was true in every detail, save that he claimed the source of the tape had been Anatoly Krivoi.

'Krivoi, yes, yes, know of him, of course,' said Ferndale. 'Well, now, I shall have to get this translated into English and show it to the Master. This could be very big indeed. You won't be able to return to Moscow tomorrow, you know. Do you have a place to stay? Your club? Excellent. First class. Well, now, you pop along and have a decent dinner and stay at the club for a couple of days.'

Ferndale called his wife to tell her he would not be home to their modest house at Pinner that evening, but he would be spending the night in town. She knew his job and was accustomed to such absences.

Then he spent the night working on the translation of the tape, alone in his office. He was fluent in Russian, without the ultra-keen ear for tone and pitch that Munro had which denotes the truly bilingual speaker. But it was good enough. He missed nothing of the Yakovlev report, or the brief but stunned reaction that had followed it among the thirteen Politburo members.

At ten o'clock the following morning, sleepless but shaved and break-fasted, looking as pink and fresh as he always did, Ferndale called Sir Nigel Irvine's secretary on the private line and asked to see him. He was with the director-general in ten minutes.

Sir Nigel Irvine read the transcript in silence, put it down and regarded the tape lying on the desk before him.

'Is this genuine?' he asked.

Barry Ferndale had dropped his bonhomie. He had known Nigel Irvine for years as a colleague and the elevation of his friend to the supreme post and a knighthood had changed nothing between them.

'Don't know,' he said thoughtfully. 'It's going to take a lot of checking out. It's possible. Adam told me he met this Krivoi briefly at a reception at the Czech embassy just over two weeks ago. If Krivoi was thinking of coming over, that would have been his chance. Penkovsky did exactly the same; met a diplomat on neutral ground and established a secret meeting later. Of course he was regarded with intense suspicion until his information checked out. That's what I want to do here.'

'Spell it out,' said Sir Nigel.

Ferndale began polishing his glasses again. The speed of his circular movements with handkerchief on the lenses, so went the folklore, was in direct proportion to the pace of his thinking, and he polished furiously.

'Firstly, Munro,' he said. 'Just in case it is a trap and the second meeting is to spring the trap, I would like him to take furlough here until we have finished with the tape. The opposition might, just might, be trying to create an incident between governments.'

'Is he owed leave?' asked Sir Nigel.

'Yes, he is, actually. He was shifted to Moscow so fast at the end of May he is owed a fortnight's summer holiday.'

'Then let him take it now. But he should keep in touch. And inside Britain, Barry. No wandering abroad until this is sorted out.'

'Then there's the tape itself,' said Ferndale. 'It breaks down into two parts. The Yakovlev report and the voices of the Politburo. So far as I know we have never heard Yakovlev speak. So no voice-print tests will be possible with him. But what he says is highly technical. I'd like to check that out with some experts in chemical seed-dressing techniques. There's an excellent section in the Ministry of Agriculture who deal with that sort of thing. No need for anyone to know why we want to know, but I'll have to be convinced this accident with the Lindane hopper valve is feasible.'

'You recall that file the cousins lent us a month ago?' asked Sir Nigel. 'The photos taken by the Condor satellites?'

'Of course.'

'Check the symptoms against the apparent explanation. What else?'

'The second section comes down to voice-print analysis,' said Ferndale. 'I'd like to chop that section up into bits, so no one need know what is being talked about. The language laboratory at Beaconsfield could check out phraseology, syntax, vernacular expressions, regional dialects and so forth. But the clincher will be the comparison of voice prints.'

Sir Nigel nodded. Both men knew that human voices, reduced to a series of electronically registered blips and pulses, are as individual as fingerprints. No two are ever quite alike.

'Very well,' he said, 'but Barry, I insist on two things. For the moment no one knows about this outside of you, me and Munro. If it's a phoney we don't want to raise false hopes; if it's not, it's high-explosive. None of the technical side must know the whole. Secondly, I don't want to hear the name of Anatoly Krivoi again. Devise a cover name for the asset and use it in future.'

Two hours later Barry Ferndale called Munro over lunch at his club. The telephone line being open, they used the commercial parlance that was habitual.

'The managing director's terribly happy with the sales report,' Ferndale told Munro. 'He's very keen that you take a fortnight's leave to enable us to break it right down and see where we go from here. Have you any ideas for a spot of leave?'

Munro hadn't, but he made up his mind. This was not a request, it was an order.

'I'd like to go back to Scotland for a while.' he said. 'I've always wanted to walk during the summer from Lochaber up the coast to Sutherland.'

Ferndale was ecstatic. 'The Highlands, the glens of Bonnie Scotland. So pretty at this time of year. Never could stand physical exercise myself, but I'm sure you'll enjoy it. Stay in touch with me, say, every second day. You have my home number, don't you?'

A week later Miroslav Kaminsky arrived in England on his Red Cross travel papers. He had come across Europe by train, the ticket paid for by Drake who was nearing the end of his financial resources.

Kaminsky and Krim were introduced and Kaminsky given his orders.

'You learn English,' Drake told him. 'Morning, noon and night. Books and gramophone records, faster than you've ever learned anything before. Meanwhile, I'm going to get you some decent papers. You can't travel on Red Cross documents for ever. Until I do, and until you can make yourself understood in English, don't leave the flat.'

Adam Munro had walked for ten days through the Highlands of Inverness, Ross and Cromarty and finally into Sutherland where the waters of the North Minch stretch away westwards to the Isle of Lewis, when he made his sixth call to Barry Ferndale's home on the outskirts of London.

'Glad you called,' said Ferndale down the line. 'Could you come back to the office? The managing director would like a word.'

Munro promised to leave within the hour and make his way as fast as possible to Inverness. There he could pick up a flight for London.

At his home on the outskirts of Sheffield, the great steel town of Yorkshire, Mr Norman Pickering kissed his wife and daughter farewell that brilliant late-July morning and drove off to the bank of which he was manager.

Twenty minutes later a small van bearing the name of an electrical appliance company drove up to the house and disgorged two men in white coats. One carried a large cardboard carton up to the front door, preceded by his companion bearing a clipboard. Mrs Pickering answered the door and the two men went inside. None of the neighbours took any notice.

Ten minutes later the man with the clipboard came out and drove away. His companion apparently stayed to fix and test the appliance they had delivered.

Thirty minutes after that the van was parked round two corners from the bank and the driver, without his white coat and wearing a charcoal-grey business suit, carrying not a clipboard but a large attaché case, entered the bank. He proffered an envelope to one of the girl clerks who looked at it, saw that it was addressed personally to Mr Pickering and took it to him. The businessman waited patiently.

Two minutes later the manager opened his office door and looked out. His eye caught the waiting businessman.

'Mr Partington?' he asked. 'Do come in.'

Andrew Drake did not speak until the door had closed behind him. When he did, his voice had no trace of his native Yorkshire, but a guttural edge as if it came from Europe. His hair was carrot red, and heavy-rimmed, tinted glasses masked his eyes to some extent.

'I wish to open an account,' he said, 'and to make a withdrawal in cash.'

Pickering was perplexed; his chief clerk could have handled this trans-action.

'A large account, and a large transaction,' said Drake. He slid a cheque across the desk. It was a bank cheque, the sort that can be obtained across the counter. It was issued by the Holborn, London, branch of Pickering's own bank, and was drawn to £30,000.

'I see,' said Pickering. That kind of money was definitely the manager's business. 'And the withdrawal?'

'Twenty thousand pounds in cash.'

'Twenty thousand pounds in cash?' asked Pickering. He reached for the phone. 'Well, of course I shall have to call the Holborn branch and – '

'I don't think that will be necessary,' said Drake and pushed a copy of that morning's London *Times* over the desk. Pickering stared at it. What Drake handed him next caused him to stare even more. It was a photograph, taken with a Polaroid camera. He recognized his wife, whom he had left ninety minutes earlier, sitting round-eyed with fear in his own fireside chair. He could make out a portion of his own sitting room. His wife held their child close to her with one arm. Across her knees was the same issue of *The Times*.

'Taken sixty minutes ago,' said Drake.

Pickering's stomach tightened. The photo would win no prizes for photo-graphic quality, but the shape of the man's shoulder in the foreground and the sawn-off shotgun pointing at his family was quite clear enough.

'If you raise the alarm,' said Drake quietly, 'the police will come here, not to your home. Before they break in, you will be dead. In exactly sixty minutes, unless I make a phone call to say I am safely away with the money, that man is going to pull the trigger. Please don't think we are joking; we are quite prepared to die if we have to. We are the Red Army Faction.'

Pickering swallowed hard. Under his desk, a foot from his knee, was a button linked to a silent alarm. He looked at the photograph again and moved his knee away.

'Call your chief clerk,' said Drake, 'and instruct him to open the account, credit the cheque to it, and provide the cheque for the twenty-thousand-pound withdrawal. Tell him you have telephoned London and all is in order. If he expresses surprise, tell him the sum is for a very big commercial promotion campaign in which prize money will be given away in cash. Pull yourself together and make it good.'

The chief clerk *was* surprised, but his manager seemed calm enough, a little subdued perhaps, but otherwise normal. And the dark-suited man before him looked relaxed and friendly. There was even a glass of the manager's sherry before each of them, though the businessman had kept his light gloves on, odd for such warm weather. Thirty minutes later the chief clerk brought the money from the vault, deposited it on the manager's desk and left.

Drake packed it calmly into the attaché case.

'There are thirty minutes left,' he told Pickering. 'In twenty-five I shall make my phone call. My colleague will leave your wife and child perfectly unharmed. If you raise the alarm before that, he will shoot first and take his chances with the police later.'

When he had gone, Mr Pickering sat frozen for half an hour. In fact Drake phoned the house five minutes later from a call box. Krim took the call, smiled briefly at the woman on the floor with her hands and ankles taped and left. Neither used the van, which had been stolen the previous day. Krim used a motorcycle parked further down the road in readiness. Drake took a motorcycle helmet from the van to cover his flaming red hair, and used the second motorcycle parked near the van. Both were out of Sheffield within thirty minutes. They abandoned the vehicles north of London and met again in Drake's flat where he washed the red dye out of his hair and crushed the eyeglasses to fragments.

Munro caught the following morning's breakfast flight south from Inverness. When the plastic trays were cleared away the hostess offered round newspapers fresh up from London. Being at the back of the aircraft, Munro missed *The Times* and the *Telegraph*, but secured a copy of the *Daily Express*. The headline story concerned two unidentified men, believed to be Germans from the Red Army Faction, who had robbed a Sheffield bank of £20,000.

'Bloody bastards,' said the English oilman from the North Sea rigs who was in the seat next to Munro. He tapped the *Express* headline. 'Bloody Commies. I'd string them all up.'

Munro conceded that upstringing would definitely have to be considered in future.

At Heathrow he took a taxi to a point near the office and was shown straight into Barry Ferndale's room.

'Adam, my dear chap, you're looking a new man.'

He sat Munro down and proffered coffee.

'Well, now, the tape. You must be dying to know. Fact is, m'dear chap, it's genuine. No doubt about it. Everything checks. There's been a fearful blow-up in the Soviet Agriculture Ministry. Six or seven senior functionaries ousted, including one we think must be that unfortunate fellow in the Lubyanka.

'That helps corroborate it. But the voices are genuine. No doubt, according to the lab boys. Now for the big one; one of our assets working out of Leningrad managed to take a drive out of town. There's not much wheat grown up there in the north, but there is a little. He stopped his car for a pee, and swiped a stalk of the afflicted wheat. It came home in the bag three days ago. I got the report from the lab last night. They confirm there is an excess of this Lindane stuff present in the root of the seedling.

'So, there we are. You've hit what our American cousins so charmingly call pay-dirt. In fact, twenty-four carat gold. By the way, the Master wants to see you. You're going back to Moscow tonight.'

Munro's meeting with Sir Nigel Irvine was friendly but brief.

'Well done,' said the Master. 'Now I understand your next meeting will be in a fortnight.'

Munro nodded.

'This might be a long-term operation,' Sir Nigel resumed, 'which makes it a good thing you are new to Moscow. There will be no raised eyebrows if you stay on for a couple of years. But just in case this fellow changes his mind, I want you to press for more; everything we can squeeze out. Do you want any help, any back-up?'

'No, thank you,' said Munro. 'Now that he's taken the plunge, the asset has insisted he'll talk only to me. I don't think I want to scare him off at this stage by bringing others in. Nor do I think he can travel, as Penkovsky could. Vishnayev never travels, so there's no cause for Krivoi to, either. I'll have to handle it alone.'

Sir Nigel nodded. 'Very well, you've got it.'

When Munro had gone, Sir Nigel Irvine turned over the file on his desk, which was Munro's personal record. He had his misgivings. The man was a loner, ill at ease working in a team. A man who walked alone in the mountains of Scotland for relaxation.

There was an adage in the firm: there are old agents and there are bold agents, but there are no old, bold agents. Sir Nigel was an old agent, and he appreciated caution. This one had come swinging in from the outfield, unexpected, unprepared for. And it was moving fast. But then, the tape was genuine, no doubt of it. So was the summons on his desk to see the Prime Minister that evening at Downing Street. He had of course informed the foreign secretary when the tape had passed muster, and this was the outcome.

The black door of Number 10, Downing Street, residence of the British prime minister, is perhaps one of the best-known doors in the world. It stands on the right, two-thirds down a small cul-de-sac off Whitehall, an alley almost, sandwiched between the imposing piles of the Cabinet Office and the Foreign Office.

In front of this door, with its simple white figures 10, and the brass knocker, attended by a single, unarmed police constable, the tourists gather to take each other's photograph and watch the comings and goings of the messengers and the well known.

In fact it is the men of words who go in through the front door; the men of influence tend to use the side. The house called Number 10 stands at ninety degrees to the Cabinet Office block and the rear corners almost touch each other, enclosing a small lawn behind black railings. Where the corners almost meet, the gap is covered by a passageway leading to a small side door, and it was through this that the director-general of the SIS, accompanied by Sir Julian Flannery, the Cabinet secretary, passed that last evening of July. The pair were shown straight to the second floor, past the Cabinet room, to the Prime Minister's private study.

The Prime Minister had read the transcript of the Politburo tape, passed to her by the foreign secretary.

'Have you informed the Americans of this matter?' she asked directly.

'Not yet, ma'am,' Sir Nigel answered. 'Our final confirmation of its authenticity is only three days old.'

'I would like you to do it personally,' said the Prime Minister. Sir Nigel inclined his head. 'The political perspectives of this pending wheat famine in the Soviet Union are immeasurable, of course, and as the world's biggest surplus wheat producer, the USA should be involved from the outset.'

'I would not wish the cousins to move in on this agent of ours,' said Sir

Nigel. 'The running of this asset may be extremely delicate. I think we should handle it ourselves, alone.'

'Will they try to move in?' asked the Prime Minister.

'They may, ma'am. They may. We ran Penkovsky jointly, even though it was we who recruited him. But there were reasons why. This time I think we should go it alone.'

The Prime Minister was not slow to see the value in political terms of controlling such an agent as one who had access to the Politburo transcripts.

'If pressure is brought,' she said, 'refer back to me and I will speak to President Matthews personally about it. In the meantime I would like you to fly to Washington tomorrow and give them the tape, or at least a verbatim copy of it. I intend to speak to President Matthews tonight in any case.'

Sir Nigel and Sir Julian rose to leave.

'One last thing,' said the Prime Minister. 'I fully understand that I am not allowed to know the identity of this agent. Will you be telling Robert Benson who it is?'

'Certainly not, ma'am.' Not only would the director-general of the SIS refuse point blank to inform his own Prime Minister, or the foreign secretary, of the identity of the Russian, but he would not tell them even of Munro who was running that agent. The Americans would know who Munro was, but never who he was running. Nor would there be any tailing of Munro by the cousins in Moscow; he would see to that as well.

'Then presumably this Russian defector has a code name. May I know it?' asked the Prime Minister.

'Certainly, ma'am. The defector is now known in every file simply as the Nightingale.'

It just happened that Nightingale was the first songbird in the N section of the list of birds after which all Soviet agents were codenamed, but the Prime Minister did not know this. She smiled for the first time.

'How very appropriate.'

Just after ten in the morning of a wet and rainy 1st August an ageing but comfortable four-jet VC-10 of the Royal Air Force Strike Command lifted out of Lyneham base in Wiltshire and headed west for Ireland and the Atlantic. It carried a small enough passenger complement: one air chief marshal who had been informed the night before that this of all days was the best for him to visit the Pentagon in Washington to discuss the forthcoming USAF-RAF tactical bomber exercises, and a civilian in a shabby mackintosh.

The air chief marshal had introduced himself to the unexpected civilian, and learned in reply that his companion was Mr Barrett of the Foreign Office who had business with the British embassy on Massachusetts Avenue and had been instructed to take advantage of the VC-10 flight to save the taxpayer the cost of a two-way air ticket. The air force officer never learned that the purpose of the RAF plane's flight was in fact the other way around.

On another track south of the VC-10 a Boeing jumbo jet of British Airways left Heathrow bound for New York. Among its 300-plus passengers it bore Azamat Krim, alias Arthur Crimmins, Canadian citizen, heading west with a back pocket full of money on a buying mission.

Eight hours later the VC-10 landed perfectly at Andrews air force base in Maryland, ten miles southeast of Washington. As it closed down its engines on the apron, a Pentagon staff car swept up to the foot of the steps and disgorged a two-star general of the USAF. Two air force police snapped to attention as the air chief marshal came down the steps to his welcoming committee. Within five minutes it was all over; the Pentagon limousine drove away to Washington, the police 'snowdrops' marched off, and the idle and curious of the air base went back to their duties.

No one noticed the modest-priced sedan with non-official number plates that drove to the parked VC-10 ten minutes later – no one, that is, with enough observation to note the odd-shaped aerial on the roof that betrayed a CIA car. No one bothered with the rumpled civilian who trotted down the steps and straight into the car moments later, and no one saw the car leave the air base.

The company man in the US embassy in Grosvenor Square, London, had been alerted the night before, and his coded signal to Langley had laid on the car. The driver was in civilian clothes, a low-level staffer, but the man in the back who welcomed the guest from London was the chief of the Western European division, one of the regional subordinates of the deputy director of operations. He had been chosen to meet the Englishman because, having once headed the CIA operation in London, he knew him well. No one likes substitutions.

'Nigel, good to see you again,' he said after confirming to himself that the arrival was indeed the man they expected.

'How good of you to come to meet me, Lance,' responded Sir Nigel Irvine, well aware there was nothing good about it; it was a duty. The talk in the car was of London, family, the weather. No question of 'what are you doing here'. The car swept along the Capital Beltway to the Woodrow Wilson Memorial Bridge over the Potomac and headed west into Virginia.

On the outskirts of Alexandria the driver pulled right into the George Washington Memorial Parkway which fringes the whole western bank of the river. As they cruised past the National Airport and Arlington Cemetery, Sir Nigel Irvine glanced out to his right at the skyline of Washington where years before he had been the SIS liaison man with the CIA, based in the British embassy. Those had been tough days, in the wake of the Philby affair, when even the state of the weather was classified information so far as the English were concerned. He thought of what he carried in his briefcase and permitted himself a small smile.

After thirty minutes' cruising they pulled off the main highway, swung over it again and headed into the forest. He remembered the small notice saying simply BPR-CIA and wondered again why they had to signpost the place. You either knew where it was or you didn't, and if you didn't you weren't invited anyway.

At the security gate in the great seven-foot-high, chain-link fence that surrounds Langley, they halted while Lance showed his pass, then drove on and turned left past the awful conference centre known as the Igloo, because that is just what it resembles.

The company's headquarters consists of five blocks, one in the centre and one at each corner of the centre block, like a rough St Andrew's cross. The Igloo is stuck on to the corner block nearest the main gate. Passing the recessed centre block, Sir Nigel noticed the imposing main doorway and the great seal of the United States paved in terrazzo into the ground in front of it. But he knew this front entrance was for congressmen, senators and other undesirables. The car swept on, past the complex, then pulled to the right and drove round the back.

Here there is a short ramp, protected by a steel portcullis, running down one floor to the first basement level. At the bottom is a select car park for no more than ten cars. The black sedan came to a halt, and the man called Lance handed Sir Nigel over to his superior, Charles 'Chip' Allen, the deputy director of operations. They too knew each other well.

Set in the back wall of the car park is a small lift, guarded by steel doors and two armed men. Chip Allen identified his guest, signed for him and used a plastic card to open the lift doors. The lift hummed its way quietly seven floors up to the director's suite. Another magnetized plastic card got them both out of the lift, into a lobby faced by three doors. Chip Allen knocked on the centre one, and it was Bob Benson himself who, alerted from below, welcomed the British visitor into his suite.

Benson led him past the big desk to the lounge area in front of the beige marble fireplace. In winter Benson liked a crackling log fire to burn here, but Washington in August is no place for fires and the air conditioning was working overtime. Benson pulled the rice-paper screen across the room to separate the lounge from the office and sat back opposite his guest. Coffee was ordered, and when they were alone Benson finally asked, 'What brings you to Langley, Nigel?'

Sir Nigel sipped and sat back.

'We have,' he said undramatically, 'obtained the services of a new asset.'

He spoke for almost ten minutes, before the director of central intelligence interrupted him.

'Inside the Politburo?' he queried. 'You mean, right inside?'

'Let us just say, with access to Politburo meeting transcripts,' said Sir Nigel.

'Would you mind if I called Chip Allen and Ben Kahn in on this?'

'Not at all, Bob. They'll have to know within an hour or so anyway. Prevents repetition.'

Bob Benson rose, crossed to a telephone on a coffee table and made a call to his private secretary. When he had finished he stared out of the picture window at the great green forest. 'Jesus H. Christ,' he breathed.

Sir Nigel Irvine was not displeased that his two old contacts in the CIA should be in on the ground floor of his briefing. All pure intelligence agencies, as opposed to intelligence/secret police forces like the KGB, have two main arms. One is Operations, covering the business of actually obtaining information; the other is Intelligence, covering the business of collating, cross-referencing, interpreting and analysing the great mass of raw, unprocessed information that is gathered in.

Both have to be good. If the information is faulty the best analysis in the world will only come up with nonsense; if the analysis is inept all the efforts of the information gathers are wasted. Statesmen need to know what other nations, friend or potential foe, are doing and if possible what they intend to do. What they are doing is nowadays often observable; what they intend to do is not. Which is why all the space cameras in the world will never supplant a brilliant analyst working with material from inside the others' secret councils.

In the CIA the two men who hold sway under the director of central intelligence, who may be a political appointee, are the deputy director (Operations) and the deputy director (Intelligence). It is Operations that inspire the thriller-writers; Intelligence is back-room work, tedious, slow, methodical, often boring but always invaluable.

Like Tweedledum and Tweedledee, the DDO and the DDI have to work hand in hand; they have to trust each other. Benson, as a political appointee, was lucky. His DDO was Chip Allen, WASP and former football player; his DDI was Ben Kahn, Jewish former chess master; they fitted together like a pair of gloves. In five minutes both were sitting with Benson and Irvine in the lounge area. Coffee was forgotten.

The British spymaster talked for almost an hour. He was uninterrupted. Then the three Americans read the Nightingale transcript and watched the tape recording in its polythene bag with something like hunger. When Irvine had finished there was a short sharp silence. Chip Allen broke it.

'Roll over, Penkovsky,' he said.

'You'll want to check it all,' said Sir Nigel evenly. No one dissented. Friends are friends, but. . . . 'It took us ten days, but we can't fault it. The voice prints check out, every one. We've already exchanged cables about the bust-up in the Soviet Agriculture Ministry. And of course, you have your Condor photographs. Oh, one last thing. . . .'

From his bag he produced a small polythene sack with a sprig of young wheat inside it.

'One of our chaps swiped this from a field outside Leningrad.'

'I'll have our Agriculture Department check it out as well,' said Benson. 'Anything else, Nigel?'

'Oh, not really,' said Sir Nigel. 'Well, perhaps a couple of small points. . . .'

'Spit it out.' Sir Nigel drew a breath.

'The Russian build-up in Afghanistan. We think they may be mounting a move towards Pakistan and India through the passes. That we regard as our patch. Now if you could ask Condor to have a look. . . .'

'You've got it,' said Benson without hesitation.

'And then,' resumed Sir Nigel, 'that Soviet defector you brought out of Geneva two weeks ago. He seems to know quite a bit about Soviet assets in our trade union movement.'

'We sent you transcripts of that,' said Allen hastily.

'We'd like direct access,' said Sir Nigel.

Allen looked at Kahn. Kahn shrugged.

'OK,' said Benson. 'Can we have access to Nightingale?'

'Sorry, no,' said Sir Nigel. 'That's different. The Nightingale's too damn delicate, right out in the cold. I don't want to disturb the fish just yet in case of a change of heart. You'll get everything we get, as soon as we get it. But no moving in. I'm trying to speed up the delivery and volume, but it's going to take time, and a lot of care.'

'When's your next delivery slated for?' asked Allen.

'Today week. At least, that's the meet. I'll hope there'll be a handover.'

Sir Nigel Irvine spent the night at a CIA safe house in the Virginia countryside, and the next day 'Mr Barrett' flew back to London with his air chief marshal.

It was three days later that Azamat Krim sailed from Pier 49 in New York harbour aboard the elderly *Queen Elizabeth II* for Southampton. He had decided to sail rather than fly because he felt he had a better chance of his main luggage escaping X-ray examination by sea.

His purchases were complete. One of his pieces of luggage was a standard aluminium shoulder-case such as professional photographers use to protect their cameras and lenses. As such it could not be X-rayed, but would have to be hand-examined. The moulded plastic sponge inside that held the cameras and lenses from banging against each other was glued to the bottom of the case, but ended two inches short of the real bottom. In the cavity were two handguns with ammunition clips.

Another piece of luggage, deep in the heart of a small cabin trunk full of clothes, was an aluminium tube with a screw-top, containing what looked like a long, cylindrical camera lens, some four inches in diameter. He calculated that if it was examined it would pass in the eyes of all but the most suspicious of customs officers as the sort of lens that camera freaks use for very long range photography, and a collection of books of bird photographs and wildlife pictures lying next to the lens inside the trunk were designed to corroborate the explanation.

In fact the lens was an image-intensifier, also called a night-sight, of the kind that may be commercially bought without a permit in the United States but not in Britain.

It was boiling hot that Sunday, 8th August, in Moscow and those who could not get to the beaches crowded instead to the numerous swimming baths of the city, especially the new complex built for the 1980 Olympics. But the British embassy staff, along with those of a dozen other legations, were at the beach on the Moscow River upstream from Uspenskoye Bridge. Adam Munro was among them.

He tried to appear as carefree as the others, but it was hard. He checked his watch too many times, and finally got dressed.

'Oh, Adam, you're not going back already? There's ages of daylight left.' one of the secretaries called to him.

He forced a rueful grin. 'Duty calls, or rather the plans for the Manchester Chamber of Commerce visit call,' he shouted back to her.

He walked through the woods to his car, dropped his bathing things inside, had a covert look to see if anyone was interested, and locked the car. There were too many men in sandals, slacks and open shirts for one extra to be of notice, and he thanked his stars the KGB never seem to take their jackets off. There was no one looking remotely like the opposition within sight of him. He set off through the trees to the north.

Valentina was waiting for him, standing back in the shade of the trees. His stomach was tight, knotted, for all that he was pleased to see her. She was no expert at spotting a tail and might have been followed. If she had, his diplomatic cover would save him from worse than expulsion, but the repercussions would be enormous. Even that was not his main worry; it was what they would do to her if she were ever caught. Whatever the motives, the term for what she was doing was high treason.

He took her in his arms and kissed her. She kissed him back, and trembled in his arms.

'Are you frightened?' he asked her.

'A bit,' she nodded. 'You listened to the tape recording?'

'Yes I did. Before I handed it over. I suppose I should not have done, but I did.'

'Then you know about the famine that faces us. Adam, when I was a girl I saw the famine in this country, just after the war. It was bad, but it was caused by the war, by Germans. We could take it. Our leaders were on our side, they would make things get better.'

'Perhaps they can sort things out this time,' said Munro lamely.

Valentina shook her head angrily. 'They're not even trying,' she burst out. 'I sit there listening to their voices, typing the transcripts. They are just bickering, trying to save their own skins.'

'And your husband's uncle, Marshal Kerensky?' he asked gently.

'He's as bad as the rest. When I married my husband, Uncle Nikolai was at the wedding. I thought he was so jolly, so kindly. Of course, that was his private life. Now I listen to him in his public life; he's like all of them, ruthless and cynical. They just jockey for advantage among each other, for power, and to hell with the people. I suppose I should be one of them, but I can't be. Not now, not any more.'

Munro looked across the clearing at the pines but saw olive trees and heard a boy in uniform shouting, 'You don't own me.' Strange, he mused, how establishments with all their power sometimes went too far and lost control of their own servants through sheer excess. Not always, not often, but sometimes.

'I could get you out of here, Valentina,' he said. 'It would mean my leaving the diplomatic corps, but it's been done before. Sasha is young enough to grow up somewhere else.'

'No, Adam, no, it's tempting but I can't. Whatever the outcome, I am part of Russia, I have to stay. Perhaps, one day . . . I don't know.'

They sat in silence for a while, holding hands. She broke the quiet at last.

'Did your . . . intelligence people pass the tape recording on to London?'

'I think so. I handed it to the man I believe represents the Secret Service in the embassy. He asked me if there would be another one.'

She nodded at her shoulder-bag.

'It's just the transcript. I can't get the tape recordings any more. They're kept in a safe after the transcriptions, and I don't have the key. The papers in there are of the following Politburo meeting.'

'How do you get them out, Valentina?' he asked.

'After the meetings,' she told him, 'the tapes and the stenographic notes are brought under guard to the Central Committee building. There is a locked department there where we work, me and five other women. With one man in charge. When the transcripts are finished the tapes are locked away.'

'Then how did you get the first one?'

She shrugged.

'The man in charge is new, since last month. The other one, before him, was more lax. There is a tape studio next door where the tapes are copied once before being locked in the safe. I was alone in there last month, long enough to steal the second tape, and substitute a dummy.'

'A dummy?' exclaimed Munro. 'They'll spot the substitution if ever they play them back.'

'It's unlikely,' she said. 'The transcripts form the archives once they have been checked against the tapes for accuracy. I was lucky with that tape; I brought it out in a shopping bag under the groceries I had bought in the Central Committee commissary.'

'Aren't you searched?'

'Hardly ever. We are trusted, Adam, the elite of the New Russia. The papers are easier. At work I wear an old-fashioned girdle. I copied the last meeting of June on the machine, but ran off one extra copy, then switched the number-control back by one figure. The extra copy I stuck inside my girdle. It made no noticeable bulge.'

Munro's stomach turned at the risk she was taking.

'What do they talk about in this meeting?' he asked, gesturing towards the shoulder-bag.

'The consequences,' she said. 'What will happen when the famine breaks. What the people of Russia will do to them. But Adam . . . there's been one since. Early in July. I couldn't copy it, I was on leave. I couldn't refuse my leave, it would have been too obvious. But when I got back I met one of the girls who had transcribed it. She was white-faced, and wouldn't describe it.'

'Can you get it?' asked Munro.

'I can try. I'll have to wait until the office is empty and use the copying machine. I can reset it afterwards so it will not show it has been used. But not until early next month; I shall not be on the late shift when I can work alone until then.'

'We shouldn't meet here again,' Munro told her. 'Patterns are dangerous.'

He spent another hour describing the sort of tradecraft she would need to know if they were to go on meeting. Finally he gave her a pad of close-typed sheets he had tucked in his waistband under his loose shirt.

'It's all in there, my darling. Memorize it and burn it. Flush the ashes down the toilet.'

Five minutes later she gave him a wad of flimsy paper sheets covered with neat, typed Cyrillic script from her bag and slipped away through the forest to her car on a sandy track half a mile away.

Munro retreated into the darkness of the main arch above the church's recessed side door. He produced a roll of tape from his pocket, slipped his trousers to his knees and taped the batch of sheets to his thigh. With the trousers back up again and belted he could feel the paper snug against his thigh as he walked, but under the baggy, Russian-made trousers they did not show.

By midnight, in the silence of his flat, he had read them all a dozen times. The next Wednesday they went in the messenger's wrist-chained briefcase to London, wax-sealed in a stout envelope and coded for the SIS liaison man at the Foreign Office only.

The glass doors leading to the rose garden were tight shut and only the whir of the air conditioner broke the silence in the Oval Office of the White House. The balmy days of June were long gone and the steam heat of a Washington August forbade open doors and windows.

Round the building on the Pennsylvania Avenue façade the tourists, damp and hot, admired the familiar aspect of the White House front entrance, with its pillars, flag and curved driveway; or queued for the guided tour of this most holy of American holies. None of them would penetrate to the tiny West Wing building where President Matthews sat in conclave with his advisers.

In front of his desk were Stanislaw Poklewski and Robert Benson. They had been joined by Secretary of State David Lawrence, a Boston lawyer and pillar of the East Coast establishment.

President Matthews flicked the file in front of him closed. He had long since devoured the first Politburo transcript, translated into English; what he had just finished reading was his experts' evaluation of it.

'Bob, you were remarkably close with your estimate of a shortfall of thirty million tons,' he said. 'Now it appears they are going to be fifty to fifty-five million tons short this fall. And you have no doubts this transcript comes right from inside the Politburo?'

'Mr President, we've checked it out in every way. The voices are real; the traces of excessive Lindane in the root of the wheat plant are real; the hatchet job inside the Soviet Agriculture Ministry is real. We don't believe there is room for any substantive doubt that tape recording was of the Politburo in session.'

'We have to handle this right,' mused the President. 'There must be no way we make a miscalculation on this one. There has never been an opportunity like it.'

'Mr President,' said Poklewski, 'this means the Soviets are not facing severe shortages as we supposed when you invoked the Shannon Act last month. They are facing a famine.'

Unknowingly he was echoing the words of Petrov in the Kremlin two months earlier, in his aside to Ivanenko, which had not been on the tape. President Matthews nodded slowly.

'We can't disagree with that, Stan. The question is, what do we do about it?'

'Let them have their famine,' said Poklewski. 'This is the biggest mistake they have made since Stalin refused to believe Western warnings about the Nazi build-up on his frontier in spring 1941. This time the enemy is within. So let them sort it out in their own way.'

'David?' asked the President of his secretary of state.

Secretary Lawrence shook his head. The differences of opinion between the arch-hawk Poklewski and the cautious Bostonian were legendary.

'I disagree, Mr President,' he said at length. 'Firstly, I don't think we have examined deeply enough the possible permutations of what might happen if the Soviet Union is plunged into chaos next spring. As I see it, it is more than simply a question of letting the Soviets stew in their own juice. There are massive implications on a worldwide basis consequent on such a phenomenon.'

'Bob?' asked President Matthews. His director of central intelligence was lost in thought.

'We have the time, Mr President,' he said. 'They know you invoked the Shannon Act last month. They know if they want the grain, they have to come to you. As Secretary Lawrence says, we really should examine the perspectives consequent upon a famine across the Soviet Union. We can do that as of now. Sooner or later the Kremlin has to make a play. When they do, we have all the cards. We know how bad their predicament is; they don't know we know. We have the wheat, we have the Condors, we have the

Nightingale and we have the time in hand. We hold all the aces this time. No need to decide yet which way to play them.'

Lawrence nodded and regarded Benson with new respect. Poklewski shrugged. President Matthews made up his mind.

'Stan, as of now I want you to put together an *ad hoc* group within the National Security Council. I want it small, and absolutely secret. You, Bob and David here. Chairman joint chiefs of staff, secretaries of defense, treasury and agriculture. I want to know what will happen, worldwide, if the Soviet Union starves. I need to know, and soon.'

One of the telephones on his desk rang. It was the direct line from the State Department. President Matthews looked enquiringly at David Lawrence.

'Are you calling me, David?' he asked with a smile.

The secretary of state rose and took the machine off its rest. He listened for several minutes, then replaced the receiver.

'Mr President, the pace is speeding up. Two hours ago in Moscow Foreign Minister Rykov summoned Ambassador Donaldson to the Foreign Ministry. On behalf of the Soviet Government he has proposed the sale by the United States to the Soviet Union by next spring of fifty-five million tons of mixed cereal grains.'

For several moments only the ormolu carriage clock above the marble fireplace could be heard in the Oval Office.

'What did Ambassador Donaldson reply?' asked the President.

'Of course, that the request would be passed on to Washington for consideration,' said Lawrence, 'and that no doubt your answer would be forthcoming in due course.'

'Gentlemen,' said the President, 'I need those answers, and I need them fast. I can hold my answer for four weeks at the outside, but by 15th September at the latest I shall have to reply. When I do, I shall want to know what we are handling here. Every possibility.'

'Mr President, within a few days we may be receiving a second package of information from the Nightingale. That could give an indication of the way the Kremlin sees the same problem.'

President Matthews nodded. 'Bob, if and when it comes, I would like it translated into English and on my desk immediately.'

As the presidential meeting broke up in the dusk of Washington, it was already long after dark in Britain. Police records later showed that scores of burglaries and break-ins had taken place during the night of 11–12 August, but the one that most disturbed the police of the county of Somerset was the theft from a sporting gunshop in the pleasant country town of Taunton.

The thieves had evidently visited the shop in daylight hours during the previous day or so, for the alarm had been neatly cut by someone who had spotted where the cable ran. With the alarm system out of commission, the thieves had used powerful bolt-cutters on the window grill in the back alley that ran behind the shop.

The place had not been ransacked, and the usual haul, shotguns for the holding up of banks, had not been taken. What was missing, the proprietor confirmed, was a single hunting rifle, one of his finest, a Finnish-made Sako

Hornet .22, a highly accurate precision piece. Also gone were two boxes of shells for the rifle, soft-nosed 45 grain, hollow-point Remingtons, capable of high velocity, great penetration and considerable distortion on impact.

In his flat in Bayswater, Andrew Drake sat with Miroslav Kaminsky and Azamat Krim and gazed at their haul laid out on the sitting room table; it consisted of two handguns, each with two magazines fully loaded; the rifle with two boxes of shells, and the image-intensifier.

There are two basic types of night-sight: the infra-red scope and the intensifier. Men who shoot by night tend to prefer the latter, and Krim, with his Western Canadian hunting background and three years with the Canadian paratroopers, had chosen well.

The infra-red sight is based on the principle of sending a beam of infra-red light down the line of fire to illuminate the target, which appears in the sight like a greenish outline. But because it emits light, even a light invisible to the naked eye, the infra-red sight requires a power source. The image-intensifier works on the principle of gathering all those tiny elements of light that are present in a 'dark' environment, and concentrating them, as the gigantic retina of a barn owl's eye can concentrate what little light there is and see a moving mouse where a human eye would detect nothing. It needs no power source.

Originally developed for military purposes, the small hand-held image-intensifiers had by the late seventies come to interest the vast American security industry and were of use to factory guards and others. Soon they were on commercial sale. By the early eighties the larger versions, capable of being mounted on a rifle barrel, were also purchasable in America for cash across the counter. It was one of these that Azamat Krim had bought.

The rifle already had grooves along the upper side of its barrel to take a telescopic sight for target practice. Working with a file and a vice screwed to the edge of the kitchen table, Krim began to convert the clips of the image-intensifier to fit into these grooves.

While Krim was working, a mile away in Grosvenor Square Barry Ferndale paid a visit to the United States embassy. By pre-arrangement he was visiting the head of the CIA operation in London, who was apparently a diplomat attached to his country's embassy staff.

The meeting was brief and cordial. Ferndale removed from his briefcase a wad of papers and handed them over.

'Fresh from the presses, my dear fellow,' he told the American. 'Rather a lot, I'm afraid. These Russians do tend to talk, don't they? Anyway, best of luck.'

The papers were the Nightingale's second delivery, and already in translation into English. The American knew he would have to encode them himself, and send them himself. No one else would see them. He thanked Ferndale and settled down to a long night of hard work.

He was not the only man who slept little that night. Far away in the city of Ternopol in the Ukraine a plain-clothes agent of the KGB left the non-commissioned officers club and commissary beside the KGB barracks and began to walk home. He was not of the rank to rate a staff car and his own private vehicle was parked near his house. He did not mind; it was a warm and pleasant night and he had had a convivial evening with his colleagues in the club.

Which was probably why he failed to notice the two figures in the doorway across the street who seemed to be watching the club entrance and who nodded to each other.

It was after midnight and Ternopol, even on a warm August night, has no life to speak of. The secret policeman's path took him away from the main streets and into the sprawl of Shevchenko Park where the trees in full leaf almost covered the narrow pathways. It was the longest shortcut he ever made. Halfway across the park there was a scuttling of feet behind him; he half turned, took the blow from the cosh that had been aimed at the back of his head on the temple and went down in a heap.

It was nearly dawn before he recovered. He had been dragged into a tangle of bushes and robbed of his wallet, money, keys, ration card and ID card. Police and KGB enquiries continued for several weeks into this most unaccustomed mugging, but no culprits were discovered. In fact both had been on the first dawn train out of Ternopol and were back in their homes in Lvov.

President Matthews personally chaired the meeting of the *ad hoc* committee that considered the Nightingale's second package, and it was a subdued meeting.

'My analysts have already come up with some possibilities consequent upon a famine in the Soviet Union next winter/spring,' Benson told the eight men in the Oval Office, 'but I don't think any one of them would have dared go as far as the Politburo themselves have done in predicting a pandemic breakdown of law and order. It's unheard of in the Soviet Union.'

'That's true of my people, too,' agreed David Lawrence of the State Department. 'The Politburo are talking here about the KGB not being able to hold the line. I don't think we could have gone that far in our prognosis.'

'So what answer do I give Maxim Rudin to his request to purchase fifty-five million tons of grain?' asked the President.

'Mr President, tell him no,' urged Poklewski. 'We have here an opportunity that has never occurred before and may never occur again. You have Maxim Rudin and the whole Politburo in the palm of your hand. For two decades successive US administrations have bailed the Soviets out every time they have gotten into problems with their economy. Every time, they have come back more aggressive than ever. Every time, they have responded by pushing further with their involvement in Africa, Asia, Latin America. Every time, the Third World has been encouraged to believe the Soviets have recovered from their setbacks through their own efforts, that the Marxist economic system works.

'This time the world can be shown beyond a doubt that the Marxist economic system does not work and never will. This time I urge you to screw the lid down tight, real tight. You can demand a concession for every ton of wheat. You can require them to get out of Asia, Africa and America. And if he won't you can bring Rudin down.'

'Would this,' President Matthews tapped the Nightingale report in front of him, 'bring Rudin down?'

David Lawrence answered, and no one disagreed with him.

'If what is described in here by the members of the Politburo themselves actually happened inside the Soviet Union, yes, Rudin would fall in disgrace, as Khrushchev fell,' he said.

'Then use the power,' urged Poklewski. 'Use it. Rudin has run flush out of options. He has no alternative but to agree to your terms. If he won't, topple him.'

'And the successor – ' began the President.

'Will have seen what happened to Rudin, and will learn his lesson from that. Any successor will have to agree to the terms we lay down.'

President Matthews sought the views of the rest of the meeting. All but Lawrence and Benson agreed with Poklewski. President Matthews made his decision; the hawks had won.

The Soviet Foreign Ministry is one of seven near-identical buildings of the wedding-cake architectural style that Stalin favoured; neo-Gothic as put together by a mad patissier, in brown sandstone and standing on Smolensky Boulevard, corner of Arbat.

On the penultimate day of the month the Fleetwood Brougham Cadillac of the American ambassador to Moscow hissed into the parking bay before the main doors, and Mr Morton Donaldson was escorted to the plush fourth-floor office of Dmitri Rykov, the veteran Soviet foreign minister. They knew each other well; before coming to Moscow, Ambassador Donaldson had done a spell at United Nations where Dmitri Rykov was a well-known figure. Frequently they had drunk friendly toasts there together, and here in Moscow also. But today's meeting was formal. Donaldson was attended by his head of chancery and Rykov by five senior officials.

Donaldson read his message, carefully, word for word, in its original English. Rykov understood and spoke English well, but an aide did a rapid running translation into his right ear.

President Matthews' message made no reference to his knowledge of the disaster that had struck the Soviet wheat crop, and it expressed no surprise at the Soviet request earlier in the month for the staggering purchase of 55,000,000 tons of grain. In measured terms it expressed regret that the United States of America would not be in a position to make a sale to the Union of Soviet Socialist Republics of the requested tonnage of wheat.

With hardly a pause, Ambassador Donaldson read on, into the second part of the message. This, seemingly unconnected with the first, though following without a break, regretted the lack of success of the Strategic Arms Limitation Talks known as SALT Three, concluded in the winter of 1980, in lessening world tension, and expressed the hope that SALT Four, scheduled for preliminary discussion this coming autumn and winter, would achieve more, and enable the world to make genuine steps along the road to a just and lasting peace. That was all.

Ambassador Donaldson laid the full text of the message on Rykov's desk, received the formal, straight-faced thanks of the grey-haired, grey-visaged Soviet foreign minister, and left.

*

Andrew Drake spent most of that day poring over books. Azamat Krim, he knew, was somewhere in the hills of Wales fine-testing the hunting rifle with its new sight mounted above the barrel. Miroslav Kaminsky was still working at his steadily improving English. For Drake the problems centred on the South Ukrainian port of Odessa.

His first work of reference was the red-covered *Lloyd's Loading List*, a weekly guide to ships loading in European ports for destinations all over the world. From this he learned that there was no regular service from Northern Europe to Odessa, but there was a small, independent, inter-Mediterranean service which also called at several Black Sea ports. It was named the Salonika Line, and listed two vessels.

From here he went to the blue-covered *Lloyd's Shipping Index* and scoured the columns until he came to the vessels in question. He smiled. The supposed owners of each vessel trading in the Salonika Line were one-ship companies registered in Panama, which meant beyond much of a doubt that the owning 'company' in each case was a single brass plate attached to the wall of a lawyer's office in Panama City, and no more.

From his third work of reference, a brown-covered book called the *Greek Owners' Directory*, he ascertained that the managing agents were listed as a Greek firm and that their offices were in Piraeus, the port of Athens. He knew what that meant. In ninety-nine cases out of a hundred, when one talks to the managing agents of a Panama-flag ship, and they are Greek, one is in effect talking to the ship's owners. They masquerade as 'agents only' in order to take advantage of the fact that agents cannot be held legally responsible for the peccadilloes of their principals. Some of these peccadilloes include inferior rates of pay and conditions for the crew, unseaworthy vessels and ill-defined safety standards but well-defined valuations for 'total-loss' insurance, and occasionally some very careless habits with crude oil spillages.

For all that, Drake began to like the Salonika Line for one reason; a Greek-registered vessel would inevitably be allowed to employ only Greek senior officers, but could employ a cosmopolitan crew with or without official discharge books; passports alone would be sufficient. And her ships visited Odessa regularly.

Maxim Rudin leaned forward, laid the Russian translation of President Matthews' negative message as delivered by Ambassador Donaldson on his coffee table, and surveyed his three guests. It was dark outside, and he liked to keep the lights low in his private study at the north end of the arsenal building in the Kremlin.

'Blackmail,' said Petrov angrily. 'Bloody blackmail.'

'Of course,' said Rudin. 'What were you expecting? Sympathy?'

'That damned Poklewski is behind this,' said Rykov. 'But this cannot be Matthews' final answer. Their own Condors and our offer to buy fifty-five million tons of grain must have told them what position we are in.'

'Will they talk eventually, will they negotiate after all?' asked Ivanenko.

'Oh, yes, they'll talk eventually,' said Rykov. 'But they'll delay as long as they can, spin things out, wait until the famine begins to bite, then trade the grain against humiliating concessions.'

'Not too humiliating, I hope,' murmured Ivanenko. 'We only have a seven to six majority in the Politburo, and I for one would like to hold on to it.'

'That is precisely my problem,' growled Rudin. 'Sooner or later I have to send Dmitri Rykov into the negotiating chamber to fight for us, and I don't have a single damned weapon to give him.'

On the last day of the month Andrew Drake flew from London to Athens to begin his search for a ship heading towards Odessa.

The same day a small van, converted into a two-bunk mobile home such as students like to use for a roving continental holiday, left London for Dover on the Channel coast, and thence to France and Athens by road. Concealed beneath the floors were the guns, ammunition and image-intensifier. Fortunately most drug consignments head the other way, from the Balkans towards France and Britain. Customs checks were perfunctory at Dover and Calais.

At the wheel was Azamat Krim with his Canadian passport and international driving licence. Beside him, with new, albeit not quite regular, British papers, was Miroslav Kaminsky.

6

Close by the bridge across the Moscow River at Uspenskoye is a restaurant called the Russian Izba. It is built in the style of the timber cottages in which Russian peasants dwell, and which are called *izbas*. Both interior and exterior are of split pine tree trunks, nailed to timber uprights. The gap between is traditionally filled with river clay, not unlike the Canadian log cabin.

These *izbas* may look primitive, and from the point of sanitation often are, but they are much warmer than brick or concrete structures through the freezing Russian winters. The Izba restaurant is snug and warm inside, divided into a dozen small private dining rooms, many of which will only seat one dinner party. Unlike the restaurants of central Moscow, it is permitted a profit incentive linked to staff pay, and as a result and in even more stark contrast to the usual run of Russian eateries it has tasty food and fast and willing service.

It was here that Adam Munro had set up his next meeting with Valentina, scheduled for Saturday, 4th September. She had secured a dinner date with a male friend and had persuaded him to take her to this particular restaurant. Munro had invited one of the embassy secretaries to dinner and had booked a table in her, not his, name. The written reservations record would therefore not show that either Munro or Valentina were present that evening.

They dined in separate rooms, and on the dot of nine o'clock each made the excuse of going to the toilet and left the table. They met in the car park and Munro, whose own car would be too noticeable with its embassy plates, followed Valentina to her own private Zhiguli saloon. She was subdued and puffed nervously at a cigarette.

Munro, as a result of handling the previous Russian defectors-in-place, knew the incessant strain that begins to wear at the nerves after a few weeks of subterfuge and secrecy.

'I got my chance,' she said at length. 'Three days ago. The meeting of early July. I was nearly caught.'

Munro was tense. Whatever she might think about her being trusted within the Party machine, no one, no one at all, is ever really trusted in

Moscow politics. She was walking a high-wire, they both were. The difference was, he had a net: his diplomatic status.

'What happened?' he asked.

'Someone came in. A guard. I had just switched off the copying machine and was back at my typewriter. He was perfectly friendly. But he leant against the machine. It was still warm. I don't think he noticed anything, but it frightened me. That's not all that frightened me. I couldn't read the transcript until I got home. I was too busy feeding it into the copier. Adam, it's awful.'

She took her car keys, unlocked the glove compartment and extracted a fat envelope which she handed to Munro. The moment of handover is usually the moment when the watchers pounce, if they are there; the moment when the feet pound on the gravel, the doors are torn open, the occupants dragged out. Nothing happened.

Munro glanced at his watch. Nearly ten minutes. Too long. He put the envelope in his inside pocket.

'I'm going to try for permission to bring you out.' he said. 'You can't go on like this forever, even for much longer. Nor can you simply settle back to the old life, not now. Not knowing what you know. Nor can I carry on, knowing you are out in the city, knowing that we love each other. I have a leave break next month. I'm going to ask them in London then.'

This time she made no demur, a sign that her nerve was showing the first signs of breaking.

'All right,' she said. Seconds later she was gone into the darkness of the car park. He watched her enter the pool of light by the open restaurant door and disappear inside. He gave her two minutes then returned to his own impatient escort.

It was three in the morning before Munro had finished reading the Plan Boris, Marshal Nikolai Kerensky's scenario for the conquest of Western Europe. He poured himself a double brandy and sat staring at the papers on his sitting room table. Valentina's jolly, kind Uncle Nikolai, he mused, had certainly laid it on the line. He spent two hours staring at a map of Europe, and by sunrise was as certain as Kerensky himself that in terms of conventional warfare the plan would work. Secondly, he was sure that Rykov too was right; thermo-nuclear war would ensue. And thirdly he was convinced there was no way of convincing the dissident members of the Politburo of this, short of the holocaust actually happening.

He rose and went to the window. Daylight was breaking in the east, out over the Kremlin spires; an ordinary Sunday was beginning for the citizens of Moscow, as it would in two hours for the Londoners and five hours later for the New Yorkers.

All his adult life the guarantee that summer Sundays would remain just plain ordinary had been dependent on a fine balance: a balance of belief in the might and willpower of the opponent super-powers, a balance of credibility, a balance of fear, but a balance for all that. He shivered, partly from the chill of morning, more from the realization that the papers behind him proved that at last the old nightmare was coming out of the shadows; the balance was breaking down.

*

The Sunday sunrise found Andrew Drake in far better humour, for his Saturday night had brought information of a different kind.

Every area of human knowledge, however small, however arcane, has its experts and its devotees. And every group of these appear to have one place where they congregate to talk, discuss, exchange their information and impart the newest gossip.

Shipping movements in the eastern Mediterranean hardly form a subject on which doctorates are earned, but in that area they do form a subject of great interest to out-of-work seamen, such as Andrew Drake was pretending to be. The information centre about such movements is a small hotel called the Cavo d'Oro, standing above a yacht basin in the port of Piraeus.

Drake had already observed the offices of the agents, and probable owners, of the Salonika Line, but he knew the last thing he should do was to visit them. Instead he checked into the Cavo d'Oro Hotel and spent his time at the bar, where captains, mates, bo'suns, agents, dockland gossips and job-seekers sat over drinks to exchange what titbits of information they had. On Saturday night Drake found his man, a bo'sun who had once worked for the Salonika Line. It took half a bottle of retsina to extract the information.

'The one that visits Odessa most frequently is the MV *Sanadria*,' he was told. 'She is an old tub. Captain is Nikos Thanos. I think she's in harbour now.'

She *was* in harbour, and Drake found her by mid-morning. She was a 5000-ton deadweight, 'tween-deck Mediterranean trader, rusty and none too clean, but if she was heading into the Black Sea and up to Odessa on her next voyage, Drake would not have minded if she was full of holes.

By sundown he had found her captain, having learned that Thanos and all his officers were from the Greek island of Chios. Most of these Greek-run traders are almost family affairs, the master and his senior officers usually being from the same island, and often inter-related. Drake spoke no Greek, but English was fortunately the *lingua franca* of the international maritime community even in Piraeus, and just before sundown he found Captain Thanos.

North Europeans when they finish work head for home, wife and family. East Mediterraneans head for the coffee shop, friends and gossip. The Mecca of the coffee shop community in Piraeus is a street alongside the waterfront called Akti Miaouli; its vicinity contains little else but shipping offices and coffee shops.

Each frequenter has his favourite shop, and they are always crammed. Captain Thanos hung out when he was ashore at an open-fronted affair called Miki's, and here Drake found him, sitting over the inevitable thick black coffee, glass of cold water and shot tumbler of ouzo. He was short, broad and nut-brown, with black curly hair and several days of stubble.

'Captain Thanos?' asked Drake. The man looked up in suspicion at the Englishman and nodded.

'Nikos Thanos, of the *Sanadria*?' The seaman nodded again. His three companions had fallen silent, watching.

Drake smiled. 'My name is Andrew Drake. Can I offer you a drink?'

Captain Thanos used one forefinger to indicate his own glass and those of his companions. Drake, still standing, summoned a waiter and ordered five of everything. Thanos nodded to a vacant chair, the invitation to join them. Drake knew it would be slow, and might take days. But he was not going to hurry. He had found his ship.

The meeting in the Oval Office five days later was far less relaxed. All seven members of the *ad hoc* committee of the National Security Council were present, with President Matthews in the chair. All had spent half the night reading the transcript of the Politburo meeting in which Marshal Kerensky had laid out his plan for war and Vishnayev had made his bid for power. All eight men were shaken. The focus was on the chairman of the joint chiefs of staff, General Martin Craig.

'The question is, general,' President Matthews asked, 'is it feasible?'

'In terms of a conventional war across the face of Western Europe from the Iron Curtain to the Channel ports, even involving the use of tactical nuclear shells and rockets, yes, Mr President, it's feasible.'

'Could the West, before next spring, increase her defences to the point of making it completely unworkable?'

'That's a harder one, Mr President. Certainly we in the US could ship more men, more hardware, over to Europe. That would give the Soviets ample excuse to beef up their own levels, if they ever needed such an excuse. But as to our European allies, they don't have the reserves we have; for over a decade they have run down their manning levels, arms levels and preparation levels to a point where the imbalance in conventional manning and hardware between the NATO forces and the Warsaw Pact forces is at a stage that cannot be recouped in a mere nine months. The training that the personnel would need, even if recruited now; the production of new weapons of the necessary sophistication; these cannot be achieved in nine months.'

'So they're back to 1939 again,' said the secretary of the treasury gloomily.

'What about the nuclear option?' asked Bill Matthews quietly.

General Craig shrugged.

'If the Soviets attack in full force, it's inescapable. Forewarned may be forearmed, but nowadays armament programmes and training programmes take too long. Forewarned as we are, we could slow up a Soviet advance westwards, spoil Kerensky's time-scale of a hundred hours. But whether we could stop him dead – the whole damn Soviet army, navy and air force – that's another matter. By the time we knew the answer, it would probably be too late anyway. Which makes our use of the nuclear option inescapable. Unless of course, sir, we abandon Europe and our three hundred thousand men there.'

'David?' asked the President.

Secretary of State David Lawrence tapped the file in front of him.

'For about the first time in my life I agree with Dmitri Rykov. It's not just a question of Western Europe. If Europe goes, the Balkans, the eastern Mediterranean, Turkey, Iran and the Arabian states cannot hold. Ten years ago five per cent of our oil was imported; five years ago it had risen to fifty per cent. Now it's running at sixty-two per cent and rising. Even the whole of continental America, north and south, cannot fulfil more than fifty-five per cent of our needs at maximum production. We need the Arabian oil. Without it we are as finished as Europe, without a shot fired.'

'Suggestions, gentlemen?' asked the President.

'The Nightingale is valuable, but not indispensable, not now,' said Stanislaw Poklewski. 'Why not meet with Rudin and lay it on the table? We now know about the Plan Boris, we know the intent. And we will take steps to head off that intent, to make it unworkable. When he informs his Politburo of that, they'll realize the element of surprise is lost, that the war option won't work any more. It'll be the end of the Nightingale, but it will also be the end of Plan Boris.'

Bob Benson of the CIA shook his head vigorously.

'I don't think it's that simple, Mr President. As I read it, it's not a question of convincing Rudin or Rykov. There's a vicious faction fight now going on inside the Politburo, as we know. At stake is the succession to Rudin. And the famine is hanging over them.

'Vishnayev and Kerensky have proposed a limited war as a means of both obtaining the food surpluses of Western Europe, and of imposing war discipline on the Soviet peoples. Reveal what we know to Rudin – it changes nothing. It might even cause him to fall. Vishnayev and his group would take over; they are completely ignorant of the West and the way we Americans react to being attacked. Even with the element of surprise gone, with the grain famine pending they could still try the war option.'

'I agree with Bob,' said David Lawrence. 'There is a parallel here with the Japanese position forty years ago. The oil embargo caused the fall of the moderate Konoya faction. Instead we got General Tojo and that led to Pearl Harbor. If Maxim Rudin is toppled now, we could get Yefrem Vishnayev in his place. And on the basis of these papers, that could lead to war.'

'Then Maxim Rudin must not fall,' said President Matthews.

'Mr President, I protest,' said Poklewski heatedly. 'Am I to understand that the efforts of the United States are now to be bent towards saving the skin of Maxim Rudin? Have any of us forgotten what he did, the people liquidated under his regime, to get him to the pinnacle of power in Soviet Russia?'

'Stan, I'm sorry,' said President Matthews with finality. 'Last month I authorized a refusal by the United States to supply the Soviet Union with the grain it needs to head off a famine. At least until I knew what the perspectives of that famine would be. I can no longer pursue that policy of rejection, because I think we now know what those perspectives entail.

'Gentlemen, I am going this night to draft a personal letter to President Rudin proposing that David Lawrence and Dmitri Rykov meet on neutral territory to confer together. And that they confer on the subject of the new SALT Four arms limitation treaty, and *any other matters of interest*.'

When Andrew Drake returned to the Cavo d'Oro after his second meeting with Captain Thanos, there was a message waiting for him. It was from Azamat Krim, to say he and Kaminsky had just checked in to their agreed hotel.

An hour later Drake was with them. The van had come through unscathed. During the night Drake had the guns and ammunition transferred piece by piece to his own room at the Cavo d'Oro in separate visits from Kaminsky and Krim. When all was safely locked away he took them both out to dinner. The following morning Krim flew back to London, to live in Drake's apartment and await his phone call. Kaminsky stayed on in a small pension in the back streets of Piraeus. It was not comfortable, but it was anonymous.

While they were dining, the US secretary of state was locked in private conference with the Irish ambassador to Washington.

'If my meeting with Foreign Minister Rykov is to succeed,' said David Lawrence, 'we must have privacy. The discretion must be absolute. Reykjavik in Iceland is too obvious; our base at Keflavik there is like US territory. The meeting has to be on neutral territory. Geneva is full of watching eyes; ditto Stockholm and Vienna. Helsinki, like Iceland, would be too obvious. Ireland is halfway between Moscow and Washington, and you still foster the cult of privacy there.'

That night coded messages passed between Washington and Dublin. Within twenty-four hours the government in Dublin had agreed to host the meeting and proposed flight plans for both parties. Within hours President Matthews' personal and private letter to President Maxim Rudin was on its way to Ambassador Donaldson in Moscow.

Andrew Drake at his third attempt secured a private conversation with Captain Nikos Thanos. There was by then little doubt in the old Greek's mind that the young Englishman wanted something from him, but he gave no hint of curiosity. As usual Drake bought the coffee and ouzo.

'Captain,' said Drake, 'I have a problem, and I think you may be able to help me.'

Thanos raised an eyebrow but studied his coffee.

'Sometime near the end of the month the *Sanadria* will sail from Piraeus for Istanbul and the Black Sea. I believe you will be calling at Odessa.'

Thanos nodded. 'We are due to sail on the 30th,' he said, 'and, yes, we will be discharging cargo at Odessa.'

'I want to go to Odessa,' said Drake. 'I must reach Odessa.'

'You are an Englishman,' said Thanos. 'There are package tours of Odessa. You could fly there. There are cruises by Soviet liners out of Odessa, you could join one.'

Drake shook his head.

'It's not as easy as that,' he said. 'Captain Thanos, I would not receive a visa for Odessa. My application would be dealt with in Moscow, and I would not be allowed in.'

'And why do you want to go?' asked Thanos with suspicion.

'I have a girl in Odessa,' said Drake. 'My fiancée. I want to get her out.'

Captain Thanos shook his head with finality. He and his ancestors from Chios had been smuggling the odd package around the eastern Mediterranean since Homer was learning to talk, and he knew that a brisk smuggling trade went into and out of Odessa, and that his own crew made a tidy living on the side from bringing such luxury items as nylons, perfume and leather coats to the black market of the Ukrainian port. But smuggling people was quite different, and he had no intention of getting involved in that.

'I don't think you understand,' said Drake. 'There's no question of bringing her out on the *Sanadria*. Let me explain.'

He produced a photograph of himself and a remarkably pretty girl, sitting on the balustrade of the Potemkin Stairway that links the city with the port. Thanos' interest revived at once for the girl was definitely worth looking at.

'I am a graduate in Russian studies of the University of Bradford,' said Drake. 'Last year I was an exchange student for six months and spent those six months at Odessa University. That was where I met Larissa. We fell in love. We wanted to get married.'

Like most Greeks, Nikos Thanos prided himself on his romantic nature. Drake was talking his own language.

'Why didn't you?' he asked.

'The Soviet authorities would not let us,' said Drake. 'Of course, I wanted to bring Larissa back to England and marry her and settle down. She applied for permission to leave and was turned down. I kept reapplying on her behalf from the London end. No luck. Then last July I did as you just suggested; I went on a package tour to the Ukraine, through Kiev, Ternopol and Lvov.'

He flicked open his passport and showed Thanos the date stamps at Kiev Airport.

'She came up to Kiev to see me. We made love. Now she has written to me to say she is having our baby. So now I have to marry her more than ever.'

Captain Thanos also knew the rules. They had applied to his society since time began. He looked again at the photograph. He was not to know that the girl was a Londoner who had posed in a studio not far from King's Cross station, nor that the background of the Potemkin Stairway was an enlarged detail from a tourist poster obtained at the London office of Intourist.

'So how are you going to get her out?' he asked.

'Next month,' said Drake, 'there is a Soviet liner, the *Litva*, leaving Odessa with a large party from the Soviet Youth movement, the Komsomol, for an off-season educational tour of the Mediterranean.'

Thanos nodded, he knew the *Litva* well.

'Because I made too many scenes over the matter of Larissa, the authorities will not let me back in. Larissa would not normally be allowed to go on this tour. But there is an official in the local branch of the Interior Ministry who likes to live well above his income. He will get her on to that cruise with all her papers in order, and when the ship docks at Venice, I will be waiting for her. But the official wants ten thousand American dollars. I have them, but I have to get the package to her.'

It made perfect sense to Captain Thanos. He knew the level of bureaucratic corruption that was endemic to the southern shore of Ukraine, Crimea and Georgia, communism or no communism. That an official should 'arrange' a few documents for enough Western currency to improve his lifestyle substantially was quite normal.

An hour later the deal was concluded. For a further $5000 Thanos would take Drake on as a temporary deckhand for the duration of the voyage.

'We sail on the 30th,' he said, 'and we should be in Odessa on the 9th or 10th. Be at the quay where the *Sanadria* is berthed by six p.m. on the 30th. Wait until the agent's water clerk has left, then come aboard just before the immigration people.'

Four hours later in Drake's flat in London, Azamat Krim took Drake's call from Piraeus giving him the date that Mishkin and Lazareff needed to know.

It was on the 20th that President Matthews received Maxim Rudin's reply. It was a personal letter, as his had been to the Soviet leader. In it Rudin agreed to the secret meeting between David Lawrence and Dmitri Rykov in Ireland, scheduled for the 24th.

President Matthews pushed the letter across his desk to Lawrence.

'He's not wasting time,' he remarked.

'He has no time to waste,' returned the secretary of state. 'Everything is being prepared. I have two men in Dublin now, checking out the arrangements. Our ambassador to Dublin will be meeting the Soviet ambassador tomorrow, as a result of this letter, to finalize details.'

'Well, David, you know what to do,' said the American President.

Azamat Krim's problem was to be able to post a letter or card to Mishkin from inside the Soviet Union, complete with Russian stamps and written in Russian, without going through the necessary delay in waiting for a visa to be granted to him by the Soviet consulate in London, which could take up to four weeks. With the help of Drake he had solved it relatively simply.

Prior to 1980 the main airport of Moscow, Sheremetyevo, had been a small, drab and shabby affair. But for the Olympics the Soviet government had commissioned a grand new airport terminal there, and Drake had done some research on it.

The facilities in the new terminal, which handled all long-distance flights out of Moscow, were excellent. There were numerous plaques praising the achievements of Soviet technology all over the airport; conspicuous by its absence was any mention that Moscow had had to commission a West German firm to build the place, because no Soviet construction company could have achieved the standard or the completion date. The West Germans had been handsomely paid in hard currency, but their contract had had rigorous penalty clauses in the case of non-completion by the start of the 1980 Olympics. For this reason, the Germans had used only two local Russian ingredients – sand and water. Everything else had been trucked in from West Germany in order to be certain of delivery on time.

In the great transit lounge and departure lounges, they had built letter boxes to handle the mail of anyone forgetting to post his last picture postcards from inside Moscow before leaving. The KGB vets every single letter, postcard, cable or phone call coming into or leaving the Soviet Union. Massive though the task may be, it gets done. But the new departure lounges at Sheremetyevo were used both for international flights and long-distance internal Soviet Union flights.

Krim's postcard therefore had been acquired at the Aeroflot offices in

London. Modern Soviet stamps sufficient for a postcard at the internal rate had been openly bought from the London stamp emporium, Stanley Gibbons. On the card, which showed a picture of the Tupolev 144 supersonic passenger jet, was written in Russian the message: 'Just leaving with our factory's Party group for the expedition to Khabarovsk. Great excitement. Almost forgot to write you. Many happy returns for your birthday on the tenth. Your cousin, Ivan.'

Khabarovsk being in the extreme orient of Siberia, close to the Sea of Japan, a group leaving by Aeroflot for that city would leave from the same terminal building as a flight leaving for Japan. The letter was addressed to David Mishkin at his address in Lvov.

Azamat Krim took the Aeroflot flight from London to Moscow and changed planes there for the Aeroflot flight from Moscow to Narita Airport, Tokyo. He had an open-dated return. He also had a two-hour wait in the transit lounge in Moscow. Here he dropped the card in the letter box and went on to Tokyo. Once there he changed to Japan Air Lines, and flew back to London.

The card was examined by the KGB postal detail at Moscow's airport, assumed to be from a Russian to a Ukrainian cousin, both living and working inside the USSR, and sent on. It arrived in Lvov three days later.

While the tired and very jet-lagged Crimean Tatar was flying back from Japan, a small jet of the Norwegian internal airline Braathens-SAFE banked high over the fishing town of Alesund and began to let down to the municipal airport on the flat island across the bay. From one of its passenger windows Thor Larsen looked down with a thrill of excitement that never left him whenever he returned to the small community that had raised him and which would always be home.

He had arrived in the world in 1935, in a fisherman's cottage in the old Buholmen quarter, long since demolished to make way for the new high road. Buholmen before the war had been the fishing quarter, a maze of wooden cottages in grey, blue and ochre. From his father's cottage a yard had run down, like all the others along the row, from the back stoop to the sound. Here were the rickety wooden jetties where the independent fishermen like his father had tied their small vessels when they came home from the sea; here the smells of his childhood had been of pitch, resin, paint, salt and fish.

As a child he had sat on his father's jetty, watching the big ships moving slowly up to berth at the Storneskaia, and he had dreamed of the places they must visit, far away across the western ocean. By the age of seven he could manage his own small skiff several hundred yards off the Buholmen shore to where old Sula Mountain cast her shadow from across the fjord on the shining water.

'He'll be a seaman,' said his father, watching with satisfaction from his jetty, 'not a fisherman, staying close to these waters, but a seaman.'

He was five when the Germans came to Alesund, big, grey-coated men who tramped around in heavy boots. It was not until he was seven that he saw the war. It was the summer and his father had let him come fishing with him during the holidays from Norvoy School. With the rest of the Alesund fishing fleet his father's boat was far out at sea under the guard of a German E-Boat.

During the night he awoke because men were moving about. Away to the west were twinkling lights, the masthead of the Orkneys fleet.

There was a small rowing boat bobbing beside his father's vessel, and the crew were shifting herring boxes. Before the child's astounded gaze a young man, pale and exhausted, emerged from beneath the boxes in the hold and was helped into the rowboat. Minutes later it was lost in the darkness, heading for the Orkneys men. Another radio operator from the Resistance was on his way to England for training. His father made him promise never to mention what he had seen. A week later in Alesund there was a rattle of rifle fire one evening, and his mother told him he should say his prayers extra hard, because the schoolmaster was dead.

By the time he was in his early teens, growing out of clothes faster than his mother could make them, he too had become obsessed with radio and in two years had built his own transmitter/receiver. His father gazed at the apparatus in wonderment; it was beyond his comprehension. Thor was sixteen when, the day after Christmas of 1951, he picked up an SOS message from a ship in distress in the mid-Alantic. She was the *Flying Enterprise*. Her cargo had shifted and she was listing badly in heavy seas.

For sixteen days the world and a teenage Norwegian boy watched and listened with bated breath as the Danish-born American captain, Kurt Carlsen, refused to leave his sinking ship and nursed her painfully eastwards through the gales towards the south of England. Sitting in his attic hour after hour with his headphones over his ears, looking out through the dormer window at the wild ocean beyond the mouth of the fjord, Thor Larsen had willed the old freighter to make it home to port. On 10th January 1952 she finally sank, just fifty-seven miles off Falmouth harbour.

Larsen heard her go down, listened to the shadowing tugs tell of her death, and the rescue of her indomitable captain. He took off his headphones, laid them down and descended to his parents who were at table.

'I have decided,' he told them, 'what I am going to be. I am going to be a sea captain.'

A month later he entered the merchant marine.

The plane touched down and rolled to a stop outside the small, neat terminal with its goose pond by the car park. His wife Lisa was waiting for him with Kristina, his sixteen-year-old daughter and Kurt, his fourteen-year-old son. The pair chattered like magpies on the short drive across the island to the ferry, and across the sound to Alesund, and all the way home to their comfortable ranch-style house in the secluded suburb of Bogneset.

It was good to be home. He would go fishing with Kurt out on the Borgund Fjord as his father had taken him fishing there in his youth; they would picnic in the last days of the summer on their little cabin cruiser or on the knobby green islands that dotted the sound. He had three weeks of leave; then Japan, and in February the captaincy of the biggest ship the world had ever seen. He had come a long way from the wooden cottage in Buholmen, but Alesund was still his home and for this descendant of Vikings there was nowhere in the world quite like it.

On the night of 23rd September a Grumman Gulfstream in the livery of a well-known commercial corporation lifted off from Andrews air force base and headed east across the Atlantic with long-distance tanks for Shannon Airport. It was phased into the Irish air traffic control network as a private charter flight. When it landed at Shannon it was shepherded in darkness to the side of the airfield away from the international terminal and surrounded by five black and curtained limousines.

Secretary of State David Lawrence and his party of six were greeted by the US ambassador and the head of chancery, and all five limousines swept out of the airport perimeter fence by a side gate. They headed northeast through the sleeping countryside towards County Meath.

That same night a Tupolev 134 twin-jet of Aeroflot refuelled at East Berlin's Schönefeld Airport and headed west over Germany and the Low Countries towards Britain and Ireland. It was slated as a special Aeroflot flight bringing a trade delegation to Dublin. As such the British air traffic controllers passed it over to their Irish colleagues as it left the coast of Wales. The Irish had their military air traffic network take it over, and it landed two hours before dawn at the Irish Air Corps base at Baldonnel, outside Dublin.

Here the Tupolev was parked between two hangars out of vision of the main airfield buildings, and it was greeted by the Soviet ambassador, the Irish deputy foreign minister, and six limousines. Foreign Minister Rykov and his party entered the vehicles, were screened by the interior curtains, and left the air base.

High above the banks of the River Boyne, in an environment of great natural beauty and not far from the market town of Slane in County Meath, stands Slane Castle, ancestral home of the family Conyngham, Earls of Mount Charles. The youthful earl had been quietly asked by the Irish government to accept a week's holiday in a luxury hotel in the west with his pretty countess, and to lend his castle to the government for a few days. He had agreed. The restaurant attached to the castle was marked as closed for repairs, the staff were given a week's leave, government caterers moved in and Irish police in plain clothes discreetly posted themselves at all points of the compass round the castle. When the two cavalcades of limousines had entered the grounds the main gates were shut. If the local people noticed anything they were courteous enough to make no mention of it.

In the Georgian private dining room before the marble fireplace by Adam, the two statesmen met for a sustaining breakfast.

'Dmitri, good to see you again,' said David Lawrence extending his hand.

Rykov shook it warmly. He glanced around him at the silver gifts from George the Fourth and the Conyngham portraits on the walls. 'So this is how you decadent bourgeois capitalists live,' he said.

Lawrence roared with laughter. 'I wish it were, Dmitri, I wish it were.'

At eleven o'clock, surrounded by their aides in Johnston's magnificent Gothic circular library, the two men settled down to negotiate. The bantering was over.

'Mr Foreign Minister,' said Lawrence, 'it seems we both have problems. Ours concern the continuing arms race between our two nations, which nothing seems able to halt or even slow down, and which worries us deeply. Yours seems to concern the forthcoming grain harvest in the Soviet Union. I hope we can find a means between us to lessen these, our mutual problems.'

'I hope so too, Mr Secretary of State,' said Rykov cautiously. 'What have you in mind?'

There is only one direct flight a week between Athens and Istanbul, the Tuesday Sabena connection, leaving Athens' Hellenikon Airport at 14.00 and landing at Istanbul at 16.45. On Tuesday, September 28th, Miroslav Kaminsky was on it, instructed to secure for Andrew Drake a consignment of sheepskin and suede jackets for trading in Odessa.

The same afternoon Secretary of State Lawrence finished reporting to the *ad hoc* committee of the National Security Council in the Oval Office.

'Mr President, gentlemen, I think we have it. Providing Maxim Rudin can keep his hold on the Politburo and secure their agreement.

'The proposal is that we and the Soviets each send two teams of negotiators to a resumed strategic arms limitation conference. The suggested venue is Ireland again. The Irish government has agreed and will prepare a suitable conference hall and living accommodation, providing we and the Soviets signal our assent.

'One team from each side will face the other across the table to discuss a broad range of arms limitations. This is the big one; I secured a concession from Dmitri Rykov that the ambit of the discussion need not exclude thermo-nuclear weapons, strategic weapons, inner space, international inspection, tactical nuclear weapons, conventional weapons and manning levels, or disengagement of forces along the Iron Curtain line.'

There was a murmur of approval and surprise from the other seven men present. No previous American-Soviet arms conference had ever had such widely drawn terms of reference. If all areas showed a move towards genuine and monitored détente, it would add up to a peace treaty.

'These talks will be what the conference is supposedly about, so far as the world is concerned, and the usual press bulletins will be necessary,' resumed Secretary Lawrence. 'Now, in back of the main conference, the secondary conference of technical experts will negotiate the sale to the Soviets at financial costs still to be worked out, but probably lower than world prices, of up to fifty-five million tons of grain, consumer-product technology, computers and oil-extraction technology.

'At every stage there will be liaison between the up-front and the in-back teams of negotiators, on each side. They make a concession on arms, we make a concession on low-cost goodies.'

'When is this slated for?' asked Poklewski.

'That's the surprise element,' said Lawrence. 'Normally the Russians like to work very slowly. Now it seems they are in a hurry. They want to start in two weeks.'

'Good God, we can't be ready for "go" in two weeks!' exclaimed the secretary of defense, whose department was intimately involved.

'We have to be,' said President Matthews. 'There will never be another chance like this again. Besides, we have our SALT team ready and briefed. They have been ready for months. We have to bring in Agriculture, Trade and Technology on this, and fast. We have to get together the team who can talk on the other, the trade/technology, side of the deal. Gentlemen, please see to it. At once.'

Maxim Rudin did not put it to his Politburo quite like that the following day.

'They have risen to the bait,' he said from his chair at the head of the table. 'When they make a concession on wheat or technology in one of the conference rooms, we make the absolute minimum concession in the other conference room. We will get our grain, comrades; we will feed our people, we will head off the famine, and at the minimum price. Americans, after all, have never been able to out-negotiate the Russians.'

There was a general buzz of agreement.

'What concessions?' snapped Vishnayev. 'How far back will these concessions set the Soviet Union and the triumph of world Marxism-Leninism?'

'As to your first question,' replied Rykov, 'we cannot know until we are negotiating. As to your second, the answer must be substantially less than a famine would set us back.'

'There are two points we should be clear on before we decide whether to talk or not,' said Rudin. 'One is that the Politburo will be kept fully informed at every stage, so if the moment comes when the price is too high, this council will have the right to abort the conference, and I will defer to Comrade Vishnayev and his plan for a war in the spring. The second is that no concession we may make to secure the wheat need necessarily remain valid for very long after the deliveries have taken place.'

There were several grins round the table. This was the sort of realpolitik the Politburo was much more accustomed to, as they had shown in transforming the old Helsinki agreement on détente into a farce.

'Very well,' said Vishnayev, 'but I think we should lay down the exact parameters of our negotiating teams' authority to concede points.'

'I have no objection to that,' said Rudin.

The meeting continued on this theme for an hour and a half. Rudin got his vote to proceed, by the same margin as before, seven against six.

On the last day of the month Andrew Drake stood in the shade of a crane and watched the *Sanadria* battening down her hatches. Conspicuous on deck were Vacuvators for Odessa, powerful suction machines like vacuum cleaners for sucking wheat out of the hold of a ship and straight into a grain silo. The Soviet Union must be trying to improve her grain unloading capacity, he mused, though he did not know why. Below the weather-deck were fork-lift trucks for Istanbul and agricultural machinery for Varna in Bulgaria, part of a transshipment cargo that had come in from America as far as Piraeus.

He watched the agent's water clerk leave the ship, giving Captain Thanos a last shake of the hand. Thanos scanned the pier and made out the figure of Drake loping towards him, his kitbag over one shoulder and suitcase in the other hand.

In the captain's day cabin Drake handed over his passport and vaccination certificates. He signed the ship's articles and became a member of the deck crew. While he was down below stowing his gear Captain Thanos entered his name in the ship's crew list, just before the Greek immigration officer came on board. The two men had the usual drink together.

'There's an extra crew man,' said Thanos as if in passing. The immigration officer scanned the list and the pile of discharge books and passports in front of him. Most were Greek, but there were six non-Greeks. Drake's British passport stood out. The immigration officer selected it and rifled through the pages. A fifty-dollar bill fell out.

'An out-of-work,' said Thanos, 'trying to get to Turkey and head for the East. Thought you'd be glad to be shot of him.'

Five minutes later the crew's identity documents had been returned to their wooden tray and the vessel's papers stamped for outward clearance. Daylight was fading as her ropes were cast off and *Sanadria* slipped away from her berth and headed south before turning northeast for the Dardanelles.

Below decks the crew were grouping round the greasy messroom table. One of them was hoping no one would look under his mattress where the Sako Hornet rifle was stored. In Moscow his target was sitting down to an excellent supper.

While high-ranking and secret men launched themselves into a flurry of activity in Washington and Moscow, the old *Sanadria* thumped her way impassively northeast towards the Dardanelles and Istanbul.

On the second day Drake watched the bare brown hills of Gallipoli slide by and the sea dividing European and Asian Turkey widened into the Sea of Marmara. Captain Thanos, who knew these waters like his own back yard on Chios, was doing his own pilotage.

Two Soviet cruisers steamed past them, heading from Sebastopol out to the Mediterranean to shadow the US Sixth Fleet manoeuvres. Just after sundown the twinkling lights of Istanbul and the Galatea Bridge spanning the Bosphorus came into view. The *Sanadria* anchored for the night and entered port at Istanbul the following morning.

While the fork-lift trucks were being discharged, Andrew Drake secured his passport from Captain Thanos and slipped ashore. He met Miroslav Kaminsky at an agreed rendezvous in central Istanbul and took delivery of a large bundle of sheepskin and suede coats and jackets. When he returned to the ship Captain Thanos raised an eyebrow.

'You aiming to keep your girlfriend warm?' he asked.

Drake shook his head and smiled. 'The crew tell me half the seamen bring these ashore in Odessa,' he said. 'I thought it would be the best way to bring my own package.'

The Greek captain was not surprised. He knew half a dozen of his own seamen would be bringing such luggage back to the ship with them, to trade the fashionable coats and jeans for five times their buying price to the black market spivs of Odessa.

Thirty hours later the *Sanadria* cleared the Bosphorus, watched the Golden Horn drop away astern and chugged north for Bulgaria with her tractors.

Due west of Dublin lies County Kildare, site of the Irish horse-racing centre at the Curragh and of the sleepy market town of Celbridge. On the outskirts of Celbridge stands the largest and finest Palladian stately home in the land, Castletown House. With the agreement of the American and Soviet ambassadors, the Irish government had proposed Castletown as the venue for the disarmament conference.

For a week teams of painters, plasterers, electricians and gardeners had been at work night and day putting the final touches to the two rooms that would hold the twin conferences, though no one knew the reason for the second conference.

The façade of the main house alone is 142 feet wide, and from each corner covered and pillared corridors lead away to further quarters. One of these wing blocks contains the kitchens and staff apartments, and it was here the American security force would be quartered; the other block contained the stables, with more apartments above them, and here the Russian bodyguards would live.

The main house would act as both conference centre and home for the subordinate diplomats who would inhabit the numerous guest rooms and suites on the top floor. Only the two principal negotiators and their immediate aides would return each night to their respective embassies, equipped as they were with facilities for coded communications with Washington and Moscow.

This time there was to be no secrecy, save in the matter of the secondary conference. Before a blaze of world publicity the two foreign ministers, David Lawrence and Dmitri Rykov, arrived in Dublin and were greeted by the Irish President and premier. After the habitual televised handshaking and toasting, they left Dublin in two cavalcades for Castletown.

At midday on 8th October the two statesmen and their twenty advisers entered the vast Long Gallery, decorated in Wedgwood Blue in the Pompeian manner and 140 feet long. Most of the centre of the hall was taken up with the gleaming Georgian table, down each side of which the delegations seated themselves. Flanking each foreign minister were experts in defence, weapons systems, nuclear technology, inner space and armoured warfare.

The two statesmen knew they were only there formally to open the conference. After the opening and the agreement of agenda, each would fly home to leave the talks in the hands of the delegation leader, Professor Ivan Sokolov for the Soviets and former Assistant Secretary of Defense Edwin J. Campbell for the Americans.

The remaining rooms on this floor were given over to the stenographers, typists and researchers.

One floor below, at ground level, in the great dining room of Castletown, with drapes drawn to mute the autumn sunshine pouring on to the south-eastern face of the mansion, the secondary conference quietly filed in to take their places. These were mainly technologists, experts in grain, oil, computers and industrial plant.

Upstairs, Dmitri Rykov and David Lawrence each made a short address of welcome to the opposing delegation and expressed the hope and the confidence that the conference would succeed in diminishing the problems of a beleaguered and frightened world. Then they adjourned for lunch.

After lunch Professor Sokolov had a private conference with Rykov before the latter's departure for Moscow.

'You know our position, comrade professor,' said Rykov. 'Frankly, it is not a good one. The Americans will go for everything they can get. Your job is to fight every step of the way to minimize our concessions. But we must have that grain. Nevertheless, every concession on arms levels and deployment patterns in Eastern Europe must be referred back to Moscow. This is because the Politboro insists on being involved in the approval or rejection in the sensitive areas.'

He forbore to say that the sensitive areas were those that might impede a future Soviet strike in Western Europe, or that Maxim Rudin's political career hung by a thread.

In another drawing room at the opposite end of Castletown, a room which, like Rykov's, had been swept by his own electronics experts for possible 'bugs', David Lawrence was conferring with Edwin Campbell.

'It's all yours, Ed. This won't be like Geneva. The Soviet problems won't permit endless delays, adjournments and referring-back to Moscow for weeks on end. I estimate they have to have an agreement with us within six months. Either that or they don't get the grain.

'On the other hand, Sokolov will fight every inch of the way. We know each concession on arms will have to be referred to Moscow, but Moscow will have to decide fast one way or the other, else the time will run out.

'One last thing. We know Maxim Rudin cannot be pushed too far. If he is, he could fall. But if he doesn't get the wheat he could fall, too. The trick will be to find out the balance; to get the maximum concessions without provoking a revolt in the Politbure.'

Cambell removed his glasses and pinched the bridge of his nose. He had spent four years commuting from Washington to Geneva on the so-far abortive SALT talks and he was no newcomer to the problems of trying to negotiate with Russians.

'Hell, David, that sounds fine. But you know how they give nothing of their own inner position away. It would be a hell of a help to know just how far they can be pushed, and where the stop-line lies.'

David Lawrence opened his attaché case and withdrew a sheaf of papers. He proffered them to Cambell.

'What are these?' asked Cambell.

Lawrence chose his words carefully.

'Eleven days ago in Moscow the full Politburo authorized Maxim Rudin and Dmitri Rykov to begin these talks. But only by a vote of seven against six. There's a dissident faction inside the Politburo that wishes to abort the talks and bring Rudin down. After the agreement the Politburo laid out the exact parameters of what Professor Sokolov could or could not concede, what the Politburo would or would not allow Rudin to grant. Go beyond the parameters and Rudin could be toppled. If that happened we would have bad, very bad, problems.'

'So what are the papers?' asked Campbell, holding the sheaf in his hands.

'They came in from London last night,' said Lawrence. They are the verbatim transcript of that Politburo meeting.'

Campbell stared at them in amazement.

'Jesus,' he breathed, 'we can dictate our own terms.'

'Not quite,' corrected Lawrence. 'We can require the maximum that the moderate faction inside the Politburo can get away with. Insist on more and we could be eating ashes.'

The visit of the British Prime Minister and her foreign secretary to Washington two days later was described in the press as being informal. Ostensibly Britain's first woman premier was to address a major meeting of the English-Speaking Union and take the opportunity of paying a courtesy call on the United States President.

But the crux of the latter came in the Oval Office where President Bill Matthews, flanked by his special security adviser, Stanislaw Poklewski, and his secretary of state, David Lawrence, gave the British visitors an exhaustive briefing on the hopeful start of the Castletown conference. The agenda, reported President Matthews, had been agreed with unusual alacrity. At least three main areas for future discussion had been defined between the two teams with a minimal presence of the usual Soviet objections to every dot and comma.

President Matthews expressed the hope that after years of frustration a comprehensive limitation of arms levels and troop deployments along the Iron Curtain from the Baltic to the Aegean Seas could well emerge from Castletown.

The crunch came as the meeting between the two heads of government closed.

'We regard it as vital, ma'am, that the inside information of which we are in possession and without which the conference could well fail, continues to reach us.'

'You mean, the Nightingale,' said the British premier crisply.

'Yes, ma'am, I do,' said Matthews. 'We regard it as indispensable that the Nightingale continues to operate.'

'I understand your point, Mr President,' she answered calmly. 'But I believe that the hazard levels of that operation are very high. I do not dictate to Sir Nigel Irvine what he shall or shall not do in the running of his service. I have too much respect for his judgement for that. But I will do what I can.'

It was not until the traditional ceremony in front of the principal façade of the White House of seeing the British visitors into their limousines and smiling for the cameras was complete that Stanislaw Poklewski could give vent to his feelings.

'There's no hazard to a Russian agent in the world that compares with the success or failure of the Castletown talks,' he said.

'I agree,' said Bill Matthews, 'but I understand from Bob Benson the hazard lies in the exposure of the Nightingale at this point. If that happened, and he were caught, the Politburo would learn what had been passed over. If that happened, they would shut off at Castletown. So the Nightingale either has to be silenced or brought out, but neither until we have a treaty sewn up and signed. And that could be six months yet.

That same evening while the sun was still shining on Washington it was setting over the port of Odessa as the *Sanadria* dropped anchor in the roads. When the clatter of the anchor cable had ceased, silence fell on the freighter, broken only by the low humming of the generators in the engine room and the hiss of escaping steam on deck. Andrew Drake leaned on the fo'c's'le rail, watching the lights of the port and city twinkle into life.

West of the ship, at the northern extremity of the port, lay the oil harbour and refinery, circled by a chain-link fencing. To the south the port was bounded by the protective arm of the great seaward mole. Ten miles beyond the mole the River Dniester flowed into the sea through the swampy marshes where five months before Miroslav Kaminsky had stolen his skiff and made a desperate bid for freedom. Now, thanks to him, Andrew Drake, Andriy Drach, had come home to the land of his ancestors. But this time he had come armed.

That evening Captain Thanos was informed that he would be brought into port and moored alongside the following morning. Port health and customs visited the *Sanadria* but they spent the hour on board closeted with Captain Thanos in his cabin, sampling his top-grade Scotch whisky, kept for the occasion. There was no rummage search of the ship. Watching the launch leave the ship's side Drake wondered if Thanos had betrayed him. It would have been easy enough; Drake would be arrested ashore, and Thanos would sail with his $5000.

It all depended, he thought, on Thanos accepting his story of bringing money to his fiancée. If he had, there was no motive to betray him, for the offence was routine enough; his own sailors brought contraband goods into Odessa on every voyage, and dollar bills were only another form of contraband. And if the rifle and pistols had been discovered the simple thing would have been to throw the lot into the sea and sling Drake off the ship once back in Piraeus. Still, he could neither eat nor sleep that night.

Just after dawn the pilot boarded. The *Sanadria* weighed anchor, took a tug in attendance and moved slowly between the breakwaters and into her berth. Often, Drake had learned, there was a berthing delay in this, the most congested of the Soviet Union's warm-sea ports. They must want their Vacuvators badly. He had no idea how badly. Once the shore cranes had started to discharge the freighter, the watchkeepers among the crew were allowed to go ashore.

During the voyage Drake had become friendly with the *Sanadria*'s carpenter, a middle-aged Greek seaman who had visited Liverpool and was keen to practise his twenty words of English. He had repeated them continuously to his intense delight whenever he met Drake during the voyage, and each time Drake had nodded furious encouragement and approval. He had explained to Constantine in English and sign language that he had a girlfriend in Odessa and was bringing her presents. Constantine approved. With a dozen others, they trooped down the gangway and headed for the dock gates. Drake was wearing one of his best suede sheepskin coats, although the day was reasonably warm. Constantine carried a duffel shoulder-bag with a brace of bottles of export-proof Scotch whisky.

The whole port area of Odessa is cordoned off from the city and its citizens by a high chain fence, topped with barbed wire and arc lights. The main dock gates habitually stand open in the daytime, the entrance being blocked only by a balanced red-and-white striped pole. This marks the passageway for lorries and trucks, with a customs official and two armed militiamen attending it.

Astride the entrance gate is a long, narrow shed, with one door inside the port area and one on the outside. The party from the *Sanadria* entered the first door with Constantine in charge. There was a long counter, attended by one customs man, and a passport desk attended by an immigration officer and a militiaman. All three looked scruffy and exceptionally bored. Constantine approached the customs man and dumped his shoulder-bag on the counter. The official opened it and extracted a bottle of whisky. Constantine gestured that it was a present from one to the other. The customs man managed a friendly nod and placed the bottle beneath his table.

Constantine clasped a brawny arm round Drake and pointed to him.

'*Droog*,' he said and beamed widely. The customs man nodded that he understood the newcomer was the Greek carpenter's friend and should be recognized as such. Drake smiled broadly. He stood back, eyeing the customs man as an outfitter eyes a customer. Then he stepped forward, slipped off the sheepskin coat and held it out, indicating that he and the customs man were about the same size. The official did not bother to try it on; it was a fine coat, worth a month's salary at least. He smiled his acknowledgement, placed the coat under the table and waved the entire party through.

The immigration officer and militiaman showed no surprise. The second bottle of whisky was for the pair of them. The *Sanadria* crew members surrendered their discharge books to the immigration officer, Drake also handing over his passport, and each received in return a shore pass from a leather satchel the officer wore over his shoulder. Within a few minutes the *Sanadria* party emerged into the sunshine beyond the shed.

Drake's rendezvous was in a small café in the dockland area of old, cobbled streets, not far from the Pushkin Memorial where the ground rises from the docks to the main city. He found it after thirty minutes of wandering, having separated himself from his fellow seamen on the grounds that he wanted to meet his mythical girlfriend. Constantine did not object; he had to contact his underworld friends to set up the delivery of his sack full of denim jeans.

It was Lev Mishkin who came, just after noon. He was wary, cautious, and sat alone, making no sign of recognition. When he had finished his coffee he rose and left the café. Drake followed him. Only when the pair had reached the wide, seafront highway of Primorsky Boulevard did he allow Drake to catch up. They spoke as they walked.

Drake agreed that he would make his first run, with the handguns stuck in his waistband and the image-intensifier in a duffel bag with two clinking bottles of whisky, that evening. There would be plenty of Western ships' crew coming through for an evening in the dockland bars at the same time. He would be wearing another sheepskin coat to cover the handguns in his belt, and the chill of the evening air would justify his keeping the coat buttoned at the front. Mishkin and his friend David Lazareff would meet Drake in the darkness by the Pushkin Monument and take over the hardware.

Just after eight that evening Drake came through with his first consignment. He saluted jovially at the customs man, who waved him on and called to his colleague at the passport desk. The immigration man handed out a shore pass in exchange for his passport, jerked his chin towards the open door to the city of Odessa and Drake was through. He was almost at the foot of the Pushkin Monument, seeing the writer's head raised against the stars above, when two figures joined him out of the darkness between the plane trees that crowd Odessa's open spaces.

'Any problems?' asked Lazareff.

'None,' said Drake.

'Let's get it over with,' said Mishkin. Both men were carrying the brief-cases that everyone seems to carry in the Soviet Union. These cases, far from carrying documents, are the male version of the string bags the women carry, called 'perhaps bags'. They get their name from the hope that each person carried with them that perhaps they may spot a worthwhile consumer article on sale and snap it up before it is sold out or the queues form. Mishkin took the image-intensifier and stuffed it into his larger briefcase; Lazareff took both the handguns, the spare ammunition clips and the box of rifle shells and put them in his own.

'We're sailing tomorrow evening,' said Drake. 'I'll have to bring the rifle in the morning.'

'Damn,' said Mishkin, 'daylight is bad. David, you know the port area best. Where is it to be?'

Lazareff considered. 'There is an alley,' he said, 'between two crane maintenance workshops.'

He described the mud-coloured workshops, not far from the docks.

'The alley is short, narrow. One end looks towards the sea, the other to a third blank wall. Enter the seaward end of the alley on the dot of eleven a.m. I will enter the other end. If there is anyone else in the alley, walk on, go round the block and try again. If the alley is empty, we'll take delivery.'

'How will you be carrying it?' asked Mishkin.

'Sheepskin coats wrapped around it,' said Drake, 'and stuffed in a kitbag, about three feet long.'

'Let's scarper,' said Lazareff, 'someone is coming.'

When Drake returned to the *Sanadria* the customs men had changed shifts and he was frisked. He was clean. The next morning he asked Captain Thanos for an extra spell ashore on the grounds that he wanted to spend the maximum time with his fiancée. Thanos excused him deck duties and let him go. There was a nasty moment in the customs shed when Drake was asked to turn out his pockets. Placing his kitbag on the ground he obeyed and revealed a wad of four ten-dollar bills. The customs man, who seemed to be in a bad mood, wagged an admonishing finger at Drake and confiscated the dollars. He ignored the kitbag. Sheepskin coats, it seemed, were respectable contra-band; dollars were not.

The alley was empty, save for Mishkin and Lazareff walking down from one end and Drake walking up from the other. Mishkin gazed beyond Drake to the seaward end of the alley; when they were abreast he said, 'Go,' and Drake hefted the kitbag on to Lazareff's shoulder. 'Good luck,' he said as he walked on. 'See you in Israel.'

Sir Nigel Irvine retained membership of three clubs in the West End of

London, but selected Brooks's for his dinner with Barry Ferndale and Adam Munro. By custom the serious business of the evening was left until they had quit the dining room and retired to the subscription room where the coffee, port and cigars were served.

Sir Nigel had asked the chief steward, called the dispense waiter, to reserve his favourite corner near the windows looking down into St James's Street, and the group of four deep, leather club chairs was waiting for him when he arrived. Munro selected brandy and water, and Ferndale and Sir Nigel took a decanter of the club's vintage port and had it set on the table between them. Silence reigned while the cigars were lit, the coffee sipped. From the walls the Dilettantes, the eighteenth-century group of men-about-town, gazed down at them.

'Now my dear Adam, what seems to be the problem?' asked Sir Nigel at last. Munro glanced to a nearby table where two senior civil servants conversed. For keen ears, they were within eavesdropping distance. Sir Nigel noticed the look.

'Unless we shout,' he observed equably, 'no one is going to hear us. Gentlemen do not listen to other gentlemen's conversations.'

Munro thought this over.

'We do,' he said simply.

'That's different,' said Ferndale, 'it's our job.'

'All right,' said Munro, 'I want to bring the Nightingale out.'

Sir Nigel studied the tip of his cigar.

'Ah, yes,' he said. 'Any particular reason?'

'Partly strain,' said Munro. 'The original tape recording in July had to be stolen and a blank substituted in its place. That could be discovered, and it's preying on Nightingale's mind. Secondly, the chances of discovery. Every abstraction of Politburo minutes heightens this. We now know Maxim Rudin is fighting for his political life, and the succession when he goes. If Nightingale gets careless, or is even unlucky, he could get caught.'

'Adam, that's one of the risks of defecting,' said Ferndale. 'It goes with the job. Penkovsky was caught.'

'That's the point,' pursued Munro. 'Penkovsky had provided just about all he could. The Cuban missile crisis was over. There was nothing the Russians could do to undo the damage that Penkovsky had done to them.'

'I would have thought that was a good reason for keeping Nightingale in place,' observed Sir Nigel. 'There is still an awful lot more he can do for us.'

'Or the reverse,' said Munro. 'If Nightingale comes out, the Kremlin can never know what has been passed. If he is caught, they'll make him talk. What he can reveal now will be enough to bring Rudin down. This would seem to be the moment the West precisely would not wish Rudin to fall.'

'Indeed it is,' said Sir Nigel. 'Your point is taken. It's a question of a balance of chances. If we bring Nightingale out, the KGB will check back for months. The missing tape will presumably be discovered and the supposition will be that even more was passed over before he left. If he is caught, it's even worse; a complete record of what he has passed over will be abstracted from him. Rudin could well fall as a result. Even though Vishnayev would probably be disgraced also, the Castletown talks would abort. Thirdly, we keep

Nightingale in place until the Castletown talks are over and the arms limitation agreement signed. By then there will be nothing the war faction in the Politburo can do. It's a teasing choice.'

'I'd like to bring him out,' said Munro. 'Failing that, let him lie low, cease transmitting.'

'I'd like him to go on,' said Ferndale, 'at least until the end of Castletown.'

Sir Nigel reflected on the alternative arguments.

'I spent the afternoon with the Prime Minister,' he said at length. 'The PM made a request, a very strong request, on behalf of herself and the President of the USA. I cannot at this moment turn that request down, unless it could be shown the Nightingale was on the very threshold of exposure. The Americans regard it as vital to their chances of securing an all-embracing treaty at Castletown that Nightingale keep them abreast of the Soviet negotiating position. At least until the New Year.

'So I'll tell you what I'll do. Barry, prepare a plan to bring the Nightingale out. Something that can be activated at short notice. Adam, if the fuse begins to burn under the Nightingale's tail, we'll bring him out. Fast. But for the moment the Castletown talks and the frustration of the Vishnayev clique have to take first priority. Three or four more transmissions should see the Castletown talks in their final stages. The Soviets cannot delay some sort of a wheat agreement beyond February or March at the latest. After that, Adam, Nightingale can come to the West, and I'm sure the Americans will show their gratitude in the habitual manner.'

The dinner in Maxim Rudin's private suite in the Kremlin's inner sanctum was far more private than that at Brooks's Club in London. No confidence concerning the integrity of gentlemen where other gentlemen's conversations are concerned has ever marred the acute caution of the men of the Kremlin. There was no one within earshot but the silent Misha when Rudin took his place in his favourite chair of the study and gestured Ivanenko and Petrov to other seats.

'What did you make of today's meeting?' Rudin asked Petrov without preamble.

The controller of Party Organizations of the Soviet Union shrugged. 'We got away with it,' he said. 'Rykov's report was masterly. But we still have to make some pretty sweeping concessions if we want that wheat. And Vishnayev is still after his war.'

Rudin grunted.

Vishnayev is after my job,' he said bluntly. 'That's his ambition. It's Kerensky who wants the war. He wants to use his armed forces before he's too old.'

'Surely it amounts to the same thing,' said Ivanenko. 'If Vishnayev can topple you, he will be so beholden to Kerensky he will neither be able, nor particularly wish, to oppose Kerensky's recipe for a solution to all the Soviet Union's problems. He will let Kerensky have his war next spring or early summer. Between them they'll devastate everything it has taken two generations to achieve.'

'What is the news from your de-briefing yesterday?' asked Rudin. He knew Ivanenko had recalled two of his most senior men from the Third World for consultations face to face. One was the controller of all subversive operations throughout Africa; the other his counterpart for the Middle East.

'Optimistic,' said Ivanenko. 'The capitalists have screwed up their Africa policies for so long now their position is virtually irrecoverable. The liberals rule still in Washington and London, at least in foreign affairs. They are so totally absorbed with South Africa, they don't seem to notice Nigeria and Kenya at all. Both are on the verge of falling to us. The French in Senegal are proving more difficult. In the Middle East, I think we can count on Saudi Arabia falling within three years. They're almost encircled.'

'Time scale?' asked Rudin.

'Within a few years, say by 1990 at the outside, we shall effectively control the oil and the sea routes. The euphoria campaign in Washington and London is being steadily increased, and it is working.'

Rudin exhaled his smoke and stubbed the tube of his cigarette into an ashtray proffered by Misha.

'I won't see it,' he said, 'but you two will. Inside a decade the West will die of malnutrition, and we won't have to fire a shot. All the more reason why Vishnayev must be stopped while there is still time.'

Four kilometres southwest of the Kremlin, inside a tight loop in the Moscow River and not far from the Lenin Stadium, stands the ancient monastery of Novodevichi. Its main entrance is right across the street from the principal Beriozka shop where the rich and privileged, or foreigners, may buy for hard currency luxuries unobtainable by the common people.

The monastery grounds contain three lakes and a cemetery, and access to the cemetery is available to pedestrians. The gatekeeper will seldom bother to stop those bearing bunches of flowers.

Adam Munro parked his car in the Beriozka car park among others whose number plates revealed them to belong to the privileged.

'Where do you hide a tree?' his instructor used to ask the class. 'In a forest. And where do you hide a pebble? On the beach. Always keep it natural.'

Munro crossed the road, traversed the cemetery with his bunch of carnations, and found Valentina waiting for him by one of the smaller lakes. Late October had brought the first bitter winds off the steppes to the east, and grey, scudding clouds across the sky. The surface of the water rippled and shivered in the wind.

'I asked them in London,' he said gently. 'They told me it is too risky at the moment. Their answer was that to bring you out now would reveal the missing tape, and thus the fact of the transcripts having been passed over. They feel if that happened the Politburo would withdraw from the talks in Ireland and revert to the Vishnayev plan.'

She shivered slightly, whether from the chill of the lakeside or from fear of her own masters he could not tell. He put an arm round her and held her to him.

'They may be right,' she said quietly. 'At least the Politburo is negotiating for food and peace, not preparing for war.'

'Rudin and his group seem to be sincere in that,' he suggested.

She snorted. 'They are as bad as the others,' she said. 'Without the pressure they would not be there at all.'

'Well, the pressure is on,' said Munro. 'The grain is coming in. They know the alternatives now. I think the world will get its peace treaty.'

'If it does, what I have done will have been worthwhile,' said Valentina. 'I don't want Sasha to grow up among the rubble as I did, nor live with a gun in his hand. That is what they would have for him, up there in the Kremlin.'

'He won't,' said Munro. 'Believe me, my darling, he'll grow up in freedom, in the West, with you as his mother and me as his stepfather. My principals have agreed to bring you out in the spring.'

She looked up at him with hope shining in her eyes.

'In the spring? Oh, Adam, when in the spring?'

'The talks cannot go on for too long. The Kremlin needs its grain by April at the latest. The last of the supplies and all the reserves will have run out by then. When the treaty is agreed, perhaps even before it is signed, you and Sasha will be brought out. Meanwhile, I want you to cut down on the risks you are taking. Only bring out the most vital material concerning the peace talks at Castletown.'

'There's one in here,' she said, nudging the bag over her shoulder. 'It's from ten days ago. Most of it is so technical I can't understand it. It refers to permissible reductions of mobile SS Twenties.'

Munro nodded grimly.

'Tactical rockets with nuclear warheads, highly accurate and highly mobile, borne on the backs of tracked vehicles and parked in groves of trees and under netting all across Eastern Europe.'

Twenty-four hours later the package was on its way to London.

Three days before the end of the month an old lady was heading down Sverdlov Street in central Kiev towards her apartment block. Though she was entitled to a car and a chauffeur, she had been born and brought up in the country, of strong peasant stock. Even in her mid-seventies she preferred to walk rather than drive for short distances. Her visit to spend the evening with a friend two blocks away was so short she had dismissed the car and chauffeur for the night. It was just after ten when she crossed the road in the direction of her own front door.

She didn't see the car, it came so fast. One minute she was in the middle of the road with no one about but two pedestrians a hundred yards away, the next the vehicle was on her, lights blazing, tyres squealing. She froze. The driver seemed to steer right at her, then swerve away. The wing of the vehicle crashed into her hip, bowling her over in the gutter. It failed to stop, roaring away towards Kreshchatik Boulevard at the end of Sverdlov. She vaguely heard the crunch of feet running towards her as passers-by came to her aid.

That evening Edwin J. Campbell, the chief US negotiator at the Castletown talks, arrived back tired and frustrated at the ambassadorial residence in Phoenix Park. It was an elegant mansion that America provided for its envoy in Dublin, and fully modernized, with handsome guest suites, the finest of

900 THE NOVELS OF FREDERICK FORSYTH

which Edwin Campbell had taken over. He was looking forward to a long, hot bath and a rest.

When he had dropped his coat and responded to his host's greeting, one of the messengers from the embassy handed him a fat manilla envelope. As a result his sleep was curtailed that night, but it was worth it.

The next day, he took his place in the Long Gallery at Castletown and gazed impassively across the table at Professor Ivan I. Sokolov.

All right professor, he thought, I know what you can concede and what you cannot. So let's get on with it.

It took forty-eight hours for the Soviet delegate to agree to cut the Warsaw Pact presence of tracked tactical nuclear rockets in Eastern Europe by half. Six hours later, in the dining room, a protocol was agreed whereby the USA would sell the USSR $200,000,000 worth of oil drilling and extraction technology at bargain-basement prices.

The old lady was unconscious when the ambulance brought her to the general hospital, the October Hospital at 39 Karl Liebknecht Street. She remained so until the following morning. When she was able to explain who she was, panicked officials had her wheeled out of the general ward and into a private room, which rapidly filled with flowers. During that day the finest orthopaedic surgeon in Kiev operated to set her broken femur.

In Moscow Ivanenko took a call from his personal aide and listened intently.

'I understand,' he said without hesitation. 'Inform the authorities that I shall come at once. What? Well, then, when she has come out of the anaesthetic. Tomorrow night? Very well, arrange it.'

It was bitter cold on the evening of the last night of October. There was no one moving in Rosa Luxemburg Street, on to which the October Hospital backs. The two long black limousines stood unobserved on the kerbside by this back entrance which the KGB chief had chosen to use rather than the grand portico at the front.

The whole area stands on a slight rise of ground, amid trees, and further down the street on the opposite side an annexe to the hospital was under construction, its unfinished upper levels jutting above the greenery. The watchers among the frozen cement sacks rubbed their hands to keep the circulation going, and stared at the two cars by the door, dimly illuminated by a single bulb above the archway.

When he came down the stairs the man with seven seconds to live was wearing a long, fur-collared overcoat and thick gloves, even for the short walk across the pavement to the warmth of the waiting car. He had spent two hours with his mother, comforting her and assuring her the culprits would be found, as the abandoned car had been found.

He was preceded by an aide who ran ahead and flicked off the doorway light. The door and the pavement were plunged in darkness. Only then did Ivanenko advance to the door, held open by one of his six bodyguards, and pass through it. The knot of four others outside parted as his fur-coated figure emerged, merely a shadow among shadows.

He advanced quickly to the Zil, engine running, across the pavement. He paused for a second as the passenger door was swung open, and died, the bullet from the hunting rifle skewering through his forehead, splintering the parietal bone and exiting through the rear of the cranium to lodge in an aide's shoulder.

The crack of the rifle, the whack of the impacting bullet and the first cry from Colonel Yevgeni Kukushkin, his senior bodyguard, took less than a second. Before the slumping man had hit the pavement, the plain-clothes colonel had him under the armpits, dragging him physically into the recess of the rear seat of the Zil. Before the door was closed the colonel was screaming, 'Drive, drive', to the shocked driver.

Colonel Kukushkin pillowed the bleeding head in his lap as the Zil screeched away from the kerbside. He thought fast. It was not merely a question of a hospital, but of which hospital for a man like this. As the Zil cleared the end of Rosa Luxemburg Street, the colonel flicked on the interior light. What he saw, and had seen much in his career, was enough to tell him his master was beyond hospitals. His second reaction was programmed into his mind and his job: no one must know. The unthinkable had happened, and no one must know, save only those entitled to know. He had secured his promotion and his job by his presence of mind. Watching the second limousine, the bodyguards' Chaika, swing out of Rosa Luxemburg Street behind him, he ordered the driver to choose a quiet and darkened street not less than two miles away, and park.

Leaving the curtained and motionless Zil by the kerbside, with the bodyguards scattered in a screen around it, he took off his blood-soaked coat and set off on foot. He finally made his phone call from a militia barracks, where his ID card and rank secured him instant access to the commandant's private office and phone. It also secured him a direct line. He was patched through in fifteen minutes.

'I must speak to Comrade Secretary-General Rudin urgently,' he told the Kremlin switchboard operator. The woman knew from the line on which the call was coming that this was neither joke nor impertinence. She put it through to an aide inside the armoury building, who held the call and spoke to Maxim Rudin on the internal phone. Rudin authorized the pass-through of the call.

'Yes,' he grunted down the line, 'Rudin here.'

Colonel Kukushkin had never spoken to him before, though he had seen him and heard him at close quarters many times. He knew it was Rudin. He swallowed hard, took a deep breath and spoke.

At the other end Rudin listened, asked two brief questions, rapped out a string of orders, and put the phone down. He turned to Vassili Petrov who was with him, leaning forward alert and worried.

'He's dead,' said Rudin in disbelief. 'Not a heart attack. Shot. Yuri Ivanenko. Someone has just assassinated the chairman of the KGB.'

Beyond the windows the clock in the tower above Saviour's Gate chimed midnight, and a sleeping world began to move slowly towards war.

The KGB has always ostensibly been answerable to the Soviet Council of Ministers. In practice it answers to the Politburo.

The everyday working of the KGB, the appointment of every officer within it, every promotion and the rigorous indoctrination of every staffer – all are supervised by the Politburo through the Party Organizations Section of the Central Committee. At every stage of the career of every KGB man he is watched, informed on and reported on; even the watchdogs of the Soviet Union are never themselves free of watching. Thus it is unlikely that this most pervasive and powerful of control machines can ever run out of control.

In the wake of the assassination of Yuri Ivanenko, it was Vassili Petrov who took command of the cover-up operation that Maxim Rudin directly and personally ordered.

Over the telephone Rudin had ordered Colonel Kukushkin to bring the two-car cavalcade straight back to Moscow by road, stopping neither for food, drink nor sleep, driving through the night, refuelling the Zil bearing Ivanenko's corpse with jerry-cans, brought to the car by the Chaika and always out of sight of passersby.

On arrival on the outskirts of Moscow the two cars were directed straight to the Politburo's own private clinic at Kuntsevo, where the corpse with the shattered head was quietly buried amid the pine forest within the clinic perimeter, in an unmarked grave. The burial party was of Ivanenko's own bodyguards, all of whom were then placed under house arrest at one of the Kremlin's own villas in the forest. The guard detailed on these men was drawn not from the KGB but from the Kremlin palace guard. Only Colonel Kukushkin was not held incommunicado. He was summoned to Petrov's private office in the Central Committee building.

The colonel was a frightened man, and when he left Petrov's office he was little less so. Petrov gave him one chance to save his career and his life: he was put in charge of the cover-up operation.

At Kuntsevo clinic he organized the closure of one entire ward and brought KGB men from Dzerzhinsky Square to mount guard on it. Two KGB doctors were transferred to Kuntsevo and put in charge of the patient in the closed ward, a patient who was in fact an empty bed. No one else was allowed in, but the two doctors, knowing only enough to be badly frightened, ferried all the equipment and medicaments into the closed ward as would be needed for the treatment of a heart attack. Within twenty-four hours, save for the closed ward in the secret clinic off the road from Moscow to Minsk, Yuri Ivanenko had ceased to exist.

At this early stage only one other man was let into the secret. Among Ivanenko's six deputies, all with their offices close to his on the third floor of the KGB centre, one was his official deputy as chairman of the KGB. Petrov summoned General Konstantin Abrassov to his office and informed him of what had happened, a piece of information that shook the general as nothing in a thirty-year career in secret police work had done. Inevitably he agreed to continue the masquerade.

In the October Hospital in Kiev, the dead man's mother was surrounded by local KGB men and continued to receive daily written messages of comfort from her son.

Finally, the three workmen on the annexe to the October Hospital who had discovered a hunting rifle and night-sight when they came to work the morning after the shooting were removed with their families to one of the camps in Mordovia, and two criminal detectives were flown in from Moscow to investigate an act of hooliganism. Colonel Kukushkin was with them. The story they were given was that the shot had been fired at the moving car of a local Party official; it had passed through the windscreen and was recovered from the upholstery. The real bullet, recovered from the KGB's guard's shoulder and well washed, was presented to them. They were told to trace and identify the hooligans in conditions of complete secrecy. Somewhat perplexed and much frustrated, they proceeded to try. Work on the annexe was stopped, the half-finished building sealed off, and all the forensic equipment they could ask for supplied. The only thing they did not get was a true explanation.

When the last piece of the jigsaw puzzle of deception was in place, Petrov reported personally to Rudin. To the old chief fell the worst task, that of informing the Politburo of what had really happened.

The private report of Dr Myron Fletcher of the Agriculture Department to President William Matthews two days later was all and more that the *ad hoc* committee formed under the personal auspices of the President could have wished for. Not only had the benign weather brought North America a bumper crop in all areas of grain and cereals, it had broken existing records. Even with probable requirements for domestic consumption taken care of, and even with existing aid levels to the poor countries of the world maintained, the surplus would nudge 60,000,000 tons for the combined harvest of the USA and Canada.

'Mr President, you've got it,' said Stanislaw Poklewski. 'You can buy that surplus any time you wish at July's price. Bearing in mind the progress at the Castletown talks, the House Appropriations Committee will not stand in your way.'

'I should hope not,' said the President. 'If we succeed at Castletown the reductions in defence expenditure will more than compensate for the commercial losses on the grains. What about the Soviet crop?'

'We're working on it,' said Bob Benson. 'The Condors are sweeping right across the Soviet Union, and our analysts are working out the yields of harvested grain region by region. We should have a report for you in a week. We can correlate that with reports from our people on the ground over there and give a pretty accurate figure, to within five per cent, anyway.

'As soon as you can,' said President Matthews. 'I need to know the exact Soviet position in every area. That includes the Politburo reaction to their own grain harvest. I need to know their strengths and their weaknesses. Please get them for me, Bob.'

No one in the Ukraine that winter would be likely to forget the sweeps by the KGB and militia against those in whom the slightest hint of nationalist sentiment could be detected.

While Colonel Kukushkin's two detectives carefully interviewed the pedestrians in Sverdlov Street the night Ivanenko's mother had been run down, meticulously took to pieces the stolen car that had performed the hit-and-run job on the old lady, and pored over the rifle, the image-intensifier and the surrounds of the hospital annexe, General Abrassov went for the nationalists.

Hundreds were detained in Kiev, Ternopol, Lvov, Kanev, Rovno, Zhitomir and Vinnitsa. The local KGB, supported by teams from Moscow, carried out the interrogations, ostensibly concerned with sporadic outbreaks of hooliganism such as the mugging of the KGB plain-clothes man in August in Ternopol. Some of the senior interrogators were permitted to know their enquiries also concerned the firing of a shot in Kiev in late October, but no more.

In the seedy Lvov working-class district of Levandivka that November David Lazareff and Lev Mishkin strolled through the snowy streets during one of their rare meetings. Because the fathers of both had been taken away to the camps, they knew time would run out for them eventually also. The word 'Jew' was stamped on the identity card of each, as on those of every one of the Soviet Union's 3,000,000 Jews. Sooner or later the spotlight of the KGB must swing away from the nationalists to the Jews. Nothing ever changes that much in the Soviet Union.

'I posted the card to Andriy Drach yesterday, confirming the success of the first objective,' said Mishkin. 'How are things with you?'

'So far, so good,' said Lazareff. 'Perhaps things will ease off soon.'

'Not this time, I think,' said Mishkin. 'We have to make our break soon if we are going to at all. The ports are out. It has to be by air. Same place next week. I'll see what I can discover about the airport.'

Far away to the north of them an SAS jumbo jet thundered on its polar route from Stockholm to Tokyo. Among its first-class passengers it bore Captain Thor Larsen towards his new command.

Maxim Rudin's report to the Politburo was delivered in his gravelly voice, without frills. But no histrionics in the world could have kept his audience more absorbed, nor their reaction more stunned. Since an army officer had emptied a handgun at the limousine of Leonid Brezhnev as he passed through the Kremlin's Borovitsky Gate a decade before, the spectre of the lone man with a gun penetrating the walls of security around the hierarchs had persisted. Now it had come out of conjecture to sit and stare at them from their own green baize table.

This time the room was empty of secretaries. No tape recorders turned on the corner table. No aides, no stenographers were present. When he had finished, Rudin handed the floor to Petrov who described the elaborate measures taken to mask the outrage, and the secret steps then in progress to identify and eliminate the killers after they had revealed all their accomplices.

'But you have not found them yet?' snapped Stepanov.

'It is only five days since the attack,' said Petrov evenly. 'No, not yet. They will be caught, of course. They cannot escape, whoever they are. When they are caught, they will reveal every last one of those who helped them. General Abrassov will see to that. Then every last person who knows what happened that night in Rosa Luxemburg Street, wherever they may be hiding, will be eliminated. There will be no trace left.'

'And in the meantime?' asked Komarov.

'In the meantime,' said Rudin, 'it must be maintained with unbreakable solidarity that Comrade Yuri Ivanenko has sustained a massive heart attack and is under intensive care. Let us be clear on one thing. The Soviet Union cannot and will not tolerate the public humiliation of the world ever being allowed to know what happened in Rosa Luxemburg Street. There are no Lee Harvey Oswalds in Russia and never will be.'

There was a murmur of assent. No one was prepared to disagree with Rudin's assessment.

'With respect, Mr Secretary-General,' Petrov cut in, 'while the catastrophe of such news leaking abroad cannot be over-estimated, there is another aspect, equally serious. If this news leaked out, the rumours would begin among our own population. Before long they would be more than rumours. The effect internally I leave to your imagination.'

They all knew how closely the maintenance of public order was linked to a belief in the impregnability and invincibility of the KGB.

'If this news leaked out,' said Chavadze, the Georgian, slowly,' and even more so if the perpetrators escaped, the effect would be as bad as that of the grain famine.'

'They cannot escape,' said Petrov sharply. 'They must not. They will not.'

'Then who are they?' growled Kerensky.

'We do not yet know, Comrade Marshal,' replied Petrov, 'but we will.'

'But it was a Western gun?' insisted Shuskin. 'Could the West be behind this?'

'I think it almost impossible,' said Rykov of Foreign Affairs. 'No Western government, no Third World government, would be crazy enough to support such an outrage, in the same way as we had nothing to do with the Kennedy assassination. Emigrés, possibly. Anti-Soviet fanatics, possibly. But not governments.'

'Emigré groups abroad are also being investigated,' said Petrov, 'but discreetly. We have most of them penetrated. So far nothing has come in. The rifle, ammunition and night-sight are all of Western make. They are all commercially purchasable in the West. That they were smuggled in is beyond doubt. Which means either the users brought them in, or they had outside help. General Abrassov agrees with me that the primary requirement is to find the users, who will reveal their suppliers. Department V will take over from there.'

Yefrem Vishnayev watched the proceedings with keen interest but took little part. Kerensky expressed the dissatisfaction of the dissident group instead. Neither sought a further vote on the choice of the Castletown talks or a war in 1983. Both knew that in the event of a tie, the chairman's vote would prevail. Rudin had come one step nearer to falling, but was not finished yet.

The meeting agreed that the announcement should be made, only within the KGB and the upper echelons of the Party machine, that Yuri Ivanenko had suffered a heart attack and was in hospital. When the killers had been identified and they and their aides eliminated, Ivanenko would quietly expire from his illness.

Rudin was about to summon the secretaries to the chamber for the resumption of the usual Politburo meeting when Stepanov, who had originally voted for Rudin and negotiations with the USA, raised his hand.

'Comrades, I would regard it as a major defeat for our country if the killers of Yuri Ivanenko were to escape and publish their action to the world. Should that happen, I would not be able to continue my support for the policy of negotiation and further concession in the matter of our armaments levels in exchange for American grain. I would switch my support to the proposal of Party Theoretician Vishnayev.'

There was dead silence.

'So would I,' said Shushkin.

Eight against four, thought Rudin as he gazed impassively down the table. Eight against four if these two shits change sides now.

'Your point is taken, comrades,' said Rudin without a flicker of emotion. 'There will be no publication of this deed. None at all.'

Ten minutes later the meeting reopened with a unanimous expression of regret at the sudden illness of Comrade Ivanenko. The subject then turned to the newly arrived figures of wheat and grain yields.

The Zil limousine of Yefrem Vishnayev erupted from the mouth of the Borovitsky Gate at the Kremlin's southwestern corner and straight across Manege Square. The policeman on duty in the square, forewarned by his bleeper that the Politburo cavalcade was leaving the Kremlin, had stopped all traffic. Within seconds the long, black, hand-tooled cars were scorching up Frunze Street past the Defence Ministry towards the homes of the privileged in Kutuzovsky Prospekt.

Marshal Kerensky sat beside Vishnayev in the latter's car, having accepted his invitation to drive together. The partition between the spacious rear area and the driver was closed and soundproof. The curtains shut out the gaze of the pedestrians.

'He's near to falling,' growled Kerensky.

'No,' said Vishnayev, 'he's one step nearer and a lot weaker without Ivanenko, but he's not near to falling yet. Don't underestimate Maxim Rudin. He'll fight like a cornered bear on the taiga before he goes, but go he will because go he must.'

'Well, there's not much time,' said Kerensky.

'Less than you think,' said Vishnayev. 'There were food riots in Vilnius last week. Our friend Vitautas who voted for our proposal in July is getting nervous. He was on the verge of switching sides despite the very attractive villa I have offered him next to my own at Sochi. Now he is back in the fold, and Shushkin and Stepanov may change sides in our favour.'

'But only if the killers escape, or the truth is published abroad,' said Kerensky.

'Precisely. And that is what must happen.'

Kerensky turned in the back seat, his florid face turning brick beneath his shock of white hair.

'Reveal the truth? To the whole world? We can't do that,' he exploded.

'No, we can't. There are far too few people who know the truth, and mere rumours cannot succeed. They can be too easily discounted. An actor looking precisely like Ivanenko could be found, rehearsed, seen in public. So others must do it for us. With absolute proof. The guards who were present that night are in the hands of the Kremlin elite. That only leaves the killers themselves.'

'But we don't have them,' said Kerensky, 'and are not likely to. The KGB will get them first.'

'Probably, but we have to try,' said Vishnayev. 'Let's be plain about this, Nikolai. We are not fighting for the control of the Soviet Union any more. We are fighting for our lives, like Rudin and Petrov. First the wheat, now Ivanenko. One more scandal, Nikolai, one more – whoever is responsible, let me make that clear, whoever is responsible – and Rudin will fall. There must be one more scandal. We must ensure that there is.'

Thor Larsen, dressed in overalls and a safety helmet, stood on a gantry crane high above the dry dock at the centre of the Ishikawajima-Harima shipyard and gazed down at the mass of the vessel that would one day be the *Freya*.

Even three days after his first sight, the size of her took his breath away. In his apprenticeship days tankers had never gone beyond 30,000 tons, and it was not until 1956 that the world's first over that tonnage took to the sea. A new class was created for such vessels, and they were called supertankers. When someone broke the 50,000-ton ceiling there was another new class, the VLCC, or very large crude carrier. As the 200,000-ton barrier was broken in the late sixties the new class of Ultra-Large Crude Carrier, or ULCC, came into being.

Once at sea Larsen had seen one of the French leviathans, weighing in at 550,000 tons, move past him. His crew had poured out on deck to watch her. What lay below him now was twice that size. As Wennerstrom had said, the world had never seen the like of her, nor ever would again.

She was 515 metres, or 1689 feet, long, like ten city blocks. She was 90 metres, or 295 feet, broad, from scupper to scupper, and her superstructure reared five stories into the air above her deck. Far below what he could see of her deck area, her keel plunged 36 metres, or 118 feet, towards the floor of the dry dock. Each of her sixty holds was bigger than a neighbourhood cinema. Deep in her bowels below the superstructure the four steam turbines mustering a total of 90,000 shaft horsepower were already installed, ready to drive her twin screws whose forty-foot-diameter bronze propellers could be vaguely seen glinting below her stern.

From end to end she teemed with ant-like figures, the workers preparing to leave her temporarily while the dock was filled. For twelve months, almost to the day, they had cut and burned, bolted, sawn, riveted, hacked, plated, and hammered her hull together. Great modules of high-tensile steel had swung in from the overhead gantries to drop into pre-assigned places and form her shape. As the men cleared away the ropes and chains, lines and cables that hung about her, she lay exposed at last, her sides clean of encumbrances, painted with twenty coats of rustproof paint, waiting for the water.

At last only the blocks that cradled her remained. The men who had built this, the biggest dry dock in the world, at Chita, near Nagoya on Ise Bay, had never thought to see their handiwork put to such use. It was the only dry dock that could take a million-tonner, and it was the first and last it would ever hold. Some of the veterans came to peer across the barriers to see the ceremony.

The religious ceremony took half an hour as the Shinto priest called down the blessings of the divine ones on those who had built her, those who would work on her yet and those who would sail her one day, that they should enjoy safe labour and safe sailing. Thor Larsen attended, barefoot, with his chief engineer and chief officer, the owner's chief superintendent (marine architect) who had been there from the start, and the yard's equivalent architect. These were the two men who had really designed and built her.

Shortly before noon the sluices were opened, and with a thundering roar the western Pacific began to flow in.

There was a formal lunch in the chairman's office, but when it was over Thor Larsen went back to the dock. He was joined by his first officer, Stig Lundquist, and his chief engineer, Bjorn Erikson, both from Sweden.

'She's something else,' said Lundquist as the water climbed her sides.

Shortly before sunset the *Freya* groaned like a waking giant, moved half an inch, groaned again, then came free of her underwater supports and rode the tide. Around the dock 4000 Japanese workers broke their studied silence and burst into cheering. Scores of white helmets were thrown into the air; the half-dozen Europeans from Scandinavia joined in, pumping hands and thumping backs. Below them the giant waited patiently, seemingly aware her turn would come in time.

The next day she was towed out of the dock to the commissioning quay where for three months she would once again play host to thousands of small figures working like the demons to prepare her for the sea beyond the bay.

Sir Nigel Irvine read the last lines of the Nightingale transcript, closed the file and leaned back.

'Well, Barry, what do you make of it?'

Barry Ferndale had spent most of his working life studying the Soviet Union, its masters and power structure. He breathed once more on his glasses and gave them a final rub.

'It's one more blow that Maxim Rudin's going to have to survive,' he said. 'Ivanenko was one of his staunchest supporters. And an exceptionally clever one. With him in hospital Rudin has lost one of his ablest counsellors.'

'Will Ivanenko still retain his vote in the Politburo?' asked Sir Nigel.

'It's possible he can vote by proxy should another vote come,' said Ferndale, 'but that's not really the point. Even at a six-to-six tie on a major issue of policy at Politburo level, the chairman's vote swings the issue. The danger is that one or two of the waverers might change sides. Ivanenko in an oxygen tent perhaps less so.'

Sir Nigel handed the folder across the desk to Ferndale.

'Barry, I want you to go over to Washington with this one. Just a courtesy call, of course. But try to have a private dinner with Ben Kahn and compare notes with him. This exercise is becoming too damn much of a close-run thing.'

'The way we see it, Ben,' said Ferndale, two days later after dinner in Kahn's Georgetown house, 'is that Maxim Rudin is holding on by a thread in the face of a fifty per cent hostile Politburo, and that thread is getting extremely thin.'

The deputy director (Intelligence) of the CIA stretched his feet towards the log fire in his red-brick grate and gazed at the brandy he twirled in his glass.

'I can't fault you on that, Barry,' he said carefully.

'We also are of the view that if Rudin cannot persuade the Politburo to continue conceding the things he is yielding to you at Castletown, he could fall. That would leave a fight for the succession, to be decided by the full Central Committee. In which, alas, Yefrem Vishnayev has a powerful amount of influence and friends.'

'True,' said Kahn. 'But then so does Vassili Petrov. Probably more than Vishnayev.'

'No doubt,' rejoined Ferndale, 'and Petrov would probably swing the succession towards himself; if he had the backing of Rudin who was retiring in his own time and on his own terms, and if he had the support of Ivanenko whose KGB clout could help offset Marshal Kerensky's influence through the Red Army.'

Kahn smiled across at his visitor.

'You're moving a lot of pawns forward, Barry. What's your gambit?'

'Just comparing notes,' said Ferndale.

'All right, just comparing notes. Actually our own views at Langley go along pretty much with yours. David Lawrence at the State Department agrees. Stan Poklewski wants to ride the Soviets hard at Castletown. The President's in the middle – as usual.'

'Castletown's pretty important to him, though?' suggested Ferndale.

'Very important. Next year is his last in office. In thirteen months there'll be a new president-designate. Bill Matthews would like to go out in style, leaving a comprehensive arms limitation treaty behind him.'

'We were just thinking. . . .'

'Ah,' said Kahn, 'I think you are contemplating bringing your knight forward.'

Ferndale smiled at the oblique reference to his 'knight', the director-general of his service.

'. . . that Castletown would certainly abort if Rudin fell from control at this juncture. And that he could use something from Castletown, from your side, to convince any waverers among his faction that he was achieving things there and that he was the man to back.'

'Concessions?' asked Kahn. 'We got the final analysis of the Soviet grain harvest last week. They're over a barrel. At least that's the way Poklewski put it.'

'He's right,' said Ferndale. 'But the barrel's on the point of collapsing. And waiting inside it is dear Comrade Vishnayev, with his war plan. And we all know what that would entail.'

'Point taken,' said Kahn. 'Actually my own reading of the combined Nightingale file runs along very similar lines. I've got a paper in preparation for the President's eyes at the moment. He'll have it next week when he and Benson meet with Lawrence and Poklewski.'

'These figures,' asked President Matthews, 'they represent the final aggregate grain crop the Soviet Union brought home a month ago?'

He glanced across at the four men seated in front of his desk. At the far end of the room a log fire crackled in the marble fireplace, adding a touch of visual warmth to the already high temperature assured by the central heating system. Beyond the bulletproof south windows the sweeping lawns held their first dusting of November morning frost. Being from the South, William Matthews appreciated warmth.

Robert Benson and Dr Myron Fletcher nodded in unison. David Lawrence and Stanislaw Poklewski studied the figures.

'All our sources have been called on for these figures, Mr President, and all our information has been correlated extremely carefully,' said Benson. 'We could be out by five per cent either way, not more.'

'And according to the Nightingale even the Politburo agrees with us,' interposed the secretary of state.

'One hundred million tons, total,' mused the President. 'It will last them till the end of March, with a lot of belt tightening.'

'They'll be slaughtering the cattle by January,' said Poklewski. 'They will have to start making sweeping concessions at Castletown next month if they want to survive.'

The President laid down the Soviet grain report and picked up the presidential briefing prepared by Ben Kahn and presented by his director of central intelligence. It had been read by all four in the room as well as himself. Benson and Lawrence had agreed with it; Dr Fletcher was not called for an opinion; the hawkish Poklewski dissented.

'We know and they know they are in desperate straits,' said Matthews. 'The question is, how far do we push them?'

'As you said weeks ago, Mr President,' said Lawrence, 'if we don't push hard enough we don't get the best deal we can for America and the free world. Push too hard and we force Rudin to abort the talks to save himself from his own hawks. It's a question of balance. At this point I feel we should make them a gesture.'

'Wheat?'

'Animal feedstuffs to help them keep some of their herds alive,' suggested Benson.

'Dr Fletcher?' asked the President.

The man from Agriculture shrugged.

'We have them available, Mr President,' he said. 'The Soviets have a large proportion of their own merchant fleet, Sovfracht, standing by. We know that because with their subsidized freight rates they could all be busy, but they're not. They're positioned all over the warm-water ports of the Black Sea and down the Soviet Pacific coast. They'll sail for the USA if they're given the word from Moscow.'

'What's the latest we need to give a decision on this one?' asked President Matthews.

'New Year's Day,' said Benson. 'If they know a respite is coming, they can hold off slaughtering the herds.'

'I urge you not to ease up on them,' pleaded Poklewski. 'By March they'll be desperate.'

'Desperate enough to concede enough disarmament to assure peace for a decade, or desperate enough to go to war?' asked Matthews rhetorically. 'Gentlemen, you'll have my decision by Christmas Day. Unlike you, I have to take five chairmen of Senate sub-committees with me on this one: defense, agriculture, foreign affairs, trade and appropriations. And I can't tell them about the Nightingale, can I, Bob?'

The chief of the CIA shook his head.

'No, Mr President. Not about the Nightingale. There are too many Senate aides, too many leaks. The effect of a leak of what we really know at this juncture could be disastrous.'

'Very well, then. Christmas Day it is.'

On 15th December Professor Ivan Sokolov rose to his feet at Castletown and began to read a prepared paper. The Soviet Union, he said, ever true to its traditions as a country devoted to the unswerving search for world peace, and mindful of its often-reiterated commitment to peaceful co-existence. . . .

Edwin J. Campbell sat across the table and watched his Soviet opposite number with some fellow feeling. Over two months, working until fatigue overcame both of them, he had developed a fairly warm relationship with the man from Moscow, as much at least as their positions and their duties would allow.

In breaks between the talks, each had visited the other in the opposing delegation's rest room. In the Soviet drawing room, with the Muscovite delegation present and its inevitable complement of KGB agents, the conversation had been agreeable but formal. In the American room where Sokolov had arrived alone, he relaxed to the point of showing Campbell pictures of his grandchildren on holiday on the Black Sea coast. As a leading member of the

Academy of Sciences the professor was rewarded for his loyalty to Party and cause with a limousine, chauffeur, city apartment, country *dacha*, seaside chalet, and access to the Academy grocery store and commissary. Campbell had no illusions that Sokolov was paid for his loyalty, for his ability to devote his talents to the service of a regime that committed tens of thousands to the labour camps of Mordovia; that he was one of the fat cats, the *nachalstvo*. But even the *nachalstvo* have grandchildren.

He sat and listened to the Russian with growing surprise.

You poor old man, he thought. What this must be costing you.

When the peroration was over Edwin Campbell rose and gravely thanked the professor for his statement, which on behalf of the United States of America he had listened to with the utmost care and attention. He moved an adjournment while the US government considered its position. Within an hour he was in his Dublin embassy to begin transmitting Sokolov's extraordinary speech to David Lawrence.

Some hours later in Washington's State Department, David Lawrence lifted one of his telephones and called President Matthews on his private line.

'I have to tell you, Mr President, that six hours ago in Ireland the Soviet Union conceded six major points at issue. They concern total numbers of intercontinental ballistic missiles with hydrogen-bomb warheads through conventional armour to disengagement to forces along the Elbe River.'

'Thanks, David,' said Matthews. 'That's great news. You were right. I think we should let them have something in return.'

The area of birch and larch forest lying southwest of Moscow where the Soviet elite have their country *dachas* covers little more than a hundred square miles. They like to stick together. The roads in this area are bordered mile after mile by green-painted steel railings, enclosing the private estates of the men at the very top. The fences and the driveway gates seem largely abandoned, but anyone trying to scale the first or drive through the second will be intercepted within moments by guards who materialize out of the trees.

Lying beyond Uspenskoye Bridge, the area centres on a small village called Zhukovka, usually known as Zhukovka village. This is because there are two other and newer settlements nearby: Sovmin Zhukovka where the Party hierarchs have their weekend villas, and Akademik Zhukovka which groups the writers, artists, musicians and scientists who have found favour in Party eyes.

But across the river lies the ultimate, the even more exclusive settlement of Usovo. Nearby the General Secretary of the Communist Party of the Soviet Union, the chairman of the Praesidium of the Supreme Soviet, the Politburo, retires to a sumptuous mansion set in hundreds of acres of rigorously guarded forest.

Here on the night before Christmas, a feast he had not recognized in fifty years, Maxim Rudin sat in his favourite button-back leather chair, feet towards the enormous fireplace in rough-cut granite blocks where metre-long logs of split pine crackled. It was the same fireplace that had warmed Leonid Brezhnev and Nikita Khrushchev before him.

The bright yellow glare of the flames flickered on the panelled walls of the study and illuminated the face of Vassili Petrov who faced him across the fire. By Rudin's chair arm a small coffee table held an ashtray and half a tumbler of Armenian brandy, which Petrov eyed askance. He knew his ageing protector was not supposed to drink. Rudin's inevitable cigarette was clipped between first finger and thumb.

'What news of the investigation?' asked Rudin.

'Slow,' said Petrov. 'That there was outside help is beyond doubt. We now know the night-sight was bought commercially in New York. The Finnish rifle was one of a consignment exported from Helsinki to Britain. We don't know which shop it came from, but the export order was for sporting rifles, therefore it was a private-sector commercial order, not an official one. The footprints at the building site have been checked out against the boots of all the workers at the place, and there are two sets of footprints that cannot be traced. There was damp in the air that night and a lot of cement dust lying around, so the prints are clear. We are reasonably certain there were two men.'

'Dissidents?' asked Rudin.

'Almost certainly. And quite mad.'

'No, Vassili, keep that for the Party meetings. Madmen take pot-shots, or sacrifice themselves. This was planned over months by someone; someone out there, inside or outside Russia, who has got to be silenced, once and for all, with his secret untold. Who are you concentrating on?'

'The Ukrainians,' said Petrov. 'We have all their groups in Germany, Britain and America completely penetrated. No one has heard a rumour of such a plan. Personally, I still think they are in the Ukraine. That Ivanenko's mother was used as a bait is undeniable. So who would have known she *was* Ivanenko's mother? Not some slogan-dauber in New York. Not some armchair nationalist in Frankfurt. Not some pamphleteer in London. Someone local, with contacts outside. We are concentrating on Kiev. Several hundred former detainees who were released and returned to the Kiev area are under interrogation.'

'Find them. Vassili, find them and silence them.' Maxim Rudin changed the subject as he had a habit of doing without a change of tone. 'Anything new from Ireland?'

'The Americans have resumed talking, but have not responded to our initiative,' said Petrov.

Rudin snorted. 'That Matthews is a fool. How much further does he think we can go before we have to pull back?'

'He has those Soviet-hating senators to contend with,' said Petrov, 'and that Catholic Fascist Poklewski. And of course he cannot know how close things are for us inside the Politburo.'

Rudin grunted. 'If he doesn't offer us something by the New Year, we won't carry the Politburo in the first week of January. . . .'

He reached out and took a draught of brandy, exhaling with a satisfied sigh.

'Are you sure you should be drinking?' asked Petrov. 'The doctors forbade you five years ago.'

'Screw the doctors,' said Rudin. 'That's what I really called you here for. I can inform you beyond any doubt that I am not going to die of alcoholism or liver failure.'

'I'm glad to hear it,' said Petrov.

'There's more. On 30th April I am going to retire. Does that surprise you?'

Petrov sat motionless, alert. He had twice seen the supremos go down. Khrushchev in flames, ousted and disgraced, to become a non-person. Brezhnev on his own terms. He had been close enough to feel the thunder when the most powerful tyrant in the world gives way to another. But never this close. This time he wore the mantle, unless others could snatch it from him.

'Yes,' he said carefully, 'it does.'

'In April I am calling a meeting of the full Central Committee,' said Rudin, 'to announce to them my decision to go on 30th April. On May Day there will be a new leader at the centre of the line on the Mausoleum. I want it to be you. In June the plenary Party congress is due. The leader will outline the policy from then on. I want it to be you. I told you that weeks ago.'

Petrov knew he was Rudin's choice since that meeting in the old leader's private suite in the Kremlin, when the now dead Ivanenko had been with them, cynical and watchful as ever. But he had not known it would be so fast.

'I won't get the Central Committee to accept your nomination unless I can give them something they want. Grain. They all know the position long since. If Castletown fails, Vishnayev will have it all.'

'Why so soon?' asked Petrov.

Rudin held up his glass. From the shadows the silent Misha appeared and poured brandy into it.

'I got the results of the tests from Kuntsevo yesterday,' said Rudin. 'They've been working on tests for months. Now they're certain. Not cigarettes and not Armenian brandy. Leukaemia. Six to twelve months. Let's say I won't see a Christmas after this one. And if we have a nuclear war, neither will you.

'In the next hundred days we have to secure a grain agreement from the Americans and wipe out the Ivanenko affair once and for all time. The sands are running out and too damn fast. The cards are on the table, face up, and there are no more aces to play.'

On 28th December, the United States formally offered the Soviet Union a sale, for immediate delivery and at commercial rates, of ten million tons of animal feed grains, to be considered as being outside any terms still being negotiated at Castletown.

On New Year's Eve an Aeroflot twin-jet Tupolev 134 took off from Lvov Airport bound for Minsk on an internal flight. Just north of the border between the Ukraine and White Russia, high over the Pripet Marshes, a nervous-looking young man rose from his seat and approached the stewardess who was several rows back from the steel door leading to the flight deck, speaking with a passenger.

Knowing the toilets were at the other end of the cabin, she straightened as the young man approached her. As she did so the young man spun her round, clamped his left forearm across her throat, drew a handgun and jammed it into her ribs. She screamed. There was a chorus of shouts and yells from the passengers. The hijacker began to drag the girl backwards to the locked door to the flight deck. On the bulkhead next to the door was the intercom, enabling the stewardess to speak to the flight crew, who had orders to refuse to open the door in the event of a hijack.

From mid-way down the fuselage one of the passengers rose, automatic in hand. He crouched in the aisle, both hands clasped round his gun, pointing it straight at the stewardess and the hijacker behind her.

'Hold it,' he shouted. 'KGB. Hold it right there.'

'Tell them to open the door,' yelled the hijacker.

'Not a chance,' shouted the armed flight guard from the KGB to the hijacker.

'If they don't I'll kill the girl,' screamed the man holding the stewardess.

The girl had a lot of courage. She lunged backward with her heel, caught the gunman in the shin, broke his grip and made to run towards the police agent. The hijacker sprang after her, passing three rows of passengers. It was a mistake. From an aisle seat one of them rose, turned and slammed a fist into the nape of the hijacker's neck. The man pitched face downward; before he could move, his assailant had snatched the man's gun and was pointing it at him. The hijacker turned, sat up, looked at the gun, put his face in his hands and began to moan softly.

From the rear the KGB agent stepped past the stewardess, gun still at the ready, and approached the rescuer.

'Who are you?' he asked. For answer the rescuer reached into an inside pocket, produced a card and flicked it open.

The agent looked at the KGB card.

'You're not from Lvov,' he said.

'Ternopol,' said the other. 'I was going home on leave in Minsk, so I had no sidearm. But I have a good right fist.' He grinned.

The agent from Lvov nodded.

'Thanks, comrade. Keep him covered.' He stepped to the speaker-phone and talked rapidly into it. He was relating what had happened and asking for a police reception at Minsk.

'Is it safe to have a look?' asked a metallic voice from behind the door.

'Sure,' said the KGB agent. 'He's safe enough now.'

There was a clicking behind the door, and it opened to show the head of the engineer, somewhat frightened and intensely curious.

The agent from Ternopol acted very strangely. He turned from the man on the floor, crashed his revolver into the base of his colleague's skull, shoved him aside and thrust his foot in the door before it could close. In a second he was through it, pushing the engineer backwards on to the flight deck. The man on the floor behind him rose, grabbed the flight guard's own automatic, a standard KGB Tokarev 9 mm, followed through the steel door and slammed it behind him. It locked automatically.

Two minutes later, under the guns of David Lazareff and Lev Mishkin, the Tupolev turned due west for Warsaw and Berlin, the latter being the ultimate limit of its fuel supply. At the controls Captain Rudenko sat white-faced with rage; beside him his co-pilot, Vatutin, slowly answered the hurried requests from Minsk control tower regarding the change of course.

By the time the airliner had crossed the border into Polish air space, Minsk tower and four other airliners on the same wavelength knew the Tupolev was in the hands of hijackers. When it bored clean through the centre of Warsaw's air traffic control zone, Moscow already knew. A hundred miles west of Warsaw a flight of six Polish-based but Soviet MiG-23 fighters swept in from starboard and formated on the Tupolev. The flight leader was jabbering rapidly into his mask.

At his desk in the Defence Ministry in Frunze Street, Moscow, Marshal Nikolai Kerensky took an urgent call on the line linking him to Soviet air force headquarters.

'Where?' he barked.

'Passing overhead Poznan,' was the answer. 'Three hundred kilometres to Berlin. Fifty minutes' flying time.'

The marshal considered carefully. This could be the scandal which Vishnayev had demanded. There was no doubt what should be done. The Tupolev should be shot down, with its entire passenger and crew complement. Later the version given out would be that the hijackers had fired within the fuselage, hitting a main fuel tank. It had happened twice in the past decade.

He gave his orders. A hundred metres off the airliner's wingtip the commander of the MiG flight listened five minutes later.

'If you say so, comrade colonel,' he told his base commander. Twenty minutes later the airliner passed across the Oder–Neisse line and began its letdown into Berlin. As it did so, the MiGs peeled gracefully away and slipped down the sky towards their home base.

'I have to tell Berlin we're coming in,' Captain Rudenko appealed to Mishkin. 'If there's a plane on the runway, we'll end up as a ball of fire.'

Mishkin stared ahead at the banks of steel-grey winter clouds. He had never been in an airplane before, but what the captain said made sense.

'Very well,' he said, 'break silence and tell Tempelhof you are coming in. No requests, just a flat statement.'

Captain Rudenko was playing his last card. He leaned forward, adjusted the channel selection dial and began to speak.

'Tempelhof, West Berlin. Tempelhof, West Berlin. This is Aeroflot flight 351. . . .'

He was speaking in English, the international language of air traffic control. Mishkin and Lazareff knew almost none of it, apart from what they had picked up on broadcasts in Ukrainian from the West. Mishkin jabbed his gun into Rudenko's neck.

'No tricks,' he said in Ukrainian.

In the control tower at East Berlin's Schönefeld Airport the two controllers looked at each other in amazement. They were being called on their own frequency, but addressed as Tempelhof. No Aeroflot plane would dream of landing in West Berlin, apart from which Tempelhof had not been West Berlin's civil airport for ten years. Tempelhof had reverted to a US Air Force base when Tegel took over as the civil airport.

One of the East Germans, faster than the other, snatched the microphone. 'Tempelhof to Aeroflot 351, you are clear to land. Straight run in,' he said.

In the airliner Captain Rudenko swallowed hard and lowered flap and under-carriage. The Tupolev let down rapidly to the main airport of Communist East Germany. They broke cloud at a thousand feet and saw the landing lights ahead of them. At five hundred feet Mishkin peered suspiciously through the streaming perspex. He had heard of West Berlin, of brilliant lights, packed streets, teeming crowds of shoppers up the Kurfurstendam, and Tempelhof Airport right in the heart of it all. This airport was right out in the countryside.

'It's a trick,' he yelled at Lazareff. 'It's the East.' He jabbed his gun into Captain Rudenko's neck. 'Pull out,' he screamed, 'pull out or I'll shoot.'

The Ukrainian captain gritted his teeth and held on course for the last hundred metres. Mishkin reached over his shoulder and tried to haul back on the control column. The twin booms, when they came, were so close together that it was impossible to tell which came first. Mishkin claimed the thump of the wheels hitting the tarmac caused the gun to go off; co-pilot Vatutin maintained Mishkin had fired first. It was too confused for a final and definitive version ever to be established.

The bullet tore a gaping hole in the neck of Captain Rudenko and killed him instantly. There was blue smoke in the flight deck, Vatutin hauling back on the stick, yelling to his engineer for more power. The jet engines screamed a mite louder than the passengers as the Tupolev, heavy as a wet loaf, bounced twice more on the tarmac then lifted into the air, rolling, struggling for lift. Vatutin held her, nose high, wallowing, praying for more engine power, as the outer suburbs of East Berlin blurred past beneath them, followed by the Berlin Wall itself. When the Tupolev came over the perimeter of Tempelhof it cleared the nearest houses by six feet.

White-faced, the young co-pilot hammered the plane on to the main runway with Lazareff's gun in his back. Mishkin held the red-soaked body of Captain Rudenko from falling across the control column. The Tupolev finally came to rest three-quarters down the runway, still on all its wheels.

Staff-sergeant Leroy Coker was a patriotic man. He sat huddled against the cold at the wheel of his air police jeep, his fur-trimmed parka drawn tight round the edges of his face, and he thought longingly of the warmth of Alabama. But he was on guard duty and he took it seriously.

When the incoming airliner lurched over the houses beyond the perimeter fence, engines howling, under-carriage and flaps hanging, he let out a 'What the sheee-yit . . .' and sat bolt upright. He had never been to Russia, nor even across to the East, but he had read all about them over there. He did not know much about the Cold War, but he well knew that an attack by the Communists was always imminent unless men like Leroy Coker kept on their guard. He also knew a red star when he saw one, and a hammer and sickle.

When the airliner slithered to a stop he unslung his carbine, took a bead and blew the nosewheel tyres out.

Mishkin and Lazareff surrendered three hours later. The intent had been to keep the crew, release the passengers, take on board three notables from West Berlin and be flown to Tel Aviv. But a new nosewheel for a Tupolev was out of the question; the Russians would never supply one. And when the news of the killing of Rudenko was made known to the USAF base authorities, they refused to lay on a plane of their own. Marksmen ringed the Tupolev; there was no way two men could herd others, even at gunpoint, to an alternative aircraft. The sharpshooters would cut them down. After an hour's talk with the base commander, they walked out with their hands in the air.

That night they were formally handed over to the West Berlin authorities for imprisonment and trial.

The Soviet ambassador to Washington was coldly angry when he faced David Lawrence at the State Department on 2nd January.

The American secretary of state was receiving him at the Soviet request, though insistence would have been a better word.

The ambassador read his formal protest in a flat monotone. When he had finished he laid the text on the American's desk. Lawrence, who had known exactly what it would be, had an answer ready, prepared by his legal counsellors, three of whom stood flanking him behind his chair.

He conceded that West Berlin was indeed not sovereign territory, but a city under Four-Power occupation. Nevertheless the Western Allies had long conceded that in matters of jurisprudence the West Berlin authorities should handle all criminal and civil offences other than those falling within the ambit of the purely military laws of the Western Allies. The hijacking of the airliner, he continued, while a terrible offence, was not committed by US citizens against US citizens or within the US air base of Tempelhof. It was therefore an affair within civil jurisprudence. In consequence the United States government maintained it could not legally have held non-US nationals or non-US material witnesses within the territory of West Berlin, even though the airliner had come to rest on a USAF air base. He had no recourse, therefore, but to reject the Soviet protest.

The ambassador heard him out in stony silence. He rejoined that he could not accept the American explanation, and rejected it. He would report back to his government in that vein. On this note, he left to return to his embassy and report to Moscow.

In a small flat in Bayswater, London, three men sat that day and stared at the tangle of newspapers strewn on the floor around them.

'A disaster,' snapped Andrew Drake, 'a bloody disaster. By now they should have been in Israel. Within a month they'd have been released and could have given their press conference. What the hell did they have to shoot the captain for?'

'If he was landing at Schönefeld and refused to fly into West Berlin, they were finished anyway,' observed Azamat Krim.

'They could have clubbed him,' snorted Drake.

'Heat of the moment,' said Kaminsky. 'What do we do now?'

'Can those handguns be traced?' asked Drake of Krim.

The small Tatar shook his head. 'To the shop that sold them, perhaps,' he said. 'Not to me. I didn't have to identify myself.'

Drake paced the carpet, deep in thought.

'I don't think they'll be extradited back,' he said at length. 'The Soviets want them now for hijacking, shooting Rudenko, hitting the KGB man on board and of course the other one they took the identity card from. But the killing of the captain is the serious one. Still, I don't think a West German government will send two Jews back for execution. On the other hand, they'll be tried and convicted. Probably to life. Miroslav, will they open their mouths about Ivanenko?'

The Ukrainian refugee shook his head.

'Not if they've got any sense,' he said. 'Not in the heart of West Berlin. The Germans might have to change their minds and send them back after all. If they believed them, which they wouldn't because Moscow would deny Ivanenko is dead, and produce a look-alike as proof. But Moscow would believe them and have them liquidated. The Germans, not believing them, would offer no special protection. They wouldn't stand a chance. They'll keep silent.'

'That's no use to us,' pointed out Krim. 'The whole point of the exercise, of all we've gone through, was to deal a single massive humiliation to the whole Soviet state apparatus. *We* can't give that press conference; we don't have the tiny details that will convince the world. Only Mishkin and Lazareff can do that.'

'Then they have to be got out of there,' said Drake with finality. 'We have to mount a second operation to get them to Tel Aviv, with guarantees of their life and liberty. Otherwise it's all been for nothing.'

'What happens now?' repeated Kaminsky.

'We think,' said Drake. 'We work out a way, we plan it and we execute it. They are not going to sit and rot their lives away in Berlin, not with a secret like that in their heads. And we have little time; it won't take Moscow forever to put two and two together. They have their lead to follow now; they'll know who did the Kiev job pretty soon. Then they'll begin to plan the revenge. We have to beat them to it.'

The chilly anger of the Soviet ambassador to Washington paled into insignificance beside the outrage of his colleague in Bonn as the Russian diplomat faced the West German foreign minister two days later. The refusal of the Federal German government to hand the two criminals and murderers over to either the Soviet or East German authorities was a flagrant breach of their hitherto friendly relations and could only be construed as a hostile act, he insisted.

The West German foreign minister was deeply uncomfortable. Privately he wished the Tupolev had stayed on the runway in East Germany. He refrained from pointing out that as the Russians had always insisted West

Berlin was not a part of West Germany, they ought to be addressing themselves to the Senate in West Berlin.

The ambassador repeated his case for the third time: the criminals were Soviet citizens, the victims were Soviet citizens, the airliner was Soviet territory, the outrage had taken place in Soviet airspace and the murder either on or a few feet above the runway of East Germany's principal airport. The crime should therefore be tried under Soviet or at the very least under East German law.

The foreign minister pointed out as courteously as he could that all precedent indicated that hijackers could be tried under the law of the land in which they arrived, if that country wished to exercise the right. This was in no way an imputation against the fairness of the Soviet judicial procedure. . . .

Was it hell, he thought privately. No one in West Germany from the government to the press to the public had the slightest doubt that handing Mishkin and Lazareff back would mean KGB interrogation, kangaroo court and the firing squad. And they were Jewish, that was another problem.

The first few days of January are slack for the press, and the West German press was making a big story out of this. The conservative and powerful Axel Springer newspapers were insisting that whatever they had done, the two hijackers should receive a fair trial, and that could only be guaranteed in West Germany. The Bavarian CSU party, on which the governing coalition depended, was taking the same line. Certain quarters were giving the press a large amount of precise information and lurid details about the latest KGB crackdown in the Lvov area from which the hijackers came, suggesting that escape from the terror was a justifiable reaction, albeit a deplorable way of doing it. And lastly the recent exposure of yet another Communist agent high in the Civil Service would not increase the popularity of a government taking a conciliatory line towards Moscow. And with the provincial elections pending. . . .

The minister had his orders from the Chancellor. Mishkin and Lazareff, he told the ambassador, would go on trial in West Berlin as soon as possible and if, or rather when, convicted, would receive salutary sentences.

The Politburo meeting at the end of the week was stormy. Once again the tape recorders were off, the stenographers absent.

'This is an outrage,' snapped Vishnayev. 'Yet another scandal which diminishes the Soviet Union in the eyes of the world. It should never have happened.'

He implied that it had only happened due to the ever-weakening leadership of Maxim Rudin.

'It would not have happened,' retorted Petrov, 'if the comrade marshal's fighters had shot the plane down over Poland according to custom.'

'There was a communications breakdown between ground control and the fighter leader,' said Kerensky. 'A chance in a thousand.'

'Fortuitous, though,' observed Rykov coldly. Through his ambassadors he knew the Mishkin and Lazareff trial would be public and would reveal **exa**ctly how the hijackers had first mugged a KGB officer in a park for his identity papers, then masqueraded as him to penetrate to the flight deck.

'Is there any question,' asked Petryanov, a supporter of Vishnayev, 'that these two men could be the ones that killed Ivanenko?'

The atmosphere was electric.

'None at all,' said Petrov firmly. 'We know those two come from Lvov, not Kiev. They were Jews who had been refused permission to emigrate. We are investigating, of course, but so far there is no connection.'

'Should such a connection emerge, we will of course be informed?' asked Vishnayev.

'That goes without saying, comrade,' growled Rudin.

The stenographers were recalled and the meeting went on to discuss the progress at Castletown and the purchase of 10,000,000 tons of feed grain. Vishnayev did not press the issue. Rykov was at pains to show that the Soviet Union was gaining the quantities of wheat she would need to survive the winter and spring with minimal concessions of weapons levels, a point Marshal Kerensky disputed. But Komarov was forced to concede that the imminent arrival of 10,000,000 tons of animal winter feeds would enable him to release the same tonnage from hoarded stocks immediately, and prevent wholesale slaughter. The Maxim Rudin faction with its hair-breadth supremacy stayed intact.

As the meeting dispersed the old Soviet chief drew Vassili Petrov aside.

'*Is* there any connection between the two Jews and the Ivanenko killing?' he enquired.

'There may be,' conceded Petrov. 'We know they did the mugging in Ternopol, of course, so they were evidently prepared to travel outside Lvov to prepare their escape. We have their fingerprints from the aircraft, and they match those in their living quarters in Lvov. We have found no shoes that match the prints at the Kiev murder site, but we are still searching for those shoes. One last thing; we have an area of palm-print taken from the car that knocked down Ivanenko's mother. We are trying to get a complete palm-print of both from inside Berlin. If they check. . . .'

'Prepare a plan, a contingency plan, a feasibility study,' said Rudin, 'to have them liquidated inside their jail in West Berlin. Just in case. And another thing, if their identity is proved as the killers of Ivanenko, tell me, not the Politburo. We wipe them out first, then inform our comrades.'

Petrov swallowed hard. Cheating the Politburo was playing for the highest stakes in Soviet Russia. One slip, and there would be no safety net. He recalled what Rudin had told him by the fire out at Usovo a fortnight earlier. With the Politburo tied six against six, Ivanenko dead and two of their own six about to change sides, there were no aces left.

'Very well,' he said.

West German Chancellor Dietrich Busch received his justice minister in his private office in the chancellery building next to the old Palais Schaumbert just after the middle of the month. The government chief of West Germany was standing at his modern picture window gazing out at the frozen snow. Inside the new modern government headquarters overlooking Federal

Chancellor Square the temperature was warm enough for shirtsleeves, and nothing of the raw, bitter January of the riverside town penetrated.

'This Mishkin and Lazareff affair, how goes it?' asked Busch.

'It's strange,' admitted his justice minister, Ludwig Fischer. 'They are being more cooperative than one could hope for. They seem eager to achieve a quick trial with no delays.'

'Excellent,' said the Chancellor. 'That's exactly what we want. A quick affair. Let's get it over with. In what way are they cooperating?'

'They were offered a star lawyer from the right wing. Paid for by subscribed funds, possibly German contributions, possibly Jewish Defense League from America. They turned him down. He wanted to make a major spectacle out of the trial, plenty of detail about the KGB terror against Jews in the Ukraine.'

'A *right*-wing lawyer wanted that?'

'All grist to their mill. Bash the Russians, etc.,' said Fischer. 'Anyway, Mishkin and Lazareff want to go for an admission of guilt and plead mitigating circumstances. They insist on it. If they do so, and claim the gun went off by accident when the plane hit the runway at Schönefeld, they have a partial defence. Their new lawyer is asking for murder to be reduced to culpable homicide if they do.'

'I think we can grant them that,' said the Chancellor. 'What would they get?'

'With the hijacking thrown in, fifteen to twenty years. Of course, they could be paroled after a third. They're young, mid-twenties. They could be out by thirty.'

'That's in five years,' growled Busch. 'I'm concerned about the next five months. Memories fade. In five years they'll be in the archives.'

'Well, they admit everything, but they insist that the gun went off by accident. They claim they just wanted to reach Israel the only way they knew how. They'll plead guilty right down the line – to culpable homicide.'

'Let them have it,' said the Chancellor. 'The Russians won't like it, but it's as broad as long. They'd draw life for murder, but that's effectively twenty years nowadays.'

'There's one other thing. They want to be transferred after the trial to jail in West Germany.'

'Why?'

'They seem terrified of revenge by the KGB. They think they'll be safer in West Germany than in West Berlin.'

'Rubbish,' snorted Busch, 'they'll be tried and jailed in West Berlin. The Russians would not dream of trying to settle accounts inside a Berlin jail. They wouldn't dare. Still, we could do an internal transfer in a year or so. But not yet. Go ahead, Ludwig. Make it quick and clean, if they wish to cooperate. But get the press off my back before the elections, and the Russian ambassador as well.'

At Chita the morning sun glittered along the deck of the *Freya*, lying as she had for two and a half months by the commissioning quay. In those seventy-five days she had been transformed. Day and night she had lain docile while the tiny creatures who had made her swarmed into and out of every part of her. Hundreds of miles of lines had been laid the length and breadth of her, cables, pipes, tubes and flexes. Her labyrinthine electrical networks had been connected and tested, her incredibly complex system of pumps installed and tried.

The computer-linked instruments that would fill her holds and empty them, thrust her forward or shut her down, hold her to any point of the compass for weeks on end without a hand on her helm and observe the stars above her and the sea-bed below had been set in their places.

The food lockers and deep-freezes to sustain her crew for months were fully installed; so too the furniture, door knobs, light bulbs, lavatories, galley stoves, central heating, air conditioning, cinema, sauna, three bars, two dining rooms, beds, bunks, carpets and clothes hangers.

Her five-storey superstructure had been converted from an empty shell into a luxury hotel; her bridge, radio room and computer room from empty echoing galleries to a low-humming complex of data banks, calculators and control systems.

When the last of the workmen picked up their tools and left her alone, she was the ultimate in size, power, capacity, luxury and technical refinement that the technology of man could ever have set to float on water.

The rest of her crew of thirty had arrived by air fourteen days earlier to familiarize themselves with every inch of her. They were made up of her master, Captain Thor Larsen, a first officer, a second mate and a third mate; the chief engineer, first engineer, second engineer and electrical engineer, who ranked as a 'first'; her radio officer and chief steward also ranked as officers. Twenty others made up the full complement: first cook, four stewards, three firemen/engine room artificers, one repair man/engine room artificer; ten able seamen/deckhands and one pumpman.

Two weeks before she was due to sail, the tugs drew her away from the quay to the centre of Ise Bay. There her great twin propellers bit into the waters to bring her out to the western Pacific for sea trials. For officers and crew, as well as for the dozen Japanese technicians who went with her, it would mean a fortnight of gruelling hard work, testing every single system against every known or possible contingency.

There was a $170,000,000 worth of her moving out to the mouth of the bay that morning and the small ships standing off Nagoya watched her pass with awe.

Twenty kilometres outside Moscow lies the touristic village and estate of Archangelskoye, complete with museum and gastronomic restaurant, noted for its genuine bear steaks. In the last week of that freezing January Adam Munro had reserved a table there for himself and an escort from the secretarial pool at the British embassy.

He always varied his dinner dates so that no one girl should notice too much, and if the young hopeful of the evening wondered why he chose to drive the distance he did over icy roads in temperatures fifteen degrees below freezing, she made no comment on it.

The restaurant in any case was warm and snug, and when he excused himself to fetch extra cigarettes from his car she thought nothing of it. In the car park he shivered as the icy blast hit him, and hurried to where the twin headlights glowed briefly in the darkness.

He climbed into the car beside Valentina, put an arm round her, drew her close and kissed her.

'I hate the thought of you being in there with another woman, Adam,' she whispered as she nuzzled his throat beneath his chin.

'It's nothing,' he said, 'not important. An excuse for being able to drive out here to dine without being suspected. I have news for you.'

'About us?' she asked.

'About us. I have asked my own people if they would help you to come out, and they have agreed. There is a plan. Do you know the port of Constanza on the Romanian coast?'

She shook her head.

'I have heard of it, but never been there. I always holiday on the Soviet coast of the Black Sea.'

'Could you arrange to holiday there, with Sasha?'

'I suppose so,' she said. 'I can take my holidays virtually where I like. Romania is within the Socialist bloc. It should not raise eyebrows.'

'When does Sasha break up from school for the spring holidays?'

'The last few days of March, I think. Is that important?'

'It has to be in mid-April,' he told her. 'My people think you could be brought off the beach to a freighter offshore by speedboat. Can you make sure to arrange a spring holiday with Sasha at Constanza or the nearby Mamaia Beach in April?'

'I'll try,' she said. 'I'll try. April. Oh, Adam, it seems so close.'

'It is close, my love. Less than ninety days. Be patient a little longer as I have been, and we will make it. We'll start a whole new life.'

Five minutes later she had given him the transcription of the early January Politburo meeting and driven off into the night. He stuffed the sheaf of papers inside his waistband beneath his shirt and jacket and returned to the warmth of the Archangelskoye Restaurant.

This time, he vowed, as he made polite conversation with the secretary, there would be no mistakes, no drawing back, no letting her go, as there had been in 1961. This time it would be forever.

Edwin Campbell leaned back from the Georgian table in the Long Gallery at Castletown House and looked across at Professor Sokolov. The last point on the agenda had been covered, the last concession wrung. From the dining room below a courier had reported that the secondary conference had matched the concessions of the upper floor with trade bargains from the United States to the Soviet Union.

'I think that's it, Ivan my friend,' said Campbell. 'I don't think we can do any more at this stage.'

The Russian raised his eyes from the pages of Cyrillic handwriting in front of him, his own notes. For over a hundred days he had fought tooth and claw to secure for his country the grain tonnages that could save her from disaster and yet retain the maximum in weapons levels from inner space to Eastern

Europe. He knew he had had to make concessions that would have been unheard of four years earlier at Geneva, but he had done the best he could in the time-scale allowed.

'I think you are right, Edwin,' he replied. 'Let us have the arms reduction treaty prepared in draft form for our respective governments.'

'And the trade protocol,' said Campbell. 'I imagine they will want that also.'

Sokolov permitted himself a wry smile.

'I am sure they will want it very much,' he said.

For the next week the twin teams of interpreters and stenographers prepared both the treaty and the trade protocol. Occasionally the two principal negotiators were needed to clarify a point at issue, but for the most part the transcription and translation work was left to the aides. When the two bulky documents, each in duplicate, were finally ready, the two chief negotiators departed to their separate capitals to present them to their masters.

Andrew Drake threw down his magazine and leaned back.

'I wonder,' he said.

'What?' asked Krim as he entered the small sitting room with three mugs of coffee. Drake tossed the magazine to the Tatar.

'Read the first article,' he said. Krim read in silence while Drake sipped his coffee. Kaminsky eyed them both.

'You're crazy,' said Krim with finality.

'No,' said Drake. 'Without some audacity we'll be sitting here for the next ten years. It could work. Look, Mishkin and Lazareff come up for trial in a fortnight. The outcome is a foregone conclusion. We might as well start planning now. We know we're going to have to do it anyway, if they are ever to come out of that jail. So let's start planning. Azamat, you were in the paratroopers in Canada?'

'Sure,' said Krim. 'Five years.'

'Did you ever do an explosives course?'

'Yep. Demolition and sabotage. On secondment to the engineers for three months.'

'And years ago I used to have a passion for electronics and radio,' said Drake. 'Probably because my dad had a radio repair shop before he died. We could do it. We'd need help but we could do it.'

'How many more men?' asked Krim.

'We'd need one on the outside, just to recognize Mishkin and Lazareff on their release. That would have to be Miroslav here. For the job, us two plus five to stand guard.'

'Such a thing has never been done before,' observed the Tatar doubtfully.

'All the more reason why it will be unexpected, therefore unprepared for.'

'We'd get caught at the end of it,' said Krim.

'Not necessarily. I'd cover the pull-out if I had to. And anyway the trial would be the sensation of the decade. With Mishkin and Lazareff free in Israel, half the Western world would applaud. The whole issue of a free Ukraine would be blazoned across every newspaper and magazine outside the Soviet bloc.'

'Do you know five more who would come in on it?'

'For years I've been collecting names,' said Drake. 'Men who are sick and tired of talking. If they knew what we'd done already, yes, I can get five before the end of the month.'

'All right,' said Krim, 'if we're into this thing, let's do it. Where do you want me to go?'

'Belgium,' said Drake. 'I want a large apartment in Brussels. We'll bring the men there and make the apartment the group's base.'

On the other side of the world while Drake was talking, the sun rose over Chita and the IHI shipyard. The *Freya* lay alongside her commissioning quay, her engines throbbing.

The previous evening had seen a lengthy conference in the office of the IHI chairman, attended by both the yard's and the company's chief superintendents, the accountants, Harry Wennerstrom and Thor Larsen. The two technical experts had agreed that every one of the giant tanker's systems was in perfect working order. Wennerstrom had signed the final release document, conceding that the *Freya* was all he had paid for.

In fact he had paid for five per cent of her on the signature of the original contract to build her, five per cent at the keel-laying ceremony, five per cent when she rode water and five per cent at official handover. The remaining eighty per cent plus interest was payable over the succeeding eight years. But to all intents and purposes, she was his. The yard's company flag had been ceremoniously hauled down, and the silver-on-blue winged Viking helmet emblem of the Nordia Line now fluttered in the dawn breeze.

High on the bridge, towering over the vast spread of her deck, Harry Wennerstrom drew Thor Larsen by the arm into the radio room and closed the door behind him. The room was completely soundproof with the door closed.

'She's all yours, Thor,' he said. 'By the way, there's been a slight change of plan regarding your arrival in Europe. I'm not lightening her offshore. Not for her maiden voyage. Just this once, you're going to bring her into Europort at Rotterdam fully laden.'

Larsen stared at his employer in disbelief. He knew as well as either of them that fully loaded ULCCs never entered ports; they stood well offshore and lightened themselves by disgorging most of their cargo into other, smaller tankers in order to reduce their draught for the shallow seas. Or, they berthed at 'sea islands', networks of pipes on stilts, well out to sea, from which their oil could be pumped ashore. The idea of a girl in every port was a hollow joke for the crews of the supertankers; they often never berthed anywhere near a city from year's end to year's end, being flown off their ship for periodical leave. That was why the crew quarters had to be a real home from home.

'The English Channel will never take her,' said Larsen.

'You're not going up the Channel,' said Wennerstrom. 'You're going west of Ireland, west of the Hebrides, north of the Pentland Firth, between the Orkneys and the Shetlands, then south down the North Sea, following the twenty-fathom line, to moor at the deep-water anchorage. From there the pilots will bring you down the main channel towards the Maas Estuary. The tugs will bring you in from the Hook of Holland to Europort.'

'The Inner Channel from KI Buoy to the Maas won't take her fully laden,' protested Larsen.

'Yes, it will,' said Wennerstrom calmly. 'They have dredged this channel to a hundred and fifteen feet over the past four years. You'll be drawing ninety-eight feet. Thor, if I was asked to name any mariner in the world who could bring a million-tonner into Europort, it would be you. It'll be tight as all hell, but let me have this one last triumph. I want the world to see her, Thor. My *Freya*. I'll have them all there waiting for her. The Dutch government, the world's press. They'll be my guests, and they'll be dumbfounded. Otherwise no one will ever see her; she'll spend her whole life out of sight of land.'

'All right,' said Larsen slowly. 'Just this once. I'll be ten years older when it's over.'

Wennerstrom grinned like a small boy.

'Just wait till they see her,' he said. 'First of April. See you in Rotterdam, Thor Larsen.'

Ten minutes later he was gone. At noon, with the Japanese workers lining the quayside to cheer her on her way, the mighty *Freya* eased away from the shore and headed for the mouth of the bay. At 2 p.m. on 2nd February she came out again into the Pacific and swung her bow south towards the Philippines, Borneo and Sumatra at the start of her maiden voyage.

On 10th February the Politburo in Moscow met to consider, approve or reject the draft treaty and accompanying trade protocol negotiated at Castletown. Rudin and those who supported him knew that if they could carry the terms of the treaty at this meeting, then barring accidents thereafter it could be ratified and signed. Yefrem Vishnayev and his faction of hawks were no less aware. The meeting was lengthy and exceptionally hard-fought.

It is often assumed that world statesmen, even in private conclave, use moderate language and courteous address to their colleagues and advisers. This is not true of several recent US presidents, and is completely untrue of the Politburo in closed session. The Russian equivalent of four-letter words flew thick and fast. Only the fastidious Vishnayev kept his language restrained though his tone was acid, as he and his allies fought every concession line by line.

It was Foreign Minister Dmitri Rykov who carried the others in the moderate faction.

'What we have gained,' he said, 'is the assured sale to us, at last July's reasonable prices, of fifty-five million tons of grains. Without them we faced disaster on a national scale. On top we have nearly three billion dollars' worth of the most modern technology, in consumer industries, computers and oil production. With these we can master the problems that have beset us for two decades and conquer them within five years.

'Against this we have to offset certain minimal concessions in arms levels and states of preparedness, which, I stress, will in no way at all hinder or retard our capacity to dominate the Third World and its raw material resources inside the same five years. From the disaster that faced us last May, we have emerged triumphant thanks to the inspired leadership of Comrade Maxim Rudin. To reject this treaty now would bring us back to last May, but worse: the last of our 1982 harvest grains will run out in sixty days.'

When the meeting voted on the treaty terms, which was in fact a vote on the continuing leadership of Maxim Rudin, the six-to-six tie remained intact. The chairman's vote therefore prevailed.

'There's only one thing that can bring him down now,' said Vishnayev with quiet finality to Marshal Kerensky in the former's limousine as they drove home that evening. 'If something serious happens to sway one or two of his faction before the treaty is ratified. If not, the Central Committee will approve the treaty on the Politburo's recommendation and it will go through. If only it could be proved that those two damned Jews in Berlin killed Ivanenko. . . .'

Kerensky was less than his blustering self. Privately he was beginning to wonder if he had chosen the wrong side. Three months ago it had looked so certain that Rudin would be pushed too far, too fast, by the Americans and would lose his crucial support at the green baize table. But Kerensky was committed to Vishnayev now; there would be no massive Soviet manoeuvres in East Germany in two months, and he had to swallow that.

'One other thing,' said Vishnayev. 'If it had appeared six months ago, the power struggle would be over by now. I heard news from a contact out at the Kuntsevo clinic. Maxim Rudin is dying.'

'Dying?' repeated the defence minister. 'When?'

'Not soon enough,' said the theoretician. 'He'll live to carry the day over this treaty, my friend. Time is running out for us, and there is nothing we can do about it. Unless the Ivanenko affair can yet blow up in his face.'

As he was speaking the *Freya* was steaming through the Sunda Straits. To her port side lay Java Head and far to starboard the great mass of the volcano Krakatoa reared towards the night sky. On the darkened bridge a battery of dimly lit instruments told Thor Larsen, the senior officer of the watch and the junior officer all they needed to know. Three separate navigational systems correlated their findings into the computer, set in the small room aft of the bridge, and those findings were dead accurate. Constant compass readings, true to within half a second of a degree, cross-checked themselves with the stars above, unchanging and unchangeable. Man's artificial stars, the all-weather satellites, were also monitored and the resultant findings fed into the computer. Here the memory banks had absorbed tide, wind, under-currents, temperatures, and humidity levels. From the computer endless messages were flashed automatically to the gigantic rudder which, far below the stern transom, flickered with the sensitivity of a sardine's tail.

High above the bridge the two radar scanners whirled unceasingly, picking up coasts and mountains, ships and buoys, feeding them all into the computer, which processed this information too, ready to throw its hazard alarm device at the first hint of danger. Beneath the water, the echo-sounders relayed a three-dimensional map of the sea-bed far below, while from the bulbous bow section the forward sonar scanner looked three miles forward and down into the black waters. For the *Freya*, from full-ahead to crash-stop, would take thirty minutes and she would cover two to two and a half miles. She was that big.

Before dawn she had cleared the narrows of Sunda and her computers had turned her northwest along the hundred-fathom line to cut south of Ceylon for the Arabian Sea.

Two days later on the 12th eight men grouped themselves in the apartment Azamat Krim had rented in a suburb of Brussels. The five newcomers had been summoned by Drake who long ago had noted them all, met and spoken with them at great length, before deciding that they too shared his dream of striking a blow against Moscow. Two of the five were German-born Ukrainians, scions of the large Ukrainian community in the Federal Republic. One was an American, from New York, also of a Ukrainian father, and the other two were Ukrainian-British.

When they heard what Mishkin and Lazareff had done to the head of the KGB, there was a babble of excited comment. When Drake proposed that the operation could not be completed until the two partisans were free and safe, no one dissented. They talked through the night, and by dawn they had split into four teams of two.

Drake and Kaminsky would return to England and buy the necessary electronic equipment that Drake estimated he required. One of the Germans would partner one of the Englishmen and return to Germany to seek out the explosives they needed. The other German, who had contacts in Paris, would take the other Englishman to find and buy, or steal, the weaponry. Azamat Krim took his fellow North American to seek the motor launch. The American, who had worked in a leisure-boat yard in upper New York State, reckoned he knew what he wanted.

Eight days later in the tightly guarded courtroom attached to Moabit Prison in West Berlin, the trial of Mishkin and Lazareff started. Both men were silent and subdued in the dock as, within concentric walls of security from the barbed-wire entanglements atop the perimeter walls to the armed guards scattered all over the courtroom, they listened to the charges. The list took ten minutes to read. There was an audible gasp from the packed press benches when both men pleaded guilty to all charges. The state prosecutor rose to begin his narration of the events of New Year's Eve to the panel of judges. When he had finished, the judges adjourned to discuss the sentence.

The *Freya* moved slowly and sedately through the Strait of Hormuz and into the Arabian Gulf. The breeze had freshened with the sunrise into the chilly shamal wind coming into her nose from the northeast, sand-laden, causing the horizon to be hazy and vague. Her crew all knew this landscape well enough, having passed many times on their way to collect crude oil from the Gulf. They were all experienced tankermen.

To one side of the *Freya* the barren, arid Quoin Islands slid by barely two cables away; to the other the officers on the bridge could make out the bleak moonscape of the Musandam Pensinula, with its sheer rocky mountains. The *Freya* was riding high, and the depth in the channel presented no problems. On return, laden with crude oil, it would be different. She would be almost shut down, moving slowly, eyes riveted on her depth sounder, watching the map of the sea-bed pass barely a few feet beneath her keel ninety-eight feet below the waterline.

She was still in ballast, as she had been all the way from Chita. She had sixty giant tanks, or holds, three abreast in lines of twenty fore-to-aft. One of these was the slop tank, to be used for nothing else but gathering the slops from her fifty crude-carrying cargo tanks. Nine were permanent ballast tanks, to be used for nothing but pure sea water to give her stability when she was empty of cargo.

But her remaining fifty crude oil tanks were sufficient. Each held 20,000 tons of crude oil. It was with complete confidence in the impossibility of her causing accidental oil pollution that she steamed on to Abu Dhabi to load her first cargo.

There is a modest bar in the rue Miollin in Paris where the small fry of the world of mercenaries and arms sellers are wont to foregather and take a drink together. It was here the German-Ukrainian and his English colleague were brought by the German's French contact man.

There were several hours of low-voiced negotiation between the French-man and another French friend of his. Eventually the contact man came across to the two Ukrainians.

'My friend says it is possible,' he told the Ukrainian from Germany. 'Five hundred dollars each, American dollars, cash. One magazine per unit included.'

'We'll take it, if he'll throw in one handgun with full magazine,' said the man from Germany.

Three hours later in the garage of a private house near Neuilly, six submachine carbines and one MAB automatic nine-millimetre handgun were wrapped in blankets and stowed in the boot of the Ukrainians' car. The money changed hands. In twelve hours, just before midnight of 24th February, the two men arrived at their apartment in Brussels and stored their equipment in the base of the wardrobe.

As the sun rose on 25th February the *Freya* eased her way back through the Strait of Hormuz, and on the bridge there was a sigh of relief as the officers gazing at the depth-sounder saw the sea-bed drop away from in front of their eyes to the deep of the ocean. On the digital display the figures ran rapidly from twenty to one hundred fathoms. The *Freya* moved steadily back to her full-load service speed of fifteen knots as she went southeast back down the Gulf of Oman.

She was heavy-laden now, doing what she had been designed and built for – carrying 1,000,000 tons of crude oil to the thirsty refineries of Europe and the millions of family saloons that would drink it. Her draught was now at her designed ninety-eight feet, and her hazard alarm devices had ingested the knowledge and knew what to do if the sea-bed ever approached too close.

Her nine ballast tanks were now empty, acting as buoyancy tanks. Far away in the fore part the first row of three tanks contained a full crude tank port and starboard, with the single slop tank in the centre. One row back were the first three empty ballast tanks. The second row of three was amidships, and the third row of three was at the foot of the superstructure, on the fifth floor of which Captain Thor Larsen handed the *Freya* to the senior officer of the watch and went down to his handsome day cabin for breakfast and a short sleep.

On the Morning of 26th February, after an adjournment of several days, the presiding judge in the Moabit courtroom in West Berlin began to read the judgement of himself and his two colleagues. It took several hours.

In their walled dock, Mishkin and Lazareff listened impassively. From time to time each sipped water from the glasses placed on the tables in front of them. From the packed booths reserved for the international press they were under scrutiny, as were the figures of the judges while the findings were read. But one magazine journalist representing a leftist German monthly magazine seemed more interested in the glasses they drank from than the prisoners themselves.

The court adjourned for lunch, and when it resumed the journalist was missing from his seat. He was phoning from one of the kiosks outside the hearing. Shortly after three the judge reached his conclusion. Both men were required to rise, to hear themselves sentenced to fifteen years' detention.

They were led away to begin their sentences at Tegel Jail in the northern part of the city, and within minutes the court house had emptied. The cleaners took over, removing the brimming waste-paper baskets, carafes and glasses. One of the middle-aged ladies occupied herself with cleaning the interior of the dock. Unobserved by her colleagues she quietly picked up the prisoners' two drinking glasses, wrapped each in dusters and placed them in her shopping bag beneath the empty wrappers of her sandwiches. No one noticed and no one cared.

On the last day of the month Vassili Petrov sought and received a private audience with Maxim Rudin in the latter's Kremlin suite.

'Mishkin and Lazareff,' he said without preamble.

'What about them? They got fifteen years. It should have been the firing squad.'

'One of our people in West Berlin abstracted the glasses they used for water during the trial. The palm-print on one matches that from the car used in the hit-and-run affair in Kiev in October.'

'So it was them,' said Rudin grimly. 'Damn them to hell. Vassili, wipe them out. Liquidate them, as fast as you can. Give it to "wet affairs".'

The KGB, vast and complex in its scope and organization, consists basically of four Chief Directorates, seven Independent Directorates and six Independent Departments.

But the four Chief Directorates comprise the bulk of the KGB. One of these, the First, concerns itself exclusively with clandestine activities outside the USSR.

Deep within the heart of it is a section known simply as Department V (as in Victor) or the Executive Action Department. This is the one the KGB would most like to keep hidden from the rest of the world, inside and outside the USSR. For its tasks include sabotage, extortion, kidnapping and assassination. Within the jargon of the KGB itself it usually has yet another name – the department of *mokrie dyela*, or 'wet affairs', so-called because its operations not infrequently involve someone getting wet with blood. It was to this Department V of the First Chief Directorate of the KGB that Maxim Rudin ordered Petrov to hand the elimination of Mishkin and Lazareff.

'I have already done as much,' said Petrov. 'I thought of giving the affair to Colonel Kukushkin, Ivanenko's head of security. He has a personal reason to wish to succeed – saving his own skin apart from avenging Ivanenko and his own humiliation. He already served his time in "wet affairs" ten years ago. Inevitably he is already aware of the secret of what happened in Rosa Luxemburg Street – he was there. And he speaks German. He would report back only to General Abrassov or to me.'

Rudin nodded grimly.

'All right, let him have the job. He can pick his own team. Abrassov will give him everything he needs. The apparent reason will be to avenge the death of Flight Captain Rudenko. And, Vassili, he had better succeed first time. If he tries and fails, Mishkin and Lazareff could open their mouths. After a failed attempt to kill them, someone might believe them. Certainly Vishnayev would, and you know what that would mean.'

'I know,' said Petrov quietly. 'He will not fail. He'll do it himself.'

'It's the best we'll get, Mr President,' said Secretary of State David Law-rence. 'Personally I believe Edwin Campbell has done us well at Castletown.'

Grouped before the President's desk in the Oval Office were the secretaries of state, defense and treasury, with Stanislaw Poklewski and Robert Benson of the CIA. Beyond the french windows the rose garden was whipped by a bitter wind. The snows had gone but 1st March was bleak and uninviting.

President William Matthews laid his hand on the bulky folder in front of him, the draft agreement wrung out of the Castletown talks.

'A deal of it is too technical for me,' he confessed, 'but the digest from the Defense Department impresses me. The way I see it is this: if we reject this now, after the Soviet Politburo has accepted it, there'll be no renegotiation anyway. The matter of grain deliveries will become academic to Russia in three months in any case. By then they'll be starving and Rudin will be gone. Yefrem Vishnayev will get his war. Right?'

'That seems to be the unavoidable conclusion,' said David Lawrence.

'How about the other side of it, the concessions we have made?' asked the President.

'The secret trade protocol in the separate document,' said the secretary of the treasury, 'requires us to deliver fifty-five million tons of mixed grains at production costs and nearly three billion dollars worth of oil, computer and consumer industry technology rather heavily subsidized. The total cost to the United States runs to almost three billion dollars. On the other hand, the sweeping arms reductions should enable us to claw back that much and more by reduced defence expenditure.'

'If the Soviets abide by their undertakings,' said the secretary of defense hastily.

'But if they do, and we have to believe they will,' countered Lawrence, 'by your own experts' calculations they could not launch a successful conven-tional or tactical nuclear war across the face of Europe for at least five years.'

President Matthews knew that the presidential election of the coming November would not see his candidacy. But if he could step down leaving behind him peace for even half a decade with the burdensome arms race of the seventies halted in its tracks, he would take his place among the the great US presidents. He wanted that more than anything else this spring of 1983.

'Gentlemen,' he said, 'we have to approve this treaty as it stands. David, inform Moscow we join them in agreeing the terms and propose that our negotiators reconvene at Castletown to draw up the formal treaty ready for signing. While this is going on we will permit the loading of the grain ships, ready to sail on the day of signature. That is all.'

On 3rd March Azamat Krim and his Ukrainian-American collaborator clinched the deal that acquired them a sturdy and powerful launch. She was the kind of craft much favoured by enthusiastic sea-anglers on both the British and European coasts of the North Sea, steel-hulled, forty feet long, tough and second-hand. She had Belgian registration and they had found her near Ostend.

Up front, she had a cabin whose roof extended the forward third of her length. A companionway led down to a cramped four-berth resting area, with a tiny toilet and a camping-gas cooker. Aft of the rear bulkhead she was open to the elements, and beneath the deck lay a powerful engine capable of taking her through the wild North Sea to the fishing grounds and back.

Krim and his companion brought her from Ostend to Blankenberge further up the Belgian coast, and when she was moored in the leisure-boat harbour she attracted no attention. Spring always bring its crop of hardy sea-anglers to the coasts with their boats and tackle. The American chose to live on board and work on the engine. Krim returned to Brussels to find that Andrew Drake had taken over the kitchen table as a workbench and was deeply engrossed in preparations of his own.

For the third time on her maiden voyage the *Freya* had crossed the equator and 7th March found her entering the Mozambique Channel heading south by southwest towards the Cape of Good Hope. She was still following her 100-fathom line, leaving 600 feet of clear ocean beneath her keel, a course which took her to seaward of the main shipping lanes. She had not seen land since coming out of the Gulf of Oman, but on the afternoon of the 7th she passed through the Comoro Islands at the north of the Mozambique Channel. To starboard her crew, taking advantage of the moderate winds and seas to stroll the quarter mile of forward deck or lounge beside the screened swimming pool up on 'C' deck, saw Grande Comore Island, the peak of its densely wooded mountain hidden in clouds, the smoke from the burning under-growth on her flanks drifting across the green water. By nightfall the skies had overcast with grey cloud, the wind turned squally. Ahead lay the heaving seas of the Cape and the final northward run to Europe and her welcome.

The following day Moscow replied formally to the proposal of the United States President, welcoming his agreement to the terms of the draft treaty and agreeing that the chief negotiators of Castletown should reconvene jointly to draft the formal treaty while remaining in constant contact with their respective governments.

The bulk of the Soviet merchant marine fleet Sovfracht, along with the numerous other vessels already chartered by the Soviet Union, had already sailed at American invitation for the eastern seaboard of North America to load their grain. In Moscow the first reports were coming in of excessive quantities of meat appearing in the peasant markets, indicating livestock slaughter was taking place even on the state and collective farms where it was forbidden. The last reserves of feedstuffs for animals and humans alike were running out.

In a private message to President Matthews, Maxim Rudin regretted that for health reasons he would not personally be able to sign the treaty on behalf of the Soviet Union unless the ceremony was in Moscow; he therefore proposed a formal signature by foreign ministers in Dublin on 10th April.

The winds of the Cape were hellish; the South African summer was over and the autumn gales thundered up from the Antarctic to batter Table Mountain. The *Freya* by 12th March was in the heart of the Agulhas Current, pushing westwards through mountainous green seas, taking the gales from the south-west on her port beam.

It was bitter cold out on deck, but no one was there. Behind the double-glazing of the bridge Captain Thor Larsen and his two officers of the watch stood with the helmsman, radio officer and two others in shirtsleeves. Warm, safe, protected by the enshrouding aura of her invincible technology, they gazed forward to where forty-foot waves impelled by the force ten out of the southwest reared above the *Freya*'s port side, hovered for a moment, then crashed down to obscure her gigantic deck and its myriad pipes and valves in a swirling maelstrom of white foam. While the waves burst, only the fo'c's'le, far ahead, was discernible, like a separate entity. As the foam receded defeated through the scuppers, the *Freya* shook herself and buried her bulk in another oncoming mountain. A hundred feet beneath the men, 90,000 shaft horsepower pushed 1,000,000 tons of crude oil another few yards towards Rotterdam. High above, the Cape albatrosses wheeled and glided, their lost cries unheard behind the Plexiglas. Coffee was served by one of the stewards.

Two days later, on Monday the 14th, Adam Munro drove out of the courtyard of the Commercial Section of the British embassy and turned sharp right into Kutuzovsky Prospekt towards the city centre. His destination was the main embassy building where he had been summoned by the head of chancery. The telephone call, certainly tapped by the KGB, had referred to the clarification of minor details for the forthcoming trade delegation visit from London. In fact it meant that there was a message awaiting him in the cipher room.

The cipher room in the embassy building on Maurice Thorez Embankment is in the basement, a secure room regularly checked by the 'sweepers' who are looking not for dust but listening devices. The cipher clerks are diplomatic personnel and security-checked to the highest level. Nevertheless, sometimes messages come in which bear a coding to indicate they will not and cannot be decoded by the normal decoding machines. The tag on these messages will indicate they have to be passed to one particular cipher clerk, a man who has the right to know because he has a need to know. Occasionally a message for Adam Munro bore such a coding, as today. The clerk in question knew Munro's real job, because he needed to: if for nothing else, to protect him from those who did not.

Munro entered the cipher room and the clerk spotted him. They withdrew to a small annexe where the clerk, a precise, methodical man with bifocal glasses, used a key from his waistband to unlock a separate decoding machine. He passed the London message into it and the machine spat out the translation. The clerk took no notice, averting his gaze as Munro moved away.

Munro read the message and smiled. He memorized it within seconds and passed it straight into a shredder which reduced the thin paper to fragments hardly bigger than dust. He thanked the clerk and left, with a song in his heart. Barry Ferndale had informed him that with the Russian-American treaty on the threshold of signature, the Nightingale could be brought out to a discreet but extremely generous welcome, from the coast of Romania near Constanza, in the week of 16th to 23rd April. There were further details for the exact pick-up. He was asked to consult with the Nightingale and confirm acceptance and agreement.

After receiving Maxim Rudin's personal message, President Matthews had remarked to David Lawrence: 'Since this is more than a mere arms limitation agreement, I suppose we must call it a treaty. And since it seems destined to be signed in Dublin, no doubt history will call it the Treaty of Dublin.'

Lawrence had consulted with the government of the Republic of Ireland, who agreed with barely hidden delight that they would be pleased to host the formal signing ceremony between David Lawrence for the United States and Dmitri Rykov for the USSR in Saint Patrick's Hall, Dublin Castle, on 10th April.

On 16th March therefore President Matthews replied to Maxim Rudin agreeing to his place and date.

There are two fairly large rock quarries in the mountains outside Ingolstadt in Bavaria. During the night of 18th March the nightwatchman in one of these was attacked and tied up by four masked men, at least one of them armed with a handgun, he later told police. The men, who seemed to know what they were looking for, broke into the dynamite store using the night-watchman's key, and stole 250 kilograms of TNT rock-blasting explosives and a number of electric detonators. Long before morning they were gone and as the following day was Saturday the 19th, it was almost noon before the trussed nightwatchman was rescued and the theft discovered. Subsequent police investigations were intensive and, in view of the apparent knowledge of the layout of the quarry by the robbers, concentrated on the area of former employees. But the search was for extreme left-wingers, and the name of Klimchuk, employed three years earlier at the quarry, attracted no particular attention, being assumed to be of Polish extraction. Actually it is a Ukrainian name. By that Saturday evening the two cars bearing the explosives had arrived back in Brussels, penetrating the German/Belgian border on the

Aachen/Liège motorway. They were not stopped, weekend traffic being expecially heavy.

By the evening of the 20th the *Freya* was well past Senegal, having made good time from the Cape with the aid of the southeast trade winds and a helpful current. Though it was early in the year for Northern Europe, there were holidaymakers on the beaches of the Canary Islands.

The *Freya* was far to the west of the islands but just after dawn on the 21st her bridge officers could make out the volcanic peak of Monte Teide on Tenerife, their first landfall since they had glimpsed the rugged coastline of Cape Province. As the mountains of the Canaries dropped away, they knew that apart from the chance of seeing Madeira's summit they would next see the lights warning them to stay clear of the wild coasts of Mayo and Donegal.

Adam Munro had waited impatiently for a week to see the woman he loved, but there was no way he could get through to her before their pre-arranged meet on Monday the 21st. For the site he had returned to the Exhibition of Economic Achievements, whose 238 hectares of parks and grounds merged with the main Botanical Gardens of the USSR Academy of Sciences. Here, in a sheltered arboretum in the open air, he found her waiting just before noon. Because of the chance of a casual glance from a passerby he could not take the risk of kissing her as he wanted to. Instead he told her with controlled excitement of the news from London. She was overjoyed.

'I have news for you,' she told him. 'There will be a Central Committee fraternal delegation to the Romanian Party Congress during the first half of April, and I have been asked to accompany it. Sasha breaks up from school on the 29th, and we will leave for Bucharest on the 5th. After ten days it will be perfectly normal for me to take a bored little boy to the resort beaches for a week.'

'Then I'll fix it for the night of Monday the 18th of April. That will give you several days in Constanza to find your way around. You must hire or borrow a car, and acquire a powerful torch. Now, Valentina my love, these are the details. Memorize them, for there can be no mistakes:

'North of Constanza lies the resort of Mamaia, where the Western package tourists go. Drive north from Constanza through Mamaia on the evening of the 18th. Exactly six miles north of Mamaia a track leads right from the coast highway to the beach. On the headland at the junction you will see a short stone tower with its lower half painted white. It is a coast-marker for fisherman. Leave the car well off the road and descend the bluff to the beach. At 2 a.m. you will see a light from the sea: three long dashes and three short ones. Take your own torch with its beam cut down by a tube of cardboard and point it straight at where the light came from. Flash back the reverse signal, three shorts and three longs. The speedboat will come out of the sea for you and Sasha.

'There will be one Russian-speaker and two marines. Identify yourself with the phrase "the Nightingale sings in Berkeley Square". Have you got that?'

'Yes Adam, where is Berkeley Square?'

'In London. It is very beautiful, like you. It has many trees.'

'And do nightingales sing there?'

'According to the words of the song, one used to. Darling, it seems so short. Four weeks today. When we get to London I'll show you Berkeley Square.'

'Adam, tell me something. Have I betrayed my own people, the Russian people?'

'No,' he said with finality, 'you have not. The leaders nearly did. If you had not done what you did, Vishnayev and your uncle might have got their war. In it, Russia would have been destroyed, most of America, my country and Western Europe. You have not betrayed the people of your country.'

'But they would never understand, never forgive me,' she said. There was a hint of tears in her dark eyes. 'They will call me a traitor. I shall be an exile.'

'One day, perhaps, this madness will end. One day perhaps you could come back. Listen, my love, we cannot stay longer. It's too risky. There is one last thing. I need your private phone number. No, I know we agreed that I would never ring. But I will not see you again until you are in the West in safety. If there should by any remote chance be a change of plan, or date, I may have to contact you as a matter of emergency. If I do, I will pretend to be a friend called Gregor, explaining that I cannot attend your dinner party. If that happens, leave at once and meet me in the car park of the Mojarsky Hotel at the top of Kutuzovsky Prospekt.'

She nodded meekly and gave him her number. He kissed her on the cheek.

'I'll see you in London, my darling,' he told her, and was gone through the trees. Privately he knew he would have to resign and take the icy anger of Sir Nigel Irvine when it became plain the Nightingale was not Anatoly Krivoi but a woman, and his wife to be. But by then it would be too late for even the service to do anything about it.

Ludwig Jahn stared at the two men who occupied the available chairs of his tidy bachelor flat in the Wedding working-class district of West Berlin with growing fear. They bore the stamp of men he had seen once, long before, and whom he hoped never to see again.

The one who was talking was undoubtedly German, he had no doubt about that. What he did not know was that the man's name was Major Schulz, of the East German secret police, the dreaded Staatssicherheitsdienst, known simply as SSD. He would never know the name, but he could guess the occupation.

He could also guess that the SSD had copious files on every East German who had ever quit to come to the West, and that was his problem. Thirty years earlier, as an eighteen-year-old, Jahn had taken part in the building workers' riots in East Berlin that had become the East German uprising. He had been lucky. Although he had been picked up in one of the sweeps by the Russian police and their East German Communist acolytes, he had not been held. But he recalled the smell of the detention cells, and the stamp of the men who ruled them. His visitors this 22nd March three decades later bore the same stamp.

He had kept his head low for eight years after the 1953 riots, then in 1961 before the Wall was completed he quietly walked into the West. For the past fifteen years he had had a good job with the West Berlin Civil Service, starting as a warder in the prison service and rising to Oberwachmeister chief officer of Two Block, Tegel Jail.

The other man in his room that evening kept silent. Jahn would never know that he was a Soviet colonel called Kukushkin, present on behalf of the 'wet affairs' department of the KGB.

Jahn stared in horror at the photographs the German eased from a large envelope and placed before him, slowly, one by one. They showed his widowed mother, in a cell, terrified, aged nearly eighty, staring at the camera obediently, hopeful of release. There were his two younger brothers, handcuffs on wrists, in different cells, the masonry of the walls showing up clearly in the high-definition prints.

'Then there are your sisters-in-law and your three delightful little nieces. Oh yes, we know about the Christmas presents. What is it they call you? Uncle Ludo? How very charming. Tell me, have you ever seen places like these?'

There were more photographs, pictures that made the comfortably plump Jahn close his eyes for several seconds. Strange, zombie-like figures moved through the pictures, clad in rags, shaven, skull-like faces peering dully at the camera. They huddled, they shuffled, they wrapped their withered feet in rags to keep out the Arctic cold. They were stubbled, shrivelled, sub-human. They were some of the inhabitants of the slave labour camps of the Kolyma complex, far away in the eastern end of Siberia north of the Kamchatka Peninsula, where the gold is mined deep in the Arctic Circle.

'Life sentences in these . . . resorts . . . are only for the worst enemies of the state, Herr Jahn. But my colleague here can ensure such life sentences for all your family; yes, even your dear old mother, with just one single telephone call. Now tell me, do you want him to make that call?'

Jahn gazed across into the eyes of the man who had not spoken. The eyes were as bleak as the Kolyma camps.

'*Nein*,' he whispered, 'no, please. What do you want?'

It was the German who answered.

'In Tegel Jail are two hijackers, Mishkin and Lazareff. Do you know them?'

Jahn nodded dumbly.

'Yes. They arrived four weeks ago. There was much publicity.'

'Where exactly are they?'

'Number Two block. Top floor, east wing. Solitary confinement, at their own request. They fear the other prisoners. Or so they say. There is no reason. For child rapists there is a reason, but not these two. Yet they insist.'

'But you can visit them, Herr Jahn? You have access?' Jahn remained silent. He began to fear what the visitors wanted with the hijackers. They came from the East; the hijackers had escaped from there. It could not be to bring them birthday gifts.

'Have another look at the pictures, Jahn. Have a good look, before you think of obstructing us.'

'Yes, I can visit them on my rounds. But only at night. During the day-shift there are three warders in that corridor. One or two would always accompany me if I wished to visit them. But in the day-shift there would be no reason for me to visit them. Only to check on them during the night-shift.'

'Are you on the night-shift at the moment?'

'No. Day-shift.'

'What are the hours of the night-shift?'

'Midnight to eight a.m. Lights are out at ten p.m. Shift changes at midnight. Relief is at eight a.m. During the night-shift I would patrol the block three times, accompanied by the duty officer of each floor.'

The unnamed German thought for a while.

'My friend here wishes to visit them. When do you return to night-shift?'

'Monday, 4th April,' said Jahn.

'Very well,' said the East German. 'This is what you will do.'

Jahn was instructed to acquire from the locker of a vacationing colleague the necessary uniform and pass-card. At 2 a.m. on the morning of Monday, 4th April, he would descend to the ground floor and admit the Russian by the staff entrance from the street. He would accompany him to the top floor and hide him in the staff day room, to which he would acquire a duplicate key. He would cause the night duty officer on the top floor to absent himself on an errand and take over the watch from him while he was away. During the man's absence he would allow the Russian into the solitary-confinement corridor, lending him his pass-key to both cells. When the Russian had 'visited' Mishkin and Lazareff, the process would be reversed. The Russian would hide again until the duty officer returned to his post. Then Jahn would escort the Russian back to the staff entrance and let him out.

'It won't work,' whispered Jahn, well aware that it probably would.

'It had better,' he said. 'If it does not, I will personally ensure that your entire family begins a regime in Kolyma that will make the "extra-strict" regime operating there seem like the honeymoon suite at the Kempinski Hotel.'

Jahn felt as if his bowels were being sprayed with liquid ice. None of the hard men in special wing would compare with this man. He swallowed.

'I'll do it,' he whispered.

'My friend will return here at six in the evening of Sunday, 3rd April,' said the East German. 'No reception committees from the police, if you please. It will do no good. We both have diplomatic passes in false names. We will deny everything and walk away quite freely. Just have the uniform and pass-card awaiting him.'

Two minutes later they were gone. They took their photos with them There was no evidence left. It did not matter. Jahn could see every detail in his nightmares.

By 23rd March over 250 ships, the first wave of the waiting merchant fleet, were docked in thirty ports from the St Lawrence Seaway in Canada down the eastern seaboard of North America to Carolina. There was still ice in the St Lawrence, but it was broken to mosaic by the ice-breakers, aware of its defeat as the grain ships moved through it to berth by the silos.

A fair proportion of these ships were of the Russian Sovfracht fleet, but the next largest numbers were flying the US flag, for one of the conditions of the sale had been that American carriers take the prime contracts to move the grain.

Within ten days they would begin moving east across the Atlantic, bound for Archangel and Murmansk in the Soviet Arctic, Leningrad at the end of the Baltic, and the warm-water ports of Odessa, Simferopol and Novorossisk in the Black Sea. Flags of ten other nations mingled with them to effect the biggest single dry-cargo movement since the Second World War. From a hundred silos from Winnipeg to Charleston the pumps spewed a golden tide of wheat, barley, oats, rye and maize into their bellies, all destined within a month for the hungry millions of Russia.

On the 26th Andrew Drake rose from his work at the kitchen table of an apartment in the suburbs of Brussels and pronounced that he was ready.

The explosives had been packed into ten fibre suitcases, the submachine guns rolled in towels and stuffed into haversacks. Azamat Krim kept the detonators bedded into cotton wool in a cigar box which never left him. When darkness fell the cargo was carried in relays down to the group's second-hand, Belgian-registered panel-van and they set off for Blankenburge.

The little seaside resort facing the North Sea was quiet, the harbour virtually deserted, when they transferred their equipment under cover of darkness to the bilges of the fishing launch. It was a Saturday, and though a man walking his dog along the quay noticed them at work, he thought no more of it. Parties of sea-anglers stocking up for a weekend's fishing were common enough, even though it was a mite early in the year and still chilly.

On Sunday the 27th Miroslav Kaminsky bade them goodbye, took the van and drove back to Brussels. His job was to clean the Brussels flat from top to bottom and end to end, to abandon it and drive the van to a pre-arranged rendezvous in the polders of Holland. There he would leave it, with its ignition key in an agreed place, then take the ferry from the Hook back to Harwich and London. He had his itinerary well rehearsed and was confident he could carry out his part of the plan.

The remaining seven men left port and cruised sedately up the coast to lose themselves in the islands of Walcheren and North Beveland, just across the border into Holland. There, with their fishing rods much in evidence, they hove-to and waited. On a powerful radio down in the cabin, Andrew Drake sat hunched, listening to the wavelength of Maas Estuary Control and the endless calls of the ships heading into or out of Europort and Rotterdam.

'Colonel Kukushkin is going into Tegel Jail to do the job on the night of 3rd to 4th April,' Vassili Petrov told Maxim Rudin in the Kremlin that same Sunday morning. 'There is a senior warder who will let him in, bring him to the cells of Mishkin and Lazareff, and let him out of the jail by the staff doorway when it is over.'

'The warder is reliable, one of our people?' asked Rudin.

'No, but he has family in East Germany. He has been persuaded to do as he is told. Kukushkin reports that he will not contact the police. He is too frightened.'

'Then he knows already who he is working for. Which means he knows too much.'

'Kukushkin will silence him also, just as he steps out of the doorway. There will be no trace,' said Petrov.

'Eight days,' grunted Rudin. 'He had better get it right.'

'He will,' said Petrov, 'he too has family. By a week tomorrow Mishkin and Lazareff will be dead and their secret with them. Those who helped them will keep silent to save their own lives. Even if they talk, it will be disbelieved. Mere hysterical allegations. No one will believe them.'

When the sun rose on the morning of the 29th its first rays picked up the mass of the *Freya* twenty miles west of Ireland, cutting north by northeast through the eleven degree longitude on a course to skirt the Outer Hebrides.

Her powerful radar scanners had picked up the fishing fleet in the darkness an hour before and her officer of the watch noted them carefully. The nearest to her was well to the east or landward side of the tanker.

The sun glittered over the rocks of Donegal, a thin line on the eastward horizon to the men on the bridge with their advantage of eighty feet of altitude. It caught the small fishing smacks of the men from Killybegs, drifting out in the western seas for mackerel, herring and whiting. And it caught the bulk of *Freya* herself, like a moving landmass, steaming out of the south past the drifters and their gently bobbing nets.

Christy O'Byrne was in the tiny wheelhouse of the smack he and his brother owned, the *Bernadette*. He blinked several times, put down his cocoa mug and stepped the three feet from the wheelhouse to the rail. His vessel was the nearest to the passing tanker.

From behind him, when they saw the *Freya*, the fishermen tugged on the horn lanyards and a chorus of thin whoops disturbed the dawn. On the bridge of the *Freya* Thor Larsen nodded to his junior officer; seconds later the bellowing bull roar of the *Freya* answered the Killybegs fleet.

Christy O'Byrne leaned on the rail and watched the *Freya* fill the horizon, heard the throb of her power beneath the sea and felt the *Bernadette* begin to roll in the widening wake of the tanker.

'Holy Mary,' he whispered, 'would you look at the size of her.'

On the eastern shore of Ireland compatriots of Christy O'Byrne were at work that morning in Dublin Castle, for 700 years the seat of power of the British. As a tiny boy perched on his father's shoulder Martin Donahue had watched from outside as the last British troops marched out of the castle forever, following the signing of a peace treaty. Sixty-three years later on the verge of retirement from government service, he was a cleaner, pushing a Hoover back and forth over the electric blue carpet of Saint Patrick's Hall.

He had not been present when any of Ireland's successive presidents had been inaugurated beneath Vincent Waldré's magnificent 1778 painted ceiling, nor would he be present in twelve days when two super-powers signed the Treaty of Dublin below the motionless heraldic banners of the long-gone Knights of Saint Patrick. For forty years he had just kept the Hall dusted for them.

★

Rotterdam too was preparing, but for a different ceremony. Harry Wenner-strom arrived on the 30th and installed himself in the best suite at the Hotel Hilton.

He had come by his private executive jet now parked at Schiedam Airport just outside the city. Throughout the day four secretaries fussed around him, preparing for the Scandinavian and Dutch dignitaries, the tycoons from the worlds of oil and shipping, and the scores of press people who would attend his reception on the evening of 1st April for Captain Thor Larsen and his officers.

A select party of notables and press would be his guests on the flat roof of the modern Maas Control building, situated on the very tip of the sandy shore at the Hook of Holland. Well protected against the stiff spring breeze, they would watch from the north shore of the Maas Estuary as the six tugs pulled and pushed the *Freya* those last few miles from the estuary into the Caland Kanal, from there to the Beer Kanal and finally to rest by Clint Blake's new oil refinery in the heart of Europort.

While the *Freya* closed down her systems during the afternoon, the group would come back by cavalcade of limousines to central Rotterdam, twenty-five miles up the river, for an evening reception. A press conference would precede this, during which Wennerstrom would present Thor Larsen to the world's press.

Already, he knew, newspapers and television had leased helicopters to give the last few miles of the *Freya* and her berthing complete camera coverage.

Harry Wennerstrom was a contented old man.

By the early hours of 30th March the *Freya* was well through the channel between the Orkneys and the Shetlands. She had turned south, heading down the North Sea. As soon as she entered the crowded lanes of the North Sea, the *Freya* had reported in, contacting the first of the shore-based area traffic control officers at Wick on the coast of Caithness in the far north of Scotland.

Because of her size and draught, she was a 'hampered vessel'. She had reduced speed to ten knots and was following the instructions fed to her from Wick by VHF radio-telephone. All round her, unseen, the various control centres had her marked on their high-definition radars, manned by qualified pilot operators. These centres are equipped with computerized support systems capable of rapid assimilation of weather, tide and traffic density information.

Ahead of the *Freya* as she crawled down the southbound traffic lane, smaller ships were crisply informed to get out of her way. At midnight she passed Flamborough Head on the coast of Yorkshire, now moving further east, away from the British coast towards Holland. Throughout her passage she had followed the deep-water channel, a minimum of twenty fathoms. On her bridge, despite the constant instructions from ashore, her officers watched the echo-sounder readings, observing the banks and sand-bars that make up the floor of the North Sea slide past on either side of her.

Just before sundown of 31st March, at a point exactly fifteen sea miles due east of the Outer Gabbard Light, now down to her bare steerage speed of five knots, the giant swung gently eastwards and moved to her overnight position, the deep-draught anchorage located at 52 degrees north. She was twenty-seven sea miles due west of the Maas Estuary, twenty-seven miles from home and glory.

It was midnight in Moscow. Adam Munro had decided to walk home from the diplomatic reception at the embassy. He had been driven there by the commercial counsellor, so his own car was parked by his flat off Kutuzovsky Prospekt.

Halfway over the Serafimov Bridge he paused to gaze down at the Moscow River. To his right he could see the illuminated cream-and-white stucco façade of the embassy; to his left the dark red walls of the Kremlin loomed above him, and above them the upper floor and dome of the Great Tsar Palace.

It had been roughly ten months since he had flown from London to take up his new appointment. In that time he had pulled off the greatest espionage coup for decades, 'running' the only spy the West had ever operated inside the heart of the Kremlin. They would savage him for breaking training, for not telling them all along who she was, but they could not diminish the value of what he had brought out.

Three weeks more and she would be out of this place, safe in London. He would be out, too, resigning from the service to start a new life somewhere else with the only person in the world he loved, ever had loved or ever would.

He would be glad to leave Moscow, with its secrecy, its endless furtiveness, its mind-numbing drabness. In ten days the Americans would have their arms reduction treaty, the Kremlin its grain and technology, the service its thanks and gratitude from Downing Street and the White House alike. A week more and he would have his wife to be, and she her freedom. He shrugged deeper into his thick, fur-collared coat and walked on across the bridge.

Midnight in Moscow is 10 p.m. in the North Sea. By 2200 hours the *Freya* was motionless at last. She had steamed 7085 miles from Chita to Abu Dhabi and a further 12,015 miles from there to where she now lay. She lay motionless along the line of the tide; from her stem a single anchor chain streamed out and down to the sea-bed with five shackles on deck. Each link of the chain needed to hold her was nearly a yard long, the steel thicker than a man's thigh.

Because of her hampered state Captain Larsen had brought her down from the Orkneys himself, with two navigating officers to assist him as well as the helmsman. Even at the overnight anchorage he left his First Officer Stig Lundquist, his Third Mate Tom Keller, one of the Danish-Americans, and an able seaman on the bridge through the night. The officers would maintain constant anchor watch, the seaman would carry out periodic deck-inspection.

Though the *Freya*'s engines were closed down, her turbines and generators hummed rhythmically, churning out the power to keep her systems functioning. Among these were the constant feed-in of tide and weather, of which the latest reports were heartening. He could have had March gales; instead an unseasonal area of high pressure almost stationary over the North Sea and the English Channel had brought a mild early spring to the coasts. The sea was almost a flat calm, a one-knot tide ran northeastwards from the vessel towards the Friesians. The sky had been a near cloudless blue all day and, despite a touch of frost that night, bade fair to be so again on the morrow.

Bidding his officers good night, Captain Larsen left the bridge and descended one floor to 'D' deck. Here, on the extreme starboard side, he had his suite. The spacious and well-appointed day cabin carried four windows looking forward down the length of the vessel, and two looking out to starboard. Aft of the day cabin was his bedroom, with bathroom en suite. The sleeping cabin also had two windows, both to starboard. All the windows were sealed, save one in the day cabin which was closed but with screw bolts which could be manually undone.

Outside his sealed windows to forward, the façade of the superstructure fell sheer to the deck; to starboard the windows gave on to ten feet of steel landing, beyond which was the starboard rail and beyond it the sea. Five flights of steel ladders ran from the lowest 'A' deck up five floors to the bridge wing above his head, each stage of the ladders debouching on to a steel landing. All these sets of ladders and landings were open to the sky, exposed to the elements, but they were seldom used, for the interior stairwells were heated and warm.

Thor Larsen lifted the napkin off the plate of chicken and salad the chief steward had left him, looked longingly at the bottle of Scotch in his drinks cabinet and settled for a coffee from the percolator. After eating he decided to work the night away on a final run-through of the channel charts for the morning's berthing. It was going to be tight, and he wanted to know that channel as well as the two Dutch pilots who would arrive by helicopter from Amsterdam's Schiphol Airport at 0730 to take her over. Prior to that, he knew, a gang of ten men from ashore, the extra hands needed for the berthing operation called riggers, would arrive by launch at 0700.

As midnight struck he settled at the broad table in his day cabin, spread his charts and began to study. At ten minutes before three in the morning it was frosty but clear outside. A half-moon caused the rippling sea to glitter. Inside the bridge Stig Lundquist and Tom Keller shared a companionable coffee. The able seaman prowled the glowing screens along the bridge console.

'Sir,' he called, 'there's a launch approaching.'

Tom Keller rose and crossed to where the seaman pointed at the radar screen. There were a score of blips, some stationary, some moving, but all well away from the *Freya*. One tiny blip seemed to be approaching from the southeast.

'Probably a fishing boat making sure of being ready on the fishing grounds by sunrise,' said Keller.

Lundquist was looking over his shoulder. He flicked to a lower range.

'She's coming very close,' he said.

Out at sea the launch had to be aware of the mass of the *Freya*. The tanker carried anchor lights above the fo'c's'le and at the stern. Besides, her deck was floodlit and her superstructure was lit like a Christmas tree by the lights in the accommodation. The launch, instead of veering away, began to curve in towards the stern of the *Freya*.

'She looks as if she's going to come alongside,' said Keller.

'She can't be the berthing crew,' said Lundquist. 'They're not due till seven.'

'Perhaps they couldn't sleep, wanted to be well on time,' said Keller.

'Go down to the head of the ladder,' Lundquist told the seaman, 'and tell me what you see. Put on the headset when you get there, and stay in touch.'

The accommodation ladder on the ship was amidships. On a big vessel it is so heavy that steel cables powered by an electric motor either lower it from the ship's rail to the sea level, or raise it to lie parallel to the rail. On the *Freya*, even fully laden, the rail was thirty feet above the sea, an impossible jump, and the ladder was fully raised.

Seconds later the two officers saw the seaman leave the superstructure below them and begin to stroll down the deck. When he reached the ladder-head, he mounted a small platform that jutted over the sea and looked down. As he did so he took a headset from a weatherproof box and fitted the earphones over his head. From the bridge Lundquist pressed a switch and a powerful light came on, illuminating the seaman far away along the deck as he peered down to the black sea. The launch had vanished from the radar screen; she was too close to be observed.

'What do you see?' asked Lundquist into a stick microphone.

The seaman's voice came back into the bridge. 'Nothing, sir.'

Meanwhile the launch had passed round the rear of the *Freya*, under the very overhang of her stern. For seconds it was out of sight. Either side of the stern, the guard rail of 'A' deck was at its nearest point to the sea, just nineteen and a half feet above the water. The two men standing on the cabin roof of the launch had reduced this to ten feet. As the launch emerged from the transom shadow both men slung the three-point grapnels they held, the hooks sheathed in black rubber hose.

Each grapnel, trailing rope, rose twelve feet, dropped over the guard rail and caught fast. As the launch moved on, both men were swept off the cabin roof to hang by the ropes, ankles in the sea. Then each began to climb, rapidly, hand over hand, unheeding of the submachine carbines strapped to their backs. In two seconds the launch emerged into the light and began to run down the side of the *Freya* towards the courtesy ladder.

'I can see it now,' said the seamen high above. 'It looks like a fishing launch.'

'Keep the ladder up until they identify themselves,' ordered Lundquist from the bridge.

Far behind and below him the two boarders were over the rail. Each unhooked his grapnel and heaved it into the sea, where it sank trailing rope. The two men set off at a fast lope, round to the starboard side and straight for the steel ladders. On soundless rubber-soled shoes they began to race up-wards.

The launch came to rest beneath the ladder, twenty-six feet above the cramped cabin. Inside, four men crouched. At the wheel, the helmsman stared silently up at the seaman above him.

'Who are you?' called the seaman. 'Identify yourself.'

There was no answer. Far below, in the glare of the spotlight, the man in the black woollen helmet just stared back.

'He won't answer,' said the seaman into his mouthpiece.

'Keep the spotlight on them,' ordered Lundquist. 'I'm coming to have a look.'

Throughout the interchange the attention of both Lundquist and Keller had been to the port side and forward of the bridge. On the starboard side the door leading from the bridge wing into the bridge suddenly opened, bringing a gust of icy air. Both officers spun round. The door closed. Facing them were two men in black balaclava helmets, black rollneck sweaters, black track-suit trousers and rubber deckshoes. Each pointed a submachine carbine at the officers.

'Order your seaman to lower the ladder,' said one in English. The two officers stared at them unbelievingly. This was impossible.

The gunmen raised his weapon and squinted down the sight at Keller. 'I'll give you three seconds,' he said to Lundquist, 'then I'm blowing the head off your colleague.'

Brick red with anger, Lundquist leaned to the stick-mike.

'Lower the ladder,' he told the seaman.

The disembodied voice came back into the bridge. 'But, sir. . . .'

'It's all right, lad,' said Lundquist. 'Do as I say.'

With a shrug the seaman pressed a button on the small console at the ladder-head. There was a hum of motors and the ladder slowly lowered to the sea. Two minutes later four other men, all in black, were herding the seaman back along the deck to the superstructure while the fifth man made the launch fast. Two more minutes and the six of them entered the bridge from the port side, the seaman's eyes wide with fright. When he entered the bridge he saw the other two gunmen holding his officers.

'How on earth. . . ?' asked the seaman.

'Take it easy,' ordered Lundquist. To the only gunman who had spoken so far he asked in English, 'What do you want?'

'We want to speak to your captain,' said the man behind the mask. 'Where is he?'

The door from the wheelhouse to the inner stairwell opened and Thor Larsen stepped on to the bridge. His gaze took in his three crewmen with their hands behind their heads, and seven black-clad terrorists. His eyes when he turned to the man who had asked the question were as blue and friendly as a cracking glacier.

'I am Captain Thor Larsen, master of the *Freya*,' he said slowly, 'and who the hell are you?'

'Never mind who we are,' said the terrorist leader. 'We have just taken over your ship. Unless your officers and men do as they are told, we shall start by making an example of your seaman. Which is it to be?'

Larsen looked slowly around him. Three of the submachine guns were pointing straight at the eighteen-year-old deckhand. He was as white as chalk.

'Mr Lundquist,' said Larsen formally, 'do as these men say.' Turning back to the leader he asked: 'What exactly is it you want with the *Freya*?'

'That is easy,' said the terrorist without hesitation. 'We wish you no harm personally, but unless our requirements are carried out, to the letter, we shall not hesitate to do what we have to in order to secure compliance.'

'And then?' asked Lundquist.

'Within thirty hours the West German government is going to release two of our friends from a West Berlin jail and fly them to safety. If they do not, I am going to blast you, your crew, your ship and one million tons of crude oil all over the North Sea.'

11

The leader of the seven masked terrorists set his men to work with a methodical precision that he had evidently rehearsed over many hours in his own mind. He issued a rapid stream of orders in a language Captain Larsen, his own officers and the young seaman could not understand.

Five of the masked men herded the two officers and seaman to the rear of the bridge, well away from the instrument panels, and surrounded them.

The leader jerked his handgun at Captain Larsen and said in English: 'Your cabin, if you please, captain.'

In single file, Larsen leading, the leader of the terrorists next and his henchman with a submachine carbine bringing up the rear, the three men descended the stairs from the bridge to 'D' deck one flight below. Halfway down the stairs, at the turn, Larsen turned to look back and up at his two captors, measuring the distances, calculating whether he could overcome them both.

'Don't even try it,' said the voice behind the mask at his shoulder. 'No one in his right mind argues with a submachine gun at a range of ten feet.'

Larsen led them onwards down the stairs. 'A' deck was the senior officers' living quarters. The captain's suite, as ever, was in the extreme starboard corner of the great sweep of superstructure. Moving to port, next came a small chart library, the door open to reveal locker after locker of high-quality sea charts, enough to take him into any ocean, any bay, any anchorage in the world. They were all copies of originals made by the British Admiralty, and the best in the world.

Next was the conference suite, a spacious cabin where the captain or owner could if he wished receive a sizeable number of visitors all at one time. Next to this were the owner's staterooms, closed and empty, reserved for the chairman should he ever wish to sail with his ship. At the port end was another suite of cabins identical but in reverse to the captain's quarters. Here the chief engineer lived.

Aft of the captain's cabins was the smaller suite for the chief officer, and aft of the engineer dwelt the chief steward. The whole complex formed a hollow square, whose centre was taken up by the flight of stairs, going round and round, and downwards to 'A' deck three floors below.

Thor Larsen led his captors to his own cabin and stepped into the day room. The terrorist leader followed him in and quickly ran through the other rooms, bedroom and bathroom. There was no one else present.

'Sit down, captain,' he said, the voice slightly muffled by the mask. 'You will remain here until I return. Please do not move. Place your hands on the table and keep them there, palms downwards.'

There was another stream of orders in a foreign language, and the machine-gunner took up position with his back to the far bulkhead of the cabin, facing Thor Larsen but twelve feet away, the barrel of his gun pointing straight at the roll-neck white sweater Thor Larsen wore. The leader checked to see that all the curtains were well drawn, then left, closing the door behind him. The other two inhabitants of the deck were asleep in their respective cabins and heard nothing.

Within minutes the leader was back on the bridge. 'You,' he pointed his gun at the boyish seaman, 'come with me.'

The lad looked imploringly at First Officer Stig Lundquist.

'You harm that boy and I'll personally hang you out to dry,' said Tom Keller in his American accent. Two submachine-gun barrels moved slightly in the hands of the ring of men round him.

'Your chivalry is admirable, your sense of reality deplorable,' said the voice behind the leader's mask. 'No one gets hurt unless they try anything stupid. Then there'll be a blood-bath, and you'll be right under the taps.'

Lundquist nodded to the seaman.

'Go with him,' he said, 'do what he wants.'

The seaman was escorted back down the stairs. At the 'D' deck level the terrorist stopped him.

'Apart from the captain, who lives on this deck?' he asked.

'The chief engineer, over there,' said the seaman. 'The chief officer, over there, but he's up on the bridge now. And the chief steward, there.'

There was no sign of life behind any of the doors.

'The paint locker, where is it?' asked the terrorist. Without a word the seaman turned and headed down the stairs. They went through 'C' deck and 'B' deck. Once a murmur of voices came to them, from behind the door of the seamen's mess-room where four men who could not sleep were apparently playing cards over coffee.

At 'A' deck they had reached the level of the base of the superstructure. The seaman opened an exterior door and stepped outside. The terrorist followed him. The cold night air made them both shiver after the warmth of the interior. They found themselves aft of the superstructure on the poop. To one side of the door from which they emerged the bulk of the funnel towered a hundred feet up towards the stars.

The seaman led the way across the poop to where a small steel structure stood. It was six feet by six, and about the same in height. In one side of it there was a steel door, closed by two great screw bolts with butterfly nuts on the outside.

'Down there,' said the seaman.

'Go on down,' said the terrorist. The boy spun the twin butterfly handles, unscrewing the cleats, and pulled them back. Seizing the door handle he swung it open. There was a light inside, showing a tiny platform and a steel stairway running down to the bowels of the *Freya*. At a jerk from the gun, the seaman stepped inside and began to head downwards, the terrorist behind him.

Over seventy feet the stairs led down, past several galleries from which steel doors led off. When they reached the bottom they were well below the waterline, only the keel beneath the deck plating under their feet. They were in an enclosure with four steel doors. The terrorist nodded to the one facing aft.

'What's that lead to?'

'Steering gear housing.'

'Let's have a look.'

When the door was open it showed a great vaulted hall all in metal and painted pale green. It was well lit. Most of the centre of the deck space was taken up by a mountain of encased machinery, the device which, receiving its orders from the computers of the bridge, would move the rudder. The walls of the cavity were curved to the nethermost part of the ship's hull. Aft of the chamber, beyond the steel, the great rudder of the *Freya* would be hanging inert in the black waters of the North Sea. The terrorist ordered the door closed again and bolted shut.

Port and starboard of the steering gear chamber were respectively a chemical store and a paint store. The chemical store the terrorist ignored; he was not going to make men prisoners where there was acid to play with. The paint store was better. It was quite large, airy, well-ventilated and its outer wall was the hull of the ship.

'What's the fourth door?' asked the terrorist. The fourth door was the only door with no handles.

'It leads to the rear of the engine room,' said the seaman. 'It is bolted on the other side.'

The terrorist pushed against the steel door. It was rock-solid. He seemed satisfied.

'How many men on this ship?' he asked. 'Or women. No tricks. If there is one more than the figure you give, we'll shoot them.'

The boy ran his tongue over dry lips.

'There are no women,' he said. 'There might be wives next trip, but not the maiden voyage. There are thirty men, including Captain Larsen.'

Knowing what he needed to know, the terrorist pushed the frightened young man into the paint locker, swung the door closed and threw one of the twin bolts into its socket. Then he returned back up the ladder.

Emerging on the poop deck, he avoided the interior stairs and raced back up the outside ladders to the bridge, stepping in from outside where they reached the bridge-wing.

He nodded to his five companions who still held the two officers at gunpoint and issued a stream of further orders. Minutes later the two bridge officers, joined by the chief steward and chief engineer, roused from their beds on 'D' deck below the bridge, were marched down to the paint locker. Most of the crew were asleep on 'B' deck where the bulk of the cabins were situated, much smaller than the officers' accommodation above their heads on 'C' and 'D'.

There were protests, exclamations, bitter language, as they were herded out and down. But at every stage the leader of the terrorists, the only one who spoke at all, informed them in English that their captain was held in his own cabin and would die in the event of any resistance. The officers and men obeyed their orders.

Down in the paint locker the crew was finally counted: twenty-nine. The first cook and two of the four stewards were allowed to return to the galley on 'A' deck and ferry down to the paint store trays of buns and rolls, along with crates of bottled lemonade and canned beer. Two buckets were provided for toilets.

'Make yourselves comfortable,' the terrorist leader told the twenty-nine angry men who stared back at him from inside the paint locker. 'You won't be here long. Thirty hours at most. One last thing: your captain wants the pumpman. Who is he?'

A Swede called Martinsson stepped forward.

'I'm the pumpman,' he said.

'Come with me.' It was four-thirty.

'A' deck, the ground floor of the superstructure, was entirely devoted to the rooms containing the services of the marine giant. There was the main galley, deep freeze chamber, cool room, other assorted food stores, liquor store, soiled linen store, automatic laundry, cargo control room including the inert gas control, and the fire-fighting control room, also called the foam room.

Above it was 'B' deck, with all non-officer accommodation, cinema, library, four recreation rooms and three bars.

'C' deck held the officer cabins apart from the four on the level above, plus the officers' dining saloon and smoke-room and the crew club with verandah, swimming pool, sauna and gymnasium.

It was the cargo control room on 'A' deck that interested the terrorist, and he ordered the pumpman to bring him to it. There were no windows; it was centrally heated, air conditioned, silent and well-lit. Behind his mask the eyes of the terrorist chief flickered over the banks of switches and settled on the rear bulkhead. Here, behind the control console where the pumpman now sat, a visual display board nine feet wide and four feet tall occupied the wall. It showed in map form the crude-tank layout of the *Freya's* cargo capacity.

'If you try to trick me,' he told the pumpman, it may cost me the life of one of my men, but I shall surely find out. If I do, I shall not shoot you, my friend. I shall shoot your Captain Larsen. Now, point out to me where the ballast holds are, and the cargo holds.'

Martinsson was not going to argue with his captain's life at stake. He was in his mid-twenties and Thor Larsen was a generation older. He had sailed with Larsen twice before, including his first-ever voyage as pumpman, and like all the crew he had enormous respect and liking for the towering Norwegian, who had a reputation for unflagging consideration for his crew and for being the best mariner in the Nordia fleet. He pointed at the diagram in front of him.

The sixty holds were laid out in sets of three across the beam of the *Freya*; twenty such sets.

'Up here in the forepart,' said Martinsson, 'the port and starboard tanks are full of crude. The centre is the slop tank, empty now like a buoyancy tank, because we have not discharged cargo yet. So there has been no need to scour the cargo tanks and pump the slops in here. One row back, all three are ballast tanks; they were full of sea water from Japan to the Gulf, now full of air.'

'Open the valves,' said the terrorist, 'between all three ballast tanks and the slop tank.' Martinsson hesitated. 'Go on, do it.'

Martinsson pressed three square plastic controls on the console in front of him. There was a low humming from behind the console. A quarter of a mile in front of them, down below the steel deck, great valves the size of normal garage doors swung open, forming a single linked unit out of the four tanks, each capable of holding 20,000 tons of liquid. Not only air, but any liquid now entering one of the tanks would flow freely to the other three.

'Where are the next ballast tanks?' asked the terrorist. Martinsson pointed with his forefinger halfway down the ship.

'Here, amidships, there are three in a row, side by side,' he said.

'Leave them alone,' said the terrorist. 'Where are the others?'

'There are nine ballast tanks in all,' said Martinsson, 'the last three are here, side by side as usual, right up close to the superstructure.'

'Open the valves so they communicate with each other.'

Martinsson did as he was bid.

'Good,' said the terrorist. 'Now, can the ballast tanks be linked straight through to the cargo tanks?'

'No,' said Martinsson, 'it's not possible. The ballast tanks are permanent for ballast, that is, sea water or air, but never oil. The cargo tanks are the reverse. The two systems do not inter-connect.

'Fine,' said the masked man. 'We can change all that. One last thing. Open all the valves between all the cargo tanks, laterally and longitudinally, so that all fifty communicate with each other.'

It took fifteen seconds for all the necessary control buttons to be pushed. Far down in the treacly blackness of the crude oil scores of gigantic valves swung open, forming one enormous single tank containing 1,000,000 tons of crude. Martinsson stared at his handiwork in horror.

'If she sinks with one tank ruptured,' he whispered, 'the whole million tons will flow out.'

'Then the authorities had better make sure she doesn't sink,' said the terrorist. 'Where is the master power source from this control panel to the hydraulic pumps that control the valves?'

Martinsson gestured to an electrical junction box on the wall near the ceiling. The terrorist reached up, opened the box and pulled the contact breaker downwards. With the box dead, he removed the ten fuses and pocketed them. The pumpman looked on with fear in his eyes. The valve-opening process had become irreversible. There were spare fuses, and he knew where they were stored. But he would be in the paint locker. No stranger entering his sanctum could find them in time to close those vital valves.

Bengt Martinsson knew, because it was his job to know, that a tanker cannot simply be loaded or unloaded haphazardly. If all the starboard cargo tanks are filled on their own, with the others left empty, the ship will roll over and sink. If the port tanks are filled alone, she will roll the other way. If the forward tanks are filled, but not balanced at the stern, she will dive by the nose, her stern high in the air; and the reverse if the stern half is full of liquid and the for'ard empty.

But if the stem and stern ballast tanks are allowed to flood with water while the centre section is buoyant with air, she will arch like an acrobat doing a backspring. Tankers are not designed for such strains; the *Freya*'s massive spine would break at the mid-section.

'One last thing,' said the terrorist. 'What would happen if we opened all the fifty inspection hatches to the cargo tanks?'

Martinsson was tempted, sorely tempted, to let them try it. He thought of Captain Larsen sitting high above him facing a submachine carbine. He swallowed.

'You'd die,' he said, 'unless you had breathing apparatus.'

He explained to the masked man beside him that when a tanker's holds are full, the liquid crude is never quite up to the ceilings of the holds. In the gap between the slopping surface of the oil and the ceiling of the hold gases form, given off by the crude oil. They are volatile gases, highly explosive. If they were not bled off, they would turn the ship into a bomb.

Years earlier the system for bleeding them off was by way of gas lines fitted with pressure valves so that the gases could escape to the atmosphere above deck where, being very light, they would go straight upwards. More recently a far safer system was devised; inert gases from the main engine exhaust flue were fed into the holds to expel oxygen and seal the surface of the crude oil; these inert gases were mainly nitrogen.

Creating as they did a virtually oxygen-free atmosphere, the possibility of fire or spark, was banished. But every tank had a one-yard circular inspection hatch let into the main deck; if these were opened by an incautious visitor, he would immediately be enveloped in a carpet reaching to above his head of inert gas. He would die choking, asphyxiated in an atmosphere containing no oxygen.

'Thank you,' said the terrorist. 'Who handles the breathing apparatus?'

'The chief officer is in charge of it,' said Martinsson, 'but we are all trained to use it.'

Two minutes later he was back in the paint store with the rest of the crew. It was five o'clock.

While the leader of the masked men had been in the cargo control room with Martinsson, and another held Thor Larsen prisoner in his own cabin, the remaining five had unloaded their launch. The ten suitcases of explosives stood on the deck amidships at the top of the courtesy ladder, awaiting the leader's instructions for placing. These orders he gave with crisp precision. Far away on the foredeck the inspection hatches of the port and and starboard ballast tanks were unscrewed and removed, revealing the single steel ladder descending eighty feet into the black depths of musty air.

Azamat Krim took off his mask, stuffed it in his pocket, took his torch and descended into the first hatch. Two suitcases were lowered after him on long cords. Working in the base of the hold by lamplight, he placed one entire suitcase against the outer hull of the *Freya* and lashed it to one of the vertical ribs with cord. The other case he opened and extracted its contents in two halves. One half went against the forward bulkhead, beyond which lay 20,000 tons of crude. Sandbags, also brought from the launch, were packed around the charges to concentrate the blast. When Krim was satisfied that the detonators were in place and linked to the triggering device, he came back to the starlight on deck.

The same process was repeated on the other side of the *Freya*, and then twice again in the port and starboard ballast tanks close up to the super-structure. He had used eight of his suitcases in four ballast holds. The ninth he placed in the centre ballast tank amidships, not to blast a hole to the waiting sea, but to help crack the spine.

The tenth was brought down to the engine room. Here in the curvature of the *Freya*'s hull, close up against the bulkhead to the paint locker, strong enough to break both open simultaneously, it was laid and primed. If it went off, those men in the paint locker a half-inch of steel away who survived the blast would drown when the sea, under immense pressure at eighty feet below the waves, came pounding through.

It was six-fifteen and dawn was breaking over the *Freya*'s silent decks when he reported to Andrew Drake.

'The charges are laid and primed, Andriy,' he said. 'I pray to God we never set them off.'

'We won't have to,' said Drake. 'But I have to convince Captain Larsen. Only when he has seen and believed will he convince the authorities. Then they'll have to do as we want. They'll have no alternative.'

Two of the crew were brought from the paint locker, made to don protective clothing, face masks and oxygen bottles, and proceed down the deck from the fo'c's'le to the housing, opening every one of the fifty inspection hatches to the oil cargo tanks. When the job was done, the men were returned to the paint locker. The steel door was closed and the two bolts screwed shut on the outside, not to be opened again until two prisoners were safe in Israel.

At six-thirty Andrew Drake, still masked, returned to the captain's day cabin. Wearily he sat down, facing Thor Larsen, and told him from start to finish what had been done. The Norwegian stared back at him impassively, held in check by the submachine gun pointing at him from the corner of the room.

When he had finished, Drake held up a black plastic instrument and showed it to Larsen. It was no larger than two kingsize cigarette packs bound together; there was a single red button on the face of it, and a four-inch steel aerial sticking from the top.

'Do you know what this is, captain?' asked the masked Drake. Larsen shrugged. He knew enough about radio to recognize a small transistorized transmitter.

'It's an oscillator,' said Drake. 'If that red button is pressed, it will emit a single VHF note, rising steadily in tone and pitch to a scream that our ears could not begin to listen to. But attached to every single charge on this ship is a receiver that can and will listen. As the tonal pitch rises, a dial on the receivers will show the pitch, the needles moving round the dials until they can go no further. When that happens the devices will blow their fuses and a current will be cut. The cutting of that current in each receiver will convey its message to the detonators, which will then operate. You know what that would mean?'

Thor Larsen stared back at the masked face across the table from him. His ship, his beloved *Freya*, was being raped and there was nothing he could do about it. His crew was crowded into a steel coffin inches away through a steel bulkhead from a charge that would crush them all, and cover them in seconds in freezing sea water.

His mind's eye conjured a picture of hell. If the charges blew, great holes would be torn in the port and starboard sides of four of his ballast tanks. Roaring mountains of sea would rush in, filling both the outer and the centre ballast tanks in minutes. Being heavier than the crude oil, the sea water would have the greater pressure; it would push through the other gaping holes inside the tanks to the neighbouring cargo holds, spewing the crude oil upwards through the inspection hatches, so that six more holds would fill with water. This would happen right up in the forepeak, and right aft beneath his feet. In minutes the engine room would be flooded with tens of thousands of tons of green water. The stern and the bow would drop at least ten feet, but the buoyant mid-section would ride high, its ballast tanks untouched. The *Freya*, most beautiful of all the Norse goddesses, would arch her back once, in pain, and split in two. Both sections would drop straight, without rolling, twenty-five feet to the sea-bed beneath, to sit there with fifty inspection hatches open and facing upwards. A million tons of crude oil would gurgle out to the surface of the North Sea.

It might take an hour for the mighty goddess to sink completely, but the process would be irreversible. In such shallow water part of her bridge might still be above the tide, but she could never be re-floated. It might take three days for the last of her cargo to reach the surface, but no diver could work among fifty columns of vertically rising crude oil. No one would close the hatches again. The escape of the oil, like the destruction of his ship, would be irreversible.

He stared back at the masked face but made no reply. There was a deep, seething anger inside him, growing with each passing minute, but he gave no sign of it.

'What do you want?' he growled. The terrorist glanced at the digital display clock on the wall. It read a quarter to seven.

'We're going to the radio room,' he said. 'We talk to Rotterdam. Or rather, you talk to Rotterdam.'

Twenty-six miles to the east the rising sun had dimmed the great yellow flames that spout day and night from the oil refineries of Europort. Through the night, from the bridge of the *Freya*, it had been possible to see these flames in the dark sky above Chevron, Shell, BP and even, far beyond them, the cool blue glow of Rotterdam's street lighting.

The refineries and the labyrinthine complexity of Europort, the greatest oil terminal in the world, lie on the south shore of the Maas Estuary. On the north shore is the Hook of Holland, with its ferry terminal and the Maas Control building, squatting beneath its whirling radar antennae.

Here at 0645 hours on the morning of 1st April Duty Officer Bernard Dijkstra yawned and stretched. He would be going home in fifteen minutes for a well-earned breakfast. Later, after a sleep, he would motor back from his home at Gravenzande in his spare time to see the new super-giant tanker pass through the estuary. It should be quite a day.

As if to answer his thoughts the speaker in front of him came to life. 'Pilot Maas, Pilot Maas, here is the *Freya*.'

The supertanker was on channel twenty, the usual channel for a tanker out at sea to call up Maas Control by radio-telephone. Dijkstra leaned forward and flicked a switch.

'*Freya*, this is Pilot Maas. Go ahead.'

'Pilot Maas, this is *Freya*. Captain Thor Larsen speaking. Where is the launch with my berthing crew?'

Dijkstra consulted a clipboard to the left of his console.

'*Freya*, this is pilot Maas. They left the Hook over an hour ago. They should be with you in twenty minutes.'

What followed caused Dijkstra to shoot bolt upright in his chair.

'*Freya* to Pilot Maas. Contact the launch immediately and tell them to return to port. We cannot accept them on board. Inform the Maas pilots not to take off, repeat not to take off. We cannot accept them on board. We have an emergency, I repeat, we have an emergency.

Dijkstra covered the speaker with his hand and yelled to his fellow duty officer to throw the switch on the tape recorder. When it was spinning to record the conversation, Dijkstra removed his hand and said carefully, '*Freya*, this is Pilot Maas. Understand you do not wish the berthing crew to come alongside. Understand you do not wish the pilots to take off. Please confirm.'

'Pilot Maas, this is *Freya*. Confirm. Confirm.'

'*Freya*, please give details of your emergency.'

There was silence for ten seconds, as if a consultation were taking place on the *Freya*'s bridge far out at sea. Then Larsen's voice boomed out again in the control room.

'Pilot Maas, *Freya*. I cannot give the nature of the emergency. But if any attempt is made by anyone to approach the *Freya*, people will get killed. Please stay away. Do not make any further attempt to contact the *Freya* by radio or telephone. Finally, the *Freya* will contact you again at zero nine hundred hours exactly. Have the chairman of the Rotterdam Port Authority present in the control room. That is all.'

The voice ended and there was a loud click. Dijkstra tried to call back two or three times. Then he looked across at his colleague. 'What the hell did that mean?'

Officer Schipper shrugged. 'I didn't like the sound of it,' he said. 'Captain Larsen sounded as if he might be in danger.'

'He spoke of men getting killed,' said Dijkstra. 'How killed? What's he got, a mutiny? Someone run amok?'

'We'd better do what he says until this is sorted out,' said Schipper.

'Right,' said Dijkstra. 'You get on to the chairman, I'll contact the launch and the two pilots up at Schiphol.'

The launch bearing the berthing crew was chugging at a steady ten knots across the flat calm towards the *Freya*, with three miles still to go. It was developing into a beautiful spring morning, warm for the time of year. At three miles the bulk of the giant tanker was already looming large, and the ten Dutchmen who would help her berth, but who had never seen her before, were craning their necks as they came closer.

No one thought anything when the ship-to-shore radio by the helmsman's side crackled and squawked. He took the handset off its cradle and held it to his ear. With a frown he cut the engine to idling and asked for a repeat. When he got it, he put the helm hard a-starboard and brought the launch round in a semi-circle.

'We're going back,' he told the men who looked at him with puzzlement. 'There's something wrong. Captain Larsen's not ready for you yet.'

Behind them the *Freya* receded again towards the horizon as they headed back to the Hook.

Up at Schiphol Airport south of Amsterdam the two estuary pilots were walking towards the Port Authority helicopter that would airlift them out to the deck of the tanker. It was routine procedure; they always went out to waiting ships by whirlybird.

The senior pilot, a grizzled veteran with twenty years at sea, a master's ticket and fifteen years a Maas pilot, carried his 'brown box', the instrument which would help him steer her to within a yard of sea water if he wished to be so precise. With the *Freya* clearing only twenty feet from the shoals and the Inner Channel barely fifty feet wider than the *Freya* itself, he would need it this morning.

As they ducked underneath the whirling blades, the pilot leaned out and wagged a warning finger at them.

'Something seems to be wrong,' he yelled above the roar of the engine. 'We have to wait. I'm closing her down.'

The engine cut, the blades swished to a stop.

'What the hell's all that about?' asked the second pilot.

The helicopter flier shrugged. 'Don't ask me,' he said, 'just came through from Maas Control. The ship isn't ready for you yet.'

At his handsome country house outside Vlaardingen Dirk van Gelder, chairman of the Port Authority, was at breakfast a few mintues before eight when the phone rang.

His wife answered it. 'It's for you,' she called, and went back to the kitchen where the coffee was perking. Van Gelder rose from the breakfast table, dropped his newspaper on the chair and shuffled in carpet slippers out to the hallway.

'Van Gelder,' he said down the telephone. As he listened he stiffened, his brow furrowed.

'What did he mean, killed?' he asked. There was another stream of words into his ear. 'Right,' said van Gelder, 'stay there. I'll be with you in fifteen minutes.'

He slammed the phone down, kicked off the slippers and put on his shoes and jacket. Two minutes later he was at his garage doors. As he climbed into his Mercedes and backed out to the gravel driveway, he was fighting back thoughts of his personal and abiding nightmare.

'Dear God, not a hijack. Please, not a hijack.'

After replacing the VHF radio-telephone on the bridge of the *Freya*, Captain Thor Larsen had been taken at gunpoint on a tour of his own ship, peering with torch into the forward ballast holds to note the big packages strapped far down below the water-line.

Returning down the deck he had seen the launch with the berthing crew turn, three miles out, and head back for the shore. To seaward a small freighter had passed, heading south, and had greeted the leviathan at anchor with a cheery hoot. It was not returned.

He had seen the single charge in the centre ballast tank amidships, and the further charges in the after ballast tanks close by the superstructure. He did not need to see the paint locker. He knew where it was and could imagine how close the charges were placed.

At half-past eight, while Dirk van Gelder was striding into the Maas Control building to listen to the tape recording, Thor Larsen was escorted back to his day cabin. He had noted one of the terrorists, muffled against the chill, perched right up in the fo'c's'le apron of the *Freya*, watching the arc of sea out in front of the vessel. Another was high on the top of the funnel casing over a hundred feet up with a commanding view of the sea around him. A third was on the bridge, patrolling the radar screens, able thanks to the *Freya*'s own technology to see a forty-eight-mile radius circle of ocean around her, and most of the sea beneath her.

Of the remaining four, two, the leader and another, were with him; the other two must be below decks somewhere.

The terrorist leader forced him to sit at his own table in his own cabin. The man tapped the oscillator which was clipped to his belt.

'Captain, please don't force me to press this red button. And please don't think that I will not, either if there is any attempt at heroics on this ship, or if my demands are not met. Now, please read this.'

He handed Captain Larsen a sheaf of three sheets of foolscap paper covered with typed writing in English. Larsen went rapidly through it.

'At nine o'clock you are going to read that message over the ship-to-shore radio to the chairman of the Port Authority of Rotterdam. No more, and no less. No breaking into Dutch or Norwegian. No supplementary questions. Just the message. Understand?'

Larsen nodded grimly. The door opened and a masked terrorist came in. He had apparently been in the galley. He bore a tray with fried eggs, butter, jam and coffee, which he placed on the table between them.

'Breakfast,' said the terrorist leader. He gestured towards Larsen. 'You might as well eat.'

Larsen shook his head, but drank the coffee. He had been awake all night and had risen from his bed the previous morning at seven. Twenty-six hours awake, and many more to go. He needed to stay alert and guessed the black coffee might help. He calculated that the terrorist across the table from him had also been awake the same amount of time.

The terrorist signalled the remaining gunman to leave. As the door closed they were alone, but the broad expanse of table put the terrorist well out of Larsen's reach. The gun lay within inches of the man's right hand, the oscillator was at his waist.

'I don't think we shall have to abuse your hospitality for more than thirty hours, maybe forty,' said the masked man. 'But if I wear this mask during that time I shall suffocate. You have never seen me before and after tomorrow you will never see me again.'

With his left hand the man pulled the black balaclava helmet from his head. Larsen found himself staring at a man in his early thirties, with brown eyes and medium brown hair. He puzzled Larsen. The man spoke like an Englishman, behaved like one. But Englishmen do not hijack tankers, surely. Irish perhaps? IRA? But he had referred to friends of his in prison in Germany. Arab, perhaps? There were PLO terrorists in prison in Germany. And he spoke a strange language to his companions. Not Arabic by the sound it, yet there were scores of different dialects in Arabic, and Larsen only knew the Gulf Arabs. Again, Irish perhaps.

'What do I call you?' he asked the man whom he would never know as Andriy Drach or Andrew Drake.

The man thought for a moment, as he ate. 'You can call me "Svoboda",' he said after a while. 'It is a common name in my language. But it is also a word. It means "freedom".'

'That's not Arabic,' said Larsen. The man smiled for the first time.

'Certainly not. We are not Arabs. We are Ukrainian freedom fighters, and proud of it.'

'And you think the authorities will free your friends in prison?' asked Larsen.

'They will have to,' said Drake confidently. 'They have no alternative. Come, it is almost nine o'clock.'

12

'Pilot Maas, Pilot Maas, this is the *Freya*.'

Captain Thor Larsen's baritone voice echoed into the main control room at the squat building on the tip of the Hook of Holland. In the first-floor office with its sweeping picture windows gazing out over the North Sea, now curtained against the bright morning sun to give clarity to the radar screens, five men sat waiting.

Dijkstra and Schipper were still on duty, thoughts of breakfast forgotten. Dirk van Gelder stood behind Dijkstra, ready to take over when the call came through. At another console one of the day-shift men was taking care of the rest of estuary traffic, bringing ships in and out but keeping them away from the *Freya*, whose blip on the radar screen was at the limit of vision but still larger than all the others. The senior maritime safety officer to Maas Control was also present.

When the call came, Dijkstra slipped out of his chair before the speaker and van Gelder sat down. He gripped the stem of the table microphone, cleared his throat and threw the 'transmit' switch.

'*Freya*, this is Pilot Maas. Go ahead, please.'

Beyond the confines of the building, looking for all the world like a chopped-off air traffic control tower sitting on the sand, other ears were listening. During the earlier transmission two other ships had caught part of the conversation and there had been a deal of chit-chat between ships' radio officers in the intervening ninety minutes. Now a dozen were listening keenly.

On the *Freya*, Larsen knew he could switch to channel sixteen, speak to Scheveningen Radio and ask for a patch-through to Maas Control for greater privacy, but the listeners would soon join him on that channel. So he stayed with channel twenty.

'*Freya* to Pilot Maas, I wish to speak personally to the chairman of the Port Authority.'

'This is Pilot Maas. This is Dirk van Gelder speaking. I am the chairman of the Port Authority.'

'This is Captain Thor Larsen, master of the *Freya*.'

'Yes, Captain Larsen, your voice is recognized. What is your problem?'

At the other end, on the bridge of the *Freya*, Drake gestured with the tip of his gun to the written statement in Larsen's hand. Larsen nodded, flicked his 'transmit' switch and began to read into the telephone.

'I am reading a prepared statement. Please do not interrupt and do not pose questions.

'"At oh three hundred hours this morning the *Freya* was taken over by armed men. I have already been given ample reason to believe they are in deadly earnest and prepared to carry out all their threats unless their demands are met."'

In the control tower on the sand there was a hiss of indrawn breath from behind van Gelder. He closed his eyes wearily. For years he had been urging that some security measures be taken to protect these floating bombs from hijackings. He had been ignored, and now it had happened at last. The voice from the speaker went on, the tape recorder revolved impassively.

'"My entire crew is presently locked in the lowest portion of the ship, behind steel doors, and cannot escape. So far no harm has come to them. I myself am held at gunpoint on my own bridge.

'"During the night explosive charges have been placed at strategic positions at various points inside the *Freya*'s hull. I have examined these myself and can corroborate that if exploded they would blast the *Freya* apart, kill her crew instantly, and vent one million tons of crude oil into the North Sea."'

'Oh, my God,' said a voice behind van Gelder. He waved an impatient hand for the speaker to shut up.

'"These are the immediate demands of the men who hold the *Freya* prisoner. One, all sea traffic is to be cleared at once from the area inside the arc from a line forty-five degrees south of a bearing due east of the *Freya*, and forty-five degrees north of the same bearing; that is, inside a ninety-degree arc between the *Freya* and the Dutch coast. Two, no vessel, surface or submarine, is to attempt to approach the *Freya* on any other bearing to within five miles. Three, no aircraft is to pass overhead the *Freya* within a circle of five miles' radius of her, and below a height of ten thousand feet. Is that clear? You may answer."'

Van Gelder gripped the microphone hard.

'*Freya*, this is Pilot Maas. Dirk van Gelder speaking. Yes, that is clear. I will have all surface traffic cleared from the area enclosed by a ninety-degree arc between the *Freya* and the Dutch coast, and from an area five sea miles from the *Freya* on all other sides. I will instruct Schiphol Airport traffic control to ban all air movements within the five-mile radius area below ten thousand feet. Over.'

There was a pause, and Larsen's voice came back.

'I am informed that if there is any attempt to breach these orders, there will be an immediate riposte without further consultation. Either the *Freya* will vent twenty thousand tons of crude oil immediately, or one of my seamen will be . . . executed. Is that understood? You may answer.'

Dirk van Gelder turned to his traffic officers.

'Jesus, get the shipping out of that area, fast. Get on to Schiphol and tell them. No commercial flights, no private aircraft, no choppers taking pictures, nothing. Now move.'

To the microphone he said, 'Understood, Captain Larsen. Is there anything else?'

'Yes,' said the disembodied voice. '"There will be no further radio contact with the *Freya* until twelve hundred hours. At that time the *Freya* will call you again. I will wish to speak directly and personally to the Prime Minister of the Netherlands and the West German ambassador. Both must be present. That is all."'

The microphone went dead. On the bridge of the *Freya* Drake removed the handset from Larsen's hand and replaced it. Then he gestured the Norwegian to return to the day cabin. When they were seated with the seven-foot table between them, Drake laid down his gun and leaned back. As his sweater rode up Larsen saw the lethal oscillator clipped at his waistband.

'What do we do now?' asked Larsen.

'We wait,' said Drake. 'While Europe goes quietly mad.'

'They'll kill you, you know,' said Larsen. ''You've got on board, but you'll never get off. They may have to do what you say, but when they have done it they'll be waiting for you.'

'I know,' said Drake. 'But you see, I don't mind if I die. I'll fight to live, of course, but I'll die, and I'll kill, before I'll see them kill off my project.'

'You want these two men in Germany free that much?' asked Larsen.

'Yes, that much. I can't explain why, and if I did you wouldn't understand. But for years my land, my people, have been occupied, persecuted, imprisoned, killed. And no one cared a shit. Now I threaten to kill one single man, or hit Western Europe in the pocket, and you'll see what they do. Suddenly it's a disaster. But for me, the slavery of my land, that is the disaster.'

'This dream of yours, what is it exactly?' asked Larsen.

'A free Ukraine,' said Drake simply. 'Which cannot be achieved short of a popular uprising by millions of people.'

'In the Soviet Union?' said Larsen. 'That's impossible. That will never happen.'

'It could,' countered Drake. 'It could. It happened in East Germany, in Hungary, in Czechoslovakia. But first, the conviction by those millions that they could never win, that their oppressors are invincible, must be broken. If it once were, the floodgates could open wide.'

'No one will ever believe that,' said Larsen.

'Not in the West, no. But there's the strangest thing. Here in the West people would say I cannot be right in that calculation. But in the Kremlin they know I am.'

'And for this . . . popular uprising, you are prepared to die?' asked Larsen.

'If I must. That is my dream. That land, that people, I love more than life itself. That's my advantage; within a hundred-mile radius of here there is no one else who loves something more than his life.'

A day earlier Thor Larsen might have agreed with the fanatic. But something was happening inside the big, slow-moving Norwegian that surprised him. For the first time in his life he hated a man enough to kill him. Inside his head a private voice said, 'I don't care about your Ukrainian dream, Mr Svoboda. You are not going to kill my crew and my ship.'

At Felixstowe on the coast of Suffolk, the English coastguard officer walked quickly away from his coastal radio set and picked up the telephone.

'Get me the Department of the Environment in London,' he told the operator.

'By God, those Dutchies have got themselves a problem this time,' said his deputy, who had heard the conversation between the *Freya* and Maas Control also.

'It's not just the Dutch,' said the senior coastguard. 'Look at the map.'

On the wall was a map of the entire southern portion of the North Sea and the northern end of the English Channel. It showed the coast of Suffolk right across to the Maas Estuary. In chinagraph pencil the coastguard had marked the *Freya* at her overnight position. It was exactly halfway between the two coasts.

'If she blows, lad, our coasts will also be under a foot of oil from Hull round to Southampton.

Minutes later he was talking to a civil servant in London, one of the men in the department of the ministry specifically concerned with oil-slick hazards. What he said caused the morning's first cup of tea in London to go quite cold.

Dirk van Gelder managed to catch the Prime Minister at his residence, just as he was about to leave for his office. The urgency of the Port Authority chairman finally persuaded the young aide from the Cabinet Office to pass the phone to the premier.

'Jan Grayling,' he said down the speaker. As he listened to van Gelder his face tightened.

'Who are they?' he asked.

'We don't know,' said van Gelder. 'Captain Larsen was reading from a prepared statement. He was not allowed to deviate from it or answer questions.'

'If he was under duress, perhaps he had no choice but to confirm the placing of the explosives. Perhaps that's a bluff,' said Grayling.

'I don't think so, sir,' said van Gelder. 'Would you like me to bring the tape to you?'

'Yes, at once, in your own car,' said the premier. 'Straight to the Cabinet Office.'

He put the phone down and walked to his limousine, his mind racing. If what was threatened was indeed true, the bright summer morning had brought the worst crisis of his term of office. As his car left the kerbside, followed by the inevitable police vehicle, he leaned back and tried to think out some of the first priorities. An immediate emergency Cabinet meeting, of course. The press, they would not be long. Many ears must have listened to the ship-to-shore conversation; someone would tell the press before noon.

He would have to inform a variety of foreign governments through their embassies. And authorize the setting up of an immediate crisis management committee of experts. Fortunately he had access to a number of such experts since the hijacks by the South Moluccans several years earlier. As he drew up in front of the prime ministerial office building he glanced at his watch. It was half-past nine.

The phrase 'crisis management committee' was already being thought, albeit as yet unspoken, in London. Sir Rupert Mossbank, permanent under-secretary to the Department of the Environment was on the phone to the Cabinet secretary, Sir Julian Flannery.

'It's early days yet, of course,' said Sir Rupert. 'We don't know who they are, how many, if they're serious or whether there are really any bombs on board. But if that amount of crude oil did get spilt, it really would be rather messy.'

Sir Julian thought for a moment, gazing out through his first-floor windows on to Whitehall.

'Good of you to call so promptly, Rupert,' he said. 'I think I'd better inform the PM at once. In the meantime, just as a precaution, could you ask a couple of your best minds to put together a memo on the prospective consequences if she does blow up? Question of spillage, area of ocean covered, tide flow, speed, area of our coastline likely to be affected. That sort of thing. I'm pretty sure she'll ask for it.'

'I have it in hand already, old boy.'

'Good,' said Sir Julian, 'excellent. Fast as possible. I suspect she'll want to know. She always does.'

He had worked under three prime ministers, and the latest was far and away the toughest and most decisive. For years it had been a standing joke that the government party was full of old women of both sexes, but fortunately was led by a real man. The name was Mrs Joan Carpenter. The Cabinet secretary had his appointment within minutes and walked through the bright morning sunshine across the lawn to Number 10, with purpose but without hurry, as was his wont.

When he entered the Prime Minister's private office she was at her desk, where she had been since eight o'clock. A coffee set of bone china lay on a side table, and three red despatch boxes lay open on the floor. Sir Julian was admiring; the woman went through documentation like a paper shredder, and the papers were already finished by 10 a.m., either agreed, rejected or bearing a crisp request for further information, or a series of pertinent questions.

'Good morning, Prime Minister.'

'Good morning, Sir Julian, a beautiful day.'

'Indeed, ma'am. Unfortunately it has brought a piece of unpleasantness with it.'

He took a seat at her gesture, and accurately sketched in the details of the affair in the North Sea, as well as he knew them. She was alert, absorptive.

'If it is true, then this ship, the *Freya*, could cause an environmental disaster,' she said flatly.

'Indeed, though we do not know yet the exact feasibility of sinking such a gigantic vessel with what are presumably industrial explosives. There are men who would be able to give an assessment, of course.'

'In the event that it is true,' said the PM, 'I believe we should form a crisis management committee to consider the implications. If it is not, then we have the opportunity for a realistic exercise.'

Sir Julian raised an eyebrow. The idea of putting a thunderflash down the trousers of a dozen ministerial departments as an exercise had not occurred to him. He supposed it had a certain charm.

For thirty minutes the Prime Minister and her Cabinet secretary listed the areas in which they would need professional expertise if they were to be accurately informed of the options in a major tanker hijack in the North Sea.

In the matter of the supertanker herself, she was insured by Lloyd's, who would be in possession of a complete plan of her layout. Concerning the structure of tankers, British Petroleum marine division would have an expert in tanker construction who could study those plans and give a precise judgement on feasibility.

In spillage control, they agreed to call on the senior research analyst at the Warren Springs laboratory, run jointly by the Department of Trade and Industry and the Ministry of Agriculture, Fisheries and Food, at Stevenage, close to London.

The Ministry of Defence would be called on for a serving officer in the Royal Engineers, an expert in explosives, to estimate that side of things, and the Department of the Environment itself had people who could calculate the scope of the catastrophe to the ecology of the North Sea. Trinity House, head authority of the pilotage services round Britain's coasts, would be asked to inform on tide flows and speeds. Relations and liaison with foreign governments would fall to the Foreign Office, who would send an observer. By ten-thirty the list seemed complete. Sir Julian prepared to leave.

'Do you think the Dutch government will handle this affair?' asked the Prime Minister.

'It's early days to say, ma'am. At the moment the terrorists wish to put their demands to Mr Grayling personally at noon, in ninety minutes. I have no doubt The Hague will feel able to handle the matter. But if the demands cannot be met, or if the ship blows up anyway, then as a coastal nation we are involved in any case.

'Furthermore, our capacity to cope with oil spillage is the most advanced in Europe, so we may be called on to help by our allies across the North Sea.'

'Then the sooner we are ready the better,' said the PM. 'One last thing, Sir Julian. It will probably never come to it, but if the demands cannot be met, the contingency may have to be considered of storming the vessel to liberate the crew and defuse the charges.'

For the first time Sir Julian was not comfortable. He had been a professional civil servant all his life, since leaving Oxford with a Double First. He believed the word, written and spoken, could solve most problems, given time. He abhorred violence.

'Ah, yes, Prime Minister. That would of course be a last resort. I understand it is called "the hard option".'

'The Israelis stormed the airliner at Entebbe,' mused the PM. 'The Germans stormed the one at Mogadishu. The Dutch stormed the train at Assen – when they were left with no alternative. Supposing it were to happen again.'

'Well, ma'am, perhaps they would.'

'Could the Dutch marines carry out such a mission?'

Sir Julian chose his words carefully. He had a vision of burly marines clumping all over Whitehall. Far better to keep those people playing their lethal games well out of the way on Exmoor.

'If it came to storming a vessel at sea,' he said, 'I believe a helicopter landing would not be feasible. It would be spotted by the deck-watch, and of course the ship has a radar scanner. Similarly, an approach by a surface vessel would also be observed. This is not an airliner on a concrete runway, nor a stationary train, ma'am. This is a ship over twenty-five miles from land.'

That, he hoped, would put a stop to it.

'What about an approach by armed divers or frogmen?' she asked.

Sir Julian closed his eyes. Armed frogmen indeed. He was convinced politicians read too many novels for their own good.

'Armed frogmen, Prime Minister?'

The blue eyes across the desk did not leave him. 'I understand,' she said clearly, 'that our capacity in this regard is among the most advanced in Europe.'

'I believe it may well be so, ma'am.'

'And who are these underwater experts?'

'The Special Boat Service, Prime Minister.'

'Who, in Whitehall, liaises with our special services?' she asked.

'There is a Royal Marine colonel in Defence,' he conceded, 'called Holmes.'

It was going to be bad, he could see it coming. They had used the land-based counterpart of the SBS, the better-known Special Air Service or SAS, to help the Germans at Mogadishu, and in the Balcombe Street siege. Harold Wilson had always wanted to hear all the details of the lethal games these roughnecks played with their opponents. Now they were going to start another James Bond-style fantasy.

'Ask Colonel Holmes to attend the crisis management committee, in a consultative capacity only, of course.'

'Of course, ma'am.'

'And prepare the UNICORNE. I shall expect you to take the chair at noon, when the terrorists' demands are known.'

Three hundred miles across the North Sea the activity in Holland was already by mid-morning becoming frenetic.

From his office in the seaside capital of The Hague, the premier Jan Grayling and his staff were putting together the same sort of crisis management committee that Mrs Carpenter in London had in mind. The first requirement was to know the exact perspectives of any conceivable human or environmental tragedy stemming from damage at sea to a ship like the *Freya*, and the various options the Dutch government faced.

To secure this information the same kinds of experts were being called upon for their specialized knowledge: in shipping, oil slicks, tides, speeds, directions, future weather prospects and even the military option.

Dirk van Gelder, having delivered the tape recording of the nine o'clock message from the *Freya*, drove back to Maas Control on the instructions of Jan Grayling to sit by the VHF radio-telephone set in case the *Freya* called up again before twelve noon.

It was he who at 10.30 took the call from Harry Wennerstrom. Having finished breakfast in his penthouse suite at the Rotterdam Hilton, the old shipping magnate was still in ignorance of the disaster to his ship. Quite simply, no one had thought to call him.

Wennerstrom was calling to enquire of the progress of the *Freya* which, by this time, he thought would be well into the Outer Channel, moving slowly and carefully towards the Inner Channel, several miles past Euro Buoy One and moving along a precise course of oh-eight-two and a half degrees. He expected to leave Rotterdam with his convoy of notables to witness the *Freya* coming into sight about lunchtime as the tide rose to peak.

Van Gelder apologized for not having called him at the Hilton, and carefully explained what had happened at 0730 and 0900 hours. There was silence from the Hilton end of the line. Wennerstrom's first reaction could have been to mention that there was $170,000,000 worth of ship being held prisoner out beyond the western horizon, carrying $140,000,000 worth of crude oil. It was a reflection on the man that he said at length:

'There are thirty of my seamen out there, Mr van Gelder. And starting right now let me tell you if anything happens to any one of them because the terrorists' demands are not met, I shall hold the Dutch authorities personally responsible.'

'Mr Wennerstrom,' said van Gelder, who had also commanded a ship in his career, 'we are doing everything we can. The requirements of the terrorists regarding the distance of clear water round the *Freya* are being met, to the letter. Their primary demands have not yet been stated. The Prime Minister is back in his office now in The Hague doing what he can, and he will be back here at noon for the next message from the *Freya*.'

Harry Wennerstrom replaced the handset and stared through the picture windows of the sitting room into the sky towards the west where his dream ship was lying at anchor on the open sea with armed terrorists aboard her.

'Cancel the convoy to Maas Control,' he said suddenly to one of his secretaries. 'Cancel the champagne lunch. Cancel the reception this evening. Cancel the press conference. I'm going.'

'Where, Mr Wennerstrom?' asked the amazed young woman.

'To Maas Control. Alone. Have my car waiting by the time I reach the garage.'

With that the old man stumped from the suite and headed for the lift.

Around the *Freya* the sea was emptying. Working closely with their British colleagues at Flamborough Head and Felixstowe, the Dutch marine traffic control officers diverted shipping into sea lanes west of the *Freya*, the nearest being over five miles west of her.

Eastwards of the stricken ship coastal traffic was ordered to stop or turn back, and movements into and out of Europort and Rotterdam were halted. Angry sea captains, whose voices poured into Maas Control demanding explanation, were simply told that an emergency had arisen and they were to avoid at all costs the sea area whose coordinates were read out to them.

It was impossible to keep the press in the dark. A group of several score journalists from technical and marine publications, as well as the shipping correspondents of the major daily papers from the neighbouring countries, were already in Rotterdam for the reception arranged for the *Freya*'s triumphal entry that afternoon. By 11 a.m. their curiosity was aroused partly by the cancellation of the journey to the Hook to witness the *Freya* come over the horizon into the Inner Channel, and partly by tips reaching their head offices from those numerous radio hams who like to listen to maritime radio talk.

Shortly after eleven, calls began to flood in to the penthouse suite of their host, Harry Wennerstrom, but he was not there and his secretaries knew nothing. Other calls came to Maas Control, and were referred to The Hague. In the Dutch capital the switchboard operators put the calls through to the Prime Minister's private press secretary, on Mr Grayling's orders, and the harassed young man fended them off as best he could.

The lack of information simply intrigued the press corps more than ever, so they reported to their editors that something serious was afoot with the *Freya*. The editors despatched other reporters, who foregathered through the morning outside the Maas Control building at the Hook, where they were firmly kept outside the chain-link fence that surrounds the building. Others grouped in The Hague to pester the various ministries, but most of all the Prime Minister's office.

The editor of *De Telegraaf* received a tip from a radio ham that there were terrorists on board the *Freya*, and that they would issue their demands at noon. He at once ordered a radio monitor to be placed on channel twenty with a tape recorder to catch the whole message.

Jan Grayling personally telephoned the West German ambassador, Konrad Voss, and told him in confidence what had happened. Voss called Bonn at once, and within thirty minutes replied to the Dutch premier that he would of course accompany him to the Hook for twelve o'clock as the terrorists had demanded. The Federal German government, he assured the Dutchman, would do everything it could to help.

The Dutch Foreign Ministry as a matter of courtesy informed the ambassadors of all the nations remotely concerned: Sweden, whose flag the *Freya* flew and whose seamen were on board; Norway, Finland and Denmark, who also had seamen on board; the USA, because four of those seamen were Scandinavian-Americans with US passports and dual nationality; Britain, as a coastal nation and whose institution, Lloyd's, was insuring both ship and cargo; and Belgium, France and West Germany, all as coastal nations.

In nine European capitals the telephones rang between ministry and department, from call box to editorial room, in insurance offices, shipping agencies and private homes. For those in government, backing, shipping, insurance, the armed forces and the press, the prospect of a quiet weekend that Friday morning receded into the flat blue ocean where under a warm spring sun a 1,000,000-ton bomb called the *Freya* lay silent and still.

Harry Wennerstrom was halfway from Rotterdam to the Hook when an idea occurred to him. The limousine was passing out of Schiedam on the motorway towards Vlaardingen when he recalled that his private jet was at Schiedam Municipal Airport. He reached for the telephone and called his principal secretary still trying to fend off calls from the press in his suite at the Hilton. When he got through to her at the third attempt he gave her a string of orders for his pilot.

'One last thing,' he said. 'I want the name and office phone number of the police chief of Alesund. Yes, Alesund, in Norway. As soon as you have it, call him up and tell him to stay where he is and await my call back to him.'

Lloyd's Intelligence Unit had been informed shortly after ten o'clock. A British dry-cargo vessel had been preparing to enter the Maas Estuary for Rotterdam when the 0900 call was made from the *Freya* to Maas Control. The radio officer had heard the whole conversation, noted it verbatim in shorthand, and shown it to his captain. Minutes later he was dictating it to the ship's agent in Rotterdam, who passed it to head office in London. The office had called Colchester, Essex, and repeated the news to Lloyd's. One of the chairmen of twenty-five separate firms of underwriters had been contacted and informed. The consortium that had put together the $170,000,000 hull insurance on the *Freya* had to be big; so also was the group of firms covering the 1,000,000-ton cargo for Clint Blake in his office in Texas. But despite the size of the *Freya* and her cargo, the biggest single policy was the Protection and Indemnity insurance, for the persons of the crew and pollution compensation. The P. and I. policy would be the one to cost the biggest money if the *Freya* was blown apart.

Shortly before noon the chairman of Lloyd's, in his office high above the City, stared at a few calculations on his jotting pad.

'We're talking about a thousand million dollars' loss if the worst comes to the worst,' he remarked to his personal aide. 'Who the hell *are* these people?'

The leader of these people sat at the epicentre of the growing storm and faced a bearded Norwegian captain in the day cabin beneath the starboard wing of the *Freya*'s bridge. The curtains were drawn back and the sun shone warmly. From the windows a panoramic view was shown of the silent foredecks, running away a quarter of a mile to the tiny fo'c's'le.

The miniature, shrouded figure of a man sat high on the bow apron above the stem looking out and around him at the glittering blue sea. Either side of the vessel the same blue water lay flat and calm, a mild zephyr ruffling its surface. During the morning that breeze had gently blown away the invisible clouds of poisonous inert gases that had welled out from the holds when the inspection hatches were lifted; it was now safe to walk along the deck, or the man on the fo'c's'le would not be there.

The temperature in the cabin was still stabilized, the air conditioning having taken over from the central heating when the sun became hotter through the double-glazed windows.

Thor Larsen sat where he had sat all morning, at one end of his main table, with Andrew Drake at the other.

Since the argument between the 0900 radio call and 1000 there had been mainly silence between them. The tension of waiting was beginning to make itself felt. Each knew that across the water in both directions frantic preparations would be taking place; firstly to try and estimate exactly what had happened aboard the *Freya* during the night, and secondly to estimate what if anything could be done about it.

Larsen knew no one would do anything, take any initiative, until the noon broadcast of demands. In that sense the intense young man facing him was not stupid. He had elected to keep the authorities guessing. By forcing Larsen to speak in his stead, he had given no clue to his identity nor his origins. Even his motivations were unknown outside the cabin in which they sat. And the authorities would want to know more, to analyse the tapes of the broadcasts, identify the speech patterns and ethnic origins of the speaker, before taking action. The man who called himself Svoboda was denying them that information, undermining the self-confidence of the men he had challenged to defy him.

He was also giving the press ample time to learn of the disaster, but not the terms; letting them evaluate the scale of the catastrophe if the *Freya* blew up, so that their head of steam, their capacity to pressure the authorities, would be well-prepared ahead of the demands. When the demands came, they would appear mild compared to the alternative, thus subjecting the authorities to press pressure before they had considered the demands.

Larsen, who knew what the demands would be, could not see how the authorities could refuse. The alternative was too terrible for all of them. If Svoboda had simply kidnapped a politician, as the Baader-Meinhof people had kidnapped Hans-Martin Schleyer, or the Red Brigades Aldo Moro, he might have been refused his friends' release. But he had elected to destroy five coasts, one sea, thirty lives and a thousand million dollars of money.

'Why are these two men so important to you?' asked Larsen suddenly.

The younger man stared back.

'They're friends,' he said.

'No,' said Larsen. 'I recall from last January reading that they were two Jews from Lvov who had been refused permission to emigrate, so they hijacked a Russian airliner and forced it to land in West Berlin. How does that produce your popular uprising?'

'Never mind,' said his captor. 'It is five to twelve. We return to the bridge.'

Nothing had changed on the bridge, except that there was an extra terrorist there, curled up asleep in the corner, his gun still clutched in his hand. He was masked, like the one who patrolled the radar and sonar screens. Svoboda asked the man something in the language Larsen now knew to be Ukrainian. The man shook his head and replied in the same language. At a word from Svoboda the masked man turned his gun on Larsen.

Svoboda walked over to the scanners and read them. There was a peripheral ring of clear water round the *Freya* at least to five miles on the western, southern and northern sides. To the east the sea was clear to the Dutch coast. He strode out through the door leading to the bridge-wing, turned and called upwards. From high above, Larsen heard the man on top of the funnel assembly shout back.

Svoboda returned to the bridge. 'Come,' he said to the captain, 'your audience is waiting. One attempt at a trick, and I shoot one of your seamen, as promised.'

Larsen took the handset of the radio-telephone and pressed for transmit.

'Maas Control, Maas Control, this is the *Freya*.'

Though he could not know it, over fifty different offices received that call. Five major intelligence services were listening, plucking channel twenty out of the ether with their sophisticated listeners. The words were heard and relayed simultaneously to the National Security Agency in Washington, to the SIS, the French SDECE, the West German BND, the Soviet Union and the various services of Holland, Belgium and Sweden. There were ships' radio officers listening, radio hams and journalists.

A voice came back from the Hook of Holland. '*Freya*, this is Maas Control. Go ahead, please.'

Thor Larsen read from his sheet of paper. '"This is Captain Thor Larsen. I wish to speak personally to the Prime Minister of the Netherlands."'

A new voice, speaking English, came on the radio from the Hook.

'Captain Larsen, this is Jan Grayling. I am the Prime Minister of the Kingdom of the Netherlands. Are you all right?'

In the *Freya* Svoboda clapped his hand over the mouthpiece of the telephone.

'No questions,' he said to Larsen. 'Just ask if the West German ambassador is present, and get his name.'

'Please ask no questions, Prime Minister. I am not permitted to answer them. Is the West German ambassador with you?'

In Maas Control the microphone was passed to Konrad Voss.

'Here is the ambassador of the Federal Republic of Germany,' he said. 'My name is Konrad Voss.'

On the bridge of the *Freya* Svoboda nodded at Larsen.

'That's right,' he said, 'go ahead and read it out.'

The seven men grouped around the console in Maas Control listened in silence. One premier, one ambassador, one psychiatrist, a radio engineer in case of a transmission breakdown, van Gelder of the Port Authority and the duty officer. All other shipping traffic had now been diverted to a spare channel. The two tape recorders whirled silently. Volume was switched high; Thor Larsen's voice echoed in the room.

'"I repeat what I told you at nine this morning. The *Freya* is in the hands of partisans. Explosive devices have been placed which would, if detonated, blow her apart. These devices can be detonated at the touch of a button. I repeat, at the touch of a button. No attempt whatever must be made to approach her, board her or attack her in any way. In such an event the detonator button will be pressed instantly. The men concerned have convinced me they are prepared to die rather than give in.

'"I continue: if any approach at all is made, by surface craft or light aircraft, one of my seamen will be executed, or twenty thousand tons of crude oil vented, or both. Here are the demands of the partisans:

'"The two prisoners of conscience, David Lazareff and Lev Mishkin, presently in jail at Tegel in West Berlin, are to be liberated. They are to be flown by a West German civilian jet from West Berlin to Israel. Prior to this, the premier of the State of Israel is to give a public guarantee that they will be neither repatriated to the Soviet Union, nor extradited back to West Germany, nor re-imprisoned in Israel.

'"Their liberation must take place at dawn tomorrow. The Israeli guarantee of safe conduct and freedom must be given by midnight tonight. Failure to comply will place the entire responsibility for the outcome on the shoulders of West Germany and Israel. That is all. There will be no more contact until the demands have been met."'

The radio-telephone went dead with a click. The silence persisted inside the control building. Jan Grayling looked at Konrad Voss. The West German envoy shrugged.

'I must contact Bonn urgently,' he said.

'I can tell you that Captain Larsen is under some strain,' said the psychiatrist.

'Thank you very much,' said Grayling. 'So am I. Gentlemen, what has just been said cannot fail to be made public within the hour. I suggest we return to our offices. I shall prepare a statement for the one o'clock news. Mr Ambassador, I fear the pressure will now begin to swing towards Bonn.'

'Indeed it will,' said Voss. 'I must be back inside the embassy as soon as possible.'

'Then accompany me to The Hague,' said Grayling. 'I have police outriders, and we can talk in the car.'

Aides brought the two tapes, and the group left for The Hague, fifteen minutes up the coast. When they were gone Dirk van Gelder walked up to the flat roof where Harry Wennerstrom would have held his lunch by Gelder's permission, the other guests looking eagerly to seaward, as they supped champagne and salmon sandwiches, to catch the first glimpse of the leviathan.

Now perhaps she would never come, thought van Gelder, staring out at the blue water. He too had his master's ticket, a Dutch merchant navy captain until he was offered the shore job with the promise of a regular life with his wife and children. As a seaman he thought of the *Freya*'s crew, locked far beneath the waves, waiting helplessly for rescue or death. But as a seaman he would not be in charge of negotiations. It was out of his hands now. Smoother men, calculating in political rather than human terms, would take over.

He thought of the towering Norwegian skipper he had never met but whose picture he had seen, now facing madmen armed with guns and dynamite, and wondered how he would have reacted had it ever happened to him. He had warned that this could happen one day, that the supertankers were too unprotected and highly dangerous. But the money had spoken louder; the more powerful argument had been the extra cost of installing the necessary devices to make tankers like banks and explosive stores, both of which in a way they were. No one had listened, and no one ever would. People were concerned about airliners because they could crash on houses; but not about tankers which were out of sight. So the politicians had not insisted, and the merchants had not volunteered. Now, because super-tankers could be taken like piggy-banks, a captain and his crew of twenty-nine might die like rats in a swirl of oil and water.

He ground a cigarette under his heel into the tar-felt of the roof and looked again at the empty horizon.

'You poor bastards,' he said, 'you poor bloody bastards. If only they'd listened.'

13

If the reaction of the media to the 0900 transmission had been muted and speculative, due to the uncertainty of the reliability of their informants, the reaction to the 1200 broadcast was frantic.

From 1200 onwards there was no doubt whatever what had happened to the *Freya*, nor what had been said by Captain Larsen on his radio-telephone to Maas Control. Too many people had been listening.

Banner headlines that had been available for the noon editions of the evening papers, prepared at 1000 hours, were swept away. Those that went to press at 1230 were stronger in tone and size. There were no more question marks at the end of sentences. Editorial columns were hastily prepared, specialist correspondents in matters of shipping and the environment required to produce instant assessments within the hour.

Radio and television programmes were interrupted throughout Europe's Friday lunch-hour to beam the news to listeners and viewers.

On the dot of five past twelve a man in a motorcyclist's helmet, with goggles and scarf drawn round the lower part of the face, had walked calmly into the lobby of 85 Fleet Street, and deposited an envelope addressed to the news editor of the Press Association. No one later recalled the man; dozens of such messengers walk into that lobby every day.

By twelve-fifteen the news editor was opening the envelope. It contained the transcript of the statement read by Captain Larsen fifteen minutes earlier, though it must have been prepared well before that. The news editor reported the delivery to his editor-in-chief who told the metropolitan police. That did not stop the text going straight on to the wires, both of the PA and their cousins downstairs, Reuters, who put the text across the world.

Leaving Fleet Street, Miroslav Kaminsky dumped his helmet, goggles and scarf in a dustbin, took a taxi to Heathrow Airport and boarded the 1415 plane for Tel Aviv.

By two o'clock the editorial pressure on both the Dutch and West German governments was beginning to build up. Neither had had any time to consider in peace and quiet the reactions they should make to the demands.

Both governments began to receive a flood of phone calls urging them to agree to release Mishkin and Lazareff rather than face the disaster promised by the destruction of the *Freya* off their coasts.

By one o'clock the German ambassador to The Hague was speaking directly to his foreign minister in Bonn, Klaus Hagowitz, who interrupted the Chancellor at his desk-lunch. The text of the 1200 broadcast was already in Bonn, once from the BND intelligence service and once on the Reuters teleprinter. Every newspaper office in Germany also had the text from Reuters, and the telephone lines to the chancellery press office were jammed with calls.

At one forty-five the chancellery put out a statement to the effect that an emergency Cabinet meeting had been called for three o'clock to consider the entire situation. Ministers cancelled their plans to leave Bonn at the weekend for their constituencies. Lunches were ill-digested.

The governor of Tegal Jail put down his telephone at two minutes past two with a certain deference. It was not often the federal justice minister cut clean through the protocol of communicating with the governing mayor of West Berlin and called him personally.

He picked up the internal phone and gave an order to his secretary. Doubtless the Berlin senate would be in contact in due course with the same request, but so long as the governing mayor was out of touch at lunch somewhere, he would not refuse the minister from Bonn.

Three minutes later one of his senior prison officers entered the office.

'Have you heard the two o'clock news?' asked the governor.

It was only five past two. The officer pointed out that he had been on his rounds when the bleeper in his breast pocket buzzed, requiring him to go straight to a wall-phone and check in. No, he had not heard the news. The governor told him of the noon demand of the terrorists on board the *Freya*. The officer's jaw dropped open.

'One for the book, isn't it?' said the governor. 'It looks as it we shall be in the news within minutes. So, batten down hatches. I've given orders to main gate: no admissions by anyone other than staff. All press enquiries to the authorities at City Hall.

'Now, as regards Mishkin and Lazareff. I want the guard on that floor and particularly in that corridor trebled. Cancel free periods to raise enough staff. Transfer all other prisoners in that corridor to other cells or other levels. Seal the place. A group of intelligence people are flying in from Bonn to ask them who their friends in the North Sea are. Any questions?'

The prison officer swallowed and shook his head.

'Now,' resumed the governor, 'we don't know how long this emergency will last. When were you due off duty?'

'Six o'clock tonight, sir.'

'Returning on Monday morning at eight?'

'No, sir. On Sunday night at midnight. I go on night-shift next week.'

'I'll have to ask you to work right on through,' said the governor. 'Of course, we'll make up the free time to you later with a generous bonus. But I'd like you right on top of the job from here on. Agreed?'

'Yes, sir. Whatever you say. I'll get on with it now.'

The governor, who liked to adopt a comradely attitude with his staff, came around the desk and clapped the man on the shoulder.

'You're a good fellow, Jahn. I don't know what we'd do without you.'

Squadron Leader Mark Latham stared down the runway, heard his take-off clearance from the control tower and nodded to his co-pilot. The younger man's gloved hand eased the four throttles slowly open; in the wing-roots four Rolls-Royce Spey engines rose in pitch to push out 45,000 pounds of thrust and the Nimrod Mark Two climbed away from RAF station Kinloss and turned southeast from Scotland towards the North Sea and the Channel.

What the thirty-one-year-old squadron leader of Strike Command was flying he knew to be about the best aircraft for submarine and shipping surveillance in the world. With its crew of twelve, improved power plants, performance and surveillance aids, the Nimrod could either skim the waves at low level, slow and steady, listening on electronic ears to the sounds of underwater movements, or cruise at altitude, hour after hour, two engines shut down for fuel economy, observing an enormous area of ocean beneath it.

Its radars would pick up the slightest movement of a metallic substance down there on the water's surface, its cameras could photograph by day and night; it was unaffected by storm or snow, hail or sleet, fog or wind, light or dark. Its Datalink computers could process the received information, identify what it saw for what it was, and transmit the whole picture, in visual or electronic terms, back to base or to a Royal Navy vessel tapped in to Datalink.

His orders, that sunny spring Friday, were to take up station 15,000 feet above the *Freya* and keep circling until relieved.

'She's coming on screen, skipper,' Latham's radar operator called down the intercom. Back in the hull of the Nimrod the operator was gazing at his scanner screen, picking out the area of traffic-free water round the *Freya* on its northern side, watching the large blip move from the periphery towards the centre of the screen as they approached.

'Cameras on,' said Latham calmly. In the belly of the Nimrod the F.126 daytime camera swivelled like a gun, spotted the *Freya* and locked on. Automatically it adjusted range and focus for maximum definition. Like moles in their blind hull, the crew behind him saw the *Freya* come on to their picture screen. From now on the aircraft could fly all over the sky, the cameras would stay locked on the *Freya*, adjusting for distance and light-changes, swivelling in their housings to compensate for the circling of the Nimrod. Even if the *Freya* began to move, they would still stay on her, like an unblinking eye, until given fresh orders.

'And transmit,' said Latham.

The Datalink began to send the pictures back to Britain, and thence to London. When the Nimrod was overhead the *Freya* she banked to port, and from his left-hand seat S/L Latham looked down. Behind and below him the camera zoomed closer, beating the human eye. It picked out the lone figure of the terrorist in the forepeak, masked face staring upwards at the silver swallow three miles above him. It picked out the second terrorist on top of the funnel, and zoomed until his black balaclava filled the screen. The man cradled a submachine carbine in his arms in the sunshine far below.

'There they are, the bastards,' called the camera operator. The Nimrod established a gentle, rate one turn above the *Freya*, went over to the automatic pilot, closed down two engines, reduced power to maximum endurance setting on the other two and began to do its job. It circled, watched and waited, reporting everything back to base. Mark Latham ordered his co-pilot to take over, unbuckled and left the flight deck. He went aft to the four-man dining area, visited the toilet, washed his hands and sat down with a vacuum-heated lunch box. It was, he reflected, really rather a comfortable way to go to war.

The gleaming Volvo of the police chief of Alesund ground up the gravel drive of the timber-construction, ranch-style house at Bogneset, twenty minutes out from the town centre, and halted by the rough-stone porch.

Trygve Dahl was a contemporary of Thor Larsen. They had grown up together in Alesund, and Dahl had entered the force as a police cadet about the time Larsen had joined the merchant marine. He had known Lisa Larsen since his friend had brought the young bride back from Oslo after their marriage. His own children knew Kurt and Kristina, played with them at school, sailed with them in the long summer holidays.

Damn it, he thought as he climbed out of the Volvo, what the hell do I tell her?

There had been no reply on the telephone, which meant she must be out. The children would be at school. If she was shopping, perhaps she had met someone who had told her already. He rang the bell and, when it did not answer, walked round to the back.

Lisa Larsen liked to keep a large vegetable garden, and he found her feeding carrot tops to Kristina's pet rabbit. She looked up and smiled when she saw him coming round the house.

She doesn't know, he thought. She pushed the remainder of the carrots through the wire of the cage and came over to him, pulling off her garden gloves.

'Trygve, how nice to see you. What brings you out of town?'

'Lisa, have you listened to the news this morning on the radio?'

She considered the question.

'I listened to the eight o'clock over breakfast. I've been out here since then, in the garden.'

'You didn't answer the telephone?'

For the first time a shadow came into her bright brown eyes. The smile faded.

'No. I wouldn't hear it. Has it been ringing?'

'Look, Lisa, be calm. Something has happened. No, not to the children. To Thor.'

She went pale beneath the honey-coloured outdoor tan.

Carefully, Trygve Dahl told her what had happened since the small hours of the morning, far to the south off Rotterdam.

'So far as we know, he's perfectly all right. Nothing has happened to him, and nothing will. The Germans are bound to release these two men, and all will be well.'

She did not cry. She stood quite calmly amid the spring lettuce and said, 'I want to go to him.'

The police chief was relieved. He could have expected it of her, but he was relieved. Now he could organize things. He was better at that.

'Harald Wennerstrom's private jet is due at the airport in twenty minutes,' he said. 'I'll run you there. He called me an hour ago. He thought you might want to go to Rotterdam, to be close. Now don't worry about the children. I'm having them picked up from school before they hear from the teachers. We'll look after them; they can stay with us, of course.'

Twenty minutes later she was in the rear seat of the car with Dahl, heading fast back towards Alesund. The police chief used his radio to hold the ferry across to the airfield. Just after one-thirty the Jetstream in the silver and ice-blue livery of the Nordia Line howled down the runway, swept out over the waters of the bay and climbed towards the south.

Since the sixties and particularly through the seventies the growing outbreaks of terrorism caused the formation of a routine procedure on the part of the British government to facilitate the handling of them. The principal procedure is called the crisis management committee.

When the crisis is serious enough to involve numerous departments and sections, the committee, grouping liaison officers from all these departments, meets at a central point close to the heart of government to pool information and correlate decisions and actions. This central point is a well-protected chamber two floors below the parquet of the Cabinet Office on Whitehall and a few steps across the lawn from 10 Downing Street. In this room meets the United Cabinet Office Review Group (National Emergency), or UNICORNE.

Surrounding the main meeting room are smaller offices; a separate telephone switchboard, linking the Unicorne with every department of state through direct lines that cannot be interfered with; a teleprinter room fitted with the printers of the main news agencies; a telex room and radio room; and a room for secretaries with typewriters and copiers. There is even a small kitchen where a trusty commissionaire prepares coffee and light snacks.

The men who grouped under the chairmanship of Cabinet Secretary Sir Julian Flannery just after noon that Friday represented all the departments he adjudged might conceivably be involved.

At this stage no cabinet ministers were present, though each had sent a representative of at least assistant under-secretary level. These included the Foreign Office, Home Office, Defence Ministry, Department of Trade and Industry, Departments of the Environment, and of Energy, and the Ministry of Agriculture and Fisheries.

Assisting them were a bevy of specialist experts, including three scientists in various disciplines, notably explosives, ships and pollution; the vice-chief of defence staff (a vice-admiral), someone from Defence Intelligence, from MI5, from the SIS, a Royal Air Force group captain, and a senior Royal Marine colonel called Tim Holmes.

'Well now, gentlemen,' Sir Julian Flannery began, 'we have all had time to read the transcript of the noon broadcast from Captain Larsen. First I think we ought to have a few indisputable facts. May we begin with this ship, the . . . er . . . *Freya*. What do we know about her?'

The shipping expert, coming under the Trade and Industry people, found all eyes on him.

'I've been to Lloyd's this morning and secured the plan of the *Freya*,' he said briefly. 'I have it here. It's detailed down to the last nut and bolt.'

He went on for ten minutes, the plan spread on the table, describing the size, cargo capacity and construction of the *Freya* in clear, layman's language.

When he had finished the expert from the Department of Energy was called on. He had an aide bring to the table a five-foot-long model of a supertanker.

'I borrowed this, this morning,' he said, 'from British Petroleum. It's a model of their supertanker the British *Princess*, quarter of a million tons, but the design differences are few; the *Freya* is just bigger, really.'

With the aid of the model of the *Princess* he went on to point out where the bridge was, where the captain's cabin would be, where the cargo holds and ballast holds would probably be, adding that the exact locations of these holds would be known when the Nordia Line could pass them over to London.

The surrounding men watched the demonstration and listened with attention. None more than Colonel Holmes; of all those present he would be the one whose fellow marines might have to storm the vessel and wipe out her captors. He knew those men would want to know every nook and cranny of the real *Freya* before they went on board.

'There is one last thing,' said the scientist from Energy, 'she's full of Mubarraq.'

'God,' said one of the other men at the table. Sir Julian Flannery regarded the speaker benignly.

'Yes, Dr Henderson?'

The man who had spoken was the scientist from Warren Springs Laboratory who had accompanied the representative of Agriculture and Fisheries.

'What I mean,' said the doctor in his unrecycled Scottish accent, 'is that Mubarraq, which is a crude oil from Abu Dhabi, has some of the properties of diesel fuel.'

He went on to explain that when crude oil is spilled on the sea, it contains both the 'lighter fractions' which evaporate into the air, and the 'heavier fractions' which cannot evaporate and which are what viewers see washed on to the beaches as thick black gunge.

'What I mean is,' he concluded, 'it'll spread all over the bloody place. It'll spread from coast to coast before the lighter fractions evaporate. It'll poison the whole North Sea for weeks, denying the marine life the oxygen it needs to live.'

'I see,' said Sir Julian gravely. 'Thank you, doctor.'

There followed information from other experts. The explosives man from Royal Engineers explained that, placed in the right areas, industrial dynamite could destroy a ship this size.

'It's also a question of the sheer latent strength contained in the weight represented by a million tons, of oil or anything. If the holes are made in the right places, the unbalanced mass of her would pull her apart. There's one last thing; the message read out by Captain Larsen mentioned the phrase "at the touch of a button". He then repeated that phrase. It seems to me there must be nearly a dozen charges placed. That phrase "the touch of a button" seems to indicate triggering by radio impulse.'

'Is that possible?' asked Sir Julian.

'Perfectly possible,' said the sapper, and explained how an oscillator worked.

'Surely, they could have wires to each charge, linked to a plunger,' asked Sir Julian.'

'It's a question of the weight again,' said the engineer. 'The weight of that number of miles of flex would nearly sink the launch on which these terrorists arrived.'

There was more information about the destructive capacity of the oil by pollution, the few chances of rescuing the trapped crewmen, and SIS admitted they had no information that might help identify the terrorists from among foreign groups of such people.

The man from MI5 who was actually the deputy chief of C-4 department within that body, the section dealing exclusively with terrorism as it affected Britain, underlined the strange nature of the demands of the captors of the *Freya*.

'These men, Mishkin and Lazareff,' he pointed out, 'are Jewish. Hijackers who tried to escape from the USSR and ended up shooting a flight captain. One has to assume that those seeking to free them are their friends or admirers. That tends to indicate fellow-Jews. The only ones who fit into that category are those of the Jewish Defense League. But so far they just demonstrate and throw things. In our files we haven't had Jews threatening to blow people to pieces to free their friends since the Irgun and the Stern Gang.'

'Oh dear, one hopes they don't start that again,' observed Sir Julian. 'If not them, then who else?'

The man from C-4 shrugged.

'We don't know,' he admitted. 'We can notice no one on our files conspicuous by being missing, nor do we have a trace from what Captain Larsen has broadcast to indicate their origins. This morning I thought of Arabs, even Irish. But neither would lift a finger for imprisoned Jews. It's a blank wall.'

Still photographs were brought in, taken by the Nimrod an hour earlier, some showing the masked men on the lookout. They were keenly examined.

'MAT 49,' said Colonel Holmes briefly, studying the submachine gun one of the men cradled in his arms. 'It's French.'

'Ah,' said Sir Julian, 'now perhaps we have something. These blighters could be French?'

'Not necessarily,' said Holmes. 'You can buy these things in the underworld. The Paris underworld is famous for its taste for submachine guns.'

At three-thirty Sir Julian Flannery brought the meeting into recess. It was agreed to keep the Nimrod circling above the *Freya* until further notice. The vice-chief of defence staff put forward and had accepted his proposal to divert a naval warship to take up station just over five miles west of the *Freya* to watch her also in case of an attempt by the terrorists to leave under cover of darkness. The Nimrod would spot them, and pass their position to the navy. The warship would easily overhaul the fishing launch still tied by the *Freya*'s side.

The Foreign Office agreed to ask to be informed of any decision by West Germany and Israel on the terrorists' demands.

'There does not, after all, appear much that Her Majesty's government can do at the present moment,' Sir Julian pointed out. 'The decision is up to the Israeli Prime Minister and the West German Chancellor. Personally I cannot see what else they can do, except to let these wretched young men go to Israel, repugnant though the idea of yielding to blackmail must be.'

When the men left the room only Colonel Holmes of the marines stayed behind. He sat down again and stared at the model of the quarter-million ton British Petroleum tanker in front of him.

Supposing they don't, he said to himself.

Carefully he began to measure the distance in feet from the sea to the stern taffrail.

The Swedish pilot of the Jetstream was at 15,000 feet off the Friesian Islands, preparing to let down into Schiedam Airfield outside Rotterdam. He turned round and called something to the petite woman who was his passenger. She unbuckled and came forward to where he sat.

'I asked if you wanted to see the *Freya*,' the pilot repeated. The woman nodded.

The Jetstream banked away to the sea and five minutes later tilted gently onto one wing. From her seat, face pressed to the tiny porthole, Lisa Larsen looked down. Far below, in a blue sea, like a grey sardine nailed to the water, the *Freya* lay at anchor. There were no ships around her; she was quite alone in her captivity.

Even from 15,000 feet, through the clear spring air, Lisa Larsen could make out where the bridge would be, where the starboard side of that bridge was; below it she knew her husband was facing a man with a gun pointed straight at his chest, with dynamite beneath his feet. She did not know whether the man with the gun was mad, brutal or reckless. That he must be a fanatic she knew.

Two tears welled out of her eyes and ran down her cheeks. When she whispered her breath misted the perspex disc in front of her.

'Thor, my darling, please come out of there alive.'

The Jetstream banked again and began its long drop towards Schiedam. The Nimrod, miles away across the sky, watched it go.

'Who was that?' asked the radar operator of no one in particular.

'Who was what?' replied a sonar operator, having nothing to do.

'Small executive jet just banked over the *Freya*, had a look and went off to Rotterdam,' said the radar man.

'Probably the owner checking on his property,' said the crew's wit from the radio console.

On the *Freya* the two lookouts gazed through eye-slits after the tiny sliver of metal high above as it headed east towards the Dutch coast. They did not report it to their leader; it was well above 10,000 feet.

The West German Cabinet meeting began just after 3 p.m. in the Chancellery Office, with Dietrich Busch in the chair as usual. He went straight to the point as he had a habit of doing.

'Let's be clear of one thing: this is not Mogadishu all over again. This time we do not have a German plane with a German crew and mainly German passengers on an airstrip whose authorities were prepared to be collaborative towards us. This is a Swedish vessel with a Norwegian captain in international waters; she has crewmen from five countries including the US, and American-owned cargo insured by a British company, and her destruction would affect at least five coastal nations, including ourselves. Foreign minister?'

Hagowitz informed his colleagues he had already received polite queries from Finland, Norway, Sweden, Denmark, Holland, Belgium, France and Britain regarding the kind of decision the Federal government might come to. After all, they held Mishkin and Lazareff.

'They are being courteous enough not to exert any pressure to influence our decision, but I have no doubt they would view a refusal on our part to send Mishkin and Lazareff to Israel with the deepest misgivings,' he said.

'Once you start giving in to this terrorist blackmail it never ends,' put in the defence minister.

'Dietrich, we gave in over the Peter Lorenz affair years ago and paid for it. The very terrorists we freed came back and operated again. We stood up to them over Mogadishu and won; we stood up again over Schleyer and had a corpse on our hands. But at least those were pretty well all-German affairs. This isn't. The lives at stake aren't German; the property isn't German. Moreover, the hijackers in Berlin aren't from a German terrorist group. They're Jews who tried to get away from Russia the only way they knew how. Frankly, it puts us in the devil of a spot,' Hagowitz concluded.

'Any chance that it's a bluff, a confidence trick; that they really can't destroy the *Freya* or kill her crew?' someone asked.

The interior minister shook his head.

'We can't bank on that. These pictures the British have just transmitted to us show the armed and masked men are real enough. I've sent them along to the leader of GSG 9 to see what he thinks. But the trouble is, approaching a ship with all-round, over-and-under radar and sonar cover is not their area of expertise. It would mean divers or frogmen.'

He was referring by GSG 9 to the ultra-tough unit of West German commandos drawn from the border troops who stormed the hijacked aircraft at Mogadishu five years earlier.

The argument continued for an hour: whether to concede the terrorists' demands in view of the internationality of the probable victims of a refusal, and accept the inevitable protests from Moscow; or whether to refuse and call their bluff; or whether to consult with the British allies about the idea of storming the *Freya*. A compromise view of adopting delaying tactics, stalling for time, testing the determination of the *Freya*'s captors, seemed to be gaining ground. At four-fifteen there was a quiet knock on the door. Chancellor Busch frowned; he did not like interruptions.

'*Herein,*' he called. An aide entered the room and whispered urgently in the Chancellor's ear. The head of the Federal government paled.

'*Du lieber Gott,*' he breathed.

When the light aircraft, later traced as a privately owned Cessna on charter from Le Touquet Airfield on the northern French coast, began to approach, she was spotted by three different air traffic control zones, at Heathrow, Brussels and Amsterdam. She was flying due north, and the radars put her at 5000 feet, on track for the *Freya*. The ether began to crackle furiously.

'Unidentified light aircraft at position . . . identify yourself and turn back. You are entering a prohibited area. . . .'

French and English was used, later Dutch. It had no effect. Either the pilot had switched off his radio or was on the wrong channel. The operators on the ground began to sweep through the wave bands.

The circling Nimrod picked the aircraft up on radar and tried to contact her.

On board the Cessna the pilot turned to his passenger in despair.

'They'll have my licence,' he yelled. 'They're going mad down there.'

'Switch off,' the passenger shouted back. 'Don't worry, nothing will happen. You never heard them, OK?'

The passenger gripped his camera and adjusted the telephoto lens. He began to sight up on the approaching supertanker. In the forepeak the masked lookout stiffened and squinted against the sun, now in the southwest. The plane was coming from due south. After watching for several seconds he took a walkie-talkie from his anorak and spoke sharply into it.

On the bridge one of his colleagues heard the message, peered forward through the panoramic screen, and walked hurriedly outside on to the wing. Here he too could hear the engine note. He re-entered the bridge and shook his sleeping colleague awake, snapping several orders in Ukrainian. The man ran downstairs to the door of the day cabin and knocked.

Inside the cabin, Thor Larsen and Andriy Drach, both looking unshaven and more haggard than twelve hours earlier, were still at the table, the gun by the Ukrainian's right hand. A foot away from him was his powerful transistor radio, picking up the latest news. The masked man entered on his command and spoke in Ukrainian. His leader scowled and ordered the man to take over in the cabin.

Drake left the cabin quickly, raced up to the bridge and out on to the wing. As he did so he pulled on his black mask. From the bridge he gazed up as the Cessna, banking at 1000 feet, performed one orbit of the *Freya* and flew back to the south, climbing steadily. While it turned he had seen the great zoom lens poking down at him.

Inside the aircraft, the freelance cameraman was exultant.

'Fantastic,' he shouted at the pilot. 'Completely exclusive. The magazines will pay their right arms for this.'

Andriy Drach returned to the bridge and issued a rapid stream of orders.

Over the walkie-talkie he told the man up there to continue his watch. The bridge lookout was sent below to summon two men who were catching sleep. When all three returned he gave them further instructions. When he returned to the day cabin, he did not dismiss the extra guard.

'I think it's time I told those stupid bastards over there in Europe that I am not joking,' he told Thor Larsen.

Five minutes later the camera operator on the Nimrod called over the intercom to his captain.

'There's something happening down there, skipper.'

Squadron Leader Latham left the flight deck and walked back to the centre section of the hull where the visual image of what the cameras were photographing was on display. Two men were walking down the deck of the *Freya*, the great wall of superstructure behind them, the long lonely deck ahead. One of the men, the one at the rear, was in black from head to foot, with a submachine gun. The one ahead wore sneakers, casual slacks and a nylon-type anorak with three horizontal black stripes across its back. The hood was up against the chill afternoon breeze.

'Looks like a terrorist at the back, but a seaman in front,' said the camera operator. Latham nodded. He could not see the colours; his pictures were monochrome.

'Give me a closer look,' he said, 'and transmit.'

The camera zoomed down until the frame occupied forty feet of foredeck, both men walking in the centre of the picture.

Captain Thor Larsen could see the colours. He gazed through the wide forward windows of his cabin beneath the bridge in disbelief. Behind him the guard with the machine gun stood well back, muzzle trained in the middle of the Norwegian's white sweater.

Halfway down the foredeck, reduced by distance to matchstick figures, the second man, in black, stopped, raised his machine gun and aimed at the back in front of him. Even through the glazing the crackle of the one-second burst could be heard. The figure in the pillar-box red anorak arched as if kicked in the spine, threw up its arms, pitched forward, rolled once and came to rest half obscured beneath the inspection catwalk.

Thor Larsen slowly closed his eyes. When the ship had been taken over, his third mate, Danish-American Tom Keller, had been wearing fawn slacks and a light nylon windbreaker in bright red with three black stripes across the back. Larsen leaned his forehead against the back of his hand on the glass. Then he straightened, turned to the man he knew as Svoboda, and stared at him.

Andriy Drach stared back.

'I warned them,' he said angrily. 'I told them exactly what would happen, and they thought they could play games. Now they know they can't.'

Twenty minutes later the still pictures showing the sequence of what had happened on the deck of the *Freya* were coming out of a machine in the heart of London. Twenty minutes after that, the details in verbal terms were rattling off a teleprinter in the Federal Chancellery in Bonn. It was 4.30 p.m.

Chancellor Busch looked at his cabinet.

'I regret to have to inform you,' he said, 'that one hour ago a private plane apparently sought to take pictures of the *Freya* from close range, about a thousand feet. Ten minutes later the terrorists walked one of the crew halfway down the deck and, under the cameras of the British Nimrod above them, executed him. His body now lies half under the catwalk, half under the sky.'

There was dead silence in the room.

'Can he be identified?' asked one of the ministers in a low voice.

'No, his face was mainly covered by the hood of his anorak.'

'Bastards,' said the defence minister. 'Now thirty families all over Scandinavia will be in anguish instead of one. They're really turning the knife.'

'In the wake of this, so will the four governments of Scandinavia, and I shall have to answer their ambassadors,' said Hagowitz. 'I really don't think we have any alternative.'

When the hands were raised, they were in majority for Hagowitz's proposal: that he instruct the German ambassador to Israel to seek an urgent interview with the Israeli premier and ask from him, at Germany's request, the guarantee the terrorists had demanded. Following which, if it was given, the Federal government would announce that with regret it had no alternative, in order to spare further misery to innocent men and women outside West Germany, but to release Mishkin and Lazareff to Israel.

'The terrorists have given the Israeli premier until midnight to offer that guarantee,' said Chancellor Busch. 'And ourselves until dawn to put these hijackers on a plane. We'll hold our announcement until Jerusalem agrees. Without that, there is nothing we can do anyway.'

At 5 p.m. the lookouts were changed. The men from the fo'c's'le and funnel top, who had been there for ten hours, were allowed to return chilled and stiff to the accommodation for food, warmth and sleep. For the night-watch they were replaced by others equipped with walkie-talkies and powerful torches.

By agreement between the NATO allies concerned, the RAF Nimrod remained the only aircraft in the sky above the *Freya*, circling endlessly, watching and noting, sending pictures back to base whenever there was anything to show; pictures which immediately went to London and to the capital of the relevant country.

The allied agreement on the Nimrod did not extend to surface ships. Each coastal nation wanted an on-site observer from its own navy. During the late afternoon the French light cruiser *Montcalm* stole quietly out of the south and hove-to just over five nautical miles from the *Freya*. Out of the north, where she had been cruising off the Friesians, came the Dutch missile frigate *Breda*, who stopped six nautical miles to the north of the helpless tanker. She was joined by the German missile frigate *Brunner*, and the frigates lay five cable lengths away from each other, both watching the dim shape on the southern horizon.

From the Scottish port of Leith where she had been on a courtesy visit the HMS *Argyll* put to sea, and as the first evening star appeared in the cloudless sky, she took up her station due west of the *Freya*. She was a guided-missile light cruiser, known as a DLG, of just under 6000 tons, armed with batteries of Exocet missiles. Her modern gas turbine and steam engines had enabled her to put to sea at a moment's notice, and deep in her hull the Datalink computer she carried was tapped into the Datalink of the Nimrod circling 15,000 feet above in the darkening sky. Towards her stern, one step up from the after deck, she carried her own Westland Wessex helicopter.

Beneath the water, the sonar ears of the warships surrounded the *Freya* on three sides; above the water the radar scanners swept the ocean constantly. With the Nimrod above, *Freya* was cocooned in an invisible shroud of electronic surveillance. She lay silent and inert as the sun prepared to fall over the English coast.

It was five o'clock in Western Europe but seven in Israel when the West German ambassador asked for a personal audience with Premier Benyamin Golen. It was pointed out to him at once that the Sabbath had started one hour before and that, as a devout Jew, the premier was at rest in his own home. Nevertheless the message was relayed, because neither the Prime Minister's private office nor he himself was unaware of what was happening in the North Sea. Indeed, since the 0900 broadcast from Thor Larsen the Israeli intelligence service, Mossad, had been keeping Jerusalem informed, and following the demands made at noon concerning Israel the most copious position papers had been prepared. Before the official start of Sabbath at six o'clock, Premier Golen had read them all.

'I am not prepared to break *Shabbat* and drive to the office,' he told his aide, who telephoned him with the news, 'even though I am now answering this telephone. And it is rather a long way to walk. Ask the ambassador to call on me personally.'

Ten minutes later the German embassy car drew up outside the premier's ascetically modest house in the suburbs of Jerusalem. When the envoy was shown in, he was apologetic.

After the traditional greetings of '*Shabbat Shalom*,' the ambassador said: 'Prime Minister, I would not have disturbed you for all the world during the hours of Sabbath, but I understand it is permitted to break Sabbath if human life is at stake.'

Premier Golen inclined his head.

'It is permitted, if human life is at stake or in danger,' he conceded.

'In this case, that is very much so,' said the ambassador. 'You will be aware, sir, of what has been happening on board the supertanker *Freya* in the North Sea these past twelve hours.'

The premier was more than aware; he was deeply concerned, for since the noon demands it had become plain that the terrorists, whoever they were, could not be Palestinian Arabs, and might even be Jewish fanatics. But his own agencies, the external Mossad and the internal Sherut Bitachon, called from its initials Shin Bet, had not been able to find trace of such fanatics being missing from their usual haunts.

'I am aware, ambassador, and I join in sorrow for the murdered seaman. What is it that the Federal Republic wants of Israel?'

'Prime Minister, my country's cabinet has considered all the issues here for several hours. Though it regards the prospect of conceding to terrorist blackmail with utter repugnance, and though if the affair were a completely internal German matter it might be prepared to resist, in the present case it feels it must accede.

'My government's request is therefore that the State of Israel agree to accept Lev Mishkin and David Lazareff, with the guarantees of non-prosecution and non-extradition that the terrorists demand.'

Premier Golen had in fact been considering the reply he would make to such a request for several hours. It came as no surprise to him. He had prepared his position. His government was a finely balanced coalition, and privately he was aware that many if not most of his own people were so incensed by the continuing persecution of Jews and the Jewish religion inside the USSR that for them Mishkin and Lazareff were hardly to be considered terrorists in the same class as the Baader-Meinhof gang or the PLO. Indeed, some sympathized with them for seeking to escape by hijacking a Soviet airliner, and accepted that the gun in the cockpit had gone off by accident.

'You have to understand two things, ambassador. One is that although Mishkin and Lazareff may be Jews, the State of Israel has had nothing to do with their original offences, nor the demand for their freedom now made.'

If the terrorists themselves turn out to be Jewish, how many people are going to believe that, he thought.

'The second thing is that the State of Israel is not directly affected by the plight of the *Freya*'s crew, nor the effects of her possible destruction. It is not the State of Israel that is under pressure here, or being blackmailed.'

'That is understood, Prime Minister,' said the German.

'If, therefore, Israel agrees to receive these two men, it must be clearly and publicly understood that she does so at the express and earnest request of the Federal government.'

'That request is being made, sir, by me, now, on behalf of my government.'

Fifteen minutes later the format was agreed. West Germany would publicly announce that it had made the request to Israel on its own behalf. Immediately afterwards, Israel would announce that she had reluctantly agreed to the request. Following that, West Germany could announce the release of the prisoners at 0800 hours the following morning, European time. The announcements would come from Bonn and Jerusalem, and would be synchronized at ten-minute intervals, starting one hour hence. It was seven-thirty in Israel, five-thirty in Europe.

Across that continent the last editions of the afternoon newspapers whirled on to the streets to be snapped up by a public of 300,000,000 who had followed the drama since mid-morning. The latest headlines gave the details of the murder of the unidentified seaman and the arrest of a freelance French photographer and a pilot at Le Touquet.

Radio bulletins carried the news that the West German ambassador to Israel had visited Premier Golen in his private house during Sabbath, and left twenty minutes later. There was no news from the meeting, and speculation was rife. Television had pictures of anyone who would pose for them, and quite a few who preferred not to. The latter were the ones who knew what was going on. No pictures of the seaman's body, taken from the Nimrod, were released by the authorities.

The daily papers, preparing for issues starting at midnight, were holding front pages for the chance of a statement from Jerusalem or Bonn, or another transmission from the *Freya*. The learned articles on the inside pages about the *Freya* herself, her cargo, the effects of its spillage, speculation on the identity of the terrorists and editorials urging the release of the two hijackers, covered many columns of copy.

A mild and balmy dusk was ending a glorious spring day when Sir Julian Flannery completed his report to the Prime Minister in her office at 10 Downing Street. It was comprehensive and yet succinct, a masterpiece of draftsmanship.

'We have to assume then, Sir Julian,' she said at length, 'that they certainly exist, that they have undoubtedly taken complete possession of the *Freya*, that they could well be in a position to blow her apart and sink her, that they would not stop at doing so, and that the financial, environmental and human consequences would constitute a catastrophe of appalling dimensions.'

'That, ma'am, might seem to be the most pessimistic interpretation, yet the crisis management committee feels it would be rash to assume a more hopeful tone,' the secretary to the Cabinet replied.

'Only four have been seen, the two lookouts and their replacements. We feel we must assume another on the bridge, one watching the prisoners, and a leader; that makes a minimum of seven. They might be too few to stop an armed boarding party, but we cannot assume so. They might have no dynamite on board, or too little, or have placed it wrongly, but we cannot assume so. Finally, they might not be prepared actually to blow the *Freya* apart and die with her, but we cannot assume so. Your committee feels it would be wrong to assume less than the possible, which is the worst.'

The telephone from her private staff tinkled and she answered it. When she replaced the receiver, she gave Sir Julian a fleeting smile.

'It looks as if we may not face the catastrophe after all,' she said. 'The West German government has just announced it has made the request to Israel. Israel has replied that she concedes the German request. Bonn countered by announcing the release of these two men at eight tomorrow morning.'

It was twenty to seven.

The same news came over the transistor radio in the day cabin of Captain Thor Larsen. Keeping him covered all the time, Drake had switched the cabin lights on an hour earlier and drawn the curtains. The cabin was well-lit, warm, almost cheery. The percolator of coffee had been exhausted and replenished five times. It was still bubbling. Both men, the mariner and the fanatic, were stubbled and tired. But one was filled with grief for the death of a friend, and anger; the other triumphant.

'They've agreed,' said Drake. 'I knew they would. The odds were too long, the consequences too bad.'

Thor Larsen might have been relieved at the news of the pending reprieve of his ship. But the controlled anger was burning too hot even for this comfort.

'It's not over yet,' he growled.

'It will be. Soon. If my friends are released at eight, they will be in Tel Aviv by one p.m. or two at the latest. With an hour for identification and the publication on the news by radio, we should know by three or four o'clock tomorrow. After dark, we will leave you, safe and sound.'

'Except Tom Keller out there,' snapped the Norwegian.

'I'm sorry about that. The demonstration of our seriousness was necessary. They left me no alternative.'

The Soviet ambassador's request was unusual, highly so, in that it was repeated, tough and insistent. Although representing a supposedly revolutionary country, Soviet ambassadors are usually meticulous in their observance of diplomatic procedures, originally devised by Western capitalist nations.

David Lawrence repeatedly asked over the telephone whether Ambassador Konstantin Kirov could not talk to him, as US secretary of state. Kirov replied that his message was for President Matthews personally, extremely urgent, and finally that it concerned matters Chairman Maxim Rudin personally wished to bring to President Matthews' attention.

The President granted Kirov his face-to-face, and the long black limousine with the hammer-and-sickle emblem swept into the White House grounds during the lunch-hour.

It was a quarter to seven in Europe, but only quarter to two in Washington. The envoy was shown straight to the Oval Office to face a President who was puzzled, intrigued and curious. The formalities were observed, but neither party's mind was on them.

'Mr President,' said Kirov, 'I am instructed by a personal order from Chairman Maxim Rudin to seek this urgent interview with you. I am instructed to relay to you his personal message, without variation. It is: "In the event that the hijackers and murderers Lev Mishkin and David Lazareff are freed from jail and released from their just deserts, the USSR will not be able to sign the Treaty of Dublin in the week after next, or at any time at all. The Soviet Union will reject the treaty permanently."'

President Matthews stared at the Soviet envoy in stunned amazement. It was several seconds before he spoke.

'You mean, Maxim Rudin will just tear it up?'

Kirov was ramrod stiff, formal, unbending.

'Mr President, that is the first part of the message I have been instructed to deliver to you. It goes on to say that if the nature or contents of this message are revealed, the same reaction from the USSR will apply.'

When he was gone William Matthews turned helplessly to Lawrence.

'David, what the hell is going on? We can't just bully the German government into reversing its decision without explaining why.'

'Mr President, I think you are going to have to. With respect, Maxim Rudin has just left you no alternative.'

14

President William Matthews sat stunned by the suddenness, the unexpectedness and the brutality of the Soviet reaction. He waited while his CIA director, Robert Benson, and his security adviser, Stanislaw Poklewski, were sent for.

When the pair joined the state secretary in the Oval Office, Matthews explained the burden of the visit from Ambassador Kirov.

'What the hell are they up to?' demanded the President.

None of his three principal advisers could come up with an answer. Various suggestions were put forward, notably that Maxim Rudin had suffered a reverse within his own Politburo and could not proceed with the Treaty of Dublin; the *Freya* affair was simply his excuse for getting out of signing.

This idea was rejected by mutual consent: without the treaty, the Soviet Union would receive no grain, and they were at their last few truckloads. It was suggested the dead Aeroflot pilot, Captain Rudenko, represented the sort of loss of face that the Kremlin could not stomach. This too was rejected: international treaties are not torn up because of dead pilots.

The director of central intelligence summed up the feelings of everybody after an hour.

'It just doesn't make sense, and yet it must. Maxim Rudin would not react like a madman unless he had a reason, a reason we don't know.'

'That still doesn't get us out from between two appalling alternatives,' said President Matthews. 'Either we let the release of Mishkin and Lazareff go through, losing the most important disarmament treaty of our generation, and witness war within a year, or we use our clout to block that release, and subject Western Europe to the biggest ecological disaster of this generation.'

'We have to find a third choice,' said David Lawrence. 'But in hell's name, where?'

'There is only one place to look,' replied Poklewski. 'Inside Moscow. The answer lies inside Moscow, somewhere. I do not believe we can formulate a policy aimed at avoiding both the alternative disasters unless we know why Maxim Rudin has reacted in this way.'

'I think you're referring to the Nightingale,' Benson cut in. 'There just isn't the time. We're not talking about weeks, or even days. We only have hours. I believe, Mr President, that you should seek to speak personally with Maxim Rudin on the direct line. Ask him, as President to President, why he is taking this attitude over two Jewish hijackers.'

'And if he declines to give his reason?' asked Lawrence. 'He could have given a reason through Kirov. Or sent a personal letter. . . .'

President Matthews made up his mind.

'I am calling Maxim Rudin,' he said. 'But if he will not take my call, or declines to give me an explanation, we will have to assume he is himself under intolerable pressures of some kind within his own circle. So while I am waiting for the call, I am going to entrust Mrs Carpenter with the secret of what has just happened here, and ask for her help, through Sir Nigel Irvine and the Nightingale. In the last resort I will call Chancellor Busch in Bonn and ask him to give me more time.'

When the caller asked for Ludwig Jahn personally, the switchboard operator at Tegel Jail was prepared to cut the caller off. There had been numerous press calls seeking to speak with specific officers on the staff in order to elicit details of Mishkin and Lazareff. The operator had her orders: no calls.

But when the caller explained he was Jahn's cousin and that Jahn was to have attended his daughter's wedding the following day at noon, the operator softened. Family was different. She put the call through; Jahn took it from his office.

'I think you remember me,' the voice told Jahn. The officer remembered him well, the Russian with the labour-camp eyes.

'You shouldn't call me here,' he whispered hoarsely. 'I can't help you. The guards have been trebled, the shifts changed. I am on shift permanently now, sleeping here in the office. Until further notice; those are the orders. They are unapproachable now, those two men.'

'You had better make an excuse to get out for an hour,' said the voice of Colonel Kukushkin. 'There's a bar four hundred metres from the staff gate.' He named the bar and gave its address. Jahn did not know it, but he knew the street. 'In one hour,' said the voice, 'or else. . . .' There was a click.

It was 8 p.m. in Berlin, and quite dark.

The British Prime Minister had been taking a quiet supper with her husband in the private apartments in 10 Downing Street when she was summoned to accept a personal call from President Matthews. She was back at her desk when the call came through. The two government leaders knew each other well and had met a dozen times since Britain's first woman premier came to office. Face to face they used Christian names, but even though the super-security-vetted call across the Atlantic could not be eavesdropped, there was an official record made, so they stayed with the formalities.

In careful, succinct terms, President Matthews explained the message he had received from Maxim Rudin via his ambassador in Washington.

Joan Carpenter was stunned. 'In heaven's name, why?' she asked.

'That's my problem, ma'am,' came the Southern drawl from across the Atlantic. 'There is no explanation. None at all. Two more things. Ambassador Kirov advised me that if the content of Rudin's message ever became public knowledge, the same consequences to the Treaty of Dublin would still apply. I may count on your discretion?'

'Implicitly,' she replied. 'The second thing?'

'I've tried to call Maxim Rudin on the hot line. He is unavailable. Now from that, I have to assume he has his own problems right in the heart of the Kremlin, and he can't talk about them. Frankly, that has put me in an impossible position. But of one thing I am absolutely determined. I cannot let that treaty be destroyed. It is far too important to the whole of the Western world. I have to fight for it. I cannot let two hijackers in a Berlin jail destroy it; I cannot let a bunch of terrorists on a tanker in the North Sea unleash an armed conflict between East and West such as would ensue.'

'I entirely agree with you, Mr President,' said the premier from her London desk. 'What do you want from me? I imagine you would have more influence with Chancellor Busch than I.'

'It's not that, ma'am. Two things. We have a certain amount of information about the consequences to Europe of the *Freya* blowing up, but I assume you have more. I need to know every conceivable possible consequence and option, in the event the terrorists aboard do their worst.'

'Yes,' said Mrs Carpenter, 'during the whole of today our people here have put together an in-depth study of the ship, her cargo, the chances of containing the spillage, and so forth. So far we haven't examined the idea of storming her; now we may have to. I will have all our information on those aspects on their way to you within the hour. What else?'

'This is the hard one, and I hardly know how to ask it,' said William Matthews. 'We believe there has to be an explanation of Rudin's behaviour, and until we know it we are groping in the dark. If I am to handle this crisis, I have to see some daylight. I have to have that explanation. I need to know if there is a third option. I would like you to ask your people to activate the Nightingale one last time and get that answer for me.'

Joan Carpenter was pensive. She had always made it a policy never to interfere with the way Sir Nigel Irvine ran his service. Unlike several of her predecessors she had steadily declined to poke around in the intelligence services to satisfy her curiosity. Since coming to office she had doubled the budgets of both her directors, of SIS and MI5, had chosen hard-core professionals for the posts, and had been rewarded by their unswerving loyalty. Secure in that loyalty, she trusted them not to let her down. And neither had.

'I will do what I can,' she said at length. 'But we are talking about something in the very heart of the Kremlin, and a matter of hours. If it is possible, it will be done. You have my word on it.'

When the telephone was back in its cradle she called her husband to tell him not to wait for her; she would be at her desk all night. From the kitchen she ordered a pot of coffee. The practical side of things arranged, she called Sir Julian Flannery at his home, told him simply over the open line that a fresh crisis had arisen, and asked him to return at once to the Cabinet Office. Her last call was not on an open line; it was to the duty officer at the head office of the firm. She asked for Sir Nigel Irvine to be contacted wherever he was, and to be asked to come immediately to Number 10. While waiting, she switched on the office television and caught the start of the nine o'clock BBC news. The long night had begun.

Ludwig Jahn slipped into the booth and sat down, sweating gently. From across the table the Russian regarded him coldly. The plump warder could not know that the fearsome Russian was fighting for his own life; the man gave no hint.

He listened impassively as Jahn explained the new procedures, instituted since two that afternoon. In point of fact, he had no diplomatic cover; he was hiding out in an SSD safe house in West Berlin as a guest of his East German colleagues.

'So you see,' concluded Jahn, 'there is nothing I can do. I could not possibly get you into that corridor. There are three on duty, as a minimum figure, night and day. Passes have to be shown every time one enters the corridor, even by me, and we all know each other. We have worked together for years. No new face would be admitted without a check call to the governor.'

Kukushkin nodded slowly. Jahn felt relief rising in his chest. They would let him go; they would leave him alone; they would not hurt his family. It was over.

'You enter the corridor, of course,' said the Russian. 'You may enter the cells.'

'Well, yes, I am the Oberwachtmeister. At periodic intervals I have to check that they are all right.'

'At night they sleep?'

'Maybe. They have heard about the matter in the North Sea. They lost their radios just after the noon broadcasts, but one of the other prisoners in solitary shouted the news across to them before the corridor was cleared of all other prisoners. Perhaps they will sleep, perhaps not.'

The Russian nodded sombrely.

'Then,' he said, 'you will do the job yourself.'

Jahn's jaw dropped.

'No, no,' he babbled. 'You don't understand. I couldn't use a gun. I couldn't kill anyone.'

For answer the Russian laid two slim tubes like fountain pens on the table between them.

'Not guns,' he said. 'These. Place the open end, here, a few centimetres from the mouth and nose of the sleeping man. Press the button on the side, here. Death is within three seconds. Inhalation of potassium cyanide gas causes instantaneous death. Within an hour the effects are identical to those of cardiac arrest. When it is done, close the cells, return to the staff area, wipe the tubes clean and place them in the locker of another warder with access to the same pair of cells. Very simple, very clean. And it leaves you in the clear.'

What Kukushkin had laid before the horrified gaze of the senior officer was an up-dated version of the same sort of poison-gas pistols with which the 'wet affairs' department of the KGB had assassinated the two Ukrainian nationalist leaders Stepan Bandera and Lev Rebet in Germany two decades earlier. The principle was still simple, the efficiency of the gas increased by further research. Inside the tubes glass globules of prussic acid rested. The trigger impelled a spring which worked on a hammer which crushed the glass. Simultaneously the acid was vaporized by a compressed air canister, activated in the same motion of pressing the trigger button. Impelled by the compressed air, the gas vapour shot out of the tube into the breathing passages in an invisible cloud. An hour later the tell-tale almond smell of prussic acid was gone, the muscles of the corpse relaxed again; the symptoms were of a heart attack.

No one would believe two simultaneous heart attacks in two young men; a search would be made. The gas-guns, found in the locker of a warder, would incriminate the man almost completely.

'I . . . I can't do that,' whispered Jahn.

'But I can, and will, see your entire family in an Arctic labour camp for the rest of their lives,' murmured the Russian. 'A simple choice, Herr Jahn. The overcoming of your scruples for a brief ten minutes, against all their lives. Think about it.'

Kukushkin took Jahn's hand, turned it over and placed the tubes in the palm.

'Think about it,' he said, 'but not for too long. Then walk into those cells and do it. That's all.'

He slid out of the booth and left. Minutes later Jahn closed his hand round the gas-guns, slipped them in his raincoat pocket, and went back to Tegel Jail. At midnight, in three hours, he would relieve the evening shift supervisor. At 1 a.m. he would enter the cells and do it. He knew he had no alternative.

As the last rays of the sun left the sky, the Nimrod over the *Freya* had switched from her daytime F.126 camera to her nighttime F.135 version. Otherwise nothing changed. The night-vision camera, peering downwards with its infra-red sights, could pick out most of what was happening 15,000 feet beneath. If the Nimrod's captain wanted, he could take still pictures with the aid of the F.135's electronic flash, or throw the switch on his aircraft's million-candlepower searchlight.

The night camera failed to notice the figure in the anorak, lying prostrate since the mid-afternoon, slowly begin to move, crawling under the inspection catwalk and from there inching its way back towards the superstructure. When the figure finally crawled over the sill of the half-open doorway and stood up in the interior, no one noticed. At dawn it was supposed the body had been thrown into the sea.

The man in the anorak went below to the gallery, rubbing hands and shivering repeatedly. In the galley he found one of his colleagues and helped himself to a piping hot coffee. When he had finished he returned to the bridge and sought out his own clothes, the black tracksuit and sweater he had come aboard with.

'Jeez,' he told the man on the bridge in his American accent, 'you sure didn't miss. I could feel the wadding from those blanks slapping into the back of the windbreaker.'

The bridge-watch grinned.

'Andriy said to make it good,' he replied. 'It worked. Mishkin and Lazareff are coming out at eight tomorrow morning. By afternoon they'll be in Tel Aviv.'

'Great,' said the Ukrainian-American. 'Let's just hope Andriy's plan to get us off this ship works as well as the rest.'

'It will,' said the other. 'You better get your mask on and give those clothes back to that Yankee in the paint locker. Then grab some sleep. You're on watch at six in the morning.'

Sir Julian Flannery re-convened the crisis management committee within an hour of his private talk with the Prime Minister. She had told him the reason why the situation had changed, but he and Sir Nigel Irvine would be the only ones to know, and they would not talk. The members of the committee would simply need to know that, for reasons of state, the release of Mishkin and Lazareff at dawn might be delayed or cancelled, depending on the reaction of the German chancellor.

Elsewhere in Whitehall, page after page of data about the *Freya*, her crew, cargo and hazard potential was being photographically transmitted direct to Washington.

Sir Julian had been lucky: most of the principal experts from the committee lived within a sixty-minute fast drive radius of Whitehall. Most were caught over dinner at home, none had left for the countryside; two were traced to restaurants, one to the theatre. By nine-thirty the bulk of them were seated once again in the Unicorne.

Sir Julian explained that their duty now was to assume that the whole affair had passed from the realm of a form of exercise and into major crisis category.

'We have to assume that Chancellor Busch will agree to delay the release, pending the clarification of certain other matters. If he does, we have to assume the chance that the terrorists will at least activate their first threat, to vent oil cargo from the *Freya*. Now we have to plan to contain and destroy a possible first slick of twenty thousand tons of crude oil; secondly, to envisage that figure being multiplied by fifty fold.'

The picture that emerged was gloomy. Public indifference over years had led to political neglect; nevertheless, the amounts of crude oil emulsifier in the hands of the British, and the vehicles for their delivery on to an oil slick were still greater than those of the rest of Europe combined.

'We have to assume that the main burden of containing the ecology damage will fall to us,' said the man from Warren Springs. 'In the *Amoco Cadiz* affair in 1978 the French refused to accept our help, even though we had better emulsifiers and better delivery systems than they had. Their fishermen paid bitterly for that particular stupidity. The old-fashioned detergent they used instead of our emulsifier-concentrates caused as much toxic damage as the oil itself. And they had neither enough of it nor the right delivery systems. It was like trying to kill an octopus with a pea-shooter.'

'I have no doubt the Germans, Dutch and Belgians will not hesitate to ask for a joint allied operation in this matter,' said the man from Foreign Office.

'Then we must be ready,' said Sir Julian. 'How much have we got?'

Dr Henderson from Warren Springs continued. 'The best emulsifier, in concentrate form, will emulsify – that is, break down into minuscule globules which permit natural bacteria to complete the destruction – twenty times its own volume. One gallon of emulsifier for twenty gallons of crude oil. We have one thousand tons in stock.'

'Enough for one slick of twenty thousand tons of crude oil,' observed Sir Julian. 'What about a million tons?'

'Not a chance.' said Henderson grimly. 'Not a chance in hell. If we start to produce more now, we can manufacture a thousand tons every four days. For a million tons, we'd need fifty thousand tons of emulsifier. Frankly, those maniacs in the black helmets could wipe out most marine life in the North Sea and the English Channel, and foul up the beaches from Hull to Cornwall on our side, and Bremen to Ushant on the other.'

There was silence for a while.

'Let's assume the first slick,' said Sir Julian quietly. 'The other is beyond belief.'

The committee agreed to issue immediate orders for the procurement during the night of every ton of emulsifier from the store in Hampshire; to commandeer lorry tankers from the petroleum companies through the Energy Department; to bring the whole consignment to the esplanade car park at Lowestoft on the east coast; and to get under way and divert to Lowestoft every single marine tug with spray equipment, including the Port of London fire-fighting vessels and the Royal Navy equivalents. By late morning it was hoped to have the entire flotilla in Lowestoft port, tanking up with emulsifier.

'If the sea remains calm,' said Dr Henderson, 'the slick will drift gently northeast of the *Freya* on the tide, heading for North Holland, at about two knots. That gives us time. When the tide changes, it should drift back again. But if the wind rises, it might move faster in any direction, according to the wind, which will overcome the tide at surface level. We should be able to cope with a twenty-thousand-ton slick.'

'We can't move ships into the area five miles round the *Freya* on three sides, or anywhere between her and the Dutch coast,' the vice-chief of defence staff pointed out.

'But we can watch the slick from the Nimrod,' said the group captain from RAF. 'If it moves out of range of the *Freya*, your navy chaps can start squirting.'

'So far, so good, for the threatened twenty-thousand-ton spillage,' said the Foreign Office man. 'What happens after that?'

'Nothing,' said Dr Henderson. 'After that we're finished, expended.'

'Well, that's it then. An enormous administrative task awaits us,' said Sir Julian.

'There is one other option,' said Colonel Holmes of the Royal Marines. 'The hard option.'

There was an uncomfortable silence round the table. The vice-admiral and the group captain did not share the discomfort; they were interested. The scientists and bureaucrats were accustomed to technical and administrative problems, their counter-measures and solutions. Each suspected the raw-boned colonel in civilian clothes was talking about shooting holes in people.

'You may not like the option,' said Holmes reasonably, 'but these terrorists have killed one sailor in cold blood. They may well kill another twenty-nine. The ship costs one hundred and seventy million dollars, the cargo one hundred and forty million dollars, the clean-up operation treble that. If, for whatever reason, Chancellor Busch cannot or will not release the men in Berlin, we may be left with no alternative but to try to storm the ship and knock off the man with the detonator before he can use it.'

'What exactly do you propose, Colonel Holmes?' asked Sir Julian.

'I propose that we ask Major Fallon to drive up from Dorset and that we listen to him,' said Holmes.

It was agreed, and on that note the meeting adjourned until 3 a.m. It was 9.50 p.m.

During the meeting, not far away from the Cabinet Office, the Prime Minister had received Sir Nigel Irvine.

'That then, is the position, Sir Nigel,' she concluded. 'If we cannot come up with a third option, either the men go free and Maxim Rudin tears up the Treaty of Dublin; or they stay in jail and their friends tear up the *Freya*. In the case of the second, they might stay their hand and not do it, but we can entertain no hopes of that. It might be possible to storm it, but chances of success are slim. In order to have a chance of perceiving the third option, we have to know why Maxim Rudin is taking this course. Is he, for example, overplaying his hand? Is he trying to bluff the West into sustaining enormous economic damage in order to offset his own embarrassment over his grain problems? Will he really go through with his threat? We have to know.'

'How long have you got, Prime Minister? How long has President Matthews got?' asked the director-general of the SIS.

'One must assume, if the hijackers are not released at dawn, we will have to stall the terrorists, play for time. But I would hope to have something for the President by afternoon tomorrow.'

'As a rather long-serving officer, I would have thought that was impossible, ma'am. It is the middle of the night in Moscow. The Nightingale is virtually unapproachable, except at meetings planned well ahead. To attempt an instant rendezvous might well blow that agent sky-high.'

'I know your rules, Sir Nigel, and I understand them. The safety of the agent out in the cold is paramount. But so are matters of state. The destruction of the treaty, or the destruction of the *Freya*, are matters of state. The first could jeopardize peace for years, perhaps put Yefrem Vishnayev in power, with all its consequences. The financial losses alone sustained by Lloyd's and, through Lloyd's the British economy if the *Freya* destroyed herself and the North Sea would be disastrous, not to mention the loss of thirty seamen. I make no flat orders, Sir Nigel; I ask you to put the certain options against the putative hazard to one single Russian agent.'

'Ma'am, I will do what I can. You have my word on it,' said Sir Nigel and left to return to his headquarters.

*

From an office in the Defence Ministry Colonel Holmes was on the telephone to Poole, Dorset, headquarters of another service, the SBS. Major Simon Fallon was found befriending a pint of beer in the officers' mess and brought to the telephone. The two marines knew each other well.

'You've been following the *Freya* affair?' asked Holmes from London.

There was a chuckle from the other end. 'I thought you'd come shopping here eventually,' said Fallon. 'What do they want?'

'Things are turning sour,' said Holmes. 'The Germans may have to change their minds and keep those two jokers in Berlin after all. I've just spent an hour with the re-convened CMC. They don't like it, but they may have to consider our way. Got any ideas?'

'Sure,' said Fallon. 'Been thinking about it all day. Need a model though, and a plan. And the gear.'

'Right,' said Holmes, 'I have the plan here, and a pretty good model of another similar ship. Get the boys together. Get all the gear out of stores: underwater, magnets, all the types of hardware, stun grenades, you name it. The lot. What you don't need can be returned. I'm asking the navy to come round from Portland and pick up the lot – the gear and the team. When you've left a good man in charge, jump into the car and get up to London. Report to my office as soon as you can.'

'Don't worry,' said Fallon, 'I've got the gear sorted and bagged already. Get the transport here as fast as you can. I'm on my way.'

When the hard, chunky major returned to the bar there was silence. His men knew he had taken a call from London. Within minutes they were rousing the NCOs and marines from their barracks, changing rapidly out of the plain clothes they had been wearing in the mess into the black webbing and green berets of their unit. Before midnight they were waiting on the stone jetty tucked away in their cordoned section of the marine base; waiting for the arrival of the navy to take their equipment to where it was needed.

There was a bright moon rising over Portland Bill to the west of them as the three fast patrol boats *Sabre*, *Cutlass* and *Scimitar* came out of the harbour, heading east for Poole. When the throttles were open the three prows rose, the sterns buried into the foaming water, and the thunder echoed across the bay.

The same moon illuminated the long track of the Hampshire motorway as Major Fallon's Rover saloon burned up the miles to London.

'Now what the hell do I tell Chancellor Busch?' President Matthews asked his advisers.

It was five in the afternoon in Washington; though night had long settled on Europe, the late afternoon sun was still on the rose garden beyond the french windows where the first buds were responding to the spring warmth.

'I don't believe you can reveal to him the real message received from Kirov,' said Robert Benson.

'Why the devil not? I told Joan Carpenter, and no doubt she'll have had to tell Nigel Irvine.'

'There's a difference,' pointed out the CIA chief. 'The British can put in hand the necessary precautions to cope with an ecology problem in the sea off their coasts by calling on their technical experts. It's a technical problem; Joan Carpenter did not need to call a full Cabinet meeting. Dietrich Busch is going to be asked to hold on to Mishkin and Lazareff at the risk of provoking a catastrophe for his European neighbours. For that he'll almost certainly consult his Cabinet. . . .'

'He's an honourable man,' cut in Lawrence. 'If he knows that the price is the Treaty of Dublin, he'll feel bound to share that knowledge with his Cabinet.'

'And there's the problem,' concluded Benson. 'That a minimum of fifteen more people would hear of it. Some of them would confide in their wives, their aides. We still haven't forgotten the Guenther Guillaume affair. There are just too damn many leaks in Bonn. If it got out, the Dublin Treaty would be finished in any case, regardless of what happened in the North Sea.'

'His call will be through in a minute. What the hell do I tell him?' repeated Matthews.

'Tell him you have information that simply cannot be divulged on any telephone line, even a secure trans-Atlantic line,' suggested Poklewski. 'Tell him the release of Mishkin and Lazareff would provoke a greater disaster than even frustrating the terrorists on the *Freya* for a few more hours. Ask him at this stage simply to give you a little time.'

'How long?' asked the President.

'As long as possible,' said Benson.

'And when the time runs out?' asked the President.

The call to Bonn came through. Chancellor Busch had been contacted at his home. The security-vetted call was patched through to him there. There was no need of translators on the line; Dietrich Busch spoke fluent English. President Matthews spoke to him for ten minutes while the German government chief listened with growing amazement.

'But why?' he asked at length. 'Surely the matter hardly affects the United States?'

Matthews was tempted. At the Washington end Robert Benson wagged a warning finger.

'Dietrich, please. Believe me. I'm asking you to trust me. On this line, on any line across the Atlantic, I can't be as frank as I'd like to be. Something has cropped up, something of enormous dimension. Look, I'll be as plain as I can. Over here we have discovered something about these two men; their release would be disastrous at this stage, for the next few hours. I'm asking for time, Dietrich my friend, just time. A delay, until certain things can be taken care of.'

The German Chancellor was standing in his study with the strains of Beethoven drifting through the door from the sitting room where he had been enjoying a cigar and a concert on the stereo. To say he was suspicious was putting it mildly. So far as he was concerned the trans-Atlantic line, established years before to link the NATO government heads and checked regularly, was perfectly safe. Moreover, he reasoned, the United States had perfectly good communications with their Bonn embassy and could send him a personal message on that route if desired. It did not occur to him that Washington would simply not trust his Cabinet with a secret of this magnitude after the repeated exposure of East German agents close to the seat of power on the Rhine.

On the other hand, the President of the United States was not given to making late-night calls or crazy appeals. He had to have his reasons, Busch knew. But what he was being asked was not something he could decide without consultation.

'It is just past ten p.m. over here,' he told Matthews. 'We have until dawn to decide. Nothing fresh ought to happen until then. I shall re-convene my Cabinet during the night and consult with them. I cannot promise you more.'

President William Matthews had to be satisfied with that.

When the phone was replaced, Dietrich Busch stayed for long minutes in thought. There was something going on, he reasoned, and it concerned Mishkin and Lazareff, sitting in their separate cells in Tegel Jail in West Berlin. If anything happened to them, there was no way in which the Federal government would escape a howl of censure from within Germany, by the combined media and the opposition. And with the regional elections coming up. . . .

His first call was to Ludwig Fischer, his minister of justice, also at home in the capital. None of his ministers would be weekending in the country, by prior agreement. His suggestion was met with immediate agreement by the justice minister – to transfer the pair from the old-fashioned prison of Tegel to the much newer and super-secure jail of Moabit was an obvious precaution. No CIA operatives would ever get at them inside Moabit. Fischer telephoned the instruction to Berlin immediately.

There are certain phrases, innocent enough, which used by the senior cipher clerk at the British embassy in Moscow to the man he knows to be the SIS resident on the embassy staff, mean in effect, 'Get the hell down here fast; something urgent is coming through from London.' Such was the phrase that brough Adam Munro from his bed at midnight (Moscow time), 10 p.m. London time, across town to Maurice Thorez Embankment.

Driving back from Downing Street to his office, Sir Nigel Irvine had realized the Prime Minister was absolutely right. Compared to the destruction of the Treaty of Dublin on the one hand or the destruction of the *Freya*, her crew and cargo on the other, putting a Russian agent at risk of exposure was the lesser evil. What he was going to ask Munro in Moscow to do, and the way he would have to demand it, gave him no pleasure. But before he arrived at the SIS building he knew it would have to be done.

Deep in the basement, the communications room was handling the usual routine traffic when he entered and startled the night duty staff. But the scrambler telex had raised Moscow in less than five minutes. No one queried the right of the Master to talk directly to his Moscow resident in the middle of the night. It was thirty minutes later that the telex from the Moscow cipher room chattered its message that Munro was there and waiting.

The operators at both ends, senior men of a lifetime's experience, could be trusted with the whereabouts of Christ's bones if necessary; they had to be, they handled as routine messages that could bring down governments. From London the telex would send its scrambled, uninterceptable, message down to a forest of aerials outside Cheltenham, better known for its horse-races and ladies' college. From there the words would be converted automatically into an unbreakable one-off code and beamed out over a sleeping Europe to an aerial on the embassy roof. Four seconds after they were typed in London they would emerge, in clear, on the telex in the basement of the old sugar-magnate's house in Moscow.

There, the cipher clerk turned to Munro standing by his side.

'It's the Master himself,' he said, reading the code-tag on the incoming message. 'There must be a flap on.'

Sir Nigel had to tell Munro the burden of Kirov's message to President Matthews of only three hours earlier. Without that knowledge, Munro could not ask the Nightingale for the answer to Matthews' question: why?

The telex rattled for several minutes. Munro read the message that spewed out with horror.

'I can't do that,' he told the impassive clerk, over whose shoulder he was reading. When the message from London was ended, he told the clerk: 'Reply as follows: "not repeat not possible obtain this sort of answer in time-scale". Send it.'

The interchange between Sir Nigel Irvine and Adam Munro went on for fifteen minutes. There is a method of contacting N at short notice, suggested London. Yes, but only in case of dire emergency, replied Munro. This qualifies one hundred times as emergency, chattered the machine from London. But N could not begin to enquire in less than several days, pointed out Munro. Next regular Politburo meeting not due until Thursday following. What about records of last Thursday's meeting? asked London. *Freya* was not hijacked last Thursday, retorted Munro. Finally Sir Nigel did what he hoped he would not have to do.

'Regret,' tapped the machine, 'prime ministerial order not refusable. Unless attempt made avert this disaster, operation to bring out N to West cannot proceed.'

Munro looked down at the stream of paper coming out of the telex in disbelief. For the first time he was caught in the net of his own attempts to keep his love for the agent he ran from his superiors in London. Sir Nigel Irvine thought the Nightingale was an embittered Russian turncoat called Anatoly Krivoi, right-hand man to the warmonger Vishnayev.

'Make to London,' he told the clerk dully, 'the following: "will try this night, stop, decline to accept responsibility if N refuses or is unmasked during attempt, stop".'

The reply from the Master was brief: 'Agree. Proceed.' It was half-past one in Moscow, and very cold.

Half-past six in Washington, and the dusk was settling over the sweep of lawns beyond the bulletproof windows behind the President's chair, causing the lamps to be switched on. The group in the Oval Office was waiting: waiting for Chancellor Busch, waiting for an unknown agent in Moscow, waiting for a masked terrorist of unknown origins sitting on a 1,000,000-ton bomb off Europe with a detonator in his belt. Waiting for the chance of a third option.

The phone rang, and it was for Stanislaw Poklewski. He listened, held a hand over the mouthpiece and told the President it was from the Navy Department in answer to his query of an hour earlier.

There was one US Navy vessel in the area of the *Freya*. She had been paying a courtesy visit to the Danish coastal city of Esbjerg, and was on her way back to join her squadron of the Standing Naval Force Atlantic, then cruising on patrol west of Norway. She was well off the Danish coast, steaming north by west to rejoin her NATO allies.

'Divert her,' said the President.

Poklewski passed the commander-in-chief's order back to the Navy Department, who soon began to make signals via STANAVFORLANT head-quarters to the American warship.

Just after one in the morning the USS *Moran*, halfway between Denmark and the Orkney Islands, put her helm about, opened her engines to full power, and then began racing through the moonlight southwards for the English Channel. She was a guided missile ship of almost 8000 tons which, although heavier than the British light cruiser *Argyll*, was classified as a destroyer, or DD. Moving at full power in a calm sea, she was making close to thirty knots to bring her to her station five miles from the *Freya* at 8 a.m.

There were few cars in the car park of the Mojorsky Hotel, just off the roundabout at the far end of Kutuzovsky Prospekt. Those that were there were dark, uninhabited, save two.

Munro watched the lights of the other car flicker and dim, then climbed from his own vehicle and walked across. When he climbed into the passenger seat beside her, Valentina was alarmed and trembling.

'What is it, Adam? Why did you call me at the apartment? The call must have been listed.'

He put his arm round her, feeling the trembling through her coat.

'It was from a call box,' he said, 'and only concerned Gregor's inability to attend your dinner party. No one will suspect anything.'

'At two in the morning,' she remonstrated, 'no one makes calls like that at two in the morning. I was seen to leave the apartment compound by the nightwatchman. He will report it.'

'Darling, I'm sorry. Listen.'

He told her of the visit by Ambassador Kirov to President Matthews the previous evening; of the news being passed to London; of the demand to him that he try to find out why the Kremlin was taking such an attitude over Mishkin and Lazareff.

'I don't know,' she said simply. 'I haven't the faintest idea. Perhaps because those animals murdered Captain Rudenko, a man with a wife and children.'

'Valentina, we have listened to the Politburo these past nine months. The Treaty of Dublin is vital to your people. Why would Rudin put it in jeopardy over these two men?'

'He has not done so,' answered Valentina. 'It is possible for the West to control the oil slick if the ship blows up. The costs can be met. The West is rich.'

'Darling, there are thirty men aboard that ship. They too have wives and children. Thirty men's lives against the imprisonment of two. There has to be another and more serious reason.'

'I don't know,' she repeated. 'It has not been mentioned in Politburo meetings. You know that also.'

Munro stared miserably through the windscreen. He had hoped against hope she might have an answer for Washington, something she had heard inside the Central Committee building. Finally he decided he had to tell her.

When he had finished, she stared through the darkness with round eyes. He caught a hint of tears in the dying light of the moon.

'They promised,' she whispered, 'they promised they would bring me and Sasha out in a fortnight, from Romania.'

'They've gone back on their word,' he confessed. 'They want this last favour.'

She placed her forehead on her gloved hands, supported by the steering wheel.

'They will catch me,' she mumbled. 'I am so frightened.'

'They won't catch you,' he tried to reassure her. 'The KGB acts much more slowly than people think, and the higher their suspect is placed the more slowly they act. If you can get this piece of information for President Matthews, I think I can persuade them to get you out in a few days, you and Sasha, instead of two weeks. Please try, my love. It's our only chance left of ever being together.'

Valentina stared through the glass.

'There was a Politburo meeting this evening,' she said finally. 'I was not there. It was a special meeting, out of sequence. Normally on Friday evenings they are all going to the country. Transcription begins tomorrow; that is, today, at ten in the morning. The staff have to give up their weekend to get it ready for Monday. Perhaps they mentioned the matter.'

'Could you get in to see the notes, listen to the tapes?' he asked.

'In the middle of the night? There would be questions asked.'

'Make an excuse, darling. Any excuse. You want to start and finish your work early, so as to get away.'

'I will try,' she said eventually. 'I will try, for you, Adam, not for those men in London.'

'I know those men in London,' said Adam Munro. 'They will bring you and Sasha out if you help them now. This will be the last risk, truly the last.'

She seemed not to have heard him, and to have overcome, for a while, her fear of the KGB, exposure as a spy, the awful consequences of capture unless she could escape in time. When she spoke, her voice was quite level.

'You know Dyetsky Mir? The soft toys counter. At ten o'clock this morning.'

He stood on the black tarmac and watched her tail lights drive away. It was done. They had asked him to do it, demanded that he do it, and he had done it. He had diplomatic protection to keep him out of Lubyanka. The worst that could happen would be his ambassador summoned to the Foreign Ministry on Monday morning to receive an icy protest and demand for his removal from Dmitri Rykov. But Valentina was walking right into the secret archives, without even the disguise of normal, accustomed, justified behaviour to protect her. He looked at his watch. Seven hours, seven hours to go, seven hours of knotted stomach muscles and ragged nerve ends. He walked back to his car.

Ludwig Jahn stood in the open gateway of Tegel Jail and watched the tail lights of the armoured van bearing Mishkin and Lazareff disappear down the street.

Unlike Munro, for him there would be no more waiting, no tension stretching through the dawn and into the morning. For him the waiting was over.

He walked carefully to his office on the first floor and closed the door. For a few moments he stood by the open window, then drew back one hand and hurled the first of the cyanide pistols far into the night. He was fat, over-weight, unfit. A heart attack would be accepted as possible, provided no evidence was found.

Leaning far out of the window he thought of his nieces over the Wall in the East, their laughing faces when Uncle Ludo had brought the presents four months ago at Christmas. He closed his eyes, held the other tube beneath his nostrils and pressed the trigger-button.

The pain slammed across his chest like a giant hammer. The loosened fingers dropped the tube, which fell with a tinkle to the street below. Jahn slumped, hit the window sill and caved backwards into his office, already dead. When they found him, they would assume he had opened the window for air when the first pain came. Kukushkin would not have his triumph. The chimes of midnight were drowned by the roar of a lorry which crushed the tube in the gutter to fragments.

The hijacking of the *Freya* had claimed its first victim.

15

The resumed West German Cabinet meeting assembled in the chancellery at 1 a.m. and the mood when the ministers heard from Dietrich Busch the plea from Washington varied between exasperation and truculence.

'Well, why the hell won't he give a reason?' asked the defence minister. 'Doesn't he trust us?'

'He claims he has a reason of paramount importance, but cannot divulge it even over the hot line,' replied Chancellor Busch. 'That gives us the opportunity of either believing him, or calling him a liar. At this stage I cannot do the latter.'

'Has he any idea what the terrorists will do when they learn Mishkin and Lazareff are not to be released at dawn?' queried another.

'Yes, I think he has. At least the text of all the exchanges between the *Freya* and Maas Control are in his hands. As we all know, they have threatened to either kill another seaman, or vent twenty thousand tons of crude, or both.'

'Well, then, let him carry the responsibility,' urged the interior minister. 'Why should we take the blame if that happens?'

'I haven't the slightest intention that we should,' replied Busch, 'but that doesn't answer the question. Do we grant President Matthews' request or not?'

There was silence for a while. The foreign minister broke it.

'How long is he asking for?'

'As long as possible,' said the Chancellor. 'He seems to have some plan afoot to break the deadlock, to find a third alternative. But what the plan is, or what the alternative could be, he alone knows; he and a few people he evidently trusts with the secret,' he added with some bitterness. 'But that doesn't include us for the moment.'

'Well, personally, I think it is stretching the friendship between us a bit far,' said the foreign minister, 'but I think we ought to grant him an extension, while making plain, at least unofficially, that it is at his request, not ours.'

'Perhaps he has an idea to storm the *Freya*,' suggested Defence.

'Our own people say that would be extremely risky,' replied the interior minister. 'It would require an underwater approach for at least the last two miles; a sheer climb up smooth steel from the sea to the deck, a penetration of the superstructure without being observed from the funnel, and the selection of the right cabin with the leader of the terrorists in it. If, as we suspect, the man holds a remote-control detonating mechanism in his hand, he'd have to be shot and killed before he could press the button.'

'In any case, it is too late to do it before dawn,' said the defence minister. 'It would have to be in darkness, and that means ten p.m. at the earliest, twenty-one hours from now.'

At a quarter to three the German Cabinet finally agreed to grant President Matthews his request: an indefinite delay on the release of Mishkin and Lazareff while reserving the right to keep the consequences under constant review and reverse that decision if it became regarded in Western Europe as impossible to continue to hold the pair.

At the same time the government spokesman was quietly asked to leak the news to two of his most reliable media contacts that only massive pressure from Washington had caused the about-face in Bonn.

It was 11 p.m. in Washington, 4 a.m. in Europe, when the news from Bonn reached President Matthews. He sent back his heartfelt thanks to Chancellor Busch and asked David Lawrence: 'Any reply from Jerusalem yet?'

'None,' said Lawrence. 'We only know that our ambassador there has been granted a personal interview with Benyamin Golen.'

When the Israeli premier was disturbed for the second time during the Sabbath night, his tetchy capacity for patience was wearing distinctly thin. He received the US ambassador in his dressing gown and the reception was frosty. It was 3 a.m. in Europe, but 5 a.m. in Jerusalem and the first thin light of Saturday morning was on the hills of Judea.

He listened without reaction to the ambassador's personal plea from President Matthews. His private fear was for the identity of the terrorists aboard the *Freya*. No terrorist action aimed at delivering Jews from a prison cell had ever been better mounted since the days of his own youth, fighting right here on the soil where he stood. Then, it had been to free condemned Jewish partisans from a British jail at Acre, and he had been a part of that fight. Thirty-five years had elapsed and the perspectives had changed. Now it was Israel who roundly condemned terrorism, the taking of hostages, the blackmail of regimes. And yet. . . .

And yet, hundreds of thousands of his own people would secretly sympathize with two youths who had sought to escape the terror of the KGB the only way left open to them. The same voters would not openly hail the youths as heroes, but neither would they condemn them as murderers. As to the masked men on the *Freya*, there was a chance that they too were Jewish, possibly (heaven forbid) Israelis. He had hoped the previous evening that the affair would be over by sundown of the Sabbath, the prisoners of Berlin inside Israel, the terrorists of the *Freya* captured or dead. There would be a fuss, but it would die down.

Now he was learning that there would be no release. The news hardly inclined him to the American request, which was in any case impossible. When he had heard the ambassador out, he shook his head.

'Please convey to my good friend William Matthews my heartfelt wish that this appalling affair can be concluded without further loss of life,' he replied. 'But on the matter of Mishkin and Lazareff my position is this: if, on behalf of the government and the people of Israel, and at the urgent request of West Germany, I give a solemn, public pledge not to imprison them here or return them to Berlin, then I shall have to abide by that pledge. I'm sorry, but I cannot do as you ask and return them to jail in Germany as soon as the *Freya* has been released.'

He did not need to explain what the American ambassador already knew; that, apart from any question of national honour, even the explanation that promises extracted under duress were not binding would not work in this case. The outrage from the National Religious Party, the Gush Emunim extremists, the Jewish Defense League and the 100,000 Israeli voters who had come from the USSR in the past decade; all these alone would prevent any Israeli premier from reneging on an international pledge to set Mishkin and Lazareff free.

'Well, it was worth a try,' said President Matthews when the cable reached Washington an hour later.

'It now ranks as one possible third option that no longer exists,' remarked David Lawrence, 'even if Maxim Rudin would have accepted it, which I doubt.'

It was one hour to midnight; lights were burning in five government departments, scattered across the capital, as they burned in the Oval Office and a score of other rooms throughout the White House where men and women sat at telephones and teleprinters waiting the news from Europe. The four men in the Oval Office settled to wait the reaction from the *Freya*.

Doctors say three in the morning is the lowest ebb of the human spirit, the hour of weariness, slowest reactions and gloomiest depression. It also marked one complete cycle of the sun and moon for the two men who faced each other in the captain's cabin of the *Freya*. Neither had slept that night nor the previous one; each had been forty-four hours without rest; each was drawn and red-eyed.

Thor Larsen, at the epicentre of a whirling storm of international activity, of cabinets and councils, embassies and meetings, plottings and consultations that kept the lights burning through three continents from Jerusalem to Washington, was playing his own game. He was pitting his own capacity to stay awake against the will of the fanatic who faced him, knowing that at stake if he failed was his crew and his ship.

Larsen knew that the man who called himself Svoboda, younger and consumed by his own inner fire, nerves tightened by a combination of black coffee and the tension of his gamble against the world, could have ordered the Norwegian captain to be tied up while he himself sought rest. So the bearded mariner sat facing the barrel of a gun and played on his captor's pride, hoping that the man would take his challenge, refuse to back down and concede defeat in the game of beating sleep.

It was Larsen who proposed the endless cups of strong black coffee, a drink he only took with milk and sugar two or three times a day. It was he who talked, through the day and the night, provoking the Ukrainian with suggestions of eventual failure, then backing off when the man became too irritable for safety. Long years of experience, nights of yawning, gritty-mouthed training as a sea captain, had taught the bearded giant to stay awake and alert through the night watches, when the cadres drowsed and the deckhands dozed.

So he played his own solitary game, without guns or ammunition, without teleprinters or night-sight cameras, without support and without company. All the superb technology the Japanese had built into his new command was as much use as rusty nails to him now. If he pushed the man across the table too far, he might lose his temper and shoot to kill. If he was frustrated too often he could order the execution of another crewman. If he felt himself becoming too drowsy, he might have himself relieved by another, fitter terrorist while he himself took sleep and undid all that Larsen was trying to do to him.

That Mishkin and Lazareff would be released at dawn, Larsen still had reason to believe. After their safe arrival in Tel Aviv, the terrorists would prepare to quit the *Freya*. Or would they? Could they? Would the surrounding warships let them go so easily? Even away from the *Freya*, attacked by the NATO navies, Svoboda could press his button and blow the *Freya* apart.

But that was not all of it. This man in black had killed one of the crew. Thor Larsen wanted him for that, and he wanted him dead. So he talked the night away to the man opposite him, denying them both sleep.

Whitehall was not sleeping either. The crisis management committee had been in session since 3 a.m., and within an hour the progress reports were complete.

Across southern England the bulk tanker lorries, commandeered from Shell, British Petroleum and a dozen other sources, were filling up with emulsifier concentrate at the Hampshire depot. Bleary-eyed drivers rumbled through the night, empty towards Hampshire or loaded towards Lowestoft, moving hundreds of tons of the concentrate to the Suffolk port. By 4 a.m. the stocks were empty; all 1000 tons of the national supply was headed east to the coast.

So also were inflatable booms to try to hold the vented oil away from the coast until the chemicals could do their work. The factory that made the emulsifier had been geared for maximum output until further notice.

At 3.30 a.m. the news had come from Washington that the Bonn Cabinet had agreed to hold Mishkin and Lazareff for a while longer.

'Does Matthews know what he's doing?' someone asked.

Sir Julian Flannery's face was impassive. 'We must assume that he does,' he said smoothly. 'We must also assume that a venting by the *Freya* will probably now take place. The efforts of the night have not been in vain. At least we are now almost ready.'

'We must also assume,' said the civil servant from the Foreign Ministry, 'that when the announcement becomes public, France, Belgium and Holland are going to ask for assistance in fighting any oil slick that may result.'

'Then we shall be ready to do what we can,' said Sir Julian. 'Now what about the spraying aircraft and the fire-fighting tugs?'

The report in the Unicorne room mirrored what was happening at sea. From the Humber estuary tugs were churning south towards Lowestoft harbour, while from the Thames and even as far round as the navy base at Lee other tugs capable of spraying liquid on to the surface of the sea were moving to rendezvous point on the Suffolk coast.

They were not the only things moving round the south coast that night. Off the towering cliffs of Beachy Head the *Cutlass*, *Scimitar* and *Sabre*, carrying the assorted, complex and lethal hardware of the world's toughest team of assault frogmen, were pointing their noses north of east to bring them past Sussex and Kent towards where the cruiser *Argyll* lay at anchor in the North Sea.

The boom of their engines echoed off the chalk battlements of the southern coast and light sleepers in Eastbourne heard the rumble out to sea.

Twelve marines of the Special Boat Service clung to the rails of the bucking craft, watching over their precious kayaks and the crates of diving gear, weapons and unusual explosives that made up the props of their trade. It was all being carried as deck cargo.

'I hope,' shouted the young lieutenant commander who skippered the *Cutlass* to the marine beside him, the second-in-command of the team, 'that those whizz-bangs you're carrying back there don't go off.'

'They won't,' said the marine captain with confidence. 'Not until we use them.'

In a room adjoining the main conference centre beneath the Cabinet Office their commanding officer was poring over photographs of the *Freya*, taken by night and by day. He was comparing the configuration shown by the Nimrod's pictures with the scale-plan provided by Lloyd's and the model of the British *Princess* supertanker loaned by BP.

'Gentlemen,' said Colonel Holmes to the assembled men next door, 'I think it's time we considered one of the less palatable choices we may have to face.'

'Ah, yes,' said Sir Julian regretfully, 'the hard option.'

'If,' pursued Holmes, 'President Matthews continues to object to the release of Mishkin and Lazareff and West Germany continues to accede to that demand, the moment may well come when the terrorists realize the game is up; that their blackmail is not going to work. At that moment they may well refuse to have their bluff called, and blow the *Freya* to pieces. Personally, it seems to me this will not happen before nightfall, which gives us about sixteen hours.'

'Why nightfall, colonel?' asked Sir Julian.

'Because, sir, unless they are all suicide candidates, which they may be, one must assume that they will seek their own escape in the confusion. Now, if they wish to try to live, they may well leave the ship and operate their remote-control detonator from a certain distance from the ship's side.'

'And your proposal, colonel?'

'Twofold, sir. Firstly, their launch. It is still moored beside the courtesy ladder. As soon as darkness falls, a diver could approach that launch and attach a delayed-action explosive device to it. If the *Freya* should blow up, nothing within a half-mile radius would be safe. Therefore I propose a charge detonated by a mechanism operated by water pressure; as the launch moves away from the ship's side, the forward thrust of the launch will cause water to enter a funnel beneath the keel. This water will operate a trigger, and sixty seconds later the launch will blow up, before the terrorists have reached a point half a mile from the *Freya*, and therefore before they can operate their own detonator.'

There was a murmur of relief around the table.

'Would the exploding of their launch not detonate the charges on the *Freya?*' asked someone.

'No. If they have a remote-control detonator, it must be electronically operated. The charge would blow the launch carrying the terrorists to smithereens. No one would survive.'

'But if the detonator sank, would not the water pressure depress the button?' asked one of the scientists.

'No. Once under the water the remote-control detonator would be safe. It could not beam its radio message to the larger charges in the ship's tanks.'

'Excellent,' said Sir Julian. 'Can this plan not operate before darkness falls?'

'No, it cannot,' asnwered Holmes. 'A frogman diver leaves a trail of bubbles. In stormy weather this might not be noticed, but on a flat sea it would be too obvious. One of the lookouts could spot the bubbles rising. It would provoke what we are trying to avoid.'

'After dark it is, then,' said Sir Julian.

'Except for one thing, which is why I oppose the idea of sabotaging their escape launch as the only ploy. If, as may well happen, the leader of the terrorists is prepared to die with the *Freya*, he may not leave the ship with the rest of his team. So I believe we may have to storm the ship during a night attack and get to him before he can use his device.'

The Cabinet secretary sighed.

'I see. Doubtless you have a plan for that as well?'

'Personally, I do not. But I would like you to meet Major Simon Fallon, commanding the Special Boat Service.'

It was all the stuff of Sir Julian Flannery's nightmares. The marine major was barely five feet eight inches tall, but he seemed about the same across the shoulders and was evidently of that breed of men who talk about reducing other humans to their component parts with the same ease that Lady Flannery talked of dicing vegetables for one of her famous Provençal salads.

In at least three encounters the peace-loving Cabinet secretary had had occasion to meet officers from the SAS, but this was the first time he had seen the commander of the other, smaller specialist unit, the SBS. They were, he observed to himself, of the same breed.

The SBS had originally been formed for conventional war, to act as specialists in attacks on coastal installations arriving from the sea. That was why they were drawn from the marine commandos. As basic requirements they were physically fit to a revolting degree, experts in swimming, canoeing, diving, climbing, marching and fighting.

From there they went on to become proficient in parachuting, explosives, demolition and the seemingly limitless techniques of cutting throats or breaking necks with knife, wire-loop or simply bare hands. In this, and their capacity for living in self-sufficiency on or rather off the countryside for extended periods and leaving no trace of their presence, they simply shared the skills of their cousins in the SAS.

It was in their underwater skills that the SBS men were different. In frogman gear they could swim prodigious distances, lay explosive charges, or drop their swimming gear while treading water without a ripple, and emerge from the sea with their arsenal of special weapons wrapped about them.

Some of their weaponry was fairly routine: knives and cheese-wire. But since the start of that rash of outbreaks of terrorism in the late sixties, they had acquired fresh toys which delighted them. Each was an expert marksman with his high-precision, hand-tooled Finlanda rifle, a Norwegian-made piece that had been evaluated as perhaps the best rifle in the world. It could be and usually was fitted with image-intensifier, a sniper-scope as long as a bazooka and a completely effective silencer and flash-guard.

For taking doors away in half a second, they tended like the SAS towards short-barrelled pump-action shotguns firing solid charges. These they never aimed at the lock, for there could be other bolts behind the door; they fired two simultaneously to take off both hinges, kicking the door down and opening fire with the silenced Ingram machine-pistols.

Also in the arsenal that had helped the SAS assist the Germans at Mogadishu were their flash-bang-crash grenades, a sophisticated development of the 'stun' grenades. These did more than just stun, they paralysed. With a half-second delay after pulling the pin, these grenades, thrown into a confined space containing both terrorists and hostages, had three effects. The flash blinded anyone looking in that direction for at least thirty seconds, the bang blew the eardrums out, causing instant pain and a certain loss of concentration, and the crash was a tonal sound that entered the middle ear and caused a ten-second paralysis of all muscles.

During tests one of their own men had tried to pull the trigger of a gun pressed into a companion's side while the grenade went off. It was impossible. Both terrorists and hostages lost their eardrums, but they can grow again. Dead hostages cannot.

While the paralytic effect lasts, the rescuers spray bullets four inches over head height while their colleagues dive for the hostages, dragging them to the floor. At this point the firers drop their aim by six inches.

The exact position of hostage and terrorist in a closed room can be determined by the application of an electronic stethoscope to the outside of the door. Speech inside the room is not necessary; breathing can be heard and located accurately. The rescuers communicate in an elaborate sign-language that permits of no misunderstanding.

Major Fallon placed the model of the *Princess* on the conference table, aware he had the attention of everyone present.

'I propose,' he began, 'to ask the cruiser *Argyll* to turn herself broadside on to the *Freya*, and then before dawn park the assault boats containing my men and equipment close up in the lee of the *Argyll* where the lookout, here on top of the *Freya*'s funnel, cannot see them, even with binoculars. That will enable us to make our preparations through the afternoon unobserved. In case of aeroplanes hired by the press, I would like the sky cleared, and any detergent-spraying tugs within visual range of what we are doing to keep silent.'

There was no dissent to that. Sir Julian made two notes.

'I would approach the *Freya* with four two-man kayaks, halting at a range of three miles, in darkness, before the rising of the moon. Her radars will not spot kayaks. They are too small, too low in the water: they are of wood and canvas construction, which does not effectively register on radar. The paddlers will be in rubber, leather, wool undervests, etcetera, and all buckles will be in plastic. Nothing should register on the *Freya*'s radar.

'The men in the rear seats will be frogmen; their oxygen bottles have to be of metal, but at three miles will not register larger than a floating oil drum, not enough to cause alarm on the *Freya*'s bridge. At a range of three miles the divers take a compass bearing on the *Freya*'s stern, which they can see because it is illuminated, and drop overboard. They have luminescent wrist-compasses and swim by these.'

'Why not go for the bow?' asked the air force group captain. 'It's darker there.'

'Partly because it would mean eliminating the man on lookout high up on the fo'c's'le and he may be in walkie-talkie contact with the bridge,' said Fallon. 'Partly because that's a hell of a long walk down that deck, and they have a spotlight operable from the bridge. Partly because the superstructure, approached from the front, is a steel wall five storeys high. We would climb it, but it has windows, to cabins some of which may be occupied.

'The four divers, one of whom will be me, rendezvous at the stern of the *Freya*. There should be a tiny overhang of a few feet. Now, there's a man on top of the funnel, a hundred feet up. But people a hundred feet up tend to look outwards rather than straight down. To help him in this, I want the *Argyll* to start flashing her searchlight to another nearby vessel, creating a spectacle for the man to watch. We will come up the stern from the water, having shed flippers, masks, oxygen bottles and weighted belts. We will be bare-headed, barefoot, in rubber wet-suits only. All weaponry carried in wide webbing belts round the waist.'

'How do you get up the side of the *Freya* carrying forty pounds of metal after a three-mile swim?' asked one of the ministry men.

Fallon smiled. 'It's only thirty feet at most to the taffrail,' he said. 'While practising on the North Sea oil rigs, we've climbed a hundred and sixty feet of vertical steel in four minutes.'

He saw no point in explaining the details of the fitness necessary for such a feat, nor the equipment that made it possible. The boffins had long ago developed for the SBS some remarkable climbing gear. Included among it were the magnetic climbing clamps. These were like dinner plates, fringed with rubber so that they could be applied to metal without making a sound.

The plate itself was rimmed with steel beneath the rubber, and this steel ring could be magnetized to enormous strength. The magnetic force could be turned on or off by a thumb switch by the hand of the man holding the grip on the back of the plate. The electrical charge came from a small but reliable nickel-cadmium battery inside the climbing plate.

The divers were trained to come out of the sea, reach upwards and affix the first plate, then turn on the current. The magnet jammed the plate to the steel structure. Hanging on this, they reached higher and hung the second plate. Only when it was secure did they unlock the first disc, reach higher still and re-affix it. Hand over hand, hanging on by fist grip, wrist and forearm, they climbed out of the sea and upwards, body, legs, feet and equipment swinging free, pulling against the hands and wrists.

So strong were the magnets, so strong also the arms and shoulders, that the commandos could climb an overhang of forty-five degrees if they had to.

'The first man goes up with the special clamps,' said Fallon, 'trailing a rope behind him. If it is quiet on the poop deck, he fixes the rope and the other three can be on deck inside ten seconds. Now, here, in the lee of the funnel assembly, this turbine housing should cast a shadow in the light thrown by the lamp above the door to the superstructure at "A" deck level. We group in this shadow. We'll have black wet-suits, black hands, feet and faces.

'The first major hazard is getting across this patch of illuminated after deck from the shadow of the turbine housing to the main superstructure with all its living quarters.'

'So how do you do it?' asked the vice-admiral, fascinated by this return from technology to the days of Nelson.

'We don't, sir,' said Fallon. 'We will be on the side of the funnel assembly away from where the *Argyll* is stationed. Hopefully the lookout atop the funnel will be looking at the *Argyll*, away from us. We move across from the shadow of the turbine housing, round the corner of the superstructure to this point here, outside the window of the dirty linen store. We cut the plate-glass window in silence with a miniature blow-torch working off a small gas bottle, and go in through the window. The chances of the door of such a store being locked are pretty slim. No one pinches dirty linen, so no one locks such doors. By this time we will be inside the superstructure, emerging to a passage a few yards from the main stairway leading up to "B", "C" and "D" decks, and the bridge.'

'Where do you find the terrorist leader,' asked Sir Julian Flannery, 'the man with the detonator?'

'On the way up the stairs we listen at every door for sounds of voices,' said Fallon. 'If there are any, we open the door and eliminate everyone in the room with silenced automatics. Two men entering the cabin, two men outside on guard. All the way up the structure. Anyone met on the stairs, the same thing. That should bring us to "D" deck unobserved. Here we have to take a calculated gamble. One choice is the captain's cabin; one man will take that choice. Open the door, step inside and shoot without any question. Another man will take the chief engineer's cabin on the same floor, other side of the ship. Same procedure. The last two men take the bridge itself; one with grenades, the second with the Ingrams. It's too big an area, that bridge, to pick targets. We'll just have to sweep it with the Ingram and take everybody in the place after the grenade has paralysed them.'

'What if one of them is Captain Larsen?' asked a ministry man.

Fallon studied the table. 'I'm sorry, there's no way of identifying targets,' he said.

'Suppose neither of the two cabins or the bridge contain the leader? Suppose the man with the remote-control detonator is somewhere else? Out on deck taking the air? In the lavatory? Asleep in another cabin?'

Major Fallon shrugged. 'Bang,' he said, 'big bang.'

'There are twenty-nine crewmen locked down below,' protested a scientist. 'Can't you get them out? Or at least up on deck where they could have a chance to swim for it?'

'No, sir. I've tried every way of getting down to the paint locker, if they are indeed in the paint locker. To attempt to get down through the deck housing would give the game away; the bolts could well squeak, the opening of the steel door would flood the poop deck with light. To go down through the main superstructure to the engine room and try to get them that way would split my force. Moreover the engine room is vast; three levels of it, vaulted like a cathedral. One single man down there, in communication with his leader before we could silence him, and everything would be lost. I believe getting the man with the detonator is our best chance.'

'If she does blow up, with you and your men topsides, I suppose you can dive over the side and swim for the *Argyll*?' suggested another of the ministry civil servants.

Major Fallon looked at the man with anger in his suntanned face.

'Sir, if she blows up, any swimmer within two hundred yards of her will be sucked down into the currents of water pouring into her holes.'

'I'm sorry, Major Fallon,' interposed the Cabinet secretary hurriedly. 'I am sure my colleague was simply concerned for your own safety. Now the question is this: the percentage chance of your hitting the holder of the detonator is a highly problematical figure. Failure to stop the man setting off his charges would provoke the very disaster we are trying to avoid. . . .'

'With the greatest respect, Sir Julian,' cut in Colonel Holmes, 'if the terrorists threaten during the course of the day to blow up the *Freya* at a certain hour tonight, and Chancellor Busch will not weaken in the matter of releasing Mishkin and Lazareff, surely we will have to try Major Fallon's way. We'll be on a hiding to nothing by then anyway. We'll have no alternative.'

The meeting murmured assent. Sir Julian conceded.

'Very well. Defence ministry will please make to *Argyll*; she should turn herself broadside to the *Freya* and provide a lee shelter for Major Fallon's assault boats when they arrive. Environment will instruct air traffic controllers to spot and turn back all aircraft trying to approach the *Argyll* at any altitude; various responsible departments will instruct the tugs and other vessels near the *Argyll* not to betray Major Fallon's preparations to anyone. What about you personally, Major Fallon?'

The marine commando glanced at his watch. It was five-fifteen.

'The navy is lending me a helicopter from the Battersea Heliport to the after deck of the *Argyll*,' he said. 'I'll be there when my men and equipment arrive by sea, if I leave now. . . .'

'Then be on your way, and good luck to you, young man.'

The men at the meeting stood up as a somewhat embarrassed major gathered his model ship, his plans and photographs and left with Colonel Holmes for the helicopter pad beside the Thames Embankment.

A weary Sir Julian Flannery left the smoke-charged room to ascend to the chill of the pre-dawn of another spring day and report to his Prime Minister.

At 6 a.m. a simple statement from Bonn was issued to the effect that after due consideration of all the factors involved, the Federal German government had come to the conclusion that it would after all be wrong to accede to blackmail and that therefore the policy of releasing Mishkin and Lazareff at 8 a.m. had been reconsidered.

Instead, the statement continued, the Federal government would do all in its power to enter into negotiations with the captors of the *Freya* with a view to seeking the release of the ship and its crew by alternative proposals.

The European allies of West Germany were informed of this statement just one hour before it was issued. Each and every premier privately asked the same question:

'What the hell is Bonn up to?'

The exception was London, who knew already. But unofficially, each government was informed that the reversal of position stemmed from urgent American pressure on Bonn during the night, and they were further informed that Bonn had only agreed to delay the release, pending further and, it was hoped, more optimistic developments.

With the breaking of the news, the Bonn government spokesman had two brief and very private working breakfasts with influential German journalists, during which each pressman was given to understand in oblique terms that the change of policy stemmed only from brutal pressure from Washington.

The first radio newscasts of the day carried the fresh statement out of Bonn even as the listeners were picking up their newspapers, which confidently announced the release at breakfast time of the two hijackers. The newspapers' editors were not amused and bombarded the government's news office for an explanation. None was forthcoming that satisfied anyone. The Sunday papers, due for preparation that Saturday, geared themselves for an explosive issue the following morning.

On the *Freya*, the news from Bonn came over the BBC world service to which Drake had tuned his portable radio, at 6.30. Like many another interested party in Europe that morning, the Ukrainian listened to the news in silence, then burst out:

'What the hell do they think they're up to?'

'Something has gone wrong,' said Thor Larsen flatly. 'They've changed their minds. It's not going to work.'

For answer Drake leaned far across the table and pointed his handgun straight at the Norwegian's face.

'Don't you gloat,' he shouted. 'It's not just my friends in Berlin they're playing silly games with. It's not just me. It's your precious ship and crew they're playing with. And don't you forget it.'

He went into deep thought for several minutes, then used the captain's intercom to summon one of his men from the bridge. The man, when he came to the cabin, was still masked, and spoke to his chief in Ukrainian, but the tone sounded worried. Drake left him to guard Captain Larsen and was away for fifteen minutes. When he returned he brusquely beckoned the *Freya*'s skipper to accompany him to the bridge.

The call came in to Maas Control just a minute before seven. Channel twenty was still reserved for the *Freya* alone, and the duty operator was expecting something, for he too had heard the news from Bonn. When the *Freya* called up, he had the tape recorders spinning.

Larsen's voice sounded tired, but he read the statement from his captors in an unemotional tone. '"Following the stupid decision of the government in Bonn to reverse its agreement to release Lev Mishkin and David Lazareff at oh eight hundred hours this morning, those who presently hold the *Freya* announce the following: in the event that Mishkin and Lazareff are not released and airborne on their way to Tel Aviv by noon today, the *Freya* will, on the stroke of noon, vent twenty thousand tons of crude oil into the North Sea. Any attempt to prevent this, or interfere with the process, and any attempt by ships or aircraft to enter the area of clear water round the *Freya*, will result in the immediate destruction of the ship, her crew and cargo."'

The transmission ceased and the channel was cut off. No questions were asked. Almost a hundred listening posts heard the message, and it was contained in news flashes on the breakfast radio shows across Europe within fifteen minutes.

President Matthews' Oval Office was beginning to adopt the aspect of a council of war by the small hours of the morning.

All four men in it had taken their jackets off and loosened ties. Aides came and went with messages from the communications room for one or other of the presidential advisers. The corresponding communication rooms at Langley and State Department had been patched through to the White House. It was 7.15 European time but 2.15 in the morning when the news of Drake's ultimatum was brought into the office and handed to Robert Benson. He passed it without a word to President Matthews.

'I suppose we should have expected it,' said the President wearily, 'but it makes it no easier to learn.'

'Do you think he'll really do it, whoever he is?' asked Secretary David Lawrence.

'He's done everything else he promised so far, damn him,' replied Stanislaw Poklewski.

'I assume Mishkin and Lazareff are under extra heavy guard in Tegel,' said Lawrence.

'They're not in Tegel any more,' replied Benson. 'They were moved just before midnight, Berlin time, to Moabit. It's more modern and more secure.'

'How do you know, Bob?' asked Poklewski.

'I've had Tegel and Moabit under surveillance since the *Freya*'s noon broadcast,' said Benson.

Lawrence, the old-style diplomat, looked exasperated.

'Is it the new policy to spy even on our allies?' he snapped.

'Not quite,' replied Benson. 'We've always done it.'

'Why the change of jail, Bob?' asked Matthews. 'Does Dietrich Busch think the Russians would try and get at Mishkin and Lazareff?'

'No, Mr President, he thinks I will,' said Benson.

'There seems to me a possiblity here that maybe we hadn't thought of,' interposed Poklewski. 'If the terrorists on the *Freya* go ahead and vent twenty thousand tons of crude, and threaten to vent a further fifty thousand tons later in the day, the pressures on Busch could become overwhelming. . . .'

'No doubt they will,' observed Lawrence.

'What I mean is, Busch might simply decide to go it alone and release the hijackers unilaterally. Remember, he doesn't know that the price of such an action would be the destruction of the Treaty of Dublin.'

There was silence for several seconds.

'There's nothing I can do to stop him,' said President Matthews quietly.

'There is, actually,' said Benson. He had the instant attention of the other three. When he described what it was, the faces of Matthews, Lawrence and Poklewski showed disgust.

'I couldn't give that order,' said the President.

'It's a pretty terrible thing to do,' agreed Benson, 'but it's the only way to pre-empt Chancellor Busch. And we will know if he tries to make secret plans to release the pair prematurely. Never mind how; we *will* know. Let's face it: the alternative would be the destruction of the treaty, and the consequences in terms of a resumed arms race that this must bring. If the treaty is destroyed, presumably we will not go ahead with the grain shipments to Russia. In that event Rudin may fall. . . .'

'Which makes his reaction over this business so crazy,' Lawrence pointed out.

'Maybe so, but that *is* his reaction, and until we know why we can't judge how crazy he is,' Benson resumed. 'Until we do know, Chancellor Busch's private knowledge of the proposal I have just made should hold him in check a while longer.'

'You mean we could just use it as something to hold over Busch's head?' asked Matthews hopefully. 'We might never actually have to do it?'

At that moment a personal message arrived for the President from Prime Minister Carpenter in London.

'That's some woman,' he said when he had read it. 'The British reckon they can cope with the first oil slick of twenty thousand tons, but no more. They're preparing a plan to storm the *Freya* with specialist frogmen after sundown and silence the man with the detonator. They give themselves a better than even chance.'

'So we only have to hold the German Chancellor in line for another twelve hours,' said Benson. 'Mr President, I urge you to order what I have just proposed. The chances are it will never have to be activated.'

'But if it must be, Bob? If it must be?'

'Then it must be.'

William Matthews placed the palms of his hands over his face and rubbed tired eyes with his fingertips.

'Dear God, no man should be asked to give orders like that,' he said. 'But if I must . . . Bob, give the order.'

The sun was just clear of the horizon, away to the east over the Dutch coast. On the after deck of the cruiser *Argyll*, now turned broadside to where the *Freya* lay, Major Fallon stood and looked down at the three fast assault craft tethered to her lee side. From the lookout on the *Freya's* funnel top all three would be out of vision. So too the activity on their decks, where Fallon's team of marine commandos were preparing their kayaks and unpacking their unusual pieces of equipment. It was a bright, clear sunrise, giving promise of another warm and sunny day. The sea was a flat calm. Fallon was joined by the *Argyll's* skipper, Captain Richard Preston.

They stood side by side looking down at the three sleek sea greyhounds that had brought the men and equipment from Poole in eight hours. The boats rocked in the swell of a warship passing several cables to the west of them. Fallon looked up. 'Who's that?' he asked, nodding towards the grey warship flying the stars and stripes that was moving to the south.

'The American navy has sent an observer,' said Captain Preston. 'The USS *Moran*. She'll take up station between us and the *Montcalm*.' He glanced at his watch.

'Seven-thirty. Breakfast is being served in the wardroom, if you'd care to join us.'

It was seven-fifty when there was a knock at the door of the cabin of Captain Mike Manning, commanding the *Moran*.

She was at anchor after her race through the night and Manning, who had taken the bridge throughout the night, was running a shaver over his stubble. When the telegraphist entered, Manning took the proffered message and gave it a glance, still shaving. He stopped and turned to the rating.

'It's still in code,' he said.

'Yes, sir. It's tagged for your eyes only, sir.'

Manning dismissed the man, went to his wall-safe and took out his personal decoder. It was unusual, but not unheard of. He began to run a pencil down columns of figures, seeking the groups on the message in front of him and their corresponding letter-combinations. When he had finished decoding, he just sat at his table and stared at the message for a fault. He rechecked the beginning of the message, hoping it was a practical joke. But there was no joke. It was for him, via STANAVFORLANT through Navy Department, Washington. And it was a presidential order, personal to him from the commander-in-chief, US armed forces, White House, Washington.

'He can't ask me to do that,' he breathed. 'No man can ask a sailor to do that.'

But the message did, and it was unequivocal.

In the event the West German government seeks to release the hijackers of Berlin unilaterally, the USS Moran is to sink the supertanker Freya by shellfire, using all possible measures to ignite cargo and minimize environmental damage. This action will be taken on receipt by USS *Moran* of the signal 'THUNDERBOLT' repeat 'THUNDERBOLT'. Destroy message.

Mike Manning was forty-three years old, married with four children, all living with their mother outside Norfolk, Virginia. He had been twenty-one years a serving officer in the US Navy and had never before thought to query a service order.

He walked to the porthole and looked across the five miles of ocean to the low outline between him and the climbing sun. He thought of his magnesium-based starshells slamming into her unprotected skin, penetrating to the volatile crude oil beneath. He thought of twenty-nine men, crouched deep beneath the water-line, eighty feet beneath the waves, in a steel coffin, waiting for rescue, thinking of their own families in the forests of Scandinavia. He crumpled the paper in his hand.

'Mr President,' he whispered, 'I don't know if I can do that.'

16

Dyetski Mir means 'Children's World' and is Moscow's premier toyshop, four storeys of dolls and playthings, puppets and games. Compared to a Western equivalent the layout is drab and the stock shabby, but it is the best the Soviet capital has, apart from the hard-currency Beriozka shops where mainly foreigners go.

By an unintended irony it is across Dzerzhinsky Square from the KGB headquarters, which is definitely not a children's world. Adam Munro was at the ground-floor toys counter just before 10 a.m. Moscow time, two hours later than North Sea time. He began to examine a nylon bear as if debating whether to buy it for his offspring.

Two minutes after ten someone moved to the counter behind him. Out of the corner of his eye he saw that she was pale, her normally full lips drawn, tight, the colour of cigarette ash.

She nodded. Her voice was pitched as his own, low, conversational, uninvolved.

'I managed to see the transcript, Adam. It's serious.'

She picked up a hand-puppet shaped like a small monkey in artificial fur, and told him quietly what she had discovered.

'That's impossible,' he muttered. 'He's still convalescing from a heart attack.'

'No. He was shot dead last October 31st in the middle of the night in a street in Kiev.'

Two salesgirls leaning against the wall twenty feet away eyed them without curiosity and returned to their gossip. One of the few advantages of shopping in Moscow is that one is guaranteed complete privacy by the sales staff.

'And those two in Berlin were the ones?' asked Munro.

'It seems so,' she said dully. 'The fear is that if they escape to Israel they will hold a press conference and inflict an intolerable humiliation on the Soviet Union.'

'Causing Maxim Rudin to fall,' breathed Munro. 'No wonder he will not countenance their release. He cannot. He too has no alternative. And you, are you safe, darling?'

'I don't know. I don't think so. There were suspicions. Unspoken, but they were there. Soon the man on the telephone switchboard will report about your call; the gateman will tell his superiors about my drive in the small hours. It will all come together.'

'Listen, Valentina, I will get you out of here. Quickly, in the next few days.'

For the first time, she turned and faced him. He saw that her eyes were brimming.

'It's over, Adam. I've done what you asked of me, and now it's too late.' She reached up and kissed him briefly, before the astonished gaze of the salesgirls. 'Good-bye, Adam, my love. I'm sorry.'

She turned, paused for a moment to collect herself, and walked away, through the glass doors to the street, back through the gap in the Wall into the East. From where he stood with a plastic-faced milkmaid doll in his hand, he saw her reach the pavement and turn out of sight. A man in a grey trenchcoat, who had been wiping the windscreen of a car, straightened, nodded to the colleague behind the windscreen, and strolled after her.

Adam Munro felt the grief and the anger rising in his throat like a ball of sticky acid. The sounds of the shop muted as a roaring invaded his ears. His hand closed round the head of the doll, crushing, cracking, splintering the smiling pink face beneath the lace cap.

A salesgirl appeared rapidly at his side. 'You've broken it,' she said. 'That will be four roubles.'

Compared with the whirlwind of public and media concern that had concentrated on the West German Chancellor the previous afternoon, the recriminations that poured upon Bonn that Saturday morning were more like a hurricane.

The Foreign Ministry received a continual stream of requests couched in the most urgent terms from the embassies of Finland, Norway, Sweden, Denmark, France, Holland and Belgium, each asking that their ambassadors be received. Each wish was granted, and each ambassador asked in the courteous phraseology of diplomacy the same question: What the hell is going on?

Newspapers, television and radio operations called in all their staffers from weekend leave and tried to give the affair saturation coverage, which was not easy. There were no pictures of the *Freya* since the hijack, save those taken by the French freelancer, who was under arrest, and his pictures confiscated. In fact the same pictures were in Paris under study, but the shots from the successive Nimrods were just as good, and the French government was receiving them anyway.

For lack of hard news, the papers hunted anything they could go for. Two enterprising Englishmen bribed Hilton Hotel staff in Rotterdam to lend them their uniforms, and tried to reach the penthouse suite where Harry Wennerstrom and Lisa Larsen were under siege.

Others sought out former prime ministers, cabinet office holders and tanker captains for their views. Extraordinary sums were waved in the faces of the wives of the crewmen, almost all of whom had been traced, to be photographed praying for their husbands' deliverance.

One former mercenary commander offered to storm the *Freya* alone for a $1,000,000 fee; four archbishops and seventeen parliamentarians of varying persuasions and ambitions offered themselves as hostages in exchange for Captain Larsen and his crew.

'Separately, or in job lots?' snapped Dietrich Busch when he was informed. 'I wish William Matthews was on board instead of thirty good sailors. I'd hold out till Christmas.'

By mid-morning the leaks to the two German stars of press and radio were beginning to have their effect. Their respective comments in German radio and television were picked up by the news agencies and Germany-based correspondents and given wider coverage. The view began to percolate that Dietrich Busch had in fact been acting in the hours before dawn under massive American pressure.

Bonn declined to confirm this, but refused to deny it either. The sheer evasiveness of the government spokesman there told the press its own story.

As dawn broke over Washington, five hours behind Europe, the emphasis switched to the White House. By 6 a.m. in Washington the White House press corps was clamouring for an interview with the President himself. They had to be satisfied, but were not, with a harassed and evasive official spokesman. The spokesman was evasive only because he did not know what to say; his repeated appeals to the Oval Office brought only further instructions that he tell the newshounds the matter was a European affair and the Europeans must do as they thought best. Which threw the affair back into the lap of an increasingly outraged German Chancellor.

'How much longer the hell can this go on?' shouted a thoroughly shaken William Matthews to his advisers as he pushed away a plate of scrambled egg just after 6 a.m. Washington time.

The same question was being asked, but not answered, in a score of offices across America and Europe that unquiet Saturday forenoon.

From his office in Texas the owner of the one million tons of Mubarraq crude, lying dormant but dangerous beneath the *Freya*'s deck, was on the line to Washington.

'I don't care what the hell time of the morning it is,' he shouted to the party campaign manager's secretary. 'You get him on the line and tell him this is Clint Blake, ya hear?'

When the campaign manager of the political party to which the President belonged finally came on the line, he was not a happy man. When he put the machine back in its cradle he was downright morose. A $1,000,000 campaign contribution is no small potatoes in any country, and Clint Blake's threat to withdraw it from his own part and donate it to the opposition was no joke.

It seemed to matter little to him that the cargo was fully insured against loss by Lloyd's. He was one very angry Texan that morning.

Harry Wennerstrom was on the line most of the morning from Rotterdam to Stockholm, calling every one of his friends and contacts in shipping, banking and government to bring pressure on the Swedish premier. The pressure was effective and it was passed on to Bonn.

★

In London the chairman of Lloyd's, Sir Murray Kelso, found the permanent under-secretary to the Department of the Environment still at his desk in Whitehall. Saturday is normally not a day when the senior members of Britain's Civil Service are to be found at their desks, but this was no normal Saturday. Sir Rupert Mossbank had driven hastily back from his country home before dawn when the news came from Downing Street that Mishkin and Lazareff were not to be released. He showed his visitor to a chair.

'Damnable business,' said Sir Murray.

'Perfectly appalling,' agreed Sir Rupert.

He proffered the Butter Osbornes and the two knights sipped their tea.

'The thing is,' said Sir Murray at length, 'the sums involved are really quite vast. Close to a thousand million dollars. Even if the victim countries from the oil spillage if the *Freya* blows up were to sue West Germany rather than us, we'd still have to carry the loss of the ship, cargo and crew. That's about four hundred million dollars.'

'You'd be able to cover it, of course,' said Sir Rupert anxiously. Lloyd's was more than just a company, it was an institution, and as Sir Rupert's department covered merchant shipping he was concerned.

'Oh yes, we would cover it. Have to,' said Sir Murray. 'Thing is, it's such a sum it would have to be reflected in the country's invisible earnings for the year. Probably tip the balance, actually. And what with the new application for another IMF Loan . . .'

'It's a German question, you know,' said Mossbank. 'Not really up to us.'

'Nevertheless, one might press the Germans a bit over this one. Hijackers are bastards, of course, but in this case, why not just let those two blighters in Berlin go. Good riddance to them.'

'Leave it to me,' said Mossbank. 'I'll see what I can do.'

Privately he knew he could do nothing. The confidential file locked in his safe told him Major Fallon was going in by kayak in eleven hours, and until then the Prime Minister's orders were that the line had to hold.

Chancellor Dietrich Busch received the news of the intended underwater attack during the mid-morning in a face-to-face interview with the British ambassador. He was slightly mollified.

'So that's what it's all about,' he said when he had examined the plan unfolded before him. 'Why could I not have been told of this before?'

'We were not sure whether it would work before,' said the ambassador smoothly. Those were his instructions. 'We were working on it through the afternoon of yesterday and last night. By dawn we were certain it was perfectly feasible.'

'What chance of success do you give yourselves?' asked Dietrich Busch.

The ambassador cleared his throat. 'We estimate the chances at three to one in our favour,' he said. 'The sun sets at seven-thirty. Darkness is complete by nine. The men are going in at ten tonight.'

The Chancellor looked at his watch. Twelve hours to go. If the British tried and succeeded, much of the credit would go to their frogmen-killers, but much also to him for keeping his nerve. If they failed, theirs would be the responsibility.

'So it all depends now on this Major Fallon. Very well, ambassador, I will continue to play my part until ten tonight.'

Apart from her batteries of guided missiles, the USS *Moran* was armed with two five-inch Mark 45 naval guns, one forward, one aft. They were of the most modern type available, radar-aimed and computer-controlled. Each could fire a complete magazine of twenty shells in rapid succession without reloading, and the sequence of various types of shell could be pre-set on the computer.

The old days when naval guns' ammunition had to be manually hauled out of the deep magazine, hoisted up to the gun turret by steam power, and rammed into the breech by sweating gunners were long gone. In the *Moran* the shells would be selected by type and performance from the stock on the magazine by the computer, the shells brought to the firing turret automatically, the five-inch guns loaded, fired, voided, reloaded and fired again without a human hand.

The aiming was by radar; the invisible eye of the ship would seek out the target according to the programmed instructions, adjust for wind, range and the movement of either target or firing platform, and, once locked on, hold that aim until given fresh orders. The computer would work together with the eyes of radar, absorbing within fractions of a second any tiny shift of the *Moran* herself, the target, or the wind strength between them. Once locked on, the target could begin to move, the *Moran* could go anywhere she liked; the guns would simply move on silent bearings, keeping their deadly muzzles pointed to just where the shells should go. Wild seas could force the *Moran* to pitch and roll; the target could yaw and swing; it made no difference because the computer compensated. Even the pattern in which the homing shells should fall could be pre-set.

As a back-up, the gunnery officer could scan the target visually with the aid of a camera mounted high aloft, and issue fresh instructions to both radar and computer when he wished to change target.

Captain Mike Manning surveyed the *Freya* from where he stood by the rail with grim concentration. Whoever had advised the President must have done his homework well. The environmental hazard in the death of the *Freya* lay in the escape in crude oil form of her million-ton cargo. But if that cargo was ignited while still in the holds, or within a few seconds of the ship's rupture, it would burn. In fact it would more than burn – it would explode.

Normally crude oil is exceptionally difficult to burn, but if heated enough it will inevitably reach its flashpoint and take fire. The Mubarraq crude the *Freya* carried was the lightest of them all, and to plunge lumps of blazing magnesium, burning at more than 1000°C, into her hull would do the trick with margin to spare. Up to ninety per cent of her cargo would never reach the ocean in crude oil form; it would flame, making a fireball over 10,000 feet high.

What would be left of the cargo would be scum, drifting on the sea's surface, and a black pall of smoke as big as the cloud that once hung over

Hiroshima. Of the ship herself, there would be nothing left, but the environmental problem would have been reduced to manageable proportions. Mike Manning summoned his gunnery officer, Lieutenant Commander Chuck Olsen, to join him by the rail.

'I want you to load and lay the forward gun,' he said flatly. Olsen began to note the commands.

'Ordnance: three semi-armour-piercing, five magnesium starshell, two high-explosive. Total, ten. Then repeat that sequence. Total, twenty.'

'Yes, sir. Three SAP, five Star, two HE. Fall pattern?'

'First shell on target, next shell two hundred metres further; third shell two hundred metres further still. Backtrack in forty-metre drops with the five starshells. Then forward again with the high-explosive, one hundred metres each.'

Lieutenant Commander Olsen noted the fall pattern his captain required. Manning stared over the rail. Five miles away the bows of the *Freya* were pointing straight at the *Moran*. The fall pattern he had dictated would cause the shells to drop in a line from the peak of the *Freya* to the base of her superstructure, then back to the bow, then back again with the explosive towards the superstructure. The semi-armour-piercing would cut open her tanks through the deck-metal as a scalpel opens skin; the starshells would drop in a line of five down the cuts; the explosive would push the blazing crude oil outwards into all the port and starboard holds.

'Got it, captain. Fall point for first shell?'

'Ten metres over the bow of the *Freya*.'

Olsen's pen halted above the paper of his clipboard. He stared at what he had written, then raised his eyes to the *Freya* five miles away.

'Captain,' he said slowly, 'if you do that, she won't just sink; she won't just burn; she won't just explode. She'll vaporize.'

'Those are my orders, Mr Olsen,' said Manning stonily.

The young Swedish-American by his side was pale. 'For Christ's sake, there are thirty Scandinavian seamen on that ship.'

'Mr Olsen, I am aware of the facts. You will either carry out my orders and lay that gun, or announce to me that you refuse.'

The gunnery officer stiffened to attention.

'I'll load and lay your gun for you, Captain Manning,' he said, 'but I will not fire it. If the fire button has to be pressed, you must press it yourself.'

He snapped up a perfect salute and marched away to the fire-control station below decks.

You won't have to, thought Manning, by the rail. If the President himself orders me, I will fire it. Then I will resign my commission.

An hour later the Westland Wessex from the *Argyll* came overhead and winched a Royal Navy officer to the deck of the *Moran*. He asked to speak to Captain Manning in private and was shown to the American's cabin.

'Compliments of Captain Preston, sir,' said the sub-lieutenant, and handed Manning a letter from Preston. When he had finished reading it, Manning sat back like a man reprieved from the gallows. It told him that the British were sending in a team of armed frogmen at ten that night, and all governments had agreed to undertake no independent action in the meantime.

★

While the two officers were talking aboard the USS *Moran*, the airliner bearing Adam Munro back to the West was clearing the Soviet-Polish border.

From the toyshop on Dzerzhinsky Square, Munro had gone to a public call box and telephoned the head of chancery at his embassy. He had told the amazed diplomat in coded language that he had discovered what his masters wanted to know, but would not be returning to the embassy. Instead he was heading straight for the airport to catch the noon plane.

By the time the diplomat had informed the Foreign Office of this, and the FO had told the SIS, the message back to the effect that Munro should cable his news was too late. Munro was boarding.

'What the devil's he doing?' asked Sir Nigel Irvine of Barry Ferndale in the SIS office in London when he learned his storm petrel was flying home.

'No idea,' replied the controller of Soviet Section. 'Perhaps the Nightingale's been blown and he needs to get back urgently before the diplomatic incident blows up. Shall I meet him?'

'When does it land?'

'One forty-five, London time,' said Ferndale. 'I think I ought to meet him. It seems he has the answer to President Matthews' question. Frankly, I'm curious to find out what the devil it can be.'

'So am I,' said Sir Nigel. 'Take a car with a scrambler phone and stay in touch with me personally.'

At a quarter to twelve Drake sent one of his men to bring the *Freya*'s pumpman back to the cargo control room on 'A' deck. Leaving Thor Larsen under the guard of another terrorist, Drake descended to cargo control, took the fuses from his pocket and replaced them. Power was restored to the cargo pumps.

'When you discharge cargo, what do you do?' he asked the crewman. 'I've still got a submachine gun pointing at your captain, and I'll order it to be used if you play any tricks.'

'The ship's pipeline system terminates at a single point, a cluster of pipes which we call the manifold,' said the pumpman. 'Hoses from the shore installation are coupled up to the manifold. After that, the main gate valves are opened at the manifold, and the ship begins to pump.'

'What's your rate of discharge?'

'Twenty thousand tons per hour,' said the man. 'During discharge the ship's balance is maintained by venting several tanks at different points on the ship simultaneously.'

Drake had noted that there was a slight, one-knot tide flowing past the *Freya*, northeast towards the Dutch Friesian islands. He pointed to a tank amidships on the *Freya*'s port side.

'Open the master valve on that one,' he said. The man paused for a second, then obeyed.

'Right,' said Drake, 'when I give the word, switch on the cargo pumps and vent the entire tank.'

'Into the sea?' asked the pumpman incredulously.

'Into the sea,' said Drake grimly. 'Chancellor Busch is about to learn what international pressure really means.'

As the minutes ticked away to midday of Saturday, 2nd April, Europe held its breath. So far as anyone knew, the terrorist had already executed one seaman for a breach of the airspace above them, and had threatened to do it again, or vent crude oil, on the stroke of noon.

The Nimrod that had replaced Squadron Leader Latham the previous midnight had run short of fuel by 11 a.m., so Latham was back on duty, cameras whirring as the minutes to noon ticked away.

Many miles above him a Condor spy satellite was on station, bouncing its continuous stream of picture images across the globe to where a haggard American President sat in the Oval Office watching a television screen. On the TV the *Freya* inched gently into frame from the bottom rim like a pointing finger.

In London men of rank and influence grouped round a screen in the Cabinet Office briefing room on which was presented what the Nimrod was seeing. The Nimrod was on continuous camera-roll from five minutes before twelve, her pictures passing to the Datalink on the *Argyll* beneath her, and from there to Whitehall.

Along the rails of the *Montcalm*, *Breda*, *Brunner*, *Argyll* and *Moran*, sailors of five nations passed binoculars from hand to hand. Their officers stood as high aloft as they could get, with telescopes to eye.

On the BBC World Service the bell of Big Ben struck noon. In the Cabinet Office two hundred yards from Big Ben and two floors beneath the street, someone shouted, 'Christ, she's venting.' Three thousand miles away four shirtsleeved Americans in the Oval Office watched the same spectacle.

From the side of the *Freya*, amidships to port, a column of sticky, ochre-red crude oil erupted.

It was as thick as a man's torso. Impelled by the power of the *Freya*'s mighty pumps, the oil leapt the port rail, dropped twenty-five feet and thundered into the sea. Within seconds the blue-green water was discoloured, putrefied. As the oil bubbled back to the surface, a stain began to spread, moving out and away from the ship's hull on the tide.

For sixty minutes the venting went on, until the single tank was dry. The great stain formed the shape of an egg, broad nearest the Dutch coast and tapering near to the ship. Finally the mass of oil parted company with the *Freya* and began to drift. The sea being calm, the oil slick stayed in one piece, but it began to expand as the light crude ran across the surface of the water. At 2 p.m., an hour after the venting ended, the slick was ten miles long, and seven miles wide at its broadest.

In Washington the Condor passed on and the slick moved off screen. Stanislaw Poklewski switched off the set.

'That's just one fiftieth of what she carries,' he said. 'Those Europeans will go bloody mad.'

Robert Benson took a telephone call and turned to President Matthews.

'London just checked in with Langley,' he said. 'Their man from Moscow has cabled that he has the answer to our question. He claims to know why Maxim Rudin is threatening to tear up the Treaty of Dublin if Mishkin and Lazareff go free. He's flying personally with the news from Moscow to London, and he should land in one hour.'

Matthews shrugged.

'With this man Major Fallon going in with his divers in nine hours, maybe it doesn't matter any more,' he said, 'but I'd sure be interested to know.'

'He'll report to Sir Nigel Irvine, who will tell Mrs Carpenter. Maybe you could ask her to use the hot line the moment she knows,' suggested Benson.

'I'll do that,' said the President.

It was just after 8 a.m. in Washington but past 1 p.m. in Europe when Andrew Drake, who had been pensive and withdrawn while the oil was being vented, decided to make contact again.

By twenty past one Captain Thor Larsen was speaking again to Maas Control, from whom he asked at once to be patched through to the Dutch premier, Mr Jan Grayling. The patch-through to the Hague took no time; the possibility had been foreseen that sooner or later the premier might get a chance to talk to the leader of the terrorists personally and appeal for negotiations on behalf of Holland and Germany.

'I am listening to you, Captain Larsen,' said the Dutchman to the Norwegian in English. 'This is Jan Grayling speaking.'

'"Prime Minister, you have seen the venting of twenty thousand tons of crude oil from my ship?"' asked Larsen, the gun barrel an inch from his ear.

'With great regret, yes,' said Grayling.

'"The leader of the partisans proposes a conference."'

The captain's voice boomed through the premier's office in The Hague. Grayling looked up sharply at the two senior civil servants who had joined him. The tape recorder rolled impassively.

'I see,' said Grayling, who did not see at all but was stalling for time. 'What kind of conference?'

'"A face-to-face conference with the representatives of the coastal nations and other interested parties,"' said Larsen, reading from the paper in front of him.

Jan Grayling clapped his hand over the mouthpiece.

'The bastard wants to talk,' he said excitedly, and then, down the telephone he said, 'On behalf of the Dutch government, I accept to be host to such a conference. Please inform the partisan leader of this.'

On the bridge of the *Freya* Drake shook his head and placed his hand over the mouthpiece. He had a hurried discussion with Larsen.

'Not on land,' said Larsen down the phone. 'Here at sea. What is the name of that British cruiser?'

'She's called the *Argyll*,' said Grayling.

'"She has a helicopter,"' said Larsen at Drake's instruction. '"The conference will be aboard the *Argyll*. At three p.m. Those present should include yourself, the German ambassador, and the captains of the five NATO warships. No one else."'

'That is understood,' said Grayling. 'Will the leader of the partisans attend in person? I would need to consult the British about a guarantee of safe-conduct.'

There was silence as another conference took place on the bridge of the *Freya*. Captain Larsen's voice came back.

'No, the leader will not attend. He will send a representative. "At five minutes before three the helicopter from the *Argyll* will be permitted to hover over the helipad of the *Freya*. There will be no soldiers or marines on board. Only the pilot and the winchman, both unarmed. The scene will be observed from the bridge. There will be no cameras. The helicopter will not descend lower than twenty feet. The winchman will lower a harness and the emissary will be lifted off the main deck and across to the *Argyll*. Is that understood?" '

'Perfectly,' said Grayling. 'May I ask who the representative will be?'

'One moment,' said Larsen and the line went dead.

On the *Freya*, Larsen turned to Drake and asked: 'Well, Mr Svoboda, if not yourself, who are you sending?'

Drake smiled briefly.

'You,' he said. 'You will represent me. You are the best person I can think of to convince them I am not joking either about the ship or the crew or the cargo. And that my patience is running short.'

The phone in Premier Grayling's hand crackled to life.

'I am informed it will be me,' said Larsen, and the line was cut.

Jan Grayling glanced at his watch.

'One forty-five,' he said. 'Seventy-five minutes to go. Get Konrad Voss over here; prepare a helicopter to take off from the nearest point to this office. I want a direct line to Mrs Carpenter in London.'

He had hardly finished speaking before his private secretary told him Harry Wennerstrom was on the line. The old millionaire in the penthouse above the Hilton in Rotterdam had acquired his own radio receiver during the night and had mounted a permanent watch on channel twenty.

'You'll be going out to the *Argyll* by helicopter,' he told the Dutch premier without preamble. 'I'd be grateful if you would take Mrs Lisa Larsen with you.'

'Well, I don't know. . . .' began Grayling.

'For pity's sake, man,' boomed the Swede, 'the terrorists will never know. And if this business isn't handled right, it may be the last time she ever sees him.'

'Get her here in forty minutes,' said Grayling. 'We take off at half-past two.'

The conversation on channel twenty had been heard by every intelligence network and most of the media. Lines were already buzzing between Rotterdam and nine European capitals. The National Security Agency in Washington had a transcript clattering off the White House teleprinter for President Matthews. An aide was darting across the lawn from the Cabinet Office to Mrs Carpenter's study in 10 Downing Street. The Israeli ambassador in Bonn was urgently asking Chancellor Busch to ascertain for Prime Minister Golen from Captain Larsen whether the terrorists were Jews or not, and the German government had promised to do this.

The afternoon newspapers, radio and TV shows across Europe had their headlines for the 5 p.m. edition and frantic calls were made to four navy ministries for a report on the conference if and when it took place.

★

As Jan Grayling put down the telephone on Thor Larsen, the jet airliner carrying Adam Munro from Moscow touched the tarmac of runway One at London's Heathrow Airport.

Barry Ferndale's Foreign Office pass had brought him to the foot of the aircraft steps and he ushered his bleak-faced colleague from Moscow into the back seat. The car was better than most that the firm used; it had a screen between driver and passengers, and a telephone linked to head office.

As they swept down the tunnel from the airport to the M4 motorway, Ferndale broke the silence.

'Rough trip, old boy?' He was not referring to the aeroplane journey.

'Disastrous,' snapped Munro. 'I think the Nightingale is blown. Certainly followed by the opposition. May have been picked up by now.'

Ferndale clucked sympathy.

'Bloody bad luck,' he said. 'Always terrible to lose an agent. Damned upsetting. Lost a couple myself, you know. One died damned unpleasantly. But that's the trade we're in, Adam. That's part of what Kipling used to call the Great Game.'

'Except this is no game,' said Munro, 'and what the KGB will do to the Nightingale is no joke.'

'Absolutely not. Sorry. Shouldn't have said that.' Ferndale paused expectantly as their car joined the M4 traffic stream.

'But you did get the answer to our questions? Why is Rudin so pathologically opposed to the release of Mishkin and Lazareff?'

'The answer to Mrs Carpenter's question,' said Munro grimly. 'Yes, I got it.'

'And it is?'

'She asked it,' said Munro, 'she'll get the answer. I hope she'll like it. It cost a life to get it.'

'That might not be wise, Adam, old son,' said Ferndale. 'You can't just walk in on the PM, you know. Even the Master has to make an appointment.'

'Then ask him to make one,' said Munro, gesturing to the telephone.

'I'm afraid I'll have to,' said Ferndale quietly. It was a pity to see a talented man blow his career to bits, but Munro had evidently reached the end of his tether. Ferndale was not going to stand in his way; the Master had told him to stay in touch. He did exactly that.

Ten minutes later Mrs Joan Carpenter listened carefully to the voice of Sir Nigel Irvine on the scrambler telephone.

'To give the answer to me personally, Sir Nigel?' she asked. 'Isn't that rather unusual?'

'Extremely so, ma'am. In fact it's unheard of. I fear it has to mean Mr Munro and the Service parting company. But short of asking the specialists to require the information out of him, I can hardly force him to tell me. You see, he's lost an agent who seems to have become a personal friend over the past nine months, and he's just about at the end of his tether.'

Joan Carpenter thought for several moments.

'I am deeply sorry to have been the cause of so much distress,' she said. 'I would like to apologize to your Mr Munro for what I had to ask him to do. Please ask his driver to bring him to Number Ten. And join me yourself immediately.'

The line went dead. Sir Nigel Irvine stared at the receiver for a while. That woman never ceases to surprise me, he thought. All right, Adam, you want your moment of glory, son, you'll have it. But it'll be your last. After that it's pastures new for you. Can't have prima donnas in the Service.

As he descended to his car Sir Nigel reflected that however interesting the explanation might be, it was academic, or soon would be. In seven hours Major Simon Fallon would steal aboard the *Freya* with three companions and wipe out the terrorists. After that Mishkin and Lazareff would stay where they were for fifteen years.

At two o'clock, back in the day cabin, Drake leaned forward towards Thor Larsen and told him: 'You're probably wondering why I set up this conference on the *Argyll*. I know that while you are there you will tell them who we are and how many we are. What we are armed with and where the charges are placed. Now listen carefully, because this is what you must also tell them, if you want to save your crew and ship from instant destruction.'

He talked for over thirty minutes. Thor Larsen listened impassively, drinking in the words and their implications. When he had finished the Norwegian captain said: 'I'll tell them. Not because I aim to save your skin, Mr Svoboda, but because you are not going to kill my crew and my ship.'

There was a trill from the intercom in the soundproof cabin. Drake answered it and looked out through the windows to the distant fo'c's'le. Approaching from the seaward side, very slowly and carefully, was the Wessex helicopter from the *Argyll*, the Royal Navy markings clear along her tail.

Five minutes later, under the eyes of cameras that beamed their images across the world, watched by men and women in subterranean offices hundreds and even thousands of miles away, Captain Thor Larsen, master of the biggest ship ever built, stepped out of her superstructure into the open air. He had insisted on donning his black trousers and had buttoned his merchant navy jacket with the four gold rings of a sea captain over his white sweater. On his head was the braided cap with the Viking-helmet emblem of the Nordia Line. He was in the uniform he would have worn the previous evening to meet the world's press for the first time. Squaring his wide shoulders, he began the long, lonely walk down the vast expanse of his ship to where the harness and cable dangled from the helicopter a third of a mile in front of him.

17

Sir Nigel Irvine's personal limousine, bearing Barry Ferndale and Adam Munro, arrived at 10 Downing Street a few seconds before three o'clock. When the pair were shown into the anteroom leading to the Prime Minister's study, Sir Nigel himself was already there. He greeted Munro coolly.

'I do hope this insistence on delivering your report to the PM personally will have been worth all the effort, Munro,' he said.

'I think it will, Sir Nigel,' replied Munro.

The director-general of the SIS regarded his staffer quizzically. The man was evidently exhausted and had had a rough deal over the Nightingale affair. Still, that was no excuse for breaking discipline. The door to the private study opened and Sir Julian Flannery appeared.

'Do come in, gentlemen,' he said.

Adam Munro had never met the Prime Minister personally. Despite not having slept for two days, she appeared fresh and collected. She greeted Sir Nigel first then shook hands with the two men she had not met before, Barry Ferndale and Adam Munro.

'Mr Munro,' she said, 'let me state at the outset my deep personal regret that I had to cause you both personal hazard and possible exposure to your agent in Moscow. I had no wish to do so, but the answer to President Matthews' question was of a truly international importance, and I do not use that phrase lightly.'

'Thank you for saying so, ma'am,' replied Munro.

She went on to explain that even as they talked the Captain of the *Freya*, Thor Larsen, was landing on the after deck of the cruiser *Argyll* for a conference; and that, scheduled for ten that evening, a team of SBS frogmen was going to attack the *Freya* in an attempt to wipe out the terrorists and their detonator.

Munro's face was set like granite when he heard.

'If, ma'am,' he said clearly, 'these commandos are successful, then the hijack will be over, the two prisoners in Berlin will stay where they are, and the probable exposure of my agent will have been in vain.'

She had the grace to look thoroughly uncomfortable.

'I can only repeat my apology, Mr Munro. The plan to storm the *Freya* was only devised in the small hours of this morning, eight hours after Maxim Rudin delivered his ultimatum to President Matthews. By then you were already consulting the Nightingale. It was impossible to call that agent back.'

Sir Julian entered the room and told the premier: 'They're coming on patch-through now, ma'am.'

The Prime Minister asked her three guests to be seated. In the corner of her office a box speaker had been stood, and wires led from it to a neighbouring anteroom.

'Gentlemen, the conference on the *Argyll* is beginning. Let us listen to it, and then we will learn from Mr Munro the reason for Maxim Rudin's extraordinary ultimatum.'

As Thor Larsen stepped from the harness at the end of his dizzying five-mile ride through the sky beneath the Wessex on to the after deck of the British cruiser, the roar of the engines above his head was penetrated by the shrill welcome of the bo'sun's pipes.

The *Argyll*'s captain stepped forward, saluted and held out his hand.

'Richard Preston,' said the navy captain. Larsen returned the salute and shook hands.

'Welcome aboard, captain,' said Preston.

'Thank you,' said Larsen.

'Would you care to step down to the wardroom?'

The two captains descended from the fresh air into the largest cabin in the cruiser, the officers' wardroom. There Captain Preston made the formal introductions.

'The Right Honourable Jan Grayling, Prime Minister of the Netherlands. You have spoken on the telephone already, I believe . . . His Excellency Konrad Voss, ambassador of the German Federal Republic . . . Captains Desmoulins of the French Navy, de Jong of the Dutch Navy, Hasselmann of the German Navy, and Captain Manning of the US Navy.'

Mike Manning put out his hand and stared into the eyes of the bearded Norwegian.

'Good to meet you, captain.' The words stuck in his throat. Thor Larsen looked into his eyes a fraction longer than he had for the other naval commanders, and passed on.

'Finally,' said Captain Preston, 'may I present Major Simon Fallon of the Royal Marine commandos.'

Larsen looked down at the short, burly marine and felt the man's hard fist in his own. So, he thought, Svoboda was right after all.

At Captain Preston's invitation they all seated themselves at the expansive dining table.

'Captain Larsen, I should make plain that our conversation has to be recorded, and will be transmitted in uninterceptable form directly from this cabin to Whitehall where the British Prime Minister will be listening.'

Larsen nodded. His gaze kept wandering to the American: everyone else was looking at him with interest; the US Navy man was studying the mahogany table.

'Before we begin, may I offer you anything?' asked Preston. 'A drink perhaps? Food? Tea or coffee?'

'Just coffee, thank you. Black, no sugar.'

Captain Preston nodded to a steward by the door who disappeared.

'It has been agreed that to begin with I shall ask the questions that interest and concern all our governments,' continued Captain Preston. 'Mr Grayling and Mr Voss have graciously conceded this. Of course anyone may pose a question that I may have overlooked. Firstly, may we ask you, Captain Larsen, what happened in the small hours of yesterday morning.'

Was it only yesterday, Larsen thought. Yes, three a.m. on Friday morning; and it was now five past three on Saturday afternoon. Just thirty-six hours. It seemed like a week.

Briefly and clearly he described the takeover of the *Freya* during the night watch, how the attackers came so effortlessly aboard and herded the crew down to the paint locker.

'So there are seven of them?' asked the marine major. 'You are quite certain there are no more?'

'Quite certain,' said Larsen. 'Just seven.'

'And do you know who they are,' asked Preston. 'Jews? Arabs? Red Brigades?'

Larsen stared at the ring of faces in surprise. He had forgotten that outside the *Freya* no one knew who the hijackers were.

'No,' he said. 'They're Ukrainians. Ukrainian nationalists. The leader calls himself simply Svoboda. He said it means "freedom" in Ukrainian. They always talk to each other in what seems to be Ukrainian. Certainly it's Slavic.'

'Then what the hell are they seeking the liberation of two Russian Jews from Berlin for?' asked Jan Grayling in exasperation.

'I don't know,' said Larsen. 'The leader claims they are friends of his.'

'One moment,' said Ambassador Voss. 'We have all been mesmerized by the fact that Mishkin and Lazareff are Jews and wish to go to Israel. But of course they both come from the Ukraine, the city of Lvov. It did not occur to my government that they could be Ukrainian partisan fighters as well.'

'Why do they think the liberation of Mishkin and Lazareff will help their Ukrainian nationalist cause?' asked Preston.

'I don't know,' said Larsen. 'Svoboda won't say. I asked him; he nearly told me, but then shut up. He would only say that the liberation of those two men would cause such a blow to the Kremlin, it could start a widespread popular uprising.'

There was blank incomprehension on the faces of the men around him. The final questions about the layout of the ship, where Svoboda and Larsen stayed, the deployment of the terrorists, took a further ten minutes. Finally, Captain Preston looked round at the other captains and representatives of Holland and Germany. The men nodded. Preston leaned forward.

'Now, Captain Larsen, I think it is time to tell you. Tonight Major Fallon here and a group of his colleagues are going to approach the *Freya* under-water, scale her sides and wipe out Svoboda and his men.'

He sat back to watch the effect.

'No,' said Thor Larsen slowly, 'they are not.'

'I beg your pardon?'

'There will be no underwater attack unless you wish to have the *Freya* blown up and sunk. That is what Svoboda sent me here to tell you.'

Item by item, Captain Larsen spelled out Svoboda's message to the West. Before sundown every single floodlight on the *Freya* would be switched on. The man in the fo'c's'le would be withdrawn; the entire foredeck from the bow to the base of the superstructure would be bathed in light.

Inside the accommodation, every door leading outside would be locked and bolted on the inside. Every interior door would also be locked, to prevent access via a window.

Svoboda himself, with his detonator, would remain inside the super-structure, but would select one of the more than fifty cabins to occupy. Every light in every cabin would be switched on, and every curtain drawn.

One terrorist would remain on the bridge, in walkie-talkie contact with the man atop the funnel. The other four men would ceaselessly patrol the taffrail round the entire stern area of the *Freya* with powerful torches, scanning the surface of the sea. At the first trace of a stream of bubbles, or someone climbing the vessel's side, the terrorist would fire a shot. The man on top of the funnel would alert the bridge-watch, who would shout a warning down the telephone to the cabin where Svoboda hid. This telephone line would be kept open all night. On hearing the word of alarm, Svoboda would press his red button.

When he had finished, there was silence round the table.

'Bastard,' said Captain Preston with feeling. The group's eyes swivelled to Major Fallon, who stared unblinkingly at Larsen.

'Well, major?' asked Grayling.

'We could come aboard at the bow instead,' said Fallon.

Larsen shook his head. 'The bridge-watch would see you in the flood-lights,' he said. 'You wouldn't get halfway down the foredeck.'

'We'll have to booby-trap their escape launch anyway,' said Fallon.

'Svoboda thought of that, too,' said Larsen. 'They are going to pull it round to the stern where it is in the glare of the deck lights.'

Fallon shrugged.

'That just leaves a frontal assault,' he said. 'Come out of the water firing, use more men, come aboard against the opposition, beat in the door and move through the cabins one by one.'

'Not a chance,' said Larsen firmly. 'You won't be over the rail before Svoboda has heard you and blown us all to kingdom come.'

'I'm afraid I have to agree with Captain Larsen,' said Jan Grayling. 'I don't believe the Dutch government would agree to a suicide mission.'

'Nor the West German government,' said Voss.

Fallon tried one last move.

'You are alone with him personally for much of the time, Captain Larsen. Would you kill him?'

'Willingly,' said Larsen, 'but if you are thinking of giving me a weapon, don't bother. On my return I am to be skin-searched, well out of Svoboda's reach. Any weapon found, and another of my seamen is executed. I'm not taking anything back on board. Not weapons, not poison.'

'I'm afraid it's over, Major Fallon,' said Captain Preston gently. 'The hard option won't work.'

He rose from the table.

'Well, gentlemen, barring further questions to Captain Larsen, I believe there is little more we can do. It now has to be passed back to the concerned governments. Captain Larsen, thank you for your time and your patience. In my personal cabin there is someone who would like to speak with you.'

Thor Larsen was shown from the silent wardroom by a steward. Mike Manning watched him go with anguish. The destruction of the plan of attack by Major Fallon's party now brought back to terrible possibility the order he had been given that morning from Washington.

The steward showed the Norwegian captain through the door of Preston's personal living quarters. Lisa Larsen rose from the edge of the bed where she had been sitting, staring out of the porthole at the dim outline of the *Freya*.

'Thor,' she said. Larsen kicked back and slammed the door shut. He opened his arms and caught the running woman in a hug.

'Hallo, little snow-mouse.'

In the Prime Minister's private office in Downing Street, the transmission from the *Argyll* was switched off.

'Blast,' said Sir Nigel, expressing the views of them all.

The Prime Minister turned to Munro. 'Now, Mr Munro, it seems that your news is not so academic after all. If the explanation can in any way assist us to solve this impasse, your risks will not have been run in vain. So, in a sentence, why is Maxim Rudin behaving in this way?'

'Because, ma'am, as we all know his supremacy in the Politburo hangs by a thread and has done so for months. . . .'

'But on the question of arms concessions to the Americans, surely,' said Mrs Carpenter. 'That is the issue on which Vishnayev wishes to bring him down.'

'Ma'am, Yefrem Vishnayev has made his play for supreme power in the Soviet Union and cannot go back now. He will bring Rudin down any way he can, for if he does not, then following the signature of the Treaty of Dublin in eight days' time Rudin will destroy him. These two men in Berlin can deliver to Vishnayev the instrument he needs to swing one or two members of the Politburo to change their votes and join his faction of hawks.'

'How?' asked Sir Nigel.

'By speaking. By opening their mouths. By reaching Israel alive and giving an international press conference. By inflicting on the Soviet Union a massive public and international humiliation.'

'Not for killing an airline captain no one had ever heard of?' asked the PM.

'No. Not for that. The killing of Captain Rudenko in that cockpit was genuinely an accident. The escape to the West was indispensable if they were to give their real achievement the worldwide publicity it needed. You see, ma'am, on the night of 31st October last, in a street in Kiev, Mishkin and Lazareff assassinated Yuri Ivanenko, the head of the KGB.'

Sir Nigel Irvine and Barry Ferndale sat bolt upright as if stung.

'So that's what happened to him,' breathed Ferndale, the Soviet expert. 'I thought he must be in disgrace.'

'Not disgrace, a grave,' said Munro. 'The Politburo knows it, of course, and at least one, maybe two, of Rudin's faction have threatened they will change sides if the assassins escape scot free and humiliate the Soviet Union.'

'Does that make sense, in Russian psychology, Mr Ferndale?' the Prime Minister asked.

Ferndale's handkerchief whirled in circles across the lenses of his glasses and he polished furiously.

'Perfect sense, ma'am,' he said excitedly. 'Internally and externally. In times of crises, such as food shortages, it is imperative that the KGB inspire awe in the people, especially the non-Russian nationalities, to hold them in check. If that awe were to vanish, if the terrible KGB were to become a laughing-stock, the repercussions could be appalling – seen from the Kremlin of course.

'Externally, and especially in the Third World, the impression that the power of the Kremlin is an impenetrable fortress is of paramount importance to Moscow in maintaining its hold, and its steady advance.

'Yes, those two men are a time-bomb for Maxim Rudin. The fuse is lit by the *Freya* affair, and the time is running out.'

'Then why cannot Chancellor Busch be told of Rudin's ultimatum?' asked Munro. 'He'd realize that the Treaty of Dublin, which affects his country massively, is more important than the *Freya*.'

'Because,' cut in Sir Nigel, 'even the news that Rudin has made the ultimatum is secret. If even that got out, the world would realize the affair must concern more than just a dead airline captain.'

'Well, gentlemen, this is all very interesting,' said Mrs Carpenter, 'fascinating indeed. But it does not help solve the problem. President Matthews faces two alternatives: permit Chancellor Busch to release Mishkin and Lazareff, and lose the treaty; or, require these two men to remain in jail, and lose the *Freya* while gaining the loathing of nearly a dozen Europen governments and condemnation of the world.

'So far, he has tried a third option: that of asking Prime Minister Golen to return the two men to jail in Germany after the release of the *Freya*. The idea was to seek to satisfy Maxim Rudin. It might have, it might not. In fact Benyamin Golen refused. So that was that.

'Then we tried another way: storm the *Freya* and liberate her. Now that has become impossible. I fear there are no more options, short of doing what we suspect the Americans have in mind.'

'And what is that?' asked Munro.

'Blowing her apart by shellfire,' said Sir Nigel Irvine. 'We have no proof of it, but the guns of the *Moran* are trained right on the *Freya*.'

'Actually, there *is* a third option. It might satisfy Maxim Rudin, and it should work.'

'Then please explain it,' commanded the Prime Minister.

Munro did so. It took barely five minutes. There was silence.

'I find it utterly repulsive,' said Mrs Carpenter at last.

'Ma'am, with all respect, so did I betraying my agent to the KGB,' Munro replied stonily. Ferndale shot him a warning look.

'Do we have such devilish equipment available?' Mrs Carpenter asked Sir Nigel.

He studied his fingertips. 'I believe the specialist department may be able to lay its hands on that sort of thing,' he said quietly.

Joan Carpenter inhaled deeply.

'It is not, thank God, a decision I would need to make. It is a decision for President Matthews. I suppose it has to be put to him. But it should be explained person to person. Tell me, Mr Munro, would you be prepared to carry out this plan?'

Munro thought of Valentina walking out into the street, to the waiting men in grey trenchcoats.

'Yes,' he said, 'without a qualm.'

'Time is short,' she said briskly, 'if you are to reach Washington tonight. Sir Nigel, have you any ideas?'

'There is the five o'clock Concorde, the new service to Boston,' he said. 'It could be diverted to Washington if the President wanted it.'

Mrs Carpenter glanced at her watch. It read 4 p.m.

'On your way, Mr Munro,' she said. 'I will inform President Matthews of the news you have brought from Moscow, and ask him to receive you. You may explain to him personally your somewhat macabre proposal. If he will see you at such short notice.'

Lisa Larsen was still holding her husband five minutes after he entered the cabin. He asked her about home, and the children. She had spoken to them two hours earlier; there was no school on Saturday, so they were at home with the Dahl family. They were fine, she said. They had just come back from feeding the rabbits at Bogneset. The small talk died away.

'Thor, what is going to happen?'

'I don't know. I don't understand why the Germans will not release those two men. I don't understand why the Americans will not allow it. I sit with prime ministers and ambassadors, and they can't tell me either.'

'If they don't release the men, will that terrorist . . . do it?' she asked.

'He may,' said Larsen thoughtfully. 'I believe he will try. And if he does, I shall try to stop him. I have to.'

'Those fine captains out there, why won't they help you?'

'They can't, snow-mouse. No one can help me. I have to do it myself, or no one else will.'

'I don't trust that American captain,' she whispered. 'I saw him when I came on board with Mr Grayling. He would not look me in the face.'

'No, he cannot. Nor me. You see, he has orders to blow the *Freya* out of the water.'

She pulled away from him and looked up, eyes wide.

'He couldn't,' she said. 'No man would do that to other men.'

'He will, if he has to. I don't know for certain, but I suspect so. The guns of his ship are trained on us. If the Americans thought they had to do it, they would do it. Burning up the cargo would lessen the ecological damage, destroy the blackmail weapon.'

She shivered and clung to him. She began to cry.

'I hate him,' she said.

Thor Larsen stroked her hair, his great hand almost covering her small head. 'Don't hate him,' he rumbled. 'He has his orders. They all have their orders. They will all do what the men far away in the chancelleries of Europe and America tell them to do.'

'I don't care. I hate them all.'

He laughed and he stroked her, gently reassuring.

'Do something for me, snow-mouse.'

'Anything.'

'Go back home. Go back to Alesund. Get out of this place. Look after Kurt and Kristina. Keep the house ready for me. When this is over, I am going to come home. You can believe that.'

'Come back with me. Now.'

'You know I have to go. The time is up.'

'Don't go back to the ship,' she begged him. 'They'll kill you there.'

She was sniffing furiously, trying not to cry, trying not to hurt him.

'It's my ship,' he said gently. 'It's my crew. You know I have to go.'

He left her in Captain Preston's armchair.

As he did so the car bearing Adam Munro swung out of Downing Street, past the crowd of sightseers who hoped to catch a glimpse of the high and the mighty at this moment of crises, and turned through Parliament Square for the Cromwell Road and the motorway to Heathrow.

Five minutes later, Thor Larsen was buckled by two Royal Navy seamen, their hair awash from the rotors of the Wessex above them, into the harness.

Captain Preston, with six of his officers and the four NATO captains stood in a line a few yards away. The Wessex began to lift.

'Gentlemen,' said Captain Preston. Five hands rose to five braided caps in simultaneous salute.

Mike Manning watched the bearded sailor in the harness being borne away from him. From a hundred feet up, the Norwegian seemed to be looking down, straight at him.

He knows, thought Manning with horror. Oh, Jesus and Mary, he knows.

Thor Larsen walked into the day cabin of his own suite on the *Freya* with a submachine carbine at his back. Svoboda was in his usual chair. Larsen was directed into the one at the far end of the table.

'Did they believe you?' asked the Ukrainian.

'Yes,' said Larsen. 'They believed me. And you were right. They were preparing an attack by frogmen after dark. It's been called off.'

Drake snorted.

'Just as well,' he said. 'If they had tried it, I'd have pressed this button without hesitation, suicide or no suicide. They'd have left me no alternative.'

At ten minutes before noon, President William Matthews laid down the telephone that had joined him for fifteen minutes to the British premier in London, and looked at his three advisers. They had each heard the conversation on the amplivox.

'So that's it,' he said. 'The British are not going ahead with their night attack. Another of our options gone. That just about leaves us with the plan of blowing the *Freya* to pieces ourselves. Is the warship on station?'

'In position, guns laid and loaded,' confirmed Stanslaw Poklewski.

'Unless this man Munro has some idea that would work,' suggested Robert Benson. 'Will you agree to see him, Mr President?'

'Bob, I'll see the Devil himself if he can propose some way of getting me off this hook,' said Matthews.

'One thing at least we may now be certain of,' said David Lawrence. 'Maxim Rudin was not overreacting. He could do nothing other than he has done, after all. In his fight with Yefrem Vishnayev, he too has no aces left. How the hell did those two in Moabit Jail ever get to shoot Yuri Ivanenko?'

'We have to assume the one who leads that group on the *Freya* helped them,' said Benson. 'I'd dearly love to get my hands on that Svoboda.'

'No doubt you'd kill him,' said Lawrence with distaste.

'Wrong,' said Benson. 'I'd enlist him. He's tough, ingenious and ruthless. He's taken ten European governments and made them dance like puppets.'

It was noon in Washington, 5 p.m. in London as the late-afternoon Concorde hoisted its stiltlike legs over the concrete of Heathrow, lifted its drooping spear of a nose towards the western sky and climbed through the sound barrier towards the sunset.

The normal rules about not creating the sonic boom until well out over the sea had been overruled by orders from Downing Street. The pencil-slim dart pushed its four screaming Olympus engines to full power just after take-off and 150,000 pounds of thrust flung the airliner towards the stratosphere.

The captain had estimated three hours to Washington, two hours ahead of the sun. Halfway across the Atlantic he told his Boston-bound passengers with deep regret that the Concorde would make a stopover of a few moments at Dulles International Airport, Washington, before heading back to Boston, due to the cover-all 'operational reasons'.

It was 7 p.m. in Western Europe but 9 in Moscow when Yefrem Vishnayev finally got the personal and highly unusual Saturday evening meeting with Maxim Rudin for which he had been clamouring all day.

The old dictator of Soviet Russia agreed to meet his party theoretician in the Politburo meeting room on the third floor of the Arsenal building.

When he arrived, Vishnayev was backed by Marshal Nikolai Kerensky, but he found Rudin supported by his allies Dmitri Rykov and Vassili Petrov.

'I note that few appear to be enjoying this brilliant spring weekend in the countryside,' he said acidly.

Rudin shrugged. 'I was in the midst of enjoying a private dinner with two friends,' he said. 'What brings you, Comrades Vishnayev and Kerensky, to the Kremlin at this hour?'

The room was bare of secretaries and guards; it contained just the five power bosses of the union in angry confrontation beneath the globe lights in the high ceiling.

'Treason,' snapped Vishnayev. 'Treason, Comrade Secretary-General.'

The silence was ominous, menacing.

'Whose treason?' asked Rudin. Vishnayev leaned across the table and spoke two feet from Rudin's face.

'The treason of two filthy Jews from Lvov,' hissed Vishnayev. 'The treason of two men now in a jail in Berlin. Two men whose freedom is being sought by a gang of murderers on a tanker in the North Sea. The treason of Mishkin and Lazareff.'

'It is true,' said Rudin carefully, 'that the murder last December by these two of Captain Rudenko of Aeroflot constitutes – '

'Is it not also true,' asked Vishnayev menacingly, 'that these two murderers killed Yuri Ivanenko?'

Maxim Rudin would dearly have liked to shoot a sideways glance at Vassili Petrov by his side. Something had gone wrong. There had been a leak.

Petrov's lips set in a hard, straight line. He too, now controlling the KGB through General Abrassov, knew that the circle of men aware of the real truth was small, very small. The man who had spoken, he was sure, was Colonel Kukushkin, who had first failed to protect his master, and then failed to liquidate his master's killers. He was trying to buy his career, perhaps even his life, by changing camps and confiding in Vishnayev.

'It is certainly suspected,' said Rudin carefully. 'Not a proven fact.'

'I understand it *is* a proven fact,' snapped Vishnayev. 'These two men have been positively identified as the killers of our dear comrade Yuri Ivanenko.'

Rudin reflected how intensely Vishnayev had loathed Ivanenko and wished him dead and gone.

'The point is academic,' said Rudin. 'Even for the killing of Captain Rudenko, the two murderers are destined to be liquidated inside their Berlin jail.'

'Perhaps not,' said Vishnayev with well-simulated outrage. 'It appears they may be released by West Germany and sent to Israel. The West is weak, it cannot hold out for long against the terrorists on the *Freya*. If those two reach Israel alive, they will talk. I think, my friends, oh, yes, I truly think we all know what they will say.'

'What are you asking for?' said Rudin.

Vishnayev rose. Taking his example, Kerensky rose too. 'I am demanding,' said Vishnayev, 'an extraordinary plenary meeting of the full Politburo here in this room tomorrow night at this hour, nine o'clock. On a matter of exceptional national urgency. That is my right, Comrade Secretary-General?'

Rudin's shock of grey hair nodded slowly. He looked up at Vishnayev from under his eyebrows.

'Yes,' he growled, 'that is your right.'

'Then until this hour tomorrow,' snapped the theoretician, and stalked from the chamber.

Rudin turned to Petrov.

'Colonel Kukushkin?' he asked.

'It looks like it. Either way, Vishnayev knows.'

'Any possibility of eliminating Mishkin and Lazareff inside Moabit?'

Petrov shook his head.

'Not by tomorrow. No chance of mounting a fresh operation under a new man in that time. Is there any way of pressuring the West not to release them at all?'

'No,' said Rudin shortly, 'I have brought every pressure on Matthews that I know how. There is nothing more I can bring to bear on him. It is up to him now, him and that damned German Chancellor in Bonn.'

'Tomorrow,' said Rykov soberly, 'Vishnayev and his people will produce Kukushkin and demand that we hear him out. And if by then Mishkin and Lazareff are in Israel. . . .'

At 8 p.m., European time, Andrew Drake, speaking through Captain Thor Larsen from the *Freya*, issued his final ultimatum.

At 0900 the following morning, in thirteen hours, the *Freya* would vent 100,000 tons of crude oil into the North Sea, unless Mishkin and Lazareff were airborne and on their way to Tel Aviv. At 2000 unless they were in Israel and identified as genuine, the *Freya* would blow herself apart.

'That's bloody well the last straw,' shouted Dietrich Busch when he heard the ultimatum ten minutes after it was broadcast from the *Freya*. 'Who does William Matthews think he is? No one, but no one, is going to force the Chancellor of Germany to carry on with this charade. It is over.'

At twenty past eight the Federal German government announced that it was unilaterally releasing Mishkin and Lazareff the following morning at 8 a.m.

At 8.30 p.m. a personal coded message arrived on the USS *Moran* for Captain Mike Manning. When decoded it read simply: 'Prepare for fire order 0700 tomorrow.'

He screwed it into a ball in his fist and looked out through the porthole towards the *Freya*. She was lit like a Christmas tree, flood and arc lights bathing her towering superstructure in a glare of white light. She sat on the ocean five miles away, doomed, helpless; waiting for one of her two executioners to finish her off.

While Thor Larsen was speaking on the *Freya*'s radio-telephone to Maas Control, the Concorde bearing Adam Munro swept over the perimeter fence at Dulles Airport, flaps and undercarriage hanging, nose high, a delta-shaped bird of prey seeking to grip the runway.

The bewildered passengers, like goldfish peering through the tiny windows, noted only that she did not taxi towards the terminal buildings, but simply hove-to, engines running, in a parking bay beside the taxi track. A gangway was waiting, along with a black limousine.

A single passenger, carrying no mackintosh and no hand luggage, rose from near the front, stepped out of the open door and ran down the steps. Seconds later the gangway was withdrawn, the door closed and the apologetic captain announced that they would take off at once for Boston.

Adam Munro stepped into the limousine beside the two burly escorts and was immediately relieved of his passport. The two presidential Secret Service agents studied it intently as the car swept across the expanse of tarmac to where a small helicopter stood in the lee of a hangar, rotors whirling.

The agents were formal, polite. They had their orders. Before he boarded the helicopter Munro was exhaustively frisked for hidden weapons. When they were satisfied, they escorted him aboard and the whirlybird lifted off, heading for Washington across the Potomac, and the spreading lawns of the White House. It was half an hour after touchdown at Dulles, three-thirty on a warm Washington spring afternoon, when they landed barely a hundred yards from the Oval Office windows.

The two agents escorted Munro across the lawns to where a narrow street ran between the big, grey Executive Office building, a Victorian monstrosity of porticos and columns intersected by a bewildering variety of different types of window, and the much smaller, white West Wing, a squat box partly sunken below ground level.

It was to a small door at the basement level that the two agents led Munro. Inside, they identified themselves and their visitor to a uniformed policeman sitting at a tiny desk. Munro was surprised; this was a far cry from the sweeping façade of the front entrance to the residence on Pennsylvania Avenue, so well-known to tourists and beloved of Americans.

The policeman checked with someone by house-phone, and a female secretary came out of a lift several minutes later. She led the three past the policeman and down a corridor, at the end of which they mounted a narrow staircase. One floor up, they were at ground level, stepping through a door into a thickly carpeted hallway, where a male aide in charcoal-grey suit glanced with raised eyebrows at the unshaven, dishevelled Englishman.

'You're to come straight through, Mr Munro,' he said, and led the way. The two Secret Service agents stayed with the girl.

Munro was led down the corridor, past a small bust of Abraham Lincoln. Two staffers coming the other way passed in silence. The man leading him veered to the left and confronted another uniformed policeman sitting at a desk outside a white, panelled door, set flush with the wall. The policeman examined Munro's passport again, looked at his appearance with evident disapproval, reached under his desk and pressed a button. A buzzer sounded and the aide pushed at the door. When it opened, he stepped back and ushered Munro past him. Munro took two paces forward and found himself in the Oval Office. The door clicked shut behind him.

The four men in the room were evidently waiting for him, all four staring towards the curved door now set back in the wall where he stood. He recognized President William Matthews, but this was a President as no voter had ever seen him; tired, haggard, ten years older than the smiling, confident, mature but energetic, image on the posters.

Robert Benson rose and approached him.

'I'm Bob Benson,' he said. He drew Munro towards the desk. William Matthews leaned across and shook hands. Munro was introduced to David Lawrence and Stanislaw Poklewski, both of whom he knew from their newspaper pictures.

'So,' said President Matthews, looking with curiosity at the English agent across his desk, 'you're the man who runs the Nightingale.'

'Ran the Nightingale, Mr President,' said Munro. 'As of twelve hours ago, I believe that asset is blown to the KGB.'

'I'm sorry,' said Matthews. 'You know what a hell of an ultimatum Maxim Rudin put to me over this tanker affair? I had to know why he was doing it.'

'Now we know,' said Poklewski, 'but it doesn't seem to change much, except to prove that Rudin is backed right into a corner, as we are here. The explanation is fantastic, the murder of Yuri Ivanenko by two amateur assassins in a street in Kiev. But we are still on that hook. . . .'

'We don't have to explain to Mr Munro the importance of the Treaty of Dublin, or the likelihood of war if Yefrem Vishnayev comes to power,' said David Lawrence. 'You've read all those reports of the Politburo discussions that the Nightingale delivered to you, Mr Munro?'

'Yes, Mr Secretary,' said Munro. 'I read them in the original Russian just after they were handed over. I know what is at stake, on both sides.'

'Then how the hell do we get out of it?' asked President Matthews. 'Your Prime Minister asked me to receive you because you had some proposal she was not prepared to discuss over the telephone. That's why you're here, right?'

'Yes, Mr President.'

At that point the phone rang. Benson listened for several seconds, then put it down.

'We're moving towards the crunch,' he said. 'That man Svoboda on the *Freya* has just announced he is venting a hundred thousand tons of oil tomorrow morning at nine European time, that's four a.m. our time. Just over twelve hours from now.'

'So what's your suggestion, Mr Munro?' asked President Matthews.

'Mr President, there are two basic choices here. Either Mishkin and Lazareff are released to fly to Israel, in which case they talk when they arrive there and destroy Maxim Rudin and the Treaty of Dublin; or they stay where they are, in which case the *Freya* will either destroy herself or will have to be destroyed with all her crew on board her.'

He did not mention the British suspicion concerning the real role of the *Moran*, but Poklewski shot the impassive Benson a sharp glance.

'We know that, Mr Munro,' said the President.

'But the real fear of Maxim Rudin does not really concern the geographical location of Mishkin and Lazareff. His real concern is whether they have the opportunity to address the world on what they did in that street in Kiev five months ago.'

William Matthews sighed.

'We thought of that,' he said. 'We have asked Prime Minister Golen to accept Mishkin and Lazareff, hold them incommunicado until the *Freya* was released, then return them to Moabit Jail, even hold them out of sight and sound inside an Israeli jail for another ten years. He refused. He said if he made the public pledge the terrorists demanded, he would not go back on it. And he won't. Sorry, it's been a wasted journey, Mr Munro.'

'That was not what I had in mind,' said Munro. 'During the flight I wrote the suggestion in memorandum form on airline notepaper.'

He withdrew a sheaf of papers from his inner pocket and laid it on the President's desk.

The United States President read the memorandum with an expression of increasing horror.

'This is appalling,' he said when he had finished. 'I have no choice here. Or rather, whichever option I choose, men are going to die.'

Adam Munro looked across at him with no sympathy. In his time he had learned that, in principle, politicians have little enough objection to loss of life, provided that they personally cannot be seen publicly to have had anything to do with it.

'It has happened before, Mr President,' he said firmly, 'and no doubt it will happen again. In the firm we call it "the Devil's Alternative".'

Wordlessly President Matthews passed the memorandum to Robert Benson who read it quickly.

'Ingenious,' he said. 'It might work. Can it be done in time?'

'We have the equipment,' said Munro. 'The time is short, but not too short. I would have to be back in Berlin by seven a.m. Berlin time, ten hours from now.'

'But even if we agree, will Maxim Rudin go along with it?' asked the President. 'Without his concurrence the Treaty of Dublin would be forfeit.'

'The only way is to ask him,' said Poklewski, who had finished the memorandum and passed it to David Lawrence.

The Bostonian secretary of state put the papers down as if they would soil his fingers. 'I find the idea cold-blooded and repulsive,' he said. 'No United States government could put its imprimatur to such a scheme.'

'Is it worse than sitting back as thirty innocent seamen in the *Freya* are burned alive?' asked Munro.

The phone rang again. When Benson replaced it he turned to the President.

'I feel we may have no alternative but to seek Maxim Rudin's agreement,' he said. 'Chancellor Busch has just announced Mishkin and Lazareff are being freed at oh eight hundred hours, European time. And this time he will not back down.'

'Then we have to try it,' said Matthews, 'But I am not taking sole responsibility. Maxim Rudin must agree to permit the plan to go ahead. He must be forewarned. I shall call him personally.'

'Mr President,' said Munro, 'Maxim Rudin did not use the hot line to deliver his ultimatum to you. He is not sure of the loyalties of some of his inner staff inside the Kremlin. In these faction fights, even some of the small fry change sides and support the opposition with classified information. I believe this proposal should be for his ears alone, or he will feel bound to refuse it.'

'Surely there is not the time for you to fly to Moscow through the night and be back in Berlin by dawn?' objected Poklewski.

'There is one way,' said Benson. 'There is a Blackbird based at Andrews which would cover the distance in the time.'

President Matthews made up his mind.

'Bob, take Mr Munro personally to Andrews Base. Alert the crew of the Blackbird there to prepare for take-off in one hour. I will personally call

Maxim Rudin and ask him to permit the airplane to enter Soviet airspace and to receive Adam Munro as my personal envoy. Anything else, Mr Munro?'

Munro took a single sheet from his pocket.

'I would like the company to get this message urgently to Sir Nigel Irvine so that he can take care of the London and Berlin ends,' he said.

'It will be done,' said the President. 'Be on your way, Mr Munro. And good luck to you.'

18

When the helicopter rose from the White House lawn, the Secret Service agents were left behind. An amazed pilot found himself bearing the mysterious Englishman in rumpled clothes, and the director of the CIA. To their right, as they rose above Washington, the Potomac River glittered in the late-afternoon sun. The pilot headed due southeast for Andrews air force base.

Inside the Oval Office Stanislaw Poklewski, invoking the personal authority of President Matthews in every sentence, was speaking to the base commander there. That officer's protestations died slowly away. Finally, the National Security Adviser handed the phone to William Matthews.

'Yes, general, this is William Matthews and those are my orders. You will inform Colonel O'Sullivan that he is to prepare a flight plan immediately for a polar route direct from Washington to Moscow. Clearance to enter Soviet airspace unharmed will be radioed to him before he quits Greenland.'

The President went back to his other telephone, the red machine on which he was trying to speak directly to Maxim Rudin in Moscow.

At Andrews base, the commander himself met the helicopter as it touched down. Without the presence of Robert Benson, whom the air force general knew by sight, it was unlikely he would have accepted the unknown Englishman as a passenger on the world's fastest reconnaissance jet, let alone his orders to allow that jet to take off for Moscow. Ten years after it entered service, it was still on the secret list, so sophisticated were its components and systems.

'Very well, Mr Director,' he said finally, 'but I have to tell you in Colonel O'Sullivan we have one very angry Arizonan.'

He was right. While Adam Munro was taken to the pilot clothing store to be issued with a G-suit, boots, and goldfish-bowl oxygen helmet, Robert Benson found Colonel George T. O'Sullivan in the navigation room, cigar clamped in his teeth, poring over maps of the Arctic and eastern Baltic. The director of central intelligence may have outranked him, but he was evidently in no mood to be polite.

'Are you seriously ordering me to fly this bird clean across Greenland and Scandinavia, and into the heart of Rooshia?' he demanded truculently.

'No, colonel,' said Benson reasonably, 'the President of the United States is ordering you to do it.'

'Without my navigator/systems operator? With some goddam Limey sitting in his seat?'

'The goddam Limey happens to bear a personal message of President Matthews to President Rudin of the USSR which has to reach him tonight and cannot be discussed in any other way,' said Benson.

The air force colonel stared at him for a moment.

'Well,' he conceded, 'it better be goddam important.'

At twenty minutes before six, Adam Munro was led into the hangar where the aircraft stood, swarming with ground technicians preparing her to fly.

He had heard of the Lockheed SR-71, nicknamed the Blackbird due to its colour; he had seen pictures of it, but never the real thing. It was certainly impressive. On a single, thin nosewheel assembly, the bulletlike nosecone thrust upwards at a shallow angle. Far down the fuselage wafer-thin wings sprouted, delta-shaped, being both wings and tail controls all in one.

Almost at each wingtip the engines were situated, sleek pods housing the Pratt and Whitney JT-11-D turbofans, each capable with afterburner of throwing out 32,000 pounds of thrust. Two knifelike rudders rose, one from atop each engine, to give directional control. Body and engines resembled three hypodermic syringes, linked only by the wing.

Small white US stars in their white circles indicated its nationality; otherwise the SR-71 was black from nose to tail.

Ground assistants helped him into the narrow confines of the rear seat. He found himself sinking lower and lower until the side walls of the cockpit rose above his ears. When the canopy came down it would be almost flush with the fuselage to cut down drag effect. Looking out, he would only see directly upwards to the stars.

The man who should have occupied that seat would have understood the bewildering array of radar screens, electronic counter-measure systems and camera controls, for the SR-71 was essentially a spyplane, designed and equipped to cruise at altitudes far beyond the reach of most interceptor fighters and rockets, photographing what it saw beneath.

Helpful hands linked the tubes sprouting from his suit to the aircraft's systems; radio, oxygen, anti-G-force. In front of him he watched Colonel O'Sullivan lower himself into the front seat with accustomed ease and begin attaching his own life-support systems. When the radio was connected the Arizonan's voice boomed in his ears.

'You Scotch, Mr Munro?'

'Scottish, yes.' said Munro into his helmet.

'I'm Irish,' said the voice in his ears. 'You a Catholic?'

'A what?'

'A Catholic, for Christ's sake!'

Munro thought for a moment. He was not really religious at all.

'No,' he said, 'Church of Scotland.'

There was evident disgust up front.

'Jesus, twenty years in the United States Air Force and I get to chauffeur a Scotch Protestant.'

The triple-perspex canopy capable of withstanding the tremendous air pressure differences of ultra-high altitude flight was closed upon them. A hiss indicated the cabin was now fully pressurized. Drawn by a tractor some-where ahead of the nosewheel, the SR-71 emerged from the hangar into the evening light.

From inside, the engines once started made only a low whistle. Outside, ground crew shuddered even in their ear-muffs as the boom echoed through the hangars.

Colonel O'Sullivan secured immediate clearance for take-off even while he was running through his seemingly innumerable pre-take-off checks. At the start of the main runway the Blackbird paused, rocked on its wheels as the colonel lined her up, then Munro heard his voice:

'Whatever God you pray to, start now and hold tight.'

In the rear seat Munro braced himself.

Something like a runaway train hit him squarely across the broad of the back; it was the moulded seat in which he was strapped. He could see no buildings to judge his speed, just the pale blue sky above. When the jet reached 150 knots, the nose left the tarmac; half a second later the main wheels parted company, and O'Sullivan lifted the undercarriage into its bays.

Clean of encumbrances, the SR-71 tilted back until its jet efflux pipes were pointing directly down at Maryland, and it climbed. It climbed almost vertically, powering its way to the sky like a rocket, which is almost what it was. Munro was on his back, feet towards the sky, conscious only of the steady pressure of the seat on his spine as the Blackbird streaked towards a sky that was soon turning to dark blue, to violet and finally to black.

In the front seat Colonel O'Sullivan was navigating himself, which is to say, following the instructions flashed before him in digital display by the aircraft's on-board computer. It was feeding him altitude, speed, rate of climb, course and heading, external and internal temperatures, engine and jet-pipe temperatures, oxygen flow rates and approach to the speed of sound.

Somewhere below them, Philadelphia and New York went by like toy towns; over northern New York State they went through the sound barrier, still climbing and still accelerating. At 80,000 feet, five miles higher than the Concorde, Colonel O'Sullivan cut out the afterburners and levelled his flight attitude.

Though it was still not quite sundown, the sky was a deep black, for at these altitudes there are so few air molecules from which the sun's rays can reflect that there is no light. But there still enough such molecules to cause skin friction on a plane like the Blackbird. Before the state of Maine and the Canadian frontier passed beneath them, they had adopted a fast-cruise speed of almost three times the speed of sound. Before Munro's amazed eyes, the black skin of the SR-71, made of pure titanium, began to glow cherry red in the heat.

Within the cockpit, the aircraft's own refrigeration system kept its occu-pants at a comfortable body temperature.

'Can I talk?' asked Munro.

'Sure,' said the laconic voice of the pilot.

'Where are we now?'

'Over the Gulf of St Lawrence,' said O'Sullivan, 'heading for Newfound-
land.'

'How many miles to Moscow?'

'From Andrews base, four thousand, eight hundred and fifty-six miles.'

'How long for the flight?'

'Three hours and fifty minutes.'

Munro calculated. They had taken off at 6 p.m. Washington time, 11 p.m.
European time. That would be 1 a.m. in Moscow on Sunday, 3rd April. They
would touch down at around 5 a.m. Moscow time. If Rudin agreed to his
plan, and the Blackbird could bring him back to Berlin, they would gain two
hours by flying the other way. There was just time to make Berlin by dawn.

They had been flying for just under one hour when Canada's last landfall at
Cape Harrison drifted far beneath them and they were over the cruel North
Atlantic, bound for the southern tip of Greenland, Cape Farewell.

'President Rudin, please hear me out,' said William Matthews. He was
speaking earnestly into a small microphone on his desk, the so-called hot
line, which in fact is not a telephone at all. From an amplifier to one side of
the microphone the listeners in the Oval Office could hear the mutter of the
simultaneous translator speaking into Rudin's ear in Moscow in Russian.

'Maxim Andreivitch, I believe we are both too old in this business, that we
have worked too hard and too long to secure peace for our peoples, to be
frustrated and cheated at this late stage by a gang of murderers on a tanker in
the North Sea.'

There was silence for a few seconds, then the gruff voice of Rudin came
down the line, speaking in Russian. By the President's side a young aide from
State Department rattled off the translation in a low voice.

'Then William, my friend, you must destroy the tanker, take away the
weapon of blackmail, for I can do no other than I have done.'

Bob Benson shot the President a warning look. There was no need to tell
Rudin the West already knew the real truth about Ivanenko.

'I know this,' said Matthews into the mike. 'But I cannot destroy the
tanker either. To do so would destroy me. There may be another way. I ask
you with all my heart to receive this man who is even now airborne from here
and heading for Moscow. He has a proposal that may be the way out for us
both.'

'Who is this American?' asked Rudin.

'He is not American, he is British,' said President Matthews. 'His name is
Adam Munro.'

There was silence for several moments. Finally the voice from Russia came
back grudgingly.

'Give my staff the details of his flight plan – height, speed, course. I will
order that his airplane be allowed through and will receive him personally
when he arrives. *Spakoinyo notch*, William.'

'He wishes you a peaceful night, Mr President,' said the translator.

'He must be joking,' said William Matthews. 'Give his people the Blackbird's flight path, and tell Blackbird to proceed on course.'

On board the *Freya* it struck midnight. Captives and captors entered their third and last day. Before another midnight struck, Mishkin and Lazareff would be in Israel, or the *Freya* and all aboard her would be dead.

Despite his threat to choose a different cabin, Drake was confident there would be no night attack from the marines and elected to stay where he was.

Thor Larsen faced him grimly across the table in the day cabin. For both men the exhaustion was almost total. Larsen, fighting back the waves of weariness that tried to force him to place his head in his arms and go to sleep, continued his solo game of seeking to keep Svoboda awake too, pin-pricking the Ukrainian to make him reply.

The surest way of provoking Svoboda, he had discovered, the surest way of making him use up his last remaining reserve of nervous energy, was to draw the conversation to the question of Russians.

'I don't believe in your popular uprising, Mr Svoboda,' he said. 'I don't believe the Russians will ever rise against their masters in the Kremlin. Bad, inefficient, brutal they may be; but they only have to raise the spectre of the foreigner, and they can rely on that limitless Russian patriotism.'

For a moment it seemed the Norwegian might have gone too far. Svoboda's hand closed over the butt of his gun, his face went white with rage.

'Damn and blast their patriotism,' he shouted, rising to his feet. 'I am sick and tired of hearing Western writers and liberals go on and on about this so-called marvellous Russian patriotism.

'What kind of patriotism is it that can only feed on the destruction of other people's love of homeland? What about *my* patriotism, Larsen? What about the Ukrainians' love for their enslaved homeland? What about Georgians, Armenians, Lithuanians, Estonians, Latvians? Are they not allowed any patriotism? Must it all be sublimated to this endless and sickening love of Russia?

'I hate their bloody patriotism. It is mere chauvinism and always has been, since Peter and Ivan. It can only exist through conquest and slavery of other surrounding nations.'

He was standing over Larsen, halfway round the table, waving his gun, panting from the exertion of shouting. He took a grip on himself and returned to his seat. Pointing the gun barrel at Thor Larsen like a forefinger he told him:

'One day, maybe not too long from now, the Russian empire will begin to crack. One day soon, the Romanians will exercise *their* patriotism, and the Poles and the Czechs. Followed by the Germans and Hungarians. And the Balts and Ukrainians, the Georgians and Armenians. The Russian empire will crack and crumble, the way the Roman and British empires cracked, because at last the arrogance of their mandarins became insufferable.

'Within twenty-four hours I am personally going to put the cold chisel in to the mortar and swing one gigantic hammer on to it. And if you or anyone else gets in my way, you'll die. And you'd better believe it.'

He put down the gun and spoke more softly.

'In any case, Busch has acceded to my demands and this time he will not go back on it. This time Mishkin and Lazareff *will* reach Israel.'

Thor Larsen observed the younger man clinically. It had been risky, he had nearly used his gun. But he had nearly also dropped concentration; he had nearly come within range. One more time, one single further attempt, in the sad hour just before dawn. . . .

Coded and urgent messages had passed all night between Washington and Omaha, and from there to the many radar stations that make up the eyes and ears of the Western Alliance in an electronic ring round the Soviet Union. Unseen eyes had watched the shooting star of the blip from the Blackbird moving east of Iceland towards Scandinavia on its route to Moscow. Fore-warned, the watchers raised no alarm.

On the other side of the Iron Curtain, messages out of Moscow alerted the Soviet watchers to the presence of the incoming plane. Forewarned, no interceptors scrambled to intercept it. An air highway was cleared from the Gulf of Bothnia to Moscow, and the Blackbird stuck to its route.

But one fighter base had apparently not heard the warning; or hearing it had not heeded it; or had been given secret orders from somewhere deep inside the Defence Ministry, countermanding the Kremlin.

High in the Arctic, east of Kirkenes, two MiG-25s clawed their way from the snow towards the stratosphere on an interception course. These were the 25-E versions, ultra-modern, better powered and armed than the older version of the 1970s, the 25-A.

They were capable of 2.8 times the speed of sound, and with a maximum altitude of 80,000 feet. But the six 'Acrid' air-to-air missiles that each had slung beneath its wings would roar on, another 20,000 feet above that. They were climbing on full power with afterburner, leaping upwards at over 10,000 feet per minute.

The Blackbird was over Finland, heading for Lake Ladoga and Leningrad when Colonel O'Sullivan grunted into the microphone.

'We have company.'

Munro came out of his reverie. Though he understood little of the tech-nology of the SR-71, the small radar screen in front of him told its own story. There were two small blips on it, approaching fast.

'Who are they?' he asked, and for a moment a twinge of fear moved in the pit of his stomach. Maxim Rudin had given his personal clearance. He wouldn't, surely? But would someone else?

Up front, Colonel O'Sullivan had his own duplicate radar scanner. He watched the speed of approach for several seconds.

'MiG Twenty-fives,' he said. 'At sixty thousand feet and climbing fast. Those goddam Rooshians; knew we should never have trusted them.'

'You turning back to Sweden?' asked Munro.

'Nope,' said the colonel. 'President of the US of A said to git you to Moscow, Limey, and you are going to Moscow.'

Colonel O'Sullivan threw his two afterburners into the game; Munro felt a kick as from a mule in the base of the spine as the power increased. The Mach counter began to move upwards, towards and finally through the mark representing three times the speed of sound. On the radar screen the approach of the blips slowed and halted.

The nose of the Blackbird rose slightly; in the rarefied atmosphere, seeking a tenuous lift from the weak air around her, the aircraft slid through the 80,000 feet mark and kept climbing.

Below them, Major Pyotr Kuznetsov, leading the two-plane detail, pushed his two Tumansky single-shaft jet engines to the limit of performance. His Soviet technology was good, the best available, but he was producing 5000 pounds less of thrust with his two engines than the twin American jets above him. Moreover he was carrying external weaponry, whose drag was acting as a brake on his speed.

Nevertheless the two MiGs swept through 70,000 feet and approached rocket range. Major Kuznetsov armed his six missiles and snapped an order to his wing-man to follow suit.

The Blackbird was nudging 90,000 feet and Colonel O'Sullivan's radar told him his pursuers were over 75,000 feet and nearly within rocket range. In straight pursuit they could not hold him on speed and altitude, but they were on an intercept course, cutting the corner from their flight path to his.

'If I thought they were escorts,' he said to Munro, 'I'd let the bastards come close. But I just never did trust Rooshians.'

Munro was sticky with sweat beneath his thermal clothing. He had read the Nightingale file, the colonel had not.

'They're not escorts,' he said. 'They have orders to see me dead.'

'You don't say?' came the drawl in his ear. 'Goddam conspiring bastards. President of the US of A wants you alive, Limey. In Moscow.'

The Blackbird pilot threw on the whole battery of his electronic counter-measures. Rings of invisible jamming waves radiated out from the speeding black jet, filling the atmosphere for miles around with the radar equivalent of a bucket of sand in the eyes.

The small screen in front of Major Kuznetsov became a seething snowfield like a television set when the main tube blows out. The digital display showing him he was closing with his victim and when to fire his rockets was still fifteen seconds short of fire-time. Slowly, it began to unwind, telling him he had lost his target somewhere up there in the freezing stratosphere.

Thirty seconds later the two hunters keeled on to their wing-tips and dropped away down the sky to their Arctic base.

Of the five airports that surround Moscow, one of them, Vnukovno II, is never seen by foreigners. It is reserved for the Party elite and their fleet of jets maintained at peak readiness by the air force. It was here, at 5 a.m. local time, that Colonel O'Sullivan put the Blackbird on to Russian soil.

When the cooling jet reached the parking bay it was surrounded by a group of officers wrapped in thick coats and fur hats, for early April is still bitter in Moscow before dawn. The Arizonan lifted the cockpit canopy on its hydraulic struts and gazed at the surrounding crowd with horror.

'Rooshians,' he breathed. 'Messing all over my bird.' He unbuckled and stood up. 'Hey, get your mother-loving hands off this machine, ya hear?'

Adam Munro left the desolate colonel trying to prevent the Russian Air Force from finding the flush-caps leading to the re-fuelling valves, and was whisked away in a black limousine, accompanied by two bodyguards from the Kremlin staff. In the car he was allowed to peel off his G-suit and dress again in his trousers and jacket, both of which had spent the journey rolled up between his knees and looked as if they had just been machine-washed.

Forty minutes later the Zil, preceded by the two motorcycle outriders who had cleared the roads into Moscow, shot through the Borovitsky Gate into the Kremlin, skirted the Grand Palace and headed for the side door to the Arsenal building. At two minutes to six Adam Munro was shown into the private apartment of the leader of the USSR, to find an old man in a dressing gown, nursing a cup of warm milk. He was waved to an upright chair. The door closed behind him.

'So you are Adam Munro,' said Maxim Rudin. 'Now what is this proposal from President Matthews?'

Munro sat in the straight-backed chair and looked across the desk at Maxim Rudin. He had seen him several times at state functions, but never this close. The old man looked wearied and strained.

There was no interpreter present. Rudin spoke no English. In the hours while he had been in the air, Munro realized, Rudin had checked his name and knew perfectly well he was a diplomat from the British embassy and spoke Russian.

'The proposal, Mr Secretary-General,' Munro began in fluent Russian, 'is a possible way whereby the terrorists on the supertanker *Freya* can be persuaded to leave that ship without having secured what they came for.'

'Let me make one thing clear, Mr Munro, there is to be no more talk of the liberation of Mishkin and Lazareff.'

'Indeed not, sir. In fact I had hoped we might talk of Yuri Ivanenko.'

Rudin stared back at him, face impassive. Slowly he lifted his glass of milk and took a sip.

'You see, sir, one of those two *has* let something slip already,' said Munro. He was forced, to strengthen his argument, to let Rudin know that he too was aware what had happened to Ivanenko. But he would not indicate he had learned from someone inside the Kremlin hierarchy, just in case Valentina was still free.

'Fortunately,' he went on, 'it was to one of our people, and the matter has been taken care of.'

'Your people?' mused Rudin. 'Ah, yes, I think I know who your people are. How many others know?'

'The director-general of my organization, the British Prime Minister, President Matthews and three of his senior advisers. No one who knows has the slightest intention of revealing this for public consumption. Not the slightest.'

Rudin seemed to ruminate for a while.

'Can the same be said for Mishkin and Lazareff?' he asked.

'That is the problem,' said Munro. 'That has always been the problem since the terrorists, who are Ukrainian emigrés by the way, stepped on to the *Freya*.'

'I told William Matthews, the only way out of this is to destroy the *Freya*. It would cost a handful of lives, but save a lot of trouble.'

'It would have saved a lot of trouble if the airliner in which these two young killers escaped had been shot down,' rejoined Munro.

Rudin looked at him keenly from under beetle eyebrows.

'That was a mistake,' he said flatly.

'Like the mistake tonight in which two MiG Twenty-fives almost shot down the plane in which I was flying?'

The old Russian's head jerked up.

'I did not know,' he said. For the first time Munro believed him.

'I put it to you, sir, that destroying the *Freya* would not work. That is, it would not solve the problem. Three days ago Mishkin and Lazareff were two insignificant escapees and hijackers, serving fifteen years in jail. Now they are already celebrities. But it is assumed their freedom is being sought for its own sake. We know different.

'If the *Freya* were destroyed,' Munro went on, 'the entire world would wonder why it had been so vital to keep them in jail. So far no one realizes that it is not their imprisonment that is vital, it is their silence. With the *Freya*, her cargo and crew destroyed in order to keep them in jail, they would have no further reason to stay silent. And because of the *Freya*, the world would believe them when they spoke about what they had done. So simply keeping them in jail is no use any more.'

Rudin nodded slowly.

'You are right, young man,' he said. 'The Germans would give them their audience; they would have their press conference.'

'Precisely,' said Munro. 'This then is my suggestion.'

He outlined the same train of events that he had described to Mrs Carpenter and President Matthews over the previous twelve hours. The Russian showed neither surprise nor horror, just interest.

'Would it work?' he asked at last.

'It has to work,' said Munro. 'It is the last option. They have to be allowed to go to Israel.'

Rudin looked at the clock on the wall. It was past 6.45 a.m. Moscow time. In fourteen hours he would have to face Vishnayev and the rest of the Politburo. This time there would be no oblique approach; this time the Party theoretician would put down a formal motion of no confidence.

His grizzled head nodded. 'Do it, Mr Munro,' he said. 'Do it and make it work. For if it doesn't, there will be no more Treaty of Dublin, and no more *Freya* either.'

He pressed a bell-push and the door opened immediately. An immaculate major of the Kremlin praetorian guard stood there.

'I shall need to deliver two signals, one to the Americans, one to my own people,' said Munro. 'A representative of each embassy is waiting outside the Kremlin walls.'

Rudin issued his orders to the guard major, who nodded and escorted Munro out. As they were in the door, Maxim Rudin called:

'Mr Munro.'

Munro turned. The old man was as he had found him, hands cupped round his glass of milk.

'Should you ever need another job, Mr Munro,' he said grimly, 'come and see me. There is always a place here for men of talent.'

As the Zil limousine left the Kremlin by the Borovitsky Gate at 7 a.m. the morning sun was just tipping the spire of St Basil's Cathedral. Two long black cars waited by the kerb. Munro descended from the Zil and approached each in turn. He passed one message to the American diplomat and one to the British. Before he was airborne for Berlin, the instructions would be in London and Washington.

On the dot of eight o'clock the bullet nose of the SR-71 lifted from the tarmac of Vnukovno Airport and turned due west for Berlin, a thousand miles away. It was flown by a thoroughly disgusted Colonel O'Sullivan, who had spent three hours watching his precious bird being refuelled by a team of Soviet Air Force mechanics.

'Where do you want to go now?' he called down the intercom. 'I can't bring this into Tempelhof, ya know. Not enough room.'

'Make a landing at the British base at Gatow,' said Munro.

'First Rooshians, now Limeys,' grumbled the Arizonan. 'Dunno why we don't put this bird on public display. Seems everyone is entitled to have a good look at her today.'

'If this mission is successful,' said Munro, 'the world may not need the Blackbirds any more.'

Colonel O'Sullivan, far from being pleased, regarded the suggestion as a disaster.

'Know what I'm going to do if that happens?' he called. 'I'm going to become a goddam cab driver. I'm sure getting enough practice.'

Far below, the city of Vilnius in Lithuania went by. Flying at twice the speed of the rising sun, they would be in Berlin at 7 a.m. local time.

It was half-past five on the *Freya*, while Adam Munro was in a car between the Kremlin and the airport, that the intercom from the bridge rang in the day cabin.

The man called Svoboda answered it, listened for a while and replied in Ukrainian. From across the table Thor Larsen watched him through half-closed eyes.

Whatever the call was, it perplexed the terrorist leader, who sat with a frown, staring at the table, until one of his men came to relieve him in the guarding of the Norwegian skipper.

Svoboda left the captain under the barrel of the submachine gun in the hands of his masked subordinate and went up to the bridge. When he returned ten minutes later he seemed angry.

'What's the matter?' asked Larsen. 'Something gone wrong again?'

'The German ambassador on the line from the Hague,' said Svoboda. 'It seems the Russians have refused to allow any West German jet, official or private, to use the air corridors out of West Berlin.'

'That's logical,' said Larsen. 'They're hardly likely to assist in the escape of the two men who murdered their airline captain.'

Svoboda dismissed his colleague who closed the door behind him and returned to the bridge. The Ukrainian resumed his seat. 'The British have offered to assist Chancellor Busch by putting a communications jet from the Royal Air Force at their disposal to fly Mishkin and Lazareff from Berlin to Tel Aviv.'

'I'd accept,' said Larsen. 'After all, the Russians aren't above diverting a German jet, even shooting it down and claiming an accident. They'd never dare fire on an RAF military jet in one of the air corridors. You're on the threshold of victory; don't throw it away for a technicality. Accept the offer.'

Svoboda regarded the Norwegian, bleary-eyed from weariness, slow from lack of sleep.

'You're right,' he conceded, 'they might shoot down a German plane. In fact, I have accepted.'

'Then it's over bar the shouting,' said Larsen, forcing a smile. 'Let's celebrate.'

He had two cups of coffee in front of him, poured while he was waiting for Svoboda to return. He pushed one halfway down the long table; the Ukrainian reached for it. In a well-planned operation it was the first mistake he made. . . .

Thor Larsen came at him down the length of the table with all the pent-up rage of the past fifty hours unleashed in the violence of a maddened bear.

The partisan recoiled, reached for his gun, had it in his hand and was about to fire. A fist like a log of spruce caught him on the left temple, flung him out of his chair and backwards across the cabin floor.

Had he been less fit, he would have been out cold. He was very fit, and younger than the seaman. As he fell, the gun slipped from his hand and skittered across the floor. He came up empty-handed, fighting, to meet the charge of the Norwegian, and the pair of them went down again in a tangle of arms and legs, fragments of a shattered chair and two broken coffee cups.

Larsen was trying to use his weight and strength, the Ukrainian his youth and speed. The latter won. Evading the grip of the big man's hands, Svoboda wriggled free and went for the door. He almost made it; his hand was reaching for the knob when Larsen launched himself across the carpet and brought both his ankles out from under him.

The two men came up again together, a yard apart, the Norwegian between Svoboda and the door. The Ukrainian lunged with a foot, caught the bigger man in the groin with a kick that doubled him over. Larsen recovered, rose again and threw himself at the man who had threatened to destroy his ship.

Svoboda must have recalled that the cabin was virtually soundproof. He fought in silence, wrestling, biting, gouging, kicking, and the pair rolled over the carpet among the broken furniture and crockery. Somewhere beneath them was the gun that could have ended it all; in Svoboda's belt was the oscillator which, if the red button on it were pressed, would certainly end it all.

In fact it ended after two minutes; Thor Larsen pulled one hand free, grasped the head of the struggling Ukrainian and slammed it into the leg of the table. Svoboda went rigid for half a second, then slumped down. From under his hairline a thin trickle of blood seeped down his forehead.

Panting with weariness, Thor Larsen raised himself from the floor and looked at the unconscious man. Carefully, he eased the oscillator from the Ukrainian's belt, held it in his left hand and crossed to the one window in the starboard side of his cabin which was secured closed with butterfly-headed bolts. One-handed, he began to unwind them. The first one flicked open; he started on the second. A few more seconds, a single long throw, and the oscillator would sail out of the porthole, across the intervening ten feet of steel deck and into the North Sea.

On the floor behind him the young terrorist's hand inched over the carpet to where his discarded gun lay. Larsen had the second bolt undone and was swinging the brass-framed window inwards when Svoboda lifted himself painfully on to one shoulder, reached round the table and fired.

The crash of the gun in the enclosed cabin was ear-splitting. Thor Larsen reeled back against the wall by the open window and looked first at his left hand, then at Svoboda. From the floor the Ukrainian stared back, in disbelief.

The single shot had hit the Norwegian in the palm of his left hand, the hand that held the oscillator, driving shards of plastic and glass into the flesh. For ten seconds both men stared at each other, waiting for the series of rumbling explosions that would mark the end of the *Freya*.

They never came. The soft-nosed slug had fragmented the detonator device into small pieces, and in shattering it had not had time to reach the tonal pitch needed to trigger the detonators in the bombs below decks.

Slowly the Ukrainian climbed to his feet, holding on to the table for support. Thor Larsen looked at the steady stream of blood running from his broken hand down to the carpet. Then he looked across at the panting terrorist.

'I have won, Mr Svoboda. I have won. You cannot destroy my ship and my crew.'

'You may know that, Captain Larsen,' said the man with the gun, 'and I may know that. But they . . .' he gestured to the open porthole and the lights of the NATO warships in the pre-dawn gloom across the water '. . . they don't know that. The game goes on. Mishkin and Lazareff *will* reach Israel.'

19

Moabit Jail in West Berlin is in two parts. The older part pre-dates the Second World War. But during the sixties and early seventies, when the Baader-Meinhof gang spread a wave of terror over Germany, a new section was built. Into it were included ultra-modern security systems, the toughest steel and concrete, television scanners, electronically controlled doors and grills.

On the upper floor, David Lazareff and Lev Mishkin were woken in their separate cells by the governor of Moabit at 6 a.m. on the morning of Sunday, 3rd April 1983.

'You are being released,' he told them brusquely. 'You are being flown to Israel this morning. Take-off is scheduled for eight o'clock. Get ready to depart; we leave for the airfield at seven-thirty.'

Ten minutes later the military commandant of the British Sector was on the telephone to the governing mayor.

'I'm terribly sorry, Herr Burgomeister,' he told the West Berliner, 'but a take-off from the civil airport at Tegel is out of the question. For one thing the aircraft, by agreement between our governments, will be a Royal Air Force jet, and the re-fuelling and maintenance facilities for our aircraft are far better at our own airfield at Gatow. For a second reason we are trying to avoid the chaos of an invasion by the press, which we can easily prevent at Gatow. It would be hard for you to do this at Tegel Airport.'

Privately the governing mayor was somewhat relieved. If the British took over the whole operation, any possible disasters would be their responsibility; and with the regional elections coming up, Berlin was included.

'So what do you want us to do, general?' he asked.

'London has asked me to suggest to you that these blighters be put in a closed and armoured wagon inside Moabit, and driven straight into Gatow. Your chaps can hand them over to us in privacy inside the wire, and of course we'll sign for them.'

The press was less than happy. Over four hundred reporters and cameramen had camped outside Moabit Jail since the announcement from Bonn the previous evening that release would take place at eight. They desperately wanted pictures of the pair leaving for the airport. Other teams of pressmen were staking out the civilian airport at Tegel, seeking vantage points for their telephoto lenses high on the observation terraces of the terminal building. They were all destined to be frustrated.

The advantage of the British base at Gatow is that is occupies one of the most outlying and isolated sites inside the fenced perimeter of West Berlin, situated on the western side of the broad Havel River, close up against the border with Communist East Germany which surrounds the beleaguered city on all sides.

Inside the base there had been controlled activity for hours before dawn. Between three and four o'clock an RAF version of the HS 125 executive jet, which the air force calls the Dominie, had flown in from Britain. It was fitted with long-range fuel tanks which would extend its range to give it ample reserves to fly from Berlin to Tel Aviv over Munich, Venice and Athens without ever entering Communist airspace. Its 500 m.p.h. cruising speed would enable the Dominie to complete the 2200-mile journey in just over four hours.

Since landing, the Dominie had been towed to a quiet hangar where it had been serviced and re-fuelled.

So keen were the press on observing the jail of Moabit and the airport at Tegel that no one noticed a sleek black SR-71 sweep over the East Germany–West Berlin border in the extreme corner of the city and drop on to the main runway at Gatow just three minutes after seven o'clock. This aircraft too was quickly towed to an empty hangar where a team of mechanics from the USAF at Tempelhof hurriedly closed the doors against prying eyes and began to work on it. The SR-71 had done its job. A relieved Colonel O'Sullivan found himself at last surrounded by his fellow-countrymen, next destination his beloved US of A.

His passenger left the hangar and was greeted by a youthful squadron leader waiting with a Land-Rover.

'Mr Munro?'

'Yes.' Munro produced his identification which the air force officer scanned closely.

'There are two gentlemen waiting to see you in the mess, sir.'

The two gentlemen could, if challenged, have proved that they were low-grade civil servants attached to the Ministry of Defence. What neither would have cared to concede was that they were concerned with experimental work in a very secluded laboratory whose findings, when such were made, went immediately into a Top Secret classification.

Both men were neatly dressed and carried attaché cases. One wore rimless glasses and had medical qualifications, or had had until he and the profession of Hippocrates parted company. The other was his subordinate, a former male nurse.

'You have the equipment I asked for?' said Munro without preamble.

For answer, the senior man opened his attaché case and extracted a flat box no larger than a cigar case. He opened it and showed Munro what nestled on a bed of cotton wool inside.

'Ten hours,' he said. 'No more.'

'That's tight,' said Munro. 'Very tight.'

It was seven-thirty on a bright, sunny morning.

The Nimrod from Coastal Command still turned and turned 15,000 feet above the *Freya*. Apart from observing the tanker, its duties also included that of watching the oil slick of the previous noon. The gigantic stain was still moving sluggishly on the face of the water, still out of range of the detergent-spraying tugs who were not allowed to enter the area immediately round the *Freya* herself.

After spillage the slick had drifted gently northeast of the tanker on the one-knot tide towards the northern coast of Holland. But during the night it had halted, the tide had moved to the ebb and the light breeze had shifted several points. Before dawn the slick had come back, until it had passed the *Freya* and lay just south of her, two miles away from her side in the direction of Holland and Belgium.

On the tugs and fireships, each loaded with their maximum capacity of emulsifier-concentrate, the scientists loaned from Warren Springs prayed the sea would stay calm and the wind light until they could move into operation. A sudden change in wind, a deterioration of the weather, and the giant slick could break up, driven before the storm towards the beaches either of Europe or Britain.

Meteorologists in Britain and Europe watched with apprehension the approach of a cold front coming down from the Denmark Strait, bringing cold air to dispel the unseasonal heatwave, and possibly wind and rain. Twenty-four hours of squalls would shatter the calm sea and make the slick uncontrollable. The ecologists prayed the descending cold snap would bring no more than a sea fog.

On the *Freya*, as the minutes to eight o'clock ticked away, nerves became even more strained and taut. Andrew Drake, supported by two men with submachine guns to prevent another attack from the Norwegian skipper, had allowed Captain Larsen to use his own first-aid box on his hand. Grey-faced with pain, the captain had plucked from the pulped meat of his palm such pieces of glass and plastic as he could, then bandaged the hand and placed it in a rough sling round his neck. Svoboda watched him from across the cabin, a small plaster covering the cut on his forehead.

'You're a brave man, Thor Larsen, I'll say that for you,' he said. 'But nothing has changed. I can still vent every ton of oil on this ship with her own pumps, and before it's halfway through, the navy out there will open fire on her and complete the job. If the Germans renege again on their promise, that's just what I'll do at nine.'

At precisely seven-thirty the journalists outside Moabit Prison were rewarded for their vigil. The double gates of Klein Moabit Strasse opened for the first time and the nose of a black-sided armoured van appeared. From apartment windows across the road the photographers got what pictures they could, which were not very much, and the stream of press cars started up, to follow the van wherever it would go.

Simultaneously, outside broadcast units rolled their cameras and radio reporters chattered excitedly into their microphones. Even as they spoke, their words went straight to the various capital cities from which they hailed, including that of the BBC man. His voice echoed into the day cabin of the *Freya* where Andrew Drake, who had started it all, sat listening to his radio.

'They're on their way,' he said with satisfaction. 'Not long to wait now. Time to tell them the final details of their reception in Tel Aviv.'

He left for the bridge; two men remained to cover the *Freya*'s captain, slumped in his chair at the table, struggling with an exhausted brain against the waves of pain from his bleeding and broken hand.

The armoured van, preceded by motorcycle outriders with howling sirens, swept through the twelve-foot-high steel mesh gates of the British base at Gatow and the pole-barrier descended fast as the first car bulging with pressmen tried to follow through. The car stopped with a squeal of tyres. The double gates swung to. Within minutes a crowd of protesting reporters and photographers were at the wire clamouring for admittance.

Gatow not only contains an air base; it has an army unit as well, and the commandant was an army brigadier. The men on the gate were from the military police, four giants with red-topped caps, peaks down to the bridge of the nose, immovable and immune.

'You cannot do this,' yelled an outraged photographer from *Spiegel*. 'We demand to see the prisoners take off.'

'That's all right, Fritz,' said Staff Sergeant Farrow comfortably, 'I've got my orders.'

Reporters rushed to public telephones to complain to their editors. They complained to the governing mayor, who sympathized earnestly and promised to contact the base commander at Gatow immediately. When the phone was quiet, he leaned back and lit a cigar.

Inside the base, Adam Munro walked into the hangar where the Dominie stood, accompanied by the wing commander in charge of aircraft maintenance.

'How is she?' Munro asked of the warrant officer (Technical) in charge of the fitters and riggers.

'Hundred per cent, sir,' said the veteran mechanic.

'No, she's not,' said Munro. 'I think if you look under one of the engine cowlings, you'll find an electrical malfunction that needs quite a bit of attention.'

The warrant officer looked at the stranger in amazement, then across to his superior officer.

'Do as he says, Mr Barker,' said the wing commander. 'There has to be a technical delay. The Dominie must not be ready for take-off for a while. But the German authorities must believe it's genuine. Open her up and get to work.'

Warrant Officer Barker had spent thirty years maintaining aircraft for the Royal Air Force. Wing commander's orders were not to be disobeyed, even if they did come from a scruffy civilian who ought to be ashamed of the way he was dressed, not to mention being unshaven.

Prison Governor Alois Bruckner had arrived in his own car to witness the handover of his prisoners to the British and their take-off for Israel. When he heard the aircraft was not yet ready, he was incensed and demanded to see it for himself.

He arrived in the hangar escorted by the RAF base commander, to find W/O Barker head and shoulders into the starboard engine of the Dominie.

'What is the matter?' he asked in exasperation.

Warrant Officer Barker pulled his head out.

'Electrical short circuit, sir,' he told the official. 'Spotted it during test run of the engines just now. Shouldn't be too long.'

'These men must take off at eight o'clock, in ten minutes' time,' said the German. 'At nine o'clock the terrorists on the *Freya* are going to vent a hundred thousand tons of oil.'

'Doing my best, sir. Now, if I could just get on with my job,' said the warrant officer.

The base commander steered Herr Bruckner out of the hangar. He too had no idea what the orders from London meant, but orders they were and he intended to obey them.

'Why don't we step across to the officers' mess for a nice cup of tea?' he suggested.

'I don't want a nice cup of tea,' said the frustrated Herr Bruckner. 'I want a nice take-off for Tel Aviv. But first I must telephone the governing mayor.'

'Then the officers' mess is just the place,' said the wing commander. 'By the way, since the prisoners can't really remain in that van much longer, I've ordered them to the military police station cells in Alexander Barracks. They'll be nice and comfortable there.'

It was five to eight when the BBC radio correspondent was given a personal briefing by the RAF base commander about the technical malfunction in the Dominie, and his report cut clean into the 8 a.m. news as a special flash seven minutes later. It was heard on the *Freya*.

'They'd better hurry up,' said Svoboda.

Adam Munro and the two civilians entered the military police cells just after eight o'clock. It was a small unit, only used for the occasional army prisoner, and there were four cells in a row. Mishkin was in the first, Lazareff in the fourth. The junior civilian let Munro and his colleague enter the corridor leading to the cells, then closed the corridor door and stood with his back to it.

'Last-minute interrogation,' he told the outraged MP sergeant in charge. 'Intelligence people.' He tapped the side of his nose. The MP sergeant shrugged and went back to his orderly room.

Munro entered the first cell. Lev Mishkin, in civilian clothes, was sitting on the edge of the bunk bed smoking a cigarette. He had been told he was going to Israel at last, but he was still nervous and uninformed about most of what had been going on these past three days.

Munro stared at him. He had almost dreaded meeting him. But for this man and his crazy schemes to assassinate Yuri Ivanenko in pursuit of some far-off dream, his beloved Valentina would even now be packing her bags, preparing to leave for Romania, the Party conference, the holiday at Mamaia Beach and the boat that would take her to freedom. He saw again the back of the woman he loved going through the plate-glass doors to the street of Moscow, the man in the trenchcoat straighten up and begin to follow her.

'I am a doctor,' he said in Russian. 'Your friends the Ukrainians who have demanded your release have also insisted you be medically fit to travel.'

Mishkin stood up and shrugged. He was unprepared for the four rigid fingertips that jabbed him in the solar plexus, not expecting the small canister held under his nose as he gasped for air, unable to prevent himself from inhaling the aerosol vapour that sprayed from the nozzle of the can as he inhaled. When the knock-out gas hit the lungs his legs buckled without a sound and Munro caught him beneath the armpits before he reached the floor. Carefully, he was laid on the bed.

'It'll act for five minutes, no more,' said the civilian from the ministry, 'then he'll wake with a fuzzy head but no ill effects. You'd better move fast.'

Munro opened the attaché case and took out the box containing the hypodermic syringe, the cotton wool and a small bottle of ether. Soaking the cotton wool in the ether he swabbed a portion of the prisoner's right forearm to sterilize the skin, and held the syringe to the light and squeezed until a fine jet of liquid rose into the air, expelling the last bubbles.

The injection took less than three seconds, and ensured Lev Mishkin would remain under its effects for almost two hours, longer than necessary but a period that could not be reduced.

The two men closed the cell door behind them and went down to where David Lazareff, who had heard nothing, was pacing up and down full of nervous energy. The aerosol spray worked with the same instantaneous effect. Two minutes later he also had his injection.

The civilian accompanying Munro reached into his breast pocket and took out a flat tin. He held it out.

'I leave you now,' he said coldly. 'This isn't what I'm paid for.'

Neither hijacker knew or would ever know what had been injected into them. In fact it was a mixture of two narcotics called pethidine and hyacine by the British, or meperidine and scopolamine by the Americans. In combination they have remarkable effects.

They cause the patient to remain awake, albeit slightly sleepy, willing and able to be obedient to instructions. They also have the effect of telescoping time, so that coming out from their effects after almost two hours, the patient has the impression of having suffered a dizzy spell for several seconds. Finally, they cause complete amnesia so that when the effects wear off the patient has not the slightest recall of anything that happened during the intervening period. Only a reference to a clock will tell him that time has passed at all.

Munro re-entered Mishkin's cell. He helped the young man into a sitting position on his bed, back to the wall.

'Hello,' he said.

'Hello,' said Mishkin and smiled. They were speaking in Russian, but Mishkin would never remember it.

Munro opened his flat tin box, extracted two halves of a long torpedo-shaped capsule called a Spansule, such as are often used as cold remedies, and screwed the two ends together.

'I want you to take this pill,' he said and held it out with a glass of water.

'Sure,' said Mishkin, and swallowed it without demur.

From his attaché case Munro took a battery-operated wall clock and adjusted a timer at the back. Then he hung it on the wall. The hands read eight o'clock but were not in motion. He left Mishkin sitting on his bed and returned to the cell of the other man. Five minutes later the job was finished. He repacked his bag and left the cell corridor.

'They're to remain in isolation until the aircraft is ready for them,' he told the MP sergeant at the orderly room desk as he passed through. 'No one is to see them at all. Base commander's orders.'

For the first time Andrew Drake was speaking in his own voice to the Dutch premier, Jan Grayling. Later, English linguistics experts would place the tape-recorded voice as having originated within a twenty-mile radius of the city of Bradford, England, but by then it would be too late.

'These are the terms for the arrival of Mishkin and Lazareff in Israel,' said Drake. 'I shall expect no later than one hour after the take-off from Berlin an assurance from Premier Golen that they will be abided by. If they are not, the release of my friends will be regarded as null and void.

'One: the two are to be led from the aircraft on foot and at a slow pace past the observation terrace on top of the main terminal building at Ben Gurion Airport. Two: access to that terrace is to be open to the public. No controls of identity or screening of the public is to take place by the Israeli security force. Three: if there has been any switch of the prisoners, if any look-alike actors are playing their part, I shall know within hours. Four: three hours before the airplane lands at Ben Gurion, the Israeli radio is to publish the time of its arrival and inform everyone that any person who wishes to come and witness their arrival is welcome to do so. The broadcast is to be in Hebrew and English, French and German. That is all.'

'Mr Svoboda,' Jan Grayling cut in urgently, 'all these demands have been noted and will be passed immediately to the Israeli government. I am sure they will agree. Please do not cut contact. I have urgent information from the British in West Berlin.'

'Go ahead,' said Drake shortly.

'The RAF technicians working on the executive jet in the hangar at Gatow Airfield have reported a serious electrical fault which developed this morning in one of the engines during testing. I implore you to believe this is no trick. They are working frantically to put the fault right. But there will be a delay of an hour or two.'

'If this is a trick, it's going to cost your beaches a deposit of one hundred thousand tons of crude oil,' snapped Drake.

'It is not a trick,' said Grayling urgently. 'All aircraft occasionally suffer a technical fault. It is disastrous that this should happen to the RAF plane right now. But it has; and it will be mended, is being mended, even as we speak.'

There was silence for a while as Drake thought.

'I want take-off witnessed by four different national radio reporters, each in live contact with his head office. I want live reports by each of that take-off. They must be from Voice of America, Voice of Germany, the BBC and France's ORTF. All in English and all within five minutes of take-off.'

Jan Grayling sounded relieved.

'I will ensure the RAF personnel at Gatow permit these four reporters to witness the take-off,' he said.

'They had better,' said Drake. 'I am extending the venting of the oil by three hours. At noon we start pumping one hundred thousand tons into the sea.'

There was a click as the line went dead.

Premier Benyamin Golen was at his desk in his office in Jerusalem that Sunday morning. The Sabbath was over and it was a normal working day; it was also past ten o'clock, two hours later than in Western Europe.

The Dutch Prime Minister was barely off the telephone before the small unit of Mossad agents who had established themselves in an apartment in Rotterdam were relaying the message from the *Freya* back to Israel. They beat the diplomatic channels by more than an hour.

It was the premier's personal adviser on security matters who brought him the transcript of the *Freya* broadcast and laid it silently on his desk. Golen read it quickly.

'What are they after?' he enquired.

'They are taking precautions against a switch of the prisoners,' said the adviser. 'It would have been an obvious ploy; to make up two young men to pass for Mishkin and Lazareff at first glance, and effect a substitution.'

'Then who is going to recognize the real Mishkin and Lazareff here in Israel?'

The security adviser shrugged.

'Someone on that observation terrace,' he said. 'They have to have a colleague here in Israel who can recognize the men on sight; more probably someone whom Mishkin and Lazareff can recognize.'

'And after recognition?'

'Some message or signal will presumably have to be passed to the media for broadcasting, to confirm to the men on the *Freya* that their friends have reached Israel safely. Without that message, they will think they have been tricked and go ahead with their deed.'

'Another of them? Here in Israel? I'm not having that,' said Benyamin Golen. 'We may have to play host to Mishkin and Lazareff, but not to any more. I want that observation terrace put under clandestine scrutiny. If any watcher on that terrace receives a signal from these two when they arrive, I want him followed. He must be allowed to pass his message, then arrest him.'

On the *Freya* the morning ticked by with agonizing slowness. Every fifteen minutes Andrew Drake, scanning the wave-bands of his portable radio, picked up English-language news broadcasts from Voice of America or the BBC World Service. Each bore the same message: there had been no take-off. The mechanics were still working on the faulty engine of the Dominie.

Shortly after nine o'clock the four radio reporters designated by Drake as the witnesses to the take-off were admitted to Gatow base and escorted by military police to the officers' mess where they were offered coffee and biscuits. Direct telephone facilities were established to their Berlin offices, from whence radio circuits were held open to their native countries. None of them met Adam Munro who had borrowed the base commander's private office and was speaking to London.

In the lee of the cruiser *Argyll* the three fast patrol boats *Cutlass*, *Sabre* and *Scimitar* waited at their moorings. On the *Cutlass* Major Fallon had assembled his group of twelve Special Boat Commandos.

'We have to assume the powers-that-be are going to let the bastards go,' he told them. 'Some time in the next couple of hours they'll take off from West Berlin for Israel. They should arrive about four and a half hours later. So during this evening or tonight, if they keep their word, those terrorists are going to quit the *Freya*.

'Which way they'll head, we don't know yet, but probably towards Holland. The sea is empty of ships on that side. When they are three miles from the *Freya*, and out of possible range for a small, low-power transmitter-detonator to operate the explosives, Royal Navy experts are going to board the *Freya* and dismantle the charges. But that's not our job.

'We're going to take those bastards, and I want that man Svoboda. He's mine, got it?'

There was a series of nods and several grins. Action was what they had been trained for, and they had been cheated of it. The hunting instinct was high.

'The launch they've got is much slower than ours,' Fallon resumed. 'They'll have an eight-mile start, but I reckon we can take them three to four miles before they reach the coast. We have the Nimrod overhead, patched in to the *Argyll*. The *Argyll* will give us the directions we need. When we get close to them we'll have our searchlights. When we spot them, we take them out. London says no one is interested in prisoners. Don't ask me why; maybe they want them silenced for reasons we know nothing about. They've given us the job, and we're going to do it.'

A few miles away Captain Mike Manning was also watching the minutes tick away. He too waited on news from Berlin that the mechanics had finished their work on the engine of the Dominie. The news in the small hours of the morning, while he sat sleepless in his cabin awaiting the dreaded order to fire his shells and destroy the *Freya* and her crew, had surprised him. Out of the blue, the United States government had reversed its attitude of the previous sundown; far from objecting to the release of the men of Moabit; far from being prepared to wipe out the *Freya* to prevent that release, Washington now held no objection. But his main emotion was relief; waves of pure relief that his murderous orders had been rescinded, unless. . . . Unless something could still go wrong. Not until the two Ukrainian Jews had touched down at Ben Gurion Airport would he be completely satisfied that his orders to shell the *Freya* to a funeral pyre had become part of history.

At a quarter to ten, in the cells below Alexander Barracks, Gatow base,

Mishkin and Lazareff came out from the effects of the narcotic they had ingested at eight o'clock. Almost simultaneously the clocks Adam Munro had hung on the walls of each cell came to life. The sweep hands began to move round the dials.

Mishkin shook his head and rubbed his eyes. He felt sleepy, slightly muzzy in the head. He put it down to the broken night, the sleepless hours, the excitement. He glanced at the clock on the wall; it read two minutes past eight. He knew that when he and David Lazareff had been led through the orderly room towards the cells, the clock there had said eight exactly. He stretched, swung himself off the bunk and began to pace the cell. Five minutes later at the other end of the corridor Lazareff did much the same.

Adam Munro strolled into the hangar where Warrant Officer Barker was still fiddling with the starboard engine of the Dominie.

'How is it going, Mr Barker?' asked Munro.

The long-service technician withdrew himself from the guts of the engine and looked down at the civilian with exasperation.

'May I ask, sir, how long I am supposed to keep up this play-acting? The engine's perfect.'

Munro glanced at his watch.

'Ten-thirty,' he said. 'In one hour exactly I'd like you to telephone the aircrew room and the officers' mess and report that she's fit and ready to fly.'

'Eleven-thirty it is, sir,' said W/O Barker.

In the cells, David Lazareff glanced again at the wall clock. He thought he had been pacing for thirty minutes, but the clock said nine. An hour had gone by, but it had seemed a very short one. Still, in isolation in a cell, time plays strange tricks on the senses. Clocks, after all, are accurate. It never occurred to him or Mishkin that their clocks were moving at double-speed to catch up on the missing hundred minutes in their lives, or that they were destined to synchronize with the clocks outside the cells at eleven-thirty precisely.

At eleven Premier Jan Grayling from The Hague was on the telephone to the governing mayor of West Berlin.

'What the devil is going on, Herr Burgomeister?'

'I don't know,' shouted the exasperated Berlin official. 'The British say they are nearly finished with their damn engine. Why the hell they can't use a British Airways airliner from the civil airport I don't understand. We would pay for the extra cost of taking one out of service to fly to Israel with two passengers only.'

'Well, I'm telling you that in one hour those madmen on the *Freya* are going to vent a hundred thousand tons of oil,' said Jan Grayling, 'and my government will hold the British responsible.'

'I entirely agree with you,' said the voice from Berlin. 'The whole affair is madness.'

At eleven-thirty Warrant Officer Barker closed the cowling of the engine and climbed down. He went to a wall phone and called the officers' mess. The base commander came on the line.

'She's ready, sir,' said the technician.

The RAF officer turned to the men grouped around him, including the governor of Moabit Jail and four radio reporters holding telephones linked to their offices.

'The fault has been put right,' he said. 'She'll be taking off in fifteen minutes.'

From the windows of the mess they watched the sleek little executive jet being towed out into the sunshine. The pilot and co-pilot climbed aboard and started both engines.

The prison governor entered the cells of the prisoners and informed them they were about to take off. His watch said 11.35. So did the wall clocks.

Still in silence, the two prisoners were marched to the MP Land-Rover and driven with the German prison official across the tarmac to the waiting jet. Followed by the air quartermaster sergeant who would be the only other occupant of the Dominie on its flight to Ben Gurion, they went up the steps without a backward glance and settled into their seats.

At 11.45 Wing Commander Jarvis opened both the throttles and the Dominie climbed away from the runway of Gatow Airfield. On instructions from the air traffic controller, it swung cleanly into the southbound air corridor from West Berlin to Munich and disappeared into the blue sky.

Within two minutes all four radio reporters were speaking to their audiences live from the officers' mess at Gatow. Their voices went out across the world to inform their listeners that forty-eight hours after the demands were originally made from the *Freya*, Mishkin and Lazareff were airborne and on their way to Israel and freedom.

In the homes of thirty officers and seamen from the *Freya* the broadcasts were heard; in thirty houses across the four countries of Scandinavia mothers and wives broke down and children asked why mummy was crying.

In the small armada of tugs and detergent-spraying vessels lying in a screen west of the *Argyll* the news came through and there were sighs of relief. Neither the scientists nor the seamen had the slightest doubt they could never have coped with 100,000 tons of crude oil spilling into the sea.

In Texas oil tycoon Clint Blake caught the news from NBC over his Sunday morning breakfast in the sun and shouted, 'About goddam time, too.'

Harry Wennerstrom heard the BBC broadcast in his penthouse suite high over Rotterdam and grinned with satisfaction.

In every newspaper office from Ireland to the Iron Curtain the Monday morning editions of the dailies were in preparation. Teams of writers were putting together the whole story from the first invasion of the *Freya* in the small hours of Friday until the present moment. Space was left for the arrival of Mishkin and Lazareff in Israel, and the freeing of the *Freya* herself. There would be time before the first editions went to press at 10 p.m. to include most of the end of the story.

At twenty minutes past twelve, European time, the State of Israel agreed to abide by the demands made from the *Freya* for the public and identifiable reception of Mishkin and Lazareff at Ben Gurion Airport in four hours' time.

In his sixth-floor hotel room at the Avia Hotel, three miles from Ben

Gurion Airport, Miroslav Kaminsky heard the news on the piped-in radio. He leaned back with a sigh of relief. Having arrived in Israel on the late afternoon of the previous Friday, he had expected to see his old fellow partisans arrive on the Saturday. Instead, he had listened by radio to the change of heart by the German government in the small hours, the delay through Saturday and the venting of the oil at noon. He had bitten his fingernails down, helpless to assist, unable to rest, until the final decision to release them after all. Now for him too the hours were ticking away until touchdown of the Dominie at four-fifteen European time, six-fifteen in Tel Aviv.

On the *Freya*, Andrew Drake heard the news of the take-off with a satisfaction that cut through his weariness. The agreement of the State of Israel to his demands thirty-five minutes later was in the way of a formality.

'They're on their way,' he told Larsen. 'Four hours to Tel Aviv and safety. Another four hours after that, even less if the fog closes down, and we'll be gone. The navy will come on board and release you. You'll have proper medical help for that hand, and you'll have your crew and your ship back. . . . You should be happy.'

The Norwegian skipper was leaning back in his chair, deep black smudges under his eyes, refusing to give the younger man the satisfaction of seeing him fall asleep. For him it was not over; not until the poisonous explosive charges had been removed from his holds, not until the last terrorist had left his ship. He knew he was close to collapse. The searing pain from his hand had settled down to a dull, booming throb that thumped up the arm to the shoulder, and the waves of exhaustion swept over him until he was dizzy. But still he would not close his eyes.

He raised his eyes to the Ukrainian with contempt. 'And Tom Keller?' he asked.

'Who?'

'My third officer, the man you shot out on the deck on Friday morning.'

Drake laughed. 'Tom Keller is down below with the others,' he said. 'The shooting was a charade. One of my own men in Keller's clothes. The bullets were blank.'

The Norwegian grunted. Drake looked across at him with interest.

'I can afford to be generous,' he said, 'because I have won. I brought against the whole of Western Europe a threat they could not face, and an exchange they could not wriggle out of. In short I left them no alternative. But you nearly beat me; you came within an inch of it.

'From six o'clock this morning when you destroyed the detonator, those commandos could have stormed this ship any time they pleased. Fortunately, they don't know that. But they might have done if you'd signalled to them. You're a brave man, Thor Larsen. Is there anything you want?'

'Just get off my ship,' said Larsen.

'Soon now, very soon, captain.'

High over Venice Wing Commander Jarvis moved the controls slightly and the speeding silver dart turned a few points east of south for the long run down the Adriatic.

'How are the clients?' he asked the quarter-master sergeant.

'Sitting quietly, watching the scenery,' said the QMS over his shoulder.

'Keep 'em like that,' said the pilot. 'The last time they took a plane trip, they ended up shooting the captain.'

The QMS laughed.

'I'll watch 'em,' he promised.

The co-pilot tapped the route chart on his knee.

'Three hours to touch-down,' he said.

The broadcasts from Gatow had also been heard elsewhere in the world. In Moscow the news was translated into Russian and brought to the table in a private apartment at the privileged end of Kutuzovsky Prospekt where two men sat at lunch shortly after 2 p.m. local time.

Marshal Nikolai Kerensky read the typed message and slammed a meaty fist on to the table.

'They've let them go,' he shouted. 'They've given in. The Germans and the British have caved in. The two Jew-boys are on their way to Tel Aviv.'

Silently Yefrem Vishnayev took the message from his companion's hand and read it. He permitted himself a wintry smile.

'Then tonight, when we produce Colonel Kukushkin and his evidence before the Politburo, Maxim Rudin will be finished,' he said. 'The censure motion will pass, there is no doubt of it. By midnight, Nikolai, the Soviet Union will be ours. And in a year, all of Europe.'

The marshal of the Red Army poured two generous slugs of Stolichnaya vodka. Pushing one towards the Party theoretician, he raised his own.

'To the triumph of the Red Army.'

Vishnayev raised his glass, a spirit he seldom touched. But there were exceptions.

'To a truly Communist world.'

20

Off the coast south of Haifa the little Dominie turned its nose for the last time and began dropping on a straight course for the main runway at Ben Gurion Airport inland from Tel Aviv.

It touched down after exactly four hours and thirty minutes of flight, at four-fifteen European time. It was six-fifteen in Israel.

At Ben Gurion the upper terrace of the passenger building was crowded with curious sightseers, surprised in a security-obsessed country to be allowed free access to such a spectacle.

Despite the earlier demands of the terrorists on the *Freya* that there be no police presence, the Israeli Special Branch were there. Some were in the uniform of El Al staff, others selling soft drinks, or sweeping the forecourt, or at the wheels of taxis. Detective Inspector Avram Hirsch was in a newspaper van, doing nothing in particular with bundles of evening newspapers that might or might not be destined for delivery to the kiosk in the main concourse.

After touch-down the Royal Air Force plane was led by a ground-control jeep to the apron of tarmac in front of the passenger terminal. Here a small knot of officials waited to take charge of the two passengers from Berlin.

Not far away an El Al jet was also parked, and from its curtained portholes two men with binoculars peered through the cracks in the fabric at the row of faces atop the passenger building. Each had a walkie-talkie set to hand.

Somewhere in the crowd of several hundred on the observation terrace Miroslav Kaminsky stood, indistinguishable from the other innocent sightseers.

One of the Israeli officials mounted the few steps to the Dominie and went inside. After two minutes he emerged, followed by David Lazareff and Lev Mishkin. Two young hotheads from the Jewish Defense League on the terrace unfurled a placard they had secreted in their coats and held it up. It read simply 'Welcome' and was written in Hebrew. They also began to clap, until several of their neighbours told them to shut up.

Mishkin and Lazareff looked up at the crowd on the terrace above them as they were led along the front of the terminal building, preceded by a knot of officials and with two uniformed policemen behind them. Several of the sightseers waved; most watched in silence.

From inside the parked airliner the Special Branch men peered out, straining to catch any sign of recognition from the refugees towards one of those at the railing.

Lev Mishkin saw Kaminsky first and muttered something quickly in Ukrainian out of the side of his mouth. It was picked up at once by a directional microphone aimed at the pair of them from a catering van a hundred yards away. The man squinting down the riflelike microphone did not hear the phrase; the man next to him in the cramped van, with the earphones over his head, did. He had been picked for his knowledge of Ukrainian. He muttered into a walkie-talkie, 'Mishkin just made a remark to Lazareff. He said, quote there he is, near the end with the blue tie, unquote.'

Inside the parked airliner the two watchers swung their binoculars towards the end of the terrace. Between them and the terminal building the knot of officials continued their solemn parade past the sightseers.

Mishkin, having spotted his fellow-Ukrainian, diverted his eyes. Lazareff ran his eyes along the line of faces above him, spotted Miroslav Kaminsky and winked. That was all Kaminsky needed; there had been no switch of prisoners.

One of the men behind the curtains of the airliner said, 'Got him,' and began to talk into his hand-held radio.

'Medium height, early thirties, brown hair, brown eyes, dressed in grey trousers, tweed sports jacket and blue tie. Standing seven or eight from the far end of the observation terrace, towards the control tower.'

Mishkin and Lazareff disappeared into the building. The crowd on the roof, the spectacle over, began to disperse. They poured down the stairwell to the interior of the main concourse. At the bottom of the stairs a grey-haired man was sweeping cigarette butts into a trash can. As the column swept past him, he spotted a man in tweed jacket and blue tie. He was still sweeping as the man strode across the concourse floor.

The sweeper reached into his barrow, took out a small black box and muttered, 'Suspect moving on foot towards exit gate five.'

Outside the building Avram Hirsch hefted a bundle of evening newspapers from the back of the van and swung them on to a trolley held by one of his colleagues. The man in the blue tie walked within a few feet of his, looking neither to right nor left, made for a parked hire-car and climbed in.

Detective Inspector Hirsch slammed the rear doors of his van, walked to the passenger door and swung himself into the seat.

'The Volkswagen Golf over there in the car park,' he said to the van driver, Detective Constable Bentsur. When the rented car left the park en route for the main exit from the airport complex, the newspaper van was two hundred yards behind it.

Ten minutes later Avram Hirsch alerted the other police cars coming up behind him. 'Suspect entering Avia Hotel car park.'

Miroslav Kaminsky had his room key in his pocket. He passed quickly through the foyer and took the lift to his sixth-floor room. Sitting on the edge of the bed he lifted the telephone and asked for an outside line. When he got it he began to dial.

'He's just asked for an outside line,' the switchboard operator told Inspector Hirsch, who was by her side.

'Can you trace the number he's dialling?'

'No, it's automatic for local calls.'

'Blast,' said Hirsch. 'Come on.' He and DC Bentsur ran for the lift.

The telephone in the Jerusalem office of the BBC answered at the third ring.

'Do you speak English?' asked Kaminsky.

'Yes, of course,' said the Israeli secretary at the other end.

'Then listen,' said Kaminsky. 'I'll only say this once. If the supertanker *Freya* is to be released unharmed, the first item in the six o'clock news on the BBC World Service, European time, must include the phrase "no alternative". If that phrase is not included in the first news item of the broadcast, the ship will be destroyed. Have you got that?'

There were several seconds of silence as the young secretary to the Jerusalem correspondent scribbled rapidly on a pad.

'Yes, I think so. Who is that?' she asked.

Outside the bedroom door in the Avia, Avram Hirsch was joined by two other men. One had a short-barrelled shotgun. Both were dressed in airport staff uniform. Hirsch was still in the uniform of the newspaper delivery company, green trousers, green shirt and green peaked cap. He listened at the door till he heard the tinkle of the telephone being replaced. Then he stood back, drew his service revolver and nodded to the man with the shotgun.

The gunner aimed once, carefully, at the door lock and blew the whole assembly out of the woodwork. Avram Hirsch went past him at a run, moved three paces into the room, dropped to a crouch, gun held forward in both hands, pointed straight at the target, and called on the room's occupant to freeze.

Hirsch was a sabra, born in Israel thirty-four years earlier, the son of two immigrants who had survived the death-camps of the Third Reich. Around the house in his childhood the language spoken was always Yiddish or Russian, for both his parents were Russian Jews.

He supposed the man in front of him was Russian; he had no reason to think otherwise. So he called to him in Russian. '*Stoi.* . . .' His voice echoed through the small bedroom.

Miroslav Kaminsky was standing by the bed, the telephone directory in his hand. When the door crashed open he dropped the book, which closed, preventing any searcher from seeing which page it had been open at, or what number he might have called.

When the cry came, he did not see a hotel bedroom outside Tel Aviv; he saw a small farmhouse in the foothills of the Carpathians, heard again the shouts of the men in the green uniforms closing in on the hideaway of his group. He looked at Avram Hirsch, took in the green peaked cap and uniform, and began to move towards the open window.

He could hear them again coming at him through the bushes shouting their endless cry: '*Stoi . . . Stoi . . . Stoi. . . .*' There was nothing to do but run, run like a fox with the hounds behind him, out through the back door of the farmhouse and into the undergrowth.

He was running backwards, through the open glass door to the tiny balcony when the balcony rail caught him in the small of the back and flipped him over. When he hit the car park fifty feet below it broke his back, pelvis and skull. From over the balcony rail, Avram Hirsch looked down at the broken body and turned to Constable Bentsur.

'What the hell did he do that for?'

The service aircraft that had brought the two specialists to Gatow from Britain the previous evening returned westwards soon after the take-off of the Dominie from Berlin for Tel Aviv. Adam Munro hitched a lift on it, but used his clearance from the Cabinet Office to require that it drop him off at Amsterdam before going on to Engand.

He had also ensured that the Wessex helicopter from the *Argyll* would be at Schiphol to meet him. It was half-past four when the Wessex settled back on to the after deck of the missile cruiser. The officer who welcomed him aboard glanced with evident disapproval at his appearance, but took him to meet Captain Preston.

All the navy officer knew was that his visitor was from the Foreign Office and had been in Berlin supervising the departure of the hijackers to Israel.

'Care for a wash and brush-up?' he asked.

'Love one,' said Munro. 'Any news of the Dominie?'

'Landed fifteen minutes ago at Ben Gurion,' said Captain Preston. 'I could have my steward press your suit, and I'm sure we could find you a shirt that fits.'

'I'd prefer a nice thick sweater,' said Munro. 'It's turned damn cold out there.'

'Yes, that may prove a bit of a problem,' said Captain Preston. 'There's a belt of cold air moving down from Norway. We could get a spot of sea-mist this evening.'

The sea-mist when it came, just after five o'clock, was a rolling bank of fog that drifted out of the north as the cold air followed the heatwave and came in contact with the warm land and sea.

When Adam Munro, washed, shaved and dressed in borrowed thick white sweater and black serge trousers, joined Captain Preston on the bridge just after five, the fog was thickening.

'Damn and blast,' said Preston. 'These terrorists seem to be having everything their own way.'

By half-past five the fog had blotted out the *Freya* from vision and swirled around the stationary warships, none of whom could see each other, except on radar. The circling Nimrod above could see them all, and the *Freya*, on its radar, and was still flying in clear air at 15,000 feet. But the sea itself had vanished in a blanket of grey cotton wool. Just after five the tide turned again and began to move back to the northeast, bearing the drifting oil slick with it, somewhere between the *Freya* and the Dutch shore.

★

The BBC correspondent in Jerusalem was a staffer of long experience in the Israeli capital and had many and good contacts. As soon as he learned of the telephone call his secretary had taken, he called a friend in one of the security services.

'That's the message,' he said, 'and I'm going to send it to London right now. But I haven't a clue who telephoned it.'

There was a chuckle at the other end.

'Send the message,' said the security man. 'As to the man on the telephone, we know. And thanks.'

It was just after four-thirty when the news flash was broadcast on the *Freya* that Mishkin and Lazareff had landed at Ben Gurion.

Andrew Drake threw himself back in his chair with a shout.

'We've done it,' he yelled at Thor Larsen. 'They're in Israel.'

Larsen nodded slowly. He was trying to close his mind to the steady agony from his wounded hand.

'Congratulations,' he said sardonically. 'Now perhaps you can leave my ship and go to hell.'

The telephone from the bridge rang. There was a rapid exchange in Ukrainian, and Larsen heard a whoop of joy from the other end.

'Sooner than you think,' said Drake. 'The lookout on the funnel reports a thick band of fog moving towards the whole area from the north. With luck we won't even have to wait until dark. The fog will be even better for our purpose. But when we do leave, I'm afraid I'll have to handcuff you to the table leg. The navy will rescue you in a couple of hours.'

At five o'clock the main newscast brought a despatch from Tel Aviv to the effect that the demands of the hijackers of the *Freya* in the matter of the reception at Ben Gurion Airport of Mishkin and Lazareff had been abided by. Meanwhile, the Israeli government would keep the two from Berlin in custody until the *Freya* was released safe and unharmed. In the event that she was not, the Israeli government would regard its pledges to the terrorists as null and void, and return Mishkin and Lazareff to jail.

In the day cabin on the *Freya*, Drake laughed.

'They won't need to,' he told Larsen. 'I don't care what happens to me now. In twenty-four hours those two men are going to hold an international press conference. And when they do, Captain Larsen, when they do, they are going to blow the biggest hole ever made in the walls of the Kremlin.'

Larsen looked out of the windows at the thickening fog.

'The commandos might use this fog to storm the *Freya*,' he said. 'Your lights would be no use. In a few minutes you won't be able to see any bubbles from frogmen underwater.'

'It doesn't matter any more,' said Drake. 'Nothing matters any more. Only that Mishkin and Lazareff get their chance to speak. That was what it was all about. That is what makes it all worthwhile.'

The two Jewish-Ukrainians had been taken from Ben Gurion Airport in a police van to the central police station in Tel Aviv and locked in separate cells. Prime Minister Golen was prepared to abide by his part of the bargain – the exchange of the two men for the safety of the *Freya*, her crew and cargo. But he was not prepared to have the unknown Svoboda play him a trick.

For Mishkin and Lazareff it was the third cell in a day, but both knew it would be the last. As they parted in the corridor, Mishkin winked at his friend and called in Ukrainian, 'Not next year in Jerusalem – tomorrow.'

From an office upstairs the chief superintendent in charge of the station made a routine call to the police doctor to give the pair a medical examination, and the doctor promised to come at once. It was half-past seven Tel Aviv time.

The last thirty minutes before six o'clock dragged by like snails on the *Freya*. In the day cabin Drake had tuned his radio to the BBC World Service and listened impatiently for the six o'clock newscast.

Azamat Krim, assisted by three of his colleagues, shinned down a rope from the taffrail of the tanker to the sturdy fishing launch that had bobbed beside the hull for the past two and a half days. When the four of them were standing in the launch's open waist, they began preparations for the departure of the group from the *Freya*.

At six o'clock the chimes of Big Ben rang out from London and the evening news broadcast began.

'This is the BBC World Service. The time is six o'clock in London, and here is the news, read to you by Peter Chalmers.'

A new voice came on. It was heard in the wardroom of the *Argyll* where Captain Preston and most of his officers grouped around the set. Captain Mike Manning tuned in on the USS *Moran*; the same newscast was heard in Downing Street, The Hague, Washington, Paris, Brussels, Bonn and Jerusalem. On the *Freya*, Andrew Drake sat motionless, watching the radio unblinkingly.

'In Jerusalem today, Prime Minister Benyamin Golen said that following the arrival earlier from West Berlin of the two prisoners David Lazareff and Lev Mishkin, he would have no alternative but to abide by his pledge to free the two men, provided the supertanker *Freya* was freed with her crew unharmed. . . .'

'"No alternative",' shouted Drake. 'That's the phrase. Miroslav has done it.'

'Done what?' asked Larsen.

'Recognized them. It's them all right. No switching has taken place.'

He slumped back in his chair and exhaled a deep sigh.

'It's over, Captain Larsen. We're leaving, you'll be glad to hear.'

The captain's personal locker contained one set of handcuffs, with keys, in case of the necessity physically to restrain someone on board. Cases of madness have been known on ships. Drake slipped one of the cuffs round Larsen's right wrist and snapped it shut. The other went round the table leg. The table was bolted to the floor. Drake paused in the doorway, and laid the keys to the handcuffs on top of a shelf.

'Good-bye, Captain Larsen. You may not believe this, but I'm sorry about the oil slick. It need never have happened if the fools out there had not tried to trick me. I'm sorry about your hand, but that too need not have happened. We'll not see each other again, so good-bye.'

He closed and locked the cabin door behind him and ran down the three flights of stairs to 'A' deck and outside to where his men were grouped on the after deck. He took his transistor radio with him.

'All ready?' he asked Azamat Krim.

'As ready as we'll ever be,' said the Crimean Tatar.

'Everything OK?' he asked the American-Ukrainian who was an expert in small boats.

The man nodded. 'All systems go,' he replied.

Drake looked at his watch. It was twenty past six.

'Right. Six forty-five Azamat hits the ship's siren, and the launch and the first group leave simultaneously. Azamat and I leave ten minutes later. You've all got papers and clothes. After you hit the Dutch coast, everyone scatters. It's every man for himself.'

He looked over the side. By the fishing launch two inflatable Zodiac speedboats bobbed in the foggy water. Each had been dragged out from the fishing launch and inflated in the previous hour. One was the fourteen-foot model, big enough for five men. The smaller ten-foot model would take two comfortably. With the forty-horsepower outboards behind them, they would make thirty-five knots over a calm sea.

'They won't be long now,' said Major Simon Fallon, standing on the forward rail of the *Cutlass*.

The three fast patrol boats, long since invisible from the *Freya*, had been pulled clear of the western side of the *Argyll* and now lay tethered beneath her stern, noses pointed to where the *Freya* lay, five miles away through the fog.

The marines of the SBS were scattered, four to each boat, all armed with submachine carbines, grenades and knives. One boat, the *Sabre*, also carried on board four Royal Navy explosives experts, and this boat would make straight for the *Freya* to board and liberate her as soon as the circling Nimrod had spotted the terrorist launch leaving the side of the supertanker and achieving a distance of three miles from her. The *Cutlass* and *Scimitar* would pursue the terrorists and hunt them down before they could lose themselves in the maze of creeks and islands that make up the Dutch coast south of the Maas.

Major Fallon would head the pursuit group in the *Cutlass*. Standing beside him, to his considerable disgust, was the man from the Foreign Office, Mr Munro.

'Just stay well out of the way when we close with them,' Fallon said. 'We know they have submachine carbines and handguns, maybe more. Personally, I don't see why you insist on coming at all.'

'Let's just say I have a personal interest in these bastards,' said Munro, 'especially Mr Svoboda.'

'So have I,' growled Fallon. 'And Svoboda's mine.'

Aboard the USS *Moran*, Mike Manning had heard the news of the safe arrival of Mishkin and Lazareff in Israel with as much relief as Drake on the *Freya*.

For him, as for Thor Larsen, it was the end of a nightmare. There would be no shelling of the *Freya* now. His only regret was that the fast patrol boats of the Royal Navy would have the pleasure of hunting down the terrorists when they made their break. For Manning the agony he had been through for a day and a half parlayed itself into anger.

'I'd like to get my hands on that Svoboda,' he told Commander Olsen. 'I'd happily wring his bloody neck.'

As on the *Argyll*, the *Brunner*, the *Breda* and the *Montcalm*, the ship's radar scanners swept the ocean for signs of the launch moving away from the *Freya*'s side. Six-fifteen came and went and there was no sign.

In its turret the forward gun of the *Moran*, still loaded, moved away from the *Freya* and pointed at the empty sea three miles to the south of her.

At ten past eight, Tel Aviv time, Lev Mishkin was standing in his cell beneath the streets of Tel Aviv when he felt a pain in his chest. Something like a rock seemed to be growing fast inside him. He opened his mouth to scream, but the air was cut off. He pitched forward, face down and died on the floor of the cell.

There was an Israeli policemen on permanent guard outside the door of the cell, and he had orders to peer inside at least every two or three minutes. Less than sixty seconds after Mishkin died, his eye was pressed to the judas-hole. What he saw caused him to let out a yell of alarm, and he frantically rattled the key in the lock to open the door. Further up the corridor, a colleague in front of Lazareff's door heard the yell and ran to his assistance. Together they burst into Mishkin's cell and bent over the prostrate figure.

'He's dead,' breathed one of the men. The other rushed into the corridor and hit the alarm button. Then they ran to Lazareff's cell and hurried inside.

The second prisoner was doubled up on the bed, arms wrapped round himself as the paroxysms struck him.

'What's the matter?' shouted one of the guards, but he spoke in Hebrew, which Lazareff did not understand. The dying man forced out four words in Russian. Both guards heard him clearly and later repeated the phrase to senior officers, who were able to translate it.

'Head . . . of . . . KGB . . . dead.'

That was all he said. His mouth stopped moving; he lay on his side on the cot, sightless eyes staring at the blue uniforms in front of him.

The ringing bell brought the chief superintendent, a dozen other officers of the station staff and the doctor who had been taking a coffee in the police chief's office.

The doctor examined each rapidly, searching mouths, throats and eyes, feeling pulses and chests. When he had done, he stalked from the second cell. The superintendent followed him into the corridor; he was a badly worried man.

'What the hell's happened?' he asked the doctor.

'I can do a full autopsy later,' said the doctor, 'or maybe it will be taken out of my hands. But as to what has happened, they've been poisoned, that's what happened.'

'But they haven't eaten anything,' protested the policeman. 'They haven't drunk anything. They were just going to have supper. Perhaps at the airport . . . on the plane . . . ?'

'No,' said the doctor, 'a slow-acting poison would not work with such speed, and simultaneously. Body systems vary too much. Each either administered to himself, or was administered, a massive dose of instantaneous poison, which I suspect to be potassium cyanide, within the five to ten seconds before they died.'

'That's not possible,' shouted the police chief. 'My men were outside the cells all the time. Both prisoners were frisked and searched before they entered the cells. Mouths, anuses, the lot. There were no hidden poison capsules. Besides, why would they commit suicide? They've just arrived in freedom.'

'I don't know,' said the doctor, 'but they both died within seconds of that poison hitting them.'

'I'm phoning the Prime Minister's office at once,' said the chief superintendent grimly, and strode off to his office.

The Prime Minister's personal security adviser, like almost everyone else in Israel, was an ex-soldier. But the man whom those within a five-mile radius of the Knesset called simply 'Barak' had never been an ordinary soldier. He had started as a paratrooper under the para commander Rael Eytan, the legendary Raful. Later he had transferred, to become a major in General Ark Sharon's elite 101 Unit, until he stopped a bullet in the kneecap during a dawn raid on a Palestinian apartment block in Beirut.

Since then he had specialized in the more technical side of security operations, using his knowledge of what he would have done to kill the Israeli premier and then reversing it, to protect his master. It was he who took the call from Tel Aviv and entered the office where Benyamin Golen was working late to break the news to him.

'Inside the cell itself?' echoed a stunned premier. 'Then they must have taken the poison themselves.'

'I don't think so,' said Barak, 'they had every reason to want to live.'

'Then they were killed by others?'

'It looks like it, Prime Minister.'

'Then who would want them dead?'

'The KGB, of course. One of them muttered something about the KGB, in Russian. It seems he was saying the head of the KGB wanted them dead.'

'But they haven't been in the hands of the KGB. Twelve hours ago they were in Moabit Jail. Then for eight hours in the hands of the British. Then two hours with us. In our hands they ingested nothing; no food, no drink, nothing. So how did they take in an instant-acting poison?'

Barak scratched his chin, a dawning gleam in his eye.

'There is a way, Prime Minister. A delayed-action capsule.'

He took a sheet of paper and drew a diagram.

'It is possible to design and make a capsule like this. It has two halves; one is threaded so that it screws into the other half just before it is swallowed.'

The Prime Minister looked at the diagram with growing anger.

'Go on,' he commanded.

'One half of the capsule is of a ceramic substance, immune both to the acidic effects of the gastric juices of the human stomach, and to the effects of the much stronger acid inside it. And strong enough not to be broken by the muscles of the throat when it is swallowed.

'The other half is of a plastic compound, tough enough to withstand the digestive juices, but not enough to resist the acid. In the second portion lies the cyanide. Between the two is a copper membrane. The two halves are screwed together; the acid begins to burn away at the copper wafer. The capsule is swallowed. Several hours later, depending on the thickness of the copper, the acid burns through. It is the same principle as certain types of acid-operated detonators.

'When the acid penetrates the copper membrane, it quickly cuts through the plastic of the second chamber, and the cyanide floods out into the body system. I believe it can be extended up to ten hours, by which time the indigestible capsule has reached the lower bowel. Once the poison is out, the blood absorbs it quickly and carries it to the heart.'

Barak had seen his premier annoyed before, even angry. But he had never seen him white and trembling with rage.

'They send me two men with poison pellets deep inside them,' he whispered, 'two walking time bombs, triggered to die when they are in our hands? Israel will not be blamed for this outrage. Publish the news of the deaths immediately, do you understand, at once. And say a pathology examination is under way at this very moment. That is an order.'

'If the terrorists have not yet left the *Freya*,' suggested Barak, 'that news could reverse their plans to leave.'

'The men responsible for poisoning Mishkin and Lazareff should have thought of that,' snapped Premier Golen. 'But any delay in the announcement, and Israel will be blamed for murdering them. And that I will not tolerate.'

The fog rolled on. It thickened, it deepened. It covered the sea from the coast of East Anglia across to the Walcherens. It embalmed the flotilla of dispersant tugs sheltering west of the warships, and the navy vessels themselves. It whirled around the *Cutlass*, *Sabre* and *Scimitar* as they lay under the stern of the *Argyll*, engines throbbing softly, straining to be up and away to track down their prey. It shrouded the biggest tanker in the world at her mooring between the warships and the Dutch shore.

At six forty-five all the terrorists but two climbed down into the larger of the inflatable speedboats. One of them, the American-Ukrainian, jumped into the old fishing launch that had brought them to the middle of the North Sea, and glanced upwards.

From the rail above him, Andrew Drake nodded. The man pushed the starter button and the sturdy engine coughed into life. The prow of the launch was pointed due west, her wheel lashed with cord to hold her steady on course. The terrorist steadily increased the power of the engine, holding her in neutral gear.

Across the water keen ears, human and electronic, had caught the sound of the motor; urgent commands and questions flashed from the warships to each other, and from the *Argyll* to the circling Nimrod overhead. The spotter plane looked to its radar, but detected no movement on the sea below.

Drake spoke quickly into his hand-held radio, and far up on the bridge Azamat Krim hit the *Freya*'s siren button.

The air filled with the booming roar of sound as the siren blew away the silence of the surrounding fog and the lapping water.

On his bridge on the *Argyll* Captain Preston snorted with impatience.

'They're trying to drown the sound of the launch engine,' he observed. 'No matter, we'll have it on radar as soon as it leaves the *Freya*'s side.'

Seconds later the terrorist in the launch slammed the gear into forward and the fishing boat, its engine revving high, pulled violently away from the *Freya*'s stern. The terrorist leapt for the swinging rope above him, lifted his feet and let the empty boat churn out from under him. In two seconds it was lost in the fog, ploughing its way strongly towards the warships to the west.

The terrorist swung on the end of his rope, then lowered himself into the speedboat where his four companions waited. One of them jerked at the engine's lanyard; the outboard coughed and roared. Without a wave, the five men in it gripped the handholds and the helmsman pushed on the power. The inflatable dug its motor into the water, cleared the stern of the *Freya*, lifted its blunt nose high and tore away across the calm water towards Holland.

The radar operator in the Nimrod above spotted the steel hull of the fishing launch instantly; the rubber-compound speedboat gave no reflector signal.

'The launch is moving,' he told the *Argyll* below him. 'Hell, they're coming straight at you.'

Captain Preston glanced at the radar display on his own bridge.

'Got 'em,' he said, and watched the blip separating itself from the great white blob that represented the *Freya* herself.

'He's right, she's boring straight at us. What the hell are they trying to do?'

On full power and empty, the fishing launch was making fifteen knots. In twenty minutes it would be among the navy ships, then through them and in the flotilla of tugs behind them.

'They must think they can get through the screen of warships unharmed, and then lose themselves among the tugs in the fog,' suggested the first officer beside Captain Preston. 'Shall we send the *Cutlass* to intercept?'

'I'm not risking good men, however much Major Fallon may want his personal fight,' said Preston. 'Those bastards have already shot one seaman on the *Freya*, and orders from Admiralty are quite specific. Use the guns.'

The procedure that was put into effect on the *Argyll* was smooth and practised. The other four NATO warships were politely asked not to open fire, but to leave the job to the *Argyll*. Her fore and aft five-inch guns swung smoothly on to target and opened fire.

Even at three miles, the target was small. Somehow it survived the first salvo, though the sea around it erupted in spouts of rising water when the shells dropped. There was no spectacle for the watchers on the *Argyll*, nor for those crouched on the three patrol boats beside her. Whatever was happening out there in the fog was invisible; only the radar could see every drop of every shell, and the target boat rearing and plunging in the maddened water. But the radar could not tell its masters that no figure stood at the helm, no men crouched terrified in her stern.

Andrew Drake and Azamat Krim sat quietly in their two-man speedboat close by the *Freya* and waited. Drake held on to the rope that hung from her rail high above. Through the fog they both heard the first muffled boom of the *Argyll*'s guns. Drake nodded at Krim, who started the outboard engine. Drake released the rope and the inflatable sped away, light as a feather, skimming the sea as the speed built up, its engine noise drowned by the roar of the *Freya*'s siren.

Krim looked at his left wrist where a waterproof compass was strapped, and altered course a few points to south. He had calculated forty-five minutes at top speed from the *Freya* to the maze of islands that make up North and South Beveland.

At five minutes to seven the fishing launch stopped the *Argyll*'s sixth shell, a direct hit. The explosive tore the launch apart, lifting it half out of the water and rolling both stern and aft sections over. The fuel tank blew up and the steel-hulled boat sank like a stone.

'Direct hit,' reported the gunnery officer from deep inside the *Argyll* where he and his gunners watched the uneven duel on radar. 'She's gone.'

The blip faded from the screen, the illuminated sweep arm went round and round, but only showed the *Freya* at five miles. On the bridge four officers watched the same display, and there were a few minutes of silence. It was the first time for any of them that their ship had actually killed anybody.

'Let the *Sabre* go,' said Captain Preston quietly. 'They can board and liberate the *Freya* now.'

The radar operator in the darkened hull of the Nimrod peered closely at his screen. He could see all the warships, all the tugs, and the *Freya* to the east of them. But somewhere beyond the *Freya*, shielded by the tanker's bulk from the navy vessels, a tiny speck seemed to be moving away to the southeast. It was so small it could almost have been missed; it was no bigger than the blip that would have been made by a medium-sized tin can; in fact it was the metallic cover to the outboard engine of a speeding inflatable. Tin cans do not move across the face of the ocean at thirty knots.

'Nimrod to *Argyll*, Nimrod to *Argyll* . . . .'

The officers on the bridge of the guided missile cruiser listened to the news from the circling aircraft with shock. One of them ran down to the wing of the bridge and shouted the information down to the sailors from Portland who waited on their patrol launches.

Two seconds later the *Cutlass* and the *Scimitar* were away, the booming roar of their twin diesel marine engines filling the fog around them. Long white plumes of spray rose from their prows, the noses rose higher and higher, the sterns deeper in the wake as the bronze screws whipped through the foaming water.

'Damn and blast them,' shouted Major Fallon to the navy commander who stood with him in the tiny wheelhouse of the *Cutlass*. 'How fast can we go?'

'On water like this, over forty knots,' the commander shouted back.

Not enough, thought Adam Munro, both hands locked to a stanchion as the vessel shuddered and bucked like a runaway horse through the fog. The *Freya* was still five miles away, the terrorists' speedboat another five beyond that. Even if they overhauled at ten knots, it would take an hour to come level with the inflatable carrying Svoboda to safety in the creeks of Holland where he could lose himself. But he would be there in forty minutes, maybe less.

Cutlass and *Scimitar* were driving blind, tearing the fog to shreds, only to watch it form behind them. In any crowded sea it would be lunacy to use such speed in conditions of zero visibility. But the sea was empty. In the wheel-house of each launch, their commanders listened to a constant stream of information from the Nimrod via the *Argyll*; their own position and that of the other fast-patrol launch; position in the fog ahead of them of the *Freya* herself; position of the *Sabre*, well away to their left, heading towards the *Freya* at a slower speed; and the course and speed of the moving dot that represented Svoboda's escape.

Well east of the *Freya*, the inflatable in which Andrew Drake and Azamat Krim were making for safety seemed to be in luck. Beneath the fog the sea had become even calmer, and the sheet-like water enabled them to increase speed even more. Most of their craft was out of the water, only the shaft of the howling engine being deep beneath the surface. A few feet away in the fog, passing by in a blur, Drake saw the last remaining traces of the wake made by their companions ten minutes ahead of them. It was odd, he thought, for the traces to remain on the sea's surface for so long.

On the bridge of the USS *Moran*, lying south of the *Freya*, Captain Mike Manning also studied his radar scanner. He could see the *Argyll* away to the northwest of him, and the *Freya* a mite east of north.

Between them, the *Cutlass* and the *Scimitar* were visible, closing the gap fast. Away to the east he could spot the tiny blip of the racing speedboat, so small it was almost lost among the milky complexion of the screen. But it was there. Manning looked at the gap between the refugee and the hunters charging after it.

'They'll never make it,' he said, and gave an order to his executive officer. The five-inch forward gun of the *Moran* began to traverse slowly to the right, seeking a target somewhere through the fog.

A seaman appeared at the elbow of Captain Preston, still absorbed in the pursuit through the fog as shown by his own scanner. His guns, he knew, were useless; the *Freya* lay almost between him and the target, so any shooting would be too risky. Besides, the bulk of the *Freya* masked the target from his own radar scanner, which could therefore not pass the correct aiming information to the guns.

'Excuse me, sir,' said the seaman.

'What is it?'

'Just come over the news, sir. Those two men who were flown to Israel today, sir. They're dead. Died in their cells.'

'Dead?' queried Captain Preston incredulously. 'Then the whole bloody thing was for nothing. Wonder who the hell could have done that? Better tell that Foreign Office chappie when he gets back. He'll be interested.'

The sea was still flat calm for Andrew Drake. There was a slick, oily flatness to it that was unnatural in the North Sea. He and Krim were almost halfway to the Dutch coast when their engine coughed for the first time. It coughed again several seconds later, then repeatedly. The speed slowed, the power reduced.

Azamat Krim gunned the engine urgently. It fired, coughed again, and resumed running but with a throaty sound.

'It's overheating,' he shouted to Drake.

'It can't be,' yelled Drake. 'It should run at full power for at least an hour.'

Krim leaned out of the speedboat and dipped his hand in the water. He examined the palm and showed it to Drake. Streaks of sticky brown crude oil ran down to his wrist.

'It's blocking the cooling ducts,' said Krim.

'They seem to be slowing down,' the operator in the Nimrod informed the *Argyll*, who passed the information to the *Cutlass*.

'Come on,' shouted Major Fallon, 'we can still get the bastards.'

The distance began to close rapidly. The inflatable was down to ten knots. What Fallon did not know, or the young commander who stood at the wheel of the racing *Cutlass*, was that they were speeding towards the edge of a great lake of oil lying on the surface of the ocean. Or that their prey was chugging right through the centre of it.

Ten seconds later Azamat Krim's engine cut out. The silence was eerie. Far away they could hear the boom of the engines of *Cutlass* and *Scimitar* coming towards them through the fog.

Krim scooped a double handful from the surface of the sea and held it out to Drake.

'It's our oil, Andrew, it's the oil we vented. We're right in the middle of it.'

'They've stopped,' said the commander on the *Cutlass* to Fallon beside him. 'The *Argyll* says they've stopped. God knows why.'

'We'll get 'em,' shouted Fallon gleefully, and unslung his Ingram sub-achine gun.

On the USS *Moran* Gunnery Officer Chuck Olsen reported to Manning, 'We have range and direction.'

'Open fire,' said Manning calmly.

Seven miles to the south of the *Cutlass* the forward gun of the *Moran* began to crash out its shells in steady, rhythmic sequence. The commander of the *Cutlass* could not hear the shells, but the *Argyll* could, and told him to slow down. He was heading straight into the area where the tiny speck on the radar screens had come to rest, and the *Moran* had opened fire on the same area. The commander eased back on his twin throttles, the bucking launch slowed, then settled, chugging gently forward.

'What the hell are you doing?' shouted Major Fallon. 'They can't be more than a mile or so ahead.'

The answer came from the sky. Somewhere above them, a mile forward from the prow, there was a sound like a rushing train as the first shells from the *Moran* homed in on their target.

The three semi-armour-piercing shells went straight into the water, raising spouts of foam but missing the bobbing inflatable by a hundred yards.

The starshells had proximity fuses. They exploded in blinding sheets of white light a few feet above the ocean surface, showering gentle, soft gobbets of burning magnesium over a wide area.

The men on the *Cutlass* were silent, seeing the fog ahead of them illuminated. Four cables to starboard the *Scimitar* was also hove-to, on the very edge of the oil slick.

The magnesium dropped on to the crude oil, raising its temperature to and beyond its flashpoint. The light fragments of blazing metal, not heavy enough to penetrate the scum, sat and burned in the oil.

Before the eyes of the watching sailors and marines the sea caught fire; a gigantic plain, miles long and miles wide, began to glow, ruddy red at first, then brighter and hotter.

It only lasted for fifteen seconds. In that time the sea blazed. Over half of a spillage of 20,000 tons of oil caught fire and burned. For several seconds it reached 5000°C. The sheer heat of it burned off the fog for miles around in a tenth of a minute, the white flames reaching four to five feet high off the surface of the water.

In utter silence the sailors and marines gazed at the blistering inferno starting only a hundred yards ahead of them; some had to shield their faces or be scorched by the heat.

From the midst of the fire a single candle spurted, as if a petrol tank had exploded. The burning oil made no sound as it shimmered and glowed for its brief life.

From the heart of the flames, carrying across the water, a single human scream reached the ears of the sailors.

'*Shche ne vmerla Ukraina.* . . .'

Then it was gone. The flames died down, fluttered and waned. The fog closed in.

'What the hell did that mean?' whispered the commander of the *Cutlass*. Major Fallon shrugged.

'Don't ask me. Some foreign lingo.'

From beside them Adam Munro gazed at the last flickering glow of the dying flames.

'Roughly translated,' he said, 'it means "Ukraine will live again".'

Epilogue

It was 8 p.m. in Western Europe but 10 in Moscow, and the Politburo meeting had been in session for an hour.

Yefrem Vishnayev and his supporters were becoming impatient. The Party theoretician knew he was strong enough; there was no point in further delay. He rose portentously to his feet.

'Comrades, general discussion is all very well, but it brings us nowhere. I have asked for this special meeting of the Praesidium of the Supreme Soviet for a purpose, and that is to see whether the Praesidium continues to have confidence in the leadership of our esteemed Secretary-General, Comrade Maxim Rudin.

'We have all heard the arguments for and against the so-called Treaty of Dublin, concerning the grain shipments the United States had promised to make to us, and the price – in my view the inordinately high price – we have been required to pay for them.

'And finally we have heard of the escape to Israel of the murderers Mishkin and Lazareff, men who it has been proved to you beyond a doubt were responsible for assassinating our dear comrade Yuri Ivanenko. My motion is as follows: that the Praesidium of the Supreme Soviet can no longer have confidence in the continued direction of the affairs of our great nation by Comrade Rudin. Mr Secretary-General, I demand a vote on the motion.'

He sat down. There was silence. Even for those participating, for more for the smaller fry present, the fall of a giant from Kremlin power is a terrifying moment.

'Those in favour of the motion. . . .' said Maxim Rudin.

Yefrem Vishnayev raised his hand. Marshal Nikolai Kerensky followed suit. Vitautas the Lithuanian did likewise. There was a pause of several seconds. Mukhamed the Tadjik raised his hand. The telephone rang. Rudin answered it, listened and replaced the receiver.

'I should not, of course,' he said impassively, 'interrupt a vote, but the news just received is of some passing interest.

'Two hours ago Mishkin and Lazareff both died, instantaneously, in cells beneath the central police station of Tel Aviv. A colleague fell to his death from a hotel balcony window outside that city. One hour ago the terrorists, who had hijacked the *Freya* in the North Sea to liberate these men, died in a sea of blazing petrol. None of them ever opened their mouths. And now none of them ever will.

'We were, I believe, in the midst of voting for Comrade Vishnayev's resolution. . . .'

Eyes studiously averted themselves; gazes were upon the tablecloth.

'Those against the motion?' murmured Rudin.

Vassili Petrov and Dmitri Rykov raised their hands. They were followed by Chavadze the Georgian, Shushkin and Stepanov.

Petryanov, who had once voted for the Vishnayev faction, glanced at the raised hands, caught the drift of the wind and raised his own.

'May I,' said Komarov of Agriculture, 'express my personal pleasure at being able to vote with the most complete confidence in favour of our Secretary-General.' He raised his hand.

Rudin smiled at him. Slug, thought Rudin, I am personally going to stamp you into the garden path.

'Then with my own vote the issue is denied by eight votes to four,' said Rudin. 'I don't think there is any other business?'

There was none.

Twelve hours later, Captain Thor Larsen stood once again on the bridge of the *Freya* and scanned the sea around him.

It had been an eventful night. The British marines had found and freed him twelve hours before, on the verge of collapse. Navy demolitions experts had carefully lowered themselves into the holds of the supertanker and plucked the detonators from the dynamite, bringing the charges gently up from the bowels of the ship to the deck, whence they were removed.

Strong hands had turned the steel cleats to the door behind which his crew had been imprisoned for sixty-four hours and the liberated seamen had whooped and danced for joy. All night they had been putting through personal calls to their parents and wives.

Gentle hands of a navy doctor had laid Thor Larsen on his own bunk and tended the wounds as best the conditions would allow.

'You'll need surgery, of course,' the doctor told the Norwegian. 'And it'll be set up for the moment you arrive by helicopter in Rotterdam, OK?'

'Wrong,' said Larsen, on the brink of unconsciousness. 'I will go to Rotterdam, but I will go in the *Freya*.'

The doctor had cleaned and swabbed the broken hand, sterilizing against infection and injecting morphine to dull the pain. Before he was finished, Thor Larsen slept.

Skilled hands had piloted the stream of helicopters that rose and landed on the *Freya*'s helipad amidships through the night, bringing Harry Wennerstrom to inspect his ship, and the berthing crew to help her dock. The pumpman had found his spare fuses and repaired his cargo control pumps. Crude oil had been pumped from one of the full holds to the vented one to restore the balance; the valves had all been closed.

While the captain slept, the first and second officers had examined every inch of the *Freya* from stem to stern. The chief engineer had gone over his beloved engines foot by foot, testing every system to make sure nothing had been damaged.

During the dark hours the tugs and fireships had started to spray their emulsifier-concentrate on to the area of sea where the scum of the vented oil still clung to the water. Most had burned off in the single, brief holocaust caused by the magnesium shells of Captain Manning.

Just before dawn Thor Larsen had woken. The chief steward had helped him gently into his clothes, the full uniform of a senior captain of the Nordia Line that he insisted on wearing. He had slippped his bandaged hand carefully down the sleeve with the four gold rings, then hung the hand back in the sling round his neck.

At 8 a.m. he stood beside his first and second officers on the bridge. The two pilots from Maas Control were also there, the senior pilot with his independent 'brown box' navigational aid system.

To Thor Larsen's surprise the sea to the north, south and west of him was crowded. There were trawlers from the Humber and the Scheldt, fishermen up from Lorient and St Malo, Ostend and the coast of Kent. Merchant vessels flying a dozen flags mingled with the warships of five NATO navies, all hove-to within a radius of three miles and outwards from that.

At two minutes past eight the gigantic propellers of the *Freya* began to turn, the massive anchor cable rumbled up from the ocean floor. From beneath her stern a maelstrom of white water appeared.

In the sky above, four aircraft circled, bearing television cameras that showed a watching world the sea goddess coming under way.

As the wake broadened behind her, and the Viking helmet emblem of her company fluttered out from her yardarm the North Sea exploded in a burst of sound.

Little sirens like tin whistles, booming roars and shrill whoops echoed across the water as over a hundred sea captains commanding vessels from the tiny to the grand, from the harmless to the deadly, gave the *Freya* the traditional sailor's greeting.

Thor Larsen looked at the crowded sea about him and the empty lane leading to Euro Buoy Number One. He turned to the waiting Dutch pilot.

'Mr Pilot, pray set course for Rotterdam.'

On Sunday, 10th April, in Saint Patrick's Hall, Dublin Castle, two men approached the great oak refectory table that had been brought in for the purpose, and took their seats.

In the Minstrel Gallery the television cameras peered through the arcs of white light that bathed the table and beamed their images across the world.

Dmitri Rykov carefully scrawled his name for the Soviet Union on both copies of the Treaty of Dublin and passed the copies, bound in red Morocoo leather, to David Lawrence, who signed for the United States.

Within hours the first grain ships, waiting off Murmansk and Leningrad, Sebastopol and Odessa, moved forward to their berths.

A week later the first combat units along the Iron Curtain began to load their gear to pull back from the barbed wire line.

*

On Thursday the 14th the routine meeting of the Politburo in the arsenal building of the Kremlin was far from routine.

The last man to enter the room, having been delayed outside by a major of the Kremlin Guard, was Yefrem Vishnayev. When he came through the doorway, he observed that the faces of the other eleven members were all turned towards him. Maxim Rudin brooded at the centre place at the top of the T-shaped table. Down each side of the stem were five chairs, and each was occupied. There was only one chair left vacant. It was the one at the far end of the stem of the table, facing up the length of it.

Impassively, Yefrem Vishnayev walked slowly forward to take that seat, known simply as the penal chair. It was to be his last Politburo meeting.

On 18th April a small freighter was rolling in the Black Sea swell, ten miles off the shore of Romania. Just before 2 a.m. a fast speedboat left the freighter and raced towards the shore. At three miles it halted and a marine on board took a powerful torch, pointed it towards the invisible sands and flashed a signal: three long dashes and three short ones. There was no answering light from the beach. The man repeated his signal four times. Still there was no answer.

The speedboat turned back and returned to the freighter. An hour later it was stowed below decks and a message was transmitted to London.

From London another message went in code to the British embassy in Moscow. 'Regret. Nightingale has not made the rendezvous. Suggest you return to London.'

On 25th April there was a plenary meeting of the full Central Committee of the Communist Party of the Soviet Union in the Palace of Congresses inside the Kremlin. The delegates had come from all over the union, some of them many thousands of miles.

Standing on the podium beneath the outsized head of Lenin, Maxim Rudin made them his farewell speech.

He began by outlining to them all the crises that had faced their country twelve months earlier; he painted a picture of famine and hunger to make their hair stand on end. He went on to describe the brilliant feat of diplomacy by which the Politburo had instructed Dmitri Rykov to meet the Americans in Dublin and gain from them grain shipments of unprecedented size, along with imports of technology and computers, all at minimal cost. No mention was made of concessions on arms levels. He received a standing ovation for ten minutes.

Turning his attention to the matter of world peace, he reminded one and all of the constant danger to peace that was posed by the territorial and imperial ambitions of the capitalist West, occasionally aided by enemies of peace right here within the Soviet Union.

This was too much; consternation was unconfined. But, he went on with an admonishing finger, these secret co-plotters with the imperialists had been uncovered and rooted out, thanks to the eternal vigilance of the tireless Yuri Ivanenko, who had died a week earlier in a sanatorium after a long and gallant struggle against heart ailment.

There were cries of horror and condolence for the departed comrade, who had saved them all, when the news of his death broke. Rudin raised a regretful hand for silence.

But, he told them, Ivanenko had been ably assisted before his heart attack last October, and replaced since his infirmity began, by his ever loyal comrade in arms, Vassili Petrov, who had completed the task of safeguarding the Soviet Union as the world's first champion of peace. There was an ovation for Vassili Petrov.

Because the conspiracies of the anti-peace faction, both inside and outside the Soviet Union, had been exposed and destroyed, Rudin went on, it had been possible for the USSR, in its unending search for détente and peace, to curb its arms-building programmes for the first time in years. More of the national effort could thenceforward be directed towards the production of consumer goods and social improvement, thanks solely to the vigilance of the Politburo in spotting the anti-peace faction for what they were.

This time the applause extended for another ten minutes.

Maxim Rudin waited till the clapping was almost over before he raised his hands, and dropped his speaking tone.

As for him, he said, he had done what he could, but the time had come for him to depart.

The stunned silence was tangible.

He had toiled long, too long perhaps, bearing on his shoulders the harshest burdens, and it had sapped his strength and his health.

On the podium, his shoulders slumped with the weariness of it all. There were cries of 'No . . . no. . . .'

He was an old man, Rudin said. What did he want? Nothing more than any old man wanted. To sit by the fire's corner on a wintry night and play with his grandchildren. . . .

In the diplomatic gallery the British head of chancery whispered to the ambassador: 'I say, that's going a bit strong. He's had more people shot than I've had hot dinners.'

The ambassador raised a single eyebrow and muttered back: 'Think yourself lucky. If this was America he'd produce his bloody grandchildren on the stage.'

And so, concluded Rudin, the time had come for him to admit openly to his friends and comrades that the doctors had informed him he had only a few more months to live. With his audience's permission he would lay down the burdens of office and spend what little time remained to him in the countryside he loved so much, with the family who were the sun and the moon to him.

Several of the women delegates were crying openly by now.

One last question remained, said Rudin. He wished to retire in five days, on the last day of the month. The following morning was May Day, and a new man would stand atop Lenin's Mausoleum to take the salute of the great parade. Who would that man be?

It should be a man of youth and vigour, of wisdom and unbounded patriotism; a man who had proved himself in the highest councils of the land, but was not yet bowed with age. Such a man, Rudin proclaimed, the peoples of the fifteen socialist republics were lucky to have, in the person of Vassili Petrov. . . .

The election of Petrov to succeed Rudin was carried by acclamation. Supporters of alternative candidates would have been shouted down had they tried to speak. They did not even bother.

Following the climax of the hijack in the North Sea, Sir Nigel Irvine had wished Adam Munro to remain in London, or at least not to return to Moscow. Munro had appealed personally to the Prime Minister to be allowed one last chance to ensure that his agent, the Nightingale, was safe at least. In view of his role in ending the crisis, his wish had been granted.

Since his meeting in the small hours of 3rd April with Maxim Rudin, it was evident that his cover was completely blown and that as an agent in Moscow he could not function.

The ambassador and head of chancery regarded his return with considerable misgivings, and it was no surprise when his name was carefully excluded from any diplomatic invitations, nor that he could not be received by any representative of the Soviet Ministry of Foreign Trade. He hung about like a forlorn and unwanted party guest, hoping against hope that Valentina would contact him to indicate she was safe.

Once he tried her private telephone number. There was no answer. She could have been out, but he dared not risk it again. Following the fall of the Vishnayev faction, he was told he had until the end of the month. Then he would be recalled to London, and his resignation from the Service would be gratefully accepted.

Maxim Rudin's farewell speech caused a furore in the diplomatic missions, as each informed its home government of the news of Rudin's departure and prepared position-papers on his successor, Vassili Petrov. Munro was excluded from this whirl of activity.

It was, therefore, all the more surprising when, following the announcement of a reception in St George's Hall in the Kremlin Great Palace on the evening of 30th April, invitations arrived at the British embassy for the ambassador, the head of chancery, and Adam Munro. It was even hinted during a phone call from the Soviet Foreign Ministry to the embassy that Munro was confidently expected to attend.

The state reception to bid farewell to Maxim Rudin was a glittering affair. Over a hundred of the elite of the Soviet Union mingled with four times that number of foreign diplomats from the Socialist world, the West and the Third World. Fraternal delegations from Communist parties outside the Soviet bloc were also there, ill-at-ease among the full evening dress, military uniforms, stars, orders and medals. It could have been a tsar who was abdicating rather than a leader of a classless workers' paradise.

The foreigners mingled with their Russian hosts beneath the 3000 lights of the six spreading chandeliers, exchanging gossip and congratulations in the niches where the great tsarist war heroes were commemorated with the other Knights of St George. Maxim Rudin moved among them like an old lion, accepting the plaudits of well-wishers from 150 countries as no more than his due.

Munro spotted him from afar, but he was not included in the list of those presented personally, nor was it wise for him to approach the outgoing Secretary-General. Before midnight, pleading a natural tiredness, Rudin excused himself and left the guests to the care of Petrov and the others from the Politburo.

Twenty minutes later Adam Munro felt a touch at his arm. Standing behind him was an immaculate major in the uniform of the Kremlin's own praetorian guard. Impassive as ever, the major spoke to him in Russian.

'Mr Munro, please come with me.'

His tone permitted no expostulation. Munro was not surprised; evidently his inclusion in the guest list had been a mistake, it had been spotted and he was being asked to leave.

But the major headed away from the main doors, passed through into the high, octagonal Hall of St Vladimir, up a wooden staircase guarded by a bronze grille and out into the warm starlight of Upper Saviour Square.

The man walked with completely confident tread, at ease among passages and doorways well known to him although unseen by most.

Still following, Munro went across the square and into the Terem Palace. Silent guards were at every door; each opened as the major approached and closed as they passed through. They walked straight across the Front Hall Chamber and to the end of the Cross Chamber. Here, at a door at the far end, the major paused and knocked. There was a gruff command from inside. The major opened the door, stood aside and indicated that Munro should enter.

The third chamber in the Terem Palace, the so-called Palace of Chambers, is the Throne Room, the holy of holies of the old tsars, most inaccessible of all the rooms. In red, gilt and mosaic tiles, with parquet floor and deep burgundy carpet, it is lush; smaller and warmer than most of the other rooms. It was the place where the tsars worked or received emissaries in complete privacy. Standing staring out through the Petition Window was Maxim Rudin. He turned as Munro entered.

'So Mr Munro, you will be leaving us, I hear.'

It had been twenty-seven days since Munro had seen him before, in dressing gown, nursing a glass of milk, in his personal apartments in the arsenal. Now he was in a beautifully cut charcoal-grey suit, almost certainly made in Savile Row, London, bearing the two Orders of Lenin and Hero of the Soviet Union on the left lapel. The Throne Room suited him better this way.

'Yes, Mr President,' said Munro.

Maxim Rudin glanced at his watch.

'In ten minutes, Mr ex-President,' he remarked. 'Midnight I officially retire. You also, I presume, will be retiring?'

The old fox knows perfectly well that my cover was blown the night I met him, thought Munro, and that I also have to retire.

'Yes, Mr President, I shall be returning to London tomorrow, to retire.'

Rudin did not approach him or hold out his hand. He stood across the room, just where the tsars had once stood, in the room representing the pinnacle of the Russian Empire, and nodded.

'Then I shall wish you farewell, Mr Munro.'

He pressed a small onyx bell on a table, and behind Munro the door opened.

'Good-bye, sir,' said Munro. He had half turned to go when Rudin spoke again.

'Tell me, Mr Munro, what do you think of our Red Square?'

Munro stopped puzzled. It was a strange question for a man saying farewell, Munro thought, and answered carefully.

'It is very impressive.'

'Impressive, yes,' said Rudin, as if weighing the word. 'Not perhaps as elegant as your Berkeley Square, but sometimes, even here, you can hear a nightingale sing.'

Munro stood motionless as the painted saints on the ceiling above him. His stomach turned over in a wave of nausea. They had got her, and, unable to resist, she had told them all, even the code-name and the reference to the old song about the nightingale in Berkeley Square.

'Will you shoot her?' he asked dully.

Rudin seemed genuinely surprised.

'Shoot her? Why should we shoot her?'

So, it would be the labour camps, the living death, for the woman he loved and had been so near to marrying in his native Scotland.

'Then what will you do to her?'

The old Russian raised his eyebrows in mock surprise.

'Do? Nothing. She is a loyal woman, a patriot. She is also very fond of you, young man. Not in love, you understand, but genuinely fond. . . .'

'I don't understand,' said Munro. 'How do you know?'

'She asked me to tell you,' said Rudin. 'She will not be a housewife in Edinburgh. She will not be Mrs Munro. She cannot see you again – ever. But she does not want you to worry for her, to fear for her. She is well, privileged, honoured, among her own people. She asked me to tell you not to worry.'

The dawning comprehension was almost as dizzying as the fear. Munro stared at Rudin as the disbelief receded.

'She was yours,' he said flatly, 'she was yours all along. From the first contact in the woods, just after Vishnayev made his bid for war in Europe. She was working for you. . . .'

The grizzled old Kremlin fox shrugged.

'Mr Munro,' growled the old Russian, 'how else could I get my messages to President Matthews with the absolute certainty that they would be believed?'

The impassive major with the cold eyes drew at his elbow; he was outside the Throne Room and the door closed behind him. Five minutes later he was shown out, on foot, through a small door in the Saviour Gate on to Red Square. The parade marshals were rehearsing their roles for May Day. The clock above his head struck midnight.

He turned left towards the National Hotel to find a taxi. A hundred yards later, as he passed Lenin's Mausoleum, to the surprise and outrage of a militiaman, he began to laugh.